FORTUNATA AND JACINTA

Benito Pérez Galdós was born in 1843 in the Canary Islands. He left home at nineteen to study law in Madrid – a city that proved so fascinating for him that he abandoned any attempts to study properly. By 1865 he was writing articles on various subjects for *La Nación*, and he published his translation of Dickens's *Pickwick Papers* in 1868. He was appointed editor of *La Revista de España* in 1870, and in the same year his first novel appeared. Galdós then embarked on his great work, a series of historical novels, to which he gave the comprehensive title of *Episodios Nacionales*. His aim was to awaken a new national conscience, but in doing so he incurred bitter opposition. The first novel of the series appeared in 1873; the forty-sixth and last in 1912. Galdós was also concerned with an analysis of contemporary society, which he examined in what he termed his contemporary novels. *Fortunata and Jacinta* (1887) is the seventh and longest of these. In 1892 his first successful play, *Realidad* (adapted from his novel), was resoundingly received and in 1901 *Electra* provoked the same extremes of opinion with its attack on the clergy and even resulted in violence in the streets. At the age of sixty-four Galdós entered the political arena as a Republican but became very disillusioned with the party and by 1912 had faded from the scene. His old age brought increasing difficulties, as he went blind and his financial position became very precarious, partly because of his many mistresses and their children. An attempt to nominate him for a Nobel Prize was quashed on the grounds that he had caused too much strife. The play *Marianela* (1916) brought him one more success before he died in 1920, unquestionably one of Spain's greatest writers.

·

Agnes Gullón is a professor of Spanish at Temple University. She has also published critical studies of the works of such Spanish novelists as Unamuno and Miguel Delibes.

BENITO PÉREZ GALDÓS

Fortunata and Jacinta

Two Stories of Married Women

Translated with an Introduction
by Agnes Moncy Gullón

PENGUIN BOOKS

PENGUIN BOOKS

Published by the Penguin Group
Penguin Books Ltd, 27 Wrights Lane, London W8 5TZ, England
Penguin Books USA Inc., 375 Hudson Street, New York, New York 10014, USA
Penguin Books Australia Ltd, Ringwood, Victoria, Australia
Penguin Books Canada Ltd, 10 Alcorn Avenue, Toronto, Ontario, Canada M4V 3B2
Penguin Books (NZ) Ltd, 182–190 Wairau Road, Auckland 10, New Zealand

Penguin Books Ltd, Registered Offices: Harmondsworth, Middlesex, England

First published in Spain, under the title *Fortunata y Jacinta*, 1886–7
This English translation first published in the USA by the University of Georgia Press 1986
First published in Great Britain by Viking 1987
Published in Penguin Books 1988
009

Copyright © the University of Georgia Press, 1986
All rights reserved

Printed in England by Clays Ltd, St Ives plc

www.greenpenguin.co.uk

MIX
Paper from
responsible sources
FSC
www.fsc.org   FSC® C018179

Penguin Books is committed to a sustainable
future for our business, our readers and our planet.
This book is made from Forest Stewardship
Council™ certified paper.

To Germán and Christina

Contents

Fortunata and Jacinta
VOLUME ONE

VOLUME TWO

VOLUME THREE

VOLUME FOUR

Acknowledgments

IN THE COURSE OF TRANSLATING this book, I incurred many debts. The first was to the person who suggested the idea—Keith Botsford, then Director of the National Translation Center in Austin, Texas. With the aid of an N.T.C. Fellowship Grant, I began work in 1968. Completing the first draft was possible largely because of Ricardo Gullón; he gave freely of his vast knowledge, thereby clarifying a multitude of difficult items in the original text.

To Rodolfo Cardona, for his unflagging enthusiasm for all Galdosian endeavors and for his significant support in having this translation published, I owe special gratitude.

Various organizations made publication feasible with their generous grants. The Spanish Ministry of Culture and specifically, one of its directors, Jaime Salinas, cleared the way with his staunch personal and official support. The Comité Conjunto Hispano-Norteamericano para la Cooperación Cultural y Educativa, headed by Ramón Bela in Madrid, and Antonio Ramos Gascón, Secretary of the U.S.-Spain Committee for Cultural Exchange of the Spanish Ministry of Culture in the United States, assisted readily. I also thank the College of Arts and Sciences of Temple University.

In preparing the manuscript, a number of people were helpful, and I hope that each understands my appreciation, even though not all are individually acknowledged here. For their multifaceted improvement of my text, I wish to thank Mrs. Ona Kay Stephenson, Peter G. Earle, Karen O. Austin, Lester Clark, Stefanie Woodbridge, and DuPont Guerry IV, M.D. Noel M. Valis and Mary Hill both read the entire manuscript with great care, and their editorial assistance was invaluable.

To my husband, Germán Gullón, I am grateful not only for his enduring encouragement, but also for the delicate and rather painstaking task he performed. He listened to several volumes read aloud while checking Galdós' Spanish, thereby catching errors and expressions that did not yet fit into the kind of text I aimed to create: a modern American version.

The University of Georgia Press, under the clear direction of Malcolm L. Call and the able management of Ellen Harris, has been a pleasure to deal with at every stage of this joint venture. I am particularly thankful for such courtesy and guidance.

In closing, a few words about the cover. The idea of using the Ramón Casas painting, *La Madeleine*, came from my friend Pablo Beltrán de Heredia, a true connoisseur of Spanish art. And finally, Padre Laplana, Director of the Museo de Montserrat in Barcelona, generously gave permission to reproduce the painting, thus making it possible to illustrate Galdós' masterpiece with an evocative image of Fortunata.

A.M.G.

Introduction

TO INTRODUCE BENITO PÉREZ GALDÓS to anyone at all acquainted with Spanish literature would be superfluous; this formidable, yet comfortably familiar author whose novels fill long shelves and memorable places in the experience of so many readers should hardly need an introduction. Yet the necessity of introducing Galdós to our English-speaking world is, ironically enough, real. In America, as in England, Spain's greatest nineteenth-century novelist is still largely unknown. Several of his works were translated in his own time, and recently he has begun to be translated again, with success in some cases; on the whole, though, Galdós continues to be an unfamiliar name for most, associated vaguely with Balzac, perhaps, or other European realists, such as Dickens and Dostoevsky. In a word, a "remote" author.

Born in 1843 in Las Palmas on the Canary Islands to Don Sebastián Pérez, a lieutenant colonel, and his wife, Doña Dolores Galdós, Benito grew up in a home ruled by an authoritarian mother. As a boy he was reportedly silent and timid, quick to observe and slow to participate in games with his schoolmates. The young boy's father, who has emerged in biographies as a weak-willed, well-meaning man, was more like a grandfather to him, and they were very close. Traces of Don Sebastián may be found in some of Galdós' characters, and remnants of the tales he told his son about his experiences in Spain's War of Independence appear in the series of historical novels, the *Episodios nacionales*. But it was Galdós' mother, or rather her resolution to send him to Madrid when he was nineteen, that had the most decisive effect on his life as a writer. Doña Dolores' fear of the consequences of her son's passionate love for the illegitimate daughter of her brother's former lover, an American named Adriana Tate, was greater than her desire to keep her cherished son at home, so she separated Benito from his idol Sisita by sending him to study law at the University of Madrid.

"Madrid was the enormous page where Galdós learned to know Spanish society" (Ricardo Gullón, *Galdós novelista moderno* (Taurus, 1960), p. 14). First as a student, mainly in cafés or wandering around the city, then as a fledgling writer and journalist strongly attracted to the popular lower-class neighborhoods, Galdós gradually gained his encyclopedic knowledge of the city and, more significantly, of people in general. Characteristically quiet and observant, Galdós found a wealth of detail to absorb him in the cosmopolitan atmosphere of Spain's capital, and all that he witnessed or experienced he used, evolving over the years a complex novelistic world that radiates out from Madrid and extends into various provinces.

During the early years of his literary life (1865 to 1870), Galdós became acquainted with the works of the two writers who by his own admission influenced him the most: Charles Dickens and Honoré de Balzac. The Madrid newspaper he worked for, *La Nación*, published his translations of *Pickwick Papers*, which until then had not been rendered in Spanish. Before going to France, Galdós had read some Balzac, but it was along the banks of the Seine that his enthusiasm grew; he began to buy the novels one by one, eventually acquiring and reading the complete works. He acknowledged Balzac and Dickens as his masters even during those first years, when he was wavering between journalism and the theater. After that initial period of varied attempts and experiments, he channeled his creativity into the genre that would become his, the novel, and once his mind was made up he settled into an extremely methodical life of writing. Working daily on his drafts, he usually wrote several pages one day and revised them the next. His productivity—over one hundred works of fiction—was due partly to his inventive genius and desire to forge a full novelistic world of his own; but what kept him artistically fertile, it seems, was the uninterrupted, almost programmatic contact with that imaginary cosmos. Regularity, solitude, and daily rereading of his work excited his imagination, constantly revitalizing his literary creations.

For about twenty years Galdós sustained a remarkable pace, developing a reputation and an audience who really read his novels. Other major writers of the time, notably the critic Marcelino Menéndez Pelayo and the novelist José María de Pereda, esteemed his art and liked him personally despite political differences, an infrequent state of affairs in a country where tolerance was not (and has not been until recently) in the air. In this case, intelligence triumphed over political partisanship, but unfortunately for Galdós and for Spain the friendly climate that these few writers fomented hardly improved the national one. Hostility toward Galdós' achievements, resentment against his greatness, envy of his success, political quibbling marring literary judgments—these were the essential components of the atmosphere concentrated in Madrid and diffused throughout the provinces, and anyone living in Spanish literary circles was caught in the conflict. In 1883 and again in 1889, he was barred from membership in the Royal Academy; on both occasions, political or "personal" criteria determined the vote. But thanks to Menéndez Pelayo (a conservative, unlike his liberal friend), who was able to persuade some of the Academy members that literary values and the good of the nation should take priority over more subjective issues, Galdós was finally elected, later in 1889.

Signs of recognition increased, and so did the predictably unfavorable reactions from jealous critics and younger pretenders to the literary throne that the Academy represented (and still represents). The most incredible show of opposition came in 1912, when Galdós was nominated as Spain's candidate for the Nobel Prize. Spaniards, unfortunately, were the first to defeat themselves, the first to spread the politically born idea that Galdós' prestige was questionable. Faced with adverse comments in the Spanish press and even a declaration from the Association of University Students stating their protest against Galdós' being awarded the prize, the committee in Sweden preferred to drop the case. Galdós' political enemies thus prevented him from being considered for a prize that they realized should have been his and that, moreover, he sorely needed to cover certain expenses in his private life. In *Pérez Galdós, The Liberal Spanish Crusader* (University of Wisconsin, 1948), H. Chonon Berkowitz explores the major political and private conflicts.

The intensely charged atmosphere in Spain probably contributed to Galdós' wish to reach a foreign audience. In countries where readers were unaware of (or indifferent to) factors influencing Spanish readers, Galdós hoped that he would be judged solely as an artist and that opinions on his work would be more reliable, more representative of posthumous judgments. In Latin America he was very popular, but success there didn't satisfy him as proof of his artistic worth, for he considered the southern Hispanic countries provinces oriented only to Spain's literary life. (At the time, he was right; the contemporary situation is obviously quite different, not to say nearly opposite, in all the arts.) The test, he felt, would be to reach an audience in a different language. His hypothesis raised a question that he had undoubtedly posed before while translating Dickens: could a good translation have intrinsic value and also reflect the particular quality of the original? To say that a definitive evaluation of a work of art may come from a translation sounds like a contradiction in terms. Yet Galdós apparently ranked an impartial reading over knowledge of Spanish as a requisite for judging his work artistically. Perhaps the near lack of impartiality in Spain made him crave a clearer (that is, unprejudiced) response to his fiction, and, indeed, it's not surprising that someone beset by pettiness should have desired communication with more receptive minds. The irony of his wish is that his use of the Spanish language is probably his most distinctive feature. Michael Nimetz, in *Humor in Galdós* (Yale University Press, 1968), studies the subject very well. Much could be said about other elements of his fiction, such as techniques of character creation, sense of plot, use of historical background, novelistic structures, narrative devices, etc.; but style, in my opinion, is his greatest achievement.

GALDÓS AND EUROPEAN REALISTS

Comparing one element of the novel to its counterpart in the two writers who resemble him most, Balzac and Dickens, should give some idea of the novelist

Galdós in relation to the other two. Character creation is, I believe, the element that reveals most fully an author's concept of man's humanity, and if we relate our understanding of these concepts to the novelistic techniques used to develop characters, we could scale the authors from simple to complex: Dickens, Balzac, Galdós, and, approaching the other extreme, Dostoevsky. But although a scale may help to assess the psychological profundity of these novelists, it does not tell us anything about the artistic success of the techniques used. I add this to avoid a possible misunderstanding of the word "simple" as applied to Dickens. His characters seem simple because they do not usually reflect our essential human trait, ambiguity. He offers instead symbols of the good and the bad. Unbelievable heroes and unredeemable villains are common Dickensian figures, often functioning in pairs, as if their creator had felt a need to approximate the extremes even though he did not admit their coexistence in a single individual. This absolute view of character determines Dickens' treatment of change, too; when the author needs a character to change, a disproportionate event must occur, and the character virtually turns inside out: if he was evil, he becomes not only good, but thoroughly washed of all traces of his former evil. Extreme good and bad can succeed each other, but not even relative good and bad coexist. Dickens excels in handling change and development in one type, though: the child, as both narrative portraits and children's views of reality in his fiction confirm.

Balzac's picture is more nuanced. He too tends to exaggerate, creating simplistic literary types, but one of his distinctive techniques (which Galdós quickly picked up), that of having certain characters reappear from book to book, adds a dimension lacking in Dickens. Balzac does not elaborate on the transition from the Vautrin, for example, who appears in *Illusions perdues* to the Vautrin we meet in *Splendeurs et misères des courtisanes*; but merely by inserting the same character in two worlds and allowing us to see him act within different structures, the author shows us more of Vautrin's essence. "Circumstances," or the changed fictional surroundings, flash to us anew our image of the character as he functioned in the earlier work. If the image doesn't coincide with what we find upon renewing contact with the character, we may feel disoriented; but if it does, we may feel a vital triumph of sorts, as if assured of the durability of an inner essence. Such renewed contacts suggest the complexity of change in fiction: how much, in the Balzacian example, is Vautrin's? how much the world's? how much the reader's? The mixture is palpable but ultimately perplexing, because no one identifiable agent controls the change perceived.

I mention Vautrin as an example because he is one of Balzac's more dynamic, enigmatic figures in whom change is inherent, unlike most of the French realist's characters, whose temperamental steadiness (not to say flatness, to use E. M. Forster's term) makes them clearly and instantly recognizable when they reappear.

There is one character in Balzac whose essence seems un-Balzacian. Not a fixed type (like the romantic heroes) or a man given to dramatic change (like Vautrin), César Birotteau starts out as a slightly ridiculous, insignificant pharmacist. Slowly —and pace is the point—he evolves into a genuine yet very un-Balzacian hero. Without resorting to sudden transformations or using the reappearance technique, the author describes a character-in-change. What occurs is not a maturing process, but rather a radical alteration of the self; initially undetected areas of his person materialize in print. The development of César Birotteau is truly masterful. Like Michelangelo's David from the block of stone, or Rodin's head of Balzac from the amorphous body, a type emerges from unshaped mass. And in this case it is a mass of conflicting detail, detail that must have resisted the mold originally planned for it: that of the insignificant pharmacist, the man who didn't count and could be overlooked.

Evolution is precisely what marks Galdós' concept of fictional characters and, by extension, man. He does not divide them into heroes, villains, and in-betweens, but is fascinated by the admixtures that more often comprise human beings and their literary analogues. Naturally, though, like Dickens and Balzac he feels the tug of extremes: the temptation to create a character and then, out of that material, shape an angel or a devil, a hero or a villain—"sensational" substance. What he grasps better than either Balzac or Dickens is the mechanism of idealization: not just how to project an idealized character, but why and how we idealize and, vice versa, why and how we condemn.

Various techniques serve to show the ambiguity of Galdosian characters. Reappearance is one. Another, typical of nineteenth-century realism, is the use of several viewpoints besides the narrator's, thereby stimulating the reader to form an impression "independently." This call for collaboration from the reader, common enough now, was innovative then, of course. In an earlier novel, La sombra (The shadow), the narrator begins by expressing his wish to set the record straight as far as the protagonist's true character is concerned; the latter's reputation as a madman is a mistake, it is claimed. While conflicting opinions on what someone is like may be taken for granted in everyday life, they present a delicate issue in fiction, where the context requires that the actors function coherently; that is, in keeping with plot, structure, and other elements.

Who are "the good" and "the bad" in Galdós' fiction? Even his most extreme types, such as the saintly Guillermina and the sinful Mauricia in Fortunata and Jacinta, resist definitive classification. Usually, Guillermina may be labeled saintly, but in her weaker moments of spiritual imperfection we are reminded of how very human she is; and her saintliness is perhaps more convincing for not being artificially sustained throughout the long novel. Similarly, Mauricia has moments of goodness and generosity when it would be impossible to regard her as a symbol of evil.

Fortunata's, not the narrator's, view of these characters is the simplifying one.

And she herself alternately acts as saint, then sinner. Her irregular conduct provokes others to brand her, and because their values differ, the labels collect. Those who obey the demands of conventional middle-class Spanish society (the Samaniego women, Estupiñá, Doña Lupe) call her a devil; those who respect society's order, but with less personal commitment (Feijóo, Guillermina) do not consider her angelic, but neither do they condemn her: she violates laws that they too reject, although inwardly; those who openly defy society (Mauricia, Maximiliano) consider themselves in extreme terms but fluctuate in their opinions of her; and those who experience her blind love or hope to (Juanito and Segismundo) idealize her. Fortunata herself, during most of the story, is persuaded that she is bad, incorrigibly bad; in the last volume, however, breaking out in anguished claims of innocence, she repeatedly affirms her angelic nature. And there is a moment at the very end when her angelic quality—unselfish love—is proclaimed in eulogistic tones by Segismundo Ballester. With words that seem to summarize the author's feelings about his literary heroine, Ballester tells a friend how he envisions Fortunata, adding that she is "an angel, an angel in disguise." So in the end, Galdós yields to the sublime, his realism gives way to romanticism. But how subtly! The idealization, or crystallization, is the work not of the narrator but of the only character whose grief permits the excess. That his first name should be that of the protagonist of a Renaissance drama by Calderón, *La vida es sueño* (Life is a dream), seems intentional. Segismundo's dream, like Ballester's image, fixes a final picture in the reader's mind. If the narrator had ventured the lofty comparison, it would have been inconsistent; he has shown the futility of moral classifications all along the way in his story.

Dostoevsky, like Galdós, delves into the workings of the psyche, and his novels present our darker motives so graphically (and convincingly) that superficial aspects of the self can even seem unworthy of depiction. Dostoevsky is interested in the maze beyond the mirror, whereas Galdós, like Stendhal, is more interested in the mirror itself, in reflecting as clearly as possible the engrossing surface of life. That Dostoevsky's interest is almost more psychological than esthetic (though the two are perhaps irrevocably intertwined) is evident in his use of point of view; discrepancies about a character serve more to indicate an essential multiplicity in the one than to indicate diversity, realistically. (Mikhail Bakhtin's use of the term polyphony is crucial for understanding in critical language what the Russian novelist demonstrates in his art.) Galdós is curious about the multiplicity in both senses (constitution of character plus opinions about him), whereas Dostoevsky tends to concentrate on the multiple interior more than the views of it. Also, Dostoevskian characters do not reappear; change signifies differently in his fiction.

A third technique I would like to mention is an important one in *Fortunata and Jacinta*: biographical versus abiographical presentation. Stephen Gilman has treated this in his excellent study, "The Birth of Fortunata" (in *Galdós and the Art of the European Novel: 1867–1887*, Princeton University Press, 1981), in which he traces the antecedents of Juanito Santa Cruz, pointing out their formative influence and contrasting the lavish frame for the male protagonist with the lack of one around Fortunata's sudden entrance in the text. In typical Victorian style, Galdós devotes much of Volume I to a scrupulous study of the antecedents of his male protagonist. We are told everything, which may sound like too much until we realize later in the story the artistic function of the background material. We are spared no names of relatives, no growth periods in the Santa Cruz family history. And once we have been packed with all these facts concerning Juanito and Jacinta, we abruptly meet the real protagonist, Fortunata, who appears to Juanito *ex nihilo*: no last name, no home, no immediate family. The switch is so rapid and radical that we may wonder if Galdós is confronting more than two individuals of diverse social origin. He is; he is uniting literary characters from realms not normally mixed. Juanito, a stereotypical hero introduced in traditional fashion, literally runs into a girl who, within the operative literary conventions, is not "ideal," who cannot, by definition, be a "heroine." Their union is one of the novel's artistic accomplishments: a new type of heroine is born, without vilification or rejection of the old. The novel's title hints at the underlying harmony— Fortunata *and* Jacinta, in alphabetical order, rather than one instead of, or in opposition to, the other.

Creating a new type of heroine in a traditional literary atmosphere naturally affected other elements of the novel too, and each of the ones mentioned previously could be examined in this light. The one that seems most pertinent in introducing a translation is language.

THE TRANSLATION

In *Fortunata y Jacinta*, language is rich. Metaphors, colloquialisms, neologisms, allusions, rhetorical devices, technical vocabulary, linguistic deformations—each could be considered at length. In the process of translating Galdós, it becomes clear that this stylistic wealth largely determines the value of the original. Each character speaks in his or her own way, and the author respects their particular speech patterns by incorporating them all in his book, whose substantial linguistic texture is the result. There is the narrator's elegant prose, precise and engaging; the pretty but empty words from Juanito; the correct yet casual speech of most of the novel's middle-class characters (the Santa Cruzes, the Samaniegos, the Corderos . . .); the exalted style of Ido del Sagrario; Aparisi's affectedness; the comical malaprops and mispronunciations of José Izquierdo; his sister Segunda's marketplace tongue; Mauricia's colorful blasphemies; the nuns' mincing expressions;

Feijóo's verbal economy; Guillermina's graphic speech; Doña Lupe's didacticism; Maximiliano's oscillations between the bombastic and the humble; and Fortunata's linguistic insecurity, which causes her timid use of "proper" speech and consequent lapses into vulgar slang.

Variety, then, is one of the novel's outstanding stylistic features; one of the major difficulties for a translator. Achieving the uniformity of the Spanish text is impossible, of course, because no matter how scrupulously one reflects, the second language is bound to stimulate in the reader associations and connotations that do not fit into the nineteenth-century Madrid captured in the novel's pages. This problem was foremost in my mind when I debated about what type of translation to do. At first, a period piece seemed desirable: if I could relocate *Fortunata y Jacinta*, group it with English Victorian novels, and aim through language at a similar literary atmosphere, retention of the original would be possible, I thought. But while the choice was pleasing in theory, I realized that it would violate what I considered most important: letting foreign readers communicate with Galdós' world as freely as possible. Rather than assemble Victorian equivalents, which might over-Anglicize Galdós' work, I wanted to deliver it as unchanged in spirit as an English version would permit. Just as a writer of fiction creates a suspension of disbelief, I hoped to be able to create a suspension of unfamiliarity with certain of the work's foreign aspects. The issue is a delicate one, because in Galdós there are several types of familiarity and unfamiliarity at play. I have mentioned his wish to reach a foreign audience, together with the fact that he was read mainly by a most unforeign public. The proximity of his contemporary readers made a familiar tone viable: their acquaintance with the countless details of Spain's sociopolitical panorama gave the author a chance to chat comfortably with them from his pages, assured of their shared context. An English-speaking reader sits in a very different chair, though; for us, Galdós' world is full of novelties, exotic elements, unfamiliar customs, etc., many of which are simply extraneous material in need of some sort of explanation.

Besides the difficulty of recreating the familiar air of the original in a period piece, there was the problem of slang. To do his style justice, the translation would have to include a multitude of metaphorical expressions, but finding and handling Victorian equivalents seemed out of the question. I finally chose to do a modern translation, not exactly contemporary, but free enough of period flavor that a reader today (for several decades?) could sense a "nowness" in the English version. Naturally this choice implied considerable relativity. Certain modern expressions were inappropriate because they referred to things like lunar trips, communes, cars, etc. (Analyzing current slang, one realizes the force of technology on contemporary language.) I have attempted a mixture in this area (colloquial language), hoping to leave the characters a little bit more room by not Anglicizing them excessively and consequently causing them to sound like somebody else. Reading a modern translation of Homer's *Odyssey* years ago, I was amused yet disappointed to hear the nurse speak exactly like an Irishwoman I knew; the pronunciation, vocabulary, and style all seemed to belong to that distinctly Irish person, not to Homer's ancient character.

Attempting a mixture meant losing vividness, and the prospect was not encouraging. Why translate an author if you suspect that the results will not be pleasing? The question is usually followed by the logical reaction: what can be saved outweighs the loss.

After the basic decision came minor ones. Among these, there are five I would like to mention. The first is the least tangible, the least perplexing technically, but, nevertheless, a difficulty: the psychological gap between certain features of Spanish and their counterparts in English. The distinction between *tú* (you, familiar form) and *usted* (you, formal) is expressive in Spanish, and in *Fortunata y Jacinta* it plays an important part in the characters' speech, especially at the end of Volume II and during Volume III, when Fortunata uses *usted* with someone she had previously addressed as *tú*. In the original, the pronoun alone signals their changed relationship, whereas in the translation an explanation is necessary. Another distinction made in Spanish but lacking in English is between the two forms of "to be": *ser* (permanent) and *estar* (temporary). Also, there are nuances of the subjunctive mood that simply do not translate.

The second point is names and nicknames. Perhaps only the Russians have as much enthusiasm as the Spanish for names. Volume I sometimes reads like a registrar, which can be trying for a twentieth-century reader until it becomes clear that all the names are necessary to permit a full view of the protagonists' genealogical trees. Names are sometimes hard, too: long in many cases, followed by compound last names, or nicknames resisting a convincing American equivalent. This point merits some reflection, because like many novelists, Galdós gives his characters expressive and frequently symbolic names.

The Santa Cruz names may be treated collectively. Each generation displays a particular linguistic pattern. Baldomero and Barbarita, the parents' names, both start with *B* and consist of four syllables, accented on the third. The children constitute another pair. Their names both start with *J* and have three syllables, accented on the second. This similarity could have been mere chance, but whether it was or was not doesn't really matter: it affects our impression of the Santa Cruz family, described several times as "more like two couples" than a family with a daughter-in-law, or two couples in separate realms, or father and son plus wives, or some such combination. Indeed, the tight phonetic symmetry leaves no space for the desired heir. When he does come, his name will not fit the pattern; it will be the beginning of another. Observation of the vowel structure in these four names reveals the same symmetry: *a-o-é-o* and *a-a-í-a*, and *a-í-o* and *a-í-a* (*i* being the vowel that suggests littleness, moreover, because of its frequent use in Spanish diminutives). When we recall Juanito's confession (his love for Jacinta is inhibited by his childhood memories of her as a sister), the twinning of their names acquires a significance enforced by the fact that Juanito's best friend's name is Jacinto.

Juan*ito* Santa Cruz is a little Don Juan; that is, not a grand seducer. Jacinta, or "Hyacinth," is as pure as the flower after which she is named; the most common metaphor attached to her is "angel," and the blue and red of the flower are the traditional colors of the Virgin's robes. (Outwardly, the symbolism seems simple; for a careful probing of this character's structural importance in the novel, see Harriet S. Turner's essay, "Family Ties and Tyrannies: A Reassessment of Jacinta," in *Hispanic Review* (Winter 1983). And the surname Santa Cruz? It is ironic. In the growing capitalism of the late nineteenth century, business was becoming the "holy cross" (*santa cruz*) of the bourgeoisie, and money its God. The Santa Cruzes' fortune was built on Baldomero's religious devotion to work, work that eventually yielded a perfect "end product": Juanito Santa Cruz. Galdós emphasizes Juanito's perfection in Volume I, leading us to expect marvels of him. Soon, however, we see that he who has been given everything will give nothing in return.

"Nothing" is probably the key word for Fortunata. Unintroduced and unexpected, she simply appears, standing near a staircase sucking on a raw egg, the origins of life in a powerful visual symbol. Fortunata, an uncommon name in Spanish, combines two ideas: born (*nata*) of chance or fortune (*fortuna*). Marginal in the early design, she eventually becomes the center. The dramatic meaning of her first name together with the omission of a surname add to her archetypal quality, and this seems to have been intentional on Galdós' part, because he names her relatives more fully. The last name shared by her Aunt Segunda and Uncle José is Izquierdo (left), and this offcenters them.

Proceeding from Fortunata's relatives to their friends, we come to José Izquierdo's pal, José Ido del Sagrario. Translated literally, his last name means "gone from the sanctuary." The religious overtones are strengthened by the two men's first name, José (Joseph, father of Jesus). "Gone" in the head, Ido suffers from a persecution complex and fabricates rambling erotic novels that grow out of his hunger and neurotic suspicions about his weary wife, Nicanora. The humor in these names is rich in the original. Artists fight over Izquierdo, a model who "does heroes and saints" (once the saintly Guillermina discovers his vocation); his laziness leads him to call all work except holding a pose "inappropriate to his dignity." And his nickname, Platón, means both Plato and "big plate."

Plays on words are deliciously rampant, as are interrelated meanings. Two main clusters of names remain: Guillermina's and her nephew's, and the Rubíns'. Scholars have documented that Guillermina was named after a saintly bourgeois lady of Madrid, Ernestina Manuel de Villena. Galdós seems to have split her main attributes between two fictional figures: Guillermina Pacheco, merciful founder of charitable institutions, and Manuel Moreno-Isla, personification of bourgeois luxury and atheism. Together, their names evoke that of the real life model: Guillermina/Ernestina, Manuel/Manuel, and Moreno/Villena. The equation is not complete, though (Pacheco has no correlation), nor is the symbolism. Late in the novel, Moreno, who has long enjoyed the hedonistic escape of life in England as a wealthy bachelor, returns from that *isla* (island) and confronts poverty (or, rather, is moved by it for the first time) when a beggar, to stir the rich man's soul, thrusts his stump at him. The incident prompts Moreno to self-inquiry, and he discovers that in addition to romantic failure he is filled with awful loneliness. He turns to Guillermina and her faith, there is a brief but aborted attempt to unite the extremes, and the denouement, true to Galdós' vision of character, ensues.

The head of the Rubín family, the widow Doña Lupe, is Señora de Jáuregui to acquaintances and "the turkey woman" to friends. The narrator designates her frequently with this nickname, which fits into the novelistic organization of bird imagery. Of Doña Lupe's three nephews, the eldest needs little comment—Juan Pablo is a common name and his is a minor role. The second nephew, Nicolás, is a priest, but, unlike his namesake Saint Nicholas, he prefers receiving to giving. That Fortunata's counselor and corrector should be the voracious, slovenly Nicolás, and that one of his clerical friends should be called León Pintado (painted lion), hints at Galdós' satire on the clergy. (An earlier version of the manuscript dubs the priest Anacleto, which reveals that the author's original intention was to treat Fortunata's reform more soberly.) The youngest nephew is Maximiliano, Maxi for short. Filled with visions of military splendor and dazzled by the figure of the Emperor Maximilian of Austria, poor Maxi's daydreams distress him when he must accept his sickly constitution and prosaic life, which includes being taunted even by the little servant in his house, Papitos. In him Galdós touches the essence of the pathetic and the sublime in us all, showing how grand dreams can mock achievements and even endanger existence. Aspiring to everlasting love, Maxi is crushed by his own disproportionate passion.

Connected with names is a third difficulty: exclamations. Personal names have connotations that apply, in varying degrees, to the characters who bear them. Exclamations pose a different kind of problem; they may refer to an unfamiliar background, something requiring an explanation (for example, games, saints' lives, jokes, local history, etc.); some obvious reality in Spanish but one that loses force if it enters the English reader's mind through a footnote.

The fourth difficulty is deformation of language. The most outstanding example is the surrealistic dialogue between Izquierdo and Ido in Volume I in which the heap of curses, colloquial terms, drunken mispronunciations, misnomers, puns, partial quotations, and made-up words is astounding. Sustained imitation of such speech is possible, but can become tedious. Fortunately, Galdós provides entertaining samples rather than an exhaustive reproduction of such verbal aberrations. Reading this dialogue, I was reminded of one of Balzac's characters, the Baron de Nucingen (in *Splendeurs et misères des courtisanes*), whose German accent is represented orthographically and in italics. The solution is convincing, but after the first few lines, the invasion of italics and strange phonetics disturbs the reading process. There are many passages in *Fortunata y Jacinta* with such irregularities, and I have tried to render them as faithfully as I could.

The fifth and last point is hyperboles. For a translator into English, the language of the understatement, Galdós' generous use of the hyperbole presents a problem of gradation: how much can the English ear tolerate without finding that it is uncalled for, given the specific content of a scene or statement? This question arose in my mind again and again, each time, in fact, that a superlative sounded too superlative, or the use of "always" and "never" became, or seemed to become, too endemic. Wishing to reflect, not criticize or interpret (although of course any act of translation implies interpretation), to retain stylistic texture, I also found that the process of encoding in English required that I measure the effect of such hyperboles in the psychic space occupied by English. A slight attenuation seemed preferable.

These, then, were the main difficulties. Precisely because it bristles with challenges, Galdós' language is a pleasure to translate, regardless of the final results. Hardly ever is there a page in his novel that could have been simultaneously interpreted adequately, because Galdós is hardly ever conventional.

What lies beyond the translation itself and yet must be considered, even if only sketchily, is the historical background, because it is pertinent.

HISTORICAL BACKGROUND

The chronological time covered, the novel's present, can be stated quite precisely: December of 1869 to the year 1876. These years, like most of the nineteenth century in Spain, were turbulent; there had been a succession of civil wars, pronunciamentos, conspiracies, coups, etc., and the political unrest can be felt in Galdós' novel.

In September of 1868, a revolution dethroned Queen Isabel II, and at the end of the year, the Federal Republicans rebelled against the provisional government. When members of the courts were elected in 1869, they drafted a new constitution (the most liberal one the nation had ever had) and established a regency that was to last until the new king was crowned. It was not easy to find one, but finally the Duke of Aosta, under the name of Amadeo I, was proclaimed king of Spain. Three days before he arrived in Spain, General Prim, head of the government and the strongest supporter of the new king, was assassinated.

The reign of Amadeo I was short and stormy: he arrived in Madrid on January 3, 1871, and on February 11, 1873, he abdicated, convinced that it was impossible, at least for him, to control the incessant machinations of both the Monarchists and the Republicans, to save the economy, and to end the civil war.

On the same evening that Congress accepted Amadeo I's abdication, the Republic was proclaimed; but for the same reasons that the king had failed, and due to further dissensions among political parties, the Republic was short-lived. Four presidents took office in less than a year. On January 3, 1874, General Pavia and his troops attacked Congress. General Serrano took over as head of state. The continuous wars and conspiracies impeded political and economic stability, and Spain's progress was negligible during these years.

During General Serrano's rule, a new conspiracy (whose members included both civilians and the military) formed and began to gain popularity, especially among the Conservatives. On December 29, 1874, General Martínez Campos proclaimed a new king of Spain: near Valencia, in Sagunto, the young son of Queen Isabel II was crowned as Alfonso XII (his posthumous son, Alfonso XIII, was the grandfather of King Juan Carlos, the present head of state). The pronunciamento was the beginning of the Restoration, whose political head was Cánovas. On January 9, 1875, the new king arrived in Barcelona, and on January 14, 1875, he entered Madrid. This is the Restoration to which Galdós alludes frequently.

In *Fortunata and Jacinta*, as in several other of the author's novels, notably *La de Bringas* (The spendthrifts), parallels may be drawn between certain characters and historical figures in the background, just as the novel's events sometimes reproduce on a smaller scale larger events recorded in history. Galdós was interested in the effects that a political situation can have on men's thoughts, actions, and very essence. But this point, like many others mentioned, deserves ample study elsewhere. My sole purpose here has been to introduce Galdós, his novel, and his times and to supply a bit of relevant material about the book, so that whoever opens it may feel oriented enough to enjoy reading it.

AGNES MONCY GULLÓN

VOLUME ONE

VOLUME ONE

1. Juanito Santa Cruz

I

THE OLDEST INFORMATION I HAVE on the person who bears this name comes from my friend Jacinto María Villalonga, and it dates back to the time when he and other friends (among them Zalamero, Joaquinito Pez, and Alejandro Miquis) were at the University. They weren't all in the same class, and although they did study under Camús together, they split up in Roman Law: the Santa Cruz boy studied under Novar, and Villalonga under Coronado. Nor were they equally studious. Zalamero, with the sense and care that characterize few, was the kind of student who sits in the first row looking up with a contented expression and nodding in discreet agreement to everything being said by the professor. On the other hand, Santa Cruz and Villalonga always sat at the back of the lecture hall wrapped in their cloaks, looking more like conspirators than students. They would spend the time making remarks under their breath, reading novels, doodling, or whispering the day's lesson to the one the professor called on. One day Juanito Santa Cruz and Miquis took a frying pan (I don't know whether it was to Novar's classes or Uribe's, on metaphysics), and they fried a couple of eggs. Villalonga has an impressive repertoire of these pranks, but I won't record them here so as not to delay our story. The whole group, except for Miquis, who died in 1864 dreaming of the glory of Schiller, was thoroughly rambunctious in the famous riot on the Eve of San Daniel. Even Zalamero, the calm one, lost his self-control on that noisy occasion, catcalling and screaming like a savage, for which he earned himself two slaps from a veteran cop—but nothing more than that, fortunately. Villalonga and Santa Cruz had a worse time of it. Villalonga was left with a saber wound in his shoulder that incapacitated him for two eternal months, and Santa Cruz was picked up near the corner of the Royal Theater and hauled off to a police station along with various other "respectable students" and some bonafide bums. For over twenty hours they kept the poor fellow behind bars, and his captivity would have lasted even longer if his papá, a most respectable and well-connected citizen, hadn't gotten him out the next day.

The fright all this gave Don Baldomero and Barbarita Santa Cruz can scarcely be imagined. What an anguished night, from the 10th to the 11th! Both thought they would never again see their beloved baby, their only child, whom they treasured and coddled with the boundless pleasure of parents whose attachment was senile, although they weren't actually old. When Juanito finally came home, pale and hungry, his charming face awry, his clothes torn and smelling of the streets, his mamá couldn't decide whether to scold him or shower him with kisses. The distinguished Santa Cruz, who had gotten rich honorably in the textile business, was a somewhat reserved member of the old progressive party, but not a member of the riotous new faction, because Olózaga's and Prim's anti-dynastic tendencies were not to his liking. His group had their club in the parlor of a friend and relative where Don Manuel Cantero, Don Cirilo Alvarez, and Don Joaquín Aguirre met almost every night, and Don Pascual Madoz joined them occasionally. So Don Baldomero could not, in view of this, be suspected by the authorities. I think it was Cantero who accompanied him to the Department of the Interior to see the minister, González Bravo, and the latter started the wheels turning to grant the revolutionary, the anarchist, the shirtless Juanito his liberty.

While the boy was in the final years of his studies, one of those critical changes so common at that age took place in him. Mischievous and unruly, he suddenly became so calm that he outdid even Zalamero. He suddenly had a compulsion to perform his scholarly duties religiously and to improve himself further by reading voraciously and engaging in heated debates and discussions with his friends. Not only did he go to class ever so punctually and armed with notes, he also sat in the first row to take in every word, never letting his gaze wander for a second, like an adoring fiancée, approving of the professor's explanations with slight nods of his head as if to say, "Oh yes, I *know* what you mean, and more, too." When class was over, he was the type who stops the departing professor to consult him on an obscure point in the text or to express a doubt of his own, thereby declaring his frenzied interest the way such students usually do.

When he was away from the University, his thirst for knowledge bothered him considerably. In those days it still wasn't customary for precocious scholars to go to the Atheneum. Juanito would get together with other fledglings over at Gustavito Tellería's, where they had great rows. The finer points of philosophy, history and law, metaphysics and other speculative sciences (experimental studies weren't in style yet, nor was transformationalism, Darwin or Haeckel) were to them what tops and kites were to their peers. What strides of progress there have been in the amusement of the young! When one stops to think that those same youngsters, had they lived in ancient times, would have gone around sucking their thumb, or doing and saying all sorts of silly things . . .

All the money Juanito received from his father he took directly to Bailly-Baillière, to pay for the books he was constantly buying from that store. Villalonga recalls that one day Barbarita appeared there, bursting with satisfaction and pride, and after paying the bill her child had run up, she told them to give him whatever bulky volumes he wanted, even if they were expensive and as big as Church Bibles. The kind and angelic lady tried to curb the expression of her maternal pride. She feared that if she let the supremacy of her son over all sons, born as well as unborn, show, she might offend others. And she didn't wish to degrade that special, intimate feeling of hers (which we could call "Barbarita's maternal mysteries") by making it public. Nevertheless, it did come to light occasionally, as when apparently out of carelessness she let escape exclamations like these: "Oh, what a boy! . . . He reads so! Heads like his must have something, yes, something, which others lack. Oh well, it might as well be this."

Santa Cruz took his degree in law, and then went on to earn another in liberal arts. His parents were very rich and didn't want their child to go into business, nor was there any reason why he should—they themselves were no longer in the commercial world. Just after completing his studies, Juanito underwent another major change, a second growth crisis, the kind that marks the mysterious transition from one stage to another in an individual's life. He lost his enthusiasm for those furious oratorical debates in which he had defended a mere degree of difference in opinion on some point of philosophy or history. He began to think it was ridiculous to have taken such pains to prove that "in Oriental civilizations the power of the sacerdotal castes was slightly more unlimited than that of the kings" to Gustavito Tellería, who maintained while banging his fist on the table that it was "very slightly less." He also began to think that it made no difference at all whether or not "consciousness was the total intimacy of a rational being with himself," or some such notion that Joaquinito Pez, swelling with angry conviction, wanted to prove. So it wasn't long before he got bored with his compulsive reading and reached the point of reading nothing. Barbarita believed in all seriousness that her son had stopped because he had drunk dry the fountain of knowledge.

Juanito was twenty-four then. I met him one day at Federico Cimarra's, at a lunch he gave for friends. I've forgotten the exact date, but it must have been around 1869, because I remember a lot of talk about Figuerola and his reforms and other events from that period. Don Baldomero's son was very good-looking and likeable, the kind who get by on their looks before captivating with their personality and who make more friends in an hour of conversation than others who actually do favors. Because of his appealing way of saying things and his charming opinions, he seemed to know more than he really did. Paradoxes from his lips sounded more beautiful than truths. He dressed elegantly and had such good manners that it was easy to forgive him for talking too much. His education and extremely sharp wit put him head and shoulders above the rest of the group, and although at first glance he bore a certain resemblance to Joaquinito Pez, once you made their acquaintance profound differences were noticeable. The Pez boy, beneath his frivolity and garrulity, was a blundering fool.

Barbarita worshiped her son, but her discretion and delicacy kept her from praising him in front of friends; she was afraid other women would be jealous. While this maternal passion made Barbarita ineffably happy, it also awoke anxieties and suspicions in her soul. She feared that God would punish her for her pride; she feared that her beloved son would fall ill overnight and die like so many others of lesser physical and moral worth. After all, there was no reason to believe that his merit would make him immune. Quite the contrary. The grossest, ugliest, and most perverse of men are the ones who gorge themselves on life; not even death seems interested in having anything to do with them. Barbarita's shield against the storm that these ideas stirred up was her ardent religious faith. As she prayed, an inner voice, an exquisite murmuring (her guardian angel gossiping, she fancied), whispered that her son would not die before she did. The care that that good lady lavished on her boy was elaborate, yet it did not reach that overniceness that makes the affection of some mothers an obnoxious obsession for whoever has to witness it and harm for the creature who experiences it. She did not spoil her son. She used her tenderness wisely, frequently clothing it in gentle severity.

And why did everyone—as almost everyone still does—call him Juanito Santa Cruz? God knows. In Madrid you hear a lot of this use of a diminutive or a nickname, even for people who are well along in years. Until just recently, the illustrious author of *Pepita Jiménez* was addressed by his friends (and some who weren't his friends) as *Juanito* Valera. In Madrid society, the most pleasant in the world because it knows how to blend courtesy with informality, there are some Pepes, Manolitos, and Pacos who even after achieving a celebrity of sorts are still referred to with this democratic familiarity that testifies to the simplicity of the Spaniard's soul. Perhaps this has to do with the Spaniard's home atmosphere, or perhaps it comes from his humble manners, which somehow extend into society. In some people's names, the diminutive can be related to their destiny. There are, indeed, Manuels who were born to be Manolos till their dying day. Whatever the reason, people called Don Baldomero Santa Cruz' and Doña Bárbara Arnáiz's fortunate son Juanito, and Juanito is what he is called now and will always be called, perhaps until his hair turns gray and the people who knew him as a child pass away, gradually causing the comfortable custom to change.

Knowing the person and his happy circumstances, it should be easy to understand which direction young Santa Cruz's thoughts took when he saw himself on the threshold of life with so many possibilities of success. Nor should it surprise anyone that a good-looking man, master of the arts of pleasing and dressing, an only child of wealthy parents, an intelligent, educated, and seductive talker with ready replies, witty and spontaneous in his judgments—a young man, in short, whom society would label "brilliant"—should conclude that it was useless and even ridiculous to ascertain whether or not there once existed a single primitive language, whether Egypt was a Brahmanic colony, whether China was absolutely independent from a particular Asian civilization, along with other subjects that had robbed him of sleep for several years but no longer mattered to him, especially when he reflected that whatever he himself didn't figure out, somebody else would. "And anyway," he would say, "let's suppose that these matters never are laid to rest. So what?"

The tangible world seduced him more than studying, which was an incomplete knowledge of life, rarely attained in a brilliant flashing of ideas from the brain or in sparks flying from the percussion of the learner's strained will. Juanito ended up declaring in private that he who lives *not wanting to learn* knows more than he who *wants to learn without living.* Living was relating to others, enjoying and suffering, desiring, hating and loving. Reading was artificial borrowed life, benefiting from ideas and sensations transmitted cerebrally, acquiring the treasures of human truth by purchase or swindle, not by work. Juanito's philosophical theories didn't end here; he made another comparison that was not wholly inaccurate. He claimed that the difference between these two ways of living was like the difference between eating a chop yourself and having someone tell you how and when someone else ate it, making the story a really good one of course—describing the expression on the person's face, his pleasure from chewing the meat, his satisfaction upon swallowing it, and then his placid digestion.

2

A new season of fear soon began for Barbarita. If her prayers had once acted as lightning rods to keep typhus and smallpox from striking Juanito, they now endeavored to free him from other no less atrocious enemies. She dreaded the scandals caused by unpleasant involvements, passions that ruined one's health and degraded one's soul, awful extravagances, moral, physical, and financial disorder. The worthy lady resolved to remain firm and keep a close watch over her son. She became prying, fault-finding, nosy. Sometimes sweetly, sometimes with a harshness she could not suppress, she inquired into the young man's activities, jabbing him with questions such as, "Where are you off to now? Where have *you* been? Why were you out until three in the morning last night? How did you spend the thousand *reales* I gave you yesterday? Hmmm, what's that rubbed off on your face, perfume?" The delinquent acquitted himself the best he could, plundering his imagination for answers that would have some semblance of logic even though they had to be formulated in a flash. He became an expert at half-truths, at categorical replies dipped in wheedling and flattery. He knew the enemy's soft spot only too well. But Barbarita, who had as much spunk as heart, held her ground and knew how to ward him off. Sometimes the onslaught of affectionate gestures was so fierce that the dear mother found herself on the verge of surrendering, worn out from her disciplinarian staunchness. But oh no, she was *not* about to give in. She went right back to her guns, quizzing him, taking note of every step her little pet had taken across the dangerous zones of society. To be truthful, I must add that Juanito's whims weren't anything out of the ordinary. In this, as with all evils, our progress has been so great that the pretty boy's rakish act of fifteen years ago would strike us as rather mild or even exemplary today.

It was about this time that our charming young man was given the opportunity to make his first trip to Paris, where Villalonga and Federico Ruiz were also being sent, commissioned by the government, the former to buy farming equipment and the latter to purchase astronomical instruments. Don Baldomero thought the trip was a fine idea—the boy would see something of the world. Barbarita didn't oppose it, although the mere thought that her son would experience stormier times in the French capital than he had in Madrid mortified her greatly. Added to her grief at not seeing him was her fear that he would be exploited by the French and those femmes fatales who were so clever at skinning a foreigner and casting a spell on even the most level-headed young man. She knew very well that over there they were masters of the art of taking advantage of human weaknesses and that Madrid, compared to Paris, was a city of abstinence and suffering. Thinking this over one day, she grew so sad and envisioned so vividly her beloved son's imminent perdition and the horrible nets that would catch her inexperienced boy that she left the house resolved to beseech divine mercy with the greatest solemnity of which she was capable or, rather, which her means permitted. First she decided to have the priest at San Ginés say lots of masses, and when this didn't seem quite enough, she came up with the idea of ordering His Divine Majesty to be put on display for the duration of her child's stay in Paris. Once she was inside the church, she reconsidered her plan; the display might be carrying it a bit far, and for the same reason would be irreverent, perhaps. No, she would save this last resort for a serious case—illness or mortal danger. As for the masses, though, she stood her ground: she ordered heaps of them, and she also gave more alms than usual that week.

When she confessed her fears to Don Baldomero, he laughed and said, "He's a good boy. Let him have some fun and get around. Today young men need to wake up and really see the world. These times aren't like mine, when no boy from a merchant's family got to go anywhere; they kept us tucked in till they married us off. What a difference between customs then and now! Civilization, my dear, is just so much talk. What father would think of slapping his twenty-year-old today because he had worn his new shoes on a workday? Or would you even dream of suggesting to one of these fellows that he should say the rosary with the family? Young people today have a freedom and a right to have fun that they didn't have years ago. And believe me, don't think they're any the worse for it. If you really want to know how I feel, I think it's better for boys not to be as bashful as they used to be. I remember when I was a kid. God, what a simpleton! I was already twenty-five and still didn't know what to say to a woman or a lady except 'Have a nice day.' And no one could get me past that. After all, I spent my whole childhood and the better part of my youth in the store and the warehouse. My father was so strict we weren't allowed to make a single mistake. So that's the way I grew up, that's the way I turned out: full of ideas about righteousness and hard work. Ideas! Humph! That's why I believe so much now in getting a few knocks. They were my real teachers. As for social graces, I was a savage. Since my parents didn't allow me to associate with anyone except other boys who were as prudish as I was, I never got into any kind of mischief or saw a woman except from a distance. I didn't know any games, and couldn't talk about anything that was normal and fun. On Sundays my Mamá had to put on my tie and stick my hat on my head because my best clothes seemed to be anxious to get off my body. You remember, don't you? And you, you laughed at me too! When my parents informed me—just like that, out of the blue—that I would be marrying you, cold shivers ran up and down my spine. I still remember how I dreaded you. Our parents gave it to us all cut and dried. They married us off like cats. It turned out well in our case, but more often than not this way of making families turns out miserably. What a laugh! Tp think that what frightened me most when my mother spoke about my getting married was the fact that I had to talk to you! I didn't have any choice, I *had* to say something to you. Holy smokes, what a sweat I was in! I remember wondering what I could say; the only thing I knew was 'Have a nice day.' Other than that I was lost. I've already told you dozens of times about the bitter drool I had to swallow—God above!—when my mother ordered me to put on my black corduroy frock coat so she could take me to your house. I guess you'll never forget my famous frock coat, how bad it looked on me and how awkward I was in your presence, incapable of uttering a word unless someone helped me. For the first few days you filled me with absolute terror, and I would spend hours thinking about how I would walk in and what I would say, plotting schemes that would make my silences seem less ridiculous. You may say whatever you wish, dear, but that upbringing was not good. Today you can't bring up children like that. What can I say? I don't think Juanito will fail us in what counts. He's well bred, it's in his blood. That's why I'm not worried and don't disapprove of his waking up to the world, of acquiring some savoir faire."

"Well, the last thing my son needs is savoir faire. He was born with it. It's not that. It's not a question of manners or savoir faire, but of those vultures devouring him."

"Look, dear: if young men are going to learn to resist temptation and vice, they have to get to know them, have a taste of them; yes, dear. There's nothing worse for a man than to spend half his life dying for a taste and not being able to, either because he's shy or because he's imprisoned at home. There aren't many cases like mine, you know, a fellow who never had an affair with a woman, either before or after getting married. No, there are very few. Every man's a product of his times. Juanito, in his, couldn't be any better than he is, and if you insist on making an anachronism or a curiosity piece out of him, like his father, you might destroy him."

This reasoning did not convince Barbarita, whose *idée fixe* was the dangers and pitfalls of the Parisian Babylon. She had heard all sorts of horror stories about what happened there. The great city was swarming with attractive and elegant women who looked like duchesses at first glance, dressed in the prettiest and latest fashions. But when you got a bit closer and heard them, they turned out to be drunken and money-hungry, gluttons and harpies who skinned and drained whatever poor creatures fell into their clutches. She had heard these things from the marquis of Casa-Muñoz, who went abroad every summer.

That peerless lady's afflictions came to an end with Juanito's return. And who would have guessed it! He came back looking better than ever. All that fuss about Paris, and just when Barbarita was expecting to see our little Juanito looking a sorry sight, all emaciated and anemic, she finds him handsomer and brighter than before, with better color, eyes livelier, much happier; in short, more manly, and with such a breadth of ideas and such a discerning mind that he left everyone speechless. Paris, eh? The marquis of Casa-Muñoz explained it to Barbarita: "Let's keep things *straight*. Paris is very bad, but it's also very good."

II. Santa Cruz and Arnáiz

A Historical View of Madrid's Business World

I

DON BALDOMERO SANTA CRUZ was the son of another Don Baldomero Santa Cruz who at the turn of the century had owned a fabric store on Sal Street, at the same location occupied subsequently by Don Mauro Requejo. Our Baldomero's father had started out on the lowest rung of the commercial ladder, but ten or fifteen years into the new century, the clerk of 1796 became, by dint of hard work, perseverance, and orderliness, the head of one of the royal city's most reputable firms dealing in domestic and imported fabrics. In 1848, Don Baldomero II (which we must dub him in order to distinguish him from the founder of the dynasty) inherited the substantial warehouse, solid credit, and Don Baldomero I's highly respectable firm, and after keeping up its traditions for twenty years, he retired with the tidy sum of fifteen million *reales*, turning over the business to two young men employed there, one a relative of his and the other of his wife's. Since then the firm has been known as "Santa Cruz and Nephews" and Don Baldomero and Barbarita fell into calling these nephews "the boys."

During the reign of Don Baldomero I, from the beginning until 1848, the firm dealt more in domestic than imported fabrics. Escaray and Pradoluengo stocked them with certain materials, the baize came from Brihuega, and wool scarves from Antequera. It was toward the end of this first reign that the firm began to deal in fabrics "from the outside," the customs reform of 1840 spurring Don-Baldomero on to bigger ventures. He not only drew up contracts with the Béjar and Alcoy factories in order to give domestic products a better chance, he also introduced the famous *Sedanes* for frock coats, and the fabrics that sold so well from '45 to '55, those serge wools, linsey-woolseys, and chinchillas illustrated in histories of modern tailoring. The firm made its biggest profits on its line of capes and uniforms sold to the army and the National Guard, although it also made a considerable amount on "the stuff for capes," the typical Spanish overcoat that has weathered all changes in fashion, just as the garbanzo has persisted on Spanish tables. Santa Cruz, Bringas, and "Tubs" Arnáiz had a monopoly on Madrid's fabric business; they supplied all the shop owners on Atocha, Cruz, and Toledo streets.

However, none of these gentlemen—neither Santa Cruz, nor Arnáiz, nor even Bringas—signed his name to the contracts written up with the army and the National Guard. The contractor who turned up was a Belgian named Albert who had started out in Spain by bringing in foreign fabrics without much success. This Albert was just the right man for the contracts: active, alert, and reliable in his deals, even though they weren't in writing. He was Casarredonda's extremely efficient assistant in the valuable contracts on the Galician linen bought for the troops. The white pants soldiers wore forty years ago have been the source of immense fortunes. In fact, the bales from Coruña and Viveros brought more money to Casarredonda and Albert than the wide capes and military frock coats from Béjar earned the Santa Cruz and Bringas families, although to be completely honest, the latter didn't have much to complain about. Albert died in '55 and left a huge fortune to his daughter, married to Muñoz's heir, owner of the immemorial hardware store on Tintoreros Street.

During the reign of Don Baldomero II, the commercial practices strayed very little from the inherited routine. An advertisement in the paper was unheard of, and traveling salesmen who could extend the sales to nearby provinces were not employed. The motto that "good things sell themselves" was as true as the gospel in that solid, reputable business. Retailers didn't have to be snared or bamboozled with a charlatan's tricks. They knew only too well how to get to the store, its methodical and honest customs, its steady prices, the discounts available if payment was prompt, the installment periods, and all the other details necessary for a good state of affairs between salesman and customer. The accounting desk never altered certain venerated traditions passed on from the laborious reign of Don Baldomero I. They never used those letter copiers that mechanically reproduce handwriting. Correspondence was copied by hand, the hard way, by an employee who sat for forty years in the same seat at the same lectern, and had learned to copy an entire letter after a mere glance at the original. Until Don Baldomero put the business in his nephews' hands, no one in the store knew how much a meter was; they had stuck to the traditional measurements. And until a few years before the change in ownership, Santa Cruz didn't use envelopes; a letter was folded so that the reverse side showed the address.

Such routine practices were not a sign of stubbornness and backwardness. On the contrary, the second Santa Cruz's intelligence and common sense fostered his belief that every man belongs to his own times and milieu and should act exclusively within those limits. He understood very well that business would undergo a profound transformation and that he would not be the one to guide it along the broader avenues that were opening up. For this reason and because he was anxious to retire, he handed the business to "the boys," who were indebted to him and had clerked there for twenty years. Both were hard-working and very intelligent. They alternated on trips abroad for novelties, the soul of the fabric trade. Competition got tougher every year, and they had to think up new ways to attract customers, to receive and send out buyers, to pamper the clientele, and to let the steady customers, especially the female ones, open long-term accounts. Since "the boys" had also begun to deal in flannel, merino wools, light fabrics for ladies' dresses, scarves, ready-made items, and other articles of feminine use, they opened a retail shop that sold by the yard. This forced them to experience the inconvenience of the delinquencies and insolvencies that hamper business so greatly. Luckily for them, the firm had excellent credit.

The store that Tubs Arnáiz owned was relatively modern. He had become a clothier in order to sell the bolts of material Albert had given him to pay off a loan in 1843. He dealt exclusively in imported fabrics, and by the time Santa Cruz left his business to "the boys" Arnáiz was inclined to do the same; he was already quite rich, obese, old, and beyond any desire to work. As it was, he handled bills of exchange with London and represented two insurance companies, which was enough to keep him from getting bored. He was an excellent person—a rabid freetrader, and Anglophile, and a bachelor who shook the building with his coughing fits. There was never any rivalry between the Santa Cruz and Arnáiz firms; they helped each other as much as possible, behaving like brothers in social life and very dear companions in the trade, except for an acrid argument every now and then on importation problems. Arnáiz had taken it into his head to read Bastiat and visit the stock exchange, not exactly to listen quietly, but to give a speech that almost always disintegrated into a choking cough. He attacked any tax that tended to keep out foreign goods, whereas Don Baldomero, always the moderate, tried to reconcile conflicts between trade and industry. "Those Catalonians don't make anything except stuff that shows bad taste," Arnáiz would object between coughs, "and they hand out sixty percent dividends to the stockholders."

"Good Lord, there you go again," Don Baldomero would reply. "Well, I can prove that . . . "

He usually didn't prove anything, and his friend didn't either; each stuck to his own opinion. But they did while away the time relishing their arguments. These two respectable gentlemen were also related by marriage. Doña Bárbara, Santa Cruz's wife, was a cousin of Arnáiz and daughter of Bonifacio Arnáiz, the one with the Chinese shawl business. A scrutiny of their family trees would quickly disclose that the very same sap, the Trujillo sap, ran through various branches of the Arnáiz and Santa Cruz families. "We're all alike," Arnáiz once said in one of his more festive, expansive moods, which brought out his democratic sincerity. "We're both bonafide Trujillos—you on your mother's side and me on my grandmother's. We're descendants of Matías Trujillo, who owned the packsaddle shop on Toledo Street back in the days of the cloak and dagger revolution. I'm not making it up, I have the documents at home. That's why I told our relative Ramón Trujillo yesterday—who, as you probably know, has been made a count—I told him to use a yoke and a headstall for a coat of arms and write underneath it, '*I belonged to Babieca, El Cid's great horse.*'"

2

Barbarita Arnáiz was born on Postas Street, on the corner of San Cristóbal Lane, in one of those dreary rowhouses that look more like shoe boxes because of their miniature scale. You could touch the ceiling with your hand and had to climb the stairs with your heart in your mouth; the rooms seemed to be destined for the premeditation of some sort of crime. Some of the dwellings had to be entered by way of the kitchen, others had slanting floors, and all were so thin-walled that you could hear the neighbors breathing. In some you could see the masonry supporting the staircase, and the excessive plaster in the construction was as obvious as the scarcity of iron and lumber. Four-panel doors, blurry tiles, useless locks, and leaded glass windows were typical. Many of these defects have disappeared in renovations during the last twenty years, but the cramped dimensions persist.

Barbarita grew up in an atmosphere redolent of sandalwood and Oriental fragrances and saturated with the vivid colors of Chinese shawls, all of which strongly influenced her childhood impressions. In fact, she cherished sweet memories of two Oriental figures whom she still loved as if they had been members of the

family: the two life-size mannequins dressed as mandarins that stood in the store.
Looking at them, her eyes learned to see. When she was still in her nursemaid's
arms, the first thing to stimulate the baby girl's visual concentration were these
two hulking figures with their blank, insipid faces and their magnificent mulberry-
colored robes. And there was another person in the store, too, whom the child
used to stare at and who gazed back at her with eyes full of Chinese candor. It was
the portrait of Ayún, full-length and life-size, drawn and painted crudely but very
expressively. In Spain this foreign artist's name is not well known, although his
works have been and still are in plain sight, as familiar to us as works by our own
artists. He is the genius of embroidery in Manila shawls, the inventor of the most
striking and elegant type of branched flower designs, the extremely fertile poet of
those madrigals in crêpe de chine composed in flowers and rhymed in birds. Spanish women owe to this illustrious Chinaman the very handsome, characteristic
shawl that suits their beauty so well, and also the embroidered silk Manila shawl,
as majestic as it is common, worn by great ladies and gypsies alike. Wrapping this
shawl around one's shoulders is like dressing up in a painting. Modern industry
will never invent the likes of the naive poetry in this flower-splashed shawl, flexible yet smoothly clinging, its silken fringe reminiscent of the tangles of a daydream, its brilliant colors once making entire crowds sparkle when it was in style.
This beautiful garment is gradually being exiled. Only the common people, with
their admirable instinct, have saved it, taking it out of trunks for the big occasions
in life, baptisms and weddings; just as when one sings a joyful hymn to the wind, a
stanza is devoted to one's country. Such shawls would be vulgar garments if they
contained only the science of design; they are not, because they preserve something of primitive and folk art, like legends or stories from childhood, candid and
richly colored, easily understood and resistant to the whims of fashion.

And yet this garment, this national work of art that has come to seem as
Spanish as tambourines and bulls, is not really ours at all, except for our use of it.
We owe it to an artist who was born on the other side of the world, a man named
Ayún who devoted his entire life and all his labors to us. The good fellow was so
grateful for the trade we gave him that he sent his Spanish sales agents a portrait
of himself, and then, later on, portraits of his fourteen wives, some of them stiff
pale ladies like the kind painted on teacups, with incredibly tiny feet and incredibly long nails.

Barbarita's faculties developed with the contemplation of such images, none of
which impressed her more than the embroidered flowers done in bright cord; they
looked so fresh you could almost see the dew on them. When a great many were
sold, on days when ladies crowded the store and clerks unfolded hundreds of
shawls on the counter, the gloomy place turned into a garden. Barbarita used to
think that handfuls of flowers could have been gathered to make bouquets or
wreaths to fill baskets and decorate her hair. She used to fancy that if the outer

leaves were plucked, the flowers would actually have a scent. And it was true in a way, because they did give off that slight fragrance which Asiatic packings have, a mixture of sandalwood and exotic resins that evoke Buddhist mysteries.

Gradually, the little girl began to appreciate the beauty and variety of the fans, one of the main sources of the shop's income. She was awed to see her mamá's swift fingers lifting them out of their perfumed boxes and opening them as most dealers of this item do, with a clever carelessness that without damaging the fan, allows the viewer to see its lightness and hear the soft clicking of its ribs as it is opened. Barbarita would look on like a rabbit, all eyes, as her mamá, having sat the child on the counter, showed the fans—no touching, now. She was enchanted by those lovely figures who didn't look like regular people at all, but like Chinese: their round, smooth faces like tiny rose petals, all of them smiling inanely, but so pretty, just like their houses, open on all sides, and their trees, which looked like basil shrubs . . . And to think that those little trees made tea, of all things, and their twisted little leaves had the juice you took for a tummy ache!

Afterward, other charming objects claimed first place in the tender heart and innocent dreams of Don Bonifacio Arnáiz's daughter, objects that her mamá showed her from time to time, always admonishing her not to touch. They were carved in ivory, and must have been the kind of toys angels had in heaven. There were multidecked towers, tiny boats with unfurled sails and lots of oars sticking out from either side; there were also tiny cases and boxes for gloves and jewels, and darling little chess sets. The respect with which her mama took them out and put them away made Barbarita think that they must surely contain something like the viaticum given to dying people or whatever people are given in church when they receive Communion. Many nights she'd go to bed feverish because they hadn't let her satisfy the urge to pick up those adorable things herself. She would have been content—being so strictly forbidden to do anything—just to touch the top of one of the towers with the tip of her finger, but not even that was allowed . . . The only thing she was allowed to do was to touch the chessboard in the grilled window (there were no display windows then) and arrange the pieces of that particular set—not the most delicate ones, either; only the white ones that were red on the back.

Barbarita and her older brother Gumersindo were Don Bonifacio Arnáiz's and Doña Asunción Trujillo's only children. When she was old enough, she went to Doña Calixta's school, located on Imperial Street, where the Fiel Contraste* was. The two little girls who became her best friends were her age, and both came from the same neighborhood; one was from the Moreno family (who owned the pharmacy on Carretas Street) and the other was a daughter of Muñoz, the hardware

---

*This was an office that officially checked weights and measures used by all types of merchants in Madrid.

merchant on Tintoreros Street. Eulalia Muñoz was very vain, and used to say that there was no store like theirs and that it was wonderful to see it, all full of iron things that were so big, "as big as Doña Calixta's cane," and so, so heavy that not even five hundred men could pick them up. Then there were thousands of hammers, hooks, kettles, "so, so big . . . bigger than this room." And as for the packets of nails—what could be nicer? And the keys, they looked like silver; and the irons and the braziers, and other great stuff? She claimed that she didn't need her parents to buy her dolls because she could make them out of hammers and dress them up with towels. And as for the needles in their store: you couldn't even count them, there were so many. Everyone in Madrid went there to buy needles from them, and her papá and the manufacturer wrote important letters to each other. Her papá got thousands of letters every day, and the letters smelled of iron. They came from *England*, where everything's made of iron, even the roads. "Oh yes they are, my papá says so. The roads are paved with iron, and the carriages go speeding over them and sparks fly everywhere."

Her pockets were always stuffed with gadgets that she used to show off to dazzle her friends. She had gold-headed tacks, hook-and-eye snaps, gun-metal rings, buckles, scraps of sandpaper, leftover samples, and other broken or damaged items. But what she treasured most, and for this reason didn't take it out except on certain days, was her collection of labels, small pieces of green paper removed from useless packages that bore England's famous coat of arms—the garter, the lion, and the unicorn. On all of them was written "Birmingham." "See? This Mr. *Birmingán* is the one who writes my father every day, in English. And they're such good friends that he's always telling him to come see him, and just a little while ago he sent my father a smoked ham that smelled sort of burned, right with the nails, and also a huge meat pie as big as this, look, as big as Doña Calixta's brazier, and it had lots of teeny raisins in it, and it was hot as a Guinea pepper but it was so good, m-mm."

The Moreno girl staked her vanity on scraps of paper with little figures and colored letters that told about pills and varnishes or ingredients for hair dyes. She would show these one by one, but save her best item for last. Suddenly pulling out a handkerchief and thrusting it at the nostrils of her friends, she would say, "Smell it." And indeed, they almost passed out from the strong smell of cologne. Their admiration momentarily silenced them, but gradually they recovered, and Eulalia, whose pride rarely admitted defeat, would produce a headless gold screw or a piece of foil with which she was planning to make a mirror. It was hard to erase the pleasant sensation and success of the perfume. The little ironmonger, somewhat abashed, had to put away her junk after hearing remarks that were really unfair. The girl from the pharmacy would turn up her nose, saying, "Ugh, what a stink, Eulalita. Put those awful things away!"

The next day, Barbarita (who didn't want to be outdone by her friends) brought some very strange pieces of cardboard-backed paper all written over with Chinese-like scrawls. After making a big to do, pretending that she was going to show what she had and then hiding it again—all of which increased the others' curiosity to the point of nervous irritation—she suddenly thrust the paper at her friends' noses, exclaiming triumphantly, "And how about *this?*" Castita and Eulalia were overwhelmed by the Asiatic fragrance, wavering between admiration and envy. But finally they had no other choice; they had to swallow their pride when Arnáiz's little girl produced that faint scent, and they begged her for another whiff. Barbarita didn't like to squander her treasure, so when she had scarcely put the paper under their snubbed noses, she withdrew it with a cautious and greedy movement, fearful that the fragrance would disappear into her friends' respiratory organs like smoke up a chimney flue. The suction of those olfactory systems was powerful. Eventually, her two little friends, along with others who had approached them out of curiosity, and even Doña Calixta herself, who deigned to be friendly with her richer pupils, admitted, above all feelings of envy, that no one had nicer things than the girl from the Philippines shop.

3

On May 3, Barbarita and other little girls from the neighborhood, all dressed up by their respective mamas (their hair combed in the Maja style with a back comb and flowers, Manila shawls, the fitted type, draped over their shoulders), gathered in the entrance hall of an apartment house on Postas Street to collect for a charitable association, the Cruz de Mayo. The donated coins chinked onto the silver tray on the red damask-covered table. The house, called "The Portico of the Virgin" because of the owners' well-known devotion to the Virgin Mary, was the scene of a lively fiesta that day. It was being held next to the entrance to the workshop, where spoons and coffee mills were made; the owners had set up an altar and a cross adorned with branches, many candles, and some nativity figures. They had also decorated the Virgin (still worshiped there) with aromatic herbs, and the spoon-maker, who was from Galicia, was wearing his regional cloth cap and red vest. If the kids could catch the grown-ups off guard, they'd break the rules and run out into the street in fierce competition, skipping from one sidewalk to the other, stopping the gentlemen passing by and harassing them until they got the prized penny. We've heard Barbarita herself say that there was nothing she liked better than collecting for the Cruz de Mayo, and that gentlemen were much more gallant about it in those days than they were now, because they would never ignore any well-dressed little girl tugging at their coattails.

Bonifacio Arnáiz's daughter had already completed her education, which was simple enough in those days (consisting of reading aloud in an expressionless voice, writing without knowing how to spell, reciting her numbers, and embroidering on a sampler), when she lost her father. Serious occupations followed his death, strengthening her soul and making her character more substantial. Her mother and brother, aided by Tubs Arnáiz, started to take inventory, for the business was not exactly in good order. The books lacked accurate figures to confirm how many shawls were in stock, and, upon counting them, they discovered more than they had expected. In the cellar there were several unopened crates, dead as doornails. In addition to this, the Cádiz import firms of Cuesta and Rubio announced that two fair-sized shipments were already on the way. There was nothing they could do except take on all that excess material, a true obstacle at a time when ready-made overcoats seemed to be growing in popularity and there was a tendency among the lower classes to imitate the middle class. The Manila shawl was on its way out. The fitted shawls, which were the cheapest, were selling fast in Madrid (especially on San Lorenzo Day) and had a ready market in Valencia and Málaga, while the great shawls, the rich shawls that cost three, four, or five thousand *reales*, hardly sold at all; months would go by without a single client asking for one.

Upon taking inventory of the firm's assets (which totaled no less than fifty thousand *duros* in shawls alone) Arnáiz's heirs realized that a crisis was imminent. They spent three or four months classifying, ordering, pricing, checking Don Bonifacio's notes against the correspondence and the bills of sale sent directly from Canton and forwarded by the branch stores in Cádiz. The late Arnáiz had no doubt used poor judgment in sending out so many orders. He must have been enthralled by some sort of financial hallucination; or perhaps his "love for the product" had been too ardent, and he had behaved more like an artist than a businessman. He had been a clerk and a member of the Philippines Company, liquidated in 1833, and when he started handling Cantonese shawls and materials himself he thought he knew the business better than anyone. As a matter of fact, he did; but he put too much faith in the perpetual appeal of that garment and certain superstitious ideas about the Spanish people's taste for those splendid crêpes with their multicolored branched designs. "The gaudier they are," he used to say, "the better they sell."

Meanwhile, in the Far East, a new artist appeared, a genius who truly impressed Don Bonifacio. This innovator was Senquá, of whom it may be said that he was to Ayún in the art of Chinese embroidery what Beethoven was to Mozart in music. Senquá modified Ayún's style by giving it more breadth, varying the tones, in short: by turning those graceful, poetic, and elegant sonatas into powerful symphonies made of new combinations and an admirable vitality. Seeing the first samples of Senquá's style and being overwhelmed were one and the same for

Don Bonifacio. "This is heaven above!" he exclaimed. "This man is *really* Chinese!" And the consequences of this enthusiasm were his imprudent orders and serious miscalculations, but the excellent man was not destined to witness all this, for death took him first.

The inventory of fans, Nipponese cloth, raw silk, Madras weaves, and ivory objects revealed very high figures in that category too, and it was done minutely. All the beautiful things that had seemed like toys to Barbarita in her childhood and had been so exciting passed through her hands now. In spite of her maturity and consequently better judgment, she could never look dispassionately at these knickknacks; even today she declares that if one of those delicate ivory bell-towers happens to come into her hands, she feels like stashing it away or running off with it. By her fifteenth birthday, Barbarita had become a very pretty girl: nicely curved, fresh and rosy-cheeked, with a humorous, restless, somewhat playful nature. She hadn't had a boyfriend yet, nor would her mother permit it. Several young bucks pursued her, but in vain. Mamá had *her* plans, and she began to pull the right strings to execute them. The Santa Cruz and Arnáiz families were on nearly intimate terms and, what's more, had family ties with the Trujillos. Don Baldomero I's wife and the late Arnáiz's wife were second cousins, flowery branches from that knotty trunk, the packsaddle-maker on Toledo Street whose story Tubs Arnáiz knew so well. The two cousins had a happy thought that they exchanged, amazed to discover that it had been mutual. "Of course, it was so natural . . . " And congratulating each other, they resolved to turn it into a joyful reality. All the descendants of the man from Extremadura, the specialist in "donkey equipment," distinguished themselves by their way of drawing a very short, straight line between idea and action. The idea was to wed Barbarita to Baldomerito.

Arnáiz's daughter had seen Santa Cruz's son many times, but it had never crossed her mind that he was to be her husband, for not only had the boy never breathed a romantic word to her, he didn't even look at her the way a person who wants to be looked back at does. Baldomero had good judgment and a good complexion; he was very good-looking and well-built. He was also very dull, a wet noodle really, and so nearly incommunicative that you could count the words in his vocabulary. His shyness didn't go with his hefty looks. He had a loyal and affectionate expression in his eyes, "the kind a huge spaniel has." He was the personification of honesty, and went to Mass whenever the Church required it; he even said the rosary with the family. He worked over ten hours a day without ever looking up from his desk, and never spent the money his parents gave him. Despite these rare qualities, Barbarita, if she ever ran into him in the street, in the Arnáiz shop, or at home (which hardly ever happened), considered him as interesting as a sack of coal or a bundle of cloth. So she was dumbfounded when her mother—on their way home together from the Santa Cruz church where they had gone to confession and Communion on a religious feast day—proposed that she marry Baldomerito. And her mother didn't beat around the bush or try to be diplomatic. She went straight to the heart of the matter in plain language, decisively . . . the famous Trujillo straight line.

Although Barbarita had a good mind, ready answers, and an ability to ignore anything that bothered her, in this grave situation she went limp and was too embarrassed to tell her mama that she couldn't care less about Santa Cruz's son. She was prepared to say so, but her mother's face suddenly looked like stone. She saw that short, straight line, that Trujillo steel, where her mother's brow was, and the poor girl was afraid, oh, so afraid! She knew only too well that if she dared to suggest any notions of her own concerning her future husband, her mother would greet them savagely. So she didn't say a word, keeping as quiet as she did in church, and to whatever her mama said that day and the next few days on the subject of the instant marriage she replied with humbly acquiescent signs and words. She probed the depths of her heart, where she found both sorrow and consolation. She didn't know what love was; she only had a hunch. The truth was that she didn't love her fiancé. But neither did she love anyone else. If it was a case of loving someone, then it might as well be Baldomero.

The strangest part of it was that once the wedding was arranged and Baldomero was seeing his fiancée regularly, he didn't have a single romantic word for her, even though her mama's brief absences (which were of course intentional) gave him the opportunity to shine in his courting. Not a word. The handsome dullard was incapable of anything except the most trivial, routine conversation. His shyness was as ceremonious as his black frock coat, Sedan's best, which on him looked like an advertisement for the store's quality fabrics. He would talk about the gas lamps that the marquis of Pontejos had installed, the cholera epidemic that had broken out the year before, the beheading of the priests, and the many magnificent houses that were going to be built on the sites of demolished convents. It was all fine for a *tertulia** at the shop, but it sounded like the droning of a fly in the heart of a young lady who, not being in love, at least wished to be.

Hearing her fiancé talk, Barbarita mused that it must all be happening inside, and that, despite seeming so grown-up and being so large, the poor boy didn't *have* a soul to show. "Does he love me?" she would ask herself. Soon she was to discover that if Baldomero did not speak explicitly about love, it was simply because he was bashful and didn't know how to break the ice. Actually, he was head over heels in love, but he was confining his declaration to delicate gestures, his compliance, and his punctuality, all of which were most expressive. Without a

---

* A *tertulia* is a conversation group; it may either form spontaneously or gather at regular intervals at an agreed time and place. Usually, *tertulias* in Spain are at cafés, although formerly they were held in the shops.

doubt, the most sublime love is the most discreet, and the most eloquent lips are those that nothing can unseal. Yet the young girl could not calm herself with this sort of reasoning, and her fright and uncertainty kept her on pins and needles. "What if I love him too, without even knowing it?" she wondered. "Oh, no!" Questioning and answering herself in all truthfulness, she discovered that she did not love him at all. True, she didn't hate him either, so we are getting somewhere.

Several months of this incredibly insipid engagement passed, after which Baldomero relaxed a bit and began to perk up. Little by little, his lips were unsealed until there finally burst from them, as if from a ripened chestnut, their tasty fruit. Chestnut after chestnut burst open, elaborate thoughts that he had guarded religiously, just as nature hides her budding life. Finally, the day set for the wedding, May 3, 1835, arrived. They were married in the Santa Cruz church without any fanfare and moved into the husband's house, one of the best in the neighborhood, on Leña Square.

4

Two months passed. Then, after a short spell during which Barbarita appeared somewhat distracted, melancholic, and on the verge of tears, to the great alarm of her mother, the marriage that had been arranged under such unfavorable conditions began to show signs of being idyllic. Baldomero was a new man. He hummed at his desk and was always looking for an excuse to leave, to go home and chat a bit with his wife, whom he would grab in the hall or wherever he found her. He also made mistakes in his accounting, and when he signed correspondence he gave the lines of the store's traditional rubric a grandiose flourish, stroking upward as if expressing his gratitude to the heavens. He hardly ever went out, and told his close friends that he wouldn't trade places for all the world with a king, or with his famous namesake General Espartero, because there was no happiness like his. Through her discreet contentment, Barbarita made it clear to her mother that Baldomero didn't give her the slightest reason to complain, that their temperaments were harmonizing perfectly, that he was pure gold and that he was quite talented, with a talent that showed itself when it should, on the right occasions. She couldn't stay at her mother's for more than ten minutes without becoming intolerably restless; she would look for excuses to leave, saying, "I've got to go now, my husband's all alone."

The idyll became more noticeable every day. Barbarita's mother finally remarked (disguising her satisfaction), "But dear, at this rate, Romeo and Juliet won't be anything next to the two of you." The couple went out for a walk every afternoon. Don Baldomero II was never seen at the theater without his wife. Every day, every month, and every year, they seemed more like lovebirds, and it was true: their love and mutual respect did nothing but grow. After years of marriage, they looked as if they were on their honeymoon. The husband has always treated his wife as if she were a sacred creature, and Barbarita has always seen in her husband the most complete man, more deserving of love than anyone else in the whole world. Understanding how those two temperaments meshed so well and how the miraculous union of those two souls came about would take a long time. Sr. and Sra. Santa Cruz, who are still alive, and may they thus continue for a thousand years, make the happiest and most admirable couple of the century. Their names should be inscribed in gold in the insipid halls of religious institutions as eternal models for future generations; in fact, there ought to be a law that whenever a priest reads Saint Paul's epistle, he include a short paragraph in Latin or Spanish about this sublime married couple. Doña Asunción Trujillo, who passed away in 1841, a sad day in Madrid because General León was executed the same day, left this world with the bold thought that to attain everlasting glory, she needed only to claim authorship of this Christian marriage and make sure that Juana Trujillo, Baldomero's mother (who had died the year before), did not dispute her glory. Asunción was prepared to prove to the celestial chanceries that *she* had had the sublime idea before her cousin.

Neither time nor life's petty concerns ever weakened this blessed couple's profound and mutual affection. When they both had gray hair Don Baldomero was still telling anyone who would listen that he loved his wife "as if it were the first day." Together on their walks, together in the theater, neither enjoyed a performance if the other didn't see it too. They celebrate each day that marks some fortunate family event by exchanging little presents, and to top it off, they're both in splendid health. Sr. Santa Cruz's last wish is that they die together on the same day and at the same time, in their conjugal bed.

I met them in 1870. Don Baldomero was already seventy, Barbarita was fifty-two. He was a very nice looking gray-haired gentleman, cleanly shaven, ruddy-cheeked, fresh, more youthful than many men at forty. His teeth were all in fine condition. He was in good form, even-tempered, generally cheerful, and yet always had a doleful look that made him vaguely resemble a Saint Bernard. His wife, to be quite frank, struck me as attractive; I'd even say adorable. Her face had the freshness of a rose just gathered, not yet wilted, and the only cosmetic she used was clear water. She still had ideal teeth and a figure that even without a corset made many a conceited lady who hid her fat look pitiful. Her hair had turned completely white and was more becoming than it had been while it was graying. It looked like powdered hair à la Pompadour, and since it was so curly and well parted from her forehead, quite a few people claimed that underneath there was no gray at all. If Barbarita had been conceited, she would have been able to trim her fifty-two years down to thirty-eight very easily without anyone being the wiser, because her face and expression were youthful and graceful, lit up by a smile that was pure honey. Well, I mean if she'd wanted to be conceited with some malicious thought in mind, you know . . . If she hadn't been what she was, a highly respectable and divinely charming matron, you would have seen men buzzing around her like flies around fruit that's just beginning to wrinkle because it's so ripe, with its nectar running out onto the skin.

And Juanito?

Well, Juanito had been expected from the very first year of that peerless marriage. The happy couple expected him to turn up one month, the next, and the one after that, and they envisioned his coming and wished for it just as the Jews had awaited their Messiah. Sometimes they despaired at his delay, but their faith restored them. After all, sooner or later he had to come, it was just a question of patience. And the little rascal really tried them on that score, because he spent ten years out there tantalizing them. He presented himself to Barbarita only in dreams, in various childlike stances—nibbling on his clenched fists, or his face in a lace-trimmed bonnet, or as a slim boy with a toy shotgun over his shoulder and mischief twinkling in his eyes. Finally, when husband and wife were beginning to complain about Providence and say that they had been cheated, the Lord delivered him in flesh and blood. It was a day of jubilation, that September day in 1845 when Juanito Santa Cruz appeared, taking his place in the happiest of homes. The baby's godfather, Tubs Arnáiz, said to Barbarita, "Don't try to pull the wool over my eyes. There's something fishy here. You've sneaked him in from the orphanage and you're tricking us . . . Ah, these protectionists are only smugglers in disguise."

They brought him up luxuriantly, with exquisite care but without spoiling him. Don Baldomero didn't have the willpower to restrain his boisterous paternal affection or to stick to educational discipline and bring up the boy the way he'd been brought up himself. If his wife had permitted it, Santa Cruz would have reached the point of letting the boy have his way all the time. And why, having been brought up so strictly by Don Baldomero I, was he so soft with his son? It was a consequence of the evolution in education, which paralleled the evolution in politics. Santa Cruz had hardly forgotten his father's disciplinary rigor: the punishments he'd been dealt and the denials he'd been made to suffer. Every night of the year he had had to say the rosary with the firm's employees. Until he was twenty-five he never went out alone, only if accompanied by those employees. He didn't get a taste of the theater except at Easter, and they had a new suit made for him once a year that he didn't wear except on Sundays. They kept him working at his desk or in the warehouse from nine in the morning until eight at night, and he had to take his turn at everything, whether it was moving crates or writing letters. At nightfall his father used to fly off the handle at him for having lit the four-wicked oil lamp before it was completely dark. As for games, he never learned any except one, a card game called *mus*, and his pockets didn't know what a small coin was until long after he'd started to shave. It was work, work, work. But the funny part about it was that while Don Baldomero thought that such a system had been extremely effective in bringing *him* up, he considered it deplorable when it came to his own son. It wasn't a logical inconsistency, but a practical consecration of the reigning idea of the times: progress. "What would become of the world without progress?" Santa Cruz reflected, and when he did, he felt like letting his son follow his instincts freely. More than once he'd heard the economists who went to the *tertulia* at Cantero's repeat the famous words *laissez-aller, laissez-passer*. Tubs Arnáiz and his friend the economist Sr. Pastor held that all great problems work themselves out, and Don Pedro Mata shared this opinion, applying this "self-healing" to society and politics. Nature cures itself; you only have to let it happen. The powers of regeneration do it all, helped by the air. Man educates himself because his conscience, aided by the social environment, constantly plants assumptions in his mind. Don Baldomero didn't say it in so many words, but his vague ideas on the subject boiled down to a fashionable expression, heard constantly: "The world goes on."

Luckily for Juanito, there was his mother, in whom heart and mind were beautifully balanced. She knew how to use discipline when there was need of it, and she knew how to be indulgent at the right times, too. While it never crossed her mind to force a boy already at the University studying metaphysics with Salmerón to say the rosary, she nevertheless did not excuse him from more elemental religious duties. The boy was clearly aware that if he tried to play hooky from Sunday Mass, there would be no theater that evening, and that if he didn't get good marks in June, there would be no pocket money, or bullfights, or trips to the country with Estupiñá (I'll tell you about this character later) to hunt birds with a net or a slingshot, or any other kind of fun that rewarded his studiousness.

During the time he was at the Massarnau school (where he ate at midday), his mother went over his lessons with him every night, stuffed them into his brain by fistfuls, like wool into a cushion. So you can see how the good lady turned into a sibyl, interpreting all the human sciences. She deciphered the obscure points in the books and cleared up all of her son's doubts with whatever God-given explanations dawned on her. To give you an idea of the extent of Doña Bárbara's encyclopedic knowledge (with which her maternal love endowed her), suffice it to say that she even translated his Latin compositions, although never in her life had she studied a word of that language. It's true that it was a free translation or, rather, a liberal, even demagogic one, but Phaedrus and Cicero wouldn't have been displeased if they could have looked over the teacher's shoulder and seen the immense amount she made of the little her pupil knew. She also trained his memory, clearing it of useless clutter, and helped him to grasp the problems of

elementary arithmetic with the aid of garbanzos or beans—she wasn't very comfortable with those abstractions any other way. To explain natural history, the
teacher often resorted to the lion in the Retiro Park. It was only chemistry that
left them both stumped, looking at each other blankly. She ended up by forcing
the formulas to stick to his memory, remarking that only pharmacists understood
such things, and that it all boiled down to whether you put in a greater or smaller
amount of well water. In sum, when Juan finished high school, Barbarita declared
laughingly that with all their ups and downs, she had unknowingly become a
bluestocking and a regular tutor, like Doña Beatriz Galindo, the famous Latin
professor.

5

In this interesting period of the heir's upbringing, from '45 on, the Santa Cruz
business underwent a transformation caused by the times. It was only external,
though; in essence, things continued unchanged. The first gas lamps appeared in
the office and warehouse around 1849, and the famous four-wick oil lamp received
such a critical blow from the hard hand of progress that it disappeared altogether.
The first bank notes issued by the San Fernando Bank were already in the cash
register. They were used strictly for transactions with other merchants, though,
because the public was still wary of them. People talked about hard currency, not
bills, and the operation of counting any sum, no matter how small, was a task fit
for Pythagoras or another great mathematician. What with *doblones, ochentines,*
Catalonian *pesetas,* Spanish *pesetas, duros, onzas,* and the bootleggers' money, it
was an awful mess. Neither postage stamps nor envelopes nor other such marks of
progress were yet to be seen. The employees had, however, already begun to
throw off their shackles. They were no longer the social pariahs they had been in
Don Baldomero I's times, when they weren't permitted to go out except on Sundays and in a group, wearing clothes cut from the same pattern so that they'd seem
uniformed, like schoolboys or prison inmates. Now they were allowed to go to
outdoor dances at Villahermosa or indoor ones by lamplight, whichever they
wished. But there was no liberalizing of that pious atavism: making them say the
rosary every night, a custom that became history only after the business was
turned over to "the boys." As long as Don Baldomero headed the firm, it stuck to
the basics, revolving on the diamantine axis on which it had been set by his
father, whom we may dub Don Baldomero the Great. If progress did manage to
modify the work of that extraordinary man (whose portrait by Don Vicente López
we have contemplated approvingly in his illustrious descendant's living room), it
was because Madrid itself was changing: the government's sale of Church proper-

ties had caused a new city to rise from the ruins of the convents, the marquis of Pontejos—then mayor—was to continue the rehabilitation, the tariff reforms of '49 and '68 turned every business in Madrid upside down, the great financier Salamanca built the first railroad, and, with the help of the steam engine, Madrid was now only forty hours from Paris. There were, in sum, many wars, revolutions, and great upheavals in individual fortunes.

Gumersindo Arnáiz, Barbarita's brother, also saw his business through great crises and changes after Don Bonifacio's death. Two years after his sister's marriage to Santa Cruz, Gumersindo married Isabel Cordero, the daughter of Don Benigno Cordero* and a woman of great ability whose gift for business made her the savior of that accredited firm. In straits from '40 to '45 (a result of the late Arnáiz's final errors), the shop stayed afloat thanks to its nankeen, that fresh, light material that was worn so much till '54. Chinese material was obviously going out. Modernized vehicles were bringing Parisian novelties to Madrid faster and faster every day, and if you looked you could see the beginnings of the slow, tyrannical invasion of mixed or secondary colors, which presume to be a sign of refinement. Spanish society began to flatter itself by fancying that it was "serious," that is to say, it began to dress mournfully: our happy empire of bright colors was plainly fading away. Manila shawls went the way of red cloaks. The aristocracy haughtily relinquished them to the middle class who, wishing to be aristocratic, cast them off to the proletariat, whose loyalty to bright colors was eternal. That sparkle, that prodigious color imitating nature's joy shining in the Mediterranean sun, began to peter out, although the people, with their instincts of colorists or poets, defended the Spanish garment just as they had defended Monteleón Park and the Zaragoza outposts against Napoleon's troops. Little by little, the shawl began to slip from the shoulders of beautiful women; society insisted on looking serious, and there was nothing better for being serious than wrapping oneself in nuanced, melancholic tones. We're under the influence of northern Europe, and the blasted North imposes on us the grays that it gets from its smoky gray sky. A top hat makes any face respectable, and there's hardly a man who doesn't think he's important once he has a chimney stack on his head. The ladies don't consider themselves ladies unless they wear soot, ash, snuff, bottle green, or Corinthian raisin. Bright tones "cheapen" them, they think, because the common people love vermilion, linden yellow, chalk white, and straw green. A love of color is so deeply rooted in the populace that "the serious look" hasn't been able to conquer them unconditionally. They have accepted the somber cloaks because they can at least line them in red. They have consented to those capes without using the hoods, keeping their mantillas and loud scarves as headwear. They have compromised on overcoats and even on the bustle in exchange

*Literally, "benign lamb."

for pastel kerchiefs, mainly light blue, pink, or bright yellow. Crêpe is what has fallen off since 1840, owing not only to the above-mentioned evolution toward the European "serious look" that has swept us off our feet, but for economic reasons that can hardly be dismissed.

Speedy communications brought us messengers from powerful Belgian, French, and English industries that were searching for a market. It still wasn't stylish to hunt for one in Africa, so they came here, giving us glass beads in exchange for gold nuggets or, in other words, light wools, cretonnes, and merino wools for cash or works of art. Other messengers sacked our churches and our palaces, carrying off the antique brocades to be found in the vestments and altar hangings, embroidered tissues and velvets with appliqué work, and other extremely rich samples of Spanish craftsmanship, and, at the same time, they whisked away the splendid Manila shawls that had gradually been handed down to the gypsies. The effects of another commercial phenomenon and child of progress could be felt here, as they were everywhere else. I refer to the huge monopolies that the English were able to develop with the growth of their enormous navy. The effects soon became evident in those humble shops on Postas Street, in the sudden depreciation of Chinese materials. Nothing could be simpler than this depreciation. When the English discovered a great commercial opportunity in Singapore, they monopolized Asian traffic and ruined the business we had along the Cádiz and Cape of Good Hope route to those remote places. Ayún and Senquá, best friends of ours till then, made friends with the English. The successor of those artists, the prolific and inspired King-Cheong, writes to our merchants in English and quotes his prices in pounds sterling. Ever since Singapore became one of the western world's ports, the material from Canton and Shanghai stopped arriving in those heavy frigates built by the Cádiz outfitters: the Fernández de Castros, the Cuestas, and the Rubios. And the lengthy crossing of the Cape, like an appendix to Vasco da Gama's and Albuquerque's fabulous deeds, became history. The new route was traced by English steamboats and the Suez railroad.

By 1840, the shops that received Cantonese materials directly from China could no longer compete with the ones that ordered through Liverpool. Any peddler on Postas Street could stock these items himself, without bothering to rely on the two or three wholesalers left in Madrid. Later on, the trend changed, and after many years, Spain started to send for King-Cheong's works directly; this return to a former practice was a consequence of the pick-up in business after the revolution in '68 and the stabilization of capital that we've seen in our times.

Gumersindo Arnáiz's firm was threatened with bankruptcy; the three or four stores whose specialty was inherited or transferred from the Philippines Company couldn't keep their monopoly on shawls and other Chinese crafts. Madrid was being flooded with material that cost less than what Don Bonifacio Arnáiz's invoices showed, so Gumersindo had to sell out. To make up for having gotten "burned," they had to set up another business quickly and head in another direction. This was where Doña Isabel Cordero, Gumersindo's wife (who had more spunk than he did), showed her special gifts. Without knowing a whit of geography, she understood that there was a Singapore and a Suez Canal.

She guessed what was happening in business, though she couldn't have given it a name, and instead of cursing the English as her husband did, she devoted herself to figuring out the best solution. What trend should they follow? The most marked one was toward novelties, admitting the influence of French and Belgian industries, which obeyed the law of the northern grays—invading, conquering and annihilating our colorful and picturesque character. Dress anticipated thought, and when poetry had not yet been exiled by prose, wool had ripped silk to shreds.

"Well, we might as well face the novelties," Isabel said to her husband, observing the obsession with fashion that this society was beginning to display together with the insistent desire of all Madrilenians to be "seriously" elegant. And on top of that, it was the era when the middle class was beginning to come into its own, taking up the jobs created by the new political and administrative system, buying up all the properties (of which the Church had held the title) with installment plans, thus making itself the chief landowner and beneficiary of the budget; in a word, gathering the spoils of absolutism and clericalism to found the empire of the frock coat. The frock coat is of course the symbol, but the most interesting thing about this empire is the dress of its ladies, the powerful energies that flow from private into public life and decide the course of great events. Clothes, ah! Is there anyone who doesn't see in them one of the main sources of the energy of our times, perhaps even a generative cause of movement and life? Think a bit about what they represent, what they're worth, the wealth and ingenuity that the most industrious city of the world spends on producing them, and your mind is bound to catch, between the pleats of fashionable materials, a glimpse of our whole mesocratic system, the huge pyramid at whose peak sits the top hat: the entire politico-administrative machine, the public debt and the railroads, the budget and the national income, the paternalistic State and socialist trends in Parliament.

But Gumersindo and Isabel had arrived a bit too late. The novelties were in the hands of clever merchants who already knew the road to Paris. Arnáiz went to Paris too, but having no taste, he brought back horrible stuff that nobody wanted. Isabel, however, didn't let her spirits flag. While her husband began to lose his good judgment, she began "to see a few things." She saw that customs were rapidly changing in Madrid; that this proud court city, this indecent country town, would soon become a civilized capital. For all its ridiculous vanity, Madrid was a metropolis in name only. It was a bumpkin in a gentleman's coat buttoned over a torn, dirty shirt. But the bumpkin was about to become a real gentleman.

Isabel Cordero, who was ahead of her times, predicted that water would be brought from the Lozoya during those roasting summers when the Town Hall refreshed and replenished the two main fountains of Madrid, the Berro and the Teja, with its buckets of well water, stored there; when entrance halls of buildings were regular bilges, and the occupants went from one room to another, pan in hand, asking, "Please, can you spare a little water for me to shave with?"

The perspicacious woman saw the future; Bravo Murillo's great project to channel water into Madrid was like something she had already envisioned. Finally, within a few years, Madrid would have torrents of water distributed through the streets and squares and its people would get into the habit of bathing, at least their hands and face. When these parts were washed, the others would follow. She envisioned this Madrid, which was still in the future then: all social classes wearing clean shirts, ladies accustomed to changing their clothes every day, and gentlemen who would be the soul of impeccability. From these visions came the idea of devoting the store to white materials, and once she got a good hold on the idea, it slowly became a reality. With Don Baldomero's and Arnáiz's help, Gumersindo began to order very delicate batistes from England; Dutch, Scottish, and Irish linens; percales; nainsook and Alsatian crêpes; and the firm—not without some effort—began to get on its feet again and eventually enjoyed relative prosperity. Complementing this business that they did "in white" were the heavy damasks, mattress ticking, and the Courtray table linen, which turned out to be the shop's specialty, as a placard affixed to an old sign said. Lace trimmings and machine-made lacework came later, and Arnáiz's orders were so big that one Swiss factory worked exclusively for him. Finally, the business made a good profit on crinolines. Isabel Cordero, who had predicted the Lozoya Canal, also predicted hoop-skirts, which the French called *Malakoffs*, an absurd invention that looked like the product of an overwrought brain that had thought too much about balloons.

All that was left in the shop of the shawls and Asiatic items were some religiously preserved traditions. There were still some little ivory towers and a goodly number of expensive shawls in delightful boxes. In all Madrid, Gumersindo was perhaps the person who had the greatest talent for folding them; and talent it was, for as everyone must know, folding crêpe is as hard as opening an umbrella in the wind. No one could do it except people who had handled the item for a long time, which is why many ladies who wore such shawls to masquerade balls would send them in boxes on the following day to Gumersindo Arnáiz, to be folded in the traditional way: with the criss-crossed border and the fringe hidden and the main design centered on the top fold. The two mannequins dressed as mandarins were also kept in the shop. There was some talk of putting them away, for the poor things looked as if they'd been in some kind of wreck, but Barbarita was against it; not being able to see them there, matching Sr. Ayún's honorable, blank face, would be like burying one of the family. And she guaranteed that if her brother insisted on removing them, she would take them to her house and put them on the sideboard in the dining room.

6

Isabel Cordero de Arnáiz, a truly great woman, had all the gifts of a clever business woman and the shrewdness of a housekeeper. She was also blessed by Heaven with a prodigious fertility. In 1845, when Juanito was born, she already had five children, and she kept on bearing them as regularly as a tree bears fruit. To the first five we must add twelve, arriving at a total of seventeen, births that she remembered by associating them with famous dates in Isabel II's reign: "My first son," she used to say, "was born when the Carlist troops besieged Madrid. My Jacinta was born when the queen was married, give or take a few days. My Isabelita came into the world the very same day that the priest Merino knifed Her Majesty in the back, and I had Rupertito on St. John's Day in '58, the same day the waterworks were christened."

The narrowness of their house suggested that the law of incommunicability of masses was the excuse death used to make that biblical flock dwindle. If the seventeen kids had lived, it would have been necessary to put them out on the balconies like flower pots or hang them in the birdcage with the partridges. Croup and scarlet fever gradually thinned out that plentiful crop, and by 1870 there were only nine left. The first two perished soon after they were born, and from time to time a fully grown one would die, so the rows became more distinctly etched. In one year—I can't recall which—three died at four-month intervals. But those who made it past ten usually grew up quite normally.

I said that nine survived. What I neglected to point out is that of those nine, seven belonged to the female sex. What a plague for poor old Don Gumersindo! What could he possibly do with seven girls? He would need an army to guard them when they grew up. And how could he marry off *all* of them well? Whenever this was discussed, Gumersindo made a joke of it, trusting in his wife, who had a knack for everything. "You'll see," he'd say, "she'll come up with seven first-rate sons-in-law."

His resourceful wife was not quite so sure of this. Whenever she thought of the future awaiting her daughters, she grew sad and felt pangs of remorse for having given her husband a family that was a financial problem. Whenever she talked this over with her sister-in-law Barbarita, she regretted having borne so many females, as if the responsibility had been solely hers. In the course of her prolific campaign from '38 to '60 she always became pregnant four or five months after each birth. Barbarita never bothered to ask her if she was; she took it for granted. "This time," she'd say, "you're going to have a boy." And Isabel would curse her fecundity, replying, "Male or female, these gifts should be for you. God should give *you* a little addition to the family every year."

The firm's earnings weren't paltry, but the Arnáiz couple could not call themselves rich; what with all those births and deaths and that brood of females, the business didn't manage to flourish as it might have. Even though Isabel worked miracles with the budget, the hefty daily expenditures drained the business of most of its sap. Gumersindo never failed to meet his commercial obligations, though, and while he didn't have much capital, neither did he have any debts. The crucial thing was to see that the seven girls were well matched, for as long as this tremendous matrimonial campaign was not crowned with brilliant success, there could be no great savings.

Twenty years ago, Isabel Cordero was an emaciated, pale woman, misshapen, like people who seem to have gone to seed and no longer have their body parts in the right places. You could hardly tell that she had been pretty. People who knew her couldn't imagine her in any state except the one called delicate; a huge belly seemed as normal on her as the color of her skin and the shape of her nose. In such condition and considering she had scarcely any leisure, her activity was remarkable: till the day she fell into bed, she ran around like a chicken with its head cut off, tirelessly managing that complicated household. She worked in the kitchen as well as at the desk; no sooner had she prepared a huge frying pan of crumbs for dinner, or a pot of potatoes, than she would drop in at the shop so that her husband could show her what bills he'd just received or tell her what installments were due. She took special pains to keep her daughters from becoming idle. The younger ones and the boys went to school; the elder ones worked at home, helping their mother mend clothes or alter the father's cast-offs to fit the sons. One of the girls was good at ironing. They also helped with the washing in the kitchen tub, and they darned, and they patched. What they all excelled in was flaunting whatever trinkets they had. On Sundays, when their mother took them out for a walk in a long parade, they were so nicely turned out that it was a pleasure to see them. When they went to Mass, they filed in amidst admiring looks from the congregation, for it must be added that they were very attractive. From the two eldest, who were already young ladies, down to the last of them, who was a tiny thing, they made an extremely interesting bevy, drawing attention because of its unusual size and neat scale. Their arrival prompted acquaintances to murmur, "Here comes Doña Isabel with her sample case." The mother, wearing the simplest hairdo, no adornment whatsoever, flaccid, freckled, and devoid now of any personal charm except respectability, guided her flock like a turkey dealer at Christmas time.

And what straits the poor woman was always in to play that demanding role!

She usually confided in Barbarita. "Listen, some months I go through such agony that I'm fit to be tied. God's watching over me, but if he weren't . . . You just don't know what it's like to clothe seven daughters! The boys, with their hand-me-downs from their father, get along all right. It's the girls! And with the styles we have now, with all they involve! Remember that piece of blue merino wool? Well, it wasn't enough. I had to get ten yards more. And I couldn't begin to tell you about the quantities of shoes! Thank goodness that anybody who tries to wear anything except rope-soled slippers around the house knows that he'll get a piece of my mind. I manage to fill them up on potatoes and breadcrumbs. I've had to cut out stews this year. I know the clerks who eat with us grumble about it, but I don't care. Let them go somewhere else where they'll be treated better. Would you believe that fifty kilos of coal go up in smoke just like that? I bring home ten gallons of oil, and in a few days . . . You'd think the owls had siphoned it off. I have Estupiñá bring fifty or sixty pounds of potatoes and my dear, I tell you, it's as if he hadn't brought any."

There were two tables in their home. At the first sat the head of the house, his wife, the girls, the clerk who'd been with them the longest, and some relative or other, such as Primitivo Cordero when he came to Madrid from his farm in Toledo, where he lived. The second was occupied by the lesser clerks and the two sons, one of whom was an apprentice to Segundo Cordero, whose shop sold blond lace. In short, a total of seventeen or eighteen mouths.

Managing such a household, which would have done in most women, did not visibly tire Isabel. As the girls grew up, their mother was relieved of some of the physical work, but whatever time she gained to rest she spent in extreme vigilance over her flock, which was beginning to be pursued more avidly by wolves and was exposed to countless snares. It's not that they weren't "nice girls," it's just that they were young, and not even God Himself could have avoided their peering out from the only balcony or from the window that gave onto San Cristobal Street. Love notes started to seep into the house, and innocent little intrigues—games of love, not love itself—began. Doña Isabel always watched them like a hawk and never let them out of her sight for a second. In addition to this exhausting maternal espionage, she was obliged to perform yet another task, that of showing off her sample case in hopes of interesting a buyer, that is, a husband. It was necessary to "push the item," and that great woman, dealing in daughters, had no choice but to dress up and appear with her "product" at this or that gathering at friends' houses, because if she didn't, her babies would pout until they became intolerable. The Sunday morning family promenade was part of the ritual too. The girls, neatly attired with more ingenuity than expense; the mama, very stiff in her gloves (which made her fingers useless), which were cut rather long (which made her hands hot), and sporting her good cashmere. Without being old, she looked it.

At long last, in appreciation of the merits of this heroine who never faltered in her social struggle, the Lord cast a benevolent gaze on the sample case and blessed it. The first girl to be married was the second eldest, Candelaria, though to tell the truth it wasn't a particularly brilliant match. The fiancé was a nice boy, a clerk in the haberdashery that belonged to Aparisi's widow. His name was Pepe Samaniego, and his fortune consisted solely of his willingness to work and his proven honesty. His last name was on many signs of small businesses. An uncle of his was a druggist on Ave María Street. One of his cousins was a fisherman, another a tent-maker on Cruz Street, another a moneylender, and the rest, like his brothers, were clerks. The Arnáizes' first thought was to oppose the marriage, but they quickly reasoned as follows: "This isn't the time to be too choosy in this business of husbands. We've got to take whatever we can get, because there are seven to marry off. It's enough that the boy's intentions are good and he's hardworking."

Then the eldest, named Benigna after her grandfather (the hero in Boteros), was wed, and hers was a really good match. Her fiancé was Ramón Villuendas, the eldest son of the famous banker on Toledo Street; his was a great house and a solid fortune. A widower with two sons, his relatives presented a shocking variety in their financial status. His uncle, Don Cayetano Villuendas, was married to Eulalia, a sister of the marquis of Casa-Muñoz, and he had millions. On the other hand, there was a Villuendas who was a tavern keeper, and another who had a hole in the wall where he sold percale and baize, a shop called Good Taste. The relationship between the poor and rich sides of the family was a bit hard to decipher, but relatives they were and many of them got on well together and were on familiar terms.

The third daughter, Jacinta, would catch a husband the following year. And what a husband! But I see that at this point I must snip the thread of my story and return to certain events that precede Jacinta's wedding.

III. Estupiñá

I

IN ARNÁIZ'S SHOP, next to the grilled window that faced San Cristóbal Street, there are three bentwood chairs that years ago replaced a bench covered in black oilcloth, and that bench's predecessor was a large chest or empty box. Here, the store's immemorial *tertulia* had its headquarters. There wasn't a shop without a *tertulia*, just as there couldn't be one without a counter and its guardian angel. This was a supplementary service that business performed for society before there were any casinos. It's true that there *were* secret societies, clubs of sorts, and more or less patriotic cafés, but the great majority of peaceful citizens didn't frequent them, preferring to chat in the shops. Barbarita still has vague recollections of the *tertulia* held there during her childhood. Its members included a skinny priest, Father Alelí by name, a tiny bespectacled gentleman (Isabel's papá), some military men, and other characters whom she confused in her memory with the two mannequins.

Conversation wasn't limited to politics and the civil war; it touched on business matters too. The lady remembers having heard something about the first matches put on the market, and even having seen them. They were like small bottles into which you stuck a wax taper, and when you pulled it out, the thing lit up. She also heard talk about the first pile rugs, the first spring mattresses, and the first railroads, which someone or other in the *tertulia* had seen abroad—there wasn't a hint of them here yet. Something was also said about the new bank notes, which in Madrid didn't become common currency till years later, and then only in big-scale banking. Doña Bárbara remembers seeing the first bill brought to the shop as a curiosity piece and everyone agreeing that a gold ounce was better. Gas came long after that.

The shop underwent a transformation, but the *tertulia* remained the same over the slow course of the years. Some talkers left, others came. We wouldn't know how to date statements such as these, which Barbarita (already married by then) happened to overhear when she stopped in at the shop to rest on her way home from a stroll or shopping: "Weren't the fusileers of the third regiment a great sight this morning with their new pompoms!" "The duke went to Mass at the Calatravas church today. He was with Linaje and San Miguel." "You know what they're saying now, Estupiñá? They say that the English are planning to make boats out of iron."

The man called Estupiñá must have been indispensable to the *tertulias* in all the shops, because when he didn't go to Arnáiz's somebody always asked, "What have you heard about Plácido?" When he appeared, they would receive him with happy exclamations; his mere presence enlivened the conversation. In 1871 I met this man whose vanity rested on his "having seen all of Spain's history" in the nineteenth century. He was born to the world in 1803, and dubbed himself Mesonero Romanos'[*] "birth twin" because they were both born on July 19 of that year. A single sentence of his is enough to prove his immense knowledge of the kind of history one can learn simply by looking around: "I saw José I the same as I'm seeing you right now." And he seemed to lick his chops whenever he replied to a question like "Did you get to see the duke of Angulema and Lord Wellington?" "You bet I did." His answer never varied: "The same as I'm seeing you right now."

---

[*] Ramón de Mesonero y Romanos (1803–1882), Spanish author known chiefly for his writings on Madrid.

He was annoyed if someone interrogated him skeptically. "Did I actually *see* María Cristina when she arrived to marry the king? Why, that was just the other day!"

To substantiate his ocular erudition, he used to talk about "the way Madrid looked" on September 1, 1840, as if it had been a week ago. He had seen Canterac die and Merino being executed—"on his own scaffold, no less"—for being one of those Samaritans who comfort prisoners condemned to death. He had seen Chico (the chief of police) being killed; . . . well, not exactly seen him, but he'd heard the shots from where he was, on Velas Street. He had seen Fernando VII on July 7 when he appeared on the balcony to tell the militiamen to "shake up" the Royal Guard. He had seen Rodil and Sergeant García haranguing from another balcony, back in '36. He had seen O'Donnell and Espartero when they embraced. And Espartero once, greeting the people. And O'Donnell doing the same; all on balconies. And finally, he had seen another historical character on a balcony not long ago, proclaiming in a high-pitched voice that it was all over for the kings. The history Estupiñá knew was written on the balconies of Madrid.

This man's business biography is as curious as it is simple. He was very young when he started out as a clerk at Arnáiz's. He served there many years, always highly regarded by the owner for his unfailing honesty and great interest in everything concerning the firm. Yet despite such virtues Estupiñá was not a good clerk. When he made a sale, he kept the customers too long, and when he was sent on an errand or a commission to the Customs House, it took him so long that in many instances Don Bonifacio thought he'd been put in jail. The reason why Plácido, even with all his shenanigans, was indispensable to the shop's owners was that he inspired blind trust. With him in charge of the shop and the cash register, Arnáiz and his family could forget about the business. Plácido's loyalty was as great as his modesty; they could scold him or insult him all they wanted—it didn't bother him a bit. That's why Arnáiz was very sorry when Estupiñá left in 1837; he'd inherited some money and gotten the idea of striking out on his own. His boss, who knew him well, made dire predictions about the commercial future awaiting Plácido once he was his own boss.

Plácido's outlook was more favorable. He had high hopes for the baize and domestic fabric shop he set up on the Plaza Mayor, next to the bakery. He didn't hire any clerks, because the small scale of the business didn't allow it, but his *tertulia* was the liveliest and most talkative in the neighborhood. Notice here the secret of why the business earned so little, and the justification of Don Bonifacio's prediction. Estupiñá had a chronic, hereditary vice that all his inner energies tried to fight off, a vice that was all the more engulfing and terrible for appearing less harmful than it actually was. It wasn't drinking, it wasn't women, or gambling, or a love of luxury; it was conversation. Estupiñá was capable of letting the best deal in the world slip through his fingers just for a bit of chit-chat. Once he was engrossed in a conversation, the sky might well come crashing down; it would have been easier to cut off his tongue than the thread of his talk. The most frenetic talkers went to his shop, for evil of course attracts evil. If someone came in to buy something during the juiciest part of the session, Estupiñá would glare at him as if the poor soul were asking for a handout. If the material sought was lying on the counter, he showed it to the customer impatiently, hoping that the interruption would soon end. But if it was on a top shelf, he'd look up wearily, like someone begging the Lord for patience, saying, "Yellow baize? There it is. I think it's too narrow for what you need." Other times he doubted or seemed to doubt that he had what they wanted. "Boys' caps? Do you want the kind with an oilcloth visor? I may have a few, but they're not wearing that kind any more."

If he was playing *tute* or *mus*, the only two card games he knew and had mastered, the world could come to an end before he'd take his eyes off his cards. His urge to talk and be sociable was so strong, his body and soul needed it so vehemently, that if talkers didn't come to the shop, he couldn't resist his craving for conversation. He'd lock up, slip the key into his pocket, and go off to another shop in search of the verbal spirits that inebriated him. At Christmas time, when stalls were being set up on the plaza, the poor shopkeeper didn't have the willpower to stay in his dark hole in the wall. The sound of human voices, the light, the murmuring sounds from the streets were as vital as air. He'd lock up and go make conversation with the women in the stalls. He knew all of them, and asked about what they were selling and how things were at home. Estupiñá belonged to that breed of shopkeepers—scarcely extant now—whose dual role in the business world seems to have been that of attenuating the evils created by a surplus market and dissuading consumers from their unhealthy inclination to spend. "Don Plácido, do you have any blue velveteen?" "Blue velveteen? What do you want so much luxury for? Yes, of course I do. But it's too expensive for you." "Show it to me. And how about a discount?" Then he'd make a huge effort, as if he were sacrificing himself and his most cherished ideals to duty, and he would climb up the ladder to get the material. "All right, here's your cloth. But look, if you're not planning to buy it, if it's all just a game, what do you want to see it for? Do you think I haven't got anything better to do?" "Don't you have anything better than this?" "What I always say: these women are enough to drive a saint crazy. Yes, ma'am, there's another kind. Do you want it or don't you? It's twenty-two *reales*, not a cent less." "But let me get a good look at it. Oh, you men! Do you think I'm going to eat the material or something?" "Twenty-two *reales* even." "Humph! You can go to the devil!" "*You* can, you snippy old hag . . . "

He was very refined with upper-class ladies. His affability was evident: "Worsted wool? Yes, of course. Do you see the bolt way up there? It seems to me, madam, that it's not quite what you had in mind; that is, in my opinion. Not that I want to impose my ideas . . . Thin stripes are fashionable now, but I don't have any. I'm waiting for a shipment to arrive next month. Yesterday I saw the girls with Don Cándido. My, they've certainly grown up. And how has the major been lately? I haven't seen him since we were in the tower of the San Ginés church together!"

After four years of this way of doing business, you could count on one hand the people who crossed the shop's threshold in a week. After six years, not even the flies went in. Estupiñá opened up every morning, swept and watered down the sidewalk in front, put on his green sleeve-guards, and sat down behind the counter to read the *Diario de avisos*. Little by little, his real friends arrived, those soul mates who, to Plácido in his solitude, seemed like harbingers; but they brought more than an olive branch in their beaks: they brought him words, the exquisitely delicious fruit and flower of life, the alcohol of the soul that bewitched him. They'd spend the whole day telling stories, commenting on political events and politicians such as Mendizábal or Calatrava, the queen, María Cristina, and even God Himself in familiar terms, outlining campaign routes on the counter, drawing extravagant strategic lines, demonstrating that Espartero simply had to go this way and Villarreal that way, and gabbing about incidents in the business world, the arrival of this or that material, the affairs of the Church, the army, women, and court intrigues, along with everything else that gets into human chatter. Meanwhile, the register wasn't opened once, and the measuring stick, in total peace, was on the verge of sprouting flowers, like Saint Joseph's staff. Since month after month went by without his renewing the stock, there was nothing but shopworn junk there. The shock was hard and sudden: one day his creditors seized everything, and Estupiñá walked out of the shop with as much grief as dignity.

2

The great philosopher did not give in to despair. His friends found him quiet and resigned. He had something of Socrates in his aura, in the calm of his face—if one can imagine Socrates talking for seven hours straight. Plácido had defended his honor, which was the important thing, by religiously repaying everyone with what was left. He didn't have a cent to his name, only the shirt on his back. And the only furniture he salvaged was the measuring stick. So he was forced to look for some kind of job. What could he do? In what line of business could he use his great talents? Turning the question over in his mind, he finally concluded that in his great poverty he nevertheless did have a capital of sorts, a capital that many would surely envy him: his connections. He knew all the wholesalers and shopkeepers in Madrid; all their doors were open to him, and he was well received everywhere because of his honesty, good manners, and, above all, that gift of gab with which God had blessed him. So his connections and these qualities gave him the idea of becoming a fabric seller. Don Baldomero Santa Cruz, Tubs Arnáiz, Bringas, Moreno, Labiano, and other wholesalers of fabrics, draperies, or novelties gave him samples to take around to the shops. He earned a two percent commission on his sales. Good Lord, what a delicious life, and what a splendid idea it had been! Nothing could have been more suited to his temperament than constantly being on the go, coming and going through dozens of doors, saying hello in the street to all sorts of people and inquiring about their families. *That* was life, and all the rest was death. Plácido hadn't been born to stay cooped up in a store. His element was the street, fresh air, discussions and making deals, doing errands, coming and going, making inquiries, shifting gracefully from being serious to cracking jokes. Some mornings he covered Toledo Street from end to end, and Concepción Jerónima, Atocha, and Carretas streets too.

Several years passed this way. As his personal needs were very limited, for he had neither a family to support nor a vice (unless you counted the saliva he squandered), the pittance his sales brought him was enough to live on. Besides, many rich businessmen helped him out now and then. One might give him a cloak; another, material for a suit; another, a hat, or maybe food and sweets. Some of the most "top drawer" families, as he called them, invited him to dine with them, and not due to friendship alone but to egoism: it was amusing to hear him relate such a variety of things with that picturesque precision and charming sense of detail. His entertaining chatter had two main characteristics: he never declared himself ignorant of anything, and he never said a mean word about anyone. If by chance he allowed himself an offensive word or so, it was invariably against Customs, but he didn't personalize his accusations.

During the period Estupiñá was selling fabrics, he was also a smuggler. You couldn't begin to count the huge bundles from Hamburg that he got past the city gates with his clever tricks. No one outdid him at crossing certain streets at night with a bundle under his cloak, pretending to be a beggar carrying a child. Nobody had such a knack for slipping the inspector a tip at the crucial moment; he handled these deals so well that the big stores called on him to get them out of trouble with the Treasury Department. And fiscal crimes like these didn't get onto government records, no matter how hard some officials tried. Public sentiment was against the notion—more so then than now—that cheating on the Treasury was a sin, and this naturally being Estupiñá's criterion, he felt no compunctions when he crowned a business deal with success. According to him, what the Treasury calls "its own" is not its own but the nation's, that is, Juan Pérez's; so cheating on the Treasury is really returning to Juan Pérez what is rightfully his. This idea, sustained by the common folk with turbulent faith, has also had its heroes and martyrs. Plácido believed in it no less enthusiastically than any Andalusian highwayman, except that he smuggled on foot, not on horseback, and besides, he didn't kill anybody. His conscience, which was totally blind to fiscal wrongdoing, was pure and luminous when it came to private property. He would have denied himself conversation for a month before keeping a penny that wasn't his.

Barbarita was very fond of him. He had been around the house for as long as she could recall. Her father's esteem of him and her own experience confirmed the great talker's excellent traits and loyalty. When she was little, Estupiñá used to take her to school, which was at the corner of Imperial Street, and at Christmas time he used to take her to see the Nativity scenes and stalls on Santa Cruz Square. When Don Bonifacio Arnáiz became fatally ill, Plácido remained at his side, both while he was ill and after he had died; not until the burial did he leave. Of the people who took part in the family's sorrows and joys, Plácido was always the most sincere. His status in this most noble family fell between that of friend and servant; Barbarita invited him to dine with them often, but most of the time she entrusted him with errands, which he did impeccably. She used to send him to the Cebada marketplace for a vegetable that had just come into season, or to Cava Baja to deal with the employees who had shipped orders for the shop, or maybe to Maravillas, where the shop's lacemaker and the ironer lived. Señora Santa Cruz had such power over that simple soul, and he respected and obeyed her so blindly, that if Barbarita had said, "Plácido, do me a favor and jump off the balcony," the poor man wouldn't have hesitated a second.

The years went by, and when Plácido was already getting old and didn't do any more door-to-door selling or smuggling, he fulfilled a very delicate function in the Santa Cruz household. As he was so close and piously devoted to the family, Barbarita trusted him to take Juanito to Massarnau's school and bring him home, or take the boy for a walk on Sundays and holidays, feeling sure that Plácido watched over him like a father, and she knew very well that he would have to be killed a hundred times over before he'd let anyone touch a hair on Juanito's head. Her Dauphin (as she used to call him) was already giving himself grown-up airs when Estupiñá took him to a bullfight, initiating him in the mysteries of the art that, being a good Madrilenian, he prided himself on knowing. The boy and the old man both got excited during the ferocious and colorful spectacle, and on the way out Plácido told him about his own bullfighting skills, for you know, way back, when he was young, he had done some turns and passes himself, and had had a sequined outfit of his own, and had fought young bulls with real style, never breaking a single rule. If Juanito expressed curiosity to see this bullfighting suit, Plácido told him that years ago his sister, the seamstress, God bless her soul, had used it to make a tunic for a Nazarene figure in the Duganzo de Abajo church.

Except for talking, Estupiñá had no bad habits; nor did he ever associate with uncouth or vulgar types. Only once in his life had he had anything to do with out and out scoundrels, and it had been inevitable. It was at the christening of the son of a nephew of his who was married to a woman butcher. The disagreeable incident, which he rued for the rest of his life, was this: his nephew, the little rascal, in cohorts with his buddies, managed to get him drunk by fooling him with some Chinchón anise that would have made an ox pass out. It was a stupid binge, the first and last of his life, and the memory of his degradation always depressed him whenever it flashed through his mind. What a disgrace, to have made fun of a man who was the spirit of moderation! Just imagine what they did to our friend: blatantly deceived him, made him down those abominable drinks, and then they didn't even hesitate to ridicule him grossly and cruelly. They asked him to sing "La Pitita" and there's reason to believe that he did, although he flatly denies it. In the midst of his confusion he realized what a state they'd put him in, and propriety inspired him with the idea of escaping. He darted out of there thinking that the night air would clear his head, but although he felt some relief his faculties still betrayed him. When he reached the corner of Cava de San Miguel, he saw the night watchman or, rather, saw the night watchman's lantern, which was heading toward the corner of Cuchilleros Street. He thought it was the Eucharist and, falling on his knees and taking off his hat, as was his custom, he said a short prayer, and then: "May God bless you with whatever your heart desires." The guffaws of his mean tormenters, who had followed him, restored him to his senses, and when he realized his plight he took refuge in his house, a few steps away. He fell asleep, and the next day it seemed as if nothing had happened. But he felt awfully sharp pangs of remorse that for some time made him sigh and fall silent. Nothing afflicted his honorable soul more than the thought that Barbarita might hear the joke about the Eucharist. Luckily, either she never heard a word, or if she did, never let on that she had.

3

When I personally met this illustrious child of Madrid he was on the brink of his seventieth birthday, but he carried his years very well. He was of less than average height, stocky and somewhat bent with age. Those who wish to know what his face was like may look at portraits of Rossini in his old age as engravings and pictures of the great musician have depicted him; with these images before them, they may say that they have beheld the divine Estupiñá. The shape of his head, the smile, the profile, and, above all, the hooked nose, the sunken mouth, and picaresque eyes, were a faithful image of those rather arrogant looks that his wrinkles had emphasized enough to suggest a resemblance to Punch. Age gradually made Estupiñá's profile look somewhat like that of a parrot.

Toward the end of his life, from 1870 on, his way of dressing acquired a certain originality due not exactly to poverty—the Santa Cruzes saw to it that he lacked nothing—but to his traditional spirit and strong reluctance to admit novelties to his wardrobe. He wore an old-fashioned hat, wide brimmed and low, from a time that hat-makers could no longer recall, and a heavy green cloak that he didn't take off except for the days between July and September. He had very little hair, none really, but he didn't wear a wig. To protect his head from the cold drafts in church, he used to keep a black wool cap in his pocket that he would put on as he entered. He was a devout early riser. At the crack of dawn, in the cool air, he was off to Santa Cruz Church, then to Santo Tomás, and finally to San Ginés. After attending several Masses at each of these churches, his cap pulled down to his ears, and after chatting awhile with other churchgoers or sextons, he would flit from chapel to chapel saying various prayers. Upon leaving, he waved good-bye to the statues as one waves to a friend up on a balcony, blessed himself with holy water, and off with the cap and out to the street.

In 1869, when the Santa Cruz church was demolished, Estupiñá went through trying times. Neither a bird whose nest has been destroyed nor a man who's been thrown out of the house where he was born would have shown the grief Estupiñá showed upon seeing the debris in clouds of dust. Since he was a man and all that, he didn't cry. If Barbarita, who had grown up in the shadow of that venerable tower, did not cry at seeing such a sacrilegious spectacle, it was because anger blocked her tears. Nor did she understand why her husband said that the man responsible, Don Nicolás Rivero, was a truly great person. When the temple was gone, when it had been razed to the ground and a house had been built on the sacred lot years later, Estupiñá still refused to acknowledge it. He wasn't one of those accommodating people who accept consummated acts. For him, the church was always there, and every time my good man went past the exact spot where the door had been, he made the sign of the cross and took off his hat.

Plácido was a member of the Peace and Charity Association, which had its headquarters in that demolished neighborhood. So he used to assist the prisoners sentenced to death, making conversation with them at the crucial hour, telling them how pointless life is, how generous God is, and how wonderful it would feel to be in glory. What would the poor fellows have done if they hadn't had someone to give them a bit of sweet-talk before sticking their necks out to the executioner!

At ten in the morning, Estupiñá invariably ended what we could call his religious workday. After ten, the gloomy seriousness he displayed in church disappeared from his Rossinian countenance, and he again became the affable, garrulous, pleasant man he was at the *tertulias* in the shops. He'd have lunch at the Santa Cruzes' or Villuendases' or Arnáizes', and if Barbarita didn't need anything, he'd go back to his job of "breadwinning"; he always pretended he was working like a dog. His purported occupation during this period was that of employment agent for clerks, and he claimed that he found them jobs for a fee. It is true that he did some of this, but for the most part it was pure farce. And when he was asked if his business was going well, he would answer as if he were a sly merchant disguising the extent of his fat profits: "Well, we're making ends meet; there're no complaints. This month I've placed at least thirty boys, or maybe forty."

Plácido lived on Cava de San Miguel Street. His building had two entrance levels: one on the Plaza Mayor and the other on the Cava. As the foundations of his and the adjacent buildings were much lower than the ground level of the plaza, one got the impression upon approaching that the plaza was a walled-in fortress. Plácido's apartment was on the fourth floor, counting from the plaza, and on the seventh, counting from the Cava. There are no higher buildings in Madrid. To get to the top of these structures, one has to climb a hundred and twenty steps, "every one of them stone," Plácido used to say proudly, being unable to praise anything else about his dwelling. The fact that they are "all stone" gives the staircases in those houses a lugubrious, monumental air, reminiscent of a castle in a fairy tale, and Estupiñá could not forget this circumstance, which somehow made him interesting. After all, it isn't the same to approach your home on a staircase like the one at El Escorial as it is to climb the vile lumber steps any old tenant has.

His pride in climbing those worn-out stone steps didn't exempt him from the fatigue resulting from such ascents, so my friend exploited his contacts to minimize his effort. Dámaso Trujillo, the owner of a shoestore on the plaza, gave him access to the staircase through his shop, whose sign read "to 'The Lily Stem.' " There was a door that opened onto the Cava staircase, and by using this door Plácido saved himself thirty steps.

The talker's home was a mystery to everyone. No one had ever been to see him for the simple reason that Don Plácido was never at home unless he was asleep. He had never had an illness that had prevented him from going out during the day. He was the healthiest man in the world. But old age was not willing to belie itself, and one day in December of '69 our great man's absence was noticed in the circles he usually frequented. Word quickly circulated that he was ill, and everyone who knew him was most concerned. A number of shop clerks ran up those stone steps for news of the charming patient afflicted with acute rheumatism in his right leg. Barbarita dispatched her doctor immediately, and, deeming this insufficient, she ordered Juanito to visit him, which the Dauphin did very willingly.

And now our attention must shift to the Dauphin's visit to his family's friend and humble servant, for if Juanito Santa Cruz had not paid that visit, this story would not have been written. Another story would surely have been written, because wherever man goes he carries his novel with him; but it would not have been this one.

4

Juanito spotted number 11 on the door of a poultry shop. It was undoubtedly the way in, he thought, stepping over feathers and crushed eggshells. He asked two women who were plucking hens and chickens, and they answered by pointing to a screen door, the entrance to the staircase to number 11. The main entrance and the shop were one and the same in that characteristic building of old Madrid. And then it dawned on Juanito why Estupiñá often turned up with feathers from different birds stuck to his boots: he must have picked them up on his way out, just as Juanito was picking them up now, no matter how carefully he tried to avoid them. It was painful to see the anatomy of those poor birds; they'd hardly been plucked when they were strung from their heads, their tail feathers still jaunty, like a sarcastic remark on their miserable fate. To the left of the entrance the Dauphin saw boxes packed with eggs, the business' supply. Man's voracity is limitless, and sacrifices not only the present but also future gallinaceous generations. To the right of that lugubrious square space, in another area, a paid assassin besmirched with blood was executing the hens. He wrung their necks with the speed and cleverness that come from experience, and when he had scarcely let go one victim and turned the agonizing creature over to the pluckers, he would grab another to caress her in the same way. There were enormous cages all over the place full of chickens and roosters whose red heads, thirsty and tired, poked between the bamboo bars to get some air; even in there, the poor prisoners pecked fiercely at one another as if to say, "Well, you stuck *your* beak out farther than me" or "Now it's *my* turn to stick out my bloody neck."

Having absorbed this gruesome spectacle (the smell of the corral and the noise of fluttering wings, the pecking and clucking of so many victims), Juanito turned to the sooty, worn, famous granite staircase. As a matter of fact, it did seem like the ascent to a castle or a state prison. The stairwell was covered in plaster, with inane or obscene graffiti scratched on it. On the side near the street, heavy iron grillwork completed the feudal aspect of the building. On the next level, as Juanito went past the door to one of the rooms, he saw it was open and naturally peeked in, because everything about the place greatly stirred his curiosity. He didn't expect to see anything, and he suddenly saw something that impressed him: a pretty woman, young and tall . . . She seemed to be spying too, moved by a curiosity similar to his, waiting to see who the devil was coming up the blasted staircase at that time of day. The girl wore a light blue scarf on her head and a large, heavy shawl over her shoulders, and the minute she saw the Dauphin she swelled up at him, I mean, she put her hands on her hips and raised her shoulders with that characteristic gesture that low-class women of Madrid have, filling out their shawls with a movement that reminds you of a hen ruffling her feathers and swelling out before coming down to normal size again.

Juanito didn't suffer from shyness, and when he saw the girl and observed how pretty she was and how fine her boots were, he had an urge to get closer.

"Does Sr. Estupiñá live here?" he asked her.

"Don Plácido? Yes, way up, on top of the top floor," the young woman answered, taking a few steps toward the door.

And Juanito thought, "You're coming out so I can see your pretty feet. Nice boots." As he was thinking this, he noticed that the girl was taking a red mittened hand from her shawl and raising it to her mouth. Young Santa Cruz craved to treat her in a familiar way, and couldn't resist asking:

"What are you eating, sweetheart?"

"Can't you see?" she replied, showing it to him. "An egg."

"A raw egg!"

Very gracefully, the girl lifted the broken egg to her mouth for the second time and sucked it again.

"I don't know how you can eat that raw drool," said Santa Cruz, not finding a better way to make conversation.

"They're better raw. Want some?" she replied, offering the Dauphin what was left in the shell.

The jellyish, transparent drool slipped through the girl's fingers. Juanito was tempted to accept the offer, but no; raw eggs were repulsive.

"No, thank you."

Then she finished sucking the egg and threw away the shell, which smashed against the wall one flight beneath them. She was wiping off her fingers with her handkerchief and Juanito was figuring out what he'd say next, when an awful voice from below ripped the silence with: "Fortunaaá!" The girl leaned over the banister and broke out with an "I'm comin'!" so shrill that Juanito thought it had broken his eardrums. The "I'm," especially, sounded like the screech of steel on steel. And as she emitted that sound, a call worthy of such a bird, she tore down the stairs so fast she seemed to go rolling down. Juanito saw her disappear, heard the noise of her clothes against the stone steps, and feared she was going to fall and break her neck. Finally, all was quiet, and the young man resumed his painful ascent. He didn't meet anyone else on the stairs, not even a fly, nor did he hear any noise except that of his own steps.

When Estupiñá saw him enter, he felt so happy that he practically recovered. The talker wasn't in bed; he was in a chair, for he detested sickbeds. The lower half of his body was invisible because it was bound up mummy-fashion in various blankets and rags. His head, including his ears, was covered by the black knitted cap he wore in church. His rheumatic pains annoyed him less than the lack of a person to talk to; the woman who worked for him, a Doña Brígida, a housekeeper of sorts, was very peevish and close-mouthed.

Estupiñá didn't own a single book, for he didn't need them to educate himself. His library was society, and his texts, fresh words from the living. His notion of science was his religious faith, and he didn't even need prayerbooks or collections of saints' sayings, since he knew all the prayers by heart. As far as he was concerned, printed matter was just reams of nothing—useless scrawls. One of the men Plácido admired least was Gutenberg. But the boredom of his illness had made him wish for the company of some of those mute speakers we call books. So there was a general search, but no printed matter turned up. Finally, in a dusty old chest, Doña Brígida found a bulky tome that had belonged to a secularized monk who had lived in the building back in 1840. Estupiñá opened it respectfully. Hmm, what was it? The eleventh volume of the *Ecclesiastical Bulletin of the Diocese of Lugo*. So he put up with it because, after all, there wasn't anything else. And he devoured it from cover to cover, not leaving out a single letter, pronouncing every syllable correctly, in a low voice, as if he were praying. No obstacle kept him from reading; when he came across long, obscure passages in Latin, he sank his teeth into them resolutely. The pastorals, synodals, papal bulls, and other entertaining things in the book were the only remedy he had for his loneliness, and the best part is that he eventually developed a taste for such a flavorless dish and re-read certain paragraphs, chewing on the words with a smile that would have made an uninformed observer think that the author of the fat book was Paul de Kock.

"It's really good," said Estupiñá, putting away the book when he saw that Juanito was laughing.

And he was so thankful for the Dauphin's visit that all he did was look at him, basking in his handsome face, his youth, and his elegance. If Juanito had been his own son twenty times over, he couldn't have looked upon him more lovingly. He patted him on the knee and made profuse inquiries about everyone in the family, from Barbarita, first on his list, all the way down to the cat. After satisfying his friend's curiosity, the Dauphin, in turn, asked him about the occupants of the building.

"They're good souls," replied Estupiñá. "There're only a few tenants who make a lot of noise at night. The property belongs to Sr. Moreno Isla, and I'll probably be his rent collector starting next year. He wants me to; your mother's already spoken to me about it, and I told her that I'd do whatever she'd like. It's a good piece of real estate; it's got a rock foundation that's top notch, and a stone staircase—you must've noticed it—except that it's a bit long. The next time you come, if you want to save yourself thirty steps, go into The Lily Stem, the shoestore on the plaza. You know Dámaso Trujillo. If you want, tell him 'I'm here to see Plácido,' and he'll let you in through the shop."

Estupiñá was laid up for over a week, and the Dauphin went to see him every day—*every day!*—which made my good man happier than a lark. But instead of entering through the shoestore, Juanito, who undoubtedly was more than equal to the staircase, always went in by way of the egg business in the Cava.

iv. The Perdition and Salvation of the Dauphin

I

AFTER SEVERAL DAYS, WHEN Estupiñá had already recovered and begun to get about again (albeit rather lamely), Barbarita began to notice certain new inclinations and tricks in her son that displeased her. She observed that the Dauphin—about twenty-five by now—would swing from hours of childish happiness to days of moodiness and brooding. And these weren't the only changes. With keen vision, the mother thought she discerned a change in the young man's habits and the company he kept when he went out; she discovered this in his voice and language, which had acquired certain very distinct inflections. He dragged certain syllables in a low-class way and had picked up some colorful expressions and uncouth words, which hardly charmed his mother. She would have given anything to follow him at night and see with what kind of people he was associating. The fact that they were not refined was glaringly evident.

And this change, which Barbarita didn't hesitate to classify as corruption, began to show in his clothes. The Dauphin had taken to wearing a short cape with a tippet and lots of trimming and braid. At night he put on his Andalusian hat (which, to be sure, looked very good on him) and combed his hair so that shocks of it fell loosely over his forehead. One day there appeared at the house a tailor who looked like a sexton; the kind of tailor who makes tight clothes for bull-fighters, rakes, and carousers; but Doña Bárbara didn't let him take out his measuring tape and all but threw him down the stairs. "Is it possible," she queried her child, without disguising her anger, "that you want to wear those tight pants that make men's legs look like a stork's?" And once she'd broken the ice, the lady launched a whole series of accusations against her son based on his new way of talking and dressing. He laughed at what she said and tried to evade her questions, but his inflexible mamá blocked his escape with more direct questions: Where did he go at night? Who were his friends? He replied that they were the same as usual, which wasn't true, because except for Villalonga, who accompanied him decked out in the same kind of short cape and Andalusian hat, his old classmates didn't visit the house anymore. And Barbarita reminded him of it: Zalamero, Pez, the Tellerías' boy . . . How could she help but compare? Zalamero at twenty-seven was already a congressman and under secretary of the interior, and the word was that Rivero wanted to give Joaquinito Pez the governorship of a province. Gustavito was always coming out with a critical article or a study on the origins of something or other and they were simply wonderful. And meanwhile Juanito and Villalonga were sitting around doing what? *What?* Picking up vulgar habits and going around with a bunch of lazy bullfighters. By 1870 the Dauphin had become so fascinated by bullfighting that he didn't miss a single fight or bull penning, and sometimes he'd even go out to the pasture ground.

Doña Bárbara was in a state of constant anxiety, and when someone told her that he'd seen her darling in the company of a practitioner of the taurine art, she'd hit the ceiling and said, "Look, Juan, I don't think you and I are going to stay on friendly terms for long. If you so much as bring home *one* of those characters in tight pants and a short jacket and spats, I'm really going to let you have it. I'll do what I've never done before: I'll take a broom to both of you and you'll be out of here in no time." These outbursts of fury usually ended up in laughter, kisses, promises from him to mend his ways, and affectionate reconciliations, for Juanito knew exactly how to humor his mother.

When the good lady found out that her son frequented the Puerta Cerrada, Cuchilleros, and Cava de San Miguel neighborhoods, she told Estupiñá to keep a close watch, and he did so very willingly, bringing her stories that he whispered in a melodramatic voice: "Last night he had dinner in the pastry shop that belongs to Botín's nephew, on Cuchilleros Street. Does the señora know where I mean? Sr. Villalonga was there too, and someone I don't know, a character who was sort of . . . how shall I put it? Well, one of those bullfighter types that wear fancy capes. It was hard to say whether he was a pickpocket or a nice boy like Juanito in disguise. He could've been either."

"And . . . women?" Barbarita asked anxiously.

"Two, Señora, there were two," said Plácido, corroborating with the same number of fingers held straight up what his voice stated. "I couldn't say what they looked like. They were the kind you see in dark shawls, blue aprons, nice boots, and with a scarf on the head; you know, the wild kind."

The next week there was more.

"Señora, Señora—"

"What?"

"Yesterday and the day before yesterday the boy went into a shop on Concepción Jerónima Street where they sell filigree work and the kind of coral jewelry that nursemaids wear."

"And?"

"Well, he spent most of the afternoon and half the night there. I got it from Pepe Vallejo, who works in the cord shop across the street. I told him to stay on the lookout."

"A filigree and coral shop?"

"Yes, Señora. Just a hole in the wall, they haven't even got twenty *duros* worth of stuff. I've never been in; it just opened a little while ago. But I'll find out about it. Looks poor. It has a glass door that's also used as the main door to the building, and they've put a sign on the glass that says: 'Gifts for Nursemaids—Our Specialty.' There used to be a watchmaker there called Bravo who died of colic."

Suddenly Estupiñá had no more stories. Barbarita intensified her questioning, but the great talker didn't know a thing. And mind you, the man's discretion had merit, because it was the greatest of sacrifices; having to say "I know nothing, absolutely nothing" was like having his tongue cut off. Sometimes it seemed that his insignificant and ambiguous revelations were aimed more at hiding the truth than revealing it: "Well, I saw Juanito in a hack, Señora; alone, around the Puerta del Sol—I mean at Angel Square. He was with Villalonga . . . They were in gales of laughter about something that had struck them funny." And all the other denunciations were the same: silliness, subterfuges, evasiveness . . . Either Estupiñá knew nothing or he didn't want to say what he knew so as not to upset the lady.

Ten months passed in this way—Barbarita interrogating Estupiñá, he not wanting or not having anything to reply—until May of '70, when Juanito began to break those uncouth habits that disturbed his mother so. Observing him most attentively, she noticed symptoms of the slow and fortunate change in a multitude of incidents in the young man's life. There is no need to say how happy this made her. And although no one could say when, there came a time when Barbarita lost her curiosity and was even willing to ignore her son's escapades as long as he was reforming. Gradually, the Dauphin started to regain his normal personality. After a night when he came in late and thoroughly exhausted and had a headache and vomited, the change seemed more pronounced. The mamá suspected that on that unknown page of her heir's history were some rather libertine attachments, vulgar orgies, jokes, and perhaps quarrels. But she forgave all, every little thing, since the trouble had passed, as the indispensable crises of every age do. "It's a kind of measles, all the boys catch them nowadays," she said. "Now mine's getting over them, and I pray to God that he'll come out of this all right."

She also noticed that the Dauphin worried a lot about certain messages or notes that were brought to the house; he seemed more fearful than desirous of them. He often ordered the servants to say that he wasn't in and not to accept any letters or messages. He was somewhat restless, and his mother said to herself with pleasure, "It looks like pursuit, but he seems to want to break loose. It's getting better." She discussed this with her husband, Don Baldomero, whose progressive spirit hadn't affected his taste for authority (the sign of the times), and he proposed a defensive plan that won her approval. "Look, dear: the best thing is for me to speak to the governor today, with no further delay; he's our friend. He'll send us a couple of policemen, and the minute a suspicious-looking character comes around here with a note or a message, they'll cart him or her off to jail."

Better than this was a plan of her own. They had taken a house in Plencia for the summer, and had set their departure for the 8th or 10th of July. With that certainty of a superior mind that at a given moment makes and enacts lifesaving decisions, Barbarita faced Juanito squarely and announced out of the blue: "We're leaving tomorrow for Plencia."

As she said this, she scrutinized his face. The first emotion the Dauphin revealed was happiness. Then he became pensive. "But give me a couple of days. I have to attend to several matters."

"What do you have to do, Juan? You're just stalling. And if you *do* have something to do, believe me, it's better to leave it as it is."

Said and done. The parents and their son left for the North on San Pedro's Day. Barbarita was very content, thinking she was already the victor, and said to herself on the way, "This time I'm going to tie up my little chicken so he won't get loose again." They installed themselves in their palatial summer residence, and words simply cannot describe how happy and healthy they were. The Dauphin, who had grown rather wan, recovered immediately, regained his good color and cheerful talk, and put on a few pounds. His mamá was waiting for the right moment. When the opportunity came, she knew exactly how to "tie up her chicken," for she was clever and knew what tricks to expect from birds who were to be caught. The Lord was undoubtedly on her side, because the chicken didn't offer much resistance.

"Yes," she said after a conversation that had been carefully thought out beforehand. "I think you should get married. I've already found the woman for you. You're such a baby, everything has to be done for you. What will you do when I'm gone? That's why I want to leave you in good hands. No, don't laugh; it's true that I have to see to everything: from sewing on your buttons to choosing the woman who's to be your lifelong companion, who'll be there to spoil you when I die. How could you imagine that I'd propose anything if it weren't for your own good? Now just hush and put your future in my hands. We mothers—some of us, anyway—have a special instinct. In certain cases we make no mistakes; we're as infallible as the Pope."

The wife whom Barbarita proposed to her son was Jacinta, his cousin, the third of Gumersindo Arnáiz's daughters. And just imagine! The day after the above-mentioned conference, Gumersindo and Isabel Cordero arrived on the scene with the youngest ones of their ménage. Candelaria was in Madrid and Benigna had gone to Laredo.

Juan wouldn't commit himself to a yes or no. He limited his remarks to formulas, saying that he would think it over; but a voice from within whispered to him that the great woman who was his mother had dealings with the Holy Ghost and that her plan was a true instance of infallibility.

2

Jacinta was a girl with excellent qualities: modest, delicate, affectionate, and very pretty too. Her lovely eyes were already announcing the readiness of her soul to fall in love and be loved. Barbarita was very fond of all her nieces, but she simply adored Jacinta. She almost always had the girl nearby, and showered her with attentions and little considerate gestures without anyone, not even Jacinta's own mother, remotely suspecting that she was grooming her for the role of daughter-in-law. All their relatives presumed that the Santa Cruzes had set their sights on one of the Casa-Muñoz girls, the Casa-Trujillos, or some other rich and titled family. But Barbarita had no such thoughts. When she presented her plan to Don Baldomero it warmed his heart, for the very same thing had occurred to him.

As I've said, the Dauphin promised to consider the matter, though with this he was probably only showing the need we all feel to pretend that we have an opinion on serious issues. In other words, pride, which swayed him more than his conscience ruled him, demanded that if he was not going to choose freely, he at least must pretend to. So he not only said that he would consider it, he pretended to by going for solitary walks through the rocky countryside, even deceiving himself as he mused, "Aren't I pensive!" For in truth, it was no laughing matter . . . hmmm! It called for *great* reflection, and he must turn it over in his mind ve-ry carefully. What the big faker was doing was savoring what was to come, wondering how he'd break it to his mother in the most philosophical language possible: "Mamá, I have given the matter deep thought. I have weighed the advantages and the disadvantages with utmost care, and I can truthfully say that although it is a case with both positive and negative aspects, I am willing to please you."

It was all a farce, a game to create the impression that he was a man who pondered his actions. His mother had regained the same complete control that she had had before the escapades I've mentioned; and like the prodigal son whose misfortunes show him how much his own acts and thoughts have harmed him, he found respite from his baneful adventures by thinking and acting with his mother's mind and will.

The worst of it was that it had never occurred to him to marry Jacinta, whom he had always regarded more as a sister than a cousin. When they were both very young (she was a year and several months younger), they had slept in the same bed and cried their tears together and accused each other—she him for having hidden her dolls, and he her for having thrown his wax soldiers into the fire so they'd melt. Juan made her furious by messing up her doll house, so there! and she took her revenge by throwing his horses into a pan of water so they'd drown. "Serves you right!" One of his Wise Men figures, the black one to be precise, had caused scenes that had ended in double spankings: Barbarita would beat their bottoms alternately, like a drummer, and all because Jacinta had cut off the tail of the camel that belonged to the black king, a tail made of real bristles, mind you. Juanito: "You're just jealous." Jacinta: "Tattle tale!" . . . They had already reached the age at which a mysterious mutual respect kept them from kissing, although they continued to be affectionate, like brother and sister. On Tuesdays and Fridays, Jacinta spent the entire day with Barbarita, who had no objection to leaving her son and niece alone together for hours at a time, because while each of them had reached the normal maturity of a twenty-year-old, put together they still acted like young adolescents, never dreaming that fate would join them when they least expected it.

The step from this sibling relationship to that of lovers did not strike young Santa Cruz as an easy one to take. He who was so daring when he was away from the parental nest was intimidated by the flower that had been nurtured in his own home. It seemed impossible for their cradles to be joined and turned into a wedding bed. But for everything except death there's a remedy, and Juanito, to his astonishment, found that soon after attempting the metamorphosis the difficulties dissolved like salt in water. What had seemed like a mountain was only a molehill; the passage from brotherhood to romance was "as smooth as silk." His sweet little cousin, also feigning surprise at first and then even embarrassment, echoed Juan: she would have to think it over. There's reason to believe that Barbarita had already helped her to think it over. Anyway, the fact is that four days after the ice was broken there was nothing left to teach them about being engaged. You'd think they hadn't done a thing in their lives except chatter away all day long. The countryside and its atmosphere were conducive to this new life. Formidable rocks, waves, shell-covered beaches, green meadows, hedges, flowery lanes lined with shrubs and lichen, paths that led to unknown endings, rustic cottages sending up blue smoke at sunset from their craggy roofs, pale gray clouds, sunbeams gilding the sand, sails of fishing boats crossing the immense sea, now blue, now greenish, terse one day, fleecy another, haze rising from the horizon, the sky tinged with smoke, a cloudburst in the mountains, and other accidents of nature in that admirable and poetic background favored the lovers, constantly supplying them with new examples of that great law that they were obeying.

Jacinta was of medium height, more graceful than beautiful; she had what's called "a sweet face." Her delicate complexion and her eyes, which radiated happiness and feeling, gave her a very appealing face. And when she spoke, her charm was greater than when she was silent due to the vitality of her face and ability to register many emotions in her features. The relative straits in which the numerous Arnáiz family lived didn't permit her to vary her clothes much, but she knew how to accent them, and whatever she wore proclaimed that she was a woman who, if she so wished, could be quite elegant. We'll get to that later. Her delicate proportions and figure and porcelain face revealed that she was one of those beauties to whom nature concedes a short period of splendor, after which they fade quickly, as soon as they are touched by maternity or the first grief in life.

Barbarita, who had virtually brought her up, was very familiar with her moral qualities and the treasures of her loving heart, which always generously rewarded the affection it was given, and because of all this, Juan's mother took pride in her choice. Even a certain tenacity of Jacinta's (which had been a defect in childhood) pleased her when the child grew up, because it isn't good, after all, for women to be only sweetness and light; they need a store of energy for certain trying times.

The news of Juanito's proposal hit the Arnáiz family like a bomb whose explosion disperses not disasters and death but hope and good luck. You must remember that the Dauphin, because of his fortune, qualities, and talent, was considered a divine creature. Gumersindo Arnáiz didn't know what had hit him; he couldn't believe his eyes. And even though the couple was quite thick, it seemed to him that they weren't thick enough, that they should get much thicker. Isabel was so overjoyed that once she was back in Madrid, she declared that her poor constitution could not bear so much happiness. This marriage had been her dream for several years, a dream too good to be true. She had never even dared to mention it to her sister-in-law because she had always feared that it might sound overly ambitious and bold.

The good lady couldn't spread the news of the happy event quickly enough to her friends. It was all she could talk about, and though worn and weakened from work and childbirth, she found strength to devote herself fully to the wedding preparations, the trousseau, and all the rest. What a flurry of planning and activity and premonitions! But in the midst of her huge task, she kept having pessimistic thoughts that she voiced sadly to herself: "Can it really be true? . . . And to think I won't be here to see it." And this presentiment, being about a bad thing, came true in the end; her restless happiness was like a secret combustion devouring the scant life left in her. One morning, toward the end of December, while she was in the dining room, Isabel Gordero fell as if struck by lightning. She had violent cerebral hemorrhaging and died that night, surrounded by her husband and grief-stricken children. She did not regain consciousness after the attack, not even enough to utter her name; nor did she seem to complain. She passed away without any pain, quietly and swiftly, "like a little bird," as is commonly said. Neighbors and friends said that it had been "more happiness than she could bear." That great woman, heroine and martyr to her duty, authoress of seventeen Spaniards, had gotten drunk on happiness after only a whiff, succumbing to her first binge. And famous dates continued to pursue her on her deathbed as they had pursued her at childbirths, as if history were still hounding her, trying to have something to do with her. Isabel Cordero and Don Juan Prim* expired only a few hours apart.

v. The Honeymoon

I

THE WEDDING TOOK PLACE in May of '71. Don Baldomero said, showing very good judgment, that it was customary for the bride and groom to leave after receiving the blessing to see something of the world. But he didn't see why it had to be a trip to France or Italy when there were so many places worth seeing in Spain. He and Barbarita hadn't been out of Madrid, because in their time a bride and groom remained at home, and the only Spaniard who permitted himself the luxury of traveling was the duke of Osuna, Don Pedro. Times had really changed! Now even Periquillo Redondo, the fellow with the tie stand at the corner of the post office, had been to Paris. Juanito said he completely agreed with his papá. After the ceremony and wedding luncheon—en famille and kept simple because they were in mourning—had taken place uneventfully, except for an attempt at a toast from Estupiñá cut off abruptly by Barbarita before he had scarcely opened his mouth, and after the farewells, the weeping, and the kissing, the newlyweds left for the station. The first stop on their trip was Burgos, where they arrived at three in the morning cheery and talkative, laughing at everything, at the cold and the darkness. In Jacinta's soul, however, the happiness didn't blot out a certain fear that at times she experienced as terror. The noise of the coach on the bumpy surface of the streets, the climb to the inn up the

---

*Juan Prim y Prats (1814–1870), prominent Spanish politician who was assassinated.

narrow staircase, the room with its tacky furniture, a mixture of city castoffs and small-town luxury, increased that invincible cold and awful expectancy that sent shivers down her spine. And loving her husband so much! How could she reconcile two such different desires: for him to leave her alone and yet to be near her? For the thought of his going away and leaving her alone was worse than death; and yet the thought of his approaching and passionately embracing her was also frightening, making her tremble. She would have liked for him not to leave her, but to be nice and quiet.

Quite late the next day, they went to the cathedral. Jacinta already knew several terms of endearment that she hadn't used yet, except in the discreet vagueness of her own mind, which was still reluctant to reveal itself. She was not embarrassed to say that she idolized him—yes, that was the word, precisely—or to ask him over and over if it was true that she had become his idol and would continue to be forever and ever. And the one whose turn it was to answer the question that had become as frequent as blinking would say, "Yeth," lisping to make the word sound childish. Juanito had taught her this "Yeth" that night, just as he had taught her to say "D'ya *luv* me?" in a special way along with other silly childishness, all in the most serious of tones. Right there in the cathedral, when the sexton who was showing them a chapel or a cloistered treasure took his eyes off them for a minute, the newlyweds snatched the opportunity to steal a few kisses in front of the holy altars or behind the reclining statue on a sepulcher. Juanito was a rascal, greedy and bold. These profanities scared Jacinta, but she consented and tolerated them, turning her thoughts to God and trusting in Him, the source of all love, to disregard them with His proverbial indulgence.

Everything made them happy. Contemplating an artistic marvel excited them, and out of pure enthusiasm they laughed, just as they did at any minor annoyance. If the food was bad, they laughed; if the carriage taking them to the Cartuja hit all the potholes in the road, they laughed; if the sexton at the Huelgas church told them absurd stories, like the one about the abbess who wore a miter and ruled all the priests, they laughed. Everything Jacinta said, even the most solemn comment, seemed incredibly funny to Juanito. And no matter what he said, his wife burst out laughing. The colorful street slang that Santa Cruz came out with every now and then was what she liked best, and she repeated some of it, trying to memorize it. When not too gross, these expressions are fairly amusing, being caricatures of language.

Time doesn't exist for lovers and people in ecstasy. Neither Jacinta nor her husband kept track of the fleeting hours. She, especially, had to think for a moment whether it was the third or fourth day of this blissful existence. Yet even though it cannot gauge the passing of the days very well, love aspires to dominate time, like everything else, and when it triumphs over the present, it longs to own the past, or at least to inquire into its events and see if they are favorable, since it can neither destroy them nor turn them into lies. Keenly aware of her present triumph, Jacinta began to be disheartened when her husband's past did not admit her as the owner of all he had felt and thought before marrying her. Since all she had of those preterit actions were slight hints, her curiosity about them made her restless. Their confidentiality grew with their mutual affection; it began innocently and gradually took the liberty of inquiries, finally reaching the stage of revelations. It wasn't that her curiosity mortified Juanito; Jacinta was purity itself. She hadn't even had one of those beaux who do nothing but ogle their beloved and wear a pained look. Because of this, she had a vast area over which to exercise her critical spirit. There shouldn't be any secrets between husband and wife. This is the first law laid down by curiosity before it gains the status of inquisitor.

As Jacinta called her husband "Baby" (which he taught her to do), when she asked him the first question, he couldn't help but feel a bit annoyed. They were walking along one of the poplar-lined avenues in Burgos, a straight and indefatigable stretch, like a path through a nightmare. His reply was affectionate but evasive. All he could tell his "Baby" was: mere flirtations, nonsense! Things boys will do. A man's education nowadays wasn't complete if he didn't deal with people from all classes, have a look at all the possible ways there are to live, have a taste of every passion. Just to educate himself. It wasn't a question of love, because as for love—and *he* knew what he was talking about—he had never known what it was until he had been smitten by the woman who was already his wife.

Jacinta believed this, but faith is one thing and curiosity is another. She didn't doubt her husband's love a bit, but she wished to know, yes, she wished to find out about certain little adventures. There should never be any secrets between husband and wife, should there now? As soon as there are, marital peace is on its way. She wanted to read very carefully certain little pages of her husband's life before their marriage. And since such stories help matrimonial training considerably . . . When women know them by heart they're more on their guard, so when their husbands have barely begun to slip—snap!—they're caught.

"Come on, you've got to tell me *everything*. If you don't I won't give you a moment's peace."

This was said on the train that ran and whistled through the narrow pass of Pancorvo. Juanito saw an image of his conscience in the landscape. The track that crossed it, revealing the muddled shady areas, was Jacinta's intelligent inquiry. The sly rascal laughed to himself, promising that, sure, he'd tell her . . . later. But the truth is that he didn't tell her anything that mattered.

"You've got to, you're cheating! Or at least you *think* you can. But I know more than you realize. There are things I saw and heard that I remember perfectly well. Your mother was very cross because you'd gotten very vulgar; yes, that's what you did."

The husband stayed on guard, but this hardly angered Jacinta. Her feminine intuition told her plainly that impertinent obstinacy yields precisely the effects one wishes to avoid. Another woman might have been provoked to serious pouting. She wasn't, because she grounded her success on perseverance combined with artful and diplomatic affection. Entering a tunnel in Rioja, she asked:

"Do you want to bet that without your telling me a single word I'll discover everything?"

And at the exit of the tunnel, the enamored spouse, after clasping her in a somewhat theatrical embrace, the smacking of his kisses lost in the bellowing of the fuming engine, cried out:

"What can I hide from such a sweet little doll? I'm going to devour you, you hear, devour you. Nosy, prying little rat-face. You want to know? Then I'll tell you, so you'll love me all the more."

"More? What a joke! *That* would be hard."

"Wait till we get to Zaragoza."

"No, now."

"Right now?"

"Yeth."

"No, . . . in Zaragoza. It's such a long, boring story."

"Good. First tell it, and then we'll see."

"You're going to laugh at me. Well, back in December of last year . . . no, the year before. See? You're already laughing!"

"No, I'm not, I promise. I'm as serious as can be."

"All right, that's better. Well, as I was saying, I met a woman . . . You know what I mean, one of those flings. But let me start at the beginning. Once upon a time there was an ancient gentleman very much like a parrot, called Estupiñá, who fell ill and . . . naturally, his friends went to see him; and one of those friends, climbing up the stone staircase, came upon a woman who was eating a raw egg . . . How's that for a beginning?"

2

"A raw egg! Ugh!" exclaimed Jacinta, spitting slightly. "What can you expect from somebody who falls in love with a woman who eats raw eggs?"

"As a matter of fact, I'll have you know she was attractive. Are you mad yet?"

"Me mad? Go on. She was eating the egg, and she offered you some and you accepted . . ."

"No, nothing happened that day. I went back the next day and I found her again."

"Admit it. She liked you, so she was waiting for you."

The Dauphin didn't wish to be very explicit, so he talked along general lines, smoothing over rough details and touching on the dangerous passages as if they were live coals. But Jacinta had an instinctive knack for handling a probe and always managed to extract some of what she wished to know. Part of what Barbarita had tried in vain to discover bubbled up to the surface now. Who was the one with the egg? "Oh, an orphaned girl who lived with her aunt, an egg dealer and a chicken raiser on San Miguel Street. Aha! Segunda Izquierdo, alias la Melaera, and wild as they come. Gossipy, and was she ever greedy! A widow 'involved,' as they say, with a picador. But that's enough side-tracking for now. The second time I went to the house I found her sitting on those same stone steps, crying."

"The aunt?"

"No, dear; the niece. The aunt had just bawled her out, and from down below you could still hear the beast raging. I consoled the poor girl with a few words and sat down beside her on the stairs."

"What a nerve."

"We began to talk. There was no one on the stairs. The girl was gullible, naive, the kind who say all they feel, the good with the bad. Anyway, on the third day I met her on the street. From a distance I could tell that she'd started to smile when she saw me. We exchanged a few words and then I went back with her and managed to worm my way into the house. I made friends with the aunt and we talked. One afternoon the picador appeared out of a pile of huge baskets where he'd been taking a nap, all full of feathers, and when he came up to me he grabbed me, I mean, he put out his enormous hand and I took it, and he asked if I'd like to have a few drinks with him, and I said yes and we drank together. It didn't take Villalonga and me long to make friends with their friends. Don't laugh. It was Villalonga who dragged me into that kind of life, because he took up with another girl in the neighborhood, the way I did with Segunda's niece."

"And which was prettier?"

"Mine!" the Dauphin hastened to reply, letting his enormous vanity show for a second. "Mine . . . an adorable little wild thing, a savage girl who didn't know how to read or write. What a way to be brought up! Poor low classes! We say they have brutal passions, when it's really our fault. We should look at these things closely. Yes, my dear, we should put our hand on the people's heart; it's healthy, but sometimes it's not really a heartbeat, it's a kicking. That poor girl! As I said, she's a wild thing, but with a good heart, a good heart . . . Poor *baby!*"

When she heard this affectionate exlamation spring from the Dauphin so spontaneously, Jacinta frowned. She had inherited the special word and it bothered her already; it smacked of the leftovers of a former passion, a dress or a jewel dirtied with use, and she showed her distaste by slapping Juanito with a slap that, coming from a wife, and jokingly, resounded quite loudly.

"You see? You're already mad. And for no reason. I'm telling you things the way they happened. But that's enough. I won't tell you any more."

"No, no; I'm not mad. Go on, or I'll hit you again."

"I don't feel like it. Can't you see that what I want is to erase a past I think is vile? I don't want to keep *any* memories of it. It's an episode that has its ridiculous and shameful sides. But youth is an excuse for such crazy episodes, provided one comes out of them all right, with a healthy heart, and honorably. Why do you force me to repeat what I want to forget, when remembering it only makes me feel I don't deserve the bliss I'm basking in today: you, darling."

"I forgive you," said the wife, fixing the hair Santa Cruz had messed up as he punctuated his subtle and passionate expressions. "I'm not impertinent. I don't demand the impossible. I know all too well that men have to run around before getting married. I warn you, I'll be very jealous if you ever give me reason to be. But I'll never harbor any jealousy of your past."

All this was as reasonable and discreet as one could hope, but Jacinta's curiosity didn't diminish; on the contrary, it only grew. It revived vigorously in Zaragoza, after the newlyweds attended Mass at the Pilar Church and visited the old cathedral, the Seo.

"If you'd like to tell me a little bit more about it . . . " Jacinta suggested as they roamed through the lonely, romantic streets that branch out behind the cathedral.

Santa Cruz frowned.

"Silly! I only want to know so I can laugh about it, that's all. What did you think, that I'd get mad? You silly thing! It's just that your escapades amuse me. They're so *chic*. I thought about them last night, and I even dreamed about the girl with the raw egg, and the aunt, and that other character. I wasn't angry, believe me, I was in stitches; it was so funny to see you in the midst of such aristocrats, so 'gentlemanlike,' 'a decent person,'—you know what I mean— 'proper.' Now *I'm* going to take over telling the story. Well dear, you courted her after a fashion and she took you on for real. You freed her from her aunt's clutches and the two of you went off to a love nest, on Concepción Jerónima Street."

Juanito stared at his wife, then burst out laughing. That wasn't guesswork. She had obviously heard something, at least the name of the street. Thinking it was wiser to keep up the joking front, he said:

"You already knew the name of the street, so don't try to sound like a swami. Estupiñá used to spy on me and report stuff to my mother."

"Tell me more about your conquest. You were saying that—"

"It only took a few days. With the common folk, my dear, proceedings are brief. Look at the way they kill each other. Love's the same. One day I said to her, 'If you want to prove you love me, run away with me.' I thought she'd say no."

"Well, you thought wrong, especially if they beat her at home."

"Her answer was to grab her shawl and say, 'Let's go.' She couldn't leave by way of the street. We had to go through a shoestore called The Lily Stem. As I already said, that's the way those people are, ready and willing and opposed to formalities."

Jacinta looked down at the ground rather than at her husband.

"And then came the usual little promise," she said, facing him squarely, watching his uncertainty.

Although Jacinta didn't personally know any victims of these "promises," she had formed a clear idea of such diabolical pacts from what she had seen of them in plays and even operas, where they were used as a theatrical device to make the audience laugh or cry. She looked at her husband again, and noticing a rather smug, man-of-the-world smile on his face, she pinched him and voiced these rather angry thoughts:

"Yes, the promise to marry her with the mental reservation that you wouldn't keep it, a trick, a swindle, a vile deception. Men! And then they say . . . And that fool didn't tear your eyes out when she realized she had been used? If it'd been me—"

"If it had been you, you wouldn't have torn out my eyes either."

"Oh yes I would have, you scoundrel, you little cad. Let's forget it, I don't want to know anything else. Don't tell me any more."

"What did you ask for then? If I tell you I didn't love her, you get mad at me and take her side. But suppose I tell you I did love her, that just after taking her away from home, the foolish thought of keeping my promise entered my mind."

"You rat, you!" exclaimed Jacinta with a teasing, though not entirely teasing, anger. "Just be glad we're in public, because if we weren't, I'd start pulling your hair this minute and I'd get a handful every time. So you thought of marrying her, and you tell me!"

The guffaw Santa Cruz hurled into the silent, hollow space of the deserted square echoed so strangely that the couple was startled by the sound. That corner of the square was constituted by huge ancient houses of Mudejar-styled bricks; on the doors, stone giants or savages with clubs on their shoulders; on the cornices, carved wooden eaves; and all of it the same dreary, dusty color. No sign of a soul anywhere. Behind the rusty iron grillwork, behind the wooden window blinds, there wasn't even a crack through which human eyes might have peeped.

"My dear, this place is so deserted," said the husband, taking off his hat and laughing, "that you could make the biggest scene in the world and no one would ever know it."

Juanito began to run. Jacinta went after him, her parasol raised. "I bet you can't catch me." "I bet I can." "I'll kill you!" And they ran all over the grass-grown, lumpy pavement, Juanito laughing loudly, Jacinta flushed, her eyes moist. Finally, bam! she whacked him with her parasol, and when Juanito rubbed himself, they paused, panting, choking on their laughter.

"Over here," said Santa Cruz, pointing to an arcade, which was the only way out.

And as they went through the tunnel, at the end of which could be seen another little square as lonely and mysterious as the preceding one, the lovers silently embraced, holding each other tightly, kissing for well over a minute, and whispering the tenderest of words.

"Marvelous, isn't it? Who would have thought that in the middle of the street you could . . . "

"But if someone were to see us," murmured Jacinta, blushing; for it's true that that spot in Zaragoza may have been as deserted as you like, but it was by no means a bedroom.

"Let them, all the better if they do. What do I care?"

And back to hugging and sweet words.

"There's not a soul around," he said. "In fact, I don't think anybody's ever been here. No human being has looked at these walls for at least two centuries."

"Shhh, I think I hear steps."

"Steps? . . . Really?"

"Yes, steps."

Someone was coming. Although they couldn't place it, they could hear the sound of feet dragging over the cobblestones. Suddenly, between two houses, a black figure appeared. It was an old priest. The married couple linked arms and moved on, feigning complete composure. As he passed, the clergyman stared at them.

"It seems to me," the wife observed, holding onto her husband's arm more firmly and pressing hard against him, "that he's seen it in our faces."

"Seen what?"

"That we were . . . fooling around."

"Psh! So what?"

"Look," she said when they arrived at a less deserted place, "don't tell me any more stories. I don't want to know anything else. Period."

She burst out laughing, so hard that the Dauphin had to ask her repeatedly the cause of such hilarity, finally receiving the following reply:

"You know what I'm laughing about? Thinking what your mother's reaction would have been if you had turned up with a daughter-in-law who wore a shawl and cheap rings and a scarf on her head; a daughter-in-law who said *see ya' later* and couldn't read."

3

"So we're agreed: there'll be no more stories."

"No more. I've already laughed enough at your silliness. Frankly, I thought you were smarter. Beside, I can imagine anything you could tell me. That you got bored after awhile. It's only natural. A well-bred man and a common woman aren't compatible. When his ardor cools, what's left? She smells of onions and uses foul language. And as for him, I can almost see it: he's revolted, and then the quarrels start. The common people are dirty. No matter how much she scrubs herself, a low-class woman is always low class. All you have to do is see the insides of their houses. Their bodies are just the same."

Later that afternoon, after seeing the door of the Carmen Church and the eloquent walls of Santa Engracia (mute witnesses to their presence), they wandered around the Torrero grove. Leaning heavily on her husband's arm, for indeed, she was a bit tired, Jacinta said:

"I just want to know one thing, just one, and after that I'll keep my mouth shut. Which house was it on Concepción Jerónima Street?"

"What difference does it make, dear? Oh, all right, I'll tell you. There's nothing special about it. An uncle of hers lived in the house, the egg dealer's brother —a real character, and as uncouth as they come. A man who's been everything: a convict and a rioter, a revolutionary, a pseudo-bullfighter, and a cattle dealer. Ah, José Izquierdo! You'd laugh if you saw him and heard him talk. A poor old gal got carried away with him, the widow of a silversmith, and he married her. In their own way they were priceless. There they were, the whole blasted day, arguing. You know, just quibbling. And the shop! What chaos, what scenes there were! First he'd get drunk by himself; then they'd take turns. Ask Villalonga, he's the one who really knows how to tell it and mimic them. I can hardly believe that I used to enjoy those scandals. What a man will do! But I was blind. I was crazy about the common people then."

"And her aunt, when she saw that her niece had been dishonored, she must have been furious, wasn't she?"

"At first, yes. You see . . . " replied the Dauphin, trying to veer away from a sticky explanation. "Well, she was angrier about her running away than about her dishonor. She wanted to have the poor girl around the house at her beck and call. Those people are atrocious. Their morals are so weird! That is, they don't have any. Segunda started off by turning up in the shop on Concepción Jerónima every day to make a scene in front of her brother and sister-in-law. 'You so-and-so, you're a—' I can hardly believe it. Villalonga and I, who heard the uproar from the floor above, just laughed. It's amazing how degraded one can get if he lets himself be dragged down! I was so stupid that I thought I'd always be living around that scum. There are things I wouldn't wish to tell you, my darling . . . One day the picador, Segunda's lover-boy, showed up. That gentleman and my friend Izquierdo could hardly stand the sight of each other. The things they said! It was worth selling seats for it."

"I can't imagine why you found that savagery so amusing."

"I can't either. I must not have been myself: what I had been and what I am again. It was like a parenthesis in my life. But let's not dwell on it, darling, it was just a blasted whim that I had for that plebian girl—some sort of artistic enthusiasm, a temporary madness that I can't explain."

"You know what I'd like now?" Jacinta said brusquely. "For you to be quiet, dear; quiet. It's revolting. You're right. You weren't yourself then. I try to imagine what you were like and I can't. My loving you and your being what you yourself describe are two things I can't fit together."

"You've said it very well. Love me madly, and let bygones be bygones. But wait a minute: to finish the story, I have to add something that will surprise you. Two weeks after that bickering and so much wrangling and so many scenes between the Izquierdo brothers and between Izquierdo and the picador, and between the aunt and the niece, everyone made up, and the quarreling was over and it was all friendliness and pats on the back."

"That really is odd. What people!"

"Common people don't know what dignity is. They're only moved by passions or self-interest. Since Villalonga and I were well-heeled for wine and flamenco sessions, they took a liking to our pockets, and pretty soon the time came when all that was done around there was drinking, clapping, guitar playing, 'oléing,' and eating. It was a continuous orgy. No selling in the shop; no work in either of the houses. When there wasn't a picnic out in the country, there was dinner at the house that lasted till dawn. The neighborhood was scandalized. The police were on our tails. And Villalonga and I, like a pair of fools—"

"Oh, what rascals! But dear, it's raining; there's a drop on the tip of my nose, see? Hurry up, we're getting wet."

The weather turned foul, and all the way to Barcelona it kept on raining. Pressing against the window, husband and wife looked at the rain, a curtain of tiny oblique lines that kept coming from the sky without ever falling, it seemed. When the train stopped, they could hear the water dripping off the roofs of the cars onto the running boards. It was cold, but even if it had not been, the travelers would have been cold from seeing the stations in puddles, the soaked employees, and the peasants with sacks covering their heads who were boarding the train. The locomotives gushed water and fire, and on the canvas laid over the open freight cars rain pockets formed like little ponds from which the birds could have drunk, if they had been thirsty that day.

Jacinta was content and so was her husband, in spite of the landscape's weepy melancholy. However, since there were other passengers in the compartment, the newlyweds couldn't spend their time kissing. When they arrived, they both laughed at how formal they had been on the trip. In Barcelona, Jacinta was fascinated by the liveliness and fertile buzzing of that great human beehive. They spent very pleasant hours visiting Batlló's and Sert's superb factories and constantly admiring in workshop after workshop the marvelous weapons that man has devised to control nature. For three days, the story about the raw egg, the seduced woman, and the family of louts that placated itself with orgies was completely forgotten or lost in a labyrinth of noisy and smoky machines or in the clattering of looms. Jacquard's, with their incomprehensible sets of punched cardboards, absorbed Jacinta's imagination and kept her in suspense; the miracle was right before her eyes, yet she still couldn't believe it. It was fantastic! "One sees things every day and never stops to wonder how they're made. We're so dumb that when we see a sheep, we don't realize that our overcoats are in it. And who would ever guess that nightgowns and slips come from plants? Cotton, ha! And how about dyes? Red was a little bug, and black a bitter tasting orange, and greens and blues, stone coal. But the strangest thing of all is that when we see a donkey, the farthest thing from our mind is that drums come out of his hide. And how about matches, coming from bones, and the sound of a violin being the product of a horse's tail soaked in a goat's innards?"

The observer didn't end her remarks here. On that instructive excursion through the field of industry, her generous heart overflowed with philanthropic sentiments, and her good judgment confronted social problems clearly. "You have no idea," she said to her husband as they were leaving a workshop, "how sorry I am for those poor girls who come here to earn a measly salary that's not even enough to live on. They don't have any education; they're like machines, and they become so stupid. But more than stupidity, it must be boredom. They become so stultified, as I was saying, that they let themselves be seduced by the first rascal who comes along. And it's not that they're evil; it's that the time comes when they say, 'It's better to be an evil woman than a good machine.'"

"My, but we're philosophical, aren't we?"

"Oh, go on. I know I haven't said anything special. Anyway, let's not talk about it anymore. Tell me if you love me, yes or no; but tell me now, right away."

The next day, up at Tibidabo, looking down at the immense city spread out on the plains, sending up from its hundreds of chimneys the black breath that declared its vehement activity, Jacinta moved away from her husband's side and said:

"Satisfy my curiosity. For the last time."

And the minute she said this she regretted it, for while what she wished to know made her itch with curiosity, it also hurt her modesty. If she could only find a delicate way of asking the question! She ransacked her mind for every expression she knew, but couldn't come up with any formula that felt right on her lips. Yet "it" was natural enough. Either she had thought of it or she had dreamed about it the night before. She wasn't sure which, but it was a consequence that would have occurred to anyone. Her thoughts ran in this order: "How long did my husband's involvement with that woman last? I don't know. But whatever it was, it could well have been that . . . a child was born." This was the hard word to say: child. Jacinta didn't dare, and even though she tried to substitute it with "family," or "heir," she could not bring herself to say it.

"No, it's nothing."

"You said you were going to ask me something."

"It was silly, never mind."

"If there's one thing I can't bear, it's having someone say he's going to ask you something and then not ask it. You're left up in the air, imagining all sorts of things. Go ahead, keep it carefully locked up, so there won't be any flies on it. Please, darling, if you're not going to shoot, don't take aim."

"I'll fire . . . There's plenty of time, dear."

"Tell me now. What can it possibly be?"

"Nothing. It wasn't anything."

He looked at her and grew serious. He seemed to be reading her mind. The look in her eyes and her playful little smile were such that you could practically see the word she was thinking written on her face. They looked at each other, laughed, and that was it. The wife said to herself: "Things will ripen in time. There'll be days when we'll be more intimate, and we'll talk then, and I'll find out whether or not there's a little 'egg dealer' somewhere."

4

Jacinta wasn't very learned. She had read very few books. She was completely ignorant in matters of artistic geography, but nevertheless she appreciated the poetry of that area along the Mediterranean coast spreading before her as they advanced from Barcelona to Valencia. Small fishing villages paraded by to the left of the tracks between the blue sea and splendid vegetation. Every now and then the landscape blued because of the silvery leaves on the olive trees. Further back, the vineyards brightened it with the green gala of their tendrils. The triangular sails of the boats, the low white houses, the absence of pointed roofs, and the predominance of horizontal lines in the constructions made Santa Cruz recall ideas on Hellenic art and nature. Following the routine pattern of people who have read a few books, he also talked about Constantine, Greece, the bars on

Aragón's coat of arms, and the tiny fish that were said to have it painted on their gills when the Mediterranean virtually belonged to the province of Aragón. Mention of the Phoenician colonies naturally came next. Jacinta didn't have the vaguest idea of what they were, nor did she miss knowing about them. Then came Prócida and the Sicilian Vespers, Don Jaime de Aragón, Roger de Flor and the Oriental Empire, the duke of Osuna and Naples, Venice and the marquis of Bedmar, Massaniello, the Borgias, Lepanto, Don Juan de Austria, the galleys and the pirates, Cervantes and the Fathers of Mercy who rescued the great writer.

Entertained by the comments he made in his cursory view of the Mediterranean coast, Jacinta condensed her knowledge in these or similar expressions: "And the people who live here, I wonder if they're happy, or as miserable as the townspeople inland who have never had anything to do with the Great Turk or Don Juan de Austria's flagship? The people who live here probably don't appreciate the fact that they live in paradise—a poor man is just as poor in Greece as in Getafe."

They had an extremely pleasant day watching the sunny countryside unfold before their eyes—the great River Ebro, the salt marshes of the delta, and finally the splendor of the Valencian countryside, proclaiming itself in the clusters of carob trees that seemed to come forth to meet the train from every direction. They made Jacinta dizzy when she stared at them. Now they approached, brushed against the window with their bushy crowns; now they retreated, up a hill; now they ducked behind a knoll to reappear, figures keeping time to a minuet in a succession of steps; or they played hide-and-seek with the telegraph poles.

The weather, which hadn't treated them very well in Barcelona and Zaragoza, improved that day. Wondrous sun gilded the fields, and its radiance reached into the couple's hearts. Jacinta laughed at the carob trees' dance and the birds perched in a row on the telegraph wires. "Just look at them up there! Clever little things! They're making fun of the train, and of us.

"Look at the wires now. They're like a musical staff—look at how they go up and down. They look like ink lines engraved on the blue sky, and the sky seems to be moving, as if it were a stage curtain still coming down.

"It seems to me," continued Jacinta in an amused tone, "that it's all very poetic. There are lots of pretty new things, but there's nothing to eat. I confess, my sweet husband, that I'm so hungry I could eat a horse. This early morning country air has given me quite an appetite."

"I didn't want to say anything so as not to make you lose heart. We'll come to a station with a restaurant soon. If we don't, we'll buy something, even if it's only some doughnuts or dry bread. Traveling has its little inconveniences. Kiss me now, and keep your chin up. Being hungry isn't so bad when you're in love."

"We've already passed three. At the next one we come to, take a good look, darling, to see if we can find something. You know what I would like now?"

"A steak?"

"No."

"What, then?"

"A steak and a half."

"You'll be lucky to have an orange and a half."

They passed more stations and still no restaurant appeared. Finally, at some station or other, a woman appeared behind a little table covered with liqueurs, doughnuts, pastries decorated with ants, and some . . . what were they? "Fried birds!" cried Jacinta, as Juanito was about to step off the train. "Get a dozen. No, wait: two dozen."

And the train started to move again. They settled down, their knees touching, put between them the greasy paper containing that pile of "fried corpses," and began to eat at the speed their great hunger dictated.

"They're delicious! Look at that breast! This nice big plump one is for you."

"No, you take it, it's for you."

Her hand was his fork and his, hers. Jacinta said that she had never had such a tasty meal.

"This one's really in its prime. Poor soul! The poor thing was probably perched up on the wire yesterday with his friends all plump and pretty, watching the train go by and saying, 'There go those beasts,' till the beastliest one of all came along, a hunter, and—bang! All so that we could treat ourselves today. They *are* tasty. I really liked this lunch."

"I did too. Let's see the pastries now. Formic acid is good for digestion."

"What kind of acid?"

"Ants, darling. Don't think about them, just go to it. Have a bite. They're scrumptious."

Their strength regained, well-being overflowed in their souls. "The carob trees don't make me dizzy anymore," said Jacinta; "dance, dance. Look over there— grape arbors! And those, what are they, orange trees? What a scent!"

They were alone. What luck they were having, always alone! Juan sat next to the window with Jacinta on his lap. He had his arm around her waist. They chatted from time to time, she making candid observations on whatever she saw. But then there were spells when neither of them said a word. Suddenly Jacinta turned to her husband, and putting an arm around his neck she fired this at him:

"You haven't told me her name."

"Whose?" asked Santa Cruz, somewhat stunned.

"Your adored torment, your . . . What her name was, or is. Because I suppose she's still alive."

"I don't know, and I don't care. What a thing to come up with now!"

"I just happened to be thinking about her a while ago. It suddenly occurred to me. Do you know why? I saw some pink corsets spread out to dry on a bush. You probably wonder what they have to do with her. Nothing, of course; but who knows how ideas connect in your mind? This morning I also thought of her when the baggage carts went screeching by. And last night I remembered her too— guess when? When you turned off the light. The flame looked like a woman saying 'Oh!' and then she died. I know it's probably foolish, but very peculiar things go on in one's mind. So how about it, baby, are you going to tell me?"

"What?"

"Her name."

"Don't bother me about names."

"What an uncooperative gentleman!" she exclaimed, embracing him. "All right, keep your little secret. I beg your pardon for even asking about it. Make sure that no one steals your treasure. You're right: either we'll be reserved about this or we won't. It's all the same to me. Don't worry, I don't really care if you tell me or not. What would I gain by adding one more name to my files?"

"It's a very ugly name. Please don't make me think about what I want to forget," Santa Cruz replied irritably. "I'm not telling you a thing, you hear?"

"Thank you, one and all. Anyway, look; if you think that I'd be jealous, you're wasting your time. That's just what you'd like: to feel important. I'm not jealous. There's no reason to be."

I don't know what it was that distracted them from this conversation. The landscape was more and more enchanting, and the countryside, gradually turning into a garden, revealed all the refinements of an agricultural civilization. Everything expressed nobility: the orange trees, with their brilliant perennial leaves, heavily scented blossoms, and golden fruit; those illustrious trees that have been one of the most dependable clichés among poets and have endured the worst in Valencia because, being so abundant, even poets dismiss them there, as if they were thistles. Tilled land delights the eye with the neat correctness of its rows. Vegetables edging the rows outline the ground, which in some spots looks like hemp. The various greens resemble the work of an artist's brush, not the result of nature's invisible labors. And everywhere flowers, young shrubs; at the stations, gigantic acacias spread their branches over the railway tracks. The men, in coarse bloomers with kerchiefs tied round their heads, remind you of the Moors. and the women are fresh and graceful, dressed in calico, their curly hair framing their faces.

"And which," inquired Jacinta, wanting to learn, "is the *chufa* tree?"*

Juan couldn't say, because he didn't know where the devil *chufas* came from. Valencia was getting closer now. Several people entered the compartment, but

---

* Earth almond tree.

the couple remained in their seats next to the window. At times the sea came into view, so very, very blue that the retina was tricked into thinking the sky was green.

"Sa-gun-to!"

Oh, what a name! Newly painted in uneven letters on the station sign, it looks like a joke. It's not an everyday sight: such a famous historical name shrouded in locomotive smoke. Juanito, who always grabbed any opportunity he could to play the doleful scholar, got a bit too carried away at the sight of the sign.

"What is it, hmm?" asked Jacinta, piqued by the theatrics. "Oh, Sagunto, of course. A name. No doubt there was some sort of scuffle here. But a lot of water has gone over the dam since then. Don't get so excited, dear, take it easy. Why so much oohing and ahing? Just because those brutes—"

"What did you say, dear?"

"Yes, sweetheart, those brutes*—and I won't take back what I said—made a monstrous mess. Call them heroes if you wish, but hush now. And don't let your mouth keep hanging open like that, you're reminding me of the priest in Burgos."

Back to more of the agricultural garden of greens, and the straw huts with a cross at the peak of their roofs. Up their thatched walls there grew some very strange plants: solitary stalks with huge leaves that Jacinta found intriguing.

"Look what a horrible tree! Do you suppose it's a prickly pear?"

"No, darling, prickly pears come from that other cactuslike plant, the short one covered with thistles. And over there is a maguey, that's where rope comes from."

"And which kind does matweed come from?"

"That I couldn't tell you. They must be somewhere nearby."

The train drew a very wide curve. The travelers noticed a large group of buildings whose whiteness was vivid against so much green. Groves of trees would block it from sight for stretches and then reveal it again.

"Well, we're in Valencia now, darling. Look at it over there." Valencia has the best location in the world for a city, according to one keen observer, because it was built in the middle of the countryside.

A bit later, packed into a two-wheeled carriage, the couple entered the rustic city's narrow, crooked streets. "Goodness, what a place! It reminds me of a scene painted on a screen . . . Where do you suppose the man's taking us?"

"The inn, no doubt."

At midnight, when they retired to their rooms exhausted from having wandered through the streets and then heard half of the opera La Africana at the Princess Theater, Jacinta, without knowing how or why, suddenly felt that little itch to know again; and the thought that was haunting her took the form of a mild

---

* A reference to Hannibal's siege of the town and the resistance of the townspeople.

sorrow, which she disguised as curiosity. Juan avoided satisfying her curiosity, defending himself with: "Don't make my head spin, dear. I've already told you, I want to forget it . . . "

"But the name, baby, just the name. What harm can it do to open your mouth for a second? Don't worry, I won't be mad, silly."

As she said this, she took off her hat, then her coat, then her jacket, her skirt, and her bustle, laying them out meticulously over the chairs and armchairs in the room. She was exhausted, and could hardly wait to feel the mattress under her tired body. The husband was throwing off his clothes too. He seemed to be in a good mood, although Jacinta's curiosity had really begun to irritate him by now. Finally, unable to resist his wife's coy interest, he resolved to oblige her. Their heads were already on the pillow when Santa Cruz lazily uttered these words:

"I'm going to tell you, but under the condition that never again in your whole life, your *whole* life, will you ever mention the name, nor make the slightest reference to it. Is that clear? Well . . . her name is—"

"Thank goodness."

It was very hard for him to say it. She helped him.

"Her name is *For*—"

"*For . . . narina.*"

"No. *For . . . tu-na*—"

"*Fortunata.*"

"That's right. Are you satisfied now?"

"You've been a perfect dear. I love you when you're like this."

Minutes later, she was deep in angelic slumber. Soon they were both asleep.

5

"You know what I've been thinking?" Santa Cruz asked his wife two days later at the station in Valencia. "It seems foolish to go back to Madrid so soon. Let's go on to Seville. I'll wire home."

This immediately saddened Jacinta. She was already eager to see her sisters, her papá, her aunts and uncles and in-laws. But the thought of extending the trip, which was so much fun, quickly conquered her. To go on like this, on the wings of the train! They always are somewhat like dragons out of fairy tales for young people. It was so wonderful and so entertaining!

They saw the opulent banks of the Júcar; they crossed Alcira, covered with orange blossoms; Játiba, which was really charming; then came Montesa, feudal-looking; and Almansa, in a cold bare region. Vineyards grew scarcer and scarcer until the severity of the land announced that they had reached austere Castille. The train hurtled through the dismal countryside like an enormous greyhound, sniffing the track and barking at the slow night gradually descending on the endless plain. Sameness, telegraph poles, goats, puddles, heaths, gray land, horizontal immensity that appeared to be just recently flooded by the sea, the smoke from their locomotive receding in puffed mouthfuls to the horizon, women at the crossings signaling with green flags to go ahead on that road to infinity, low-flying flocks of birds, and stations where they had to wait a long time, as if something good would finally emerge from them . . . Jacinta fell asleep, and so did Juanito. The famous region of La Mancha was like a drug. Finally they got off at Alcázar de San Juan at midnight, shivering with cold. They waited there for the train to Andalusia, had hot chocolate, and were on their way again, through another part of La Mancha, the most famous of all, the area around Argamasilla.

The couple spent a bad night on that barren plain, and tried to shut out the cold by cuddling up together under a single blanket. At last they arrived in Córdoba, where they were able to rest, and they saw the mosque the next day, because one day wasn't enough for both. They were dying to get on, to the incomparable Seville! Back on the train. It must have been nine in the evening when they pulled into the romantic happy city and found themselves in the thick of that sibilant Andalusian grace and humor. They were there for eight or ten days, I think, enthralled, not bored for a minute as they beheld the architectural and natural wonders and were smitten by the good spirits that fill the air in Seville, there for the taking from the faces of its people. One of the things that charmed Jacinta most was how patios were turned into furnished gardens where the azalea branches swept so caressingly close to the piano keys they seemed to be showing their desire to play. Jacinta was also pleased that all the women—even the old ones begging for alms—wore a flower in their hair. If they don't have a flower, any green leaf will do: they walk down the street radiating life.

One afternoon they had lunch at a humble tavern in the outskirts of Seville. According to Juanito, you had to see everything close up and rub elbows with these original people: they were born artists, poets whose words nearly paint what they say, having the divine gift of a very practical philosophy; seeing the funny side of everything so that life, turned into a joke, becomes more bearable. The Dauphin had drink after drink, claiming (and thus showing his considerable common sense) that in order to assimilate Andalusia, really feel it inside, you had to let your system absorb all the manzanilla it could take. Jacinta didn't have more than a taste, finding it harsh and acid; nor did she manage to appreciate the faint bouquet of a Ronda pear that the drink supposedly has.

They headed back to the inn in high spirits, and upon arriving saw a crowd of people in the dining room. It was a wedding feast. The bride and groom were Anglicized Spaniards from Gibraltar. The Santa Cruzes were invited to join them, but they declined, though they did have a little champagne to be polite. Then a boor of an Englishman who made a mess of Castillian Spanish with his pursed lips and teeth that tightened their grip on whatever words he spoke, insisted that they have some wine. "No, really . . . but thank you very much." "*Ooooh, sí!*" The dining room was bubbling with joy and laughter at jokes, some of which began to be in questionable taste. Santa Cruz's only alternative was to give in to the bloody Englishman's persistence, and, accepting a drink, he muttered under his breath: "You're stoned out of your mind." But the Englishman didn't understand. Jacinta saw that things were taking a bad turn. The Englishman cried out for order, and directing himself to the youngest ones in the crowd he told them with his pursed lips to "be *seriohs, seriohs.*" He needed this advice more than anyone else, and what he needed most of all was for someone to stop his drinking. By now that was no longer just a mouth, it was a funnel. Jacinta sensed that a quarrel might start, so, acting quickly, she tugged at her husband's arm just as he was starting to tease the Englishman.

"I'm so glad," said the Dauphin as his wife led him upstairs, "that you got me out of there, because you have no idea how that Englishman was getting on my nerves with his clenched white teeth and his friendly ways and his silly flat shoes. If I'd stayed another minute I would've smacked him one. My blood was already boiling . . . "

They went into their room and, sitting opposite each other, commented on the funny characters in the dining room and the puns they had heard. Juan didn't talk very much and seemed rather restless. Suddenly he wanted to go back downstairs. His wife opposed the idea. They argued. Finally Jacinta had to lock the door.

"You're right," said Santa Cruz, collapsing into a chair. "It's better for me to stay because if I do go down and that *Mister* starts up again with his fine manners, I'll hit him. I know how to box, too."

He shadow-boxed around the room. Then his wife really did scowl at him.

"You should go to bed," she said to him.

"It's too early. We can sit and talk for a while, all right? You're not sleepy, are you? I'm not either. I'll keep my better half company. That's what my duty is and that's just what I'll do, yes sir. Because I'm a slave to my duty . . . "

Jacinta had taken off her hat and coat. Juanito sat her on his lap and started to bounce her up and down the way you play horsey with children. And he went on and on about being a slave to his duty, and the family being the most important thing there is. The long ride her husband was taking her on was beginning to annoy Jacinta, who dismounted and went back to the chair she had been sitting in before. Then he started to pace the room nervously.

"My greatest pleasure is being with my adorable baby," he said without looking at her. "'*I love you madly,*' as they say in plays. Bless my sweet mother . . . for marrying me to you."

He knelt before her and kissed her hands. Jacinta watched him warily, without batting an eye, trying to laugh but not succeeding. Santa Cruz chose a plaintive tone to say:

"And I was so stupid I couldn't see what you were worth! Staring at you day in, day out, like a donkey at a flower he doesn't dare eat! And I ate the thistle! Oh, forgive me, *forgive* me. I was blind, depraved; I was so *cañí*—that means gypsy, my love. Vice and crudeness had left a scab on my heart. Let's just call it a crust . . . Jacintilla, don't look at me that way. What I'm telling you is the absolute truth. If I'm lying, may I be struck dead this minute. I can see all my mistakes clearly tonight. I don't know what's gotten into me, but I feel inspired. I can see things better, believe me. I love you, my angel, my little dove, and I'm going to build an altar of gold to adore you."

"Goodness, aren't we poetic!" exclaimed the wife, no longer able to hide her anger. "Why don't you go to bed?"

"Go to bed? Me? When I have so many things to tell you, my little chick!" added Santa Cruz who, having already tired of kneeling, had drawn up a footstool to sit at his wife's feet. "Please forgive me for not having been honest with you. I was ashamed of revealing certain things to you. But I can't go on anymore like this. My conscience has got to clear itself, like a jug that has to be knocked over, yes, yes, and let it all come spilling out. You'll forgive me when you've heard me out, won't you? Say you will. There are times during mankind's existence, I mean in a man's life, terrible times, my love. You understand, don't you? I didn't know you then. I was like humanity before the Messiah's coming, in the dark, the lights out . . . yes, that's it. Don't condemn me, no, don't; don't condemn me before you've heard me out."

Jacinta didn't know what to do. For a while they stared at each other, each riveting his eyes on the other, until Juan said in a quieter tone:

"If only you could've seen her! Fortunata's eyes were like stars, almost like the ones on the Virgin in Carmen Church who used to be in Santo Tomás Church and who's in San Ginés now. Ask Estupiñá. Ask him if you don't believe me. Let's see . . . Fortunata's hands were rough from working so hard. Her heart was pure innocence. Fortunata hadn't had any education. Such a pretty mouth, and it left out letters right and left and mixed up others. She used to say 'indilgences,' 'goin,' 'sorta.' She spent her childhood taking care of the 'cattle.' You know what the 'cattle' were? Hens. And she nursed the baby doves herself. Since baby birds won't eat anything that doesn't come from their mother's beak, Fortunata would take them to her bosom—and oh, if you could see what a lovely bosom—except that there were a lot of scratches on it, from the birds' feet. Then she'd have a mouthful of water and a few grains of carob beans, and putting their beaks into her mouth, she'd feed them. She was the mother dove for all the birdlets. Then she'd warm them with her own heat, cradling them, saying 'shhhhhh,' and sing them lullabies. Poor Fortunata, poor Pitusa!* . . . Did I tell you that they called her *la Pitusa*? No? Well, now I've told you. So there . . . I lost her, yes, and that's that; everyone must bear his share in life. I lost her. I tricked her, I told her hundreds of lies, I made her think that I was going to marry her. You see what I mean? I really *am* a cad! Let me laugh a little. Oh, yes, she fell for every phony line I handed her. The common people are very naive, they're just plain stupid. They'll believe anything you tell them as long as you use pretty words. She fell for me, hook, line, and sinker, and I just walked off with her honor—thought nothing of it. Men, us *señoritos* I mean, are a rotten lot; we think that the honor of a village girl is just a toy for us. Don't look at me like that, darling. I know you're right. I'm no good, I deserve your scorn, because . . . as you yourself would say, any woman is always one of God's creatures, isn't she? And after having my fun with her, I left her to fend for herself, in the gutter . . . like a bitch. Didn't I?"

6

Jacinta was in a state of shock, half dead with fear and grief. She didn't know what to do or say. "Juanito," she exclaimed, wiping the perspiration from her husband's forehead, "you're not well! Calm down, for heaven's sake. You're delirious."

"No, I'm not delirious, I'm repenting," said Santa Cruz who, practically collapsing as he tried to move, braced himself with his hands on the floor. "Do you think that maybe it was the wine? Oh, no, my dear. Don't underrate me. It's my conscience that has gone to my head, and it weighs so much it throws me off balance. Let me prostrate myself and and place all my guilt at your feet so that you'll forgive me. Don't move, don't leave me, for God's sake. Where are you going? Can't you see how upset I am?"

"What I see is . . . Oh my God, Juan, for the love of God, try to calm down; stop saying such absurd things. Lie down. I'll make you a cup of tea."

"Tea? What good can tea do me?" he queried in such a broken voice that tears welled up in Jacinta's eyes. "You offer me tea, when what I need is your forgiveness, all humanity's forgiveness, for having insulted and trampled on another human being. Say you will. There are times in people's existence, I mean in men's lives, when one should have a thousand mouths so that all at once, with all of

---

* Juanito's nickname for Fortunata is a word that means "little, graceful, or pretty" and is usually applied to a child.

them, one could . . . express the, uh . . . it would be a chorus, yes, that's it. Because I've been wicked, don't say I haven't been. No, don't say it."

Jacinta saw that her husband was sobbing. But was he really sobbing or was it all a joke?

"Juan, for God's sake, please! You're torturing me!"

"No, my darling," he replied, seated on the floor, keeping his face covered with his hands. "Can't you see that I'm crying? Take pity on a poor man. I've been perverse. Because Pitusa worshiped me. Let's face it."

Then he raised his head and looked a bit calmer.

"Let's face it; the truth should come first, before everything else. She worshiped me. She thought I wasn't like everyone else; that I was the essence of a gentleman, and breeding, and decency, and nobility, in person; the end-all of men . . . Nobility! What a joke! Nobility in my lies. It can't be, I tell you. It simply can't. Decency because you wear something called a frock coat! What a farce humanity is. The poor always the underdogs, the rich doing as they please. I'm rich. I'm frivolous, I know it. The picturesque charm was wearing off. If it's charming, crudeness is seductive for a while, but then it makes you sick to your stomach. The burden I'd taken on was heavier every day. The smell of garlic was starting to disgust me. I even wished—and believe me, it's the truth—that Pitusa were worthless so that I could give her the gate . . . but no, she wasn't one of those. Her worthless? Not on your life. If I'd told her to throw herself into a fire she would've plunged in head first. Pandemonium every day in that house. One day it would end off all right, the next day it wouldn't. Singing, guitar playing . . . José Izquierdo, the one they called Plato* because he ate from a plate as big as a dishpan, would throw gravel at the picador. Villalonga and I would egg them on or help them make up, depending on what suited us best. Pitusa would tremble whether they were happy or sulking. Do you know what was entering my head? Not to have anything more to do with that cursed house. Finally Villalonga and I decided to disappear into thin air and never go back. One night there was such a row that they even took out their knives and it nearly ended up in a bloodbath for all of us. I can hear their refined words now: 'Slob, cheat, snake-in-the-grass, crap, louse.'

"That kind of life wasn't possible. Admit it. I was so fed up I couldn't stand it. Pitusa became hateful to me, just like the disgusting words they used. One day I said, 'I'll be back,' and I never went back. As Villalonga put it, 'Make a clean break.' My conscience bothered me though, as if a fine thread in it were tugging at me to go back there. I snipped it. Then Fortunata started to pursue me. I had to play hide and seek. She'd be in one place and I'd be in another. Oh, I was as slippery as an eel. She wasn't going to catch me, no sir. The last one of the bunch I saw was

---

* In the original, the character is called Platón, which means both 'big plate' and the name Plato.

Izquierdo. I met him one day on the staircase, going up to my house. He threatened me. He said Pitusa had 'gotten big,' five months along . . . five months! I shrugged my shoulders. He made a few remarks, I made a few, then I swung at him and crash! Izquierdo fell down a whole flight of stairs at once . . . another blow and crash! down the next flight, head over heels . . . "

He was visibly disturbed as he told this. He remained seated on the floor, legs extended, one arm resting on the seat of the chair. Jacinta was trembling. She felt a deathly cold, and her teeth were chattering. She remained standing in the middle of the room like a statue, contemplating the incredibly pitiful figure that her husband made, not daring to ask him anything or request that he clarify any of the strange parts of what he was revealing to her.

"For the love of God, for your mother's sake!" she cried at last, moved by love and fear, "don't tell me any more. You *must* lie down and try to go to sleep. Be quiet now."

"Be quiet? Be quiet? Ah, my good wife, my angel, my Savior and Messiah . . . you forgive me, don't you? Say you do."

He leaped up and tried to walk. He couldn't. He spun around and collapsed on the sofa, covering his eyes and saying in a hollow voice: "What a nightmare!" Jacinta approached him, put her arms around his neck, and lulled him to sleep as one would a child.

Overcome at last by its own excited state, the Dauphin's brain lapsed into a dull stupor. His nerves, which were beginning to be calmed, fought the sedation. Suddenly he moved, as if something were jumping inside him, and he uttered several syllables. But the sedation was winning, and he finally fell into a deep sleep. At midnight, not without considerable effort, Jacinta was able to carry him to bed and tuck him in. He dropped off to sleep again as if he'd fallen down a well, and his wife spent a miserable night tormented by the unpleasant recollection of what she had seen and heard.

The next day Santa Cruz was somewhat embarrassed. He was vaguely aware of the foolish things he had said and done the night before, and his self-esteem suffered terribly at the thought that he had looked ridiculous. He didn't dare bring it up to his wife and she, being the soul of prudence, besides not breathing a word about it, was as pleasant and affectionate as usual. Eventually, though, my friend couldn't resist a craving to explain his conduct, so preparing the ground with oozing flattery, he said:

"Sweetie, you'll have to excuse me for the bad time I gave you last night. I must've been an awful bore. I felt so sick! Nothing of the sort has ever happened to me before. Tell me the foolish things I said to you, because I can't remember them."

"Oh, there were so many, *so* many . . . Thank goodness I was the only one in the audience."

"Come on, be frank: I was unbearable."

"Well, you're right about that."

"It's just that I don't know . . . Never before in my life, I assure you, *never* have I gotten so smashed. It was the damned Englishman's fault, and he's going to pay for it. God, I must've been a sight! What did I say? Don't pay any attention to whatever it was, dear, because I probably said hundreds of things that weren't true. What a mess! Are you mad? Don't be, please; there's no reason to be."

"Of course not. Since you were . . . "

Jacinta didn't dare say "drunk." The awful word refused to cross her lips.

"Say it, sweetie. Say 'tipsy.' It sounds better, and it makes what I did seem less serious."

"Well, since you were a bit tipsy, you weren't responsible for what you said."

"Why, did I say anything offensive?"

"No, just a half-dozen elegant words, the kind one uses in only the best society. I didn't understand them very well. The rest was crystal clear, though; *too* clear, really. You cried for your beloved Pitusa, and you called yourself a cad for having abandoned her. Believe me, you were impossible."

"Oh, go on, dear. Now that my head's clear I want to tell you some more so that you won't think that I'm worse than I am."

They went for a walk down the Delicias, and sitting on a lonely bench facing the river, they chatted for a while. Jacinta's eyes devoured her husband, guessing his words before he actually said them and checking them against the expression in his eyes to see if they were sincere. Was Juan telling the truth? There was a bit of everything. His declarations were a recasting of the truth, as in ancient comedies; his vanity kept him from giving her a true account of the facts. Well, when he got back from Plencia, engaged to be married and in love with his fiancée, he was curious to know what had become of Fortunata, from whom he hadn't had any news in a long time. He wasn't moved by any feelings of tenderness, but by compassion and the desire to lend her a hand if she was in a bad way. Plato was out of town and his wife had kicked the bucket. No one knew where the devil the picador was keeping himself, but Segunda had closed the poultry shop and set up again right in the Cava, a bit lower down, near the Steps, in a cavelike hole she called "the establishment," where she lived and sold coffee every morning to the market people. The furnishings consisted of a table, two chairs, and a few pieces of crockery. The rest of the day she lent her services at a nearby tavern. Her physical and economic condition had changed so drastically that her former pal hardly recognized her.

"And what about the other woman?" *This* was what mattered.

7

It took Santa Cruz some time to muster up the answer she had requested. He drew lines on the ground with his cane. Finally he put it this way:

"I gathered that she had—"

Jacinta's mercy saved him from finishing the sentence; she supplied the words herself. The Dauphin felt relieved of a burden.

"I tried to see her. I looked all over for her . . . no luck. But wait a minute, you believe me, don't you? I couldn't do anything. And then your mother died. For a while I didn't even think about it, and I must say that I felt a sort of prickling here, in my conscience. Sometime in January this year, when I was preparing to make further inquiries, a friend of Segunda's told me that Pitusa had left Madrid. Where? With whom? I didn't know then and I still don't know. And I swear that I haven't seen her since or heard a word from her."

His wife heaved a deep sigh. She didn't know why, but her soul was still heavy; her scrupulous character made her feel that she should bear some of her husband's responsibility for that evil deed. For it was, beyond all doubt, an evil deed. Jacinta could not regard the fact of his abandoning Fortunata from any other standpoint, even though his action had meant the triumph of legitimate love over criminal love, marriage over an illicit relationship. But they couldn't spend any more time talking, because they were planning to leave for Cádiz that afternoon and still had to pack and buy a few souvenirs. There was to be a souvenir from each city for each person. With all the activity of leaving, shopping, and saying their farewells, both of them were so distracted that by afternoon all the unpleasant thoughts had vanished.

Not until three days later did Jacinta again experience that gnawing sensation. It came upon her suddenly, provoked by Lord knows what, perhaps by one of those mysterious initiatives of one's memory that seem to appear out of nowhere. We remember things for no logical reason, and sometimes the linking of thoughts is extravagant, even ridiculous. Who would have ever thought that Jacinta would remember Fortunata when she heard someone shout, "Fresh anchovies from Cádiz!" A curious observer might ask, and rightly so, what in the world anchovies had to do with that woman. Nothing, nothing at all.

The couple returned from Cádiz on the mail train. They didn't plan to make any stops, but to go directly to Madrid. They were very content, anxious to see the family and give each one his or her trinket. Although she still felt that same gnawing, Jacinta had resolved not to bring up the subject again, but to bury it in her memory until every trace of it was erased by time. Upon arriving at the station in Jerez, however, something happened that unexpectedly revived what they both were trying to forget. It was like this: they saw the darned Englishman come out of the station restaurant, and he immediately recognized them, walking over to greet them very politely and gallantly inviting them to join him for a few drinks. As soon as they were able to shake him off, Santa Cruz cursed him vehemently and said that some day he'd get the chance to give him the black eye he deserved. "That creep's the one who's to blame for my acting the way I did that night and telling you all those awful things."

At this point, the conversation began to get involved again, until it touched on "the sore spot." Jacinta didn't want to leave her conviction bottled up inside, so at the first opportunity she poured it out:

"Poor women!" she exclaimed. "They always get the worst of it."

"You must judge things more carefully, darling, examine the circumstances . . . study the environment," stated Santa Cruz, rounding up his mental gimmicks for a conventional dialectic, the sort that will prove anything you want.

Jacinta let herself be caressed. She wasn't angry. But in her soul, a phenomenon very new to her was taking place. She felt two different feelings shuffling, superimposing themselves, one, then the other. Since she adored her husband, she was proud that he had scorned the other woman for her. This pride is primordial and will always persist, even in the most perfect of beings. The other feeling stemmed from the virtue underlying her noble soul, and it inspired her to protest against his having abused and pitilessly abandoned the unknown woman. Try as he might to deny it, the Dauphin had abused humanity. Jacinta could not pretend that he had not. The victory of her vanity didn't prevent her from seeing that underneath the trophy lay a crushed victim. Perhaps the victim did deserve it; but whether the woman deserved her fate or not was not Jacinta's concern, and on the altar of her soul there was a tiny flame of compassion burning.

With perspicacity, Santa Cruz understood this and tried to free his wife from the burden of having compassion for someone who clearly did not deserve it. In order to persuade her, he used all the rational apparatus he could command (it was very shiny, but not terribly solid), marshaling all the arguments he had learned in his dealings with human frivolities and superficial readings. "Look, dear, you've got to face reality. There are two worlds, the one you *can* see and the one you *can't* see. Society isn't governed by ideas alone. Some fix we'd be in if it were . . . I'm not as guilty as it seems at first glance; follow me closely, now. Differences in education and background always establish a great difference in conduct in human relations. This isn't in the Decalogue; it's reality. Social conduct has its laws, laws that are not written down anywhere, but that you're aware of and don't break. I made a few mistakes—who would say I didn't?—but what if I'd gone on with those people, if I'd 'kept my word' with Pitusa? Just imagine! I see you're smiling, which proves that it would've been absurd, crazy, to have stayed on what appeared to be the straight and narrow road then. From our viewpoint, it's altogether different. When it comes to morals, things are right or wrong, depending on how you look at them. So you see, to save myself all I could have done was what I did. Survival of the fittest. That's life. Because I *did* have to save myself, you'll agree on that, won't you? Well, if I was going to do it, I had to jump off the sinking ship. There's always someone who drowns in a shipwreck. And as for abandoning her, there's a lot that hasn't been said about that, either. Some words don't mean anything out of context. You've got to consider the facts. I looked for her, to help her out, but she chose not to appear. Everyone gets what he deserves. What she got was for not showing up when I was looking for her."

No one would dream that the man who was reasoning in this fashion, so subtly and paradoxically, was the same man who, several nights before, under "the influence," had poured out his heart and soul with a brutal sincerity that can be compared only to the physical vomiting induced by a powerful emetic. Afterward, when his head cleared and he was once again master of the tricks that his well-read, worldly self knew, he didn't allow a single uncouth word to cross his lips, nor any spontaneous expression like those he knew but kept hidden away, like the parts of a gaudy costume stashed into a corner by someone who was once a comedian, even though only an amateur. All that could be found in him now were conventional phrases and clever sentences dressed up in intellectual airs, in a frock coat cut from ready-made ideas with the lapels of language pressed flat.

Jacinta, who was still quite unworldly, was dazzled by her husband's seductive speech. And she loved him so much—perhaps for that very gift and for others— that she didn't need to strain her mind in the slightest to believe everything he was saying, although it's true that she believed him more out of faith, which is feeling, than out of conviction. They talked for a long time, blending arguments with discreet signs of affection (more people entered the compartment in Seville and they had to forget about their "cuddling," as they put it). And when night fell over Spain, which they were crossing swiftly, they fell asleep somewhere around the Despeñaperros mountain pass; they dreamed about how much they loved each other, and they finally awoke in Alcázar with the pleasant thought that they would soon be in Madrid with the family again, telling them all the details of their trip (except for the little scene that night) and giving the presents they'd bought.

They were bringing Estupiñá a cane that had a parrot's head for a handle.

VI. Still More Details about the Distinguished Family

I

MONTHS WENT BY, YEARS WENT BY, and all was peace and harmony in that happy home. There never was a family in Madrid that got along as well as the two Santa Cruz couples. Nor can one imagine two such compatible souls as Barbarita and Jacinta. I've seen mother-in-law and daughter-in-law together many times and swear that you could hardly tell the difference in their ages. At fifty-three Barbarita still had a marvelous freshness, a perfect figure, and amazingly good teeth. It's true that her hair was almost white, but it looked more as if it had been powdered Pompadour style than whitened by age. Yet what really made her youthful more than anything else was her constant affability, that charming and kind smile that gave her face a special radiance.

Those four people certainly had no reason to complain about their fate, and yet there are cases like theirs: individuals and families to whom God owes nothing and who nevertheless ask Him for more. One of the vices of human nature is begging, there's no doubt about it. Just look at the Santa Cruzes—in perfect health, rich, respected by everyone, and devoted to one another. What didn't they have? Nothing, you'd say. But one of the four was begging. Somehow, when circumstances bless a man with most of what he wants and deprive him of only one thing, the principle of discontent, always animating us earthly beings, kindles a desire for that little bit that was not granted. Health, wealth, love, peace, and other advantages did not satisfy Jacinta's soul. After a year of marriage, and even more so after two, she fervently desired what she lacked. Poor girl! She had everything, except children.

This sorrow, a minor annoyance at first, impatience really, soon became a painful feeling of emptiness. It wasn't very Christian, as Barbarita said, to despair at the lack of a successor. The Lord, who had been so good to them, had merely denied them that wish. There was nothing that they could do but resign themselves and praise the hand of the power who proves His omnipotence as much by giving as by taking away.

In this manner she consoled her daughter-in-law, who seemed more like a daughter to her; but deep inside she shared Jacinta's wish for a child to appear to perpetuate the Santa Cruz line and make them all happy. She kept this ardent desire to herself in order not to increase Jacinta's sorrow, anxiously watching in the meantime for anything that might possibly be a sign of hope for a successor. But none came. A year went by, then two, and still nothing, not even any of those vague presentiments typical of women who wish to become mothers, making their heartbeat quicken and sometimes making their words and actions appear foolish.

"Don't be in such a hurry," Barbarita would say to her niece. "You're very young. Don't worry about having children—you'll have them in time. You'll have a whole family on your hands, and you'll be as bored with them as your mother was, and you'll beg the Lord not to give you any more. You know something? We're better off as we are. All children do is mess everything up and give you a headache. The measles, then croup . . . And the nursemaids, what a nuisance *they* are! And then you become a slave: Are they eating what they should? Will they digest it? What if they fall and split open their heads? Then they start to show their own ways. What if they're bad seeds, and don't study either? Heaven only knows what they may bring!"

This didn't convince Jacinta. She wanted little ones no matter what, even if they turned out rickety and ugly; or grew up to be pranksters, perverts or daredevils; or nearly killed her with trouble when they got older. Her two older sisters gave birth every year, like their mother. But she didn't bear anything, not even hope. More contradictory yet was the fact that Candelaria, who was married to a poor man, had had twins! And she, who was rich, hadn't even had half a child! God must be in his dotage, she figured.

Let's turn to something else. Being a rich and terribly respectable family, the Santa Cruzes were very well connected and had friends in all spheres, from the highest to the lowest. It's strange to see how our times, which are unfortunate in other ways, present us with a happy confusion of social classes or, rather, their harmony and reconciliation. In this respect our country is ahead of others, where serious historical suits for equality are awaiting a verdict. The problem has been solved here simply and peacefully, thanks to the democratic spirit of Spaniards and our less vehement concern about aristocratic status. A huge national defect, "employomania," has also had its part in this great conquest. Offices have become the trunk onto which historical branches have been grafted, and from these branches friendships have sprung up between the fallen nobleman and the plebian swollen with a university degree, and such friendships have led to blood relations. This confusion is good. Thanks to its existence, we aren't terrified of being afflicted by class wars; we already have a mild, inoffensive form of socialism in our blood. Imperceptibly, and aided by bureaucracy, poverty, and education, all classes have gradually mixed; the members of one migrate to another, making a strong network that holds together and toughens the national fabric. Birth means nothing to us, and comments on ancestral lineage are only conversation. There are no differences other than the essential ones based on good versus bad breeding, on stupidity versus discretion, on the spiritual inequalities that are as old as the soul itself. The other positive class distinction, money, is based on economic principles as immutable as the laws of physics, and trying to alter them would be like trying to swallow the sea.

The friends and relations of the Santa Cruz and Arnáiz families may serve as an example of that merry scrambling of social classes. But who in the devil would dare to make statistics out of the branches of such an extensive and labyrinthine tree? That tree is like a climbing vine whose branches crisscross, shooting up and down, disappearing into pockets of thick shrubbery. Such a venture can be undertaken only with the help of Estupiñá, who knows all the ins and outs of the stories of all the business families in Madrid and all the liaisons there have been for half a century. Tubs Arnáiz knows a lot too. He always has a craving to talk about family backgrounds and hunt for relationships, discovering the humble origins of some proud fortunes and emphasizing the inequality in certain marriages that, to tell the truth, are responsible for having laid the democratic ground on which Spanish society stands. The following information is from a conversation between Arnáiz and Estupiñá:

2

We already know that Don Baldomero Santa Cruz's and Gumersindo and Barbarita Arnáiz's mothers were related and were descendants of Trujillo, the Extremaduran who made donkey saddles. The present-day bank Trujillo and Fernández, a pillar of respectability and reliability, descends from the same line. So Barbarita is related to the director of that bank, although her relationship is somewhat distant. The first count of Trujillo is married to one of the daughters of the famous merchant Casarredonda, who made a colossal fortune selling sackcloth from Coruña and Vivero for uniforms for the troops and the National Guard. Another one of the marquis of Casarredonda's daughters was the duchess of Gravelinas. With this we have a perfect link between the old aristocracy and the modern business world.

But in Cádiz there is an ancient and wealthy family of merchants that has tangled the social skein more than any other family. The daughters of the shawl importer, later banker and wine specialist, the famous Bonilla, were married: one to Sánchez Botín, the landowner (and their children were General Minio's wife, the marquise of Tellería, and Alejandro Sánchez Botín); the next to one of the Morenos of Madrid, co-founder of the Five Unions and the San Fernando Bank;

the third to the duke of Trastamara, and their union produced Pepito Trastamara. Bonilla's only son married a Trujillo.

Let's turn now to the Morenos, originally from the Mena Valley, one of the most widespread families of all, offering the most inequalities and contrasts because of their countless scattered members. Arnáiz and Estupiñá have argued (without reaching an agreement) over whether the trunk of the Moreno family tree was in a drugstore or a furrier's. There's a certain obscurity in this that won't be cleared up until it attracts one of those fanatic researchers who are capable of telling Noah how many hairs he had on his head and the number of moves he made when he went on that first escapade in the annals of history. What is known is that a Moreno married an Isla-Bonilla at the beginning of the century, which is how the banking house originated. From 1819 to 1835 it was located near the Plaza Mayor, next to the church, and afterward it moved to Pontejos Square. About the same time, we hear of a Moreno in the Supreme Court, another in the armada, another in the army, and another in the Church. The banking house was no longer called Moreno in 1870, but instead Ruiz-Ochoa and Company, although a principal associate was Don Manuel Moreno-Isla. The ancient Moreno family tree branches off in many directions, into the Moreno-Islas, the Moreno-Vallejos, and the Moreno-Rubios; in other words, into the rich Morenos and the poor Morenos, so far removed from each other by now that they scarcely have any contact, and do not even consider themselves related. Castita Moreno (Barbarita's conceited friend at the Imperial School) was born on the rich side, but life's vicissitudes made her end up on the poor side. She married a pharmacist from the interminable Samaniego family, who also have a role in this. One of the rich young Moreno girls married a Pacheco, a second son of an aristocrat, brother to the duke of Gravelinas, and from this union came Guillermina Pacheco, whom we shall meet later. So notice how a branch of the Morenos gets into the Gravelinas shrubbery, where there is also a Trujillo branch that had already gotten snarled with Arnáiz branches in Madrid and Bonilla branches in Cádiz, making a tangle whose threads are almost impossible to follow.

There's more yet. Don Pascual Muñoz, the owner of a highly accredited store on Tintoreros Street and a progressive with great prestige in the southern districts and genuine electoral and political power in Madrid, married a Moreno from some branch or other, I don't recall which, thus marrying into the Mendizábals and Bonillas from Cádiz. His son, who was to become the marquis of Casa-Muñoz, married a girl whose father was Albert, the front man who handled the wool and canvas contracts with the government. Eulalia Muñoz, also a daughter of Don Pascual and sister of the marquis, married Don Cayetano Villuendas, a rich real estate agent and a progressive from way back. We'll tie these loose ends later.

The Samaniegos, like the Morenos, were natives of Mena, and are also quite a tribe. We already know that Gumersindo Arnáiz's second daughter, Jacinta's sister, married Pepe Samaniego, the son of a bankrupt druggist on Concepción Jerónima Street. There are lots of Samaniegos with small businesses; reading the instructive book made up of shop signs, we discover a Samaniego's Pharmacy on Ave María Street (owned by Castita Moreno's husband), and a Samaniego's Meat Market on Maldonadas Street. There are also Morenos without signs: a moneylender knowledgeable in legal matters; a bill collector at a bank; another who sells silk in a shop on Botoneras Street; and, finally, several salesclerks who are cousins of the stockbroker Samaniego.

Gumersindo Arnáiz's eldest daughter married Ramón Villuendas, the widower with two children, a well-known banker on Toledo Street whose firm was the busiest in Madrid. A brother of his married Aparisi's widow's daughter. Aparisi at one time owned a haberdashery where Pepe Samaniego worked as a clerk. Their uncle, Don Cayetano Villuendas, a staunch progressive and wealthy landlord, was Eulalia Muñoz's husband, and his huge fortune came from tanning leather, before Céspedes' time. So there are no longer any loose ends.

Now we're faced with some branches that seem to go off in different directions, but actually intertwine. Who, though, can say exactly how and where they intersect the complicated crisscrossed stems of this colossal climbing plant? Who can tell whether Dámaso Trujillo, who set up The Lily Stem on the Plaza Mayor, belongs to the line of the aforementioned Trujillos? Who would set himself the task of determining whether or not the owner of a tiny blanket shop on Encomienda Street called Good Taste is a bona fide relative of the rich Villuendases? There are those who say that Pepe Moreno-Vallejo, a cordmaker on Concepción Jerónima Street, is first cousin to Don Manuel Moreno-Isla, one of the Morenos for whom life is a bowl of cherries; and it's also said that a lowly paid employee named Arnáiz is a relative of Barbarita's. There's a Muñoz y Aparisi, a tripemonger in the vicinity of the Rastro Market, who's said to be a second cousin of the marquis of Casa-Muñoz and his sister, Aparisi's widow. And finally, it must be added that there's a certain Trujillo—a Jesuit—who has claimed a place on this distinguished plant; and we must certainly make room for His Illustrious Bishop of Plasencia, Fray Luis Moreno-Isla y Bonilla. The Trujillo name also appears on Sra. Zalamero's family tree: she is the wife of the under secretary of the interior, but her maiden name is Ruiz-Ochoa, and she is the daughter of the distinguished person who directs the Moreno bank today.

Barbarita wasn't in touch with all the individuals who appear on this complicated climbing plant. She avoided many because she considered them too high up; she was hardly aware of others because they were too far down. Her true friendships, like her acknowledged relatives, were not very numerous, although they did constitute a large circle in which all hierarchies mingled. In the same day, on a walk or a shopping trip, she exchanged variously affectionate greetings

with Zalamero's wife, with Señora Minio (the general's wife), with Adela Trujillo, with a rich Villuendas, with a poor Villuendas, with Samaniego's fishmonger
relative, with the duchess of Gravelinas, with a Moreno-Vallejo who was a judge,
with a Moreno-Rubio who was a doctor, with a Moreno-Jáuregui who was a
haberdasher, with an Aparisi in the clergy, with various clerks—in short, with
such different people that someone with less tact would have mixed up their
names and ways of greeting them.

Even the most competent mind would be incapable of tracing the labyrinthine
offshoots of this colossal tree of Madrid families and keeping them separate.
Threads cross, get lost, and reappear where you'd least expect them. After a
thousand or so turns upward and about as many downward, they join, then separate, and from their intersection or bifurcation come new ties, new skeins and
tangles. The way in which the extremities of these multitudinous branches meet is
curious indeed; as, for example, when Pepito Trastamara, who bears the name of
Don Alfonso XI's illegitimate offspring, asks for a loan from Cándido Samaniego,
a usurious moneylender and member of the Society for the Protection of Gentlemen in Distress.

3

The Santa Cruzes owned the apartment house in which they lived. It was on
Pontejos Street, facing the little square of the same name; they'd bought the
building from the late Aparisi, one of the associates of the Philippines Company.
The owners occupied the first floor, which was immense; its twelve balconies
overlooked the street and it had a very comfortable interior. Barbarita wouldn't
have traded it for any of the modern townhouses where you find nothing but
staircases and you have to live open to the wind on all four sides. She had plenty
of rooms, and they were all off the same hall that led from the living room to the
kitchen. Nor would she have exchanged her neighborhood, that "corner of
Madrid" where she had been born, for any of the flamboyant sections of town that
enjoyed the reputation of being airier and cheerier. No matter what they said, the
Salamanca neighborhood was country. The good lady was so fond of the suburb
that was her native land that in her mind she wasn't really living in Madrid unless
she could hear the concave noise of the water buckets being dipped into the
Pontejos well in the morning, the uproar of the mail coaches every morning and
afternoon, the constant echo of the hubbub on Postas Street, the beating of
tambourines in Santa Cruz Square, the chiming of the post office clock, which
sounded as if it were in her very own house, the collectors going by ladened with

money, and the mailmen filing out to make their rounds. Barbarita had grown accustomed to the neighborhood noises; they were somewhat like friends without whose company she couldn't live.

Their house was so large that the two couples lived in comfort, with plenty of extra room. They had a rather old-fashioned living room with three balconies. Then behind it to the left was Barbarita's parlor, another room, and the bedroom. To the right of the living room was Juanito's "study," as it was called, not because he did any work there, but because it had a desk with an inkwell and two beautiful bookcases. It was a very comfortable and well-furnished room. Jacinta's parlor, which adjoined it, was the prettiest and most elegant room in the house and the only tapestried one (all the others had wallpaper whose artistic value was somewhat dubious, the predominating colors being gray, pearl, and gold). The room had some very delicate watercolors that Juanito had bought and two or three pastels, all fine pieces with decent signatures. Within the limits of what was popular, Santa Cruz had good taste. The furniture was covered in satin or some stylish combination of plush and silk, its main feature being that it didn't strike you as either original or conventional. Next came the young couple's bedroom, distinguishable from their parents' room in that the latter had a double bed, whereas the former had very elegant twin beds with blue silk canopies. The parents' bed looked like massive mahogany scaffolding with a dark forbidding headboard and bedposts like columns in a Maundy Thursday ciborium. The "youngsters' room" was adjacent to the dressing rooms, and then came two large rooms Jacinta intended to use for the children . . . when the Lord granted them, that is. They were furnished with leftovers from redecorated rooms and had a mixed look about them. But Jacinta's imagination had already foreseen down to the last detail all that would be put there when the time came.

The dining room was an interior room with three windows overlooking the courtyard; it had an enormous table and walnut sideboards full of delicate china, some of those ubiquitous leather-backed chairs, and on the walls imitation oak wallpaper, paneled. There were some still lifes in oil, not bad really, with the inevitable slice of watermelon, dead rabbit, and a couple of slices of hake painted so graphically that they almost smelled. Don Baldomero's study was also an interior room.

The Santa Cruz family had a rented carriage at their disposal and were seen in it when they went for their drives, although theirs was the kind that "wasn't conspicuous." From time to time Juan rented a phaeton or a tilbury, which he drove very well, and he also had a riding horse; but he had such a craving for variety that he had scarcely mounted one horse, when he began to find fault with it and wanted to exchange it for another. The two couples didn't deprive themselves of anything, but they weren't conceited and always shrank from the limelight and from letting the newspapers call them "Hosts." They ate well. They were informal at home and their meals had a certain patriarchal benevolence about them, because they sometimes invited humble people together with some very decent impoverished ladies and gentlemen. They didn't have one of those white-hatted chefs, they had an old cook, a woman with quite a repertoire who could have held her own against any chef; she was assisted by two kitchen maids who were more like apprentices.

At the beginning of every month Barbarita received a thousand *duros* from her husband. Don Baldomero enjoyed an income of twenty-five thousand *duros*, partly from rentals, partly from his shares in the Bank of Spain, and the rest from what stock he still had in his former shop. In addition to this, he gave his son two thousand *duros* a semester for his personal needs, and on a number of occasions offered him some capital to start a business of his own. But the boy was happy with his golden indolence and didn't want any worries. Don Baldomero invested the rest of his income, purchasing more shares every year or accumulating a sum with which to buy another apartment house. Of the thousand *duros* his wife was allotted each month, she gave the Dauphin two or three thousand *reales* which, combined with what his papá gave him, put him in seventh heaven. The seventeen thousand *reales* left over were for daily household expenses, and the two ladies managed their funds very well, without there ever being the slightest question over a *duro* more or a *duro* less. Both of them supervised the domestic situation, particularly the mother-in-law, who was a bit inclined to be an enlightened despot. The daughter-in-law had the delicate art of respecting this, and when she noticed something she had ordered being changed by the autocrat, she did not protest. When it came to household matters, Barbarita was general manager; even her husband, after he'd assigned the money to her, was free of handling any domestic affairs except perhaps their summer trips. The lady paid for everything, from the carriage rental down to the monthly *peseta* for the newspaper *El Imparcial*, and she didn't even need to keep track of her complicated accounts. She had such a good head for numbers that she never once crossed that faint line which the rich cross so easily. When the end of the month came there was always extra, her "surplus," which she donated to several charitable associations that will be mentioned later in our story. Jacinta always spent much less than the sum her mother-in-law gave her for miscellaneous expenses. She wasn't particularly interested in constantly wearing something new or in making the dressmakers rich. The thrifty habits she had acquired as a child were so deeply ingrained that although she could have done differently, she hired a seamstress to come to the house for alterations and remodeling; other ladies who weren't as wealthy sent their things out to be done. Luckily for her, she didn't have to bother about thinking up ways of using the "surplus," because her sister Candelaria was always there: poor, and with an ever growing brood. Jacinta's younger unmarried sisters were also frequent recipients of her gifts: the latest hat, or fichus, or a shawl, or even entire outfits fresh from Paris.

Their season ticket for an orchestra box at the Royal Theater was Don Baldomero's idea; he couldn't have cared less about going to the opera, but he wanted Barbarita to go to them so that when they were retiring, or after they were already in bed, she could relate to him what she had seen at that "fabulous coliseum." It just so happened that she didn't find the Royal particularly exciting either, but she gladly accepted so that Jacinta could go. Jacinta, in turn, wasn't much of a theater-goer, but she was delighted to be able to take her unmarried sisters to the Royal; if it weren't for her, she knew they'd never get a glimpse of a stage. Juan, who was very fond of music, had reserved a box higher up and close to the stage where he sat with six friends at all performances.

The Santa Cruz women didn't dress conspicuously for the theater. Any looks in their direction were intended for the younger chicks, symmetrically arranged in the most noticeable seats. Barbarita usually sat in the front row so that she could aim her opera glasses squarely at the audience and be able to tell Baldomero something more than the details of the opera's plot and the stage effects. The two married sisters, Candelaria and Benigna, went from time to time. Jacinta went almost always, but it wasn't much fun for her. Pampered by our good Lord, who had surrounded her with tenderness and well-being and ensconced her in a most healthy, appealing, and serene environment (unusual in this valley of tears), she nevertheless used to say in a plaintive tone that she "didn't enjoy anything." She, who was envied by everyone, envied any poor barefoot beggarwoman she saw go by with a bundle, a little suckling wrapped in rags. Her eyes followed children in whatever shape or form they took, whether they were rich ones dressed in sailor suits and led along by an English nanny, or runny-nosed poor ones wrapped in yellow flannel, dirty, with dandruff in their hair and a crust of drooly bread in their hand. She didn't yearn for just one; she wanted to be surrounded by a whole mob, from the talkative and mischievous five-year-old scamp down to the babe in arms who spends the day laughing like a fool, guzzling milk, and making a fist.

Her affliction declared itself constantly, as much when she met a gang of kids on their way to school, slates on their shoulders and bookbags all dirty, as when a precocious beggar crossed her path, exposing his bare flesh and chilblained feet to stir her compassion. When she saw the pupils of the Pía School in their gallooned uniforms and gloves, so clean and in such complete attire that they resembled miniature gentlemen, her eyes couldn't get their fill. The little girls dressed in pink or blue, playing hoops in the Prado Park, like blossoms just fallen from spring's trees; the poor kids with torn kerchiefs tied around their heads; the toddlers daring to take their first steps, leaning against a shop door, then bracing themselves against the wall; others sucking at their mother's breast, looking out of the corner of their eye at whoever stares at them; the little ragamuffins in street fights; the boys in an empty lot, throwing stones or tearing their clothes and making their mothers despair; the tiny girls dressed up as gypsies at Carnival time, parading about with their hands on their hips; the ones collecting for the Cruz de Mayo; the beanpoles, already sporting a cane and winning prizes at school; the ones at the matinees who let out a shriek during the crucial scene, distracting the actors and infuriating the audience . . . All of them, in a word, interested her equally.

4

Her desire to be a mother began to absorb her so fully that she soon began to take her advantages for granted. They became invisible, as invisible as the basic medium of our life, the air, is to us all. What was the Lord up to, not sending her a single one of the countless babes He had at His disposal? What did His Divine Majesty have in mind? To think of Candelaria, who hardly had enough to live on—she got a new one every year! And the things people said about the Divine Power's sense of equity . . . Justice up there was fair all right, oh yes, we have plenty of proof of that, but . . . Her grief did have strange intermissions, but after these long periods of calm it boomeranged again, hitting her like a chronic illness always lying in wait, ready to spring when you least expect it. Sometimes a meaningless word heard in the street or at home or perhaps the sight of some object flashed the subject through her mind and left her feeling oppressed, inexplicably frightened.

She forgot her affliction by taking care of (and spoiling) her sisters' children, whom she loved dearly. But there was always a distance between herself and her nieces and nephews that she couldn't bridge. They weren't hers, she hadn't *had* them; she didn't feel the bond, that mysterious thread. The only children she really felt bound to existed in her mind, and she had to keep her thoughts lit, like a forge, to get the maternal happiness they gave her. One night she left Candelaria's house just before dinner and headed home. She and her sister had disagreed over a trivial point, that Jacinta was spoiling Pepito, the Samaniegos' three-year-old, their first-born. She bought him expensive toys, she let him hold—and break—the china figures in the living room, and she allowed him to stuff himself with sweets. "Ah, if you were a real mother, you wouldn't do that." "Well, if I'm not, so much the better. And besides, what difference does it make to *you?*" "None. I'm sorry. But what a temper!" "You're the one who's mad, not me." "Well, you *are* spoiled!"

Nonsense like this was inconsequential; ten minutes later they had usually

made up. But when she left that night, she felt like crying. Her desire to have
children had never shown itself so imperiously before. Her sister had humiliated
her, been angry that she loved her little nephew so much. After all, if it wasn't
jealousy, what was it? If and when *she* had a little boy, she wouldn't let anyone so
much as look at him. She went from Hileras Street to Pontejos Street in an
extremely agitated state, oblivious of everyone. It was sprinkling, but she didn't
remember to open her umbrella. The gas lamps in shop windows were already lit,
but Jacinta, who usually stopped in on her way home to see what was new, didn't
stop once. When she got to the corner of Pontejos Square and was about to cross
the street and enter her house, she heard something that made her hesitate. A
chill ran through her body like a knife. She came to a halt, ears perked for the
murmuring sound that seemed to come from the ground, from in between the
cobblestones. It was a wail, an animal's cry begging for help and protection
against desertion and death. And the cry was so piercingly sharp, so cutting, that
it sounded less like the voice of a living creature than the treble sound of a violin
faintly played on its highest note: *meeeeee* . . . Jacinta looked down at the ground;
the whining was undoubtedly rising from the depths of the earth. She felt it pierce
her to the core, penetrate her heart like a needle. She looked all about her and
saw at last, next to the sidewalk by the square, a grate in the curb where rainwater
drains into the sewer. So that was where the sounds were coming from . . . And
those laments were upsetting, producing a painful flood of pity in her. All the
maternal emotions of which she was capable and all the tenderness she had experienced until then in her dreams of being a mother were activated by that cry.
That underground *meeeeee* echoed plaintively in her soul.

To whom could she turn for help? "Deogracias!" she cried out, summoning the
doorman. Fortunately, the doorman was nearby, on the corner of Paz Street talking with one of the coachmen, and he immediately heard his mistress' voice. A
few strides and he was at her side.

"Deogracias, that . . . that noise over there . . . go and see what it is," she
said, trembling and pale.

The doorman listened carefully, then got down on all fours, looking at his
mistress with a rather wheedling, jovial expression.

"It must be . . . Aha! It's some kittens that got thrown into the sewer."

"Kittens! Are you sure? Are you positive that they're kittens?"

"Yes, Miss; and they must belong to the cat in the bookstore across the way.
She gave birth last night and can't nurse 'em all."

Jacinta leaned over to hear better. The *meeeeee* had grown so faint that it was
hardly audible now.

"Get them out of there!" the lady commanded, unusually authoritative.

Deogracias got down on all fours again, rolled up one sleeve, and put his arm into the hole. Jacinta didn't detect the incredulous, almost mocking expression on his face. It was raining harder and water started running into the opening, gushing and bubbling as if it were in a frying pan, so loudly you could hardly hear the thin *meeeeee*-ing any more. Nevertheless, the Dauphin's wife heard it distinctly. The doorman looked up with his dullard's face as if to invoke the heavens and, smiling, said:

"I can't, Miss. They're deep down . . . really deep down."

"Can't you take up this paving stone?" she said, stamping on it.

"Paving stone?" Deogracias repeated, standing up and looking at his mistress as one looks at someone whose sanity is in doubt. "As for taking it up, yes, it could be done. You could notify city hall. The lieutenant mayor, Sr. Aparisi, is a neighbor. But—"

They both perked up their ears.

"Can't hear anything anymore," Deogracias commented stubbornly. "They're drowned."

The brute never suspected that he was driving a dagger into his mistress' back with those words. Jacinta, however, thought she could hear the wailing deep down. But this couldn't go on. She began to realize what a lack of proportion there was between the vastness of her pity and the smallness of its object. The rain came driving down, and by now the opening was swallowing a thick wave that made a gargling noise as it hit the walls of that gullet. Jacinta broke into a run toward the house and dashed up the stairs. Her nerves were so rattled and her heart so heavy that her in-laws and husband thought she was sick. And all night long she suffered the ineffable annoyance of constantly hearing that *meeeeee* from the sewer opening. She knew it was nonsense, perhaps a nervous disorder, but she couldn't help it. And if her mother-in-law should find out from Deogracias what had happened in the street, wouldn't she laugh at her! Jacinta was ashamed at the mere thought of it, blushing as she imagined Barbarita saying in her sarcastic way: "Really my dear, can it be true that you told Deogracias to go down into the sewer to save some abandoned children?"

She confessed the kitten incident to her husband, "swearing him to secrecy." Jacinta couldn't hide anything from him; and she derived a certain pleasure from confiding even the most trivial nonsense on her mind if it was related to the subject of motherhood. Juan, showing good judgment, was indulgent with these consequences of her childless motherhood: her craving for affection. She dared to tell him everything that had happened. And many things that she wouldn't have dared to utter by day surfaced in their intimacy and solitude; they seemed to fit in then. She could say them easily, let them "say themselves." Her remarks on their having a successor were, after all, based on her renewing the probability of their having one.

5

Barbarita was very, and I mean very, wrong to laugh at her daughter-in-law's obsession. As if she didn't have her own, and a good one at that! She had a considerable advantage over Jacinta, though, in that she could satisfy her thoughts by making them real. She was spoiled and got bored with things as soon as she acquired them, whereas her daughter-in-law suffered horribly because she was never able to possess what she most desired. The satisfaction of a desire exasperated Barbarita as much as its denial exasperated Jacinta.

Barbarita's craze was buying. She cultivated art for art's sake, or in other words, buying for buying's sake. There was nothing she liked better than going on a shopping spree and coming home laden with purchases that, though not exactly superfluous, weren't absolutely necessary either. But she never went beyond her means, and her masterful art of being a rich customer stemmed precisely from this control.

The vice had its depravities. Señora Santa Cruz patronized not only the expensive shops, but also the various markets, and she covered every last stall on San Miguel Square, the poultry shops on Caza Street, and the good veal butchers on Santiago Street. "Doña Barbarita" was so well-known in the district that the market women fought for her business and got into brawls over who would have dibs on the illustrious customer.

For the markets as well as the shops, she had an invaluable assistant who looked things over first and took these matters so seriously you'd think he was saving his soul: Plácido Estupiñá. Since he lived in the Cava de San Miguel, from the moment he got up in the first light of day he'd watch the plaza stalls like a hawk. When everyone else was still enjoying the morning in the taverns and sidewalk cafés, he'd go out and look over the stands, getting an idea of the market and how prices were that day. Then, wrapped in his cloak, he'd go off to San Ginés, sometimes arriving there before the sexton had unlocked the door. He'd chat for a while with the women who were already there, some of whom had brought their hot chocolate and gas burners, and he'd make his breakfast at the door. When it was opened, they all rushed in so hurriedly you would have thought they wanted to get a seat at a full house performance. Then Mass started. Barbarita didn't come till the third or fourth Mass; as soon as he saw her appear, Estupiñá slowly slid over to where she was, gliding from pew to pew like a shadow and coming to a stop at her side. The Señora prayed quietly, moving her lips. Plácido always had a lot to tell her, so he interrupted his praying every now and then to squeeze in what he could:

"Don Germán's Mass is next, in the Dolores chapel . . . They're getting in some conger at Martínez's today; they showed me the fresh fish from Laredo—'full of grace, the Lord is with thee'—There's no cauliflower yet, the muleteers from Villaviciosa haven't come because the roads are in awful shape. It's this blasted rain!—'And blessed is the fruit of thy womb, Jesus.'"

On some days neither of them said a word; she at one end of the pew, he at a certain distance behind, now kneeling, now sitting. Estupiñá got bored sometimes, no matter how well he disguised it, and he liked for a late churchgoer or an unctuous face to consult him about the stage the Mass was at: "Would he make this one?" Estupiñá replied either yes or no very courteously, and if his answer was negative, he always added something to console the questioner: "But don't worry; Father Quesada will be saying one in no time, and he's a live wire." What he wanted was to start a conversation.

After a long spell of silence dedicated to devotion, Barbarita turned to him and said with a haughtiness improper in that holy place:

"Hmph! Your friend the Deaf Man has put a good one over on us!"

"What do you mean, Señora?"

"I told you to order half a sirloin, and you know what he sent? A huge piece of fat from the flank and a piece of back, all scraps and tendons. What a way to treat his customers! We'll never go back there again. It's your fault. So that's what your 'protégés' are like . . . "

When she'd said this, Barbarita went back to praying and Plácido began to silently curse the Deaf Man, a butcher he had . . . He was not his protégé, but he *had* recommended him, it's true. Was he going to tell off the Deaf Man now! Other families to whom he had also recommended the Deaf Man complained that they had been given shoe leather, the worst meat instead of the real thing . . . These days nobody had any morals; you couldn't recommend anyone. Other mornings he'd have gibberish like this: "You should see the market near my house! What partridges, Señora! They're divine, really divine."

"No more partridge. Today we have to see whether Pantaleón has some good baby goat. I'd like a nice juicy cow's tongue too, and maybe some tender veal if he has any."

"There's some that's so tender, Señora, it's almost like hake."

"Fine. Tell them to send me a good loin cut and some veal chops. And remember, don't try to come up with anything like the other day."

"Don't worry, I won't. Will the Señora be having guests tomorrow?"

"Yes. And as for fish, what is there?"

"I told them to hold some salmon for us if it comes in tomorrow. What they do have today is tons of lobster."

When the Masses were over, they went down Mayor Street in search of the pure and innocent emotions that the one's amiable officiousness and the other's copious supply of money afforded them. The subject wasn't always food. Many a time Estupiñá had stories such as:

"Señora, Señora, you mustn't miss the cretonnes that Sobrino's 'boys' got in today. They're glorious!"

Barbarita interrupted an Our Father to say (keeping the religious expression on her face), "Flowered, and shot with gold? Yes, and they're in now, too."

At the door, where Plácido was already waiting for her, she said, "Let's go see them."

Besides the cretonnes, the "boys" showed Barbarita some flowery cotton sateen that was the latest thing. The capricious woman couldn't buy a dress fast enough for her daughter-in-law, who was sure to pass it on to one of her sisters.

Another day:

"Señora, Señora, it's too late for this Mass. But pretty soon the priest's nephew will say one. He polishes them off in no time. Pla has already gotten in that cheese you wanted. I forget what it's called."

"'Now and at the hour of our death'—Has he? Well, if it's like the English doughnuts you made me buy the other day that smelled so stale . . . they looked like leftovers from Saint Isidore's wedding feast."

Despite this scolding, and also the fact that they went off to Pla's intending to buy no more than two pounds of Corynthian raisins for a plum cake, the Señora got so caught up in buying that she ended up leaving about eight or nine hundred *reales* in the shop. While from behind the counter Estupiñá admired the novelties in that universal Museum of Edibles, giving his expert opinion on everything, sampling perhaps an almond cookie that tasted almost like Toledan marzipan, or praising the excellent aroma of the tea or spices, the lady stepped aside with one of the employees, a Samaniego, and . . . that was it. Barbarita kept saying, "That will be all," but after the collection of purées came the "Nizam pearls," then special bread, English sauces, "sea turtle broth," the dozen bottles of Saint-Emilion, which Juanito was so fond of, the jar of "supreme mushrooms" to please Baldomero, the canned anchovies, truffles, and other gourmet items. Out of Barbarita's purse (always well stocked) came the payment, and if it amounted to a little more than a round sum, she took the liberty of disregarding the fraction.

"Eh, boys: deliver it to the house, right away!" Estupiñá said despotically, pointing to the goods as he said good-bye.

"Good-bye and thank you," Doña Bárbara said, rising from her chair to leave as the owner appeared from the back of the shop, greeting his customer effusively and taking off his silk cap.

"We've been fine, thank you. Goodness, one *does* get robbed in this shop! I'm never coming here again. Bye now."

"Till tomorrow, Madam. At your service. And best wishes to Don Baldomero. God be with you, Plácido."

"Maestro, I wish you well."

They always bought certain items wholesale and, if possible, directly from the producers. Barbarita had business in her bones, and always craved a "good deal." But oh, how remote from reality those attempts would have been if she had not been assisted by that exemplary agent, Estupiñá the Great! The ground that that saintly man covered to discover fresh eggs in large quantities! Every egg-dealer along the Cava knew his face, and he gave himself no small importance, saying things like: "Either we're serious about this or we're not. Let's 'xamine the item, and then we'll talk . . . relax, friend, relax." Which meant holding the eggs up to the light one by one, weighing them and making endless remarks on their probable antiquity. If one of those characters tried to cheat him, he might as well pray for the Lord's protection, because Estupiñá would spring on him like a wild beast threatening to bring in the deputy, municipal inspection, and even the gallows.

For wine, Plácido went to the dealers on Cava Baja who do their buying in Arganda, Tarancón, or La Sagra. He had a middleman to set aside so many bottles from a shipment, and he had a trusted cart-driver deliver them. It had to be good stuff, 'pletely unwatered. One of the items that stirred the greatest activity and zeal in him was chocolate; once Barbarita gave him an order for this, he had no rest. He bought high quality cocoa, sugar, and cinnamon at Gallo's, and a boy whom Plácido never let out of his sight carried all this on his back to the house, where it was prepared. The Santa Cruzes couldn't stand industrially produced chocolate; the kind they bought had to be made by hand. As the chocolateer worked, Estupiñá hovered over him and stayed all day long to see that it was being done *conshenshusly* . . . You can't be too careful in matters like these, you know.

There were days when the purchases were big, and days when they were small, but there were never days when there were none at all. If she didn't need anything basic, the luxuriant lady brought home gloves, safety pins, metal cleanser, a package of hair pins, or whatever else had struck her fancy at a penny bazaar. She brought her son endless little gifts: ties he didn't wear, sets of buttons he never wore. Jacinta gladly accepted whatever her mother-in-law brought her and passed it on to her married or single sisters, except for certain things that they did not permit her to give away. White clothes and linens aroused true passion in Señora Santa Cruz's heart. From her brother's shop she brought home entire bolts of fine chambray, batiste, and madapollam. Don Baldomero II and Don Juan I had enough clothes to last them a century.

Barbarita supplied them with tobacco, too. The husband smoked cigars and the son cigarillos. Estupiñá took charge of securing these dangerous items from a sharpster who sold them undercover, and as he traipsed through the streets of Madrid with the boxes under his green cloak, his heart would beat pleasurably at the thought of the Treasury, and he was nostalgic for the beautiful times of his youth. In those liberalish years, 1871 and '72, things were already changing . . . Public inspectors didn't nose around much now. Yet the bold smuggler would have relished a real run-in to show the world that he was still capable of making the government go bankrupt if he wanted to. Barbarita examined the boxes and brands, haggled over the price, sniffed the tobacco, chose what seemed best, and paid handsomely. Don Baldomero always had an assortment as varied as it was excellent, and the worthy gentleman kept the habit—among other tenacious ones of a former salesclerk—of saving his best cigars for Sunday.

VII. Guillermina, Virgin and Founder

I

OF ALL THE PEOPLE WHO CAME to the house, the one who received the most attention from the entire Santa Cruz family was Guillermina Pacheco. She lived next door, was Moreno-Isla's aunt and Ruiz-Ochoa's cousin; these gentlemen were the principal partners in the old Moreno banking house. The bay windows of the two houses were so close that Doña Bárbara could communicate with her friend through them—a little rap on the glass was enough to establish contact.

Guillermina was completely at home with the Santa Cruzes, and besides, etiquette and formality were all but absent there. She already had her place in Barbarita's parlor, a low chair; she would sit down and pick up her mending or sewing in the same breath (she always brought a big bundle or workbasket) and, putting on her glasses and picking up her instruments, she was set for the rest of the evening. Whether or not there were formal visitors in the other rooms, she neither budged an inch nor had anything to do with anybody. Frequent visitors, such as the marquis of Casa-Muñoz, Aparisi, or Federico Ruiz, considered her a permanent fixture. Outsiders and insiders alike were respectful and even worshipful of this illustrious lady who looked like a nativity scene figure: tiny and graceful, her hair quite gray, though not as gray as Barbarita's, rosy cheeks, a pleasant mouth, quiet and charming speech, and very modest attire.

Sometimes she came for lunch. She would usually take a little soup, but would only peck at the rest of the meal. Don Baldomero would get annoyed and scold her with: "My dearest friend, when you wish to do penance don't come to my house. I notice that you aren't even eating what you like best. Don't come to me with stories. I have a good memory. I heard you say many times in my father's house that you like quail, and here it is and you're not even touching it. You're not in the mood for it! A dish like this is always appealing. And I see that you haven't touched your bread. Come now, Guillermina, we're going to lose our friendship."

Barbarita, who knew her friend well, didn't harp on the subject like Don Baldomero; she let her eat whatever she felt like eating or nothing at all. If by chance Tubs Arnáiz was at the table, he allowed himself a few quips on this terribly ancient style of sainthood that consisted of fasting. "Things that go into your mouth don't hurt your soul. Saint Francis himself said so." The Pacheco woman, who had a quick tongue, replied wittily to the jokes without ever becoming irritated. With the meal over, the diners scattered—some to the study for coffee and a game of ombre, others to form lively gossipy groups, and Guillermina to her little chair and the clicking of her needles. Jacinta usually sat at her side and often assisted in those labors so much to her liking: Guillermina made camisoles, pants, and tunics for her hundred or so children of both sexes.

The person who could tell you all about this renowned lady is Zalamero, who's married to one of the Ruiz-Ochoa girls. He has promised to write us his sublime relative's biography after she dies, and in the meantime he doesn't object in the slightest to supplying whatever information is asked of him, or to correcting the generally accepted versions of the reasons why a passion for beneficence awoke in Guillermina twenty-five years ago. Someone has ventured to say that unhappiness in love plunged her first into devotion and then into propagandistic and militant charity. Zalamero assures us, however, that this opinion is as foolish as it is false. Guillermina, who was once pretty and even a bit conceited, never had a romantic attachment of any sort, and if she did, absolutely nothing is known about it. The secret is buried deep in her heart. What the family does admit is that her mother's death made such a vivid impression on her that she must have secretly proposed "to not serve another master or mistress who could die on her." This peerless woman wasn't born to lead a contemplative life. She had a temperament at once dreamy, active, and enterprising, a mind of her own with masculine initiative. She didn't find discipline hard going on the spiritual side, but she did on the material side, which is why she never considered affiliating herself with any of the rather severe religious orders. She didn't think she had enough patience to coop herself up all day and yawn through mournful funereal singing, or to fight on the valiant squads of the Sisters of Charity. The vivid flame that burned in her breast didn't inspire her to passive submission; instead, it spurred her on to initiate activities that required her total freedom. She was strong-willed and had a wealth of gifts for supervising and organizing, gifts that some of the men who decide the world's fate would have been pleased to possess. She was the kind of woman who when she decided something went straight to it like a bullet, persisting in an almost grandiose way, without wavering or hesitating for a second, always inflexible and serene. If she encountered thorns on this straight and narrow path, she stepped right over them and kept on going, bloody feet and all.

She started out by joining a number of her friends, aristocratic ladies who had founded associations to aid needy households. Guillermina soon outdid her companions. They did such things out of vanity, sometimes without even liking the work, whereas she toiled ardently and energetically, and she used up half of her inheritance. After two years of living in this manner, it was apparent that she had completely given up dressing and adorning herself according to fashion's dictates. She adopted a plain dress of black merino, a cloak, a large dark shawl when it was cold, and some awful clodhoppers. This was to be her uniform for the rest of her days.

The charitable society to which she belonged cramped her enterprising spirit. She wanted to reach higher, attempt truly difficult things, things generally thought of as impossible. And this is when she revealed her talents as a founder, frightening the whole lot of her friends, who didn't know how to break away from their routines. Some of them told her plainly that she was crazy, because it *was* mad to think of founding an orphanage, and even crazier to endow it on a permanent basis. But the tireless initiator never faltered. "It could be done." And it was, supported for the first three years of its shaky existence by part of the remainder of Guillermina's income and by donations from rich relatives. Then the institution suddenly began to grow, swelling up and spreading out like human misery, and its necessities increased at a terrifying speed. The lady mortgaged the rest of her inheritance, and then she was forced to sell. Thanks to her relatives she didn't find herself in the awful spot of having to put the orphans in the street to beg for themselves and their founder. At the same time, she was also periodically doling out substantial alms to the poor in the hospital and orphanage districts. She clothed many children and old people, gave medicine to the sick, food and miscellaneous aid to everyone. In order to continue this assistance and keep the orphanage afloat, she had to find new resources. Where? How? She had already exploited her friends and relatives; pulling on those strings a bit more might make them snap. The most generous ones were starting to frown on her, and the miserly ones, when she tried to collect their quotas, "were not at home."

"There came a day," said Guillermina, dropping her work to tell various friends of Barbarita's about it, "when things looked really bad. The sun came up that morning and those twenty-three little creatures of the Lord whom I had picked up out of the streets and put up in that damp, low house on Zarzal Street— put them up like rabbits—didn't have a thing to eat. I could scrounge up enough here and there for one day, but how about the next? I was completely out of money and there was nobody to give me any more. I was in debt for goodness knows how many bushels of beans, twelve dozen pairs of *alpargatas*,* and so many

---

* Rope-soled slippers, or espadrilles of the plainest sort.

liters of olive oil. The only thing I had left to pawn or sell was my rosary. My cousins, who'd gotten me out of a tight spot so many times already, were impossible . . . I was ashamed to ask them again. My nephew Manolo, who was usually an ear for my problems, was in London. And even supposing that my cousin Valeriano agreed to feed my twenty-three mouths (plus my own, twenty-four) for a few days, what would I do next? No, there was nothing to do but scratch the earth and hunt for money somewhere else.

"That day was a trial for me. It was the Friday of the Virgin of the Seven Swords, and believe me, they were all stabbing me right here . . . I felt as though I'd been struck by lightning. What I needed was a guiding thought; but what I needed even more was courage, yes, courage to strike forth. And then suddenly I felt the courage I was longing for flooding through me, tremendous courage, like the kind soldiers have when they hurl themselves at the enemy's cannons. I threw on my cloak and left. Don't worry: I'd made up my mind already and was as happy as could be, because I knew what I had to do. Up until then I had asked my friends for money; but from that moment on I asked every living soul; I'd go from door to door with my hand out . . . The first bell I rang put me in the house of a foreign duchess I'd never seen before. She received me rather distrustfully—she took me for a schemer of some sort, you see. But what did I care? She gave me alms, and immediately afterward, to build up my courage and fill up the chalice quickly, I spent two days climbing stairs and ringing bells without stopping once to rest. One family recommended me to another; I wouldn't want to tell you about how I was humiliated, and how doors slammed in my face, and the things that were said to me. But the manna was raining down now, drop after drop. In a little while I saw that business was going better than I expected. Some people practically rolled out a red carpet for me, but most of them were cold, mumbling apologies and looking for an excuse not to give me a penny. 'There are so many things to give to, you see . . . we hardly have anything . . . the government takes it all in taxes.' I reassured them. 'Just a few pennies . . . a few pennies is all I need.' And they gave me one here, or a larger coin there . . . or sometimes a five- or ten-*real* note, or nothing at all. But I always kept smiling. Ah, my friends, this job has a lot of things that are hard to bear. One day I climbed up to a room on a second floor that someone or other had recommended to me. The recommendation turned out to be a stupid joke. There I am ringing the bell, I go in, and then a couple of hussies appear. Good Lord! They were women of the streets. The minute I saw them I felt like running away. 'But no,' I said to myself, 'I'm not leaving. Let's see if I can get something out of them.' I'd hate to tell you the way they insulted me; one of them disappeared and came back with a broom to hit me. And what do you think I did? Get scared? Hah! I stood my ground. I gave *them* a piece of my mind, and I mean it. Humph! Trying to meddle with me, with *my* temper!

And just imagine: I got some money out of them! Can you believe it? The nerviest one—the one who'd come lunging at me with the broom—came to my house two days later with a gold coin.

"So you see how it is. This habit of begging has gradually given me this lovely poker face I have now. Rejections just don't work on me. In fact, I don't know what it is to blush anymore. Nothing embarrasses me. My skin doesn't know what it is to redden, and my ears are no longer scandalized by words that are not exactly refined. They can call me a 'Jewish bitch' if they want; it's the same as if they'd called me the 'Pearl of the Orient'; it all sounds the same to me. All I see is my objective, and I go straight to it and don't let anything stop me. I've gotten so plucky I'll dare anything. It's as easy to beg from the king as it is from the lowliest worker. Just listen to this: one day I said: 'I'm going to see Don Amadeo.'* I request an audience, I arrive, I'm shown in, he receives me very solemnly. I wasn't fazed at all; I told him about my orphanage and said that I hoped to receive some assistance from his royal munificence. 'An orphanage for old people?' he asked me. 'No, sir; for children.' 'Are there many?' And that's all he said. He looked at me affably. What a man! What a giver! He ordered for me to be given six thousand *reales*. Then I saw the queen, Doña María Victoria, an excellent lady. She had me sit down beside her and treated me like an equal. I had to give her all sorts of information about my orphanage, tell her all the particulars. She wished to know what the little ones ate, how I dressed them. And we became friends. She insisted that I visit her every day. The next week she sent me heaps of clothes and bolts of material and she had her own children become members of the association, with a monthly pledge.

"So you see, with a little bit here and a little bit there, my orphanage has managed to keep bread on the table. The permanent subscription of members increased so much that a year later I was able to move to the house on Albuquerque Street; it has a big courtyard and lots of space. I've set up a cobbler's shop so that the older boys can work, and two schools so that they can get some education. Last year there were sixty, and now there are already a hundred and ten. We have our hard times, but we come out all right. One day we're badly off, and the next we're showered with provisions. When I see the pantry empty, I 'take to the streets,' as the revolutionaries say, and by nightfall I'm back with enough bread for the mouths I have to feed. And there are even days when they're not denied their treat—what did you think, that they were? Today I gave them a rice pudding as good as the one that all of you listening to me have. We'll see whether or not, in the long run, I get my way; it won't be easy. Nothing less than putting up a new building, a real palace with all the necessary space and the right kind of layout: an

---

* Amadeo was king of Spain from 1871 to 1873.

area for this, an area for that, and with room enough for two or three hundred orphans, so they'll be able to live nicely and be well brought up and become good Christians."

2

"A building *ad hoc*," the marquis of Casa-Muñoz, one of those present, remarked incredulously.

"*Ad . . . hoc*, yes, sir," replied Guillermina, emphasizing the two Latin words. "You're up to date, aren't you? Did you know that I have the land and the blueprints, and that they're already starting to clear the lot? Do you know the place? It's down from the Micaelas' house of correction. The architect and the draftsmen aren't charging me. And I'm hunting not just for money, but also for medium- and hard-baked bricks. So if—"

"Do you already have enough stone?" asked Aparisi with an interested air, for he was strong in the stone business.

"Yes, sir. Do you want to give me something?"

"I'll give you," said Aparisi, accompanying his generosity with an imperialistic gesture, "a chunk of sixty cubic meters of ashlar that I have in Guindalera."

"For how much?" asked Guillermina, squinting and pointing her needle at him.

"For nothing. The stone's yours."

"Thank you, may God reward you. And the marquis, what will he give me?"

"Well . . . Would you like two double T iron beams left over from the house on La Carrera?"

"Do I want them! I take everything, even an old key, for when the building's finished. Do you know what I brought home yesterday? Four kitchen tiles, a faucet, and three packages of iron rings. You can use everything, you know. If they give me a couple of bricks at a tile-works, I take them and find a way to use them. Have you ever noticed how birds make their nests? Well, that's how I'm going to build my palace: gathering a branch here and a branch there. I've already told Barbarita she isn't to throw away a thing; not even a nail, not even if it's crooked; or a board, even if it's broken. Used stamps can be sold, and so can matchboxes. How do you think I bought the big sink we have at the orphanage? Melting together candle stubs and selling them by the ounce. The other day someone offered me a Russian leather cigarette case. 'What could I use that for?' you gentlemen may be wondering. Well, I used it as a gift for one of the draftsmen on the project. Do you see the marquis of Casa-Muñoz who's listening to me and has offered me two double T beams? Fine. How much do you want to bet that I can coax more out of him? After all, do you think the Sr. Marquis has his big plaster factories in Vallecas just so that he can see what fixes I get into and not help me out of them?"

"Guillermina," said Casa-Muñoz somewhat moved, "count on two hundred sacks of the white kind, that's nine *reales* a sack."

"See? Good. And Señor Ruiz, what will he do for me?"

"My dear friend, I don't have a nail or a splinter to my name. But I swear to God that I'll go to the outskirts of Madrid some Sunday and steal a tile for you. I'll steal two or three or a dozen tiles. And what's more, if you'd like my two plays, my pamphlets on "Iberian Unity" and "The Organization of Swiss Firemen," and my work called *Castles*, they're all at your disposal. Ten copies of each, so that you'll have some prizes for a charity raffle."

"See what I mean? The manna comes raining down. All you have to do is put your mind to it. My friend Baldomero will give me something too."

"The chapel bells," said the renowned merchant. "And maybe the lightning rod and the weather vanes too. Now that my friend Aparisi wants to start the building, I want to finish it."

"No one will keep me from laying the cornerstone," said Aparisi, swollen with pride.

"We'll give a bit more, won't we, Baldomero?" asked Barbarita. "For example, the whole chapel—the organ, the altars, statues . . . "

"All you want, dear. Even though the Micaelas have already carried off a good chunk. We put up almost half of their building. But now it's Guillermina's turn. She knows she can count on us."

The group around the founder gradually broke up. Some of them, persuaded that it had been mere conversation, went into the living room to talk "seriously" about politics and business. Don Baldomero, who wanted to play a hand of *mus*, the classic and traditional card game of Madrid merchants, waited for Pepe Samaniego, a past master, to come and start the game. For a long while nothing was heard from the living room except "I bid my lows" . . . "I bid evens" . . . The works!"

The three ladies were left alone for a minute, talking about Guillermina's project. She sewed on, stitch after stitch, aided by Jacinta. Some time ago, Jacinta had grown very enthusiastic about the Pacheco woman's enterprises, and besides saving all the money she could for her, she pricked her fingers sewing long hours. She felt somewhat consoled, you see, by making children's clothes, knowing that the sleeves would cover bare little arms. She had already paid two visits to the orphanage on Albuquerque Street and accompanied Guillermina once on her rounds to the miserable pigsties where her poor lived.

Jacinta's comments after her first visit to the neighborhoods in the southern section of Madrid were worthy of being heard: "What inequalities!" she said, not realizing that she was touching on society's main problem. "Some have so much, others so little. Things are unbalanced; the world seems to be coming to an end. Everything would be all right if the people who had a lot gave away what they didn't need to the people who don't have anything. But what don't they need? Who knows." Guillermina assured her that one needed great faith to face the spectacles presented by poverty. "For there are good souls, oh yes," she said, "but there's also a lot of ingratitude. The lack of education is a bigger disadvantage for a poor man than his poverty. And then too, human misery attacks and corrupts many of them. They've insulted me. They've thrown fistfuls of manure and cabbage stalks at me. They've called me 'an old witch.'"

That night Barbarita was in the mood to talk about architecture, and she took every opportunity there was. Moreno-Isla came in during this and they welcomed him with cries of delight. The Señora called to him, "Do you have any rubble?"

All three of them laughed at Moreno's surprise and confusion; he was a bachelor, an excellent person, about forty-five and extremely rich, so fond of anything English that he spent most of the year in London; tall, thin, very poor color due to his health, which was very delicate.

"Do I have any rubble, she says . . . ! For you?"

"Answer me, now, and don't be like the Galicians, who answer a question with another question. Since you tear things down, do you have any rubble, yes or no?"

"Yes, as a matter of fact I do . . . and some magnificent flint. Sixty *reales* the cartful, all you want. The rubble is eight *reales* a— Oh, I'm so stupid! Now I know what it's all about. The great saint is bamboozling you with stories about the orphanage she's going to build. You've got to be careful with her tricks, very careful. Before she's laid the first stone she'll have us all in the poorhouse."

"Shhh! We all know how stingy you are. I'm not asking you for anything anyway, you old miser. You can have your carts of flint. They'll put them on the scales with you when the final accounting starts; you know, when the trumpets start to play. Oh yes, and then when you see how much your stinginess weighs on the scales, you'll say, 'Lord, take away these cartloads of stone and rubble that are plunging me into Hell,' and we'll all say, 'Oh, no. Pile it on, because he's very wicked.'"

"All I have to do is put the money you've squeezed out of me on the other side of the scales and I'm saved," Moreno laughed, patting her face.

"Don't humor me, my dear nephew. That won't get you anywhere, you big cheat, swindler, miser!" Guillermina was smiling, and her tone was benevolent. "Men! You always want more, even when you're skinning the poor by tearing down a block of old houses to make nice new ones."

"Don't pay any attention to the churchmouse—or rather, church *rat!*" said

Moreno, sitting down between Barbarita and Jacinta. "She's leaving me bankrupt. I'm going to have to go live in a small town somewhere so she'll leave me in peace. I can't turn my back for a minute. At home, I'm getting dressed and I hear a murmur, like a burglar's steps; I look, I see a blurry shape and I scream. But it's just the rat; she's crept in and she's skittering around the room. I rush over, but no matter how fast I am, my beloved aunt has already rifled my clothes on the rack and emptied my waistcoat pockets."

The founder broke into convulsive hysterics, laughing from the bottom of her heart.

"Come here, you rascal," she said, drying her tears of laughter. "The right way of doing something isn't any good with you. Come on, you know as well as I do that whoever robs a thief deserves to be spared his grief . . . deserves to go to heaven."

"Where you're going to go is jail."

"Hush, you silly, stop denouncing me or you'll be even worse off than you are now . . . . "

This dialogue, which promised to be entertaining, was interrupted by an energetic and insistent call for Moreno's presence in the living room. From Barbarita's parlor they could hear lively talking and the hubbub of voices, among which those of Juan, Villalonga, and Zalamero (for they had just entered) could be distinguished.

Moreno left to join the men, and Guillermina, still laughing, said to her friends:

"He's an angel. You have no idea of the divine stuff that man's heart is made of."

Barbarita couldn't rest until she knew why there was such a commotion in the living room. She went in to see and returned with this:

"Girls, the king is leaving."

"What did you say?"

"It seems that Don Amadeo is tired of fighting people off and he's about to throw his crown out the window and say, 'Somebody else can have the headache.'"

"May it be God's will," declared Guillermina, heaving a sigh and returning imperturbably to her work.

Jacinta went to the living room, not so much to hear the news as to see her husband, who had not lunched at home that day.

"Pssst," Guillermina said secretively as she stopped her, whereupon they exchanged conniving looks. "If you can squeeze twenty duros out of him, that'll do."

3

"No one knew anything at the stock exchange. I heard it at a stockbrokers' meeting at ten o'clock," said Villalonga. "Then I went to the casino with the news. When I got back to the meeting, consolidated stock was going for 20."

"We'll see it drop to 10, gentlemen," said the marquis of Casa-Muñoz, Hamlet-like.

"The bank stock at 175!" cried Don Baldomero, putting his hand on his forehead and looking down in consternation.

"I beg your pardon, my friend," Moreno-Isla corrected him. "It's at 172, and if you'd like to buy mine at 170, I'll hand them to you this minute. I don't want any more paper from our dear country. I'm going back to London tomorrow."

"Yes," said Aparisi, with a prophetic air, "what we're about to witness is going to be out of this world."

"Gentlemen, let's not be too impressionable," said the marquis of Casa-Muñoz, always fond of seeing a situation objectively. "The poor man is worn out. It's the least we could have expected; he's simply said: 'There it is.' I would've done precisely the same thing if I'd been in his shoes. Things will be unstable for a while; there'll be a short-lived republic; but we all know that nations don't die."

"The blow came from the outside," declared Aparisi. "I could see it coming. France—"

"Let's not 'involute' the issues, gentlemen," said Casa-Muñoz, wearing a very parliamentary expression. "And frankly, for my part, a republic doesn't scare me. What scares me is republicanism."

He looked at everyone's reaction to his sentence. There could be no doubt but that the murmuring with which it was received was laudatory.

"My dear Marquis," stated Aparisi, piqued into rivalry, "the Spanish people are a dignified people . . . who when faced with danger, know how to be—"

"—And what does one have to do with the other?" sprang the vexed marquis, annihilating his opponent with a glance. "Don't 'involute' the issues."

Aparisi, a property owner and councilman by profession, was a man who prided himself on "dotting his i's," but his competence did not suffice with the marquis because the latter tolerated no impositions on his ideas and was, moreover, capable of dotting even h's. Their tacit rivalry showed in the former's emulation of the latter's way of throwing succinct observations into the arena. A mutual look of profound dislike was the only thing that sometimes allowed others a glimpse of the spiritual belligerence of those two mental athletes. Villalonga, who was a very playful observer, once asserted that he had discovered the antagonism or competition between Aparisi and Casa-Muñoz in how they used certain choice words. One would challenge the other to prove whose speech was more refined; so while the marquis did all sorts of things with "involute," "*ad hoc*," "*sui generis*," and other Latin expressions, his opponent would immediately rack his brain for such select phrases as "the concatenation of ideas." Aparisi sometimes appeared to be the winner, as for example when he declared that something or other was the "*bello ideal*" of the people; but Casa-Muñoz took off from there, slaying his opponent with "the desideratum."

Villalonga says that years ago Casa-Muñoz's way of speaking was ridiculous. He swears up and down that he once heard him say (before he became a marquis) that the "doors were hermetically open"; but this hasn't been confirmed. Joking aside, it should be added that the marquis was an extremely pleasant person—very normal, very affable, a perfect gentleman with his family and friends. He was the same age as Baldomero, but he didn't carry his years as well. His teeth were false and his dyed sideburns had a slightly reddish tint that contrasted with the undyed hair on his head. Aparisi was much younger; he was conceited about his small feet and fine hands; he had a ruddy face, a chestnut-colored mustache that drooped Chinese-style, large eyes, and on his head a bald spot, the kind their owners wear like a diploma certifying their talent. The most characteristic feature of the perennial councilman was his facial expression: he seemed to be detecting a very disagreeable odor. The expression was caused by his way of contracting the muscles of his nose and upper lip. Other than this, he was a good sort who owed nobody anything. He had once owned a lumber business, and it was often said that during a certain period of his life he had "made heaps" on the pine groves of Balsaín. He was a man without a formal education, and precisely because he had not learned anything, he liked to pretend that he had.

Villalonga—the rascal—has told about when Aparisi used to use Galileo's *e pur si muove* when he still didn't interpret it correctly; he thought the famous saying meant "just in case," and he was heard using it with this meaning more than once: "It doesn't seem as if it'll rain, but I'll take my umbrella *e pur si muove*."

Jacinta took her husband by the arm and led him aside.

"What's happening, baby, are there barricades?"

"No, dear, none. Don't worry."

"You won't go out again tonight, will you? You know I'll be very scared if you do."

"Well, I won't go out then. What . . . what are you looking for?"

Jacinta, laughing, her hand sliding along the lining of his frock coat, was hunting for the inside pocket.

"Oh! I was trying to see if I could get your wallet without your noticing it."

"You're a sneaky little pickpocket, aren't you?"

"Ha! I wish I could be. The one who really knows how to do this is Guillermina. She takes the change out of Manolo Moreno's coat pocket without his even feeling it. Let's see . . . "

With the wallet in her hands now, Jacinta opened it.

"Will you be mad if I take this twenty *duro* bill? Do you need it?"

"No, not at all. Take whatever you want."

"It's for Guillermina. Mamá gave her two and she just needs a tiny bit more to pay the quarterly rent on the orphanage tomorrow."

The Dauphin replied by pressing her hands together very effusively and wrinkling the bill into them.

As soon as Guillermina had snared what she needed to complete the sum, she dropped her sewing and threw on her cloak. With hurried good-byes to the two ladies, she hastily crossed the living room.

"That's the one, there she goes!" cried Moreno. "She's taking something with her for sure! Gentlemen, check to see that you still have your watch. Bárbara, do you see that bumpy shape under the 'church rat's' cloak? Weren't there some silver candlesticks here?"

In the midst of the jovial uproar caused by the joking, Guillermina walked out, sending them all an ineffable smile like a blessing.

They immediately returned to the juicy subject of the king's departure and they all vehemently set forth their opinions like prophets, as if they had never done anything but correctly foretell the future. Villalonga could already envision Don Carlos entering Madrid, and the marquis of Casa-Muñoz talked about "the liberticidal exaggerations" of the red demagoguery and the white demagoguery as if they were painted on the wall before his eyes; the ex–under secretary of the interior, Zalamero, saw King Alfonso's name clearly written across the future, while the councilman sustained that "Alfonsism was still in the cloudiness of the unknown." Aparisi and Federico Ruiz sang their prophecies in the same key. By God, *they* weren't afraid of the republic. They could almost see it now: nothing would happen. It's just that we're all very impressionable, the slightest trouble makes us think the sky's falling in. "I can assure you," proclaimed Aparisi, his hand on his chest, "that absolutely nothing is going to happen. You have no idea of what the Spanish people are like. I'll vouch for them. I'd even put my head on the block for them." Moreno didn't predict anything; all he did was say: "Just in case it turns out badly, I'm leaving for London tomorrow." The rich bachelor boasted of having a total lack of patriotic feeling, and he was such a rabid expatriate that nothing Spanish seemed good to him. Playwrights or meals, trains or small industries—they all seemed pathetically inferior to him. He used to say that shopkeepers here don't know how to wrap up a pound of anything. "You buy something and after they've misweighed it and overcharged you, the wrapping comes undone on your way home. There's no point in beating around the bush. We're as awkward a race as can be."

In sad tones, Don Baldomero made a very sensible remark: "If only Don Juan Prim were alive . . . !" Juan and Samniego withdrew from the huddle and talked with Jacinta and Doña Bárbara, trying to calm their fears. There wouldn't be any shooting, or any rumpus . . . It wouldn't be necessary to get any provisions. Ah, our Barbarita! She was already dreaming of buying the provisions. The next morning, if there weren't any barricades, she and Estupiñá would take care of it.

Gradually they all left. It was midnight. Aparisi and Casa-Muñoz went to the stockbrokers' *tertulia* for news, not without showing yet another sign of their rivalry before leaving. The councilman was in such a state that the contraction of his snout was more pronounced than usual, as if that imaginary odor were of some terribly fetid substance. Zalamero, who was going to the Ministry of the Interior, wanted to take the Dauphin with him, but the latter's wife, holding onto his arm, refused to let him go. "My wife won't let me."

"My namesake," remarked Villalonga, "is becoming very anticonstitutional."

Finally the family was alone. Don Baldomero and Barbarita kissed their children and retired. Jacinta and her husband kissed their parents and did the same.

VIII. Scenes from Private Life

I

SHORTLY AFTER GETTING INTO BED, Jacinta noticed that her husband was sleeping deeply. She herself was wide awake and watched him steadily from her bed. Was he talking in his sleep? No, it was just his usual inarticulate moaning, probably due to lying in the wrong position. Political thoughts related to the conversations that evening quickly vanished from Jacinta's mind. What difference did it make to her if they had a republic or a monarchy, or if Don Amadeo returned to Italy or stayed in Spain? She was more concerned about the conduct of the ungrateful soul sleeping so peacefully beside her. She had no doubt about it: Juan had something on his mind. His parents didn't notice it for the simple reason that they never saw him at such close range as she did. The perfidious creature kept up appearances so well that nothing he said or did outwardly revealed anything but consistent and extremely correct behavior. He treated his wife so affectionately that . . . well, one would have thought he really *was* in love with her. Alone together behind the bedroom door, it was plain that it was all a dirty trick; only she, who was aware of certain negative facts, could destroy the halo that the outside world and the family had hung on the glorious Dauphin. His mamá said that he was the perfect husband. The big rascal! And the wife couldn't say a word to her mother-in-law when the latter came out with remarks like these. How could she tell her: "Well, he's *not* the perfect husband, and I know what I'm talking about."

Jacinta spent part of the night thinking about this, tying together loose ends to see if she could make some sense of the disconnected facts. In truth, these facts didn't cast much light on what remained to be proved. On such and such a day at such and such a time, Juan had left the house brusquely after seeming very, very pensive for a while. On such and such a day at such and such a time, Juan had received a letter that had put him in a bad mood. No matter how hard she had tried, she hadn't been able to find it. On such and such a day at such and such a time, walking along Preciados Street with Barbarita, they ran into Juan, who was in a hurry and lost in thought. He was taken aback at seeing them, but he knew how to control himself instantly. None of these facts proved anything, yet there was no doubt: her husband was playing games.

From time to time these trivial objections ceased; Juan knew how to handle himself so that his wife would not reach the point of knowing that she was right, thereby becoming discontented. Like a wound that has had fresh balm put on it, Jacinta's grief was assuaged. But somehow the days and nights slowly brought her back to the same painful situation. And it was very odd. She would be completely at peace, entirely oblivious to it, when the slightest incident—a word or a meaningless reference—attacked her mind like a dart shot from afar by a stranger's hand, piercing her very brain. Jacinta was observant, prudent, and wise. Her husband's most insignificant gestures, the inflections of his voice—she secretly observed everything, smiling when she was at her most attentive, disguising her vigilance with a thousand sweet words, just as naturalists hide and disguise the lens through which they examine bees at work. She knew how to ask crafty questions, design traps and camouflage them. But he was hardly one to let himself be caught!

And the ingenious culprit had pretty words for everything: "A perpetual honeymoon is a contradiction in terms, it's . . . even ridiculous. Enthusiasm is a childish state, improper for serious people. A husband thinks about his business; a wife, about her domestic affairs, and they treat one another more as friends than as lovers. Even doves, my dear, even doves, when they've passed a certain age, show their affection like this—sensibly." Jacinta laughed at this, but she didn't admit such compromises. The funniest part of it was that he talked as if he were a busy man. What a clown! He didn't do a thing except parade around and have fun! His father had worked like a dog all his life to insure this happy laziness for the prince of the house . . . Well, anyway, no matter what it was, Jacinta resolved never to abandon her humble and discreet manner. She firmly believed that Juan would never create a scandal, and as long as there wasn't a scandal, things would be all right. Every living being has some little worm inside, a parasite that gnaws at its existence and lives at its expense, and she had two: her husband's periodic estrangements and the disconsolation of not being a mother. She would bear both burdens patiently as long as nothing worse descended on her.

Out of respect for herself, she had never mentioned this to anyone, not even to the Dauphin. But one night he was so communicative, bantering, and teasing that Jacinta's mouth brimmed with sincerity and word after word, everything she had been thinking, poured out. "You're deceiving me, and it's not something new, it's been going on a long time. If you think that I'm dumb . . . You're the dumb one."

Santa Cruz's first reply was to burst out laughing. His wife covered his mouth so that he wouldn't make too much noise. Then the rascal began to justify his explanations, dressing them up seductively. But they sounded hollow to Jacinta, who was a better connoisseur than he of the dialectics of the heart because she really knew how to love. Then it was her turn to laugh and pick apart his flimsy excuses. But sleep, sweet and mutual sleep, overtook them, and they both sank happily into it . . . And just imagine! Juan reformed—or at least he seemed to be reforming.

Santa Cruz possessed a number of the tricks necessary for the art of living; he was one of those people who know how to use things in the best possible way, to systematize and refine their well-being. He got something out of everything, extending his pleasures and adjusting them to those mysterious tides of the human appetite that, when its ebb and flow is great, signifies a propensity to vice. In the depths of human nature there is also—as there is on the social surface—a succession of styles, periods during which one must change his tastes. And Juan had his "times." Almost periodically he got fed up with running around, and then his wife, who was so adorable and affectionate, attracted him as if she were somebody else's wife, which is how the very old and well known is renewed. A text that one knows so well that he scorns it regains interest when it fades in one's memory; it can stimulate one's curiosity again. In this case, the extremely tender love that Jacinta felt for Juan aided him, for there was no farce, or vile interest, or anything studied about her love. So it was truly luck for the Dauphin to be able to return to his port after so many storms at sea. He seemed to be restored by that affection that was so pure and loyal and so much his own, for indeed, no one else in the world could claim it.

In honor of the truth, it should be added that Santa Cruz loved his wife. Not even in the days when his tides of infidelity ran highest did that special spot for Jacinta disappear from his heart, which had so many nooks and winding streets. Nor did the variety of his affinities and whims exclude an unmovable feeling for his legal and religious companion. Perfectly aware of her moral worth, he admired in her the virtues he lacked and that, according to his criterion, he didn't particularly need either. For this last reason he didn't commit the humble act of confessing that he wasn't worthy of such a gem; his self-love always came first, and he thought he deserved whatever good fortune he enjoyed or might enjoy in this vile world. A discreet lover of vice, a sybarite and a man of talent aspiring to the erudite knowledge of all pleasures and equipped with fairly good taste when it came to spiritualizing material things, he couldn't content himself with bought or conquered beauty, charm, wit, extravagance; he also wanted virtue, not exactly defeated virtue—which has ceased to be virtuous—but pure virtue, which attracted him precisely because of its purity.

2

From what has been said, it may be gathered that the Dauphin was a completely idle man. When he got married, Don Baldomero proposed several times that he take a few thousands and invest them in some way, either by playing the stock exchange or in another kind of speculation. The young man accepted, but the attempt didn't satisfy him and he flatly renounced an involvement in business that would cause him a lot of worry and sleepless nights. Don Baldomero hadn't been able to disengage himself from that very Spanish concept, to wit: parents must work so that their children may rest and enjoy themselves. That worthy gentleman delighted in his son's indolence just as an artist delights in his work; the more the hands that made it grow pained and tired, the more he admires it.

But it should also be said that the young man was not a spendthrift. He spent money all right, but never recklessly, and his pleasures were no longer pleasures when they began to demand dissipation. In cases such as these, virtue appeared to him with a calm and seductive face. He had a certain inborn respect for his pocket, and if he could buy something for two *pesetas*, he certainly wasn't one to spend three. Shelling out a huge quantity was never easy for him, as it is for big spenders, who seem to be freeing themselves of a burden when they pay. And since he knew the value of money so well, he knew how to acquire his pleasures in a very prudent and almost commercial way. No one could squeeze a five- or twenty-*duro* bill the way he could. The sum that supplied a prodigal spender with one pleasure always supplied Santa Cruz with two.

By dint of his clever financing, he could pass himself off as a generous person when he had to. He never did anything wild, and if his appetites led him to certain extremes, he knew how to hang on and keep from slipping. One of the purest satisfactions that the Santa Cruzes had was knowing for a fact that "their son had no debts," unlike most sons in those depraved times.

Don Baldomero would have been rather pleased if the Dauphin had let it be known that he had an extraordinary talent for politics. Oh, if he would only go into politics—he would surely shine! But Barbarita discouraged him. "Politics, politics! Aren't we seeing all they are now? A farce. It only amounts to talk and not doing anything that needs to be done." What slightly puzzled Don Baldomero II was that his son didn't have any firm ideas of his own, like his father, whose ideas in 1875 were the same as they had been back in '45; namely, that there should be plenty of liberty and a nice big stick behind it, that liberty gets along very well with religion, and that everyone who goes into politics for self-gain should be persecuted and reprimanded.

Juan, though, was the spirit of inconsistency. In Prim's times, he enthusiastically supported the duke of Montpensier's candidacy. "He's the man we need, don't kid yourselves. A man who knows the household expenses like the palm of his hand; a model father." Then Don Amadeo came along and the Dauphin turned so republican that his opinions were frightening. "The monarchy's impossible, we've got to convince ourselves of it. They say the country's not ready to be a republic—well, they can get it ready. It's like thinking a man should know how to swim before he's decided to get in the water. Either we like it or lump it. Hard times will teach us. And if you don't think so, look at France with her prosperity, her intelligence, her patriotism . . . the way she can pay up the five thousand millions." Well, friends, the 11th of February came around and at first Juan thought it was going to be peaches and cream. "It's great. Europe is dumbfounded. They can say what they want, but we Spanish have a lot of common sense." Two months later, however, pessimistic ideas had completely overtaken him. "This is ridiculous, it's shameful. Every country gets the government it deserves, and the only person who can rule this country is somebody with a club in his hand!" Very gradually Juanito started to warmly defend Prince Alfonso's ideas. "By God, son," Don Baldomero said innocently, "that can't be." And he reminded them of all the "Nevers!" uttered by Prim. Barbarita sided with the exiled prince, and since feeling plays such a big part in the destiny of countries, all the women supported the prince and defended him with arguments they pulled out of their hearts. Jacinta left Don Alfonso's strongest enthusiasts way behind. "He's a child!" . . . And she gave no other reasons for her support.

The Santa Cruz heir considered himself a great person. He was self-satisfied, as if he had created himself and was pleased with the results. "Because as for me," he would say, trying to be at once truthful and modest, "I'm not the worst humanity has to offer. I realize that there are people who are better than I am, my wife for example; but then there are so many, many people who are inferior!" Physically, he *was* very attractive, and declared himself in his private soliloquies: "I'm so handsome! My wife is so right when she says that there's no one who's as witty as I am. The poor little thing worships me . . . and I worship her, it's only fair. I cut a perfect figure, I dress well, and as for my manners and my personality, well . . . I guess I'm really special." At home, the only opinion that counted was his; he was the oracle of the family and he charmed them all, not only because of how much they loved and pampered him, but because of the spell of his imagination, his charming way of speaking and ingratiating himself. The most subjugated of them all was Jacinta, who wouldn't have dared to declare to the family that white was white if her dearly beloved husband maintained that it was black. She loved him with true passion, not a small part of which was determined by his good looks and intellectual polish. As for the moral perfections that the whole family declared were Juan's, Jacinta had her doubts. I'll say she did. But seeing that she was alone in her doubts, she sadly mused to herself: "Is it possible that I'm complaining for the sake of complaining? Am I really, as people say, the happiest woman of all and I just haven't realized it?"

With these thoughts, she thrashed and mortified her anxiety, hoping to placate it, just as penitents whip their bodies to reduce themselves to obeying their souls. What she could not accept, though, was the idea of not having children; "because I can bear anything," she said to herself, "except that. If I had a child, I'd amuse myself with him and I wouldn't think about certain things." As a result of musing so much on this, her mind fell prey to hallucinations and delirium. On some nights during the first phase of sleep, she felt something hot on her breast and then a mouth sucking it. The licking made her wake with a start and then with the terribly sad impression that it was all false, she heaved a sigh and her husband would say from his bed: "What is it, baby, a nightmare?" "Yes, dear, a very bad dream." She didn't want to tell the truth because she was afraid that Juan would laugh at her.

The corridors of their huge house seemed lugubrious to her simply because they didn't resound with the clatter of childish steps. The unused rooms destined for the babies, *if there were any*, filled her with such sadness that on the days when she was especially upset by her obsession, she simply avoided them. When she saw Don Baldomero come home at night looking so jovial and kind, always wearing a smile, dressed in very fine black wool and so clean and rosy-cheeked, she couldn't help but think of the grandchildren that that man should have if there was any justice in the world, and she said to herself, "What a grandfather they're losing!"

One night she went to the Royal Theater; she didn't feel at all like going. She had spent the whole day and the night before at Candelaria's, where the littlest girl was sick. Sleepy and in a bad mood, she hoped that the opera would be over soon, but unfortunately, being one of Wagner's, it was very long. Excellent music, according to Juan and everyone who had taste, but it didn't appeal to her in the slightest. She didn't understand it. The only music that existed for her was Italian, and the simpler and the more from a hand organ, the better. She had the "samples" of the family women sit in the front row, taking the chair farthest back herself. The three chicks—Barbarita II, Isabel, and Andrea—were very pleased as they felt arrows dart at them from young men sitting in the peanut gallery or in boxes. They also got a few good looks from orchestra seats. Doña Bárbara wasn't there. When they reached the fourth act, Jacinta was bored. She glanced at her husband's box very often but didn't see him. Where was he? Thinking of this, her charming head bowed politely to the great Wagner and remained thus, drooping over her breast. The last thing she heard was a descriptive piece in which the orchestra was imitating the buzzing with which mosquitoes amuse mankind on a summer night. Lulled by this music, the lady fell into a deep sleep and had one of those intense and brief dreams in which the brain recreates reality in high relief, showing an admirable histrionic sense. The impression left by these lethargies is usually much stronger than that produced by many external phenomena. Jacinta found herself in a place that was and was not her house . . . Everything was lined in the white flowered satin that she and Barbarita had seen the day before at Sobrino's shop. She was sitting on a puffy cushion and a beautiful little boy was climbing up over her knees, first touching her face, then putting his hand on her breast. "Stop it, stop it! It's a dirty thing, it's bad. You don't want to touch *that!*" But the little boy wouldn't stop. He was wearing a shirt of fine Dutch linen, and his delicate flesh slid over the silk of his mamá's bathrobe. It was the powder-blue bathrobe she had given to her sister Candelaria weeks ago . . . "No, no; don't do that! It's dirty . . . " But he went right on insisting, stubborn and adorable. He wanted to unbutton her bathrobe and put his hand inside. Then he pushed his head against her breast. Seeing that this didn't get him anywhere, he became serious, so extraordinarily serious that he seemed like a grown man. He looked at her with huge intense eyes, moist now, expressing with them and his mouth all the sorrow of which humanity is capable. Adam wouldn't have looked otherwise on the good he was losing when he was banished from Paradise. Jacinta wanted to laugh but she couldn't because the little boy pierced her soul with his burning gaze. A long time passed in this way, the child-man looking at his mother, and slowly melting her firmness with the power of his eyes. Jacinta felt something tearing inside her. Not knowing what she was doing, she unbuttoned one button, then another. But the boy's face didn't lose its seriousness. The mother was alarmed and . . . then the third button . . . still nothing; the child's face and expression remained stern, with a beautiful gravity that was becoming terrible. The fourth button, the fifth, all the buttons slid through their buttonholes making the material strain. She lost count of the buttons she'd undone. There were a hundred, maybe a thousand. But not even with that many . . . His face began to seem distrustful, immobile. Finally, Jacinta put her hand into her robe, took out the breast the boy wanted, and looked at it, feeling sure that he wouldn't be mad anymore when he saw such a pretty, full bosom. But no. Then she took the boy by his head and drew him up to her, putting her breast into his mouth . . . But his mouth was insensitive and his lips didn't move. His whole face looked like a statue's. The touch Jacinta felt on this very delicate area of her skin was the horrifying friction of chalk, friction from a rough, dusty surface. This contact made her shudder and left her dumbfounded for awhile; then she opened her eyes and realized that her sisters were there; she saw the large, heavy, painted curtains flanking the stage, the crowded side sections of the upper gallery. It took her awhile to register where she was and what nonsense she had been dreaming, and she put her hand on her breast with a modest and fearful gesture. She heard the orchestra, which was still imitating mosquitoes, and upon looking at her husband's box she saw Federico Ruiz, the great music lover, his head thrown back, his mouth half open, listening and savoring every bit of the delicious music from the muted violins. It seemed as if the clearest and sweetest and finest stream imaginable was being poured into his mouth. The man was in ecstasy. The lady saw other rabid music lovers in the boxes; but the fourth act was already over and Juan hadn't appeared.

3

If everything that happens to exceptional people deserved commemoration, the following little paragraph might easily have appeared on the page of a calendar that corresponded to December 1873: "Such and Such a Day: Juanito Santa Cruz's bad cold. The impossibility of leaving the house puts him in an incredibly bad mood." He was sitting next to the fireplace, wrapped up from the waist down in a blanket that looked like a tiger skin, a knitted cap pulled down over his ears, a newspaper in his hand, and in the chair next to him three, four, lots of newspapers. Jacinta joked with him about his confinement and he, finding her teasing entertaining, made believe that he wanted to punch her; he grabbed her by the arm, nipped at her chin with his fingers, shook her head, then dealt her a few blows—hard blows—and pummeled her all over and pinched her or stabbed her, keeping his index finger very stiff. After she was riddled with his stabs, he cut off her head by threshing her neck, and as if this weren't fierce enough, he started tickling her with extreme cruelty, accompanying each new blow with more ferocious tickling. "My little baby's becoming quite a tease, isn't she! But I'm going to teach my little clown how to be *really* funny, and I'm going to give her a spanking that's going to take away any urge she has to . . . "

Jacinta practically split her sides laughing and the Dauphin, speaking slightly more seriously, continued: "You know very well that I don't hang around in the streets. Why should you complain? I know husbands who as soon as they put a foot in the street don't come back for days. I ought to be a model for them."

"Aren't we a goodie-goodie!" replied Jacinta, drying the tears that the laughter and tickling had made her shed. "I know there are others who are worse, but I wouldn't stake my life on your being the best."

Juan shook his head threateningly. Jacinta put herself out of his reach in case he decided to repeat the ferocious tickling.

"It's just that you demand too much," said the husband, lamenting the fact that his wife didn't consider him the most perfect creature in the world.

Jacinta made a winsome face, wrinkling her eyebrows and lips, which meant: "I don't want to get into an argument with you because I'd come out of it by giving up." And it was true; the Dauphin was capable of very clever sleights of hand.

"All right," she said. "Let's stop fooling around. What do you want for lunch?"

"That's exactly what I've come about," said Doña Bárbara, appearing at the door. "You may have whatever you want, but I'd like to inform you, if it's going to affect your choice, that I've brought home some absolutely delicious larks. They're *divine*, as Estupiñá would say."

"Bring me whatever you want—I'm so hungry I could eat a horse."

When the two ladies had left, Santa Cruz thought about his wife for a little while, formulating a mental panegyric. What an angel! He'd hardly finished doing something wrong when she was already forgiving him. In the days preceding the cold, my man was going through a change, being borne along on one of those tides of his inconstant nature that made him forget about adventure and brought him closer to his wife. The people who are most accustomed to illegal living occasionally feel a strong desire to abide by the law briefly. The law tempts them in exactly the same way whims do. When Juan found himself in this situation he even reached the point of wanting to stay in it; what's more, he even thought he *would* stay in it. And the Dauphin's mate was content. "I've won him back again," she thought. "If only it would last! . . . If I could only win him back forever and defeat every last one of the enemy!"

Don Baldomero came in to see his son before going into the dining room. "What's this, son? I told you so! You don't dress warmly enough. You and Villalonga are the limit! Standing at ten o'clock at night on the corner of the Ministry of the Interior. I saw you. I was with Cantero; we'd been at the board meeting at the bank. We don't know what we're going to do. Who knows what this anarchy will come to? The shares at 138! Come in, Aparisi . . . It's Aparisi, he's having lunch with us."

The councilman came in and greeted the Santa Cruzes.

"Which newspapers have you read?" his father asked, slipping on his bifocals, which he used only for reading. "Here, take *La Epoca* and give me *El Imparcial.* Things are in fiiine shape, oh, yes . . . Poor Spain! With shares at 138, and consolidated stock at 13."

"What do you mean, 13? It'd be nice if it were," observed the perennial councilman. "Last night they were giving it away at 11 at the stockbrokers' meeting and no one wanted it. This is the end of us."

And greatly exaggerating that expression of his that suggested that he was smelling something awful, he added that he had foreseen all these events, and that there was no discrepancy between them and what he had predicted all along, "day by day." Without paying much attention to his friend, Don Baldomero read the news—which was getting to be like a refrain—out loud: "The X party entered the town of Y, burned the municipal archives, appropriated supplies of rations, and left . . . The X column actively pursued the leader of Y, and after taking supplies of rations—

"Huh," he said without finishing, "let's look for some rations ourselves. The marquis isn't coming. We're not going to wait any longer for him."

At this point Juan's servant, Blas, entered with a small table, already set for the patient's lunch. Soon after, Jacinta appeared bringing in dishes. After greeting her, Aparisi said:

"Guillermina gave me a message for you . . . There won't be any 'philanthropic odyssey' today to the 'parish crawling with lice' because she's out hunting for a certain kind of brick for the foundation. She already has the site cleared for the building, and it cost her next to nothing. Some of the wagons did piecework, others didn't charge her; one would go for half a day, another for a couple of hours, with the result that each cubic meter cost her less than five *reales*. That woman has something about her. When she goes to inspect the work, it seems as if even the mules that pull the wagons know her and pull harder to make her happy. I didn't use to think that the building was 'practicable,' but frankly, I'm beginning to see . . . "

"A miracle, a miracle," noted Don Baldomero on his way to the dining room.

"And you?" Juan asked his spouse when they were left alone. "Are you having lunch here or there?"

"Do you want me to have lunch here? I'll have it in both places. Your mamá says that I'm pampering you too much."

"Here, have a bite," he said, handing her his fork, with a piece of omelette on it.

After eating it, the Dauphine ran off to the dining room. In a little while she came back laughing.

"I've saved this lark's breast for you. Here, open your mouth, baby."

His baby took the fork and after eating the breast started to laugh again.

"Well, someone's in a good mood!"

"It's because the marquis has come, and from the minute he sat down at the table, he and Aparisi have been at each other's throats."

"What did they say?"

"Aparisi said that the monarchy wasn't 'practicable' and then he came out with an *ipso facto* and other lovely stuff."

Juan let out a loud laugh. "The marquis must be furious."

"He's eating in silence, thinking about how he'll take his revenge. I'll tell you what happens. Do you want some hake? Or beef steak?"

"Bring me whatever you want as long as you come back right away."

And she didn't take long to come back, with a dish of fish.

"He slayed him."

"Who?"

"The marquis. He slayed Aparisi. Really left him speechless."

"Tell me about it."

"Well, he'd no sooner started to answer when he came out with a '*delirium tremens*' just like that, and then without giving him a chance to get his breath, a '*mane tegel fare.*' The other one's stunned by the blow. We'll soon see what *he* comes up with."

"What a show! We'll have coffee together," said Santa Cruz. "Come right back. You're so flushed!"

"It's from laughing so much."

"If I were to tell you that it appeals to me . . . "

"I'll be back in a minute. I'm going to see what's going on there. Aparisi is indignant about Castelar, and he says that Salmerón's having the trouble he's having because he didn't take his advice."

"Aparisi's advice!"

"Yes. And what's keeping the marquis hanging by a thread is whether or not 'the working masses' will revolt."

Jacinta went back to the dining room, and the last story she brought him was this:

"Boy, if you were there you'd die laughing. Poor Muñoz! The other one's back on his feet and he's coming up with some choice ones. Imagine. He's saying that he's seen one of those projectiles that are shot from rifle cases, and the Berdan gun . . . He doesn't say holes, he says 'orifices.' Everything's an 'orifice,' and the marquis doesn't know what's hit him."

She couldn't continue because Muñoz came in, smoking a huge cigar to visit the patient.

"Hello, Juanín. So we've been 'cloistered'? What do you have, a head cold? It's good for your system; if your nose has to eliminate fluids, then let it eliminate them. Well, I'm—" He was going to say "I'm off," but when he saw Aparisi come in (or so Jacinta and her husband thought) he said: "I'm going to absent myself."

At about three o'clock, husband and wife were alone in the study: he was in the armchair reading newspapers and she was straightening up the room, which was rather messy. Barbarita had gone shopping. The servant announced that there was a man who wished to speak with "the young gentleman."

"You know that he's not receiving anyone," the young lady said, and taking the card from Blas' hands, she read: "José Ido del Sagrario, Domestic and Foreign Publications Salesman."

"Send him in, send him in immediately," ordered Santa Cruz, wriggling in his chair. "He's the funniest madman you can imagine. Just wait, you'll see how he'll make us laugh. When we're tired of him we can throw him out. A really amusing character! I saw him at Pez's a few days ago, and we nearly died laughing."

A few minutes later a man entered the study. He was very skinny, with a sickly face full of lobes and caruncles; bushy, stiff, reddish hair that looked like the mane of a mop; prehistoric clothes, very threadbare; an unraveling red tie; boots so creased they seemed to have been made that way. In one hand he carried a hat, an opera hat that had been around since that kind of hat was invented, the first of the opera hats without a shadow of a doubt; and in the other, a bundle of samples of the books for subscriptions to deluxe editions, so worn that the filth had darkened the gold finish on the binding. The compassionate Jacinta was painfully impressed by this picture of poverty in decent dress, and she felt more pity when he greeted them urbanely, without shrinking, as if he were very comfortable in all social situations.

"Hello, Sr. Ido. It's so nice to see you," said Santa Cruz, feigning sincerity. "Sit down, and tell me what brings you here."

"With your permission . . . Would you like *Famous Women?*"

Jacinta and her husband looked at each other.

"Or *The Women in the Bible?*" continued Ido, showing them book prospectuses. "As Sr. Santa Cruz said to me the other day at Sr. Pez's house that he wished to see some of the publications of the Barcelona companies that I have the honor of representing . . . Or would you like *Famous Courtesans, Religious Persecutions, Sons of Labor, Great Inventions, Pagan Gods? . . .* "

4

"Enough, enough; don't quote me any more titles or show me any more. I've already told you that I don't like books by installments. The shipments get lost, and it's a mess. I prefer to take a complete work. But I'm in no hurry. You must be tired from making so many rounds. Would you like a drink?"

"Thank you very much. I never drink."

"You don't? Well, the other day, when we saw each other at Joaquín's, he said you were slightly hazy . . . you know, a little high."

"I beg your pardon, Sr. Santa Cruz," Ido replied, embarrassed. "I never become inebriated; I have never been inebriated. Sometimes, without my knowing how or why, I'm subject to a certain excitement, and I get this way, nervous, as if I were shooting off sparks . . . I get electric. You see? I am already. Look closely, Sr. Don Juan, and notice how my left eyelid and this muscle on the same side of my jaw twitch. See? It has already started. Frankly, it's impossible to live like this. The doctors tell me to eat meat. I eat meat and I get worse. Ah, I'm like a watch spring. With your permission, I'll leave."

"Heavens no; stay and rest. It'll be over soon. Would you like a glass of water?"

Jacinta was sorry that Juan didn't let him leave, because the thought of that man fainting and having a fit filled her with repugnance and fear. As Juan was insisting on the glass of water, his wife said to him under her breath: "What this poor man needs is something to eat."

"Sr. Ido," the lady indicated, "could you eat a small chop?"

Don José gave her a tacit reply expressing profound incredulity. His eyes looked stranger all the time, and the twitching in his eyelid and cheek was getting more and more pronounced.

"I beg your pardon, Madam. When my thoughts get away from me, I can't seem to focus on anything. Did you ask me if I could eat a—"

"A little chop."

"I'm not in my right mind. I forget the names of people and things. What do you call a chop?" he added, putting his hand to his stiff mane, through which his memory escaped and the electricity flowed in. "By any chance, is what you call . . . whatever it is, is it a piece of meat with a short tail of bone?"

"Exactly. I'll have them bring you one."

"Don't trouble yourself, madam. I'll go order it."

"Have them bring him two," said the Señorito, enjoying the thought of seeing a starved man eat.

Jacinta left the room, and while she was gone Ido talked about his bad luck.

"In this country, Sr. Don Juanito, arts and letters aren't supported. I, who have been a primary school teacher; I, who have written amusing literary works, have to devote myself to selling publications from door to door so that I can bring bread home to my children. Everyone tells me that if I had been born in France, I'd already have a villa of my own."

"Undoubtedly. Can't you see that there's no one who will read here, and the few who do have no money?"

"Naturally," Ido said again and again, throwing anxious looks about him to see if the chop had appeared yet.

Jacinta came in, a dish in her hand. Behind her came Blas with the same small table on which the Señorito had had his lunch, a place setting, a napkin, a roll, a glass, and a bottle of wine. Ido looked at these things in a ravenous stupor ill-

disguised by courtesy, and he broke out in a nervous laugh, a sign that he was close
to the peak of that state that he called electric. The Dauphine sat down next to her
husband and looked at the unfortunate Don José with an expression somewhere
between fear and compassion. He left his samples and opera hat (which never
folded as it should) on the floor and attacked the chops like a tiger. Mumbled
between bites, disconnected words and sentences left his mouth. "Extremely grateful . . . Frankly, it would have been bad manners not to have accepted . . . It's not
that I'm hungry, of course . . . I had a substantial lunch, but how can I be disrespectful? Very, very grateful . . . "

"I've been noticing something, my dear Don José," said Santa Cruz.

"What?"

"That you don't chew what you eat."

"Oh! Would you care for me to chew?"

"No, not necessarily."

"You see, I don't have any back teeth. I eat the way turkeys do. Naturally . . . it's better for me that way."

"And you're not going to drink anything?"

"Just half a glass. Wine isn't good for me; but I'm very grateful, very grateful . . . " And as he ate, his eyelid and muscle danced on and started to look as if
they'd gone on strike. His arms and body shuddered spasmodically, as if someone
were tickling him.

"This man before your eyes," said Santa Cruz, "has gotten for himself one of the
most attractive women in all Madrid."

He made a sign to Jacinta that meant: "Just wait; the best part's coming."

"Really?"

"Yes. He doesn't deserve her. You can see that he's as homely as they come."

"My wife . . . Nicanora . . ." Ido murmured thickly, already taking his last
bite, "the Venus de Medici . . . satiny flesh . . . "

"Oh, would I love to meet that famous beauty!" cried Juan.

There was nothing left on his plate except the bone. Then he heaved a very deep
sigh, and, putting his hand on his breast, uttered the following words in a gruff
voice:

"Only outer beauty, that's all . . . a whitened tomb . . . a heart full of snakes."

His glance instilled such terror in Jacinta that she made signs to her husband to
let him leave. But since Juanito wanted to have more fun, he kept needling the poor
madman so that he would reach the breaking point.

"Come here, my dear Don José. What do you have to say against your wife?
She's a saint."

"A saint!" repeated Ido, his chin on his chest and throwing at the Dauphin a
look that, had it come from another face, would have seemed ferocious. "Very well,
sir. And what makes you assert that without proof?"

"It's common knowledge."

"Well, common knowledge is wrong!" shouted Ido, stretching his neck and gesticulating energetically. "People don't know what they're talking about."

"But don't get so upset about it, my poor man," Jacinta dared to say. "We don't care what your wife is."

"You don't care," replied Ido in the tragic tone of a melodramatic actor. "I know very well that nobody cares about these things except me, the abused husband, the man who knows how to place his honor above all else."

"It's clear that it should be mainly his concern," said Santa Cruz, harassing him further, "and that this Sr. Ido has a slow temper."

"So that you, Madam," added the miserable man, looking at Jacinta in such a way that she began to tremble, "may appreciate the just indignation of an honorable man, I'll have you know that my wife is . . . a*dulll*terous!"

He said this word with a horrible scream, getting up from his chair and extending both arms, as opera tenors usually do when they curse someone. Jacinta put her hands to her head. She could no longer stand the disagreeable spectacle. She called the servant to usher out the wretched salesman of literary works. But Juan, who still wanted to have fun, tried to calm him down.

"Sit down, Sr. Don José, and don't get so upset. You have to be patient with things like this."

"Be patient, be patient!" exclaimed Ido, who in his electric state always repeated the last sentence said to him, as if he were chewing on it, despite the fact that he had no teeth.

"Yes, my good man; there's no choice but to take these things as they come. They make you a bit bitter, but as someone has said, a man finally learns to take them."

"Take them! And how about honor, Sr. Santa Cruz?"

And again he sank his chin on his chest, looking out with eyes half back into their sockets, and suddenly shutting them, as bulls do when they lower their heads to charge. The caruncles on his neck were so inflamed that they almost eclipsed the red of his tie. He looked like a turkey in the excitement of a fight; he was beginning to look wild.

"Honor," said Juan. "Bah! Honor is a purely conventional sentiment."

Ido approached Santa Cruz step by step and touched him on the shoulder very gently, piercing him with his alarmed turkey eyes. After a long pause, during which Jacinta clung to her husband's side as if to defend him from an aggressive act, the poor man said the following, beginning very quietly, as if he were secreting it, and gradually raising his voice until he finished stentorially:

"And if you discovered that your wife, the Venus de Medici of the satiny flesh, and swan's neck, and eyes like stars; if you discovered that the divine being whom you madly adore, that lady who was so pure; if you discovered, I repeat, that she was failing to fulfill her obligations and having mysterious appointments with a duke, with one of the grandees of Spain, yes: with the duke of ____ himself . . . "

"That's very serious, my friend; *ve-ry* serious," stated Juan, looking graver than a judge. "Are you sure of what you're saying?"

"Am I sure of it! I've seen it . . . I've seen it."

He sounded oppressed as he said this, as if he were about to burst into tears.

"And you, my dear Sr. Don José," said Santa Cruz, pretending to be not merely serious but distressed now, "why is it that you don't ask the duke for satisfaction?"

"A duel . . . me in a duel!" Ido replied sarcastically. "They're for fools. They aren't the way to settle these things."

And he started off again in a low voice and ended up shouting:

"I'll do justice, I swear I will . . . I'm waiting to catch them *flagrante delicto* again, Sr. Don Juan, *flagrante delicto*. Then you'll see the two corpses slashed by a single sword. Vengeance will be done! My honor will be upheld . . . a single sword . . . And I'll be as calm as can be, as if nothing had happened. And I'll be able to go out in the world and show my hands, stained by their adulterous blood, and shout to everyone: 'Husbands, learn from me to defend your honor. Look at these hands that have done justice; look at them and kiss them . . . ' And they'll all come . . . every one of them, to kiss my hands. And there will be a kissing of my hands, for there are so many who have been wronged; so, so many . . . "

When he reached this stage of his pathetic attack, there was nothing that the poor man could hold onto. He gestured wildly in the middle of the room, going from one side to the other, he stood before the husband and wife with no sign of respect, turned quickly on one heel, and had all the appearances of a man who is entirely unaccountable for his words and deeds. The servant in the doorway was laughing, waiting for his master to order him to put the ridiculous character in the street. At last, Juan gave Blas the signal and said to his wife under his breath, "Give him a couple of *duros*." Poor Don José let himself be led to the door without saying a word or taking leave. Blas put the first of all opera hats on his head; in one hand, the smudged samples; and in the other, the two *duros* that the lady had given him. The door was shut, and the heavy, unsteady steps of the electric man could be heard going down the stairs.

"I don't think it's funny," declared Jacinta. "It scares me. Poor man! Poverty and hunger must have made him get like that."

"He wouldn't hurt a fly. Whenever he goes to Joaquín's house, we egg him on so he'll talk about the adulteress. His delusion is that his wife sleeps with a grandee of Spain. Other than that, he's reasonable and very accurate. What in God's name could be the cause of it? As you say, not eating. The man has also been a novelist, and from writing about so much adultery, and living on beans, he's gone soft in the head."

And nothing more was said about the madman. That night Guillermina came, and Jacinta, who had kept the dirty card with Ido's address on it, gave it to her friend so that she would give him some aid on one of her rounds. Indeed, the publications salesman's family (they lived at 12 Mira el Rio Street) deserved concern from someone. Guillermina knew the house and had many "customers" there. After visiting it, she painted her friend a very pathetic picture of the misery that reigned in the Idos' hole. The wife was a pitiful soul, a slave to her work and always exhausted, humble, her health ruined, ugly as sin, disheveled. He earned very little, next to nothing really. The family lived on the earnings of the eldest son, who was a typesetter, and those of the daughter, a good-looking girl who was an apprentice hairdresser.

One morning, two days after Ido's visit, Blas announced that the man with the stiff hair was in the vestibule. He wished to speak to the lady. "He was in a very subdued mood." Jacinta came out to see him, and before she had reached the vestibule, she was already opening her change purse.

"Señora," stated Ido as he accepted what she was giving him, "I am extremely grateful for your kindnesses, but oh, the lady doesn't realize that I'm naked . . . I mean, the clothes that I'm wearing are falling apart at the seams. And naturally, if the lady by any chance were to have any trousers that Sr. Don Juan had perhaps cast off . . ."

"Oh, yes. I'll take a look. Come again."

"Because Señora Doña Guillermina, who is so good, gave us some meat and bread coupons, and she gave Nicanora a blanket that's been heaven sent, because before we used to keep warm in bed by putting our clothes on top of the sheets."

"Don't worry, Sr. del Sagrario; I'll find some clothes that are in good condition. You're the same height as my husband."

"And it honors me . . . so grateful, Señora; but believe me, and I tell the lady this with my hand on my heart: I could use children's clothes more than men's clothes, because I don't mind if I'm naked, so long as the children have something to wear. All I have is one shirt, which Nicanora, naturally, washes for me on certain set nights while I sleep so that it'll be clean when I put it on in the morning; but I don't mind. If my children are dressed, pneumonia can strike me dead for all I care."

"I don't have any children," the lady said as painfully as the other one had said, "I don't have a shirt."

Jacinta marveled at how reasonable the salesman was. She didn't notice a single sign of his extravagances from the other day.

"The lady doesn't have any children. What a pity!" exclaimed Ido. "The Lord doesn't know what he's doing . . . And I'd like to know this: if the lady doesn't have any children, who should have them? As I say, God may be as wise as they say, but he does certain things that I won't stand for."

This seemed so well reasoned to the Dauphine that she fancied that the best philosopher in the world was standing before her eyes, and she gave him more money.

"I don't have any children," she repeated, "but now I remember. My sisters do . . . "

"A thousand and a thousand quadrillion thanks, Señora. We could do with some heavy clothes, like the ones Doña Guillermina gave to my neighbors' children."

"Doña Guillermina distributed things to your neighbors and not to you? Don't worry—I'll give her a good scolding."

Encouraged by this show of benevolence, Ido began to get familiar. He advanced a few steps into the vestibule, and lowering his voice, said to the lady:

"Doña Guillermina gave out some little hooded wool cloaks, some stockings, and other stuff; but we didn't get anything. The best things were for the Señá Joaquina's kids and 'Pitusín,' that little boy . . . does the lady know who I mean? . . . the little kid who lives with my neighbor Pepe Izquierdo. A good man, as wretched as we are. I don't want to keep Pitusín from being her favorite. I realize he should get the best, because he's one of the family."

"What did you say? Who are you talking about?" asked Jacinta, suspecting that Ido was getting electric. And as a matter of fact, she did think that she noticed his eyelid starting to twitch.

"Pitusín," Ido continued, becoming more familiar and lowering his voice, "is a three-year-old, and a very cute one at that, son of a so-called Fortunata, a bad woman, Señora; very bad . . . I saw her once, only once. She's good-looking, but wild. My neighbor told me everything . . . Well, as I was saying, poor little Pitusín wins you over . . . smarter than a fox, and mischievous! He's got the whole neighborhood around his little finger. I love him as if he were one of my own. Sr. Pepe picked him up somewhere, I don't know where, because his mother wanted to get rid—"

Jacinta was stunned, as if she'd just received a sharp blow on the head. She heard Ido's words but was unable to ask him plain questions. Fortunata, Pitusín! . . . Could this be another extravagant invention of that novelistic brain?

"But wait, let's see," the lady said at last, beginning to get hold of herself. "All this that you're telling me: is it the truth or some crazy story of yours? Because I've been told that you've written novels, and that by writing them and eating badly, you've lost your wits."

"I swear to the Señora that what I'm telling her is the holy truth," replied Ido, putting his hand on his breast. "José Izquierdo is a serious person. I don't know if the Señora knows him. He used to have a silversmith's shop on Concepción Jerónima, a big place; its specialty was gifts for nursemaids. I don't know if it was there that Pitusín was born; what I do know, naturally, is that he's the son of your husband, Señor Don Juanito Santa Cruz."

"You're crazy," exclaimed the lady in a fit of anger and scorn. "You're a liar. Get out of here!"

She pushed him toward the door, looking every whichway to see whether there was anyone in the vestibule area or the corridors who had heard this nonsense. There was no one around. Don José gushed reverent expressions; but he didn't get upset at being called crazy.

"If the lady doesn't believe me," he limited himself to saying, "she can find out for herself in the neighborhood."

At this she detained him. She wanted him to say more.

"You say that José Izquierdo . . . But I don't want to hear anything else. Go on, leave."

Ido crossed the threshold and Jacinta slammed the door just as he was opening his mouth, perhaps to add an interesting detail to his revelations. The lady fought against wanting to call him back. She thought she could see through the wood, as if it were glass, Ido's twitching eyelid and his turkey face, which by now was as hateful to her as that of a harmful beast's. "No, no, I won't open . . . " she thought. "He's a snake. What a horrid man! He pretends he's crazy so that people will feel sorry for him and give him money." When she heard him go down the stairs she again felt the desire for more explanations. At that very same moment Barbarita and Estupiñá were coming up loaded with packages of purchases. Jacinta saw them through the peephole and fled to the back of the house, fearful that they would see in her face the turmoil that that cursed man had created in her soul.

5

What a day the poor thing had! She didn't comprehend what was said to her; she didn't see or hear anything. It was like moral blindness and deafness that were almost physical. The snake that had coiled up inside her, from her breast to her brain, ate at all her thoughts and sensations and almost blocked out external life. She wanted to cry, but what would the family say when they saw her flood of tears? She'd have to explain why. She didn't lack strong, temporary reactions to grief, and when the wave of consolation came, she felt momentary relief. It was all a hoax after all, and the man was crazy! He was an author of bad novels, and not being able to write them for the public anymore he tried to fill real life with the products of his tubercular imagination. Yes, that was it, of course! It couldn't be anything else: his fantasy was consumptive. It's only in bad novels that unexpected children turn up, when they're needed to thicken the plot. But if his revelations might conceivably be a hoax, they might also not be one . . . This thought punctured her relief and the snake, instead of uncoiling further, re-tightened around her heart.

That day—it must have been the work of the devil—Juan's cold got much worse. He was the most impertinent and finicky patient imaginable. He wouldn't let his wife leave his side, and when he noticed an unusual sadness about her, he said to her in an annoyed tone: "Is there something wrong? What's the matter with you? A fine way to be. Here I am, a wreck, all bored and at the mercy of my cold and *you* come along with a face like a judge. Smile, for heaven's sake." And Jacinta was so good that she finally made an effort to seem happy. The Dauphin had no patience when it came to putting up with the nuisance of a simple cold, and he despaired when he was beset by that sneezing that seems to go on forever, like unending rosary beads. He was intent on clearing his head of heavy conges-tion by blowing his nose loudly and angrily.

"Be patient, my son," his mother said to him. "What would you do with a serious illness?"

"Shoot myself, Mamá. I can't stand this. The more I blow my nose, the more congested my head gets. I'm sick of drinking watery concoctions. To the devil with them! I don't want any more brews. My stomach's like a pool. And they tell me to be patient! I could run out of patience any minute. I'm going out tomor-row."

"Not unless we let you."

"You could at least be cheerful and tell me something to amuse me. Jacinta, sit beside me. Look at me."

"I'm already looking at you. You look adorable with your little scarf tied around your head, your nose all red, your eyes like tomatoes . . . "

"Go ahead, make fun of me. That's just what I wanted . . . I wish you had a cold like mine. No, I don't want any more candy. All your candy has turned my body into a confectionery. Mamá!"

"Yes?"

"Will I be well tomorrow? For God's sake, have pity on me, make this bearable for me. I'm on the rack. I can't stand to sweat. If I take something off, I cough; if I put more on, I start dripping. Mamá, Jacinta, get my mind off this. Send for Estupiñá so I can kill some time laughing with him."

When she was alone again with her husband, Jacinta returned to her own thoughts. She looked at him from behind the armchair in which he was seated. "Oh, how you've deceived me! . . . " She was beginning to think that the mad-man, as far gone as he was, had told a few truths. The unequivocal hunches that she had assured her that the disagreeable story about Pitusín was true. Unfortu-nately, there are things that are necessarily true, especially bad things. And the poor wife was suddenly caught off guard by *such* rage! It was the sort of rage that fills doves when they start to fight. Seeing her husband's head very near her, she had the urge to pull his hair, which cropped out between the folds of the silk scarf. "I'm so furious at him," thought Jacinta, clenching her extremely pretty teeth, "for having kept such a serious thing from me! Having a child and abandoning it that way! . . . " She was blinded by rage; everything looked black. She felt as if she was about to have a convulsion. That unknown and mysterious Pitusín, that creation of her husband's, without its being as it should have been, *her* creation too, was the real snake coiling up inside her. "But why should I blame the poor child?" she thought afterward, transformed by pity. "This, . . . this cad!" She looked at his head, and oh, how she craved to pull out a shock of his hair, hit him really hard on the head! Once? No, twice, three or four times, give him a few big lumps so that he'd learn to stop deceiving people.

"What are you doing back there behind me, dear?" he murmured without turning his head. "As I said: you seem dumb today. Come here, dear."

"What do you want?"

"Darling, do me a little favor."

These sweet words made the Dauphine's furious urge to hit him vanish. She unclenched her teeth and walked around the chair to stand facing him.

"Do me a favor and cover me with another blanket. I think I've gotten a chill."

Jacinta went to look for a blanket. On the way out she said to herself: "In Seville he told me that he'd taken steps to help her. He wanted to see her and wasn't able to. Mamá died; time passed; he never heard anything more from her. In the name of God the Father, I'll find out what's behind this, and if" (she choked when she reached this point in her thoughts) "if it's true that the children I'm not having with him are being borne by another woman . . . "

As she put on the blanket she said to him:

"Keep warm, scoundrel."

And her solemnity, as she said this, didn't escape Juanito. In a little while he took up a pampering tone again.

"Jacintilla, my treasure, the angel in my life, come over here. You don't pay attention to your shameless little hubby anymore."

"I'm glad you recognize yourself. What do you want?"

"Love me and pamper me. That's the way I am. I realize I'm impossible. Bring me some sugared water . . . nice and warm, you know. I'm thirsty."

After giving him the water, Jacinta touched his forehead and his hands.

"Do you think my forehead's too hot?"

"As hot as roast chicken. All you have is a fresh tongue. You're worse than a child."

"Look, sweetie, lamb; when *La Correspondencia* comes, read it to me. I want to know what's becoming of Salmerón. Then read me *La Epoca*. You're so good!

You're right here, yet I still can't believe that I have an angel like you for a wife. And no one's going to rob me of such a bargain. What would I do without you, sick and prostrate!"

"Some illness! If it were what you make it sound like with your complaints—"

Doña Bárbara came in, saying authoritatively:

"To bed, child, to bed. It's already dark and you'll get chilled in that chair."

"All right, Mamá; I'm going to bed. I haven't said a word—all I do is obey my tyrants. I'm as gentle as a lamb. Blas! Blas! Where in the devil does that man disappear to?"

Lord above, what a struggle it was to put him to bed! Luckily for them, they knew how to humor him. "Jacinta, put a silk scarf around my neck. But don't make it so tight, you're strangling me. Never mind, you don't know how. Mamá, you tie the scarf. No, take it off, neither of you knows how to tie a scarf. What a useless pair!"

A little while later:

"Mamá, has *La Correspondencia* come?"

"No, dear. Don't take anything off. Put those arms *in*. Jacinta, cover his arms."

"All right, all right, my arms are in. Do you want me to put them in further? That's it, they insist that I suffocate. They've put a Saratoga trunk on top of me. Jacinta, take off some of that tonnage; so much weight is exhausting me. Wait a minute, not so much; pull up the quilt a bit, my neck's frozen. Mamá, didn't I tell you so, they don't want to help. I'll never get well this way. And now everyone's going off to eat. And am I going to be left all alone with Blas?"

"No, silly; Jacinta will eat here with you."

While his wife was eating, he didn't stop pestering her for a second.

"You're not eating, you're not hungry; something's wrong with you; you're hiding something . . . You can't fool me. Frankly, I can never relax. Always wondering whether you'll get sick on us. Well, you have to eat; make an effort. Are you not eating because you want to make me mad? Come over here, silly, rest your head here. *I'm* not mad, I love you more than my own life. If I could see you happy I'd sign a contract for a lifelong cold right now. Give me a taste of that apple. Ooh, it's good! Let me lick your fingers."

Friends of the family who often came in the evening were arriving.

"Mamá, for all of Christ's sores and nails, don't bring Aparisi in here. Everything has to be 'obvious' now. This is *obvious*, that's *obvious*. If you bring him in to see me, I'll throw him out and I won't mince any words."

"Oh, stop that nonsense. He may come in to say hello, but he'll leave right away. Who just came? . . . Ah! I think it's Guillermina."

"I don't want to see her either. She'll bore me with her building. What a laugh! That woman is crazy. Last night she gave me a migraine with that bit about getting six-foot planks for only thirty-eight *reales*, and foot-and-a-quarter strips for sixteen *reales* a foot. So much chatter about feet, it felt as if my head had been bashed in. Don't let them send *her* in. I couldn't care less about the cost of baked bricks and doorframes. Mamá, keep watch, and don't let anyone in except Estupiñá. Have Placidito come so he'll tell me about his glorious actions when he went to the Gil Imón gates to smuggle in contraband stuff, and the San Ginés crypt, where he slashed his flesh to shreds with a whip . . . Have him come so I can say: 'Hey, Parrot, give me your claw.'"

"What impertinence! You know very well that poor Plácido goes to bed between nine and ten. He has to be on his feet at five in the morning, since he has to wake the sexton at San Ginés who's such a heavy sleeper."

"And I have to give up my pleasure just because the San Ginés sexton likes to sleep? Have Estupiñá come over and talk to me. He's the only one who amuses me."

"For the love of God, dear, put your arms under the covers."

"Huh! Well, if Rossini doesn't come, I won't put them in and I'll put my whole body out."

And Plácido came, and told him hundreds of funny things that I'm afraid I can't reproduce here. This not being enough, Juanito wanted to have fun at his expense, and, recalling a passage in Estupiñá's life that he had heard about, he said:

"Let's see, Plácido; tell us about the time you went down on your knees before the night watchman thinking he was the viaticum . . ."

When he heard this, the generous and talkative old man was disconcerted. He replied awkwardly, stuttering negatives and: "Who told you that fib?" Juan would probably spring this at him now: "But tell me, Plácido, haven't you ever had a girl friend?"

"Well, well," said Estupiñá, getting up to leave, "Juanito feels like seeing a comedy today."

Barbarita, who held her good friend in such high esteem, was, as they say, on the lookout for this teasing; it annoyed her very much. "Dear, don't be such a bore; let Plácido leave now. Since you sleep till eleven in the morning, you forget that there are people who have to get up early."

Meanwhile, Jacinta had left the bedroom for a bit. She saw several people in the living room—Casa-Muñoz, Ramón Villuendas, Don Valeriano Ruiz-Ochoa, and someone else—talking politics with such a tragic air that they looked more like conspirators. In Barbarita's parlor and in the habitual corner, she found Guillermina darning stockings with heavy duty thread. In the short time she sat with her she told her about the plan she had devised for the following day. They would go together to Mira el Río Street, because Jacinta was particularly interested in helping the eccentric subscriptions collector's family. "I'll tell you about it later; we have to talk about it at length." They had a whispering session that had lasted at least a quarter of an hour when Barbarita appeared.

"For the love of God, child, go see him. He's been calling you for some time now. Don't leave his side. He has to be treated like a baby."

"What a way to go off and leave me. You have no heart!" cried the Dauphin upon seeing his wife enter the room. "What a way to take care of someone. Huh . . . I could be a dog for all you care."

"But darling, I left you with Plácido and your mother. I'm sorry. I'm back now."

Jacinta seemed happy. God only knows why . . . She leaned over the bed and began to caress her husband as one caresses a three-year-old.

"My, but this little boy's getting naughty! I'm going to give him a spanking. Here—this one from your mother, this one from your father, and this big one . . . from your closest relative."

"Sweetie!"

"But you don't love me."

"Go on, you flatterer. You're the one who doesn't love me."

"Not at all, by the grace of God."

"How much do you love me?"

"This much."

"That's not enough."

"Well, from here to the post office, then. No—to the sky. Are you satisfied?"

"Yeth."

Jacinta grew serious.

"Fix this pillow for me."

"Like this?"

"No, higher."

"Is it all right now?"

"No, a little bit lower . . . perfect. Now scratch my back."

"Here?"

"Lower down . . . a bit higher . . . there; hard. Oh, what a glorious angel you are! I'm so lucky to have you!"

"It's when you're sick that you tell me these things. But you'll have to pay me back for everything."

"I know, I'm a rascal. Hit me."

"Here, take that."

"Go ahead and gobble me up."

"Don't worry, I will, and I'm taking a mouthful now."

"Ow! Not so much, for heaven's sake. If anyone were to see us!"

"They'd think we were idiots," Jacinta observed with a certain melancholy. "This silliness isn't for anyone else's eyes."

"Are you closing your eyes? Go to sleep; shhhh . . . "

"I know. You want me to go to sleep so you can run off and wind up your maniac friend Guillermina. You're responsible for her going out of her mind, because you bring up the subject of her building. You're already hoping I'll close my eyes so you can leave. You like chatting with her more than being with me. You know what I think? That if I go to sleep, you have to stay here, keeping watch, to make sure that my covers don't slide off."

"All right, all right. I'll stay."

He grew drowsy, but he opened his eyes immediately, and the first thing he saw was Jacinta's eyes, fixed on him with loving attention. When he really did fall asleep, the sentry abandoned her post and hastened to Guillermina's side to resume their most interesting conference.

IX. A Visit to the Slums

I

THE NEXT DAY THE DAUPHIN was more or less the same. That morning, while Barbarita and Plácido were walking through the streets, yielding to the pleasures of Christmas shopping, Jacinta left the house with Guillermina. She had left her husband in Villalonga's care after telling the white lie that she was going to the Virgen de la Paloma Church to attend Mass as she had promised. The two ladies' attire was so different that they looked like mistress and maid. Jacinta was wearing her raisin-colored *pardessus*, and Guillermina was in her usual extremely modest clothes.

Jacinta was so rapt in her thoughts that the hubbub on Toledo Street didn't distract her from her inner world. The half-set-up stands along the sidewalk, from the gates to San Isidro, the trinkets, the tambourines, the cheap crockery, the lacework, the Alcaraz copper, and the hundreds of thousands of knickknacks visible in those niches with their badly nailed boards and more clumsily stretched canvas passed by without her being able to tell exactly what they were. All that registered on her was a blurry image of the diverse objects that paraded past them; I say it this way because it was as though she were standing still and the picturesque route were being drawn past her like a curtain. On that curtain were clusters of dates hanging from a rack; strips of white lace attached to a rod and waving gently, like stems of a climbing vine; lumps of overripe figs in blocks; pieces of nougatlike stone cut out of a quarry; olives oozing out of barrels; a woman seated on a chair in front of a cage, showing off two little trained birds; and heaps of gold—oranges in panniers or piled up in the ditch. The ground was an obstacle course: piles of earthenware jugs, bowls, and vases at the feet of the rushing crowd, and the vibration of the cobblestones as wagons rumbled over them seemed to make the people and earthen pots dance. Men with strings of multicolored scarves approached passersby like bullfighters provoking bulls. Strident women practically broke your eardrums with their emphatic cries, harassing the public and giving it the alternative of buying or dying. Jacinta saw bolts of material unfurled in waves along the walls: blue, red, and green percales stretched from door to door, and her dizzy eyes exaggerated the curves of those cloth rubrics. Hanging from them, attached with common pins, were small shawls in the bright, basic colors that appeal to primitive people. Orange blazed out in some areas, screeching like an ungreased axle; native vermilion, scratching one's eyes; carmine, as bitter as vinegar; then cobalt blue, vaguely suggesting poison; lizard-belly green; and linden yellow, which mixed poetry and consumption, as in *La Traviata*. The mouthlike openings of the stands—open spots in that ruffled facade of rags—revealed the interiors, which were just as motley as the exteriors. Clerks were leaning forward over the counters, or beating the dust out of their materials with their yardsticks, or chatting. Some of them swung their arms as if they were swimming in a sea of scarves. The picturesque instinct of those standowners shows in everything. If there's a post in the stand, they decorate it with pink, black, and white corsets and make pleasing visual combinations with petticoats.

Jacinta ran into various ceremonious individuals. They were mannequins dressed up as ladies in huge bustles, or gentlemen in flannel outfits. Then caps, scads of caps placed high on racks and aligned with a stick; sheepskin jackets and other garments that looked rather—yes, indeed—rather like legless and headless human beings. Eventually Jacinta didn't look at any one thing. All she noticed were some yellow men hanging from pitchforks, swaying in the breeze. They were matching shirts and trousers sewn together that all of a sudden looked like sulfur people. There were red ones too. There was so much red everywhere that blood seemed to be the religion of these people. Red material, red harnesses, red collars and yokes with berry-shaped tassels, Arabic style. The doors to the taverns were blood-colored too. And not just one or two of them. Jacinta was frightened at seeing so many, and Guillermina couldn't resist exclaiming: "Oh, perdition, perdition! Every other door leads into a tavern. That's where the crimes start."

When she approached the end of her journey, the Dauphine centered her attention exclusively on the small children she came across. Señora Santa Cruz was astonished by the quantities of mothers there were in these neighborhoods; at every step she ran into one with a suckling in her arms, nicely tucked under her cloak. All that could be seen of these future citizens were their heads over their mothers' shoulders. Some of them looked backward, showing their little round faces and lively eyes framed by bonnets, and laughed as if they were sharing a private joke with the passersby. Others looked disgruntled, like people who mistrust everything and everyone from the minute they're born. Jacinta also saw not one but two or even three being taken in boxes to the cemetery. She imagined that they were very still and wax-colored in those boxes, carried by anyone at all, like shotguns.

"Here it is," said Guillermina, after walking a stretch on Bastero Street and turning a corner. They soon found themselves in a rectangular patio. Jacinta looked up and saw two rows of low-walled open-air corridors and large wooden pilasters painted ochre, quantities of clothes hanging, lots of yellow underskirts, lots of undressed sheepskin stretched out to dry, and she heard a buzzing, as if from swarms. In the patio, which except for a few stone-covered spots was the ground itself, were children of different sexes and ages. As a head covering an overgrown girl was wearing a red shawl with holes—*orifices*, as Aparisi would say—in it; another, a white shawl; another had left her rat's nest exposed. This last one was wearing cloth slippers; and the first, delicate white boots, but they were creased now and the heels were crooked. There were various types of boys. There was the type who always goes to school with his book bag, and there was the barefoot prankster who does nothing but waste time. They differed very little in their dress, and even less in their language, which was rough and had slovenly inflections.

"*Hey,* kid . . . looka this. I'll push ya' face in. Get what I *mean* . . . ?"

"See the one that's bragging so much?" Guillermina said to her friend. "She's one of Ido's daughters. That one, over there, who's jumping around like a grasshopper. Hello! Little girl! . . . They don't hear us. Come here!"

All the kids, male and female, started to look at the two ladies and stopped talking, half in fun, half out of respect, not daring to approach them. Who did approach them step by step were seven or eight brown pigeons with rainbow-hued necks; they were very pretty and plump, striding toward them very trustingly, swaying from side to side like coquettes, pecking at what they found on the ground. And they were so tame that they went right up to the ladies without being frightened. Suddenly they rose in flight and perched on the roof. In some doorways women were airing mats and chairs and tables. Something like heavy smoke curled out of others: it was the dust from sweeping. There were tenants combing their black oily braids or long blond mops; and their thickets hung over their faces like curtains. Others came out, dragging their feet in squashed-heeled shoes over the God-forsaken stones, and when they saw the strangers, ran back to their lairs to tell their neighbors, and the news went around, and in the grilled windows combed or partly combed heads started to appear.

"Hey, kids! Come here," Guillermina repeated. And they gradually approached, in echelons, as when there's going to be an attack. Some of the more daring ones, with their hands behind their backs, looked at the two ladies in a very insolent way. But one of the bunch, who undoubtedly had gentlemanly instincts, removed from his head a rag that was playing the role of a cap and asked them whom they were looking for.

"Are you Sr. Ido?"

The young boy replied that he was not, and at the same time the long-legged girl with the exposed rat's nest and cloth slippers stood forth from the group by pushing aside all the other boys and girls who were already clustering around the ladies.

"Is your father upstairs?" The girl replied that he was, and from that moment on she became a regular policeman. She wouldn't let anyone approach them; she wanted all the urchins to step back, to guide the two ladies upstairs herself. "They're such a nuisance! . . . They want to stick their noses in everything. Back, you guys, step back . . . Get outta the way; let us through!"

Her desire was to lead. She would have liked to have had a bell to ring as she went through those corridors so that everyone would know about the important visit.

"Little girl, you don't have to go with us," said Guillermina, who didn't like for anyone to make such a fuss over her. "It's enough to know that they're at home."

But longlegs ignored this. There was a woman sitting on the bottom step of the staircase selling strings of dried figs, and longlegs practically stepped on her face with her cloth slippers. And all because she wouldn't budge to make way for them. "What a place you had to pick to sit, you old witch! Outta the way, or I'll knock ya down!"

They went up, not without Jacinta's still craving to get a good look at all the kids in the patio. She had glimpsed two little boys and a little girl behind the others. One of them was blond and about three years old. They were playing with mud, the cheapest toy there is. They packed it to make cakes, like big coins. The girl, who was older, had made an oven with pieces of brick, and to her right there was a stack of bread, rolls and cakes, all of the same stuff, which was so abundant. Señora Santa Cruz observed this group from a distance. Was he one of them? Her heart was in her mouth; she didn't dare ask the long-legged girl. On the top step of the staircase they met with another obstacle: two girls and three babies, one of them in a mantilla, intercepted them. They were playing with the "best" sand, the fine kind used for scouring. The suckling was swaddled on the floor with his paws out, bellowing for all he was worth, and being completely ignored. The two girls had spread out the sand on the floor, and here and there they had placed various little sticks with strings and rags. It was an imitation clothesline.

"God, what a bunch!" longlegs exclaimed as indignant as a public warden, but having no effect. "Careful where you sit. Out, out! . . . And you, you little squirt, pick up your brother or we'll make mincemeat out of him."

These warnings from such a zealous authority were received with insolent scorn. One of the pups dragged his belly across the floor with all fours stuck out;

the other one picked up fistfuls of sand and washed his face with it, which was perfectly logical, for the sand represented water.

"Come, children, move out of the way, " Guillermina said to them as longlegs destroyed the washing place with her foot, shouting:

"You should be ashamed! Don't you have some place else to play? What a stupid bunch . . ." and she struck forth resolved to destroy any obstacle she found in her path. The other little girls picked up the pups as if they were dolls and, putting them on their hips, dashed away down those corridors.

"Come on," Guillermina said to her guide. "Don't scold them so much. You're not so perfect yourself."

2

They continued through the corridor, and at every step something blocked their way. Either a brazier that was being lit, with the iron pipe over the live coals so that it would catch, or a pile of undressed sheepskin, or mats, or a basket of clothes, or a jug of water. From all the open doors and windows came voices: arguments or festive clamor. They could see the kitchens: pots set on the stove, the washtub next to the door, and, further back, in the adjoining small room, the indispensable bureau covered with oilcloth, the brass lamp, its green shade, and on the wall a sort of altar made of various prints, a chromo or so from a prospectus or satirical newspaper, and numerous photographs. They went through a residence that was a cobbler's workshop, where the shoemakers' hammering on soles together with their off-key singing made an infernal racket. Farther away they could hear the convulsive tick-a-tack-a-tick of a sewing machine, and the faces and busts of curious women peering out of windows. Here they saw a sick man lying in a broken-down bed, there, a married couple shouting at each other. Some of the women knew Doña Guillermina and greeted her respectfully. In other quarters Jacinta's elegant looks caused admiration. A bit further away, cutting or disrespectful remarks were being exchanged from door to door. "Seña Mariana, have you noticed that we're carrying the sofa on our rump? Ha, ha, ha!"

Guillermina stopped, looking at her friend. "That chaff doesn't get anywhere with me. You can't imagine how these people hate bustles; it shows that they have a—what do you call it?—an *aesthetic* instinct that is better than what those stupid French have, always inventing so much heavy stupid stuff."

Jacinta was somewhat abashed, but she laughed too. Guillermina retreated several steps, saying:

"All right, ladies, mind your own business, and don't bother people who don't bother you."

Then she stopped at one of the doors and rapped on it with her knuckles.

"Señá Severiana isn't in," said one of the neighbors. "Would the Señora like to leave a message?"

"No; I'll come again another day."

After going up and down both sides of the main corridor they penetrated into a sort of tunnel in which there were more numbered doors. They climbed about six steps, always preceded by the long-legged girl, and found themselves in a corridor bordering another patio, much uglier, dirtier, and more dismal than the one before. Compared with the second, the first was rather aristocratic and might have been taken as a refuge for "distinguished" families. Between the two patios, which belonged to the same owner and for this reason were joined, there was a social step, the distance between what are called "echelons." The dwellings on that second level were more cramped and shabbier than those on the first; the stucco was chipping off, which made it seem as if the marks on the walls had been scratched more angrily; the penciled lines on some of the doors were more stupid and obscene; the wood, more faded and filthy; the air, more foul; the fumes escaping through the windows and doors, thicker and more revolting. Jacinta, who had visited various other tenement houses, had never seen such a gloomy and foul-smelling one.

"What, does it scare you, my pretty one?" said Guillermina. "After all, what did you expect, that it would be like the Royal Theater or Fernán-Núñez's house? Take heart. To come here you need two things: charity and a strong stomach."

Looking up to the top of the roof, the Dauphine saw an area where leather pieces, tripe, and other spoils were spread out to dry. From that area and wafted-in gusts of air came a nauseating smell. Walking over the uneven rooftops were ferocious-looking cats—skinny, angular haunches, drowsy-eyed, fur standing on end. Others came down to the corridors and stretched out in the sun; but the really wild ones lived and even nourished themselves up there, pursuing the tasty rat around the drying area.

Ragged figures, blind men tapping sticks on the floor, crippled creatures with furry heads, soldier's pants, and horrible faces, passed the two ladies. Jacinta pressed against the wall to make way for them. They met women wrapped in scarves and brown cloaks, covering their mouths with a hand wrapped in a fold of the cloak itself. They looked like Moors; all that could be seen of them was an eye and part of a nose. Some were graceful, but most of them were skinny, pale, paunchy, and aged before their time.

Through the open windows, along with the smell of fried food and the querulous atmosphere, came the murmur of coarse conversations in which the last syllables were muted and dragged. This way of speaking, saying *chicooo* instead of *chico*, originated in Madrid from a mixture of the Andalusian accent (which the soldiers made popular) and the Aragonese accent; both are assimilated by men who want to brag about their masculinity.

Another barricade of kids blocked their way. Upon seeing them, Jacinta and even Guillermina, despite her experience of strange sights, were astonished and would have been horrified by what they saw had the laughter not dispelled the terrifying spectacle. It was a bunch of savages, made of two awkward-looking beanpoles who were about ten and twelve, a younger girl, and two other small fry whose age and sex were unascertainable. They all had their faces and hands full of black stains from what must have been tar or the strongest kind of Japanese varnish. One had painted stripes on his face; another, glasses; still another, a mustache, eyebrows, and sideburns so clumsily that his face looked as if it had been dipped in the dregs of an inkwell. The little things didn't look as if they belonged to the human race. With that grimy soot spread and rubbed into their faces and hands, they looked more like monkeys, miniature devils, or some such infernal offspring.

"Damn you!" shouted longlegs when she saw those horrid faces. "What a nerve, to make yourselves look like that, you indecent pigs, hogs!"

"In the name of the Father!" exclaimed Guillermina, making the sign of the cross. "Can you believe it?"

They contemplated the ladies silently and with extreme excitement, secretly enjoying the surprise and terror that their frightful looks produced in such refined, delicate ladies. One of the little ones tried to clutch at Jacinta's coat, but longlegs began to scream at them:

"Get outta here, go away, you dirty little pigs! You're getting these ladies dirty with your paws."

"God above! . . . They look like cannibals. Don't touch us. It's not your fault, it's your mothers' for letting you do such things . . . And if I'm not mistaken, these two loafers are your brothers, child."

The two alluded to smiled, showing their milk-white teeth and redder-than-cherry lips in the surrounding blackness; they replied that they were, nodding their savage heads. They were beginning to feel ashamed and didn't know what to do. At that very moment a big woman came out of the nearest door, and, grabbing one of the besmeared little girls, she pulled up her petticoats and began to give her such a beating on the appropriate spot that it could be heard from the first patio. In no time another furious mother appeared, one who looked more like a wolf than a woman, and she got started on another of the devils, slapping at his dirt, with no fear of dirtying herself too. "You little savages, stinkers, look what you've done!" And more irritated mothers poured out. What a scene! Soon there were tears streaming over the tar, and their grief blackened. "I'm going to kill

you, you big rascal, thief . . . " "It's the blasted varnish that Señá Nicanora uses.
Holy Jesus, Señá Nicanora, why do ya let these youngsters . . . ?"

One of the noisiest of the women calmed down when she saw the two ladies—
Señora Ido del Sagrario, whose face had smudges and stains of that same tar the
Caribbeans use and hands that were entirely black. She was a bit abashed by the
visit: "Please come in, ladies . . . I'm an awful mess."

Guillermina and Jacinta entered Ido's mansion, which consisted of a narrow
hall and two interior rooms, still more oppressive and gloomy, which made
whoever entered them shudder. The ubiquitous bureau and illustration of Christ
as "The Great Power," faded pictures of members of the family, including deceased children, were there too. The kitchen was a cold lair full of ashes, turned-
over pots, broken jars, and a washtub heaped with stiff, dry rags and dust. In the
small room where they were the loose tiles played like piano keys under their feet.
The walls looked as if they belonged to a coal shed, and in certain spots they had
been punched with lime, which made a fantastic chiaroscuro of them. One would
have thought there were ghosts around—or at least shadows from a magic lantern. The Victorian sofa was one of the most alarming pieces of furniture imaginable. All you had to do was look to realize that it wouldn't vouch for the safety of
whoever sat on it. The two or three chairs also looked quite suspicious. The one
that looked best would probably fool you too. Jacinta saw posters of illustrated
books, packages of cigarette paper, and cardboard covers of old American alma-
nacs that no longer had any pages; and there were those fantastic walls.

But what stirred both ladies' curiosity most was a large drawing board in the
middle of the room, taking up almost all the empty space; it was a table set up on
benches, like the kind document writers use, and on top were quires of fine writing paper. On one side the stacked quires contained compact white reams; on the
other, those same reams with newly painted black borders became mourning
paper.

Ido spread out the unfolded sheets of paper on the drawing board. A girl (probably Rosita) counted the sheets that were already "in mourning" and made the
quires. Nicanora asked the ladies for permission to continue her work. She was an
aged rather than old woman, and it was plainly evident that she had never been
beautiful. At one time she must have been well rounded, but now her sagging
body was wrinkled and bumpy, like an empty shepherd's pouch. In fact, you
couldn't tell what was breast and what was belly on her. Her face was snoutish and
disagreeable. If it expressed anything, it was a very bad temper and an acrid
disposition; but in this, her face, like so many others, was deceiving. Nicanora
was a miserable woman, kinder than she was intelligent, worn out by the trials of
life, which for her had been a battle with neither victories nor rest. All she had
left was patience. Facing adversity so long must have given her that drawn-out snout
which considerably uglified her. The "Venus de Medici" had sickly red eyelids

deprived of eyelashes and, since they were always damp, people said that "she cried for her father with one eye and for her mother with the other."

Jacinta didn't know whom to pity more, Nicanora for being what she was, or her husband for believing that she was Venus when he got "electrified." Ido was very inhibited in the presence of the two ladies. When the chair that Doña Guillermina had sat in so often began to squeak in protest, announcing that it would perhaps collapse, Don José ran out to look for another in the neighborhood. Rosita was graceful, but decayed and chlorotic, greenish-colored. Her hairdo was what one noticed first: ringlets that had been teased and stiffened with quantities of lacquer.

"But what are you up to with that paint, woman?" Guillermina asked Nicanora.

"It's my work; it's *mourning*."

"It's *morning!*" said Ido, smirking, very satisfied at having the opportunity to crack his joke, which was as old as the hills and had been used on many a previous occasion.

"What is he saying!" said Guillermina, miffed by his joke.

"Be quiet, stop saying stupid things," Nicanora instructed him. "I'm in the mourning business; I paint mourning paper. When I don't have something else to do, I bring home a few reams and turn them into mourning paper, as the ladies can see. The salesman pays a *real* a ream. I pay for the dye, and working all day long, I make six or seven *reales*. But times are bad, and there's not much 'dyeing' to be done. All of us are out of a job because naturally, either not many people are dying, or they're not announcing it. José," she said to her husband, making him tremble, "what are you doing with your mouth hanging open? Start the *dissembling*."

Ido, listening to his wife as if she were a brilliant orator, awoke from his ecstasies and started to "dissemble." This was their word to describe stacking the folded sheets one on top of another, graduating the edges so as to leave equal borders on each, which they then dyed all at once. Since Jacinta was carefully observing Don José's work, he took pains to do it especially perfectly and deftly. It was a pleasure to see those borders, whose equality made them look as if they had been aligned by a compass. Rosita piled up folds and reams without a word. Nicanora made a sign to Jacinta that, because of her glance at Ido, meant: "He's all right today." Then with a brush she began to stroke the paper quickly.

"And the serial subscriptions," asked Guillermina, "do they bring in enough to eat?"

Ido opened his mouth to emit a prompt and sensible answer to the question, but his wife quickly took the floor, while he stood for quite awhile with his mouth hanging open.

"The subscriptions," declared the Venus de Medici, "are a calamity. José, here, doesn't have much luck . . . He's so honest anybody can cheat him. The public's a bad thing, ladies, and there are subscribers that can't be dragged to pay. And then, since *this here*" ("this here" was her husband) "lost a four hundred *real* bill last month, the man in charge of the subscriptions is collecting it, discounting it from the premiums he gets. And naturally this has made us get way behind, and the little we can hold onto goes to the landlord."

After the bit about the lost bill had been mentioned, Ido didn't take his eyes from his work again. He was as ashamed of that carelessness as if it had been a crime.

"Well, the first thing that you have to do," la Pacheco pointed out, "is put those two beanpoles and that tomboy daughter of yours in school."

"I don't send them because I'm ashamed to have them leave the house in such rags."

"It doesn't matter. Besides, my little friend and I will give you some clothes for the boys. How about the oldest one, does he earn anything?"

"He earns five *reales* for me at a printing press. But he's not serious. Whenever he feels like it he leaves his job and goes off to the calf-killings in Getafe or Leganés and doesn't show up for days. He wants to be a bullfighter and he's killing us with it. He goes to the slaughterhouse in the afternoons when they do the beheading, and when he's home asleep he talks about whether he stuck the banderillas in *a la porta-gayola* or some other way."

"And you," Jacinta asked Rosita, "what do you do?"

Rosita blushed crimson. She was just about to answer when her mother, who spoke for the whole family, replied:

"She's a hairdresser. She's learning from a neighbor who teaches. She already has a few customers. But they don't pay her, of course. She's so dumb—if they don't put the money in her hand it's all the same to her. I tell her not be such a ninny and get mad; but . . . look at her. Just like her father: if one person doesn't cheat them, the next does."

After taking out various coupons, including theater tickets, and giving the unfortunate family enough to supply them with garbanzos, bread, and meat for half the week, Guillermina said she was leaving. But Jacinta wasn't ready to leave so soon. She had come with a purpose and would not retreat for anything in the world unless she at least tried to accomplish it. Several times she had the word on the tip of her tongue to ask Don José about it, and he looked at her as if to say, "I'm dying for you to ask me about Pituso." Finally the lady decided to break the ice on this capital point and, rising, she took several steps in Ido's direction. That was all he needed. Seeing her approach, he quickly left the room and returned a few minutes later holding a little creature by the hand.

3

"In the name of God! . . ." exclaimed la Pacheco as she saw the outlandish little figure come in. And the others let out similar exclamations when they saw the child, whose face was so thoroughly blackened that the true color of his skin couldn't be seen anywhere. His hands were dripping with tar and the other boys had wiped off their disgusting hands on his clothes. Pitusín had black hair. His red lips against that asphalt were finer than the purest coral. His little teeth shone like glass. The tongue he stuck out (because he thought that to be like a black boy he should stick out his tongue as far as possible) looked like a rose petal.

"What a mess! Oh, you rascals! Good God, look what they've done to him—covered him with that vile stuff!" The neighbors clustered in their doorways laughing and making a rumpus. Jacinta was astonished and grieved. Strange thoughts crossed her mind: the stain left by the sin had spread its shadow over innocence itself; and the cursed little boy laughed behind his infernal mask, happy that everyone was paying attention to him, even if it was to make fun of him. Nicanora left her printing to run after the rascals and longlegs, who also had probably had a part in the offense. The little black boy's boldness knew no limits, and he stretched out his sticky hands toward the pretty lady who was looking at him. "Hey, hands off, brat! . . . take your hands off," they shouted at him. When he saw that they wouldn't let him touch anybody, and that his looks made them laugh, the boy stamped his feet in the middle of the ring of people, sticking out his tongue and showing his ten fingers as if they were claws. This way, he thought, he'd look like a very evil beast that would eat people up . . . or would like to, anyway.

Then came the sound of a beating; Nicanora, incensed with anger, was flogging her children, who whimpered. Pitusín was soon bored with his role of hoodlum, because this business of not being allowed to hit anybody wasn't any fun. The best he could do in his awkward situation was to put his fingers in his mouth, but that black brew tasted so awful he quickly took them out.

"Do you suppose it's poison?" inquired Jacinta, alarmed. "He should be washed. Why don't they wash him?"

"You're a fine sight, Juanín," Ido said to him. "And look at this lady, who wanted to give you a kiss."

Greedy for a touch of him, the Dauphine grabbed a shock of his hair, the only part of him that was free of paint. "Poor little thing, what shape you're in!" Suddenly Juanín felt like crying. He didn't show his tongue anymore; all he did was sigh.

"But how about Sr. Izquierdo, isn't he here?" Jacinta asked Ido, taking him aside. "I must speak with him. Where does he live?"

"Señora," Ido replied in a refined way, "the door to his residence is sealed . . . hermetically, very hermetically."

"Well, I want to see him; I want to speak with him."

"I'll put you in touch with him," answered the publications salesman, who liked to use bureaucratic language when the occasion called for it.

"Come on, let's be on our way, it's late," said Guillermina impatiently. "We'll come again another day."

"Yes, we'll come back . . . But have him washed. Poor child! He must be suffering like a martyr with his face plastered like that. Tell me, silly, do you want to be washed?"

Pituso nodded yes. His affliction was growing and he was practically on the verge of tears. All the neighbors admitted that he should be washed, but some didn't have any water and others didn't want to use it on a thing like that. At last a gypsylike woman in a very long-waisted flowered percale skirt, a scarf fallen on her shoulders, straight hair, and a coarse, terra cotta complexion, suddenly appeared and wanted to show up her neighbors in front of the ladies, saying that she had plenty of water to "clean up" and "beautify" the little angel. They carried him off in a farcical procession, with him at the head of it, isolated by his soot and so bereft of his dignity that he began to whimper; the kids at the back were making an infernal racket, and the hag with the hard bun was threatening to clobber them if they didn't get out of the way. The masqueraders disappeared up a filthy narrow staircase off one corner of the corridor. Jacinta wanted to follow them up, but Guillermina harassed her not to, reminding her of their hurry:

"Do you realize what time it is?"

"Yes, we'll go. We're already leaving; I'm ready," the other one replied, looking at the roof, where all she could see was the horrible area where the pieces of leather were hanging out to dry. Meanwhile, despite her great rush, the orphanage founder had gotten into a brief conversation with Don José.

"Don't you have anything left to do at home?"

"Nothing at all, Señora. The last reams are already 'dissembled.' I thought I'd go out for a bit of fresh air and a walk."

"Exercise is good for you . . . very good. Listen: while you're out airing yourself, you can do me a favor."

"I'm at the Señora's disposal."

"Go out to Ronda Street; head down past the gas company. You know the one I mean? . . . Do you know where the Pulgas train station is? Good; well before you get to it, there's a house under construction. The frame's up and now they're building a very high chimney flue. It's going to be a sawmill. Do you follow me?

You can't miss it. Well, go in and ask for the superviser, who's called Pacheco, just like me. Tell him: 'I've come for Doña Guillermina's bricks.'"

Ido repeated, like a child who's memorizing his lesson, "I've come for the bricks, etc."

"The owner of that factory has given me about seventy bricks, which is all he had left—not much, but I can use anything. So pick up the bricks and take them to the construction site. They're for my project."

"Project? What project?"

"In Chamberí, my friend . . . my orphanage . . . Are you with me?"

"Oh! Please excuse me, Señora . . . when I heard 'project,' I immediately thought it was a literary project."

"If you can't do it in one trip, make two."

"Or three or four . . . with great pleasure. If it were necessary, I'd naturally make as many trips as there are bricks."

"And if you do the errand well, you can count on a bowler that's practically brand new. It was given to me yesterday, and I'm keeping it for a friend who helps me. So you'll do it? You help me, I'll help you. Well, so long."

Ido and his wife outdid themselves in compliments and escorted the ladies through the corridors to the front door. On Toledo Street they took a hansom to save time, and the simple-minded Ido went off on the assignment the founder had given him. It wasn't by any means a delicate mission, as he would have liked; but the charitable principle on which the act was based transformed it from the prosaic into the sublime. My man spent the whole doggoned afternoon transporting bricks, and he had the satisfaction of not having a single one of the seventy bricks break along the way. The contentment flooding his soul made him forget his exhaustion; his pleasure came almost exclusively from the fact that Jacinta, in the moment she had taken him aside, had given him a *duro*. He hadn't put the coin in his vest pocket, where Nicanora might discover it, but is his waistband, very well hidden in a girdle he wore against his skin to keep his stomach warm. It's a good idea, after all, to keep things tucked away. That *duro*, given to him in private, far from the starved faces of the rest of the family, was his alone. That had been the lady's intention, and Don José considered it offensive to his benefactress to interpret it in any other way. So he would put his treasure away and use every last resource he had to guard it against Nicanora's eyes and nails, because if *she* discovered it, holy saints above . . . !

He worried all night long. He was afraid that his wife with her sharp eye would discover what he had smuggled into his waist. Damned woman, she seemed to have a nose for silver. It was because of this that he was so upset and didn't feel safe in any position, thinking that she would see the coin through his clothes. They were all very happy during dinner; it had been a long while since they had eaten so well. But when Ido was going to bed he was tormented again by his fears, and he had no choice but to cower all night with his hands crossed over his waist, because if during their tossing and turning on that lumpy mattress his wife's hand were to touch the *duro* he would have to be awake to remove it. He slept very badly, always with one eye open and alertly guarding the contraband item. The worst of it was that when his wife saw him in such a tangle, circled up like an S, she thought that he was having one of his spasmodic pains, and as the best remedy for them was rubbing, Nicanora suggested it, and when Ido heard the suggestion he trembled, imagining himself found out and lost. "Now we've really done a good job of it," he thought. But his wits supplied him with a reply: he said he didn't have the slightest pain; that he was cold; and without further explanation turned his back to the wall, affixed himself like paste, and pretended he was asleep. Finally day came, and with it, calm in his heart. He scrubbed and washed most of his face and straightened his red tie somewhat conceitedly.

It was already ten in the morning, for this business of washing thoroughly had taken some time. Rosita had delayed in bringing the water, and Nicanora had given herself the immense treat of going shopping. So the members of the family, when they met each other, burst out laughing, and the one who wore the biggest smile of all was Don José, because . . . if they only knew!

4

My good man charged into the street and headed for Mira el Río Baja Street, which is so steep that one has to be a trapeze artist to keep from falling head first over the bumpy stones. Ido went down it almost like a child—in one breath— and once he reached the esplanade called "New World" his soul expanded like a bird taking off into the open sky. He started huffing and puffing as if he wanted to get more air than would fit in his lungs and he shook his body the way hens do. The slight prickling of the sun on his skin pleased him, and the contemplation of that blue sky, incomparably clean and clear, gave wings to his light soul.

Candid and impressionable, Don José was like a child or a true poet; his sensations were always extremely vivid, images in extraordinary relief. He saw everything hyperbolically enlarged or dwarfed, depending on the circumstances. When he was happy, objects took on a marvelous beauty; everything "smiled" on him, as he liked to say. On the other hand, when he was upset—which was more apt to be the case—even the most beautiful things became ugly and black and had a film over them . . . He thought it was more accurate to call it "a shroud."

Today, though, he was in high spirits, and his excitement at his luck made him more childlike and poetic than ever. For this reason the New World area, which is the most forsaken and ugly spot on the globe, looked like a pretty plaza to him. He continued to Ronda and looked at various places with an artistic eye. There was the Toledo Gate—a fantastic piece of architecture! In another direction the gas company. Oh, the prodigies of industry! . . . Then there was that splendid sky and Carabanchel in the distance, almost invisible in such immensity, which seemed to be imitating and even carrying the murmuring of the sea . . . the sublime works of Nature! Oh! Walking on, he was suddenly overcome with such vehement zeal to "educate the public" that he almost dropped his jaw when he saw the asinine signs all around him.

"NO PEDLING CLOTHES AND NOR NALING NALES" it said on one wall, and Don José exclaimed, "How awful! What ignorance, using two copulative conjunctions! You stupid beasts, don't you know that the first one naturally connects the clauses affirmatively, and the second one, negatively? And to think that a man who could teach grammar to all Madrid and correct these linguistic crimes has to starve! . . . Why can't the government, let's see, why can't it put me in charge—and give me an adequate fee for my services—of supervising signs? You blockheads—I'd *really* fine you! Here's another: 'RUMES FOR RINT.' So you like your o's so much you gobble them up with your rice? Ah, if the government would only appoint *me* Official Speller, you'd see . . . Ha, here's another one: PROHIBBITID. I'd say braying was prohibited."

He was immersed in the most entertaining part of his, shall we say, literary criticism—so appropriate in his business—when he noticed three characters heading toward him in tight pants, high boots, short coats, caps, their hair combed forward, hanging over their brash faces. They were very Madrilenian types and belonged to the pickpocket set. One was a sneak thief, another a two-finger specialist, and the third was a virtuoso. Ido knew them; they lived next to the same patio he did when they weren't Saladero's tenants (that is, in the city jail), but he didn't want to have anything to do with such scum. He would've been happy to kick them you know where, but he didn't dare. It's one thing to reform the public's spelling and quite another to take certain corrective measures with the human species. "There goes 'Good morning,'" the bums said gaily to him, and Ido broke out in gooseflesh because he thought of the *duro* and was afraid they'd nab it if he got into a conversation with them. Passing by them, he said very politely: "God be with you, gentlemen . . . Take care"; and broke into a run. His heart wouldn't stop pounding till he saw that they were out of sight.

"I have to treat myself to something," thought the penman, and he silently reviewed the dishes he liked most. Near the Toledo Gates he came across the honey vendor from Alcarria who lived in his building too. They were talking when a tambourine painter, also a neighbor, came up; they both invited him to have a few drinks. "Go to the devil, you vulgar fools!" thought Ido, and he thanked them, immediately leaving them. Walking further, he saw a wretched little roadhouse on the right side of Ronda Avenue. "Eat in a tavern!" The idea stuck in his mind. For some time, Ido del Sagrario stood in front of the establishment called El Tartera, looking at the two 'vonimus* shrubs coated with dust. Signs indicated that bowling and hopscotch were allowed inside; a black hand with a stiff forefinger pointed to the door; he couldn't make up his mind to obey the pointing finger. Meat had such a bad effect on him! Whenever he ate it, he got that strange sickness, and took it into his head that Nicanora was the Venus de Medici. Nevertheless, he recalled that the doctor always prescribed meat, and the rarer the better. From the depths of his soul came a howling, a begging, for meat, meat, meat! It was a voice, an irresistible craving, an imperious biological necessity like what drunks feel when they're denied the fire and stimulation of alcohol.

He couldn't resist it any longer; he slipped into the tavern, and, taking a seat at one of the faded tables, began to clap for the waiter. The waiter was Tartera himself, a corpulent man wearing a Bayona vest and a green and black striped apron. Not far from where Ido sat were some embers in an enormous brazier and, on top, a grill almost the size of a window grating. The veal steaks were broiled there, and as they were singed by such intense heat they gave off an appetizing aroma. "Steaks," said Don José, and at that moment he noticed a friend coming in, a man who had seen him and was undoubtedly coming in for that reason.

"Hello, Izquierdo. God be with you."

"I saw you go by, maestro, and so I says, 'Well, well, if it ain't my namesake. I'll have to shoot the bull with him.'"

He sat down with no further ado and, putting his elbows on the table, stared at his namesake. Either looks express nothing or that character's were a solemn petition for an invitation. Ido was such a gentleman that he couldn't extend the invitation quickly enough, although he did add these prudent words: "But, namesake, I must tell you that I only have a *duro*. So don't go overboard . . . " The other made a reassuring gesture, and when Tartera set the table (if you could call a couple of horn-handled knives, a dirty napkin, and a saltshaker a setting) and asked what they would like in the way of wine, he said, "Take me for a hick, eh? No *sir*. Bring us the *best!*"

Ido del Sagrario assented to everything and continued to contemplate his friend, who looked like a bored *grand homme* embittered by the endless struggles of life. José Izquierdo looked about fifty; he was arrogantly tall. One seldom sees a

---

* Euonymus

head as beautiful as his, such a noble and masculine expression. He looked more Italian than Spanish, and it's no wonder that in the epoch following '73, well into the Restoration, he was the favorite model of our most famous painters.

"I'm glad to see you, namesake," said Ido as the steaks were being put on the table, "because I had some important things to tell you. You see, yesterday Doña Jacinta, Sr. Don Juanito Santa Cruz's wife, was at the house and asked after the boy, and saw him. Well . . . she didn't exactly *see* him, 'cause he was all done up in black. And then she said where were you, and since you weren't in, she said she'd be back . . . "

Izquierdo must have had to catch up on his hunger, because when he saw the steaks his eyes pounced on them as if to say: "Charge!" And without so much as a reply to his friend, who was talking, he viciously attacked them. And Ido began to gulp down big pieces without even chewing them. For a while they were silent. Izquierdo broke the silence by loudly banging his knife-handle on the table and saying:

"Fuck the Republic! It's a lot of *garbage!*"

Ido assented by nodding his head.

"Republickins, ha! You're a stew of chopped lungs is what *you* are, ya bunch of smart alecks. You're worst than slavish, worst than *mod*-irates!" added Izquierdo, wildly exalted. "Not give *me* a job—*me*, the endivid'al that worked the hardest for the Republickins in this fuckin' country . . . It's just like they say: 'Give 'em the milk of human kindness and . . .' Oh, Señor Martos, Señor Figueras, Señor Pi—try to tell *me* you don't know poor ole Izquierdo, just because you don't like my clothes. Ha! Before, when Izquierdo had *enfl*ince in the Inclusa district, and when Bicerra came around to see 'im with that bit about going into the streets, *then* . . . Fuck it! So we've lost our prestige and we don't have any money. But if we get back up there again, I swear to those stuff shirts, we'll have a real 'yection'!"

5

Ido kept commiserating with him, although he didn't understand the bit about the "yection," nor could anyone have understood it. For Izquierdo, the word implied a bloody collision, a row or something of the sort. He drank glass after glass without its going to his head, which had a notable capacity.

"'Cause look, maestro, what gets 'em is that I was there *pers*nally in Cartagena. And damn it, I say it's to my credit. Only us *real* libbrals was there. And lemme tell you somethin' else, namesake: all I've done all my life is spill my blood for fuckin' liberty. In '54 whaddid I do?—throw myself at the barricades like a decent endivid'al. They can ask poor ole Don Pascual Muñoz who's dead now, bless 'im; the guy that had the hardware store, the marqués de Casa-Muñoz's father; he had more pull than anybody in these parts, and you know what he said to me? Said: 'Plato, friend, give me your hand.' So then I go to the Palace with Don Pascual himself, and he goes up to talk to the queen, and pretty soon he comes down with the paper with the queen's signachure. Wow! That really let them modirates have it. And Don Pascual tole me to put a white handkachiff at the end of a stick and go first sayin': 'Cease fire, cease fire!'

"In '56 I was a militia lootinint and Genrul O'Donnell got scared a me, and when he talked to the troops he said, says, 'If there's nobody that can get me Izquierdo, then we haven't done a damned thing.' In '66, when there was the artillery thing, me and my buddy Socorro were shootin' from the corner of Leganitos Street. In '68, when things really blew up, I was on guard at the bank so they wouldn't rob it, and lemme tell *you*, if some goddam robber so much as shown his face around there, I'd of suicided 'im . . . So then it gets to be time for the pay off, and they make Pucheta a guard at the Casa del Campo, and Mochilo at the Pardo—and they give *me* a kick in the pants. And all I wanted was a lil' job, carryin' the mail somewheres, and pfft! Then I go see Bicerra, and do you think he knows me? Not on your life! I tell him I'm Izquierdo, my nickname's Plato, and he shakes his head. It's just like they say: they forget about the fuckin' step as soon as they've climbed up it.

"Well, so then I got married and we made out okay, more or less. But when the fuckin' Republick came, my Demetria died on me, and I didn't have a thing to eat. I went to see Señor Pi and I said, I says to him: 'Señor Pi, I've come 'bout a position.' Not on your life! I tell ya, the man must of hated my guts, 'cause he jumped up and said he didn't have no positions. And a fuckin' doorman shows me out! God damn his stinkin' guts! If only Calvo Asensio was alive! *There* was a man that knew how to handle things and treat real people. What a friend I lost! The whole district was ours, and at 'lection time not even God would of sneezed at us. Not even God, damn it! There was a man for you. Oh, yeah. He'd take me by the arm and we'd go into a café or a tavern for a couple—'cause he was real simple, and libbraler than the blessed Virgin. But the ones we've got now? It's like they say: they're not libbrals, they're not republickins, they're *nothin'*. Look at Pi—a pipsqueak. And Castelar? Another pipsqueak. And Salmerón? Another pipsqueak. Roque Barcia? 'Xactly the same. And then, time comes they need us, they'll come around beggin' for our help. But me? I won't lift a finger. I've had my fill of 'yections.' If the Republick sinks, let it sink; and if everybody's gonna sink, they can fuckin' well sink."

He drained his glass again, and the other José admired both his fluency and his capacity. Then Izquierdo let out a sarcastic laugh and continued as follows:

"They say they're bringin' in Alifonso. Ha! let em! It's like they was really gonna bring the Terso.* But me, I don't give a tinker's damn. Here's the best part, though: last year, when I was in Alcoy, the Carlists pulled one on me. I ran over to the Callosa de Ensarriá group and fired a bunch of shots at the Nashnull Guard. What a 'yection'! They was jumpin' all over the place! But pretty soon I was makin' as if I didn't know what was up, because they'd made a deal with me to pay me half a *duro* a day, and the dough didn't show up no how. I said to myself: 'José, you'd better turn libbral, 'cause this Carlist business ain't worth it.' One night I slipped out and went straight to Barcelona, where I practilly started bitin' people, I was so hungry. Oh, namesake, if I hadn't a had the luck to run inta my niece Fortunata there, I wouldn't a been here to tell the story. She helped me out. She's a good girl, and with the money she gave me, I hopped the fuckin' train for Madrid."

"So then," said Ido, tired of the incoherent story and grotesque vocabulary, "you took in that adorable child."

Ido was hunting for a novel on that garrulous page of contemporary history, but Izquierdo, having a shrewder mind, scorned the novel and resumed his serious history:

"I go up and have an interview with the committee men and don't mince my words: 'But gentlemen, are we gonna declare ourselves an endepindint canton or not? Because if we don't, there's gonna be a 'yection' here.' Oh, they laughed at me—the bums! After all, they'd sold out to the modirates. You know what those pipsqueaks threw in my face, namesake? That I couldn't read or write. That's not the whole truth, fuck it! 'Cause I *can* read some, even if I can't keep it up as long'z I should. As for writin'—I don't write 'cause the ink runs down my fingers . . . Bah! It's like they say: the ones that write books and newspapers, and the publicaishunners have ruined the fuckin' country with their tiologies, maestro."

Ido, being who he was, was naturally hesitant to corroborate this, but Izquierdo squeezed his arm so tightly that he finally had no choice but to nod his assent, with the mental reservation that he was giving his authoritative vote on such a horrible statement only because violent pressure had been exerted.

"So, my dear namesake, seein' that they wanted to put me in the clink and get me mixed up with the police, I took a powder. We headed for Cartagena. Jesus, what a sweet life that was! They wanted to make me menistir of the enterior; but I gave 'em a no. I don't like bein' a big wig. You can bet your life we got outta there in friggits—crossed that holy sea. And like it or not, they talked me into bein'

---

* Don Carlos, pretender to the throne.

ship's tinint, and I was right up there with Genrull Contreras himself, and he treated me like one a them. Oh, what a man, and what a great ship he 'ad! He was the spittin' image of the great Turk, with that red cap a his. It was glory. Alicante, Aguilas! Gunnin' 'em here, gunnin' 'em there. If they only woulda let us, name-sake, we'd a gone all over the whole bloody world and made a canton of every damned place. Orán—what a hole! And that damned *vu* the French use—they ain't nobody can understand it. I cleared outta there as fast I could and came back to good ole Spain. Came to Madrid real quiet-like, casual as can be . . . whaddid I care? And I went up to those tiologists—the pipsqueaks—and I says to them: 'Here I am in person: the endivid'al that spent his whole bloody life fightin' like a dog for those fuckin' liberties. Kill me, damn it, go ahead and kill me. Still don't wanna gimme a job, do ya?' Didya *hear* me? Well, they didn't. You can talk your head off at the Congress and the whole bloody country could blow up for all they care. And I say we've gotta make Madrid a canton, set fire to the congress, the royal palace, and the fuckin' ministrees, the banks, the Nashnull Guard barricks and the water lines, and then string up a rope and hang 'em high—Castelar, Pi, Figueras, Martos, Bicerra, and the rest, 'cause they're *modirates, modirates, modirates* . . ."

6

He said " 'cause they're *modirates*" at least six times, raising his voice gradually; the last cry could have been heard from the Toledo Gates. The other José was very distressed by this fierce talk from the *grand homme*, the unluckiest hero of all and the most unrecognized of martyrs. His mask of misanthropy and tone of a persecuted genius were a natural consequence of having spent half a century without finding his niche in life. After all, thirty years of trying and failing is enough to crush the hardiest soul. Izquierdo had been a horsetrader, a wheat dealer, a revolutionary, a guerrilla leader, a candlemaker, a hired gambler, and owner of a gambling joint, he had been married twice to rich women, and in none of these various circumstances had fate been kind. One way or another, married or single, working for himself or for someone else, things had never worked out . . . never worked out, damn it!

His restless life, sudden appearances and disappearances, and his having been "in stripes" at different times enveloped him in mystery and gave him a deplorable reputation. Awful things were said about him. They said he'd killed his second wife, Demetria, and committed other nefarious crimes. It was all false. It must be said that part of his bad reputation was due to his bravado and all those revolutionary clouds of smoke in his head. The majority of his political adventures were imaginary, and now only a very few of his listeners believed him, and of these, Ido del Sagrario was the most gullible.

To complete his portrait, I ought to add that he had never been to Cartagena. From thinking so much about that famous rebellion, he undoubtedly came to believe that he *had* been there. Talking up his sleeve about those tremendous 'yections' and giving details that deceived a lot of fools probably convinced him. The bit about the Callosa skirmish does appear to be true.

It can also be said without fear that a historical fact may prove the opposite; that Plato was not courageous, and that despite so much bragging he was beginning to lose his reputation for bravery, just as all glory based on uncertainty is lost. During the time I have been referring to, his discredit was such that even his own "platonic" vanity was deeply wounded. He was in the process of becoming a nobody, and when he got carried away in one of those desperate soliloquies, usually after some vile act that had gotten him money but had turned out badly, he ridiculed himself in all sincerity, saying: "I'm worst than a mule; I'm dumber than a doornail; I'm a good for nothin'." The thought that he'd turned fifty without having learned to write and could read only by fits and starts gave him a highly unflattering image of himself as an "endivid'al." He didn't hide the pain that this caused him, and that day he revealed it to his namesake with heartfelt ingenuity.

"It's really a jam, this business of not knowing how to write . . . Damn it! If I only knew how. Believe me, that's the reason why Pi can't stand me."

Don José didn't answer. He was doubled over in pain himself, for digesting the two enormous steaks that he'd wolfed down was no small order. Izquierdo didn't notice that his friend's eyelid was terribly twitchy, and that the caruncles on his neck and warts on his face, turgid and inflamed, looked ready to burst. Nor did he notice Don José's restlessness—he was squirming around in his chair as if there were thorns in it. And lamenting his fate again, he permitted himself to say, "Because they just don't care about truthful men of merit. All those pipsqueaks with the jobs and us—me and you, namesake—two high quality men, nobody gives a damn about us. But you can bet it's their loss, because you—damn it! you'd be as smart as a fox in Public 'Destruction,' and me, . . . *me!*"

Just as it was swelling to its fullest, Plato's vanity suddenly burst, and since he couldn't find an adequate function for his personality, he crashed headlong into the awareness of his incompetence. "Me . . . I'd be good for pulling a heavy cart," he thought. Then he let his gallant and manly head fall on his breast, and he meditated for some time on the reasons for his horrible luck. Ido was entirely oblivious to the compliment his friend had paid him, and was lost in a dark lake of sadness, doubts, fears, and suspicions. Izquierdo felt pessimism gnawing at him. The burden of alcohol in his stomach had no small part in that terrible depression, during which he saw parading before him the thirty years of failures that constituted his life's history. The most peculiar thing was that in his sadness he heard a sweet voice whispering: "You're good for something . . . don't let yourself be dragged down . . . " But he couldn't be persuaded. "If a man could tell me," he thought to himself, "what the hell this mess of a man is good for, I'd love 'im to death, love 'im more than my own father." The unfortunate man was, like many other beings who spend most of their life out of place, drifting, drifting, without ever stopping in the square on the chessboard that fate has marked for them. Some die never reaching it; Izquierdo was to arrive, at the age of fifty-one, at the position fate had reserved for him in this world, and we could well call it a glorious one. A year after the events being related, that wandering planet—and I have proof of it—took its place in the cosmos. Plato at last discovered the law of his destiny, the thing that he was "intirely" and exclusively good for. And he knew calm and had bread, and was useful and played a great role, and even became a celebrity who was fought over and applauded. There is no human being, no matter how despicable he may seem, who cannot stand out in something, and that unlucky hunter, after a half-century of mistakes, has, thanks to his extremely handsome figure, come to be *the* model in contemporary historical painting. You should see the nobility and arrogance that form on his face when they put a nicely made suit of armor on him, or put him in doublets and satin cassocks, and have him "do" the duke of Gandía when he was struck by the notion of becoming a saint, or the marquis of Bedmar before the Council of Venice, or Juan de Lanuza on the gallows, or the great Alba subduing the Flemish people. The oddest thing is that that mule of a man who was ignorance and coarseness personified had a remarkable instinct for posing. He could sense the looks of a character very deeply and knew how to translate them into gestures and certain expressions on his admirable face.

But at that time all this was in the future, and the only inkling Plato had of it in his brutish mind was a vague presentiment of glory and prosperity. The hero breathed a sigh, which the poet reciprocated even more tempestuously. Looking squarely at his friend, Ido coughed a few times, and in a faint, metallic voice said, putting his hand on his shoulder:

"You are unfortunate because they haven't done you justice; but I am more so, namesake. There is no worse fate than that of being dishonored."

"A republick for pigs, for hogs!" Plato brayed, banging his fist on the table so hard that the whole tavern shook.

"Because everything is bearable," said Ido, lowering his voice lugubriously, "except matrimonial infidelity. It's terrible to speak of this, my dear namesake, and terrible that this dishonored mouth should proclaim its own ignominy. But naturally there are times when, frankly, one cannot be silent. Silence is a crime; yes, indeed. Why should society fling this at me when I am not guilty? Am I not a model husband and father? After all, when have I been adulterous? When? Let them name an instance."

Suddenly, and bouncing up as if he were made of rubber, the electric man got up. He felt an anxiety strangling him, a fury that made his hair stand on end. In this exceptionally disconcerted state, he nevertheless remembered to pay, and after giving his *duro* to Tartera, picked up the change.

"Noble friend," he whispered into Izquierdo's ear, "don't escort me. I value your offer to help for all it's worth. But I must go alone, completely alone, yes. I'll catch them in the act. Silence! Shhh! . . . The law authorizes me to punish them . . . Oh, but it's horrible, incredible! Silence, I say!"

And he darted out. Seeing him run off, Izquierdo and Tartera laughed. The miserable Ido made a beeline for where he was going without noticing any of the obstacles. He practically knocked down a blind man and did upset a woman's basket of peanuts and piñon nuts. He crossed Ronda Avenue, the New World Plaza, and took Mira el Río Baja Street, going straight up the steep incline without pausing to catch his breath. He went along wildly, gesticulating, his eyes flashing, his lower lip protruding. Without stopping to notice anyone or anything, he entered the house, climbed the stairs, went down one corridor after another, and soon arrived at his door. It was closed but unlocked. He crouched, his ear at the keyhole, and suddenly, throwing the door wide open, he bellowed in a deafening voice: "Adulllteress!"

"Christ! Here he is again having one of his blasted fits!" cried Nicanora, gathering her wits about her immediately. "Poor thing, today he's really gone . . ."

Don José entered in long measured strides, striking the pose of a professional comedian, his eyes popping out of their sockets. And he repeated the fearsome word in a cavernous tone: "Adulllteress!"

"For the love of God," said the wretched woman, putting aside her work, which was sewing, not painting, this time, "you've had something to eat, haven't you? Oh, we've done a *fine* job of it."

She looked at him with more pity than anger and with a certain relative calm, as one looks at very familiar chronic illnesses.

"The attack's pretty bad . . . Oh, what a state you're in today, love! Some joker has invited you out. If I get my hands on him . . . Look, José, you should lie down."

"For God's sake, Papá," said Rosita, who had followed her father in, "don't scare us. Get those notions out of your head."

He pushed her aside brusquely and continued to lurch forward, taking tragicomic steps that revealed his disconcerted state. He seemed to be inspecting the house; he peered into the fetid bedrooms, spun on his heel, felt up and down the walls, looked under the chairs, rolling his eyes fiercely and making such a fuss that he would have made people double over with laughter if compassion hadn't stopped them. The neighbors, who had a great time with poor Ido's fits, began to congregate out in the corridor. Nicanora went to the door.

"It's atrocious today. If I could only lay my hands on the jerk that invited him to have some meat."

"Come here, you unfaithful lady!" said the frenetic spouse, grabbing her by the arm.

It must be noted that not even at the most furious moment of his access was he brutal. Whether because he had very little strength or because his gentle nature was never conquered by the fever of that incredible distemper, the fact is that his hands hardly ever caused offense. Nicanora held him down with both arms, and while shaking and kicking, he discharged his anger in these hoarse words:

"You can't deny it now . . . I've seen him, I've seen him, I have."

"Who have you seen, love? Oh, yes! I know: the duke. Yes, here he is . . . I'd forgotten: the naughty duke, who wants to take away this cursed wife of yours!"

Once he was out of his wife's hands, which had gripped him like a pair of pliers, Ido went back to his mimicry and Nicanora, knowing that there was no way of placating him except by giving free rein to his insane mania so that the attack would end sooner, put in his hand a drumstick that the children had left lying around and, pushing him along . . . "You can make mincemeat of us," she said. "Go on, go on, we're in bed all cuddled up . . . Hard, son, hit us hard, and beat the living daylight out of us."

Stumblingly, Ido entered one of the bedrooms and, bracing his knee on the lumpy bed, began to beat with the stick, sluggishly pronouncing these words: "Adulterers, expiate your crime!" The people who could hear him out in the corridor nearly cracked up with laughter, and Nicanora remonstrated with the audience, saying: "It'll be over soon; the worse it is, the less it lasts."

"There, take that! Both of you, dead . . . a puddle of blood . . . Me revenged, my honor wa . . . washed clean," he mumbled, the blows getting weaker and weaker, until he collapsed face down on the mattress. His legs hung off the bed; his face was pressed against the pillows; and in this posture he mumbled slurred words that gradually faded, turning into snores. Nicanora turned him over on his back so that he'd be able to breathe easily, she put his legs into the bed, handling him as if he were a corpse, and she took the stick out of his hand. She fixed the pillows and loosened his clothes. He had entered the second stage, the comatose, and although he was still delirious, he didn't move a finger and kept his eyelids tightly shut, afr. l of the light. He was drunk on meat.

When the "Venus de Medici" left their lair, she noticed that among the people peering through the window was Jacinta, accompanied by her maid.

7

Jacinta had witnessed part of the scene, and she was terrified. "The worst is over," said Nicanora, coming out to receive her. "A very bad attack . . . But he doesn't hurt anyone. Poor angel! He gets this way when he eats."

"How odd!" said Jacinta, entering.

"When he eats meat. Yes, ma'am. The doctor says his brain's sort of in shock because for a long time he was writing things about evil women, without eating anything except those blasted beans . . . Poverty, ma'am. This dog's life. And if you only knew how good he is! When he's calm he doesn't act up at all, and he'd never tell a lie . . . wouldn't hurt a fly. He could go for a couple of years without touching bread as long as his children have some. So the lady can see how miserable I am. It was two years ago that José started having these notions. He used to spend the nights awake, dreaming up stories . . . all about unfaithful ladies, real pretty ones, who'd go off on the sly with adulterous dukes . . . and the husbands were enraged all the time. The stuff he thought up! And in the morning, he'd make a clean copy, on demy paper, in handwriting that was so pretty it was nice just to look at it. Then he got typhus, got so sick they gave him the last sacrament, and we thought he was a goner. He got over it, but he was left with these brain fevers, these fits he has whenever he eats anything substantial. He has his periods, Señora. Sometimes the attack's very mild, and other times he gets so carried away; all he has to do is go by a slaughterhouse and his eyelid starts twitching and he starts to say foolish stuff. They're so right, Señora, when they say that meat is one of the soul's enemies . . . Just look at what it brings out: that I'm an adulteress, and that I'm sleeping with a duke! Imagine—me, with this puss . . . "

The sad tale didn't interest Jacinta as much as Nicanora thought, and since the former realized that Nicanora was not getting to the end, the lady had to make one.

"Excuse me," she said, softening her tone as much as possible, "but I have very little time. I would like to speak with the gentleman whom they call *Don* . . . José Izquierdo."

"At your command," said a voice at the door. Upon looking, Jacinta came face to face with the extremely formidable figure called Plato, who didn't look as fierce as he was said to be.

The Dauphine said that she wished to speak with him, and he invited her as courteously as he knew how to come to his room. The mistress and her maid directed themselves to number 17, Izquierdo's dwelling.

"Where is Pituso?" Jacinta inquired along the way.

Izquierdo looked at the patio where various children were playing and, not seeing him anywhere, he let out a loud growl. Near number 17, at one of the turns in the corridor, there was a group of five or six individuals who were neither big nor small, in the middle of which was a boy about ten, blind, sitting on a bench and playing the guitar. His arm wasn't long enough to reach the end of the neck. He was playing it backward, playing the chords with his right hand and strumming with his left, the guitar on his knees, the face and strings upward. The blind boy's pretty small hand grazed the strings gracefully, plucking sweet arpeggios and those somber sounds that reveal so clearly the deep, primitive sensitivity of the common people. The musician's head moved from side to side, as if it were on one of those dolls whose neck is a steel coil, and the dead globes of his coagulated eyes turned back and forth, without a moment's rest. After a long warming up, he broke into song in a shrill voice:

"Pepa the little Gyyyyp . . ."

That y sound seemed to last forever; it swirled up and down, like a rubric traced by sound. The listeners were almost breathless when the blind boy decided to perch on the end of the sentence:

"sy—when she was born from her mother . . ."

Expectancy, as the musician voiced some "ays" and growls that came from his depths, grew; he sounded like a dog whose tail is being pinched. "Ay, ay, ay! . . ." Finally he concluded:

"in her nose alone
she had seven cramps"

Laughter, hubbub, stamping . . . Next to the child singer there was another blind person, a leathery old man with a face like a cork, a goatskin cap pulled over his head, his body wrapped in a brown cloak with more patches than cloth. His satisfied chuckle denounced him as the author of the celebrated stanza. He was also the blind boy's teacher, perhaps his father, and he was teaching him the business. Jacinta took a quick look at the group, and among the respectable individuals in the ring of people she discerned one whose presence made her quiver. It was Pituso, who was peering between the blind man and the boy, lost in the

music, with one hand on his waist and the other in his mouth. "There he is," said
Señor Izquierdo, instantly removing him from the group. The strangest part was
that while Pituso's face was smeared, Jacinta thought that she detected a strong
resemblance to Juanito Santa Cruz, but now that she saw Pituso's face in its
natural state (though it wasn't actually clean), the resemblance had vanished.

"He doesn't look like him," she thought, feeling at once happy and discouraged, when Izquierdo showed her the door for her to go in.

Jacinta and her maid say that when they saw themselves in that tiny, filthy,
God-forsaken cell and observed that the so-called Plato was closing the door, they
were seized by such fear that it occurred to both of them to run to the window and
cry for help. The lady looked sideways at her maid to see if she had her wits about
her; but Rafaela looked more dead than alive. "This character," thought Jacinta,
"is going to break our necks without even giving us a chance." She was somewhat
relieved to hear the guitar playing nearby and the bustle of the crowd around the
blind boy. Izquierdo offered them the two chairs in the room, and he sat on a
trunk, putting Pituso on his knee.

Rafaela says that at that moment she thought of a foolproof plan to defend
themselves against the monster in case he should attack them. The moment she
saw him make a hostile gesture, she'd pull his beard. If at the very same moment
and faster than you could say jackrabbit, her mistress had enough skill to grab a
spit very near her hand and stick it in his eyes, they would be saved.

There was no furniture there except for the two chairs and the trunk. No
bureau, no bed, no anything. In the dark bedroom there must have been some
sort of excuse for a bed. On the wall there was hanging a large and beautiful
engraving, behind the glass of which could be seen two black braids of real hair,
very beautiful ones, coiled like snakes, and between them a silk ribbon with these
words: "My daughter!"

"Whose hair is it?" Jacinta asked brightly, and her curiosity alleviated her fear
momentarily.

"My wife's daughter's," Plato replied gravely, casting a scornful glance at the
framed braids.

"I thought that it was . . ." stammered the lady, not daring to finish the sentence. "And the young girl whose braids they were—where is she?"

"In the cemetery," grunted Izquierdo, making a sound that was more animal
than human.

Jacinta examined the little Pituso and . . . of all things, she again noticed a
resemblance to the big "Pituso." She looked at him steadily; the more she looked
at him, the greater the resemblance. Good God! She called him, and Señor
Izquierdo said to the child with a certain attenuated harshness that, coming from
him, could pass as sweetness: "Go on, mousie, give the lady a kiss." The child,

standing now, refused to step forward. He looked frightened as he fixed his starlike eyes on the lady. Jacinta had seen pretty eyes, but she had never seen any like those. They were like the eyes of Murillo's Baby Jesus. "Come on, come here," she said to him, calling him with that movement of both hands that she had learned from mothers. He looked at her very gravely, his cheeks flushed with the childish bashfulness that so easily turns into nerve.

"He's not shy. It's just that he's real scared of refined people," said Izquierdo, pushing him to within reach of Jacinta.

"Oh, but he's a little gentleman," the lady declared, kissing his dirty face, which still smelled of the accursed paint. "Why are you so serious today, when yesterday you laughed so hard and stuck out your little tongue at me?"

The words dissolved Juanín's seriousness. She had scarcely said them when he broke into an angelic smile. Jacinta laughed too, but she felt something like a sudden blow in her heart, and her vision blurred. The resemblance that the lady thought she had detected reappeared vividly, magically really, when the winsome child laughed. It seemed to her that the Santa Cruz looks had come out in his face, just as the redness of childish blushing had come out a bit earlier. "He is, he is . . . ," she thought with profound conviction, devouring the boy's face with her eyes. She saw those beloved features in it; but there were some unknown ones too. Then she was seized by one of those little fits of anger that from time to time disturbed the placidity of her soul; and her eyes, bright with slight rancor, tried to detect the abhorred, guilty beauty of the mother in the innocent face of the child. She spoke, and the timbre of her voice was entirely different. It sounded somewhat like the low notes on a guitar: "Señor Izquierdo, do you, by any chance, have a picture of your niece?"

Had Izquierdo replied that he did, you can imagine how Jacinta would have descended on it! But there was no such picture, and it was better that there was not. For a while the lady was silent, feeling that lump in her throat forming again, that unmistakable symptom of her immense grief. Meanwhile, Pituso was quickly making headway on the road to familiarity. He began by shyly touching the antique coin bracelet Jacinta was wearing, and, seeing that he wasn't being scolded for this disrespect, that, on the contrary, the pretty lady was drawing him to her, he decided to examine the clasp, the fringe of her cloak, and especially her muff, that nice, soft fur thing with a hole in it where you put your hand and it got so warm.

Jacinta sat him on her knee and tried to bury her discouragement, stimulating in her soul the compassion and affection that the destitute child inspired in her. A quick scrutiny of his clothes revived her sorrow. To think that her husband's son had his tender flesh exposed, his feet almost bare! . . . She ran her hand through his curly hair, promising her noble conscience that she would love another woman's child as if he were her own. The child fixed his savage attention on the lady's gloves. He didn't have the slightest notion that there were such things as those "fake hands," inside which were real ones.

"Poor little thing!" exclaimed Jacinta with sharp pain, observing that Pituso's pathetic clothes were full of holes. One of his shoulders was exposed, and one of his buttocks was also unprotected against the elements. Oh, how lovingly she ran her hand along that smooth flesh that she imagined had never known the warmth of a motherly hand and was as freezing cold at night as it was during the day!

"Touch him," she said to the maid. "Freezing to death." And to Señor Izquierdo: "Why is this child so skimpily dressed?"

"I'm poor, Señora," grumbled Izquierdo with his usual surliness. "They won't gimme a job . . . 'cause I'm decent."

He was about to plunge into his political woes, but Jacinta ignored him. Juanín, whose audacity was growing by leaps and bounds, dared nothing less than to touch her face (although showing great respect, that much is true).

"I'm going to bring you some very pretty boots," said his aspiring adoptive mother, tossing the words into his dirty ear with a kiss.

The boy lifted a foot—and what a foot! Far better if no one had seen it: a shapeless mass of ropesole and revolting rags, full of mud, with a big hole through which a row of tiny pink toes showed.

"Holy God!" exclaimed Rafaela, bursting out laughing. "Señor Izquierdo, are you so poor that you don't have enough for . . . ?"

" 'Xactly."

"I'm going to make you look so cute . . . ! You'll see. I'm going to put a pretty dress on you, and a little hat, and patent-leather boots."

Grasping what was in store for him, the sly little thing widened his eyes and looked . . . ! Of all human weaknesses, the first recorded in a child—and that thereby heralds the man—is vanity. Juanín understood that they were going to make him handsome and he burst out in a laugh. But ideas and sensations change quickly at this age, and without any warning, Pituso clapped his hands and heaved a deep sigh. It's a special way children have of saying: "This is boring me; I'd rather leave." Jacinta restrained him, using force.

"Let's see, Señor Izquierdo," the lady said, posing the issue decisively. "I already know from your neighbor who the mother of this child is. It's obvious that you can't bring him up or educate him. I'm taking him."

Izquierdo prepared to reply.

"I'd like to tell the lady . . . I . . . that is, I really have the law on my side. I love 'im, if it comes to that, like a son . . . Won't the lady help 'im, being who she is, by gettin' me a job, and let me keep 'im."

"No. Those arrangements don't suit me. We'll be friends, but under the condition that I take this poor little angel home with me. What do you want him for?

So that he'll grow up in these unhealthy patios among hoodlums? . . . I'll protect you. What do you want, a job? a sum?"

"If the lady," Izquierdo insinuated grimly, releasing the words after ruminating a long time, "gets something for me . . ."

"What is it you have in mind?"

"The lady can cross paths with Castelar and Pi . . . who can't stand the sight of me."

"Never mind all this business about *pi* and *pa* ⁎ . . . I can't give you any sort of job."

"Well, if they don't let me be a 'menistrater at the Pardo, the boy stays here . . . damn it!" declared Izquierdo in the harshest way, getting up. His reply was more in his gallant stance than in his language.

"Nothing less than the administration of the Pardo! Oh yes, that's just the thing for you. I'll speak to my husband, who will identify Juanín as his son and claim him legally, because his mother has abandoned him."

Rafaela says that when Plato heard this, he was rather disconcerted. But he didn't give up, and, taking the boy in his arms, caressed him in his own way: "Who loves you, little gypsy? And who do *you* love, my little mousie?"

The boy flung his arms around his neck.

"I'm not preventing you nor will I prevent you from continuing to love him, nor from seeing him from time to time," the lady said, looking dumbly at Juanín. "I'll be back tomorrow, and I hope to convince you . . . And as for the administration of the Pardo, don't think that I'm telling you no. It might work out . . . I don't know."

Izquierdo relented a bit.

"No, it's useless," thought Jacinta. "This man's a typical horse trader. I don't know how to treat people like this. I'll come back tomorrow with Guillermina, and then . . . , *then* I want to see you." "The best thing for you," she said out loud, "would be a sum. I think your pocket's got a hole in it."

Izquierdo sighed and put the boy down. "An endivid'al that spent his bloody life fightin' his head off so Spaniards could be free . . ."

"But for heaven's sake, my dear man, do you want them even freer?"

"No . . . it's like they say: put yourself out for them, and they walk all over you. I'll have you know that Becerra, Castelar, and other pipsqueaks too—they owe it all to me—everything they've got."

"How very odd."

The noise of the guitar and the blind men's songs grew considerably louder, adding to the racket of the Christmas drums.

⁎ "*Pi* and *pa*" means "blah-blah," but it's also a spontaneous substitute, probably inspired by the sound of one of the names Izquierdo mentions, Pi.

"Don't you have a drum?" Jacinta asked the youngster, who, when he'd scarcely heard the question, was already answering that he didn't by shaking his head.

"How awful! Imagine not having a drum . . . ! I'm going to buy you one today, right away. Will you give me a kiss?"

Pituso didn't have to be coaxed. He was shameless by now. Jacinta produced a package of candy and he, showing the instincts of someone with a sweet tooth, rushed to see what the lady was taking out of the paper wrappings. When Jacinta put a piece of candy in his mouth, Juanín laughed gleefully.

"What d'ya say?" Izquierdo asked him.

The question was useless; he didn't know that when one receives something, one gives thanks.

Jacinta picked him up again and looked at him. The resemblance was fading again. If he wasn't . . . ! It would be a good idea to find out for sure and not rush into anything. Guillermina would take care of it. Suddenly the little rascal looked at her and, taking the candy out of his mouth, he offered it to her to suck.

"No, silly, I've got some more."

Then, seeing that his gallantry had gone unappreciated, he stuck out his tongue.

"Well, you big rascal—making *fun* of me!"

And getting excited, he stuck out his tongue again and spoke for the first time during that conference, saying very clearly: "Big whore."

Mistress and servant burst out laughing, and Juanín giggled in a captivating way, repeating the expression and clapping his hands together as if to applaud himself.

"The things you teach him!"

"Come on, son, don't use bad langigge . . . "

"Do you love me?" the Dauphine asked, pressing him to her.

The boy fixed his eyes on Izquierdo.

"Tell 'er ya do, except that ya won't go away with 'er . . . ya see . . . ya won't go away with 'er, 'cause ya love your papa Pepe more, mousie . . . and they have to give your papa the 'menistration."

The barbarian picked him up again and Jacinta said good-bye, firmly resolving to return enforced by the presence of her friend.

"Bye-bye, Juanín, till tomorrow," and she kissed his hand, for his face was impossible—candy all over it.

" 'Bye, precious," said Rafaela, pinching the toes sticking out of the shoe with the ventilation system.

And they left. Izquierdo, who, although he knew he was a mule, prided himself on being a gentleman, accompanied them to the main door, the little one in his arms. And he moved the little hand to make Pituso wave good-bye to the two women until they turned the corner of Bastero Street.

8

At nine the next morning mistress and maid were there again, waiting for Guillermina, who had agreed to meet them as soon as she finished certain errands at the Pulgas Station. She had received two wagons of ashlar and arranged with the director of the Northern Company to have them unloaded at no charge. The steps she had had to take for this! But she finally got her way. She wanted the company to take care of transporting the goods too. "They earned enough, and they could afford to give the helpless orphans a few truck trips."

As soon as Jacinta and Rafaela came in, they saw Juanín playing in the patio. They called him, but he didn't want to come. He looked at them from a distance, laughing, with half his hand stuck in his mouth; but as soon as they showed him the drum they'd brought him—just as people provoke a bull by showing him the banderillas with which they'll gore him—he came like lightning. He was so excited he practically had a conniption, and so impatient that it took Jacinta some effort to hang the drum on him. With a stick in each hand he started to beat the drum, running all around that dump, envied by the others, and unconcerned about everything except making as much of a racket as he could.

Jacinta and Rafaela went upstairs. The maid was carrying a bundle of things, the lady's offerings to the needy in that severely poor neighborhood. Women came out, moved by curiosity, the whispering started, and soon, in the murmuring circles that were forming, news and remarks went around: "She's brought a lambswool cloak to Señá Nicanora; and a hat and a wool undershirt to Uncle Dido; and she put five *duros*, like five suns, in Rosa's hand . . ." "She gave the crippled woman in number 9 a blanket, and one of those flannel things to Señá Encarnación for her rheumatism, and some salve in a big jar to Uncle Manjavacas, the kind they call *pitofufito*, you know, the kind I gave my little girl last year, but it didn't stop her from dying on me . . ." "I can already see Manjavacas pawning it or exchanging it for a few drops of alcohol." "I heard she wants to buy the kid off Señó Pepe, and that she's giving him thirty thousand *duros* . . . and making him governor . . ." "Governor of what? . . ." "You must be stupid or something . . . Governor of the Republic's stables."

Jacinta was growing impatient because her friend hadn't arrived, and in the meantime three or four women, all talking at once, were expounding their needs to her in a hyperbolic fashion. This one had both her children barefoot; the next didn't have them barefoot or shod: they'd all died on her, and she'd been left with an anguish, a tightness in her chest that they called "eroisim." And another one had five children and one in the oven, which was confirmed by the promontory that lifted her skirts half a yard from the ground. In such a state she couldn't go to the tobacco factory, and it was making the family go through "real creases." The relative of the next one couldn't work because he'd fallen off the scaffolding and had been in a cot for three months with a big bruise on his chest and lots of pains, spitting blood. So many, many tales of woe oppressed Jacinta's heart, suggesting very broad ideas on the extent of human misery. Living at the heart of prosperity as she did, she had never been able to realize the vastness of the kingdom of poverty, and now she saw that no matter how much it was explored, one would never reach the ends of that vast continent. She consoled them all and promised to protect them as much as her means allowed, for while it was true that they weren't small, they were perhaps insufficient to handle so many, many needs. The circle around her was closing in on her, and the lady was beginning to feel smothered. She took a few steps, but at every step she was confronted by a new reason for compassion; before her luminous charity, human misfortunes sprang up, claiming the right to her mercy. After visiting several houses and leaving them brokenheartedly, she found herself in the corridor again, very worried now by her friend's delay, when she noticed a gentle tugging at her cashmere shawl. She turned and saw a child, a very pretty girl, about five or six, very clean, and wearing an euonymus leaf in her hair.

"Señora," the little girl said in a sweet and timid voice, pronouncing the word impeccably, "would you like to see my apron?"

Taking her apron by the border, which was of blue cretonne, freshly ironed and spotless, she showed it to the lady.

"Yes, I see it," said the latter, admiring such grace and coquettishness. "You're very pretty and the apron is . . . magnificent."

"I'm wearing it today for the first time . . . I won't get it dirty, because I don't go down to the patio," she added, her tiny nostrils flaring with pleasure and vanity.

"Whose child are you? What's your name?"

"Adoración."

"Aren't you cute . . . and so friendly!"

"This little girl," said one of the neighbors, "is the daughter of a very bad woman they call 'the hard-hearted Mauricia.'* She's lived here twice before, but they put her in the Arrecogidas and she escaped, and now no one knows where she is."

"Poor child! . . . Her mother doesn't love her."

"But she has her Aunt Severiana for a mother, who looks after like she was her own daughter, and she's raising her. Doesn't the lady know Severiana?"

"I've heard my friend mention her."

"Yes, Señorita Guillermina is very fond of her . . . After all, she and Mauricia

---

* *Mauricia la dura.*

are the daughters of the woman that irons for them . . . Severiana! . . . Where is that woman?"

"Shopping," replied Adoración.

"Well, you certainly are a little Miss."

When she heard herself called "Miss," Adoración could hardly contain her satisfaction.

"Señora," she said, charming Jacinta with her silvery voice and divine pronunciation, "I didn't paint my face the other day . . . "

"Of course not, you *wouldn't!* I could tell. You're very clean."

"Oh, *no, I* didn't paint myself," she repeated, emphasizing the "no" so strongly with her head that she looked as if she'd break her neck. "Those big pigs wanted to paint me, but I wouldn't let them."

Jacinta and Rafaela were enchanted. They had never seen such a pretty, well-mannered, and endearing little girl. It was a pleasure to see how clean her clothes were. Her skirt was patched, but thoroughly clean; her shoes were old, but they stood up all right; her apron was a masterpiece of pulchritude.

At this point Adoración's aunt and adopted mother arrived. She was a handsome woman, tall and graceful, the wife of a man who wall papered, and she was the most orderly or, if you will, the most powerful tenant in that hive. She lived in one of the best rooms off the first patio and had no children of her own, which made it all the more probable that Jacinta would feel comfortable with her. As soon as they met, they understood one another. Severiana appreciated the lady's kindness toward the little one; she invited her in and offered her a chair, which in those hovels struck Jacinta as opulence itself.

"And Doña Guillermina?" Severiana asked. "I know that she comes every day. Don't you know me? My mother ironed for the Pachecos . . . My sister Mauricia and I were brought up there."

"I've heard Guillermina speak of you and Mauricia . . ."

Severiana put down her shopping basket, which was well packed; she threw off her cloak and scarf, and couldn't resist the urge to be vain. Among the inhabitants of tenement houses, it's typical for the one who's come back from the plaza loaded with purchases to show them off to the admiration and envy of her neighbors. Severiana started to take out her goods, and, extending her hand, she showed them at the door. "Look, broccoli . . . a quarter-pound of flank steak . . . a snout with jaw meat . . . escarole . . . " and last of all came the big sensation; Severiana displayed it like a trophy, swollen with pride. "A rabbit!" clamored half a dozen voices . . . "Well! You've really gone overboard!" "Sure, because I can, and I got it for seven *reales.*" Jacinta thought that courtesy obliged her to flatter the lady of the house by showing great interest in the provisions, praising their quality and reasonable price.

Then they talked about Adoración, who had sewn herself to Jacinta's skirts, and Severiana began to relate:

"This child is my sister Mauricia's. Doña Guillermina put my sister in with the Micaelas, but she ran away—climbed the wall. And now we're looking for her to shut her up there again."

"I know that order very well," said Señora Santa Cruz, "and I'm very good friends with the Micaela mother superiors. They'll set her straight there. Believe me, they do miracles . . ."

"Yes, but she's very bad, Señora, . . . very bad," replied Severiana, heaving a sigh. "She left me with this creature, but she's no burden, because she's as deep in my heart as if I'd borne her myself. Being as how all mine were born dead; and my Juan Antonio has gotten so fond of the kid that he can't live without her. She's a show-off, it's true. And she does give trouble. Being as how she started to grow up around bad women, who taught her to daydream and put powder on her face. When she walks along the street she has a way of swinging her little hips that . . . I tell her I'll break her neck if she doesn't stop it. Ah, you'll see, you'll see, lazybones! The good thing about her is that she doesn't make a mess of her clothes, and she likes to wash her hands, her arms, her snout, and even her body, Señora. As soon as she lays hands on a piece of perfumed soap it's gone. And her hair! She's already broken three mirrors on me, and one day—what does the lady think she was doing?—painting her eyebrows with some burnt cork."

Adoración turned beet red, ashamed of the vile things being told about her.

"She won't do it anymore," said the lady without tiring of stroking the child's face, so smooth and pretty. And changing the subject (thereby greatly pleasing the little girl), she started to observe and praise the nice arrangement of the room.

"Your house is very attractive."

"It'll do for our needs. Naturally, it's at the Señora's disposal. It's too big for us, but I've got a friend sharing it with us—Doña Fuensanta, the widow of a military commander. My husband's as good as the best gold. He earns fourteen *reales* for me, and he doesn't have any vices. We live real well."

Jacinta admired the bureau, burnished from so much rubbing, and the altar on top of it, which consisted of hundreds of knickknacks and photographs of soldiers, with their trousers painted red and buttons yellow. Christ the King and the Virgin of the Doves were two of the beautiful paintings; there was a large print of the *Numantia* sailing over a dark, mossy sea, and another small, bordered picture of "two hearts in love," a sampler bound with a ribbon.

It was getting late, and Jacinta was no longer calm. Finally, as she was exiting to the corridor, she saw her friend, huffing and puffing . . . "Don't scold me, child; you have no idea how dizzy those nincompoops at the Pulgas Station have made me. They say they can't do a thing until they get an express order from the council. They didn't pay any attention at all to the card that I had, and I have to go back this afternoon, and there are the chairs—just sitting there, and my project's held up. But, anyway, let's do what we came to do. Where's the little creature that everyone's so taken with? Good-bye, Severiana. I can't stop now. We'll talk later."

They advanced in search of Izquierdo's den, constantly surrounded by the women of the neighborhood. Adoración followed them, holding onto Jacinta's skirts as if she were a page carrying the train of a king's robe; and preceding them, clearing the way like a beater, was longlegs, who on that day seemed to have more developed shins and wilder shocks of hair. Jacinta had brought her some boots, and the girl was most annoyed because her mother wouldn't let her wear them until Sunday.

The door to 17 was ajar, and Guillermina pushed it open. It was no surprise to her to suddenly confront not Señor Plato, whom she had expected to find, but instead a huge, ugly woman dressed in loud colors, very long-waisted, her face looking dyed, her greasy hair so black it looked blue. The freakish figure guffawed, showing teeth whose whiteness could have been compared to snow, and she told the ladies that "Don" Pepe wasn't in, that he'd be back any minute. She was the tenant in the garret, commonly known as "the chicken woman" because she had a chicken and fried foods stand on the corner of Arganzuela. She lent her domestic services to the decadent gentleman in that dwelling, sweeping the room once a month, beating the mattress, and giving Pituso a good scrubbing when the crust of filth on his angelic face got too thick. And she also usually prepared a few exquisite dishes for the *grand homme*, such as a half-pound of gizzards, half-pound of fried blood, and sometimes an escarole salad with plenty of garlic and cumin.

Izquierdo wasn't long in coming, and when he did come he threw out that scarecrow woman (who had horrified Rafaela and made her say a silent Our Father for her to leave soon). The barbarous man came in huffing and puffing as if he were all worn out from all the tasks he'd been doing, and, tossing his Andalusian hat in the corner and wiping the sweat from his extremely noble forehead with a scrunched-up handkerchief, he let out this growl:

"I'm comin' from seein' Bicerra . . . Did you receive me this morning? Well, neither did he, the big jerk, the ——! It's my fault for lowerin' myself to such insignifyin' endivid'als."

"Calm down, Señor Pepe," advised Jacinta, feeling brave in her friend's company.

Since there were only two chairs, Rafaela had to sit on the trunk, and the misunderstood *grand homme* remained standing. But later on he took an empty basket, turned it upside down, and made his respectable person comfortable.

9

From the moment the first words were exchanged in that conference (which I wouldn't hesitate to call memorable), Izquierdo realized that he was pitted against a much abler diplomat. Despite her reputation as a saint and her good little face, Doña Guillermina gave him a pain in the neck. He knew beforehand that she'd get him all rattled with her "tiologies," because that woman was undoubtedly a "conserv'tiv," and the truth was that he didn't know how to treat conservatives.

"So, Señor Izquierdo," the founder proposed smilingly, "as you know, this friend of mine wants to take in the poor child who's so badly off with you. There are two acts of charity here: you see, we'll be helping you too, as long as you don't expect too much . . ."

"Fuck the old hag!" Plato mumbled unintelligibly, mixing his words with grunts. And then, out loud: "Well, as I said to the Señora, if the Señora wants Pituso she'll hafta approach Castelar . . . "

"Oh, sure, so they'll make you a minister. Señor Izquierdo, don't give us any of that nonsense. Do you think we're stupid? You've tried the wrong people . . . You can't be given a post—you don't know how to *read.*"

Such a tremendous blow to Izquierdo's vanity left him speechless. Striking a noble pose, with his hand on his breast, he replied:

"Señora, as for this not knowin' how, that's not the whole truth . . . it's not the whole truth I tell you, it's a lie. It's just name calling, 'cause we're poor. Poverty ain't dishonor."

"Certainly it's not, in itself; but it's not honor either, is it? I know very honorable poor people, but there're also some who are fine specimens."

"I'm as decent as they come . . . Agreed?"

"Oh, yes! We're all decent, but just try to prove it. Let's see: how have you spent your life? Trading horses and mules; then conspiring and setting up barricades . . . "

"And I'm proud of it, proud of it! . . . Goddamit" the horse dealer shouted, jumping up enraged. "Jesus, what a bunch of harpies!"

Jacinta's teeth chattered. Rafaela wanted to call for help, but her own fear had paralyzed her legs.

"Ha, ha, ha. He's calling us 'harpies'!" exclaimed Guillermina, bursting into laughter as if she'd just heard an innocent joke. "Well, well, look what the exemplary gentleman says . . . And does he think, we're going to get mad at this compliment? Humph! I'm used to these refinements. They said worse to Christ."

"Señora . . . Señora, don't take away my dignity, 'cause I'm really puttin' up with a lot . . . a lot."

"We're putting up with more."

"I'm an endivid'al . . . just like—"

"We know very well what you are: a lazy bum and an animal. Oh yes, I know what I'm saying, I don't take it back. Do you think I'm afraid of you? Come on, take out your switchblade."

"I don't use it on women."

"Or men either . . . If this pompous ass thinks he's going to intimidate us with his looks . . . Sit down and stop making faces—it might work on the kids, but not on me. Besides being an animal you're a fibber, because you weren't in Cartagena or anywhere near it, and everything you say about revolutions is just because you feel like talking. Someone who knows you very well has filled me in . . . Oh, you poor man! Do you know what you make us feel? Pity, so much pity I couldn't begin to tell you how much . . . "

Completely dazed, as if he'd been hit on the head with a hammer, Izquierdo sat down on the basket and looked vacantly at the floor. Rafaela and Jacinta breathed deeply, astonished at their friend's courage; they considered her a supernatural creature.

"So, let's see," continued Guillermina, squinting her eyes as she always did when she was expounding on an important matter. "We'll take the boy, and we'll give you a sum to make up—"

"And what am I s'posed to do with a piddling sum? Do you think I'd sell myself?"

"Oh, all this is splitting hairs. What do you mean, sell yourself? Not till there's someone who'll buy you. And this isn't a sale, it's charity. You can't say you don't need it . . . "

"Look, to cut this short . . .," José retorted brusquely, "if you gimme the 'menistration . . .'"

"A sum, and that's that."

"Well, I just don't feel like a sum, I plain don't, dammit!"

"All right, all right, don't shout so much, we're not deaf. And don't be so refined, because these refinements aren't proper in a revolutionary man who's so . . . ferocious."

"You make my blood boil."

"So it's either a job or nothing, then? If that's how it has to be, that's how it'll be. The man's really cut out to be an administrator. Señor Izquierdo, let's stop joking. I'm very sorry for you because—and I'm speaking in all sincerity—you don't seem to be as bad as people think. Do you want to know the truth? It's this. You're just a poor soul that never had a part in any sort of crime or even a half-baked scheme for one."

Izquierdo lifted his eyes from the floor and looked at Guillermina without a trace of rancor. His sincere gaze seemed to confirm what the founder had declared.

"And I mean it: this child of God is not a bad man. They go around saying you murdered your second wife. Humbug! They say you've robbed out on the highways. It's a lie! And they say you've shot at people with a blunderbuss when you were in the barricades. Stuff and nonsense!"

"Talk, talk, talk," murmured Izquierdo bitterly.

"You've spent your life fighting for fodder to fill your belly, and not knowing how to win. It couldn't be helped . . . The truth is, this bluff is a man with very little aptitude: he doesn't know anything, he doesn't work, and his noggin isn't good for anything except for making up fish stories and saying he eats children raw. Lots of talk about the republic and the cantons, and the man's not even any good for the lowliest jobs there are. How about it? Am I wrong? Is that a faithful portrait of you, yes or no?"

Plato didn't say a word. His impressive gaze traveled over the tiles of the floor as if it wanted to sweep them. Guillermina's words rang in his soul like those eternal truths that human sophistry tries in vain to refute.

"Then," added the saint, "the poor man had to use hundreds of shady means to stay alive, because one *must* live. One must be indulgent with misery and grant him a minuscule right to evil."

During the brief pause following Guillermina's words, the miserable man plunged into his conscience as if it were a well, and there he saw himself as he really was, stripped of the tinseled front that his self-pride had set up. He thought what he had thought at other times: "I know I'm a real mule, a good Johnny that wouldn't hurt a fly; that damn saint has the Eternal Father in her."

Guillermina didn't take her eyes off him. Her winking made them roguish. It was amazing how she read his mind. It's hard to believe, but it's a fact, that after another solemn pause the Pacheco woman said:

"Because this business of Castelar getting you a job is just talk. You yourself wouldn't even dream of it. You say it to dumbfound Ido and other fools like him. And besides, what sort of job are they going to give a man who signs his name with an X? You, who brag about having started so many revolutions, and having founded the canton of Cartagena—that's why it turned out the way it did! You, who go around acting persecuted and call us conservatives scornfully, and go around publishing that they're going to make you some sort of tycoon, you'd be satisfied—let's say it frankly—you'd be satisfied if they gave you a job as a doorman."

Izquierdo's heartbeat quickened, and the change in his mood was so clear to Guillermina that she burst out laughing. Patting him on the knee, she repeated:

"Isn't it true that you'd be satisfied? Come on, son, confess it by the passion and death of our Redeemer, in whom we all believe."

The horse dealer's eyes lit up. A slight smile crossed his lips and he said brightly:

"Doorman at the ministry?"

"No, son, not so high . . . Typically Spanish—always shooting high and wanting to serve the state. I'm talking about being a doorman for a private house."

Izquierdo frowned. What he wanted was to put on a braided uniform. With a single dive, he submerged into his conscience again and did somersaults around being-doorman-for-a-private-house. Him, he was fed up by now, fighting all the time for a dog's life. What could be a better rest than what the "harpy," who must have been a niece of the Holy Virgin, was offering him? . . . After all, he was starting to get old and he didn't feel like putting up with much anymore. The offer meant bread on the table, easy work, and if the job was at a big place, nothing would keep him from wearing a uniform. His mouth was already open to deliver an "Agreed" bigger than the house at which he hoped to be doorman, when his self-pride, which was his worst enemy, mutinied, and the braggadocio he had cultivated so many years ruffled his calm. He was lost. He began to shake his head contemptuously, and casting scornful looks hither and thither, he said, "A doorman! That's not enough."

"Evidently not. You can't forget that you've been a minister of the interior; that is, that they wanted to appoint you . . . although it seems to me that we agreed that it was all a figment of your great imagination. I can see that between you and Don José Ido, who's another great mind, you could invent some lovely novels. Ah! Poverty, lack of food, what they do to these poor brains! To sum it up, Señor Izquierdo—"

He had risen and started to pace the room, his hands in his pockets, and he voiced his magnanimous thoughts as follows:

"My dignity and caliber won't let me . . . I mean, it's like they say—I'd like to, but it can't be done; nope, it can't be done. If you really wanna help me out, 'cause you're takin' away little mousie here, I'll stick to the honoraries."

"God be praised! So we've finally settled for a sum! . . ."

Jacinta thought the way was clear now. But they met another obstacle when from out of a corner the brute spoke these fateful words, which echoed in a sinister fashion:

"Eh . . . well . . . a thousand *duros* and it's a deal."

"A thousand *duros!*" cried Guillermina. "Holy Mother of God! We wouldn't mind having them ourselves. It would have to be a bit less."

"I won't come down a cent."

"You want to bet? Because you may be a horse dealer and a haggler, but so am I."

Jacinta wondered how she could possibly get together a thousand *duros*, which sounded like a huge sum at first, then a small one, and she spent some time considering the figure with different criteria.

"I'm not comin' down, not the slightest bit. I don't care whether you give it to me in gold or bank notes. But make sure of the number, 'cause I'm not comin' down a cent."

"That's it, that's it; let's be firm . . . You're not pretentious, are you? You and all your kind aren't worth a thousand *cuartos*, never mind a thousand *duros* . . . Oh, go on. Do you want two thousand *reales?*"

Izquierdo made a scornful gesture.

"What, getting mad on us? All right, keep your little angel. What did you think anyway, you jerk, that we'd swallow the bit about Pituso being the son of this lady's husband? How can you prove it?"

"I don't have nothin' to do with it. But it's plain enough he's the natural father," answered Izquierdo, ill-humoredly now, "natural father of my niece's son, namely, Juanín."

"Do you have the baptismal papers?"

"I've got 'em," said the savage, looking at the trunk on which Rafaela was seated.

"No, don't get out any papers—they don't prove anything either. As for the 'natural' fatherhood, as you call it, either it's true or it's not. We'll get the information from the people who have it."

Izquierdo scratched his forehead as if he were trying to scratch up an idea. The allusion to Juanito had undoubtedly made him recall the time he had rolled ignominiously down the staircase of the Santa Cruz residence. Meanwhile, Jacinta wanted to reach a settlement by offering half; but Guillermina, who detected conciliatory desires in her friend's face, imposed silence, and, rising from her chair, she declared:

"Señor Izquierdo, you can keep your gypsy boy; you're not going to swindle us."

"Señora . . . God dammit! I'm an honest man and no conserv'tiv can make me nothin' else. Right?" he replied with that superficial rage of his that was only word deep.

"You're very kind . . . You're so refined that it's really not possible for us to reach an understanding. If you think this lady really cares about appropriating the boy! . . . It's a whim, nothing more than a whim. This simple creature is determined to have some kids—a stupid obsession, because when God doesn't grant them, He must have His reasons. She saw Pituso and felt sorry for him; she liked him. But the little animal is very expensive. They give them away for nothing in these patios, and let you have your choice . . . and on top of it they're grateful. What did you think, that your 'little mousie' is the only one there is? There's that precious little Adoración. We could have her whenever we wanted, because Severiana's will is as good as mine. So. What do you have to say to that? Oh, I can just hear it: that Pituso is related by blood to the Santa Cruzes. Maybe so and maybe not . . . Right now we're going to explain the case to my friend's husband, who has a lot of influence and is on familiar terms with Pi and has lunch with Castelar and was nursed by the same woman as Salmerón. He'll decide what he wants to do. If the child's his, he'll take him away from you: and if he's not, God help you. If that's the case, you brute, there'll be no money, no doorman's job, no nothing."

Izquierdo looked bewildered at this rush of harsh, bruising words. In these great oratorical crises, Guillermina used the familiar *tú* form with everyone. After pushing Jacinta and Rafaela toward the door, she turned back to the miserable, speechless man, and, starting to laugh with angelic kindness, she spoke to him:

"Forgive me for having treated you harshly, as you deserve. I'm that way. And don't go thinking that I'm mad. But I don't want to leave without giving you alms and advice. Here, take this to buy a little bread."

She extended her hand, offering him two *duros*, and, seeing that he didn't take them, she put them on one of the chairs.

"Here's the advice: you're not good for a thing in the world. You don't know any trade, you can't even be a laborer because you're a loafer and don't like to carry weights. You're not any good as a street sweeper, or even at carrying a sign to advertise something. And yet, you unfortunate man, there's nothing made by God that doesn't have its wherefore in this admirable workshop which the universe is. You've been born to render great service, one that will give you a lot of glory, and bread every day. Can't you see that, you numskull? You're so thick! Tell me the truth, now: haven't you ever looked in the mirror? Hasn't it ever occurred to you? You must be dumb . . . Well, I'll tell you: what you're good for is being an artist's model. Don't you get it? *They're* the ones who'll dress you up as a saint, or a knight, or the Eternal Father, and do your portrait. Because you've got a wonderful figure: face, body, expression—everything that isn't soul in you is noble and beautiful. You have a treasure, a real treasure in your lines. Come on, I'll bet you don't understand me."

The poor simpleton's vanity increased his perplexity. He felt hints of glory, like hot lashes across his forehead. He glimpsed a brilliant future. Him, a subject for painters! And paid at that! And he'd earn *cuartos* just for dressing up, and making faces, and ah! Plato looked at himself in the glass pane over the coiled braids. But he couldn't see himself very well . . .

"So don't forget, now. Drop by any studio and you've made it. With your mousie on your back, you'd make the most beautiful Saint Christopher one could hope to see. Good-bye, good-bye . . . . "

x. More Scenes from Private Life

I

ON HER WAY OUT, in the corridor, Guillermina said to her friend: "You're so naive. You don't know how to handle these people. Leave it to me and don't worry, Pituso will be yours. I know what I'm doing. If that scoundrel had caught you alone, he would've gotten more out of you than what all the kids in the Inclusa plus their parents are worth. What did you plan to offer him? Ten thousand *reales?* Well, you can give them to me, and if I get him for less, the difference is for my projects."

After chatting awhile with Severiana at the latter's place, they left, escorted by various divisions and members of the patio gangs. No matter how hard Jacinta and Rafaela looked, they didn't see Juanín anywhere.

That day, which was the 22nd, the Dauphin got worse due to his impatience and insistence on hurrying Nature, thereby interfering with her remedies. Shortly after getting up, he had to go back to bed, complaining about purely illusory aches and pains. His family, who knew his tricks very well, was not alarmed, and Barbarita repeatedly prescribed sheets and resignation. He spent a bad night; but he slept all morning on the 23rd, which allowed Jacinta to go off on another little jaunt (Rafaela escorting her) to Mira el Río Baja Street. This visit had so little to it that the lady came home feeling very sad. She had not seen either Pituso or Señor Izquierdo. Severiana told her that Guillermina had been there earlier and given the "endivid'al"—who had the boy on his shoulders, undoubtedly rehearsing a Saint Christopher—a long sermon. The only thing Jacinta gained from the excursion that day was new proof of the popularity she was beginning to gain with the tenants of those houses. Men and women surrounded her and practically lifted her into the air. One voice was heard to shout: "Long live her kindness!" and they sang couplets that were in doubtful taste but had very good intentions. The Idos cried out above everyone else in that concert of praises, and it was a pleasure to see Don José looking so elegant in the decent garments Jacinta had given him including his almost new, coffee-colored derby. The firstborn of opera hats became the object of a series of puny transactions until it was finally acquired for two *cuartos* by one of the residents of that same house whose specialty at Carnival time was to go around jiggling a long stick with candy dangling from the end.

Adoración clung to Doña Jacinta from the moment she saw her come in. Her affection was idolatrous, really. She became ecstatic and speechless in the lady's presence, devoured her with her eyes, and if Jacinta touched her face or kissed her, the poor little girl quivered with emotion and began to look feverish. Her way of expressing her feelings was to rub her head against her idol's body, nestle it in the folds of the cloak and press hard, as if she wanted to bore a hole in the cloth. Doña Jacinta's departure made Adoración despair, and Severiana had to be a bit gruff to make the child behave reasonably. That day the lady brought her some very pretty boots and promised to bring more garments—earrings and a ring with a lovely diamond as big as a garbanzo or bigger: the size of a hazelnut.

When she got home, the Dauphine was eager to know whether Guillermina had accomplished anything. She called to her from the balcony, but the founder wasn't in. She probably wouldn't be back until evening, said the maid, because she had had to go to Pulgas Station for the third time, to the construction site, and to the orphanage on Albuquerque Street.

A happy event occurred that day in the Santa Cruz household. Don Baldomero came in from the street when they were just about to sit down for lunch, and in the most natural tone imaginable declared that he'd won the lottery. Barbarita received the news calmly, almost sadly, because the whims of luck, that insane creature, did not particularly amuse her. Fortune had not shown herself to be, shall we say, very clever in this: they had no need whatsoever to win the lottery. It even seemed like a nuisance to receive a prize that logically should have been for the wretched souls who play to improve their lot. There were so many people cursing the devil that day for not having gotten back even the pitiful amount they'd played! When the long list was posted on the 23rd, Madrid was a land of disillusionment because—it was so odd—no one had won! And you've got to see a winner if you're to believe, at least, in the rewarded ones.

Don Baldomero was serene. This stroke of luck didn't affect him one way or the other. He bought a whole series ticket every year; it was a routine or a vice, perhaps an obligation, like renewing one's identification papers or some other document that certifies one officially as a Spaniard. He had never won more than tidbits, a reimbursement or very small prizes. But this year he won two hundred and fifty thousand *reales*. As always, he had split up the ticket among just about as many people, which meant that the sum would be distributed to a multitude from all walks of life. And while it was true that some rich participants would carry off good chunks, lots of poor ones would get a share too. Santa Cruz took the list into the dining room and read it off as he ate, estimating the winnings of each. He sounded like the children from the San Ildefonso school when they pick a number at the charity raffle and call it out to the public.

"The 'boys' played two *décimos* and they've made fifty thousand *reales*. Villalonga, one *décimo*: that makes twenty-five thousand. Samaniego, half that."

Pepe Samaniego appeared at the door the minute Don Baldomero announced his name and prize, and the overjoyed man began to embrace everyone there, including the servants.

"Eulalia Muñoz, one *décimo*: twenty-five thousand *reales*. Benignita, half a *décimo*: twelve thousand five hundred *reales*. Now we come to the small change. Deogracias, Rafaela, and Blas each played ten *reales*. They win one thousand two hundred and fifty each."

"How about the coal dealer?" asked Barbarita, who was interested in the players in the lowest division.

"The coal dealer laid down ten *reales*; our illustrious cook, twenty; the butcher, fifteen. Let's see, let's see: Pepa the kitchenmaid, five *reales*, and the same goes for her sister. They win six hundred and fifty *reales*."

"How piddling!"

"It's not my doing, dear, it's what the figures say."

The participants gradually arrived, attracted by the aroma of the news, which spread quickly; and the cook, the kitchenmaids, and others on the staff dared to commit a breach of etiquette, penetrating as far as the dining room door and showing their overjoyed faces, waiting to hear their master call out the amount of all that money they'd won. Señorita Jacinta was the first to congratulate the winners in the kitchen. The kitchenmaid fainted, because she thought that her measly five *reales* had won her at least three million. As soon as he knew what was going on, Estupiñá shot out into the street in search of the other lucky winners to give them the news. It was he who informed Samaniego, and when he could no longer find anyone who had been personally affected by the lottery, he pestered every acquaintance and friend he ran into. And he hadn't won anything!

Barbarita mentioned this to her husband with the discreet seriousness the case required.

"Poor Plácido—he's very down at heart, dear. He can't disguise his feelings. He's running out to tell the news just so we won't see how dejected he feels about it."

"But dear, it's not my fault. Remember that he was standing there with the half *duro* in his hand, offering it and taking it back until finally his greed was stronger than his ambition and he said: 'For what I'd get out of it, I'd rather use my money for licorice.' So he had his licorice!"

"Poor thing! . . . Put him on the list."

Don Baldomero looked at his wife rather sternly. That violation of a mathematical law was serious in his eyes.

"Add his name, dear, go ahead. What difference does it make to you? Make everyone happy."

Don Baldomero smiled with that patriarchal kindness of his, and, taking out the list and pencil again, said out loud:

"Rossini, ten *reales*: he wins one thousand, two hundred and fifty."

Everyone present hastened to congratulate the rewarded man while he simply stood there in suspense, convinced that they were pulling his leg.

"But I didn't—"

Barbarita cast him a look that stopped him in mid air. When the Señora looked at him that way, there was no choice but to be silent.

"This blessed Plácido is a born winner," said Don Baldomero to his daughter-in-law. "He wins at the lottery without even playing!"

"Plácido," said Jacinta, laughing very contentedly, "is the one who brought us good luck."

"But I . . .," murmured Estupiñá, who had a very clear sense of justice, as long as it didn't concern contraband.

"Silly! What a state you must be in," said Barbarita very forcefully, "not to even remember that you gave me half a *duro* for the lottery!"

"I . . . when you say so . . . well, the truth is, my head's 'pletely, you know, sort of off . . ."

I have a feeling that Estupiñá reached the point of believing beyond a doubt that he *had* given her the coin.

"Didn't I say that that number was one of the luckiest of all?" Don Baldomero declared proudly. "As soon as the lottery men gave it to me I had a hunch that it was the one."

"As for being a lucky one . . . ," added Estupiñá, "there's no doubt about that."

"It had to win; I knew it would," Samaniego asserted with pleasurable conviction. "Three fours in a row, then a zero, and ending in an eight! It just had to be the one."

Samaniego himself was the one who thought of celebrating the great event with tambourines and Christmas carols, and Estupiñá proposed that all the winners go into the kitchen and make a commotion banging pots and pans together. But Barbarita prohibited any sort of uproar, although when she saw Federico Ruiz, Eulalia Muñoz, and one of the "boys," Ricardo Santa Cruz, come in at that moment, she ordered half a dozen bottles of champagne opened.

All this hubbub could be heard from Juan's bedroom, where he was being entertained by his wife and his servant, who were keeping him posted, especially about Estupiñá's prize. It goes without saying that he laughed heartily over these incidents. But the prison to which he was so annoyingly confined soon put him in a bad mood again; he was becoming very quarrelsome now, saying to his wife: "Go ahead and leave me alone again; you can go right back and have fun with those idiots and make more of a racket. The lottery! What a way for a country to stay retarded! It's one of the things that should be suppressed: it discourages saving; it's a way out for good-for-nothings. There can't be any public prosperity with a lottery. What? Are you leaving again? A nice way to take care of a sick man! And anyway, what have you been doing out in the streets all morning? Come on, explain it, I want to know, because it's getting to be a regular habit."

Smiling and calm, Jacinta made excuses. But she had to tell a little white lie. She'd gone out that morning "to buy Nativity scenes, colored candles, and other knickknacks, for Candelaria's children."

"Then," replied Juanito, tossing between the sheets, "I'd like to know what Mamá and Estupiñá are for, because all they do is make the shopkeepers' heads spin, and they know the stands on Santa Cruz Plaza by heart. So, come on, give me an explanation . . . "

The commotion made by the winners was dying down a bit, but then it got louder with the arrival of Guillermina, who heard the news at her house and came in, crying out: "Every one of you must give me twenty-five percent for my building. If you don't, God and Saint Joseph will make your prizes turn to dust."

"Twenty-five percent is a lot for the small winners," said Don Baldomero. "Consult with Saint Joseph and you'll see that he agrees."

"Heretic!" retorted the lady, feigning anger. "You big heretic. After you squeeze out the nation's money—which is the Church's money—you want to refuse to contribute to my work, to the poor. Twenty-five percent, and fifty percent from you. Period. Either this or you can answer to the Lord. So take your choice."

"No, my dear. If it were up to me, I'd give you all of it . . . "

"And that's exactly what you will do, you greedy man. Things are going *just* beautifully—ha! A hundred bricks were ten *reales* last week, and now they want eleven and a half, and the brown ones are at ten and a half. I'm about to jump out of my skin. Materials are sky-high."

Samaniego insisted that the saint have a glass of champagne.

"What do you think I am—full of vices like you? Me drink that repulsive stuff? When do you collect, tomorrow? Well, prepare yourself. I'll be there like the Rock of Gibraltar. I won't give you a moment's peace."

Shortly afterward Guillermina and Jacinta, far from indescreet ears, conferred in private.

"You don't have to worry anymore," Guillermina told her. "Pituso is yours. I closed the deal this afternoon. You have no idea how I fought with that Judas. I don't know how many times the blasphemous brute said 'God dammit!' He pulled the baptismal certificate out of the trunk—filthy old papers. The document doesn't prove a thing. The boy may be, and then again, he may not be . . . Who knows? But since you have this whim, which you have because you're spoiled, to heck with God. It all seems irregular to me. You should have spoken to your husband first. But you like little surprises and dramatic effects. We'll see what will come of it. Remember now, a deal is a deal. It's taken me God and more to make Señor Izquierdo reasonable. He finally settled for six thousand five hundred *reales*. What's left over from the ten thousand is for me, and I've certainly earned it . . . So tomorrow afternoon I'll go and get him. You come too, with the 'holy dough.' "

Jacinta was most pleased. She had turned her wish into a reality; she had her toy. It might very well have been childish, but she had her reasons for acting as she did. The plan she had conceived for introducing Pituso and making him a member of the family revealed a certain astuteness. She thought that for the moment she should say nothing to the Dauphin. She would stash her treasure at Candelaria's house until she made him presentable. Then she would explain that he was a little orphan from the streets, that she had taken him in . . . Not a word as to who his mother might be, not the slightest hint about his father. The whole point was to observe the expression on Juan's face when he saw the little doll. Would the mysterious rush of their blood tell him anything? Would he recognize in the poor child's features those of . . . ? Jacinta sacrificed the advantages of a more proper procedure to this dramatic element. Imagining what would happen— the infidel's confusion, her forgiveness, and dozens of other novelistic details that she anticipated—she felt a pleasure similar to that of the artist who creates and composes a work, and also a touch of revenge; that is, the type that a soul as noble as hers was capable of.

2

When she went to the Dauphin's room, Barbarita made him drink a big cup of tea flavored with cognac. The noise kept up in the dining room, but people's spirits were calming down. "Now," said the mamá, "they've gone on to politics— Samaniego says that until they behead several hundred people there won't be any peace. The Marquis isn't in favor of spilling blood, and Estupiñá was asking him why he had declined to be a representative. He turned crimson and said he couldn't get mixed up with—"

"That's not what he said," sprang Juanito, holding the hot drink in mid air.

"Yes, he did, son; he said he didn't want to get mixed up with those . . . I don't know."

"Mamá, he did *not* say that. Don't you change the facts too."

"But son, I heard him."

"Even if you did, I insist that he couldn't have said that."

"Well, then?"

"The Marquis couldn't have said 'get mixed up with' something. I bet you anything he said 'embroiled' in something. I ought to know how *refined* people talk."

Barbarita laughed loudly.

"Why, yes . . . you're right; that's what it was, he didn't want to be *embroiled*."

"See? Jacinta!"

"What do you want, you spoiled boy?"

"Give Aparisi a message. Tell him to come here immediately."

"What for? Do you know what time it is?"

"The minute he hears, he'll come running."

"But what for?"

"Oh, nothing at all! Do you think he's going to let that bit about being 'embroiled' pass just like that? I want to see how he gets himself out of this one."

The two ladies expressed their approval of the joke as they straightened the bed. Guillermina had left without saying good-bye, and the others were leaving little by little. By midnight all was quiet, and after the elder Santa Cruzes had reminded Jacinta to watch over the Dauphin very carefully to see that he stayed covered, they retired to their room. He seemed to be sleeping deeply; his wife lay down sleeplessly, more disposed to keep watch than to rest. An hour hadn't gone by when Juan woke up, apparently uneasy, and started talking somewhat irrationally. Jacinta thought he was delirious and sat up in bed. But it wasn't delirium; it was worry, and a slight impertinence. She tried to calm him with affectionate words, but he wouldn't let her. "Do you want me to call someone?" "No, it's late, and I wouldn't want to alarm them. I'm just nervous. I had a dream that scared me. I can see why—all day long with this boredom. These sheets are burning and my body's cold."

Jacinta put on her robe and sat on the edge of her husband's bed. It seemed to her that he had a slight fever. The worst was that he had put his arms out and pushed back the covers. Fearing he would get chilled, she tried her best to soothe him. Seeing that this didn't work, she took off her robe and got into bed with him, prepared to spend the night seeing to it that he stayed covered, and she lulled him to sleep. And this did soothe him somewhat, because he liked to be pampered and have people make a fuss over him and chat with him when he couldn't sleep. And oh, what a baby he became when his wife, deliciously maternal and gentle, took him in her arms and pressed him to her breast, burying him in affection and giving him her own body heat! It wasn't long before Juan fell into a lethargy, thanks to this honeyed treatment. Jacinta didn't take her eyes off his; she watched steadily and attentively to see whether he was sleeping, or murmuring some complaint, or perspiring. In this state she clearly heard the bells at the Puerta del Sol strike one, one thirty, two, so distinctly that they seemed to be striking inside the house. The porcelain lamp diffused soft light into the bedroom.

And when a long while had passed without his moving, Jacinta began thinking again. She took thoughts out of her mind the way a miser takes his coins out when nobody is there to see him, and she began to count and examine them, checking to see whether any of them were false. Suddenly she remembered the mean trick she intended to play on her husband, and her soul trembled pleasurably at the thought of this childish revenge. And she was struck by a vision of Pituso. She could just see him! His unfamiliar features—their likeness to his mother's features—were what upset Jacinta the most and clouded over her pious happiness. It was then that she felt the tickling—for it didn't deserve to be called anything else—the tickling of that childish rage that possessed her from time to time; and she also felt a certain urge to squeeze him, squeeze him hard so the unfaithful man would feel her dovelike fury.

But in fact, she didn't squeeze him at all for fear of disturbing his slumber. When he seemed to be shivering with chills she did squeeze him—yes, gently, wrapping herself around him to provide as much warmth as she could. When he moaned or breathed very hard, she lulled him, patting him lightly on the back; she never withdrew her hands from that duty, and whenever she wanted to know if he was perspiring, she put her nose and cheek against his forehead.

It must have been three in the morning when the Dauphin opened his eyes and looked at his wife, whose face was only two or three nose-lengths away.

"I feel so much better now!" he said sweetly. "I'm sweating; I'm not cold anymore. And how about you, haven't you slept? Ah, of all the prizes in the lottery, I won the grand prize. You're the grand prize. You're so good!"

"Does your head hurt?"

"Nothing hurts. I'm well. But I've woken up and I'm not sleepy anymore. If you're not either, talk to me. Let's see, tell me where you went this morning."

"'Well, this little piggy went to market . . .' That's what Mamá used to tell us when my sisters and I asked her where she'd been."

"Give me a straight answer. Where were you?" Jacinta giggled, suddenly thinking she would play a very droll joke on her husband. "You're in a great mood, aren't you! What are you laughing about?"

"You . . . Men are so odd! Good heavens, they want to know everything."

"Naturally, and we have a right to."

"One can't even go shopping . . . "

"Don't give me that about shopping. Competing with Mamá and Estupiñá? Impossible. You didn't go shopping."

"I did too."

"Then what did you buy?"

"Material."

"For shirts for me? But I've got . . . twenty-seven dozen, I think."

"Shirts for you, yes; but I'm going to make little tiny ones."

"Tiny ones!"

"Yes, and I'm making you some bibs too—they're adorable."

"Bibs! Bibs for *me*?"

"Yes, silly, in case you drool."

"Jacinta!"

"Oh, go on . . . And you laugh, silly. Wait till you see the shirts! Except that the sleeves are like this. Only your fingers would fit in them."

"Are you really . . . ? Come on, be serious. If you giggle, I won't believe a word you say."

"See how serious I am? It's just that you make me laugh. Oh well, I'll say it formally. I'm filling a basket with little things."

"Come off it, I don't want any of your teasing."

"But it's true."

"But . . . "

"Would you like me to tell you? Tell me if you want to know."

A little while passed, during which they looked at each other. Their smiles were like a single smile, leaping from mouth to mouth.

"What a bore! Come on, tell me."

"All right, here goes: I'm going to have a baby."

"Jacinta! What are you saying? These things are not to joke about," said Santa Cruz, so joyfully that his wife had to restrain him.

"Eh, careful. If you get uncovered, I won't talk."

"You're just joking . . . Huh! If it were true, you would never have made such a secret of it . . . as eager as you are! You would've told everyone, even the deaf. But go on, does Mamá know?"

"No. No one knows yet."

"Really? Let go, I'm going to ring."

"Silly . . . crazy! Be quiet, or I'll hit you."

"Let's wake up the whole household so they'll know. Wait a minute, though. Is this a farce? Yes—I can see it in your eyes."

"If you're not quiet, I won't tell you anything else."

"All right, then; I'll be quiet. But answer me: are you just presuming this, or—?"

"It's a fact."

"Are you sure?"

"As sure as if I were seeing him and hearing him run through the halls. He's so funny and so mischievous . . . ! As beautiful as an angel and a scoundrel, just like his father."

"Hail Mary, full of grace, what precocity! It still hasn't been born, and you already know that it's a boy and that he's as big a scoundrel as I am."

The Dauphine couldn't contain herself. They were so stuck together that Jacinta seemed to be laughing with her husband's lips and he seemed to be perspiring through the pores of his wife's temples.

"Well, well, just look at what my good wife was keeping from me!" Juan added incredulously.

"Are you glad?"

"Shouldn't I be? If it were true, I'd have the whole family on their feet this minute so they'd know; Papá would be sure to grab his hat and tear out like a shot to find a Nativity scene. But wait a minute; explain this. When will it be?"

"Soon."

"In six months? In five?"

"Sooner."

"In three?"

"Much, much sooner . . . It's just about to drop, any time now."

"Bah! Look, these jokes are impertinent. Do you mean that it's so close you can't even say when? Well, it doesn't show."

"Because I hide it."

"Sure, that's *exactly* what you'd do. What you'd really do, with your craving for kids, is go out so that everyone could see you with your bass drum, and you'd send Rossini over to *La Correspondencia* with an announcement."

"Well, it could be any day now. When you see him, you'll be convinced."

"But whom am I going to see?"

"Your . . . your little son, your beloved little baby."

"Well, I'll tell you frankly that you're confusing me no end, because this is getting awfully serious for a joke, and if it *were* true, you wouldn't have kept it such a secret till now."

As Jacinta realized that she couldn't carry the joke any further, she tried to back out, and she encouraged him to go to sleep: the excitement of this conversation might be harmful because of his condition.

"There's plenty of time to talk about it," she said, "and you'll . . . you'll be convinced, little by little."

"*All right,*" he replied with childish charm, adopting the tone of a child who's being lulled to sleep.

"Try to go to sleep now . . . Close your little eyes. You love me, don't you?"

"More than my own life. But darling, you're so strong! You're squeezing me so hard!"

"If you deceive me, I'll grab you like this, and . . . like this."

"Ow!"

"I'll squeeze you into crumbs, like a cake."

"Oooh, it feels nice!"

"And now, sleepy-sleepy . . ."

This sort of baby-talk never failed to amuse them; their intimacy and solitude lent a certain charm to expressions that would have sounded ridiculous in the light of day and in front of other people. After a little while, Juanito opened his eyes, saying in a manly tone:

"Are you really going to have a baby?"

"Yeth . . . and *sleepy-sleepy* now, *baaaby*."

She hummed him a lullaby, patting him on the back.

"It's so nice to be a *bebé*," murmured the Dauphin; "be in your mother's arms, and feel the warmth of her breathing and . . . !"

Another stretch of time, and then Juan, waking up and imitating the whimper of a tender infant being nursed, bleated:

"Mamá . . . Mamá . . . "

"What?"

"Nipple."

Jacinta stifled a laugh.

"Not now . . . it's bad . . . dirty . . ."

They both found such silly phrases amusing. It was a way of killing time and showing their affection.

"Here, my nipple," said Jacinta, putting a finger in his mouth; and he sucked it, saying it was delicious and other foolish things, justified only by the occasion, the night, and their sweet intimacy.

"If someone were to hear us, just think how they'd laugh at us!"

"But since no one can . . . Four o'clock—it's gotten so late!"

"Early, you mean. Pretty soon Plácido will be getting up to go wake the sexton at San Ginés. He must be so cold!"

"We're so much better off here, all snuggled up!"

"I think I'm going to sleep now, dear."

"Me too, darling."

They slept like angels, their cheeks touching.

3

December 24th.

Barbarita asked Jacinta to do some domestic duties that morning, which annoyed her; but staying at home gave the young woman a chance to take a step that had always worried her. Barbarita told her to stay at home all day, and since she had to go out at some point, she had no other choice but to tell her mother-in-law about the intrigue she was caught up in. She begged her forgiveness for not having confided the secret sooner, and she noticed with immense grief that her mother-in-law was not at all enthused by the idea of possessing Juanín.

"Do you realize how serious this is? Just like that, out of the blue . . . a son raining down on us. And are there any proofs that he is a son? Are you sure it's not a swindle? Do you really think he looks like him? Isn't it just an illusion of yours? Because it's all very vague . . . Finding lost sons like this only happens in novels."

The Dauphine was very disappointed. She had expected an outburst of joy from her mother-in-law. But it had turned out differently. Worried and scowling, Barbarita said coldly:

"I don't know what to think of you; but anyway, bring him and hide him until we see . . . This is no laughing matter. I'll tell your husband that Benigna is sick and you've gone to see her."

After this conversation, Jacinta went to her sister's house and confided the secret to her too; they agreed that she would deposit the child there until Juan and Don Baldomero were told.

"We'll see how they take it," she added, heaving a deep sigh.

Jacinta was beside herself that afternoon. She felt as if she had borne Pituso herself, and had grown so accustomed to the idea of possessing him that she was indignant when her mother-in-law didn't entirely agree.

Rafaela joined her mistress at Benigna's house, and the next thing you know they were walking down Toledo Street. They had small change to dole out to the poor, and a few odds and ends, among them the ring that the Señorita had promised Adoración. It was a superb jewel, purchased that morning by Rafaela at one of the bazaars having a "Close-out Sale—Everything for a *real* and a half," and it had a diamond so large and so well cut that the king himself would have been dazzled by such splendor. The makings of this superb gem included the best chip left from a broken glass.

When they'd scarcely reached the corridors that surround the first patio, clusters of women and kids rushed up to them, and to avoid resentment and jealousy Jacinta had to put something in every hand. Who would get a *peseta*, who a *duro*, or a half-*duro* . . . ? Some, like Severiana (already the possessor, we might add, of a magnificent head of cabbage, pickled ribs, and porgy for dinner that night), were content with an affectionate greeting. Others didn't show any satisfaction with what they'd received. Jacinta asked all of them what they had to make dinner with that night. Some of them came over holding a porgy by the gills; others hadn't been able to bring home more than scraps. She saw lots of women go upstairs with pitchers of milky almond water that had been given to them at the Café de Naranjeros, and from almost all the kitchens came the odor of fried food and the clang of metal. One kissed the *duro* the Señorita had given him; another threw it up in the air to catch it gleefully, saying: "Come on, off to the market!" And they ran down the stairs, off to various stores. There were those who prepared their Christmas feast with a snout and jawmeat, a pound of shank meat, or other disdained cuts of a steer. The most opulent gave themselves airs with a piece of hard nougat, the kind that needs to be hammered apart, and whoever brought back a pomegranate made sure that everyone saw it. But there was no inhabitant in that poverty-stricken region as joyful as Adoración, nor as envied by her friends, because the rich gem on her finger that she displayed (thrusting out her fist) was refined and legitimate and had cost a mint. Even the little ones showing off new shoes, thanks to Doña Jacinta's charity, would have exchanged them for that monstrous, bedazzling stone. Its possessor, after running the length of both corridors to show it off, clung to the Señorita again, rubbing against her like a cat.

"I won't forget you, Adoración," said the Señorita, who with this sentence seemed to be announcing that she would not be back soon.

In both patios the noise of drums was so loud that you had to shout to be heard. When the clanging of oil cans was added to the drumbeats, the fragile houses looked as if they were about to collapse. During the few minutes the "toccata" abated, they could hear the tune (which is all that's left of it now) of the famous liberal hymn by Riego being whistled. A crank organ was being played on Mira el Río Baja Street, and on Bastero Street another, and between the two they made quite a musical row; their notes sounded like nails scratching at each other in a furious fight. The polka and the pathetic andante were like two frenzied cats in a clench. This and the drums and the old woman screaming "Figs for sale!" and the uproar of the excited neighborhood and the laughing of the children and the barking of the dogs made Jacinta dizzy.

The alms distributed, she proceeded to number 17, where Guillermina was already impatient because of her delay. Izquierdo and Pituso were there too, the former pretending to be deeply grieved by the separation. The founder had already handed over the "miserable stipend."

"Come on, let's move it," she said as she grabbed the boy, who looked terrified.

"Do you want to come with me?"

"*Shit on ya,*" Pituso replied zestily, laughing at his own wit.

The three women laughed heartily too at such a refined utterance, and Izquierdo, scratching his noble forehead, said:

"The lady . . . I guess now she'll teach 'im not to use bad langigge."

"He needs it all right . . . Well, let's go."

Juanín resisted at first, but finally let himself be led away, seduced by the promise that they would buy him a Nativity scene and lots of good things he could eat his fill of.

"I've already promised Sr. Izquierdo," said Guillermina, "that we'll find him a position, and in the meantime I've given him my card to show to one of the most famous artists in Madrid who's painting a magnificent Saint Dimas now. Well . . . God be with you."

The future model bid them farewell with all the urbanity he could muster, and they left. Rafaela carried the boy in her arms. As the days are so short toward the end of December, by the time they left the house night was falling. The cold was intense, penetrating, and treacherous; the sky, burnished and terribly bare; its few stars were so forlorn that their twinkling looked more like shivering. On Bastero Street Pituso rebelled. The frown on his beautiful forehead seemed to say: "Where are these women taking me?" He began to scratch his head, calling for his "*Papá Pepe* . . ."

"What do you care about your Papá Pepe? Do you want a rebec? Tell me what you want."

"Want 'livs,"* he replied, pouting more. "No, not 'livs. A fish."

"A fish? . . . All right," said his future mamá, who was extremely nervous and could feel those glacial vibrations of the stars in her own soul.

On Toledo Street the weary organs started up again, and there also two of them clawed at each other, one doing a light tune from the *Mascota* and the other a symphonic theme from *Semiramis*. They cranked away furiously, about thirty steps apart, tearing out hair, biting and collapsing together in the cacophony of their sounds. Finally *Semiramis* won, resounding proudly and emphasizing its noble accents while the notes of its rival extinguished, whimpering more and more faintly until they were lost in the tumult of the street.

It was hard for the three women to walk rapidly because of the crowd hurrying along in the opposite direction, almost home and anxious to get there. The workers carried small sacks, their week's wages; the women, some scrap or other they'd just bought. The boys, scarves wrapped around their necks, lugged rebecs, prehistorically crude Nativity scenes, or drums that were worn thin before they even got them home. The girls were in groups of two or three, heads covered with shawls, each one of them talking more than seven put together. This one carried a bottle of wine; that one a little pitcher of almond milk; others came bounding out of food stores or stopped to look at stalls with tambourines, which they tapped discreetly to hear how they sounded. In the fish stalls, Maragatos cleaned porgy, tossing the scales at passers-by as an errand boy dressed in the typical uniform—baggy black trousers and green-striped apron—cried out at the door: "Alive 'n' kickin'!" An enormous lantern with very clean panes illuminated heaps of flounder, sardines, and mullet. From the butcher shops came the deafening thud of cleavers and the repeated creak of scales going up and down, making a mysterious noise as they hit the marble counter; somehow it sounded like happiness. Some of the shop owners in those neighborhoods show off not only their exquisite products but also their exuberant imagination; to catch people's attention and make them buy they use fantastic theatrical devices. From outside Jacinta could see barrels of olives in pyramids one story high, altars made of marzipan boxes,

---

*Olives.

trophies of raisins, and triumphant arches decked with clusters of dates. High and low there were Spanish flags with poetic inscriptions that read: "A Marzipan Deluge" or "Nougat from Earthly Paradise." Further away were "Mantecadas* from Astorga Blessed by His Holiness Pius IX." At the very door, a couple of salesmen, dressed ridiculously in tails and top hat, their hands dirty and faces sooty, shouted out the virtues of their goods, giving out samples to everyone who went by. A nougat vendor in the street had thought up a unique advertisement to squash his competitors—the proud, established shop owners. What could he say? Saying that his nougat was very good didn't mean a thing. So on his biggest block of almonded stuff, my man had pinned a little banner that said: "Hygienic Nougat." The public could draw their own conclusions . . . The other nougat might be the tastiest and sweetest there was, but it wasn't "hygienic."

"Want a fish," grumbled Pituso, rubbing his eyes ill-humoredly.

"Look," Rafaela said, "your mamá's going to buy you a fish made of sweets."

"*Papa Pepe,*" the boy repeated, crying.

"Do you want a tambourine? Yes, a great big tambourine that makes lots of noise?"

The three women tried to soothe him by offering him everything that could be had. After the drum had been bought, the boy said that he wanted an orange. They bought him oranges, too. Night was falling, and it was getting hard to keep going because the sidewalk was narrow, slippery and damp now, and they kept bumping into people as the crowd thickened.

"Wait till you see the Nativity scene we have for you," Jacinta said to calm him. "It's so pretty! And the children are adorable! And there's a big fish, a huge one, all marzipan so you can eat every bit of it."

"A big one, *big!*"

At times he would calm down, but suddenly he'd have another tantrum and start kicking. Rafaela, who was very feeble, couldn't hold him any longer. Guillermina took him out of her arms, saying:

"Here, give him to me . . . You can hardly stand up yourself. Eh, little gentleman; you're to be quiet, hear?"

Pituso socked her in the head.

"Watch out now, or I'll give it to you. Wait till you see the spanking you're going to get. And the little monster's so *fat!* Who would've thought it!"

"Want a caney . . . damn!"

"A cane? . . . We'll buy you that too, son, if you're quiet. Where can we find a cane, now?"

---

* A type of butter bun, made in the northern city of Astorga, whose inhabitants are called "Maragatos."

"I could really use one," said Guillermina, "and of hardwood, the kind that really stings, to teach him not to be naughty."

In this fashion, they reached the arcades and then Villuendas' house; it was already night. They went in by way of the shop, and in the back room Jacinta, who was exhausted, collapsed on a big sack of coins. Guillermina deposited Pituso on a voluminous bundle that contained . . . a thousand ounces of gold!

4

The employees who were counting the money and preparing the balance sheets put the rolls of gold coins and packets of bank notes, secured with elastic bands, into iron chests. Another, at a table, counted the *pesetas* that had worn thin and then scooped them up like lentils. He handled the "goods" with absolute indifference, as if the sacks contained potatoes and the bundles of bills were scrap paper. It scared Jacinta to see all this; she always entered that room with a certain respect, similar to the kind church inspired in her, because the fear of leaving with a four thousand *real* bill accidentally stuck to her skirt made her nervous.

Ramón Villuendas wasn't in. But Benigna came down instantly, and the first thing she did was to carefully observe the dirty face of the Christmas gift her sister had brought.

"What is it, don't you see the resemblance?" said Jacinta, somewhat piqued.

"As a matter of fact . . . I don't know what to say."

"He's the living image of him," Jacinta asserted, trying with this firm opinion to end any doubts that might arise.

"He could be . . ."

Guillermina prepared to leave, first asking an employee to change three gold coins she had for bills.

"You should reward me for giving you gold," she said. "Three *reales* for every hundred. If you don't, I'll go to the Lonja del Almidón, where they're more charitable."

At this point the owner of the house came in and, examining the coins, said with a smile:

"They're fake . . . they don't ring true."

"You're the one who doesn't ring true," joshed the saint, and the others laughed too. "A reward of a *peseta* for every one of them."

"Raising your price, no less! You cutthroat!"

"Just what you deserve, publicans."

From a nearby pile, Villuendas took two *duros* and added them to the bills he had given her in exchange for the gold.

"Oh, well . . . just so you won't grumble."

"Thank you. I always knew that you . . . "

"Wait a minute, Doña Guillermina, don't leave yet," added Ramón. "Is it true, what they've told me? That when you don't get enough money in subscriptions you hang a brick around San José's neck so he'll see to it that you get some more?"

"San José doesn't need for us to hang anything around his neck, because he always does what we want. Good night. You have the little gentleman now. The first thing you ought to do is put him in to soak so those layers of filth will soften up."

Ramón looked at Pituso. His face didn't express a very profound conviction of the resemblance either. Benigna smiled; if it hadn't been for the consideration she had toward her beloved sister, she would have said the same thing about Pituso that her husband had said about the coins that didn't ring true: "He's a fake." Or at least, "Something's fishy."

"First we should wash him."

"He's not going to let us," said Jacinta. "He's never even seen water. Let's go upstairs."

They took him upstairs and, like it or not, they divested him of the rags he was wearing and brought in a huge tub of water. Jacinta tested it with her finger, saying fearfully, "Do you think it's too cold? Is it too hot? Poor lamb, what a bad time he's going to have!" Benigna didn't worry so much about such things and splash! she ducked him and held down his arms and legs. Lord! Pituso's screams could be heard at the Plaza Mayor. They lathered him and scrubbed him without fussing over him in the slightest, paying as much attention to his screams as they would have to shrieks of joy. Only Jacinta, more piously, stirred up the water, trying to persuade him that it was all a lot of fun. When he was relieved at last from that torture, well wrapped in a bath towel, Jacinta pressed him to her breast and told him that he was really handsome now. Her gentle warmth calmed his irritable screams, turning them into sobs, and the reaction, together with his cleanliness, animated his face, tinging it with that pure dawn pink that infants have when they emerge from the water. They rubbed him dry, and his rounded arms, delicate complexion, and beautiful body inspired one exclamation of admiration after another: "He's a baby Jesus . . . he's divine, this little doll!"

Then they began to dress him. One of them put on his stockings, another put him into an exquisite little shirt. Bothered by being dressed, his bad mood returned, and they brought him a mirror so that he could see himself, to see whether his vanity would make him forget his peevishness.

"Now, supper! Would you like that?"

Pituso opened his enormous mouth and let out some yawns that described the approximate size of his appetite.

"Oh, isn't the child hungry! Just wait. You're going to have some delicious things to eat . . . "

"Potatoes!" he shouted with famished ardor.

"What do you mean, potatoes? Marzipan, almond milk . . . "

"Potatoes, damn!" he repeated, kicking.

"All right, potatoes then; anything you want."

Now he was dressed. Good clothes suited him so well that it looked as if he had worn them all his life. There was no small uproar when the Villuendas children saw him enter the room where their Nativity scene was. First they were collectively surprised; then it seemed as if they were glad to see him; finally feelings of fear and distrust took over. There were five children: two older girls, daughters of Ramón's first wife, and Benigna's three, two of whom were boys.

Juanín was dumbfounded, speechless before the Nativity scene. The first demonstration he gave of his ideas of human liberty and collective property was to reach for the colored candles. One of the little girls took his disrespect so badly and screamed so loudly that it sounded like the Battle of San Quintín starting again.

"Oh, my God!" exclaimed Benigna. "We're going to have trouble with this little savage . . . "

"I'll buy him lots of candles," Jacinta declared. "You want candles, don't you, sweetheart?"

What he mainly wanted was for them to fill his belly, because he started yawning again, deep yawns that moved Jacinta.

"Time for supper, time for supper," said Benigna, calling the entire troop.

And she prodded them all ahead of her like a herd of turkeys. The meal had been prepared for the children only because their parents were having dinner at their Uncle Cayetano's that night.

Jacinta had forgotten about everything else, even about going home, and had no idea of the time it had taken to bathe and dress Pituso. When she realized how late it was, she threw on her cloak and said good-bye to Pituso, kissing him effusively. "You're taking it so seriously, dear!" her sister said, smiling. And she was right to a certain point, because Jacinta was on the verge of tears.

And Barbarita—what had she done on the morning of the 24th? Let's see. The minute she entered San Ginés Church, Estupiñá ran up to her like a hound dog ready to attack and, rubbing his hands, said to her:

"The Galician oysters have come! The salmon gave me a scare—I didn't sleep a wink last night. But it's ours for sure. It's coming in on the train today."

No matter how energetically the great Rossini maintains that he heard Mass devotedly that day, I don't believe it. What's more, it can be said with certainty that not even when the priest raised his hands to the sacramented God was Plácido as edified as on other occasions, nor did his beating on his breast resound as much as usual in his thoracic cavity. His mind wandered off to fickle thoughts of shopping, and the Mass seemed so, so long to him that he would have dared to tell the priest in private to "move it." At last the Señora and her friend departed. Then he tried to make what was really a pleasure for him sound like a painful task accomplished. He stressed everything and exaggerated the difficulties.

"I've got a feeling," he said in the same tone that Bismarck must have used to tell William, the emperor of Prussia, that he didn't trust Russia, "that the turkeys they're selling on the plaza steps haven't been as well fed as we've been led to believe. When I left the house today I weighed them one by one, and frankly, my opinion is that we should buy them from González. His capons are really good . . . I weighed them too. Well, it's up to you."

They spent two hours on Cuchilleros Street picking up and putting down animals, harassed by the vendors, whom Plácido treated like dirt. He claimed that he had such a precise sense of weight that he wasn't off by even an nth of an ounce. After leaving a considerable amount of money there, they went off in another direction. They went to Ranero's place to pick out some rounds of genuine Labrador marzipan. And they still had another hour's worth of shopping.

"What the Señora should've done today," Estupiñá said breathlessly, pretending to be more out of breath than he was, "was bring a list; that way we wouldn't have forgotten anything."

They went home at ten thirty because Barbarita wanted to know how Juan had slept the night before, and it was then that Jacinta revealed the Pituso business to her mother-in-law, who was as surprised as she was unenthusiastic, as has been said. Satisfied with Juan's progress (he was much better that day), Doña Bárbara went back to the streets with her squire and chancellor. She still had a few odds and ends to buy, most of them presents for friends or relatives. The daughter-in-law's words stuck in the lady's mind. What sort of grandchild was he? Because after all, this was serious . . . A son of the Dauphin! Could it be true? Holy Mother of God, what wonderful news! A little grandchild behind the Church's back! Ah, the outcome of that affair a long time ago. She had been afraid of this . . . But suppose it was a figment of Jacinta's imagination and her angelic heart? Oh well, when she went to bed that night, she'd tell Baldomero everything.

More purchases were made during that second morning session, and as they were heading home, both of them loaded with packages, Barbarita stopped at the Santa Cruz Plaza and examined the Nativity scenes with the concentration of a potential buyer. Estupiñá was puzzled; he didn't understand why the Señora was examining the stalls so interestedly, because all the children in the Santa Cruz clan had already been "supplied with that item." Plácido's amazement increased when he saw that after treating one of the prettiest Nativity scenes half seriously, she bought it. Respect sealed his mouth just as it started to open to say, "And who is that one for, Señora?"

Her ancient friend's confusion and curiosity reached a peak when, as they were going upstairs to the house, Barbarita said somewhat mysteriously, "Give me those packages and put this bulky thing under your cloak. Don't let anyone see it when we go in." What was the meaning of these subterfuges? Bring in a crèche as if it were smuggled goods! And being an expert smuggler, Plácido did a remarkably clean job of contrabanding. The Señora took it out of his hands and, carrying it into her bedroom with minute precautions so that no one would lay eyes on it, she hid it on the highest shelf of her mirror-doored wardrobe, covering it carefully with a scarf.

For the rest of the day the illustrious lady was very busy, and Estupiñá was kept coming and going because just when they thought they had everything, they realized that they'd forgotten the most important thing of all. When night came, Jacinta's delay disturbed Barbarita, and when she saw her come in exhausted, her dress wet and looking a sight, she went in with her while she changed and said severely:

"Have you gone crazy? . . . What a thing to come up with . . . bringing me grandchildren . . . This afternoon I had it on the tip of my tongue to tell Baldomero about your escapade, but I didn't dare . . . So you can imagine how serious I think it is . . . "

It was cruel to speak this way; my friend Doña Bárbara should have remembered that they matched each other, purchase for purchase, obsession for obsession. And the sharp reproofs didn't end here. Immediately afterward she made the following observation, which chilled poor Jacinta to the bone:

"All right, let's suppose I grant you that this creature is my grandchild. Fine. But hasn't it occurred to you that his nuisance of a mother might claim him and get us involved in a suit that could ruin us?"

"How can she claim him if she abandoned him?" replied Jacinta, her face flushed, trying to feign an immense scorn for difficulties.

"Oh, you can be sure of that . . . You're hopelessly naive."

"Well, if she claims him, I won't give him back," declared Jacinta with such resolve that it bordered on savageness. "I'll say that he's my son, that I gave birth to him, and let them prove otherwise . . . Let's see how they can prove it."

Exalted and beside herself, Jacinta, who was dressing as fast as she could, dropped her clothes and beat on her breast and stomach. Barbarita tried to be serious, but could not.

"No, you're the one who has to prove what you've given birth to . . . But don't think wild things, and relax now; we'll talk about it tomorrow."

"Oh, Mamá!" said the daughter-in-law, becoming tender. "If only you could see him! . . ."

Barbarita, who already had her hand on the doorknob to leave, turned back to her daughter-in-law to say:

"But is there a resemblance? . . . Are you sure he looks like him?"

"Do you want to see him, yes or no?"

"All right, child, I'll have a look. It's not that I think . . . I need proof, very clear proof. I don't trust a resemblance that may be an illusion, and until Juan clears up my doubts, I'll keep thinking that where your Pituso should go is to the orphanage."

5

What an excellent and happy dinner there was that evening in the home of the affluent Santa Cruz family! It wasn't really dinner,* but a late main meal, because the family didn't like to stay up late and therefore fell under the jurisdiction of the most rigorous abstention. The turkey and capon were for the next few days; everything served that evening belonged to the kingdom of Neptune. Meat was served only to Juan, who was better now and could come to the table. It was a banquet fit for a king with its overabundance of fish, shellfish, and everything else that comes from the sea, all of it so delicately prepared and well presented that it was truly glorious.

There were twenty-five people at the table and, I might add, the guests offered a perfect sampling of all social classes. The climbing plant described earlier had brought together its most diverse stems. From the financial aristocracy there was the marquis of Casa-Muñoz; from the old aristrocracy there was an Alvarez de Toledo, brother of the duke of Gravelinas and married to a Trujillo. Somehow the conjunction of the two noblemen had an ironic harmony, for one of them was a descendant of the great duke of Alba and the other was a successor of Don Pascual Muñoz, the respectable hardware dealer on Tintoreros Street. On the other hand, there was Samaniego, who was practically a clerk, sitting very near to Ruiz-Ochoa; that is, to higher banking circles. Villalonga represented parliament; Aparisi, the municipal council; Joaquín Pez, the bar; and Federico Ruiz represented many things simultaneously: the press, literature, philosophy, music criticism, the firemen, welfare societies, archaeology, and chemical fertilizers.

And as for Estupiñá in his new frock coat of good wool—what did he represent? Business as it was years ago, no doubt; the traditions on Postas Street,

---

* Dinner is usually a late, light meal in Spain.

contraband, and perhaps "the faith of our forefathers" because he was so sincerely pious. Don Manuel Moreno-Isla wasn't present on that occasion, but Tubs Arnáiz was, and Gumersindo Arnáiz too, with his three daughters, Barbarita II, Andrea, and Isabel. But Jacinta eclipsed her three sisters that night; she looked beautiful in a very simple dress with black and white stripes on a red background. Barbarita was a fine sight too. From his seat at the end of the table, Estupiñá darted looks at her whenever compliments traveled from mouth to mouth on those absolutely sumptuous dishes and the unheard-of variety of fish. When the great Rossini wasn't looking at his idol, he talked uninterruptedly to people sitting near him, restlessly turning his parrotlike profile from side to side.

Nothing worth reporting occurred during dinner. It was a session of unclouded happiness and unfaltering appetites. The mischievous Dauphin urged Aparisi and Ruiz to drink to make them tipsy, because wine made them both very amusing; finally, with champagne, he got what he hadn't been able to get out of them with sherry. Whenever he got tipsy, Aparisi displayed an exalted enthusiasm for national glories. His binges always brought on floods of patriotic tears; he wept over everything he said. He toasted to "the heroes of Trafalgar,"* to "the heroes of Callao,"† and many other naval heroes. And all this moved him so and made his olfactory muscles contract so much that you would have thought that the two greatest sea heroes of all, Churruca and Méndez Núñez,‡ were his parents and that they smelled awful.

Ruiz went in for heroes and patriotism too, but he was inclined to stick to terrestrial heroes and speak in a rather savage tone. He brought in Tetuán and Zaragoza, tearing all foreigners to shreds, saying, in sum, that "our future lies in Africa" and that "the Strait is a Spanish ditch." Suddenly, the great Estupiñá rose, glass in hand. Words cannot describe the expectant air and solemn silence that preceded his brief speech. Moved almost to tears, even though he wasn't tipsy, he toasted the noble group, the noble ladies and gentlemen of the house, and—here there was an emotional pause and a fond look directed at Jacinta—the noble family's having a successor soon, as he hoped, and suspected, and believed, they would.

Jacinta blushed deeply and everyone present, including the Dauphin, greatly celebrated Estupiñá's felicitous remarks. Then they adjourned to the living room, where they had a great *tertulia*. Shortly after midnight, they had all retired. Jacinta slept restlessly, and the next morning, when her husband was still asleep, she left for Mass at San Ginés. Then she went to Benigna's house, where she found scenes of desolation. All of her little nieces and nephews were upset beyond consolation, and the moment they saw her they ran up to her demanding justice.

---

*The English defeated the Spanish fleet in the Battle of Trafalgar, 1805.
†The storming of Callao, Perú, in 1866, by the Spaniards.
‡Churruca died in Trafalgar, and Méndez Núñez led the Callao expedition.

Look what Juanín had done to them! . . . Look how "careful" he'd been with their things! He had begun by breaking off the heads of their Nativity figurines, and the worst part was that he had laughed while he was doing it, as if it were funny. Humph, some joke! He was a brat, a meanie, a murderer. Isabel, Paquito, and the others all testified this in confused, incoherent words; their indignation was so great they couldn't express themselves clearly. They all fought to get the floor and tugged at their auntie, standing on tiptoe. And where *was* the rascal? Jacinta saw his sly, intelligent face appear. When he saw her, he looked somewhat perturbed and he sidled up to the wall. Jacinta approached him gravely, suppressing her urge to laugh. She asked him to account for his horrid crimes. Breaking off the figurines' heads! Pituso hid his face, terribly ashamed, and put his finger in his nose. His adopted mother was not succeeding in getting an answer from him, and the accusations were verging on frenzy. The most execrable crimes were flung in his face, and they ridiculed him and his disgusting habits.

"You know what, Auntie?" Ramona said laughing. "He eats orange peels."

"Pig!"

Another childish voice testified with greater solemnity that it knew more. That morning, Juanín had been in the kitchen chewing on potato peels; that was *really* disgusting.

To the great stupefaction of the other children, Jacinta kissed the delinquent.

"Well, your apron's in a fine state." Juanín's apron looked as if it had been used to scrub floors. All his clothes were just as dirty.

"Auntie," said Isabelita, pretending to be offended. "If you could've seen him! All he does is drag himself around and kick like a donkey. He gets into the garbage and he grabs fistfuls of ashes to throw in our faces . . . "

Benigna came in from Mass and corroborated all the denunciations, although in an indulgent tone.

"Dear, I've never seen such a savage! Poor little thing. You can tell what sort of people he's grown up among."

"All the better. We'll simply tame him."

"And his language! Ramón hurts from laughing. You have no idea how his muleteer's tongue amuses him. Last night he gave us a bad time because he kept asking for his Pa Pepe and being homesick for that hole he's lived in. Poor little thing! This morning he urinated in the living room. I came in and found him with his skirts up. Thank goodness he didn't feel like doing it on my pouf! . . . He did it in the coke bin. I've had to close off the living room because he was ruining everything. Have you seen what he did to the Nativity? Ramón thought it was very funny . . . and he went out to buy more figurines, because if he hadn't, we wouldn't have been able to stand this racket. You have no idea what it was like last night. All of them crying at once, and him grabbing the figurines and smashing them on the floor."

"Poor little thing!" exclaimed Jacinta, lavishing caresses on her adopted son and also the others to avoid an outbreak of jealousy. "Can't you see that he's been brought up differently? He'll learn good manners. Won't you, my little son?" Juan nodded that he would and examined one of Jacinta's earrings. "Yes, but don't tear off my ear. You must all be good friends and be like brothers and sisters. Isn't it true, Juan, that you won't break any more figurines? Right? He's a good boy. Ramoncita, you're the oldest; teach him, instead of scolding him."

"He's so fresh. He wanted to eat a candle too," said Ramoncita implacably.

"Candles are not to be eaten, no. They're to be lighted. You'll see how fast he learns everything. Don't think he isn't smart."

"There's no way to make him eat unless we let him use his hands," Benigna commented laughingly.

"But dear, how do you expect him to know? He's never seen a fork in his life. But he'll learn . . . Can't you see how clever he is?"

Villuendas came in with the figurines.

"Well, well, let's see if these escape the guillotine."

Pituso looked at them with a malicious smile, and the rest of the children appropriated them, taking all sorts of precautions to keep them out of the destructive hands of the savage, who clung to his adopted mother's side. Instinct, as strong and precocious in young human creatures as it is in young animals, told him to cling to Jacinta and never leave her side while she was in the house. He was like a puppy who quickly distinguishes his master in a group and stays close to him, looking up and rubbing against him.

Jacinta felt like a mother, and experiencing that ineffable pleasure inside her, was inclined to love the poor child with all her heart. It's true that he was another woman's child. But this thought, which interposed itself between her happiness and Juanín, was gradually losing its force. What did she care if he was another woman's child? She had perhaps died, and if she was alive, it was all the same, because she had abandoned him. It was enough for Jacinta that he be her husband's son for her to love him blindly. Didn't Benigna love the children of her husband's first wife as if they were her own? Well, she'd love Juanín as if she herself had carried him in her womb. And that was it. Forget everything, and none of this retrospective jealousy. Stirred by her affection, the lady began to entertain a rather daring scheme in her mind. "With Guillermina's help," she thought, "I'll give them the story that I got this child from the orphanage so they won't ever be able to take him away from me. She'll fix it and make up a document that's as legal as it has to be . . . We'll be forgers and God will bless our fraud."

She kissed him effusively, instructing him to be good and not to do anything disgusting. Juanín had hardly been put on the floor when he grabbed Villuendas' cane and made a beeline for the Nativity with an alarming expression on his face.

Villuendas laughed without stopping him and cried, "Hey! . . . Help! Police!"

Unanimous screaming and desolation filled the house. Ramoncita, in all seriousness, said that they should call in the Guardia Civil.

"Come *here*, you little rascal; that's not done!" shouted Jacinta, rushing over to restrain him.

One thing pleased the young woman very much. Juanín would not obey anyone except her. But he only half-obeyed, looking at her maliciously and suspending his attack.

"He already knows me," she thought. "He already knows that I'm his mother, that I really will be the one. I'll bring him up as he ought to be brought up, in time."

The oddest part was that when she said good-bye, Pituso wanted to go with her. "I'll be back, dear, I'll be back. You see how he loves me? See? . . . So behave properly, all of you, and don't fight. I don't love anyone who's bad."

6

Barbarita wasn't fit for anything until she satisfied her curiosity by seeing the jewel that her daughter had bought her: a grandson. Whether he was apocryphal or genuine, the lady wanted to meet and examine him, so as soon as Juan had company, she and her daughter-in-law found an excuse to leave, and they headed for Benigna's. On the way, Jacinta explored Barbarita's state of mind, but to her great sorrow she found that her mother-in-law was just as severe and suspicious as she'd been the day before. "Baldomero doesn't like the looks of this one bit. He says we need guarantees. And frankly, I think you've been very rash."

When she entered the house and saw Pituso, her severity, far from diminishing, seemed to increase. Without a word to her so-called grandson, Barbarita contemplated him and then looked at her daughter-in-law, who was on pins and needles and had an awful lump in her throat. But all of a sudden, just as Jacinta was bracing herself for a categorical denial, the grandmother uttered a cry of joy, saying:

"My dear little boy, my love! Come here, come to grandmother."

And she squeezed him so energetically that Pituso could hardly help but protest with a scream.

"My child! Sweet little baby . . . Isn't he handsome! You adorable little dear, give grandmother a kiss."

"Does he look like him?" asked Jacinta, barely able to speak because she was, as the vulgar expression goes, drooling with pleasure.

"Does he look like him!" remarked Barbarita, devouring him with her eyes.

"He's the living image of him, child. How can there be any doubt? It's like seeing Juan when he was four."

Jacinta started to cry.

"And as for that woman," added the lady, examining the boy's features more closely, "this mirror certainly indicates that she's attractive . . . This child is perfection."

And she embraced and kissed him again.

"So come on, dear," she added resolutely, "let's take him home."

It was all Jacinta could have wished for. But Barbarita immediately checked her own spontaneity, saying:

"No, we mustn't rush into this. Your husband has to be told first. Be sure to tell him tonight, and I'll take charge of sounding out Baldomero. He's the living image, I tell you!"

"And to think you doubted it!"

"What do you expect? I had to doubt it; these things are very delicate. But the whole business was in my mind. Would you believe that I dreamt about this little doll? Yesterday, without realizing what I was doing, I bought a Nativity scene. I bought it automatically, for some inexplicable reason. I guess my bad habit of buying got worse from my constantly thinking about him."

"I was sure that when you saw him . . . "

"My goodness! And the stores are closed today!" exclaimed Barbarita in consternation. "If they were open, I'd leave this minute to buy him a sailor suit with a cap saying 'Numantia.' It'd look so cute on him! Come here, sweetheart . . . Don't run away; I love you. I'm your grandmother! These sillies say that you broke the black king's camel. It's all in pieces, darling, all broken. But I'll buy my little boy dozens of camels and black kings and white kings and kings in every color."

Jacinta was already jealous, but she was consoled by seeing that Juanín didn't want to stay in his grandmother's lap and slipped out of her arms to return to his real mother. At this point, more accusations and reports were given on various barbarous acts committed by Juanín. The five prosecuters clustered around the two ladies, each one of them formulating his or her complaint in the most defamatory terms possible. The things he had done! He had taken one of Isabelita's boots and thrown it into a sink of water so it would swim like a duck. "Oh, how cute!" cried Barbarita, smothering him in kisses. Then he had taken off his own shoes, because he was a pig who liked to put his paws on everything and run wild all over the house. "Oh, how cute!" He took off his stockings too, and ran after the cat and pulled its tail and rolled it over and over . . . That's why the poor creature was in such a bad mood. Then he climbed up on the dining room table to hit the lamp with a stick. "Oh, how cute!"

"It certainly is a shame," repeated Señora Santa Cruz, heaving a deep sigh, "that the stores are closed today! Because we *must* buy him clothes, lots of clothes. At Sobrino's there are stockings in different colors and little knitted suits that are adorable. Come to granny, lamb. Ah! The sly little thing already knows what you've done for him, and he doesn't want to be with anyone except you."

"That's right," Jacinta said proudly. "But no; he's a good boy, isn't he? And he loves his granny too, doesn't he?"

When they left and were in the street, one was as giddy as the other. It was agreed: that very night, each would speak to her respective husband.

That day, which was the 25th, there was a great feast; Juanito left the table and retired early, saying that he was very tired and had a headache. His wife didn't dare broach the subject, and kept it for the next day. She had the whole speech so well prepared that she felt confident of delivering it in its entirety without stumbling over anything or getting upset. On the morning of the 26th, Don Baldomero entered his son's room when the latter had just gotten up, and they shut themselves up in there for half an hour. In the study, the two ladies impatiently awaited the results of the conference. There was nothing encouraging in Barbarita's words. "Baldomero doesn't seem very promising, dear. He says it has to be proven, just as I feared, and that the resemblance is probably only a delusion. We'll see what Juan says."

Both of them were so anxious that they went over to the bedroom door to see if they could catch a few syllables of what father and son were saying. But nothing could be heard. The conversation was calm, and at times it sounded as if Juan were laughing. But the ladies were destined to be imprisoned by that cruel doubt for longer than they wished. It seemed as if the devil himself had a hand in it, because just as Don Baldomero was leaving his son's room, Villalonga and Federico Ruiz appeared in the study. The former descended on Santa Cruz to tell him about the loans he'd given the Treasury from his own and others' money, earning a hundred percent on them in a few months; and Ruiz charged into the Dauphin's room. Jacinta didn't have a chance to speak with Juan; she was greatly surprised by his cheerful mood and by the malicious, somewhat mocking look that he gave her.

They all went to lunch and the mystery continued. Jacinta says that she had never in her life felt such a strong urge to knock someone down and crush him. She felt like ripping Federico Ruiz to shreds, because that insubstantial, dizzying chatter of his, like a bee buzzing around, kept interposing itself between her husband and herself. The blasted man had an obsession with castles at the time; he was making inquiries about all the relatively ruined castles in Spain in order to write a great heraldic, archaeological work, a sentimental catalog that, although well done, would be of no use whatsoever. He made people's heads spin with his emotional displays over whether certain ruins were Byzantine, Muhammadan, or Lombardic with Mozarabic influence and Romanesque lines. "Ah, the Coca castle! And how about the Turégano one in Segovia? But none could hold a candle to the Bierzo castles. Ah, el Bierzo! The treasures in that region were astonishing!" It turned out that the so-called treasures consisted of caved-in walls, rotted eaves, and bastions that were crumbling stone by stone. Then he looked up in ecstasy, clasped his hands devoutly, and scrunched his shoulders up to his ears, saying: "There's a window in the castle at Ponferrada that . . . well . . .I simply couldn't begin to describe it to you." You would have thought that the Eternal Father and the entire celestial court were visible from that window. "Confound the window," thought Jacinta, whose lunch wasn't settling well. "I'd *really* like that window if I could throw you and all your blasted castles out of it."

Villalonga and Don Baldomero did not pay the slightest attention to their insufferable friend's enthusiasm and busied themselves with more substantial matters.

"Just imagine . . . the director of the Treasury accepts a loan in consolidated stock, that's at 13 . . . and makes out a promissory note for the *full* nominal value—100—with 12 percent interest. So you can draw your own conclusions."

"It's scandalous . . . Poor country!"

Juanito and his wife found themselves alone for a few minutes and able to exchange a few words. Jacinta wanted to ask him a question, but he jumped the gun on her, leaving her petrified with this terribly cruel statement, which he pronounced in an affectionate tone: "Come here, baby . . . So we have kids, do we?"

Further explanation was not possible, because the *tertulia* got going and other friends arrived, laughing and joking, pulling Federico Ruiz's leg about his castles and asking him seriously if he had studied every one of them without overlooking a single one. Then the conversation turned back to politics. Jacinta despaired, and whenever she could, she exchanged a few words with her mother-in-law, who said very disconsolately: "This is bad business, child, bad business."

That evening, guests came for dinner. Then there was conversation, and more visitors arrived. The martyrdom lasted until midnight. They finally left, one by one. Jacinta could have thrown them out—opened every window and brushed them out with a napkin, like flies. When she and her husband were left alone, the house seemed like paradise; but her anxiety was so great that she could not savor their sweet isolation. Alone in their bedroom! At last . . .

Juan grabbed his wife as if she were a doll and said to her:

"Darling, your feelings are angelic, but your mind's up in the clouds; it lets itself be deluded. They've deceived you; they've put a big one over on you."

"For God's sake, don't say that," murmured Jacinta after a pause in which she wanted to speak but could not.

"If you'd told me at the beginning . . . ," added the Dauphin very affectionately. "But no, you went ahead, and here's the result of your subterfuge. Oh, women! They all go around with a novel in their heads and when what they imagine doesn't turn out to be true in real life—which is usually the case—they take out their little compositions . . . "

The poor woman was so upset that she didn't know what to say. "That José Izquierdo—"

"—Is a scoundrel. He's cheated you in the worst way. Only you, being innocence itself, could fall into such a poorly made trap . . . What shocks me is that Izquierdo could have had an idea like this. He's such a dumb brute that a scheme like this couldn't have entered his head. He's such a blockhead that he seems honest without being honest. No, he wasn't the one who thought up this charming little hoax. Either I'm wrong or this is the product of a novelist who lives on beans."

"Poor Ido, he's incapable—"

"—Of cheating someone on purpose, yes, that's true. But don't doubt it for a second. The original notion that this child was my son must have been his. It probably came to him as a hunch, some sort of artistic-flatulent inspiration, and the other guy probably said to himself: 'Hmm . . . I could get something out of this.' Plato couldn't have thought this thing up all by himself. I'm sure of that."

Annihilated, Jacinta tried to defend her argument at all costs.

"Juanín is your son. Don't deny it," she replied, crying.

"I swear to you, he's not. How do you want me to swear it to you? . . . Oh, good God! It just occurred to me that the poor child belongs to Izquierdo's stepdaughter. Poor Nicolasa! She died in childbirth. She was a fine girl. Her son is the same age, with three months' difference, as mine would be if he were alive."

"If he were alive!"

"If he were alive . . . yes . . . So you see, I'm making things plain. This means that he's not alive."

"You never mentioned this to me," Jacinta declared sternly. "The last thing you told me was . . . I don't know. I don't like to remember these things. But they cross my mind anyway. 'I never saw her again; I never heard a word from her; I tried to help her but I couldn't find her.' Wasn't that what you told me?"

"Yes, and it was the truth, the absolute truth. But later on, there was another episode, one that I never mentioned to you because there was no reason to. When it happened, you and I had already been married a year; we were living in peace and harmony . . . There are certain things that a husband shouldn't tell his wife. No matter how discreet and prudent a woman is—and you're very discreet—she still makes a fuss in these cases. She doesn't take circumstances into account; she doesn't consider the motives behind the acts. So I was silent then, and I firmly believe that I was right to be silent about it. What happened doesn't reflect badly on me. I could have told you about it. But what if you had misinterpreted it? Now, the occasion to tell you has come of its own accord, and we'll see what you think. What I *can* assure you is that there was nothing after that. What I'm about to tell you is the last paragraph of something I've been telling you like a serial story. This will be the end. A closed case . . . But it's late, dear. Let's go to bed now and sleep, and tomorrow . . ."

7

"No, no!" cried Jacinta, more angrily than impatiently. "Right now. Do you think I can sleep when I'm this anxious?"

"Well, as for me, sweetheart, I'm going to bed," said the Dauphin, preparing to do so. "If you think I'm going to tell you something that's going to make your hair stand on end . . . and yet it isn't anything, really. I'm going to tell you the story because it's proof that they cheated you. I see that you're putting on a very sad face. Well, if it weren't for the fact that it is a pretty sad incident, I'd say that you'd laugh. You'll be so convinced! And don't worry about your blunder, dear. That's what happens when people are too good. Since angels are used to flying, they can hardly take a step on earth without stumbling."

Jacinta had grown so used to the idea of making Juanín hers, of bringing him up and teaching him manners as if he were her own son, that it hurt to feel him torn from her by a proof, a plot that involved the abhorred woman whose name she wanted to forget. The strangest part was that she still loved Pituso, and her affection and self-pride rebelled against the thought of throwing him out into the street. She would not abandon him now, even if her husband, her mother-in-law, and the whole world laughed at her and considered her crazy and ridiculous.

"And now," continued Santa Cruz, snuggled under his covers, "say good-bye to your novel, that great invention of two wits: Ido del Sagrario and José Izquierdo. And picking up where we left off . . . The last thing I told you was—"

"—Was that she had left Madrid and that you couldn't find out where she had gone. You told me this in Seville—"

"What a memory! Well, time went by, and after we'd been married a year, suddenly one day, bam! You come into the study and give me a letter."

"Me?"

"Yes, a note that was addressed to me. I open it, and it leaves me in a bit of a daze. You ask me what it is and I say: 'Nothing, it's poor old Valledor's mother asking me for a recommendation to the mayor.' I grab my hat and leave."

"She was coming back to Madrid—looking for you, writing you," observed Jacinta, seated on the edge of the bed, her eyes steady, her voice lowered.

"That is, she had someone else write me, because the poor thing doesn't know how . . . 'Well, all I can do is go to her.' You can believe that your poor husband went very much against his will. You can't imagine how irritated I was by that resurrection of a thing I thought was dead and gone forever. 'What's she after this time? Why had she gotten in touch with me?' And I also said to myself: 'She's had a baby, for sure.' It really bothered me. 'But, oh well, what can I do?' I thought as I climbed those dark stairs. It was a house on Hortaleza Street, apparently a boarding house. On the ground floor there's a coffin maker. And what did I find? That the poor woman had come to Madrid with her son . . . with mine—why not come out and say it?—and with a man who was very badly off, which wasn't surprising. The poor child had arrived and gotten sick all at once. The poor woman was in a terrible spot. Whom to go to for help? It was natural: to me. I told her, 'You were perfectly right . . .' The saddest part is that the croup had come on so suddenly that by the time I got there—and this will make you very sad, as it did me—well, by the time I got there, the poor child was dying. And I told her, when I saw her there in a pool of tears: 'Why didn't you tell me sooner?' Because naturally I would have brought in a couple of good doctors, and who knows? We might have been able to save him."

Jacinta was silent. Terror kept her from articulating a single word.

"And you didn't cry?" was the first thing she thought to say.

"I assure you, I spent a . . . oh, what a time it was for me! And having to hide it from you at home! You were going to the Royal Opera that night. I went too; but I swear that I've never in my whole life felt such sorrow in my heart as I did that night. You wouldn't remember . . . You didn't know a thing about it."

"And?"

"Nothing else. I bought him the prettiest blue coffin there was in the shop downstairs and he was taken to the cemetery in a deluxe hearse drawn by two plumed horses. No one was at the cemetery, except Fortunata's lover and the boarding house owner's husband or whatever he was. On the Red de San Luis— imagine, what a coincidence—I met Mamá. She said to me, 'You look so pale!' 'It's because I've just come from Moreno Vallejo's house, and they cut off his leg today.' As a matter of fact, they had cut off his leg, due to a fall from a horse. And as I was telling this to Mamá, I saw the hearse with the little blue coffin disappear down Montero Street . . . That's the way life is. Let's see, now, if I'd told you this, wouldn't it have brought on all sorts of quarrels and jealousy and unpleasantness?"

"Perhaps not," said his wife, heaving a deep sigh. "It would depend on what followed. What happened next?"

"Everything else is dull. Once the little creature was in the ground, my only desire was to see the mother off. You can believe me when I say that she didn't interest me in the slightest. The only thing I felt was compassion for her misfortunes. It wasn't exactly fun to live with that brute—a gross character who mistreated her terribly; he didn't give her a moment's peace. Poor woman! I said to her while he was at the cemetery: 'How can you live with that beast and put up with him?' And she answered: 'I have nowhere to go. I have to live with that animal. I can't stand him; but my gratitude . . .' It's a sad thing to live like that—hating and being grateful.

"So you see how much unhappiness and misery there is in this world, my dear. Well, to go on. That wretched couple gave me a pain in the neck. He was one of those peddlers that put up stalls at fairs and he had taken it into his head to be an accountant in a municipal treasury in a town. What a beast! He harassed me with his demands and even with threats, and I caught on soon enough: what he wanted was to get money out of me. Poor Fortunata, not a peep out of her. The beast wouldn't allow her to see me unless he was present, and when he was around, she hardly ever raised her eyes from the floor, she was so terrified of him. One night, the boarding house owner told me that the brute had tried to kill her. You know why? Because she had looked at me. That's what he said . . . Believe me, as this is night, Fortunata didn't arouse anything in me but pity. She had deteriorated a lot physically, and she hadn't gained anything spiritually. She was skinny, dirty, wearing smelly rags; poverty and the dog's life she led—and being around that beast—had robbed her of most of her charm. After three days the brute's demands were unbearable and I agreed to everything. I had no choice but to say, 'A silver bridge for my enemy's departure'; as long as they left, I didn't care how they sponged off me. I was soft about the amount, but on the condition that they leave immediately. And then it was peaceful and glorious again. And that's the end of my story, my dear child, because I haven't heard another word from that respectable couple since, which fills me with pleasure."

Jacinta's eyes were fixed on the pattern on the bedspread. Her husband took her hand and squeezed it hard. All she did was say, "Poor Pituso, poor Juanín!" Suddenly, an idea slashed her mind like a whiplash and shook her out of her discouragement. It was a final conviction, flapping furiously in the agony of defeat. There is nothing that resigns itself to dying, and error is perhaps that which defends itself from death most fiercely. When error sees itself threatened by the ridicule that is commonly called "making a blunder," it makes disproportionate efforts, stimulated by self-pride, to prolong its existence. So from the ruins of her wrecked illusions, Jacinta scavenged for one more sword, and she wielded it vigorously, perhaps because she had no other. "All that you've said is probably true; I don't doubt it. But all I have to say is: what about the resemblance?"

Hearing this and bursting into laughter were one and the same for the Dauphin.

"The resemblance! There is no such resemblance; there can't be. It's all in your mind. Kids that age look like anyone you want them to look like. Observe him closely now; examine his features impartially; I mean, be consciously impartial, you know? And if you still detect a resemblance after that, there's witchcraft in this."

Jacinta contemplated him with her mind's eye, as impartially as he had recommended, and . . . in truth . . . the resemblance remained, although it was a wee bit blurry and was gradually disappearing. In despair at her inevitable defeat, the lady dug up yet another argument:

"Your mother saw a strong resemblance too."

"Because you set her up. You and Mamá are a couple of lovely, beguiled ladies. I admit that we need a baby in this house. I want one as much as you two do. But this, my dear, is not something you can go shopping for; nor should Estupiñá smuggle it in under his cloak like boxes of cigars. Look, silly: you've got to realize that the resemblance is merely an exaltation of that confounded novel of yours about finding a lost son. And you can be sure of one thing: that story—which is utterly false—is also a bad novel. If you're not convinced, think back on the people who helped you with it: Ido del Sagrario, who's got a bad case of verborrhea; José Izquierdo, a crank, and as stupid as a mule; Guillermina, a loony saint, and in the last analysis, a nut. Then there's Mamá; when she sees you daffy, she gets daffy too. Her kindness dulls her good sense, just as yours does; you're both so good that sometimes, believe me, you ought to be tied down. No, no, don't laugh. With people who are so, so good, there comes a time when there's no choice but to tie them down."

Jacinta smiled sadly and her husband caressed her over and over, trying to soothe her. He begged her so insistently to go to bed that she finally agreed.

"Tomorrow," she said, "you'll come with me to see him."

"Who, Nicolasa's kid? Me?"

"Even if it's only out of curiosity. Think of him as a purchase that your obsessive wife and mother made. If we had bought a puppy, wouldn't you want to see it?"

"All right. I'll go. If Mamá lets me go out tomorrow. And it would do me good, because this confinement is getting on my nerves."

Jacinta went to bed, and a little while later she noticed that her husband was sound asleep. She wasn't very sleepy and mused on what she had just heard. What a sad picture, and what a vision of human misery! She also thought a lot about Pituso. "I think I may love him more now. Poor little thing—so adorable, so cute, and not looking like Juan! But I'm still sure that he does. A delusion, ha! How could it be a delusion? Don't try to pull anything over on me. Those little wrinkles in his nose when he laughs . . . that place between his eyebrows . . ." and she went on like this until very late.

On the morning of the 28th, already back from Mass, Barbarita entered the young couple's bedroom to tell them that it was a lovely day and that the patient could get up and go out if he dressed warmly. "Take the hack and go for a ride in the Retiro Park." This was exactly what Jacinta and the Dauphin wanted. Except that instead of going to the Retiro, they presented themselves at Ramón Villuendas' house. He was in the office downstairs, but when he saw them come in, he took them upstairs because he wanted to witness the recognition scene, which he hoped would contain pathos and drama. Benigna and he were quite taken aback when they saw the calm indifference with which Juan regarded the little creature, not showing the slightest sign of fatherly affection.

"Hi, handsome," said Santa Cruz, sitting down and picking up the boy. "Well, he really *is* handsome! Too bad he's not ours. But don't worry, dear. The real Pituso will come along, the legitimate one, the one the stork will bring us . . . You know, the one we'll make."

Benigna and Ramón looked at Jacinta.

"Let's see," continued the husband, setting up a trial. "All of you come here and say impartially, in all fairness and judging freely, whether or not this boy looks like me."

Silence. Benigna broke it to say:

"Actually . . . I . . . never saw any resemblance."

"And you?" Juan asked Ramón.

"I . . . well, I agree with Benigna."

Jacinta could not hide her disturbance.

"You can say what you like, but I . . . It's just that you aren't looking closely. And, anyway, do you deny that he's absolutely adorable?"

"Oh, no; not that . . . Or that he's a mischievous little devil. He has someone to take after on that score. His father was an employee at the gas company first, then a bookie in a gambling joint."

"A 'bookie'! What's that?"

"Oh, it's a great position . . . This child's father, if I'm not mistaken, is probably 'taking a walk in Ceuta'—in the penitentiary, I mean."

"No! That's not so," Jacinta said angrily. "Do you want to insult my child too? Give him to me. Isn't it true, dear, that your father isn't . . . .?"

They all burst out laughing. She consoled herself in her embarrassing situation by kissing him and saying:

"Look how much he loves me. No, I'm not going to abandon him, no; I don't care who orders me to. He's mine."

"Since *you* paid for him."

8

The boy flung his arms around her neck and looked at the others rancorously, as if he were indignant at the infamous mark being made on his lineage. The other children carried him off to play, but not without Jacinta's first fawning over him, which made Benigna say that "she shouldn't take him so seriously."

"Be quiet. I tell you I won't abandon him. I'm taking him home with me."

"Are you crazy?" the Dauphin inquired severely.

"Oh no, I'm perfectly sane."

"Come now, be reasonable. I don't say that we should throw him out either; but if he's well recommended, he shouldn't have a bad time in the orphanage."

"In the orphanage!" exclaimed Jacinta, very red-faced. "Where they'll send him to funerals for people he doesn't even know . . . and he'll have to eat hogwash!"

"But what do you expect? You're so naive. Where did you get the idea that you can simply take over other people's children? What romanticism!"

Benigna and her husband indicated by nodding energetically that the bit about romanticism had been well said.

"After all, I want to protect him too," Juan asserted, appreciating his wife's sentiments and condoning her exaggeration. "He's lucky to have fallen into our hands and be freed of Izquierdo. But let's not confuse the issue. It's one thing to protect him and quite another to take him home with us. Even if I did please you, we'd still need my father's consent. Your good heart makes you forget about reality, isn't that so, Benigna? I've said that people who are very, very good sometimes have to be tied down. She's an angel, and angels make the foolish mistake of thinking that the world is heaven. The world isn't heaven, is it, Ramón? And our actions can't respond to angelic criteria. If everything thought and felt by angels like my wife were put into practice, life would be impossible, absolutely impossible. Our ideas should come from generally accepted ideas, for they make up the moral atmosphere in which we live. I know very well that we should aspire to perfection, but not if it means kicking at the harmony of the world—a fine spot we'd be in then! And the harmony of the world, for your information, is a grandiose mechanism of imperfections that are admirably balanced and combined. Well, let's see; have I convinced you, yes or no?"

"More or less," replied Jacinta, very sad and a bit perplexed by her husband's paradoxes. Jacinta thought so highly of the Dauphin's talent and knowledge that she hardly ever failed to be floored by them, even though she did have stowed away a number of personal opinions that modesty and feminine subordination did not permit her to express. Scarcely ten seconds after her acquiescence they heard loud screams. "What is it, what's the matter?" What could it be, except some outrageous act of Juanín's? Or at least Benigna thought so, running in alarm toward the dining room, the source of the fearsome uproar.

"Hurray for the brave little fellows!" said Santa Cruz as Ramón Villuendas headed back to his office downstairs. Jacinta ran to the dining room and in a few seconds came back terrified.

"Do you know what he's done? There was a platter of rice pudding in the dining room, and Juanín climbed up on a chair and grabbed the pudding in fistfuls . . . more and more till he filled himself up, and then he threw it on the floor and wiped his hands on the curtains."

Benigna's enraged voice could be heard crying out:

"I'm going to kill you, you indecent savage!"

The other children came in screaming. Jacinta scolded them:

"Sillies! Couldn't you see what he was up to? Why didn't you warn us? Or do you just let him get into trouble so you can laugh about it and throw these scenes?"

"Jacinta! Take him away; take this little monster out of my house for good," said Benigna, coming in very agitatedly. "Mother of God, my platter of rice pudding!"

The Villuendas kids jumped up and down gleefully.

"It's your fault, you silly things, because you egg him on," said their auntie, who had to take out her anger on someone.

"You must wash him," stated Benigna, whose rage hadn't let up at all, "you, you. What a mess he's made of my curtains!"

"All right, dear, I'll wash him. Don't worry."

"—And change his clothes. I can't. I've got enough with my own . . . And that's all."

"Oh, come on, don't make such a fuss; it's not that important."

Jacinta and her husband went into the dining room, where they found him in a sorry state. Face, hands, and clothes were covered with that sticky stuff.

"Hurray, hurray for the brave," cried Juan in the beast's presence. "Into the rice pudding! This boy amuses me."

"I'm going to kill you, you rascal," said his adopted mother, kneeling before him and suppressing her laughter. "You've made a fine mess of yourself . . . Wait till you see the scrubbing you're going to get."

While he was being washed, the younger Villuendases clustered around their uncle, climbing onto his knees and hanging from his arms to tell him about the piggish things that Juanín, the little beast, had done. Not only did he eat candles, he licked his plate, an' then . . . he threw his fork on the floor. When their daddy reprimanded him, he stuck out his tongue and said "damn" and other bad words, an' then . . . he did something else too, that was really filthy: he lifted up his dress in back and turned around laughing, to show his little behind.

Santa Cruz couldn't keep a straight face. Jacinta finally came back, holding the delinquent by the hand; he had been washed and was in clean clothes now. Shortly afterward Benigna came in, completely placated, and, facing her brother-in-law, asked him in dead seriousness: "Do you by chance have a duro? I don't have any change." Juan hastened to take out a duro, and just as he put it in Benigna's hand, Jacinta and the children burst out laughing. Then it dawned on him:

"You've put one over on me. I forgot that today was Día de Inocentes.* That was a good one, hmm—very good! I thought it was a bit odd that there was no change in this money-house."

"Here," Benigna said to the children, "your uncle's treating you to sweets."

"There's a good practical joke for you," said Juan laughing, "the one my wife wanted to play on us."

"Not on me," replied Benigna. "We've talked this over pretty well now, and as a matter of fact, he might be genuine; but she couldn't pull the wool over our eyes when it came to his resemblance. So it turns out that the precious little beast is not one of the family. I'm glad, and I'd like to ask you to do me the favor of getting him out of my house. My own give me enough headaches as it is."

Jacinta and her husband begged her, upon leaving, to keep him one more day so that they could decide what to do with him.

Jacinta was to hear some very cruel things that day, but none caused her such astonishment and discouragement as these words that Barbarita whispered into her ear:

"Your joke has annoyed Baldomero. Juan spoke plainly to him. There's no such son, not even a thousand leagues away. The truth is, you rushed into it; and as for the resemblance . . . Frankly, dear, he doesn't look a bit like Juan, not a bit."

That was all Jacinta needed to hear.

"But you . . . for the sake of the Virgin Mary! You, too . . . ," she dared to say, aghast. "But you agreed with me . . ."

"No. Your delusion infected me," replied her mother-in-law, attempting to excuse her error. "Juan says it's an obsession—I call it hopeful illusion—that's as contagious as smallpox. All fixed notions are contagious. That's why I'm so scared of crazy people—scared to be around them. When someone starts to make faces, I start doing the same thing. We imitate one another like monkeys. Well, anyway, you can be sure that the resemblance is only an optical illusion, and both of us— I'll say it in a whisper—we've both made an incredible blunder. And now what can we do? Don't let it enter your head that you'll bring him home. Baldomero wouldn't consent to it, and he's very right. I . . . . if you want to know the truth, I've grown fond of him. Oh, how his savage pranks amuse me! And he's so cute. What eyes! And how about the little wrinkles in his nose, and that little mouth, and those lips? The way he pouts, especially. Come see the Nativity scene I bought for him."

She took Jacinta into her dressing room, and after showing her the scene she said:

"There's more contraband here. Look. This morning I went shopping and . . .

---

* April Fool's Day, on December 28 in Spain.

here, look: colored stockings, a blue knit suit, English style. Look at the cap that says 'Numantia.' It's a whim I had. He'll look divine. I swear that if I don't get to see him with that little sign on his forehead, I'm going to be upset."

Jacinta heard and saw this melancholically.

"If you only knew what he did this morning!" she said, and she told her the rice pudding incident.

"Oh, my goodness, how funny! It's enough to make you want to eat him up. To tell you the truth, I'd bring him home, if it weren't for the fact that Baldomero and Juan don't like this sneaking around. Oh, I really mean it: one can't live without having a little creature around to adore. Dear, it's a terrible shame for us all that *you* haven't given us one."

This sentence drove into Jacinta's heart, where it quivered a while and enlarged the wound, like an arrow that doesn't make a clean cut.

"Yes, this house is very . . . very dull. It needs a child who would shriek and make a racket; who'd get into mischief; who'd make our heads spin. When I tell this to Baldomero, he laughs at me; but anyone can see that he's ready to get down on all fours and put the kids on his back."

"Since Benigna doesn't want him," said the daughter-in-law, "and we can't have him here either, we'll keep him at Candelaria's. I'll give my sister enough every month so that the guest won't be a burden . . . "

"That seems very well thought out—very well indeed. You're like a cat with her new kittens, hiding them here today, there tomorrow."

"What other choice do I have? Because as for the orphanage, he's not going there. Don't even consider it. The things that occur to my husband! Naturally, since he's never been forced to go to funerals through the mud in the rain and the cold, it seems very natural to him that the poor little thing be brought up around coffins. Well, he'll never live to see the day."

"I'll take charge of paying his lodging at Candelaria's house," said Barbarita, whispering to her daughter as if they were a couple of children plotting mischief. "I think I should start by buying him a bed. What do you think?"

She replied that it sounded like a very good idea, and was greatly consoled by this conversation and scheming and imagining of maternal pleasures. But her bad luck intervened that very day or the next, when Don Baldomero clipped her wings by calling her into his study for the following sermon.

"Darling, Bárbara has told me that you're very confused because you don't know what to do about the boy. Don't worry, it'll all be worked out. You needn't fear—we're not going to put him in the street. For the future, don't get carried away by your good impulses and rush into things; everything should be in moderation, dear, even sublime impulses. Juan says—and he's so right—that angelic procedures upset society. If we all concentrated on being perfect, we wouldn't be able to stand each other, and we'd go around with our fists out, hitting people . . . . Well, anyway, as I was saying, the poor child will be under my care; but he won't be brought here, because it wouldn't be fitting, nor will he stay with anyone in the family, because it will seem as if there's some sort of cover up."

Jacinta did not agree with these pronouncements, but the respect that her father-in-law inspired took the wind out of her sails, making it impossible for her to express all the good ideas that had occurred to her.

"Therefore," continued the respectable gentleman, taking his daughter-in-law's hands, "the little gentleman you bought for us will be put in Guillermina's orphanage. No need to frown. He'll be in heaven there. I've already spoken to the saint. I'll support him, and he will be given an education and a suitable upbringing. He'll master a trade, and who knows—maybe he'll even have a profession. It all depends on whether he's gifted. It looks as if my idea doesn't enthuse you. But reflect on it a bit, and you'll see that it's the only solution. He'll be so well cared for there—eating well, dressing warmly . . . Yesterday I gave Guillermina four bolts of Spanish wool to make them jackets. You'll see how handsome she'll make them look. And she fills their bellies, by God! Otherwise, why would they have such plump little faces and be so apple-cheeked? There are many children whose parents spend a lot on clothes and whose mothers run around with their noses in the air who would love theirs to shine and be as well dressed as Guillermina's are."

Jacinta was being persuaded, and she felt less and less inclined to oppose that excellent man's reasoning.

"Here you've got me before you," Santa Cruz added jovially, "someone else who's fond of the little doll. I mean, I didn't escape being infected by the obsession you and Bárbara have with bringing children into the house. When Bárbara told me about it, she was so convinced that he was my grandson that I fell for it too. It's true that I demanded proof . . . But before there was any proof, I went off my rocker too. It must be because I'm old! I spent the whole day making great plans. I tried not to lead Bárbara on, or be swayed by her, and I said to myself: 'Let's keep our head, now, and not start doting till we see . . .' But thinking about it—I'll confess it to you now, in private—I went out laughing to myself, and without realizing what I was doing, I went into the Union Bazaar and—"

His fatherly smile becoming more marked, he opened one of his desk drawers and took out an object wrapped in paper.

"—And I bought him this: it's an accordion. I planned to give it to him when you brought him home. Look at what a lovely instrument it is, and how nice it sounds. For twenty-four *reales*."

Picking up the accordion by its two lids, he began to open it and close it, making it go *whee, whush, whee, whush.* Jacinta laughed, and at the same time a tear rolled out of each eye. Then Barbarita came in unexpectedly, saying:

"What's making that music? Let's see."

"Nothing, dear," the good man declared, accusing himself frankly. "It's just that I got carried away too. I didn't want to say it. When you told me that this grandson business was out of a novel" (*whee, whush*) "I thought I'd throw this music out without anyone seeing it; but since it was bought for him" (*whee, whush*) "he might as well enjoy it. Don't you think so?"

"Let's see, give it to me," said Barbarita, very content and anxious to play the toy instrument. "Ah, you reckless fellow, so that's how you spend your money—on vices. Here, give it to me. Let me play it" (*whee, whush*). "Oh! It has something about it. It's so nice to hear! It seems to make the whole house sound happy."

And she went out playing it in the halls and saying to Jacinta:

"A pretty toy, isn't it? Put on your cloak—we're going to take it to him this minute . . ." *whee, whush.*

xi. The End, Which Turns Out to Be the Beginning

I

WHATEVER THE BOSS SAYS, GOES. The Pituso matter was handled according to Don Baldomero's instructions, and one morning Guillermina herself carried him off to her orphanage, where he remained. Jacinta visited him very often, and her mother-in-law almost always accompanied her. The child was so spoiled that the founder had to step in, severely admonishing her friends and closing the door to them more than once. In the last days of that inauspicious year, Jacinta was attacked by melancholia, and with good reason; the unsuccessful, ridiculous denouement of the "Pitusian novel" would have crushed the heartiest soul.

And there were other things, too, trivialities if you will, but since the spirit forced to bear them was already broken, they seemed heavier than they actually were. From the moment he was well and took to the streets again, Juan stopped being as expansive, mushy, and overnice as he had been during his confinement, and there were no more of those nocturnal scenes in which their familiarity imitated the language of innocence. The Dauphin adopted the serious air and level-headedness that behooved a man of his talent and reputation; but he emphasized the pose so much that he seemed to be trying to erase with sensible conduct the childishness of his catarrhal period. He made a point of always being affable and attentive to his wife, but cold, and sometimes he was even a bit scornful. Jacinta swallowed this bitter pill without a word to anyone. Those former fears began to hound her again, and connecting one thing with another and observing details, she tried to locate the cause of her husband's distraction.

First she thought of the Casa-Muñoz girls' governess, because of certain little things she had happened to see and a few sentences she had overheard in a conversation between Juan and his confidant Villalonga. Then she considered it nonsense and concentrated on a friend of hers (married to Moreno-Vallejo), a novelty shop owner whose fortune was very slim. The lady in question raised eyebrows for spending money ostentatiously. There was obviously a lover involved. Jacinta suspected that the Dauphin was the lover, and she yearned for a word, a tone, any sort of detail that would confirm it. More than once she felt the tickling sensation of that childish rage that would suddenly overtake her, and she would stamp the floor and struggle to keep from pulling his hair and saying: "Cad, scoundrel!" and anything else that usually gets said in a married couple's quarrel.

What tormented her the most was that she loved him even more when he seemed so sensible and played the decorous role of a person who obeys society in order to set an example of moderation and good judgment. Jacinta was never as jealous as when her husband put on those airs of formality, because experience had taught her to know him, and it was perfectly clear to her: when the Dauphin showed off his gift for turning a phrase and bewitched the family with the incense of his paradoxical reasoning, there was undoubtedly "someone in the picture."

Days came when the history of Spain was marked by resonant events, and that happy family, like the rest of us, discussed those events. January 3, 1874! General Pavía's coup d'etat against the republic. Nothing else was talked of (or should I say, there wasn't anything better to talk about). This theatrical switch of institutions and the throwing over of a situation like a ballot box with fake votes appealed to the Spanish temperament. It had been admirably done, according to Don Baldomero, and the army had "once again" saved the unfortunate Spanish nation. Government bonds had dropped to 11, and the Bank of Spain shares to 138. There was no credit. War and anarchy weren't over yet. We had reached "the algid stage of the conflagration," as Aparisi said, and soon, very soon, whoever had a *peseta* would exhibit it like a curiosity piece.

They all wished that Jacinto Villalonga would come and tell them about the memorable session that took place on the night of the 2nd; he had witnessed it from one of the parliamentary benches. But the congressman didn't show up at the Santa Cruzes! He finally appeared on the morning of the 6th, Three Kings' Day.* Jacinta was crossing the hall when the family friend entered.

"Good morning, namesake. How's the family? And the monster—is he up yet?"

---

*The celebration of this holiday marks the end of the Christmas season in Spain. Children traditionally receive their gifts from the Kings on January 6.

Jacinta couldn't stand her dear little namesake. This antipathy was grounded on her belief that Villalonga was the one who had corrupted her husband and influenced him to be unfaithful.

"Papá has gone out," she said, not looking particularly pleased. "He'd be so sorry to miss hearing you tell about it! Were you very scared? Juan says you hid under a bench."

"Oh, how funny! Has Juan gone out too?"

"No; he's getting dressed. Go on in."

And she followed him, because whenever the two friends shut themselves in, she went to great lengths to hear what they said; she put her little pink ear to the crack of the badly closed door. Jacinto waited in the parlor and she went in to announce him.

"What, has that wretch already come?"

"Yes, you clown. Here I am."

"Come on in, you rake. Well, 'what a pleasant surprise!' as they say."

The old chum went in. Jacinta noticed some sort of mischief in his eyes. She would have loved to have hidden behind a curtain to snatch those rascals' secrets. Unfortunately, she had to go to the dining room to carry out some orders Barbarita had given her. But she'd be back and try to catch wind of something . . .

"Out with it, boy, out with it. We've been dying to see you."

And Villalonga began his tale in Jacinta's presence. But as soon as she left, the narrator's face filled with malice. They both looked at the door; Juan's crony made sure that the wife was gone, and, turning back to the Dauphin, he said in the hushed voice that small-time conspirators use:

"Boy, you don't know . . . the news I'm bringing you! If you only knew who I've seen! Can your wife hear us?"

"Nah, don't worry about it," replied Juan, putting the studs in his shirt front. "Make yourself clear, fast."

"Well, I've seen the person you'd least expect . . . Here."

"Who?"

"Fortunata. But you have no idea how she's changed. What a transformation! She's so attractive, so elegant. My jaw almost dropped when I saw her."

Jacinta's steps could be heard. When she appeared, raising the curtain, Villalonga took a brusque turn in his speech: "No, no; you don't understand; the session started in the afternoon and there was a recess at eight o'clock. During the recess they tried to reach an agreement. I went up to all those groups to get a whiff of the stew . . . hmmm—bad, all right; the Palanca government was cooking slowly . . . And meanwhile—imagine how blind those men must be!—meanwhile, outside parliament they were setting up the machinery to snare them. Zalamero and I took turns carrying the news to a house on Greda Street where Serrano, Topete, and the others were. 'General, sir, they haven't reached an agreement. It's like floating oil . . . boiling. They want to overthrow President Castelar. Anyway, we'll soon see.' 'Go back. Will there be any voting?' 'I think so.' 'Bring us the results.'"

"And the results of the voting," remarked Santa Cruz, "were against Castelar. Tell me: what if they'd been *for* him?"

"Nothing would have been done. You can be sure of that. Well, as I was saying, Castelar spoke . . ."

Jacinta paid close attention to this, but Rafaela came in to ask her something and she had to leave.

"Thank God we're alone again," said Juan's crony once she had left. "Can she hear us?"

"How do you think she's going to hear us? You're becoming so timid! Hurry up. Where do you see her?"

"Well, last night . . . I was at the Café Suizo till ten. Then I went to the opera for a while, and as I was leaving, it occurred to me to stop in at the Praga to see if Joaquín Pez was there, because I had to tell him something. I go in, and the first thing I see is a couple—at one of the tables on the right. I stopped and stared like a fool. It was a gentleman and a woman dressed very . . . how shall I put it? . . . a woman whose clothes had an improvised elegance about them. 'I know that face' was the first thing that crossed my mind. And a couple of seconds later it struck me. 'It's that confounded Fortunata!' But no matter what I say, you couldn't *begin* to conceive of the metamorphosis . . . You have to see her for yourself. She looks fantastic! She's been to Paris for sure, because there are certain things in her transformation that couldn't have come from anywhere but Paris. I got as close as possible, hoping to hear her speak. 'How will she speak?' Because dressmakers can manage a good fit and a corset easily enough if there's quality inside, but as for speech . . . . You should see her, you'd drop your jaw, the way I did. You'd say her elegance is put-up and that she doesn't really look like a lady. Agreed; she is not a lady, but she doesn't need—but that doesn't keep her from looking ravishing. Why, she could . . . She's enough to drive you mad. You remember that incomparable body, that statuesque bust—the type that come from the *pueblo* and die in obscurity unless civilization searches for them and 'presents' them. How many times did we say it: 'If that bosom only knew how to exploit itself . . . !' Well, it wasn't just words, it's been perfectly exploited already. Do you remember what you used to say? 'The *pueblo* is a quarry with great ideas and great beauties. And then the working hand comes with intelligence and art to cut out a block . . . ' Well, there it is, finely carved. What graceful lines! Of course, she'd be sure to put her foot in it if she opened her mouth. I approached her unobtrusively. I realized that she'd recognized me and that my glances were inhibiting her. Poor thing! Her elegance didn't disguise her coarseness, that certain something that smacks of *pueblo*, a sort of shyness that somehow combines with effrontery, an awareness of being worth very, very little, morally and intellectually, and yet the assurance that they can enslave—ah, the wretches!—men like us, who are better than they are. I mean, it's not that I dare to say that we're better, except insofar as social appearances go . . . Well, anyway, to sum it up, she's enough to set you on fire. I wonder how much water she used for that transformation. But, ha! Women learn fast. They're like the devil himself when it comes to assimilating everything there is in the kingdom of the toilette. On the other hand, I'd be willing to bet that she hasn't learned to read. That's how they are. Hmph! And they go around saying that we pervert them. Well, getting back to the point, the metamorphosis is complete. What with water, fashion plates, and learning in no time how to be well groomed— plus silk, velvet, and a hat . . . "

"A hat!" exclaimed Juan at the peak of his stupefaction.

"Yes; and you can't imagine how well it suits her. She looked as if she'd worn one all her life . . . Remember the little scarf she used to wear that puffed up into a peak, and how she tied it under her chin? Who'd ever guess it now! What a transformation! It's like I say: the ones that have a gift for it learn in no time. The Spanish race is fantastic, I tell you, when it comes to assimilating anything that belongs to the realm of appearances. But you simply have to see her for your- self! . . . As for me, I admit it: I was stunned, dazzled, struck—"

"Oh, for heaven's sake!" Jacinta came in and Villalonga was forced to change the subject immediately.

"—I tell you I was struck dumb! Salmerón's speech was admirable, really admi- rable. I can still see that face, that 'Arab on the desert' look, and that horizontal movement of the eyes, and the gallantry of his gestures. A great man. But I said to myself: 'Your philosophy won't do you any good; you've gotten yourself into a fine one and soon we'll see what we've cooked up for you.' Then Castelar spoke. What a speaker! What a brave man! You should've seen how he grew in our eyes! I thought he'd reach the ceiling. When he finished, there were shouts: 'Questions, questions!' "

Jacinta left again without a word. Perhaps she suspected that the rascals were talking about something else in her absence, and she walked away with the urge to sneak back to the door.

"And that man you mentioned—who was he?" asked the Dauphin, burning with feverish curiosity.

2

"I'll tell you . . . from the moment I saw her, I said to myself: 'I know that face.' But I couldn't figure out who it was. Pez came in and we talked. He, too, tried to recall who the man was. We all racked our brains. Finally we realized that we'd seen the character two days before in the Director of the Treasury's office. I think he was there about a payment for some guns ordered from England. He has a Catalonian accent, wears a mustache and a goatee . . . about fifty . . . a rather unpleasant sort. Well, anyway, since Joaquín and I were staring at her, the fellow got irked. She didn't flirt at all; she just seemed embarrassed. And blushing made her so pretty! Remember that pale little mug, and her stringy black hair? Well, it looks much better now, because it's fuller; her face and body are fuller now."

Santa Cruz was somewhat bewildered. Barbarita's voice was heard; then she came in with her daughter-in-law.

"I charged out of there," continued Villalonga, "to tell our friends that the voting had started.—Nice to see you, Barbarita . . . Fine, thank you; and you? I was just telling Juanito that I started to run—"

"Toward Greda Street."

"No. Our friends had moved to a house on Alcalá Street—Casa-Irujo's; the windows look out on the park, near the War Ministry. Well, I found them very discouraged. We looked out the windows that face the park, and I couldn't see anything. 'What are they waiting for? What could they be planning?' Frankly, I thought the coup had been a flop and that Pavía didn't dare dispatch the troops into the streets. Serrano, who was impatient, was wiping off the steamy lenses of his glasses to see better. But there was nothing to be seen down there. 'General,' I said to him, 'I see a black band—which in the darkness of the night looks like a socle to me. Look closely: could it be a row of men?' 'Then what are they doing stuck to the wall like that?' 'Look sir, look; the socle's moving. It looks like a snake coiling around the building, and now it's uncoiling . . . see? Its tail is stretching toward the ramps in the park.' 'They're soldiers all right,' said the general in a low voice, and at the same time Zalamero rushed in all out of breath and said: 'They're still voting; Salmerón's not ahead anymore. Castelar is winning by the same margin now. Nine votes. But half the congress still hasn't voted.' Anxiety on everyone's face. Then I had to go and tell them the final results of the voting. Zoom! I took off down Turco Street and as I was going into congress, I ran into a reporter on his way out. 'The proposal is winning by ten votes. We'll get the Palanca government.' Poor Castelar! I went in. The upper rows were already voting. I took a look and left. I went around the bend thinking of what I'd just seen at the War Ministry: that black ribbon wound around the building . . . I met Figueras on the clock staircase and he said to me: 'What do you think—will there be a skirmish tonight?' And I replied: 'No cause to fear, maestro; nothing's going to happen.' 'It seems to me,' he said sardonically, 'that the devil is going to walk off with it.' I laughed. A few seconds later, a doorman goes by and says to me as calm as can be that he's seen troops on Florín Street. 'Really? You must be dreaming. Troops, shroops!' I pretended to be surprised. I stuck my head out the door near the clock. 'I'm not budging an inch,' I thought, looking at the table. 'Now you're going to see a real beaut.' They were reading off the results of the voting. They called off the names of all the voters without skipping a single one. Suddenly, several privates sent by an officer appear at the Fernando el Católico corner and install themselves next to the stairway by the table. They looked like a bunch of theater extras. An old colonel in the Guardia Civil came in through the other door."

"Colonel Iglesias," said Barbarita, who wanted the story to end. "The country was lucky to get out of that one. Fine. Well, Jacinto, I presume you'll stay for lunch."

"You bet your life he will," said the Dauphin. "I'm not letting him out of my sight today; and hurry, Mamá—it's late."

Barbarita and Jacinta left.

"How about Salmerón—what did he do?"

"I watched Castelar, and I saw him put his hand over his eyes and say: 'What ignominy!' There was an awful row at the table—shouting, protests. From where I was near the clock I could see masses of people standing. I couldn't even see the president. The privates, stock-still . . . Suddenly, bang! A shot in the corridor."

"And they disbanded. But tell me something else. I can't get it out of my mind . . . Did you say she was wearing a hat?"

"Who? . . . Oh! You mean her? Yes, a hat, and in very good taste," said Juan's crony, as emphatically as if he were continuing his narration of the historical event. "And a terribly elegant blue dress and a velveteen coat—"

"Are you kidding? A velveteen coat?"

"Oh yes, and it was trimmed with fur. A splendid coat. It suited her so well that—"

Without any warning whatsoever, Jacinta appeared. They hadn't heard the sound of steps or anything else. Villalonga spun away from this last topic like a weathervane hit by a strong gust of wind.

"The coat I was wearing—my fur overcoat, I mean—well, they yanked off one of the lapels in that riot . . . I mean they tore the fur off the lapel."

"As you were crawling under the bench."

"I didn't hide under any bench, namesake. What I did do was find a safe place, like everybody else. As a precaution."

"Look, my dear wife," said Santa Cruz, pointing to his waistcoat, which he took off as soon as he'd put it on. "Look, the bottom button is loose. Do me a favor and sew it on, or tell Rafaela to sew it. Or if worse comes to worst, call in Colonel Iglesias."

"Give it to me," said Jacinta ill-humoredly, leaving again.

"What a close call that was, comrade," said Villalonga, suppressing his laughter. "Do you suppose she understood? Well, anyway, here's another detail: she was wearing some turquoise earrings that were absolutely divine on that pale but dark complexion of hers. Those ears look like the work of God. And what turquoises! Those ears looked good enough to eat. When we saw them get up to leave, we decided to follow them to see where they lived. Everyone in the Praga was looking at her; she seemed more mortified than proud. We left . . . zoom! down Alcalá to Peligros, Caballero de Gracia, them in front, us behind. Finally they stopped; it was on Colmillo Street. They called the night watchman, he opened the door for them, they went in. The house is on the north side of the street, between the plaster figurine shop and the donkey milk place . . . right there."

Jacinta came in with the waistcoat.

"Is there anything else his grace wishes?"

"Nothing else, dear. Thank you very much. This monster says he wasn't a bit scared and that he walked out as calm as can be. I don't believe it."

"Scared of what? After all, I was in the thick of things. I'll tell you one more detail that will astonish you. The cannons that General Pavía put at the intersections weren't loaded. And you know what went on inside. Two shots fired into the air. Just like birds perched on a tree, flying off the minute you clap your hands a few times; the republic's parliament disbanded."

"Lunch is on the table. You can come now," said the wife, leading them in and feeling very worried.

"Stomachs, to the front!"

The Dauphine had overheard a few words that did not, in her mind, have any relationship whatsoever to the story about congress, Colonel Iglesias, and the Palanca government. Their conversation smacked of something—or someone—else: an enemy who had to be discovered, pursued, and annihilated at all costs.

At the table conversation centered on the same subject, and Villalonga, telling the tale again with all its ins and outs for Don Baldomero's benefit, added some new details that made the story even more colorful.

"Ah, Castelar struck some admirable blows." "And how about the federal constitution?" "You killed that in Cartagena."

"Touché!"

"The only one who put up any resistance was Díaz Quintero, who started to shout and struggle with the Guardia Civil. The representatives and the president abandoned the assembly room, leaving by way of the clock door, and waited in the library to be allowed to leave. Castelar left with two friends by way of Florín Street and went home, where he had a bad bout with his bile."

These references or stray pieces of news were, in that sad story, like the loose grapes left in the bottom of a basket after the clusters have been taken out. They were the ripest, and perhaps for that reason, the tastiest.

3

In the next several days, the observant and suspicious Jacinta noticed that her husband came home tired, as if he had walked a lot. He was the perfect picture of a door-to-door salesman who comes and goes and climbs stairs and combs the streets without succeeding in his business. He was crestfallen, like people who lose money; he was like the impatient hunter who exhausts himself by going from hill to hill without catching sight of any worthwhile game; like a forgetful artist who feels that the special idea or image worth worlds to him is escaping him. His wife attempted to determine the cause by dropping into him a plumb of curiosity whose lead was her jealousy, but the Dauphin kept his thoughts hidden deep within, and when he noticed her plummeting, his thoughts sank even deeper.

Juanito Santa Cruz was being subjected to the horrible torture of having an obsession. He went out, searched, and searched again, but that woman, the unlikely vision that had upset Villalonga, was nowhere to be found. Could it have been a dream or a vain invention of his friend? The concierge of the house that Jacinto had mentioned offered as much information as Juanito wished, but the only useful facts that he got from her obliging indiscretion were that a gentleman and a lady—" she was a looker"—had stayed in the boarding house on the second floor for two days—"that was all." Then they had disappeared. The concierge declared with notable astuteness that, in her opinion, the gentleman had "beat it" on the train and the "dame," lady, or whatever she was "was somewhere around Madrid." But where the devil was she? This was what he had to figure out. For all his talent, Juan couldn't account satisfactorily for this interest of his, this curiosity or amorous yearning for a person toward whom he had felt indifferent; a person who had even revolted him two years ago. Appearances, the tricksters, and the soul of the world were to blame. The unfortunate young woman—abandoned, miserable, and maybe smelling bad—had only to become an elegant, clean, and seductive adventuress for his disdain to turn into an ardent desire to appreciate for himself that admirable transformation and prodigy of this, our age of silk.

"It's just curiosity, pure curiosity," Santa Cruz said to himself, making his troubled soul all the more overwrought. "I'm sure it won't affect me in the slightest when I see her; but I want to see her anyway, and until I do, I don't believe in the transformation."

And this idea ruled him so exclusively that his fruitless search caused unspeakable pain, and he got more and more wrought up, until at last he envisioned himself as having to bear a huge, irreparable misfortune. To clinch his disturbance and boredom, Villalonga appeared one day with some new reports. "I've discovered that that man is a schemer of some sort. He's no longer in Madrid. The business about the guns was a hoax: the papers were forged."

"But how about her?"

"Joaquín Pez saw her yesterday. Calm down, man, don't have a fit. Where? On some street or other, I don't know. The street doesn't matter. She was dressed as humbly as could be. You're probably wondering, as I did, what happened to the velveteen coat? and the hat? and the turquoise earrings? I seem to recall that Joaquín told me she was still wearing the earrings. No, no, he didn't say that; because if she'd been wearing them, he wouldn't have seen them anyway. She had a scarf on her head, tightly tied under her chin, and a black cloak—quite worn at that—and a big bundle of clothes under her arm. Does it make any sense to you? No? Well, it does to me. The bundle contained the coat, and maybe other clothes too . . . "

"I can just see her," said Juan, catching on quickly. "Joaquín saw her go into a pawn shop."

"You're a wizard, man! Two and two make—"

"But didn't he see her come out? Didn't he follow her afterward to see where she lives?"

"That's up to you. He would have done it too, but just remember, my dear Christian soul, that Joaquín is on the Board of Tariffs and Appraisals, and there was a meeting that same afternoon, and our friend was on his way to the ministry with all the punctuality of a Pez."

This news put Juan into a worse and more pensive mood because he felt symptoms of the ailment from which he was suffering and that was lodged mainly in his mind: a spiritual sickness mixed with nervousness aggravated by obstacles. Why did he scorn her when he had her as she was, and pursue her when she became so different? Ideals trick you, and then, too, there's always the eternal question: "What's she like now?"

Poor Jacinta, with all this, was racking her brains to figure out what blasted desire or obsession was controlling her intelligent husband's soul. He always made a point of being considerate and affectionate toward her (he didn't want to give her any reason to complain); but to manage this, he had to resort to his wounded imagination, invest his wife with a form she didn't have, imagine that she was fuller in the shoulders, taller, more womanly, paler . . . and wearing those turquoise earrings. If Jacinta had discovered this terribly well-hidden arcanum in the soul of Juanito Santa Cruz, she surely would have filed for a divorce. But these things were very deep inside him, in caves deeper than those at the bottom of the sea, and Jacinta's plumb would never reach them, not even with all the lead in the world.

More obsessed every day by his investigative frenzy, Santa Cruz visited various houses, some of worse reputation than others, some mysterious, others open to everyone. Not finding what he was looking for at the seemingly highest level, he gradually descended, visited places where he had been several times before and others he had never been to. He came across familiar and friendly faces, unfamiliar and repulsive faces, and he asked them all for news, searching for a remedy for that typhoid, curiosity, that was consuming him. He knocked on every door he thought might conceal the shameful lost woman as well as the shame of losing himself again. His search seemed like something else, due to his ardor and his endowing it with a humanitarian character. He seemed like a father or brother searching desolately for the loved one who has vanished into the black labyrinth of vice. And he tried to whitewash his uneasiness with philanthropic and even Christian reasoning. And that mind *was* rich in sophistry: "It's a moral case. I cannot consent to her sinking into poverty and abjection. I'm responsible for this. Oh, may my wife forgive me! But a wife, no matter how intelligent she is, cannot appreciate the moral—yes, moral—motives that I have and that force me to proceed in this manner."

And when he combed the streets at night, every black or dark brown mass seemed to be the one he was looking for. He ran up, got a close look . . . but no . . . Sometimes he thought he spied her in the distance; then the shape disappeared, like a drop into water. Human silhouettes that vanished almost magically around corners and into doorways in the chiaroscuro of a shifting crowd startled him and nearly made him lose his mind. He saw lots of women—here, in the dark, there, lit up by the shop lights. But his did not appear anywhere. He checked all the cafés; he even went into several taverns, sometimes alone, sometimes with Villalonga. He was convinced that he would find her in this place or that, but as soon as he arrived, his image of her—being, as it was, a creation of his own eyes—vanished. "It seems that no matter where I go," he said with profound weariness, "I make her disappear, and that I'm fated to drive her out of my sight precisely because I want to see her!"

Villalonga told him to be patient, but he could not be. He was losing his calm, and lamented that a man as serious and level-headed as himself should be so upset by a mere whim, by persisting and yet not having his curiosity satisfied. "Nerves, wouldn't you say, Jacintillo? It's this rascal of an imagination that I have. It's like getting sick and delirious, waiting for a card that never turns up. Frankly, I thought I was stronger; that I wouldn't be so horribly neurotic about a card that won't turn up."

One very cold night, not especially late, the Dauphin came home in a lamentable state. He felt bad, yet he wasn't able to say exactly what it was. He collapsed into an armchair and leaned to one side, showing signs of terribly intense pain. His loving wife rushed to his side, very frightened by his condition; she heard his pitiful groans and saw an ugly expression, easily forgivable in a suffering man. "What's wrong, baby?" The Dauphin pressed his hand against his left rib-cage. It suddenly occurred to Jacinta that her husband had been stabbed. She screamed. She looked. There was no blood . . .

"Oh, does it hurt you? Poor little baby! It must be the cold. Wait, I'll put some warm flannel over it; we'll rub you with . . . with arnica."

Barbarita was alarmed at the sight of her son; but before making a decision of any sort, she gave him a good scolding for not protecting himself from the awfully raw, dry, north wind that had been blowing for several days. Then Juan started to shiver, teeth chattering. The cold that had attacked him was so intense that the words of his complaints disintegrated. Mother and wife looked at each other in terror, consulting in silence on the seriousness of his symptoms. Madrid is too much: a man goes hunting in its streets night after night. Where could the game be? Try this way, that way; nothing. No game anywhere. And just when the hunter least suspects it, up creeps a case of pneumonia. Quietly, from behind. It takes aim, fires, and plugs him in the heart.

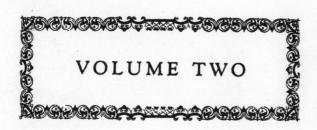

VOLUME TWO

1. Maximiliano Rubín

I

THE VENERABLE SHOP OF GOLD-PLATED bellpulls that had stood for time immemorial in the arcades on Platerías Street between La Caza and San Felipe Neri streets disappeared, if I am not mistaken, at the outbreak of the revolution in 1868. So in the same year, two secular orders fell: the throne of the Bourbons and this shop, which if it was not as old as the Spanish monarchy, was older than the Bourbons, for it had been founded in 1640, as a very badly painted sign on a case of shelves announced. Said establishment had only one door, above which was this brief sign: *Rubín*.

Federico Ruiz, who years ago was obsessed with writing articles on "The Obscure but Unquestionable Remains of the Israelites in Modern Spain" (articles that the editors of a magazine collected for a pamphlet they published at no charge to him), maintained that the surname Rubín was Jewish and had been used by certain converts who stayed here after the expulsion. "Lodging on Milaneses, Mesón de Paños, and Platerías streets were various *ex deicidal* families whose youngest descendants are alive today and whose 'physiognomical' and 'ethnographic' character is gone." Thus wrote the prolific publicist, and he devoted half the article to proving that the Rubíns' real surname was Rubén. Since no one contradicted him, he devoted himself to proving whatever he wanted, with the good intentions and honorable enthusiasm certain wise men of our times profess to have for erudite works that people don't read and editors don't pay for—they do enough to publish them. I wouldn't want to be wrong, but it seems to me that all my friend's Judaism was just a cold in the head or in his brain, which eliminated those troublesome substances like so many others, depending on the weather and the circumstances. And I am sure that Don Nicolás Rubín, the late possessor of the aforementioned shop, was a Christian from way back, and that it had never crossed his mind that his ancestors might have been Pharisees with tails or bignosed executioners like the ones in Holy Week processions.

The death of this Don Nicolás Rubín and the shop's closing were simultaneous. For quite a while, debts had been making the house sink; it had been kept afloat thanks to the creditors' considerate treatment of the owner. The reason for the ruin, according to all the family's friends, was the wife's misconduct. Nicolás Rubín's wife was an extravagant and scandalous woman who lived in a style beyond her means and who caused a lot of talk with her love affairs and intrigues. There were diverse and inexplicable ups and downs in that marriage, no sooner made by law than broken in fact, and the husband oscillated between the most barbarous violence and the most shameful tolerance. Five times he threw her out, and he took her back just as many, after paying off all her debts. They say that Maximiliana Llorente was a beautiful woman who enjoyed being appealing, one of those women who feel cramped by the vulgar narrowness of a shop. God took her in 1867, and the following year poor old Nicolás Rubín went on to a better life too (a case of ruptured varicose veins); the only inheritance he left his sons was his deplorable domestic and commercial reputation plus huge debts, paid off painfully with what was left of the shop. The creditors carried off everything, even the shelves, which were only good for firewood. They dated back to the count duke of Olivares.

The unfortunate businessman had three sons. Take note of their names and the age of each when their father died:

Juan Pablo, twenty-eight years old.

Nicolás, twenty-five.

Maximiliano, nineteen.

They bore no resemblance to each other, either in their appearance or physical constitution; and only by trying in good faith could one detect a vague family likeness among the brothers. It was undoubtedly the heterogeneity of those three faces that gave rise to the malicious rumor that they were sons of different fathers. Perhaps it was calumny, perhaps not; but in any case, the point should be mentioned so that you, my dear reader, may draw your own conclusions. They did have one thing in common, now that I think of it: they all suffered from severe and terribly upsetting headaches. Juan Pablo was handsome, affable, and very well built, of good height; he had a pleasing and easy way of speaking, also an alert and flexible mind. Nicolás was ungainly, uncouth, red-faced, pockmarked by a bad case of smallpox, and so ridden with hair that tufts of it even sprouted out of his nostrils and ears. Maximiliano was rickety, weak, lymphatic, and completely devoid of physical charm. After all, he had been born at seven months and then brought up on a bottle and goat's milk.

When the father of these three boys died, Nicolás, or "the hairy one" (so we can begin to keep them straight), went off to Toledo to live with his uncle, Don Mateo Zacarías Llorente, a chaplain at the Noble Maidens School, who put him in a seminary and made a priest of him. Juan Pablo and Maximiliano went to live with their paternal aunt, Doña Guadalupe Rubín, Sr. Jáuregui's widow, commonly known as Doña Lupe, "the turkey woman," who at first lived in the Salamanca section of Madrid and later in Chamberí. She was a lady surrounded by such noteworthy circumstances that she well deserves all the attention I shall later give her. The Rubín brothers had a maternal aunt in a town in the province of Alcarria, a childless rich widow, but since she was the picture of health, the inheritance she would one day leave them was only a remote hope.

There was no choice but to work, and Juan Pablo started to look for a way to earn a living. He detested bellpull shops so much that when he walked past one he would feel one of his headaches coming on. He finally went into the fish business, joining up with a man who offered to sell him fresh and pickled fish wholesale at the station or at Cebada Square; but he had so many differences with his partner during the first few months that he gave up the fish business and became a traveling salesman. He rode trains for a couple of years, lugging his sample boxes wherever he went. From Barcelona to Huelva, from Pontevedra to Almería, there wasn't a town he hadn't seen; he stopped over in Madrid for as long as he could. He dealt in felt hats and shoes, and scattered these and other items all over the Peninsula the way you sprinkle sand on a freshly written page to dry the ink. During another period he sold chocolate, handkerchiefs, and shawls, canned foods, prayer books, and even toothpicks. Because of his diligence, honesty, and punctuality in turning over his earnings, his suppliers held him in high esteem. But for some reason or other he was always (as he used to say) "poorer than a churchmouse," and he lamented his perverse luck in elaborate, pessimistic language. Everything he earned just "slipped through his fingers" because he frequented cafés in his free time, invited his friends constantly, and lived as well as possible in the towns he visited. He attributed the unsuccessful results of this system to "having been born under an unlucky star." The very heterogeneity and quantity of the items he sold quickly sapped the profits from his trips, and some firms started to lose confidence in him. And so the bored salesman, forever in a bad mood and cursing the merchants, aspired to a change in life and a more lucrative, noble occupation.

It was a memorable day for Juan Pablo when he ran into an old friend from his childhood, a classmate of his at San Isidro. The friend was one of those government employees called *cimbros*,* and Juan Pablo, who had a gift for expressing his thoughts, made such a miserable picture of his boredom with business life and such a fine one of his background for administrative work that his friend believed him, and before he knew it had given him a job. The next month Rubín was a police inspector in some province or other. But his "unlucky star" dogged him: in three months, the political situation changed and my friend Rubín joined the ranks of the unemployed. He had developed a taste for seeing his name on a payroll, and he could no longer be anything but a salaried man or an aspirant to such. I don't quite know why it is, but being unemployed seems to have a bitter charm for certain temperaments; the emotions involved in aspiring to a post seem to invigorate these people, and for this reason there are many who die the day they're given a job. Irritability gives them life, whereas abrupt sedation kills them.

---

*Cimbros: Equivalent of 'congressmen,' and called *cimbros* because of their tendency to bend, or sway, with dominant political trends.

Juan Pablo took incredible pleasure in going to the café, maligning the government, predicting who would be appointed, nosing around the ministries, stalking his protector on the corners of the Ministry of the Interior or at the exit of congress, pouncing on him as soon as he came into sight. At last the credentials came. But confound it, he always had the same cursed luck! The jobs they gave him were the most unpleasant ones imaginable. When they didn't involve the secret police, they had something to do with jails and penitentiaries.

Meanwhile, he took care of his little brother, of whom he was very fond and whom he pitied, too, because the poor boy was forever getting sick. After turning twenty he started to grow a bit stronger, but he continued to have his spells. Seeing that Maxi was now sturdier, Juan Pablo decided to help him learn a profession so that *he* wouldn't fail in life too, going astray at the age when a man's future is decided. The oldest of the Rubíns chalked up his own misfortunes to the incompatibility between his natural talent and his limited means for developing it. "Oh, if only my father had given me a profession," he would muse, "I'd *be* somebody in the world today!"

Before long he was dealt another blow: just when he was dreaming about being promoted, the place was cleaned up again. So once again we find our friend walking around Madrid with his hands in his pockets or sitting in a café staring into space, talking about "the situation" (always about "the situation"), the war, and how indecent and grotesque and infamous Spanish politicians were. It was hard on him, all right! Disturbed and tormented souls unburden themselves with fierce criticism. But this time, there was no hope for Juan Pablo: the people on his side, the ones he so emphatically called "my" people, were low on the totem pole, and there had been what they call a hiring streak in bureaucratic circles. Sometimes in his misery the dismissed public officer explored his conscience, and he was amazed not to find anything there on which to base his political affiliations. As for any firm notions of his own . . . unless God gave him a few, he was dry; he had read very little and nourished his mind on what he heard in cafés and read in the papers. He didn't actually know if he was a liberal or not, and with the greatest outspokenness called anyone at all "doctrinaire," not even knowing what the term meant. All of a sudden, without the slightest clue as to the reason, he would be frenetically enthusiastic about man's rights; and just as suddenly, his soul would be overjoyed at hearing that the government was going to "crack down" and tell those "rights" to go to the devil.

In the midst of this situation, Nicolás Rubín turned up unexpectedly in Madrid. Our hairy little priest had a few dreams himself; he wanted to join the ranks of the clergy, in the army or the cathedral, I'm not sure which, and the brothers had private talks on this matter in the outskirts of Madrid, where they discussed it at length on their strolls. After one such talk, Juan Pablo appeared one day at the café with a peculiarly animated look, sounding very relaxed in his political judgments and even giving himself the airs of a prophet, voicing more haughtily than ever his scorn for the present situation. People who behave this way in cafés are treated with respect and even a certain amount of envy, which arise from the common suspicion that these people must know classified secrets or have inside information on a huge intrigue.

"Our friend Rubín," Don Basilio Andrés de la Caña, one of the regulars at the table, said in his absence," is not, it seems to me, being aboveboard with us. If they're going to give him a position, why doesn't he come out and say so! Is the federal republic going to take over or what? All this *mystery*! Or do you suppose that he reports back to Don Práxedes?* Well, let him. Spying doesn't bother me."

This happened toward the end of 1872. Suddenly Rubín said that he was leaving the country to take up his work as a traveling salesman again. He disappeared from Madrid, and some months later it was whispered in the *tertulia* that he was "on the other side," and that Don Carlos, the pretender to the throne, had appointed him as his accountant or treasurer or something of the sort at the Royal Headquarters. It was learned later that he had gone to England to buy guns; that he was in charge of contrabanding near Guetaría; that he came back to Madrid incognito, going on to La Mancha and Andalusia in the summer of '73, when the Peninsula, burning up everywhere, was an immense pyre to which every Spaniard had taken his torch and the government fanned the flames.

2

Juan Pablo had always made mistakes in his own life and had taken the crooked path himself, but he hit the mark when he decided that his little brother should study to be a pharmacist. Many people who do nothing but lumber along in their own lives have this clear-headedness when it comes to counseling others; though missing their own calling by a long shot, they nevertheless discern clearly that of others. Someone else had a considerable part in this decision too, a close friend of their deceased father and indeed, of the whole family: the pharmacist Samaniego, who owned a pharmacy on Ave María Street. He promised to take Maximiliano under his wing as an errand boy or apprentice with the understanding that in time he would let him run the business.

Maximiliano began his studies in '69. His aunt and brother pointed out that being a pharmacist was very nice and that he'd earn lots of money, because medicines were quite expensive and the raw materials for making most of them were quite cheap: well water, ashes, flowerpot soil, and so on. The poor boy, who was

---

* Práxedes M. Sagasta, head of the Liberal party.

very docile, agreed to everything. As for being enthusiastic about the enterprise, we might as well come out and say it—he wasn't, not about that profession or any other; he hadn't yet experienced the great urges or burning curiosity that herald the coming of knowledge. And he was so feeble that he was ill most of the time; his mind never really saw clearly into the heart of science, nor could he grasp an idea except after tying it up like a boat. He used his poor memory as if it were a falcon, to catch ideas; but the falcon usually flew off and left him with his mouth hanging open, staring up at the sky.

The first steps he took in his career were excruciating. Laziness and weakness made him linger in bed too long in the morning, and poor old Doña Lupe had a terrible time of it trying to get him up. She rose very early herself, and would bang on the brass mortar near the sleeping boy's head, but as a rule he showed no sign at all that he had heard the racket. Then she would tickle him, put the cat in bed with him, and pull back the covers—carefully, so that he wouldn't get a chill. Sleep ensconced itself so deeply in that body (his system did need it) that waking up the student was a task worthy of the Romans and one that required the greatest energy and constancy on Doña Lupe's part.

The boy *did* study, and he wanted to complete his assignments, but he could not overcome his limitations. Doña Lupe helped him with his homework and gave him courage when he was downhearted, and when she saw him grow nervous and anxious toward exam time, she would throw on her mantilla and go visit his teachers. She told them such impressive stories that the boy passed, although with low grades. Unless he was ill, he never missed a class, and he was the type who lugged around more notes and notebooks than anybody else. He would enter the classroom burdened with that stack of notes, and never missed a syllable of what the teacher said.

He was small, not very well built, and so puny that it seemed the wind would blow him away; his head was flat; his hair, lank and thin. Seeing him with his brother Nicolás, one would have thought of suggesting to the latter that he give his extra hair to the former. All the hair had gone to Nicolás, whose usurping of the family hair made it clear that Maximiliano would be bald before thirty. His skin was shiny and fine, baby skin, with the transparency one sees in emaciated, chlorotic women. The bone in his nose was sunken and blunt, like a soft substance that had been hit hard; it not only looked ugly, it also obstructed his nasal passages, which is probably why he went around with his mouth hanging open. His teeth were so uneven that each tooth seemed to have made its appearance on a whim. It wouldn't have been so bad if those blasted bones of his hadn't bothered him, but the poor boy had toothache after toothache, such bad ones that he screamed his head off. He also suffered from head colds; one overlapped the next, giving him a chronic cold, his pituitary gland forever swelling and his nose forever running. As he gradually learned his trade, he started to mix his own remedies, doctoring himself with potassium iodide in all possible forms; he went around with a little stick of it in his mouth, reeking of pitch or God knows what.

No matter how you looked at it, Rubín was not attracted to pharmacology. Yet the young man whom Nature had favored so stingily that he seemed to be made of physical and moral leftovers had no lack of lofty aspirations in his soul. Two or three years into his profession, our mollusk began to sense the vibrations of manhood and even catch a glimpse now and then of the great glories of life to which he had been blind since birth. Doña Lupe lived in the part of Salamanca known as Pajaritos. From his third floor window Maximiliano could see the military students (when the school was at 40 Serrano Street, according to the old numbering), and words simply cannot describe the admiration he felt for those students, nor his ecstasy upon seeing their blue-striped trousers, their caps, their long coats with oak leaf–embroidered collars, and their swords. Some were so young, and yet already carried a sword! Many a night Maximiliano dreamed that he had a sword, a mustache, and uniform, and he talked in his sleep. Awake, he was delirious too: he thought he had grown inches taller, that his legs were straight and his body didn't slump so badly, that his nose was better, that his hair was growing in thicker, and that his appearance was much more impressive. What a rotten lot! If he hadn't gotten stuck with such an awkward body and if they had sent him to military school, oh, how he would have applied himself! Just handling the books would surely have ignited his talent, the way fire comes from rubbing two sticks together.

On Saturday afternoons, when the students drilled with their guns on their shoulders, Maximiliano followed them to watch their maneuvers, and his fascination with the spectacle lasted until Monday. Even in class, which with its quietness and monotony invited napping, he toyed with his fantasies and concocted illusions. The result was total ecstasy. During an explanation of the therapeutic qualities of natural dyes, he envisioned the military students in their tactical field study as someone else would look at a landscape through a stained glass window.

The boys in botany class amused themselves by giving each other nicknames based on Linnaeus' nomenclature. One named Anacleto—who considered himself very elegant and gentlemanly—was dubbed *Anacletus obsequiosissimus;* they called Encinas, who was very short, *Quercus gigantea.* Olmedo was very slovenly, so *Ulmus sylvestris* fit him perfectly. Narciso Puerto was ugly, dirty, and smelly, so they called him *Pseudo-Narcissus odoripherus.* Another boy who was very poor and had a little job on the side received the name *Christophorus oficinalis.* And finally Maximiliano Rubín, who was terribly homely, clumsy, and dull-witted, was called *Rubinius vulgaris* throughout his career as a student.

At the beginning of 1874 Maximiliano was twenty-five, and he still didn't look a day over twenty. He had no mustache, although plenty of pimples were sprinkled all over his face. At twenty-three he developed a fever due to his nervous condition and it almost took his life, but when he got over it he seemed a bit stronger: his breathing wasn't so heavy, his head colds were less persistent, and even that blasted pain in the roots of his teeth was more civilized. He didn't use iodine or tar sticks as much as before, and only the headaches persisted, like boring friends whose periodic visits fill us with terror. Juan Pablo was at the Royal Headquarters then, and Doña Lupe let Maximiliano go out whenever he wished; she considered him vice-proof because of his poor physique, apathetic nature, and shyness, this last being a result of his overall condition. In addition to his liberty, she gave him spending money for his boyish pleasures, confident that he would be quite prudent in how he used it. The boy tended to save his money; he had a clay piggy bank where he kept the silver coins and occasional gold ones his brothers gave him when they came to Madrid. He was most concerned about clothes and enjoyed being outfitted in inexpensive but fashionable suits, suits of which he took such exquisite care that one could only conclude that they were his prized possessions. His manner of dressing led him to take a certain amount of pride in his appearance, thanks to which his build didn't look as bad as it really was. He owned a good red-lined cloak; at night he wrapped himself in it, took a streetcar, and rode around, usually till eleven, occasionally till twelve. Meanwhile, Doña Lupe had moved to Chamberí—always in search of cheaper lodgings—and Maximiliano eventually forgot about the military students.

Far from diminishing with the years, his shyness seemed to grow. He thought that everyone made fun of him and considered him insignificant, useless. He undoubtedly exaggerated his inferiority, but his dejection led him to avoid social contacts. When he had to make a visit, the house he had to enter terrified him, even from the outside, and he would pace the street before finally deciding to launch his attack. He was afraid of meeting someone who might give him a malicious look, so he planned beforehand what he would say; usually, however, he ended up not saying anything. Certain people filled him with a respect verging on panic, and whenever he saw one of these approach, he would cross the street. They had not harmed him in any way; on the contrary, these people were friends of his father, or Doña Lupe, or Juan Pablo. At a café with his friends, he was fine if there were just two or three in the group. His tongue even loosened up a bit under such circumstances and he was able to talk on almost any subject. But as soon as the number rose to six or eight, he clammed up; he was incapable of an opinion on anything. If he was forced to speak, either because they wanted to tease him or ask him something in all sincerity, my poor friend's face turned red and he could only stutter.

So he preferred, when the weather wasn't too cold, to wander through the streets wrapped warmly in his cloak, looking at shop windows and the people passing by, or to pause outside a courtyard to hear a blind man singing, to peer into café windows. He could last for two hours on these excursions without getting tired; from the moment he set out he felt transported, as if to a rarefied zone where he fancied he was seeking adventure and was quite different from his real self. With their hubbub and variety, the streets were a great incentive to that imagination that, having blossomed late, displayed the kind of energy found in seriously ill people. At first he didn't observe the women he met, but soon he began to distinguish the pretty ones from the ones who weren't, and he would pursue one for the sheer ecstasy of the adventure until he found a better one; then he would follow her too. Soon he was able to distinguish women by their social class; he developed such a keen eye that he could tell in a flash which ones were decent and which ones were not. His friend *Ulmus sylvestris*, who sometimes accompanied him, persuaded him to overcome the reserve that his bashfulness imposed on him, so Maximiliano met some of the women whom he had seen more than once and had judged very attractive. But his soul remained serene in the midst of his ventures into vice; the same women with whom he spent pleasant times he later found revolting, and he avoided them if he crossed paths with them again in the street.

He preferred to wander around alone rather than in Olmedo's company, for his friend distracted him, and Maximiliano's pleasure consisted of thinking and musing at his own free will, conjuring up realities and flying straight through the space of what was possible . . . although improbable. Walking, walking, and dreaming in time to his legs, as if his soul were echoing a music whose rhythm decided his pace—ah, this he enjoyed. And when he found pretty women, whether alone, in pairs, or in groups, wearing a kerchief or a shawl, he took great pleasure in asserting silently that "*they* were decent," and he would follow them to their destination. "A decent woman! If only a decent one loved me!" That was his dream . . . But better not to yearn for such things. The mere thought of addressing a decent woman made him shake in his boots. Ha! When Rufina Torquemada or Señora Samaniego with her daughter Olimpia came to call, he hid in the kitchen to get out of greeting them!

3

So it was that our misanthrope took to using his internal vision more than his external vision. The same young man who had resembled an oyster had grown into something like a poet. He lived two lives: one based on bread and the other on dreams. At times, this latter life was so splendid and rarefied that when he fell from those heights down to his bread-life, he was all battered and bruised. Maximiliano had moments when he believed that he was, indeed, someone else; they always occurred at night, during the loneliness of his roamings. He became either an army officer and was inches taller, with an aquiline nose, great muscular strength, and a head . . . a head that never hurt. Or he became a lofty, gallant civilian who chatted away, not fazed by anything, capable of flattering the surliest of women and as comfortable in their presence as a fish in water. Well, as I've said, he got so wound up he believed all this. And if it had lasted, he would have gone as mad as any of the inmates in Leganés.* His luck was that it all passed, like a headache; but the hallucination reconquered its kingdom while he slept, when he relived all this nonsense—the ins and outs of adventures that were usually very touching and refined, complete with abnegations, sacrifices, heroism, and other sublime phenomena of the soul. Upon awakening, when normal thoughts weave together with deceitful images from dreams and the brain is a twilight zone holding a vague discussion on the true versus the untrue, that deception lingered a bit, and Maximiliano did what he could to preserve it by closing his eyes again in an effort to attract the scattering images.

"Actually," he said to himself, "why should one thing be more real than another? Why shouldn't daytime events be a dream and whatever happens at night be real life? It's a question of terms, of our having taken it upon ourselves to call *sleeping* what is really *waking,* and *going to bed, getting up.* Why shouldn't I, as I'm getting dressed, say: "Maximiliano, now you're getting ready to go to sleep. You're going to have a bad night, with a nightmare and everything, I mean, a class on 'Animal Matter in Pharmaceutical Preparations.'"

Ulmus sylvestris was a pleasant boy, a good sort, cheerful and rather frivolous. Of all *Rubinius vulgaris'* friends, he was the fondest of Maxi, and Maxi repaid him with an affection tinged with respect. Olmedo led a very unexemplary life, moving every month to a new rooming house, spending his nights in sinful places, and doing all the crazy things students do as if they were part of a compulsory program. Lately he'd been living with a so-called Feliciana, a funny and very experienced woman, and he felt important because of her, as if keeping a woman were a profession one must study to deserve the title of "real man." He gave her what little he had, and she did what she could with it, one day in straits, the next in the lap of luxury, and always with her devil-may-care attitude. He took this kind of life seriously, and when he had enough money, he invited his friends "for codfish" at his "*hôtel,*" putting on airs to convince them that *he* was a man of the world and a rascal. But it was only a poor imitation of the affected Parisian insouciance as he perceived it in Paul de Kock's novels. Feliciana was from Valencia, for which reason her rice was very good; but the presentation and table itself left something to be desired. Olmedo did everything so intensely and so strictly by the book that he would go out and get drunk even though he didn't like wine; he sang flamenco without knowing how to sing; he murdered the guitar and committed all the other

---

* A mental institution in Madrid.

senseless acts that in his mind constituted the rites of the debauchee. For he deeply wanted to be a debauchee, just as others want to be masons or crusaders; he needed to play a role, to be somebody. If there had been a uniform for debauchees, Olmedo would have worn it enthusiastically; he regretted that there was no sort of distinctive sign—a ribbon, plume, or galloon—that he could have worn to announce tacitly: "Look at what a debauchee I am." And underneath it all, he was just a poor devil. All his cavorting was no more than the typical prolonging of adolescence.

Maximiliano never went to the gala events his friend hosted, although he was always invited. Nevertheless, he was kept posted on Feliciana's health, as if she had really been a lady. Olmedo took things seriously, saying things like: "My Felicianita is a bit indisposed. Today I told Orfila to drop by." Orfila, a young student in his last year of medical school, had the same name as the famous doctor and he cured (that is to say, he wrote prescriptions for) his friends and their girlfriends.

On the way out of class one day, Olmedo said to Rubín:

"Drop by if you want to see a real woman. She's a friend of Feliciana's who's staying at our *hôtel* for a few days while she looks for a job."

"Is she decent?" asked Rubín, his tone revealing the importance he attached to decency.

"Decent! What a laugh!" exclaimed the debauchee, laughing. "Do you really think there's a woman who's . . . who's really decent?"

He said this with philosophical aplomb, his hat tilted to the right as if to emphasize his slanted ideas on human depravity. There were no decent women left—this came from a profound connoisseur of society and vice. Olmedo's skepticism was actually a sign of his childishness, his incomplete transition into manhood, rather like a second teething. It all amounted to a lot of drool, after which the man, with other ideas and another view of life, would step forth.

"Not decent!" remarked Maximiliano, who desired that all females be decent.

"What did you expect, my friend? She's a nice little piece! She came to Madrid not long ago with a good-looking character, a gun dealer, I think, and did they come in style! I saw her one night—a real killer! I swear she looked straight out of Paris. But then something happened—heck, I don't know what it was. The man pulled a dirty trick on her; he ran off one morning and left her to foot the bill— and it wasn't a small one—at the rooming house, and another bill somewhere else, and so on: bills, bills, bills. So the poor thing had to pawn all her clothes and all she had left was what was on her back—when she had it on, that is. Feliciana found her somewhere or other drowning in tears and said, 'Come home with me.' And now, there she is! She makes her little expeditions, on the quiet side, you know, and Feliciana lends her clothes for them. But don't get the wrong idea; she's a very nice girl. There's something special about her . . . ."

That night Maximiliano went to Feliciana's "*hôtel*" on the third floor on Pelayo Street, and when he entered, the first thing he saw was—well, you see, next to the front door there was a little room where the guest lived, and just as Rubín was entering, she was emerging from her nook. Feliciana had come to open the door and was holding a lamp that she was taking to the living room, and in the brilliant light of the unshaded oil lamp Maximiliano stood face to face with the most extraordinary beauty his eyes had ever beheld. She looked at him as though he were an oddity, and he at her as though she were a supernatural vision.

Rubín went into the living room and, putting his cloak down, sat on an oilcloth chair whose springs assassinated whatever part of your body sat there. Olmedo wanted his friend to play cards with him, but since Maximiliano declined, he started a game of solitaire. Feliciana worked on the lamp, assembling a shade out of pages from fashion magazines showing models on which she had pasted remnants as clothes, and then she sank lazily into the armchair, snuggling up in her big heavy shawl.

"Fortunata!" she called out to her friend, who was running about the house—she seemed to be hunting for something. "What did you lose?"

"My blue scarf."

"Are you going out already?"

"Yes. What time is it?"

Rubín was glad to have the opportunity to serve such a beautiful woman and, taking out his watch with great solemnity, he said:

"Seven . . . and a half minutes before nine."

The time could not have been told more accurately.

"You see," said Feliciana, "you have time, till ten. If you leave here by quarter of ten . . . what's your scarf doing over there? Look at it, on the chair next to the dresser."

"Oh, for goodness sake! If it had been a dog, it would've bitten me."

She wrapped it around her head, looking into the black-framed mirror over the dresser, and then sat down to wait. Maximiliano got a better look at her. He simply couldn't get his fill, and a singular obstruction formed in his chest, interrupting his breathing. What could he say? Because he had to say *something*. The presence of her beauty left the poor young man more abashed than having to face the most distinguished person alive.

"You'd better dress warmly," Feliciana advised her friend. And Rubín saw the sky open up, for this permitted him to remark in a sententious tone:

"Yes, it's a bit chilly tonight."

"Take the key," added Feliciana. "And remember, the night watchman's name is Paco. He's usually in the tavern."

Her friend didn't say a word. She seemed to be in a bad mood. Maximiliano gazed, dumbstruck by those eyes. That incomparable brow, that perfect nose . . . !

He would have given anything for her to have deigned to look at him in some other way than how one looks at odd creatures. "What a pity she's not decent!" he thought. "But who knows if she is; I mean, if she has kept her spiritual honor in the midst of . . ."

This notion of there being two kinds of honor, or decency, was firmly planted in his mind, but whether they harmonized or not is unsure. Fortunata said very little; what she did say was trivial and certainly not worth recording for posterity: that it was very cold, that one of her mittens was coming apart at the seams, that the key looked like a steam hammer, that on her way home she'd be stopping at the pharmacy to buy some cough drops.

Maximiliano was fascinated. Not daring to open his mouth, he assented with a smile, his ecstatic eyes glued to that angelic countenance. And whatever she said was (for him at least) a bouquet of wonderfully clever thoughts. "She's an absolute angel! She hasn't said a single uncouth word. And the tone of her voice! I've never heard such music. What must this woman sound like when she says 'I love you,' when she puts her heart and soul into it?" The thought rattled him for quite a while. A cold shiver ran up and down his spine and his nose began to itch as if he'd just drunk soda water.

Tired of solitaire, Olmedo started telling dirty jokes that Maximiliano thought were in poor taste. He had heard similar anecdotes on other nights and laughed; but tonight he turned all shades of red, wishing that his cursed friend would shut up. "What impudence—telling such filthy stories in front of people who were . . . decent; yes, decent!" Rubín was just as disconcerted as if the two women present had been prudes or pupils in a nun's school; his shyness, however, kept him from ordering Olmedo to be quiet. Fortunata didn't laugh at the stupid jokes either, but she seemed more indifferent than indignant. She was distracted, thinking of her own affairs. What could they be? Just to know what they were, Maximiliano would have given . . . his piggy bank with all it contained. Remembering his treasure gave him another shock, and he wriggled in his chair, hurting himself quite a bit on those blasted springs.

"But the juiciest story of all, damn it," said Olmedo, "is the one about the baker. Have you heard it? When the bishop went on his pastoral visit and lay down in the priest's bed, you see—"

Fortunata got up to leave. It occurred to Maximiliano to follow her to see where she was going. It was his special way of courting her. With his dreamy nature, he vaguely believed that following her would establish a mysterious, perhaps magnetic, communication between them. Yes, he'd follow her, watch from afar with a language or telegraphic code *sui generis*; and the person being followed, even though she didn't turn back, would probably sense the effects of the "attracting fluid." Fortunata left, saying good-bye rather coldly, and two minutes later Maximiliano left too, still in hopes of catching up with her at the main door. But that cursed *Ulmus sylvestris* stopped him by grabbing his hand and squeezing it with crude boasts of his muscular strength so that he could enjoy hearing squeaks of pain from poor *Rubinius vulgaris.*

"What a nincompoop you are!" exclaimed the latter, finally withdrawing his crushed hand, its fingers still stuck together. "Very funny! This and telling dirty stories are your strong points. You'd do better to open your books for a change."

"Goody-goody, prudy, do me a favor and wipe my nose."

"Don't try to be coarse," Rubín said kindly. "You're not, you can't even pretend to be."

This hurt Olmedo's pride more than a shower of insults; he could take anything in good grace except being downgraded a hair from the degree of debauchery that he attributed to himself. Rubín's indulgence annoyed him so much that he followed him to the door, calling out, among other foolish things:

"You damned hypocrite! Damn it! These big saints have probably tricked you."

4

Maximiliano went downstairs like an eight-year-old whose toy has fallen out the window. He arrived at the main door breathless, doubting whether to turn right or left. His heart told him to head for San Marcos Street. He quickened his pace, figuring that Fortunata probably didn't walk very fast and that he'd soon catch up with her. Was that her? He thought he saw the blue scarf, but when he got closer, he saw that it was not the fair lady his eyes were seeking. When he saw a woman who looked like Fortunata, he slowed down so as not to get too close; not getting too close made the charm of pursuit all the more mysterious. He walked down street after street, he backtracked, he went around one block after another, but his "lady of the night" was nowhere to be seen. He had never felt so afflicted in his life. If he *had* found her, he would have even been capable of addressing her and saying something bold. He was so shaken by this wandering pursuit that by eleven o'clock he could barely stand up, and he leaned against a wall to rest. To go home without having found her and perhaps even having strolled around with her a little . . . being just thirty steps away . . . it depressed him. But finally it grew so late and he was so weary that there was no choice but to take the streetcar for Chamberí and head home. Once there, he went to bed, anxious to turn off the light and dream on his pillow. He was crushed. Sad thoughts filled his mind, making him feel like crying. He hardly slept that night, and the next morning he resolved to go back to Feliciana's "*hôtel*" as soon as class was over.

He did as planned, and that day was able to partially overcome his shyness. Feliciana helped by stimulating him artfully, and with her help Rubín managed to say a few things that, in his effort to hide his real feelings, he uttered maliciously.

"You came in rather late last night. You still weren't back at eleven."

He offered other simple observations of this sort, which Fortunata heard indifferently and answered disdainfully. Maximiliano was saving the purity of his soul for a more propitious occasion. Obeying a fortunate instinct, he decided to feel his way along, as if he were just one of the regulars, only interested in a little fun. Feliciana—the sly witch—left them alone, and Rubín cowered at first, but suddenly he got hold of himself. He wasn't the same man anymore. The faith that swelled in his soul, the passion born in innocence and developed overnight like a miraculous tree risen from the ground laden with fruit, stirred and transfigured him. Even his cursed shyness had shrunken into a purely external phenomenon. He looked at Fortunata evenly, and, taking her hand, said to her in a trembling voice:

"If you would love me . . . I'd love you more than my life itself."

Fortunata looked at him too, surprised. She couldn't believe that the "odd creature" was speaking like this. She looked into his eyes and found a loyalty and honesty that astounded her. Then she reflected for a moment, trying to keep her balance by resigning herself to pessimistic thoughts. She'd been made fun of so often that what she was witnessing now could only be another joke. He was undoubtedly trickier and a bigger cheat than the rest. The consequence of these thoughts was a loud laugh in the remorseful face of a man who was all soul. But this did not disconcert him; the fact that he had been listened to attentively inspired him with singular strength. Courage!

"If you'll love me, I'll adore you, I'll idolize you—"

The woman revealed a deep-rooted skepticism; she didn't take the young man's passion seriously at all.

"And if I were to prove it?" inquired Maximiliano in grave tones that—who would have dreamed it?—made him suddenly appear handsome, "if I were to prove it to you beyond a doubt?"

"What?"

"That I'll idolize you! No, that I already *do* idolize you."

"What a laugh! Idolize *me?* Ha!" she repeated, returning the word "idolize" like a ball in a game.

Maximiliano didn't persist with such expressive words, realizing that ridicule was hovering over him. All he said was:

"All right, then we'll be friends. I'll settle for that today. I'm just a poor fool, I mean, I'm a good sort. I've never loved a woman till now."

Fortunata stared at him. Frankly, she couldn't get used to that snub nose, that insipid mouth, and that puny body: it looked as if it would fall apart at a puff of air. Why did it always have to be his type that fell for her! Obliged as she was to disguise her emotions and play certain roles (although the truth is that she didn't play them very well), she kept the conversation going.

"Tonight I want to speak to you," Rubín said categorically. "I'll be here at eight thirty. Will you give me your word that you won't go out? That you'll wait, to go out with me?"

She gave him the word he so urgently requested, and with it the interview concluded. Rubín went running home.

What a boy! He wasn't the same. He noticed that something had broken open inside, like a sealed chest spewing forth a wealth of objects that had been compressed, buried; it was a crisis, more gradual or unnoticed in others, but violent and explosive in him. He even believed he was healthy! He even seemed to have talent! And that afternoon he *did* have magnificent thoughts and surprisingly original opinions. Previously, he had held a very unfavorable view of his own intelligence, but one of the effects of his sudden love was his conviction that he could confront anyone. Modesty gave way to a certain pride that was gaining ground in his soul. "But what if she doesn't love me?" he mused, losing heart and crashing to the ground on broken wings. "She'll simply have to love me . . . This isn't the first time . . . Once she gets to know me . . ."

All at once his apathy and laziness were conquered. He was full of new itchings and urges, desires to do something, to prove his willpower with huge, difficult deeds. He went along the street entirely oblivious to everything, bumping into passers-by, and almost walking into a tree on Luchana Street. As he stepped onto Raimundo Lulio Street he saw his aunt sitting on the balcony basking in the sun. Seeing her and experiencing real fear, immense fear, were one and the same. "If my aunt ever found out . . ." But his fear spawned courage, and he clenched his fists under his cloak so hard that his fingers hurt. "If my aunt's against it, let her go ahead and be against it and go to the devil." Never, not even in his innermost thoughts, had Maximiliano spoken of Doña Lupe so disrespectfully. But the old pattern was broken now. Everything belonging to his existence preceding this wholly new state dispersed like darkness around the rising sun. Aunt, brothers, family, anybody—nothing existed any longer; whoever barred his way would be an outright enemy. Maximiliano's fit of anger was so vehement that his image of Doña Lupe, his veritable mother, took on a detestable aura. Going upstairs to his home, he relaxed at the thought that his aunt knew nothing; but if she did, she could just—so there! "What a strong will I'm developing," he reflected as he sequestered himself in his room.

He shut the door carefully and picked up the piggy bank. His first impulse was to smash it on the floor, break it open to get at the money, and he already had it in his hand to carry out this uneconomical deed when he was beset by fear that his aunt would hear the noise and come in and make a scene. He recalled how proud Doña Lupe was of her nephew's piggy bank. When people came to visit, she showed it off like a curiosity piece, shaking it and letting them hold it to see how heavy it was so that they'd all be amazed at what an orderly and prudent child he was. "This is what's called being responsible. There are very few boys like him."

Maximiliano figured that to carry out his plan he would have to buy another earthenware piggy bank of exactly the same type and fill it with small change so that it would make a sound and weigh . . . He snickered at the thought of how he was going to trick his aunt. He, who'd never gotten into mischief in his life! The only thing he'd ever done, years ago, was to steal buttons from her for his collection. He had a collector's instinct, which is a form of greed. He'd even cut buttons off her dresses, but he got such a spanking that he never felt like doing it again. Except for that, his record was clean. He'd always been the soul of meekness and so thrifty that his aunt loved him, perhaps more because of this virtue than any of the others.

"All right; let's go to it. In the crockery shop on Santa Engracia there are piggy banks exactly like mine. I'll buy one; I'll take a good look at this one first to get an idea of its proportions."

Maximiliano was standing there holding the piggy bank, studying it from different angles as if to do its portrait, when the door opened and a girl of about twelve came in, thin and wiry, sleeves rolled up, face decked and adorned with rings and spit curls, wearing an apron that hung down to her feet. The mere sight of her was so upsetting to Maximiliano that you'd think he'd been caught red-handed in a shameful act.

"What do you want here, you nosy little runt?"

Her reply was to stick out several inches of tongue at him, squinting and making the most grotesque faces imaginable.

"Aren't you cute! Get out of here or you're going to get it!"

She was the family maid. Doña Lupe detested huge, older women and always hired young girls so that she could bring them up and in the process train them to know her tastes and habits. They called her Papitos for some reason or other. She was livelier than a firecracker, active and diligent when she chose to be, lazy and sly at other times. Her body was slim, her hands rough from work and cold water; she had a mischievous face with bulging eyes that she used to make people laugh; an appealing pouting little mouth; and her lips and glistening white teeth seemed made to order for the most extravagant grimaces. Her two front teeth were enormous, real buck teeth, and always in sight because even when she was pouting, her mouth did not completely close.

Maximiliano's threats made Papitos brasher. That's the way she was. The more she was threatened, the more insufferable she became. She stuck out an incredible amount of tongue again and then started to taunt him with "Ugly, ugly . . ." thirty or forty times. This opinion, which was far from contradicting reality, had never inspired Rubín with anything but scorn; this time, however, it made him so indignant that he would have been perfectly willing to cut off all that tongue she was sticking out at him.

"If you don't clear out of here, you're going to get a real kick—"

He went after her, but Papitos escaped. She seemed to have wings. From the end of the corridor at the kitchen door she repeated her taunts, making monkey faces at him. He went back to his room very annoyed, and a little while later she came in again.

"What do you want here?"

"I've come to prepare the lamp."

The reason she said this with a certain degree of calm and self-assurance was that she heard Doña Lupe coming and calling out in her formidable voice:

"Watch out, Papitos, or I'll come—"

"Auntie, come . . . She's picking a fight."

"Tattle-tale!" the girl said to him under her breath as she took the lamp. "Mmmm, ugly face!"

"It's your own fault!" Doña Lupe added severely from the doorway, "because you go and play with her and this is what comes of it. When you want her to respect you she doesn't. She's very spoiled."

Aunt and nephew exchanged a few words.

"Will you be coming home late tonight, too? Remember, the nights are cold now. These frosts are cruel. You're not up to them."

"I don't feel a thing. I've never felt better," said Rubín, sensing that his shyness was winning out again.

"Don't do anything silly. It's terribly cold. What a bad winter! Would you believe that I couldn't get warm till dawn last night? And that was with four blankets on. It's just awful! We're going 'right through the heart of old man winter,' as my Jáuregui used to say."

5

"Are you going to Doña Silvia's tonight?" Rubín asked her.

"I plan to. If you're going out you can escort me and then pick me up at eleven sharp."

This bothered Maximiliano because she was encroaching on his time, but he didn't say anything.

"And are you going out this afternoon too?" he asked her, hoping that his aunt would leave before lunch so that he could switch the piggy banks while she was out of the house.

"I may go over to Paca Morejón's for a little while."

"I'll take you. I have to go see Narciso to borrow his notes. I'll take you to Habana Street."

Doña Lupe went to the kitchen and scolded Papitos for having let the main course burn. But the girl was used to this and everything else, and wasn't fazed in the slightest. After being called all sorts of insulting names and receiving a pinch that practically tore off some flesh, she stood behind her mistress making faces and sticking out her tongue as she rubbed her pained arm.

"If you think I can't see what you're up to, you're wrong, you scamp," said Doña Lupe without turning around, half-smilingly and half-angrily. Actually, she couldn't get along without Papitos. She needed to have a child around to reprimand and teach.

Doña Lupe put on her cloak and left with Maximiliano. She went as far as Arango Street, and he went on to buy the piggy bank and headed home. The time had come to commit the crime; but for some reason, having displayed such courage during the premeditation, he was intensely restless when the critical moment drew near. He began by defending himself from Papitos' curiosity, locking the door as soon as he had turned on the light. But how could he find protection from his own conscience? It was starting to react, you see, registering this misbehavior as a nefarious crime. He compared the two piggy banks, observing with satisfaction that they were exactly the same size, the same shade of terra-cotta. It would be impossible to detect the substitution. So on with it. The first step was to break the original and take out the gold and silver; then transfer the coins to the new one, adding the two *pesetas* in change that he had gotten at the foodstuffs store. Breaking the piggy bank noiselessly was an impossible feat. He sat for a while in a chair next to the bed where he had put both piggy banks and softly stroked the one destined to become the victim. His eyes fixated vaguely on the light, as if trying to discover an idea in it. The lamp illuminated the bedside table on whose black oilcloth cover stood his school books, covered in newspaper and neatly arranged by Doña Lupe; beside them were a few medicine bottles, an inkwell, and several issues of *La Correspondencia*. The young man's gaze wandered around the narrow room as if tracing the arcs of a fly in flight, going from the table to the rack, where molds of himself hung: his underwear, his coat, which reproduced his torso, and his trousers, which were his own legs, hanging as if stretching out. Then he looked at the dresser, the trunk, and the boots lying on it: his own feet cut off, but ready to walk. A happy gesture and the animation in his face indicated that Maximiliano had caught the idea he was chasing. He was so right: love had suddenly turned him into a man of talent. He got up, and picking up a boot he went to the kitchen, where Papitos was singing.

"Will you give me the pestle? This boot has a nail in it that's so huge it's crippling me."

Papitos took the pestle and pretended she was going to bash in the Señorito's head.

"Come on, be a good girl or I'll tell Auntie. She told me to watch you, and to whack you on the head if you left the kitchen."

Papitos started to chop some endive and kept on making faces.

"And me, I'll tell her," she replied. "I'll tell her what her scheming little nephew does."

Maximiliano trembled.

"Silly! What do I do?" he said, hiding his anxiety.

"Shut yourself up in your room—*olé!*—so nobody will see you. But *I* saw you through the keyhole—*olé, olé!*"

"What?"

"Writing letters to your girl friend."

"That's a lie. *Me?* Get out of my way, you nosy brat!"

He went back to his room with the pestle, and once he'd locked the door again, he plugged the keyhole with a handkerchief.

"She won't spy on me, but just in case it does occur to her . . ."

Time was short and Doña Lupe might come home. When he picked up the full piggy bank his heart started to thump and it was hard to breathe. He felt sorry for the victim, and to control his compassion, which might frustrate the act, he did what criminals do: he struck the first blow frenetically in order to conquer his fear and calm his conscience, preventing himself from turning back. He grabbed the piggy bank and with a feverish hand whacked it hard. The victim sighed weakly. It had cracked, but had not broken yet. Since he dealt this first blow on the floor, it sounded so loud that he thought it would be better to put the wounded pig on the bed. He was so terrified he practically hit the empty pig instead of the full one, but he collected his wits and said: "What a fool I am! Why shouldn't I do whatever I want with it? After all, it's mine." And this spurred him on. The poor victim, his loyal old friend, a model of honesty and trust, groaned at the savage blows and at last broke into several big chunks. Its gold, silver, and copper innards scattered all over the bed. In the midst of the silver, which predominated, the gold coins sparkled like yellow melon seeds in a pulpy white mass. His hands trembling, the assassin took everything except the small change and put it in his pants pocket. The broken shell looked like pieces of a skull, and the fine red clay dust dirtying the white bedspread was stains of blood in the criminal's eyes. Before thinking about erasing the traces of the breakage, he thought of putting his money in the new piggy bank, and this he did so hastily that the coins got clogged in the slot and some were hard to get through; the slot was a bit narrower than the dead pig's. Then he put in the copper coins he had received for his two *pesetas*.

There was no time to lose. He heard steps. Was Doña Lupe already coming upstairs? No, it wasn't her; but she would be back soon and he had to finish up. Those broken pieces—what could he do with them? This was a problem that made the assassin's hair stand on end. The best thing would be to wrap up the bloody debris in a handkerchief and throw it into the street when he went out. And the blood? He cleaned the bedspread as best he could by blowing off the dust. Then he noticed that his right hand and cuff still showed traces of the crime, and he busied himself with carefully erasing them. The pestle needed a good cleaning too. And how about his clothes—did they have any traces on them? He looked himself over from head to toe. There wasn't a sign on him. Like all killers in these circumstances, he was scrupulous in his examination, but those unfortunate souls always forget something; where they least suspect it, they leave the incriminating evidence that sheds the necessary light for the eyes of the law to detect them.

What disconcerted Rubín when he thought his deed had been concluded was his apprehension that the new piggy bank didn't resemble the sacrificed one at all. How could they have looked so alike before the crime? A perceptual error. The difference he noticed now might be an error too. Had he been wrong before or was he wrong now? In the great turmoil of his mind he was incapable of deciding. "All you have to do is look," he said to himself, "to see that this piggy bank isn't that one. The clay's more baked on this one, it's darker, and it has a black spot here. You can tell at a glance that it's not the same pig. God help me! And their weight? This one seems lighter . . . No, heavier; much heavier. This *would* have to happen!"

He stood staring at the light for some time and envisioned Doña Lupe picking up the piggy bank and saying, "I don't know . . . somehow this piggy bank just doesn't seem the same." Heaving a deep sigh, he quickly proceeded to wrap up the remains of the victim in a handkerchief and put them in his dresser for when he would be ready to leave. He put the new piggy bank in the usual place, the top drawer of his dresser; he opened the door, pulling the handkerchief out of the keyhole, and after depositing the treacherous tool in the kitchen, he returned to his room intending to count the money. Why all this worry and fear? It was his, wasn't it? He hadn't stolen anything from anybody and yet he was acting like a thief. It would be more straightforward to tell his aunt what he had done instead of sneaking around like this. Ha! He could just imagine how Doña Lupe would react if he told her about his adventure and what he planned to use his savings for! It was better to keep things quiet and forge ahead.

He had no opportunity to entertain himself by counting his treasure because Doña Lupe came in and headed straight for the kitchen. Maximiliano paced around his room waiting to be called to eat, and as he did so he made a mental estimate of the unknown sum that weighed so much. "It must be a lot, a heck of a lot," he mused, "because once I put in a big coin, and another time, too. And when I had to take that medicine that tasted so awful my aunt gave me two *duros*, and every time I had to take a purgative, a *duro* or half *duro*. There must be over fifteen *duros* altogether."

He felt a resurgence of his courage. But when they called him to the table and he entered the dining room and faced his aunt, he thought that she could read in his face what he'd done. She looked at him with the same expression as on that cursed day he had torn the buttons off her clothes and hidden them. And so her nephew was perturbed, and saw danger where there was none. "I don't think I got the spread clean enough," he worried as he swallowed his soup. "Darn it, I forgot something, something really important: to look and see whether there were any pieces lying around anywhere. Now I remember, I heard a tinny noise the minute I broke the piggy bank, as if a little piece had hit the iodine flask. On the floor, maybe . . . And my aunt sweeps every day! Oh, the way she's looking at me! Could she suspect anything? All I need now is for her to have stopped in at the shop on her way home from the Morejóns' and the shopkeeper to have said: 'Your nephew was here asking for change for two *pesetas*.'"

Doña Lupe's scrutinizing stare didn't have anything special about it. She was in the habit of studying his face to check on his health, and his face was a book from which the good lady had learned more about medicine than her nephew had learned about pharmacy from textbooks.

"I don't think you're well," she said. "When I came in I heard you cough. It's these chills. For heaven's sake, be careful; let's not have to go through what we did last year when you got four colds in a row and practically had to drop out of school. Don't forget to tie your silk scarf around your head at night when you go to bed. And if I were you, I'd start taking tar water. Don't turn up your nose. It's good to keep an eye on your health. Just in case, I'm bringing home some *tolú* tablets* tomorrow."

With this the young man relaxed, for he realized that the stare was only her daily medical inspection. They ate and prepared to leave. The criminal wrapped himself snugly in his cloak and then turned off the light in his room so as to pick up the remains of the victim in the dark and sneak them out of the house. As the coins in his pants pockets weren't made of straw, they denounced themselves with their jingling. To avoid this vexing noise, Maximiliano put a handkerchief in his pocket, wadding it up so that the gold and silver coins wouldn't make any noise. And so he left, and went all the way from Chamberí to Torquemada's house without his ruse being detected by Doña Lupe, who always perked up her ears at the sound of money, like a cat at the sound of a mouse. When her nephew thought the coins were jingling, he pressed his pocket against his body as if he

---

* Prepared from substances of balsam-yielding trees native to Tolú, Colombia. They are used in cough syrups, expectorants, and tablets.

were reaching for a weapon. You would have thought a tumor had grown on his leg!

II. The Strivings and Mishaps of a Redeemer

I

GREAT INDEED WAS FORTUNATA'S ASTONISHMENT that night when she saw Maximiliano produce fistfuls of varied coins, which he counted quickly, separating the gold from the silver. But the girl's happy surprise was soon supplanted by the suspicion that her new friend had acquired the fortune in some shady manner. She surmised that he was a mamma's boy who in his passion had lost his head and foolishly walked off with the family savings. The thought mortified her no end and made her see the cruel insistence with which fate mistreated her. Ever since she had plunged into the hazards of her type of life she had found herself connected with uncouth, perverse, or deceitful men—"the worst of every lot," as she put it.

She didn't give Maximiliano a clue to her suspicions about the source of the money that, whatever its origin, could not be badly received, and little by little she relaxed, for she saw that the worthy boy boasted about his notions on thriftiness, notions that contradicted those of his predecessors.

"This," he said, showing her a little stack of gold coins, "is for getting out of hock the clothes you need most. Your dressy clothes, your velveteen coat, your hat and jewels will come later, and we'll renew the loan so that you won't lose them. For the time being, forget about anything that's just for show. The circus is over now. You'll spend only what you have, not a cent more, so there won't be any debts. Understand?"

This sensible thinking was new to Fortunata, and she began to alter considerably her original opinion of her lover; indeed, to regard him as better than the rest. In the days that followed, Olmedo confirmed her favorable opinion, ardently praising the boy's good habits and sense of responsibility.

Fortunata and her protector agreed to rent a room that happened to be available in the same building. Rubín stressed that the furniture should be modest and inexpensive because (and this should show how sensible he was) "it was wise to start out simply." Later on they would consider adding to what they had and enhancing it, and their humble home would grow and gradually become attractive. She agreed to everything without an iota of enthusiasm or idealism. She would "try it out." Maximiliano hardly appealed to her, but from the start she could tell from his words and actions that he was decent, and this was a great novelty to her. The idea of living with a decent person aroused her curiosity. It took her two days to get settled. A neighbor who had moved out rented them furniture. Rubín took care of everything so skillfully that Fortunata was awed by his admirable administrative qualities; she was completely devoid of the ingeniousness that some people have for getting the most out of their money, and she had no idea of how to cut expenses or, indeed, master any financial art of the kind Maximiliano had learned from Doña Lupe.

In his attempts to measure the affection he felt for his friend, Maximiliano found the usual verb for "to love"—querer—pale and inexpressive, and he had to resort to novels and poetry in order to find the unusual verb, amar, which is as common in grammatical drills as it is forgotten in everyday language. Even that verb seemed to fall short of expressing the tenderness and ardor of his affection. "Adore" and "idolize" and other such words were better at helping the weak-bodied, high-spirited youth declare his exalted passion.

When the lovesick boy went home he took with him the image of a trans-figured Fortunata. Indeed, there has never been a princess in an oriental tale or a lady in a romantic play who has presented herself to a gentleman's mind with attributes more ideal or features nobler and purer. Two Fortunatas existed during this period: the one of flesh and blood, and the one engraved in Maximiliano's mind. Young Rubín's extraordinary love refined his feelings so greatly that he was inspired not only to good deeds, enthusiasm, and abnegation, but also to a delicacy that even approached chastity. His puny physique hardly existed, but his soul grew robust and its new strength was compelling. All the nobility and beauty a human soul can contain erupted in his like streams of lava out of a live volcano. He envisioned redemption and regeneration, washing away stains and discovering merits in the black past of his beloved. The generous lover saw the sublimest of moral problems on that miserable woman's forehead, and finding a solution to them seemed to him the greatest enterprise a human will could undertake. His feverish enthusiasm impelled him to attempt the social and moral salvation of his idol and to devote all the energy bristling in his soul to this grandiose task. The shameful incidents in her life did not discourage him; he even derived pleasure from measuring the depth of the abyss engulfing his friend, whom he was bound to rescue. And he was going to get her out of there pure . . . or purified. In their confidential sessions, Maximiliano thought he detected a certain rectitude in the sinner and less corruption than had showed at first. Could he be mistaken? Sometimes he suspected that he was, but his good faith immediately triumphed over this suspicion. What he could maintain with no fear of erring was that Fortunata truly wished to improve her character; that is, to become decent and polished. As may be supposed, her ignorance was complete. She read haltingly and didn't know how to write.

The basic things that even children and country bumpkins know she did not know, just as other women of her humble class and even some women of a higher class do not. Maximiliano was intrigued by having to start from scratch, but correcting her along the way was something he took seriously. And she didn't try to hide her lack of culture; on the contrary, she was disarmingly sincere in showing her burning desire to acquire certain notions and learn refined, decent language. She was constantly asking what this or that word meant and informing herself on hundreds of bits of common knowledge. She didn't know what north and south were. They had something to do with the wind, she thought, but that was all. She thought that a senator was a thing in the Town Hall. On printing she had very strange notions; she thought that the authors themselves wrote those nice equal letters on the pages. She'd never read a book in her life, not even a novel. She thought that Europe was a town and England was a country inhabited by creditors. As for the sun, the moon, and the rest of the firmament, her notions were those of a primitive people. She confessed one day that she didn't know who Columbus was. She thought he was a general, "sort of like O'Donnell or Prim." She was no better at religion than she was at history. The little she had learned of the Christian doctrine she had forgotten. She had some sense of the Virgin, Christ, and Saint Peter; she considered them good people, but that was it. As for immortality and redemption, her ideas were very confused. She knew that if you repented with all your heart, you'd be saved, for sure. And no matter what she was told, nothing involving love was sinful.

Her defects in pronunciation were atrocious. It would have taken superhuman powers to make her say "fragment," "magnificent," "enigma," and other common words. She strived to overcome this difficulty, laughing and emphasizing it, but she could not. Final s sounds became h's and she didn't even notice the difference; she couldn't help it. She swallowed lots of syllables. If she had known how pretty her mouth looked when she did it, she wouldn't have tried to correct her charming defects. But Maximiliano had acquired the strictness of a schoolteacher and the conceit of an academic. He didn't give her a moment's rest and stalked after her solecisms, ready to pounce on them like a cat on a mouse.

"It's not '*deffrence*,' it's '*difference*.' It's not 'Holly Ghost' or 'indilgences.' Besides, saying you're 'fed up' sounds awful, and calling everything you don't understand 'tiology'' is terrible. And saying 'you're damned sure' every two seconds is vulgar."

The most appealing quality in Fortunata was her naiveté. Maximiliano re-

---

* *Tiología* is Fortunata's rendering of *teología* (theology). It sounds terrible to Maxi because *tío* means 'guy' or 'fellow.'

minded her repeatedly of the fact that she had been dishonored, since it was an important point in his plan of moral regeneration. The inspired young man stressed vigorously how bad señoritos were and how much Spaniards needed a law like the English one to protect innocent girls from seducers. Fortunata didn't have an inkling as to what these laws were about. All she maintained was that said Juanito Santa Cruz was the only man she had ever really loved, and that she would always love him. Why claim anything else? Avowing, like a gentleman, that her feelings were praiseworthy, Maximiliano nevertheless felt pricklings of jealousy that momentarily interfered with his redemptive plans.

"And do you love him so much that you'd save him if you saw he was in danger?"

"Of course—you can be sure of it. If I saw he was in danger, I'd get him out even if it meant that I had to die. I can only say what I've got in my heart. If it's not true, may God strike me down tonight."

She looked so attractive as she made this declaration that Rubín looked at her for a long time before commenting:

"No, don't swear to it; you don't have to. I believe you. Tell me something else: if he were to come in the door this minute and say, 'Fortunata, come with me'—would you go?"

Fortunata looked at the door. Rubín swallowed saliva and felt for a mustache to twist, but finding only a few thin hairs, he martyrized them cruelly.

"That depends . . . ," she said, her brow wrinkling. "I might go and I might not."

2

Maximiliano wanted to know everything. He was like a good doctor who asks his patient about the most insignificant details related to the illness being suffered and wants a complete history so as to know how to treat the case. Fortunata did not hide anything—which was good—and her loving doctor sometimes found that he had perhaps more information than was necessary for the prodigious cure. And how horrible it was, hearing how badly that beauty's seducers had behaved! The scrupulously honest pharmacologist's apprentice didn't see how there could be such evil men; all the tortures in hell weren't punishment enough, in his opinion. A more perverse criminal than assassins and thieves, this señorito who had seduced a poor girl, made her think he was planning to marry her and then ditched her with a baby, or the makings of one. What price would he, Maximiliano Rubín, have to be paid to do that? Juanito Santa Cruz was the most infamous, execrable, vile man imaginable. Yet the offended woman herself wasn't as severe as one would have expected in her fulminations against her seducer; this doubled Maximiliano's fury and led him to call Juanito a monster and other uncomplimentary names. Fortunata realized that she must repeat the names, but there was no way to make her utter the word "monster." It got stuck inside somehow, like so many others, and finally, after dozens of attempts (which made her feel nauseous), she emitted the word from her extremely pretty teeth and mouth as if she were spitting it out.

She preferred to relate details from her childhood. Her deceased father had owned a stand in the square, and he was an honest man; her mother, like Segunda, her paternal aunt, was in the egg business. They had called her "Pitusa" ever since she'd been a little girl because she was very rickety and weak until she was twelve; then suddenly she blossomed overnight into a graceful, seductive woman. Her parents died when she was twelve. Maximiliano listened to these details with pleasure. But soon he told her to get to the heart of the matter, the serious things, like the baby she had had. Halfway through the story, the young man felt tears well up in his eyes; he envisioned the tender, young, fatherless creature; the poor mother's distress at finding herself abandoned—it really did make a pathetic picture. Why hadn't she protested to the authorities? That's what she should have done. Those cads had to be dealt with sternly. And another thing—why hadn't she made a scene, gone to his house, babe in arms, to tell Doña Bárbara and Don Baldomero, sparing them no details about their sweet little son's deed? But no, this wouldn't have been dignified. It was better to scorn him, let him struggle with his conscience, which would give him a good fight sooner or later.

Hearing this, Fortunata fixed her gaze on the floor and repeated mechanically, "Yes, scorning him is best." "Scorn him," repeated Maximiliano, "it would be ignominious to seek his protection." But no matter what the prize, Fortunata would not have been capable of pronouncing "ignominy." Maximiliano insisted that it had been a grave error to seek aid from Juanito Santa Cruz, the infamous wretch, when she got back to Madrid and her child was ill.

"But silly, don't you see that if it hadn't of been for him, we wouldn't of had the money to bury him?" said Fortunata, coming to the defense of her own executioner.

"I would have left him unburied before resorting to . . . Dignity, dear, comes first. Take note of it. Now what I want to know is, who was the character you joined up with afterward, the one who carted you off from Madrid and took you around from town to town like a circus?"

"He was a mean, sneaky man," Fortunata said listlessly, as if the memory of that part of her life was very disagreeable to her. "I went off with him because I felt lost, and didn't have anyplace to go; he was the brother of a neighbor of ours in the Cava de San Miguel. First he had a meat-scrap stand on the square; then he opened a junk shop. He went to all the fairs with tons of chests full of trinkets and he set up to sell his wares. They called him 'Juárez el Negro' because his skin was very dark. Seeing how bad off I was, he offered me the sun and the moon and promised to do all kinds of stuff for me. My aunt threw me out and then my uncle disappeared. I was sick, and Juárez said if I went with him he'd take me to a spa. He said he earned loads at the fairs and that I'd live like a queen. He couldn't marry me 'cause he was already married, but as soon as his wife died—and she was a drunk—he'd keep his word, he said."

And she continued to relate that ugly page of her life, quickly, so that it would be finished faster. As disastrous as it was, her tale about the señorito, Santa Cruz, was told in great detail and with a certain bitter satisfaction; but what she said about "Juárez el Negro" crossed her lips like a forced confession or testimony before a jury, the kind of confession that burns one's mouth on the way out. Oh, how she regretted having put herself in that man's hands! He was a profligate, a rascal. She would have resisted following him if her relatives hadn't pushed her into it; they didn't have the slightest desire to support her, and they let her know it. Soon she saw that the only thing Juárez el Negro had to offer was conversation. He didn't earn a penny; he picked quarrels with everyone, and all the venom he had accumulated in his depraved soul he poured onto his mistress. To make a long story short, she'd never had such a degrading life and hoped she never would again. With the money Juanito Santa Cruz gave her when she was back in Madrid and the child died, the brute would have been able to fix up his business, but what did he do? drink, drink, drink. And wine and cheap spirits in those quantities finished him off. One morning she was awakened by a loud growling, as if he were being strangled. What was it? He was dying. Terrified, she jumped out of bed and called the neighbors. There wasn't time to give him the last rites; all he got was the annointing. This happened in Lérida. Two days later she sold their few belongings and rounded up enough funds to get herself to Barcelona. She had vowed to have nothing to do with brutes again. Freedom, freedom, and more freedom was what she craved.

Put the truth above all. Why say one thing instead of another? Frankness can be a virtue when all others are lacking, and frankness obliged Fortunata to state that in the first period of this moral anarchy she had had some fun forgetting her cares, as drunks do. She had great success, and her ignorant state helped to blind her. She came to believe that if she really wallowed in vice she would be taking revenge on the men who had put her where she was, and she often thought that if that scoundrel Santa Cruz could see her in her glory, so elegant and triumphant, he'd fall in love with her again. But ha! A fine state she was in for him . . . After relating this, she described so many other things that Maximiliano felt wounded. He was forced to "drop a curtain," as the rhetoricians say, over that part of his beloved's life. The curtain had to be very thick, for Fortunata's frankness projected a glaring light on the events related, and her picturesque language made them reverberate. Then she deleted various episodes from her tale, skipping over not just words but paragraphs and entire chapters, the gist of the remainder being the following: Torrellas, the famous Cataluñan landscape artist, was so jealous that he didn't give her a moment's peace. He thought up hundreds of ways to torment her, and he set traps for her. The man became so abominable that she finally let herself fall into one of his traps. She walked into it on purpose, recognizing it for what it was, out of sheer pleasure at being able to put one over on *him*; with this she could take revenge on him for all the times he'd tried to trick her. And that was it. The result? The blasted tree painter almost killed her. What infuriated him most was that her infidelity had involved a close friend of his, also a painter, the author of a painting of *David Gazing at* . . . somebody, Fortunata couldn't remember the name, but it was somebody who was taking a bath. She didn't love either of them; she wouldn't have given two cents for either of them if they had been for sale. Their paintings were worth more than they were. From the moment she deceived the first with the second, she got the idea of putting one over on both of them, and the satisfaction of this desire was granted her by a young employee, poor and rather endearing, bearing a strong resemblance to Juanito Santa Cruz.

Another curtain. Maximiliano felt it must be drawn.

"Be quiet, do me a favor and be quiet," he said, thinking as he heard her story that it needed at least a bolt of tulle.

But she kept on talking. "Well, like I was sayin', that young man turned out to be a slippery one too." One morning, when she was asleep, he pawned all her jewels so that he could go gamble. And that was it. Then there was an old man who gave her lots of money and took her to Paris, where she dressed to the teeth and refined her taste in clothes to an extraordinary degree. *He* was an old trickster! He had been a Carlist general in the last war and had engaged in many dealings with the clergy. He was totally depraved and gave her constant headaches with his never-ending demands. One day she got mad and then he ditched her. His successor, Camps, set her up in a luxurious apartment. He seemed very rich, but later it turned out that his money was from a long-term swindle. Before coming to Madrid she "smelled somethin' rotten," and shortly after that she knew a storm was brewing. Camps had letters of recommendation addressed to the director of the Treasury and tried to collect on some false bills for guns that the government had supposedly bought. One night he came home looking all stormy, grabbed a small suitcase, filled it with clothes, asked Fortunata for all the money she had, and said he was going to El Escorial, a town north of Madrid. So he left and never showed up again. Maximiliano knew the rest very well: *he* had succeeded Camps, and the special glow in his eyes showed how proud he was of his inheritance. And Fortunata had expressed it plainly: thank God she had come across a decent person in her life!

Maximiliano thought he possessed redemptive powers akin to nature's creative powers. The world would soon see how he would make goodness and truth radiate from that miserable victim of man! Ever since he had met her and felt that the sky inhabited his soul, he was all idealism, nobility, and good deeds. What a difference there was between him and the reckless men in whose hands the poor thing had been until now! No matter how one probed into Rubín's life, all that could be found were headaches and other physical discomforts. An ignominious act? Not even misbehavior of any kind.

3

One of the things that Maximiliano considered the most important for his redemptive plan's success was Fortunata's loving him; without that, his sublime work would surely encounter obstacles. If Fortunata grew fond of him, even if only for moral reasons (which meant the smallest quantity of love possible), it wouldn't be so hard for him to convert her to goodness: her soul would be attracted to his. This prerequisite, love, caused Maximiliano to ask his idol repeatedly whether she loved him yet, or whether she was at least beginning to love him. Sometimes she said that she did love him, replying with the mechanical ease of a studious child who knows her lesson well. At other times, more sincere and pensive, she would say that being fond of someone didn't depend on one's will, and even less on logic, which is why a woman as smart as a fox could fall in love with any old simpleton and turn up her nose at a decent man. She assured Maximiliano that she was very grateful for his having treated her so well, and that this gratitude would, in time, give way to love. According to Rubín, the natural order of things in the spiritual realm allows that love be born from gratitude as well as certain other parents. His heart told him in its quiet way that Fortunata would eventually love him, and he patiently awaited the fulfillment of this sweet prophecy. Nevertheless, he felt that he was not on firm ground, because one's heart can prove to be wrong; so the poor boy spent hours of dire anguish alone at home, lost in deep thoughts on the state of his mistress' true feelings. He swung from the cruelest doubts to the boldest assertions. He could just as easily feel convinced that she didn't care a whit about him as he could that she was beginning to love him, and he found himself debating the issue constantly, analyzing her words and gestures and actions, interpreting them in one way or another. "Why did she say such and such? What did she mean with that reticence? And that little giggle—what did it mean? When she opened the door yesterday, she didn't say a word; but when I left, she told me to dress warmly."

Their apartment was in a building tucked away on what used to be called San Antón Street. At the entrance there was a glassed-in watchmaker's shop that left so little space in the entranceway that obese people had to come in sideways. On the ground floor there was a bakery that filled the house with the aroma of cinnamon and sugar. On the main floor there was a pawnshop with a lamp hanging over the street, and on certain days pawned cloaks were aired on the balconies. The floors above were divided into narrow, low-priced apartments. On each floor there was one on the right, one on the left, and two interior apartments. There were two types of tenants: loose women, and families engaged in business at the nearby San Antón marketplace. Poultry dealers and greengrocers inhabited those cramped quarters, putting their children out to play on the staircase. Feliciana lived in one of the exterior apartments on the second floor and Fortunata lived in an interior on the third floor. Rubín had rented it because of the proximity; he intended to move to a better place when their circumstances changed.

Maximiliano spent all the time he could there. He stayed until midnight, sometimes until one, and wasn't absent even when he had one of his terrible migraines. The surprise and confusion that this inspired in Doña Lupe goes without saying; nor was she satisfied with the explanations that her little nephew was feeding her. "He's keeping something from me," said the astute lady, "or, to put it bluntly, someone."

When Maximiliano went to his beloved's with a migraine, she took care of him almost as well as Doña Lupe herself and did everything possible to keep the children in the poultry shop from making a racket. Her patient was so grateful that his love grew—if something already so large could grow, that is. He noted with satisfaction that Fortunata went out as seldom as possible. Mornings she went out to shop with her basket on her arm and was back in fifteen minutes. She cooked and cleaned house herself, which occupied almost her entire day. She didn't receive any women whose conduct was reprehensible, and her own was strictly adjusted to the standards of her newly regulated life. "She's honest to the core," thought Maximiliano, overjoyed. "She's so diligent that when she finishes something she undoes it and does it over again so as not to be idle. Work is the cornerstone of virtue. There's no doubt about it: this woman was leading that bad life only because she was forced to."

Adrift in these honeyed fantasies of his enraptured soul, Maximiliano nevertheless felt sharp stabbings every now and then: the knives of reality. It was like dropping off to sleep in a pleasant haze only to be ferociously bitten by a mosquito. And no matter how much he stretched the money from his piggy bank, it would all have to end, for everything ends in this world, money going the fastest. Holy Mary! When the time he feared came . . . when the last *peseta* from the last *duro* was cashed! If the mosquito bit Maximiliano in his sleep or as he was falling asleep, he bolted upright, as wide awake as at midday, or he tossed around and overheated the bed with his feverish worrying. Sometimes he invoked the heavens, praying fervently, hoping that the generous task that he had set himself would carry weight in fate's designs on him and might free him from the mire into which the lovers would surely sink. He was not a cad; she was behaving well, and her conduct encouraged him to drop one curtain after another over her past. If fate failed to take into account such circumstances, what good was it to be well-behaved, a model of order and good faith? There couldn't be any doubt about it; and Fortunata agreed when he confided his fears to her. It simply had to be that way, or everything people said about fate was hogwash.

Soon I'll explain how they got their way, which shows that they did have someone up there—some sort of godfather protecting them. And they well deserved such protection, because he, ennobled by his affection, and she, aspiring to an honest life and embarking on one already, were two priceless individuals; or shall we at least say, worthy of receiving the funds they needed to continue their virtuous campaign.

4

The only visitors they admitted were Feliciana and Olmedo. Neither particularly pleased Maximiliano; Feliciana's commonness and base nature made her incapable of leading an honest life, and Olmedo, with his impetuosity and talkativeness, was always relishing dirty jokes and bad words. He would come in with his hat pushed back, affecting a coarseness that wasn't really in him, imitating how a drunk looks, talks, and acts, while abstaining from drink; he gave the excuse that it was bad for his stomach, but the real reason was that he got dizzy and acted giddy after the second drink. Maximiliano told Fortunata when they were alone that they ought to move away from neighbors who were so unlike the decent people they proposed to emulate.

Of all the plans our lover had for the redemption of his mistress, none seemed so urgent as that of teaching her to read and write. Every morning he made her spend half an hour practicing her penmanship. Fortunata wanted to learn, but neither her patience nor her concentration was an aid in that effort to acquire some calligraphic skill. Her fingers had become too tough for such delicate operations. Working since childhood had caused her pretty hands to become robust, as coarse as a laborer's, though not steady enough to write. The ink stained her fingers and she perspired profusely, running out of breath and then making a comely little trumpet of her mouth just as she was about to make a stroke.

"Don't make your mouth look like a little snout, dear; it's very ugly," said her professor, stroking her head. "Don't clench your fingers like that. It's so easy, it's the easiest thing in the world."

For him. But for her, never having endured such torture, writing was an insurmountable obstacle. She remarked sadly that she would never learn, and lamented that she had never been sent to school. Reading tired her too, and bored her to tears; after trying for some time to decipher a syllable, like someone slowly drawing a bucketful of water up a well, it turned out that she didn't have the foggiest notion of what the text said. She would throw down the book or newspaper scornfully, declaring that she couldn't bear it any longer.

While she showed no inclination toward literary matters, she was not only conscientious but even gifted with the social arts. The lessons Maximiliano gave her on the social graces she absorbed easily, often needing only a slight indication to assimilate an idea or cluster of ideas.

"Even though the inky stuff bothers you," he would say, "I think you are talented."

In no time at all, he taught her all the formulas suitable for formal visits: greetings for arriving and taking leave, how to make guests feel at home, and many other fine points of polite conduct. She also learned such important things as the order of the months of the year (which she didn't know) and which months have thirty and which have thirty-one days. It may be hard to believe, but this gap is a typical one in Spanish ignorance, found more in cities than in towns and more among women than men. She enjoyed household work very much and never tired of it. Her muscles were made of steel; resting didn't suit her fiery blood. Whenever possible she prolonged her tasks instead of trying to get them over with. Washing and ironing delighted her no end, and she devoted herself to these tasks with pleasure and ardor, tirelessly developing the strength in her arms. Her flesh was hard and firm, and her robust body was very agile; her grace combined with her roughness, and this mixture made her the most beautiful savage imaginable. Her body had no need of corsets to be slim. Clothed, she was a source of pride to dressmakers; nude or half-dressed, as she walked around the house hanging out the clothes on the balcony, dusting the furniture, or puffing up the mattresses as if they were cushions to be aired, she looked like a figure from another era. Or at least Rubín thought so. The only place he'd seen beauty like hers was in paintings of Amazons. At other times, he fancied she was one of the biblical women—Bathsheba, the one who bathed herself, or Magdalene* or Rebekah,—ladies he had seen in an illustrated work; but as well built as they were, they still couldn't match the healthy beauty and grace of his friend Fortunata.

At first Maximiliano neglected his studies, but as he began to express his love

---

*Although Galdós speaks of a woman of Samaria, Magdalene seems preferable in English for two reasons: to avoid the confusing image of the Good Samaritan (beauty, not virtue, is praised), and to associate Fortunata with an image of a reformed prostitute.

in this more regular life, his awareness of the moral mission upon which he had embarked stimulated him to work hard, to finish his studies and start practicing his profession. Something quite special was happening inside him: he discovered that he was more alert, more perspicacious, more curious about the secrets of science and interested in things that had previously bored him. In his private meditations, he fell into the habit of telling himself that "he had developed talent" for his work, almost as if this talent were a fever. Without a doubt, he had changed. In half an hour he could learn a lesson that used to take him two hours (and even in two hours he never really mastered it). His awe grew when he heard himself answer questions in class easily now, and he realized that his opinions made good sense. His teacher and fellow students were dumbfounded at the way *Rubinius vulgaris* had miraculously blossomed overnight. And he derived keen pleasure from certain books that had nothing to do with pharmacology, books that had never attracted his attention before. Some of his friends used to sneak in famous literary works to read in class. Rubín had never had the urge to hide, say, Goethe's *Werther* or Shakespeare's plays between the pages of his *Organic Chemical Pharmacy*; but after being shaken up by love, he acquired such a taste for great literary creations that he was engrossed by them. He devoured *Faust* and Heine's poems; and French, which had been an obstacle, soon became easy. In a word, our man had undergone a deep crisis. The amorous cataclysm had changed his inner constitution. He now regarded himself as a sleeping soul who had been awakened when fate confronted him with that special woman and the problem of redeeming her.

"When I was dumb," he would say, without disguising the scorn he had for his, shall we say, antediluvian period, "when I was dumb, I was dumb because I had no purpose in life. That's what the dumb are: people who have no mission in life."

Fortunata did not have a maid. She said that in a home as small as theirs she could handle everything and still have free time. Many afternoons while she was in the kitchen Maximiliano did his homework stretched out on the sofa in the living room. If it hadn't been for the ghost of the piggy bank that appeared to him from time to time to announce that the money was almost gone, the poor boy would have been ecstatic. Even in spite of this, though, he was seized with happiness and drunk on a love that colored all his thoughts with optimism. There were no difficulties, no dangers, no stumbling blocks. The money would come from somewhere. Fortunata was good, and her intentions to be proper were plainly clear. Things were going just as they should, and all he had to do was finish his studies and . . . When he reached this point, an idea that he had kept tucked away ever since the beginning of their relationship (for he did not want to announce it until the time was ripe) came bubbling to his lips. He couldn't keep the secret any longer; it was struggling to escape, and if he didn't tell it, he'd burst, that's all there was to it; his secret was the result of all his love, it was his soul, it expressed all the new and sublime essences in him, and such hugeness cannot be constrained by the narrow limits of discretion.

The partially redeemed sinner came into the living room (which often doubled as a dining room) to set the table, a very simple task that she did in about five minutes. Maximiliano threw himself at his mistress with that blind respect that possessed him every now and then and, chastely kissing her bare arm and taking her rough hand and pressing it to his heart, he declared:

"Fortunata, I'm going to marry you."

Incredulous, she burst out laughing; but Rubín repeated, "I'm going to marry you," so solemnly that Fortunata began to believe it.

"I thought of this some time ago," he added. "It occurred to me when I met you, a month ago. But it seemed best not to say anything until I knew you better. Either I marry you or I'll die. It's a dilemma."

"What a riot! What does dilemma mean?"

"It means this: either I marry you or I die. You're going to be mine in the eyes of God and the world. Don't you want to lead a decent life? Well, all you need to be decent is to wish to be, and to have a name. I've decided to make you decent, and you *will* be—that is, if you would like to be."

He bent over to pick up the books that had fallen to the floor. Fortunata disappeared to get what she needed to finish setting the table, and when she came back she said:

"You should think these things over . . . not for my sake, but for yours."

"Oh, I've thought it over all right, and very carefully. How about you—had it occurred to you?"

"No, I never even dreamed of it. Your family's going to be against it."

"I'll be legally of age soon," Rubín stated energetically. "They can oppose it if they wish; it's all the same to me."

Fortunata sat down next to him, the table partially set and dinner about to burn. Maximiliano embraced her and kissed her over and over; she was rather bewildered, not particularly pleased, to tell the truth, looking one way, then another. Her friend's generosity did not leave her indifferent, and to his squeezes of her hand she responded with some rather less passionate ones, and to his amorous caresses, with friendly ones. She rose to return to the kitchen, and began to weigh in her mind the idea of this marriage as she mechanically poured the soup into the tureen. "Me, get married! Not on your life! And to that pipsqueak! Live with him forever and a day, every day, every day and every *night*! But just think, Fortunata, you'd be decent, married, a señora . . . decent!"

5

Maximiliano had often mentioned the Rubíns to her, which is why she had some idea of what Doña Lupe, Juan Pablo, and the priest were like. Through the details the young man gradually revealed about his relatives, Fortunata got to know them as if she had met them herself. That night, excited by his decision to get married, he let slip something about his aunt that was perhaps indiscreet. Doña Lupe lent money through a man named Torquemada to military people, employees, and any other needy individuals. Maximiliano, in all sincerity, was not in favor of earning money like that, but what could he do about how his aunt ran her life? She loved him dearly and would probably make him her heir. She had an antique desk, an enormous old black iron thing opposite her bed where she kept her money and IOU notes. She spent only what was necessary, and her fortune grew from month to month, God knows how much. She was probably rich, very rich, because Torquemada used to bring her stacks of bills. As for his brother Juan Pablo, it was a known fact that he was on the Carlists' side and that if they took over he'd be given a very high post. His brother Nicolás would eventually become a prebendary and—who knows?—maybe even a bishop. In short, the young couple had a sunny horizon to contemplate. They spent the first night commenting on these and other details until Maximiliano departed, leaving Fortunata pensive and worried. She finally fell asleep, and had an uneasy night.

Her lover had a hard time getting to sleep too, but it was because his enthusiasm tickled the walls of his stomach and left a lump in his lungs that made it hard to breathe and, moreover, lit up his brain as if with candles. No matter how hard he tried to put them out and fall asleep, he could not. His aunt was a bit piqued. She undoubtedly suspected something and, being quick to pick up a scent, she no longer fell for the story that he had been studying, or had sick friends who needed care. Two days after the exalted youth's betrothal, Doña Lupe had a serious talk with him. The lady's face revealed suspicion and also deep grief, and when she called her nephew into the parlor he felt his courage wane. The lady took off her cloak and, folding it neatly, put it on top of the dresser. After sticking some pins into it, she looked at her nephew, making him tremble with these words:

"I have to speak with you at length."

Whenever his aunt said "at length" it meant he was in for a scolding.

"Do you have a migraine today?" Doña Lupe asked.

Maximiliano's head felt fine, but to get into a favorable position he said that he felt one coming on; Doña Lupe would pity him. He dropped into a chair and frowned.

"Well, I have some bad news," declared Jáuregui's widow. "I mean, not exactly bad, but . . . it's not good, either."

Not knowing what his aunt might be referring to, Rubín had a hunch that it had nothing to do with his clandestine love and he breathed a sigh of relief. The walls of his stomach felt less oppressed and he calmed down again upon hearing the following:

"The news won't affect you much. Why beat around the bush? Your Aunt Melitona Llorente has passed away. Look, here's the letter from the priest in Molina de Aragón. He says she died like a saint; she received all the holy sacraments and left thirteen thousand *reales* for Masses for her soul."

Maximiliano scarcely knew his maternal aunt. He'd only seen her once or twice when he was very little, and the only image he had was the ring-shaped cakes and honeyed grape syrup she used to send them every year when Don Nicolás Rubín was alive. Indeed, the news of this good lady's demise meant little to him.

"As long as it was God's will," he murmured, to say something.

Doña Lupe turned her back to open the dresser drawer, and in this posture said:

"You and your brothers are Melitona's heirs and, according to my calculations, she must have had the tidy sum of twenty or twenty-five thousand *duros*."

Maximiliano couldn't hear very well because his aunt had her back turned, but it interested him so much that he got up, leaned an elbow on the dresser, and asked her to repeat it to make sure he had heard right.

"That's the way I figure it," added Doña Lupe. "But you know how it is in small towns: you can't tell what people have or don't have. She probably lent some money, which is like throwing it to the wind. You collect long after you should and not all that you lent—if you collect anything at all, that is. So don't get your hopes up. When Juan Pablo comes to Madrid he'll go up to Molina de Aragón to find out about the will and collect what belongs to you."

"Have him go right away," said Maximiliano, slapping the dresser. "I mean, have him go and collect it at the station and take the next train out."

"He doesn't have to do it that fast. Your brother is in Bayonne. The best thing would be for him to go through Molina on his way to Madrid. I'll write to him today. You just calm yourself. You're always like that now—either all listless or a keg of gunpowder. *Now*, that is; you used to ask one foot permission to move the other. You're becoming so impetuous."

She looked at him so penetratingly that the poor boy felt his spirits flag again. As long as his aunt didn't stare at him with her beady brown eyes and make him aware of her astuteness, he was strong-willed. Under her gaze, though, he felt so lost he hastened to change the subject; he asked his aunt how old Doña Melitona was when she died. Señora Jáuregui spent some time reckoning, puckering her lower lip and nodding her head until she came up with a number that Maximiliano didn't hear. Then she went back to the subject of her nephew's transformation and made a few jokes about it that Maximiliano found very unfunny.

"I can see that with all this studying with your friends you're turning into a walking encyclopedia. Don't try to pull the wool over my eyes. You're spending your days and half the night in some sort of conspiracy. I'm not worried about your getting mixed up with women. You don't like that sort of fun and besides, you couldn't, even if you wanted to."

Hearing that "you couldn't" bothered and humiliated him so much that he almost hit her. But it didn't come to that, because Doña Lupe had more important things to do than try to find out if her nephew could or could not. Papitos was the one who saved him this time by turning his aunt's attention to her. That little monkey had her days, all right. Sometimes she did everything so diligently and cleanly that Doña Lupe said she was a gem. But there were days when she was unbearable. That day started out as one of her good ones and ended up as one of her worst. She had done her duty admirably that morning; her tongue and hands had moved freely at first, and she had grimaced and frolicked as soon as her mistress wasn't watching. The feverish activity was a sign of trouble to come. That afternoon she cracked the soup tureen cover, and from that moment on it was one disaster after another. When she sulked, she also seemed to be doing things wrong on purpose. She did the opposite of what she was told, making countless mistakes in an hour. Doña Lupe phrased it well when she said that Papitos had a streak of the devil in her and was evil, really evil; shameless, and spoiled, and a calamity—"in the full sense of the word." And the more her hair was pulled, the worse she got. So much hot water got into the stew that the vegetables drowned in the puddle. The garbanzos burned and tasted foul. And the soup! There wasn't a Christian alive who could have downed it, with all the salt that cursed little creature had dumped into it. And on top of all this she was insolent. Instead of admitting her mistakes, she would blame them on her mistress, saying: "Look, I'm not gonna hang around here for one more day 'cause nobody would treat me this bad." Doña Lupe argued vehemently with her and enforced her reprimands with cruel pinches, adding that Papitos' mother had authorized her to horsewhip her, if need be. To which Papitos replied glaringly:

"Do me a favor and stop rippin' me to shreds."

This was usually the culminating stage of the argument, which terminated with the lady giving her servant a resounding slap in the face and the girl bursting into tears. The nonsense didn't end here, though; when Papitos set the table she put the plates down without bothering to consider that they weren't made of iron. Doña Lupe threatened to lock her up, or call in a couple of policemen, or marinate and pickle her, and eventually the little savage was placated and again became as docile as a lamb.

6

Pleased that all this fuss had made his aunt completely forget him, Maximiliano sided with the household authority against Papitos. She *was* a nuisance; she was shameless . . . a menace. He fanned the flames of Doña Lupe's anger so that she wouldn't keep talking about his new habits and what he did when he went out.

That night Doña Lupe went to visit the Cañas family. Maximiliano came home at eleven. He had left Fortunata in bed, almost asleep, and was resolved to stand up to his aunt's innuendoes by declaring his intentions. Since the inheritance had appeared on the horizon, there could be no doubt but that fate was on his side, showing him the way. He had never been very religious, but that night it seemed disrespectful or even ungrateful not to dedicate a thought, if not a prayer, to divine powers. He was like a man possessed. On the way home he gazed at the stars and found them more beautiful than ever, like wide eyes brimming with messages. Without mentioning the inheritance he was due to receive from the deceased, he had told Fortunata a bit about his farmlands in Molina de Aragón and had said something about money in mortgages being the best kind. His imagination often increased the amount of the inheritance; he added zeroes "because people in small towns don't spend a cent; all they do is save, save, save."

The streetlights looked like stars, and the passers-by, excellent people whose actions stemmed from good intentions and noble sentiments. He entered his house determined to have it out with his aunt.

"Do I dare?" he wondered. "If only I dared . . . But what am I doing that's wrong? After all, what can my aunt do to me—eat me alive? If she refuses to let me make my own choice in marriage I'll tell *her* a thing or two. You never know what anybody's like till they really show it."

In spite of this belligerent preparation, though, when Papitos said that the Señora had not returned, it took a great burden off his mind; revealing the secret and then facing the music was enough to make the pluckiest person in the world cringe. His fear of being defeated didn't paralyze him, though, because his love and sense of mission gave him great courage. It would be wise to proceed with tact and diplomacy, however; to weigh cautiously what he was going to say, so as not to offend his aunt and, if possible, get her on his side in this awful business.

He followed Papitos into the kitchen. It was an old habit of theirs, talking and amusing themselves when they were alone. The year before, maid and student would while away their time there telling each other stories or riddles. The girl was good at riddles; you could hear her laughter from the street when she came up with the answer that he couldn't guess. Maximiliano would scratch his head as if to sharpen his brain, but the answer wouldn't come. Papitos called him a dodo, a blockhead, and worse, but he didn't take offense. He got back at her with stories, of which he had a huge repertoire, and she would listen in awe, her mouth hanging open and her eyes glued to the narrator. That night Papitos was in a horrible mood due to the beating she had taken, and she had a grudge against the Señorito because he hadn't sided with her in the quarrel as he usually did.

"Ugly, stupid," she said, wrinkling her snout when she saw him sit down at the pine table. "Tattletale, butterfingers . . . you silly nitwit!"

Maximiliano searched for a formula of apology that would not compromise his dignity as her master. He felt protective toward her. They *had* been playmates, after all; and despite their difference in age, both had been only children a year ago when they still entertained themselves with innocent games. But things were different now. He was a man—and what a man!—and Papitos was a frolicsome kid without an ounce of common sense. She was a good girl, and when she grew up and settled down, she'd be a priceless maid. After hurling all those insults at him, she started to mend a stocking that she had put her left hand into as though it were a glove. Her sewing kit, a cigar box, was on the table. Inside were spools, snippets of ribbon, a filthy little packet of needles, a piece of white wax, buttons, and other items pertaining to the art of sewing. A primer in which Papitos was learning to read was also there with its dirty, dog-eared pages. The kitchen lamp with its smoky unshaded glass cover lit up the maid's gypsylike face, tinging it reddish-bronze, and illuminated the master's pale, waxen face with violet circles under the eyes and pimples around the mouth.

"Do you want me to test you on your lesson?" asked Rubín, picking up her primer.

"I don't need it. Weakling, toothpick! You look like somebody *scribbled* you instead of makin' you. And I don't want any *tests*," she retorted, mimicking his voice and tone.

"Don't be a little savage. You have to learn to read, to be an educated woman," said Rubín, trying to sound sensible. "You really flew off the handle today, but it's past history now. If you're reasonable, we'll always consider you one of the family."

"Ha! Just listen to him! *The family* can go fly a kite," she shrieked, mimicking him and making one of her diabolical grimaces.

"We'll never abandon you," the youth affirmed, full of protective instincts. "You know what?—and this is the truth . . . When I get married . . . when I get married, I'll take you with me to be my wife's maid."

Papitos burst out laughing, leaning back so suddenly that the back of the chair creaked as if to break.

"Him, get married! *You!* The Señora says you can't get married. Yes, that's exactly what she said—to Doña Silvia, the other night."

The indignation Maximiliano felt at hearing this was so vivid that if he had shown it in actions, there would surely have been some kind of catastrophe. The only reply to an insult like that would have been to grab Papitos by the neck and strangle her. The only trouble was that Papitos was much stronger than he was.

"You're the most monstrous, vulgar thing I've ever seen," stammered Rubín. "If you don't grow out of this infantile state you'll never amount to anything."

Papitos pushed her left arm further into the stocking and, sticking her fingers through the holes, she grabbed the Señorito's nose and pulled it.

"Stop it! You've never really been beaten up, but I'm going to show you what it's like. What's so funny, stupid? The fact that I'm getting married? Well, I am; yes, indeed. I'm getting married because I damn well feel like it."

For a long time Maximiliano had wanted to talk to someone that way, freely declare himself without floundering. The self-confidence that eluded him with someone else came easily with the little cook; he felt himself swell after uttering the first few words.

"You're still naive," he said, putting his hand on her shoulder. "You don't know what the world is like, or what real passion is."

When he reached this point, Papitos didn't have the faintest idea of what he was talking about. It was a new language for her, like his grave face. It didn't look at all like that when he told stories.

"Look, it's like this," Rubín continued, expressing himself emotionally. "Love is the law of laws, love rules the world. If I find the right woman—and she will be half, if not all of my life—the woman who will transform me, inspiring me to noble acts and instilling in me qualities I previously lacked, why shouldn't I marry her? Let's hear a reason why not, if there is one. Even half a reason. You won't give me any silly arguments; you certainly won't share those worries that—"

When he got to this part, the orator was a bit muddled, surely not for fear of his interlocutor's dialectical skills. After being greatly amazed by the solemnity with which her master spoke and by the incomprehensible things he was coming out with, Papitos began to get bored. Maximiliano continued to discharge all that he had in him, for he knew that this opportunity to pour out his heart was unique. Finally, the girl stretched out her left arm on the table and, wearied by the emotional upheaval and pinches of that day, she used her arm as a pillow on which to rest her head. At that moment, Maximiliano, exalted by his own eloquence, permitted himself to say:

"The only reason they give me is that she has or hasn't been such and such. My reply is that it's false, absolutely false. If there have been shameful days in her life—no, I wouldn't say shameful so much as stormy, unfortunate days—it was out of necessity and poverty, not immorality. Men, señoritos, that wretched, corrupt race descended from Cain—they're to blame. I'll state it clearly and repeat it: the responsibility for so many women losing their virtue rests with men. If seducers and señoritos were punished, society . . ."

Papitos was sound asleep, her cheek on her stiff arm, which was still stuck into the stocking, her fingers poking out of the holes. Her sleep was deep and calm, her face serious, as if she were unconsciously approving of his angry words about seducers and digesting this lesson for when her turn came. Maximiliano's feverish words led him to an exaltation that seemed abnormal. He couldn't keep still or quiet. He got up and went out into the hall talking to himself under his breath and gesturing. The hall was dark; he went into his aunt's parlor, scarier than a lion's den, and in there he became twice as eloquent, his declamation bordering on frenzy. Punctuating his clauses with emphatic gestures, he thought of amazingly forceful sentences, sentences that would have floored every member of the family if they had been there to hear. What a pity his aunt wasn't there! He uttered these bold statements as though she were standing before him:

"And once and for all, I'm telling you that I can't give in, because I'm obeying the dictates of my conscience, and there's no use in trying to turn me against my conscience, Madam. Not even with that bunch of . . . stale arguments you're using. I'm getting married, I tell you; I'm getting married because I'm my own boss, and I'm legally of age, and because my conscience tells me that I should, because it's God's will. And if you give me your approval, she and I will open our loving arms to you, and you'll be our mother, our counselor, our guide . . ."

Oh, but he was sorry that she wasn't there in the flesh, sitting opposite him in the oilcloth chair; because he would have told her the same things he was telling the imaginary person; he would have told her for sure. Then he went out into the hall for a while and continued his speech, walking from one end to the other and gesturing in the dark. Solitude, the silence of night, and dim light encourage shy people in their game of being bold and talkative, using themselves as an audience and becoming quite daring due to their easy success. Maximiliano spoke in a low voice; his wild gesticulating didn't go with his low-pitched words, whose smothered vehemence made them sound as if he were rehearsing.

When Doña Lupe rang the bell, her nephew opened the door. She was shocked to see him still up.

"Some people don't need to sleep, do they!" she exclaimed with a touch of sarcasm that made the young man tremble all over. Her words suddenly erased any imprudent ideas he had had, just as lighting a lamp dispels any shadows playing on the shade. When Papitos heard the bell, she came stumbling out, rubbing her eyes. All Doña Lupe said was:

"Everybody to bed."

It was very late and Papitos had to get up early. Nephew and cook went to their respective rooms without a word, like rabbits scurrying off at the sound of the hunter.

7

Maximiliano's declaration had caused Fortunata much painful perplexity. That night and the following nights she slept poorly due to her troubled mind and its contradictory thoughts. After going to bed she had to get up; she wrapped herself in a blanket and plunked herself on the sofa in the living room. Her ruminations didn't stay behind, in bed; they accompanied her wherever she went. That first night, after a long debate, positive thoughts finally won out. "Me, get married, and marry a good man—a *decent person!*" It was all she could hope for! Having a name, not having to mix with coarse people anymore, being among ladies and gentlemen! Maximiliano was a good soul and would surely make her happy. This is what she thought in the morning, after washing and lighting the fire, as she picked up her basket to go shopping. She put on her cloak and scarf and left the house. As soon as she put her foot in the street, her ideas changed: "Oh, but to live with that boy forever . . . he's so homely! He only comes up to my shoulder, and I can pick him up like a feather. A husband who's weaker than his wife can't really be a husband. The poor boy's as good as gold, but I couldn't love him if I lived with him for a hundred years. It's probably ungrateful, but what can I do about it? I can't change how I feel."

She was so distracted that the butcher had to ask her three times what she wanted, still without getting an answer. Finally she snapped out of it.

"All I need today is half a pound of flank meat for the stew and a pork chop. Weigh it right, now, Señor Paco."

"Here you are, beautiful. What else can I do for you?"

She bought two ounces of salt pork too; then some broccoli at the vegetable stand in the butcher's shop, and at the store on the corner she bought rice, four eggs, and a can of whole pimientos. When she got home, she stoked the fire and did the cleaning and sweeping. As she dusted the furniture her mind fell back to thoughts from that morning: "It's not every day you find a man that's willing to take on a burden like me."

She made the bed and began to comb her hair. When she saw her pretty pale face in the mirror, she started to compare. "Holy Mary! If Maximiliano were to bet that he was the ugliest man alive, nobody else would win. And those medicines . . . they smelled so awful! He should've studied something else. God help me. If I had a child, I'd have company . . . but hmmph!"

After this reticence, the peremptory tone of which made it sound like the result of deep conviction, she continued contemplating and preening over her beauty. She was proud of her black eyes; they were so pretty that—as she herself said—"they would've slayed the Holy Ghost." Her complexion was divine— smooth and transparent; her flesh looked like freshly polished ivory. Her mouth was a bit large, but fresh and appealing, both when she smiled and when she pouted. And those teeth! "I have teeth," she said to herself, displaying them, "like little pieces of solid milk." Her nose was perfect. "You don't see many noses like mine." And at last, taking her comb and arranging her hair, which was black and as plentiful as evil thoughts, she said, "What *hair* God gave me!" As she was finishing, a thought that had occurred to her in the past struck her again. It was this: "I'm so much more attractive now than . . . before. I've improved a lot."

And then she grew very sad. The little pieces of solid milk disappeared under the frowning mouth, and something like a heavy cloud settled on her brow. The thought that had struck her like a ray was: "If only he could see me now!" Its weight left her mute, and her eyes stared blankly into space. Finally she awoke from this lethargy and, looking at herself again, she gathered strength from the reflection of her pretty face. "Say what they will, my best feature is my eyebrows. They're pretty, even when I'm mad. Let's see, how do I look when I get mad? Like this . . . Uh oh, somebody's at the door!"

The ringing bell called her away from her dressing table. She went to the door with her shell comb in her hand and a towel over her shoulders. It was the redeemer. He was very cheerful and told her to finish combing her hair. As she didn't have much combing left to do, she was soon finished. Maximiliano praised her for deciding not to have a hairdresser. Why couldn't women do their hair themselves? And those who didn't should learn how. Fortunata agreed. The poor boy expressed repeatedly his admiration for his future spouse's sense of order and economy, for doing a task that those brazen thieves called servants do poorly. Fortunata assured him that the habit had no particular merit because she enjoyed working.

"You're a real jewel," her lover said proudly. "As for hairdressers, they're all panderers, and once they enter a house it can't be peaceful."

They would take a servant eventually, because it wouldn't be wise for her to overwork. They would undoubtedly be better off then, and would occasionally have guests for dinner. Servants were necessary, and the day would probably come when they wouldn't be able to do without a nursemaid. When she heard this, Fortunata practically burst out laughing; but she contained herself, and concentrated on wondering in silence: "What could this poor creature want a nursemaid for?"

Immediately afterward, the young man brought up the subject of their marriage, and, hearing him talk, Fortunata couldn't help but admire his great generosity and nobility.

"Your conduct will decide your fate," he declared, "and since your conduct is going to be good—because your soul is basically good—we're approaching our goal. I'll put a crown of decency on your head; you'll do what's necessary to keep it there and wear it with dignity. What's past is past. Repentance doesn't leave a trace of a stain, not a single trace. The world can say what it wants. What's the world? If you look closely you'll see that it's nothing, except your conscience."

Fortunata's eyes moistened with tears. She was very emotional; whenever someone spoke to her solemnly, and with generosity, she was moved, even if she did not quite understand everything said. The tone, style, and expression in the speaker's eyes affected her. At this point, she thought it mandatory to make the following observation:

"Consider what you're doing," she said, "and don't, on my account, commit your . . ."

She wanted to say "dignity," but she couldn't find the word, due to the scant use she had made of such words in her life. But she managed to express the idea crudely, saying:

"Remember that people who know me are goin' to call you 'la Fortunata's husband'* instead of callin' you by your Christian name. I'm very thankful for what you're doin' for me, but since I respect you, I don't want to see you . . ."

She meant "stigmatized." But she didn't know the word, and even if she had known it, she wouldn't have been able to pronounce it correctly. "I don't want them to pull your leg 'cause of me," is what she did say, blithely hoping to convince him. But Maximiliano, as sure of his plan and conscience as if they had been an impregnable fortress, burst out laughing. He felt like the inhabitants of Gibraltar when they see attackers approach armed only with a walking stick. He could make a splendid case for the stupidity of most people. As long as his conscience said to him, "Look, son, this is the right road to take, stay on it;" the whole human race could try to stop him for all he cared; they could aim a loaded cannon at him. People didn't know it yet, but he was getting tough; he'd developed a will of steel that made any talk of his shyness mere chitchat.

"What counts is your being good, honest, and loyal. I'll take care of the rest; you just leave it to me," he said.

Shortly afterward, Fortunata was having lunch and Maximiliano was studying; they exchanged a few words every so often. All afternoon, optimistic thoughts enticed her, for he had let slip something about his inheritance, land, and mortgages in Molina de Aragón, indicating that "his vineyards might bring such and such a sum." That night they ordered coffee from Café La Paz and the waiter brought it up. Olmedo and Feliciana came to visit. They seemed peeved and were hardly speaking, an unmistakable sign of a domestic quarrel. The reason was plain: if even the most stable nation undergoes a crisis when its treasury isn't operating perfectly, a household or family or whatever can't help but be affected by the anomaly of a budget that always has a deficit. Feliciana had already pawned

---

*Use of the definite article *la* before a first name is colloquial and may be, as is the case here, a pejorative way of referring to a person.

her best clothes, and Olmedo had lost all his credit. Republics as well as monarchies can collapse because of a lack of credit. And good old Olmedo no longer had any illusions about avoiding the imminent catastrophe. His friends, who knew him well, detected less gusto in his libertine performance, and his inherent goodness often showed through the mask. Friends told Maximiliano that they'd caught Olmedo studying on the sly in the Retiro Park. When his friends saw him, he was hiding his books in the bushes, embarrassed by having them discover his weakness. He attached a great deal of importance to human actions; he thought it would dishonor him to suddenly get caught without his libertine's uniform and insignias. His friends, and younger boys who looked up to him as a model—what would they say? His situation was like that of the little boy who, trying to appear grown-up, lights a strong cigar, starts to smoke it, and gets dizzy, but tries to disguise his nausea so people won't say it was too much for him. Olmedo couldn't stand a minute more of this awful uneasiness, nausea, and vertigo, but he kept the cigar in his mouth and pretended to puff, although all he was doing, really, was chewing on it.

For her part, Feliciana had begun to have a change of heart. Honor and love were all well and good, but you couldn't survive on them. Her daredevil friend didn't loosen up his tongue that night except when the four sat down to have coffee and he said in his usual relaxed way:

"Hell, the whole demimonde is here tonight."

Fortunata and Feliciana didn't understand, but Rubín blushed crimson and was most annoyed. The idea of applying a word like that to people who intended to be joined in holy matrimony was disrespectful; it was gross and obscene, downright obscene . . . But he kept his thoughts to himself to avoid a quarrel and to keep the gathering on a careful, formal level. He reminded himself that he hadn't told his friend a word about the marriage; it was clear that Olmedo was using such "liberal" terms out of ignorance. He decided to reveal his plans to his friend at the first opportunity so that Olmedo would weigh his words more carefully in the future.

8

It was a bad night for Fortunata, too. She spent most of it speculating on whether or not *he* remembered her. It was very odd that she had never run into him. It certainly wasn't because she hadn't looked carefully in every direction. Was he sick, or had he left Madrid? Later on, when she found out that Juanito Santa Cruz had had pneumonia in February and March, she recalled that she had dreamed it, precisely that night. And it's true: she did dream it, early in the morning, when her feverish brain gradually fell asleep, surrendering to a torrent of speculations. When she awoke the next day from a deep, although brief, sleep, her mental images and thoughts had taken a full turn. "I'll stick to my pharmacist," she thought, after saying the Lord's Prayer (which she never forgot to do). "We'll be as cozy as can be." She got up, lit the fire, went out shopping, and in between stores entertained the thought that Maximiliano might somehow grow taller, with a more developed chest—in a word, become more masculine and be cured of that chronic cold that kept him blowing his nose all the time. It went without saying that he had a good heart; he was a saint, and if and when he did get married, his wife would be able to wind him around her little finger. A couple of sweet words and he'd cheerfully agree to anything. The only matter on which she should not contradict him was that business about one's conscience or those . . . missions. What did he call them? Fortunata couldn't remember the adjective; it was "sublime." But it didn't make any difference; she knew that it had something to do with goodness.

That day her shopping took a bit longer, because since Maximiliano had announced that he would be coming for lunch, she was planning to make a dish that they both liked very much and was, moreover, her specialty: rice and giblets. Hers were wonderfully tasty. It was a pity artichokes weren't in season, because she would have added them, too. But she did add a bit of lamb, which gave the dish that special flavor. She bought veal chops, two *reales* worth of chicken giblets and some pickled sardines for the second course.

Home again, she started up three separate pots, using the exquisite care that Spanish cooking requires, and started the rice in the casserole dish. There wasn't a utensil left unused that day. After frying the onion, crushing the garlic, and chopping the giblets, when nothing important had been forgotten, the sinner washed her hands and went to comb her hair, more carefully than usual. Time passed; a variety of mingled aromas wafted out of the kitchen, and it was no surprise, given all that had been done there. When Rubín arrived at noon, his girlfriend opened the door with a smile. The table was already set, because that girl could squeeze twice as much out of her time as anyone else, and without any effort, working easily and quickly. Her lover announced that he was famished, and she informed him that it wouldn't be long. She had forgotten something essential—the wine—and was about to go out for it, but Maximiliano offered to run the errand, disappearing in a flash.

Half an hour later they were seated at the table in an aura of love and companionship. But just at that moment, Fortunata was suddenly struck by thoughts so strange that she didn't know what to make of them. She herself compared her soul during those days to a weathervane. It pointed one way just as easily as another. With no warning whatsoever, as if a strong wind had suddenly blown up, the weathervane swiveled halfway around and pointed to where its tail had been. She had experienced many of these sudden reversals, but none had been so vivid as the one she was experiencing now, just as she was dipping the spoon into the rice to serve her future husband. She couldn't have said how or why the feeling overtook her; all she knew was that she looked at him and felt so horribly revolted by the poor boy that it took great pains to disguise her emotions. Maximiliano, who failed to notice anything, praised her for seasoning the rice perfectly, but she didn't say a word as she swallowed, together with the first forkfuls, a bitter medley of impressions attempting to force its way out of her heart. Deep inside she said to herself: "They can chop me to pieces like these before I'll marry *him* . . . Can't you see what he's like? He doesn't even look like a man. He even smells bad. I hate to think what'll become of me when I realize that I'll be facing that little snub nose the rest of my life."

"You seem sad, angel face," said Rubín, who had given her this affectionate nickname.

She replied that the rice hadn't turned out the way she'd hoped. As they were eating the veal chops, Maximiliano said with a certain pompous pedantry:

"One of the things I must teach you is to use your fork and knife together, not just your fork. But I'll have time to teach you that along with other things."

Being corrected so much got on her nerves too. She wanted to speak well and be a proper, refined person, but oh, how much more she would have gotten out of the lessons if the teacher had been someone else, whose nose didn't run all the time, whose face wasn't such a wet noddle, and whose body was made of real flesh instead of what his looked like—sheep guts!

This antipathy she felt didn't cancel her esteem of him, which was mixed with a deep pity for that poor soul, a gentleman in his honor and virtue and so morally superior to her. The esteem in which she held him, her gratitude and that peculiar commiseration—for superior people do not inspire compassion—were the thoughts with which she held her repugnance in check. She was not very good at hiding her emotions, and someone less befuddled than Rubín would have realized that her terribly pretty frown was disguising something. But he saw things through the prism of his own ideas, and thus perceived reality as he felt it should have been, rather than as it actually was. Fortunata was relieved when lunch was over, because keeping up a serious conversation and listening to advice and corrections hardly amused her. She preferred clearing the table, which she did as soon as they had finished their coffee. To procrastinate in the kitchen, she inspected all the pots and pans and started to chop up the salad ingredients earlier than necessary. From time to time she walked through the living room, where Maximiliano was studying. It was not easy for him to concentrate on his books that day. He was very distracted, and every time his friend came in, pharmacology faded from his mind. Nevertheless, he wanted her to be there, and he even got slightly vexed at her for staying in the kitchen so long each time.

"Don't work so hard. You'll get all tired out. Bring your work in here."

"But if I come in you won't study, and you need to study so that you'll pass," she replied. "If you don't pass you'll have to repeat a year!"

This argument had a considerable effect on Rubín's mood.

"It doesn't matter if you're here. As long as you don't talk, I'll study. When you're around I seem to understand things better; I grasp the problems better. Sit here and take up your sewing; I'll keep at my books. When I feel dumb, all I have to do is look at you and I snap out of it."

Fortunata laughed, walked out, and came back in with her sewing.

"You know what?" Rubín said as she sat down. "My brother Juan Pablo went to Molina to see about our inheritance from Aunt Melitona. My Aunt Lupe wrote him, and he stopped off there on his way to Madrid. He's written saying that there won't be any major difficulties."

"Really? Well! That's good."

"That's right. I still can't say how much each brother will get. But I'll tell you this: it makes me very happy for your sake. Complain about your fate now! You know, the more financial security you have, the easier it is to keep your honor. Half the dishonor you see in life isn't anything but poverty. God really is on our side, and if we don't behave well now, we deserve to be dragged through the streets."

Fortunata would have said, "What a moralist I ended up with!" but she didn't know the word, so what she said was, "I'm up to *here* with missionaries!," using the word in two senses, namely, that of preacher and that of agent, the agent of what Rubín called "his mission."

9

Maximiliano informed Olmedo of his wedding plans "in strict confidence," for, as he said, "it wouldn't be wise for it to get around ahead of time and cause stupid gossip." The great libertine thought his friend was crazy, and deep down inside he pitied him, although he admired the courage Maxi showed in committing the greatest and most scandalous folly imaginable. Marry a . . . ! That was the limit; you couldn't carry good intentions any further. He detected a horrendous mixture of ignominy and sublime abnegation in the act, some sort of audacity or baseness, which made Rubín transcend the mediocrity of his life. Rubín might very well be a fool, but he wasn't your ordinary fool; he was the kind who practically touch the sublime with their fingertips. It's true that such fools don't manage to possess the sublime; but they do touch it. As he plumbed the grave depths of his friend's plan, Olmedo couldn't help but admit that such a shenanigan had never even occurred to him, the professional libertine.

"Don't worry, kid; no one will find out about it from me. Hell, I'm your friend, aren't I? That speaks for itself. I give you my word of honor. Don't worry."

When *Ulmus sylvestris* gave his word on some roguish matter it was sacred. But this time the urge to gossip was stronger than his sense of roguish honor and the big secret slipped out to Narciso Puerta (*Pseudo-Narcissus odoripherus*)—confidentially, of course, and only after Narciso had sworn not to breathe a word of it.

"I can confide in you, because I know it'll stay between you and me."

"Don't even doubt it. You know I'm a tomb."

Indeed, Narciso did not tell anybody except . . . After all, what difference would it make to whisper the secret to just one person, someone who'd be sure to keep it?

"You're the only person I'm telling, because I know you're very discreet," Narciso whispered into the ear of his friend Encinas, alias *Quercus gigantea*. "Promise you won't repeat a word of it; not a word. You're the only one who knows. You've got to promise, now."

"Don't be silly, Narciso. You'd think you just met me yesterday. You know I'm a tomb."

And the tomb opened for the Cañas ladies at their house—in the strictest secrecy, you understand, and after he'd made them all solemnly swear that they would guard the secret deep in their bosom.

"Really, Encinas, the things you come out with! Do you think so little of us? You know we're not silly girls who are going to repeat your story and get you in trouble."

But one of these ladies thought it would be a mortal sin not to drop a hint to Doña Lupe; she'd have to know sooner or later anyway, and it was better to prepare her for the tremendous shock. Poor lady! It hurt, seeing her so calm, so unsuspecting of the dishonor hovering over her. In sum, the news reached Doña Lupe's sharp ears three days after it had left *Rubinius vulgaris'* timid lips.

They say that Doña Lupe sat dazed for some time after she'd been told. Then she insinuated that she had suspected something of the sort because of her nephew's irregular conduct. Marry a woman who had been involved with scores of men! Bah! Maybe it wasn't true. And if it was, she'd soon find out, that was for sure; Doña Lupe wouldn't let the bomb fizzle out inside *her*; that very night or early the next morning, Maximiliano would have to face her. That the widowed Señora de Jáuregui was beside herself was proven by the uncertainty of her step as she walked home from the Cañas' house. She talked to herself out loud, dropped her umbrella twice, and when she bent over to pick it up, her scarf fell off, and finally, instead of entering the front door to *her* building, she went into the one next door. If that little hypocrite was at home, she was really going to let him have it! But he probably wasn't in, because it was eleven o'clock and the Señorito never came in these days until midnight or one in the morning. Who ever would have guessed it! That bashful creature, that calamity of a boy, that useless, puny nephew of hers who couldn't even blow out a candle, and who at eighteen—yes, at eighteen, she knew it for a fact—didn't know what a woman was like and thought babies were brought by the stork; that sickly man to have fallen madly in love, and with a woman of the streets!

"Has the Señorito come in yet?" she asked her maid. And when Papitos told her that he had not, she pursed her lips impatiently.

Heaven only knows what stage her restless anger would have reached if she hadn't taken it out on Papitos, whose innocent head received the blows. Literally her head, and I'll explain why. Papitos was somewhat conceited, and as her best feature was her thick, black hair, she did all she could and more to make the best of it. She was precocious in the art of hairdressing; she made ringlets around her face, and to curl her bangs (not having any curling iron) she used a thick piece of red-hot wire. She would have liked doing all this in the morning, but since her mistress rose before she did, it was not possible. Evenings, when she was left alone, were the best time for her elegant hairdressing sessions. A broken mirror, a practically toothless comb, a little sticky lotion, and thick wire were enough for her. But luck would have it that on that night she had worked up a truly extraordinary hairdo. "Gee, looks like I'm goin' out to *dance!*" she said with a convulsive laugh as she inspected her face, one part at a time (since she couldn't see it all at once).

"You stuck-up little brat, swine!" cried Doña Lupe, furiously messing up all the spit curls the girl had made. "So this is how you spend your time! You ought to be ashamed, going around in clothes full of holes, and then, instead of sewing them, preening over that mane of yours! You conceited, shameless child! And how about your reading exercises? You probably haven't laid eyes on them. I'll make your hair look good. I'm going to take you to the barber and have it all shaved off so your head will look like an egg."

If she had been told she was going to have her head cut off, she couldn't have felt more terrified.

"Oh I know, now comes the sniveling and the tears, after you've made my blood boil with your indecent hairstyles. You look like the monkey in the Retiro Park. What's this? Have you used grease on your hair too?"

Doña Lupe smelled the hand with which she had sacrilegiously spoiled the criminal bangs. She put her hand to her nose so majestically that it was a shame that a good sculptor wasn't there to copy her pose.

"You pig! Look what you've done to my hand. Ugh, it's repulsive! Where did you get this garbage?"

"Sito Maxi gave it to me," Papitos answered humbly.

This brusquely reminded Doña Lupe of the real cause of her anger. It occurred to her to search her nephew's room, for which Papitos was most grateful since it let her off the hook.

"Go to the kitchen," said the Señora; and she didn't have to repeat it, because Papitos skittered off like a scared mouse.

Doña Lupe lit the lamp in Maximiliano's room and began to look around. "If only I could find a letter!" she thought. "But ha! Now I remember that they told me she doesn't know how to write. She's an animal, in the full sense of the word."

She searched one place and then another, but found nothing to confirm the awful news. She unlocked the dresser (the keys opened hers too), but found nothing there either. The piggy bank was in its place, full . . . perhaps a bit heavier than before. As for pictures, she didn't see any, anywhere. Doña Lupe was engrossed in her search, like a detective unable to find a trace of the crime, when Maximiliano came in. Papitos had let him in. On the way to his room he was surprised to see his light on. When he came face to face with his aunt, who was rummaging through the third drawer of his dresser, he realized that his secret had been discovered, and cold shivers ran up and down his spine. Doña Lupe was able to contain herself. She had good judgment and was very strategic. I mean, she didn't like to do anything at the wrong time or place, and midnight was a bad time to let her nephew have it. She knew she would undoubtedly raise her voice, and she didn't want a scandal. Also, the boy would probably get a bad migraine if he were given such an untimely scolding, and Doña Lupe did not want to torture him. The student stood dazed and speechless at the door of his room when his aunt turned toward him and casting a meaningful look, said:

"Come in, I'm leaving now. Get a good rest, and we'll have this out tomorrow."

She headed toward her room, but when she had taken only ten steps or so she turned around furiously, threatening him with her hand and shouting:

"You little rascal! But no. We'll discuss it tomorrow. Go to bed now."

Maximiliano couldn't sleep, envisioning the scene that would ensue with his aunt. First his imagination enlarged the conflict and made it as beautifully terrible as a scene from Shakespeare; then he reduced it to piddling proportions. "And what of it, my good aunt, what of it?" he said, shrugging his shoulders in bed as if he were standing up. "I've met a woman, I like her, and I want to marry her. I don't see any reason for so much . . . What do you think I am, some kind of machine? Don't I have a free will? What do you think I am?" Sometimes he felt so sure of his rights he felt like getting up, running to his aunt's room, tugging at her leg to wake her up, and flinging the following at her: "You might as well know that it's tit for tat with me. If my family insists on treating me like a child, I'll show them I'm a man." But he was petrified when he imagined what his aunt would reply, probably something on the order of: "You, a man? *You?*"

When the poor boy got up the next day, which was Sunday, Doña Lupe had already returned from Mass. Papitos brought him his hot chocolate, but he couldn't drink it because his throat had that stiff, anguished feeling, the same one he got before exams or some such scare. He was frozen with fear, and the Señora must have felt sorry for him when he came into the parlor like a criminal walking into a courtroom. The window was open, but Doña Lupe closed it so the poor boy wouldn't catch cold; justice was one thing, but his health was another. The delinquent entered with his hands in his pockets and a plaid cap on his head, wearing his new boots with the clothes he wore around the house. He looked so withered and crestfallen that one had to be made of steel not to pity him. Doña Lupe was wearing an everyday skirt covered with big patches sewn on admirably well, a blue-checked apron, a dark shawl around her arrogant bosom, a black scarf on her head, red mitts, and thick felt slippers that were so soft they muffled her steps; she sounded like a cat. The little parlor was a remarkably clean room. The main pieces of furniture were the dresser and the tall, mirror-doored armoire. The sofa and chairs had crocheted covers like the kind you see in rooming houses, and the lady of the house had made every one of them herself.

But what gave a certain grandiose air to the parlor was the portrait of Doña Lupe's deceased husband hanging in the place of honor. It was a rectangular portrait done in oil, wretchedly done, showing Don Pedro Manuel de Jáuregui, alias the "Turkey Man," in his uniform as a commander in the National Guard, with his hat in one hand and his baton in the other. A painting in worse taste was inconceivable. The artist must have specialized in signs for dairies or markets. Doña Lupe, however, maintained that Jáuregui's portrait was a masterpiece, and she pointed out the painting's two salient features to whoever contemplated it; namely, no matter where the spectator stood, the portrait gazed back; also, the watch chain, the gorget, the buttons, the helmet chin strap, and plaque; all the metallic details, that is, were painted in the most extraordinary, masterful way.

The photographs, standing like honor guards around the canvas, were numerous, and had been arranged with such a poor sense of symmetry that one would have thought they were live creatures meandering over the surface of the wall.

"Very well, Señor Don Maximiliano; very well indeed," said Doña Lupe, looking at her nephew extremely severely. "Sit down. This is going to take awhile."

III. A Portrait of Doña Lupe

I

MAXIMILIANO DID NOT SIT DOWN. Doña Lupe did, under the portrait, which hung over the middle of the sofa, as if to reinforce her words; then she repeated: "Very well, Señor Don Maximiliano" in a sarcastic tone. Generally, whenever his aunt addressed him formally, calling him "Señor Don," the poor boy knew he was in for it.

"Work myself to the bone," she continued, "all for my nice little nephew; fight off his illnesses by pampering him; give him a profession, even if it means going hungry myself; do things for him that not even most mothers would do for their own children . . . and this is what I get for it! Oh, I've been perfectly well informed already. I know who that . . . illustrious lady you wish to marry is. Hmmph—a *lovely* girl! And do you think that the family is going to consent to this dishonor? Tell me it's all just boyish foolishness and I'll forget everything."

Maximiliano couldn't say that it was, but neither could he say that it was not; and though waves of strength did surge from the depths of his soul, they crested and broke before reaching the shore of his lips. He was so abashed that he could not display the energy he felt inside; that blasted nervousness of his inhibited him. His eyes wandered over the surface of the wall, searching for support. On certain trying occasions when the soul is in a dull stupor, people tend to rivet their eyes on some insignificant detail that has nothing to do with the situation at hand. Maximiliano stared for a while at a portrait of the Samaniego girls, Aurora and Olimpia, in white mantillas, their arms linked, the former very stern, the latter sentimental. Why did he look at them? His confusion led him to fix his attention first on one detail, then another, attaching his soul to anything at all, even the heads of the nails securing the pictures.

"Explain yourself, son," added Doña Lupe, whose temper was rather short. "Is this some childish game?"

"No, Señora," replied the accused. And this denial, which was an affirmation, started to give him courage and alleviate the anguish in the pit of his stomach.

"Are you sure it's not a childish game? What notions you have of women and the world, you innocent boy! I cannot consent to letting one of those hussies inveigle you and cheat you so that she can steal your honest name the way a thief steals a watch. You have to be treated like a retarded child who's only half alert. Remember, only five years ago I still had to button up your pants in the morning, and you were afraid of the dark, even in your own room."

Such an uncomplimentary version of his personality exasperated the youth. He felt his courage mounting, but he lacked words. Where the devil were those confounded words that wouldn't come to him in this dilemma? That cursed shyness of his was the cause of his stupid silence. The boy felt a singular fascination when his aunt looked at him, which is why he could not manage to speak, although he had plenty to say. "What can I say? How should I begin?" he wondered, staring at the portrait showing Torquemada and his wife arm in arm.

"Everything will be all right," said Doña Lupe in a conciliatory tone, "if I can manage to make those clouds vanish from your head. You're noble, and you have common sense . . . But sit down. It makes me tired to see you standing."

"First, you must be properly informed of the events," stated Maximiliano as he sat down in the armchair, thinking that he had found a good little speech to start out with. "I . . . was planning to speak to you—"

"Why didn't you, then? It must be quite a story! Imagine, a frail boy like you getting mixed up with hussies! And mark my word: it'll be the end of you. When you collapse, don't come running to Auntie. Oh, I know, that's what I'm good for: for taking care of you when you're sick, you ungrateful wretch! And do you think it's fair to treat me like this, when I've had to slave so that you could get ahead in the world? Do you think it's fair to do this to me, when I've been more than a mother to you? For you to go off and marry a woman of the streets?"

Rubín turned green and felt an acid burning its way from his heart to his lips.

"That's not so, Auntie; that's not the way it is," he declared, gaining control of himself. "She's not a woman of the streets. You've been deceived."

"Oh, I've been deceived all right—by you! Making me think you were a shrinking violet. But the truth's out now. Don't think you can fool me; don't think I'm going to let you have your way. What do you take me for, you nincompoop? Oh, if only I hadn't trusted you! But I was a fool, I thought you weren't capable of even looking at a woman. You really pulled the wool over my eyes. You're a sneaky one, you are."

As Maximiliano heard this, he was enthralled by the portrait of Rufina Torquemada. He saw her, but not really. Only vaguely, and in a nightmarish confusion, was he aware of the young lady's pose: behind her was a seascape, as if she were on a ship's deck. When he snapped out of it, he thought of defending himself, but he couldn't find the weapons, that is, the words. Not for a minute did he think of giving in, though. His nerves could turn to jelly, but his will remained firm.

"You've been misinformed," he ventured awkwardly, "about the person who . . . She doesn't lead any such life, and you're on the wrong track. I had planned to tell you this: 'Auntie, I . . . love this person and . . . my conscience'—"

"Be quiet! Don't make me angrier than I am already. When I hear you say that you love a painted floozie I feel like drowning you, not because you're bad, but because you're a nincompoop. When I hear you mention your 'conscience' while you're talking about something like this, I feel like : . . Oh, God forgive me. Do you know what? From this moment on, I'm going to treat you as if you were twelve. Today you're staying in. A little bit of discipline will do the trick. And tomorrow you're to take your cod liver oil again. Go to your room and take off your boots. You're not setting foot in the street today."

Lord knows what the accused was about to reply. He had just opened his mouth when the arrival of a visitor cut him short. It was Sr. Torquemada, a close friend of the family who upon arriving always went straight to the parlor, the kitchen, the dining room, or wherever the Señora was. The man's physionomy was puzzling. Only Doña Lupe, by virtue of her long experience, could read the hieroglyphics on that plain, shrunken face that somehow smacked of a military man with a clerical touch. In his youth Torquemada had been a halberdier, and as he had kept his mustache and goatee, now graying, he had an ecclesiastical air about him; it was undoubtedly his affected, cloying meekness and his habit of raising and lowering his eyelids that softened his innately gross face. His head was always tilted to the right. He was tall, but not arrogantly so; being nearly bald, his fat, scaly scalp was visible beneath that clumsily wrought grill of hair. Since it was Sunday, his shirt collar was almost clean, but he was wearing his everyday cloak with its greasy borders and threadbare trim. His trousers, shriveled because the cloth had stretched over the knees, rode up so much that he looked as if he had been horseback riding without gaiter straps. His boots (again, since it was Sunday) had been blackened, and squeaked so loudly you could hear them a mile away.

"And how is the family?" he inquired as he sat down, having offered his hand—always sweaty—to Doña Lupe and her nephew.

"Perfectly fine," said the Señora, anxiously observing Torquemada's face. "And yours?"

"Nothing new, thank goodness."

That day Doña Lupe was expecting news on a matter that interested her greatly. Since she always expected the worst (so that misfortunes wouldn't catch her off guard), she thought that her agent was coming to bring her bad news. She was afraid to ask. All that showed in the quasi–military man's face was a marked interest in the family. At last, Torquemada (who did not like to waste time) said:

"Well, well, Doña Lupe. Today's our day. I bet you can't guess what I've come to tell you. A little incident."

The Señora's face lit up; she knew that an "incident" meant an unexpected payment. He chuckled and put his hand in the inside pocket of his jacket.

"Oh, Don Francisco, don't tell me he's paid!" exclaimed Doña Lupe incredulously, clasping her hands.

"You can see for yourself. I didn't expect it either; last night I went over to tell him that I'd seize his possessions on Monday. This morning, while I was getting dressed to go to Mass, he comes in to see me. I thought he was going to ask me for another extension. Since he's always cheating us, saying he'll pay today and then tomorrow, I don't believe a word he says, not even if it's the Gospel truth. He's always making up alibis. But never mind, I wish there were godsends like this every day. 'Señor Torquemada,' he says to me, all serious, 'I've come to pay you back.' I almost dropped my jaw, as they say, since I wasn't expecting this *incident*. Finally, after he gave me the stuff—eight thousand *reales*, that is—he picked up his IOU and was off."

"I told you so," observed Doña Lupe, nearly speechless from the happiness stuck in her throat. "Joaquinito Pez is a decent person. He just goes through these straits, like any boy from a well-off family who leads a high life—plenty one day and none the next. I bet he gambles . . ."

Torquemada divided the bills, giving Doña Lupe the majority of them.

"Six thousand *reales* for you, . . . two thousand for me. Some stroke of luck! I'd given up on them, because I'd heard that Joaquinito was up to his neck. I wonder who he's sponging off now. Not that it makes any difference to us."

"Since we're not going to let him borrow from us again—"

"Look, Doña Lupe," said Torquemada, making a perfect o with his thumb and index finger and showing it to his interlocutor.

2

Doña Lupe contemplated the o in veneration and listened.

"Look, Señora, those dissolute dandies are good customers, because they take no notice of the materialism there is in premiums and installments. But they get caught in the end, and how! You've got to keep an eye on them. Having their possessions seized scares them at first, but once they've been through it, they don't care what happens. You can advertise it in *La Gaceta* and it rolls right off their backs. Take the little marquis of Casa-Bojío; I repossessed him last month and sold every last thing he had, down to the engraving of his family tree. Well, at long last, three days later, I see him go by in a carriage—just like that, he passed right by—and the wheels splashed mud on me. It's not that I mind the materialism of the mud; I'm telling you just so you'll see what they're like. Well, believe it or not, he found somebody else to borrow from. It was at four percent monthly, but even if it had been at five, it would have been a giveaway, as they say. It's true they don't bother you, and if it's no inconvenience, when they're asking for an extension they'll keep you happy by getting your nephew some sort of job, the way the Pez boy did for me. But the materialism of a job isn't what counts; they'll probably pull a big one on you in the end and they do a master job of it. So if he comes knocking on my door, I know where I'll tell him to go."

At this point Torquemada took out his greasy cigarette case. Since he was on such close terms with the family, he thought he'd have a cigarette. He offered one to Maximiliano, but Doña Lupe answered brusquely for him, saying scornfully:

"He doesn't smoke."

The preparatory operations for smoking took some time because Torquemada rerolled his cigarettes, using his own paper. Then he lit a match, striking it against his thigh.

"Another sure bet," he continued, "although he gives me a lot of work, is the boy from the ready-made clothes store, José María Vallejo. I show up there the first of the month, every month, like a hound dog. He's got a thousand *duros* of mine, and all I collect every month in interest is twenty-six. So he's behind? 'Look, son, I've got big commitments and I can't wait for you.' So I take half a dozen capes and I cart them off like nothing. And I don't do it because of the materialism, you know, the capes, but just so he'll be sure to remember the next installment. It's the only way, Señora. You have to treat them like that because they have no consideration for us. They think your money's for them to go out and spend. Remember those students that gave us such a hard time? It was the first time I lent money for you. That Cienfuegos boy, and Arias Ortiz! What a bunch of rascals! If it hadn't've been for me, nobody would've collected. And they were such louses that they'd come crying for an extension and then I'd see them in the café filling themselves up on steak . . . and 'Bring on the rum and maraschino!' Just like the shopkeeper, the fellow named Rubio, the one with the furrier shop on Mayor Street, remember? One day he finally brings me his watch, his wife's earrings, and twelve boxes of furs and muffs, and that same afternoon—imagine, Señora—that very same afternoon, I see him at the Puerta del Sol climbing into a carriage to go to the bullfight. That's the way they are; they want the money for the materialism of throwing it away, so to speak. That's why I spend the whole doggone day watching over José María Vallejo, who's a good man—not to say others aren't. I go to the store and see if there's anybody there, if there's any action, I take a look at the register, I find out if the boy who collects the bills has any money, I give the owner a sermon and some advice: I tell him to crucify whoever doesn't pay. It's the truth, it's the only way! In the end, if you're soft on them, they step on you. And they don't thank you for it, Señora; oh, no. You should see their faces when I come in! They forget the fact that they're getting along on *my* money. And what does it all add up to? They're a bad lot, that's what. Just because they give me twenty-six *duros* a month they think they've done their duty. They say it's a lot to pay, and I say they should be grateful, because times are bad, really bad."

Throughout the years of the nineteenth century that coincided with Don Francisco Torquemada's long usurious existence, he was not once heard to say that times were good. They were always "bad, really bad." Even so, by '68 Torquemada already owned two houses in Madrid, and he had started his business with the twelve thousand *reales* that his wife had inherited in '51. In a couple of lustrums he had increased Doña Lupe's once puny capital a hundredfold. (She was his only associate in these shady dealings.) He charged her a nominal fee, and showed as much interest in her affairs as he did in his own because of his great friendship with the deceased Jáuregui.

"So I've left my load and I'll hit the road," he said, getting up and adjusting his cloak, which was slipping off his left shoulder.

"So soon?"

"Señora, I still haven't been to Mass. Like I said, when I was getting dressed to go, Joaquinito came and there was the big incident."

"Yes, it *was* big, wasn't it!" exclaimed Doña Lupe, pressing to her breast the hand that clutched the bills so tightly that the paper could not be seen between her fingers.

"God be with you," Torquemada said to Maximiliano, whose reply to the greeting was an indistinct "Uh-huh."

And he exited to the hall, accompanied by Doña Lupe; Maximiliano could hear them whispering at the door. Finally the loud boots of the ex-halberdier could be heard going downstairs, and Doña Lupe reappeared in the parlor. The joy she felt at having recovered money she had given up as lost was so great that her brown eyes shone like hot coals and a smile played around her lips. From the moment he saw her enter, Maximiliano knew that her wrath had been placated. Money, or "the stuff," as Torquemada called it, couldn't help but sweeten her, and approaching the delinquent, who had not budged from his armchair, she put one hand on his shoulder and, tightly clutching the bills in the other, she said to him:

"Now don't get rattled, and don't take it so seriously. I'm telling you these things for your own good."

"No, really," Maximiliano replied with a serenity that surprised him even more than Doña Lupe; "I'm not upset, I'm calm, because my conscience—"

Here he went astray again. Doña Lupe didn't give him time to find his way because she went into her bedroom and closed the glass door. Maximiliano could hear her moving things around. She was putting away the money. Then, opening the door but staying in her bedroom, the Señora continued her talk with her nephew:

"You heard what I told you. You stay in today. And starting tomorrow, you'll take your cod liver oil again, because all this nonsense is just a vitamin deficiency. After awhile, we'll start you on phosphate again. You shouldn't have stopped taking it."

Since his aunt was out of sight, Maximiliano allowed himself a derisive smile. He directed it to his uncle, Sr. Jáuregui, who was looking back at him, naturally. He couldn't help but note that his aunt's worthy spouse was hideous, and he was puzzled that Doña Lupe could actually stay all alone with the portrait at night and not be scared to death of it.

"So now you know," she said, appearing at the door and buttoning up her black wool jacket, for she was getting dressed to go out. "You can go take off your boots. You're my prisoner."

The youth went to his room without a word, and Doña Lupe thought "how docile" he was. Her rigorous authority, which the boy had always greatly respected, would be the right remedy for the chaos in his mind. She had said so before: "All I have to do is raise my voice and he scurries off like a scared rabbit. Those wolves will have him over my dead body."

"Papitos!" cried the Señora, and the girl was immediately heard galloping down the corridor like a horse at the racetrack.

She appeared with a potato in one hand and a knife in the other.

"Listen," her mistress said in a low voice, "make sure you watch Señorito Maxi carefully while I'm out, to see if he writes a letter or anything."

With her monkey face she showed she understood and went leaping back to the kitchen.

"Let's see," said the Señora, talking to herself. "Have I forgotten anything? Ah, my change purse! What do I need? Noodles, sugar . . . nothing else. Oh, yes, and the cod liver oil; I won't spare him that. This thing has to be cured by spoonfuls. And there's not going to be a little penny prize for taking it this time, either. He's a man now. I mean, he's not a little boy anymore."

One can imagine Doña Lupe's astonishment when she saw her nephew walk into the living room, not in his slippers or in the clothes he wore around the house, but dressed to go out, in his cloak with the red lining, his blue jacket, and coffee-colored Derby. The young man's disobedience angered and stupified her so extremely that she could hardly stammer a protest. "B . . . But . . ."

"Aunt," said Maximiliano in an altered, trembling voice, "I . . . cannot obey you. I've grown up. I'm twenty-five. I respect you; respect me."

And without waiting for a reply, he spun on his heel and left the house hastily, because he was afraid that his aunt would grab him by the skirts of his cloak.

He explained his conduct well enough to himself with the following silent mumblings: "I don't know how to defend myself with words; I can't speak—I get all flustered and upset the minute my aunt looks at me; but I can defend myself with actions. My nerves give me away, but my will is stronger; there's no doubt about that: my will is good and strong now. The whole human race can try to stop me now; they can go ahead and try to change my mind, and I won't argue with them, I won't say a word. But I'm going where I want to go, and whoever steps in my way, no matter who it is, will get trampled, and I'll keep right on going."

3

Doña Lupe didn't know what had hit her.

"Papitos, Papitos! No, I'm not calling you, run along. But did you see how insolent he was? It's not like him, he's not like that. They've turned him inside out; they've cast a spell on him. Have you ever seen such a rascal? I've a good mind to follow him and tell a pair of policemen to stop him . . . But we'll see what's what tonight. Because you'll be back, you have to come back, you hypocritical premature baby, you seven monther! Papitos! Here, go get the noodles and sugar. I'm not going out, I can't. I think I'm going to faint. Look, go by the pharmacy and ask for a bottle of cod liver oil—the kind I used to get. They know which one. Tell them I'll pay for it later. Wait—don't bring it. What for, when he won't want to take it? Bring a switch or a stick . . . No, don't bring a yardstick either. Go by the drugstore and ask for ten cents worth of bloodroot. I feel something coming on . . ."

She was subject to high blood pressure, and this time with good reason. She had never seen her nephew show a sign of independence comparable to that which she had just witnessed. He had always been such a milksop who stayed put exactly where she said. He had never had a will of his own. She had never had to lay a hand on him, because a frown had always been enough to bring him around. What had happened to that sheep to turn him into something more like a baby lion? Doña Lupe's mind could not decipher such great mystery. Her anger and confusion were succeeded by a drained feeling; she felt as worn out physically as if she had spent the whole morning at some painful task. Between pauses she took off the Sunday clothes she had started to put on, and called the girl Papitos again to say:

"Don't make anything except garlic soup. The 'Señoritingo'* won't be home for lunch, and if he does come, he'll be too busy being scolded by me to have lunch."

Taking the little chair she sat in to sew, she placed it near the balcony. In her midriff she felt pain, and as she sat down, she exhaled a deep sigh. She always

---

* The suffix -ingo makes the word extremely contemptuous.

wore her glasses for sewing. Putting them on and taking some work out of her basket, she began to mend sheets. Working on Sunday wasn't repugnant to Doña Lupe because Jáuregui, after many years of progressive propaganda, had freed her of her religious scruples. So she sat down to her reweaving in the usual place, next to the balcony window. There were a few flowerpots on the balcony, and between their dry branches she could see the street. As the room was on the second floor, it was a very good place from which to watch people pass by, if any did. But her street, Raimundo Lulio, and the one it intersected, Don Juan de Austria, had very little traffic. It might as well have been in a small town. Doña Lupe's only pastime in her hours of solitude consisted of seeing who entered the carriage repair shop next door or the printer's across the street, and whether or not Doña Guillermina de Pacheco passed, on her way to the orphanage on Albuquerque Street. The time and place were admirably suited to meditating: work in lap, needle in hand, glasses in place, basket of clothes nearby, the cat curled up in a ball asleep at its mistress' feet. That day, more than ever, Doña Lupe had food for thought.

"Sacrifice myself all my life, and for this! He doesn't know it—how could he? He's such a dunce. He sits down to his supper and has no idea of the pains I've taken to feed him. If he knew that some time ago there were days when every garbanzo was worth a pearl, because of what it took to put it on the table . . . I don't know what would have become of me if it hadn't been for Sr. Torquemada. Or what would have become of Maxi, without me. A fine life he would have had if he'd been left to his brothers' care! I'd like to know what would have become of you, you numskull, if I hadn't worked like a dog to keep the ship afloat and bring home the bread; if I hadn't racked my brains the way I did and used every resource God gave me to keep things going; what would have become of you, you ungrateful pipsqueak! Oh, if only my Jáuregui were alive!"

The memory of her deceased husband, which always became more vivid when she had to cope with a conflict of some sort, gave her solace. In all her afflictions, what always consoled her was the sweet memory of her conjugal bliss, for Jáuregui had been the best of men and a first-rate husband. "Oh, Jáuregui!" she exclaimed, pouring her soul into a sigh.

Don Pedro Manuel de Jáuregui had served in the Royal Halberdier Corps. Then he devoted himself to business, and he was so honest, so insipidly honest, that all he left when he died was five thousand *reales*. A native of the northern province of León, he received crates of eggs and other products, especially poultry. All the turkey vendors from León, Zamora, and Segovia deposited in his hands the money they earned for him to send on to the towns that raised the turkeys, whence came his nickname, given to him in Madrid at Puerta Cerrada and inherited by Doña Lupe. During the Christmas season, Jáuregui also received shipments of the famous *mantecadas*, cookies from Astorga, a city in northern Spain and all the sales agents from that region who were in Madrid used to go to his house for orders and payments. Don Pedro played a great role in politics; he was a rank and file member of the National Militia, and so tactful that he never rebelled except once, and to the magical cry of "Long live the Queen!"

But the blessed man perished in time, and Doña Lupe would have died too, if grief could kill. The little widow had no lack of suitors, though. Among others, there was Don Evaristo Feijoo, an army colonel who pursued her hotly. But loyalty to the memory of her homely, honest Jáuregui overpowered all her earthly interests. Then came bringing up and caring for her nephew, a very healthy distraction for a distressed soul. Torquemada and their business also helped her to fill her life and bear her grief. Time passed, she earned money, and gradually her present situation, which I have described, came about. Doña Lupe was bordering on fifty now, but she was so well preserved that she didn't look a day over forty. In her youth she had had a fresh, plump body and a thin face and had vaguely resembled Juan Pablo. Her brown eyes still had the spark of youth in them, but there was a certain legal sternness about her face now, emphasized by its wrinkles and lack of color. Above her upper lip, which was thin and violet, like the edge of a recent wound, grew an ever so faint down, the kind precocious boys have, a peach fuzz that by no means detracted from her looks; on the contrary, it was perhaps the only graceful stroke on that medieval countenance. And the down had a charming way of disappearing at the right corner of her mouth, next to a small wart from which there sprouted several reddish hairs that shone in the light like twisted copper threads. Her bosom was beautiful, although, as will be seen later on, it contained something (some things, in fact) that falsified the truth.

Doña Lupe stood out for her intelligence and her urge to display it whenever she could. Just as self-pride inspires other women to be conceited, the conviction of her intellectual superiority and her desire to control other people's conduct made Jáuregui's widow give advice on any and every practical, gubernatorial matter. She was one of those people who, not having had any education at all, seem to have had an excellent one because they are so articulate, so firmly assertive, and so clever at disguising the brutality of human egoism with social rhetoric.

She turned from thoughts of her Jáuregui to her nephew. They were her two loves. Nudging her glasses back up (for they had slipped down to the tip of her nose), she continued: "Well, he's not going to play games with me. I'll put him in the street, just as sure as three and two are five. It will be hard, because I love him as if he were my own child. And to think I hoped to marry him to Rufina, or at least Olimpia! No, I like Rufina Torquemada much more. I really am a fool. When he acted so unsociable and hid when Doña Silvia came to call with her daughter, I thought that talking about women to that boy would be like mentioning the cross to the devil. It just goes to show that you can't trust appearances. And now it turns out that he's been keeping a woman for months and spends all day long with her and—I've got to see it to believe it. And there's something else:

how does he manage to support her? The piggy bank weighs as much as it ever did."

At this point Doña Lupe became engulfed in such abstruse speculations that it would be impossible to follow; her mind submerged and surfaced like a piece of driftwood in the surf. The good lady spent the whole afternoon this way. When night came, she ardently hoped that her nephew would return so that she would be able to pour off onto him all the lava that her volcanoed breast could not contain. The seven monther came in very late, when his aunt was already at the table and had served herself some stew. Maximiliano sat down in silence, looking very serious and somewhat abashed. He started to eat the cold soup hungrily, glancing inquisitively and worriedly at his aunt, who avoided his gaze. "To prevent a quarrel . . . I had better restrain myself," she thought, "until he has eaten. Hmm, it looks as if he has a good appetite." From time to time, the young man sighed deeply and looked at his aunt as if he wanted to come to terms with her. More than once Doña Lupe wanted to break out into insults, but her nephew's silence and composure restrained her and made her fear that he would repeat the masculine reaction he had had that morning. Finally, the youth had a few raisins for dessert and, leaving the table, went to his room. Doña Lupe no sooner saw his back turned than her spirit crested again in fury, and she ran after him, holding back the words that rushed to her mouth. The poor boy was lighting the lamp in his room when the Señora appeared at his door crying out shrilly:

"Nitwit!"

Maximiliano did not react, not even when Doña Lupe called him a nitwit four or five times. And this word seemed to be the lid on her rage, because it was followed by a thick flow of complaints about what the boy had done that morning.

"I'm not interested in your reasons right now," she added, "for taking up with that woman—and she's probably the one who's showing you bad manners. I want to speak to you about that nonsense this morning. Do you think your aunt is an old rag or something?"

The boy sat down in the chair next to the bed and endured the scolding without looking at his judge. He had a toothpick in his mouth, and he nervously shuffled it from side to side. He had gotten over the great fear his father's sister had always inspired in him. Just as certain cowards turn courageous the minute they've fired the first shot, Maximiliano, once he had opened fire with his manliness that morning, felt that his will had been freed from the restraints that his shyness had placed upon it. Said shyness was a purely nervous phenomenon, although his routine subordination and self-effacement had played no small part in it. As long as a powerful force was lacking in his soul, those habits and his nervous constitution formed the crust, or appearance, of his personality; but energy welled up inside him, fought for some time to display itself, and broke the crust. His shyness, or false humility, hardened this crust, and as that interior energy found no assistance in words (for his habitual submission and shyness had not permitted him to master discursive language), it took some time for the crust to break. Finally, what words could not do, an action did. Once the crust had broken, Maximiliano discovered he was more courageous and readier to face the beast than he thought. A mountain was only a molehill.

Calmly, he listened to his aunt's outpourings. There were so many arguments that could have opposed the ones his aunt fired at him more ardently than logically. But as for arguing with words—forget it! He wasn't strong enough yet. He would argue with actions. He could handle that with no trouble. When his aunt paused for a breather and collapsed into the chair next to the table, Maximiliano picked up where she'd left off. But it wasn't reasoning; it was as though he'd taken his heart and poured its contents onto the bed, just as he had poured out the contents of the piggy bank once he had smashed it open.

"I love her so much," he said without looking at his aunt and finding, relatively easily, words to express his feelings. "I love her so much that my whole life depends on her, and neither the law, nor my family, nor the whole world can keep me from her. If I had to choose between death and giving up loving her, I'd prefer death a thousand times over; killing myself or being killed. I loved her from the moment I first saw her, and the only way I can stop loving her is to stop living. So it's foolish to oppose my plans, because I'm going to overcome everything; if there's a wall in front of me, I'll ram right through it. Have you seen how the horsemen at the Price Circus crash through the paper hoops when they jump? Well, that's what I'll do too, if someone puts a wall between me and her."

4

This simile was to make a vivid impression on the great Doña Lupe, who sat looking at her nephew with more pity than anger.

"I've been disappointed before," she said, nodding her head like a doll with a wire spring in its neck, "but never like this. You've done a professional job of it. It's true that I don't have any influence over you now. If you lose your way, you'll be lost for good. And don't come sidling up to me then. I brought you up, I educated you, I've been a mother to you. Don't you think you might have said: 'Well, Aunt, such and such has happened'?"

"Of course," Maximiliano hastened to reply, "but I couldn't, Aunt. Now that I'm not so inhibited it seems like the easiest thing in the world. I beg your pardon for this error; I realize that I've behaved badly. But my tongue got all caught up whenever I tried to say something, and I would break out in a cold sweat. I got used to not talking to you except to say that I had a headache, or that I'd lost a button, or that it was raining, or some such silly thing. Listen to me now, please; after having left so much unsaid I feel as if I'll burst unless I tell you everything. I met her three months ago. She was poor, and had been very unfortunate."

"Yes, I know; I've heard that she has run around quite a bit. You'd fall for anything," declared Doña Lupe cruelly.

"Don't pay any attention to things you've heard. Men are very evil. Don't you agree? And say—isn't it a noble act to lead a good lost soul back to the straight path?"

"The idea! You—" shrieked the Jáuregui widow, making the sign of the cross, "fancying yourself a shepherd!"

"Wait a minute, Aunt. Don't judge so quickly," Maximiliano insisted, worried by his inability to express himself correctly. "She has repented! And she's not as bad as they say. She's an angel—"

"Oh yes, right from a cornice! Well, good luck!"

"Believe me, when you meet her—"

"Me? Meet her? She won't have to worry about that. I repeat, good luck with your sheep, or rather, your stray goat."

"But that's not how it is; it's just that I don't know how to express myself. Tell me something: isn't wanting to be decent the same as being decent? It's not? Well, that's not the way I see it."

"How can wanting to be something be the same as being it?"

"In the realm of morality, it is. If she's a decent woman *with* me and she might not be without me, how do you expect me to tell her, 'Good-bye, and go to the devil if you choose.' Isn't it more natural and human of me to take her under my wing and save her? After all, should great . . . Christian works be considered egoistically?"

The poor boy thought that this argument would work, and he studied its effect on his aunt. The truth is that Doña Lupe did feel rather confused for a minute and didn't know what to reply. Finally she answered scornfully:

"You're crazy. These things don't occur to anyone who has any brains. I'm leaving, because if I stay, I'll hit you. My only choice is to break the broomstick on you. And you know, while you're not much of a man for all that sublime love, you're even less of one when it comes to taking a beating."

Maximiliano held onto her dress and made her sit down.

"Listen, Aunt. I love you very much, I owe you my life, and even if you insist on quarreling with me, you're not going to. Now. What's making you so mad, as I'm beginning to see, is a noble act; my conscience approves of it, and I'm as satisfied as if God himself were inside me saying: 'Good, good. . . .' You can't make me believe we were brought into this world just to eat, sleep, digest our meals, and walk around. No. We're here for something else. And if I feel a huge—and I mean huge—force inside that fills me with the desire to save a soul, I'm going to do it, even if the world comes to an end."

"What you have inside," said Doña Lupe, trying to stick to her role, "is so much foolishness that it's coming out all over. And that's all. You won't wheedle me with pretty words. Hmmph! Overnight, you've picked up some fancy language that leaves me speechless. You're a regular poet, in the full sense of the word. I've always considered them big cheats, the crazy fools. You're no longer the little nephew I brought up. What deceit! A woman, a mistress, bedlam! And now you come up with marriage, and Lord knows what else. Look, I don't love you anymore; I'm not your Auntie Lupe any more. I won't throw you out, because I feel sorry for you, and because I hope you'll repent and beg my forgiveness."

Completely serene now, Maximiliano nodded his head doubtfully.

"I already asked to be forgiven when I kept silent; I don't have to ask for your forgiveness anymore. And there's still something you don't know that I want to tell you. How did I support her for three months? Oh, Auntie! I broke my piggy bank. It had over three thousand *reales* in it, enough to support her in a modest way—she's extremely thrifty, Aunt, and doesn't spend a cent more than she has to."

This revelation made Doña Lupe's anger flag momentarily. So she was thrifty! The young man picked up the piggy bank and, showing it to his aunt, revealed his deed as if it had been the most natural thing in the world. He reenacted it.

"See? I took the old piggy bank, after bringing home this one, which is identical. I smashed the full one; I took out the gold and the silver and transferred the copper to this one, adding two *pesetas* in change so it would weigh the same. You want to see how?"

Before Doña Lupe could reply, Maximiliano dashed the piggy bank against the floor, the copper pieces scattering all over.

"Oh, I can see that you've got a whole bag of tricks now," observed Doña Lupe, picking up the coins. "And when you run out of money, do you expect to come to me for more? Well, you're wrong if you do."

"When I run out, God will come to my aid in one way or another," Maximiliano declared fervently.

He was overexcited and his face gleamed. Doña Lupe had never seen those eyes shine so, or that face look so animated. When they had finished picking up the fallen coins, she wrapped them in an issue of *La Correspondencia* and, flinging the packet onto the dresser, she said contemptuously:

"Here, that's for a wedding present."

Maximiliano put the heavy packet in the dresser and then donned his cloak. Doña Lupe didn't dare restrain him, for although her heart was full of haughtiness and authority, she couldn't translate any of it into exteriors; the minute she tried to, a mysterious brake stopped her. She felt her authority over the enamored youth waning; she sensed that a true, revolutionary strength was overpowering her usual strength, and while she was not afraid of Maximiliano, it is undeniable that his sudden display of willpower had inspired in her a certain respect.

That very woman who slept like a baby after having strangled, in concert with Torquemada, a wretched debtor, was beset by the moral problems that her nephew had posed so candidly. If he loved the woman so much, what right did she have to oppose the marriage? And if the woman was inclined to be honest (and her being so thrifty was a good sign), who had the right to deter her from the road to reform? Doña Lupe suddenly had numerous scruples. She was not depraved, except insofar as loans were concerned. She was like people who have one vice, people who when freed of their fever are reasonable, prudent, and discreet.

The next day, after another argument with her nephew, vague thoughts of compromise crept into her mind. There was no longer any room for doubt: Maximiliano's passion was profound and tenacious; it gave him a unique energy. Confronting it was like standing in front of a huge wave just about to break. Doña Lupe meditated deeply all day, and because she had an uncommonly good hold on reality, she began to acknowledge the strong effect of consummated acts and the weakness of thoughts that try to oppose them. This matter of Maxi's love was nonsense: she still considered it an atrocious stupidity; but it was a fact, and there was no choice but to recognize it as such. Then she tactfully concluded that when a private or public realm is disrupted by a powerful revolutionary impulse that is also logical, deep-rooted, and aided by circumstances, it is absurd to attempt to counteract it; a more practical course is to go along with it, albeit elusively, in hopes of eventually channeling it into the desired direction. Thus, she proposed to control her domestic revolution. Stamping it out was impossible now; whoever tried would be crushed. These reflections made her relatively tolerant toward her nephew during their second confidential session; that evening, she pumped him for facts and details about his fiancée cleverly, without showing any curiosity, and she even dared to give him some advice. She did get in a few insults here and there, but she took care not to let Maxi see what she was really doing.

"Don't count on me for anything. Go your own way. I've already told you, I don't care whether your fiancée's eyes are black or yellow. Don't try to butter me up. I'm listening out of consideration; but I couldn't care less. And you want me to meet her? What a fresh one you are!"

Maximiliano's transformation had gifted him with intermittent insights. At times he had the quick, sure vision of a superior mind; at other times he was so blind he couldn't see three men on a donkey. Exalted passions produce these awesome differences in one's faculties and make men dull or sharp, as if their minds were under a lunatic influence of some sort. That day the young man was able to read Doña Lupe's mind, where he discovered a willingness to make peace despite the studied phrases with which she tried to disguise her willingness. More-over, his reasoning demonstrated the brilliance he had acquired in moments of true inspiration; he could now guess what was at the back of other people's minds. His reasoning went as follows: "My aunt is yielding; she's going to accept things. And since Fortunata doesn't owe her any money, nor will she ever—because I'll be around to prevent that—the day will come when they'll be friends."

5

Doña Lupe matched the image in her nephew's mind perfectly: she was sensi-ble, reasonable, she cast a somewhat skeptical eye on human weaknesses, and she was capable of forgiving insults and even abuse; but as for a debt, she never forgave a debt. There were two different people in her, the woman and the money lender. Whoever wanted to be on good terms with her and enjoy her friendship had to be sure to keep her two natures separate. A mere promissory note, made out and signed in the most cordial manner conceivable, was enough to convert the friend into a mortal enemy, the Christian into an Inquisitor.

This lady's dual personality had an external mark on her body, a fatal sign and a work of surgery which in this case was an accusing and just science. One of Doña Lupe's breasts was missing; it had been removed because of a tumor while her husband was alive. Since she took pride in her good figure (she even wore a corset around the house), she substituted for her missing part a well-made ball of raw cotton. Fully clothed, she appeared to have a nice figure, but underneath her clothes only half of her bosom was flesh and blood; the other half was insensitive, and a dagger could have been driven through it without causing her any pain at all. Her heart was just the same—half flesh, half cotton. The type of relationship she had with a person determined which half would predominate. When a prom-issory note was not involved, dealing with that lady was a pleasure, but whoever was forced by circumstances to owe her money had something in store for him.

She wasn't like that while her husband was alive. It's true, however, that during that happy period of her life the only money she handled was whatever Jáuregui gave her to manage the house. After becoming a widow and seeing that she had been left with a couple of odds and ends and five thousand *reales*, she considered starting a rooming house, but Torquemada dissuaded her, offering to invest her money at a good interest rate and as safely as possible. Success and earnings attracted Doña Lupe, who gradually and rapidly acquired all the marks of the perfect usurer, and when it came to collecting her money on time, she thrust forward that cotton breast implacably. Her first years as a usurer were hard, be-cause although the profits were good, they still failed to provide the lady with enough to run the house. By dint of organization and thrift, though, she managed to keep the ship afloat and even performed true miracles, obtaining medicines for Maximiliano and defraying the cost of his education. She loved her nephew dearly and bent over backward to give him everything he needed. This great merit of hers was undeniable. What she said about a garbanzo being worth a pearl was quite true. But what was not was that she had practiced usury solely in order to give the seven monther an education. She told herself that this was so in her soliloquies, but it was just one of those sophisms that human egoism uses to put an honest, noble veneer on things. Doña Lupe "lent money at a rate" for the sheer pleasure of it, a pleasure that Torquemada had taught her. Without a nephew or any financial needs, she would have done precisely the same.

When better years came along and the widow's capital increased to two thousand *duros*, she had a streak of good luck that was soon to become incredible prosperity. Into the joint nets of the two moneylenders fell a poor gentleman, more unfortunate than perverse, who had been a high official in a ministry and lived in style despite the fact that he couldn't pay for the shirt on his back, and they gave him a treatment I'd rather not describe. Doña Lupe's two thousand *duros* swelled like foam for three years; she renewed her loan contracts and accumulated the interest, which she raised every year from two percent monthly (her original rate) to four. Torquemada got a lot more out of the poor victim: he carried off his ornate furniture for a song; but the "so-and-so" had it coming to him. He built his fortune up again during a stint in Cuba as a government official, but then he lost it again, and headed for the Philippines to build it up once more; now he's in the vampires' clutches for the fourth time. Since there's no more money left in the colonies, it doesn't seem likely that the poor wretch will make a fifth pile. "America for the Americans," they say . . . Ha! America is for the moneylenders in Madrid.

Our story catches Doña Lupe when she had already amassed a small fortune—ten thousand *duros*, some of which were shares she owned in the Bank of Spain and others were loans given with certified promissory notes for sums much larger than the debtors' actual borrowings. The ex-halberdier was opposed to "the materialism" of legally insured mortgages at reasonable interest rates. Risky loans with very high returns were his delight, because even though one might not collect until the night before the Last Judgment, most of the victims fell foolishly into the trap for fear of scandal, and the money doubled itself quickly. He could smell a punctilious person a mile off and knew who would rather lose his skin than get a bad name. These were the ones he dug into and glutted himself on.

Little by little, he transmitted his way of being, working, and feeling to his crony, just as marks on a sheet of paper may be impressed on another sheet by tracing or stenciling. Every time Don Francisco brought money of hers that he had collected, a problem in usury solved and concluded, it made the little widow so happy that her pores opened up, and in flowed Torquemada's personality to possess hers, stocking it with yet more of his traits.

Torquemada's wife was so much like him that Doña Lupe listened to her and treated her as though she were Don Francisco himself. And since the two ladies saw a lot of each other, Doña Silvia got to be a strong influence, and she too grafted some of her moral traits onto Doña Lupe. She was mannish and outspoken, and when she stood akimbo, a formidable spectacle. More than once she sprang on a debtor in the street to insult him mercilessly in front of other people. The Jáuregui woman never went that far; a certain delicacy in her nature and upbringing kept her above such usurious rancor. Once, however, she did accompany Doña Silvia to see a poor widow who owed them money, and, after trying in vain to pressure her into paying them back, they cast greedy looks at her furniture. The two harpies exchanged a few words in front of the victim, who almost died of fright.

"You could use this brazier," said Doña Silvia, "and I could use that dresser."

They had porters come to carry away the items as soon as they had emptied the dresser drawers and put out the fire in the brazier. The debtor agreed to everything just so that the terrifying, infernal women would leave.

The brazier was in Doña Lupe's living room, but it was never lit. Maximiliano knew its origins, just as he knew those of the *bargueño** and the handsome wardrobe in his aunt's bedroom. The table where the student worked had come into the house the same way, and their good china, which they saved for special occasions, had been purchased for a fifth of its value as payment of a small debt contracted by one of Doña Lupe's close friends. Doña Silvia had handled the deal to spare Doña Lupe, who would not have ventured to go so far. A sterling silver centerpiece, two silver trays, and a teapot that the lady exhibited proudly had been pawned by another close friend and were now in her home for good, thanks to insolvency. Maximiliano knew many particulars about his aunt's dealings. The jewels, dresses, lace, and Manila shawls that had come into her possession after long captivity she sold through an agent called Mauricia "la Dura,"† who used to come by frequently; but she hardly worked as a vendor anymore. Doña Lupe sorely missed her, for although she was excitable and dissolute, she had always done a good job. So Maximiliano had observed in his own home how implacable his aunt could be with debtors, and from that knowledge came this inspired resolution: "If I marry Fortunata and fate isn't kind to us, I'd sooner beg for alms in the streets than ask my aunt to lend me two *pesetas*. The closer we are, the clearer things have to be."

---

* A *bargueño* is an antique wooden desk or cabinet, usually with handsome carved ornamentation.
† "*La Dura*" means "the Tough One."

iv. Nicolás and Juan Pablo Rubín Propose New Methods of Redemption

I

DEEP DOWN INSIDE, DOÑA LUPE was in favor of the gradual change being forced on her by the circumstances, but she wished neither to let her arm be twisted nor to appear to relent in her prudent intransigence until Juan Pablo arrived and she had a chance to discuss this shocking family event with him. One morning, when Maximiliano was still in bed dozing, he heard noises from the stairs and then the hall. First came the clatter of feet and porters shouting; then the voice of his brother Juan Pablo, which awoke in his soul that insidious fear he thought he had conquered.

The last thing he felt like doing was getting up. He could hear his aunt haggling with the porters over a price for their services. Then he thought he heard Juan Pablo and his aunt talking in the dining room. She was probably telling him all about it, because she loved to make a story out of everything; she didn't like certain things to get stale inside her. Then he heard his brother washing up in the room next to his, and when Doña Lupe went in to bring him some towels, they started whispering; they whispered a long time. Maximiliano imagined that they were talking about the inheritance, but he couldn't be sure. He tried to brace himself by remembering that his brother was the most likable one in the family, the most talented one, and the best at taking charge of things.

At last he forced himself to get up. He washed and dressed, but hesitated to leave his room, standing with his hand on the doorknob for a little while. Doña Lupe knocked on the door, and then he had no choice but to open. He was pale; a pitiful sight. He embraced his brother and could tell instantly from Juan Pablo's expression and the tone of his voice that he knew the incredible story. The young man had no desire to get involved in explanations and arguments at that hour of the morning, and as it was a bit late, he hurried off to class. But he found no rest there, nor did he cease to wonder what his brother would say and do. This perplexity expressed itself in sighs. Fear, that rascal fear, was his worst enemy. His best course would be to unmask himself before his brother as he had done before Doña Lupe, for until he did this, he would not be able to regain control of his will. If Juan Pablo took it badly it might be better, because that way Maximiliano wouldn't have to be polite to him; but if he reacted with diplomatic astuteness, pretending to give in but actually resisting passively, then . . . This, alas, was what he feared most of all.

Soon, he was to be freed from doubt. When Maximiliano returned for lunch, Juan Pablo was already seated at the table, and shortly afterward Doña Lupe appeared with a platter of fried eggs and ham. The lady was content that day because Papitos was behaving properly, which she always did when there was more work.

"That chatterbox!" she said. "Whenever there's a lot to be done, she performs miracles. What *she* wants is to show off; really, whenever she has the chance, she's as good as gold. When there's not much to be done, though, she's an impossible little monkey. She was a savage when I took her in, but little by little I'm making her drop her bad habits. She used to taste everything she could get her fingers into, and whenever I sent her shopping I had to check on her. Would you believe that she ate raw noodles? I picked her up from a dump near Cuatro Caminos—starved and ragged. She used to go begging, which is why she had all those lazy habits. But with my techniques I'm straightening her out. A slap here, a slap there. I'll make a woman of her yet—in the full sense of the word."

"Getting good help is so hard in Madrid," observed Juan Pablo, "that you shouldn't make so much of her faults."

All through lunch they talked about servants, and they looked at Maximiliano after everything they said, as if to entreat his approval. The youth observed that his older brother was serious with him; the seriousness indicated that he considered him a man, for up until now he had always treated him like a child. The student had expected to be jeered at (which was what frightened him most) or paternally reprimanded. Neither attitude was visible in Juan Pablo's cold, indifferent language. After finishing lunch, Juan Pablo said he felt a migraine coming on and he retired, ill-humoredly, to rest. All afternoon and part of the evening he was locked in the clutches of that discomfort, more a nuisance than an illness. His attacks were not as painful as Maximiliano's, and he was usually able to easily avoid the hemicranial pain by going to sleep. He was well aware that his exhaustion from the consecutive trips had caused the attack, and that the migraine would be gone in the morning; but this did not make him any more patient. He cursed his bad luck until late that night, and finally sank into a calm sleep.

Meanwhile, Doña Lupe mused on the indifferent disdain with which Juan Pablo had received the news. He had frowned, commented that his brother was crazy, and finally, shrugging his shoulders:

"What does it have to do with me? He's of age. To heck with him."

Both Maximiliano and his aunt had noticed that Juan Pablo was sad. First they attributed it to his exhaustion, but later they noticed that after twelve hours of sleep, he was even sadder. He didn't participate in their conversation. He didn't seem to be interested in anything, not even the inheritance, which he hardly cared to discuss, although he did speak his mind plainly.

"Did you know that your brother took it calmly?" Doña Lupe said to Maxi one night.

"What?"

"Your affair. I've spoken to him twice, and do you know what he does?—Shrug his shoulders, flick the ashes from his cigarette and say that he couldn't care less."

The enamored youth listened joyfully to these words, which were a great consolation to him. Juan Pablo was undoubtedly obeying the wise rule of respecting others' feelings and plans so that his own would be respected. He spoke so little that Doña Lupe had to pull the words out of him like teeth. "Either he's serenading someone too," she said to herself, "or something's wrong with him. A fine time my nephews give me, brooding like this. At least Maxi is frank and says what he wants."

Doña Lupe would have prodded her eldest nephew for the cause of his sadness, but since she presumed that it was political, she didn't want to touch on this delicate point for fear of getting into a quarrel with Juan Pablo, who was—or had been—a Carlist, whereas she was a Liberal and, strange to say, a Liberal "in the full sense of the word." After having served Don Carlos in an administrative military position, Rubín had been expelled from the Royal Headquarters. His close friends heard him speak of calumnies and "treasonous traps," but nothing definite was known. He uttered angry exclamations, vows to take revenge and scorn for his own lack of judgment: "I was asking for it, getting mixed up with people like that!" When he came to Madrid, thrown out of Don Carlos' court, he always stayed at his aunt's house, but he was hardly ever there. He slept elsewhere, and ate out too, almost always in cafés or at some girlfriend's house, and Doña Lupe was uneasy about it, for she thought—and rightfully so—that such a lifestyle wasn't conducive to good moral and financial habits. Suddenly, the misanthrope went north again, saying that he would return soon, and while he was away, they learned of Melitona Llorente's death. The first that Juan Pablo heard of the inheritance was a letter from his paternal aunt, who wrote to him in Bayonne. He was preparing to come back to Spain, and the letter hastened his return. He came by way of Santander, went to Zaragoza by way of Miranda, and from there to Molina de Aragón. He spent ten days in the town, where no major difficulties prevented him from collecting the inheritance. It amounted to thirty thousand *duros*, including real estate and money in farm mortgages, and deducting the legacies and inheritances taxes, twenty-seven thousand *duros* were left. Each brother would receive nine thousand. Upon arriving in Madrid, Juan Pablo wrote

Nicolas, asking him to come too, so that the three brothers could meet to divide the inheritance.

I have said that Doña Lupe avoided discussing politics with Juan Pablo. Actually, she didn't have the vaguest notions about politics, and if she was a Liberal it was for emotional reasons, as a tribute to the memory of her Jáuregui and out of respect for the military uniform that he proudly sported in his portrait. But if she had been asked to explain the essentials of the Liberal dogma, she would have found herself in a tight spot. All she knew was that those blasted Carlists were indecent sorts who wanted to start the Inquisition all over again, complete with chains. That lady had breathed such progressive air in her childhood and the glorious twenty years of her union with Jáuregui that she didn't wish to hear any talk of absolutism. She didn't understand how her nephew, such a clever boy, had made the blunder of becoming a subject of that big oaf, Don Carlos, that gross character and tyrant—in the full sense of the word.

On religious issues, Doña Lupe adapted her ideas to the criterion held by her deceased husband, a most sensible man who knew how to "give God what was God's and Caesar . . ." etc. The widow proudly repeated this refrain whenever she had the chance, adding that she believed in whatever the Holy Church commanded but that the less you had to do with priests, the better. She went to Mass on Sunday and to confession from time to time, and no one could have changed her routine.

Ever since the day that she had argued with her nephew on the subject and they had practically started throwing things at each other, Doña Lupe eschewed any mention of the Carlists in Juan Pablo's presence. So when she saw him return, humiliated and shamed from the Royal Headquarters, the lady was so overjoyed that it was hard to disguise it. She remembered her Jáuregui and the wise, opportune remarks he had made about the unfortunate people who got involved with priests; it was like going to bed with a child, he had said. "But Juan Pablo won't learn," thought Doña Lupe. "He'll probably take the same steps again, and be there to brush the flies off that drone Carlos the Seventh."

2

Maxi was lulled to sleep by hope that night. It was a symptom of the reconciliation that his aunt no longer spoke to him in an angry voice and even seemed to regard him as a fully grown man. At times she even seemed to respect him. There's nothing like being tough and firm to gain the respect of others! And Doña Lupe once again cared for him with her usual solicitude. She made his favorite dishes and saw to it that he had all the comforts he might wish in his room. In a word, the poor boy was satisfied; he felt the ground firming up under his feet and he began to feel like the master of his fate, almost triumphant in this huge battle against the family.

As for Juan Pablo, there was nothing to fear. The two brothers had very few occasions to talk at length, because the older one usually left after lunch for one of the cafés at the Puerta del Sol to fritter away his time there. In the evening, he returned very late or not at all. Maxi relished the thought that his brother was off with a woman somewhere; "now" he mused, "we'll see who's well-behaved; whose morals are better; he'd better not try to seem holier-than-thou with me."

In short, ever since the showdown with his aunt that morning, our Maxi found himself respected and esteemed. The only person who did not share in any of this respect was Papitos, whose vulgar familiarity with him got worse every day.

"Ugly, tick-face, wet noodle!" she jeered, sticking out an incredible amount of tongue. "Some ladies' man you are! Just wait and see—they're not gonna let you get married. Ha, what a laugh! You stupid dunce."

Maximiliano overtly despised her:

"Get out of my sight, you brat, or I'll knock out your teeth."

"You? Ha! If I socked you, you'd land on the roof."

It was better to ignore her. She didn't know any better. Papitos was cleaning up Sito Maxi's room, where she had set up a bed for the priest, who was due to arrive the following morning. The student took a dim view of this arrangement because whenever his brother Nicolás came to Madrid and slept in the same room, his snoring deprived Maxi of his sleep. His throat and nasal passages sounded like the trumpet of Jericho, or worse. Maxi got so nervous that he sometimes had to get out of bed and leave the room. What irritated him most was that the next morning the priest claimed that "he hadn't slept a wink."

Maxi suggested to Doña Lupe that she free him from this martyrdom by putting Nicolás in another room. Where, though, when there were no other rooms in the house? The Señora promised to put the bed in her own room if the priest snored too much the first night.

"Now that I think of it, I snore too . . . Oh well, we'll arrange something. Even if you have to sleep in the living room."

Nicolás Rubín arrived the next morning, and Maxi viewed his arrival as that of one more enemy he would have to fend off. His brother's priestly aura impressed him, for no matter how much he and his aunt disapproved of reactionaries, a priest is always an authority in any family. Maxi was not as fond of Nicolás as he was of Juan Pablo, doubtlessly because he had not lived with him during childhood.

The two older brothers had lunch together; they did not, however, touch on politics so as not to shock Doña Lupe. It was none other than Nicolás who had made Juan Pablo jump through the Carlist hoop by promising him mansions and castles. He had given him letters of recommendation addressed to the top brass at the Royal Headquarters and also some calvary chaplains in Bayonne. But none of this was discussed at the table. They knew very well that their aunt wished that due respect be paid to her Jáuregui, whose presence was always felt as a mental fiction, tangibly symbolized by the ugly portrait in the parlor. They talked about the weather, about how bad it was living in Toledo, about how the wind had blown away the best of the apricot crop, and about other light subjects, all the while bodily appreciating the good meal.

After lunch, Juan Pablo proposed that since they were gathered together they review a few aspects of the inheritance that needed clarification. He preferred not to have any country property, so if his brothers approved, he would take his share in cash and mortgages. Other mortgages and land would go to Nicolás and Maximiliano. They agreed to their brother's proposal, at which point Doña Lupe felt like speaking up, but she did not dare intervene in business that did not concern her. Her only choice was to swallow her words for now. Later she said to Maximiliano:

"You were both fools. Your brother wants his share in cash so that he can spend it right away. Money slips through his fingers like water. I have nothing to gain from telling you this, but if I were you, I would have taken my share in cash so I could have invested it for you, and it would have brought you a nice little income. Otherwise, you'll see. I'd like to know how you're going to manage all those olive trees and vineyards and that piece of a mountain they say is yours. The same as that fool Nicolás—agreeing to everything. First of all you'll have to get an administrator, who'll cheat you for all you're worth and send you bills that'll make you shake in your boots. What a pair of idiots! I kept looking at you and making signs for you to resist him, but you just sat there like a bump on a log. And then you go around thinking you've got a mind of your own! Well, you've chosen a fine road; oh yes, a fine one."

The eldest brother had also proposed something else that the others had accepted with pleasure. When Don Nicolás Rubín died, all the creditors appropriated what was left of the shop, except for one, who had been the best and most loyal friend the deceased had had, in fair or foul weather. This creditor was Samaniego, the pharmacist on Ave María Street, and the debt to him, counting the six percent interest, amounted to over fifteen thousand *duros*. Juan Pablo proposed that in honor of justice and the memory of their beloved father they repay Samaniego, and it was unanimously approved. Doña Lupe herself approved of this measure that, if it somewhat reduced the capital in the inheritance, was also an act of loyalty and a posthumous consecration of her poor brother's honesty. Samaniego had never mentioned the debt, and this delicacy of his influenced the Rubíns' desire to repay him. The families visited each other frequently, were on the best of terms, and it was even said that Juan Pablo had an eye for the pharmacist's eldest daughter, Aurora, whose virtue, cleverness, and readiness to work Doña Lupe extolled highly.

Thus, with the approval of Nicolás and Maximiliano, the debt to Samaniego was paid off.

Maximiliano felt increasingly sure of himself after participating in such matters. He had sat on the family council and made decisions; therefore, he was a man. If he had a personality legally, why shouldn't he have one otherwise? He had the impression that something was developing inside him, and he even imagined that if he were put on a scale he would weigh more now. His physique was probably more robust, his muscles tougher, his lungs stronger. Nevertheless, he was waiting on pins and needles to hear what his priest-brother would say. It might very well be that just when everything was going smoothly, Nicolás would come up with some of the "mysticking" typical of his trade; pull God out of his sleeve and start another commotion.

The evening of the day the inheritance was discussed, Nicolás was informed of the recent events; he didn't take them as calmly as Juan Pablo. His first reaction was to be indignant. He adopted a worried, pensive pose, playing the role of the level-headed man who, far from being scared by difficulties, faces them squarely with no effort at all. Nicolás and the widow, whose relationship had been chilly up until two months before the events, were on very cordial terms now—not because aunt and nephew had any temperamental affinity, but because the temporary coincidence in their financial status had erased their considerable personal differences. Nicolás had never appealed to Doña Lupe; first, because cassocks in general didn't please her, and second, because this particular nephew wasn't exactly likable. He didn't have Juan Pablo's personal charm or the little one's humility. He wasn't physically attractive; his hairiness has been mentioned. Doña Lupe had put it plainly when she said that the eldest had gotten all the talent in the family, whereas Nicolás had walked off with all the hair. The day after he shaved, his face was black. Freshly shaved, his jaws were slate gray. The hair on his hands and arms was like grass on a fertile field, and thick tufts of it protruded from his ears and nostrils, rather like ideas that had tired of the darkness in his brain and had peeped out onto the balconies of his nose and ears to see what was going on in the world.

His sermonistic pretensions and uncouthness, combined with his clerical haughtiness, greatly irritated Doña Lupe, and their relationship had always been purely perfunctory until Nicolás, on one of his trips to Madrid, had the brainstorm of giving his savings to his aunt for her to invest. Note how this produced a conventionally pleasant relationship that was to evolve into friendship. They were like two countries separated by essential racial differences and antagonistic customs united later by a commercial treaty. A long time ago, she had been fond of him and had valued his great personal qualities, but her fondness gradually faded. She couldn't forgive his wasteful habits and squandering of money. He had never given her a cent to invest. He was always broke, and whenever he could get anything out of his aunt, using the craftiest means imaginable, he did, and it made the widow's blood boil. Yet we've seen how she ended up getting along best with him, the least likable of her nephews.

3

Informed of the terrible news, Nicolás lost no time; he launched into a soporific sermon interrupted only by Papitos' serving the salad. Nicolás Rubín positively could not sleep unless he had a lettuce or escarole (depending on the season) salad at eleven at night; well-dressed and tossed, with that indispensable touch of garlic rubbed into the salad bowl, and the special treat of celery too, when it was in season. So the priest ate his salad with gusto—a fact not worth recording, for no one can remember a day in the year when he didn't. His stomach was a veritable gristmill. Three hours after being filled it was ready to be filled to capacity again.

"It's this debility I have," he'd say, putting on a grave and sometimes worried face. "You have no idea how I've tried to improve my condition. The doctor says I should eat lightly but often."

He attacked the forage of greens, leaning over his food like an animal over a manger full of hay.

"You know, Aunt," he mumbled between grunts, as well as his chewing allowed, "I don't eat much, even though it may seem like it."

"You could eat more. Eat, son; eating isn't a mortal sin."

"You know, Aunt . . ."

He didn't specify what, because chewing the juicy stems of the escarole absorbed all his attention. His thick lips shone with the goo, and it trickled down the sides of his mouth in threads that would have run straight to his throat if the thick stubble on his badly shaved chin hadn't stopped them. He was wearing a black wool cap with a pom-pom that jounced forward whenever he bent over his plate and jounced back when he raised his head again. Nicolás' table manners revolted Doña Lupe—she couldn't help it; she thought he would be much better off if he knew less theology and more manners. Since the two of them were alone, she teased him about "eating lightly but often," but he hastened to change the subject to Maxi's affair.

"It's very serious, Aunt, and I mean serious."

"It certainly is; but I think it's going to be hard to change his mind."

"I'll take care of that. Oh, if only I didn't have other mountains to move too," said the priest, pushing away the salad bowl (which didn't have a leaf left in it). "You'll see; you'll see . . . I'll make him backtrack. I'm the world's best at—"

He didn't finish the sentence, because from the pit of his stomach there emerged such a voluminous quantity of gas that the words had to scurry aside to let it escape. The burp was so loud that Doña Lupe had to turn away, even though Nicolás had put the palm of his hand in front of his mouth to act as a shield. This was one of his few relatively polite habits.

"—best at these things," he concluded, when the fluids had dissolved into the dining room. "You'll see: as soon as he comes in, I'll let him have it. It's my specialty. Oh, I think I hear him now."

The bell rang, and Doña Lupe herself went out to greet her nephew. The minute he entered the dining room, he knew from the impertinent expression on his brother's face that Nicolás had been told about "it." The priest gave him no time whatsoever to collect himself; skipping over the preliminaries, he thrust these words at him:

"Sit down here, my little man; we have things to talk about. Well—I've just heard something that's stunned me. A fine story. So—"

The stiff hand put itself in front of his mouth again just as the words were getting pushed aside and his head vibrated.

"So, around here everybody does what he darn well wants without taking into consideration divine and human laws; and makes what he wants of religion, and the dignity of the family."

Maximiliano, who was crushed from the start by this reprimand, suddenly collected himself, and all the strength he possessed emerged in a virile burst. This was the characteristic symptom of the "new man" in him. Now that the formidable subject had come out into the open, the ice was broken, and his great courage in defending it came to the fore. He couldn't argue, but he *could* defend himself with actions, or at least demonstrate his firm decision to be independent with brief, emphatic words.

"Bah!" he exclaimed, turning away from his brother with a scornful nod. "I don't want to hear any sermons. I know very well what I should do."

And speaking thus, he rose to leave for his room.

"All right, all right," murmured the priest, abashed; he looked from Doña Lupe to Papitos, who was astounded at being looked to for advice. "What bad manners, and what a temper my little brother has developed! Fine, indeed!"

A cubic meter of gas rushed to his mouth with such vehemence that Nicolás had to stiffen up to let it escape, and in spite of his anger, he made sure that his hand did its duty. Doña Lupe looked indignant too, although if that worthy lady's innermost thoughts had been carefully examined, it would have been seen that amidst the anger that dignity obliged her to show, she was secretly relishing an odd joy at having witnessed Maxi's independence. So her nephew really *was* a whole man! It had always disturbed her that he was so shy and self-effacing. Why shouldn't she be pleased at this sign of some determination to be himself? "I want to see what this little devil will be up to next," she mused somewhat mischievously. "And what a temper he's turning out to have!"

"Fine, indeed," said the priest, resting his hands on the arms of his chair so as to straighten his body. "You'll see, you cockeyed fool; I'll straighten you out. Good night, Aunt. Now comes the showdown. He and I will talk once we're in bed."

Nicolás shut himself up in his room (his brother's, that is) and they retired. Doña Lupe stationed herself nearby to eavesdrop. At first all she heard was the creaking of the priest's iron bed, which was very flimsy and made music of its occupant's every move, music that, combined with the noise of those veteran springs, would have kept anybody but Nicolás Rubín from getting a wink. Then Doña Lupe heard Maxi's voice—blurry, but firm and solid; Nicolás didn't let him get a word in edgewise, but Maxi held his ground. It was a terrible duel, between the sermon and the sincere language of the heart! Doña Lupe paid special attention to the seven monther's voice; she would have been delighted to hear him say something exceptional, categorical, out of the ordinary, but she couldn't distinguish the words very clearly because Maxi's voice was very low; it seemed to be coming from deep inside a bottle. On the other hand, the priest's words were plainly audible from the hall. "The things he brings in!" thought Doña Lupe, turning away in scorn. "What in the world do Saint Thomas or Father Suárez have to do with . . . . !" At last the priest's cavernous voice was heard no more; instead, there was a rhythmic whistling, soon followed by a roaring, like air rushing through the ruins of a fortress tower.

"He's already snoring away," thought Doña Lupe, retiring to her room. "What a bad night poor Maxi's going to have!"

It was about nine o'clock the next morning when Nicolás asked Papitos to bring him his hot chocolate. He emerged from the room, his face washed so badly that parts of it looked as if they hadn't seen water since his christening.

"My hot chocolate?" he asked in the dining room, rubbing his hands together as if he wanted to start a fire.

"Coming up."

His hot chocolate was to have cinnamon, it was to be made with milk (naturally), and it was to have no less than two ounces of chocolate. It was to come with a big roll, several little cakes, and sugared water. And Nicolás even went so far as to say that he had chocolate "not because he liked it" but so that he could "smoke a cigarette" afterward.

"So what happened last night?" asked Doña Lupe as she set the cargo he called breakfast in front of him.

"Nothing. No one can tell him anything," replied the priest, dunking the first cake into the thick liquid. "It's like you said: his mind can't be changed. We can do one of two things: either kill him or leave him alone, and since we're not going to kill him . . . We finally agreed that I'd meet the . . . wild woman today."

"I don't think it's a bad idea."

"And depending on my impression of her, we'll decide what to do."

"Are you going together?"

"No, I'm going alone; I prefer to. Besides, he has a migraine today."

"A migraine? Poor dear!"

Doña Lupe ran in to see how he was. Maximiliano had started dressing but he had been forced to go back to bed. Provoked, undoubtedly, by the emotional stress he was under, the long debate with his brother, and more so, perhaps, by Nicolás' insufferable snoring, the feared attack had materialized. From midnight on, Maxi felt that peculiar deadening in his head, accompanied by the warning. The debility continued along with his frustrated desire to sleep, and then he felt the darting pain behind his left eye that he relieved a bit by pressing the skin below his eyebrow. The patient tossed and turned, searching for a more comfortable position. Then the sharp pain grew heavy, spreading itself like an iron blockade advancing through his skull. The general malaise developed shortly thereafter: anxiety, nausea, restlessness, and then an intense need to rest. It couldn't go on like that and finally he was overcome by that epileptic uneasiness of his, that cursed tingling he felt all over. When he tried to get up, he felt as if his head were splitting in several places, just as his piggy bank had split open when he smashed it with the pestle. He heard his aunt come in. Doña Lupe knew the illness so well that at a glance she could tell what stage he was in.

"Is it splitting yet?" she asked him softly. "I'll put laudanum on you."

He felt something like a nail, a hot iron rod, crossing from his left eye to the crown of his head. Then the torture shifted to his right eye, somewhat milder this time. As affectionate as always, Doña Lupe applied the laudanum and freshened his bed. Closing the blinds, she then went to make him a cup of tea; he had to have something. The sick boy told his aunt that if Olmedo should come by on his way to class, to send him in so that he could ask him to do a favor. Olmedo did come, and Maximiliano begged him to warn Fortunata of the priest's visit.

"Listen. Tell her to be very careful of what she says, but not to be afraid; to speak sincerely, that's enough. Tell her how I am, and that I won't be able to see her till tomorrow."

4

The warning about the priest's visit, punctually relayed by Olmedo, threw Fortunata into a state of confusion. First it struck her as a considerable honor, then as a commitment: being visited by such a respectable person meant that Maxi's plan was legitimate. But she didn't regard herself as sufficiently refined to receive such an authoritative figure. "An ecclesiastical clergyman! I'm going to be so ashamed! I just know he's going to ask me the kind of things they ask when you go to confession. What should I wear? Should I put on my best clothes or just any old thing? Maybe it'd be best to be in rags—look poor so he won't . . . No, that's not proper. I'll wear something decent and modest." Once she had done the most urgent household tasks, she combed her hair very simply; she put on a black dress, her new boots; she also put on her dark wool scarf, and held it together with a white swallow-shaped pin and, looking in the mirror, she approved of her perfect semblance of an honest woman. Before getting dressed she had a quick lunch, though with a poor appetite, because she didn't like such serious visits; she didn't know what she was expected to say on such occasions. The thought of making a blunder or not giving a straight answer to what she was asked took away her appetite. And anyway, why did she have to be visited by a priest? But she scarcely had time to think about this when all of a sudden—rrrring! It was approximately one thirty.

She ran to open the door. Her heart was in her mouth. The black figure advanced through the hall on his way to the living room. Fortunata was so nervous she couldn't find words to invite him to sit down and take off his hat. Maxi, who when talking about his family was swayed by pride rather than prompted by sincerity, had told her dozens of exaggerated stories about Nicolás, depicting him as a very talented, virtuous person, and she had believed him. Therefore she was somewhat disillusioned upon seeing that coarse-looking country priest with his badly shaved chin and abundance of black body hair that seemed to be there for a harvest. He had a disagreeable face, a big mouth that was too far from his crooked little nose, a spacious though not noble forehead, a stout body, long dark hands that had hardly ever seen soap, and dark, rough, oily skin. The priest's black clothes revealed slovenliness, and this detail, well observed by Fortunata, restored her hopes for the man's saintliness, for in her ignorance she assumed that cleanliness was never next to godliness. Shortly afterward, noticing that her future brother-in-law smelled (and not of amber) confirmed her notion.

"You seem to be somewhat frightened," said Nicolás with a cold clerical smile. "Don't be frightened of me. I don't eat people. Do you know why I've come?"

"Yes, sir . . . no. I mean, I have some idea. Maximiliano—"

"Maximiliano is madder than a hatter," stated the clergyman with the brash self-confidence of someone who senses that his interlocutor is too weak to reply, "and you must know it as well as I do. Now he's come up with this nonsense of marrying you. I'm not angry; don't worry, I'm not going to scold you. I'm all for peace, my friend, and I've come here to iron things out. My idea was to see whether you're a sensible person, and if you are, you must realize that this business of marriage is utter nonsense. If you *can* see it—and here's my idea—then you're precisely the one to change his mind. That's all."

Fortunata was familiar with *La Dame aux Camélias*; she had heard it read aloud. She recalled the scene in which the priest begs the lady to make the boy forget the foolish love that was degrading him, and she derived a certain pride from discovering herself in a similar situation. More out of a desire to flirt with virtue than from an inclination to self-abnegation, she accepted the role being offered her. And it was a nice one! Since it didn't require any effort to play (because she was far from being in love), she replied in sweet, grave tones:

"I'm ready to do anything you wish."

"Good, very good indeed," said Nicolás, proud of what he believed had been the triumph of his personality, which had only to display itself to command others. "That's the way I like people to be. And if I order you to never see my brother again, to escape tonight so he won't find you here tomorrow?"

Fortunata hesitated at this.

"I'll do it, sir," she answered at last, hastening to find loopholes in the priest's plan. "But where can I go so he won't follow me? He'd go to the ends of the earth to find me. You have no idea how mad he is about me."

"Oh, I know all about it. You don't know who you're telling. So you think we won't get anywhere by leaving him in the lurch? This is what counts."

"Nowhere, sir," she declared, already disliking the role, for while marrying Maximiliano was not a particularly pleasant solution, living in the street terrified her so much that anything seemed better than going back to that life.

"Good, very good," stated Nicolás, imitating a very ponderous person who reasons things mathematically. "We already have our point of departure, which is your willingness to cooperate. That's what counts. Tell me this: Don't you have anyone you can go to if you break up with my brother?"

"No, sir."

"You have no family?"

"No, sir."

"Well! You are in a spot. So," he said, crossing his arms and leaning back, "in that case you have no choice but to . . . take up the good life . . . er, free love . . . You know what I mean."

"Yes, sir; I understand. It's my only choice," the young woman declared humbly.

NEW METHODS OF REDEMPTION

"What a tremendous responsibility for me!" exclaimed the priest, nodding his head and looking down. And he repeated this as many as five times in a tone he saved for the pulpit.

At that moment he was struck by thoughts other than those that he had entertained on his way over and that were more in keeping with his towering clerical haughtiness. His aim had been to break those ties if his brother's fiancée proved cooperative, but when he saw how humble and resigned she was to her sad lot, it whetted his appetite for designing a compromise that would show off his skill as a reweaver of a torn moral fabric. "This is my chance to shine," he thought. "If I win this battle, it'll be the greatest, most Christian victory a priest can brag about. Just think how I'll look, if I can turn this Magdalene into an exemplary lady, a better Catholic than the best of them." Nicolás imagined himself saying this to his colleagues. His duty of fishing for souls was something he took seriously, and the truth is that he'd never been offered a fish like this. If he rescued it from the waters of corruption, "what a victory, gentlemen! What a catch!" In other similar, although less important, cases that he had handled with all his apostolic tricks, he had won such showy success that he had become an enviable object among the Toledan clergy. Oh, yes—Father Rubín had rescued two marriages he had found on the rocks, he had saved a pretty girl from prostitution, he had forced three seducers to marry their victims, and all with the persuasive power of his dialectics. "I'm made to order for this business," was his last private thought as he swelled with vanity and happiness at the prospect of winning this great battle. Then he rubbed his hands together vigorously, murmuring: "Good, very good; this is shaping up." The gesture was reminiscent of a laborer's loosening up his hands just before starting on a rude task, or a tiller's spitting on them before picking up his hoe. Then he said brusquely, smilingly:

"Do you mind if I have a cigarette?"

"Not at all; please go right ahead, Father," replied Fortunata, who was awaiting the results of his meditations and hand rubbing.

"Yes, indeed," Nicolás declared gravely, inhaling the smoke, "I lack the courage to throw you back to a low life; that is to say, charity and my priestly office forbid me to do so. When a shipwrecked man wants to be saved, is it human to stand on the shore and give him a kick? No. The human response is to hold out your hand or a stick he can hang onto. Yes, that's it."

"Yes, sir," said Fortunata gratefully. "And I'm a shipwr—"

She was going to say "a shipwrecked woman," but since she feared that she would not be able to pronounce the word correctly, she saved it for another occasion, saying to herself: "Let's not put our foot in it if we can help it."

"What I need now," added Rubín, playing with his skirts and gesturing like a man who needs to have his arms freed for a colossal task, "is to see in you clear signs of repentance and the desire to lead a regular, decent life; what I need now is to read what's in your mind and your heart. So. How long has it been since you last confessed?"

Fortunata blushed, for it embarrassed her to admit that it had been at least ten or twelve years since she'd gone to confession. At last she declared it.

"Splendid," said Nicolás, drawing his chair up to the sofa where the young woman was seated. "I warn you, I'm very experienced at this. I've been hearing confessions for five years, and I can spot things in no time. I mean, no woman can fool me."

Fortunata was scared, and Nicolás drew up his chair closer. Even though they were alone, there are certain things that ought to be said in a whisper.

"Let's see: who was the first man?" the presbyter inquired, putting his stiff hand to his mouth, for certain gases were trying to exit with the questions.

She told him about Juanito Santa Cruz, not without embarrassment, and related the story incoherently.

"Be brief. There are many details that I already know by heart, just like the catechism—that he promised to marry you, and you were dumb enough to believe him. That he caught you off guard one day, when you were alone. Bah! The same old story. Then you knew lots of other men—approximately how many?"

Fortunata looked up at the ceiling and made a mental estimate.

"It's hard to say . . . It depends on what you mean by 'knowing.'"

The priest smiled to himself.

"I mean on intimate terms with; men you lived with for a month or two . . . You know. I'm not referring to the ones you knew in passing. That will come later."

"Well, there were . . ." she said, very uncomfortable by now.

"Come on, don't be frightened by the number."

"Well, there were about eight or so . . . Give me a minute to remember."

"That'll do; eight's the same as twelve or eight hundred and twelve. Is the memory of those scandals repulsive to you?"

"Oh, yes, sir! Believe me—"

"You can't stand the sight of them. I believe you. The rascals! However, tell me this: would you have a relationship with any of them if they asked you again?"

"With none of them," said Fortunata.

"Really? Think carefully."

Fortunata thought carefully, and after a few minutes the loyalty and good faith in which she was making her confession showed in this declaration:

"With one of them . . . I don't know . . . But it can't be."

"Never mind whether it can or can't be. That one, that exception to your disgust, is the first—that so-called Don Juanito. You don't have to confirm it. I know these stories like the palm of my hand. Remember, child, I was the father confessor at the Repented Women's in Toledo for five long years."

"But it's impossible. He's married, he's very happy, and doesn't even remember me."

"Maybe not, maybe so. But anyway, you say that he's the only one you really love, the only one who really appeals to you and makes you feel the way you women do . . ."

"The only one."

"And the rest can go to the devil."

"They can go wherever they want."

"And my brother? This is what counts."

The abruptness of the question disturbed the contrite woman. She wasn't expecting it, and poor old Maxi was the furthest thing from her mind at that moment. Being so sincere, she didn't think for a minute of altering the truth. Things were as they were. Besides, that priest seemed pretty smart, and if she told him one thing instead of another, he'd notice the difference.

"I don't care what happens to him either."

"Fine," said the priest, pushing his chair as close as it would go.

5

So that no malicious soul will misinterpret these brusque approaches of Nicolás Rubín's chair to his interlocutor's seat, let me make it clear once and for all that he was a terribly strong-willed, or rather cold-blooded, man. Feminine beauty did not move him, or moved him only slightly, which is why his chastity lacked merit. The flesh that tempted him was of another breed—a calf's, for example, or a pig's, in thick slices; rib steaks or a sirloin nicely done with peas. His eyes brightened more readily at the sight of ham than hips, no matter how succulent, and the "skirt" or flank he liked best was the kind found in stews. He bragged about how he was never hungry for women, making a colossal virtue of it; but he didn't have to fight off the devil to triumph. Being bold with his chair was simply a habit he had acquired from hearing confessional secrets.

"As for loving him," said Fortunata, making an effort to express herself clearly, "I mean love, you know?—no. But esteem, respect—yes."

"So you have no 'romantic' feelings?"

"No, sir."

"But you do feel a quiet fondness, which is often the beginning of a constant friendship, of that pure, calm affection that brings happiness in marriage."

Fortunata didn't dare answer plainly. What the priest was saying seemed to overstate the truth. If some of it were trimmed off, it would be more acceptable.

"I could learn to love him . . ."

"Good. Because there's something you have to see clearly: what people call 'romance' is pure gibberish—for fools. Falling in love with a fellow because his eyes are this or that color, because his little mustache looks just so, or because he has a nice way of talking and stands up straight is typical of primitive females. Loving in that sense isn't loving; it's perversion, my child. Vice. True love is spiritual, and the only way to love is to fall in love with someone's spiritual qualities. Women today let themselves be perverted by novels and false ideas that other women give them about love. Lies and indecent propaganda! It's Satan's doing, and he uses poets, novelists, and other lazy men to spread it. They'll tell you that love and physical beauty are brothers, and they'll tell you about Greek and pagan naturalism. Don't pay any attention to those lies, my child; don't believe in any love except spiritual love, that is, the affinity one soul feels for another."

His listener sensed the meaning of all this, but she didn't really comprehend it; what he was saying ran against her feelings. But since a learned man was speaking, she had no choice but to assent to everything. Seeing that she was nodding in the affirmative, the priest's spirits rose, and he added emphatically:

"To maintain anything else is to deny Catholicism and go back to mythology. Yes, that's it."

"Of course," she remarked. But inside, she was wondering what he meant by "mittollogy." . . . It couldn't have anything to do with mittens, could it?

This clergyman, who specialized in mending consciences and considered himself a physician of lovesick hearts, was perhaps the most inept person in the world for the job he did so unstintingly, thanks to his own sterile and glacial virtue, that negative condition that, if it protected him from danger, also shut his eyes to the reality of the human soul. He practiced his apostleship with routine formulas or rancid aphorisms from books written by saints like himself, and he had done immeasurable harm to humanity by dragging gullible maidens off to the loneliness of a convent, concocting marriages between people who weren't in love, and, in short, upsetting the admirable works that human passions are. He was like doctors who have studied the human body in an anatomy text. He had a charlatan's prescriptions for everything, and he gave them out recklessly, causing havoc wherever he went.

"Thus, my child," he added fatuously, "there are cases of beautiful women who deeply love ugly men. True love—make a mental note of this—is love between souls. All the rest comes from the imagination, the madwoman in the house."

This figure of speech amused Fortunata.

"Who pays any attention to his imagination?" he continued, listening to himself and feeling very satisfied by the effect he thought he was producing. "When the madwoman upsets you, just ignore her, child. Would you pay any attention to a person speaking nonsense in the street? Well, it's exactly the same thing. You must treat your imagination scornfully and do the opposite of what she inspires you to do. I realize that because of the bad life you've led and the lack of good examples you won't be able to control the madwoman for some time; but here I am to teach you how. You have me now, and I think I know what I've got on my hands. So let's start. If you're going to be worthy of marrying a proper man, the first thing you have to do is turn to religion, and start by edifying your inner constitution."

"Yes, sir," the woman replied humbly. She understood what he meant by religion, but not the "edifying" business. To her, edifying meant building houses.

"Good. Are you prepared to put yourself in my hands and do everything I tell you?" proposed the priest, swollen with the conceit he felt when he played that sublime role of mender of broken souls.

"Yes, sir."

"And how are we on Christian doctrine?"

He said this with a tinge of impertinent superiority, the way some doctors say, "Let's see your tongue."

"I, um . . . I'm very bad on 'doktrim,'" replied the penitent, trembling. "I don't know anything."

The chaplain didn't look astonished. On the contrary, he preferred that his catechumens start from scratch so that *he* could teach them everything. Then he meditated a bit, twiddling his thumbs. Fortunata looked at him in silence. She couldn't doubt that he was very learned in worldly things and human weaknesses, and she thought it would be wise to put herself in his hands. She was still under the influence of superstitious notions she had acquired as a child on religion and the clergy. Her catechism was pretty basic; it amounted to a couple of incomplete notions: there was heaven and hell, suffer here to be happy there, or vice versa. Her moral knowledge was purely personal and intuitive; it had nothing to do with the little she remembered of Christian doctrine. She formed a good impression of Maxi's brother because he hardly washed and knew a lot and didn't scold sinners like herself, but instead treated them gently, offering them marriage and salvation and talking to them about the soul and other very nice things.

"It all depends on whether you can tell the madwoman to leave you alone," continued Nicolás, coming down from the abstract. "Remember what Christ said to the Samaritan woman when he spoke to her at the well, in circumstances somewhat like ours."

Fortunata smiled, making believe she knew the quotation; but she was in the dark.

"If you want to reform and edify yourself inside so that you'll acquire the necessary strength, here I am to help you. After all, what are we here for? When I think you're safely on your way to self-reform I might not object so much to my brother's plans. The poor boy's crazy about you. He told me last night that if we don't let him marry you, he'll die. My aunt wants to change his mind, but I said to her: 'Calm down, Aunt; you've got to take a good look at things. Let's not be hasty.' And that's why I'm here. I'll commit myself to curing you of that sickness of the imagination that consists of your passion for the unworthy man who was your perdition. When that's done, you'll love the man who's to be your husband, and you'll love him with spiritual, not sensual, excitement. That's how it'll be. Oh, I've won so many victories like this! I've saved so many people who thought they were damaged for good! You can be sure of it: in this, as in other things, it's just a question of starting. Just think how happy you'll be when we've reformed you: you'll be contented and respected, you'll have a respectable name, and you'll have someone who adores you, not for your physical charms—they don't mean a thing—but for your spiritual ones, the ones that really count. At first it will be a little hard for you; you'll have to forget about your pretty little face. That will probably be the hardest part. But let's remember that the only true beauty is that of the soul, my child, because the beauty of the body goes to the worms."

This sounded right to the sinner, who assented with a nod.

"Well, let's go to it. Do you want to establish the possibility,—this is the issue—the possibility of marrying a Rubín?"

"Yes, sir," Fortunata replied rather fearfully, still frightened by the mention of the worms.

"Then you'll have to submit yourself to the following test," said the priest, covering a yawn, for it was already four o'clock and he wouldn't have minded a snack. "There's a religious institute in Madrid of the most useful kind; its function is to take in girls who have gone astray and convert them to the truth through praying, working, and a cloistered life. Some of them who've been disillusioned by the meager substance there is in pleasure stay there forever; others leave, 'edified,' either to get married or to work in the homes of respectable people. Very few of them go back to their old life. Decent ladies go there too, to expiate their sins; frivolous wives who've pulled one on their husbands. And then there are others who go into seclusion to search for the happiness they couldn't find in the hubbub of the outside world."

Fortunata kept nodding. She had heard of the place; it was the convent run by the Micaela nuns.

"Good. That's right. So. You'll go there and we'll keep you locked up there for three or four months. The house chaplain is such a close friend of mine, it's as if he were me. He will take charge of your spiritual direction, because I can't do it; I've got to go back to Toledo. But whenever I come to Madrid, I'll come to take your pulse and check on your education. This won't keep me from giving you some sessions on Christian doctrine before I leave, so you won't enter the convent completely green. If, after a reasonable length of time, you seem spiritually ready to be worthy of being my sister-in-law, you may perhaps become that person. You can count on this: as soon as this humble priest says the word, the whole family will bow."

He said this simply and sweetly. It was one of his best and most studied recipes, and for its delivery he used a tone of mild conviction that had a strong effect on the inexpert people he usually addressed.

Its effect on Fortunata was so strong that she could barely keep from bursting into tears. Without a doubt, the interest that that kind apostle of Christ was taking in her was something to be very grateful for. And all this with no scolding, no throwing up of his hands, treating her the way a good shepherd treats his beloved flock. Despite this excellent disposition of her soul, the poor girl hesitated. On the one hand, a retired, silent, Christian life in the cloisters sounded appealing. It might well be that the wound in her heart would be completely healed there. There was no harm in giving it a try. But on the other hand, she was terrified by the unknown, the nuns . . . What would the nuns be like? How would they treat her? But Nicolás anticipated her fears, telling her that they were the most indulgent, affectionate ladies imaginable. Fortunata's eyes welled with tears; she envisioned herself transformed into a lady, her imagination freed of the evil that was destroying her, her conscience rebuilt, her mind illuminated by the hundreds of lovely things she would learn. Her imagination itself, which her teacher had depicted as awful, was what kindled the enthusiasm in her soul and instilled in her the pride of becoming a new woman.

"Yes, yes; I *do* want to go to the Micaelas," she asserted vigorously.

"Well, then, on with the purification. You see how well we've understood each other?" said the priest happily, getting up now. "When I was tired of arguing with my brother, I said to him: 'If your passion is so strong that you can't fight it, put the matter in my hands, silly; I'll fix things. It's my business; it's all I can do. What would I be good for unless I straightened out lost souls?'"

Pride oozed from every pore like sweat; his eyes shone. He picked up his hat, saying:

"I'll be back. I'll speak to my brother and my aunt. We already have a lot to work with: your agreement to do whatever this poor priest commands."

Fortunata took his hand and kissed it.

The final words spoken during the visit were about the bad weather, about his not being able to stay in Madrid for more than two weeks, and, finally, about Maxi's migraine.

"It's a family illness. I have them too, but what really kills me is a tricky stomach ailment I have . . . debility, they say it's debility. I have to eat very often, small amounts. It comes from overworking myself. Well, that's life! By this time of day I feel as if there's a puppy inside biting me. And if I don't throw him something, he gives me a bad time, the little pest."

"If you'd like . . . wait, I—" said Fortunata, recollecting what she had in her poor cupboard.

"No, no; I wouldn't hear of it, my dear. Do you think I can't bear it? It's not that I feel like anything, it's even repulsive to me; but it's good for me, I realize that."

"If you'd like, I could go get . . . I don't have anything in the house, but I could go down to the store—"

"No, I wouldn't hear of it; don't give it another thought. Well, good-bye, my child. And take care. There's pneumonia about now."

The priest left and went to a friend's house, where at that critical hour he was usually given the remedy for his stomach's debility.

6

On the night of that memorable day, and when his migraine had subsided, Maxi learned that his brother had been to Pelayo Street and had come away with an impression that "wasn't bad," as the priest put it. Nicolás always made a lot of his apostleship, and whenever a deal to conquer a soul fell into his lap, he exaggerated the difficulties and dangers to enhance his victory. Maxi was itching to know the details, but all he could get out of Nicolás were hints. "We'll see . . . This is no laughing matter, you know. I've already got my hands in the dough. It's not bad dough, but it has to be kneaded. That's the point. I'll be going back again. You have to be patient—what do you expect?" That night seemed eternal; the poor boy could hardly wait till the next day to hear the details from her. Fortunata saw him come in about ten o'clock, pale as a ghost, convalescing from his migraine (which had left him dizzy), disturbed and weak all over. He stretched out on the sofa, his friend covered him up to the waist with a blanket, she put a couple of pillows under his head, and as she did these things she placated his curiosity by telling him everything all at once.

The plan of sending her to a convent to be purified struck Maxi as splendid proof of his brother's great catechizing talent. Something similar had vaguely occurred to him, but he hadn't managed to formulate it. What a remarkable man, Nicolás! To have thought of that! Sifted by religion, Fortunata would be screened into society free of her dust and straw. Who would dare to cast aspersions on her honor then? The seven monther's soul, scrambled from top to bottom by his passion, was like a sea torn by a furious hurricane; it flowed, as it were, from one direction to another, spreading itself over any idea that appeared. So the presentation of the religious idea and his rush toward it and splashing it with a fresh, impetuous wave were one and the same. Religion—what a wonderful thing! And he was such a dimwit; he'd never thought of it! It wasn't dimwittedness, though; it was distraction. And in his eyes, his woman, who was more like his fiancée now, was wearing a shining halo and had ideal qualities. The love she inspired in him seemed to be on the verge of becoming even more refined, as subtle as they say Dante's love for Beatrice was, or Petrarch's for Laura, for it too was of the very finest variety.

Maximiliano had never taken much interest in religion, but all of a sudden he felt his soul devastated by such a burningly pious ardor and desire to get on familiar terms with Christ or the Holy Trinity or even with any other saint that he didn't know what had hit him. Love led him to devotion as easily as it would have led him to impiety, had things chanced to turn in that direction. His brother's plan pleased him so greatly that he had a relapse, though not a serious one. Pressing two of his fingers against his left eyebrow, he told Fortunata how good the Micaela nuns were, how pretty the convent would be, the lovely, useful things she would learn there, and how she would miraculously break out of her hard shell and grow into a lady, a lady so decent that others might be *as* decent, but none *more* decent than she—none.

His enthusiasm infused her with high spirits. Religion! She hadn't thought of it either. Imagine, not to have thought of something so obvious! Curiously enough, she regarded her purification the way a believer conceives of a miracle: it would be like turning water into wine, or making four fish forty.

"Tell me something," she said to Maxi, remembering that she was beautiful. "Will they let me wear a white hood?"

"Perhaps," he replied seriously. "I can't assure you that they will, but it's very probable."

Fortunata picked up a towel and, throwing it over her head, went to look at herself in the mirror. Then she remembered something essential, namely, that in her new existence, physical beauty wouldn't be worth two cents and that what counted and had merit was spiritual beauty. Observing Maxi's face that day and seeing it so pale, she decided that his moral features had become more pronounced and had made him less unattractive. Her way of looking at things, she surmised, was about to undergo a radical change. "Who knows," she mused, "what will happen after being in there with the nuns, praying and looking at the monstrance all day! I'm bound to turn into somebody else without even noticing it. I figure that good things can happen to me by remembering all the bad ones that've already happened. This must be like when you're afraid of the worst thing in the world happening and you say to yourself: 'That'll never happen to *me!*' Well, it'll be the same with the good. You say, 'I'll never get that high up,' and without knowing how, you find yourself up there."

Maximiliano stayed for lunch. But his weak stomach and poor appetite forced him to practice the most prudent frugality. She, on the other hand, had a good appetite, because she had worked hard that morning and, perhaps too, she was happy and excited. The sight of her made the redeemer recall and mention how much his brother ate. This somewhat disillusioned Fortunata; she looked blankly at her lover, holding her fork in midair for a minute. She'd always thought that the mark of priests who knew a lot and were virtuous was that they hardly used soap and water and ate only unsalted boiled greens.

The lovers spent all afternoon talking about her going to the convent and details related to the material aspects of their future existence.

"The will," Maximiliano said with marked emphasis, "provides that some country farms are for me. My aunt was angry because she wanted me to have the cash, but I disagreed with her. I prefer the real estate."

Fortunata nodded her assent, although she wasn't sure what "real estate" meant and didn't want to ask. It was probably something to do with the state. Maxi cleared up her doubts later when he talked about his olive groves and vineyards and the good harvest predicted that year. She gathered that real estate meant trees. She, too, preferred property in the country to any other kind of wealth. After her lover had left, she continued to think about his fortune; and the olive trees, grapevines, and pin oaks dancing in her head kept her awake until very late. Meanwhile, she further improved her plans for an honest life.

"Well, what's she like? Is she attractive?" Doña Lupe had asked Nicolás with intense curiosity.

Although the remarkable clergyman did not experience certain passions, his eyes *were* able to appreciate the quality of the goods. He put together the tips of the fingers on his right hand and, bringing them up to his mouth as if to kiss them, then taking them away, he said:

"She's quite a woman."

Doña Lupe was disconcerted. So to the already familiar dangers of matrimony there was added this one: superior beauty.

"Married women shouldn't be especially beautiful," said the widow (the sentence was proclaimed in a profoundly convinced tone).

She asked him dozens of other questions to satisfy her intense curiosity: how Fortunata dressed and wore her hair, how she talked, how her apartment was decorated. Nicolás supplied answers to show how observant he was. His impression of her was not bad, and even though he didn't have enough facts to judge her character, he could, because of his experience, vouch for her basic goodness and a certain way about her that was promising. This sharpened Doña Lupe's curiosity all the more; she wouldn't be able to relax now until she stuck her own nose into the stew. Visiting the so-called fiancée didn't seem dignified, since she had made such a scene about her; but not seeing her for many days and guessing what her faults were—if she had any—would be impossible. She would have loved to see her through a keyhole. The lady didn't want to give in to her nephew, so she persevered in her intolerance, although less ardently now. She liked the idea of the girl being purified at the Micaelas', and although she said nothing to anyone, she inwardly regarded that path as the only one that might lead to a solution. She was simply dying to get a look at the "basilisk," as she called her, and since her nephew did not suggest that she visit Fortunata, the silence intensified her impatience. One day she was no longer able to contain herself and, catching Maxi off guard in his room, she suddenly rammed this down his throat:

"Don't think I'm going to lower myself to that—"

"To what, Aunt?"

"To visiting your . . . . There are certain words I cannot utter. It doesn't seem fitting for me to go there, despite all the religious reprimanding you plan to do."

"But, Aunt, I haven't asked you to—"

"I won't go, I tell you; I won't."

"But, Aunt—"

"Calling me Aunt is no good. You haven't asked me, but that's what you want. Do you think I can't read your mind? You'll never be able to hide your thoughts from me! Well, you're not going to have it your way. I'm not going unless my hands and feet are tied and I'm dragged."

"Well, then, we'll tie you up and drag you there," said Maxi, laughing.

She wanted to go, all right; but since she had already set her standards and traced an unswerving line of conduct for herself, she didn't attach much importance to the possible outcome of the visit. Notice how the turn of events placed Doña Lupe in a subordinate position and how the poor boy, who months earlier never dared to contradict her, could look her in the eye now. The dignity of his passion had made the boy become a man, and like the plebeian who is ennobled, he regarded the former autocrat with respect, but not with fear.

Since Nicolás visited Fortunata several times to teach her Christian doctrine, Doña Lupe was furious. All that coming and going turned her stomach, she said. But what really upset her was her envy at seeing Nicolás go when she couldn't. Because of this, aunt and nephew were at odds with each other. They were well into March now, and on Saint Joseph's Day, the 19th, Nicolás said at the table:

"The first strawberries are in now, Aunt."

But the hint had no effect on the thrifty widow. The priest brought up the subject again on various occasions:

"What delicious looking strawberries I saw today! Aunt, how much are strawberries selling for now?"

"I don't know and I don't care," she replied, "because I don't plan to buy any till they're down to three *reales.*"

Nicolás heaved a sigh as Doña Lupe said to herself: "If the only strawberries you eat are the ones I'm going to give you, then you're in a bad way, you big glutton."

Since Doña Lupe had a sweet tooth herself, she smuggled in a paper cone of strawberries under her cloak one day. But she didn't put them on the table. After lunch, while Nicolás was reading *La Correspondencia* or *El Papelito* in the dining room, Doña Lupe shut herself up in her room to eat the strawberries, generously sprinkled with súgar. As soon as the priest left for the street, Doña Lupe came out of her hiding place to offer Maximiliano some of the tasty fruit; she appeared in his room with dish and spoon. The boy appreciated this special treatment very much, and ate the fruit. His aunt watched him expectantly, and when there were only six or seven berries left, she took the dish from him, saying:

"Those are for Papitos. Her eyes almost popped out when she saw them."

The girl ate the strawberries and then licked the plate absolutely clean.

7

Juan Pablo paid very little attention to Maximiliano's affairs and the other family business as well, except for the inheritance. He was anxious to collect his share so that he could pay his debts. He came in very late at night and almost always ate out, for which Doña Lupe was very grateful, because Nicolás with his punctual voracity upset her household budget. The misanthropy that had possessed Juan Pablo ever since he had been gracelessly kicked out of the Royal Headquarters didn't weaken during the days following the inheritance. He spoke very little, and when Doña Lupe mentioned Maxi's wedding to him, using it like a pin to keep a person awake, he shrugged his shoulders, said a few scornful words about his brother, and that was it. "It's his pipe, so he can smoke it. What do I care?"

Carlism was not discussed because Doña Lupe did not permit it. But one morning the two elder brothers got so involved in a conversation, or rather dispute, that they completely ignored their aunt. Juan Pablo was washing up in his room, Nicolás went in to say something or other, and they got more and more entangled over whether the priest Santa Cruz[*] was a murderer or a madman until—

"You want to know something?" shouted the firstborn, all upset. "It's *your*

---

[*]Manuel de Santa Cruz (1842–1926) was a Basque Jesuit who defended Don Carlos. Juan Pablo attacks him because Santa Cruz was considered a corrupt politician.

fault, the priests' fault, that Don Carlos hasn't triumphed yet. You have to be on the scene the way I was to know what goes on with you skirted men who want everything for yourselves and are only interested in discrediting the real workers with your slander and gossip. I couldn't stand it there; it stifled me. I said to Dorregaray*: 'General, I don't know how you can stand it'; and he shrugs his shoulders and gives me a look . . . ! A day didn't go by when the skunks didn't report to Don Carlos that Dorregaray was making a deal with Moriones† to surrender, or that Moriones had offered him ten million *reales*; all kinds of indecent stories. When I heard they were accusing me of having gone to Moriones' headquarters with a message from my chief I flew off the handle, and that same afternoon when they found me in their nest in the atrium of the San Miguel Church, I went all out—practically started a riot. 'The only traitors here are you. The trouble with you is that you envy the traitor—if there *is* one, that is—for what he gets out of his treason. Not for ten million, but for ten thousand cents you'd sell the king and all his descendants. Thieves, slanderers, traitors!' Anyway, if Colonel Goiri (who's very fond of me) hadn't happened to come by and yank me out of there and get me home, I would've ripped open a priest so his guts could see the sun set that afternoon. I had to stay in bed three days, on the verge of a stroke. When I got up, I requested an audience with His Majesty. His answer was to put my passport and papers in my hand and tell me to make for the border. In short, they just kept brandishing their rosaries and let me have it because I wasn't willing to cooperate with their schemes against people who had been loyal and courageous. Cassocks were the end of Carlos V, and Carlos VII didn't profit by the lesson. What the hell. So he didn't want any religion? Well, he's got it. He can stuff himself and get sick on priests till he bursts."

"That's your opinion," said Nicolás, moderating his anger, "and it doesn't seem to be very well founded. That's the point."

"Do you think you have any idea of the world and reality? You're in limbo."

"And you're off your rocker, I'd say. You've certainly come out with some nonsense. Shut up, stupid," said Nicolás, fuming.

"You know what my answer to that is?" shouted Juan Pablo, raising his voice arrogantly. "Nobody orders me to shut up, understand? I've had the honor of telling the bishop of Persépolis a few things, and if I'm not afraid of purple skirts, why should I be afraid of black ones?"

"Well, I'm telling you," added Nicolás, in a state of consternation, trembling, and not knowing whether to threaten him with his fist or simply with words, "that what you are is a puny jerk!"

---

*General Antonio Dorregaray (1823–1882) started and ended his military career as a Carlist, but for about fifteen years he switched to Espartero's side.
†General Domingo Moriones (1823–1881), a Carlist enemy.

"What's this fuss all about?" cried Doña Lupe, coming in to make peace. "What a nuisance you gentlemen are! I've already told you weekend patriots: when you want to have an argument, have it in the street. I don't want any scandals in my house."

"You can't talk with this beast," said Nicolás, who could hardly breathe, he was so vexed.

Juan Pablo didn't say anything and kept on dressing, his back turned on his brother.

"What a temper you've developed!" said Doña Lupe. "You might remember your brother is a priest. And above all, don't try to pretend you're such a big shot. Just because your pass at the 'infamous party' failed and you had to come home with your tail between your legs, we're not to blame."

Juan Pablo didn't deign to reply. Doña Lupe took the priest by the arm and led him out of the room, fearing another row. In the dining room, Maximiliano was already seated, waiting for lunch. He had heard the quarrel, but didn't care a whit who won. To heck with them. Nicolás' tantrum hadn't dulled his appetite; no spiritual disturbance, no matter how serious, could deprive him of his most characteristic organic manifestation. The three heard someone shouting in the street and Doña Lupe listened closely, expecting it to be an "Extra!" announcing the Liberals' triumph over the Carlists. In those days of 1874, extras were fairly common and kept the neighborhood in constant suspense.

"Papitos," said the Señora, "here—go buy the *Gaceta* Extra. You'll see—it'll be all about the good beating they've given the Carlists."

Nicolás, who had very sharp ears, after making everybody be quiet, said:

"But, Aunt—don't be silly. They aren't shouting 'Extra!' What's being shouted is plain as day—it's 'Frresh *strawberries*!'"

"Maybe so," replied Doña Lupe, whisking her change purse out of sight. "But they're so green they're like vinegar."

"May it be God's will," sighed Nicolás. "Christ had it worst: he asked for water and they gave him gall."

Chewing his last mouthful, Maximiliano left for class carrying his load of books; Juan Pablo had lunch much later, alone. Serving separate lunches at different times annoyed Doña Lupe immensely. What did her nephews think the house was—an inn? The only one who was considerate, the one who gave her a minimum of trouble and ate the least, was Maxi, with his angelic ways, he was always polite, even after a woman's eyes had rattled him. Doña Lupe reflected on this that afternoon as she sat sewing in her little chair next to the balcony accompanied by the cat.

"No matter what you say, he's the best of the three," she thought, pushing the needle through and pulling it out. "Better than that big egotist Nicolás, better than that madcap Juan Pablo. And he wants to marry a—? Well, you have to look into these things. You can't pass judgment without hearing the case. Maybe she's not . . . There *are* instances . . . Oh, go on! He's madly in love with her. And what can we do about it? I only hope God will help us through this."

Nicolás came in from the street, and in response to Doña Lupe's question said that he had been at the "basilisk's" house. That day he seemed more satisfied, and even claimed that his catechumen had grasped religious issues quite well and that, regarding moral issues, she seemed to be made of "good stuff," which heightened the widow's curiosity to a peak. She could no longer continue to play the scornful role she had assigned herself.

"You're insisting on it so much," she said to the student that night, "that you're finally going to succeed."

"With what, Aunt?"

"With making me go in person to see that—. But remember: if I go, it'll be against my will."

Maximiliano, who was kind and wanted to stay on good terms with her, didn't want to reveal his indifference.

"Well, Aunt, if you do go, we'll be grateful to you for the rest of our lives."

"I don't need your gratitude—if I do decide to go, which I still don't know . . ."

"Yes, Aunt."

"I'm not going because you're thanking me for it (that is, if I *do* go), but because I want to gauge with my own eyes just how deep the abyss is that you want to throw yourself into, and because I still want to see if there's a way of getting you away from it."

"Tomorrow, then, Aunt. I'll escort you," the boy said enthusiastically. "You'll see my abyss for yourself, and when you do, you'll push me."

And Doña Lupe did go the next day, in her Sunday best because she had first attended a ceremony at Doña Guillermina's orphanage at the latter's invitation, which had pleased her considerably. She wanted to be impressive, and since she had so much self-control and spoke so fluently, she expected it to be easy to shine during the visit.

That, indeed, was what happened. Few times in her life, even including the best of Jáuregui's days, had Doña Lupe swelled so much as during that interview, for as the "basilisk" was so weak in the social arts and felt so inhibited by her situation and bad reputation, the other woman led the show and gloried in it to an incredible degree. Doña Lupe treated her niece-to-be urbanely, but kept her distance. It was to be made clear even in the most minor details that the person being visited was a girl with a shady reputation and commendable aspirations to decency, whereas the visitor was a lady, and not just any lady, but the Señora de *Jáuregui*—the most honorable, clean-living man who had ever resided in Madrid, or at least in their neighborhood. And the proof that she was a lady came when, after having done everything possible in the first half of her visit to indicate a certain severity in her principles, she deemed in the second half that it would behoove her to adopt a slightly more indulgent attitude. People with true seignoriality never take pleasure in humiliating their inferiors. Doña Lupe experienced such a vivid protective impulse toward Fortunata that she gave her countless pieces of advice and rules of conduct. The fact is that she had a craving to protect, direct, advise, and rule someone . . .

One of the things that touched her most in Fortunata was her shyness in expressing herself. It was immediately apparent that she did not speak like a refined person; that she was afraid of a blunder and was ashamed. This was to her credit in Doña Lupe's opinion, because to her, a loose tongue would have indicated a disorderly will.

"Don't worry," the widow said to her, tapping the girl's knee familiarly with her fan. "Learning to speak as we do takes more than a day. It will come with time and practice and knowing us. No one should be ashamed of mispronouncing a word; the person who hasn't received a good education isn't to blame."

The extremely formal visit was sheer torture for Fortunata. She blushed one color and then another, not knowing how to answer Doña Lupe's questions or whether to smile or be serious. What she wanted was for the lady to leave, fast. They talked about her entering the convent, a decision that Maxi's aunt praised highly in the finest words and the most euphuistic phrases she knew. She carried this to such extremes that Fortunata was left fasting during most of the conversation. At last it was time for the farewells, which Fortunata feared and yet anxiously desired; she thought she would not be capable of clearly and calmly pronouncing those final formulas and offering her home to her visitor. The Jáuregui woman was adept at it; Fortunata stuttered and said everything backward.

Maximiliano said very little during the visit. All he did was to stay on the lookout to rush forth and, supplying the words, help Fortunata "ward off the bull." When Doña Lupe left, he thought he ought to escort her to the street, which he did. "She's such a dumb little thing," the widow said to her nephew. "Just like you. She looks as if she's just been lassoed. In an intelligent person's hands, that woman could straighten out, because she must be good underneath it all. But I doubt that you . . ."

8

Doña Lupe had good taste and instantly appreciated the "basilisk's" beauty without adding any "buts" as women generally do. Even those who lay no claim to beauty themselves are apt to be reticent in proclaiming another's beauty. "She's truly pretty," the widow said to herself on her way home. "But she's a savage and needs to be tamed." Fortunata's avowed desire to learn pleased the widow greatly and awoke in her an urge to activate her gifts as teacher, adviser, protector, and head of the family. Doña Lupe had an educator's attitude and vanity; in her mind, supreme glory meant having someone on whom to exercise her authority. Maxi and Papitos were at once her children and pupils, and she always made the inferior beings whom she was educating fond of her. People say that Jáuregui himself had been as much a disciple as he was a husband.

So Maximiliano's aunt headed home concocting grand plans. Her domesticating instincts had been aroused by the sight of that magnificent animal in search of a tamer. Stirred by different passions, aunt and nephew came to coincide in their desires; the tyrant of the house ended up by casting a benevolent eye on the very person she had defamed so vociferously. The young man was very grateful for this; he had a hunch that Doña Lupe's indulgence stemmed from her having liked Fortunata, but the strict truth is that it resulted from that imperious need that we human beings have to exercise every great faculty we have. The widow thought constantly about what a fine product she could make of Fortunata, how she would sand her down and polish her until she became a lady, and she envisioned a victory comparable to the one Maximiliano expected to win in another area. It wouldn't be easy—the animal was probably ridden with bad habits. But the bigger the obstacles, the more the teacher would shine. Suddenly, sharp misgivings overtook Señora de Jáuregui and she thought: "But it can't be: she's too much of a woman for a half-man. If they weren't so darned different physically, he with his love and I with all I know could tame the beast; but that girl's going to cheat on us some day; there's no doubt about it."

She struggled with this half the week, now wanting to give in so that she could take over as teacher, now persevering in her original fears and inclining not to intervene at all. But with her friends she had to play another role, for she was vain in public and disliked finding herself in an ungraceful or ludicrous position. She was always very careful to tower over others, which forced her to exaggerate and beautify her surroundings. She was one of those people who always overpraise their own possessions. Everything she had was always good: her house was the best on the street, the street was the best in the neighborhood, and the neighborhood was the best in town. Whenever she moved, this residential supremacy moved with her, no matter where she was going. If an ungraceful or ridiculous thing happened to her, she kept it secret; but if something flattering happened, she practically rang bells to spread the news. Therefore, when friends of the family got word that the seven monther wanted to marry a jezebel, the "turkey woman" didn't know what pose to strike. It was a rather ticklish problem, and not even all her wits sufficed as they had on other occasions to make black appear to be white.

For several evenings she was totally abashed at the Cañas sisters' *tertulia*. But from the day she met Fortunata she regained her composure, convinced that she had found a cornerstone on which to reconstruct her optimism. And what do you suppose she used to persuade them that nothing daunted her? Fortunata's beauty. No matter how well they imagined it, they "simply had no idea of what it was really like." In short, she had seen attractive women, but *none* like that. Fortunata was divine—"in the full sense of the word."

Her friends listened open-mouthed, and Doña Lupe took advantage of their amazement, slipping in the following strategic item:

"And as for her shady past, there's a lot to be said about *that*. It wasn't as bad as they say. I dare say it was a lot less."

When questioned about the divinity's moral qualities and character, Doña Lupe was a good deal more reserved and conditional.

"I really can't say, I've spoken with her only once. She seemed humble and weak-willed—the type who's easy to handle if you know how."

When she mentioned that they were sending her to the Micaelas, all the women present praised the resolution, and Doña Lupe staunchly upheld her vanity, saying that it had been her brainstorm and, indeed, the condition on which she had yielded. After a period of life in a religious atmosphere, the girl would be admitted to the family. Things shouldn't be carried too far; it was easy enough to thunder at Maximiliano and claim that she would disinherit him, but it was something else to actually do it.

Meanwhile, the date set for sending the "basilisk" to the Micaelas was drawing near. Nicolás Rubín had spoken to the chaplain (his classmate from the seminary), who spoke to the mother superior, an illustrious lady, a close friend and distant relative of Guillermina Pacheco's. Fortunata's admission was arranged within the institution's rules, and they had only to wait for Holy Week to pass. On Thursday, Maxi and his friend went out to pray at a few stations of the cross and very early Friday morning they went to church, after which they took a long walk along San Bernardino. Fortunata with religion was like a child with new shoes. She wanted her lover to explain the meaning of Maundy Thursday and the Tenebrae, the Easter lily, and other symbols. Maxi had a hard time getting out of the spot; he explained things as best as he could, filling in the gaps with imaginative patches. The religion he was experiencing during that spiritual crisis was too lofty and couldn't inspire him with true interest in any cult; but he was quite sure that Fortunata's intelligence would not be able to rise above the tops of the towers of Catholic churches. His did; his went far, very far, on the wings of feeling rather than meditation, and although his ideas were not based on study, he conceived of the causes of universal order that give the physical as well as the moral world a solemn, regular, mathematical movement. "All that should happen, happens," he mused, "and all that should be, is." He had developed blind faith in providence's direct effect on the mechanism of daily life. Providence dictated not only public history, but also private history. Beyond this, what did symbols mean?

Nothing. But he didn't want to destroy Fortunata's love of images, rituals, and all the theatrical pomp of religion, because, as they all knew, the poor girl's mind hadn't been trained sufficiently to grasp certain things, and as she was a sinner, it was best to confine her temporarily to observation, that relatively low conceptual level that is somewhat like moral hygiene.

The young woman was experiencing an enthusiasm like that produced by a newly arrived fashion. The two lovers walked along the knolls of Vallehermoso, now through the tileworks, now along paths in the barley field, and at last they tired of so much religious talk. Rubín had run out of liturgical knowledge, and one of Fortunata's feet had started to bother her because the boot was too tight. Tight shoes are torture, and the resultant physical disturbance clips the wings of the mind. They passed "the cemeteries of the north," as they were called, then stopped at the reservoir; Fortunata sat down on a stone block and took off her boot. Maximiliano pointed out how good the view of Madrid was from there—all those houses crammed together, so many domes, and, behind it all, an immense horizon that looked like the sea. Then he pointed eastward to a huge mass of red bricks under construction, and told her that they were the convent where she would be staying. The building and its location looked pretty to Fortunata, and she expressed her desire to enter soon—that very day if possible. Then a sad thought struck Rubín. Things were well enough as they were. Too much piety might be a disaster for him . . . suppose she got very ardent about religion and turned into a true saint who didn't want to hear about the world anymore? Who'd rather stay locked up worshiping the Eucharist the rest of her days! The thought crushed the poor redeemer so badly that his face reddened. And it might very well come to pass; some of the women who went in burdened with sins reformed so radically and began doing penance so ardently that they didn't want to leave, and mentioning marriage to them was like invoking the devil. But no, Fortunata wouldn't be like that. She didn't look as if she'd become a saint "in the full sense of the word," as Doña Lupe would say. If she did, Maximiliano would die of grief; he'd become a Protestant, a Mason, a Jew, an atheist.

He did not disclose these fears to his beloved, one of whose feet was shod, the other bare, as she sat scrutinizing the comings and goings of a procession of ants. He merely said:

"There's time yet. It's not wise to take it too seriously, either."

They had to go on. She put her boot back on and—oh, what pain! The worst of it was that being Holy Friday, there were no carriages; the only way to get home was to walk.

"We've strayed quite far," said Maximiliano, offering her his arm. "Lean on me, and you won't limp so. You know what you look like, being dragged along like this? A pregnant woman who's so overdue she can hardly move. And I look like the husband who's about to become a father."

This thought couldn't help but make her laugh, and, recalling the previous night, when Maximiliano in an epileptic effusion of love had said something about their successor, she mumbled to herself:

"That's one thing that won't happen to you."

The following Thursday, Fortunata was taken to the Micaelas.

v. The Micaelas, from Without

I

IN MADRID THERE ARE THREE CONVENTS devoted to reforming women. Two of them are in the old quarter; one is in the new northern section, the favorite zone of new religious institutes and communities expelled from downtown because their historic houses were seized by the revolutionary government. Along this northern belt of the city religious buildings are so numerous that it would be hard to count them. There are places both for secluded nuns and for the ones who stay in touch with the world, keeping up their tough battle with human misery, these latter constituting modern orders derived from the Saint Vincent de Pauls, whose mission consists in sheltering all people, helping the sick, or educating children. We have seen huge brick structures rise miraculously in that zone; their architectural value is dubious, but they do prove how positive religious propaganda can be and how practical the results of spiritual savings, or alms are, when managed well. The "Little Sisters of the Poor," the "Servants of Mary," and others highly esteemed in Madrid for their tangible aid to city residents have built their houses in this zone as rapidly as if they had been under contract. There is only one institute for the priests—a big old thing, vulgar and dreary as a community settlement. The Royal Salesa nuns, who were thrown out of the convent that the queen, Doña Bárbara, built them, also have new quarters, and other historic nuns—the ones who gathered and saved King Pedro's bones—are camped there too, in the hills of the borough called Salamanca.

The flat part of Chamberí, from Los Pozos and Santa Bárbara to beyond Cuatro Caminos, is where the new orders prefer to build. It was there that the constant and extraordinary Guillermina Pacheco built her orphanage, and it is there that the Micaelas are located. The buildings have a somewhat improvised air, and all of them, combining low cost with haste, have unplastered brick surfaces, which give them a Mudejar mixed with French Gothic look. The churches with their fragile stucco interiors copy the effeminate attempt at elegance that marks the style of the Lourdes basilica. Thus they combine a tidy orderliness (very pleasing to the eye) with a deplorable architectural manner. The new imported, pious styles, such as the one at the Sacred Heart, and those hordes of Christian brothers with their bibs expelled from France, have brought us something good—tidiness in places marked for worship, but also something bad—a perversion of taste in religious decoration. Granted, Madrid could scarcely have defended herself against this invasion; the churches in this city, in addition to being filthy, are simply awful artistically. So we can't protest too loudly. The graceless Baroque of our churches, the dirty partitions in chapels covered with horrid dusty stucco figures, and all the rest that adds to the indecorum and vulgarity of Madrilenian temples, can't throw any stones at the affected pomposity of the brand new monumentalism. And while the latter does use crumbly plaster and has too much gold and tempera paintings, at least it gives off a clean smell and has the decorum of being anointed by soap, water, and a broom.

The Micaelas was higher up than Guillermina's establishment; it was up where there was much more uncultivated land. In the spaces between the houses one can see luminous, steppelike horizons, the walls of cemeteries crowned with cypress trees, narrow factory chimneys that look like branchless palm trees, great expanses of badly sown land used as grazing pastures for milk-carting donkeys and goats. The houses are low, as they are in villages; some have walkways and numbered rooms whose doors can be seen from behind neighboring walls. The Micaelas' building, formerly a private home, had a new interior L-shaped wing on two sides of the garden, forming a half-cloister, and a church was now being added on the opposite side. It was a spacious church, being done in the style popular at the time—unplastered brick, modeled in the Mudejar fashion; Novella stone ogival arches decorated the surface. Since the church was only half-built, services took place in a provisional chapel, a low-ceilinged space left of the door.

The decoration in the provisional temple testified to the good intentions, neatness, and artistic innocence of the excellent ladies who constituted the community. The walls were stuccoed (like many of our bedroom walls), both because it was inexpensive to finish walls this way in Madrid and because it was a considerable aid to cleanliness. At the extreme end was the altar, which, predictably enough, was white and gold and whose style was so familiar and standard that it seemed copied from a book. On the right and the left in big, loud chromos were two Sacred Hearts, and above them, two narrow windows that peaked in ogival arches; their red, white, and blue windowpanes and rhomboid designs were like those found in staircase windows in modern houses.

Near the door was a wooden grillwork that separated the nuns from the public on visiting days, Thursdays and Sundays. From the grillwork inward, the floor was covered in sturdy oilcloth, and flanking what could be designated as the nave were rows of prayer stools. To the right of the nave were two medium-size doors: one led to the sacristy and the other to the room used for the choir, from which came the flutelike sounds of a reed organ being candidly played in tonic and dominant chords and with the most elemental modulations. The exalted tones of two or three singing nuns also floated out of that room. The music was worthy of the architecture; it sounded like the stuff played in Zarzuelas* or the songs that fashion magazines send out to their subscribers. This is what grandiose ecclesiastical chants have come to, thanks to the neglect of those responsible for these matters and to the increasing permissiveness with novelties in the severe Catholic church.

The sinner was taken to the Micaelas a few days after Easter Sunday. That day, from the moment he awoke, Maxi had such a huge lump in his throat that he thought it would block everything. During exams he usually experienced the same thing, but not as intensely. Fortunata seemed contented; she wished that the time would come to bring their expectancy and perplexity to an end. They were both at a loss for words. She, at any rate, couldn't think of a thing to say to him, and he, although many impressions were crowding his mind, had an innate aversion to theatricality; he disliked outpourings on certain occasions. If the truth be told, Maxi inspired in his fiancée a sweet, calm affection faintly tinged with pity that day. He tried to inject a familiar tone into the conversation, commenting on the weather or reminding the young woman not to forget any important item of clothing. Nicolás, who was present, would not have permitted any sweetness or display of affection anyway; he helped collect and form a pile of everything that was to be taken, adding such practical observations as: "Remember, now—no perfume or jewelry or frills are allowed there. All worldly baggage is left at the door."

When the boy hired to transport the trunk came, Fortunata was prepared to depart, dressed in the utmost simplicity. Maximiliano glanced at his watch repeatedly without registering the time. Nicolás, who was more severe, looked at his own and said that it was late. The three left the house and walked in ponderous silence toward Hortaleza Street to find a cab. The young man took the folding seat in front, not without some effort, for his future spouse's skirts and the clergyman's long habit cluttered the entrance and exit; if the trip had been longer, those six unaccommodated legs would have been in for great martyrdom. The neophyte looked out the cab window, her attention vaguely attracted by people passing by. One would have thought she was looking out to avoid looking in; Maximiliano devoured her with his eyes, while the presbyter tried in vain to perk up the conversation with a couple of unfunny jokes.

At last they arrived at the convent. At the door there were a few old women begging for alms, which Maximiliano had no time to give. He noticed a terribly bitter taste in his mouth; his weak voice came out gaspingly, as if he were asthmatic. His distress forced him to seek refuge in ordinary subjects: "What a bore

---

*Sentimental musical comedies.

these poor people are! Mass must be in progress, because you can hear the bell ringing for people to stand. The place is pretty and cheerful. Very cheerful."

They entered a room off to the right, across from the chapel. It was here that the nuns and also the secluded women received visits; the latter were allowed to see their families on Thursday afternoons for an hour and a half in the presence of two holy mothers. Decorated with a simplicity verging on poverty, all that the room contained was a few prints of saints and a large oil portrait of Saint Joseph that looked like the work of the same hand that had done the Jáuregui portrait at Doña Lupe's. The floor was tile, thoroughly scrubbed and polished, and protected against the cold only by two mats, one in front of each of the two facing benches. The benches, chairs, and a piano-legged sofa were from different ensembles, which clearly indicated that all the dingy household furniture had come from donations or alms.

They didn't have to wait even five minutes; two nuns (who were expecting them) appeared very shortly, and following them almost on their heels came the chaplain, a very hearty man who laughed at everything. His name was León Pintado,* but his appearance had nothing to do with his name. Nicolás Rubín and that massive, jovial figure embraced and exchanged greetings using the familiar *tú* form. One of the nuns was young, flushed, with a graceful mouth and eyes that would have been extremely pretty if she had not needed to squint. The other looked withered and middle-aged, wore glasses, and made it plain that she wielded more authority in the house than her companion. To their remarks, basted in that cloying sweetness characteristic of the style and tone of religious women of that era, the neophyte intended to respond with some sort of appropriate sentence, but she was tongue-tied, and the only thing that left her lips was a sound—*huhu*—that the others didn't understand. The session was brief. Doubtlessly the Micaelan mothers did not like to waste time. "Say good-bye," the dried-up one commanded her, taking her by the arm. Fortunata shook Maxi's and then Nicolás' hand without distinguishing which was which and let herself be led away. *Rubinius vulgaris* took a step, leaving behind the two priests, who shook each other's cloak tassels as they talked, and he witnessed the disappearance of his beloved, his idol, the light of his life through the white door that connected the visiting room to the rest of the religious dwelling. It was a door, like any other, but when it closed this time, the enamored boy thought it looked quite different from any other door in the vast kingdom of doors.

---

* "The Painted Lion."

2

Maxi set out for Madrid on the dusty road that crosses the former Campo de Guardia and glanced at his watch again mechanically, not seeing what time it was. He wasn't aware that his brother and Don León Pintado, engaged in an interesting conversation and stopping every ten words or so, had lagged behind. They were discussing the competitive exams for a position in the cathedral at Siguenza and the quarrels that the exams had occasioned. The chaplain, being a rejected candidate, was smearing the diocesan bishop's name and the other priests in the cathedral. Not noticing their pauses, Maximiliano kept on walking until he discovered that he was home. Doña Lupe opened the door and asked him several questions: "How was she—happy?" These interrogations revealed as much interest as curiosity, and, stimulated by the benevolence he observed in his aunt, the young man conversed with her and even pulled out some of the sharp thorns scratching his heart so that she could see them. He had a vague foreboding that he would never see Fortunata again, not because she was going to die, but because in the convent, caught up by the nuns' piety, she might be carried away by divine things and fall in love with the spiritual life and no longer want a husband of flesh and blood, preferring Christ, the Husband who really breaks hearts among the holiest nuns. He expressed this irreverently, leaving out a word here and there; but Doña Lupe got the gist of it.

"That very well might happen," she said with a conviction that increased Maximiliano's disturbance. "And it wouldn't be the first case of bad—I mean, easy—women converting overnight and becoming so unlike what they were that the only choice has been to canonize them."

The redeemer felt a chill in his heart. Fortunata canonized! This thought, despite its sheer absurdity, tormented him all morning.

"Frankly," he said at last, after lengthy meditation, "it wouldn't come to canonization. But she might very well get mystical and not want to leave, and I'd be left empty-handed." Lord above! The thought terrified him. If it *did* happen, all he could do would be to turn into a saint too, devote himself to the Church, and become a priest. Lord, what madness—a priest! What for? His mind jumped from one thing to the next until finally it sank into an upsetting whirlpool where he had to let his thoughts drown to keep from being tortured by them. He tried to study . . . Impossible. Then it occurred to him to write to Fortunata, recommending that she ignore what the nuns said about the spiritual life. Divine grace and mystic love were just a lot of nonsense. At last he regained his calm, and his mind felt some of the mist clearing.

It must have been eleven when (from his room) he heard Doña Lupe and Papitos quarreling fiercely. The cause of this household spat was Nicolás' tragic idea of inviting his friend Father Pintado to lunch, and the worst part wasn't the idea, but his blasé way of executing it. With that clerical nerviness he possessed so much of, he simply brought in his comrade, never stopping to consider whether there was enough food in the house for two mouths of those dimensions.

Doña Lupe couldn't say anything in the other clergyman's presence, but her blood was boiling. Her pride didn't permit her to let the prestige of her home be lowered by putting out a big pot of cheap stuff to fill them up, and, spitefully coping with her problem, she muttered things that would have made the entire religious profession's hair stand on end. "I don't know what this Heliogabalus* thinks he's doing, treating my house like the Peine Inn. He eats his way up to one of my elbows and then he brings in a cohort to eat up to my other one. And from the looks of him, he must have a scary set of choppers and a stomach like the reservoir. My God, what a bunch of egoists these priests are! What I should do is send him the bill, and then—ha!—*then* he wouldn't be back with guests, because he's as stingy as they come and doesn't like to fork out unless it's somebody else's money."

The volcano smoldering in Señora Jáuregui's breast could spew its lava on only one person: Papitos. That's what she was there for. The little monkey had started off doing things right that day, but her mistress scolded her so unfairly that—the devilish girl!—she ended up doing everything backward. If she was told to pour off water from a cooking pot, she put in more. Instead of chopping onion she crushed garlic. They sent her to the store for a can of sardines and she came back with four pounds of Scottish cod. She broke a bowl and performed so many other shenanigans that Doña Lupe practically bashed in her skull with the pestle. "It's my own fault—the beast!—for trying to tame pack animals and make human beings out of them. You're going home today, to your little hut in the rubbish heap at Cuatro Caminos where you were before, with the pigs and chickens— that's the kind of society you're fit for." And she poured out more insults in the same vein. Poor Papitos! She sighed, tears ran down her face. She was so confused now that she didn't know what she was doing.

Meanwhile the two priests were in the living room smoking, their hats on chairs, grossly sprawled in the two armchairs and still discussing the same subject—the Siguenza exams. It was all the dean's fault; he was just a no-good who wanted to save the prebendary for his nephew. A couple of scoundrels is what they were. The uncle had given rationalist speeches, but when the "Gloriosa" revolution broke out he had cheered Admiral Topete and Prim at the Democrats' meeting. Doña Lupe finally came in, vehemently contorting the muscles of her face to produce a smile, and she informed them that lunch was served but that they would have to overlook many things and suffer a bit.

*Voracious Roman emperor.

As they were sitting down, she looked in terror at her nephew's friend; he was like an ox standing on its hind legs; if his appetite matched his size, not even everything on the table would be enough to fill him up. Luckily, Maxi's appetite that day was so poor that he hardly ate. Doña Lupe declared that she wasn't hungry either, so the problem was solved; there was no dilemma to fear. Father Pintado, despite his voluminosity, was not much of an eater, and he added a pleasant note to the gathering by telling them what had happened during . . . the Siguenza exams. To be polite, Doña Lupe said that it was disgraceful that they hadn't given him the prebendary.

Señora Jáuregui's anger was not diminished a bit by the happy success of her luncheon; she kept on hammering away at poor little Papitos who, I might add, had a temper of her own and was inwardly seething with rage and a desire for revenge. "Look at the old witch," she said to herself, drinking back her tears, "with only one teat! She'd be better off if she wore a cloth one instead of pretending so people will think they're both real like everyone else's and like mine will be any day now." That afternoon, when the lady went out, having ordered Papitos to do the laundry, the little servant concocted her terrible revenge, and it was the kind that is never forgotten. It occurred to her to hang from the balcony the bodice of a dress that had stuck to it the "false thing" with which Doña Lupe deceived the outside world. In her malice, Papitos imagined that if she put the proof of what her mistress was missing on the balcony, people passing by would see it and get a good laugh. But things didn't turn out as she expected; no passer-by noticed the false breast, which looked more like a bladder made out of butter, so she finally brought it in, figuring—with common sense—that if Doña Lupe saw that accusal of her defect hanging from the balcony she would fly into a rage and be capable of cutting off "the two real ones" her servant was about to sprout.

3

The next morning Maximiliano headed for the convent, not to enter it (for this was impossible) but to see the walls behind which his beloved was breathing. It was a delightful morning—not a cloud in the sky, the trees along Santa Engracia just beginning to bud. The young man stopped in front of the Micaelas and looked at the new church under construction; it was already half way up to the ogival arches over the main nave. Backing away to the sidewalk facing the convent, climbing some mounds of hardened dirt, and looking over the half-built church, a long corridor in the convent could be seen, and he could even make out the heads of the nuns or inmates who were walking down the corridor. But as the construction progressed rapidly, less could be seen each day. Maxi observed on the following days that each new layer of bricks was discreetly covering up that interesting part of the nunnish interior, like clothes being spread out to cover bare flesh. The day came when all he could see were the socles on the beams supporting the roof above the corridor, and one day the massive construction covered everything, leaving in sight only the chimneys, and even then it was necessary to stand at a great distance to discern them.

To the north there was a badly sown barley field. Facing that public land, where there was a post with a sign announcing lots for sale, were the convent's garden walls, which were very high. The tops of a few pagoda trees and an Indian water chestnut rose above them. But what was most visible, and what captivated the disconsolate young man, was a windmill that stood on an apparatus that was taller than the convent roofs and the neighboring houses. The immense disk, rather like a Japanese parasol without convexity, revolved on its axis, either slowly or rapidly, depending on the force of the wind. The first time Maxi noticed it, the disk was revolving with majestic slowness, and it was so beautiful to see with its armor of red and white boards that his sad eyes fixed on it for a full quarter of an hour. The southern side of the garden ended at a partition wall, behind which was an ink factory, and the eastern side ended at the shed roof over the quarry works where hard work went on. Just as Maxi's eyes were fascinated by the pump disk, his ears were prisoners, as it were, of the continuous and forever unchanging music the stonecutters made as they chiseled away at the hard rock. One would have thought they were engraving on memorial stones a legend that an inconsolable poet was dictating to them out of his heart. Behind this toccata reigned the august silence of the countryside, like the immensity of the sky behind a cluster of stars.

He also wandered around the by-roads without losing sight of the convent; he came and went along the paths that had been beaten by human feet, killing the grass; and sometimes he sat in the sun, when it wasn't too strong. Far off, heaps of manure and straw broke the uniformity of the ground; here and there, dusty brick walls, industrial signs on plaster strips, houses unsuccessfully attempting to surround themselves with a bit of a garden; further away, rooftops and the lead-colored huts of the city's cargo inspectors; and everywhere the eye could see, a profound sense of expectant solitude. It was interrupted only by an occasional shrewd dog—the kind that flees from the strychnine in city pounds and sniffs around out there without once raising its snout from the ground. Sometimes the young man went back to the main pond and headed north for quite a distance, but he had no desire to see people and turned off again, crossing the countryside until he caught sight of the arches of the Lozoya aqueduct. The sight of the far-off mountains distracted and even bewitched him momentarily with strokes of incredibly bright blue and those snowcaps; but after awhile he looked south, searching for the scaffolding and bulk of the Micaelas, which were hard to distinguish amidst the more eccentric houses in Chamberí.

Every morning before class, Rubín went on this little jaunt out to the country. He was like a devout man attending Mass or visiting the remains of his beloved in a cemetery. From the moment he passed the Chamberí church, he could see the windmill, and he didn't take his eyes off it until he got close. When the disk revolved swiftly, the lover, unwittingly obeying an impulse in his blood, quickened his step. He couldn't say exactly why, but the machine's speed said to him: "Hurry up, come on; there's news." But then he got there and nothing had happened, except that the wind was blowing harder that day. From the garden wall could be heard the soft whooshing of the disk, somewhat like the sound made by a kite, and the creaking of the mechanism that transmits the wind's energy to the piston rod could be felt. Other days it was motionless, drowsily resting in the arms of the wind. For some unknown reason, the young man stopped; but then he kept walking slowly on. He would have expelled all the air in his lungs to make the machine run. It was silly, but he couldn't help it; when the motor stopped, it seemed to augur misfortune.

But what tormented Maximiliano most were the varying impressions he formed on Thursdays, when he visited his future wife. Nicolás always escorted him, and since the two nuns were always there too, it was impossible to say anything in private. The first Thursday he found Fortunata very contented; the second Thursday she was pale and a bit sad. As she hardly smiled at all, she didn't have that bewitching expression that fascinated her lover, that way of contracting her lips. Their conversation centered on the convent, which Fortunata praised highly, extolling her progress in reading and writing and boasting about how fond the nuns had grown of her. Since on one of the following Thursdays she mentioned how much she had enjoyed celebrating Pentecost (the most important holy day in that community), the conversation turned to religious subjects again, and the neophyte expressed herself quite ardently. Maximiliano was again stricken by the thought that his beloved might become a mystic and fall madly in love with such a formidable rival as Christ. He was struck by the extravagant notion of taking advantage of the nuns' momentary distraction to secretly whisper to his beloved "not to believe in that Pentecost business—just an allegorical story was all it was—because there never were nor could there ever have been any 'tongues of fire' or a God to make it up," adding, if he could, that "the contemplative life is the most sterile imaginable, even as a preparation for immortality, because struggling in this world and carrying out our social duties was what purified and ennobled the soul most." Needless to say, he kept these scandalous doctrines to himself, for it would have been embarrassing to voice them in front of the nuns.

VI. The Micaelas, from Within

I

WHEN THE TWO NUNS, the cross-eyed one and the withered-looking one, led her in, Fortunata felt very moved. Her first sensation was that admixture of fear and bashfulness that besets a schoolboy facing the classmates who will soon be his friends but who view him at first with hostile and jeering eyes. The inmates she met on her way in stared at her so impertinently that she blushed deeply and didn't know what to register on her face. The nuns, who had ushered countless sinners into that place, didn't seem particularly interested in or impressed by the new inmate's beauty. They were like doctors whose experience numbs them to the pathological horrors they handle in the clinic. Quite some time passed before the young woman was able to collect herself and exchange a few words with her quarantined companions. But the ice breaks faster among women than schoolboys, so word after word, and then cordial feelings, sprouted, laying the ground for future friendships.

As she had expected and hoped, she was given a white wimple to wear; but there were no mirrors in the convent to tell her whether it was becoming. Then she was instructed to put on a very simple, coarse, black wool dress. These garments, she was told, were indispensable only in the chapel or for prayer hours; during work hours, she would be permitted to wear an old skirt of her own with a blouse, also wool and very decent, which she would be given for that purpose. The inmates were divided into two groups: the "Filomenas" and the "Josefinas." The first consisted of women there to be reformed; the second, of young girls sent there by their parents to be educated, though more often than not they'd been sent by stepmothers who didn't want them around. These two groups or families did not meet on any occasion. Needless to say, Fortunata belonged to the Filomenas. She noticed that most of their time was devoted to religious exercises: prayers in the morning, doctrine in the afternoon. Later she learned that on Thursdays and Sundays the host was worshiped in extremely long, entertaining rituals accompanied by music. For this exercise and morning Mass, the inmates as well as the nuns wore a veil that was almost as big as a sheet. The inmates picked up their veils in a room adjoining the entrance to the chapel, and after the service the veils were folded and put back.

Being used to rising at nine or ten in the morning, it was excruciating for the sinner to get up at the crack of dawn every day in the convent. At five o'clock, Sor Antonia was already ringing her way into the dormitories with a bell that shattered the poor sleepers' eardrums. Rising early was one of the best disciplinary and educational methods the nuns used, and staying up late was a bad habit they fought vigorously, as if it were as noxious to the soul as it was to the body. Because of this, the night watch-nun patrolled the dormitories at different hours of the night, and if she caught any whispering, she dealt out extremely severe punishments.

The work varied in nature, and was sometimes rough. The religious teachers took special care to subdue vice-ridden types or fiery tempers by exhausting them, thus mortifying the flesh and ennobling the spirit. Delicate tasks, such as sewing and embroidery (for which there was a special workroom), were the least appealing to Fortunata, who was hardly fond of needlework and whose fingers were very clumsy. She was happier when she was ordered to wash, polish the tile floors, clean the windowpanes, or do other jobs suited to scrub maids. She was bored to death when they had her sit and sew nametags on clothes. Another duty she liked was being kitchenmaid for the nun who was cook; it was amazing to see how she scrubbed and polished all the copper and crockery—better and faster than two or three of the most diligent inmates.

Considerable vigor and vigilance characterized the nuns' handling of the inmates' relationships, regardless of whether they were Filomenas or Josefinas. The nuns were sharp sentries when it came to supervising budding friendships and couples that formed as a result of mutual fondness. The veteran inmates whose submissiveness was known were instructed to accompany those new inmates who were considered suspect. There were some who were not allowed to speak to their companions except in the main group during recess.

In spite of the severity exercised in preventing intimate couples or groups, there were always sly violations of the rule. It was impossible in a group of forty or fifty women to prevent two or three of them from getting together to talk when they were able to meet during their duties. One Saturday morning Sor Natividad, who was the mother superior (alias the withered-looking one), ordered Fortunata to polish the tile floor of the visiting room. Sor Natividad was from a northern province and was extremely zealous about the care of the convent; she always kept it as clean as a whistle, and if she saw a speck of dust or any other kind of dirt, she became frenetic and shrieked for all she was worth, as if a great calamity had befallen the world or original sin had been committed anew. Whoever obeyed her fanatical doctrine of cleanliness she pampered and favored, whereas she hurled awful curses at whoever prevaricated, even venially, in that closed morality of hers. One day she threw a scene because they hadn't cleaned the—imagine—the gold-plated heads of the nails that fastened the prints to the wall in the visiting room. As for the prints, they were to be taken down, and the backs as well as the fronts were to be cleaned.

"You don't know what the soul is, and you haven't got even a drop of the grace of God in you," she said. "And you'll be condemned, not because you're bad, but because you're filthy."

That Saturday she ordered the floor to be polished, instructing Fortunata and another inmate to leave it as bright "as the face of the sun."

For Fortunata this work was not only easy, it was fun. She enjoyed putting the thick swab of cloth around her right foot and dragging it with the left foot, going from one end of the vast room to the other, doing dance steps or pretending to skate, with her hands on her hips and flexing her muscles with these enjoyable gymnastics till she was perspiring freely, her face flushed and waves of pleasure titillating her body. The companion assigned to her for that task by Sor Natividad was a Filomena whose face was hauntingly familiar to the neophyte. She had undoubtedly seen her somewhere, but she couldn't remember where or when. The first time, they stared at each other as if desirous of an explanation; but neither ever spoke to the other. What Fortunata knew was that the woman plagued the nuns with trouble because of her quarrelsome and uneven temper.

From the moment the mother superior left them alone, the familiar-looking one started skating and talking all at once. Stopping in front of Fortunata, she said:

" 'Cause we know each other, don't we? They call me Mauricia la Dura. Don't you remember seeing me at Paca's house?"

"Oh . . . yes!" said Fortunata, and, shifting her weight to her right foot, she headed off in another direction, rubbing the floor with Amazonic strength.

Mauricia la Dura looked thirty or slightly older, and her face was familiar to anyone knowledgeable in historical iconography, for it was the image of Napoleon Bonaparte's face before he became first consul. That singular woman, beautiful and handsome, had short hair, always somewhat tangled and badly combed. When she moved a lot in her work, shocks of her hair came loose and fell to her shoulders, at which point her resemblance to the precocious leader of Italy and Egypt was perfect. Not everyone who met Mauricia liked her, but whoever saw her once never forgot her and felt the urge to see her again. Whoever observed her was strangely fascinated by those straight, marked eyebrows; the large, fever-ish eyes, sunken but ready to spring out of that frontal concavity; the pupils, avid and restless; the prominent cheekbones; the thin cheeks; the robust jawbone; the Roman nose; the emphatic mouth ending energetically; and finally that dreamy, melancholy air of hers. But as soon as Mauricia spoke, the illusion vanished. Her voice was harsh, more a man's than a woman's, and her language was extremely vulgar, revealing a chaotic personality that oscillated mysteriously between de-pravity and affability.

2

After they recognized each other they were silent for a while; both worked eagerly. Then, growing tired, they sat on the floor to rest. Dragging herself over to her companion, Mauricia said:

"That day—you know when I mean?—when you'd just left, Juanito Santa Cruz came to Paca's house."

Fortunata looked at her in terror.

"What day?" was all she said.

"Don't you remember? The day *you* were there; the day I met you, stupid. I was in a fight with Visitación, who stole a handkerchief off me, the nervy thief. I grabbed at her and rrrip!—I tore her ear and pulled off her earring, and some flesh came off with it. I almost took off half her face. She bit my arm; look—you can still see the mark—but I shut one of her eyes good and tight. She still hasn't opened it. And I tore off a strip of skin from up here on her forehead down to her chin. If they hadn'ta separated us—if you hadn'ta grabbed me by the waist and Paca hadn't grabbed her—I woulda pulled her apart . . . believe me."

"Now I remember . . . . that brawl," said Fortunata, looking at her companion fearfully.

"Nobody gets away with pullin' one on *me*. I don't know if you know, but that curvy blond called Matilde—"

"No, I don't know her."

"Well, she comes up to me with some big rumors—'cause I was 'friendly' with the Tellería boy then, and—well, one day I grabbed hold of her, knocked her down on the floor, and walked right over her as many times as I felt like it. Then I took a shovel and the first time I hit her I banged a hole in her head the size of a coin. They took her to the hospital. They say you could see her gray stuff through the hole I made in her. I really beat her up good. Another day, when I was in jail, this brassy-looking woman, really nervy, said I was this and that and the other, you know, and wow! The first punch I gave her, she was down rollin' on the floor. They had to tie me up. Well, anyways, goin' back to what I was sayin'—the day I had that fight with Visitación—"

They heard the mother superior approaching and quickly got up and started polishing again. The nun inspected the floor and left. Shortly after that, the two repentant women resumed their conversation.

"You didn't show up around there anymore. Then I asked Paca if the Santa Cruz guy had come back and she said, 'Shhh! Last night they said he's got nu-moanya.' Poor kid, he almost didn't make it. He was on the borderline for awhile. I asked Feliciana about you one afternoon when I went to show her the Manila shawls I was sellin', and she told me you were gonna marry a pharmacist. I know his aunt, Doña Lupe, the turkey woman. And oh, if you only knew how well I know her. Just ask her. I've sold her more jewels than the hairs I've got on my head. Oh, was I doin' fine in those days! But then all of a sudden I got sick and my stomach was so weak I couldn't eat a thing; if you just put a drop of water or a bite of food in my mouth, it still did the same thing—set my stomach on fire. And my sister Severiana, who lives on Mira el Río Baja Street, took me home with her, and when I was there I got such bad cramps I thought it was all over for me. And one night, when I saw that things weren't gettin' any better, I tore out of there and went to a tavern, and I downed three straight whiskies just like that—glug, glug, glug—and I left, and then I collapsed in the middle of the street and some kids gathered around me, and then the cops came and I ended up in the clink. Severiana wanted to take me home again, but a lady we know called Doña Guillermina—you must've heard of her—took charge of me and brought me to this 'establishment.' Doña Guillermina is one of those kinds that choose to be poor, you know what I mean? She asks for charity and she's buildin' a big palace for orphans. Me and my sister grew up in her home—the Pachecos have a big house. They're real rich, you should see 'em. My mother ironed for 'em. That's why Doña Guillermina is so good to us. Whenever she sees I'm in a bad way, she helps me out and tells me that the worst I am, the more she'll help me. Well, like it or lump it, here I am. They put me in here before, but I was only here a week 'cause I escaped over the garden wall like a cat."

This story, related with such terrifying sincerity, deeply impressed the other Filomena. They continued to dance across the room, gliding over the polished floor like ice skaters, and Fortunata, who felt slighted by what Mauricia la Dura had said about her, wished to clarify an important point. She said:

"I only went to Paca's house twice, and if it had been up to me I wouldn't have gone at all. Being poor, you know . . . I never went back again, because I started going out with the boy I'm going to marry."

After a pause during which many past events crowded into her mind, she deemed it opportune to say something related to the thoughts that the mention of that house had evoked in her:

"And why was that man looking for me anyway? Why? To ditch me again. Once is enough."

"Men are fickle," Mauricia la Dura said philosophically. "When they've got you at their beck and call, they treat you like a piece of furniture; but if you pay attention to somebody else, they start to cuddle up, you know, like you were candy they were gonna steal from him. Well, anyway, if you set yourself to being what they call decent, the cads don't go for it; and if you start to pray a lot, and go to confession and Communion, they start burnin' with love and crave for us the minute we take up this religious life. Do you think Juanito hasn't been sniffin' around this convent from the moment he found out you were in it? Don't be a fool. You can count on it—one of those carriages you hear out there is his."

"Don't be silly. That's foolish," replied Fortunata, growing pale. "It can't be . . . because look, he had pneumonia in February—"

"You seem to know a lot."

"I heard it from Feliciana, and she got it days ago from a gentleman friend of Villalonga's. So you see, he got pneumonia in February, and in the meantime I met the boy I'm seeing now. He was very sick for two months, right on the borderline. Finally he got over it, and in March he went to Valencia with his wife."

"And?"

"And he's probably not back yet."

"You must be stupid. Wait, that's just my way of talking. If he's not back yet, he'll be back. I mean, when he gets back and finds out you're on your way to becomin' a *saint* he'll be hot on your tail."

"You're the one that's stupid. Leave me alone. And suppose he does come chasing me. What do I care?"

Sor Natividad examined the polished floor and saw that "their work was good." Her little withered face shone with the satisfaction of an artist. She looked up at the ceiling, trying to discover some tiny speck left by a fly, but there were none, and even the nailheads (cleaned the day before) shone like tiny gold stars. The mother superior aimed her glasses in every direction, hunting for something to criticize, but she found nothing worthy of her strict reprimands. She stated that all the furniture was to be cleaned and rubbed down before being brought back in so that any dust on it would remain outside. She stressed that they were to follow "the grain of the wood" in their cleaning, but since the two workers weren't sure what this meant, she herself picked up a cloth and soberly demonstrated her system. When they were alone again, Mauricia said to her friend:

"You've got to keep that nut happy; she's a good person, and if her furniture's polished 'along the grain' like she says, she'll bend over backwards for you."

Mauricia had her days. The nuns thought she was literally a lunatic, because while she could be made to obey them easily most of the time if she was put to work, she was sometimes suddenly seized by a fit of madness, speaking utter nonsense and acting strangely. The first time it happened, the nuns were alarmed, but once they saw that they could tame her without resorting to force and had handled several such attacks peacefully, they didn't worry much about her occasional unruliness. It was an imposing and even entertaining spectacle for the staff, and it usually took place every fifteen or twenty days. The first time Fortunata witnessed it, she was in mortal terror.

Mauricia's disturbance broke out like other illnesses: the faint but infallible

symptoms gradually became more pronounced, eventually signaling the onset of
the whole morbid process. The prodromal stage was usually brought on by a trivial
incident—an argument with another inmate about whose hot chocolate was
whose, or someone bumping into her "on purpose" as they were leaving the dining room. The nuns would intervene and Mauricia would finally fall silent and be
taciturn for a few hours, sulking and doing the opposite of what she was told. Her
astounding diligence gave way to slovenliness, and if the nuns reproached her, she
wouldn't answer them to their faces, but as soon as they turned their backs she
growled and muttered vulgar words. This stage was usually followed by a noisy,
carnivalesque prank to make the Filomenas laugh and the nuns indignant.
Mauricia would take advantage of the silence in the sewing room by tying a
chocolate pot to the cat's tail and flinging it into the middle of the room, or she
would perform some other more childish than adult act. Sor Antonia, who was
the soul of kindness, looked at her, mustering up all the severity her angelic
nature could, and Mauricia returned her look insolently, saying:

"I didn't do it. What're you starin' at *me* for? You want to paint a picture of me
or somethin'?"

That day Sor Antonia called in the mother superior, who was a calm Basque
woman, and upon entering she said:

"So the enemy's loose again?"

And she decreed that the enemy be locked up in the room that served as a jail
for insubordinate inmates. Then came the explosion.

"Lock me up? Oh, *really*? Come on, don't gimme that, dearie."

"Mauricia!" the nun said with masculine strength in her voice. "Stop this
hullabaloo, and do as I say. You know your shenanigans don't scare us. We're not
afraid of wild women here. We won't throw you out, because we're compassionate
and charitable. Come on, child, stop all this and do as you're told."

Mauricia's jaw quivered and her eyes darkened with that sinister look cats get
when they're about to pounce. The other inmates looked at her fearfully, and
some of the nuns surrounded the mother superior in an effort to force Mauricia to
respect her.

"Look what the nut comes up with now! Lock me up in a room! Where I'm
goin' is home—giddyap!—home, where these brazen witches took me from and
cheated me, yeah, cheated me! 'Cause I was as decent as they come, and all they
teach you here is hogwash. Ha, ha, ha! To the devil with these virtuous ladies, all
saintlike! Ha, ha!"

These guttural monosyllables were emitted in her thickest voice in such a
sarcastic, derogatory tone and so grossly that they would have exasperated people
less patient than Sor Natividad and her companions. They were so accustomed to
this treatment and had tamed such formidable beasts that insults no longer had
any effect on them.

"Come on," said the mother superior, frowning, "quietly now, down to the courtyard."

"Well, well, well—just look at the Traviatas in the church will you! Ha!" cried the notorious woman, standing with her arms akimbo and looking at the inmates who had gathered around. "They lock themselves up here so they can fool around all they want with the priests. Ha, ha! What a bunch of harpies!"

Many of the inmates covered their ears. Others, their hands resting on their embroidery frames, looked at the nuns, dumbfounded by their serenity. At that moment a strange figure appeared in the room. It was Sor Marcela, a lame old nun, practically a dwarf, and the most pitiful version of a woman one could imagine. Her face (which looked as if it were made of cardboard) was dark, hard, flat, almost Mongolian; her eyes, expressive and affable, resembled those of some species of the quadrumanous race. Her body did not have a womanly shape, and when she walked it seemed to lose its balance and sink to the left, stamping the floor with a hard blow that might have been from her wooden leg or the stump itself. Her ugliness was equaled only by the compassionate composure with which she regarded Mauricia.

Sor Marcela had a large key in her right hand, and pointing it at the delinquent's breastbone, she clucked her tongue and merely said:

"Out."

The beast quickly removed her wimple, shook her hair loose, and went out into the corridor hurling insolent remarks as she left. The lame one again pointed the way and Mauricia, rotating her arms as if she were a windmill, cried out:

"Hogwash and garbage! Well, aren't you tryin' to dishonor me like I was a criminal? Shrews! If I feel like it, I can knock you across the room with a couple of punches!"

Despite these wild exclamations, the lame nun guided her as calmly as one might lead a furiously barking dog who probably won't bite. Halfway downstairs the harpy turned back, and, looking with enraged eyes at the nuns still standing in the corridor, she called out stridently:

"Thieves, worse than thieves! You big whores!"

This said, the lame one gently put her hand on Mauricia's back and nudged her along. In the courtyard she had to take her by the arm to keep her from going back upstairs.

"They're not listening to you, silly," she said. "It's not you who's speaking, it's the devil in your mouth now. Be quiet for the love of God, and stop making our heads spin."

"You're the one that's the devil," replied the beast, who in her highly exalted state didn't seem to be responsible for the nonsense she was uttering. "Ugly, hideous—"

"Spit it out, all of it," murmured Sor Marcela, opening the door to the cell.

"You'll get over the fit sooner that way. In with you, now, and tomorrow you'll be soft as putty. When night comes I'll bring you something to eat. Be patient, child."

Mauricia barked for a little while longer, but despite all the fury in her words she didn't really put up much of a fight, so that the poor old invalid handled her like a child. All she had had to do was take her arm and lead her into the cell. Sor Marcela turned the key in the lock twice and put it in her pocket. Her face, whose resemblance to a Japanese mask was so marked, remained imperturbable. As she was crossing the courtyard heading toward the stairs, she heard a few "ha, ha, ha!'s" from Mauricia, who was peering through one of the two little windows in the upper part of the door. The nun didn't pause to heed the insults the beast was flinging at her.

"Hey, cripple! Turtle! Come on back and see how I'm gonna crown you one! What a face! . . . Stump foot!"

3

Toward sunset, the livid Napoleonic countenance, hair tangled, appeared behind the bars again. And Sor Marcela passed by the dungeon a number of times after she had checked the hens' nests to see if they had laid any eggs or after watering the pansies and buttercups that she grew in a corner of the garden. The courtyard, which was small and separated from the garden by a wooden gate that was almost always open, was very badly paved; consequently, the lame nun's steps across it were so irregular that her swaying body looked like a small vessel on a choppy sea. Sor Marcela was in that area very often, for she had the keys to the woodbin and the coal pile, the dungeon, and another room where old furniture from the convent and the church was kept.

It was just before nightfall, as I have said, and Mauricia pressed her face to the cell bars so that she could talk to the nun whenever she passed by. Her tone had lost its angry harshness; she was hoarser now and spoke in a pained, miserable tone, begging for mercy. The beast had been tamed. Clutching the bars tightly with both hands, her face pressed against them, opening her mouth wide so that she would be heard better, she said in a plaintive voice:

"My little lame one, my little bird seed, I love you so much! There goes the little duck, waddlin' by—one, two, three. Our bright light in the convent—come, listen; I wanna tell you a little secret."

These tender phrases mixed with affectionate mockery drew no response whatsoever from the nun, who continued on her way without so much as a glance. And the other woman continued:

"Uh oh! My sweet little turtle's mad at me, and I love her so much! Just say one little word, Sor Marcela, just one. You shouldn't let me out of here 'cause I deserve to be locked up. But oh, my dear little one, if you could see how awful I feel! It feels like they're pullin' out my stomach with hot tongs. It's from all the fuss this morning. I feel like hangin' myself from these bars with a rope made out of my petticoat. And I'm gonna do it, too; I'm gonna hang myself if you don't look at me and say one little word, at least . . . Funny face, limpy dwarf, listen to me: if you want me to love you more than my own life and obey you like a dog, do me a favor. Just bring me a tiny teardrop of that divine glory you have, you know— the stuff the doctor prescribed for your belly-aches. Come on, be an angel; I'm askin' you with all my heart, because this little pain I have won't go away and I feel like I'm gonna die. Come on, sweetie, angel bird seed, bring me what I'm askin' you for, and God'll give you the heavenly after-life you deserve, and three more, and the angels will crown you with glory when you get to heaven on your little lame foot . . ."

The nun walked by—thump, thump—wounding the cobblestones with that hard foot of hers that must have been like a chair leg; she conceded neither a look nor a reply to the prisoner. When night fell, she descended with the prisoner's supper, and, opening the door, penetrated the murky room. At first she didn't see Mauricia, who was huddled up on some boards, her knees against her chest, hands crossed over them, her chin resting on her hands.

"I can't see. Where are you?" murmured the lame one, sitting on another pile of boards.

Mauricia answered with a growl, like a mastiff who has been kicked awake. Sor Marcela put a bowl of stew and some bread next to her.

"The mother superior," she said, "didn't want me to bring you anything except bread and water, but I spoke in your behalf. You don't deserve it. Even though I resolve to be firmer, I can't. I handle you my own way, and I know that the worse you're treated, the angrier you get. And just so that you can see how lenient I am, child—" she added, taking out an object from under her cloak.

One would have thought Mauricia had sniffed it, because she suddenly raised her head, her face lighting up so vividly it looked like *his* when he pointed to the pyramids and said that bit about "forty centuries." The low-ceilinged dungeon was dark, but the last light of day was streaming in through the door, and the two women in there could discern each other, although each seemed more like a bulky shape than a person. Mauricia stretched out her hands eagerly until she touched the bottle, when she uttered truncated, stammered words to express her gratitude; but the nun withdrew the coveted object.

"Eh! keep your hands to yourself. If you're not polite, I'm leaving. You can see I'm no tyrant, and that I'm carrying charity to an extreme that may be unwise. But I say, 'If I give her a little bit, just a few drops, I'll console her, and there can't be any harm in it.' I know what a weak stomach is, and how much it makes you suffer. Always refusing a sinner everything he asks for can't be good. The Lord wouldn't want it. Let's have mercy, and console man in his sadness."

Saying this, she took out a small glass and prepared to pour a limited serving of the precious liqueur, which was a very good cognac she used to combat her rebellious dyspepsia. Then it occurred to her that Mauricia should eat her stew first. The prisoner understood and hastened to devour her supper.

"What I'm giving you," added the nun, "is to quiet your nerves and invigorate your spirits. Don't think I'm doing this behind the mother superior's back; she just now authorized me to give you this treat, as long as I made a distinction between necessity and appetite and remedy and pleasure. I know this picks up your spirit and makes you cheerful enough to do your duty well. What some people think is bad is good if it's in reasonable amounts."

Mauricia was so grateful that she couldn't find words to thank the nun, who poured about a finger's width into the glass, tipping the bottle with an extraordinarily steady pulse so that no more than was suitable would flow out; and as she gave it to the prisoner, she repeated the sermon. Did the other lick her lips when she finished! And how good it tasted! She knew the little turtle too well to dare to ask for more. She knew from experience that Sor Marcela never went beyond the limits set by her kindness and charity. She was as good as an angel when it came to conceding something, but she knew when to stop and was firm about it.

"I know," she said, carefully stopping up the bottle, "that with this consolation for your nerves, you'll feel better, and curing the body helps the soul."

Indeed, Mauricia began to feel cheerful, and with her cheerfulness came a readiness to obey orders and work. She felt such a strong urge to do a good deed that she even wanted to pray, confess, and perform exaggerated acts of piety like Sor Marcela who, according to the inmates, wore a hairshirt.

"For God's sake, tell the mother superior that I've repented and to forgive me; that when 'the spirit' calls and I start shootin' off my mouth, I'm just a parrot— my tongue gets carried away. Get me out of here fast and I'll work like never before, and if they tell me to scrub the house from top to bottom, I'll do it. Give me lots of penances and I'll do 'em in a flash."

"I'm glad to see you're so reasonable," the nun said, picking up the dish. "But you're not leaving here tonight. Meditate, meditate on your sins, pray for a long time and ask the Lord and the Holy Virgin to enlighten you."

Mauricia thought she was already illuminated enough, for in her excited state her mind felt sharper and she experienced a peculiar enthusiasm; after exercising a bit by hanging from the bars (because she needed to stretch her limbs), she started to pray with all the devotion of which she was capable, struggling with the various distractions that made her mind wander, and eventually she fell asleep on the hard bed of boards. She was released from this confinement early the next day and went to work in the kitchen immediately, without a word, submissive and marvelously active. After serving a sentence, which she did without fail every thirty or forty days, the Napoleonic woman seemed inhibited and embarrassed in front of her companions and she concentrated wholeheartedly on her work, displaying a zeal and obedience that delighted the nuns. For four or five days she did the work of three women without any effort or exhaustion. After two weeks of this regime, they noticed that she was beginning to tire; her work no longer exemplified that admirable perfection and diligence; mistakes, forgetfulness, and signs of carelessness crept into it, and when she began to repeat the same mistakes, they knew that another outburst was imminent.

After the violent scene that I have described, Mauricia renewed her friendliness to Fortunata and the two talked for hours in the kitchen while they peeled potatoes or scrubbed pots and pans. They enjoyed a certain amount of liberty there, freed of their wimples and wearing instead uniforms ordinarily worn by household maids.

"I have a little girl," Mauricia announced in one of their confidential sessions. "I named her Adoración. She's the cutest thing! She's with my sister Severiana 'cause with my temper I'm a bad example to her, you know? I can't help it . . . and the little angel's better off with Severiana than with me. Doña Jacinta—the wife of your Señor—is very fond of my little girl and buys her clothes, and she took it into her head to take her home with her; she's just dyin' to have a kid, but just imagine: the Lord doesn't want to give her any! He's done wrong, don't you think? 'Cause kids should be for the rich, not the poor, who can't support 'em."

Fortunata said she agreed. She'd heard something about that lady's enormous desire to have children, and Mauricia told her more about it, including the business of Pituso, whom Jacinta had wanted to adopt, believing him to be the child of her husband and Fortunata. The story of this incredible case of maternal delirium and unsatisfied passion affected Fortunata so deeply that she couldn't get it out of her mind for three days.

4

From the upstairs corridor there was a partial view of the Campo de Guardias, the Lozoya Reservoir, the San Martín Cemetery, and the cluster of houses at Cuatro Caminos, and behind all this the stark tones of the Moncloa landscape and the admirable horizon that looks like the sea: gentle wavy lines from whose apparent unsettledness there rose like the masts of a boat towers of nearby towns. When the sun set, that magnificent western sky was streaked with splendid flames, and after it set, the sky faded with infinite grace, fusing with the pale underlying shades of opal. The dark clouds cut strange figures that accommodated themselves to the melancholic, pensive imagination that noticed them. And when it was night in the streets and houses, a soft light shone on in that part of the sky, like the tail of the fleeing day, slowly leaving too.

These beauties were to be completely excluded from the Filomenas' and Josefinas' view when the new church—which was being worked on constantly— was finished. Every day the growing mass of bricks covered up another thin layer of the landscape. With every row that was laid, it seemed as if the builders were erasing rather than adding. From the ground up, the panorama was gradually disappearing, like a world being flooded. The houses along Santa Engracia sank, then the reservoir, then the cemetery. When the bricks had grazed the lovely line of the horizon, the far-off towers of Húmera and the tops of the cypress trees in the cemetery still stood out. The day came when the inmates had to stand on tiptoe or jump up to see a bit more and say good-bye to those friends who were leaving for good. At last the roof of the church swallowed everything, and all that could be seen was the clear light of the sunset, the tail of the day being dragged away by the sky.

But if nothing could be seen any longer, things could be heard: the clinking of the stonecutters' chisels seemed to form part of the atmosphere surrounding the convent. It had become a familiar music, and when it ceased on Sundays its absence was the best sign the inmates had that it was a holiday. On Sunday afternoons from two o'clock on, they could hear the drum that was played in time to the merry-go-round and see-saws near the reservoir. This hubbub and the sounds of the crowds flocking to the taverns at Cuatro Caminos and Tetuán lasted until late into the night. Some of the nuns were very annoyed by the drum at first, not only by the heavy-handed way it was played, but by the thought of how much sinning went on to the sound of that mundane instrument. But they got used to it, and eventually the sound of the merry-go-round on Sundays had the same effect on them as the clinking of the stonecutters on workdays. Sometimes on a holiday afternoon when the boarders were strolling in the garden or the patio, the nuns' tolerance reached the extreme of allowing them to dance a wee bit—within the limits of decency, you understand—to the beat of that popular music. What a torrent of memories and sensations reawakened in those few steps and turns! How vividly the poor inmates recalled the polkas they had danced with clerks in the Alhambra Dance Hall in the afternoon, kicking up clouds of dust, their hands perspiring, eating stale candy. And the worst of it, what had really been their downfall, was that those poor clerks had come with good intentions. Good intentions plus not such good means were precisely what brought on the bad endings. Afterward, the good intentions and the beginnings and the lady were gone; what were left were shame and misery.

The nun who pleaded the most insistently that they be allowed to dance a few steps was Sor Marcela, whose lameness and looks made her seem incapable of appreciating the aesthetic side of dancing. But that little woman with the flat Oriental face knew a lot about the world and human passions. Her heart overflowed with tolerance and charity, and she upheld the following thesis: absolutely refusing to satisfy appetites developed by fairly vicious habits is the worst remedy of all because it engenders despair, and curing bad habits is better accomplished by allowing their owners to indulge themselves from time to time, to a carefully limited degree.

One day she caught Mauricia in the coal bin smoking, which was indeed unbecoming and improper for a woman. The lame one didn't hasten to take the cigarette out of her mouth, as one might have expected. She merely said:

"What a pig you are! I don't know how you can smoke like that. Doesn't it make you dizzy?"

Mauricia laughed, and, closing one eye tightly (for smoke was getting into it), she looked at the nun with the other and handed her the cigarette, saying:

"Try it, Señora."

Lo and behold! Sor Marcela took a puff, and then she flung the cigarette to the ground, turning up her nose, spitting a lot, and making a face as ugly as one of those monstrous Malayan fetishes. Mauricia picked it up and kept chewing it, first closing one eye, then the other, looking at the nun. Then they discussed the source of the cigarette. Mauricia didn't want to confess, but the little nun who knew so much ventured:

"The masons threw it to you. Don't deny it. I saw you making eyes at them. If the mother superior finds out you're sending messages back and forth, you'll be in for it . . . and you deserve it. Throw away that tobacco, you pig. Ugh, it's disgusting! It's ruined my mouth. I don't see how you can like that burning thing in your throat. Men are always inventing new vices—as if they didn't have enough already."

Mauricia dropped the cigarette and stamped on it.

After she had been there a month, Fortunata developed another close friendship with Doña Manolita, who was a married lady; she assisted the nuns in their reading and writing classes, and she made a special effort to teach Fortunata, which is how their friendship started. The nuns allowed this particular boarder a measure of freedom from the rules; she was permitted to be alone with one or two Filomenas for long periods of time, either in the classroom or the garden; she was permitted to visit the Josefinas' section too, and as she had a separate room and paid well for it, she enjoyed more comforts than her companions.

Once she and Fortunata got to know each other, they lost no time in confiding their respective stories. The story we already know was told without frills, but Manolita embellished hers so much and tried to make it sound so pathetic that no one would have recognized it. According to her, she hadn't sinned at all. It had all been a big mistake; her husband, who was a brute, was to blame. Yes, he was to blame for her mistakes or evil temptations, and he had simply thrown her into the convent. Since this lady had enjoyed considerable social rank, she had charming tales of the world and its pomp, the parties she had attended, the many good dresses she used to wear. Her husband dealt in *nouveautés* and was her social inferior (her papá was a clerk in the Treasury). Hearing these haughty declarations, Fortunata concluded that her friend's papá's job must be "really classy."

But the best part was that an extremely interesting subject suddenly came up in their conversation. Manolita knew the Santa Cruzes. Know them? Her husband, Pepe Reoyos, was one of Don Baldomero's closest friends. And she herself had visited Doña Bárbara many times. Then they went on to talk about Jacinta. Ah! Jacinta was adorable; she had everything: kindness, beauty, talent, and virtue. That rogue Juan didn't deserve such a gem; he was too much of a ladies' man. But except for that, he was an excellent boy and he was most likable, really.

"You probably already know," she said later, "that he caught pneumonia last February. He almost died. The convent—for it owes a lot to the Santa Cruzes— put the Lord on display, and when he was over the dangerous stage, Jacinta financed some solemn services. The assistant bishop came and said Mass—"

"*Really?* That's funny."

"Really. You don't know what you missed! Jacinta is one of the ladies who's helped support this convent most. You can see why . . . since she doesn't have any children, she doesn't know what to spend money on. Have you noticed those nice big branches with the gold tissue flowers and silver leaves?"

"Yes," replied Fortunata, who was all ears. "The ones they put on the altar at Pentecost?"

"Exactly. Well, they were a gift from Jacinta. And the Virgin's cloak—the brocade flowered cloak that's so nice—she donated that too, as a token of her gratitude for her husband's recovery."

Fortunata exclaimed in astonishment. It was the strangest thing! Just a few days ago she had had that very cloak in her hands, to remove a few drops of wax; the very same cloak that had paid, as it were, for the recovery of the Santa Cruz boy! And nevertheless, it was all very natural. It was just that her mind got muddled and she had started thinking, not of the incident itself, but of the coincidence: that she should have unwittingly held in her hands objects related to him.

"Well, you haven't heard the best part," Manolita added, relishing her friend's astonishment, which seemed more like horror. "You know the monstrance, where the Lord himself is put? Well, it came from them too. It was a gift from Barbarita, who promised it to the nuns if her son got well. Don't go thinking it's made of gold; it's gold-plated silver. But it's adorable, don't you think?"

Fortunata's thoughts had sunk so deep that she missed hearing the incredibly ludicrous word Manolita used for the monstrance: "adorable."

5

For many days she couldn't get her mind off the things Doña Manolita had told her. I might add parenthetically that Fortunata didn't particularly like her informant, and that what absorbed her most was not the knowledge that the mantle and monstrance were gifts of the Santa Cruzes, but the coincidence. "That's funny." If she had entered the convent a few days earlier, she would have attended the solemn Mass, bishop and all, that was given for the recovery of that . . . This would have been even funnier. For her part, Fortunata, who knew how to forgive an offense, would have willingly joined the rest of the inmates in prayers for him. And that was even funnier.

What did completely upset her soul was the sight of Jacinta in flesh and blood. She neither knew her nor had ever seen a picture of her, but since she had thought about her so much, she had formed an image of her that, faced by reality, turned out to be all wrong. The ladies who sponsored the convent, supporting it with cash or donations, were allowed to visit the interior rooms whenever they wished, and on certain solemn days the convent was cleaned from top to bottom till it shone like a mirror, although no attempt was made to disguise its needs so that the protectoresses would be able to see clearly where their generosity was needed. On Corpus Christi, after High Mass, the visitors, who came all afternoon, started to arrive. Marquises and duchesses in emblazoned carriages and others who had no titles but lots of money filed in through those rooms and corridors where the fanatic instructions of Sor Natividad and the rough hands of the inmates had attained such prodigious cleanliness that the floors—as the saying goes—were clean enough to eat from, without a tablecloth. Embroidery done by the Filomenas, calligraphy samplers done by the Josefinas, and other accomplishments of both groups were on display, receiving a constant stream of congratulations. The ladies came and went, leaving the house scented with a worldly perfume that more than one inmate's nose inhaled greedily. The curiosity of those two groups was stirred by the dresses and hats worn by that elegant, free crowd, some of whom, in fairness, had sinned more—far, far more—than the worst in the convent. Manolita didn't fail to whisper this mischievous observation into her friend's ear. In the midst of the parade, Fortunata saw Jacinta, and Manolita (emphasizing this one exception to her social criticism) took pains to point out Señora Santa Cruz's charm, the elegance and simplicity of her dress, and that modest air she had that won everybody over. From the moment Jacinta appeared at the end of the corridor, Fortunata's eyes were glued to her, anxiously examining her face and the way she walked, her manners and her dress. Lost in the group of inmates next to the dining-room door, Fortunata's eyes followed her, and she crouched next to the stairs to get a good look when she came down. She was left with the appealing image Jacinta presented, and it impressed her memory vividly.

The moral impression received was so complex that Fortunata couldn't understand her own feelings. Undoubtedly, her primitive, passionate nature made her feel envy first. That woman had taken away what was hers, what in her mind was rightfully hers. But this feeling somehow blended strangely with another very different and sharper one; namely, a burning desire to look like Jacinta, to be like her, to have her air—that particular kind of sweetness and composure. For of all the ladies she saw that day, none seemed to be as much of a lady as Jacinta; none had decency so clearly written in her face and gestures. If the sinner had been offered at that moment to transmigrate into the body of someone else, she would have automatically, unhesitatingly said that she wished to be Jacinta.

What started out as resentment in her soul gradually turned into pity, for Manolita repeated *ad nauseum* that Jacinta endured terrible scorn and disrespect from her husband. She even set down as a general rule that all husbands love their, shall we say, temporary wives more than their permanent ones, although there were exceptions. So Jacinta, in the last analysis, and despite the vows of matrimony, was as much of a victim as Fortunata. Once this thought had interposed itself between Fortunata and Jacinta, the sinner's rancor was milder and her desire to resemble the victim stronger.

For the next few days she kept seeing Jacinta in her mind's eye or expecting her to appear in any doorway at any moment. Thinking so much about her in the solitude of the convent led her to have hallucinatory dreams at night in which she envisioned Señora Santa Cruz with the texture she actually had in reality. Now she dreamed that Jacinta came to her in tears to tell her the foul things her husband had done; now that the two of them wondered which of them suffered more; now, finally, that they exchanged identities, Jacinta taking on Fortunata's appearance and Fortunata, Jacinta's. These absurdities disturbed the reformed woman's brain so much that when she woke up she continued to imagine similar, if not more extreme, nonsense.

These thoughts were cut short by Maximiliano's visits every Thursday and Sunday between four and six in the afternoon. The young woman looked forward to these visits with pleasure; she desired and anticipated them, for Maximiliano was the only real tie with the outside world that she had and even though religious sentiments had conquered part of her, they had not detached her from her worldly interests and affections. On this score good old Rubín had no need to worry; not once, not even in her greatest moments of fervent piety, did it enter the sinner's head to become a saint. So she was glad to see Maximiliano, and even found that time flew by as she listened to him talk about Doña Lupe and Papitos or make predictions about what was to come. It is true that the worthy boy was physically displeasing to her; but it is also true that she was gradually getting used to him, that his defects no longer seemed so huge, and that her gratitude had become deeply implanted in her soul. If she examined her heart, she discovered that as far as love for her redeemer went, she had gained very little; but her esteem and respect were surely greater, and what had certainly grown and taken root in her mind was the suitability of the marriage; it would secure her an honorable position in the world. At times she asked herself in all sincerity how and why that notion had become so firm, but she found no reply. Was it perhaps that the silence and peace of this new life had engendered and developed her common sense? If so, she didn't realize it; the only thing her primitive mind was able to formulate was this: "It's just that from thinking so much I've gotten smarter, the way Maximiliano did from loving me, and this new talent tells me I should get married; that I'm a dumb fool if I don't."

Seeing that his beloved did not reject the idea of shortening her stay and setting the wedding for an earlier date, the good pharmacy student considered himself the happiest man alive. By now her soul was undoubtedly cleaner than pure water. The trouble was that that idiot Nicolás, after the poor girl had been in the convent for five months, said it wasn't enough; that they should at least wait out the year. Maximiliano got furious and Doña Lupe, when consulted on the issue, gave her approval to the girl's leaving the convent. Although she had visited the "basilisk" several times (escorted by her nephew), she hadn't been able to tell whether she was thoroughly cleansed of those spots from the past; but she wished to exercise her educational faculties, and any delay in bringing Fortunata under her jurisdiction meant that the great experiment would have to wait. The worthy lady was somewhat distrustful of the efficacy of religious institutions in setting straight people who had gone astray. What they learned there, she said, was the art of disguising their bad habits under hypocritical manners. Out in the world, in the thick of things, was where faulty characters should be corrected, under wise direction. Oh, it was very good and saintly to fortify rickets with remedies, but Doña Lupe's opinion was that they were worthless unless accompanied by exercise and gymnastics, fresh air. And this is what she wanted to try out: the world, life, and, at the same time, principles.

6

Fortunata had no contact at all with the Josefinas. They were five-, ten-, or twelve-year-old girls who lived in separate quarters in the front rooms. They dined before the others, in the same dining room, and went into the garden when it was their turn, just as the Filomenas did. All morning long the little girls sang their lessons aloud in unison in high mournful voices that could be heard all over the house. In the afternoon they sang the doctrine. When they went to church, they left their section two by two, in a procession, wearing black scarves on their heads, and they stood on either side of the chancel captained by the two nun teachers.

As Fortunata made new friendships every day among the Filomenas, I should like to mention two of them (perhaps the youngest in the group) who stood out because of their exaggerated show of religion. One of them was practically a child, with a remarkably delicate figure, blonde, and the possessor of a lovely voice. Being in the choir, she sang the refrains (in very dubious taste) that celebrate the presence of a transubstantiated God. Her name was Belén, and in the time she had spent there she had given unmistakable proof of her desire to mend her ways. Her sins could not have been great in number, for she was very young; but be that as it may, the girl seemed prepared to wipe all trace of them from her soul, judging by the dog's life she led, the atrocious penance she did, and the frenzy with which she consecrated herself to pious tasks. It was said that she had been a chorus girl in musical comedies and had gone from that to a worse life until a charitable soul had rescued her from the mire and delivered her to the protected place she now inhabited. Her inseparable companion was Felisa, somewhat older, also possessed of a nice figure and a ladylike air. The two got together whenever they could—working on the same embroidery frame and eating from the same plate, forming an inseparable couple during recess. Felisa's background was very different from her friend's. Her connection with the theater had been indirect (she had been a famous actress' maid), and she had gone astray in the theater too. She had been brought to the Micaelas by Doña Guillermina Pacheco, who "caught" her in the streets of Madrid, told two policemen to grab her, and, with no reason except her will, appropriated the girl. That was how Guillermina operated, and what she'd done to Felisa she had done to many others, with no explanations given for her violation of their civil rights.

All one had to do to annoy Felisa and Belén was to suggest that they go back into the world. After managing to escape from it! They were as cozy as could be in the convent and gave no thought to what they had left behind except to feel sorry for the poor girls who were still caught in the devil's clutches. There wasn't a soul in the house except the nuns who prayed as much as they did. If it had been up to them, they would have spent the whole day in the chapel. The long pious exercises conducted at different times of the year—the corpus octave, sermons during Lent, the Vespers to the Virgin in May—always left them hungry for more. Belén exercised her musical faculties ardently for God, singing couplets until her voice grew hoarse, and she would have sung unto death. They both went to confession often and consulted the chaplain about very subtle doubts they had in their consciences, and in this were like conscientious students who corner the professor when class is over to have a difficult point cleared up. The nuns were satisfied with them, but although pleased by such piety, they were experienced souls who knew what youth was like, so they watched the couple very closely and made sure that they were never left alone. Felisa and Belén, together all day long, separated at night, for they slept in different dormitories. The nuns took scrupulous care to separate by night the girls who tended, out of instinctive congeniality, to stick together by day.

The bonds between Fortunata and Mauricia were very strange. When the latter had one of her "attacks," she terrified the former; Fortunata was infuriated by her friend's audacity, yet la Dura must have had some diabolical power over her because Fortunata preferred her to everyone else and delighted in their private conversations. She was undoubtedly captivated by Mauricia's frankness and ability to find a reason to explain everything. Mauricia's looks—her grave, sad expression, that beautiful paleness, and her profound, intent eyes—fascinated Fortunata and led her to consider her an authority on matters of love and the definition of the exceedingly odd morals they both professed to have. One day they were put to work doing laundry in the orchard. They were wearing their work clothes, heads bare, feeling the bite of the sun and the cool of the air on their robust necks. Fortunata revealed to her friend a few details about her imminent departure and the person she was to marry.

"I get the picture. It's just what you needed. Shoot! I know Doña Lupe like the back of my hand. When you see her, ask her about Mauricia la Dura and you'll see—she'll praise me to the skies. Oh, the dough I've handled for her! They call me 'the tough one'; but they should call her 'close-fists.' It's true, that's what she's like . . ." Saying this, she closed her fist tightly and showed it to her friend. "But she's got a head on her shoulders and knows how to steer herself all right. You know what? She's got millions hidden in the bank and in pawnshops. Huh! That woman knows more than the president! I've seen the nephew a couple of times. I heard he's dumb and no good at anything. All the better; you couldn't have asked for a better piece of luck. And you can count on what I'm telling you, 'cause I've got a good lantern. I mean, I can see a lot. Believe me, if your husband's a ninny—you know what I mean, if he lets himself be run by you, and you wear the pants—you can sing hallelujahs, 'cause that and being in heaven are just the same. Even if it only means you'll be decent, this is the thing for you."

Because of the lively interest the two women had in this dialogue, their vigorously busy arms sometimes stopped in the water and their reddened hands momentarily ignored the soaking clothes that hissed faintly when the suds were squeezed through them. Standing on opposite sides of the washtub they faced each other squarely during those short intermissions and then went back to work, wagging their tongues all the while.

"Even if it only means being decent," repeated Fortunata, pushing all her weight into her hands to knead a roll of clothing as if it were dough. "There's nothing to say on that score, because you can be sure of this: once I get married, I have to be decent. I don't want any more bedlam."

"Yeah, that's best if you want to get along in the world," said Mauricia. "But we don't know things'll work out . . . 'cause you know, you say 'I want this,' and you start to do it, but bang!—you wanted a fish and it turns out to be a frog. You're in luck, kid. God's on your side. You can make the Santa Cruz boy stew in his juices, 'cause as soon as he sees you've turned into a decent person he'll be after you like a cat smelling fish. Believe me, that's how it'll be."

"Come on, stop it; he probably doesn't even remember the saint I'm named after."

"Are you kidding? How much do you want to bet that as soon as they give you the holy blessing he loses his head? You just don't know him."

"You'll see—it won't happen."

"You want to bet? Sure, you wouldn't believe it, but he's on your tail right this minute. I can just see him. And you think I don't know that you think about him? You can't fool me! When you're shut up with all this religion, going to Mass all the time with a sermon here, a sermon there, always looking at the monstrance and breathing in that nun smell and lights and incense, it seems like all the bad and good things that've happened to you start creeping out like ants from a hole when the sun goes down, and what religion does is freshen up your head and soften your heart."

Spurred by this declaration, Fortunata admitted that she did indeed think about him and sometimes had extravagant dreams at night. She'd dream that she was walking along the arcade on Fresa Street and wham! all of a sudden she'd run smack into him. Other times she saw him coming out of the Treasury. Neither of these places meant anything to her as far as she could remember. Then she dreamt that she was the wife and Jacinta the mistress, whom he at times had abandoned and others had not. The natural wife was the one who wanted children and the legal wife was the one who had them. Until one day . . . "I felt so sorry for her I said, 'Okay, take one of my kids so you won't cry anymore.'"

"What a riot!" exclaimed Mauricia. "That's a good one. Dreams sure have something strange about them."

"What a lot of nonsense! It's just like I say—it's as if I was seeing him. I was the wife in the eyes of the Church, and she was the wife behind its back, and the strangest part is that I didn't have a grudge against her; I felt sorry for her, because I had a kid every year and she . . . she didn't even have that. The next night I had the same dream, and that day I thought about it. What a laugh! What do I care if Jacinta's wild to have a baby and can't, and I—?"

"—And you have 'em all the time and whenever you feel like it. Go on, say it, silly; don't be a coward."

"I mean, while I've already had one and could easily have one again."

"Sure! And some stew she'll be in when she sees that what she can't do is duck soup for you. Look, kid, don't be stupid, don't lower yourself, don't take pity on her, 'cause she didn't take any on you when she snatched what was yours—and I mean yours. But if you're born poor nobody respects you, and that's the way this crummy world is. Whenever you can foul her up do it, for Christ's sake. Don't let 'em laugh at you 'cause you were born poor. Take back what she took from you, and let 'er guess who did it."

Fortunata did not reply. These words and others of Mauricia's always aroused in her feelings of love or despair that lay dormant in the most recondite part of her soul. When she heard them a horrid chill ran up and down her spine and she sensed that her companion's insinuations concurred with feelings that she kept carefully hidden away like dangerous weapons.

7

Surprised by a nun in this juicy conversation that made them slacken their work, they were forced to keep silent. Mauricia drained the dirty water and Fortunata turned on the faucet to fill the tub with clean water from the metal tank as if she were vicariously bringing clean thoughts into their rather impure conversation. It took a long time to fill the tub because there wasn't much water in the tank. The large disk that transmitted the strength of the wind to the pump was very lazy that day and moved only at intervals with indolent majesty; after groaning for a second as if to say it didn't feel like working, the apparatus came to a halt in the silent countryside. The two inmates still felt like chatting, but the nun wouldn't let them and wanted to check on how they were rinsing the clothes. Then the friends were forced to separate because it was Thursday and Fortunata had to get dressed for the Rubíns' visit. Mauricia stayed and hung up the wash.

That afternoon Maximiliano stated categorically that with his family's agreement and the mother superior's consent, Fortunata's seclusion would come to an end in September and she would leave the convent to be married. The nuns had no complaints about her and praised her humility and obedience. She didn't excel like Belén and Felisa in their ardent religious zeal, which indicated that she had no vocation for the cloistered life, but she performed her duties punctually and that was sufficient. She had made considerable progress in reading and writing and knew Christian doctrine backward and forward, and the Micaelas deemed that their disciple's religious knowledge would illumine her sufficiently to guide her on the straight or crooked paths in the world. They were confident that the possession of those principles gave their students incredible strength to face all doubts. In these matters one had to consider the person's nature, his spiritual frame, that inner, lasting shape that usually manages to superimpose itself on all the outer transfigurations produced by education; in respect to Fortunata, none of the nuns, not even the ones who knew her well, had any reason to believe that she was bad. They considered her empty-headed, tame, and easy to manage. In truth, though, the nuns hardly exercised their educational faculties in the immense kingdom of the passions, either because they were unfamiliar with that kingdom or because they were too wary to approach its frontiers.

It should be mentioned that when Maximiliano spoke to his betrothed that afternoon about her imminent departure, she recoiled from the idea. Leave the Micaelas, get married! At that moment her blessed fiancé seemed more disagreeable than ever, and she reflected fearfully that in the solitude and holiness of the convent she had not, as Nicolás Rubín had predicted, discovered those magnificent regions of the beauty of the soul despite all the praying and so many, many sermons. What the chaplain said in the pulpit was that we should do everything in our power to save our soul, that we should be good and not sin, also that we should love God above all things, and that God is beauty itself and is just as the soul sees him; but she figured that underneath all this the heart was free for worldly love, which we feel instinctively because we like someone, and whether or not the person we love looks like a saint makes no difference. Thus, Nicolás' doctrine fell apart at the seams. The priest knew as much about love as he knew about branding mosquitoes.

In short, the incorrigible woman's feelings toward her future husband had not changed at all. Nevertheless, when Maximiliano told her that he had already picked out a house to rent and he consulted her on what furniture to buy, pride in having a decent home awoke in Fortunata a sense of dignity; it encouraged her to unite with the man who was redeeming and regenerating her. And so she came to show great contentment at the prospect of leaving soon, and made dozens of helpful comments about the furniture, the china, and even the kitchen utensils.

They parted in high spirits, and Fortunata retired with her mind set on what they had discussed. A decent, quiet home! It's what she had wanted all her life! She had never cared for luxury or expensive, sinful living. What she had always desired was anonymity and peace, but her cursed fate had made her life scandalous, constantly afflicted. Her fondest dream had always been to be surrounded by a little circle of beloved people and live as God would wish—loving one's own and being loved by them, going through life easily. She'd been thrown into the bad life, left in the lurch against her will, and she didn't like it one bit. After thinking this over, she examined her conscience and asked herself what she had gained from religion in the convent. If she hadn't taken much of a liking to the soul's attractions, she had gained in another way. She enjoyed a certain peace of mind that had been unknown to her before, a peace of mind disturbed only by Mauricia's malignant whisperings. And that wasn't the only victory. She found that a new idea had taken root in her: resignation and the conviction that we should take things as they come in life, receive joyfully what is given us and not aspire to completely satisfy our desires. She heard this as she knelt before the monstrance. It was a "white idea"* that seemed to radiate from the monstrance itself. The trouble was that in those long, sometimes boring hours she spent kneeling in front of the Sacrament, its head draped in a huge veil that hung like a mosquito net, the sinner usually paid more attention to the monstrance framing the sacred form than the form itself because of the associations that the jewel awakened in her mind.

And the simple girl reached the point of believing that the host, the "white idea," was speaking to her in a language just like her own: "Don't look so hard at this ring of gold and gems around me, look at Me, 'cause I'm the Truth. I've given you the only good thing you could hope for. It's not much, but it's more than you deserve. Take it and don't ask me for the impossible. Do you think we're here to have things our way, to change the laws of society just because a fool like you happens to want it? The man you're asking me for is a high-class gentleman and you're a poor girl. Do you think it's easy for me to marry young gentlemen to maids or turn country girls into ladies? Really! The things that occur to you, child! And besides, silly, can't you see that he's married, married in my religion and at my altar? And look who to! To one of my female angels. Do you think that all that's got to be done is to make a man a widower to satisfy the whim of a flighty girl like you? It's true that it'd suit me, like you say, to bring Jacinta up here. But that's none of your business. And suppose I do bring her up here; suppose he's a widower. Bah! Do you think he'd marry *you*? Oh sure, he's just your type. Well, he wouldn't marry you even if you hadn't lost your honor, never mind now that it's lost! It's what I always say: you all seem as if you're off your rocker and vice had dried up your brains. You ask me for such crazy things, I don't even know why I listen. What counts is turning to me with a clean heart and good intentions like your chaplain told you yesterday; he's not a genius or anything but he's a good man and he does his duty. My indulgence singled you out, Fortunata; I don't treat every girl who's gone astray like that. But since you listened to me sometimes, and I saw that you meant well and wanted to reform . . . Now you come up with 'oh yes, you'll be decent,' as decent as I want, as long as I give you a man that suits

---

*The author does not explain this concept, but at the end of section 8 it is associated again with divine inspiration, or what Fortunata thinks is divine inspiration.

your fancies. Some promise! But I don't want to get mad. What's said is said: I'm infinitely merciful with you, giving you something you don't deserve, supplying you with a decent husband who adores you, and you're still quibbling and asking me for more, more, more . . . You can see why I get tired of saying yes to everything. These miserable girls don't take stock of things, they don't think. You manage to give someone the idea of reforming them, and then they come along saying 'but' to everything. They either say he has to be handsome or he has to be such-and-such and if not, forget it. Look, my dear child: I can't change what I've done or play tricks on my own laws. A fine time to ask for handsome men! So resign yourselves, my children; your Shepherd won't abandon you just because you're black sheep; follow the example set by the sheep you live with. And you, Fortunata, thank me sincerely for the immense good fortune I'm giving you and you don't deserve, and stop being so finicky and asking for the moon, because otherwise I won't give you anything and you'll be back where you started. So be careful, now . . ."

When the inmates took off their veils on their way out, the ones nearest to Fortunata noticed that she was smiling to herself.

8

It is very annoying to a storyteller to be obliged to mention many childish details and circumstances that are more apt to arouse scorn than curiosity in the reader, for although these trivialities later turn out to be woven into the scheme of things, they do not because of this seem worthy of being included in a serious, accurate narration. So you can see why I think that whoever reads that Sor Marcela was afraid of mice will laugh, and it will doubtless be in vain to add that the little old lame nun's fear was huge and horrible and occasioned disagreeable incidents and even tragic consequences. If in the solitude of her cell she heard the skittering of that cursed animal, she couldn't get a wink of sleep for the rest of the night. She went into such a rage that she couldn't even pray; this rage was directed not so much at the mice as it was at Sor Natividad, who insisted that there be no cats in the convent because the last one they had had didn't share her concern for cleanliness in every corner of the house.

One August night a tiny rodent waged such war on the little nun that she got up the next morning firmly resolved to catch him and give him the most terrible of punishments. He was so insolent that he calmly scampered around the cell in broad daylight and looked at Sor Marcela with his playful black eyes.

"You wait and see, you'll see," she said, climbing onto the bed with great difficulty, because the thought of the mouse getting close to one of her feet—even if it was the wooden one—filled her with terror. "Today you're not getting away. Just take it easy and rest; I'll get to you."

She called Fortunata and Mauricia and briefly informed them of the situation. Both inmates, particularly la Dura, wanted action; either they crushed the enemy or they weren't worth their salt. Sor Marcela went down to the chapel and the two women launched their attack. Not an item was left untouched. To move the bureau, which was terribly heavy, they had to make masculine efforts for about a quarter of an hour; they didn't finish sooner because their laughter weakened them. Finally, they worked so hard that when Sor Marcela came out of the chapel, a nun gave her the happy news that the mouse had been caught. The dwarf went up to her cell, and the clamor she could hear on the way announced that Mauricia was into her mischief: she had the live mouse in her hand and was scaring her companions with it.

It took some effort to restore order and have Mauricia end the victim's life and throw it away. Sor Marcela ordered them to put things back in place in the cell, and here ends the story of the mouse.

The next day was one of the hottest that summer. It was impossible to stay in the rooms that faced south because there was no air in them. Wherever the sun shone, the dry, still, burnt atmosphere roasted them. Not even the highest branches on the trees in the orchard stirred, and the parson's disk stared, immobile, like a coagulated moribund pupil, at the immensity. From twelve to three, all work in the house was suspended because no body or soul could stand the heat. Some of the nuns retired to their cells for a nap; others went to the chapel because it was the coolest place in the convent and, sitting on the benches and leaning against the wall, they either prayed sleepily or simply drowsed.

The Filomenas were exhausted too. Some went to their rooms and others stretched out on the floor in the sewing room or the classroom. The nuns who supervised them permitted this violation because they couldn't stand the heat either. And gently dropping their lids and lulling themselves into a placid trance, they wore their teacherly expressions like a mask, thus doing their duty of keeping order.

In the classroom there were two or three groups of women sitting on the benches resting their heads and bosoms on the table. Some snored noisily. The nun had fallen asleep too, her head thrown back and her mouth hanging open. At one of the desks, two inmates kept watch: Belén, who was reading her prayer book, and Mauricia la Dura, who leaned on her closed fist on the desk. At first Belén thought she was praying, because she heard murmuring and an occasional syllable. But then she noticed that Mauricia was actually crying.

"What's wrong, Mauricia?" asked Belén, lifting up her friend's face energetically.

The sinner made no reply, but the other could see her face bathed in tears, as if someone had emptied a bucket of water on it, and her eyes were swollen, making her wet face look just like the Magdalene's—or at least Belén thought so. Belén asked her so many questions and was so affectionate that she finally obtained an answer from the desolate woman, who looked truly inconsolable, as if she would never ever stop crying.

"What could be wrong with me, miserable old me," she exclaimed at last, drinking in her tears, "except that today, for some unknown reason, I see myself the way I really am; I'm rotten, rotten, worse than rotten, and suddenly I remember all the sins I've ever committed, from the first down to the very last . . ."

"But look," argued Belén in that mellifluous voice she had learned that fit her angelic face and demure way so well, "you can be sure that even if you've committed as many crimes as all the sand on the shores, God will forgive you if you repent."

Hearing this, wailing, and crying another flood of tears was all one for Mauricia.

"No, no," she murmured between big, choking sobs. "He can't forgive me, not me, because I've been so, so contemptible. Whatever sins there are, I've committed them. And if not, name one, any one, and I've got it in me for sure."

"What nonsense," observed Belén very worriedly, for she recalled her life as a chorus girl; visions of the Zarzuela Theater filled her with horror. "Others have committed ugly sins too, very ugly ones, but they've cried over them like you and they've been forgiven."

Mauricia had a handkerchief in her hand, but it was like a damp ball from her crying and perspiring. She scrunched it up and wiped her anguished forehead with it.

"But how did this . . . so suddenly?" the other asked confusedly. "Oh, God touches our hearts when we least expect it. Cry, Mauricia, get it out of your system and don't be scared. You know what you're going to do? Tomorrow you're going to confession. Maybe you've got something left to say from last time— because somehow or other there's always something that doesn't get said, and they're the dregs that torment you the most . . . So tell him everything, gather it all together. That's what I did, and until I did I had no peace. Then that dog Satan was after me for revenge, and when Mass started it was like the curtain going up, and when I burst out singing, the song I had on the tip of my tongue was one from a musical, one that goes, 'We are real, live mannequins.' And one day I almost blurted it out. Tricks the devil plays on you . . . But he couldn't get ahold of me, not with my faith, and I worked so hard at it that I finally had him wound around my little finger. Let him dare something now—but he won't, he doesn't dare. Have a good cry, Mauricia, cry all you want; God will show you the way and give you His grace."

Not even this did it. The more Belén consoled her friend, the more inconsolable her friend became, and the bigger the flood of tears. Sor Antonia (who was in charge) woke up, and to cover up for her own delinquency she talked loudly, showing very little concern for her sleeping charges, and added that it was terribly hot. A minute later, Belén and the nun were whispering, undoubtedly about Mauricia, at whom they were looking. Belén had sway over the nuns because of her humility and devotion and because of her prompt reports on her companions' actions and words.

It was Sunday, and at four o'clock the entire community went to the chapel for religious exercises and a sermon. The Filomenas took their places behind the nuns. The Josefinas stayed in the room used for the choir. Belén and the other members of the choir sang innocent romanzas during the exposition of the Sacrament, romanzas that said their breasts "were burning in flames of love" and such. When the singing stopped, some tasteless ritornellos came from the harmonium. But despite these artistic profanities, the church was "adorable," as Manolita would say—quiet, mysterious, and relatively cool, filled with the fragrance of natural flowers.

Fortunata ended up beside Mauricia. The future Señora Rubín observed, glancing at her companion through her veil, such an odd expression on Mauricia's face that she was dumbfounded. When Mauricia came in she was crying; but after awhile she looked more as if she were suppressing devilish laughter. Fortunata could not understand the reason for this and thought that the dark veil must be disfiguring her friend's true expression. She looked again, pretending that she had turned to brush off a fly, and . . . it might have been an illusion, but Mauricia's eyes looked like live coals. Well, perhaps it was her own apprehension.

Don León Pintado climbed up to the pulpit and gave a sermon full of the mannerisms he used in his oratory. What he said that afternoon he had already said on other afternoons, and certain sentences were old favorites of his. He thundered on, as always, against free thinkers—whom he called "the apostles of error"—over and over. Leaving church, Fortunata glanced as usual at the people behind the wooden gate and she saw Maximiliano, who was present every Sunday for their silent amorous appointment. She looked fondly at him, noting with pleasure that the worthy young man's physical defects were beginning to lose importance in her eyes. Could this be the beginning of her love for the beauties of his soul? Fortunata's greatest consolation was her hope, becoming firmer every day; the chaplain had told her not a few times in the confessional box that when she got married and lived piously with her husband, obeying divine and human laws, she would love him, not in any old way, but with true warmth and from the depths of her soul. The "form"—the "white idea" inside the monstrance—also told her this.

9

When night fell and the Josefinas were all in their dormitory, the nuns allowed the Filomenas to stay in the orchard a little later than usual to let them cool off if they could. It was already nine o'clock but the ground was still hot, the air was absolutely still, and the stars looked closer because of their brightness, and more of the smaller ones could be seen than usual; so many were visible that it seemed as if silver dust had been scattered all across that intensely deep blue sky. The new moon soon disappeared into the horizon like a sickle with a whitish halo that announced more heat for the next day.

The inmates were seated in groups on the ground and on the wooden stairs leading to the main corridor, and they took off their wimples to let their skin breathe. Some of them looked at the wind motor, which was immobile. Beside the pool at the foot of the motor were three women—Fortunata, Felisa, and Doña Manolita. They were sitting on the brick wall enjoying the cool air from the nearby water. It was the best place, but they didn't say so, because their egoism warned them that if all the women came to cluster there, the slight cool from the water would have to be shared and each would get less. On the other side of the orchard, the most isolated and ugliest place, there was a shed under which were empty or broken flowerpots, a heap of manure that looked like coffee grounds, two wheelbarrows, hoses, and other assorted garden tools. There had once been a lair there, and in it a pig fed on left-overs, but the town hall had ruled that the animal had to be removed, so the lair was empty now.

At nightfall Mauricia la Dura settled there by herself on the pile of manure; since it was the hottest place of all no one wanted to accompany her. One of the inmates went over to ridicule her, but couldn't get her to say a word. She was sitting Moorish style, arms hanging down, head high, looking more Napoleonic than ever as she stared blankly into space with a dreamy expression on her face. She looked numb or, on second thought, somewhat like one of those Hindustani penitents who sit for days staring at the sky without even blinking, in a state somewhere between drowsiness and ecstasy. It was already late when Belén sat down beside her. She looked at her closely, asked her what she was doing, what she was thinking about, and at last Mauricia parted her sphinxlike lips to pronounce the following words, which sent shivers up and down Belén's spine:

"I've seen Our Lady."

"What? What's wrong, Mauricia?" the ex–chorus girl inquired anxiously.

"I have seen the Virgin," Mauricia repeated with an assurance and poise that plunged the other woman into total confusion.

"Are you sure of what you're saying?"

"May I be struck dead if I'm lying. I swear it on the Holy Cross," said the radiant woman in a quivering voice, kissing her hands, which she had crossed for her vow. "I have . . . seen her. She came down over there, by the mill wheel. She came down wrapped in a kind of—how can I put it?—a light you can't imagine; it was like pure honey—"

"Like honey?" echoed Belén, failing to understand.

"And . . . so sweet that . . . Then she came walking, walking over to here, and she stood right there in front of me. She passed right by the rest of you, and you didn't see her. Only I saw her. She didn't have the Baby Jesus in her arms. She took a few more steps and then she stopped again. Look, see that little rock? Well, right there. And she kept looking at me . . . I couldn't breathe."

"And did she say anything to you, did she?" asked Belén, all eyes, pale as a ghost.

"Nothing. But she cried when she looked at me. If you could've seen the big tears in her eyes! She wasn't carrying the Baby Jesus; it looked like they'd taken him away from her. Then she turned and went back the other way, and she walked right past all of you and not one of you saw her, till she reached that tree. I saw lots of little angels all around it, climbing up and down, all over, from the trunk to the branches and—"

"—From the branches to the trunk—"

"—And then I didn't see anything . . . I felt like I was blind, I mean really blind; for a while I couldn't see a thing. I couldn't move. I felt something here, inside me, some sort of thing . . ."

"Like grief."

"No, not like grief; pleasure, relief—"

Fortunata came up at that moment and they both fell silent.

"If it's a secret, I'll leave."

"I think," said Belén after a serious pause, "that you should ask the confessor about this."

Mauricia got up and slowly headed for the room where she slept and kept her clothes. The other two thought she was going to bed and stayed where they were, remarking on the strange case, which Belén had related to Fortunata down to the last detail. Belén believed in it, or pretended to; Fortunata did not. Soon they saw la Dura coming back, taking up her place again on the manure pile. They looked at her suspiciously and retreated.

Suddenly the orchard was filled with the sound of a long contented "Ah!," the kind a crowd ejaculates when fireworks are set off. All the inmates looked at the mill wheel, which solemnly started to move, rotated twice, then stopped again. "Air, air!" cried several voices. But the motor made only a half-turn more and stopped again. The iron piston rod screeched for a second, and the inmates sitting beside the pool heard a slight regurgitation from the depths of the pump. The pipe spit out some water like saliva, and then all was as despairingly still as before.

Belén had started to chat quietly with a nun called Sor Facunda, who was the convent's walking encyclopedia—very well read and gifted at writing, as kind and innocent as could be, the director of all their special performances, lady-in-waiting for the Virgin and all the saints who needed attendance, dearly beloved by the Filomenas and more so by the Josefinas, and so naive that she believed everything she was told (especially if it was good), as if it were the Gospel truth. Let it suffice as praise of this lady's *sancta simplicitas* that she never had anything to accuse herself of in confession, but since she considered it ungracious to come empty-handed to the court of penitence, she racked her brains for something that might at least be tinged with evil, and she combed her conscience for what were, in fact, such insubstantial sins that the chaplain couldn't help but secretly chuckle at her naiveté. Since poor old Don León Pintado made his living on hearing sins, he listened seriously and pretended to be carefully weighing those superfine sins that no Christian in his right mind would have been able to comprehend. The nun was most punctilious, promising that she wouldn't do it again, and he—the rascal—said, yes, "she had better be careful not to let it happen again," and so on. Such was Sor Facunda, an illustrious lady from the highest aristocracy who had abandoned her wealth and position to take up this life; a tiny woman, not good looking, affable and affectionate, very touched by the girls' fondness of her. She was always followed about during recess by a flock of precociously mystical girls—all inquisitive and pious—whose conduct, words, and enthusiasm indicated that they had an adolescent infatuation with holiness.

It would be hard to pinpoint exactly what happened in the huddle formed by Sor Facunda and her little friends. The fact is that Belén, trembling with emotion, her face anxious, declared to the nun:

"Mauricia has seen the Virgin . . ."

And shortly afterward, the others repeated with ineffable awe:

"She's seen the Virgin!"

Sor Facunda, followed by her convoy, approached Mauricia, at whom she stared for some time in silence. The poor woman was still in the same Moorish position, her head resting on her knees. She seemed to be crying.

"Mauricia," the nun said in a tearful tone with good intentions, which in her were like divine grace. "Just because you have been very bad, don't think that God will refuse to forgive you."

A loud cry sounded, as if from a wild animal, and the inmate raised her grief-stricken face. She uttered a few unintelligible words from which Sor Facunda and company learned nothing. Suddenly she rose. In the moonlight her face had a grandiose beauty that was lost on those present. Her eyes shone with inspiration.

She clasped her breast with both hands, much in the way sculptors have shown some saints, and in moving tones uttered these words:

"Oh, my lady! I'll bring him to you, I'll bring him back . . ."

Breaking into a run, she headed for the stairs and soon disappeared. Sor Facunda spoke to the other nuns. Then, obeying the mother superior's call, everyone gathered and left the orchard, slowly climbing upstairs to their rooms (most of the women went unwillingly, for the heat of the night made the fresh air inviting). Word went around that the visionary had retired.

Fortunata, who had been transferred to Mauricia's dormitory several days earlier, saw that her friend had lain down dressed and barefoot. She approached her and, hearing her deep breathing, thought she was sound asleep. That singular state her friend was in gave her reason to worry; she hoped that Mauricia would soon come around as she had on other occasions. She stayed awake for a long time thinking about this and related things, and around midnight, when peace and quiet reigned throughout the house, she noticed that Mauricia was getting up. She didn't dare say a word or try to stop her for fear of disturbing the peaceful dormitory, which was very faintly lit. Mauricia crossed the room like a shadow and left. Shortly after, Fortunata felt drowsy and began to drop off to sleep; but in that twilight zone between sleeping and waking, she thought she saw her companion come back into the dormitory without a sound, crawl under her bed (where she kept a trunk), and rummage around between the mattress and springs. Then Fortunata lost track of everything because she really did fall asleep.

Mauricia went out to the corridor and, walking to the end of it, sat down on the first stair. "I tell you I will dare . . ."

With whom was she speaking? No one, for she was completely alone. All she had for company in that solitude were the stars, high in the sky.

"What did you say?" she asked, like someone participating in a conversation. "Speak up; I can't hear you with the organ playing. Phh! Now I get it. Don't worry—even if they kill me, I'll bring him back to you. You must know who Mauricia la Dura is—the woman that's not afraid of God. Ha, ha, ha! Tomorrow, when the chaplain comes and those hypocrites go down to the chapel, what a shock they're gonna get!"

Snickering insolently, she rushed downstairs. What the devil was going on in that brain? She went through the little door connecting the courtyard to the long inside corridor and, once inside, went straight into the vestibule, finding her way by feeling the walls, for it was pitch black. She ground her teeth and uttered a few guttural monosyllables that might have signified laughter or anger. Finally she arrived at the door to the chapel and, groping for the lock, she began to scratch the iron. The key wasn't there. "Aw, dammit! Where could the blasted key be?" she muttered contemptuously. She tried to force the lock, then she tried to pick it, but neither attempt got her anywhere. The door to the sacred spot was tightly shut. The miserable woman whimpered like a dog locked out of his house who wants to be let in. After half an hour of futile efforts she collapsed on the threshold and, leaning her head to one side, fell asleep. The sleep she fell into was like instant death. Her head hit the wall like a falling stone, and the crooked posture that her body took when she collapsed suddenly obstructed her respiratory passages, making the air sound like sharp whistling when she inhaled and noisy boiling liquids when she exhaled.

In a profoundly lethargic state, Mauricia did what she had not been able to do awake: she continued the action interrupted by the locked door. Nothing actually happened, but the action was firmly rooted in Mauricia's will. The shrew entered the chapel, not bumping into anything because the lamp on the altar gave off enough light to show her the way. Unwaveringly she headed for the main altar, saying along the way: "I'm not going to hurt you, my little God; I'm just going to take you to your Mamma, who's out there crying for you and waiting for me to get you out of here . . . What is it? Don't you want to go to your Mamma? She's waiting for you, and she's so pretty, and looks so nice, all dressed up in that cloak full of little stars, with her feet up there on the moon. Just wait—you'll see what a nice job I'll do of getting you out of here. 'Cause I love you so, I really do. You know me, don't you? I'm Mauricia la Dura; I'm your friend."

Even though she was walking very fast, it was taking her a long time to get to the altar because the chapel, which was so small, had become very big. There was at least half a league from the door to the altar. And the more she walked, the further it was. Finally she reached it, climbed up the two, three, four stairs, and felt so odd there, seeing the table covered with delicate, snowy-white linen, and seeing it at such close range that for some time it kept her from taking the last step. When she put her hand on the Holy Communion table, she was overtaken by a fit of convulsive laughter. "Who would've said it? Oh my God, oh God; that I . . . hee, hee, hee!" She removed the crucifix from in front of the ciborium door, then stretched out her arm; but since it didn't reach far enough, she stretched it more and more until it hurt her from straining so much. At last, thank God, she was able to open the door touched only by the priest's anointed hands. Lifting the curtain, she fumbled for a moment in that holy, worshiped, mysterious hollow . . . But there was nothing there! She felt this way, then that way, and found nothing. Then she remembered that that wasn't where the monstrance was. It was kept higher up. She climbed onto the altar, put her feet on the Communion table, looked this way, then that way . . . Ah! Finally her fingers touched the metallic base of the monstrance. Oh, but it was cold! So cold it burned. Contact with the metal sent an icy chill down her spine. She hesitated. Should she take it or not? Oh, yes; a hundred time yes; even if she died she had to do this. With exquisite care, but very decisively, she clutched the monstrance and descended a staircase that hadn't been there before. Pride and happiness filled the daring woman's soul as she saw the tangible representation of God in her own hands. Oh, how the gold rays on the glass pane shone! And what mysterious, placid majesty there was in the pure host's being safely behind the glass—white, divine, and somehow seeming like a person, yet it was really only fine bread!

With incredible arrogance Mauricia descended, entirely unaware of any weight. She lifted the monstrance as a priest does, for the faithful to adore it. "See how I've dared," she thought. "Didn't you say it couldn't be done? Well, it could and it was!" She continued on her way out of the chapel. The most pure host was faceless, yet it looked out as if it had eyes. And the sacrilegious woman, approaching the place under the chair, began to be afraid of that look. "No; I'm not letting you go. You're not going back there. Home to Mamma, all right? Baby's not crying 'cause he wants his mother, is he, now?" Saying this, she dared to take the holy form to her bosom as if it were a baby. And then she noticed that the holy form not only had profound eyes as luminous as the sky, but also a voice, a voice that echoed pitifully in her ears. The material quality of the monstrance had completely vanished; all that remained were the essentials: the representation, the pure symbol; and these are what Mauricia pressed furiously to her breast. "Girl," the voice said, "don't take me. Put me back where I was. Don't do anything crazy. If you let me go, I'll forgive your sins, which you have so many of that they can't be counted; but if you persist in trying to take me away from here, you'll be condemned. Let me go and don't worry—I won't say a word to Don León or the nuns. They won't scold you. Mauricia, what are you doing, woman? Are you eating me?"

And that was all. What raving madness! No matter how absurd something is, there's always room for it in the bottomless pit of the human mind.

10

Early the next morning, the mother superior and Sor Facunda ran into each other as they were leaving their respective cells.

"Believe me," said Sor Facunda, "there's something extraordinary about it. I'm going to consult with Don León. Mauricia's case ought to be examined with great care."

Sor Natividad, who was very knowing and accustomed to her companion's puerile enthusiasm, merely smiled kindly. She felt like saying, "How silly of you, Sor Facunda." But she said nothing and, taking out a bunch of keys, headed for the wardrobe.

"Where is that crazy woman?" she later asked.

"She hasn't been seen anywhere," said Fortunata, who at Sor Marcela's orders had come down to search for her friend. "She's not upstairs."

There was great activity in the Filomenas' dormitories. They were all washing their hands and faces, fighting over the water and quibbling over whose towel was whose. "No; this water's mine!" Another took a crust of stale bread from under the bed and started to eat it. "Am I ever hungry! When it's this hot, you really sweat; you can hardly breathe. And to have to wear a wimple!"

Sor Antonia came in, silenced them, and hurried them up. The chapel bell was ringing. The sexton had stuck his head out the gate between the sacristy and the vestibule several times by now and said: "Don León isn't here yet." Then, "Here he is." Then, "He's getting dressed now." The whole community could be heard on the second floor, heading for the chapel to attend morning Mass. The Josefinas led the way sleepily, still yawning and bumping into one another. Next came the Filomenas in a rather orderly fashion, the most diligent prodding the lazier ones. Whenever there are a lot of women around, schoolgirlish whispering is inevitable and ignores the most severe discipline. Amid joking and laughing could be heard: "Did you hear about Mauricia? Last night she saw the Virgin face to face." "Oh, come off it." "Word of honor. Ask Belén." "Bah, you can't give us that." "The Virgin?" "Sure; it was probably Our Lady of Whiskey."

Sor Facunda and her entourage went downstairs saying that it might be false, but then again it might not be; the fact that Mauricia sinned a lot meant nothing, because God had worked his wonders on women far more perverse than she was.

Mass was said by Don León, who was an expert at polishing them off in no time. He had been a priest for the troops, and the nuns never completely approved of their chaplain's martial briskness. Later on, Mass was given by Don Hildebrando, one of those French abbots and the opposite of Pintado; his Masses were unbelievably long.

As the community was leaving the chapel, Doña Manolita (who had been among the last to rush in) approached the mother superior and told her that Mauricia was in the orchard on the manure pile.

"Humph . . . with the filth," replied Sor Natividad, frowning. "Just where she belongs."

The inmates went down to the refectory for hot chocolate and a slice of bread. A worldly gaiety dominated the frugal breakfast tables, and even though the nuns tried to create an austere atmosphere, they could not.

"This plate's mine." "Give me my napkin." "I tell you it's mine!" "Jesus, is this bread *hard*!" "This piece is left over from San Isidro's wedding for sure!"

"Quiet!"

Some had voracious appetites and would have eaten three times as much if it had been offered.

Immediately after breakfast the troop of women was divided like soldiers being sent off to their respective regiments. Some down to the kitchen, others up to the classroom and sewing room, and yet others, taking off their wimples and putting on their work clothes, set about cleaning house.

The mother superior was talking with Sor Antonia in the doorway of a cell when an inmate rushed up, exclaiming:

"I told her to come and she wouldn't. She wanted to hit me. If I hadn't run away . . . ! Then she picked up some of that scum and threw it at me. Look!"

The inmate showed the nuns her manure-stained shoulder.

"I'll have to see to this. Oh, what a woman! The trouble she gives us!" said the mother superior. "Where's Sor Marcela? Tell her to bring the key to the dungeon. Today we're in for it. She's loonier than ever. May God give us patience."

"And Sor Facunda just told me," said Sor Antonia, laughing candidly and squinting her eyes more narrowly, "that Mauricia has seen the Virgin!"

The mother superior responded to the laugh with a less candid one. Three or four of the most mannish Filomenas went down to the orchard with the express order to capture the visionary.

"Poor woman! She goes completely off her rocker!" remarked Sor Natividad to the circle of nuns forming. "A nervous disorder, that's what it is."

And as she said this, her eyes met Sor Facunda's; the latter was approaching the group with a terribly afflicted expression on her face.

"Haven't you discussed this case with the chaplain yet?" she asked.

"Yes," replied Sor Natividad in a slightly amused tone. "And the chaplain said to put her in the doghouse."

"Lock her up because she's crying!" exclaimed the other woman who, being shy, did not dare to contradict the mother superior. "The case deserved to be examined."

"Just to stay on the safe side," stated the northern nun, "we'll inform the doctor too."

"What does the doctor have to do with it? Oh, I don't know, though. You're the one who's in charge. It seems to me . . . that her nerves might have caused it. But what if it was something else? If Mauricia actually did—I'm not saying she did, but I wouldn't dare deny it, either. That constant crying—what could it have been except repentance? Who knows what paths the Lord takes . . ."

And she retired to her cell. She very nearly ran headlong into Sor Marcela, who was on her way to the circle of nuns, lurching along and thumping with her wooden foot. Her face, distorted by anger, was uglier than ever; she was in such a rush she could hardly catch her breath, and her first few sentences came out shredded by anger:

"Oh yes, we know all about it! Great God above, what a faker she is! Who would have thought . . . Oh my God, it's enough to drive you mad!"

She exchanged a few words very quietly with the mother superior, whose visible reaction was a formidable face.

"I . . . you know very well," stammered Sor Marcela. "I had it for my weak stomach, the best cognac."

"That cursed woman! But, how . . . ? This is—Oh my God, I'm horrified! When?"

"Very simple. The day before yesterday, when she was in my cell moving things around to catch the mouse."

Before the mother superior could prevent it, a slight smile crossed her lips. But she immediately put on a poker face again. And the dwarfish nun hurried over to the inmates and repeated to Fortunata what she had told Sor Natividad without making any effort to control her anger.

"Have you ever heard of such an awful thing? What about it? We're all horrified."

Fortunata said nothing; her face grew very stern. Perhaps the nun's declaration didn't surprise her. Obeying Sor Marcela, she went up to the dormitory for proof of the nefarious crime attributed to her friend.

"So you see," the mother superior said to those nearest her, "the kind of vision that brazen woman saw . . . Humph! I wonder what she *didn't* see! And she *still* isn't back? I swear she won't pull another one of these on us. She has to be told what's what."

The lame nun joined the circle again, this time holding the enormous key to the dungeon. She wielded it like a pistol, with homicidally threatening eyes. She was really furious, and when her hard foot thudded against the floor, it sounded exceptionally violent and resonant. Meanwhile, Fortunata arrived with a bottle, which Sor Marcela snatched from her.

"Empty, completely empty!" she exclaimed, holding it up to the light. "And it was almost full; I had just—"

Then she put her snub nose to the open bottle, intoning piteously:

"All she left is the smell! The big cheat. Huh! Come ask me for a drink *now*."

The body of the crime passed from Sor Marcela's nose to Sor Natividad's nose, whence it passed to all the other nearby noses, and the whiff of its aroma embittered the comments made on the crime.

"How disgusting! She certainly had her fill, didn't she?" exclaimed the mother superior. "Oh, what a state she must be in now, with all that burning liquid in her! Nothing like this has ever happened here. We'll fix her, we'll fix her all right. But what's keeping her?"

She was on the verge of going downstairs, resolved to delay no longer the act of justice, when a great commotion broke out. The three sturdy women who had gone to fetch the delinquent came running out of the orchard into the courtyard through the little green door, fleeing in fear and screaming in panic. A loud report, of a stone hitting the door, was heard.

"She'll kill us, she'll kill us!" cried the three, gathering up their skirts in order to hasten their escape upstairs. The nuns peered over the banister in the corridor where it bordered the courtyard and they saw Mauricia, barefoot, hair wild, glazed eyes burning—all the marks, in short, of a madwoman. The mother superior, who had quite a temper of her own, could not contain herself and from up above shouted:

"Rebel! Wretch! If you don't behave, you'll see what's coming to you!"

"We'll call in the police, we will!" a few nuns chimed in.

"No, wait. I can handle this myself," said the mother superior, boasting that she was the one for this. "She won't try anything on *me*."

Mauricia leaped up to the corner of the corridor where the nuns were, and staring at them insolently she stuck out her tongue and made uncouth faces and obscene gestures.

"Sluts!" she screamed. And bending over quickly, she gathered stones and pieces of brick from the ground and began to throw them with as much vigor as aim. Other nuns and inmates, hearing the racket, rushed out in hordes to the first and second floor corridors and broke out in loud cries. It looked as if the world was coming to an end. God, what pandemonium! The wild woman met their screaming with her howling.

Some of them ducked behind the banister when a rock came flying; others peered out for a second and hid again. More and more projectiles were coming in, and with them, more outcries from the fiendish woman. She looked like an Amazon. One of her breasts was half-exposed, the bodice of her dress was tattered, and her loose hair whipped across her face as she threw back her right shoulder to hurl something. She looked hideous to the nuns; but the strict truth is that she was beautiful and looked more arrogant, handsome, and Napoleonic than ever.

Sor Marcela valiantly attempted to make it downstairs, but three steps down she got scared and hurried back up. Her Philippine face had turned the color of English mustard.

"You just wait—if I come down, you infamous devil!" was her warcry. But she did not go down.

Behind the sacristy grate that opens into the courtyard there appeared the face of the sexton, and shortly thereafter, that of Don León Pintado. Two nuns on duty at the main entrance also peered at the event from another low window. But no sooner did Mauricia see them than she started to hurl rocks at them too, so they had to retreat. Being frightened, the poor things wanted to call for help. At that moment, someone rang the bell at the main door, and a few seconds later a lady visitor entered, went to the receiving room, and, informing herself of what was going on, peered out of the low window. It was Guillermina Pacheco, who crossed herself when she saw the tragedy that was unfolding.

"In the name of . . . ! You! Mauricia! What's the meaning—? What are you doing? Are you mad?"

The nuns watching the door couldn't restrain her; Guillermina went straight out into the courtyard through the vestibule door.

"Guillermina!" cried Sor Natividad from above. "Don't come out. Be careful, she's wild. Some gem you brought us! Go back, for heaven's sake; she's crazy and doesn't know what . . . Please go find a pair of policemen."

"A pair of policemen?" remonstrated Guillermina. "Mauricia! How do you dare—"

Before she could finish the question, a rock grazed her face. If it had hit her squarely, it would have bashed in her head.

"Good Lord! . . . But no, it's nothing."

And putting her hand on the wounded place, she shrieked:

"You wretch! Throwing things at *me!*"

Mauricia laughed wickedly.

"At you, yes, and the whole human race!" she shouted in a voice so hoarse it was scarcely intelligible. "You sugary old witch . . . Get outta here—fast!"

The horrified nuns threw up their arms; some were crying. Meanwhile, Don León had—with no small effort—forced open the sacristy grate and lunged into the courtyard (the only way to the convent) and, flinging himself on Mauricia, restrained her by the arms.

"Let go of me, León, you dames' chaplain!" bellowed the visionary.

But Pintado had hands of iron (although not much courage), and once he had darted into his heroic act he not only managed to hold down Mauricia, he also gave her a couple of loud slaps. It was a repugnant scene. The acolyte had come out on the chaplain's heels, and while the two of them were coping with la Dura, the nuns, seeing the enemy subdued, risked coming down and hastened over to Guillermina, who was stopping the flow of blood from her slight wound. With a certain tranquility, and more smilingly than angrily, the foundress said to her friends:

"Things certainly take a strange course! I came to ask you for some left-over bricks and debris, and look how soon I got what I wanted. Oh, well . . . Put her out in the street and let her go to the fifth floor of hell—that's where she belongs."

"This very minute. Don León—don't mistreat her," said the mother superior.

"You sissy! I hope you get stabbed to death!" stormed Mauricia, who had very little strength left by now and had fallen to the ground. "A priest hitting a . . . lady!"

"Have her clothes brought down," cried Sor Natividad. "Hurry, now. I can hardly believe she's leaving."

Mauricia no longer defended herself. Her savage strength had waned, but her face still looked ferocious and showed signs of derangement.

Then a pair of boots and a cloak were thrown down from the second floor corridor.

"Bring them down, children," said the mother superior from the courtyard, her composure regained now. Fortunata brought down a bundle of clothes and, picking up the boots, she gave everything to Mauricia; that is, she put the bundle down in front of her. The dreadful scene had made a disagreeable impression on the young woman, who felt deep compassion for her friend. If the nuns had permitted it, she might have calmed the beast.

"Here are your clothes and your boots," she said in a soft, quiet voice. "Oh, what a state you're in! Don't you see now that you were upset?"

"Get outta my way, you slut! Outta the way or I'll—"

"Leave her alone," said the mother superior. "Don't say another word to her. To the street with her, period."

With great difficulty, Mauricia rose from the ground and picked up her clothes. When she stood up, she seemed to recover some of her fury.

"You're forgetting your bundle."

"The boots, the boots."

The wild woman gathered it all up. She was already on her way out when Guillermina looked at her severely.

"What a woman! She doesn't even know how to leave decently."

She was barefoot, holding her boots by the straps.

"Put on your boots," ordered the mother superior.

"I don't feel like it. So long. You're all a bunch of stinkin' hypocrites!"

"Patience, sisters, patience. We need a lot of patience," Sor Natividad said to her companions, covering her ears.

The doors swung wide open. Some frightened souls used them as shields, just as when the doors of the bullring are flung open for the wild beast to charge in, some people take cover. The last to speak with her was Fortunata, who, following her into the vestibule and moved by pity and friendship, wanted to extract some sort of declaration of repentance. But Mauricia was deaf to her friend's entreaty; she was out of her mind, and pushed her friend away so roughly that if Fortunata hadn't leaned against the wall, she would have been knocked down.

The madwoman left triumphantly, casting haughty, scornful looks in all directions. When she saw the street, her eyes lit up with joy and she cried, "Oh, my ever-lovin' street!" She stretched luxuriantly and then clasped her arms as if she were trying to embrace all that her eyes could see. Then she breathed heavily; she stopped and looked around confusedly, like a bull that has just entered the ring.

Then, getting her bearings, she thrust forth downhill. It was a sight worth seeing—that barefoot woman, bold and wild-haired, her eyes agleam with savagery, a bundle under her arm, boots dangling by their straps from her hand. The few people passing by looked at her in awe. When she reached the city's warehouses, she passed several boys, street sweepers who were sitting on their carts, brooms in hand. They took her for a nobody, and they burst out laughing in her Napoleonic face.

"Hey—you've really hung one on. *Olé!*"

And turning arrogantly to them, she raised her free arm and said:

"Apostles of error!"

She broke into stupid laughter and went on her way. Finding the "apostles" bit very amusing, the sweepers put their brooms into their carts and trailed Mauricia, pushing their carts and looking like a ludicrous artillery squad, making an infernal racket and firing gross insults at her.

VII. The Wedding and the Honeymoon

I

AT LAST IT WAS AGREED THAT Fortunata would leave the convent to be married toward the end of September. The date was very near now, and although the inmate did not really know yet what to expect from her new life, she had no doubt but that her decision to get married was good for her; she realized that one should not aspire to the best, but be contented with the attainable good that fate wisely assigns us. On his last visits, Maxi talked of nothing but her imminent good fortune. One day he told Fortunata that he had already picked out their home—a lovely apartment on Sagunto Street near his aunt's. Another day he entertained her with the juicy details of his arrangements for their move. They had already bought most of the furniture. Doña Lupe, who was unbeatable at this game, had checked daily on the private sales advertised in *La Correspondencia,* and she had acquired bargain after bargain. The double bed was the only item that had been bought in a shop, but Doña Lupe had gotten it for such a good price that it too had been a real bargain. And they not only had a home and furniture, they had a maid as well. Torquemada had recommended one who could do anything and cooked very well besides; a middle-aged woman, serious, clean, and dependable. It could well be said of her that she was a bargain too, for service in Madrid was a problem, and no small one either. Her name was Patricia, but Torquemada called her Patria because he was so thrifty that he even saved letters from words, and was very fond of abbreviations because they saved him saliva when he talked and ink when he wrote.

Another afternoon Maxi had a beautiful surprise for her. When Fortunata entered the convent, the pawn notes for her jewelry and dress clothes had passed into his hands, and he had vowed to get them out of hock as soon as he had the means. Well, now he was able to tell his beloved with ineffable pleasure that when she entered their new home she would discover the garments and jewels she had been forced to cast overboard the day of her shipwreck. Incidentally, the jewelry greatly appealed to Doña Lupe for its value and elegance. She also remarked that if it were altered here and there, the velveteen coat would be a splendid piece. This led him quite naturally to discuss the inheritance. He had already received his share, and with the little cash that came with it had redeemed the clothes. He already owned real estate, which was worth more than cash. And on the subject of the inheritance, he added, his eldest brother and Doña Lupe had had loud, bitter disagreements. Juan Pablo had used his full share to pay off numerous debts and the balance of what he still owed to the Carlist administration. Since his share wasn't enough for all this, he had had the gall to ask Doña Lupe to lend him a sum, and when she heard the request she flew off the handle. In short, they had had a big spat and were no longer on speaking terms, and Juan Pablo had gone off to live with his mistress. Long live morality! And look at our traditionalist now!

Another day they chatted about the apartment, which was lovely and had a fine view. You could see a tiny corner of the reservoir from the parlor balcony. It had new wallpaper, a stuccoed bedroom, was on a quiet street without too many neighbors (two units per floor), and there were only two floors. Besides these many advantages, everything was nearby: a place to buy coal downstairs, the meat market just a few steps away, and on the next corner a grocery store.

Meanwhile, they couldn't forget the important matter of *Rubinius vulgaris'* career. In mid-September he took his final exams, and he planned to take his degree as soon as possible. Then he would work as a pharmacologist's assistant to Samaniego, who was seriously ill; if the latter died, his widow would have to turn the pharmacy over to two pharmacists. In time, Maximiliano would become the senior pharmacist and eventually the owner of the establishment. In a word, things were going smoothly and the future smiled on them.

These facts gave Fortunata happiness and hope, increasing her newly born sense of peace, order, and domestic regularity. And common sense helped to nudge her along in that direction, making her glad to have a home, a name, and respectability.

Two days before leaving, she confessed with Father Pintado. It was a lengthy expurgation, an overall review of her conscience from way back. It was like a final exam for a degree, and the chaplain handled her case with great care and attentiveness. The realms that the penitent woman's sincerity could not reach were explored by the probing questions of her confessor. He was an old hand at it. Since there was nothing prudish about him, the confession ended up as a conversation between friends. He gave her healthy, practical advice; he used obvious and sometimes funny examples to convince her that one is lost if one gives in to the senses, and he painted the advantages of a controlled, modest life oblivious to the vain excesses and chaos of carnal appetites. Descending from these spiritual heights to the terrain of utilitarian philosophy, Don León pointed out to the penitent that it is always advantageous to behave well; that eventually, evil, even though accompanied with brilliant triumphs, ends up penalizing one in this life, not to mention the inevitable penalties awaiting us in our afterlife. "Realize too," he said, "that you're a new woman; that you've died and have been reborn to another world. If some day you happen to run into the people who dragged you into the gutter in your past life, consider them ghosts, shadows, and nothing more, and don't even look at them." Last of all, he recommended that she pray to the Blessed Virgin as a healthful spiritual exercise and a way of predisposing herself to good deeds. The penitent emerged very contented, and when she went to Communion, observed herself with a totally new tranquility.

Her farewells to the nuns were heartfelt. Fortunata burst into tears. Her friends Belén and Felisa kissed her good-bye, gave her holy stamps and medals, and assured her that they would remember her in their prayers. Doña Manolita was envious and dejected. She, too, would be leaving—she was only there because of an error; things would soon be cleared up; her ass of a husband would soon come and beg her forgiveness and get her out of there. Sor Marcela, Sor Antonia, the mother superior, and the other nuns were most affable, declaring that she was one of the inmates who had caused them the least trouble. They were visibly sorry to see her go, but they gave her best wishes for her wedding and congratulated her on the fine conclusion of her stay there.

Maximiliano and Doña Lupe, who had been waiting for her in the reception room, gathered up her things and led her out to a rented carriage. It had been arranged previously that she would be taken to her fiancé's house, which was truly a bit odd, but as she had no relatives in Madrid (that they knew of, anyway), Doña Lupe could find no better solution to the problem of her lodging. The wedding was to be held on the first Monday in October, two days after she left the Micaelas.

Señora de Jáuregui was experiencing that ineffable joy of the eminent sculptor who has been given a block of wax and told to model it as best as he can. Her educational talent now had soft material to work with. In her hands, a savage "in the full sense of the word" would become a lady modeled on her own image and likeness. She would have to teach her everything: manners, language, conduct. The poorer the student's previous education, the greater the teacher's delight in her plan. That very day, as they were having lunch, she had the first occasion (which she secretly relished but reacted to with a dignified face) to apply her teachings.

"Not *shrimps*, dear; *shrimp*. You must get used to speaking the language as God intended."

Doña Lupe wanted Fortunata to recognize *her* as the director of her moral and social acts, so she displayed from the start a severity tinged with tolerance like that found in teachers who perform their duties perfectly.

Fortunata was assigned a room next to the Señora's, a room that the latter used for storage. There was so much bric-a-brac that the newcomer could hardly move around in it. But anything would do for a couple of days. During this period, the young woman felt very inhibited in the presence of her aunt-to-be, for Doña Lupe never stepped down from the podium or relented in her corrections; when Fortunata opened her mouth, the other woman almost always made some comment on her pronunciation or behavior, and always in an authoritarian tone, although with a studied gentleness.

"The convents," she said, "correct many faults, but they also make their residents become too shy. Be more open, and when you greet visitors, do it easily. Don't get all choked up."

These things put Fortunata in a bad mood and made her even shyer.

She reminded herself that when she got into her own house she would be freed from this annoying tutelage. She would be diplomatic though, because Doña Lupe struck her as a particularly useful woman who knew a lot and gave some very sound advice.

Visitors annoyed Fortunata. She had the feeling that they came only out of curiosity. Doña Silvia, for one, hadn't been able to resist her curiosity; she appeared on the very same day the fiancée left the convent. The next day brought Paquita Morejón, Don Basilio Andrés de la Caña's wife; Fortunata found both ladies impertinent and nosy. Their refinement seemed affected, as if they were common but determined not to appear that way.

The visitors gave her best wishes for her wedding. You could almost read their thoughts in their eyes, though: "Some bargain you got!" Don Basilio's wife repeated her visit the second day. Being pretentious, she was wearing poorly pieced together silk remnants. She was cloyingly sweet, overly familiar, and praised Fortunata's beauty so as to hint at the fiancée's moral deficiencies.

Another notable visit was Juan Pablo's; Nicolás brought him. Doña Lupe and the eldest Rubín had not been on speaking terms since the squabble over the inheritance. To the fiancée's great surprise, he was affectionate toward her. One would have thought he was trying to make his aunt mad by conceding his benevolence to the very person whom she had criticized so strongly. During his visit (which was not short) Fortunata sat perched on the edge of the chair like a stick, somewhat dazed and at a loss for words with this man who was so articulate. As he was leaving, Juan Pablo clasped her hand warmly and said that he would come to their wedding.

Then aunt and niece went to see the couple's new home. Doña Lupe showed her the furniture piece by piece, pointing out how good it was and how the arrangement (hers, incidentally) couldn't be better. Decisions on every detail had already been made by Doña Lupe, so that all that was left for the other woman to say was "Yes, yes . . . that's true."

Late in the afternoon, on their way back to Raimundo Lulio Street, they busied themselves with planning the next day's activities. Maximiliano had left to invite some friends out and Doña Lupe left too, saying that she would return before nightfall. Fortunata was alone, and set herself the task of making a few minor alterations on the black twill silk dress that she was to wear for the ceremony. All she had for company was Papitos, who abandoned the kitchen so as to be near the Señorita, whose beauty she admired greatly. Her hair style was what stupified the girl the most—she would have given one of her fingers just to be able to copy it. She sat at Fortunata's side and didn't tire of contemplating her, overcome with joy when the Señorita asked for assistance, even if it was only for a minor detail. Someone rang the front doorbell. Papitos ran to open the door. Fortunata was dumbfounded. It was Mauricia la Dura.

2

The emotions which that woman had aroused in her at the Micaelas—that inexplicable medley of terror and attraction—were suddenly reborn with new force. Mauricia inspired fear, yet at the same time an irresistible, mysterious liking; she somehow stirred up ideas that were at once reprehensible and pleasing to Fortunata's heart. Mauricia looked at her friend in silence as if to say: "What you least expected was to see me here now."

"Is it really you?"

She noticed that Mauricia was wearing some very pretty yellow shoes tied with blue laces that ended in berry-shaped tassels.

"Hmm—some shoes!"

"Whaddya 'spect?"

Then she looked at her face. It was very pale; her eyes looked larger and more treacherous and seemed to be lying in ambush in their deep violet hollows under those straight black brows. The nose looked like ivory; the mouth seemed more emphatic than ever, and the two creases marking its limits, more energetic. Her whole face exuded melancholy and a certain pensive air, or at least Fortunata thought so, although she couldn't say why. Mauricia was wearing a new cloak, a turquoise and red striped silk scarf, a checked apron, and a plaid skirt, and in her hand was something bulky tied up with the four corners of a handkerchief.

"Isn't Doña Lupe in?" she asked, sitting down with no further ceremony.

"I already told you, no," Papitos replied, scowling at her.

"Nobody asked you, you nosy little brat. Go back to your kitchen and leave us alone."

Papitos left grumblingly.

"What are you doing around here?" asked Fortunata, who from the moment she had seen Mauricia felt butterflies in her stomach.

"Nothing much. I'm peddling again, and I've got some cloaks to show that sweet-talking old bitch."

"What language! Watch your tongue. Have you already forgotten about what you did at the convent? What a scandal! I was very sorry for your sake. It even made me get sick that day."

"Kid, don't remind me of it . . . I really was upset. But everybody gives in to a temptation. Did I come out with lots of awful beauts? I don't remember. I wasn't in my right mind—didn't know what I was doin'. All I remember is that I saw the Pure and Holy One, and then I wanted to get into the church and take the Holy Ghost . . . I dreamt I ate it . . . I've never had a worse one, kid. The things you think of when the devil gets into your head! Believe you me, and I *know* what I'm talkin' about: when I got calmed down again, I was sick to my stomach about it. The only one I still had a grudge against was that chaplain character. I could've devoured him. Not the ladies. I felt like goin' and apologizin', but I got my 'dinnity,' and it kept me from goin' back. What really bothered me was that I'd thrown that big brick at Doña Guillermina. I can't forgive myself for that; nope, I just can't . . . And I'm so scared of her now that when I see her come down the street, I get beet red and I cross over so she won't see me. She told my sister she forgives me, you know, and she still wants to help me out."

"You're terrible," said Fortunata. "If you don't stop that habit, you're going to end up in a really bad way . . ."

"You don't have to tell me; ever since I left the Macaelas I haven't touched a drop of the stuff. You might say I'm like a new woman. I don't want to live with my sister 'cause me and Juan Antonio don't get along so good; but there's not a decent person that can outdo me now. And you can count on it, 'cause I say so: I'll never take another drop in my life. You'll see, just wait. Well, to move on to somethin' else: I hear you're gettin' married tomorrow."

"How did you find out?"

"Hmmm . . . Everything gets said," la Dura replied maliciously. "Well, so you won the grand prize. I'm glad, 'cause I really like you."

As she said this, she bent over abruptly and picked up a small object from the floor. It was a button.

"A good omen. Look," she said, showing it to Fortunata, "a sign that you're gonna be lucky."

"Don't believe in that witchcraft."

"You don't believe in it? You act like you're dumb. When you find a button, it means that somethin's gonna happen to you. If it's a button like this—white with four holes—it's a good sign; but if it's black, and it has three, it's bad business."

"That's absurd."

"Gospel truth, kid. I've tried it loads of times. You're in for somethin' big. Know what?"

She said these last words so purposefully that Fortunata, whose anxiety was for some unknown reason growing, sensed that there was something terribly serious and confidential behind that "Know what?".

"What?"

"You're gettin' warm."

"What do you mean, I'm getting warm?"

"Just that: you're gettin' warm. You like things to be clear, right? Well, here goes. He came back from Valencia all well and he's dyin' to see you. Just like I told you, kid: the minute he found out you were at the Micaelas bein' such a Catholic and all he started to get the hots for you and he'd go past there every afternoon in his carriage. Men are like that; they scorn what they've got, but when they see somethin' under lock and key—now *that* takes their fancy."

"Stop it, stop it!" said Fortunata, trying to seem serene. "Don't try to hand that to me."

"You'll see for youself."

"What do you mean, I'll see for myself? The things you come up with!"

Mauricia burst out laughing in that forthright way of hers that struck her friend as beautiful, tempting, devilish. That satanic laughter framed these words, which made Fortunata's hair stand on end:

"Should I tell you? . . . Should I, huh?"

"Tell me *what?*"

They looked at each other. From their purplish hollows, Mauricia's pupils stared out ferociously, like those of a bird of prey.

"Should I tell you? Well, he knows how to go out and get what he wants. He's a smart one—fast. He's set a trap for you and you're gonna fall right in it. You've already put your foot in."

"Me?"

"Yes, you. He's rented the apartment next to the one you're gonna have; yours is on the right."

"Bah! Don't say such foolish things," replied Fortunata, trying to seem unperturbed.

The black twill skirt she was altering slipped from her knees to the floor.

"You heard right, kid. There he is. From the minute you go through the door to your place, you'll be hearin' him breathe."

"Stop it, stop it! I don't want to listen to you."

"I oughta know what I'm talkin' about. Get this: just a half hour ago I was talkin' to him at a friend's house. If you don't fall into his trap, I think the poor guy's gonna crack up, he's so wild about you."

"Next door . . . On the left as we go in; mine on this side, so . . . Don't drive me crazy."

"A woman by the name of Cirila has rented it for him. You don't know her; I do. She's been a jewelry peddler, and she had a boarding house. She's married to a plainclothesman, and now your friend has set her up workin' for the railroad."

Fortunata felt congested. Her head burned.

"Oh, go on—that's a pack of lies. You think I'm going to fall for that? He doesn't even remember me! Or have to."

"You'll see for yourself. Oh, what a boy! It'd break your heart to see 'im, so wild about you and so sorry for the bad deal he gave you. If he could fix it up, he would—believe me."

In the midst of this, Papitos appeared with the excuse that she wanted to ask the Señorita something, but actually it was to stick her nose in things. No sooner did Mauricia see her than she reproached her in the most despotic manner.

"Look, kid, if you don't beat it, you just wait—"

She threatened her with a movement of her arm, but the little monkey stood her ground, screaming:

"I don't feel like it. What do you care, anyhow?"

Fortunata said:

"Go to the kitchen, Papitos." And the girl obeyed, although very sulkily.

"Well, I . . . ," proceeded Fortunata. "If it's true, I'll tell my husband to take another apartment."

"You'd have to tell him the reason."

"I'll tell him. So there."

"Nice scandal you'd make. And anyway, they'll set a trap anywhere you go, and snap! You'd be in the same fix."

"Well, then, I won't get married," said the bride-to-be, totally confused.

"Nah! No matter how stupid you are, you won't do that. Do you think things like this fall in your lap every day? Forget it. Once you're a nice little married lady you can do as you please—and keep the fringe benefits that go with 'properness.' A single woman's a slave; she can't even go where she wants. The ones that get themselves an excuse for a husband have carte blanche for everything."

Fortunata kept silent, looking vaguely at the floor, her chin resting on her hand.

"What're you lookin' at?" asked la Dura, bending over. "Ah! another button. And this one's black with three holes. A bad sign, kid. It means that if you don't get married you deserve to be beaten."

Picking up the button, she looked at it closely. It was getting dark, and the room was too. Soon, all Fortunata could see was her friend's silhouette and the yellow shoes. She was beginning to be frightened of her, yet she didn't want her to leave; she wanted her to talk on and on, on the same fearful subject.

"I tell you I won't get married," the young woman repeated, her horror of marrying the Rubín boy reawakening in her soul.

And the ideas that had been so laboriously constructed at the Micaelas suddenly lost ground. That frail altar built by meditation and rational gymnastics was beginning to crack, as if the ground underneath had begun to give way.

"The one on the left . . . So it's like being sold. One door here, the other one there."

"Like I say, one paw in the trap; all you have to do is put in the other."

And she burst out laughing again with the insolent frankness that pleased Fortunata, strange to say, and aroused her instincts to be deliciously perverse.

"I just won't get married; I won't—so there!" declared the bride, rising and pacing up and down as if hoping to gain the energy she lacked.

"If you say that once more . . . ," added Mauricia with a mock threat. "Do you think there are bargains like these around every corner? No, kid, you've gotta get married. Others would like to be in your shoes. And for the last time: get married, kid, and try not to fall in the trap. Go ahead and lead a clean life. Remember, we started out bein' nothin'. Listen to what I tell you, 'cause it's straight outta the Gospel, it's the Gospel truth."

Fortunata paused in front of her friend, who forced her to sit down beside her again.

"You're gettin' married, and that's that. 'Cause it's your salvation. If you don't, you'll go from one man to the next till the end of time. Don't be stupid; if you want to be decent, be it, kid. Don't worry, nobody's gonna pull a knife on you to make you sin."

"Yes, that's right," said Fortunata, her spirits rising. "What do I care about the trap? Unless I want to fall into it . . ."

"Sure. With him right beside you . . . To heck with him! What do you care? Say 'I'm decent,' and nobody can lay a hand on you. A couple of days after movin' in, tell your husband you don't like the house and move out."

"Yes. We'll take another house, and that'll be the end of the trap," declared the bride, taking her friend's advice seriously.

"It's true that that won't stop him, and he'll stay on your tail no matter where you go. Believe me, he's nuts about you. And I'll tell you somethin' else: your maid, that Patricia—the one Torquemada recommended to Doña Lupe—she's workin' for him."

"Working for him? Oh!" exclaimed Fortunata, her terror renewed. "So that's why I didn't like that woman when I saw her this morning. She kept flattering me and being too nice. Ugh, she was a real snake in the grass. Well, I'll just tell my husband I don't like her and I'll fire her tomorrow."

"Sure. And hurray for having a firm hand. Now listen to me: if you want to be decent, go ahead and be decent. But not get married? Don't even think of it!"

Fortunata seemed to be relieved by this exhortation from her friend, for it was expressed with affectionate sisterliness.

"Something else has occurred to me," she added with the joy of a drowning man who sees a board drifting his way. "I'll tell my husband I'm sick and to take me to live in that small town where he got the inheritance from."

"A town! What're you gonna do in a *town?*" objected Mauricia disconsolately, like a mother concerned about her daughter's future. "Now listen—and you'd better believe it, 'cause *I'm* tellin' you—it's a lot harder to be decent in a small town than in these big cities where there's lots of people; 'cause you get bored in a town, and since there's only two or three men with good manners and you see 'em all the time—heck! you end up likin' one of 'em. I know what it's like in a small town. It turns out it's the mayor, and if it's not the mayor it's the doctor, or it's the judge—if there is one—that appeals to you, and I hate to tell you what happens. Or you get so bored you get touched in the head and fall for the priest."

"Stop it! How awful!"

"Well, don't consider leavin' Madrid, kid," she added, taking Fortunata by the arm and making her sit on her lap. "Who cares about ya? *I* do. Whatever I tell you is for your own good. Let yourself go. Get married, and if there's a trap, well, there's a trap. What oughta happen happens. Let yourself go, and listen to me, 'cause I've gotten fond of you and I talk to you like I was your mother."

Fortunata was about to reply when the bell rang; it was Doña Lupe. When she came in, she already knew from Papitos who was there.

"Where is that madwoman?" she asked, entering. "Oh, it's so dark! I can't see a thing. Mauricia—"

"Here I am, my lady Doña Lupe. We could use a light."

Fortunata went to look for a lamp; meanwhile, the widow said to her saleswoman:

"What are you doing here? It's been ages! How are you? Have you reformed? Father Pintado told Nicolás horrid things about you."

"Don't pay any attention to him, Señora. Don León's got a good imagination and shoots off his mouth too much. It was just a tantrum I had."

"Some tantrum! And what have you brought?"

Fortunata came in with the lamp, and Mauricia began to show Doña Lupe Manila shawls, a Japanese tapestry, a mesh bedspread, and some chenille.

"Look—just look at these treasures. This shawl belonged to the Señá Marquesa de Tellería. She's givin' it away for beans. Come on, Señora, why don't you make a gift of it to your niece for tomorrow and let it be the start of all their happiness."

"Oh, be off with you! What does she want with a shawl? That's all we needed! How much is it? Fifty *duros*! Ha, ha, ha—what a riot! The ones I have—and they're real Senquás—have lots more flowers than yours, and I sell them for twenty-five."

"I'd like to see them. You know what?—and may I drop dead in this very spot if it's not true—I had an offer for thirty-eight, and I didn't wanna let go of it. I swear it on the cross."

And making a cross with two fingers, she kissed it.

"Fine place you've come to! I'm up to my neck in shawls."

"But I bet they're not like this one."

"They're better, a hundred times better. But I'm glad you came. I'm going to give you some jewelry to sell."

And they went on gabbing until Maximiliano came home, when Doña Lupe ordered the soup served. The bridegroom, gathering that there was a visitor in the living room, approached the door cautiously to see who it was.

"It's Mauricia," said his betrothed, crossing his path.

They went into the dining room and waited there for their aunt to finish with her saleswoman. When the latter got up to leave, Fortunata did not go out to say good-bye for fear that Mauricia would say something embarrassing.

3

Maximiliano told his bride-to-be who the guests would be. Fortunata listened, but it went in one ear and out the other. The young man didn't notice her distraction, for he was in a highly exalted state. As he was so idealistic, he wanted to play the role of fiancé according to all the accepted rules, so even though he found himself alone with her in the dining room, he treated her with the delicacy dictated by the most exquisite respect. He did not even kiss her, preferring to save that for once they were blessed by the Church; nor did he caress her once, enjoying the illusion that he had not yet done so. Fortunata felt drowned in sadness as they ate, and took great pains to disguise it. Her imminent status filled her with such fear and repugnance that she considered escaping, and she said to herself: "They're getting me to the church over my dead body!" Doña Lupe, who relished posturing and imposing social correctness on every action, did not want the engaged couple to be left alone for a minute. This moral fiction was her tribute to morality, proof of the importance we must concede to form in all our actions.

That night was a sleepless one for Fortunata. At times she wept like Mary Magdalene and tried to recollect everything Father Pintado had told her; she sought solace in prayer to the Blessed Virgin. She finally fell asleep while praying and dreamt that the Virgin was marrying her not to Maxi, but to her own true man, the man who was hers in spite of everything. She awoke startled, saying: "This isn't what we decided." In the delirium of her feverish insomnia, she thought that Don León had deceived her and that the Virgin was siding with the enemy. "Well, if this is how it is, I could've saved myself some of those Our Father's and Hail Mary's." The next morning she laughed at such nonsense and her thoughts were calmer. She saw clearly that it was madness not to take the road designated for her; that it was undoubtedly the best. "On with it! Decency, no matter what. I'll protect myself from any traps they set for me."

Doña Lupe left her lazy feathers at five in the morning, when it was still dark, and she dragged Papitos out of bed, pulling her by the ear to get her to light the fire. No small order that day—lunch for twelve! She called Fortunata so that she would start dressing early, and they agreed to let Maxi sleep until the last minute; getting up early didn't agree with him. Doña Lupe gave the bride instructions on what was to be done in the kitchen and went out shopping with Papitos, taking with her the biggest basket in the house.

What Doña Lupe called "tidbits" were excellent: sautéed kidneys, brains, hake or red sea bream (if there was any), veal chops, a London broil . . . The widow paid for it all and Fortunata offered to make a paella. At eight o'clock Doña Lupe was back like a shot, her activity feverish by then. After all, they had to leave for church at ten. "But no, I won't go, because if I do Papitos is sure to botch it up." Luckily, Patricia came by, so Doña Lupe decided to attend the ceremony.

The bride put on her black silk dress, and Doña Lupe insisted on pinning an artificial orange blossom to her bosom. There was some dispute over this, but Don Basilio's wife had brought the corsage and they couldn't offend her. After all, it was the very same corsage that she had worn at her wedding. Fortunata looked ravishing, and Papitos hunted for all sorts of excuses to go into the parlor to admire her, even if only for a moment. "This one sure doesn't have any cotton stuck inside her front," she thought.

The Jáuregui woman wore elaborate glass beads with her short dress cape, and Doña Silvia appeared in a Manila shawl, which rather displeased the widow because it made the wedding look like a small-town affair. Torquemada looked quite dapper; he was wearing a new bowler (his collar was a bit dirty, as usual) and a black threadbare tie with a tie pin displaying a magnificent pearl that had belonged to the marquise of Casa-Bojío. His rattan walking cane and trousers gone baggy at the knees completed the characterization. Being a humorous sort, he had a deck of jokes on the weather. When it was pouring, he'd come in saying: "It's horribly dusty out there." That day it was quite hot and dry, reason enough for my man to shine: "What a blizzard!" Only Doña Silvia and Doña Lupe laughed at these jokes.

Maxi was wearing his new frock coat and top hat for the first time. He felt very awkward in this unfamiliar paraphernalia, and even more so when he saw its shadow, because it looked two or three feet high. Inside the house he felt as if he was touching the ceiling. But as for top hats, the most remarkable one was Don Basilio Andrés de la Caña's; it was at least fourteen styles behind and dated back to when Bravo Murillo had appointed him payroll director. His boots envied his hat's shine. Nicolás Rubín was less unkempt than usual; he regretted that he had not been able to bring Don León. *Ulmus sylvestris, Quercus gigantea,* and *Pseudo-Narcissus odoripherus* all looked very dashing in their frock coats, several of them in brand new gloves; they clustered around the bride, wished her well, and even cracked a few jokes that she was hard pressed to answer. At last Doña Lupe gave the command and they were off to the church.

Fortunata's mouth felt extremely bitter, as if she'd been chewing medicinal bark. Entering the church, she was overcome with horrible fear. She suspected that her enemy was hiding behind a pillar. If she heard steps, she thought they were his. The ceremony took place in the sacristy and was brief. The bride was greatly impressed by the symbols of the Sacrament. And at the same time, she felt a new light within herself, as if she had been shaken, jolted by the dignity entrancing her soul. The idea of becoming a lady fortified her mind, which was leaning like a column about to tip over. Married! Decent, or about to be! She felt changed. These thoughts, originating perhaps in a spasmodic phenomenon, comforted her; but upon leaving the church she was seized by that fear again. What if the enemy should appear! Mauricia had told her that he was stalking her, he was stalking her for sure. The Virgin would aid her. But to think that the Virgin might be on *his* side! Of all things! She could not rid herself of this extravagant notion. How could the Blessed Virgin defend sin? What utter nonsense! But nonsense or not, she could not ban the thought from her mind.

Once she was back home, Doña Lupe was like three women, busily attending to so many and such different things. Now she was quietly advising Fortunata not to be so peevish with Doña Silvia, now she was running to the dining room to set the table, now she was involved with Patricia and Papitos; she seemed to be in the kitchen, the living room, the pantry, and the halls all at once. You would have thought there were three or four Jáuregui widows in the house. Her mind was plagued by the thought that her luncheon might not go well. But if it *did* turn out well—what a triumph! Her heart beat furiously, communicating its feverish heat to the rest of her, and even the cotton ball seemed to be receiving its share of life, throbbing and taking on some of the pain. Finally, everything was ready. Juan Pablo, who had not been at the church but who had joined the wedding party at home, was looking for an excuse to leave. He entered the dining room as the guests were taking their places, and to the sound of their scraping chairs, he announced:

"I'm leaving so as not to make it thirteen."

Some of the guests objected to this superstition; others applauded it. Don Basilio said that it was out of place in their enlightened century and Doña Lupe agreed, although she made a point of not restraining her nephew (her ill-will still being strong) and Juan Pablo departed, leaving the soothing sum of twelve guests at the table.

During lunch, which was long and fastidious, Fortunata continued to feel very inhibited, hardly daring to speak and doing so very awkwardly when she was forced to reply to someone. She was afraid that her table manners would not be refined enough and would reveal her poor upbringing. Her fear of seeming vulgar caused words to stick to her lips just as she was about to pronounce them. Doña Lupe, who was sitting beside her, was on the alert to help if necessary, and she usually answered for her or discreetly prompted her niece's replies.

Fortunata and Doña Lupe both noticed at the same time that Maximiliano was not feeling well. The poor boy tried in vain to ignore it and behave bravely, but he finally gave in.

"You have a migraine," his aunt said.

"Yes, you're right, I do," he replied downheartedly, putting his hand over his eyes. "I wanted to see if it would go away if I ignored it. But it's useless; there's no escape now. My head's splitting. I knew it would happen—with yesterday's excitement and the bad night I spent—because at three in the morning I woke up thinking it was time to get up, and I couldn't go back to sleep."

There was a chorus of sympathy around the table. Everyone looked piteously at the poor migraine victim and some of the guests suggested extravagant remedies.

"It's a family illness," remarked Nicolás. "Nothing helps. I've had such bad ones that the days I had them I couldn't help but compare myself to Saint Peter when he had the axe in his head. For some time now I've been curing them with ham."

"How? Putting a slice on your forehead?"

"No, dear; by eating it."

"Ah, internal use!"

"It'd be better for you to lie down," said Fortunata to her husband, whose suffering was increasing by the minute.

Doña Lupe was of the same opinion, and Maximiliano asked permission to be excused, which he was granted in the form of another chorus of lamentations. Lunch was drawing to a close; Fortunata rose to accompany her husband, and, needless to say, regretting the reason, she was nevertheless happy to leave the table because it freed her of etiquette and the torture of being ogled by so many people. Maxi lay down, his wife covered him up well, and closing the door, went to the kitchen to make him a cup of tea. There she ran into Doña Lupe, who said:

"Coffee first. They're waiting for it. Help me, and then you can make tea for your husband. What he needs is rest."

After-dinner talk lasted a long time. Don Basilio and Don Nicolás had a long session on Carlism and the war and its probable solution, and a hot debate got going because the pharmacists, who were atrociously liberal, intervened and they all practically started throwing plates at one another. Torquemada tried to calm them down because they were making a racket that was disturbing the sick man. Finally, at about four in the afternoon, the party started to break up. The bride had to listen to their mixture of cloying sympathy and jokes in poor taste and make replies as well as she could. Maxi had a very bad afternoon; he vomited and had that epileptic tingling, which caused him more discomfort than anything else. When night fell, he insisted on leaving for their new apartment, and his wife and aunt couldn't get the idea out of his head.

"Look, you'll get worse. Sleep here and tomorrow—"

"No; I don't want to. I feel better. The worst part is already over. The pain is weaker now, and in half an hour it will be on the right side and leave the left side free. We're going home; I'll lie down and go through the rest of it there."

Fortunata insisted that he not move, but he got up and put on his cloak. There was no choice but to set out for their apartment.

"Aunt," said Maxi, "don't forget the flask of laudanum. Fortunata, go get it. When I go to bed, I'll try to sleep, and if I can't, put six drops—measure carefully, now—six drops of this medicine in a glass of water and give it to me to drink."

When he was warmly dressed, his head well protected from the cold, they took him to the couple's new home, which was christened under hardly flattering conditions. The distance between the dwellings was very short. As she crossed Santa Feliciana Street, Fortunata thought she saw . . . she could have sworn . . . A cold gust of air chilled her to the bone. She didn't dare look back to make sure. It was probably nothing but delirium and the confusion in her soul, stimulated by the hundreds of lies Mauricia had told her.

They arrived, and since everything was ready for them to spend the night, they didn't lack anything. The only thing they had forgotten was some candles, which Patricia went out to get. Once Maxi was in bed, what they had feared happened: he got worse and had more vomiting and spasms.

"You wouldn't listen to me. It would have been so much better if you'd slept at home tonight! This is what your stubbornness has done."

After thus expressing her authoritarian opinion, Doña Lupe, seeing that her nephew was calmer and seemingly drowsy, began to give Fortunata instructions for managing the house. She didn't advise; she commanded. For the sake of giving orders, she even told her what to have brought from the market the next day and the next and the next.

"And be sure to check what the girl spends, down to the last cent, because Torquemada says he can't vouch for her. So we shouldn't trust her yet. If you're lacking any kitchen utensil, don't buy it; I'll buy it, because they'll gyp you. And let's not have any fuel oil in cans—I'm scared to death of fires. Starting tomorrow, my oilman will come, and you can order what you need for the day. Potatoes and laundry soap: you'll need about twenty-five pounds of each. Be careful not to spend over sixteen *reales* a day; seventeen at the most. When you have extra expenses, tell me. I'll go to the San Ildefonso Plaza with Papitos and bring you what I think you need. As you know, Maxi's to have two soft-boiled eggs and some very light soup tomorrow. Otherwise, the usual—his chop with french fries. Never buy hake in the Chamberí marketplace. Papitos will buy it for you. Keep a sharp eye on the butcher—he's worse than Judas. If you have any trouble with him, just mention my name and watch him shake in his boots."

And on she went, admonishing and advising with all the airs of a true house-keeper and administrator of the whole family. Luckily she soon departed.

It must have been ten o'clock when the bride was left alone with her husband and Patricia. Maxi's condition didn't improve, which made it necessary to resort to the extreme: laudanum. The patient himself asked for it from between the sheets in whimpers so faint they didn't seem to fit the magnitude of the bed. Fortunata picked up the eyedropper and, drawing up the lamp, she prepared the potion. Instead of six drops she added only five. The medicine frightened her. Maxi took it, and in a short while fell asleep open-mouthed, making a grimace that could have been interpreted as one of irony or pain.

4

Asleep, her husband looked as if he was withdrawing from her; she felt alone, surrounded by treacherous silence and deceitful quiet. She walked through the house a few times, her mind always on the walls that separated their room from the adjacent one; she fancied that they were transparent, like thin gauze revealing everything on the other side. Tiptoeing through the hall and into the living room, she heard the murmur of voices. If she had dared to put her ear to the wall, she might have been able to hear them distinctly; but she didn't dare. Through the dining room window that faced the inner courtyard there could be seen an identical window with curtains. A green-shaded lamp shone, and around it moved shapes, shadows, blurry images of people whose faces couldn't be distinguished.

After these observations she went into the kitchen, where the maid was readying utensils and such for the following day. She was very industrious and so experienced that she surprised even Doña Lupe, for she did things in a wink without a mistake. Fortunata didn't like her because of that cloying way of hers, beneath which she suspected treachery.

"Patricia," said her mistress, affecting an idle curiosity. "Do you know who lives next door?"

"Señorita," said her maid, without letting her finish, "since I've been here since the day before you left the convent, I already know the whole neighborhood, you know? A very refined lady called Doña Cirila lives in that apartment. Her husband has something to do with trains. He's got a braided cap with letters on it. Tonight, when I went out for the candles, I met the lady in the store and she asked after the Señorito. She said if you need anything—you know? She's very friendly. Yesterday she came over to see the apartment, and I went to hers. She says she'd really like to call on you."

"Me!" replied Fortunata, sitting on the kitchen chair next to the white pine table. "Aren't we familiar! And as for you: what business do you have barging in over there? How do you know whether or not I want to get acquainted?"

"Señorita, I . . . thought that—"

"I've been bought, that's all there is to it," thought Fortunata. "This woman's worse than the devil himself."

She thought for a while until Patricia, as she was putting the garbanzos in water to soak, snapped her out of her musings with these clever words:

"Doña Cirila said you were very pretty, you know? That she saw you in church this morning and liked you right off. You'll see, when you get to know her, that she's likable too. She says she'd be very glad to have you come see her whenever you want, and she means it. She says they play cards till midnight."

"Have me go there? Me!"

"Sure. You could go right now, tonight, because the Señorito's asleep and it's only ten o'clock. If you want to have a little fun, that is."

"What do you think you're saying? Me, have fun!"

Fortunata would have acted on her first angry impulse if another permissive impulse and a certain relaxation of her conscience hadn't been born in her at the same time. She remained silent, and at that moment, someone knocked at the door.

"A visitor! Don't open the door," she said, sensing danger close by.

"Why not, Señorita? What are you scared of? I'll look through the peephole."

And she went toward the door. From the kitchen, Fortunata could hear whispering. It didn't last long, and the maid came back, saying:

"The people next door. It was Señorita Cirila herself. All she wanted was to borrow some sugar. I told her no. She asked how the Señorito was getting along. I told her he's sleeping like a log."

Fortunata left the kitchen frowning; her lips were trembling. She went into the bedroom and observed her sleeping husband; in his opiate delirium he mixed amorous words with pharmacological terms: "Idol . . . a centigram of morphine acetate . . . My heaven! Chlorohydrate of ammonia, three grams, to be dissolved—"

Returning to the kitchen, she ordered the maid to go to bed, but Señora Patricia wasn't sleepy.

"Until the Señorita goes to bed, why should I? Something might come up."

And the mischievous woman tried to start a conversation with her mistress; but the latter did not reply to anything. Fortunata's thoughts were centered on the trap she suspected had been set for her, and suddenly, she thought she heard a noise at the door. It sounded as if someone was cautiously trying keys in the lock. Frightened to death, she headed for the door, and as she approached it, the noise ceased. She wasn't sure of herself and called Patricia:

"I'd swear somebody is tinkering with the lock. What's this? Didn't you bolt the door?"

Indeed, the door was unbolted, so she very carefully bolted it without making any noise.

"Well! If I had trusted you to lock up! Listen. Don't you hear a little noise, like someone trying to force the lock? See? Now they're pushing. What is it?"

"It's only the wind blowing up the stairs, Señorita. Don't be such a scaredy-cat."

The oddest part was that as she was bolting the door so carefully, Fortunata felt somewhere in the depths of her soul a mischievous desire to unbolt it. It could have been an illusion, but she thought she could see—as if the door had been made of glass—the person standing on the other side. She could tell who it was, strange to say, by the way the door was being pushed and the lock picked; the way a wrong key was being tried. For a while, the Señora and her maid did not look at each other. The former's hands were trembling and her mind was in a tumultuous state. The maid fixed her feline eyes on the Señora and laughed, and her ironic laugh seemed to be the only comic element in the scene and also the most terrible, dramatic one. Then all of a sudden, inexplicably, maid and mistress exchanged a look of understanding. Patria said with her little clawing eyes: "Open up, you fool, and forget your scruples." Her mistress' look said: "Do you think I should open the door? Do you think . . . ?"

But suddenly Fortunata was overtaken by a sense of decorum, and her honor and dignity rebelled.

"If this keeps up," she said, "I'll wake my husband. Ah! It sounds as if the thief's leaving. Because it must have been a thief."

She felt the lock to make sure that it was tight and went into the living room. Patricia went back to the kitchen.

"In any case, it's too soon," thought Fortunata, sitting in a chair to think things over. It was rather like a concession to the evil thoughts emerging so quickly from her brain, like a long procession of busy, black ants coming out of an anthill. Then she attempted to regain her composure.

"Tomorrow I'll tell my husband that I don't like the house and that we simply have to move. And I'll dump that nervy woman in the streets."

The things that happen! Unexpectedly, obeying an irresistible movement, almost mechanically or fatally, Fortunata got up and walked to the front door. In that act, all that constituted a moral entity disappeared; in the eclipsed soul of that unfortunate woman all that was left was a physical impulse, and what little spirituality remained she tried to interpret as mere curiosity. She put her ear to the little opening. Yes—the person, the thief, or whatever he was, was still there. Instinctively, like a person about to commit suicide putting his finger on the trigger, she put her hand on the lock, and like the suicidal person who just as instinctively is seized with fear and doesn't shoot, she withdrew her hand from the lock, whose hard handle pointed like a finger.

Then through the openings in the grillwork, from the outside in, came these words, as if they were passing through a very fine screen: "Oh baby, baby. Now you'll never escape from me!"

Fortunata stood still as a statue. She thought she was alone, but then she saw Patria coming stealthily toward her. With that feline face of hers and mouth that always seemed to have just swallowed its prey, she seemed to say:

"Señorita, open up and stop pretending. If you're going to open up tomorrow, why not open up tonight?"

As if replying to audible words, the Señora said:

"No; I won't open the door."

"For God's sake."

Long, fearful silence followed this. Then they heard the door to the next apartment open and close. Fortunata breathed a sigh of relief. "He" had gotten tired of waiting and left.

"For God's sake," repeated Patria, as if she were saying: "All this hemming and hawing when you're only going to give in later."

Fifteen minutes later, they heard the door on the left open again. Fortunata ran to the peephole, peered out cautiously, and—he was walking out, throwing his red-lapeled cloak over his shoulders. The emotion she felt when she saw him was so great that she was petrified and lost track of where she was. It had been

three years since she had seen him. She noticed a very disagreeable detail: when
he left, he didn't look at her door as one would have expected. He was probably
angry.

Moved again by the same mechanical impulse, Señora de Rubín ran to the
living room balcony and softly opened the glass door. She saw him cross the street
and turn the corner onto Don Juan de Austria Street. He hadn't glanced up at the
balcony either, unlike the defeated stormer of a plaza who naturally looks back at
the walls upon retreat.

Patricia took the liberty of putting her hand on her mistress' shoulder and said:

"Now we can go to bed. What a scare we had!"

Fortunata responded:

"Me, scared? Humph!"

All this was said in cautious whispers, and even if there had not been a sick
man to respect, it still would have been said in whispers. The maid glided smoothly
through the dark halls and her mistress went into the bedroom. Seeing her husband gave her the impression that what had been a hundred miles away was
suddenly right next to her. Maxi had tossed around some and was now sleeping
like a bird with its head under its wing. His puny body was lost in that huge bed; it
was so roomy that he looked as if he was in limbo.

The wife did not lie down. Drawing a chair up to the bed and dropping into it,
she closed her eyes. During the early morning she was conquered by sleep; her
brain became a painful tumult of locks and doors being opened, transparent walls
that men walked through to get into her house.

5

The next morning Maxi was better, but exhausted. He was a pathetic sight—
pale as death, his tongue white, his body weak, no appetite. They gave him
something to eat and Fortunata was of the opinion that he should stay in bed until
that afternoon. This appealed to him, because he derived a certain childish pleasure from that enormous bed where he could roll freely. His wife cared for him,
treating him like a child; the thought that he was a man had vanished from her
mind.

Doña Lupe came by very early, and once she had seen for herself that Maxi was
well, she started to give orders and was irritated because certain things hadn't
been done according to her instructions. She went from the living room to the
kitchen and from the kitchen to the living room, dictating her rules for good
household management. Maxi complained that his wife spent more time outside
the bedroom than in it and he called for her constantly.

"Thank God you're here. You haven't even kissed me. What a wedding day, and what a night! This cursed migraine . . . But it's over now, and I won't have another for at least two weeks. Well! So you're itching to get back to the kitchen again. Isn't that Señora Patria there?"

"She's gone shopping. Who is there is you aunt, and by the way, she's giving so many orders I don't know which to obey first."

"Let her say what she wants. You say yes to everything and then do what you want, pigeon. Come here. Let Patria work; that's what she's here for. She serves well, doesn't she? She's a very smart woman."

"Oh yes, that's for sure."

"Are you really going?"

"Yes, because if I don't, you aunt's going to bawl me out."

"Humph! I like *that*! Then I'm getting up, and I'll go to the kitchen too. I want to look at you till I've had my fill. You're mine now; I'm your sole possessor and I rule you."

"I'll be back in a second, sweetheart."

"Those seconds annoy me," he said, swimming in the sheets as if they were waves.

All morning Fortunata's mind was on the apartment next door. While she was having lunch alone, she looked out the window that gave onto the courtyard, but she didn't see anyone. It looked like a vacant dwelling. Whenever she went through the living room, Señora de Rubín threw furtive looks at the street. Not a soul. The trap was undoubtedly set at night.

That afternoon, finding herself alone with Patricia in the kitchen, she had it on the tip of her tongue to say: "And how about the people next door?" But she didn't unseal her lips. That cursed cat-woman must have been able to read her mistress' mind, for as if she were answering a question, she suddenly came out with:

"Well, as a matter of fact, when I went down to the butcher's, you know, I ran into Señorita Cirila. She asked after the Señorito and said she'd come see you, but she didn't say when."

"Don't come to me with stories about that . . . that woman," answered Fortunata, whose spirits were calm enough to adopt this correct attitude. "What do I care?"

Maximiliano got up and walked around a little, but he was so weak that he had to go back to bed. She, meanwhile, was on the alert. No noise was to be heard. That night, the same silence. It was as if the earth had swallowed up Doña Cirila, her husband with the letters on his cap, and the friends who visited them. Fortunata felt so sad and upset that she didn't know what was wrong. One might have thought that it nettled her not to see anyone next door, hear no steps, no sound of doors, nothing. Maximiliano, who from mid afternoon on had been swimming in the surf of his sheets and was as impertinent as a sick child who has started to recover, told his wife at about ten o'clock to go to bed and she obeyed him; but her soul was steeped in such imperious repugnance and loathing that it took quite an effort to hide the fact. And the poor boy wasn't in any condition to express his measureless love except in declarations springing solely from his head and heart. Ardent words with no echo in any corporeal cavity, affectionate impulses that were properly ideal—he didn't go beyond this, or rather, couldn't. Fortunata said in sisterly, consoling tones:

"Look, go to sleep; rest and don't get overexcited. You were very ill last night and you need a few days to get back in shape. Make believe I'm not here, and go to sleep."

Whether or not she calmed him down is not known, but the fact is that she fell asleep and didn't wake up until seven the following morning.

Maxi stayed in bed longer to get his fill of sleep; it was the repair that his damaged constitution needed. Fortunata put the house in order and sent Patricia shopping, when who should appear but Doña Lupe, at her wits' end.

"You'll never guess what happened. A mess! Let me sit down, I'm all out of breath. My nephews certainly don't give me a dull moment. Last night Juan Pablo was arrested. Don Basilio came just now to tell me. The police raided the house of that woman he's been living with, and after searching everything and taking some papers, they tied up my nephew and took him off to jail. So! What am I supposed to do now? Frankly, he's behaved very badly with me; he's ungrateful and wasteful. If it were only a question of keeping him in jail a few days, I'd even be glad, so he'd learn his lesson and not go back where he's not wanted. But Don Basilio told me that everybody they arrested last night—and they grabbed lots of people—is going to be sent to the Mariana Islands no less; and although Juan Pablo's had this cruise coming to him, well, frankly, he's my nephew, and I ought to do everything in my power to set him free."

Maxi, who heard some of this from the bedroom, called them in and Doña Lupe repeated her story, adding:

"You must get up immediately and go see the people who might take an interest in your brother. He more than deserves this slap on the wrist, but what can we do? Go see Don León Pintado and ask him to introduce you to Dr. Sedeño, who will introduce you to Don Juan de Lantigua, who's a reactionary, but he does have influence because he's so respectable. I plan to see Casta Moreno to ask her to put in a word for Juan Pablo to Don Manuel Moreno-Isla, who in turn will speak to Zalamero, who's married to Ruiz-Ochoa's girl. Each one of us is going to pull, and if we pull hard enough, we'll keep them from shipping him off to the Marianas."

The young man got dressed as hastily as possible and Doña Lupe, in the meantime, said that lunch was not to be made in Fortunata's kitchen, but that the couple would lunch with her so that they'd be together and ready on this busy day. Maxi went out after breakfast, and his aunt and wife went to the other house. Along the way, Doña Lupe said:

"It's a pity Nicolás has gone to Toledo, and just two days ago, because if he were here he'd take steps to help his brother and would surely have gotten him out of jail today, because priests are the biggest conspirators of all and they have the most pull with the government. They set up a conspiracy and then they manage to get the ministers' hands tied when it comes time to be punished. The country's in a sorry state. Everything's corrupt . . . and there's so much poverty! And potatoes are going at six *reales* for the twenty-five-pound sack; it's unheard of."

The widow lunged into the courageous activity that had made her so successful in life, and Fortunata and Papitos were left in charge of making lunch. At lunch time Doña Lupe came home exhausted, saying that Samaniego (Casta Moreno's husband) was in critical condition and that nothing could be done in that department. Casta wasn't in any mood to take her anywhere. So she would have to knock on someone else's door—Señor Feijóo's, for he was a friend of hers and had once wanted to marry her and was on excellent terms with Don Jacinto Villalonga, who was a close friend of the secretary of the interior. Shortly thereafter, Don Basilio came to say that Maxi would not be home for lunch.

"He's with Don León Pintado seeing someone or other and it'll take time."

Fortunata decided to go home because she had things to do; so repeating the autocrat's instructions to Papitos, she put on her cloak and headed for the street. She wasn't in a hurry, so she decided to go for a walk and bask in the beautiful day and let her mind go round and round like a merry-go-round, up and down and around. She strolled down Santa Engracia Street and stopped at a shop to buy some dates, which she liked very much. And continuing on her wandering way, she savored the intimate pleasure of liberty, of being alone and free, even though for a short while only. The idea of being able to go wherever she wanted excited her and stimulated her circulation, and her good spirits soon became a philanthropic sentiment: she gave away all her small change to the poor people she met, and she met a number of them.

As she walked along it occurred to her that she didn't have the slightest desire to go home. What would she do there? Nothing. It would be good for her to stretch her legs and get some fresh air. She had had enough slavery, being shut up in the Micaelas. What a pleasure it was, to go from one end clear to the other, of a street as long as Santa Engracia! The chief pleasure of her walk was being alone, free. Not Maxi, nor Doña Lupe, nor Patricia—no one was there to count her steps or watch her or stop her. She could have gone on like that for God knows how long. She looked at positively everything with that exhilirating curiosity experienced by people freed after a long captivity. Her thoughts acquired grace in that sweet freedom, and her mind entertained itself with its own ideas. How pretty life was without worries, living with people who loved her and whom she loved.

She observed the houses in the Virtudes neighborhood; poor people's houses always aroused her affectionate interest. The poorly dressed women in the doorways and the dirty children playing in the street attracted her attention, because the quiet life, even if it was obscure and needy, made her envious. She couldn't lead such a life; it wasn't in her blood. She had been born to work hard, and she didn't mind working "like a dog" as long as she possessed what she had a right to. But someone had lifted her out of that first mold and set her in a different life; then other hands took her this way and that. And finally yet others insisted on making a lady of her. They put her in the convent to be remolded; then they married her off. And more of the same! She felt that she was a living doll controlled by an invisible, unknown power she could not name.

She wondered if she would ever have some pluck, some initiative of her own; if she would ever do what "was in her." Rapt in this thought, she reached the Campo de Guardias next to the reservoir. She sat down on one of the many benches there and began to eat some dates. Whenever she threw away a pit, it was as if she were hurling into the immensity of mankind's thoughts an idea of her own—hot, like a spark thrown into a haystack to make it catch fire.

"Everything turns out wrong for me. God ignores me. And he really gives me a hard time. Why didn't I fall in love with a poor mason? No; it had to be a rich señorito who would deceive me and couldn't marry me. Then, the natural thing would've been for me to hate him. But no; the worst always has to happen: I love him more. Then the natural thing would've been for him to leave me alone and I would've gotten over it. But no, sir; the worst again: he's on my trail and he's setting a trap for me. And it also would've been natural if no decent person wanted to marry me. But no, Maxi comes along and bang! they rush me into marriage, and before I know what's happened, the holy vows have been said. Am I *really married?*"

6

She looked at the pit of the date she had just eaten; it seemed to say "yes, you're married," and she echoed disconsolately, "I'm married, all right!" Her thoughts had gone so deep that she forgot where she was. But suddenly she got up and walked downhill with the unmistakable air of a person obsessed with an idea. She had come up that long street like a stroller—gay, light-hearted, eyes wandering; she went back down it like a monomaniac. When she arrived at the front of the church, she was jolted out of this state by the sound of steps behind her.

"That step is his," she thought. "Well, for my part, I'm not going to turn around. What'll I do? Hurry up now."

Her curiosity got the best of her and she looked; it wasn't him. Further on, she heard persistent steps again and saw a shadow paralleling her own. It was surely . . . Should she look? No. Better to ignore it. Finally, though, her curiosity . . . She looked, and it wasn't him this time either. When she got home she was calmer, and when Patria opened the door, she asked:

"Has anyone come? Is the Señorito in?"

"The Señorito won't be back until nighttime. He left word for you not to wait up for him."

And the cunning cat smiled so unctuously that Fortunata couldn't help but ask her:

"Who's in there?"

Patricia smiled again with infernal malice.

"But what . . . ?" stammered the Señora, tiptoeing to the door to the living room.

She pushed it gently until it cracked open. She couldn't see anything. She opened it more, and a bit more . . . Her face was so pale it looked drained of its blood. She pushed the door further open, then once and for all: on the living room sofa, sitting there calmly . . . Oh, God! It was *him!* Fortunata practically fainted. Something like a veil being lowered or lifted blurred her vision. She said nothing. He rose, pale too, and said clearly:

"Over here, baby."

Fortunata didn't stir. Suddenly (only the devil could explain it) she felt an insane joy, an outburst of infinite longing that had been locked in her soul. And she threw herself into the Dauphin's arms, uttering this wild cry:

"Baby! Holy God!"

Oblivious to everything, the lovers met in a long embrace. Fortunata was the first to speak:

"Baby, I'm dying for you."

"Come here," said Santa Cruz, taking her by the arm.

She let herself be led as though it were the most natural thing in the world. They opened the front door, which was unlocked. And the one next door—what a coincidence!—also unlocked. After they'd gone in, someone locked it. Treacherous discretion reigned over that dwelling. Juan took her to a nicely furnished room, next to which was a perfectly arranged bedroom. They sat on the sofa and embraced again. Fortunata was drunk with emotion and felt slightly deranged; she had lost her memory of recent events. All her ideas on morality had disappeared like a dream vanishing from the brain upon waking. Her marriage, her husband, the Micaelas—all this had receded into the distance, become so incredibly remote that it was beyond her mind's grasp. Her lover said in an enticing voice:

"We have so much to talk about!"

And she was overtaken by convulsive laughter.

"Ha, ha, ha—three years! No, longer. It's been longer because—ha, ha, ha—see how I'm trembling? I don't know what's wrong with me. Yes, it's been longer, because when I was here with Juárez el Negro, I saw you, yet I didn't really, with him always there. And one day when I told him I loved you he pulled a big knife on me—ha, ha, ha—and he wanted to kill me. I was dying to talk to you, and him saying no, no . . . Our little baby dead and I was even deader—ha, ha—and in Barcelona I thought of you and blew kisses to you, and in Zaragoza I blew more kisses to you—ha, ha—and in Madrid it was the same. And when they put me in the convent, too—blowing kisses to you—and you never giving me a thought, you cad."

"Forgetting you! Ever since I came back from Valencia I've been hunting for you. What I've been through! I'll tell you all about it. And finally I've caught you. Ah, what a slippery one! Now you'll pay for it all. The suffering you've caused me! The curses I've hurled at that convent! Oh, but you're looking beautiful, baby!"

"Yeth."

"You're divine."

"Yeth . . . for you."

Her feverish chill suddenly became burning heat, and the convulsive laughter, a flood of tears.

"This isn't a time to cry; it's time to be happy."

"Do you know what I'm remembering? My little baby boy—he was so cute. If he'd lived, you would've loved him, wouldn't you? I can see them now, taking him away in that little blue coffin. It was the same night that Juárez el Negro pulled that big knife on me and said, in that booming voice of his, 'Humph! It's eight o'clock. Do all your praying now, 'cause I'm going to kill you before nine.' He was in a jealous rage. I was scared to death."

"We've got so much to tell each other! Both of us. I already know that you got married. You did the right thing."

This "you did the right thing" fell on Fortunata's heart like a cold drop, brusquely reminding her of reality. Drying her tears, she remembered Maxi and her wedding. Her house, which had seemed a hundred million leagues away, was suddenly there again, gloomy and unattractive. This private recoiling from her real situation immediately stopped her tears.

"And why did I do the right thing?"

"Because this way you're freer and you've got a name. You can do what you like as long as you're discreet. I've heard that your husband is a good chap—a dreamer."

Upon hearing this, her self-image, or rather, the specter of her own perversity, flashed before her. What she had just done hardly deserved a name, it was so irregular and abnormal a human iniquity. The place and circumstances made her act even uglier, and she realized this in a swift review of her conscience. But her old yet forever new passion had such thrust and vigor that the specter vanished, leaving not a single trace. Fortunata felt like a blind mechanism activated by a supernatural hand. In her mind, what she had done had been to obey the mysterious forces that determine the greatest phenomena in the universe—the rising of the sun and the falling of weighted bodies. She could neither refrain from it, nor argue against its inevitability, nor try to lessen her responsibility, which she could not distinguish very clearly anyway. Even if she had been able to, she was so set on her course that she was not prepared to stop, no matter what the consequences; she "was resigned"—for this was her notion—"to ending up in hell."

"My renting the apartment next to yours," said Santa Cruz, "was reckless, and it would have been unforgivable if I hadn't been so crazed with this desire to see you and talk to you, baby. When I heard that you'd come back to Madrid I nearly went mad. My heart had a debt to you, and the love I owed you weighed on my conscience. I almost lost my mind. I looked for you the way we look for what we love the most in the world. I didn't find you; pneumonia was just around the corner, waiting to spring on me, and it did—"

"My poor little Juan! I heard about it. I also heard that you'd looked for me. God reward you for it! If I'd known before, you would've found me."

She looked around the room. Its relative elegance didn't affect her. In a miserable tavern, in a cellar full of cobwebs, in any old fetid underground place she would have been just as happy, as long as she was with him. Her eyes couldn't get their fill.

"You're so handsome!"

"How about you? You're ravishing! Much better now than before."

"Oh, no," she replied, rather coquettishly. "Do you say that because I've been tamed a bit? Tssh! Don't believe it. I'm not going to be tamed. I don't want to be. I'll always be one of the people. I want to be the way I was before, like when you roped me in."

"The people! That's what it is," Juan observed somewhat pedantically. "In other words, the essence of humanity, raw material, because when civilization allows great feelings and basic ideas to be lost, it's necessary to go back to the rock, the quarry, the people."

Fortunata didn't quite understand the concepts involved, but she had some inkling of what he meant.

"I can hardly believe that I have you here with me," he said, "lassoed again, my little beast; and I can beg you to forgive me for all the harm I've done you."

"Oh, go on. *Forgive* you?" she exclaimed, drowning in her own generosity. "If you love me, what does the past matter?"

At that very moment she raised her forehead, and with a satanical conviction that had a certain beauty because it was a conviction and because it was satanical, she allowed these arrogant words to escape her lips:

"*You're* my husband. All the rest is . . . . rubbish!"

Santa Cruz's conscience was flexible, but not so flexible as to exempt him from a shiver of terror when he heard this bold declaration. To reciprocate, he was going to say, "You're my wife," but he sheathed his lie, like a prudent man who saves his weapons for really serious occasions.

7

It was already dark when Fortunata reentered her house. Her husband had not yet come home. While she waited for him, the sinner saw that specter of her perversity again. But this time she saw it more clearly and was not able to make it vanish so easily. "They've deceived me," she thought. "They roped me into marriage the way you take an animal to the slaughterhouse, and when I wanted to think it over it was too late—they'd stabbed me. Why blame myself for this?" The house was dark, so she lit a lamp. The match she threw away was still aflame when it hit the floor, and Fortunata looked at it with lively curiosity, recalling one of the superstitions she had been taught as a child. "When the match falls lighted," she recalled, "with the flame pointing toward you, it's good luck."

Maxi came in tired and distracted, but when he saw his wife, he cheered up. A whole day without seeing her! He'd brought her some pastries. And Juan Pablo? He would undoubtedly be spared the Mariana Islands, but they might keep him in jail fifteen or twenty days.

"He deserves it. Why does he always insist on taking on more than he can handle?"

As they ate, Fortunata contemplated her husband, more mentally than perceptually; her examination produced an overwhelming tedium and her old dislike, but it was so much stronger now that it could not be greater. And the perverse woman didn't try to combat this feeling; she took pleasure in it, as though it had some sort of monstrous, yet seductive, appeal.

"Darling," said her husband as they finished eating, "I'm glad to see that you have a good appetite. Would you like to go to a café now?"

"No," she replied curtly. "I'm exhausted. Can't you see that I can barely keep my eyes open? What I'd like is to go to sleep."

"Fine, all the better; I want to, too."

They went to bed, and until she fell asleep, Fortunata spent the time making comparisons. Maxi's emaciated body made her twitch nervously whenever it touched hers. And she thought how trying it was going to be to lead two different lives, one true and the other false, like an actress. Roles and pretending were very hard for her and, remembering this, she felt considerably more tormented. "I won't be able to; I can't," she thought as she fell asleep, "play this part very long." The next morning she awoke after a deep restoring sleep; but she started to cry when she envisioned—in notably graphic detail—the scenes there would be, and she pitied herself for not being able to see her lover all the time.

On the following days her escapades next door took place at various hours— whenever Maxi was out. He was studying with a friend for final exams (after which he would receive his degree) and he usually went to Samaniego's pharmacy too. It was already agreed that there would be a place for him in the business. Even though his absences were guaranteed, the criminals decided to build their nest further away. In the meantime, Patricia did as she pleased. Fortunata's and even Doña Lupe's orders were just so many words to her. She was stealing shame-lessly, and her mistress didn't dare to reprimand her. Santa Cruz, who was respon-sible for the whole mess, didn't know what to suggest when his friend consulted him. The wisest course was to rent another place, fire Patricia, and give her a good tip to keep her quiet.

The Dauphin offered his lover gifts and money several times, but she didn't want anything. She had gotten a most peculiar notion into her head, an obsession really, that they both laughed over heartily when she explained it. It was that Juan "shouldn't be rich." For things "to be right," he should be poor and she should work "like a dog" to support him.

"If you'd been a mason or a carpenter or, let's say, a cargo inspector, it would've been a different story for me."

"What a thing to come up with."

"That's all."

There was no way to dissuade her from this correction of fate's designs.

"In other words," he said, "you're a sweet little fool. But say, don't you like luxury?"

"When I'm not with you I like it some—not much; I've never been wild about clothes. But when I have you, gold and brass are all the same to me. Give me silk or cotton, I don't care which it is."

"Speak frankly. Don't you need anything?"

"No, nothing; believe me."

"That poor simpleton gives you everything you need?"

"Everything, believe me."

"I want to give you a dress."

"I won't wear it."

"And a hat."

"I'll use it for a fruit basket."

"Have you vowed to be poor?"

"I haven't vowed anything. I love you because I love you, that's all I know."

"Completely primitive," thought the Dauphin. "She's from that quarry, the people, where you have to go to find the feelings that civilization has lost because it refines them too much."

One day they talked about Maximiliano.

"Poor boy!" said Fortunata. "The hatred I've begun to feel for him isn't really hatred; it's pity. I never liked him. I let myself be put in the Micaelas and I let myself be married. You know what it was like? Like when they 'hipnetise' somebody and do what they want with you. It's exactly the same. When it's not a question of love, I don't have any willpower. They can lead me around by the nose. And now, believe me, I've got my regrets for cheating on him. That poor boy wouldn't hurt a fly. Sometimes I feel like telling him the truth and . . . But I just can't caress him; my whole self refuses; it's not in me. I ask the Blessed Virgin to give me strength to speak up."

"The Virgin! *You* believe in her?" Santa Cruz asked amazed, for he had pegged Fortunata as a nonbeliever.

"And why shouldn't I? What she always advises me when I pray to her with my eyes closed is to love you very much and let you love me. You've got her on your side, kid. Why are you so surprised? Well, anyway, I pray to the Virgin and she protects me, even though I'm bad. Who knows what will come of it, if things will turn out like they should. If you want to know the truth, sometimes I doubt that I'm so bad. Yeah, I do. Maybe I'm not. My conscience turns this way, then that. I'm always doubting, and I always end up telling myself: *to love the person you love can't be wrong.*"

"Listen," said the Dauphin, amused by these weird notions. "Suppose your husband found out and wanted to kill me?"

"Oh, don't say that! Not even as a joke. I'd throw myself on him like a lion and tear him apart. You know how you take a crayfish and pull out its claws and crack its shell and take out what's inside? Well, that's what I'd do."

"But wait a minute, baby. Don't you hold a grudge against me for having abandoned you? For leaving you poor and pregnant and in el Negro's clutches?"

"No grudge at all. I was furious then. Being furious and poor are what made me go off with Juárez el Negro. Know something? You probably won't believe it, but I went off with him because I hated him so much. Strange, isn't it? And since I didn't even have a crumb of bread to put in my mouth and he was offering to feed me, well, there you have it. I said to myself: 'I'll get my revenge by going off with this animal.' When I had my little boy, that consoled me, but then he died on me, and when Juárez blew up, since I thought you didn't love me anymore, I said: 'Well, now I'll really get my revenge by being as bad as I can.'"

"But what's your idea of getting revenge?"

"Don't ask me. I don't know. Getting revenge is doing what you're not supposed to . . . the ugliest, the most—"

"And whom do you take revenge on that way, dear?"

"On God, on . . . oh, I don't know. Don't ask me, because I'd have to be educated like you to explain it, and I don't know beans about anything, and I can't learn either, even though Doña Lupe and the nuns have polished me up a little by rubbing me to death. And taught me not to talk so much nonsense."

Santa Cruz was pensive for a long time.

One day they talked about Jacinta too. Juan did not like the conversation to enter this realm, but whenever Fortunata had a chance, she went straight at it. He answered her questions evasively:

"Look, baby, leave my wife at home."

"Well, promise me you don't love her."

"I do love her. Why deceive you? . . . But in a very different way from the way I love you. I'm as considerate of her as she deserves, and she deserves a lot. You can't imagine how good she is."

Fortunata kept asking about their conjugal intimacy with an annoying curiosity, but he eluded her queries gallantly and, to the extent that it was possible in that criminal colloquy, kept the sacred character of his wife intact.

"The poor dear," he said at last, "has a passion, or rather an obsession, that upsets her."

"What is it?"

"An obsession with children. It's not God's will, yet she insists on it. Her sterility has caused her so much grief that she's beginning to deteriorate; she's gotten thin, and for some time now her hair has been turning gray. It's become a matter of life and death to her. Did you hear about what happened? They swindled her. Your uncle José Izquierdo, in cahoots with another madman, made her believe that a three-year-old child he had with him was our Juanín. My wife got all excited, wanted to adopt him, and just imagine: bring him home to live with us. Even though we didn't lose any time finding out about the deal, it was too late to prevent your uncle from robbing her of six thousand *reales*."

"A funny story. Yeah, I knew about it. The kid must be Nicolasa's; she's Uncle Pepe's step-daughter. He was born six days after ours; he's the son of a lamplighter. But there's something I don't understand. It seems to me that your wife should've loved that little boy because she thought he was yours, and hated him for being another woman's. At least that's how I see it."

"Quiet, silly. My wife is crazy about every child in the world, no matter whose it is; just thinking that Juanín was mine was enough to make her adore him. She's like that; you have no idea how good she is. If she ever had a child! Holy Christ, I don't want to even think about it. She'd be sure to lose her mind and make the rest of us go mad too. She'd love our child more than me; more than the whole world put together."

Hearing this, Fortunata looked pleased and pensive. What was that extravagant mind concocting now? This:

"Listen, baby; I've just had an idea, a great idea, you'll see. I'm going to offer to make a deal with your wife. Will she accept?"

"Depends on what it is."

"It's very simple. Let's see what you think of it. I give her your child and she gives me her husband. All it is, is exchanging a little baby for a big baby."

The Dauphin laughed at that singular pact, which she had expressed rather wittily.

"Will she agree to it? What do you think?" asked Fortunata in utmost sincerity, which became enthusiasm as she said, "Well, look; you can laugh all you want, but it's a great idea."

The illustrious young man plunged into a sea of thought.

8

The visits at Cirila's apartment continued for two weeks, but it became quite clear that they could not go on, so they rented another room. Patricia had become unbearable and Doña Lupe, who descended on them whenever she wanted to stick a finger in the pie, complicated her niece's escapes. Meanwhile, Fortunata wasn't inconsiderate to Maximiliano, but her coldness would have frozen fire itself. He would have preferred a thousand times over for his wife to have thrown things at him than be treated with that scornful, icy courtesy. Only very rarely did she caress him, and even then, only after Maxi practically petitioned for it; and what he got was more like charity. Fortunata wasn't any good at being a courtesan. Her pretenses were pitifully awkward.

The young pharmacist had moments of terrible sadness when he was filled with dark thoughts. After this brooding, he began to observe things, and he developed his powers of observation to an astounding degree. When he was at home, he glued his eyes to his wife, studied her movements, her looks, her way of walking, and even her breathing. When they dined, he examined the way she ate; when they were in bed, the way she slept.

Fortunata never looked at him. This fact, which he had carefully noted, produced unspeakable melancholy in the poor boy. To have bought those eyes with his hand, his honor, and his name, and for them to look at a chair rather than at him! It was dreadful, simply dreadful. One day an insane fury shook him to the core. But he didn't want to show it, and he vented his feelings when he was alone, gnawing at his fists.

"Why don't you look at me?" he asked her one night with a frown.

"Because . . ."

She said no more; she swallowed the rest of the sentence. God only knows what she had planned to say.

The miserable boy did everything in his power to make her love him. He invented as many subtleties as the obsession or sickness that love is has to offer. He inquired feverishly into the recondite reasons why one is "appealing," and not being able to come up with anything useful in the physical realm, he scrutinized the spiritual realm, searching for a remedy. He imagined that he could make his wife fall in love with him by spiritual means. He, already good, was ready to become a saint, and he carefully studied what pleased his wife so as to better accomplish his aims. She liked to give alms to the poor. Well, he would give more than she gave—much more. She was prone to admire cases of abnegation. Well, he would find an opportunity to be heroic. She liked to work. Well, he would work himself to death. In this way, the poor youth ravished his soul, picking all its good, noble, and beautiful roses for her, the ungrateful girl, just as one gathers from a garden all the best flowers for a single bouquet.

"You don't love me anymore," he said to her one day, revealing his immense sadness. "Your heart's flown away like the little bird that flies away when the door to its cage is left open. You don't love me anymore."

And she replied that she did, but . . . It would have been better to have plainly said no.

"Why are you so distant with me? I seem to horrify you. When I come in, you turn glum; when you think I'm not noticing you, you're lost in private thoughts and smile as if you were talking to someone."

Something else mortified him. When they went out for a walk, everyone noticed Fortunata, admired her beauty; then they looked at him. Maxi assumed that what they all observed was that he wasn't man enough for so much woman. Some permitted themselves insolent glances at him. If they went to a café, they were only there a short while because their friends clustered around Fortunata without paying the slightest attention to her husband, who swallowed a lot of bile. What disoriented Maxi the most was that she "didn't make eyes" at anyone and whenever he said, "Let's go," she was ready to leave.

The pharmacist searched for something on which to base the conjectures that were beginning to obsess him, but he found nothing. He thought of asking his aunt's advice, but he didn't want to risk her criticism; he feared that Doña Lupe would say, "You see? I told you you should have listened to me!" Jealous. But of whom? Fortunata was as cold to everyone else as she was to him. She cast melancholic looks about the street, among the crowd, but not at any one person, as though she were looking for someone who was eluding her. And then she grew distracted again and was sadder.

The praise his friends had for her also tormented the young man.

"What a wife you have!" said *Pseudo-Narcissus odoripherus*.

And *Quercus gigantea* whispered these funereal words into his ear:

"She's a lot of woman for you, old boy. Keep your eyes open."

Doña Lupe, however, imbued him with optimism. Who ever would have thought . . . ! More than once, the knowing, perspicacious, experienced Señora de Jáuregui remarked to her nephew:

"Your wife is so diligent! Whenever I come over, I always find her washing or ironing. Frankly, I didn't expect . . . She'll certainly be a help to you. And she's so quiet. There are days when I don't hear a peep out of her."

Between one thing and another, the poor boy could hardly study and had to take great pains to prepare himself for his final examinations. He had already been assured of a position in the pharmacy; Samaniego died at the end of October and his widow reorganized the staff so as to make room for Maxi. Doña Casta Moreno and Doña Lupe agreed that once the boy took his degree he would receive a fixed salary, and that after a year of apprenticeship he would share in the profits. Financially, things were great, because until the day he started his profession, he would be able to live fairly well on the modest income from the inheritance. The bad part was that once he started work at the pharmacy, he would have to be out of the house all day, and the thought of this kept him on pins and needles. Then it occurred to him—as it occurs to any jealous person—to leave one day, saying that he was going to the pharmacy, and return immediately. He did this once and didn't discover anything. Fortunata was in the kitchen. He tried the trick again to no avail: she was sewing. The third time she had left. Two hours later, she returned with a package in her hand.

"Where have I been? Buying a few things. Didn't you say you wanted a tie? Look, here it is."

One night Maximiliano came home in a rather excited state. He took his wife's hand and, making her sit down beside him, he blurted out:

"Today I met that scoundrel who dishonored you."

Fortunata's face fell.

"But . . . isn't he ill?"

This spontaneous reaction escaped before she could repress it. For a week, Santa Cruz had not been keeping his engagements with her and had sent word through Cirila that he had fallen off his horse in the Casa del Campo and had injured his arm.

"Ill?" said Maxi, nailing his enlightened eyes on her. "As a matter of fact, he did have his arm in a sling. But how did you know?"

"No, no—I didn't know," replied Fortunata, completely rattled.

"You're the one who said it!" exclaimed Rubín with a terrible look. "How did you know?"

She turned crimson, then pale. She was hunting for a way out, and at last she found one:

"Ah!"

"What?"

"You want to know how I knew it, silly? It's very simple. It was in the newspaper. Your aunt read it out loud last night. Look, here it is—it says he fell off his horse while riding in the Casa del Campo."

And regaining her composure, she rummaged through the things on the table and found El Imparcial, which did, indeed, contain the news.

"Look—you see? This should convince you."

After reading it, Maxi continued:

"Well, I saw him in jail, where that pig ought to be for the rest of his life. Olmedo, who was with me, pointed him out to me. I was there to see my brother; he had gone to see a man named Moreno-Vallejo, another prisoner, for conspiracy. That Santa Cruz is really an annoying character."

Fortunata covered her face with the newspaper, pretending to read. Maxi tore it away from her.

"You look . . . dazed or something."

"Leave me alone," she retorted with a coldness that cut him to the quick.

"Manners, child! Not even considerate anymore, are you?"

Fortunata's mouth looked as if it had been sealed. They ate without a word; then he sat down to study and she to sew, lugubrious silence enveloping them. They went to bed. More of the same. She turned her back on her husband, insensitive to his sighs. For a long while they both lay awake, each on one side, very close physically but miles apart spiritually.

Several days later, coming back from jail (where he had gone to tell his brother that he'd soon be released) Maximiliano saw a phaeton heading up Santa Engracia Street. The arm was healed now. Santa Cruz looked at Maxi, who looked back at him. From afar, for the carriage was going quite fast, Rubín observed that it was turning onto Raimundo Lulio Street. Would it turn onto Sagunto next? Never had the exalted youth wished so keenly to have wings. He walked as fast as he could, and when he reached his street . . . God! Just what he'd feared . . . Fortunata on the balcony, looking toward Castillo Street, which the carriage had undoubtedly taken on its way to La Habana Avenue. The young pharmacist climbed the stairs so fast that he was out of breath when he got to the top. You've got to have good lungs to be jealous, you know. He collapsed rather than sat in a chair, and his wife and Patricia hastened to his side, thinking that he'd had some sort of accident. He couldn't speak, and he banged his fists against his head. When his wife was left alone with him, Rubín felt his frantic wrath turn into cowardly fear. His soul tore away from him, shook, rejected the anger in his breast. His eyes filled with tears, his knees caved in. Falling to his wife's feet, he covered her hands with kisses.

"Take pity on me," he said with an affliction that was more childlike than manly. "For your own sake: the truth, the truth! That man . . . and you waiting for him . . . he was coming to see you. You don't love me, you're deceiving me; you love *him* again. You've seen him somewhere. The truth . . . I'd rather die of grief than shame. Fortunata, I took you out of the gutter and you're covering me with mud. I gave you my honor pure, and you're giving it back defiled. I gave you my name, and you've made a mockery of it. The last favor I beg of you . . . The truth, tell me the truth."

9

Fortunata's tongue moved and she parted her lips. She had the truth on the tip of her tongue, and for a few seconds she doubted whether to come out with it or push it back in. The truth wanted to come out. The words lined up side by side, mutely, and said: "Yes, it's true that I hate you. Living with you is death. And I love him more than my own life."

The battle was brief; Fortunata sent the terrible truth back into the depths of her soul. Maxi's affliction required lies, and his wife had to tell them. Lies that inspire vivid compassion in the person who tells them, offering only a paltry consolation to the person who hears them. She delivered them like a nurse administering useless medicine to a suffering patient.

"Say it differently and I'll believe you," implored Rubín. "Say it with feeling, even if it's not much—the way you used to say it to me. You don't know the harm you're doing me. You're making me believe that there's no God; that it doesn't make any difference at all whether one's behavior is good or bad."

The delinquent was overcome by compassion. She was so affectionate that afternoon and evening that she finally pacified Maximiliano. The poor creature was fated to endure the worst, though, for just as his spirits were picking up, a migraine started. It was a cruel night, and Fortunata took pains to attend to him well. In the midst of his migraine pain, the young man overtaxed his poor brain even more by thinking up remedies or palliatives for the anxiety that ruled him. Shortly after vomiting, he said to his wife:

"I've got an idea that will solve the difficultires. We'll go to Molina de Aragón, where I have my property. I'll give up my profession and devote myself to farming. Do you want tó—yes or no? I'll be able to live in peace there."

Fortunata agreed, although she remembered what Mauricia had said about life in a small town. They'd have to cut her to pieces before she'd go live in the country. That night, however, she had no choice but to say yes to everything.

The next few days, poor Maxi noted that he was languishing more and more, alarmingly so, and in great fear he consulted his friend Augusto Miquis, who told him that it would have been better if he had consulted him before getting married, for he would have given him strict orders to stay single. This increased his sorrow. But when Miquis proposed a country life as the only remedy for his illness, he took heart; this strengthened his resolve to leave Madrid and bury himself forever in his country estates.

The second time he spoke of this to his wife, he did not find her so receptive.

"How about your studies, and your career? Ask your aunt's advice; she'll tell you that what you're considering is nonsense."

Maxi was quite perturbed by certain things he had noticed in his wife. For days she had hardly taken her eyes off the floor, and when she did look at him, her eyes revealed great sorrow. Then all of a sudden, coming home from the pharmacy one afternoon, he heard her singing as he was going upstairs. He went in, and Fortunata's face was radiant with happiness and life. What had happened? Maxi couldn't figure it out, although his jealousy, which sharpened his intelligence, gave him some ideas that could well have had some truth in them. The truth was that the sinful woman had received a note (via Patria) announcing a reopening of the amorous session that had been interrupted for fifteen days. "This happiness," mused Maxi. "What could be the reason for it?" And his jealous instinct made him realize that he was flinging cold water on that happiness when he said:

"It's been decided. We're going to Molina de Aragón. I've consulted my aunt, and she approves."

It wasn't true that he had consulted Doña Lupe, but he said so to give his proposition unquestionable authority.

"Maybe *you're* going . . . ," she said, smiling.

"No," he added, repressing the bitterness that overflowed from his soul, "both of us are."

"You've gone mad," remarked Fortunata, laughing rather impudently. "I thought . . . Are you serious?"

"Well, well, well! Didn't you say that you'd go too, and that you wanted to be a country hick?"

"Yes, but I thought we were just talking. *Me* shut myself up in a small town! What brainy ideas you have!"

The young man's face changed color so suddenly that Fortunata, who was just about to make another joke on the subject, restrained herself. Maxi didn't say a word and before she knew it he'd shot out of the house, slammed the door, and bounded down the stairs four at a time. Fortunata was frightened. Peering out from the balcony she saw him dash down Sagunto Street, heading for Santa Engracia. Then she left, heading in the opposite direction, toward Cuatro Caminos.

It must have been six in the evening when Rubín returned. He was livid, then green, when Patricia told him that the Señora had gone out shopping. Under the spell of his insane jealousy, he interrogated the maid, but she was the last person who would help. Patria had the discretion of a traitor, and any and all she said was intended to convince Maxi that his wife practically deserved canonization. When the criminal came in, her husband had already ordered the lamps lit and he was sitting next to the table in the living room.

"Where have you been?" he asked.

"I seem to remember telling you," she retorted, "that I was going out to buy this twill."

She showed him the package, then several smaller ones too:

"See? The vegetable soup that you like so much."

"This afternoon," Maximiliano said in a somewhat sinister manner, "I bought you a little present too. Look."

He reached under the table and took out something he had hidden there when he got home. It was an object wrapped in paper that he slowly unwrapped as she bent forward smilingly to see what it was.

"Let's see. What is it? Oh!! A revolver!"

"Yes, to kill you and me," said Maxi in a tone that was not as gloomy as he wished, because the weapon was beginning to frighten him; he'd never handled anything like it in all his life.

"The things you come up with!" she said, turning pale. "You don't realize what you're getting yourself into. You must be dumb. Kill me? Why?"

She gave him a sweet, penetrating look, the look that she had used to make him her slave. The poor boy felt as though his soul had been shackled.

"Really, the stuff you come up with, Maxi. I scare easily. Just looking at that thing makes me shake. A fine way you picked to make me love you!"

Timidly, she touched the butt of the gun.

"You can hold it, it's not loaded," said Maxi, whose fury had subsided instantaneously and given way to pity.

"You're a child," she declared, taking the weapon. "And you have to be treated like one. I'll take care of this thing; I'm going to put it away in case thieves try to break in."

And she carried it off without any resistance on his part. After locking it up in a trunk full of old stuff, she returned to her husband's side; he was still there, self-absorbed, undoubtedly measuring the distance between the impetus of his will and the inefficacy of his miserable actions.

Nothing happened that night, but the next afternoon *Pseudo-Narcissus odori-*

pherus went to Samaniego's pharmacy to tell Maxi that Fortunata was meeting a gentleman in a house on Santa Engracia, just beyond the city warehouses at La Villa.

IO

Maxi took a cab home. After being informed that the Señorita was not at home, he walked slowly toward the church, and as he passed and saw the iron cross in the atrium, it occurred to him that he should have brought his revolver. He backtracked, and halfway home recalled that his wife had hidden the weapon. What a fool he was, to have let her! He headed north again, experiencing the unspeakable torture produced by harboring simultaneously two such opposite feelings: a yearning to know the truth and a horror of knowing it. When he saw the mill wheel jutting up above the Micaelas, he couldn't repress a choked pained feeling in his throat that made him sob. The disk was not turning.

The young man went beyond the city warehouses and examined the tall one-story buildings. As he didn't know which one of them was shielding the adulterers, he decided to keep watch over all of them. Night was falling and Maxi wished it would come more swiftly so that he would stop seeing the wheel, which looked to him like the witnessing eye of a jester expressing all the sarcasm there is in this world. A sacrilegious curse escaped him when he realized that the site of his dishonor and the sanctuary where the infamous pill of his hopes had been sugared were so close together. He had come to find the sacramental host and had been given instead a mill wheel. And the worst was that he had swallowed it anyway.

After walking around for quite some time, he saw Santa Cruz's phaeton driving by slowly, as if to keep the horses from getting cold. There could no longer be any doubt about it: the carriage was waiting for its owner. He saw it go as far as Cuatro Caminos, where it stopped and the lackey lighted the lamp. Then it came back, and when it reached the warehouses it turned around again. Maxi didn't lose sight of it. The coachman made it plain that he was bored and impatient. On one of the turns, Rubín caught the coachman looking at one of the houses. "So that's the one." He planted himself nearby, his watchful walk closer now. It was seven o'clock.

Finally, as Maxi was heading north, he saw a man leaving the house. It was Santa Cruz himself, wearing a suit coat and a derby. He paused in the doorway to look for his carriage. The two lights shone further up the street. He headed for Cuatro Caminos . . . Behind him, quickening his step, was hatred itself, personified in Maximiliano.

It was a lonely street. Very few people went by and it was quite chilly. The

Dauphin heard steps behind him and felt inexplicably apprehensive; it was his conscience, perhaps, which told him whose they were. He turned around just as a trembling voice said:

"Listen, you."

Santa Cruz stopped dead in his tracks, and even though he didn't know the other man well, he instantly guessed who he was.

"What is it?"

"Cur! Pig!" exclaimed Rubín with more ferocity in his tone than in his appearance.

Santa Cruz didn't wait to hear more, nor did his self-love permit him to give any explanations, and with a vigorous movement of his right arm, he pushed aside his assailant. More than a sock, it was a push, but Rubín's puny skeleton couldn't take it; he lost his balance and fell to the ground, crying out:

"I'm going to kill you . . . and her too!"

He struggled on the ground. For a minute he flayed his arms and legs, crying out between moans:

"Thief, scoundrel . . . Just wait!"

Santa Cruz stood gazing at him for a while with the cold calm of a momentarily confused assassin, and then, seeing that his enemy was finally managing to get up, he went toward him and grabbed him fiercely by the neck as if he really did want to strangle him. Holding Maxi down, he hurled these words at him:

"Stupid . . . flabby. You want me to beat you up?"

From the miserable youth's throat came a faint moan, the croaking of asphyxiation. His bulging eyes were riveted on his executioner, sparking electrically like the eyes of a rabid, dying cat. All that the underdog could resort to was his nails, which he dug into the arms, legs, any part of his victor that he could reach, and in his nervous rage he managed to gain enough of an advantage to throw off his enemy. Once the two of them were down it might be more even a match. Poor reason, crushed by pride! Where is justice? Where is the vengeance of the weak? Nowhere.

The Dauphin's fury was not so great as to blind him to the danger of homicide, which lurked in a use of his superior strength. "After all, this is a man even though he looks like an insect," he thought. So out of pitying scorn he freed his prey, who fell to one side of the street into a sort of hole or rut. When he saw his victim—a shapeless mass—Juan was somewhat scared. "Could I have killed him unintentionally? In any case . . . it was in self-defense." But the victim exhaled a groan and, wriggling around epileptically, he repeated:

"Thief . . . assassin!"

The Dauphin approached him and, stepping gingerly on Rubín's chest, said:

"If you don't shut up, I'll squash you like a cockroach."

Rubín leaped up. He was all nails and teeth. He used the weak man's weapons, but so fiercely that if he had gotten hold of the other man he would have torn off his skin. Santa Cruz hastened to defend himself.

"I tell you I'll kick you if you so much as—"

He picked him up like a feather and hurled him violently to where he had fallen before—a badly plowed field or vacant lot beyond the last house. The victim lost consciousness, and the barbarous Señorito took advantage of the opportunity to call his carriage (which was passing by), jump into it, and giddy up! the horses were off.

A man had stopped in front of the combatants toward the end of the brawl; he walked over to Maxi and looked at him suspiciously. Thinking that the man was fatally wounded, he didn't want to get involved with the law. When he heard him speak, he drew closer.

"What is it, my good man? Poor boy! But he looks like an old man, not a boy. The idea! Knocking down a poor old man!" Then another man appeared out of the crowd of workers going up the street. With the latter's assistance, Maxi managed to get up, and he ran quite some distance down the street, shouting:

"Thief! He's the one, the assassin!"

But the carriage was already past the church. A circle of four, six, ten people of both sexes formed around the victim. He looked at them as though they were friends who should side with him, recognize that justice had been offended and humanity outraged. He looked like a madman. His distressed face inspired fear, and his quavering voice struck people as very peculiar.

The fight had somehow relaxed his larynx so as to give him a completely falsetto voice. He sounded as if he hadn't even reached puberty yet.

"Where's he hiding? Where? It's true, isn't it, friends, that he's a bum and a kidnapper? He took what was mine, he robbed me and left her in the gutter. I picked her up out of it and washed her clean; he took her away again and threw her back, back in the gutter again. Vile scum! I have to kill two people, I do. I'll go to the gallows. I don't mind going to the gallows, friends. I mean, I want to go. But them first, them first."

The people standing around felt sorry for him. Not knowing the cause of the brawl, each one offered his version. "It was wine brought 'em to it." "No, it was skirts, right?" "You're both wrong. Can't you see he's a fairy?"

The women looked at him with more interest now.

"There's blood on your forehead," said one of them.

He had scraped his forehead without realizing it. He put his hand to his head and looked at it, stained with blood. He noticed that his right arm hurt terribly.

"Come on," someone said, "come along to the first-aid station."

"Sneaky cur . . ."

"Come on, fella, it's all over now. Where's your hat?"

Maxi said nothing. He was totally unconcerned about his hat. Suddenly he started howling. The bystanders could barely make out what he was saying: "smashing his heart in two isn't enough; it's got to be *pounded* to bits!"

Two men led him down the street, each holding an arm, and, looking dumbly at his guides, he repeated: "Pound it to bits!" Every now and then he stopped and burst out in insane laughter. By the time they had almost reached the church two policemen appeared; seeing Maxi in that state, they received him very badly. They thought he was a little rascal who richly deserved the blows he had received. They grabbed him by the collar with that paternal grip that characterizes the law.

"What's going on?" one of them asked him ill-humoredly.

Maxi answered with the same insane, delirious laughter, at which the flatfoot tightened his grip, as if to express the rigor that human justice should use on criminals.

"And the assailant?"

"Pound him to bits!"

They reached the first-aid station, followed by what had become a procession by now. The doctor in charge of emergencies knew Maxi, and after treating the minor wound in his head sent him home escorted by the policemen.

I I

When the ill-fated boy entered his home, Fortunata had not yet returned. No sooner did Patricia see him in that sorry state than she ran to tell Doña Lupe, who immediately appeared on the scene, worried and stricken. The first thing she did—and it was in keeping with her strong character—was to take things in hand: not cower at the sight of blood, but dictate sound preliminary orders, such as, "Put Maximiliano to bed, bring a supply of arnica, inspect his wounds, and call a doctor."

"But where's Fortunata?"

"She went shopping," said Patricia.

"That's odd! And it's eight thirty."

In vain Doña Lupe attempted to extract from the young man what had happened. All he said was "Pound it to bits!" in that falsetto voice, which was also new to his aunt. Not without some effort they managed to put him to bed and covered him with poultices. The doctor from the first-aid station came and ordered rest. He feared there was some sort of cerebral disturbance, but said that it would probably go no further than a bad migraine. He also prescribed strong doses of potassium bromide, and after the first dose the wounded man fell into a drowsy state, uttering disconnected words that Señora Jáuregui could not piece together. Meanwhile, *she* wasn't back!

Finally, at about nine thirty, after the doctor had left, Doña Lupe heard a commotion, then whispering, in the hall. Fortunata had come in and was talking to Patricia in a very low voice. The widow's mind, which up until that moment had been confused and vague, began to harbor the most peculiar notions; bold and horrifyingly pessimistic thoughts. She crept slowly toward the living room, hoping to overhear their secret conversation. Fortunata came in waxen-faced, with fear in her eyes, but Doña Lupe said nothing to her. She saw her advance toward the parlor, take a few steps toward the bedroom door, pause, and crane her neck to get a look at her husband. Why didn't she go in? What fear was preventing her?

The bedroom was almost dark, for the light from the living room lamp barely reached it. Doña Lupe carried the lamp into the parlor. She wanted to observe her niece. She was first struck by her strange attitude—it didn't jibe with the natural emotions of a wife in such a painful situation. Once she got a good look at her from a distance, Fortunata, without paying the slightest attention to someone as respectable as her husband's aunt, went back to the living room where it was very dim now and sat down. She had still not taken off her cloak and looked on the verge of leaving. Her cheek resting on her hand, she sat immobile for about fifteen minutes. The silence reigning in the three rooms was interrupted only by an occasional slurred word from Maxi and the feline steps of the servant, who crossed the living room to take her orders from the only person who was in charge that night. Had the patient's condition allowed her to raise her voice, oh, how Doña Lupe would have shook the house with the thunder of her authoritarian tones. But it couldn't be. The things her niece would have heard! Maxi's aunt resolved to let the matter rest until the following day. But her curiosity and anger were so intense that she couldn't help but creep back into the living room and say to Fortunata in a choked voice:

"Explain this to me."

"This?" she murmured, looking up, as if out of sleep.

"Yes, this: Maximiliano abused, your coming home so late and acting like a betrayer in a melodrama."

After surveying Doña Lupe from head to toe for about a minute, Fortunata leaned her head on her fist again without a word.

"Well, I like what's happening! Very nice . . ."

And she went to the bedroom, for she heard Maxi calling her. Then he could be heard vomiting. Fortunata concentrated on what was happening in there, but held her sphinxlike pose.

When the widow came back to the living room it was already past ten o'clock.

"The clock's struck ten!" she said in that severe voice that would have made a stone quiver. "And you still haven't taken off your cloak. Are you planning to go . . . shopping again? When poor little Maxi woke up awhile ago, he asked me if you were back yet and I told him you weren't. I was ashamed to say you were, because I would have had to add that you'd confessed your guilt just by the way you came in. He said: 'It's better if she doesn't come.' Don't you realize we can't go on like this? That you've got to explain this? Speak, child, speak, or I'll take the matter into my hands."

After looking at her husband's aunt with an expression that Doña Lupe could not have defined, Fortunata put her head on her hand again and, heaving a great sigh, withdrew into that lugubrious silence that would have made patience itself despair.

"This is enough to drive me crazy!" cried Doña Lupe with an irate gesture. "Do you think, do you* think your cunning will get you anywhere with me? I'll have you know—"

She was exploding with rage and made an effort to contain it by going back to the bedroom. Her agitated brain produced these thoughts: "Just what I was afraid of—it's happened. I said it would, I told them this woman would end up giving us real trouble. Oh, what a sharp eye I have! She just didn't convince me, and I always said it: with or without the Micaelas, you can't turn a bad woman into a decent wife. There she is; just look at her now and tell me whether or not I was right, whether or not I had cause to worry."

What stimulated Doña Lupe's pride most was her disappointment, for, say what she would, the fact is that she had thought Fortunata had been radically reformed. She couldn't contain herself and returned to the living room.

"Are you going to explain this—yes or no?"

Then she noticed that she was speaking to a shadow. Fortunata was not there. Doña Lupe went out to the hall and saw a light in a small interior room where Maxi's wife kept her clothes. She pushed open the door. There she was, without her cloak on now, taking clothes out of a wardrobe and putting them into a big trunk.

"Would you mind clearing up my doubts once and for all?" she said, without bothering to keep her voice down now. "This is disgraceful. If you insist on keeping mum, I'll think that the one who caused all this tragedy is you, no one else but you."

Fortunata turned toward her. She was as pale as a corpse.

"Let's see," added the Jáuregui woman, gesticulating. "If my nephew asks me again whether you're back, what should I tell him?"

"Tell him," replied the wife in a lower voice and speaking with great difficulty, "tell him that I haven't come back, because I'm leaving as soon as it's light."

---

* "You" is given as the familiar *tú* the first time; the second time the polite, or more formal, *usted* is used. The change is naturally very expressive of Doña Lupe's rejection of Fortunata, hereafter addressed as *usted*.

"I don't understand a word of this. What's happened, for God's sake? Who mistreated Maxi?"

Fortunata heaved a great sigh.

"What a farce! I'm going to tell the law about this. We'll see whether you answer the judge this way. It's obvious that you're guilty. Otherwise, why would you be leaving?"

"Because I must go," she replied, casting her eyes down.

She said nothing else. Beside herself by now, Doña Lupe grabbed Fortunata's arm and, shaking her violently, cursed her:

"Be damned, woman! It's obvious you're an imposter, an imposter in the full sense of the word . . . and that you've always been one and always will be for as long as you live. You fooled everyone except me. Not me—I saw it coming."

Crushed by her conscience, Fortunata could not respond at all. If Doña Lupe had flung herself on Fortunata and hit her, the latter would have let herself be punished.

"You're doing well to get out of here," added Doña Lupe, who was standing in the doorway now. "I won't be the one to stop you. Some trick! What a household, and what a marriage! Nothing surprises me, because—I repeat—you fooled everyone except me."

It was a lie. She had been the first to be fooled. A fine fiasco for her educational talent! The thought of this fiasco enraged her all the more, more than the crime itself that she suspected her niece had committed.

Going back to the living room, Doña Lupe checked her frenzy by deciding what had to be done. First she would spend the night there. Then she sent Patricia home for Nicolás, who had come in from Toledo that same day.

"I want my nephew here immediately. If he's sleeping, tell Papitos to wake him."

Fortunata stayed where she was, but she didn't get very far with her packing, because every now and then she would stop, sit on the trunk, and look at the floor or the candle, whose long black wick burned, giving off big drops of wax. She hadn't felt such remorse since she had started to cheat on Maxi. The ghost of her wickedness had not yet appeared to her except jokingly, and it had been very easy to scare it off. But it was different now. The ghost came and sat down with her and got up with her; when she packed, it helped her; when she sighed, it sighed; her eyes were its eyes—in short, her self and it seemed to be one and the same. And she was also tormented (besides the pangs in her conscience) by a yearning to love; a vivid desire to normalize her life as much as the passion that ruled her allowed. She recalled that her lover had offered to provide her with her own apartment and establish between them a domestic regularity within their irregular situation. But could it work? Her amorous yearnings alternated with vague fears, and at last she came to consider herself the most unfortunate woman in the world, not through any fault of hers, but because it had been so ordained by a superior force, by that spiritual mechanism that pushed her irrevocably on. She didn't expect to sleep that night and wished day would break soon so she could leave; hearing her husband's pained voice was an atrocious martyrdom. She would have given ten years of her life to erase what had happened. But she couldn't help it now. She only hoped Maxi's wounds weren't serious. Next to this her most ardent desire was to go out the door and run away from that house forever. Better to die than to keep up the farce of an impossible marriage.

She was snapped out of this meditation by Doña Lupe, who entered the room again after midnight. She was all wrapped up in a blanket, which gave her a formidable, lugubrious air, rather like that of a soul from another world.

"All poor Maxi can do now," she said, "is cry . . . He keeps asking me if you're back. Frankly, I don't know what to tell him."

"Tell him I died," replied Fortunata.

"It certainly would be better that way. Are your trunks ready yet?"

"I still have a bit more to do. Look, don't worry; I'm not taking anything that's not mine."

"How about your jewelry?" asked the widow, who kept the most valuable pieces at her house.

"My jewelry?" repeated Fortunata, hesitating at first and then becoming more decisive. "It's not mine. It's his, Maxi's; he got it out of hock. It's his, all of it."

"So all you're taking is your clothes?"

"That's all. I'm even leaving behind my change purse with the last money he gave me—here, on the bureau. See?"

The prudent lady took the change purse, which was still well stuffed, and tucked it away.

12

There is reason to believe that when Papitos entered Nicolás Rubín's room at midnight and gave him a good shake, saying, "Sir, sir, it's your aunt—she wants you over there right away," the good man bellowed at her, turned over, and fell soundly asleep again. It is probable that at Papitos' second attack he shook off some of his sloth and drove the little monkey away with another loud roar, entertaining in his groggy brain the thought that his aunt should wait until morning to disturb him. And the basis of these hypotheses is that Nicolás did not show up at his brother Maxi's house until after seven o'clock the next morning. Such sluggishness exasperated Doña Lupe, who cried:

"I'm fated to be the victim of these three idiots. Each one in his own way is consuming my life, and between the three of them they're going to be the end of me. What a family, Lord, what a family! If my Jáuregui were alive with me, it'd be a different story. My God, you're calm! I don't know why it is that with all that calm and all you eat you're not fatter. I sent for you at eleven o'clock at night and this is when you turn up. You do realize what's going on?"

She said this in the living room when she saw Nicolás come in, his eyes still testifying to how well he had slept. When she heard the colloquy, the sinner came out of her hiding place and, creeping to the living room door, she tried to eavesdrop. But aunt and nephew were talking in very low tones and she couldn't make out what they were saying. Then the priest, at his aunt's urging, went out into the hall; Fortunata ducked quickly into her hiding place to wait for him there.

The room was almost dark at that time of day. Going in, you couldn't see who was there. The candle, which had burned for most of the night, had gone out. From within, Fortunata saw the priest—a black shadow in the luminous frame of the open door—and she waited for him to come in or say something. As if wary of stepping into the den of a wild beast, Nicolás lingered in the doorway, and from his vantage point he darted these words into the darkness:

"Woman—are you there? I can't see anything."

"Yes, sir, I'm here," she murmured.

"My aunt," added the priest, "has told me about the horrors that happened last night. My brother mistreated, wounded; you coming home at an odd hour, and only to pack your clothes and leave, destroying marital harmony and leaving us all swimming in confusion. Would you like to explain all this hullabaloo to me?"

"Yes, sir," the voice replied with inexpressible confusion.

"Have you had a part in this infamy?"

"I . . . I didn't have anything to do with the wounds," the voice hastened to say.

"Let's see now," said the priest, taking a few steps into the room, his outstretched hands groping in the darkness. "A few days ago—I found out yesterday by chance—my brother suspected that you were being unfaithful to him; this is the point. Did he have any grounds for his suspicion?"

The voice said nothing, and there was a short pause of fearful expectancy.

"What? You aren't answering me?" Nicolás interrogated angrily. "What do you take me for? Remember, you're in the confessional box. I'm not asking as one of the family or a judge, but as a priest. Did the suspicion have any basis?"

After another interval that seemed longer than the first to the priest, the voice responded faintly:

"Yes, sir."

"Now I see," Rubín affirmed angrily. "You've deceived us all; first me, then the Micaelas, then my friend Pintado, and then the whole family. You are unworthy of being our sister. What a fine role we played! And I, who guaranteed you!

Nothing like this has ever happened to me in my whole life. I took you for a girl who'd gone astray, not a corrupt woman, and now I see you're what they call a monster."

He took another step forward, closed the door halfway, and touched the wall to see if he could find a chair or a bench on which to sit.

"To put it plainly, you don't love my brother. Let your conscience speak."

"No, sir," the voice said promptly and effortlessly.

"You never loved him; this is the point."

"No, sir."

"But you told me you hoped to grow fond of him in time, as you got to know him better."

"Yes, I did say that."

"But it didn't work out that way, did it? What a failure! There are cases . . . So there's no feeling on your part?"

"Nothing."

"Fine. But you forget that you're married and God says you have to love your husband; if you don't, you still have to be faithful in body and soul. Oh, this is lovely, isn't it! Nothing like this has ever happened to me. And you, trampling on honor and divine laws, losing your head over some jerk . . . Oh, it's plain to see—your licentious past has poisoned your soul, and your 'purification' rolled right off, like water off a duck. And not to have seen this, Lord! Not to have seen this!"

The priest was so furious at how badly his repair job had turned out, and his self-pride as mender of souls was so keenly wounded, that he couldn't help but vent all his spite with these wrathful words:

"Well, you might as well know you're condemned. Don't try to get around it: condemned."

It is not known whether or not these terrorist tactics had their effect, because Fortunata made no reply. The expression of her feelings about the tremendous anathema was lost in the darkness of that cavern.

"The least you can do is confess your crime, woman," said Rubín, who, slipping through the darkness, had found a box to sit on. "Don't hide anything from me. Now. How many times have you been unfaithful to your husband?"

The answer didn't come. Nicolás repeated the question as many as three times, more gently, and at last a whisper was heard:

"Lots."

Father Rubín says that that "lots" made him shiver, and that it sounded like the rustle of tiny beetles scurrying across the wall in throngs.

"With how many men?"

"Only one . . ."

"Only one! . . . Really? Did you meet him after you were married?"

"No, sir. I've known him for a long time. I've always loved him."

"Aha! I know, the same old story," said the priest, whose self-pride came to the fore upon discovering a way to seem farsighted. "Just what I was afraid of. First love! I told you so, didn't I? That's where the danger was. I've seen lots of cases. All right. And is it the same character?"

Fortunata answered in the affirmative.

"And was he the heel who took advantage of poor, weak little Maxi and mistreated him? Oh, but this world's a bitter place."

"He was the one. But Maxi provoked him," said the voice. "These things happen before you know it. I saw it from the window."

"What window?"

"The one in that house."

"Oh, so we have a house, do we? Oh yes, it's the same old story, all right. I knew it would happen. Don't think it's news to me. The love nest—the whole works! What a disgrace! And aren't you ashamed of yourself? Anybody who has a soul would be full of tribulation, but you—you're as cheeky as they come."

"I'm sorry . . . I'm so sorry. I wish this had never happened."

"Sure, so you could keep sinning on the sly. More mud. I know this kind of perversity by heart."

Fortunata fell silent. Either the priest's eyes were getting used to the dark or there was more light in the room now, but the fact is that Nicolás was beginning to be able to see his sister-in-law; she was seated on the trunk, a handkerchief in her hand. From time to time she put it to her face as if to dry her tears. Fortunata *was* crying, as a matter of fact; but sometimes the reason why the young woman covered her nose with the handkerchief was that she needed to protect herself from the unpleasant smell from the priest's terribly worn black habit.

"Those tears you're shedding—are they a sign of sincere repentance? Come now! If you really—and I mean really—repent for us, and your contrition is ardent, all this could be fixed up. But you'd have to submit to hard and conclusive proofs; this is the point. Would you go back to the Micaelas?"

"Oh no, sir!" the sinner retorted promptly.

"Well, go to the devil then!" shouted the priest with a disdainful gesture.

"Let me say this: I repent . . . but—"

"But, schmut!" Rubín declared crassly. "Curse your infamous adultery. And curse the evil man who put the devil in you."

"That . . ."

"That what? The nerve! And to say it like that, with such cynicism!"

Fortunata didn't know what *cynicism* meant, and kept silent.

"Everything leads me to believe that you're prepared to do it again, and that nobody can get you to forget that cursed dream you have."

The great sigh that she heaved confirmed the supposition better than words.

"So even though you can see you've been ruined and dishonored by the heel, you still love him. Well, lots of luck."

"I can't help it. It's *in* me; I can't control it."

"Oh, I know; it's the same old story—I know it by heart. They love *him* only, and can't get him out of their heads and diddle-dee-dee and diddle-dee-dum . . . It all comes from not having any scruples but a rotten heart and a sneaky way of sinning. What a lot you women are! You know that passions have to be controlled and uprooted, but oh no, you go right on clinging to your little dreams . . . Got to have what you want. In other words, you don't want to be saved. We put you on the road to recovery and you couldn't get off it fast enough. Off you went to your perdition! Fine and well. Explain it to God if you can. The mere thought of it makes me laugh. Because I can just see it: you're going to take up your free and easy life again in no time. Fun—ha! For the time being, maybe. The scoundrel will fix up something and look after you for a while; you'll have a house to live in . . . Now that I think of it—is the man married?"

"Yes, sir," Fortunata said sorrowfully.

"Holy Mother of God!" exclaimed the priest, throwing up both hands. "What a horror, what a society this is! Another victim: the gentleman's wife. And you, fresh as can be, sowing death and disease wherever you go . . ."

This sermonish sentence terrified Fortunata.

"You'll have your punishment, and soon. The same old story. What women will do, oh Lord! Go on off and have your adventures, dishonor your husband, upset two marriages; the explosion will come later. I wouldn't want to be in your shoes. A kept woman now, then prostitution—the abyss. Yes, the abyss: there it is. Look at it—its black mouth open already, uglier than the mouth of a dragon. And there's no stopping it now; you're heading straight into it, because that man's going to abandon you. Your days are numbered."

Fortunata's head was near her knees now. She was hunched up in a ball, and her sobs betrayed her troubled soul.

"Oh, what a pitiful woman you are!" the priest added solemnly, rising now. "You're not only a hussy, you're an idiot. Every woman who's in love is. Their brains dry up. You get them out of those purgatories of pleasure and they go right back. If that's what you want, that's what you'll get. Take it. They'll settle with you in hell. Try your sophisms and love-making down there. It's all over. There's nothing I can tell you now, and there's no place for you in this house. It's the end of the line. To the gutter, child. Have your fun. Leave, and when you do, we'll burn holy incense; yes, we'll burn holy incense. That's what we'll do."

He said this from the door and retreated with no further ado. Doña Lupe was waiting for him in the living room to find out if he had had more luck than she had in pumping out the truth. And they stayed there talking a good while. Then they heard noise; they heard Fortunata's voice; she was talking softly with Patricia, perhaps telling her how and when she would send someone for her clothes. Then aunt and nephew peered out the balcony window and saw her hurrying across the street and turning the corner without a single glance back at the home she was leaving forever.

Nicolás repeated the figure of speech he found so satisfying: "Burn incense, burn incense." And as far as lavender was concerned, it wouldn't have done *him* any harm, physically. No offense meant.

VOLUME THREE

I. The Café

I

JUAN PABLO RUBÍN DIDN'T FEEL ALIVE unless he spent half the day or almost all of it at the café. Being used to this way of life, he would have considered himself unfortunate if his work or various activities had forced him to live differently. He was an implacable, persistent assassin of time; his only deep joy consisted of watching the hours die gaspingly and the boring moments gradually give out, never to rise again. He went to the café after lunch, in the early afternoon, and stayed until four or five o'clock. After dinner, at about eight, he usually went back and stayed until past midnight or daybreak, depending on the occasion. Since his friends were not so constant, he spent part of the time alone meditating on serious political, religious, or philosophical problems and gazing absently at the plaster molding, the smoke-stained painting on the ceiling, and other such decorative details. That nook and its atmosphere had become so vital to him that only when he was there did he feel in full possession of his faculties. Even his memory failed him when he wasn't at the café. If he suddenly forgot an important name or fact in the street, he didn't try to remember it; instead, he reflected calmly, "I'll remember it at the café." Indeed, when he had barely taken his seat on the sofa, the stimulating influence of the place began to have its effect on his system. Once his sight and sense of smell were aroused, his spiritual faculties quickly revived, his memory felt refreshed, and his mental powers unnumbed. The café gave him the feeling of privacy that usually comes from one's own home. When he entered, all the objects smiled as if they belonged to him. He fancied that the people he saw there constantly—the waiters, the headwaiter, certain regular customers—were closely related to him by family ties. He even felt he had a certain spiritual kinship with the little hunchbacked woman who sold matches and newspapers at the door.

But even though Juan Pablo was so fond of the place, he had changed cafés quite a few times in five years. It was like moving to a new house, and since all cafés in Madrid look alike (just as all the houses do), Juan Pablo took his domesticity wherever he went, and after patronizing a new café for a few days he felt at home there. These moves were due to certain inexplicable emigration currents common in the society of lazy men.

Sometimes the impulse came from fickle friends who craved variety; at other times the emigration was due to a very disagreeable quarrel with "that man at the next table." Or it was because the owner of a café had "acted like a pig" in charging them for some glasses that had been broken during an argument over the real causes of the death of General Concha, or, finally, because the place had gotten progressively and intolerably worse and had made many of them anxious to try a new or remodeled establishment. Juan Pablo didn't favor starting an emigration, but he almost always followed them. A member of the group could easily get lost in one of those waves of emigration, either because he opposed the move or because his debts kept him tied to the old place, like a mortgage on his presence there. On the other hand, the group always gained a new member who refreshed their ideas and jokes.

If someone had taken the trouble to follow Rubín's steps from '69 to '74, he would have found that our man was a steady customer of the Café San Antonio, then the Café Suizo Nuevo, then Café Platerías, then Café Siglo and Café Levante; he would have seen Rubín preferring cafés with singers for a while, then hating them; he would have seen him going to the Gallo or the Concepción Jerónimo when he wanted to make himself scarce; and, finally, he would have seen him setting up shop in one of the busiest and noisiest cafés in the Puerta del Sol. In the afternoon he was always one of the last to arrive because he was a late riser; at night he was unfailingly the first. Rarely did he find Don Evaristo González Feijóo or Leopoldo Montes when he arrived. The evening *tertulia*'s set of members was different from the midday *tertulia*'s; only a few went to both. Rubín was the only fixture in both groups. They occupied three tables that the waiter set up before they arrived. Juan Pablo appeared at eight, when there were only three or four people in the whole place and the waiters were sitting at the counter talking. The owner or the headwaiter set up services, putting sugar cubes on each saucer, then stacking the saucers. The glass door opened every two minutes, admitting a customer (taking off his scarf or unwrapping his cloak as he entered), and then it shut with a loud bang, opening again immediately, its rusty hinges squeaking stridently. It was a wearisome refrain: *creeeek* . . . an individual with a cigar in his mouth, making his entrance; then *bang!* and *creeeek* . . .

From behind the counter the café owner greeted whoever passed. Most of his customers liked to be served their coffee promptly, and they clapped loudly if the boy didn't respond right away. Juan Pablo entered slowly and ponderously, like a man about to perform a sacred duty. He headed gravely toward the tables on the right and always sat in exactly the same place. Just as he was about to wipe off the table, the waiter greeted Juan Pablo, who, answering in a dignified manner, rubbed his hands together and made himself comfortable, keeping his cape on. Then he drew his glass nearer and put the sugar bowl on the right, at the discreet distance at which one places an inkwell when writing, and he watched the operation of pouring the milk and coffee into the glass, making quite sure that the proportions of these liquids were right and that the glass was filled just to the brim. This was essential. Then he took the spoon with his left hand, and with his right hand gradually added the sugar cubes to his coffee, casting indulgent looks at the people coming in. Being a veteran at the café, he knew how to have his coffee with that slowness and art that an important act demands.

It would be impossible for us to follow our man through all his café-going periods. But we can't leave out the Puerta del Sol period, when the *tertulia* members and his friends included Don Evaristo González Feijóo, Don Basilio Andrés de la Caña, Melchor de Relimpio, and Leopoldo Montes, all of them much given to politics and discussing their country as if it were one of their personal possessions. Since they all had the same mania, each one cultivated a speciality: Leopoldo Montes brought news of a political turnover almost every day; Don Basilio always had gossip about bureaucratic issues; Relimpio was precocious and malicious in his judgments; Rubín stood out for thinking he knew everything and could forecast events; and, finally, Feijóo was profoundly skeptical and took all politics with a grain of salt.

The fraternal spirit of Spaniards shone splendidly in that group, in which the Carlist and the Republican, the hard-headed progressivist and the implacable moderate, all took hands. Once upon a time, the political parties that remained separate in public were also separate in private; but progress in customs injected a certain mildness into personal relations and eventually the mildness turned into softness. Some people think we've gone from one bad extreme to another without stopping at a suitable point in between, and they detect a loss of character in this fraternizing. This business of everybody being a personal friend of everybody else is a symptom of the state we're in: ideas are becoming mere pretexts to earn or keep one's bread. There is a tacit agreement (not so tacit that it can't be discovered by scratching a politician's surface) according to which turns have been established for the right to govern. For this reason, there is no aspiration, no matter how far-fetched, which cannot be considered probable; for this reason, there is insecurity—the only constant we know—and Masonic alliances among various groups, from the clerical to the anarchist, so that jobs are given out of mercy during times of peace as easily as pardons are granted after wars and revolutions. It's somewhat like mutual insurance against punishment, which is why violent events are considered the most natural thing in the world. Political morality is like a cape with so many patches that one no longer knows which was the original fabric.

In their conversation, Feijóo and Rubín attributed this loss of character to disillusionments.

"I," said Feijóo, "am a disillusioned progressive and you are a repentant traditionalist. We have something in common—we think it's all a farce and it's only a matter of knowing who gets perks and who doesn't."

2

Don Evaristo González Feijóo deserves more than a mention in this tale. He was a bachelor well along in years who lived comfortably on his rents and retired pay as an army colonel. Shortly after the African war, he left active service. He was the only member of the *tertulia* who wasn't in straits or involved in shady financial deals. His trim, robust, pleasant appearance reflected his placid and orderly existence. His carriage proclaimed his military profession and innate nobility; he had a white mustache and a martial arrogance; a serene look, lively eyes, a smile that was at once playful and kindly; his dress was very careful and clean, and his talk was most instructive, for he had traveled and served in Cuba and the Philippines; he had had scores of adventures and seen many and quite strange things. Neither the most exaggerated nor the most demoralizing notions fazed him. He listened to a supporter of the Inquisition or a rabid radical with the same benevolent cool. He was indulgent toward enthusiasts, undoubtedly because he too had "suffered" enthusiasms. If someone expressed his views ardently and in good faith, Feijóo listened with the compassionate patience one feels for the insane. He had been crazy, too; but he had regained his ability to reason, and reasoning in politics was—according to him—a complete absence of faith.

In the *tertulias* held in cafés there are always two kinds of members: the ones who make the underbrush of a conversation by telling absurd news or gross jokes and the ones who have the last word on whatever is being debated; the latter deliver doctoral judgments, thus bringing the jokes and nonsense down to their real level. Wherever there are men there is authority, and these café authorities, who sometimes define, sometimes predict, and always influence the crowd because their opinions are apparently sound, constitute a sort of consensus that usually ends up in the press, where the consensus probably wasn't based on anything better.

So. The ones who exercise authority in the *tertulias* usually sit on the sofa, that is, their backs to the wall, as if they were presiding or constituting a jury. Juan Pablo and Feijóo belonged to this category. But Feijóo never sat on the sofa because the corduroy cover was uncomfortably warm; instead, he sat in one of the chairs, drinking his coffee at an angle to the table, with his back turned to the neighboring table.

On the other hand, Don Basilio Andrés de la Caña, who was one of the "commoners," always sat on the sofa. He liked positions that were better than what he deserved, and he rested his shiny, bald head against the mirror frame. He wore glasses, and his small nose could have passed as an emblem of his sharpness. He squinted when he gave a difficult answer, like a man who wants to marshal his ideas carefully. His forehead was extremely spacious, and his facial structure was the type that seems to reveal a profound mind capable of a clear synthesis. He bore a certain resemblance to Cavour, which is why the others teased him a bit tiresomely. We may refer to one of Melchor de Relimpio's sayings for a definition of his intelligence:

"The best business you could do these days would be—guess what? Open up Don Basilio's head, take out all that straw, and sell it."

And Don Basilio, who had his tricks, like any old donkey, exploited his deceptive looks and that air of being "somebody" that was due to his pumpkinlike baldness, his wide, curved forehead, his spectacles, and his tiny, prismatic nose. More than once, the ministers to whom he introduced himself experienced the fascination that that masklike face had over the common mob, and they took him for an unrecognized eminence. The skull and brow were a phrenological hoax. Whenever he spoke, he adopted such a solemn tone that many unwary souls listened to him out of respect. He considered laughter improper, undignified, and he had banished it almost completely from his face, taking as his model a page from a state document.

This man's life had two major phases: journalism and "employmania." At the press he was in charge of foreign affairs and matters related to the Treasury. In journalism those days it wasn't necessary to know how to write for either of these things. But La Caña took these two branches of human knowledge so seriously that from the way he worked it looked as if he were writing *The Critique of Pure Reason*. His salary at the newspaper office never rose to over thirty *duros*—when they did pay him, that is. He went back and forth, from the newspaper to the bureaucracy, so that when he was out of work and his family was starving, the muses of foreign affairs and finances were happy. My man was always "very much in line," as his friends used to say; that is, very moderate, because it was always the conservatives who employed him. Señor Mon gave him his first job, and he was connected with the Treasury off and on until the long Union liberal period started. It was his downfall, the worst times he'd known; he lived miserably on his writings, and asked at the end of every article: "What will Russia do?," answering himself in deliciously good faith: "We don't know." He always called England "Saint James' Cabinet" and France "The Tuilleries' Cabinet."

During the revolutionary period poor old Don Basilio had a wretched time of it because he didn't want to sell out or give up his ideas. He *did* consent to work for a mildly liberal journal . . . although he made it quite clear to the editor that he would "treat only financial matters, and absolutely exclude all political ideas." Said and done: every day La Caña cranked out a long article (which nobody read) criticizing the management of the Treasury, not just saying this or that, but using figures. "Figures are a serious matter," he would say, and he would start in on the budget and itemize it like a laundry bill.

"These people just don't understand," he would say in the café, swollen with authority, "that without a budget there's no politics, no country—nothing. I'm sick of telling them every single day. It's like talking to a stone wall. Gentlemen, I assure you that I've examined the figures one by one, and believe me, it doesn't make any sense that that mess should have come out of the Treasury offices. It's like I say: that man [meaning the minister] doesn't know what he's doing and he's never been in such a spot in his life. And here I've been proving it all along! But no, they don't want to listen to me."

After expressing the pity he felt for this poor country by heaving a deep sigh, he kept drinking his coffee indolently but thirstily (because it was real nourishment for Don Basilio) and he drank a brimming glassful;* he let it overflow onto the saucer as much as possible so that he could later pour this liquid into the glass. During the final years of the revolution, Don Manuel Pez gave him a little job in the governor's office, and he took it as an aid until better times came; but he was dissatisfied, not only by the pittance they paid him but because he felt his dignity had been insulted. The friends who heard him complain, comparing his meager wages to the multitude of mouths he had to feed, consoled him, each in his own way; but he invariably said: "And above all, believe me: what makes me saddest of all is not being *in my field.*" His "field" was the Treasury.

The group's conversation, which almost always started on the theme of the war, shifted imperceptibly to the subject of jobs. Leopoldo Montes, eternally out of work, Relimpio, and others who had a few scraps of the budget in their clutches flung themselves with hungry delight on that tantalizing subject:

"You, how much do you have?"

"Me? Fourteen; but I should get sixteen. So-and-so, who was behind me in the payroll office, has already got twenty, and I've had fourteen for ten years."

"Well," said Don Basilio, "when I was 'in my field,' I got up to twenty-four, little by little. With all the confusion there is now, though, you can't tell which way you're headed. When I get back into my field, I won't take anything under thirty."

"But since nobody pays any attention to the accrued benefits we're supposed to get . . . What a country! I went into the Legal Clearance Department with eight; then they sent me over to Education with ten; then, when I was out of work, I finally had to take six from the Lottery Office so I wouldn't starve to death."

"Well, as for me," murmured a voice that sounded as if it had come out of a bottle, a voice that belonged to a squalid and cadaverous face on which were stamped all the sadnesses of the nation's administration, "all I want is two months, two more months of active service so I can be retired by the Overseas Office. I've been sent to the colonies seven times. I'm drained, and I'm already due to retire, to rest with twelve. Blast my luck!"

---

*In Spanish cafés, coffee is still sometimes served in a glass.

The dismissed public employee who most deserves our sympathy is the one who asks only for a few more days of employment so that he can rest a head heavy with years, fears, and services on the pillow reserved for the retired.

3

From eight to ten the café was completely full, and the breathing, vapors, and smoke brewed up an atmosphere that congested the lungs. At nine, when *La Correspondencia* and the other evening papers arrived, there was more of a bustle. The hunchbacked lady and a brother of hers who also had a somewhat humped back came in with an armload of papers and, handing them out from a central spot among the tables, they reached everyone who wanted one. Shortly afterward the crowd began to thin; some went off to the theater, and the clusters of students broke up, for there were many who left early to study. In all the cafés, a considerable number of customers retire between ten and eleven. At midnight the place livens up again with the people on their way home from the theater who are in the habit of stopping in for hot chocolate or a light supper before going to bed. After one o'clock the only ones left are the conversation addicts, who stick to the sofa or chairs as if there were some sort of calcareous substance there; they are the true oysters of a café.

Juan Pablo didn't leave until the doors were closed, and of all his friends, the only one who kept him company at these late hours was Melchor de Relimpio. They would set out together for their neighborhood, and sometimes one escorted the other to his front door, where they kept right on chatting until the night watchman came to open up. If it was a good night, they usually kept it up for another hour, wandering through the streets.

What did those men talk about for so many, many hours? Spaniards are the most talkative creatures on earth; when they have no subject of conversation, they talk about themselves, and naturally they're always negative. In our cafés, anything under the sun is fair game for conversation. Gross banalities as well as ingenious, discreet, and pertinent ideas may be heard in these places, for they are frequented not only by rakes and swearers; enlightened people with good habits go to cafés too. There are *tertulias* made up of military men, of engineers; most often, there are *tertulias* made up of employees and students; and whatever room they leave is filled up by out-of-towners. In a café one hears the stupidest and also the most sublime things. There are people who have learned everything they know about philosophy at a café table, which leads us to suppose that there must be individuals who convert a café table into a pleasant class on philosophic systems. There are famous figures from parliament or the press who have learned all they know in cafés. Men with great assimilatory powers can reveal a considerable wealth of knowledge without ever having opened a book, and it is because they have appropriated ideas poured into these nocturnal circles by studious men who allow themselves an idle hour to scatter their knowledge in these pleasant and fraternal *tertulias*. Scholars go to cafés too; one may hear eloquent observations and pithy expositions of complex doctrines. It's not all frivolity, stale anecdotes, and lies. The café is like a grand fair where countless products of the human mind are bought and sold. Naturally there are more trinkets than anything else; but in their midst, and sometimes going unnoticed, there are priceless gems.

The table over which Juan Pablo Rubín presided was the second on the right as you entered. The one next to it belonged to the same circle of friends; then came the one occupied by "the free-lance priests," so called because it usually drew several, shall we say, stray priests who during the night and part of the day led a secular life. One of this table's regulars was Nicolás Rubín, dressed as a layman like the others; he linked this circle to the one where his brother sat. These two neighboring *tertulias* enjoyed excellent relations, and at times their worthy members even mixed. Behind the presbyters' table were two occupied by writers, journalists, and playwrights. Federico Ruiz joined them very often and, being a very talkative man, he used to butt in on the priests, the result of which was that on one side the priests got to know the "pen people" and on the other Rubín's and Feijóo's friends. After the writers came the "road boys,"[*] who took up the three corner tables. The dividing line in that vast place started there. Said dividing line marked the beginning of the café's second section, which had been invaded by students (most of them from Galicia and León), who made an infernal racket.

Since all this refers to 1874, it's only natural that the main topic of conversation in the café then was the civil war. Noteworthy events and affairs happened that year—the siege of Bilboa, General Concha's death, and, finally, the Monarchist pronunciamento in Sagunto. Seldom did a day go by without the newspapers' putting out an Extra, announcing battles, unloading of arms, movements of the troops, changes in command, and other things that usually caused endless comments.

"Have you heard, Rubín?" Feijóo said as he took his seat next to the corner of the table and took off the saucer covering his glass. "It looks like Mendiry has fled in the direction of Viana."

"Don't worry," Juan Pablo replied assuredly. "They won't get beyond the little circle of the Basque provinces and Navarre. I know them pretty well. All the chiefs are after is the loot. The day there's a government that wants to buy them, the war's over."

---

[*] Highway engineers.

"No, come now!"

"That's all there is to it. Rascals here, there, and everywhere."

"All it is is hunger—lots of it," said one of the priests, raising his voice at the next table. "The war isn't ending because the military's happy to have the hammer in its hand. They're not for peace on either side. But what can you tell *me*? I've seen it at close range; worked in the fourth regiment; I've seen the war close up . . . and it'll keep right on bothering us as long as they're squeezing a profit out of it."

"What a rage the chaplain's in!" said Feijóo smiling; he did not continue because Don Basilio arrived and in very mysterious tones declared:

"When I say there's news . . ."

After he had been served his coffee, he lowered his head and confided to his four or five friends, who were leaning forward:

"I'm telling you this in the strictest confidence."

"But, what is it?"

"*Mysteries!* . . . Sagasta's annoyed. His private secretary told me so."

"Ah! I heard that too," said Relimpio. "It's true; something's bothering him like a toothache."

"I don't know the reason," La Caña added brightly. "Think whatever you want. All I'm sure of is that he's really upset, and there's something underneath it all."

"But don't you know anything else?" Feijóo asked restlessly. "I thought you were going to give us news of the duke's conference with Elduayen, and you come tell us Sagasta's in a bad mood. God help us. But the bit about the conference—*is* it true or isn't it?"

Don Basilio usually kept a toothpick in his mouth, and now, taking it out with two fingers, he showed it to them, gesturing with it as if it were part of what he had to say.

"What I know is—" he affirmed in a pathetic tone, offering up the toothpick to the admiration of his friends, "what I know is, that things are in a very bad way. I agree with Lorenzana: 'Let us meditate.'"

The circle of heads formed again, and into it Don Basilio, like a medicine man, projected his breath before emitting his words. Said breath was scarcely pleasant to Feijóo's nose, which is why the latter discreetly recoiled.

Don Basilio wavered between his conscience, which told him to keep silent, and his desire to satisfy his friends' curiosity. Finally he came out with:

"This afternoon Romero Ortiz left the ministry at four o'clock, and as he was going along Amor de Dios Street, he saw a friend; the carriage stopped, the friend got in and they went—"

"But who was the friend?"

"I can't tell you everything . . . Oh, well—here goes: it was Romero. They went—just listen to this—to Don Antonio Canovas' house, . . . at 1 Madera Street."

This said, La Caña became very serious, relishing the effect his words were sure to have. He put the toothpick between his teeth again and looked at his friends with a certain pity.

"And?" Rubín said rudely. "I don't get it."

"Well, my friend," replied Don Basilio, using the tone of a superior man who doesn't want to put himself out, "if you don't want to 'get it,' what am I supposed to do about it?"

"What difference does it make whether or not they went to Canovas'?"

"Oh, none at all, none at all. It's perfectly irrelevant; just an insignificant detail. So they went there instead of to church or work."

Then he allowed himself to burst out laughing, which was very odd in him. "This Don Basilio . . ."

"My friend," declared Feijóo with his customary frankness, "admit to us that the news you've brought may be sheer nonsense."

"All right, Señor Don Evaristo; think what you want. I wash my hands of it."

This bit about "washing his hands" was something La Caña repeated very often, but the facts did not confirm his words, as simple observation proved.

"You can think whatever suits you," repeated the gentleman from the Treasury, attempting to make his dignity as a news-giver rise above his friends' sneers; "but what I say is, before this month's up, Prince Alfonso will be on the throne."

General laughter. Don Basilio blushed and then paled. His lips trembled as they touched the rim of his glass.

"And I say he won't," Juan Pablo said angrily. "I'd rather see the *cantonals'* back than let it come to that. We're not *that* dumb in Spain. Gentlemen, can you imagine Prince Alfonso taking over? And after him Doña Isabel? A fine future for us! Conservatism again. But what I'd like to ask," he added exaltedly, letting his cape slip off his shoulders and pushing back his hat, "is this: who does the prince have on his side, hmm? Tell me that."

Don Basilio didn't dare reply. He was content to assume the airs of a profound man who can't quite decide to release the swarm of ideas buzzing in his brain.

"Answer me."

"No one—just a couple of poor chaps," said Montes.

"The ones who didn't even know how to defend the mother when we kicked her out. And now . . . if Don Basilio is willing, let's call roll of all Alfonso's supporters. Come on, let's see who the rats are."

If it had been up to him, Don Basilio would have crawled under the table. He

---

Cantonals were rebels who declared the eastern city of Cartagena independent of the republic.

just chewed on his toothpick and grunted like a mastiff who hasn't decided to bark but doesn't want to keep quiet either.

"Alfonsism is a crime," stated Leopoldo Montes, who didn't beat around the bush when he wanted to express an opinion.

"A crime against the nation," Rubín added. "It's what I was saying last night to Relimpio, who's also leaning to that side: in times like these, when we don't know what will happen with the war! If Don Carlos weren't a fool, wouldn't he already be in Madrid?"

"But what does that prove?" Don Basilio finally argued, spying a good way out of the confusion into which his opponent had plunged him. "What does that have to do with it? Be reasonable, gentlemen."

"Nothing. It's just that he won't be coming. I bet my right arm."

"But . . ."

"No buts; he won't come. Don't try to get around it, Señor de la Caña."

"Give me reasons."

"He won't come. You'll see, in time."

"All right."

"No, I'm telling you. If you wait for when the prince returns for them to give you a job in your field, you might as well grow a beard waiting."

"It's not a question of whether I'll have time for a beard or not," declared Don Basilio, becoming slightly annoyed and showing them the pulpy toothpick.

But Rubín started talking with Feijóo, who was inquiring about his brother's inexplicable marriage to a corrupt woman. Don Basilio struck up a conversation with the chaplains and Nicolás Rubín. In that circle he received more attention than he did in his own, and he felt more at ease. Opinion was split: the chaplain of the fourth regiment was in favor of the prince, but Rubín (the priest) and the other two snorted at the mere mention of Alfonsism. Don Basilio, leaning toward them and resting on his elbow, disclosed his secrets very discreetly. All that was missing were a few finishing touches. It was all ready, and the first to fall would be General Serrano.

"You heard right. And time will tell. You'll see, soon enough."

Then he quietly pilfered all the sugar cubes he could and got up to leave, saying good-bye to each and every person, either with a hand shake or a slap on the back.

4

After his failure in Don Carlos' camp and court, Rubín had taken a vehement dislike to the men who had stayed on with the absolutists; but he had kept his authoritarian ideas and opinion that it is impossible to govern well without a big stick. He discarded the religious part of the Carlist program, retaining only the political part, for he had already learned that in practice priests spoil everything. He said that his ideal was "a stiff government"—one that would make laws and apply them without further ado, always keeping sight of justice and carrying a very big stick, raised for use. This autocratic system referred more to methods of governing than to ideas and theoretical solutions; among the latter, Rubín professed to have some notably advanced, popular, and even socialist ones. One of his themes was this: "Everyone should eat . . . , because hunger and poverty are what most impede the action of governments and instigate revolutions, keeping the nation in a restless and disorderly state." This socialism without freedom, combined with that absolutism without religion, created an infernal mess in my good man's head.

Another one of his themes was: "No more rascals and the death penalty for thieves." Or, more clearly: immediate and cruel punishment for any and every person who goes into government with the sole purpose of making shady deals. The ambitious streak that appears in every Spaniard's mind more or less frequently, making him say, "Now if I were in power," crossed Rubín's mind several times a day, more like a dream than hope; in his hours of solitude he drowsed off with that idea in his mind and gave it a workout, beat it up as one beats an egg white so that it will froth and stiffen. The upshot of this mental stirring and beating was that "what we need here is a man with guts, somebody who's really talented, who's got guts enough for everyone."

Having been in jail (for suspicion of conspiracy) had emphasized his haughtiness and dreamy moodiness and, at the same time, made his sociopolitical program more of a mess. When he walked out of jail his thoughts were more jumbled and his spirits more inflamed. And he had an urge to read, for he recognized his ignorance and the necessity of understanding the ideas of great men and the noteworthy events that had taken place in the world. He read a lot for a couple of weeks—devoured various works—and since he could assimilate easily and had a good tongue, he converted his morning readings into "paper birds" at night in the café. His thoughts were only paper birds, but this didn't prevent them from captivating Don Basilio, Leopoldo Montes, and even Feijóo.

One day he woke up thinking that he ought to cram on philosophic systems and history and religion. The reason for this was not merely his love of knowledge; rather, it was a malicious desire to learn arguments with which to squelch the priests at the next table whom he disliked simply because they were priests, even if they were of the "stray" sort; he had hated all priests ever since the skirts had played that dirty trick on him in the north.

Little by little, as he was building up his arguments, Rubín inched across the sofa until he was presiding over the chaplains. There were three of them (four when Nicolás Rubín came), and all three of them were witty and determined. None of them minced their words, no matter what the subject was. The most qualified one was a congested old Andalusian, a great narrator of anecdotes who used bad language and had a good heart. He used to retire at eleven and say Masses in the morning. The second was a chaplain who had been thrown out of his order for having violated some rule or other, and the third was an ex-chaplain from a mail steamer, expelled because he had been caught with contraband tobacco. These two were a fine pair—they knew a lot about the world, and didn't have a license to practice, so they howled with hunger; they'd been thrown out of one church after another, and couldn't find refuge anywhere. This situation had embittered them, making them seem worse than they really were. They never wore their habits, but they kept their faces shaved, as if they wanted to be ready in case they were readmitted into their profession.

I don't know what the congested old fellow's name was; everyone in the café called him Pater; even the waiter who served him used the nickname. The ex-chaplain was called Quevedo and came from the heart of Málaga, ugly as sin, pockmarked, with a perverse look in his eyes and a kidnapper's face that would have terrified any poor soul who met him in a dark alley. That cleric drank as if it were water, and his speech was a combination of Andalusian z sounds and gargly noises. His tales of battles and adventures in the barracks he told with a crude charm and frankness that were enough to make your flesh crawl. The other one was called Pedernero and was from Ceuta, the son of a woman who was related to the regiment; young and likable, much more refined than his colleagues, smart as a whip, and with such a gift for gab that it was a pleasure to hear him talk. There was nothing he didn't know about human life and youth. His companion Quevedo would wrap himself up in hypocritical formulas; not so Pedernero, who showed himself for what he was and started out by saying that the superior had done very well to revoke his license.

The so-called Pater affected a certain episcopal leadership over the other two; he reproached them when they said anything outrageous and gave them good advice, voicing the principle that everything is tolerable if it isn't taken seriously. He, for example, spoke and heard (especially heard) many bad things, but his life remained pure. He had a round face, white and cheerful, and when he wasn't wearing a hat he looked like a woman in her fifties, a canon's housekeeper. He disliked violent arguments at the table and preferred for the conversation to stick to juicy tidbits and jokes, even if they were dirty.

This, then, was the circle Juan Pablo edged into with his clericophobia and makeshift knowledge of theology and Catholic philosophy.

He would start with a few hints. Since his talk was frivolous and newsy at first, they all laughed and the Pater was in his element. But little by little, Rubín began to bring up serious issues. He tore to shreds the temporal power of the Pope, yet not a single one of the tonsured individuals formally defended it. The Pater and Quevedo reacted calmly, meeting Rubín's attacks with evasive arguments in a half-playful, half-serious style. Pedernero made a joke of the whole thing. But one night, when Rubín arrived with his "paper bird," his notion that there exist other inhabited worlds, Pedernero began to wake up. He was a doctor of theology, and even though he had chucked his books long ago he did remember a few things and, besides, was a very gifted debater. Rubín got rather badly bruised, but in his retreat he defended himself well thanks to his flexibility and acuity. Another day he came back with an arsenal of arguments against revelation. "Only the cobblestones believe that now . . ." The Old Testament was no better than a fraud, an imitation of Indian and Persian theogonies. It was all too evident—same myths, same symbols. Original sin, the expulsion from Paradise, incarnation, redemption—they were just a lot of poetic and naturalistic representations that kept being reproduced throughout the centuries, "on the banks of the Euphrates as easily as on the banks of the Nile or the Jordan."

"Is that so? Well, you just wait and see." This is what Pedernero said to himself; his pride as an outlawed theologian was deeply wounded. In a couple of days he refreshed himself on the subject, recuperated the erudition he had lost because of his trips and libertine life, and, when he was ready, he took on his opponent's challenge, equipped with some third-hand knowledge he had raked out of one of those popular little French lay editions that sell for a few cents a volume. Well, friends, one night the ex-chaplain of the mail steamer gave Rubín such a beating that the latter had to run for cover. It was a splendid sight: Pedernero transfigured, an ardent orator full of arrogant eloquence. An audience developed at neighboring tables, and even the people at the center tables pressed forth, clustering around the angry rivals. Rubín was sharp, a clever warrior in an argument; the other was master of the subject, firm and moderate in tone, secure in his dialectics.

And it didn't end here. Full of spite, Rubín racked his little penny editions for more weapons against the Church. But he had barely tried them when Pedernero smashed them to bits with his sledgehammer arguments. The Pater could hardly contain himself, he was so overjoyed; he fairly wriggled in his chair. Quevedo poked his nose into it and even dared to peep approval of his friend's admirable arguments by repeating them. The others plucked up their courage and took sides, not out of any convictions they held but to have fun and make it a better row. Besides the three priests, the following people were at the table: a wealthy stockbroker who together with the Pater had attended the café (sitting in the exact same spot) for ten years; a retired opera bass; a low-salaried employee; and the owner of an accredited chocolate factory. The priests and these four gentlemen formed the most brotherly group imaginable, each bringing a tasty tidbit to that gossip fest where they spent pleasant hours together as friends. Outside these meetings they had almost no relationship at all.

Rubín, upon finding himself defeated (even the stockbroker, who was the biggest freethinker of them all, had gone over to Pedernero's side), started to look for trouble by using malicious arguments and personalizing the debate. The opera bass felt that it was his duty to support the religious side because he had expressed it so many times with a sheet wrapped around his head, playing the respectable role of high priest. And the man from the chocolate mill egged them both on to see if he could make things so bad that they'd bite off each other's heads. Furious phrases could be heard from that part of the café, propositions that sounded as if they were coming from the pulpit, and over and above the tumult rose Pedernero's brave voice:

"I tell you that *no* holy father could have defended that nonsense. So don't be a bother. I challenge you to show me the text, and if you don't, it's proof that you're making it up."

That night things ended badly; the contenders' tones, as well as the charged atmosphere, made some of the men fear an unpleasant scene. The catastrophe took place the next night. After Rubín had been critical and reluctant several times about the reputation of the Virgin Mary, Pedernero sprang out of his chair, quivering with his loss of composure, and in a horrible state of agitation hurled such a frenzied anathema at his opponent that their friends had to restrain them.

"I'm a fresh one, I'll admit that," the chaplain shouted, trying to smother his rage. "And I'm a bad priest. But no shameless Jew's going to malign the Virgin Mary in front of me. Either you swallow those insults or I'll break your soul in half . . . now."

It would be impossible to describe what happened there. Voices, shouts, kicks, torn cloaks, glasses knocked over, sugar cubes scattered on the floor. Grabbing a bottle, Rubín aimed for the priest, but so badly that . . . the poor opera tenor got it in the head. It was a first-class row, all right. Don Basilio yanked at Rubín's coattails and practically ended up with them in his clutches. The whole café was in an uproar. The owner stepped in . . .

Emigration. From the next day on, Juan Pablo gave his business to another café.

5

The first to follow was Don Evaristo González Feijóo, who was indifferent to whatever place they chose. For the time being, they camped out in Fornos. The second night Leopoldo Montes came, and the third, Don Basilio, who found them discussing which café they should finally settle on. Don Basilio hastened to give his favorable opinion of the Café de Santo Tomás because more sugar was put out there than anywhere else. Montes replied that they needn't necessarily view the issue "through the exclusive prism" of the sugar provided; what counted was the coffee. Then the Café de la Aduana almost won, but they decided against it because they didn't want to be surrounded by Frenchmen all the time. And the Imperial was eliminated because of the bullfighters, and another because of its vulgar, pretentious patrons. Feijóo would have stayed right where they were, but Rubín disliked the military school students who arrived at Fornos early in the evening. He was also annoyed by the habit the owners had of dimming the gas lights at ten o'clock when the students left. The place was left dark, and wasn't well lit again until midnight, when the stockbrokers came to dine. And the stockbrokers, who didn't talk about anything except money, irritated Rubín too.

At last they decided to install themselves in the Café Siglo on Mayor Street, where a fair number of people they knew went. Rubín needed a few days to get used to the new spot. At first he changed tables frequently, either because there was a draft or because the neighbors were slightly bothersome. On one of his first nights there, when his friends still hadn't arrived, Rubín was alone at the table and was watching two groups next to him. In both, the conversation was lively. On the right someone was saying: "Today I sold about fifty *arrobas** at twenty-five *reales*. But business is bad. The hicks are learning a lot. Today they said they wouldn't bring any more escarole if we don't pay 'em ten for it." The group on the left, consisting of three people, offered this to Rubín's ears: "I assure you, I believe in metempsychosis as the Egyptians and the Chaldeans understood it." Rubín realized that the people on the right were food wholesalers and those on the left were café philosophers. Spiritualists had great meetings at the Siglo, and at the time, Federico Ruiz was a member of that group. Rubín saw him and joined the group to indulge in the pleasure of arguing with the most enthusiastic individuals of that sect. Juan Pablo thought that this business of going from one world to another after you died was all right, but he didn't go for the medium bit, or the idea that Socrates and Cervantes will come chat with us whenever we feel like it. That stuff's only for fools. One of the wackiest ones in the in the "school" strived to convince Rubín, adopting that slightly unctuous tone and such mannerisms as a bowed head and lowered eyes, to which every religious propagandist—no matter what his doctrine—succumbs. Feijóo pretended he believed them so as to wind them up and then hear them unwind. Federico Ruiz always frequented that circle hurriedly, because at such and such a time he had to attend a meeting about erecting a monument in honor of Jovellanos; then he had to go to another to

*Spanish weight of about twenty-five pounds.

supervise a banquet for fishermen from the provinces who were coming to the Piscicultural Conference. A busier man has never been seen in our country; since he had so many things in his head he found that in order not to forget them he had to write them down in pencil on his shirt cuffs. When he didn't have to go to the Society of Economics to defend his personal vote as a member of the informing commission on social reforms, he was headed for the Society of Sciences to give his lecture on the use of serious studies of the art of making bread. Between appointments, Ruiz spent time with his spiritualist friends and urged them to get organized, established, rent quarters, and, above all, get a column in the press. They'd get nowhere without that.

Other members of the little clique were Aparisi, whom the spiritualists had already half-convinced; Pepe Samaniego, who wouldn't let himself be taken in; and Dámaso Trujillo, the owner of the cobbler's shop called "The Lily Stem," as gullible as they come and who alone at home performed experiments with a cobbler's bench. At the next table there were employees from the Treasury, the Ministry of the Interior, the Overseas Office, and also a flock of the unemployed. *
Among them, Rubín saw the man who needed only two months' employment to be eligible for retirement. His face was contorted in the most terrible anxiety; his skin looked like a rotten lemon peel; his eyes were ghostly; and when he went up to the spiritualists' table he looked like one of those creatures that have been dead for thousands of years and have suddenly turned up in our midst, summoned by the tapping of a special stick. The Cuban and Philippine climate had juiced him, leaving only a bag of bones, and since he was all dried up, his eyes were the only live spots in him, so much so that when he looked at people he seemed bent on devouring them. Some joker in the group started to call him Ramses II, and the nickname fit so well that he became Ramses II for everyone. Scornfully bypassing the spiritualists, he would sit with the employees, to listen rather than speak, and every now and then to make an observation in an otherwordly voice that resounded from his throat like an echo from the dank caves of an Egyptian pyramid: "Two months—all I need are two months, and all I get are promises: today, we'll . . . , tomorrow . . . , we'll see . . . , there aren't any openings . . . "

Feijóo used to approach him to sympathize with him, to encourage him, and to distract him from his obsession, but Ramses II (whose real name was Villaamil) could only be consoled by putting his dry, yellow ear to the conversation and catching something about a crisis or trouble that was sure to break out soon and turn everything topsy-turvy. What he wanted was a big row, a good big one to start, to see if . . .

"But tell me—who's recommending you?" Juan Pablo asked him one night.
"Me? Don Claudio Moyano."

---

* *Cesantes;* or dismissed public employees, is the equivalent for the American "unemployed."

"Hmm, some wait you're going to have."

"They say they're bringing the prince in," said Ramses II timidly.

"Sure, sure—the Russians are bringing him, by way of Alcorcón. You're barking up the wrong tree if you're waiting for the prince to come. The only thing that's coming is social turmoil, and then God knows what. The man we need will step forth—he'll be some character with a big stick and lots of guts."

Ramses II lowered his head. Don Basilio was his only friend, because he too stood up for the prince's coming.

"Naturally," he added, "he'll be here with the stick our friend Juan Pablo mentioned."

Rubín felt comfortable in this circle. But one night he noticed sitting at one of the tables opposite his a man who completely disconcerted him. It was a friend of his who had lent him money. The secret loathing that a creditor inspires revealed itself in Rubín's soul as a hidden hatred, born perhaps from the sense of humiliation that a very susceptible, proud person feels when he contracts debts. The man was Cándido Samaniego: half legal clerk, half businessman, affable in private or social life, tough in business life. He had renewed Juan Pablo's promissory notes many times and finally pressed him rather bitterly for payment. Rubín condensed his feelings for the moneylender in one sentence: "Pay him and then bash his head in." From the moment he spotted him at the table opposite he felt really bad; his stomach hurt and he felt like flying off the handle. He got so nervous that he would have hurled a bottle at the first spiritualist who started talking about invoking Epaminondas to consult him on the Carlists' march through the Baztán.

And the perfidious "Englishman"* wandered over to their tables with the excuse that he had to talk to his cousin Pepe. But his intentions were clear enough: get closer to Juan Pablo, see what he'd do, and then exchange a few words with him. The miserable debtor put on a bold front and with a smiling face invited Samaniego to have a drink with him; but the usurer declined, thanking him, and when he had the chance he dropped a mild hint such as:

"Look, this can't go on. You're always telling me 'next week,' and frankly, . . . I'm going to be forced to take steps that . . ."

Suddenly, Rubín's coffee tasted like venom, and the *tertulia* was hell. He couldn't stand that man's presence; he couldn't ignore him—he was the living image of his disorderly life and appeared like the ghost of a victim just when he was happiest. The only delight in his sad existence was the café. And Samaniego had turned that placid dream into an anguished nightmare. He could bear it no longer, and one night, without a word, he flew off to other regions.

---

*Nickname in Spain for all creditors.

6

In this new emigration, wishing to flee as far as possible from the Café Siglo, he went to San Joaquín, on Fuencarral Street, and if he didn't go any further north, it was because there were no cafés in that part of Madrid. But in this desertion neither Don Basilio Andrés de la Caña nor Montes joined him, the latter because "San Joaquín was off the map," and the former because he was getting fed up with Rubín's persistent jokes about his prophecy that the Restoration was due to come soon. Don Evaristo Feijóo followed him ill-humoredly, stating flatly that he didn't like "piano cafés" and that in those parts one didn't find good stuff or the best society. They were alone there for a few days. They didn't see any of their friends until one night when a familiar couple showed up. It was Feliciana and Olmedo, the pharmacy student, Maxi's friend. They (Feliciana and Olmedo) didn't live together anymore because he had undergone a radical change: he had become overtly studious. He no longer hid to study, and he bragged in public—with the greatest insolence—about his firm resolve to take the exams that very year, and he was even so audacious as to write a very good paper on dextrin and aspire to a university chair. But he had found his old flame in a sorry state and so had invited her for coffee at that out-of-the-way café. For more than two hours the former lovers talked, and she let flow a steady stream of complaints about the inconsiderate man who was her master at the moment. Two nights later they reappeared at the same table, and Rubín started a conversation with them. They talked about Maximiliano's wedding and the incredible subsequent events, Juan Pablo remarking that his sister-in-law was a sly little thing.

"But, for heaven's sake," Feijóo queried his friend, "why did you let your brother get married?"

"My brother's off his rocker."

"Ah! As for being a beauty—*that* she is," Don Evaristo added rather enthusiastically. "I saw her yesterday . . . or rather, I've seen her several times."

"Where?"

"At her house. It's a long story . . . Let's leave it for some other time."

It was undoubtedly too delicate to tell with witnesses present; they were Olmedo and Feliciana, the blind pianist, who often joined that placid *tertulia* during intermissions, and a plump woman, a faithful customer of the café between nine and twelve. They called her Doña María de las Nieves [Mary of the Snows], and she was one of Madrid's most noteworthy figures of all the extremely varied series of types there are in Spanish cafés. Sometimes she came alone; other times with a woman in a lambswool cloak who looked like a well-to-do greengrocer. She wore a purple cape that she took off when she sat down, whereupon she attracted a group of men, including a janitor from the School for the Deaf and Dumb, an employee from the Auditor's Court, an old lieutenant retired from the ranks, and two characters who had meat and fruit stalls respectively on San Ildefonso Square. Doña Nieves reigned over this group as if it were a salon; she would make malicious pronouncements on the events of the day, and the others would laugh at her sarcasms. Sometimes she slid over to the next table, usually when it was very late, when her friends—who had to get up early—began to desert the place. Then a second huddle formed. Doña Nieves, who had digested her coffee by then, had chocolate, and Juan Pablo, Feijóo, the blind pianist, Feliciana, Olmedo, and perhaps someone else too joined her. The waiter himself, who had gotten on familiar terms with the group, also joined them, sitting at one end, where he listened and applauded. Doña Nieves owned a few stalls in the marketplace and rented them. This, plus the fact that she had lots of connections in different groups and lent money to some of her tenants, made her quite a boss in the marketplace. The cops respected her; she defended the weak against the strong and also people who didn't obey city statues from municipal tyranny.

The café owner paid the blind pianist seven *reales* and supper. During the day he tuned pianos. He was married, with a family of eight. He played pieces from operas and French operettas mechanically: easily, although incorrectly, with neither feeling nor taste. But in spite of this, when he played certain realistic passages imitating a storm or bells tolling disaster in a town, the audience applauded heartily, and at the end they always requested one of his Cuban dances.

If the truth be told, Juan Pablo found all this—Doña Nieves and her marketplace friends, women of shady reputation chaperoned by fake mothers, the café waiter with his over-familiar ways, and the pianist and his Cuban dances—excruciatingly boring. And to top it off, Feijóo wasn't punctual, and didn't even come many evenings. On the other hand, Feliciana and Olmedo began to appear more regularly, and she brought a friend of hers who had just gotten out of the San Juan de Dios Hospital.

In the last weeks of '74, Rubín began to crave books again. He wanted to educate himself at all costs: a hard, vast task, considering that he had no foundation on which to build. His father had instilled in him the notion that Latin gets in a businessman's way, and, acting on this, he had forbidden his son to learn anything beyond basic arithmetic and a little French. Juan Pablo didn't have a library of his own; a friend lent him books. He went to see him, chose the books whose titles intrigued him most, and devoted every moment he had—except for the time he spent in the café or sleeping—to reading. He acquired so many ideas that he had an urge to spew them all out, in propaganda. Either he preached or he'd burst. What a pity he didn't go back to Pedernero's *tertulia* to slay him! He knew enough now to tear every single theologian to shreds.

Rubín's readings were like a discovery. He had had a hunch, but did not dare to express it; he had discovered that the best organization of the state is disorganization; the best law, that which annuls all others; the only *true* government, that which purposely governs nothing, letting social energy manifest itself freely. Absolute anarchy produces true order: rational, human order. Societies naturally have ages, like people; there are societies still nursing, societies crawling on all fours, adolescent societies, youthful societies, and, finally, there are mature societies, masters of themselves; there are venerable, bearded societies, too. As for the religions and customs of these various societies, Juan Pablo was full of ideas about them. For example, he reasoned that only in society's childhood, when it's still drooling and living under parental rule, does it make any sense to support the institution called marriage, or the perpetual union of the sexes, which goes against nature's laws . . . and whatever for? Let's see now . . . nature rules everything, that's for sure. If we study life carefully, in its totality, we brush out the cobwebs the centuries have woven in our minds, and we realize that nature is the true light in our soul. The word, the legitimate messiah, not the one who will come, but the one who is always coming into our midst, is our inspiration. It made itself, in its eternal evolution, conceiving and giving birth endlessly: it's always mother and child of itself. Well, how does that sound? What do you think?

My friend discovered that he had enough dialectic strength and enthusiasm to preach and spread these truths all over the world. But since his only audience was the *tertulia* at the café, he had to be content with it. And anyway, so what? It was much better to plant the new doctrine in simple, uncultivated minds! After all, didn't Christ himself choose as disciples some simple fishermen—poor, rustic souls who didn't know anything—and also corrupted women? So you see why Doña Nieves and her female friends, Feliciana and the girl from the hospital, the waiter and the pianist were chosen to receive the first seeds of Juan Pablo's gospel *au naturel*. For many nights he dished out hot propaganda. Sometimes he couldn't help but be annoyed: they made stupid or vulgar remarks. As he could express himself very well, they all paid close attention to him, and the "good girls" eyed him hungrily. The waiter was the most enthusiastic, and would comment:

"What a tongue this Sr. Rubín has!"

The anarchy and even the marriage business went over all right, but when he got to the part about everything being nature, he stirred up great confusion in his audience, and Doña Nieves (taking it as a joke) asked him to make it plainer.

"Explain it better, Don Juan Pablo . . . because I don't quite get it when you say that 'we're all the all.'"

"First of all, my children," he said unctuously, "we must wash the *intellectus* free of errors acquired in infancy; wash it of prejudices and crutches; what comes first is *wanting to understand*. The only arguments I accept are rational arguments."

"And when we die," asked one of the hussies, "what happens?"

"Child, when we die, we fit into the grand universal scheme . . ."

"Look at 'er! Well, whad'ja want—to keep on havin' fun up there?"

"How about God?"

"God! . . . Frankly, I don't like—I mean, bearing in mind the consideration we should have toward all great historical ideas, I wouldn't want to say anything against Him. So . . . I deny him . . . respectfully."

"That's a good one! The things you come up with! So Mass isn't anything either?"

"Holy Mary! The things you say! Mass . . . is a ritual, just another ritual."

"So it doesn't make any difference if you go or not? What are Masses for the dead for?"

"They're another ritual. Look, whoever can't or doesn't know how to give nature what belongs to nature and history what belongs to history, keep quiet. Death doesn't exist, children, and those of you who have ears, listen: this is the truth; to die is to conform with a law of harmony."

"Sure—we go back to the substance of the earth and we mix with it," observed Doña Nieves.

"You're right . . . I mean, you're correct."*

"And so, in the long run, what we do when we die is water the plants. After all, what are most vegetables, if they're not people who've been converted into, let's say for example, broccoli?"

"Come off it, for God's sake!" exclaimed one of the market women, crossing herself. "What a laugh!"

"But the soul flies off to the skies—somewhere up there. To fly around. Because there's no hell. I agree with Sr. Rubín on that."

"In truth, I tell you that there is no hell, no heaven, no soul," Rubín declared in an apostolic tone. "All there is, is nature surrounding us—immense, eternal, animated by basic forces."

"By basic forces! . . . Yes, that's it," assented the waiter. "Of course."

And he made gestures as if to suggest he was lifting a great weight.

"Call it whatever you want," replied Doña Nieves. "Force, soul, or as they say, the . . . the idea."

"Doña Nieves, for the love of God," said Rubín with pedantic despair. "You're starting to sound very Hegelian."

"There's one thing I don't understand," one of the girls said most candidly. "It's this: if there's nothing up there, where do souls go?"

"What souls?"

"*Blessed* souls."

Juan Pablo burst out laughing.

"We're not going to get anywhere unless you realize that man can't call real anything that's not in nature as we perceive it. If you've got eyes, *look.*"

---

*Another instance of a speaker switching from the familiar form of address (tú) to the polite form (Ud.).

"Yes, that's right. But one thing doesn't exclude the other," observed Doña Nieves calmly, starting to drink her chocolate. "Because there can be as much nature as you want, but that doesn't mean there's no holy trinity."

"Madam, in the name of the nails driven into Christ," said the philosopher, at wit's end by now. "Let's examine the concept of nature first. What is nature?"

"The country!" the girl from San Juan de Dios offered eagerly.

"And animals," murmured the blind man, the one who spoke the least.

"Don't be silly," stated Doña Nieves. "We sinners are nature—all of us weaklings are nature. Right, Don Juan Pablo?"

"Sins are nature," another girl said. "That's why children we have in sin are called 'natural' children . . .* Of course, that's it."

"What a mess you've gotten me into!"

One of the marketplace women who was there had a large bosom, and once a priest had told her, while she was saying confession, to "be modest in her dress and not show off those 'two natures' the Lord had given her." "What, sir?" "Your . . . front." Therefore, when she heard nature and sin mentioned, she thought that they were referring to the parts that modesty should cover, and she objected, scandalized:

"What indecent things to talk about!"

"No, not indecent, child."

"What I say is," declared one of the hussies, putting her foot in her mouth, "is that this Don Juan Pablo is daffy."

Maybe he wasn't crazy, but he *was* exhausted after all his futile efforts. He couldn't have driven the light of truth into those blockheads even if he had drilled a hole for it to get in. Sliding over to the next table where the blind pianist was having his supper, he ordered a hot chocolate. The blind man turned toward him with his empty, dead eyes and face like an unlit lamp and inquired with profound sadness:

"Is it true, Don Juan Pablo—what you tell us? Do you really believe it, or do you just want to amuse yourself and have fun with us ignorant folks? You've filled me with doubts. Can it really be true that we turn into a piece of escarole after we die?"

Juan Pablo looked at the blind man and the words with which he was about to spew out his cruel philosophy froze on his lips. Rubín had a good heart, and it hardly seemed human to plunge that sad and miserable life further into the dark. But at the same time, his conscience wouldn't permit him to belie what he had just sustained. Dignity first. He struggled for a while between piety and duty, and when the blind man asked him again, insistently this time, "Is it true that when we die we turn into cabbage?" the apostle replied:

---

*The Spanish expression for bastard is *hijo natural*, or, literally, a 'natural child,' from nature.

"Well . . . There are different opinions . . . Don't pay any attention to it. If it weren't for these jokes, how would we spend our time?"

They didn't continue their philosophical conversations because the news about the Monarchist pronunciamento was brought up, and this event claimed everyone's attention in every café—from the biggest down to the smallest. Rubín was furious, and said that the government wasn't worth two cents if it didn't immediately—and he meant immediately—shoot Martínez Campos, Jovellar, and all the others who were mixed up in that business. When his friends didn't want to hear what he had to say about this he talked to himself. He categorically denied whatever news reached the café. It was all false. Before the prince came there would be a general uprising, and the Carlists would make a final effort. He denied that Prince Alfonso had arrived at Marseilles, that he was embarking for Barcelona on the *Navas de Tolosa*; and when the prince entered Madrid, he would deny that he was there. But one night, after long absences, Feijóo came to the café, and when the two were seated together alone, Feijóo said to him:

"I've seen Jacinto Villalonga and spoken to him at length. As you know, he's involved in politics and he's a very good friend of mine. Naturally he won't accept the directorship they've offered him, because he prefers to be on his own. He's close with the minister, Romero Robledo. And this brings me to what I wanted to tell you: I mentioned your name to him—"

"You did!"

"Yes. You've got to get a job. You can't go on like this."

"Look, my friend," said Rubín, chewing his words in an attempt to get out of that spot. "I can't accept . . . What about a man's integrity? All my life I've maintained—"

"It's just words."

"Well, anyway, I appreciate . . . but it can't be. I'd be offended; I would."

"So," exclaimed Feijóo in a loud voice, extending his arms and adopting a tone that was either indignant or sarcastic (it was hard to say which), "so there's no patriotism left."

"Yes, there is, but I . . ."

"Do what I say and we'll get a spot for you."

Rubín continued to feign a bad mood all night, wearing a troubled, angry face and looking like a person who's had a dagger held at his throat to carry out an act that runs against his convictions. As he left to go home, he compared himself to the Visigoth, King Wamba,* and grumbled to himself: "If that's the way it has to be . . . patience. I'll have to support the prince; I'll be forced to. What a bind! Good God, what a bind I'll be in!"

---

* King Wamba was obliged by noblemen to accept the throne.

II. The Victorious Restoration

I

JACINTA RECENTLY TOLD ME that one night she became so irritated by her jealousy, unsatisfied curiosity, and forced reserve that she was on the verge of exploding and revealing her inner state, letting the mask of tranquillity she wore for her in-laws shatter to pieces. The worst of her mortification was that she had to play the role of the happy wife and contribute with cheerful laughter to Don Baldomero's and Doña Barbarita's happiness, swallowing her bitterness in silence: She no longer had any doubts that her husband was "keeping," as they say nowadays, a woman, and his blissful parents didn't even suspect it. She knew that the wench who was stealing her husband was the same one he had had an affair with before he got married, the mother of the dead Pituso, that blasted Fortunata, who had given her so many headaches. She wanted to see her . . . , but no; it was better not to see her, not ever, because if she did, she'd surely lose control of herself.

On the night to which Jacinta was referring (a terribly sad one for her because she had just heard from a reliable source that her husband was being unfaithful to her) there was great merriment in the Santa Cruz household. That day King Alfonso XII had entered Madrid and Don Baldomero was reacting to the Restoration like a child to new shoes. Barbarita was overjoyed too, and said: "What a witty, pleasant boy the prince is!"

Jacinta had to appear gay too, despite everything she felt inside and wear a festive face for all the people who came in remarking on the event. The marquis of Casa-Muñoz presided as the palatine chamberlain. He had had the great luck of being in the palace and forming part of one of the committees, and the king had spoken to him. The marquis told them about it, taking care to stress the familiar tone in which His Majesty had addressed him: "Hello there, Marquis. How've you been?" "—As if he'd known me all his life."

Shortly thereafter, Aparisi maintained that he had foreseen everything that was now happening. He wasn't in favor of the Restoration, but one did have to respect consummate acts. Don Baldomero kept exclaiming: "*Now we'll see*, blazes! if we can *do* something; if this country *will* jump through the hoop!" Jacinta was inwardly indignant. A volcano was smoldering in her breast, and the joy the others felt mortified her. If she had had her way, she would have wept in their midst; but she had to contain herself and smile whenever her father-in-law looked at her. Tightening the rope in her heart with which she was strangling herself, she mused: "And what does this man care about the king? What difference does it make! I'm furious and I wish I could scream! But I can't cause a scandal. Oh, this is horrible!"

She found Don Alfonso disagreeable because his image was associated with the awful sorrow she was suffering. That morning she had accompanied Barbarita to Eulalia Muñoz's (who lived on Calle Mayor) to see the king's entrance. Amalia Trujillo took her aside and flattered her a bit before giving her the big shock. They were alone together on the balcony of Eulalia's bedroom and the clarions were already heralding the king's arrival when bang!—Amalia shot it out at her:

"Your husband's 'keeping' a woman called Fortunata—extremely attractive, a brunette. He's given her a very luxurious place at number o, X Street. Everyone in Madrid knows about it, and it's high time you knew too."

She stiffened. It's true that she already suspected it; but hearing it like that, with all the details—the black hair, the exact address—was a tremendous blow. From that ill-fated moment on she lost track of what was happening in the street. The king passed, and Jacinta saw him, but in a state of vague confusion mixed with the bustle of the crowds below and the racket of so many musical instruments playing at once. She saw people waving handkerchiefs and it's possible that she waved hers, not realizing what she was doing. The rest of the day she acted like a sleepwalker . . .

Guillermina came in, adding her notes of gaiety to the concert at large.

"It was about time," she said before settling into her usual corner. "As soon as he's rested up from the trip I'm going straight over there to scold him. He's got to help me finish the ground floor. And he will, because we brought him here on that condition: that he support charity and religion. God save him."

Jacinta followed her into the parlor where they had a session that lasted over an hour. Guillermina said:

"Patience, child, patience, and it will all work out; I promise you."

Toward midnight Juan came in, and his wife looked at him severely, without a word. "I'm going to detest you," she thought to herself, "unless you reform. This was all I needed. And tonight! Just wait till I get at you . . . You're not going to soften me up with your sweet talk."

Even though Juan wanted to contradict his father's and friends' optimism, he didn't dare; their opinion was too strong to combat. Until the end of 1874 he had defended the Restoration. But once it took place he was against its having been brought about by the military, and he based his criticism of the event on this aspect.

"Changes in power have always been managed that way here," Sr. Santa Cruz said with patriarchal good faith. "It's our way of doing things. And anyway, what did you expect—for congress to do it? You're naive."

Then the Dauphin maintained—with examples from France and England—that no restoration had lasted for long; but they all refused to follow him along these historical paths. Without beating around the bush, Don Baldomero made a very sensible commentary, the product of his experience and observation:

"I don't know what will happen twenty or fifty years from now. You can't see that far ahead in Spanish society. All we know is that our country alternates between two fevers, revolution and peace. At certain times we all want lots of authority. Pour it on! But then we get tired of it and we all want to step out of line. So the fun comes, but then we start sighing for it to be over. That's how we are, and that's how we'll be, as far as I can see, till frogs start shaving."*

"It's the human condition. Societies are brought up to believe this," said the Dauphin. "What *I* object to is that it's been done illegally."

"You tricky rascal!" thought Jacinta, swallowing her words, and with them the bitterness trying to escape from her. "What do *you* know about the law? Demagogue, anarchist, phony! Just look at you . . . If I didn't know you so well. . ."

When they retired to their bedroom, Jacinta tried to increase her fury; she wanted to cultivate or nourish it as one feeds a fire, throwing in more combustible matter. "Tonight I'm going to light into him. I wish I were madder than I am so I wouldn't let him soften me up. I *am* quite mad already. But I could do with a bit more rage. He's a fake, a hypocrite, and if I don't abhor him, I don't deserve forgiveness from the Lord."

As she was thinking this Juan approached her and put his arms around her waist.

"Stop it, leave me alone!" she cried. "I'm very annoyed. Can't you see how annoyed I am?"

Juan saw that she was trembling and unable to breathe.

"I beg your pardon, madam," he replied jokingly.

Jacinta had it on the tip of her tongue to say "I know everything"; but she recalled that several nights ago she and her husband had laughed heartily over that sentence, which they noticed was repeated in every situation comedy they saw. The irritated wife thought the following would be more fitting:

"I'll hate you; I'm already beginning to hate you."

Santa Cruz, who was in a good mood, humorously quoted another sentence from that type of play:

"'Now I understand everything.' But the truth, dear, is that I don't understand a thing."

Her battle plans disturbed by his affectionate mood, Jacinta burst into tears like a child. Juan caressed her at length, kissed her here and there—on her neck and

---

*An English metaphorical equivalent for this image would be: "Till the sky falls in."

her hands, her ears, and the crown of her head, and he kissed her elbow and her chin, and he accompanied all this with the most refined, tender language imaginable.

"I can't stand it anymore, I can't stand anymore," was all she could chokingly say, wetting his face and hands with so many, many tears; she was inconsolable. All her weeping came from the pretense she had kept up so long, the unmentioned suspicions, being hurt and not being able to say even "Oh! This is horrid, this is awful; no woman is as wretched as I am. And from now on I'm really going to detest you, because I can't love someone who doesn't love me. I loved you more than my life. What a fool I've been! Men can't be treated with consideration. This is all I can take; no more, no more. I'm furious, and you might as well know I won't forgive you this time; I won't!"

It took some effort on Santa Cruz's part to make his wife repeat what her friend had told her that morning. And when he denied it, the offended wife, who was deeply convinced of the authenticity of the report, grew more irritated:

"Don't try to deny it. I know it's true. I could tell a long time ago."

"How?"

"By lots of things."

"Name them," he said, becoming gruff.

"Why? So you'll keep denying it? But you can't deceive me anymore.

"What Amalia told me," Jacinta suddenly declared angrily, full of dignity, standing up and confirming her assertion with an admirable gesture, "is true. I say that it's true and that settles it."

Gazing at her seriously, the anarchist replied in a very assured tone:

"Well, then, it's true. I hereby declare that it's true."

2

Jacinta stopped in her tracks; finally, turning her back on her husband, she started to leave. He grabbed her arm and tried to embrace her. She resisted. All she could vaguely articulate as they struggled was: "I'm leaving." What irritated her most was that the cad should still, after what he had said, be in the mood for joking and look mischievously at her as if it were all just a game. He was smiling all right, and, looking calm, he said to her in a mock-serious tone:

"Go to bed, madam."

"Me?"

"I order you to. Go to bed immediately."

Then he trapped her in a tight embrace she couldn't wriggle out of, and in this second clasp she heard these affectionate words:

"Wouldn't it be better for us to clear the air like good friends? Don't you see, my little darling, if you sulk we won't be able to understand each other."

This abruptly disarmed Jacinta. She felt like a warrior in a fairy tale who sees his sword and shield turned into a needle and thimble by magic.

Toward the end of '74 the Dauphin had entered one of his tranquil periods; they invariably followed an inconstant one. This change was not actually a virtue, rather, it was boredom with sin; it did not represent a pure and regular sense of order, but a surfeit of revolution. What Don Baldomero had observed about Spain was also true of his son: he suffered alternate fevers of total liberty and absolute peace. Two months after one of the gravest periods of "distraction" in his life, he began to covet his wife as if she belonged to somebody else. Her kindness encouraged this centripetal movement (which had occurred five or six times during their marriage). On other occasions Jacinta had believed that his resumption of his conjugal duties would be definitive, but she had been mistaken, for the Dauphin, who had the devil of variety in him, tired of being good and faithful and invariably gave in to that centrifugal force. Each time, though, his wife was so happy to see him reform that she didn't stop to think that it might be a sort of rest to prepare him for another, stormier period out in the world. This paralleled another notion of Don Baldomero's; namely, "When the country yields and supports authority, it's not because it truly loves law and order, but because it has to convalesce, strengthen its blood so that it can later satisfy its appetite for squabbles more enjoyably."

Jacinta, as I have said, was thoroughly disarmed. But since she felt that her dignity demanded that she continue to be very angry, she uttered all the words necessary to show it, for example:

"I'll go to bed or not, as I wish. What do you care? It seems that I'm here . . . only to be played with, wouldn't you say? What did you think, silly? We're finished; I tell you we're finished. Now! I'll go to bed because I feel like it, not because you've ordered me to. So there!"

A little while later, the following words could be heard from their bedroom:

"Calm down, be still. Don't think I'm going to forgive you now. No, you're not softening me up. No, no warm spot for you anymore. It's over—too late to be forgiven, sir. Please! I told you . . . I don't want to see you; I don't want to hear you; I don't even care whether you love me or not. If you do, so much the better—I'll laugh when I see you suffer. So leave me alone; I'm terribly tired. Can't you see that I can't even keep my eyes open?"

It wasn't true. Far from being sleepy, she was wide awake and very nervous.

"You're not sleepy. I know you're not," he said. "Want to bet that I can wake you up in a jiffy?"

"Bet you can't. How?"

"By telling you the whole truth about what Amalia told you; by confessing everything so you'll see that I'm not as bad as you think."

"Oh, yes! Come here, darling!" she exclaimed, stretching out her bare arms to him. "Confess everything to me, but nobly—don't try to fool me with your stories . . . you're so good at them. Since I know your tricks, at least I won't fall for all of them. Are you really going to tell me everything?"

The idea of forgiving him electrified Jacinta and made her jittery. She could hardly contain herself, she was so restless thinking of how huge her forgiveness would have to be to repay him for the sincerity he was offering her. And she was so anxious that she almost jumped out of bed when Juan left her to get into his bed. "What?" she asked herself. "Is the rascal sorry for what he said? Doesn't he want to tell me anything?"

"Good-bye," she said spitefully.

"No, wait; I'll be right back . . . My wife's got quite a temper."

"If you're going to tell, tell now; and if you're not, you're just saying it to make me go to sleep. I'm not here to wait around until the Señorito decides to let me stay up all night."

"Quiet, you," And saying this he turned toward her, sat on the bed, and whispered endless tender phrases in her ear.

"Oh, this is the end," murmured Jacinta in the pauses between her husband's suffocating caresses. "Look: be still and stop smothering me. I'm not in a joking mood."

"Let's get to it, my little dove. So that I can tell you what you want to know, you have to tell me something else first. You say that you suspected, or rather guessed, this thing that's happened. What made you suspect it? What did you see and know?"

"Oh! The things this fool comes up with now! Do you think a jealous woman needs to see anything? She sniffs it, she figures it out, and she doesn't make mistakes. Her heart tells her."

"Hearts don't say anything. That's literature."

"When you start staying out, the slightest word or gesture is enough to read your mind. And do you think the way you treat me isn't proof enough? Even your way of coming in shows it. You give yourself away even when you're tender or say something affectionate, because it's plain to see that they're leftovers from somewhere else that you bring here out of duty, just to cover up for yourself. Words and caresses that are so worn out."

"Well, don't you know a lot, though!"

"You know more! No, I do. Misery teaches one . . . Many times I've kept silent to avoid a scandal; but inside I could feel something grinding and grinding away at me. My sixth sense is sharp, that's for sure. Whenever you start to stray a bit, I can tell by the perfume on your clothes. And other things too: once you came in wearing your silk scarf around your neck, and what do you suppose was on it? A long black hair. I took it off with my fingertips and examined it. It disgusted me as much as if I'd found it in my soup. I didn't say a word. Another night you talked in your sleep, said words that men say when they fight. I was scared. It was the same night you came in all upset with a pain in your arm. I had to put arnica on. You told me that as you were going along some street or other a drunk crossed your path and you had to fight him off. Your blue coat was dirty. You were very restless all night, don't you remember?"

"Yes, I remember," said the Dauphin, recalling his scuffle with Maximiliano.

"And another thing. One night when you were getting undressed, ping!—a button fell on the floor. It rolled toward my bed. It looked like an eye staring at me. It was made of nickel and had a very elaborate design. When you fell asleep I got out of bed and picked it up. It was a woman's button, the kind that's on vests now. I saved it. These ignominies should be kept so that when the day comes one can produce them and say: 'Do you deny this?' And there you were, playing a role the whole time! What I went through! . . . But I never wanted to lower myself to spying on you. I thought of asking the coachman. If I'd given him a good little tip, Manuel wouldn't have kept from me what I already knew. But out of respect for you and myself and the family I did nothing. Tell your mother about my suspicions? What for? To upset her for no good reason? Guillermina, the only one I confided in, always said 'Patience, child, patience.' And at last I learned to be patient, and meanwhile that gristmill in my heart kept grinding away, pulverizing me, and I had to bear it and keep smiling as if nothing had happened when I was all bitterness inside. This morning when Amalia told me what she told me, my blood felt poisoned and I resolved to detest you, to completely abhor you, and not forgive you even if you got down on your knees. But one is so weak! We deserve everything that happens to us! It's the worst thing in the world, to be such a fool and be at the mercy of those . . . female kidnappers who from time to time lend us our own husbands so we won't make a fuss . . ."

3

This last complaint somewhat disconcerted Santa Cruz and made him grow pensive. He was not unaware of his hardly dignified position before Jacinta, whose moral stature increased before his eyes and showed him how small he was. He was very haughty; his self-pride was stronger than either his conscience or any emotion he knew, so that nothing bothered him more than to have to recognize that he was inferior to his wife. When he had promised to confess his sins half an hour earlier, he had been moved by pride and wanted to bask in his sincerity, show off the cross he had to bear. Confessing guilt always ennobles one, and as he knew all too well that anything noble struck a chord in Jacinta's great heart, he said to himself: "This is the time for a good deed." But as the time to confess approached, the sinner was rather confused and unsure about how he would fare. What he wanted was to make a good show; climb up to his wife's loftiness and surpass her, if possible, presenting his faults as merits and retouching the whole story so that what seemed black and dishonorable, the button and the hair, would seem white and even noble. He didn't have to strain his mind much to get out of that spot because his brain had a special aptitude for such tricks. His extremely vivid imagination was clever with ideas; he shook them like dice until he got the combination he wanted. What he couldn't stand was being taken for an ordinary man like so many others. He wanted even his most trivial and common actions to pass as deliberately admirable acts that bore no resemblance whatsoever to those performed by everyone else. Rapidly, with the quick judgment of an improvising artist, he laid out his composition and set the confidential details in place. Jacinta would be stunned. She'd see what a husband she had, what a superior, extraordinary person he was.

There is a general, let's say "raw," morality, one that everybody understands, including women and children. And there is an exquisite, "refined" morality that the common people cannot appreciate; it is reserved for very sensitive palates, and . . .

"Well, let's hear your fake stories," she said.

"From everything you've said one would think that I'm a cad, an ordinary man like so many others. Well now, we'll see about that. I've been reserved with you because I thought you wouldn't understand. Let's see if you can understand now. It's true that two months ago I met—"

"Do me a favor and don't say her name," Jacinta hastened to request. "Hearing that name is like being bitten by a snake."

"All right; well, to get to it: I saw her and she was married."

"Married!"

"Yes, to a poor fool. They'd put her in a convent and then they married her off, almost by surprise. It's a long story—full of violence and intrigues—things that would horrify you."

"Poor woman!" she exclaimed, reacting as Juan had planned, for he was starting by making the other woman worthy of pity. "But she deserves it for her misbehavior."

"Wait a minute. I don't think there's ever been a more unfortunate woman."

"Or a worse one, either."

"There's a lot to be said about that. It isn't evil in her; it's a lack of morals. She's never seen anything except bad examples. She's always lived with cads and cheaters. Put the most perfect woman in the world in her place and watch what she does. No, it's not what you think. I'd go even further: if she were led to goodness, she'd be good. But consider what her lot has been: after going from one man to another, being picked up and dropped, they marry her off to a man who's not a man, a man who's not fit to be anybody's husband."

Jacinta's jaw dropped in astonishment.

"And the jerk martyrizes her so much from the day they get married that the poor woman—preferring her freedom in ignominy to that unbearable slavery—runs away and takes to the street the way she used to in her worst moments. And then I run into her and she asks me to help her."

Jacinta's mouth was still hanging open.

"In such a situation," continued Juan, finding himself in full control of his thesis and dicebox of thoughts, "I present you with the following problem: let's see, suppose you were a man. Suppose you ran into that unhappy woman; she asks you to give her a hand in her poverty and dishonor; and when you see her standing there before you, you can't help but admit that you're the author of all her misfortunes because you robbed her of her virtue; *you* caused her problems. I want you to tell me truthfully what you would do in such a situation. But close your mouth first; stop being astonished and answer me."

"Me . . . what would *I* do? Put my hand in my pocket, give her four or five *duros*, and be on my way."

"That was my first reaction. But there are certain debts, my good wife," said Santa Cruz triumphantly, "that can't be paid off with four or five *duros*."

"Well, then, a thousand, two thousand, or a hundred thousand *reales*."

"No, that wouldn't work either. I thought that I should set that miserable woman on the road to acquiring a decent and stable position. Find her a husband? Impossible: she was already married. Arrange for her to live independently and honorably? Ah, that's hard to do! She has no education. She doesn't know how to do any gainful work. All she can do is live on her beauty. But even in that there are different degrees of ignomiy. Don't try to turn away, now. You've got to look at things the way they are. So I said to her: 'All right, I'll give you a place to live, and you can manage on your own.' Stop looking so afflicted, I tell you. You've got to face reality, little girl. Don't look at it with a woman's eyes; put yourself in my place; imagine you're a man."

"I'm astonished at how clever you are at disguising your whims, and passing off as disinterested protection what was really love that you felt or feel for that cursed woman."

"I'm coming to that part now. Listen closely. I swear to you that she didn't inspire the slightest love in me; not even a thing of the moment. No one could feel as cold as I did toward her. You can believe this—she not only didn't arouse my passion, she even revolted me."

"That," said his wife, "you can feed to someone else, because as for me—"

"What a fool you are! Your disbelief comes from your mistaken idea of what she's like. You've built her up to be a seductive monster, like the kind without a scrap of education or any morality, but with countless wiles to drive men crazy and turn them into stupid slaves. That kind—of whom there are so many in France you'd think they came out of a school—hardly exists in Spain. You can count them on one hand here . . . still; but there'll be more of them—they'll come in just the way the railroad did. Well, as I was saying, Fortunata isn't one of them; all she has is her pretty face. Other than that, she's ordinary, dull, never dreams up any of the mischief that makes a man lose his head; and as for her manners—she's just as coarse as when I met her. She can't learn; nothing sticks in her head. Everything requires talent, you know, some special kind of talent, but that poor woman whom you fret about so much doesn't even have what it takes to be a siren. If they were all like her there would hardly ever be any scandals, and married couples would live in peace and the general morality would be in very good shape. In a word, Jacintilla, she's no vice-ridden seductress. She was born to be a decent woman and live an anonymous life, darning socks and looking after children."

When Juan reached this point he got scared and feared he had gone too far, realizing that if Fortunata were like his description—if she weren't ridden with vice—his responsibility for abusing her was much, much greater. Jacinta had exactly the same thoughts and promptly expressed them. But the prestidigitator hastened to defend himself.

"It's true," he said to her. "And that increased my remorse. I had no choice but to favor her as I wouldn't have favored another woman. Put yourself in my place; imagine you're me, and that everything that's happened to me happened to you. You can imagine what anguish I went through, and how I suffered at having to reconsider, and protect her, because I had my scruples; protect a woman who inspired no feeling at all in me, and who had begun to fill me with dislike. Believe me, not even the most enamored man in the world could stand Fortunata for a month. They all give up after a month; I mean, they all run off and leave her."

Jacinta had begun to kick, making the quilt over their feet puff up and down. It was her way of expressing excitement when she was in bed. If what Juan was telling her was true, her feared rival was like a scarecrow, which even birds jeer at when they examine it closely. But she still had her doubts. Was it true or wasn't it? It was too carefully told to be a lie.

"And does she still love you?" she asked with the wry humor of an examining magistrate.

Her husband asked her to repeat the question, his purpose none other than that of stalling his answer, which had to be well thought out.

"Well . . . I'd say yes, she does. She has that weakness. Other women, the licentious ones, are as vehement in their passions as they are fickle. They quickly forget the man they adore and throw off their infatuation like a dress gone out of style. Not this one."

"Not this one," repeated Jacinta, frightened by the realization that her enemy was so unlike the image she had of her.

"No. She's got this thing about always loving me just as much as when she met me for the first time. And that's another thing that affects me and makes me indulgent with her. Put yourself in my place, dear. Now if I saw that she was flirting with other men, to heck with her. But you can't knock that idea of being faithful out of her. Faithful to me! Why, for heaven's sake? I assure you, that dumb girl's made me ponder it so much . . . She's been through so many hands, and yet she's always faithful; hasn't budged an inch in her love. Neither dishonor nor marriage has cured her of that mania. Doesn't it sound like a mania to you?"

So many thoughts struggled in Jacinta's mind that she didn't know which to attend to and she ended up perplexed, not saying a word.

"There are so many men," Santa Cruz exclaimed in the tone he used for his philosophical remarks, "so many, who've been made unhappy by a woman's inconstancy; to think I have to suffer from a loyalty I didn't even ask for and don't need—and don't give a damn about!"

Jacinta heaved a deep sigh.

"But having a conscience, a deep moral sense of things," added the Dauphin, "as I do, has put me in a false position with you. I had to explain it to you. Now I have, and you will have seen that men's acts shouldn't be judged by what they appear to be; no, child, you've got to get to the bottom of things. Are you beginning to understand? One can be wrong so often! How often we think badly of someone, basing our judgment on rumors or some misleading detail such as a hair, or a button! And after we've examined the facts carefully, what do we find? That a button isn't enough to go on; that you can't hang a case on a strand of hair—it won't hold. In a word, my dear child, that what is apparently dishonorable may not be, and that instead of covering a man with shame, what it does is elevate and perhaps even honor him."

"Slowly now," his wife advised him. "I still find this obscure. It seems to me that it all fits together too neatly. I don't trust you, because no one's as good as you at building magnificent arches of words and sentences and then grandly walking through them. The fact is that you *did* give her an apartment, you've been to see her, and you've had a great time with her. Some conscience you have! Some way of repaying her for her faithfulness—being blithely unfaithful to me when you *owe* it to me! What kind of morality is that? Don't try to hide the truth. That woman's a cheater and you'd be a fool if you weren't such a rascal too."

"Wait a minute, my dear friend," Santa Cruz replied, somewhat disconcerted. "How can I best describe to you the situation I was in? It was one of the strangest predicaments you can imagine. Just so you'll see that I am sincere and loyal, I confess that I did feel a certain weakness; yes, weakness born from compassion. I didn't have the strength to resist the—what shall I call them?—the passionate suggestions from a person who idolizes me. Granted, I don't deserve it; but she does idolize me. But I swear I did it against my will, and disliking it, as if I were performing a duty, and meanwhile thinking of my wife—seeing *you* more than the woman who was so close to me, and wishing the farce would end."

Both were silent for a while. Did Jacinta believe those things or was she pretending to believe them, like Sancho when Don Quixote fed him stories about the cave of Montesinos? Juan's last words were:

"Now you judge for yourself; compare the good in what I've told you to the bad that's undoubtedly in it, too. I put myself in your hands."

"Ending, just ending forever any type of relations with that calamity is what matters," declared the Dauphine, tossing restlessly. "Don't ever see her again, don't even greet her if you see her in the street. Oh, what a woman! She's a nightmare for me."

"Consider it done—definitively, forever. I want to break up with her as much as you want it—believe me."

He said this so ingenuously that Jacinta felt very happy.

"No, I can't take any more. She can go to the devil with her loyalty."

"And if she should pursue you?"

"I'll be capable of even going to the police."

"So. You won't go back to that place? Say you won't. Tell me you don't love her."

"Bah! You know very well I don't. I won't go back except once, to say goodbye."

"No, write her a letter. Farewells in person aren't good for breaking off."

"I'll do whatever you want, whatever you tell me to do, sweetface, baby-doll. Anything my little angel wants."

4

The next morning Jacinta got up in a very gay mood, lively and full of things to talk about and laughing for no apparent reason. Barbarita, who came in from the street at ten o'clock, said:

"What a frisky mood you're in today! Listen: coming back from San Ginés I met Manolo Moreno, who got in yesterday from London. I've invited him to lunch."

Jacinta went to her dressing room. Her husband was still asleep; she began to get dressed. Shortly afterward a visitor arrived and she received her in the parlor. It was Severiana, who came twice a week to show Jacinta her protégée, Adoración. (As we know, the Dauphine couldn't adopt Pituso, and since her maternal urge had been strengthened by this frustration, she'd taken it into her head to adopt as a protégée Mauricia la Dura's adorable and affectionate daughter.) Jacinta's greatest and purest pleasure consisted of caressing a little child, giving it warmth and communicating to it the kindness that brimmed in her soul. That little girl pleased her so much that she would have kept her if her in-laws and husband had permitted it; but as this wasn't possible, she consoled herself by dressing her up to look like a little lady, paying for her schooling, and seeing her frequently. She enjoyed seeing the child's beauty, breathing in the fragrance of her innocence and looking her over to see how she was progressing.

"Hello! Come here, child. Give me a kiss and embrace me," said the lady, drawing the child to her with maternal fondness.

Adoración rubbed her face and body against her protectress' skirts.

"She says that what she prays to the Virgin for," declared Severiana with that adulation that characterizes humble people who have been given many favors and would like even more, "is to never be separated from the lady, never, so she can always look at her."

"I know she loves me, and I love her if she's being good and studying. Oh, my! Look how elegant you are! I hadn't seen your new dress."

"Last night she dreamed about her new dress," said Severiana. "And yesterday, when she put it on, all she did was look at herself in the mirror. If we so much as touched her she wanted to hit us. What she wanted was for the lady to see her so pretty, isn't that so, princess?"

"I don't approve of paying so much attention to appearances. What I want to know now is how those lessons are going. I don't have time to ask about them today, but next time, on Thursday, we'll see about your catechism."

"Oh, Madam, she knows it backwards and forwards. She's made our heads spin telling us about the people that ate the manna and the stuff about Noah's ark with all those animals he put in it. And her reading! She reads better than my husband."

"I like that. Next month I'll have her start boarding school. She's getting to be a big girl and she has to learn her manners; a little French, the piano . . . I want her to be a school teacher or a governess, isn't that so?"

Adoración looked at her ecstatically.

"And that woman?" Jacinta asked Severiana, referring to Adoración's mother.

"Don't mention her to me, Ma'am. When she first got out of the Micaelas she seemed a little better. She went back to selling Manila shawls and stuff again; she was mending her ways. But she's taken to the bottle again. Night before last we found her stiff as a board on Comadre Street. For shame!"

Jacinta seemed sorry to hear it.

"My poor little baby!" she exclaimed, embracing her protégée more tightly.

"So I wanted to speak to you, Ma'am," said Severiana, "and ask you if Doña Guillermina could put her someplace where she couldn't get out. It won't work at the Micaelas—they already had to throw her out because she was making scandals. But they could even put her in an orphanage or a loony bin; at least she wouldn't be around to set a bad example."

"We'll see," said Jacinta distractedly, getting up, for she heard her husband ringing.

Something remained to be done before Adoración left. Her benefactress always gave her sweets, but that day she had forgotten. The child stood in the middle of the parlor even after the final farewell kisses. Jacinta realized what she had forgotten.

"Wait a moment."

She presently returned with what the little girl wanted, and after repeating her recommendation to behave nicely and study, she accompanied them to the door. As Severiana and her niece were leaving, Moreno-Isla was coming up, and Jacinta, seeing him climbing the stairs, waited in the hall. He was out of breath and climbed the stairs slowly due to his heart condition. He looked much older, had an unhealthy color, and looked more foreign than before.

"Oh, heavenly door! What lovely hands open you! Please excuse me, I get terribly tired," said Moreno, greeting her in a tone as fond as it was urbane.

Estupiñá, who was coming up behind him, greeted Don Manuel heartily and permitted himself to embrace him, for they were old friends.

"You're looking dandy," Moreno said, slapping him on the back.

"I'm getting along all right. And you?"

"So-so."

"Always in 'furrin' parts! And with so many friends here!"

The outsider answered with that rather cold benevolence that well-bred superior people know how to use. They separated in the hall because Estupiñá had to go to the dining room. Moreno followed Jacinta into the living room and from there into the parlor.

"Guillermina didn't tell me you were in Madrid. I found out from Mamá today," she said, to say something.

"Guillermina! Announce my arrival with her head in that state! Do you know, every time I come to Spain I find her more daffy. Yesterday when I came home, the first thing she did while she was welcoming me back was to rifle through all my pockets. She plucked me bare. It's as I said to her, 'You hardly set foot in Spain when you meet up with bandits.' Now she's bent on getting all her relatives to pay for a whole floor."

"Poor dear! She's a saint."

Then Don Baldomero arrived, announcing himself before entering with this happy cry:

"Where's that enemy of Spain?"

When he appeared at the door open-armed, Moreno went to embrace him.

"You look like a boy again, godfather."

"And how about you, you rascal. I heard you weren't too well."

"I get terribly tired," the visitor replied, touching his heart. "There's something here . . . but they say it's nerves."

"Yes, of course; nerves," Santa Cruz stated, as if he had the science of medicine at his fingertips.

"Yes, nerves," repeated Jacinta.

And Barbarita, who was coming in at that moment, also said:

"What else could it be but nerves?"

"This wandering friend of ours," Don Baldomero said, looking hard at his friend and relative, not daring to say that he looked ill, "always such a foreigner."

"Doesn't want anything to do with us," said Barbarita, looking his clothes over. "Look—just look at his buttoned-up gray frock coat and white spats. Manolo, what clodhoppers they wear over there! And those gloves! They look like a coachman's."

Moreno burst out laughing. He had such an English air that anyone who saw him would have taken him for one of those bored millionaire lords who wander around the world trying to shake off the homesickness that consumes them. Even when he spoke he belied his Spanish origin—not because he was affected, but because he'd gotten in the habit of dragging his r's and had forgotten certain uncommon words. He had studied at the famous Eton; at thirty he had returned to England, where he now resided, except for occasional short stays in Madrid. He had mastered the art of having a good education in the most exquisite way possible: having a captivatingly easy manner. He was Don Baldomero I's godson, which is why he continued to call Don Baldomero II "godfather."

"As you know, I'm intransigent about our country," he said, smiling. "The more I visit it, the less I like it. Out of respect for my godfather I daren't say more."

That man's taste for foreign things and his dislike of his own country were the cause of many stubborn disputes with Don Baldomero, who defended "everything in their kingdom" with sincere enthusiasm. Sometimes the good Spaniard lost his perspective, sustaining that "outside it was a farce"; and Moreno, whose antipathy was intensified by this, sustained that there were only three good things in Spain: the Civil Guard, white grapes, and the Prado.

"Let me see," said Don Baldomero with irrepressible glee. "What do you have to say about the king we've crowned? *Now* we're cooking. Just wait and see how the country's going to prosper and the wars will end for good."

"He's not half bad. Several of us Spaniards who live in London escorted him on the train to Dover. I gave him a magnificent watch. He's a bright boy, very bright. Poor king! I said to him: 'Your Majesty is going to rule the country of ingratitude, but Your Majesty will conquer the hydra.' I said it to be polite; I don't think he'll be able to manage these people. He'll try to do a good job, but first they'll have to let him."

At this point Juan entered the room, and he and his relative embraced appropriately. They had only to wait for Villalonga to have lunch.

"Shall we wait for him?" asked the Dauphin. "God knows when he'll arrive. Last night it must have been three o'clock when he retired from the minister of the interior's *tertulia*, so he's probably still in bed."

They agreed not to wait any longer, and during the cordial lunch, conversation turned—like it or not—on whether or not everything in Spain is bad and whether or not everything we admire in France and England is actually good. Moreno-Isla didn't budge an inch from the antipatriotic ground on which he stubbornly stood.

"Look, speaking seriously now," he said after pressing the subject of meals and then certain cultural notions, "I've observed something that nobody will deny. From the moment you cross the border into France you're sure of not being bitten by a flea." (Laughter)

"But what do fleas have to do with it!"

"So you maintain that there are no fleas in France?"

"None. Believe me, godfather, there are none. It's a result of the general cleanliness there—the clean houses and clean people. Go to San Sebastián or anywhere in northern Spain. They'll eat you alive."

"For heaven's sake, what flimsy arguments!"

The bell rang. "There he is!" they all cried, and Barbarita looked at the empty place at the table. Villalonga arrived in a cheerful mood, greeted the family, and shook hands with Moreno.

"I beg your pardon, Madam. I flew over as fast as I could so that you wouldn't have to wait for me."

"My friend, ever since you've been a bigwig you've become invisible. Your value is sky high!"

"I don't have a moment's peace. Last night the hubbub lasted till three in the morning. Two hundred people coming in and out. And asking for the moon, all of them."

"Preparing for the elections, eh?"

"If we get started on *politics*—" said Moreno.

"No, let's not," replied Santa Cruz. "I give in on that subject."

Then there was a debate on cheeses, Don Baldomero saying that Spain's were very good too. Then they discussed the houses, which Moreno called uninhabitable. "That's why everybody lives in the street."

"Now wait a minute," said Villalonga. "The houses may be as bad as you say, but houses in other countries have a feature you could hardly call appealing. I'm referring to their lack of wooden blinds in the windows and on the balconies, which lets the light come pouring through from the moment God gets up in the morning; you can't sleep that way."

"Do you mean to tell me you think there are people out there who sleep till noon?"

Much was said about this, and the outsider then praised other things too.

"For my part, I can say that when I cross the border Spain always makes a lamentable impression on me. There's undoubtedly something to be admired, but it escapes me. All I see is crassness, bad manners, poverty, men who look like savages bundled up in blankets, skinny women . . . What shocks me the most is seeing how deteriorated we are as a people. It's rare to see a hearty, robust man and a healthy-looking woman. There's no doubt about it: our people don't eat well, and not just now; they've been hungry for centuries. I find my country quite distasteful, and as soon as I board the Irún express I start cursing. When I wake up the next morning in the Sierra and I hear them shouting 'Bottilsa milk!' I feel ill, believe me. And when I get to Madrid and see people in capes, the women in shawls, the streets badly paved, and carriage horses looking like skeletons, I can't wait to leave again."

"What absurd things you notice, Moreno!" observed Don Baldomero, continuing his apology of Spain in glowing terms that the other listened to benevolently.

As they were having coffee they all noticed that Moreno wasn't feeling well, but he tried to hide his condition, and, putting his hand on his heart, said:

"Something here . . . it's nothing; nerves, perhaps. What bothers me most is the noise of my blood circulating. That's why I enjoy traveling so much . . . With the train's noise I can't hear my own."

There was a moment of silence and sadness at the table, but it passed and they resumed their chatter. Jacinta noticed someone making signs to her from the door, raising the curtain a bit. She went out. It was Guillermina.

"No, no, I won't come in. I have to be off to the builders," she said secretively. "I've come to entrust you with speaking to him. Bring up the subject and make him realize how needy we are."

"Moreno will help you," said Jacinta, taking her friend to another room so that they could speak more freely.

"I don't know . . . he's annoyed with me. We quarreled this morning. The truth is, I got mad at him. I had to. This time he's come back more of a heretic

than ever. A man may condemn himself if he wishes, but why does he have to
criticize religion to me?"

"How awful!"

"And he made so many jokes and was so sacrilegious that—God forgive me for
it—I got angry. I told him I didn't need his money anyway and that I'd be scared
to have it in my hands because it was Satan's money. But it was just a figure of
speech."

"Of course."

"Hasn't he talked about religion here?"

"No, he hasn't even touched on it. Mamá wouldn't tolerate it. He's said that
there are more fleas in Spain than in France."

"Ha! What difference does it make if there are fleas as long as there's Christianity? The things these heretics say would make us indignant if we took them
seriously. You have no idea how Protestant and Calvinistic he's become. Just
listening to him made my hair stand on end. Oh well, he'll have to settle with
God when the time comes, and meanwhile what counts is getting him to fork up
for my project. It'll stand his soul in good stead, even if he doesn't care. So let's
see if you can bring him round."

"I'll do what I can. I mean, I'll talk to him about it."

"Don't forget, now. Good-bye, my child. I'm leaving. Tonight you can tell me
what he tells you; I don't think he'll let us down, because deep down he's a good
soul. If you just scratch that heretic's surface you discover the same angel he used
to be. God bless you."

Jacinta returned to the dining room. In time we shall see whether or not she
accomplished her mission. She was more concerned about the outcome of what
she and her husband had discussed the previous night than about collecting
money for Guillermina's orphange. So as soon as Moreno and Villalonga left, she
took the Dauphin aside to discuss further the question of his break with Fortunata.
On basic things they were agreed; they disagreed only about the most appropriate
procedure. She, as we know, was in favor of sending a letter, and he, a personal
farewell. After lengthy discussions the latter won out, as whoever continues to
read will see.

III. The Revolution Fails

I

IF ONE HAD BEEN ABLE TO CUT through the shiny thicket of fake ideas and spurious words that Juanito Santa Cruz displayed to his wife that night, one would have discovered a bare, withered mind and an absence of desire; a man who was absolutely sick of Fortunata and anxious to get rid of her as soon as possible. Why is it that we want what we don't have, and when we get it, we scorn it? When she emerged from the convent crowned with respectability and on the verge of marriage, when she bore on her bosom the lilies of religious purification and the orange blossoms of her wedding, the Dauphin considered it a worthy deed to pluck her from that life. And so he did, with more success than he had hoped; but his conquest obliged him to support his victim indefinitely, and this, after a certain time, grew boring, dull, and costly. The man was lost without variety; it was in his nature—he couldn't help it. He simply had to switch regimes every so often; when the republic was in power, the monarchy was so tempting! As he left home the afternoon after their joint decision, he reflected on this. His wife was beginning to seem more appealing now, much more than that revolutionary situation that he had created by trampling on two marriages.

"Who would doubt," he continued to think, "that it's wise to avoid a scandal? And anyway, I can't be like every Tom, Dick, and Harry—living in anarchy and gossiped about by everybody. There's another reason, too; I'm starting to get tired of her again, like last time. Poor thing can't learn, she hasn't progressed a single step in the art of pleasing, she has no instinct for seduction, doesn't have the slightest notion of how to charm a man with little things. She was born to make some good carpenter happy. She can't see beyond her pretty nose. Making me shirts now! Some shirts, ha! She's sincere, but she has no sense of humor, no wit. What a difference between her and Sofía la Ferrolana! When Pepito Trastamara brought her back from her first trip to Paris she was a veritable Spanish Du Barry. You've got to be able to assimilate in every art, no matter what, but this dumb woman I got stuck with is always herself. To think that she spent the whole afternoon praying the other day . . . and why, what for? To ask God for kids. What an infernal idea! Well, I can't take any more, so today I'm putting an end to this irregular relationship. Down with the republic!"

Thinking this, he arrived at his mistress' apartment, and the minute he reached out to ring the bell, a strange occurrence abruptly interrupted his train of thought. Before he rang, the door opened, allowing a well-dressed elderly gentleman to leave; he greeted Santa Cruz with a polite nod. Fortunata herself had opened the door and was bidding him farewell.

Juan entered. The exit of that gentleman produced in him two distinct feelings that quickly succeeded each other. The first was mild anger; the second, satisfaction—the coincidence might help him to shake off Fortunata. "I think I know that dapper gentleman. I've seen him somewhere, I know I have," he mused as he entered the living room. "Don't tell me there're shennanigans here! Wouldn't *that* be a nice surprise! But no, it's better this way."

Out loud and rudely he asked Fortunata:

"Who's the old man?"

"I thought you knew him. Don Evaristo Feijóo, a colonel or something in the military service. He's a great friend of Juan Pablo's."

"And who's Juan Pablo? All these people you're springing on me!"

"My brother-in-law."

"When did I ever meet your brother-in-law and what do I care about him? Fine state we're in. And why was that gentleman here? Feijóo, you say his name is? I think he's a friend of Villalonga's."

"He came to see me; this is the third time. He's a very good and proper gentleman. What'd you think, that he came to make love to me? Silly! But anyway, if you don't think I should see him, I won't. And let's be friends."

"No, no. See him as often as you want," he said, chainging tactics with the speed of a genius. "If he's proper, as you say, it might be a good idea for you to cultivate him."

Fortunata didn't quite understand, and he plucked up his courage when he saw her fall silent.

"You see, my child, I am bound to tell you that we can't go on like this."

The big cad thought that it would be best to make a clean break: pose the issue clearly from the outset.

The small room he was in was characterized not by true but by that newly acquired luxury in which elegant concubinage lives, timidly still, and rather as if it were rehearsing for the real thing. There was furniture covered in silk and beautiful curtains, but the former was unattractively done in a mixture of amaranth and lime green, and the latter were crookedly hung, the valances poorly placed. The rug didn't go with the rest, and the flowerstands with their paper begonias were rickety. The clock on the console table had never learned to chime. It was gilded, with pastoral figures on it, and it matched the candelabra, which were inserted in glass shades. There were little engravings with crosstree frames that had been bought at sales, and much more pretentious junk, all of it predating the transformation in taste that had taken place in the last ten years. Santa Cruz regarded the room rather proudly, finding proof of his splendor in it; but at the same time he often made fun of Fortunata for her poor taste. She had an instinct for elegance when it came to clothes, but as for furniture and interior decoration, she committed atrocities. In sum, she had as many qualities as you might desire; but as for being chic—no, she was not.

Seated on the sofa with his hat on, Juan looked lingeringly at everything in the room, relishing the thought that he was seeing it for the last time. Fortunata was standing before him; then she sat down on a footstool, fixing her eyes on her lover as if she were expecting him to say something very serious.

"If this wet noodle," thought Santa Cruz, looking at her, "could only see how gracefully Sofía la Ferrolana sits on a pouf, she'd realize how much she has to learn. This one will never to her dying day learn how to be soft and catlike, arch her body subtly and make it caress the chair. Oh, what beasts God made us!"

And out loud:

"Tell me, why aren't you wearing your silk dressing gown as I told you to?"

"Really, the things you think about! I don't want to spoil it."

"That's right," he said, laughing in her face, "save it for special occasions. I like people to be well dressed. And when I come to see you, you wear your wool robe that smells like cinnamon one day and fuel oil the next."

"That's a lie," replied Fortunata, smelling her clothes. "It's good and clean. Why do you say things that aren't so?"

"Oh, I know you: when you're at home you think, 'I've already caught him.' Fine—go ahead and look as vulgar and ordinary as you can."

"Funny, aren't you! Well, as a matter of fact I didn't put on my silk dressing gown because I had to spend the whole morning in the kitchen."

"Doing what?"

"Making pickled porgy."

"Good. I like it. Like a squirrel, aren't you? All ready for hard times," said the Dauphin with benevolent irony. "Well, child, I have to speak plainly today. I love you too much to keep you in the dark. You're reasonable, you know how things are, and you'll understand that I'm right about what I'm going to say."

This language disconcerted Fortunata because it reminded her of the other time he had used it to get rid of her. But he thought it was the time to make a show of his affection and he had her sit down beside him so that he could run his hand over her face and cajole her the way you do children when you want them to take medicine.

"Come here; don't be afraid. I only want your good. You can't say I haven't done everything in my power for you. As far as I'm concerned, we could go on like this, but my wife has found out; last night we had an awful scene—it was simply awful, you have no idea what she was like. She fainted; we had to call for the doctor. The worst of it is that my parents found out too . . . and it was one reproach after another; my father was furious; they almost ate me alive."

Fortunata was so absorbed and terrified that she was speechless.

"I've already told you, I'll do anything except hurt my parents. So last night I firmly resolved to myself: 'Even if I die of grief, this must end.' I know it will cost me my health. It will be a hard blow. A thread as fine as this can't be cut without a lot of pain. But it has to be done; that's what character is for."

As she began to whimper, Juan said to himself: "Now come the tears. It's inevitable. On your guard."

"Don't cry, silly; don't get upset," he added, kissing her. "Remember, my soul's hanging by a thread too, and if I see you weakening, I'm lost."

He tried to look as if he was about to cry; he wore a very sad face.

"Don't worry," she stammered between sobs. "I could see it coming. You've been plotting it for days . . . All right, we're finished."

"No; I'll always love you, my little squirrel. It's just that I can't visit you anymore. Well, maybe once in a great while. But not like this, as if I were living here; impossible. Madrid may seem big, but it's very small—it's a village. Everything's made public here, and in the end you have no choice but to bow your head. I'm married; so are you. We're trampling on every human and divine law there is. If there were lots like us society would be worse than a prison camp in no time. It would be hell run loose. Have you ever stopped to think it over?"

What Fortunata had thought was that love made up for any and all irregularities; or, rather, that love makes everything regular, rectifies laws, abolishes the ones that oppose it. She had expressed this in a crude fashion to her lover several times. But now, in this dilemma, it seemed ridiculous to refer to that true or false concept of love, for she instinctively knew that all his remarks about divine laws, principles, conscience, and so on were covering up the hole left by his dead love. But she wouldn't dream of following him into the realm of controversy, because she didn't know how to manipulate all those fancy words.

"I already knew it in my heart," she exclaimed, pressing her fists to her eyes.

"One cannot ignore principles," he proceeded. "Social proprieties, my child, are stronger than we are, and one cannot scorn them for long because the blow is bound to come and make us bow our heads. I wish you could grasp this. I never mentioned it, but you know at times, when I was here, my conscience troubled me so deeply that—"

Fortunata gave him a look that cut him short. A look that said, "It's a bit late for that now." "So," she thought, "after we've committed every crime there is, you start having scruples. And I pay for both of us."

"I had it coming to me," she declared in a burst of angry grief, "because we've both been bad; but I've been worse than you . . . nobody can hold a candle to *me* on that score. God, what I've done! Behave that way to Maxi's family! You said it was nothing when *I* got sad thinking about what I'd done. Oh yes, you laughed . . . you laughed."

"Yes, but—"

"I repeat: you laughed, and how! Split your seams laughing, called me a fool and I don't know what else. Well, we've said enough. You're leaving, you've had enough. All right. I'll be sorry—you can be sure of that. But I'll get over it. Bad things can't last forever. Enough!"

She quickly dried her tears, displaying a strength she did not have.

"We'll separate as friends," said Santa Cruz, taking her hand, which she promptly withdrew. "And I'll leave you with this advice—"

"What advice?" she asked, more angry than sad.

"Go back—try to go back to your husband."

"Me, do that!" exclaimed Sra. Rubín with ineffable terror. "After what I've—"

"You'll get over it, child. Time . . . ! The miracles it works! You yourself just said so: bad things can't last forever, and when the huge disadvantages of living illegally begin to chafe at us, we have no choice but to go back to the law. It sounds impossible now, but you'll go back. After all, it's the natural—the easy— way to live. We often say: 'That could never happen.' And yet it does, and it hardly even surprises us, it happens so gradually."

The young woman jumped up and disappeared into the parlor. She was half-crazed. Juan followed her, fearing that she would have an attack of despair. They met at the bedroom door, he entering, she exiting.

"You know what I have to say to you?" cried Fortunata in a voice hoarse with spite and sorrow. "You get in my way around here."

"But don't get so irritated—"

"Out, out!" she shouted, pushing him energetically.

Santa Cruz recognized her strength (which was nearly greater than his) and didn't put up much of a fight. He pretended to ward off his mistress' arms. She won out and slammed the bedroom door. The Dauphin tapped on the glass panes, saying:

"There's no reason to make such a fuss. Come on, my little squirrel, open up. Calm down; don't get all upset. Bah! It's always like this with you."

But no answer came from the bedroom; not a sound. Juan put his ear to the door, thinking he heard sobbing or stifled moans. Then in a flash he realized that he couldn't have asked for better circumstances to make a neat escape and put an end to this annoying business of an emotional split.

"But there's still something undone," he thought, putting his hand into his wallet. "I can't leave her like this . . ." After meditating a bit he put his wallet back into his pocket and said silently: "It's better for me to go. I'll send it to her in a letter. Good-bye. Jacinta can't say I . . ."

He tiptoed out as one would from a house where someone is seriously ill.

2

For the remainder of that fateful day, poor Sra. Rubín gave in to the most extravagant conduct (for indeed, acts such as refusing to eat, crying bucketfuls for three hours straight, turning on the lamp when it was still light outside, and making dozens of absurd remarks as if she were delirious may be called extravagant). The maid tried to calm her, but verbal consolation only irritated her even more. At about nine, the grieving woman resolutely rose from the sofa she had collapsed onto and groped about the dark parlor for her shawl. "They'll see; they'll see," she murmured in her epileptic agitation, and, still in the dark, she felt for her boots, which she put on. Scarf on her head, shawl clinging closely to her shoulders, she left for the street. She walked out briskly with determined steps, like someone who knows where he's going and is obeying one of those formidable impulses that lead straight to a decisive act. When Dorotea realized what her mistress was up to, it was too late to stop her: she was already opening the door and shooting out like an arrow.

It was nine o'clock in the evening. Fortunata swiftly crossed Hortaleza, then La Red de San Luis. She must not have been very upset when instead of taking Montera (where the crowds slowed traffic) she headed for Salud Street in hopes of gaining ten minutes. From Carmen Street she proceeded to Preciados without losing her sense of direction for a second. She crossed the Puerta del Sol at the Cordero house and went straight up Correos to Pontejos Square. She was almost there, and as she saw the object of her trip draw closer, it seemed as if the convulsive impulse that had made her embark on this feverish pursuit was running out. She saw the main door to the Santa Cruz residence; warily, she peered into that wide, stucco-walled cavity, illuminated by gas lamps. Seeing it and coming to a halt, with a certain chill in her soul as she felt her speed abruptly checked, were one and the same.

Her seeing the door was like a bird flying blindly into a wall. People who act on cerebral impulses, which are irresistible and mechanical, like the instincts that determine conversation, stay on course nicely so long as they don't see their goal except as their desires falsely represent it to them; but when the reality of that goal confronts them and presents it as an action subject to objective interpretation, no amount of speed can overcome their impulse to stop. What was Fortunata's purpose, and what was she going to do there? Holy blazes! She was simply going to force her way into the house, shout, and bump into everyone she met, make her way to Jacinta, take her by the knot of her hair, and . . . Well, she hadn't actually decided to grab her by the hair, but she *did* plan to cover her with horrid, bitter remarks. This is what she had planned when she had suddenly decided to dash out of the house and head for Pontejos. And as she was going down Salud

Street, she thought: "I'll get it all out of my system; every bit of it. She's the one that makes me wretched, stealing my husband. Because he's my husband: I've had a child by him and she *hasn't*. So who's got the right to him? Whose insides are worth more, hers or mine?" These mad thoughts, born from her confused state of mind, persisted after she had stopped in astonishment opposite the entrance to the Santa Cruzes' house.

"I . . . I don't know why I don't go in and make the scene I ought to make."

But a certain inexplicable respect restrained her. She retreated, and from the sidewalk across the street looked at the house, saying to herself: "The light must be on in Jacinta's parlor, where they're probably sitting and talking." But she didn't see anything. All the windows were closed and dark. "What if they're out! . . . No, they're probably all in there, making fun of me, laughing over what they've done to me. Some lot! They're all the same breed." She felt the same stupid urge again to break into the house, and took several steps toward it. But she retreated again. "Who's that coming out?" It was an old man who was stopping in the doorway to chat with Deogracias. The young woman recognized Estupiñá, who had been a neighbor of hers when she lived in the Cava, where all her endless troubles had started. Plácido wrapped himself in his cloak and headed for Vicario Viejo Street. Fortunata watched him until he was out of sight and, shortly thereafter, resumed her watch. Who was leaving now? A gentleman in spats; looked like a foreigner. The man passed her, looked at her, nearly stopped a second to get a better look at her, then continued on his way. Other people came out or went in. Even though the impossibility of entering the house was solidifying in Fortunata's mind she stayed on, nailed to the spot without understanding why. She couldn't leave, although she was beginning to realize that the idea that had propelled her to the spot was crazy, like the ideas that come to us in dreams. One of the many delirious notions that entered her head while she was standing there was that this or that man on his way out of the house was Jacinta's lover. "They can't tell me she's virtuous. The things people try to get away with! You can't believe anything. Virtuous? My foot! None of those rich married women are—they can't be. Us low-class women are the only ones with any virtue—except when they fool us. Me, for instance . . . me." She was overcome with convulsive laughter. "What're you laughin' about, stupid?" she said to herself. "You're as honest as the day's long, 'cause you've only loved one man in your whole life. But them? Ha, ha, ha. A new man every four months and 'I'm virtous.' Why? Because there're no scandals—they all cover up for each other. Oh, Señora Doña Jacinta—keep your virtue for somebody who'll believe it; you'll fall, you've got to, if you haven't already."

Suddenly she saw a carriage drawing up to the door. Was somebody inside, or was it coming for someone? Coming for someone, because nobody got out; the footman entered the house and Deogracias started talking with the coachman.

"They're going to come out," the miserable woman said to herself as she again felt the burning impulse that had made her leave home. "They won't get away from me this time. I'll pounce on them, and I'll insult both of them, the mother-in-law and the daughter-in-law—two of a kind! Oh, they're taking so long! My head's burning up, and I feel like I'm all nails."

The ladies came out. First, Fortunata saw a white-haired one, then Jacinta, then a young chick—her sister, she thought. She saw velvet, white furs, silk, jewels—all of it quickly, as if by magic. The three ladies entered the carriage and the footman closed the door. Imagine! No sooner had she seen the three ladies than Fortunata was overtaken by fear. And to think she'd planned to dig her fingers into them with fingers like steel claws! What she felt instead was more like terror, the kind that comes from a sudden, horrible danger; and her will was so imposing in this sudden panic that she broke into a run to escape without so much as daring to look back once. She heard the noise of the carriage coming down the street and even saw it pass by so fast it practically ran over her.

"Hey!" shouted the coachman.

And Señora Rubín let out a shriek, jumping out of the way. What a scare, holy God! She continued on toward Puerta del Sol, conscious of the very intense fear she had felt and wondering whether there might not be some shame in it too. But it wasn't easy to tell whether her terror was like that of the exalted Christian who sees the devil, or like that of the devil when he's shown the cross.

Letting herself be carried along by her own steps, she somehow found herself in the middle of the Puerta del Sol. Unconsciously, she sat down on the curbstone of the fountain and looked at the foaming water. A public attendant eyed her suspiciously, but she paid no attention to him and stayed where she was for a long time, watching the streetcars and carriages circling around her as if she were in the middle of a merry-go-round. The cold and the damp forced her to get up, and so she did, wrapping herself snugly in her cloak and covering her mouth. All that could be seen of her were her eyes, and since they were so pretty, quite a few men came up to her and asked if they might escort her, telling her jokes all the while. Then she remembered other unhappy times, and the thought of having to go back to them made her feel very intense pain, clearing her head of the chimeras that had filled it. Her sense of reality was slowly regaining its control of her. But reality was hateful to her, and she clung to that delirious state. One of the men who had followed her dared to stop her, calling her by name:

"My, but you've covered yourself up well . . . Fortunata."

She stopped in front of the man who had said this. Wondering who he could be, she looked at him blankly. "I know I've seen that face before," she said to herself. "Oh! It's Don Evaristo."

"Goodness, child, you certainly are distracted."

"I'm going home."

"This way?" exclaimed Feijóo. "You're headed for the Royal Theater."

"Well . . . ," she replied, looking at the houses around her, "I made a mistake. I don't know what's wrong with me."

"Let's go this way; I'll take you home," Don Evaristo said kindly. "Capellanes, Rompelanzas, Olivo, Ballesta, San Onofre, Hortaleza, Arco."

"That's the way. But don't doubt what I say."

"What, dear?"

"That I'm decent; I've always been."

Feijóo looked at his friend. Frankly, those eyes had always charmed him, but the exalted look they had tonight didn't charm him a bit.

The abandoned woman covered her mouth with her cloak again; her escort didn't say a word. But when she stopped again to repeat what she'd said, Feijóo, who was very frank, couldn't help but say:

"Listen, my friend, you're not well; I mean something has just happened to you. Confide in me; I'm a loyal friend, and I'll give you good advice."

"But do you doubt," said Fortunata, leaning against the wall, "that I've always been—"

"Decent? How could I doubt it, dear? What I do doubt is your health. You're tired, and I think we should take a carriage. Coachman!"

Sra. Rubín let herself be led along and mechanically got into the cab. She had done the same before with whomever she'd picked up in the street.

Feijóo spoke to her with fatherly affection, but she didn't reply exactly in kind. Suddenly she looked at him in the darkness of the carriage and said:

"And you, who are you? Where are you taking me? What do you take me for? Can't you tell that I'm decent?"

"Oh, my God!" the good man murmured, truly upset. "That poor head's not right, not at all."

At last they arrived. The maid opened the door.

"Now," said the pleasant retired colonel, "into bed. Would you like me to call a doctor?"

Without answering she went into her bedroom. Feijóo followed her, grieved to see her in such a sorry state. Then he and the maid conferred in whispers.

"A break. That scoundrel's given you the gate again," said Don Evaristo. "If that's all it is, the storm will pass."

He took leave until the next day and the suffering woman lay down. As her maid helped her undress, she said:

"I'm decent, and I've always been. What? You doubt it?"

"Me? . . . No, Ma'am; why should I doubt it?" her servant said, turning aside to hide her smile.

The unfortunate Sra. Rubín fell asleep very soon, but half an hour later she was wide awake and very excited. Dorotea, who was at her side, heard her sing—

softly, with her arms crossed. She was singing the mystical chants she had learned at the Micaelas.

iv. A Course in Practical Philosophy

I

THE NEXT DAY DON EVARISTO dropped in several times to inquire about Fortunata. But he wasn't permitted to see her. Dorotea told him that the lady didn't want to see anyone, and that thinking so much about being decent had given her a splitting headache. The following day the Señorita was slightly better. She had gotten up and drunk some very thin soup.

"But she's still got that same idea in her head," the girl added, not unmaliciously, with her sharp eye and sense of humor. "I'm warning you so you'll humor her, Sir, and agree with her."

"Don't worry, child," the gentleman replied. "If she's not humored, it won't be because of me. May I see her? Will I disturb her very much? Does she know I'm here?"

"Yes, she knows. Wait a few minutes; she'll be out."

After waiting fifteen minutes my man was still alone in the dining room. Dorotea told him he could go in. Fortunata was in the parlor lying on the sofa, her head resting on a blue satin pillow. She was wearing her silk dressing gown and a very delicate white scarf, tied so closely over her head that only the oval of her face could be seen. She was pale, with circles under her eyes and a very dejected look. Since Don Evaristo prided himself on knowing a bit about medicine, he took her pulse.

"It's as regular as a clock, child. You don't have a fever or anything like it. Bah, nonsense! A little tantrum, that's all it is. And aren't you pretty with that scarf around your head! You can't even see your hair or your ears. You look like a sister of charity. What ailments the lady has to endure!"

"Yesterday I felt awful," she said faintly. "My head was splitting with pain, and since I couldn't get that idea off my mind, it went on and on. The things that go through your head! I want you to know that I'm—"

"Decent, yes, I know: more than yesterday; and you'll be more decent tomorrow than today. It goes without saying."

"No, that's not what I was going to say."

"What do you mean?"

"What I am is bad, really bad; the worst woman in the world. Do you realize what I did? I got what was coming to me, all right, oh yes, 'cause I've done my share of wrong in this world."

"Come now, it can't have been that bad."

"There's something else," said the young woman, pulling her hand out from under her cloak and showing him a letter. "Yesterday he sent this."

"Who? Oh! Santa Cruz."

"I didn't read it till this morning. He says good-bye again and gives me advice and tries to sound like a saint. He put four thousand *reales* in with the letter."

"Well, he didn't exactly go overboard."

"I want to write him today," she said, livening up a bit. "No, not write him; just put these two bills in an envelope and send them back to him."

"Wait a minute, child; think it over carefully," her friend said, approaching her affectionately. "This business of returning the money is romanticism; it's out of date nowadays. The only money that has to be returned is stolen money, and you have a right to what he gave you; to that and much more. So let's not have any 'gestures' if you don't want me to start booing. The only place you'll find simple-minded acts like this are in bad plays. So. I've decided to get you away from this foolishness and put you squarely on practical ground."

"As for the money—I won't take it," declared the heartsick woman, beginning to pout like a spoiled child.

"Isn't that nice! Fine and dandy! Live on pouting," said the colonel, pouting his lips theatrically. "Give back the blasted money? He'll laugh all the harder. That's just what he wants. Do you have any savings?"

"I must have about thrity *duros.*"

"Just as I thought: nothing. What are you going to live on now?"

"I want to be decent."

"Magnificent . . . Sublime. What I can't exactly see is why being decent means not eating. Are you thinking of working, perhaps? Doing what? The four thousand *reales* will at least give you time to think about it and survive for a few months. So. Put away the paper and let's not hear any more about it."

This did not convince Fortunata, who was rather stubborn, but she did postpone returning the bills till the next day. Since the wound was still fresh, she couldn't help but talk about it.

"Some stunt he's pulled on me!" she murmured after a pause, looking at the floor. "What a way to pay me! When I went and left everything for him, and gave a kick in the pants to the people who'd made me respectable. Excuse my bad language. I'm very vulgar. It's the way I am. The family that wanted to make me refined and respectable—I threw their respectability in their faces. Ungrateful, aren't I? Oh, but I was indecent! And all because I loved him more than I should, like a tigress. And just so you can see how stupid I am, listen to this: all that man has to do is look my way and I'd forgive him; I'd be in love with him again."

"I know. Anyone can see that your heart's as soft as butter," said Don Evaristo thoughtfully.

"The rest don't even seem like men. For me, there are just two kinds of men: he's on one side, and all the rest are on the other. I wouldn't lift a finger for all of them put together. That's how I am; I can't help it."

"You're not telling me anything I don't already know. I've seen a lot in my life," Feijóo asserted with the tolerance of a priest who has heard many a confession. "People like you have a dog's life. There's nothing worse than having a heart that's too big. A big brain, big stomach, big liver—they're ailments too, but lesser ones. And if I'm worth anything I'm going to trim off some of that heart of yours so there'll be more of an equilibrium."

"Equi—?"

"Equilibrium."

"Uh huh. I can't pronounce it, but I understand what it is. And how are you going to 'trim' it?"

"Oh, it will take lessons; quite a few of them. It's the only way to keep you from being miserable for the rest of your life. Ah! This world is like bagpipes full of holes; you've got to tune them and keep tuning them if you want them to sound right. You're wet behind the ears. One would think you'd just been born and stood up on wobbly legs. You know what the trouble is? You don't know where you're going. You return money that's given to you and you lose your head two, three times over the same person. A fine future! I'm going to teach you something you don't know."

"What?"

"How to live. Living is our first duty in this vale of tears, and yet how few of us know how to! This is from a man who has seen a lot of the world and who has had—like you—an enormous heart. So! Get ready, because I'm starting on the lessons."

"And will I be happy?" Fortunata asked expectantly, as if someone were telling her fortune.

"What I want for the time being is to make you practical."

"Practical!" she uttered, wrinkling up her nose as she always did when she wanted to pretend she didn't understand something and make fun of herself at the same time. "Practical? What does that mean?"

"You mean to tell me you don't know? Don't pretend to be stupider than you are!" Don Evaristo said, wrinkling up his nose too.

"Well, then, we'll become praktickle," said Señora Rubín, ridiculing the word so as to ridicule the idea.

The visit was over soon, because Señor Feijóo didn't want to tire her. He promised to return soon. If it had been up to him, he would have been back in an hour.

"Listen, my little friend: you can't be left alone for long, because that head of yours will start spinning . . . Unless you throw me out, I'll be back again this afternoon."

And he returned before nightfall bringing flowers, and a short while later a delivery boy came up with several potted plants. Fortunata liked flowers very much, both cut and potted; her balconies were full of flowerpots, and she spent most of the morning tending them. She greatly appreciated the good gentleman's presents, which were more expensive than usual, being out of season. The cut flowers were the most beautiful, rare, and valuable that could be had in winter. From their conversation about plants that afternoon, Don Evaristo gathered that his friend's taste was a bit out of the ordinary. She didn't care for flowers that had no scent, and she especially disliked camelias. She could see no real difference in value between the best camelia and the yellowest, most ordinary sunflower. What she liked to receive was a pretty carnation, a spikenard, or a rose; in a word, whatever flowers "appeal to your nose" the minute you're near them.

"And how do we feel this afternoon?" asked Don Evaristo, leaning closer in order to get a good look at her face.

He was playing doctor, but he was examining her face because it was so pretty, not because he was searching for symptoms. And as night was falling and there was no light, he had to draw very close in order to see clearly. She was in the same place, the same pose, as that morning.

"I feel the same," she replied without moving. "I was crying the whole time you were gone."

"Well, there's no need to rack your brains for the remedy. As long as I'm here . . . But the remedy might be worse than the illness, and eventually you'd have to cry so that I'd leave. Come now, child, stop heaving such deep sighs or you'll sigh away your soul. We'll console ourselves bit by bit. Time is the best doctor for curing these things. One day I'll find my little friend happier than a lark, with everything that's upsetting her today completely forgotten. And soon, very soon . . . You should turn your thoughts to something else. Do you know how to play ombre?"

"Me? No; the only card game I know is *tute*. *He* tried to teach me ombre, but I never could catch on. You don't know how slow I am."

"Do you like the theater?"

"Oh, yes; especially plays with things that make you cry."

"Holy saints above! Plays that have lines like 'My son! . . . Father ! . . .'"

"Those, and others that have scenes where they suffer a lot and draw their swords, and an actress faints 'cause they're taking her son away."

"In the name of the Holy Ghost!" cried Feijóo cleverly. "There we differ, because as for me, no sooner do the actors start carrying on at the top of their lungs and the actresses start pouting than I start fuming in my seat and itching to leave. No tears for now. What you need is to laugh a bit, see something light at the Lara or Variety Theater. Leave dramas for reality, child. Do you like masquerades?"

"You're going to laugh," Fortunata replied, sitting up. "In the short time I was on my own in Barcelona, running around here and there, I used to go to dances. They were fun at first, then they weren't . . . Juan took me twice this year, and I went another time with a girlfriend, to see if I could catch him living it up with somebody else. Would you believe that I didn't even have this much fun? Those masks are so hot you feel like you're burning up. I always want to take them off. And then if I try something funny, it makes me laugh just to see how bad I do it. You can't imagine how dull I am. All I ever think up are these dumb things. Juan used to tell me I wasn't good for anything, and that I didn't deserve my pretty little figure. He kept trying to change me—but you can't teach an old dog new tricks. I was born *pueblo* and I'll stay *pueblo*—I mean, vulgar, you know, a savage. Oh, if you coulda seen how mad he'd get when I told him I liked stew—the kind they eat in taverns, with loin. I had to hide to eat what I liked. And how about the way he preached at me 'cause I don't have that French look that Antoñita does—she's Villalonga's—and another one they call Sofía la Ferrolana? 'They even sit differently,' he used to tell me. 'Notice that blasé air, or that lively look, depending on the circumstances; that charm, that way of walking down the street. When *you* go by wearing your veil, walking along calmly the way you do, without looking at anybody, you look as if you were going from door to door to collect donations for a Mass.' See what I mean? And then he'd insist that I wear those tight, tight dresses that make you feel like you're showing off everything God gave you."

"I'm wild about this woman," thought Feijóo, who as he listened to Fortunata experienced ineffable joy. "I must be doting—I don't know what's wrong with me. Oh my God, at my age! There's no use, I've got to speak out . . . No; control yourself, Evaristo, it's not time yet . . ."

My good man looked dazed as he listened to her talk with such enchanting sincerity. A happy, hopeful smile made his lips purse and exposed his impeccable teeth. His face, which was always rosy, brightened all the more, and in his cheeks one could see the true ardor of youth. He was, in a word, the handsomest, most pleasant, and brisk elderly man imaginable; clean as a whistle, his hair curly; his mustache pure silver; the rest of his face so well shaven it was glorious; his forehead wide and ivory-colored, its fine wrinkles neatly drawn. As for his body, most of today's young men would be delighted to have one like it. None was as straight or had better carriage than his.

"No, not today," he thought. "I'm afraid I'll put my foot in my mouth. Stay cool, Evaristo; hold back. There'll be time to spur things later. She isn't ready yet. The wound's still fresh."

2

"Well, today I'm not keeping this bottled up inside me," he thought the next day as he entered the living room, sparkling clean and reeking of cologne. "Where in blazes is she? What's keeping her so long? This woman's pure delight; that Santa Cruz character is the biggest two-legged booby there is . . . She's making me wait so long! It sounds as if she's beating the furniture with the duster. She's probably cleaning house, although today isn't Saturday. But that doesn't matter. That's what she needs: work, exercise, distractions, running around a bit. Magnificent! Yes, she's undoubtedly cleaning. That woman's a diamond in the rough. If she'd fallen into my hands instead of that simpleton's, what a surface I would have cut on her! They're still moving things around in there. That's it, hit hard. The best thing for heartsickness is sweat, lots of it. Oh, I'm so happy today! It's been a long time since you've felt this happy, Evaristo. Not since you were in the Philippines . . . It sounds as if they're moving the iron bed now. Oh, how that metal creaks! . . . Ah, at last she's coming out."

"Please excuse me, Don Evaristo," said Fortunata, appearing at the parlor door in a housedress, a huge apron, and a scarf tied around her head, "I'm cleaning."

Behind her the air was dusty and unsettled; sun poured through the wide-open balcony door and brightened the room.

"You see I've got this habit . . . When I feel like crying and I'm all miserable inside, you know what I do? I grab the duster, the brooms, a big sponge, and a pail of water. Whenever I'm real upset I attack the dust."

"Dear me, I feel sorry for you, child, because the house couldn't be cleaner."

"That's how it should be. It's my only pastime. I don't know how to do any delicate work—I can't sew, except simple stuff. I can't embroider or play the piano. And I can't paint like Antonia, Villalonga's friend; she's always got a brush in her hand. I can hardly read, I can't figure out what books say. What else can I do? Scrub and clean. At least it takes my mind off things."

"I could devour her," thought Don Evaristo, who gazed at her dumbfounded, without a word.

"So it's best if you go now and come back later. We'll get dust and trash all over you."

"No, child, I'm not leaving."

"Ooh, do you smell of cologne! There's a smell I like. But we'll make a mess of you. We're just starting in the living room."

"I don't care," the good gentleman replied with an indescribable smile. "Get dusty? Doesn't matter—I'll shake it off."

"Whatever you want. Make yourself at home, then. I don't have any albums or books to give you while you wait."

"I don't need any albums anyway. Go on, go on now—work hard. That's what's good for you. We'll talk later. I don't have a thing in the world to do."

And two hours later they were seated in the parlor, facing each other, she in the same outfit as before and rather tired.

"I must be a mess!" she said, getting up to look in the mirror over the sofa. "Holy Mary, will you look at these eyelashes, all covered with dust!"

"They wouldn't look that way unless they were so black and thick and beautiful . . ."

"I'd like to fix up a bit. It's not nice to have visitors looking like this."

"If it's for my sake, don't worry . . . I like you more as you are. Relax, and let's talk for a while. Let me ask you this: what do you plan to do now?"

Fortunata, leaning forward to hear better, let her head fall back on the headrest of the chair—the best way of expressing that she hadn't given the matter any further thought.

"Do you plan to beg your husband's forgiveness and go back to him?"

"Good God, the things you think of!" she exclaimed, throwing her hands to her head as if she'd heard the biggest nonsense.

"Well, I don't think that what I've said is so absurd."

"Before going back to Maximiliano," stated Fortunata, with the most serious face she could muster, "I'll go through anything, anything . . ."

"Including poverty, being dishonored . . ."

"Yes, sir."

"Fine. Well, that means that when the little you have runs out—and I presume that you didn't insist on returning his four thousand *reales*—when it runs out, you'll have no choice but to earn your living as best you can. You don't know how to do any respectable work that pays. So . . . if you guess what I've got in my hand I'll give you some flowers."

Fortunata frowned, and without looking up she folded and unfolded a corner of her apron.

"There are no two ways about it, my friend. Either you go home to your husband or back to the streets with any Tom, Dick, or Harry, hoping that things will work out with one of them. And there are a couple of paths leading off from this evil road, and not all of them end up in the hospital and abjection. So think it over. No matter how hard you rack your brains you won't find a way out of this dilemma."

"This what?"

"Dilemma—you know, sink or swim."

"I want to be decent," said the young woman, with the most serious expression in the world, torturing the corner of her apron.

"Decent? I think that's a fine idea. Now tell me frankly: eating while you're decent, or not eating?"

Fortunata smiled faintly, and her face lit up for a minute. But soon it was cloaked in that gloomy seriousness again, that sign of the horrible doubt in her soul.

"Being 'decent' sounds pretty," continued Feijóo. "There's nothing easier to say, but that turns out to be so hard to practice. You must have meant to say 'relatively decent' . . ."

"No. I want to be decent every inch of the way. Decent."

"Without going back to your husband?"

"Without going back to my husband."

With his lips and eyes and all the muscles of his face, Feijóo made a very expressive, human gesture that is part of the language and mime of every country in the world; a gesture that said, "Child, I don't see how . . ."

Fortunata didn't either, and it made her feel completely helpless. She was on the verge of tears.

"Come now," said the colonel, brushing aside all that captious reasoning as if it were so many flies, "let's speak plainly and be practical, and face the situation as it really is. Things are what they are, not what we want them to be. What would be nicer than your being as decent and pure as the sun! But tarde piâche, as the little bird said while he was being eaten. What we're concerned with now is how to make you as relatively decent as possible. Talking about virtue is easy enough, but how about eating and staying alive? You, my dear friend, have no choice but to agree to let a man take care of you. All you need now is for fate to put a good man in your path. Are you going to look for one you already know, or are you going to hunt for a stranger somewhere in the streets or the theaters? Which will it be? I mention this because if you want to save yourself some work . . . imagine yourself bored, out looking for a man, you throw out a line, they're biting, you pull it in, and—oh, what a surprise!—you've caught one. Here I am, fresh out of the water and flipping my tail merrily to find myself so well caught. I'm a bit old, but without being vain I think I can say that I'm good for anything, and both inside and out I'm worth more than most boys. I don't have any other obligations, I live on my own income, I'm alone in the world, I have a good life, and I can give it to whoever suits me. So you decide. Modesty aside, I can tell you that it would be a wee bit difficult for you, in your situation, to find a better arrangement. You'll understand what I mean when you get over this depression, which I hope will be soon. Your head's not clear now. And I won't hesitate to tell you this," he said, raising his voice as if he were getting annoyed, "you've won at the lottery, and not just any old prize but the grand prize."

"I want to be decent," replied Fortunata without looking at him, like a spoiled child who insists on saying an improper word because he gets scolded for it.

"I won't be the one to take that notion out of your head," said the gentleman, smiling, without doubting his victory. "And it could well be that you've discovered how to make a square circle."

"What?"

"Nothing . . . It has just occurred to me that accepting my proposal won't keep you from being as decent as you want. The more, the better . . . Well, I don't want to make your head spin, so I'll leave you alone to think over what I've said. Keep scrubbing; work; whack away at the furniture; scrub till your fingers chafe. Physical work—lots of it—and meanwhile, think it over, and tomorrow or the day after tomorrow—there's no rush—I'll be back for 'the word,' as they say."

3

Since what should happen happens, and reality plays no tricks, things came to pass according to the wishes of Don Evaristo González Feijóo. He was well aware that it couldn't be otherwise, unless the woman was mad. What way out did she have except his proposal? None. Not knowing how to work, not wanting to go back to her husband, and not at all charmed by the thought of going off to a steppe and living on roots, what sort of desirable decency could she claim? The moral: what had to happen due to the infallible linking of human necessities happened.

"And just so that you'll see that I know how to handle things and have your best interests at heart," Don Evaristo said to her one day, already using the familiar tú form, "I intend to avoid a scandal for your sake and for mine. I'll be especially careful to keep this from Juan Pablo Rubín, who introduced me to you in the street—remember?—and started our happy relationship, which we must hide as well as we humanly can. Just wait, you'll see how good it will be. I'll teach you to be practical, and when you see what it's like you'll be amazed at all the foolish things you've done in your life and how you've gone against the law of reality."

It must be said that Fortunata was not happy or anywhere near it. She felt resigned, if anything, and she consoled herself with the thought that in her unfortunate situation there was no better solution than this, and that it was better to fall on a haystack than on a pile of stones. During the first few days, she went through hours of intense melancholy in which her conscience, together with her memory, vividly presented to her all the wrong things she had ever done, particularly getting married and committing adultery only a few hours later. But suddenly, without a clue as to how or why, everything turned inside out in the unknown depths of her soul, and her acts seemed clean, and clear, and firm. She judged herself and found that she was guiltless, innocent of all the evil that had ensued, as if she had acted on impulses dictated to her by some strange, superior entity. "I'm not bad," she thought. "What is there that's bad inside here? Nothing."

Intermittent spells of a religious mania were related to these different states of mind. When she was feeling very guilty, she was seized by her fear of temporal and eternal punishments. She recalled all that Don León and the Micaelas had taught her and envisioned details of her life in the convent with extraordinary clarity. Whenever she was having one of these religious spells, she went to Mass and even to confession; but soon she was afraid to continue and put off going.

Then she would swing in the opposite direction, that is, toward the conviction of her guiltlessness, which succeeded the previous state like a mechanical reversion and banished from her mind all her hazy mystical apprehensions. For two or three days she would enjoy complete tranquillity and forget about praying, except for the Our Fathers she mumbled perfunctorily every morning. Her conscience spun on an axis that showed her first the white side, then the black. At times this abrupt rotation depended on a word, a whimsical thought that flew into her head like a bird whisking across the immensity of the sky. In no time at all, and for no real reason, Fortunata stopped thinking of herself as an evil monster and suddenly felt like an innocent, unfortunate creature. A leaf falling from an already withered stalk and landing silently on the rug could cause the change, or the neighbor's canary starting to sing, or an unidentified carriage rumbling noisily down the street.

She was very grateful to Señor Feijóo, who behaved like a gentleman and wasn't at all finicky or impertinent as men are apt to be. The first day, he read the rules to her:

"Look: I'm going to give you complete freedom. You may come and go whenever you wish, and do whatever pleases you. I'm not in favor of preventive measures. I want you to be faithful to me, as I am to you. As soon as you're bored, let me know . . . Don't ever bring a man here, because if I discover any fooling around, I'll leave and you'll never see me again. I'll do the same if I discover it outside. If you behave well, I'll provide for you even if I should have to leave you for some reason."

The truth is, Fortunata did not feel what we call "love" for her friend; but she did feel respect and the quiet affection that he had earned with his noble conduct. She considered him the most decent person she had ever known. And he knew so much! And how well he knew the world, and how clever he was at handling things!

To put into effect the discretion he had mentioned at the beginning, he told her to take a modest room; not for economical reasons—he could easily pay for an apartment like the one Santa Cruz had given her—but out of a desire to be modest. The "decency" she yearned for without knowing the exact meaning of the word was senseless; but even though she wouldn't be "being decent" she could at least appear to be, and that would be better than nothing. A modest little place in an out-of-the-way neighborhood at least meant that a scandal could be avoided.

Shortly after moving into her new home, Don Evaristo bought her a good Singer sewing machine, which she enjoyed very much. Her protector paid her a visit every day, but at no set time. Sometimes he came in the afternoon; other times at night. But he always retired to his own house for the night. He thought Fortunata should have a servant who was loyal, discreet, and relatively respectable. Feijóo spent about a month searching and finally found someone suitable.

Although Fortunata began by resigning herself to this new life, she eventually grew contented with it; Don Evaristo was most content all along.

"I'm not jealous," he said to her, "and although I wouldn't swear to any woman's being faithful, I don't think you'll disappoint me, unless that lover boy turns up again. I *am* afraid of *him.*"

And she, with her usual sincerity, declared that, indeed, she did continue to care about the blasted author of all her troubles. She couldn't help it; but if he did start pursuing her again, she'd know how to resist him and punch him in the nose with all the power of her decency. Upon hearing this, Feijóo became benevolently incredulous and said:

"Let's pray to God he doesn't look for you, just in case. I can't be too careful when it comes to him."

They lived in near isolation and never went anywhere together. Not even Feijóo's most observant friends discovered his affair. Fortunata didn't cause any talk, and her husband's family thought that she had left Madrid. Things went so well for them with this cautious, modest system they had adopted that Don Evaristo congratulated himself continuously.

"See what a paradise it is, *chulita?*[*] Like this, we manage to accomplish two things: live peacefully on the inside and keep up a decent front. Why should I let them call me a 'dirty old man'? And you—why should you have to be the butt of other people's gossip? This is what I wanted to teach you: how to be a practical person. The world must be treated ve-ry respectfully. Of course I know it's better if you can be a saint; but since that's a wee bit hard, we can at least keep up appearances and never set a bad example. Take note of this, my friend: never lose your dignity."

Talking on this subject stimulated him to the point of eloquence.

"Listen, *chulita:* I don't preach hypocrisy. In certain realms, dignity consists of not committing an act. For example, I do not condone anything that involves appropriating what is not one's own, or telling lies that hurt another man's reputa-

---

[*] In the diminutive, *chula* is an affectionate name for a colorful, low-class woman in Madrid.

tion, or anything vile and cowardly; nor do I condone underrating military discipline—I'm very severe on that. But in anything that's related to love, dignity consists in keeping of appearances because I don't understand—and never have understood—how any act derived from true love can be a sin or a crime, or even a shortcoming. That's why I never wanted to get married. Naturally, passions should be curbed a bit, and perverts shouldn't be allowed; that's why there are ten commandments instead of eight. The eight are the real ones; I simply can't grasp the other two. Oh, *chulita*, you probably think I've got a strange set of values. You know, if someone were to tell me that So-and-So had stolen, or killed, or slandered, or started some sort of row, I'd be indignant. And if I caught him, believe me, I'd strangle him. But if someone were to come and tell me that such and such a woman has been unfaithful to her husband, or that such and such a girl has run away from home with her boyfriend, it would roll right off my back. It's true that I would pretend to be shocked just for appearances' sake, and I might say something like 'Oh, how horrible!' But deep down inside it would make me laugh and I'd say to myself, 'Let the world have its way, and the species reproduce; that's what we're here for.' "

At first, all this struck Fortunata as very odd; but when she heard it the second time, she discovered that it agreed with what she thought. But . . . mightn't it be nonsense? Because it was impossible for her and Feijóo to be right when the whole world was against it.

"So now you know," added the colonel. "The day you feel like being unfaithful to me, tell me. I don't believe in absolute fidelity. I'm indulgent, I'm human, and I know very well that saying 'mankind' is the same as saying 'weakness.' If it happens, come and tell me to my face. No sneaking around. Do you think I'd come back with a gun to shoot you and then myself? A fine ass I'd be if I did! No. In the name of the human race I'll look upon you benevolently . . . Of course it's true that it would irritate me a bit. But I'd put on my hat and leave, by which I don't mean to say that I'd abandon you, because what I'd be doing would be retiring you; putting you on half pay."

"What a peculiar man, and what a way to love!" thought Fortunata.

4

That day they had lunch together—an excess that Don Evaristo allowed himself occasionally. She said that she knew how to "fix some beans" tavern style, in a stew. And Feijóo was anxious to taste them because he liked certain typical Spanish dishes. Fortunata had an admirable store of provisions and spent very little on clothes and odds and ends. He was so clever and practical that he was easily able to make her almost give up the useless and costly habit of dressing in style. In the kitchen department he gave her a free hand and recommended that she buy the best there was and choose what was in season. But she had no need of instructions from her master in this area, because as a native Madrilenian, from the Cava de San Miguel no less, she knew what to eat in every season. She wasn't gluttonous; but she was intelligent when it came to food and everything related to Madrid's well-stocked marketplace.

And the truth is that with that quiet, calm, and eminently practical life she blossomed and became so fetchingly beautiful that she made a glorious sight. Señora Rubín had always enjoyed good health, but never before had she flourished physically to that luxuriant degree. When he looked at her, Feijóo couldn't help but feel crushed. "With every day that goes by, she's prettier," he reflected, "and I'm older." And when she looked in the mirror, she couldn't help but admire her own image. Sometimes a thought that had struck her in other periods of her life seemed to reappear under the space between her eyebrows: "If only he could see me now! . . ." But she instantly tried to brush aside such thoughts, which led only to sadness and brooding.

She lived on Tabernillas Street, which the residents in the heart of Madrid considered so far out that "Christ could shout there and no one would hear him." This suburb, called Moors' Gate, is so remote it seems like a town in itself. On the whole it's a quiet, modestly comfortable neighborhood: wholesalers, marketers, traveling vendors. There are no employees, because the area is too far from any office. It has a happy, sunny look, and if you follow the road to Gil Imón, there's a view of the Manzanares lowland and the mountains. Toward the slopes that lead to El Rosario, the neighborhood isn't very distinguished, nor are the views very good, because that side runs into the military prisons and so there are women on the loose and soldiers who would like to be.

At the end of Aguila Street the neighborhood deteriorates again; along the esplanade leading to Gil Imón, which is drenched in sun all day long, there are endless portraits of human misery. Fortunata took Solana Street, where there is so much poverty, on her way to Mass at La Paloma, and it continually amazed her not to see a single familiar face. As a matter of fact, anyone from downtown or northern Madrid who visits that neighborhood has the impression that neither the houses nor the faces are Madrid. For a month Fortunata didn't wander out of Moors' Gate; when she did, she stopped in Puerta Cerrada, and when she breathed the thicker air of the capital, it scared her. She turned back to her peaceful and silent Tabernillas Street.

Once he retired, Don Evaristo lived on the second floor of a large, aristocratic house on Don Pedro Street. It was one of those grand but architecturally poor palaces built for the nobility. On the main floor there was an embassy, and whenever there was a party in the evening, they decorated the staircase with flowerpots and rolled out a rug. Feijóo had grown accustomed to the bare spaciousness of his rooms, the tall windows that rose to the ceiling, and he couldn't live in "those cardboard houses" of modern Madrid. His residence was somewhat like a convent, and his neighbor (on the left side of the second floor) was an archaeologist, the owner of magnificent collections. You could hear a pin drop in that house, for other than the quiet residents on the second floor, there was only the ambassador, who was single, on the ground floor, and unless he was giving a reception (which he did only rarely) you would have thought that no one lived there.

Aguas Street, which was a lonely one, quickly connected Feijóo with his idol. I don't take the word back, for the good man came to feel deep love for his protégée, and it did not consist entirely of romantic passion; it was also a kind of fatherly affection that grew more and more as time went on. "What a pity," he thought to himself, "that you aren't twenty years younger! It really is . . . If I'd only met her before . . . ! Just as others ruined this priceless person with their clumsy hands, I would have made something admirable of her. She's so Spanish! . . . And I'm getting so senile!"

In a month, Feijóo found that he couldn't live without increasing indefinitely the time he spent with her. Many days they dined or lunched together, and since the lovers had agreed to improve, indeed practically restore Spanish cuisine, she prepared stews and fried foods that gave off an aroma that reached San Francisco el Grande. After dinner, if they didn't play cards, the good man told his mistress about the adventures and fascinating experiences he had had in his dramatic military life. He had been in Cuba at the time of the Narciso López expedition and worked intensively on the persecution and capture of the famous insurgent. Fortunata listened in awe, her elbows on the table, her face resting on her hands, her eyes glued to the storyteller who, under the ingenuous influence of his lover, felt more eloquent, with a fresher memory and clearer head.

"You can't imagine what those moonlit nights in Cuba were like—that shiny, silvery canopy, those mangrove plantations that looked like gardens mirrored in the sea . . . Well, the night I'm describing, we were lying in ambush next to a river because we knew the revolutionaries were going to come down it. We heard splashing in the water; we thought it was an alligator gliding through the bamboos. Suddenly, bang!—a shot. The enemy! All our people grabbed their guns: ratta tat tat tat. A big black man jumps me and ugh!—I plunge my machete into his stomach and it comes out his back. I'd never been in such a spot, I tell you."

He had also been on the expedition to Rome in 1843. Oh, Rome! That was beauty for you. What a sight, to see Pius IX blessing the troops! And the conversation somehow drifted from the pope's blessing to the narrator's love affairs. This was an endless subject; from the total, it could be concluded that he had had seven affairs a year, with the specialty that he had had them all over the world; for Feijóo, who had also been in the Philippines, had been involved with women from China, Java, and even Sulu. A savage had made him lose his mind by demonstrating that on the Polynesian Islands one could find kinds of coquetry no less refined than what one found in European salons.

"Oh, what a good one!" exclaimed Fortunata, laughing with all her heart when she heard certain incidents. "It sounds like it was here! What a smart one she must've been! And then they say . . ."

Not to mention the European women. The ex-colonel related aventures with single ones and married ones that his friend could hardly believe, and in fact would not have, if they hadn't come from the lips of such a truthful, reliable person.

"Just think. If you told anyone, they wouldn't believe it. And if you wrote it down, people'd say it was fake. The things women do! No wonder they say we've got the devil in us."

I might add that Feijóo never said anything untruthful; he didn't even touch up his realistic accounts. Fortunata did the same when, prompted by her protector, she narrated chapters of the story of her life, which already contained episodes worthy of being related and even recorded. She didn't have to be begged, and since she had the virtue of being frank and had a rather coarse moral palate, which prevented distinguishing the good from the bad implications of certain facts, she disgorged everything. Sometimes her narration filled Don Evaristo with joy, other times with absolute terror; but from all of their sessions, he eventually emerged feeling sad and thinking to himself: "If only she'd crossed my path sooner; if only I'd gotten hold of her before; all those ignominious episodes could have been avoided. What a shame, Evaristo; what a crying shame! And the strangest part is that after being pawed so much, she could still have kept certain things intact—like her sincerity, which after all is something, and her constancy, loving one man only."

They both kept certain names from coming up in their conversation; but one night, for some reason or other, they began to talk about Juanito Santa Cruz.

"Huh!" said Fortunata. "He's probably tired of his dumb wife again. She'll get her revenge, though."

"I don't think so."

"Well, I do," declared the lowly woman, pretending to be convinced. "Bah! There isn't a married woman that doesn't sleep . . . Those rich ladies know how to cover up good."

"I don't like you to speak that way about anyone, dear, and least of all, her. I can understand why you don't exactly love her; but remember, she's not to blame for the dirty tricks her husband played on you."

Feijóo knew several members of the Santa Cruz family. He had never talked to Jacinta and Juan; but he had talked to Don Baldomero and briefly to Barbarita. He knew "Tubs" Arnaiz and other family friends such as the marquis of Casa-Muñoz and Villalonga; he was even vaguely acquainted with Plácido Estupiñá.

"You've got to learn," he continued in a rather severe tone, "not to pass irresponsible judgments and to avoid saying anything that could hurt or insult that respectable family. What's past is past; those people are leagues away, or dead, as far as you're concerned."

"I'll tell you something that will shock you," said Fortunata with the somber expression she adopted whenever she was going to make an extremely, almost incredibly, sincere declaration. "The day I first set eyes on Jacinta I liked her; although liking her didn't keep me from hating her. One night I went to bed so burned up with jealousy I felt I could . . . even kill her. Imagine."

"Bah! No more nonsense, now. I don't like you to speak that way. This talk of killing your rival is vulgar."

"But I haven't finished. Let me tell you the best part. I hate her and yet I like to look at her; I mean, I'd like to look like her, be like her, and let my whole self change till I was just exactly like her."

"Now, that I *don't* understand," said Feijóo, sinking into a sea of thoughts. "Whims of the heart."

And as he rose to go, bracing his hands on the arms of the chair, he noticed—oh!—that his body weighed more . . . much more than before.

5

Feijóo's awareness of his physical decline didn't end here. One morning as he was getting up he felt dizzy. He had never felt anything like it. In the street he noticed that he had to make a deliberate effort to walk in a straight line. As he passed the rotted door of the Latina convent, he couldn't help but stare as if it were a mirror. And there he saw himself clearly: a decorous vestige, preserved only by the indulgence of time. "Everything ages," he thought, "and if stone wears away, how can a man's body do less?"

The symptoms of this decay multiplied with terrifying speed. Two days later he noticed that he couldn't hear well. Sound escaped him, as if the whole world, with its hubbub and the words of men, had drifted further away. Fortunata had to shout for him to understand what she was saying. Besides being painful, the situation became ridiculous. It's true that he still walked at his usual pace; but it tired him more than before, and when he climbed the stairs he lost his breath. He looked at himself in the mirror every morning, and in these enlightening consultations he noticed that his cheeks, which had been fresh, were flaccid and

yellowish, his forehead was dry and withered, and his eyes were red and watery.
When he put on his boots, his right knee felt as if a hot needle were being driven
into the knee cap, and whenever he bent over, a muscle in his back whose name
he didn't know gave him a lacerating pain that would have been terrible if it
hadn't passed so quickly. "What deterioration, my friend . . . what deterioration! And it's going to be fast, I can tell. This time I've been caught with my
bones hardening on me and too many Christmases under my belt. But frankly, I
didn't expect it to come so soon . . ."

This physical state caused him great sadness, which at first he tried to hide
from his mistress; but one afternoon, when they were sitting next to the balcony,
his spirits sank so low that he couldn't contain his grief, and he confided to his
friend:

"*Chulita*, You've probably noticed that I . . . well . . . you've probably noticed that I'm not in good health. And incidentally, how old would you say I am?"

"Sixty," she said seriously, noting mentally that she was falling a bit short.

"A few days ago I turned sixty-nine . . . So before you know it, seventy. Do
you know that in the last two weeks I suddenly feel as if I'd put on twenty years? I
had kept the looks and energy of a fifty-year-old man, when suddenly nature said:
'I'm leaving you now . . . I can't keep this up!'"

Fortunata had noticed his decline, but naturally had not mentioned it.

"What irritates me most," Don Evaristo said angrily, banging his fist on the
arm of the chair, "is losing my good eyesight. I've always had eyes as sharp as a
fox. Just imagine: in Havana, from the castle of Atarés, I could see the lookout
signals they made in El Morro, and I could make out the colors of the flags perfectly. Well, since yesterday I've noticed something: some objects are a complete
blur, darkness, and the sun makes my eyes sting. I'm going to start wearing tinted
glasses tomorrow. Won't I make a fine sight? And as for my hearing—you know
about that. A couple of days ago, it was my left ear; now it's the right: I've come
up in the 'ranks,' I'm afraid—I *was* a 'lieutenant' but now I'm a 'captain.' Oh, I'm
having a great time of it. But it's sheer foolishness to rebel against nature. She has
her own laws, and whoever doesn't learn them pays dearly. I've been very imprac-
tical on this, even though I'm particularly practical when it comes to other things.
And since I see that I lost my head in this case, trying to be a boy at sixty-nine,
I'm going to try to find it again and prevent the consequences. What I've got to do
now is think of you, not me. I can't last very long . . ."

"No . . . that's nonsense!" said Fortunata, this time with more pity than
sincerity.

"Don't try to sweeten it for me. No matter how much I push myself, it would
only be a year or two—not to mention that I could wake up one fine morning like
a puppet, and you'd have to blow my nose and spoon-feed me. Anyway, the fact is
that I don't have much left in me, *chulita mía*, and I've got to think about you

now, because you *do* have a lot left in you: you're in full bloom, at the height of your beauty."

And another day, climbing the stairs, he noticed that he was relying more on his arms, braced on the banister, than on his legs. "This is progressing by leaps and bounds. If I don't watch out, I won't even have time to leave this poor girl protected from rascals and her own weaknesses. Poor little *chulita*! I've got to provide for her very carefully, because people can wind her around their little finger without half trying. My plan to insure her against disasters, that is, any sort of mishap, may not appeal to her; in fact I'm sure it won't. But she'll gradually see that there's no other way. Ah, one more flight to go! God help me. Whoever would have guessed . . . !"

As he entered her house, he switched imperceptibly from his soliloquy to speech, thinking out loud.

"Whoever would have guessed that I'd start caring about pharmacies! To think that I, who never swallowed a pill or a tablet or needed corpuscles, have a cabinet full of concoctions! And if I did everything the doctor tells me, I wouldn't last three days. Whoever would have guessed that I'd turn up my nose at food. I, who never asked any dish what its intentions were. My stomach wants to retire before the rest of me . . . and you know what happens when the boss leaves the office. Oh well, what can I do but accept it?"

Upon reaching this point, Don Evaristo had to raise his voice considerably in order to be heard, because down in the street someone had started to play a crank piano—polkas and waltzes. The tenants on the third floor, who were the house-keepers or nieces of the priest of the San Andrés Church (who lived there) began to dance, and shortly after that the people on the right side of the second floor started up too. On the main and second floors of the house across the street the same rumpus started, so all this plus the kids shouting in the street made a terrible racket; Don Evaristo and his friend were forced to remain silent, looking at each other and laughing.

"Well, on top of the fact that I'm deaf," said the endearing old man, "the neighborhood won't even let us hear each other. Let's not talk now; there'll be plenty of time later."

He cast his sad eyes downward, and Fortunata, who was sitting cross-armed, looked at him attentively, observing how senility was beginning to ravage his face; and down below in the street, the piquant dance rhythms grew fainter and fainter until they faded out altogether. The afternoon was dying; it would soon be night, and since Feijóo was terrified of the dark, his friend lit a lamp, which she put on the skirted table, and then she closed the shutters.

"Where did you go today?" Don Evaristo asked her as he did almost every night, not to be inquisitive but because this interrogation almost always led to a pleasant chat.

"Let's see. Today at noon I went up to the priest's house to see his nieces or whatever they are," she said, smiling and putting her arm on his shoulder. "They're cute girls and they look alike, but they're not sisters. Yesterday they came to see me and they asked me if I'd backstitch and border some strips they have for pleats for dresses. They dress up a lot and they've got tons of patterns up there. They're making two dresses now, and ooh, if you could only see them . . . I couldn't help but laugh, 'cause they're making little suits for Jesus and the virgins out of the velvet that's left over. They use everything—they even take a buckle from a hat they can't wear and stick it on at the waist of any old saint."

Fortunata had made few friends in the immediate neighborhood. She visited other tenants in the building and a family or so next door who were simple, God-fearing souls. Suffice it to say that our woman wore her cloak and a scarf on her head when she paid her visits. During the time she lived that comfortable life, she picked up her old habits that she had lost because of her contact with more refined people. Once again she put her hands on her hips almost all the time, and her way of slurring her speech and dragging certain vowels took control of her mouth again, just as one's own language streams out easily when returning to one's native land after a long absence. The people who were the most refined—or at least those who tried hardest to be—in the neighborhood were the priest's family, and the two ecclesiastical nieces made every effort to emphasize the difference between their affected speech and that of their beautiful neighbor.

"Guess what they said to me today, kid?" Fortunata continued, suppressing her laughter. "Oh, was it funny! I'll tell you so you'll have a good laugh. The oldest one—who's the most stuck-up—raised her eyebrow and, looking at me sort of pitying-like, she started to say in that voice of hers that's *so so* delikit you'd think spiders had spun it out of her, she says to me: 'And what about that gentleman—isn't he going to marry you?' I almost had a conniption. I said to her, 'Maybe.' And she went on with her sermon. Just so she'd leave me be, I finally told her that we *were* getting married; that we were already getting the papers and soon it'd be official."

"Well said. What a pair of busybodies!"

"And now I'm asking you," Fortunata said more affectionately, but much more seriously, "if I was single, would you marry me?"

"You know what my ideas are on that subject," he answered good-humoredly. "Do you think they've changed now that I'm sick, and that men think one way when their stomach runs like clockwork, and another when the machine starts to break down? It's partly true, *chulita*. It's one thing to talk about health when you're riding on the crest, and another when you're on the edge of an abyss. But as for marriage, I can assure you that my ideas haven't changed. I still think that getting married is stupid, and that I'll head for the other world without changing carriages. What can I say? I've seen a lot in this world; nobody can pull the wool over my eyes. And I know that the condition necessary for love is its not lasting, and that of all the people who commit themselves to adoring each other for as long as they live, ninety percent, believe me, consider themselves the other's prisoner after two years and would be glad to be unshackled. What people call 'infidelity' is nothing but nature's law, which tries to assert itself against social despotism, and that's why I'm so indulgent—as you know—with the men and women who rebel."

He continued with this ingenious theme; but Fortunata didn't understand these theories very well, undoubtedly because of the language that her friend used to articulate them. A little while later, she sat down to have dinner. Feijóo had only a boiled egg and some hot chocolate because his stomach could no longer stand a heavy meal at night. But he with his slight repast enjoyed watching his protégée, whose appetite was a blessing.

"Child, you have a model appetite. I look at you and even though I envy you, I congratulate myself on seeing that you've got such a strong hold on life. That's the way it should be. Don't be ashamed to eat well—as long as there's food, eat heartily, because the day will come . . . I hope not. What a contrast we make— I'm going downhill and you're going up. To think you've still got the best in life ahead of you! It would be foolish not to get as fat as you can, and let your flesh get as firm and hard as possible. With your gullet you'll be perfect for love."

After this, as Fortunata was eating innumerable raisins and almonds, taking them one by one from the dish and putting them into her mouth without looking at them, the kind, elderly man kept up his talk, rather disconcertedly now, and wandering. At times, he seemed uncomfortable and, expressing himself as if he were refuting an opinion he had just heard, he slapped the arms of his chair:

"But I've always maintained that; it's not a new opinion. Love is the claim of the species that wants to perpetuate itself, and obeying the stimulus of this necessity, which is as preservative as eating, the two sexes look for each other and unite; and choice is determined by some fatal, superior law that is alien to all the artifices of society. A man and a woman look at each other. What is it? The demand of their species to continue in a new being, and this new being, in turn, urges his probable parents to give him life. All the rest is literature, hot air, words from people who want to build a society in their studies, ignoring the immortal foundations laid by nature. It's as clear as day, don't you see? That's why I laugh at certain laws and the whole social penal code of love; all it is is a bag of foolishness invented by the ugly, monstrous, and stupid experts who never had the slightest success with a female."

Fortunata looked at him in fearful surprise, her elbow on the table, her back straight, in a grave, elegant pose, slowly taking now a raisin, now an almond, from the dish to her mouth. Feijóo took hold of her chin with his fingers and said affectionately:

"Aren't I right, *chulita?* Aren't I? Oh! What's going to become of you when I die, *chulita?* And if I don't, if my life goes on and I keep going downhill? We have to think of everything. I'm so worried lately! You're so full and beautiful and . . . I'm . . . finished, completely finished! I'm a clock that has rung its bells for the last time, and even though it still works, it doesn't tell time right."

"No," she murmured, rubbing her head against his chest. "No . . . not yet."

"Oh, wouldn't that be wonderful! But I'm finished. My stomach's begging to be retired. And something inside me has already resigned—irrevocably; my services have been rendered, my actions are history now. I must foresee . . . I have to provide for you, insure you against foolishness."

Fortunata laughed, and to calm the anxiety that his wild thoughts and apprehensions created, she lavished on him all the tender affection and care that a very loving daughter would show to the best of fathers.

6

The next day, Feijóo said as he entered:

"This is the first time I've had to take a carriage from the Plaza Mayor. Until today my legs have held up. Imagine, these legs that have marched six leagues in one night. I told the coachman to wait. Let's go out for a drive around the southern part of town."

Fortunata's only thoughts were to please him, so she accepted, although somewhat reluctantly, for whenever they went out together, even if it was to some out-of-the-way place, she was afraid of suddenly coming face to face with Maximiliano and Doña Lupe. The mere thought made her tremble.

They drove around for a good while and had no disagreeable encounters. Two days later Don Evaristo didn't come to see her; in his place came a servant with a brief note asking her to come to his house. The master had "had a very bad night" and the doctor had ordered him to stay in bed. Fortunata flew to him in great consternation and found him sitting up in bed, feigning calm and happiness.

"It's nothing, really," he said, motioning for her to sit down beside him. "The doctor insists that I stay in. But I'm not sick; I would almost say I'm slightly better than I have been lately. Except that I'm not used to being in bed . . . Not since I had yellow fever in Cuba forty years ago have I known what sheets are like at four in the afternoon. Oh, did I crave seeing you! Last night I went through such anguish; I thought I was going to die without having arranged a practical life for you. Just in case something happens, I'm going to tell you about something I've been thinking lately, some essentially practical thinking I've been doing. Listen to my plan. You may not like it at first, but there's no other choice really."

He leaned toward the young woman so as to put his mouth as close as possible to her ear and, face to face, shot these words at her:

"The result of all my thinking about you: you must return to your husband."

Contrary to what the pleasant old man expected, Fortunata was not shocked. She *did* put on a very charmingly grieved face and, raising her voice, asked:

"Is that really possible?"

"You don't have to raise your voice. I can hear much better today. Everything reaches me perfectly through my left ear, and it doesn't go out the other. You wonder if it's possible? Well, that's what has to be done: making it possible. I've already begun to think it out. Juan Pablo was here to see me this morning and I dropped him a hint. And listen to this: the day before yesterday I met Doña Lupe in the street and dropped her a hint too."

"Do they know . . . ?" Señora Rubín asked, her lips very dry.

"About us? I don't think so. Perhaps they suspect it; but they don't know anything officially."

"Well, you couldn't have suggested anything," declared the young woman, wetting her lips, which dried even faster, "*anything* that would have appealed to me less."

"I know."

"You're not going to die," Fortunata protested energetically. "You're going to get well!"

Feijóo had closed his eyes, and he was smiling faintly from the depths of his musing. His *chulita* fell silent and looked at him. His smile, which was like the kind that stays on some people's faces after they die, answered her better than words.

"And how about Nicolás—have you dropped him a hint too?" she asked after a pause, trying to liven up this lugubrious conversation.

"No; I haven't seen him. He's the biggest blockhead of the three of them. Believe me, if we win over Doña Lupe, the others will bow their heads, including your husband. Doña Lupe's the one who wears the pants in that family, and it's a lucky thing for them."

"Uh, I really doubt they'll want to . . . I double-crossed them," she stated, delighted to find an argument against the plan she disliked. "I played a really dirty trick on them. What I did is the sort of thing you don't forgive."

"Everything may be forgiven, child; everything," said the sick man with an indulgence steeped in skepticism. "No matter how big we think someone's capacity for forgetting is, it's bigger; it's a kind of substance poured over society that acts as a renewing element. Good things and gratitude are limited; they always seem to fall short of what we want. But forgetting is infinite. One way of 'starting over again' depends on this, and without it, the world would come to an end."

"Oh, no . . . it's impossible. They wouldn't be able to hold their heads up if they forgave me."

"Leave that to them. What I care about is leaving you in a correct, and above all, a practical situation. You have very few defenses in you against your enthusiasm, which continuously exposes you to the dangers of life. If I leave you on your own, even with an allowance, you'll be a slave to your passions and go back to the bad life. My little girl needs a brake, and that break, which is legality, won't bother her if she learns how to use it, if she follows the advice I'm going to give her. Silly, silly *chulita*—everything in this world depends on form, on style. Nothing is good or bad in itself. Understand? The first thing is this: keep a sharp eye on your heart. Don't let it rule you. This business of throwing everything out the window the minute Sir Heart becomes vexed is a lot of nonsense, and expensive nonsense at that. You have to give the heart little tidbits of meat; it's a savage beast, and long hunger makes it furious, but you also have to give society's beast enough to keep it from starting a fuss. If you don't, you risk everything and life becomes impossible. You're scared to live with your husband again because you don't love him."

"Not even this much; I don't love him, and I can't possibly love him—ever."

"All right. Everything will work out, child; it will all work out. Don't get upset and look so distraught. We'll talk it over slowly. I don't want you to get overexcited, or me either; I've talked enough for now and I'm beginning to feel bad. We've settled the main points."

The good man fell asleep, as might have been expected, for he hadn't been able to sleep all night long. Fortunata stayed at his side without a word or a movement, so as not to disturb him. She examined the room and would have liked to scrutinize the whole house. From what she saw in the bedroom, she concluded that the house must be well furnished. Don Evaristo, who aimed at such practicality in social life, was even more practical in his domestic life because, according to his theory of life, the first thing a man must do in this vale of tears is hunt for a good niche to live in that will serve as a perfect mold for his character. A bachelor with an income that was ample for a man without a wife or children or any immediate family, Feijóo lived in happy solitude, well attended to by faithful servants, recognized as the absolute master of his house and time, not forced to deny himself anything he wanted, and able to have all his wishes fulfilled in strict accordance with his precious will. Comfort and cleanliness, rather than luxury, were what struck you most in his home, which was ruled by a woman called Doña Paca, a Galician who had once run a guest house for distinguished, recommended individuals where Feijóo had resided for a long time. The other two members of the staff were a cook, who was fairly good, and a very laconic (and old now) manservant who had also been his master's "Filipino."

About half an hour after falling asleep, Feijóo awoke and, rubbing his eyes and grunting a bit, he was astonished to see his friend before him; he sat up straight to look at her. Seeing that she was laughing, he said:

"Hmmm—this little nap made me forget where I was, and when I woke up, I didn't remember that you were sitting there. And when I saw you just now, I said to myself in that groggy state of mind you have between sleeping and waking, 'Is that Fortunata? When and how did she come to my house?'"

He pulled his hand out from under the covers to take hers and, collecting his scattered thoughts, said:

"Mark what I'm about to say: Doña Lupe, who's the most intelligent one in the family, won't be hard to get along with if you're tactful. What Doña Lupe wants is to stick her nose into everything; rule the house and set herself up as everyone's adviser and teacher. You've simply got to let her; let her pry all she wants. She can run the house much better than you anyway, because she knows what it's all about. I had some contact with her when her husband was alive. He was a friend of mine, from the same town. Which reminds me: when she became a widow, she took it into her head to go around saying I was making passes at her. Half-cocked notion of hers! Well, anyway, she likes to direct everybody. So if you give her a free rein on household matters and let her have her way in that area, you'll be able to keep your independence in everything else. I'm not sure you follow me, but I'll explain it to you more fully later on. In any case, if you ever have any disagreements with her, stand your ground and say: 'Eh, Señora; I don't meddle in your business. Don't meddle in mine.'"

It had grown dark by now, and the two interlocuters could not see each other. Feijóo rang for the servants to bring a lamp, and when Doña Paca came in with one, she took advantage of its first shining into the room to rapidly inspect her master's friend's face, musing to herself: "So this is the scheming hussy that's gotten our master all upset." This suspicious nosiness of a servant hoping to inherit was followed by a variety of excuses for her prolonged presence in the room; she just might "pick up something" from the conversation . . . But as long as Paca was in the room, pretending that she was putting things in order, moving his medicines around and checking their labels, Don Evaristo didn't open his mouth. He looked at his housekeeper with a malicious smile that seemed to say, "You'll get tired of this."

And she did. The servant left, and Don Evaristo picked up where he had left off.

"The first thing you must always, *always* bear in mind at every moment and under any circumstances is that you must keep up appearances. Look, *chulita*, I'm not dying until I'm sure I've planted this notion firmly in your head. Learn my words by heart and say them every morning right after the Lord's prayer."

Like a language teacher who repeats a declination to his pupils, hammering in the syllables one by one as if he were nailing them into their brains, Don Evaristo, right hand raised, as if it were a hammer pounding steadily against a wall, slowly nailed these words into his pupil's mind:

"*Keeping . . . up . . . appearances; following . . . the rules; showing . . . the respect . . . we owe each other . . . and above all . . . never losing control, you hear? . . . never losing control*" (as the teacher repeated this last rule, his hand was suspended in the air; his eyebrows arched halfway up his forehead; and his eyes, which were extremely bright, emphasized the importance he placed on this part of the lesson), "*never losing control, you can do whatever you like.*"

Then he had a coughing spell. Doña Paca materialized in their midst, grumbling that his cough was from talking too much, which was against the doctor's orders.

"It's not sickness that's going to kill you; it's conversation. You should take the syrup and close your mouth."

To alleviate the effect of this rather discourteous outburst in the presence of a visitor, the woman directed a forced smile to the intruder. Which of them would give the sick man his spoonful of cough syrup? The housekeeper wanted to, but Fortunata was quicker. The other one retaliated with a remark full of disdainful authority:

"Sure, sure—give him the chloral instead of the cough syrup and then we'll be doing—"

"But isn't this the right medicine?"

"That one? Yes, but you could have made a mistake. I'm here to see that you don't."

"Let her give me whatever she wants," Feijóo grunted with mock annoyance. "What do you care, Señora Doña Francisca?"

"It's just that—"

"Fine. And what if she did poison me? It would be better that way."

7

Once she was alone at home again, Fortunata couldn't stand the creeping thoughts that "were filling up her head like it was a box." Go back to her husband! Be Señora Rubín again! If she had heard the idea a month ago, she would have burst out laughing. The idea still had a painful unfamiliarity about it, but after hearing it from her good friend it didn't seem so absurd. Would it eventually be possible and even suitable? A whispering in her soul told her that it would, even if her dislike of the Rubín family didn't diminish at all. That Don Evaristo would die soon was doubtless; you only had to look at him to see that. What would become of her when she was denied the advice and direction of such an excellent man? Oh, but he was wise! And he knew so much; he could tell you anything offhand. And as for human nature, the "secret of life," which is so elusive for most people, it was a catechism for him, and he knew it by heart. What a man!

Just as in shows called "dissolving pictures" certain figures fade while others gradually begin to appear, their lines becoming contours, then masses of color, and finally recognizable forms, so in Fortunata's mind during the night the members of the Rubín household began to sketch themselves in, like ghosts emerging from the mistiness of sleep. Little by little, Fortunata could discern Maxi, Doña Lupe, Nicolás Rubín, and even Papitos. They came anew into the light, first as ghosts, then as real people with their respective body, life, and voice. At dawn, restless and unreceptive to sleep, she could hear them speak and recognized even the most insignificant gestures that modeled the personality of each.

The *chulita* got up very late and found that there was a note from her friend saying that he was better and would be getting up and going out, weather permitting. She awaited his visit, and in the meantime continued to muse on the same thing. Her gratitude toward Feijóo was even greater than before; she wished that her life with him could go on because, although it was somewhat tedious, it was so peaceful that she knew she shouldn't aspire to a better one. "If this lasts long, will I get sick and tired of this insipid life? I might." Her heart's appetite, its need to love intensely, made her uneasy from time to time and gave her the sad feeling that she was in jail, living on bread and water. But she had resigned herself to it; perhaps this resignation was shrinking now . . . perhaps in her imagination she was anticipating some new, unknown experience that would engage her intimately and stimulate her faculties, which were freeing themselves from numbness after a long period of inactivity.

Don Evaristo arrived in a carriage at about four in the afternoon; he was in high spirits and told Fortunata to make some hot chocolate for five o'clock. She took pains with it, and when the good man drank it heartily, he said among other things that if he continued to improve, he would speak to Juan Pablo the next day and pose the question to him.

"And something else: I don't see why your husband should be so hateful to you. He may not be charming, but he's not a bad fellow. He may not be an Adonis, but he's not a bogeyman either. Some women are married to men who are infinitely worse, and they manage to live with them; they probably have their quarrels, but they work things out and stay together. Don't be silly! You don't know what a bargain it is to have a name and a decent veneer in society. If you know how to use them you'll be happy. I'd almost say that the kind of husband you have is better than a more appealing one, because if you're clever you'll be able to wrap him around your little finger. I've heard that ever since your separation he's been very taciturn, very absorbed in his studies, and that as far as anyone knows he hasn't gotten mixed up with anyone else to forget you. No matter how much he resents what you did to him, I think he'd positively melt if someone suggested he go back to you."

Smiling, Fortunata expressed her incredulity.

"No? Oh, *chulita!* You don't know human nature. Believe what I'm telling you: Maximiliano will greet you with open arms. Can't you see that he's like you—passionate, sentimental? He idolizes you, and people who love like that—madly—crave to forgive each other. Ah, forgiving! They go wild with pleasure whenever they can outdo themselves. Let him love you, you silly fool, and open your eyes to the wide horizons he can show you—if you know how to appreciate them."

This image of a horizon sharpened the young woman's new-born yearning for the unknown, for loving intensely without knowing how or whom it would be. What she could not reconcile, however, was this hope, still so undefined, with the family life that was being recommended to her. But somehow her mind was beginning to grasp a part, or parts, of the proposal.

Feijóo improved considerably in the next few days. He regained some of his strength, and with it some of his good humor, and premonitions of dying gradually vanished from his mind. But this did not prevent him from proceeding with his plan, which had practically become an obsession and dominated all his thoughts. Resolved to speak to Juan Pablo, one morning he went to see him at the Café Madrid, where the latter usually stopped in for a brief *tertulia* before going to the office; he now had a job that paid him—alas!—only twelve thousand a year; Villalonga had given it to him after Feijóo himself had made the recommendation. The proud Rubín was far from satisfied with this, and complained that his sacred friendship with Feijóo should have forced him to accept tidbits from the government. Obviously the situation couldn't last. Cánovas didn't know what was up. In the meantime, whether Don Antonio Cánovas knew it or not, the fact is that Juan Pablo had bought a new silk hat and was planning to exchange his cloak, whose trimming was somewhat worn and whose lining was quite filthy, for a new one. So the country was at least gaining that.

But of all the finery appearing in the streets of Madrid and in political circles due to the change of government, none was as worthy of making history as the fine, brand new woolen frock coat that Don Basilio Andrés de la Caña christened six days after occupying his new position. Into the abyss of yesteryear fell his old frock coat with all its filth and shiny proof on the elbows of his many years of unemployment and the many, many times he had dragged around the editorial room. The garment's handsome look was completed by a stylish hat, and the great Don Basilio looked like the noonday sun, for he simply beamed with satisfaction. Ever since he had begun to work "in his line" and at a level "that behooved him," he could barely contain himself. He even seemed to have gained weight, to have more hair on his head, to be less nearsighted, and to have taken off ten years. He shaved every day now, which as a matter of fact made him look less like himself.

I don't want to even mention all the other new, flamboyant frock coats and overcoats that were seen in Madrid, nor the ladies who traded in their old dresses for elegant, fashionable ones. This historical phenomenon is very familiar. It explains why tailors and fabric dealers, after a long period without political change, throw up their hands and with their complaints stir up the discontented and goad the revolutionaries. "Business has come to a standstill," say the shop-keepers, and someone else fans the flames with: "Commerce and industry are not being protected by the current regime."

When Feijóo entered Café Madrid, Juan Pablo had not yet arrived, so he decided to wait for him and sat down in the place his friend usually took. Soon Don Basilio came in hastily in his new frock coat, a toothpick between his teeth, and he called out toward the counter with an authoritative air:

"Have my coffee sent to the office," looking at his watch and making a gesture that fully conveyed to those present that there would certainly be a catastrophe in the Treasury if Don Basilio were delayed a moment longer.

"Hello, Don Evaristo," he said, pausing a moment to offer his hand. "How's your health—good, I hope?—I'm glad. Take care. Very busy. A meeting in the boss' office . . . So long."

"Doing pretty well, aren't we? So much the better. I'm getting on all right. Good-bye now."

When he was left alone again, Don Evaristo wrinkled his brow; he had just thought of an obstacle that might spoil his plan. On his way to the café he had prepared the speech he was planning to spring on Juan Pablo. It started like this: "My friend, I've heard that your brother's poor wife is almost isolated and has repented for her bad conduct; also, that she's destitute, with no one to help her out" and so on. But this was a gross mistake, because if after stressing how lost and hungry Fortunata was they saw her looking so beautiful . . . No, by no means. The relation between Señora Rubín's sparkling health and her tragedy was all too clear. How could he keep her in-laws from concluding, upon seeing that firm flesh and rosy color, a careless, gay, pampered life? My friend spent some time wondering how he could prove that it's not actually strange that a disturbed person should gain weight. He had not quite figured out a logical explanation for this when Juan Pablo arrived, rubbing his hands together and letting it show in his face that the mere act of entering the café gave him intimate satisfaction. His face had that placid air you see on a worthy bourgeois' face when he steps into his own home. The two friends greeted each other with the same affection they had always felt. After bearing with all the hypocritical commonplaces that a healthy man throws at a sick man, such as "you're nervous" or "walk more" or "I had the same thing once," Feijóo took the bull by the horns. By leaps and bounds, starting off with whatever came to him first, he came to the point: that he had resolved, out of pure kindness, to bring about the reconciliation.

"Poor girl!" said Rubín, dropping the sugar cubes into his coffee one by one, with measured pauses that were sheer pleasure for him. "So you say that she's leading a hard life and deeply regrets what she did. How emaciated she must be!"

"Well, as a matter of fact, she isn't exactly emaciated; what she is, is very . . . self-absorbed. But she's as attractive as ever."

"And, uh, Santa Cruz hasn't—?"

"Please! They broke up ages ago. It was right after the trouble started. Ever since then your sister-in-law has been living quietly on her own, regretting her conduct and dipping into her savings until they ran out. Then the worst was still ahead. It was just by chance that I found out. I'll tell you how it happened. I ran into her several days ago; she told me her story. I really felt sorry for her. Try to imagine what it's like—a woman with a guilty conscience, and in that situation— she's suffered a lot."

"Oh no, Señor Don Evaristo, don't give me that. You're so clever, you can get away with murder."

Upon hearing this, the diplomatic Feijóo was alarmed; he prepared himself for the worst.

"My dear friend," he said coolly, "when I discuss things seriously, I consider joking about it very impertinent, all right? It is not particularly delicate of you to presume that I've had some sort of affair with the lady and am trying to cover up by trying to reconcile her with her husband. Really, you're a bit too smart."

"It was only an assumption," Rubín recanted.

"Well, wouldn't I have been assigned a lovely role! Thanks, thanks a lot."

"But I didn't mean—"

"Besides, you've heard me say many times that I've been out of the game for a long time."

"Yes, I know."

"And that if in my thirties and forties and even in my fifties I made some startling plays, as for now . . . Humph! A fine party-goer I'd make now, at sixty-nine and with all these aches and pains! Do me another favor: when I tell you something, believe it; that's what good friends are for—to believe you."

"You're right—I'm sorry that you couldn't see that my reticence was only a joke."

"It seeemed to me that, given the subject, and considering that it had to do with a member of your family, and that I was the one to broach it, that it wasn't a laughing matter."

Rubín believed, or at least pretended to believe this, and adopted a very philosophical air to listen to what else his friend had to say on this most important subject. Oh! Now's the time to include a fact: Juan Pablo had received from Feijóo several long term loans without repayment stipulated. Seeing his friend's difficulties, the excellent man had found a tactful way to provide him with the sum needed, freeing Juan Pablo from Cándido Samaniego, who was pursuing him like an Inquisitor. Feijóo performed these discreet kindesses quite often for friends he esteemed, thus helping them without humiliating them. Naturally, he knew that he was not lending but giving alms; and this was perhaps the most evangelical, acceptable way in the eyes of God. He never once reminded a debtor of his debt, not even those who turned out to be ungrateful and forgetful. Juan Pablo was not among these, and therefore he gladly adopted the pose of moral subordination that befits the insolvent man who has been excused from repaying his generous "Englishman." He knew all too well that a man who had done such great favors must always be believed, and that one formed a tacit pact with one's benefactor to share his opinion in a dispute and to be serious when it is recommended. Deep within, Rubín was free to think whatever he wished; but from the skin out, he played the role that fit his circumstances.

"I won't raise any objections to it. But even so . . . I have no idea what Maximiliano will think of it. Since then I haven't heard him mention his wife once. And in any case, nothing can be done if my aunt's against it. I'm not on very good terms with her at the moment. The best thing would be for you to speak to her."

Then, very cleverly, Feijóo caught up on some family news. Maxi had taken his degree and was already working in Samaniego's pharmacy under the orders of a man named Ballester, who was in charge of the place. Doña Lupe no longer lived in Chamberí; she had moved to Ave María Street. Maxi spent all his free time from the pharmacy devouring philosophical texts. So that was how he was getting it out of his system . . .

Then they talked of other things. The café philosopher told his friend that the next time he wanted to have a chat with him he shouldn't look for him in Café Madrid because he had fallen in with a group of hunters there who were beginning to bore him to death with their talk of pointers and ferrets and whether or not "a partridge was fooled by a decoy." He still hadn't decided where to move to, but he would probably go to the Old Swiss, where Federico Ruiz and some atrociously pantheistic friends of his met. The only ones in his group who still went to the Café Madrid were Don Basilio, who was unbearable with his ministerial airs, Leopoldo Montes, and the Pater. And the latter would be leaving that very night for his home town, Cuevas de Vera, to work on Villalonga's election. Juan Pablo also discussed politics a bit, and said with a lot of gall that the government "was lying in state," and that at the very most the situation would only last three or four months.

8

The first time that Don Evaristo visited his friend after this interview he embraced her gleefully and said:

"Good news! It's going beautifully."

"What is? What's going on? Good news?"

"It's golden . . . I mean, I have excellent impressions so far. Your husband—"

"Have you seen him?"

"I haven't had that satisfaction yet, but I've heard something that's extremely favorable. Just so you won't wonder about it, I'll tell you: Maximiliano has devoted himself to philosophy."

Fortunata didn't know how to react and kept looking at her friend. She did not understand, nor did she know, what philosophy was, although she suspected that it was a very involved, incomprehensible thing that "made men go off their rockers."

"I'm not surprised that you're speechless. You'll soon understand. He simply devours philosophy! And I seem to recall that Juan Pablo said he was reading spiritualist philosophy."

"Oh! You mean the ones that talk to table legs? Holy Mary!"

"No, not those. But we're lucky, anyway; no matter what sect or school has made your husband go soft in the head, it's ninety-six percent sure that he'll greet you with open arms. You'll see, in time."

Fortunata doubted this. What she had done to Maxi was too awful to be forgotten by reading books.

The next day Feijóo arrived happier and excited. His plan had come to occupy him so fully that he could think of nothing else; from morning till night he turned it over and over in his mind. His health had improved greatly, although he was much less concerned about his personal appearance now. Ever since he had adopted these paternal functions so fervently he had let his beard grow and wore a derby and a generous scarf around his neck. He rented a cab by the hour for his various errands about town. When Fortunata saw him come in that day with his derby pushed back, his eyes sparkling, his movements agile, she intuited that he had good news.

"These strokes of luck," he said, embracing her, "are rejuvenating me. Another embrace, *chulita*, another. I've just talked with none other than Doña Lupe, 'the turkey woman.'"

The mere sound of her in-law's name frightened Fortunata.

"Very good impressions," added the diplomat. "She started out very pompously, refusing to propose the reconciliation. But the more she brays against it, the surer I am that she'll do what we want. I can read her like a book. She's got her own philosophy of life and she can't fool me. I know the ins and outs of human nature better than the corners of my own house. Doña Lupe wants you back with them. I could see it in her face and in the way she said she didn't. I don't know if I ever mentioned that there was a time, shortly after becoming a widow, when she had her sights set on me; sincerely, of course. She went around saying that I was pursing her. Would you believe that every time she sees me her face shows it?"

Fortunata burst out laughing. "And tell me, when she was after you had they already cut off one of her breasts?"

"I really don't know. As far as I'm concerned, they can have both of them. Well, anyway, as I was saying: we're making progress. I told her that if there was a reconciliation, you'd live with her, because I considered it the most suitable thing. She looked so conceited when I said this that I think a new breast was budding. Now, listen to what you must do when the time comes: I'll give you a sum that you'll turn over to her the first day, asking her to invest it for you. Refuse to take a receipt. There's nothing she likes better than for people to trust her on financial matters. Oh, I can read her as easily as I read you. Don't you see, I saw her quite a bit when Jáuregui—an excellent man, by the way—was alive. I'll be giving you a long lesson on the knack of getting along with her—it's a clever mixture of submission and independence; of drawing a line, and I mean a very clear, fine one, and saying: 'From here to there you're the boss; and from there to here I am.' The only key I haven't turned yet is your husband. I've talked with him a few times; I hardly know him; but never mind, it doesn't matter . . ."

His improvement was so marked that Don Evaristo dared to go out at night, and the first thing he did was go search for Juan Pablo. He didn't find him in the Old Swiss Café, though he did see Villalonga, Juanito Santa Cruz, Zalamero, Severiano Rodríguez, Dr. Moreno-Rubio, Sánchez Botín, Joaquín Pez and others who had started the wittiest, liveliest *tertulia* that had ever existed in the cafés of Madrid. They had made up a humorous set of rules of which every member had a copy in his pocket. Their famed tables had already produced a minister, two under secretaries, and various governors. Although some were friends of Feijóo, he didn't choose to join them. Instead he went to a table that was far from theirs. Next to him, the civil engineers were discussing European politics, and to the other side, the mining engineers were discussing dramatic literature. Not far away a group of employees from the accounting office was heatedly involved in artesian wells, while two judges from the claims court together with a retired actor, a horse dealer (who supplied the bullring), and a naval officer were arguing over whether women looked prettier with bustles or without. Then Don Evaristo's attention was caught by a man who was wandering among the tables; he looked like a mummy brought to life by witchcraft. "I know that face," Feijóo said to himself. "Ah! Of course, it's the man we used to call Ramses II—poor old Villaamil. He only needed two months' work to complete his term and retire." Timidly, the wretched figure approached Villalonga, who was already getting up to leave, and with his eyes popping out of their sockets, he spoke to him about something that must have concerned the cursed two months. Jacinto shrugged his shoulders, answering with grumbling kindness. He seemed to be saying, "If only I could! I've done everything possible. We'll see . . . I've sent a note . . . Believe me, it won't be neglected because of me. Yes, I know, you just need two months." A moment later Ramses II passed by Don Evaristo, gliding between chairs and tables like an intangible shadow. Feijóo called him by his real name, and Villaamil came toward the table to see who had called him, his face yellow and burned by the sun in Cuba and the Philippines. They recognized each other. At the invitation of his friend, Villaamil bent his skeleton to sit down, and he drank some coffee, which had more milk than coffee in it.

"Oh, were you looking for Juan Pablo? Well, he suddenly switched to the Café Zaragoza. He said the engineers were getting on his nerves. Since he knew he ought to retire early, Don Evaristo did not go to the Zaragoza that night. It was about nine o'clock when he entered the place the next night and found it full, with a suffocating atmosphere so thick you could cut it with a knife and a deafening noise from the crowded hives of people that Madrilenians put up with, just as blacksmiths put up with the heat and stridency of their forges. Unwrapping his cloak, the old man advanced along the tortuous aisle left open in the middle and looked this way and that for his friend. Now he ran into a waiter laden with set-ups, now his cloak pulled off some pretentious woman's short cape, here he met with the arm of a newsboy holding out his *Correspondencias* to his customers, and there the barricade consisted of two fat men on their way out or four skinny ones on their way in. At last he spotted Juan Pablo in the corner next to the spiral staircase that leads up to the billiards room. Two people were sitting with him: one rather pretty woman, although she was past her prime, and a young man whom Don Evaristo immediately recognized as Maximiliano. The two brothers were having a very lively conversation. The woman was Juan Pablo's love, a so-called Refugio, a memorable character, although not a historical one, who had a provocative, charming face and was missing one of her upper teeth. Feijóo had never seen her, nor did the café philosopher usually appear in public with this courtesan, so Rubín was taken aback a bit when he saw his friend.

Maximiliano greeted Don Evaristo, inquiring very earnestly after his health, to which the ancient man replied very emphatically:

"I'll tell you. I've been this way for five months. One day I'm down, the next I'm up . . . *Five* months! One day the machine's going to come to a halt and say, 'This is the end of the line, my friend, and it's no use trying to make repairs or add more oil. It won't work, it simply won't work, and it's got to stop.'"

"But what do you have?" asked Maximiliano with the presumptuous air of a new doctor or an incipient pharmacist, both of whom ache to be useful to humanity.

"What do I have? Ah, a terrible illness. The worst there is: being seventy! Doesn't it sound like much to you?"

They all burst out laughing.

"My brother told me," Maxi added, "that you have trouble digesting."

"For five months my stomach has been rebelling," said the crafty old man, who no doubt wanted Maxi to remember the five months. "I don't bother about it anymore. I've given up, and I'm quietly waiting for the 'cutoff.'"

"If you'd like, I can mix you a peptonic preparation."

"Thank you. We'll see what my doctor says."

"Come now, this little illness has been well complained about," said the other Rubín, slapping him on the back.

"But you were talking about something that must have been interesting," said Feijóo. "Don't let me interrupt you."

"We were—hang on now—in ethereal regions."

"No. It's just that he wants to convince me," Maximiliano said energetically, "that everything consists of force and matter. I say this: what you call force, I call 'soul,' the Word, universal love, and we come back to the same old story—to God as creator and unity, and to the soul that emanates from Him."

Meanwhile, Don Evaristo was looking at Refugio, examining her face, her mouth, her missing tooth. The girl felt ashamed of being so closely observed and didn't know what pose to strike or what to do with her lips as she brought a spoon of ice cream to them.

"That's it, that's the sore spot," said the ex-colonel, siding with Maximiliano. "The soul! These materialists think that by changing the names of things they've turned the world upside down."

"But I've already told you—" Juan Pablo argued heatedly.

"Let me finish—"

"That's not it, blazes!"

"We're back where we started. Don't I know myself as a single, conscious, responsible being?"

"But look here—"

"Wait. If I recognize myself in the substance of my 'I'-ness . . ."

He expressed himself exaltedly, without letting his brother get a word in edgewise, and the latter, in turn, did the same, so they were constantly interrupting each other.

"Wait a minute. That's not how it is."

"I'm coming to it. I live in my conscience because of myself and before and after myself."

"Yes, but first thing we have to establish is— Look—"

"What a pair of nuts you two are!" Don Evaristo thought, looking curiously at the gap in Refugio's teeth.

"Try again," said Maxi. "That's not it. I—am I myself? Do I recognize myself; as that 'I' in all my actions?"

"No. All I am is an accident in this grand symphony; I don't belong to myself, I'm a phenomenon."

"I am a phenomenon! Holy Mother of God, what nonsense!"

"You're off the track. The permanent element isn't me, my 'I'; it's the whole. That's how I see it in the passing phenomenon of my knowledge."

And these things being said in the corner of a café, next to a customer reading La Correspondencia and another talking about the price of meat! At one of the nearby tables there was a group that looked like a gang of smugglers or something like it. To the right could be seen two tacky-looking women accompanied by a prostitute, all of them guests of a gentleman who was flattering them foolishly; opposite them, a triad was arguing in unharmonious voices and with much waving of their arms over Lagartijo and Frascuelo.* And meanwhile, customers were constantly going up or down the spiral staircase, every step thumping like a kick; and down that spiral came the sound of angry voices, the cracking of billiards, and the singing of the waiter who was taking orders.

"If I may give my opinion," said Feijóo, whose head was beginning to spin from all this clatter, "I side with the young man."

At that moment the piano, which was mounted on a platform in the middle of the café, began to be played with its triangular lid raised to make the music louder; and the toccata—a piano and violin duo—was under way. The music, the applause, the voices, and the constant rustle in the café created such an unbearable racket that my good Don Evaristo feared he would swoon and fall flat on the floor if he stayed there a quarter of an hour more. He decided to retire, dissatisfied at not having found Juan Pablo alone, for he couldn't bring up the ticklish subject in front of the pharmacist. His annoyance turned into happiness when Maxi, seeing him stand up to leave, declared that he was leaving too, because it was time to return to the pharmacy. So they left together, and before they got to the door, the

---

*Nineteenth-century bullfighters from Andalusia.

elderly man saw an emaciated, deathly figure about to cross his path. It was Ramses II, who had come in search of Feijóo.

"Señor Don Evaristo, for the love of God, please present my case to Señor Villalonga," implored the mummy, stepping in his way, as if he didn't intend to let him pass unless given a promise.

"I will, friend; I'll speak to Villalonga," said Don Evaristo, wrapping his cloak around him. "But I'm in a hurry now. I can't stop. Come on, Maxi."

And breaking through, he left with the Rubín boy.

9

To whom he said at the door:

"Where're your feet taking you?"

"Me? To Ave María Street."

"What a coincidence! I'm going in the same direction. We can go together. Wait a second while I wrap my cloak good and tight. Now. Give me your arm. My legs aren't much help to me. You know, it's been five whole months, you know, never digesting well. It's a mystery to me that I'm still alive. Since October of last year I haven't been able to stand up straight. The ideas Juan Pablo gets into his head! Who would ever guess it—in a boy with such good sense! Now *you* know where you're going . . . Yes, sir. Don't wait till you get to be an old man on the verge of death to believe that we're something more than little heaps of garbage animated by a force that's like the electricity that makes a man talk. That's for fools and reckless types, for people who don't think. You're in the right, and will be capable of noble acts; acts that, precisely because they're so far above it all, ordinary people can't understand."

Maximiliano didn't know why, but his soul felt remarkably receptive, ready to grasp any subtle point that was made; he hungered for ideal things, and meditation, study, and human solitude had made him astonishingly receptive to whatever originated from pure thought. Because of this, and with no inkling of what was being discussed, he answered humbly:

"You're so right . . . so right."

"A man who, like you," continued Don Evaristo, "doesn't let himself be lured by modern knowledge is in the position to do good—not just in any old way, but sublimely, yes sir, looking up at the sky, not down to earth."

For some time Maxi had been looking up at the sky.

"Listen, Señor Don Evaristo," he said, swelling with that spirituality he had developed by shuffling his sad feelings with learned pages. "My grief has made me turn my eyes to things one can't see or touch. If I hadn't done it, I would have died a hundred times. And if you only knew how different the world looks from up above from how it looks down below! I never dreamt that my thirst for vengeance and hatred, which had turned me into a brute, would disappear. And yet time and abstract thinking about the totality of life and the immensity of its purpose have led me to become what I am now."

"Of course. What's the point of hating others or any of that melodramatic revenge?" Feijóo asked rhetorically, relishing his progress. "It only leads to self-destruction. Fortunate are those who know how to rise above the passions of the moment and temper their soul with eternal truths!" And, muttering into his beard: "This boy's so metaphysical he fits into our plan perfectly."

"In all the ruckus of our immediate passions," Maxi went on rather emphatically, "one forgets that we also live to forgive offenses and to do good to those who have wronged us."

"You're right, son. And blessed is the man who, like you, can grasp this concept while he's still young and put it into practice in his own lifetime."

"A great sorrow, or a hard blow—they're the real teachers in life. And getting over them takes a lot of suffering, and enduring the anguish that anger leaves, and being pricked by self-pride, and swallowing all the bitterness that spews forth. Oh, Señor Don Evaristo! I can hardly believe that I feel so renewed now! I even thought I had the right to kill a man and took pleasure in planning the crime, which I finally gave up thinking about. My conscience is as clear today for not having killed as it was firm and resolved when I was planning to kill. I couldn't find God in me then; now I can. Believe me: you have to annul yourself in order to triumph; say 'I'm nothing' to be everything."

In view of Maxi's evident readiness, Feijóo plunged straight in:

"To a soul as well fortified as yours," he replied, "I can speak plainly. Has Doña Lupe said anything about a certain subject to you . . . ?"

Maximiliano turned as red as his cloak's lining and replied, perturbed and awkward, in the affirmative.

"As for me," Don Evaristo added, "I'll do everything I can to make this jell. It has to . . . It's the practical thing to do, my friend. And since you're so mystical, it might be wise for you to be a bit practical too. It's only by chance that I'm intervening in this. I can tell you this: she wants to come back—"

"She does!" exclaimed Rubín, taking off his muffler.

"So! Now we come up with that? Well, if she didn't want to, why would I get involved in such dealings? Don't you see . . . ?"

"Yes, but . . . Let's keep this straight: on a strictly spiritual, evangelical level, I've forgiven her. But as for the, shall we say, social forgiveness, which is equivalent to a reconciliation, it's impossible."

"Oh, come now, it can't be all that hard," Don Evaristo retorted, pulling up his cloak.

"It's impossible," repeated Maxi.

"Think it over carefully; talk to your pillow, my boy. I think that once you've gotten used to the idea—"

"Even if I spent ten years getting used to it, I don't think—"

"On matters like this one must be charitable; a simple criterion based on justice isn't enough. It might be wise for you to talk to her—"

"Me?! But Don Evaristo—"

"Yes; I don't take it back. Somebody with ideas like yours, blazes! Somebody who knows how to feel and think on your high level, with that spirituality and . . . naturally . . ."

"And do you think she'll be able to account—and I mean clearly—for all she's done since she left me?"

"Son, I think so; but you mustn't force things, you know. Either you forgive her or you don't. Charity first, then indulgence, and seeing whether she does, in fact, have a sincere wish to reform. From what I've heard, I'd say that she does; at least, that's my sincere impression."

"I doubt it."

"Well, I don't. Take my opinion for what it's worth. And remember, I don't have anything to gain; I intervened in this because I've decided not to die without leaving behind some good deed to atone for all the bad and meaningless ones I've done in my life. I don't like to meddle in other people's affairs, but in this case, believe me: I'm convinced that it would be good for both of you to have a reconciliation."

Now that he had entered this realm, Don Evaristo revealed more.

"Friend," he said, stopping at the pharmacy door, "your wife seems to me to be a woman with many faults. Although I've had very little to do with her, I can assure you that she's basically good, but she lacks moral fiber. She'll always be what people who know her want to make of her."

Maximiliano looked at him in astonishment. He thought the same.

"The day before yesterday I gave her a long sermon urging her to adjust to the realities of life, to control that rambling imagination of hers. 'My child, you should think before you do something, and stop your foolishness.' Looking very serious. I think I got somewhere. You'll see, my friend. It's a shame that with her basic goodness, her good heart—although it's a bit big—and none of the malice other women have, that she shouldn't have some common sense. Because if she had just this much of it—she wouldn't need more—she wouldn't have done the foolish things she's done. Oh well, son, you're probably wondering who asked me to poke my nose into this. Nobody. But you know, we old folks like to fix up young people's lives and put them on the right track so that they won't make the same mistakes we've made."

He said this last part with such a good-hearted smile that Maximiliano was plunged into uncertainty. Don Evaristo said good-bye, leaving the poor boy so confused that he was to spend many days trying to digest the aftertaste of his colloquy with the respectable old man on that cold night in March.

The next day Don Evaristo went by carriage to see Fortunata, whom he found alone, brushing her hair. Sitting down beside her and taking her arm, he drew her to him and kissed her, saying:

"The last kiss . . . The affair that Feijóo had late in his life is now history. We'll soon be in our new lives, and all that will be left of this will be what you and I remember. For the public, it didn't exist, and these ashes will hide a bit of heat only for us."

Fortunata, who had parted her thick black hair, held half in each hand, as if it were a curtain; she didn't know whether to laugh or cry.

"Have you spoken to him?" she asked, quite moved, yet at the same time smiling.

"Start getting used to addressing me in the polite form,"* he replied somewhat severely. "Don't let out any intimate words; it would ruin everything. When there are other people around, I'll use the polite form too. It's all over now. All I am is a father, Fortunata. The Feijóo who loved you as a man loves a woman doesn't exist anymore. You're my daughter. And we're not going to be playing roles either; from now on, you'll be just that—my little daughter—and I'll be your papá. I sincerely mean it. I'm not the man I was with you; I'll soon be dying and . . ."

Seeing that he was affected by what he was saying, the *chulita* couldn't bear it, and she burst into tears. Those admirable loose locks of hair made her look like one of the images of suffering on epitaphs. Feijóo reacted like a grown-up who is trying to control a childish weakness, saying:

"No, I'm not ashamed of the tears in my eyes. I swear to God, in whom I've always trusted, that it's my fatherly love that's making me shed them. The manly part, that was capable of sensual love, has disappeared; it all died, and there's nothing left. I've never been a father. Now I feel like one, and my heart is filled with a new kind of affection that's pure, so pure . . ."

The sinful woman had never seen a man so overcome by emotion. His eyes were moist; his hands trembled. She pulled her hair back and tied it at the nape of her neck with a black band; she couldn't toll bells and march in the procession all at once, comb her hair and, at the same time, amid tears and chaste handclasps, celebrate the sanctification of their relationship. Little by little they calmed down; Don Evaristo had her sit down beside him on the sofa and in a clear, firm voice spoke as follows:

"I think this is going to work out. I'd be so happy if I could die knowing that you're in a normal, decent situation! I can see that it's not going to be easy for you

---

* Usted instead of tú.

to like your husband. But that's not an insurmountable obstacle. We have to compromise, you know, and take things in life as they come. Who says that after living with him for a while you might not grow fond of him? He's good and decent. I saw him last night, and he didn't seem so rickety. He's put on weight, filled out a bit, and he even seemed to have a faintly arrogant look about him, as if he were more . . ."

Smiling sadly, the young woman expressed her incredulity.

"Well, you'll see for yourself. And anyway, you've got to resign yourself to it. Regular life and settling for social laws is so important, my child, that you have to sacrifice your personal tastes and dreams. I don't mean completely; you don't have to sacrifice everything, all your tastes and all your dreams; but you can be sure of this: you'll have to sacrifice some of them. There's a big difference between having a husband, a name, and a decent home and running around from place to place like a cab with its 'for hire' flag up, saying 'I'll take that one, leave this one . . .' A big difference, for you not to think twice about what you're doing. You have to foresee everything. I'm going to describe the two situations you can expect to encounter in your legitimate married life, and I'm going to advise you on both of them—frankly, loyally, and realistically. First, suppose that, shortly after you've gone back to Maximiliano, you see that he's treating you well, and you're starting to notice good qualities (they always show up in the little things), and suppose, too, that you're beginning to grow fond of him . . ."

Like a sword that has been driven so deeply it can't be pulled out, Fortunata's stare was riveted to a spot on the floor. Certain that she was listening, even though she wasn't looking at him, Feijóo kept talking slowly, pausing between clauses.

"Let's suppose that. Well, your duty, in that case, is to try to make that fondness—or friendship—grow as much as possible. Work on yourself to achieve this. Good behavior works miracles, my child, and good will does too. At the same time, avoid laziness, and you'll see how something that seemed so hard is really very easy. There have been numerous cases of women who, for some reason, have had to marry a man they hated and who have gradually gotten used to him, and eventually become as sweet as honey. I won't bother to mention what would happen if you had children—"

"Humph! As if that was there!" Fortunata said brusquely.

"Aren't you a silly one! What do you know? You can't be sure about things like that. Nature is full of surprises. With children you'd be halfway along on the road to peace that I'm recommending to you; bringing them up and taking care of them will take a big part of that heart God has given you, and you'll settle down and forget about your foolishness. Well, we've already talked about the first possibility. We'd better get on to the second. I'm describing it to you in case the first fails, which could well occur. So, let's get on to it."

Fortunata anxiously awaited the exposition of the second case, but Feijóo was taking it slowly; he sat thinking for a good while, staring at the floor, his brow knit.

"The best," he continued, "is the one I've just described; but when you can't do what's best, you choose the lesser of two evils. Do you understand? Suppose that you can't possibly grow fond of the poor boy, and that neither his conduct nor his good qualities make him less unappealing; suppose that life gets to be unbearable and . . . This is so rash, it takes all my strength to advise you like this. But above all, I try to see what's practical, what's possible; I can't advise anyone to let himself die or commit suicide. But no one should try to impose sacrifices that are beyond human strength to make. If your heart stays as big as it is now, if there's no way of trimming it down, if it rebels on you—we can't help it, can we? So for this let's see which would be the lesser of two evils."

Feijóo racked his brains for words more suitable than these. His thoughts strained in different directions and he had to hold them in check to keep from foundering. Sighing deeply, he smoothed his hair, looking dazedly into space. Emerging, finally, from his perplexity, he said in a cautious voice:

"And if worse comes to worst—I mean, if you find yourself about to be triggered off into infidelity—keep up appearances and you will have chosen the lesser of two evils. Appearances, good conduct, decency—they're the secret, my friend."

He stopped, scared, like a thief who's heard a noise, and he put his hand to his head again, as if invoking the dignity of his white hair. But his white hair made no reply. Then he struck forth boldly and regained his composure, saying:

"You're too inexperienced to realize how important style, or form, is in this world. Do you know what form, or rather, appearances are? Well, I won't say that they're everything, but there are cases in which they're nearly everything. Society lives on them; I wouldn't say according to its desires, but as well as it can manage. Principles are very pretty, but appearances aren't any less so. If I had to choose between a society without principles and a society without appearances, I don't know which I'd take."

10

Fortunata understood. She nodded affirmatively, and with her hands crossed on one of her knees made her body swing back and forth.

It had required considerable effort on Feijóo's part to expound his moral principles this particular time because he was aware of a lump that seemed to be hardening inside him; but all of a sudden it dissolved and he was able to evoke the principles he had practiced all his life. Having launched the most dangerous concept, he flowed on as smooth as silk, free of lumps and obstacles:

"You already know my ideas on love. It's nature's imperious claim, nature saying 'Let me grow.' There's no way to combat it. The human species clamors to grow—do you understand? Am I making myself clear? Do I need to use parables or examples?"

Fortunata understood and continued to swing back and forth, emphasizing her affirmations with her tousled head.

"Need I say more? It's a very precarious thing, this need to love; as precarious as a loaded pistol balanced on your head—you can't play with it. The first case— fidelity—is always preferable, because it allows you to satisfy both nature and the world. I've described the second situation to you *just in case*, so that if you *do* find yourself in the predicament—and mark my words, now—if your heart makes irresistible demands and you throw principles out the window, you'll know how to keep up appearances."

My friend felt that lump in his throat again, but, continuing to expound his philosophy of a lifetime, he dissolved it.

"In all events you must keep up appearances and pay society the external worship without which we'd regress to our primitive state. Our relationship will serve you as an example of the fact that if you want to, you can keep a secret. It's a question of style and skill. If I had the time now, I'd tell you about innumerable cases of little sins that have been committed in strict secrecy, without the slightest scandal, without the slightest offense to the propriety we should all show in our relations with one another. You'd be amazed. Listen closely to what I'm saying and learn it by heart. The first thing you must do is keep law and order; in other words, peace in your marriage. Respect your husband, and never let him lose his dignity. You're going to tell me that this is hard; I know it is, but here's your chance to use your talent, my friend. You'll have to figure it out as you go along. But above all, remember this: keep a firm hold on your own dignity if you want to respect someone else's. Next—"

At this point Don Evaristo moved closer to her, as if he were afraid he might be overheard, and, marking his words by pointing his finger, he said:

"The second thing is to be very careful in choosing—this is basic—be *very* careful about who . . . about the person . . ."

The rest of the sentence didn't come forth; it didn't want to. Seeing that he was in a spot, Fortunata hastened to assist him, saying:

"I understand."

"Fine; then I don't need to add anything else, because if you give in to the temptation to love a man without scruples, you can say good-bye to decency and everything that goes with it. And the last thing I have to tell you is, if you can manage to keep from giving in to that Santa Cruz idiot, your victory will be complete."

On this note, Feijóo rose and, picking up his cloak and hat, prepared to take leave. At the door he turned back to Fortunata and, lifting his cane with an authoritative gesture, said to her:

"I repeat: it's over now. I'm your father, and you're my daughter; when you speak to me, don't use the *tú* form; we're in our new roles now. So, let's learn to live a practical life. Stay calm, and finish combing your hair; it's late. I'm leaving . . . I've got a lot to do."

The original moralist climbed into his cab. No sooner had he reached Carros Square than he began to feel an inexplicable restlessness in his soul. And then this moral anxiety was succeeded by a physical malaise—trembling and chills, and superstitious fear. But he couldn't define the cause of this fear. The carriage rolled along the Cava Alta and Feijóo felt increasingly worse. Suddenly, something like a terribly intense vibration shook him, and then there was a flash, like a spear cutting through him. He thought he heard an unknown voice shouting at him: "Look what you've taught your daughter, stupid!" He put out his hand to stop the coachman and tell him to go back to Tabernillas Street; but before he could, the vibration ceased, and all was calm. "What weakness!" he exclaimed to himself. "I must be doting, that's all it is. How could I turn around and take back my words? Don't get cold feet, Evaristo; stick up for your ideas—you've always believed in them. It's the only way; it's the practical way. What would happen if I recommended absolute virtue to her? It'd be a lost sermon. This way, at least . . ."

And he rolled on, satisfied.

With all the commotion of those busy days during which he visited Doña Lupe twice and had many sessions with Juan Pablo and another very substantial one with Nicolás Rubín, who was trying desperately for a canonship, the good man had a relapse. One afternoon toward the end of March he felt so ill that he had to go home to bed. Together with the symptoms of his aggravated state, Doña Paca detected a certain feverish happiness in him. This she considered a very bad omen, for if her master was entering his second childhood or going mad in this grave state, it was a sign that the end was in sight. He tossed and turned all night long, trying to get out of bed and cursing them for holding him prisoner in that jail of sheets. At dawn his senses blurred, and when he was on the verge of losing consciousness, he took leave of the real world with the following manly statement, which could barely make its way from his brain to his lips: "Now I can die in peace for I have snatched from the demon of foolishness the soul that he had in his clutches."

Doña Paca and his manservant, convinced that their master was having a fit, started to scream; they called the doctor, they rubbed him up and down, and finally they brought him back to life. They were all awed to see him regain a cheerful face and hear him say that nothing hurt, that he felt well and happy. But in spite of this, the doctor looked very doubtful and predicted that the cerebral and nervous weakness would soon cause the patient's death. Despite his valiant efforts, Feijóo could not get up; his strength was beginning to fail him. He had no appetite. The friends at his side that day agreed to tell him as delicately as possible that he should prepare his soul for the final step so that it might be saved. Most of them thought that Don Evaristo would balk at this, because he had always bragged about being a free thinker; but to everyone's great surprise he took their advice very serenely and congenially, saying that he had his own beliefs, but that he wanted to fulfill any and all obligations that he felt the majority expected of him.

"I believe in God," he said, "and I have my own religion here, inside. Out of the respect that we all owe to each other, I want to fulfill the requirements established by the men who run a well-organized society. I've always been a slave to good manners and appearances. Bring in as many priests as you want—nothing can scare me and I'm not afraid of anything; I'd never cause a breach. Never lose your composure—that's my motto."

Everyone present marveled at his words, and that very day he was given the Holy Sacraments. Then he improved considerably, which gave them the opportunity to say what it's our custom to say: that religion is medicine for the soul *and* the body. He assured them that he was not going to die, that it had only been a spell, and that he had nine lives, like a cat, and that it was highly probable that God would let him hang on a little longer to let him see many and wondrous things. And so it was; the year 1875 ran its course without seeing the death of our practical philosopher.

During his convalescence from this attack he did not permit Fortunata to visit him. He wrote her notes from time to time, reiterating his advice and adding more for the imminent day set for the reconciliation. At the same time, he revised his will and added various charitable provisions for which several persons would be grateful. He had a small fortune divided into various loans to needy friends. Some of them had signed IOU's for a thousand, two thousand, or even three thousand *reales*. All of these slips of paper were torn up. He provided for the distribution of his valuables, some of which had considerable worth: rings with beautiful solitaires, sets of buttons, charming little ivory or sandalwood boxes he had brought back from the Philippines, a handsome sword, several gold-headed canes. By the way in which he distributed his possessions, he revealed once more his characteristic delicacy and his ability to value friendship.

Regarding Fortunata, his arrangements were impeccable. All he left her in his will, in which he referred to her as his "godchild," were several little gifts; but with the assistance of a very discreet agent at the stock exchange, he arranged a transaction which made Fortunata the buyer of a certain number of shares in the Bank of Spain; besides this, he gave her several sums in bills, in person. This did not make Don Evaristo forget about his relatives; he had two nieces, one in Astorga and the other in Ponferrada. Both were amply provided for in his will. And he also remembered, despite the many problems that distracted him that year, to send his nieces their annual sums. Doña Paca and the servants would be given their tidbits too, the day their master perished.

The priests of the parish asked whether he planned to leave something for the good of his soul, and with a kindly smile he replied that he had not forgotten any of his duties to society and, so as to leave no doubts, told them that he had left a little something for Masses too.

Villalonga visited him one afternoon, and the first thing Feijóo said as he let his friend embrace him was:

"Come now, Jacinto—are you really so mean that you won't give the canonship to the man I recommended?"

"For God's sake, my dear patriarch, be patient. I'll do what I can. I wrote Cárdenas a very strong letter and included the note. But Rome wasn't built in a day, remember. A canonship! I'd like one myself."

"And so would I. Well . . . can you or can't you? He's one of the best priests I've ever seen."

"I believe you, but—you know how it is. There's a big demand for those positions. As soon as one's open, there are four hundred priests after it with teeth this long."

"Yes, I know. But my priest is special; he's a saint, really. He fasts every day, imagine!"

"Mmm. That Father Rubín must be a big shot. And anyway, didn't we already give a prison administration job to a Rubín? It seems as if you've taken that family under your wing."

"I don't protect families, son. That's not the issue. I'm just interested in people with merit."

"Well, I won't stand in his way. I'll try Cárdenas again. But, as I said: there are hordes of people after those positions. Candidates take advantage of the influence women have on their husbands. It's almost always skirts that decide who's going to sit in the cathedrals."

"Well, suppose, my dear friend, that I'm wearing skirts; that I'm a lady—eh?"

"But it's not up to me."

"I warn you: if you don't appoint my man, I won't die; I'll torment you for months."

"Fine. Live for a thousand years."

"And how are the elections—are they going well?"

"Like a dream. I've got a priest who's worth an empire. He's fixing up a few things in the district and, I tell you, it's enough to make God and the Holy Trinity shake in their boots. That man's really worth his stuff; the kind that deserves not just a canonship, but seven miters."

"Oh yes, the Pater. I know him. He was the chaplain in my regiment."

Villalonga departed, revoicing his hopes for Nicolás Rubín's success.

"Eh, Jacinto! Wait a minute, by God, I wanted to talk to you about something else!" said Don Evaristo as his friend was about to leave. "For the love of God and all the saints, don't forget about that poor wretch Villaamil, the one they call Ramses II."

"He's already been recommended in the 'indispensable' category. That's the most I can do."

"He won't leave me in peace. He comes in here three times a day. The night they gave me the last blessing, at that very moment I looked to one side and the first person I saw was Ramses II holding a candle. You should have seen how the poor man looked at me! I think it was all his praying that kept me alive."

"Maybe. I won't forget him. Good-bye, now."

And Don Evaristo was left alone in a mildly pensive mood, savoring in his conscience the pure joy of having done unto others the greatest good possible, or of having warded off evil as well as Providence had allowed him.

v. Another Restoration

I

VERY ROUTINE AND ORDERLY PEOPLE who grow accustomed to the calm sweetness of a methodical life eventually abuse order by subjecting not only their activities but the very workings of their soul and even their most ostensibly rebellious body functions to the dictates of time. Thus, the great Doña Lupe, whose existence was very similar to that of a clock endowed with a soul, had used time so well that whenever anything of interest popped up and she wanted to think about it, she had a certain time of day and special place reserved for it. When she had something she needed to ponder because it kept buzzing in her head like a bothersome bee, either she did not think about it or she sat down in her little chair next to the window in the living room, her glasses propped on the bridge of her nose, her sewing basket in front of her, the cat stretched out comfortably on the edge of the scatter rug. This meditation was much more profound and effective if Doña Lupe put her whole left hand (up to the wrist) in a stocking, and if the hole was wide enough to allow her to weave a grating over it, making a jaillike window. This habit was so ingrained that Doña Lupe could not think in comfort unless she was sitting in that particular place, just as the best time for her numerical calculations was when she was shelling peas in the kitchen (when peas were in season), or when she was putting garbanzos in to soak. Habit had produced these marvels; as soon as she saw the garbanzos and put her hand into them, numbers rushed into her brain and she began to visualize the business on her mind: whether or not she should give a certain loan, whether or not she should keep this or that jewel. When she woke up early in the morning, she foresaw all the events and actions of the day and prepared herself for them by mentally summoning up all her energy and methodically dividing her time so as to allow for any foreseeable and/or probable events. She "wound herself up," accumulating all the intellectual strength she would need.

These routines were upset by the move, which took place in December of 1874. It goes without saying what a huge sacrifice it was for Doña Lupe. She was one of those people who hate the unknown and become very attached to their little nook. Moving her belongings made her feel as if the house would go up in flames or be torn down. But there was no choice. She had to make the change from northern to southern Madrid, because with Maximiliano's having to spend most of his time at Samaniego's pharmacy, it would be uncharitable to make him travel three-quarters of a league each way twice a day from Chamberí to Lavapiés. So Señora de Jáuregui gathered up their belongings and moved into a second-floor apartment on Ave María Street. She would have preferred living in the same building that housed the pharmacy, but none of its rooms had a "For Rent" sign. She chose an apartment next door with balconies next to those of her friend Casta Moreno, Samaniego's widow. At first she felt odd in her new home and considered it worse than the other, but soon she admitted that it was much better, more spacious, and more attractive; and as for the neighborhood, what the lady had lost in tranquillity she regained in liveliness. Little by little she got used to her new home, and when our story finds her this time, sitting next to the window, lost in thought with her hand in a stocking, sometime in March of 1875, she has forgotten about the house in Chamberí where we met her.

Her meditation and darning did not keep her from looking out the window from time to time; Ave María Street has much more traffic than Raimundo Lulio. In one of the widow's almost mechanical glances, which helped her maintain some sort of continuity as she confronted her terrible problem, she saw a person who caught her attention for a moment. It was Guillermina Pacheco. "It seems that the saint has taken to visiting this neighborhood now," murmured Doña Lupe, craning to get a better look at Guillermina. "I've already seen her go by four or five times, at different times of day. Distances certainly don't stop her . . . Now that I think of it, Casta said she's a relative of hers. I'll have to ask her . . ."

Having seen Guillermina walk down Raimundo Lulio Street so many times on her way to the orphanage had given Doña Lupe the feeling that she knew her. Whenever there was a public ceremony in the chapel of the orphanage, Doña Lupe attended, hoping to introduce herself and get to know the saint. She admired her greatly, not so much for her saintly acts as for her disregard for worldly things, her masculine activity, and the grandeur of her character. Perhaps Señora Jáuregui felt some of that autocratic ferment, burning initiative, and organizational power in her own soul, and perhaps it was this spiritual kinship that made her yearn all the more to be on close terms with the saint. She had only spoken to her once or twice at orphanage ceremonies, and these brief exchanges had been the results of her officious, intrusive manner. When she saw the saint at these events, surrounded by ladies "of the nobility" and rich important women who had their carriages at the door, Doña Lupe would have given the only breast she had to nudge elbows with that group and get in on their collection drives. For in her vanity—which, indeed, was well-founded—she was convinced that she could hold a candle to all of the ladies present when it came to breeding and manners. Besides, she knew very well that not all of them had been born with a silver spoon in their mouth, and that refinement was the substance of true aristocracy in these liberal times. There was no reason why she, who could stand up to the first of them, should not mix with these ladies who flocked after Guillermina like sheep. Furthermore, when it came to clothes, it could be said that Jáuregui's widow's were in excellent condition. With her talent and economy she had negotiated for a fur-trimmed velveteen coat that not even the best dressed of the ladies could outdo. And it had cost her next to nothing, considering what such garments usually cost. And when she appeared for the first time in the short cloak she was having altered . . . Well, let's just say it would turn heads. These thoughts grew out of Doña Lupe's other thoughts like a tangent that lengthened when she saw Guillermina pass and ended when the virgin and founder disappeared from view.

Picking up exactly where she had left off, she mused: "And even if Señor Feijóo does deny it today, it's true: he *did* start to pursue me a year after my Jáuregui died. As true as the fact that we'll all die some day. And if it's not true, then what was he doing standing on that silly corner on Tintoreros Street? That was just before the war with Africa, I remember it well . . . and if he hadn't gone off to kill Moors, who knows if . . . But that's beside the point. Where was I? There's not the slightest doubt that he's a thoroughly decent gentleman. Jáuregui thought highly of him, and used to say that the only thing he had against him was that he was a skirt-chaser. Other than that, a completely reliable man; he keeps his word as if it were the Holy Bible. Whenever he gave his word on something, it might as well have been recorded by a notary. And yet, the things he's been telling me lately sound so strange! That she's repented, that he's taken her under his wing. So he found her at a neighbor's house and took pity on her and so forth. But no matter what that saintly man tells me, her repentance doesn't convince me. And it might even be that . . . Stop it; don't let yourself be tempted by such a natural suspicion . . . Maybe Feijóo himself . . . he might . . . have had . . . and now . . . No; bury the thought. It could drive you crazy. And anyway, the truth is that the poor man has deteriorated so much. He couldn't have been up to playing around a few months ago. If what he says is true! Charity, pity, repentance; her need to be forgiven; decency; a reconciliation . . . !"

Another tangent. She looked out the window and saw Guillermina passing by again. "What's that she has in her hand? A stick and an iron hook. The things that saint turns up with! Must be something they've given her. She says she takes everything. Hmm—I could help her project by giving her half-a-dozen old keys I've got. That board she's carrying looks like a pattern. Sure, it's probably from the lumberyard on Valencia Street. She's always moving things, never lets up. Now there's what I'd like to do: build an institution, asking everybody for money. I'd make it as big as the Escorial."

End of tangent and back to the subject. "Just think of what Nicolás said this morning: that Feijóo is the finest gentleman of Madrid and that he's promised him a canonship! If he gets it, nothing will surprise me. I'd be glad; it would get that burden off my back. Goodness, what times we live in. I don't know what the government's coming to. Now if I could be in the government, if I were a cabinet member, I'd really make everybody stay on his toes. People just don't know how. It's so obvious. Imagine, giving a canonship to a young priest who comes in at one in the morning and spends his time talking at the café with disreputable characters who hang around the streets and aren't even properly authorized to say Mass. Oh well, if that's what God wants for you and you're smart enough to hook it, good luck and write when you get there, and don't show up around here anymore, you big egoist, hog . . . And as for your brother Juanito Pablo—ever since he's had that new job he hasn't bothered to come say hello. Next to the two of you, Maximiliano is an angel, a genius. And that reminds me of something else Nicolás said this morning: that Don Evaristo's so good a Catholic, and that when they gave him the last blessing, he took the wafer with such a saintly look that everybody there burst into tears. I don't know about that—they're probably exaggerating. When it comes to calling people saints you've really got to look things over carefully. Oh well, let's suppose that Nicolás is right. Where does that get us? We still don't know whether with all this Christianity he's trying to give us chalk for cheese. Pity, repentance! Dear God, I wish you'd either let me see this thing clearly or take this racket out of my head! It's enough to drive me crazy. And anyway, I don't know why I should be racking my brains, because after all—what difference does it make to me? If Maximiliano wants to humiliate himself after all the atrocious things that have happened, I shouldn't interfere. But I will. Yes, I will interfere. How can I consent to this insult? The indecent hussy. Thinking that her husband will forgive her after what she pulled on him! After her lover boy knocked down my poor little Maxi, taking advantage of how weak he is! A disgrace, I tell you! If I hadn't hammered it into him for a full month that he should forget about revenge, I hate to think of the catastrophe there would have been. He wanted to shoot him. He even thought of bundling up some dynamite and putting it inside the door of that character's house. He was delirious, poor boy. The best thing is scorn. Good-for-nothings don't deserve anything but scorn. Fine candidate my nephew is for a fight—he's scared of being in the dark by himself. Poor little Maxi! He has a heart of gold, and now that he's so caught up in his studies of the other world, he gets such peculiar ideas! Imagine what he said to me the other night: 'My dear Aunt, after much thinking and suffering, I've come to detach myself from all earthly passions, and I no longer feel hatred or revenge within me.' He says he forgives her in the Christian way, because of this and that and God knows what. But as for living together again, not even the Pope could command him to. And then he confuses me even more by asking me to go see her. 'Visit her, Aunt, find out how she is; explore her feelings and see what she has to say. What Don Evaristo says may be true.' Every night the same theme song. If he keeps up like this, I won't have any choice; I'll have to go see her. And it's no short walk, from here to Moors' Gate."

2

One Monday afternoon Doña Lupe came home at about five o'clock. She was dressed to the teeth.

"Papitos—who came while I was away?"

"That man with the white beard."

"No one else? Didn't Mauricia come?"

"No, Ma'am. This morning I saw her at the door to the wine tavern at Lavapiés Square. She lives somewhere near here. 'Señá Mauricia, my mistress wants to see you.' And she says: 'Tell the creep if she wants to sell shawls she can sell 'em herself, and if she doesn't wanna she can—' "

"What an indecent woman!" the Señora exclaimed, somewhat distractedly.

Papitos, who had been punished that morning for bringing home some bad hake from the market, thought that her mistress hadn't gotten over the tantrum yet, and she watched her hands fearfully. But Doña Lupe's corrective wrath had vanished from her heart to make way for another series of feelings and the great stupefaction that had taken hold of her about an hour before.

"Listen, Papitos," she said. "Come here, and listen closely to the instructions I'm going to give you. I have to go out again. Serve lunch to Señorito Nicolás and Señorito Maxi, who'll come home much later than his brother. Remember what I tell you now, and don't do the opposite. For the main course, the priest will have the hake you brought home this morning, hear? It stinks to high heaven. Put on lots of salt and then dredge it in flour—make the crust as thick as you can; then fry it. Use all of it—he'll gobble up everything you give him and won't even know the difference. He's like a shark—he'll take anything you throw him. Now for dessert, there are some nuts and wine-flavored honey. Put the crock on the table and let him have his fill—maybe he'll finish it for us. It's starting to get so fermented nobody can stand it. If Señorito Maxi comes in before I get back, serve him one of the two veal chops—the big one—and for dessert give him the pastries the baker brought this morning and some of the quince paste that I eat. So. Don't get it the other way around, now."

When Doña Lupe gave such proofs of her confidence in Papitos, delegating authority to her, the little imp grew inches taller, and vanity sharpened her mind so much that she was able to carry out orders in the most irreproachable fashion. Doña Lupe, who knew her like a book, was sure that her orders would be followed. Papitos nodded to show that she understood and inwardly smiled slyly, undoubtedly relishing the thought of pouring heaps of salt on Señorito Nicolás' hake.

Doña Lupe sat for a while in the living room, in the same chair she had taken when she came in, her cape still on, her cheek still resting on her hand, her mind still on the same subject. She had not yet recovered from her astonishment, nor would she recover from it for quite some time. Fortunata, from whose house she had just come, had given her a thousand *duros* for her to invest as she saw fit, and she had refused to accept a receipt. At first Señora Jáuregui suspected that the bills were fake; but oh, no, she could see that they were as real as day. This show of trust touched her deeply, for it was not only trust in her honesty, it was confidence in her ability to make money grow. And besides, in the course of the conversation Fortunata had intimated that she had some shares at the bank; she didn't say how many. How had she gotten so rich? Maybe it was Juanito Santa Cruz . . . or Feijóo . . . The oddest part was that Doña Lupe, who suddenly felt very tolerant toward Fortunata, was straining herself to think up a decent source for the fortune. What people with a good character will do if they're fascinated by money! For them, good things have to come from good things. "And why shouldn't that business of her repentance be true?" she asked herself. "But there's one thing I don't understand: that first day Feijóo told me she was poor; poor as a church mouse, and eating up her savings. Hmmm, if all those shares are the leftovers! Oh well, what's past is past, and we should look at things objectively, and not pass judgment before we know the facts. Who would dare to condemn his fellow man without hearing him out first? It'd be cruel, unjust. The notion that we should always be wary of others is monstrous. But I'm getting carried away, and it's time to leave. If I'm late, Don Francisco may not be in when I get there. He's going to ask me what we should do with all this manna."

On her way downstairs, her thoughts took another turn. "And she's looking so beautiful! Ravishing, really. And always so well-behaved, you'd think she'd never committed a sin. Whan I walked in she almost fainted. And that's not put on. You can call her whatever you like, but she doesn't play a role; it's just not in her. As for her manners—she's forgotten everything I taught her. I'll have to start all over again. And the same goes for her language. Not the slightest reference to last year's events. She probably thinks—and she's right—that it's worse to hash over them."

Doña Lupe was away for three long hours. When she came back, Nicolás had eaten and left and Maximiliano was finishing his lunch. The first question she asked Papitos concerned the orders she had given her.

"He didn't leave a scrap," the girl replied, showing her mistress the dish on which she had served the hake.

"And did he say anything?"

"He couldn't, 'cause he was chomping away the whole time."

Doña Lupe smiled faintly. She made sure that Maximiliano had been served according to her instructions, and after changing clothes she prepared her own meal, which was extremely frugal. When she entered the dining room Maxi was no longer there; half an hour later she found him in his room, in the dark, sitting at the table, his hands bracing his head, his fingers in his hair as if he wanted to pull it out. Seeing him so depressed, his aunt said:

"Come now, don't take it so seriously. Things will turn out according to the Lord's wishes. When things are unexpected, there's no way to avoid them."

"Well, have you seen her?" Maxi asked, finally changing his awkward position and looking anxiously at his aunt.

"Yes. You put me in such a state that I . . . well, I finally went. I've seen her and she hasn't gobbled me up. She's the same slow, dumb girl she always was."

"Does she look unwell?"

"Unwell? Ha! What she looks is ravishing. All the stars in the sky shine from those eyes. Poverty is becoming to some people."

"What? She's poor? and doesn't have enough to live on?" the boy asked, squirming in his chair. "That shouldn't be allowed to happen."

"I don't say she's gone hungry; maybe she even . . . She must not have very much, though. She told me that at four o'clock this afternoon all she'd eaten all day was a bit of stale bread left over from yesterday, a little piece of chocolate, and at midday a small serving of lung meat."

"Good Lord! And you consent to that? Lung meat!"

"Maybe she's doing penance," replied the widow in that naively convinced tone she used when she wanted to toy with her nephew's gullibility, like a cat with a ball of paper.

"Frankly, Aunt, to think that she's starving . . . But I won't forgive her; I can't. I assure you that I'll *never, never, never*—"

"I've already told you that it's not wise to say 'never' when it comes to human matters. Remember Don Juan Prim; look what happened to his nevers."*

"Well, what happened to Don Juan Prim won't happen to me, because I know what I'm talking about. And since the restoration depends on me, and I'm not going to agree to it . . . Anyway, that's not what we're talking about. Even if we aren't going to make peace, it hurts me that she's going hungry. We must help her."

"Well, then I'll go back. But wait: why don't you go?"

"Me!" exclaimed the exalted boy, who could feel his hair standing on end.

"Yes, you, because you're used to having everything all cooked and mashed for you. This is very delicate. I don't want to take any responsibility. You're not a child anymore, and you should decide these things for yourself."

"Me? Me go?" murmured the young pharmacist, beginning to shake and feel chilled. The mere thought of it made him ill.

"Yes, you. Forget all your fears and stop hesitating. If you want to do it, do it, and if you don't, forget about it."

"I don't have time to go," said Rubín, relaxing with this easy excuse.

Doña Lupe insisted in blunt language that he make the decision about the reconciliation; see Fortunata and proceed according to his own impressions. She preached this to him so forcefully that the poor boy finally made up his mind to go, and the next day, when he had some free time from the pharmacy, he headed for Tabernillas Street feeling more dead than alive and planning what he would say and what he would leave out; he felt as if he were about to take an exam—his stomach was full of butterflies. When he got there and saw the number of the house, he was overcome by such horror that he withdrew, fleeing from both street and neighborhood.

The next day he tried again and got as far as the main door; but when he looked through the glass panes at the staircase he stopped. The idea of going up terrified him, obliterated everything he had planned to say. He hung on for a while, struggling terribly, until this thought alarmed him: "If she comes out and finds me here . . ." And he fled down the nearest street without even daring to look back.

His third attempt on the following day met with no more success, and in his boredom and disconcertedness he finally resolved to express himself to his wife in

---

*General Prim said that the Bourbons would "never, never, never" come back to Spain. Prim was killed and the Bourbons did come back, and the Restoration took place.

a letter. Walking toward Ave María Street, he decided to make the letter very severe and give it a slight touch of indulgence, just one grain of the salt of pity to season it. He would say that he could not admit her into his home, but that in time, if she proved that she had repented . . . In short, the epistle would be just the thing. Aroused by these thoughts and plans he entered his house, and as he went toward his bedroom and heard his aunt calling to him from the living room, he felt as if his heart were being pricked by a pin. He walked into the living room and—good God, he hardly believed his eyes!—God above it was impossible! It was Fortunata, standing in the living room, livid, like a suspect awaiting trial.

By some miracle, Maximiliano didn't fall flat on his face. He said "Ah!" and stood stock still. She didn't make a sound either, and looked heavily down at the floor. At last, at the height of his confusion, the young man dared to speak, and said something like "Good afternoon" and then "I thought that . . ." and then "So it was you, Aunt . . ."

"No, it wasn't; I haven't meddled in anything," declared Doña Lupe, who was seated, as if presiding over them. "The only thing I did was to bring her here so that face to face the two of you could make up your minds. Fortunata, sit down."

This reminder of the insult made Maximiliano experience a brusque reaction against his lately acquired mysticism, which had been born more out of necessity than conviction.

"This seems premature," he said, and left the room.

Shortly afterward, his aunt followed him into the study and said:

"Your severity is fine. But under the circumstances . . . Didn't you yourself say that we simply had to give her a daily allowance for food? And do you think we're in the position to maintain two households?"

The boy's head was so confused that he couldn't follow her reasoning. If his aunt had talked about four thousand houses it would have sounded the same to him.

"Leave me alone," he said, almost sobbing. "Nothing ever works out right for me."

"Well, now that she's here she might as well stay," Doña Lupe continued in a low voice. "We can put her in the little room next to mine. And that's that. Oh, Lord! Why do I always have to be the one to iron things out? You know what? This is your chance to have it out together—insult each other all you want, or make up, if that's what you want. I'm washing my hands of it. Don't drag me into your dance . . . If you want to reach an agreement, fine; if you don't, that's fine too. I'm doing plenty to lend you my house so that you can see whether or not you want to make up. And for God's sake, don't give me any more headaches. If this thing doesn't work out in a matter of days, it never will. So please, don't give me any more headaches."

She raised her voice as she said this and started walking out into the hall, so that it was perfectly audible to Papitos at one end of the house and Fortunata at the other. The latter stayed that afternoon in a position that was far from graceful: her husband hardly spoke to her. Nicolás did all the talking at the table. The second day, Fortunata told Doña Lupe that she was leaving, which made the lady of the house go into the hall, crying, "Good Lord, don't give me any more headaches. I can't take it. Do as you please, all of you!" But in spite of this, the wife did not leave. On the third day, in the thick of the charged silence between man and wife, Maxi began to throw out a few words, then instead of words came sentences, and after icy clauses came some lukewarm ones. Finally, he allowed himself a cheerful remark or two. On the fifth day, he smiled faintly when he looked at his wife. On the sixth, Fortunata paid courteous attention when he said something; on the seventh, Maxi sided with her whenever there was a disagreement at the dinner table; on the eighth, he patted her on the shoulder from time to time; on the ninth, Señora Rubín was solicitous about her husband's dress when he went out into the cold; and on the tenth, they sat whispering for about a quarter of an hour in a corner in the living room; on the eleventh, Maxi squeezed her hand hard when he came home; and on the twelfth, like a priest proclaiming "Hosannah!," Doña Lupe exclaimed:

"Lord, you're getting thick. For God's sake, don't give me any more headaches. If you're craving to make up, why bother with all these ifs and buts? I'm smart to stay out of it, with all I have to worry about."

And so the restoration came about, and their legitimate married life was reestablished. It was one of those things that happen without anyone's knowing how; destined events in the history of a family, similar to their counterparts in the history of a nation; events that wise men foresee and experts explain, although they cannot determine the cause; events that imperceptibly take place, for although we can feel them coming, we cannot actually see the subtle mechanism that makes them occur.

3

The first few days following this great event nothing worth remembering occurred. The only thing worth mentioning took place outside the Rubín residence. Here's what it was. One afternoon Doña Lupe and Fortunata were sitting in the living room sewing rings onto some magnificent silk curtains that had become the former's property because of an unpaid loan when Papitos, who had stepped out onto the balcony to bring in the clothes that had been hung to dry, began to scream:

"Señoras! Look! Look at all the people! Somebody's been killed."

The two ladies stepped out and saw that down the street next to the San Carlos corner was a big circle of people growing thicker and thicker.

"There's a *corpse* dead down there in the middle of all those people!" cried Papitos, leaning half-way over the railing.

"I see a shape stretched out on the ground," said Doña Lupe. "Do you* see anything? It's probably a drunk. But look at the crowd that's forming. The carriages can't even get through. What happened to the police? When you need them, they're never around."

"Señora, send me out for noodles. You know we need some," said monkey-face.

"Ha! What you want is to stick your nose in things."

"Let me go," the girl begged, jumping up and down.

"Oh, all right, go ahead," agreed Doña Lupe, who was in a good mood that day. "If I don't let you, you'll go and fall off the balcony. But come right back. And be sure to wipe your feet on the mat downstairs, because it's very muddy. Don't make a mess of my rug like you did when you went to see the coal dealer."

Papitos shot out of the house and was gone about twenty minutes. Her mistress saw her coming back and went to open the door.

"Did you wipe your feet well?"

"Yes, Ma'am. Look."

"Now. Wipe them again here. You know what you should do whenever you come in? Wipe all the mud off on the neighbors' mat, the one over there."

"This one?" asked monkey-face, doing a tap dance on the mat in front of the apartment on the left.

"The less we stamp on ours the better."

"You know what, Señora?" added Papitos, who, even though she was out of breath from running so much, kept dancing on the neighbors' mat. "Guess what's going on down there? It's a woman and it looks like she's drunk . . . really drunk. And guess who it is? Señá Mauricia."

"Ooh, Fortunata, did you hear that?" Doña Lupe asked from the hall on her way back to the living room. "Mauricia drunk! So that's what's attracting all those people."

"Did you get a good look? Are you sure it's her?" asked Fortunata after a pause of astonishment.

"Yes, Ma'am; it's her."

"Child," remarked Doña Lupe, stepping out onto the balcony again with an

---

* Doña Lupe is using the familiar *tú* form again with Fortunata; she had stopped using it at the end of Volume II.

officious air, "believe me: this is a shock . . . And no policemen have come! No, wait—they're picking her up now. What a woman! Imagine getting into such a state."

"They're taking her away now. She looks like a corpse," said Fortunata, recalling the scenes she had witnessed in the convent.

"Yes, they're taking her to a first aid station, or the hospital. What? No? They're coming this way. How much do you want to bet they're taking her to the pharmacy?"

"She's split her head wide open," stated Papitos, thus giving a graphic description of the size of the wound. "And she was spouting blood all over; it was running down the street like the water when it rains."

When the lifeless body of Mauricia la Dura, carried by policemen and escorted by a crowd, passed beneath their balcony, Fortunata went inside; she didn't have the heart to witness such a spectacle. Doña Lupe and Papitos saw everything, and the latter even went so far as to ask her mistress for permission to go to the pharmacy to watch "the drunk woman" be cured. But this was asking too much, and even though the little maid thought up various excuses to go out, she did not get her way.

At lunch Maximiliano talked about it; he described the cure and issued unfavorable forecasts on the sick woman's chances for recovery.

"You're right," observed the widow. "I don't think she'll pull out of this one. Poor woman! What a vice to have! I'm really sorry; nobody can match her when it comes to selling valuables."

Then Maxi related a most intriguing and recent episode of Mauricia's life, one that had been told that very afternoon (after she'd been cured) by Señor Aparisi, one of the gentlemen who often went to the *tertulia* held in the pharmacy.

"Well, on one of her drunken sprees the hussy was picked up off the street by the Protestants, who've got a chapel and house in Las Peñuelas. Doña Guillermina heard about it—you know, the lady who goes around collecting for the orphans over on Albuquerque Street—and flew off the handle. Imagine. She went straight over to the Protestants' house after the hag. Knock, knock . . . 'Who's there?' 'It's me.' And out comes the minister—Don Horacio they call him—with his skimpy red beard; his wife came out too—Doña Malvina they call her—both good people. After all, being Protestant doesn't mean you can't be decent. By the way, they both wear what they please—they've got their own style. Doña Malvina makes Don Horacio's frock coats and Don Horacio fixes up her hats. You know how the English are—those two don't spend a penny on tailors and seamstresses. But back to my story. The ministers held their ground and so did Doña Guillermina. Religion against religion—it was getting bad. The Protestants said the woman had asked them for alms and shelter; Doña Guillermina denied it, accusing them of having gone after her and gotten her on their side. Don Horacio said it wasn't true and that he'd stand up for his Lutheran rights, even in the Supreme Court; she was miffed at that, and then Doña Malvina got out a copy of the constitution. But Guillermina said she didn't understand constitutions or knight errant novels. Finally our Catholic friend went to the governor, and the governor ordered Mauricia to be released from Pontius Pilate, that is, Don Horacio."

"You see?" remarked Doña Lupe. "That's the kind of trouble you get into with religion. My Jáuregui was so right when he said he was very liberal but didn't think much of free worship."

"Just wait. You haven't heard the best part yet. Don Horacio, who respects the law like a good Englishman, obeyed the governor's order and planned to demand his rights in court. But when he told Mauricia to leave she didn't want to and she started to call Doña Guillermina—who was there, mind you—all sorts of names. And she went on insulting all the ladies on Catholic committees."

"What impudence! She's impossible. She gets in that state and doesn't know what she's saying."

"Well, Doña Guillermina didn't cringe at this and she didn't give up the idea of taking Mauricia away. She started to leave, ve-ry softly, and sat in the doorway on a stone spur there is there. Every day she went back to the same spot, like a sentry. The minister and his wife invited her in, but she told them no, thank you. And finally yesterday the tables turned: Mauricia got furious and attacked Doña Malvina and scratched up her face. So Don Horacio calls in the police. Meanwhile the hussy's gotten into the chapel and she's breaking the pulpit, turning over the inkwell, tearing up all the books, making a barricade with the chairs, and then in the chalice they use for Communion she . . . she profanes it in the most indecent way you can imagine. It took some doing to get her out of there. Just as she was coming out, yahoo! Doña Guillermina slings a rope around her neck and drags her away. Aparisi's the one who told me all this; he knows it from Don Horacio and Doña Guillermina themselves and also because he had to step in as lieutenant mayor of the district. Mauricia was turned over to a sister who lives on Toledo Street, and it seems they couldn't hold her down either. They took her from the pharmacy to the first aid station."

This tale was too long for Maximiliano's lungs; he was exhausted when he finished telling it. Everyone was shocked at the story, and Doña Lupe said she felt sorry for la Dura and deplored the waste of a good saleswoman on such an indecent vice. As for Fortunata, she overflowed with pity and wished her husband would hurry up and finish telling these terribly sad tales so that the conversation would move on to other subjects. But it turned out differently; all they talked about until the end of the meal was Mauricia, the Protestants, and the insane vice of drinking. And toward the end Nicolás brought up the incidents that had taken place in the Micaelas, soliciting Fortunata's testimony. Very much against her will she told them the novelistic episodes of the mouse, the visions, and the brandy bottle; but she gave only a sketchy account to get it over with sooner.

4

That night they went to Varieté's, which is just a few steps from Ave María Street. Another of this neighborhood's advantages over Chamberí is that you can go out at night to see a play or drop in at a café without having to walk for miles or take a streetcar. Fortunata didn't like going to the theater or appearing in public places. She had an inexplicable fear of people looking at her; even though few or none knew her, she felt that they all knew her and that every mouth was making a remark about her. Unfortunately, there *was* something to notice. If men looked at her, it was to admire her, and if they whispered afterward, they hardly ever said anything based on a knowledge of the truth. Another source of terror for her in theaters and public places was the thought that she might see "familiar faces," and this anxiety kept her on pins and needles throughout the performance.

At home she feld comfortable. She had undoubtedly known happier times in her life, but not such blandly calm ones. She had had days—the minority of them, to be sure—in which her sun-drenched soul had simply sparkled; others of almost total darkness had come; but she had never felt herself in such a steady, calm current of warm, equal days flowing under such sweet, restoring shade. She got along very well with Doña Lupe, and the oddest thing was happening to her and Maxi. We won't say she loved him in the usual sense of the word, but she had grown very fond of him in a sisterly way. He neither was nor could be the sort of man a woman gives her life for, finding spiritual joy in the sacrifice; he was simply a creature whose well-being mattered to her. And just as one anticipates and can practically see a distant coast when still at sea, so she could glimpse loving him with firmer love and foresee spending her whole life at his side without wishing for anything better.

Instead of shirking her household duties Fortunata prolonged and multiplied them, well aware that work helped her to stay on balance—that luckless, griefless balance that made her heart feel drowsy and smoothed, as if a balm were being constantly rubbed into it. She recollected the two cases that our good friend Feijóo had described to her and wondered whether the one she considered the likelier, that is, the first, would occur. Would she grow satisfied with this life, contented with this tasteless fruit of love without hankering for a sweeter, less healthy one?

Maximiliano, on the other hand, could not control his anxiety. Yet he had no reason to suspect his wife, whose conduct was absolutely correct. Doña Lupe and he agreed that Fortunata must never go out alone, and this decree was strictly obeyed. But not even this security put his mind at ease. He had an ardent desire for children for two reasons: first, so that he could tie down his other half with new ropes; second, so that motherhood would tone down that splendid beauty, which was more dazzling every day. The lack of proportion in their heights and personal appearances mortified the poor boy so much that he made impossible—and sometimes ridiculous—efforts to cover up for it. He wore stacked-heeled shoes and took pains to dress well, copying certain stylistic details he saw stylish men wearing. Unfortunately, although Fortunata hardly worried about her appearance, the disproportion was always very plain. But Maxi noticed with pleasure that his wife did very little to emphasize her beauty and looked upon fashion rather disdainfully, which made him happy for two other reasons: this way they looked better together, and also others wouldn't notice her so much.

Ever since he had restored his domestic order, Maximiliano had completely abandoned his readings in philosophy and had begun to feel anew in his soul his poorly cured pain and vindictive hatred. All his asceticism and "finding God in himself" had been nothing but a flimsy support system for his sadness or perhaps a result of the circumstances, and now they seemed to be stuck to his mind with saliva, as if he were cramming for an exam. His new obligations in the pharmacy required a use of chemistry and pharmacological knowledge, and he devoted himself to this with a truly ardent desire to learn. Doña Lupe told him he should invent some sort of medicine, any old thing that would sound like a miracle if he gave it a good name; but he resisted the idea because he considered it scientifically unethical. Aunt and nephew had lively debates on this subject.

"As if it were a crime to invent some new pills or capsules or lozenges and give them a name! 'Hypochetropythical capsules'—vegetal or animal, it's all the same—'discovered by Dr. Rubín' . . . 'infallible'; works on anything—consumption, rabies, it doesn't matter what you pick. As long as you *discover* something and stick a label on it with a picture of yourself. Really, you're a coward. If you don't invent something I'll have to. Fortunata, tell him to invent something; convince him, child—you'll make piles of money."

Fortunata saw Sr. Feijóo very infrequently now; he came to pay ceremonious visits and stayed for about an hour, talking more with Señora Jáuregui than with Señora Rubín. The pleasant old man appeared to be happy, but his health was failing; by April he never left home without a servant. On one of his visits he was alone with his friend and spoke to her in such a fatherly way that she almost burst into tears. Everything was going quite well and he presumed that "his *chulita*" had had time to appreciate his lessons and advice. Feijóo's friendship displeased Maxi, although he couldn't have said exactly why. But the strangest part was that after a month or so of this new life, even Fortunata began to enjoy Don Evaristo's visits less. She continued to feel the same gratitude and affection for him, but she couldn't help considering the presence of her former protector in that house a monstrosity. "Could it really be," she wondered, "like what he said—that life is full of these unbelievable horrors? Just think—this is what it's like! There's the world you see and then there's another one, hidden underneath . . . and the inside is making the outside the way it is. Well, I guess it makes sense after all; it's not the face of the clock that runs, but what's inside—what you can't see."

At dark Doña Lupe came in after having wiped the mud off her feet on the neighbors' mat.

"Listen," she said to Fortunata, taking off her cloak. "I heard this afternoon that Mauricia's dying . . . Poor woman! We have to go see her. It's not far—Mira el Río Baja Street."

She had gotten the news from her friend Casta Moreno, who had heard it from Cándido Samaniego. Doña Guillermina had taken Mauricia out of the hospital to her sister's house and called in the doctor that the ladies' committee provides for the poor. Under this care and tenderness from Doña Guillermina, and because death was now threatening her, the miserable sinful woman suddenly seemed changed, cured of her wickedness and repentant "in the full sense of the word," saying that she wanted to die in the most Catholic way possible and begging forgiveness from everyone with such deep sighs and such religious fervor it practically broke their hearts.

"Let me tell you—if this is all real we'll have to get a ticket to watch her die. We're going over there tomorrow."

Doña Lupe was not going to visit Mauricia purely out of charity. For some time Guillermina had fascinated her—more because of her masterful air than her virtue—and now that the great founder was going to demonstrate her saintliness to a court of high-class ladies in a place accessible to Doña Lupe, why shouldn't she try to stick her nose into it? After all, wasn't she a "lady" too? She discussed this at length with Casta Moreno, who often dropped in with her two daughters for an evening visit, and Samaniego's widow had nothing but praise for Guillermina, saying she was out of this world, really. And to think she was a distant relative, on the Morenos' side! Doña Lupe swelled with pride and self-love as she envisaged herself mingling with all that elegant charity and taking orders from the illustrious founder. If it did come about, however, there would be one obstacle: she would have to cough up a contribution.

The next morning, as she was dressing for the occasion, Doña Lupe wondered whether or not to wear her velveteen coat, but she soon reasoned that it would be foolish. Besides the fact that it would get wet (for it was a rainy day), it wasn't suitable for the place, people, and occasion. She'd have time enough to show off her coat, hat, and other garments. She told Fortunata to dress very simply, and she put on something slightly better so as to keep what she considered a suitable distance between them.

VI. Spiritual Naturalism

I

AS THEY TURNED ONTO MIRA EL RÍO STREET they met Severiana, whom Doña Lupe had seen on various previous occasions. She was carrying a flask of medicine sealed with paper, the way it used to be dispensed. Doña Lupe questioned her, and when Severiana realized that they were on their way to see her sister she gladly offered to guide them, taking them through the dirty main door and up the no less dirty, winding staircase to the corridor. As we already know, Severiana's abode was one of the best of the tenements and because of its size and furnishings could easily pass as luxurious in that neighborhood. A woman called Doña Fuensanta, a commander's widow, lived with her, and the house reflected their partnership, for it consisted of two small, identical living rooms, each with a window facing the street. Between the door and the first room was a hall (with the washtub) that opened into the kitchen, whose grilled windows faced the large corridor. Two interior rooms completed the house. When Guillermina, realizing that Mauricia was about to die, urged Severiana to get her out of the hospital for the third time and take her home, the commander's widow offered her room for this charitable cause and moved her furniture into a neighbor's apartment. So Mauricia was moved into the second of the two rooms. Severiana's bed was in the interior bedroom and the first room was set aside for visitors, as was evident in the relative luxury of the bureau, the brand new straw chairs, the sofa, the oilcloth-covered table, the picture of the "two loving hearts," another of the *Numantia* (the Spanish ship that had sailed around the world shortly before, during the reign of Isabel II), the portraits of Severiana's brothers-in-law, who were military men, the esparto rug (as yet tightly woven, without a hole), and, finally, the large prints that Severiana had picked up at the flea market for next to nothing. They were excellent etchings, out of style now. The paper was old and stained by the humidity; the frames were mahogany. They pictured themes that weren't at all Spanish, come to think of it: battles of Napoleon I, reproduced from the once famous paintings of Horace Vernet and the baron of Gros. Who hasn't seen *Napoleon in Eylau*, and *Napoleon in Jena*, the *Bonaparte in Arcola*, the *Apotheosis of Austerlitz*, and the *Farewell at Fontainebleau?*

Preceded by Severiana, Doña Lupe and Fortunata entered the sickroom and found the patient sitting up in bed. Her hair had been cut several days ago so that her head wound could be treated, and this accentuated her Roman profile: the nose looked more delicate, the lower jaw larger, and the emaciation made her eyes larger. The graceful curves of her mouth were more flourishing, and the line between her lips, which looked as if it had been sharply drawn, gave her an air of fallen greatness or humiliation sublimely resigned. The reddened circles under her eyes spread over half her face; her eyebrows jutted out like visers; her eyes, beautiful and burning, were sunken, and, surrounded by that purple flesh, they shone more, as if they were about to ambush whatever accosted her. Her black eyebrows formed a single straight line. Her forehead was wide; a lock of black hair fell over it. In a word, la Dura completed the story told on the walls; she was *Napoleon at Saint Hélène*.

When Doña Lupe and Fortunata greeted her, she looked blankly at them as if she didn't immediately recognize them. Then she uttered their names. What a voice! Mauricia's voice had always been very hoarse, but now it had dropped to the lowest pitch possible. "Good God!" thought Fortunata after seeing and hearing her. "She looks like a man!" Meanwhile, Doña Lupe, sitting down on one of the straw chairs, murmured condolences appropriate for the occasion and added:

"I hope this will teach you . . . and you'll behave yourself from now on. We'll see whether you've learned your lesson when you get over this."

Mauricia turned to Fortunata, who had sat down next to the headboard. She stared at her without a word; then she fixed her eyes on the ceiling, grumbling:

"Yes . . . I've been bad all right, real bad."

And turning back to her friend she said:

"Listen, you: repent for your sins, but don't leave it for the end. Don't leave it because . . . it doesn't work. *Your* nose isn't clean either, and the day you decide to do some spring cleaning in your conscience you're going to need a lot of soap and water; lots of brooms and lots of rags . . ."

She said this so earnestly that Fortunata couldn't take offense. The warning struck Doña Lupe as most impertinent and discourteous. What right did the woman have to talk about other people's sins when she had so many to worry about herself? It was true that her niece-in-law hadn't been any model, but she had reformed, and there was no use in hashing over the past.

"We've heard they're treating you very well," she said to change the subject.

"Thanks to the mother of the poor," declared Severiana, who was tidying up the bed, "she has all she needs. What a lady Doña Guillermina is!"

"A saint!" exclaimed Doña Lupe in a very adulatory tone. "Don't call her anything else, because that's the name that suits her."

"But my sister here has closed her mouth on us," said Severiana. "And chameleons are the only creatures that can live without eating."

"Is she really fasting?"

"The only way we can get some broth into her is by spiking it with sherry. And in the morning, so she'll eat a little toast, we have to give her a little glass of *horchata*,* and another one at night."

"Are you really giving her that . . . vile stuff?" Doña Lupe asked, very alarmed.

"Doctor's orders. He says it's medicinal. Sounds like he's got it backward to me."

"Imagine! Wouldn't you like," Fortunata proposed to the patient, "a little drumstick, some hake, or some croquettes?"

The mere mention of food made Mauricia worse. Her hands trembled vehemently, and now and then she had an attack that made it hard for her to breathe, and she complained about the unbearable heat. While Señora Jáuregui and her niece-in-law were there, la Dura tried repeatedly to cough, but without success. The three women looked at her sorrowfully, wishing they could ease her pain.

"Drink a little water," suggested Fortunata.

But the poor woman improved and started to talk again, catching her breath after every word. "They . . . brought me the kid yesterday. She was so pretty and ladylike!"

"You mean she isn't here with you?" Rubín's wife asked.

"No, Ma'am. She's at school," replied Severiana. "She boards at Doña Visitación's school for girls."

"Yes. She's better off . . . there . . . away from me. Yesterday . . . oh, it was sad! . . . She didn't recognize me. It's been so long since she's seen me . . . she was scared of me, poor angel! Really scared . . . You'd think her mother was the bogeyman or something."

Just then they heard steps, and they all turned to the door. It was Doña Guillermina, rushing as usual, her cheeks aglow, wearing her habitual dark cloak, bulky shoes, wool skirt. Doña Lupe and Fortunata rose, and the founder greeted them with that grace and friendliness she had for everyone, from the king on down to the lowliest beggar. Doña Lupe thought that she wouldn't recognize her, because they had only spoken once, at the orphanage ceremony; but she did recognize her, and even called her by name, for Guillermina was like a great captain who has an extraordinary memory for names and faces and can speak once with a soldier and remember him forever.

"My niece," said the widow, introducing her.

And Guillermina looked at her with a smile.

"I've seen you before . . . at the Micaelas. Glad to meet you."

Then she turned to Mauricia, bracing her hands on the bed.

"Well, and how are you today? Would you like something to eat? Don't worry,

---

*Sweet drink made from a plant called *chufas*. *Horchata de cepa* is a metaphor for wine.

you'll get over this in no time. You'll be ready for Communion tomorrow. How's that conscience? We're going to give it a good scrubbing. That's what you need more than anything. I wanted to take charge of you and make you confess, because if you yourself tell the Lord about your shenanigans, He'll forgive you. So get set. Father Nones will be back this afternoon. He told me that you gave him a good confession. But I've got a feeling there're still some more dregs down there, eh? What do you say?"

Mauricia smiled, abashed. She nodded in the affirmative.

"You know you've got to get rid of the dregs, because the devil will clutch at anything," said the saint, stroking her chin. "So now you know: we're going to have a big party here tomorrow. All right? The one who made heaven and earth will be coming to visit you. You'll think you don't deserve it. Well, even if you don't, He'll be coming, and He'll have his reasons."

The vivacity, wittiness, and fervor with which Guillermina spoke impressed the four women who were listening. Severiana cried two huge tears. Fortunata felt such great admiration for Guillermina that she could have kissed the hem of her dress. "And they say that there aren't any good people left in this world," she thought. "How about her? Giving up everything—her home, her relatives, money, love—and sacrificing her youth for all this work with the poor." It frightened her to measure in her mind the enormous distance separating her from that illustrous lady; it was probably infinite and could never be shortened; even if the saint sinned and she herself did lots of charitable deeds, their two souls would never touch.

The founder, with that energetic activity that characterized all her actions, gave Severiana a few instructions on how to prepare for the ceremony to be held the next day.

"Bring in the table from the other room and put it here to make the altar. I'll have a crucifix sent over and we'll find some flowers. The sheet will have to be changed, and decorate the room the best you can."

Then she went into the living room followed by Doña Lupe, who wanted to be sure to have a hand in things.

"We'll be delighted to come tomorrow. I have a high opinion of Mauricia, who, if it weren't for that cursed vice of hers, would be a good woman—hardworking, loyal . . . Tell me, do you need someone to sit up with her during the night? I'd be glad to stay some evening, and if I can't, my niece—"

"God bless you. We'll call on you. Talk to Severiana. The commandant's wife and I stayed last night. Two people have to stay, because when she has convulsions it takes God and more to hold her down."

"Really," said Doña Lupe in a flattering way, "you set such a good example, Señora, that you make the rest of us better than what we'd be if you didn't exist."

The compliment was well expressed, so Guillermina laughed and thanked her but didn't want to accept it.

"Me set a good example! I wish I could. I'd like for someone to show me what to do. Child, I need to be taught—not to teach."

"What do you mean? You don't even like for someone to say what you're worth. Don't be so good and we won't say such nice things about you."

"Oh, come now. You're just saying that. Who knows what merciful acts you've done in this world without anyone finding out about them; maybe even for Mauricia herself! And you want to pin them on me."

"Me! Dear God! I won't say that I haven't done a few little good deeds that'll stand me in good stead later on. But compare myself with you? Please, don't even think of it."

"Well, we needn't start a quarrel about who sins the least—don't you agree?" said the founder, blending courtesy with modesty and winking in her playful way. "My motto is, 'Let everybody do what he can and knows how to do, and God will be his judge.'"

"That's exactly what I think."

"So if you'll excuse me . . . I have a lot left to do. Till tomorrow, now, and don't fail to come."

Meanwhile, Rubín's wife was alone with the sick woman because Severiana had gone to the kitchen. She fluffed the pillows and the two looked at each other. Fortunata thought of the inexplicable appeal Mauricia held for her, despite the fact that she was so crazy and evil. Was it some sort of depravity of theirs? If Mauricia said something that appealed to her, she felt it echo in her mind as if it were a truth uttered by a supernatural force. The young woman tried repeatedly to analyze this fascination that she felt, but she was never able to explain it. Mysteries of the soul that only God understands.

Mauricia seemed sad, calmed.

"What a lady!" exclaimed Fortunata. "She seems to have come from a different world than ours."

"I bet she did," said la Dura. "What a woman! The day she wanted to get me out of those Protestants' clutches, I flew off the handle and called her names. Oh, was I mean! (She almost cursed, but she stopped herself, because she was not allowed to say bad words, and it was sheer torture for her, not having many words to choose from.) She acted as if something nice had been said. Really, she's something; no one like her. After all that, to bring me here and take care of me the way she does, huh! I don't know what to say! Just look at what she does for me. She must be a first cousin to Christ; nobody can tell me she's not. It hurts to think what we are when you look at her. Us, such sinners! Even if we repent, we're not worth the ground she walks on. And the other one—she's another one from heaven."

"Who?"

"Her young friend, the one that likes my little girl."

Fortunata suddenly felt a cloud in her mind; her heart skipped a beat.

"Jacinta," she said. "Does she come here too?"

"She was here yesterday. She herself brought me my little girl, and let me tell you, when she came in, it was like a light filling the room."

Fortunata felt like running away.

"Have you still got a grudge against her? If you do, you're a mean one. Forgive her. She deserves it well enough. She took away your man, but it wasn't her fault. What the hell! Whoops, there I go again with my bad language. Don't be dumb, girl. What do you think, that your Don Juan won't suddenly fall in love with you again? Don't worry, he will. I can almost picture it. When you're about to die you see things clearly, very clearly. Death lights things up for you, and I can tell you this: your gentleman friend will come back to you. It's the way things go, kid. It can't miss. If you really want to know, he couldn't care less about Jacinta. He doesn't love her a bit. These rich married ladies that have so many things don't love their husbands. They love other men. I don't say it on her account, and God's my witness, but God knows what she does. I don't mean to say she's not an angel. She hands out charity."

Fortunata didn't say anything. The sick woman leaned toward her and, with an evangelical air, admonished her in a religious tone:

"Repent, Fortunata. Don't leave it for later. Repent for everything except for loving the man you love. That's not a sin. Don't steal, don't get drunk, don't tell lies—all right. But as for loving—be free, and too bad for the loser. As long as you live like that nobody can take away your little piece of heaven."

Fortunata was going to answer her friend but couldn't, because Doña Lupe came in, hurrying her up. It was a bit late and they had to make another stop before going home. They said good-bye, promising to come back the next day, and they left. In the street they talked about Guillermina, and Jáuregui's widow remarked:

"That woman has an electrifying effect. When you're with her, you can't help but become saintly yourself. Mauricia owed me fifty-three *reales*. I'd forgotten about it, but believe me, right now I'd be happy if she owed me at least two hundred so I could forget that much too."

2

Two hours before the time set for Mauricia to take Communion, the founder appeared.

"What's come over you, Severiana?" was the first thing she said when she stepped into the hall. "Get that tub out of here. It's hardly what you'd call decoration—dirty clothes and soapsuds."

"I was going to move it, Señorita. Come in. The neighbors said that the two pictures of Napoleon next to the altar should be taken down because they looked very Protestant—you know, Masonic, and—"

"Nonsense. How's our patient today, hmm? How do you feel?"

She was quite weak; her hands were shakier and she was breathing slowly, although not heavily, showing a marked tendency to be still and quiet, her eyes wandering over the ceiling or the opposite wall as if she were tracing the movements of a fly.

Guillermina made a detailed inquiry about how the patient had passed the night, who had stayed with her, what the doctor had said on his morning visit. Severiana filled her in on all the details, telling her that the doctor had prescribed a double dose of nux "comica," * more spoonfuls at night, the powder during the day, and a glass of sherry at regular intervals. Without failing to listen, Guillermina turned her attention to something else. In front of the window and at right angles to the bed they had put a table that was to be the altar, and kneeling on it was Juan Antonio, Severiana's husband, hammering nails into the wall so they could hang the decorative items in place.

"Stop hammering, for heaven's sake. It sounds as if the house is about to cave in. And the noise will bother her. What are you going to put there?"

Severiana came in with some remnants of red and yellow damask that had been curtains forty years ago and had since served a number of purposes. They were going to cover the wall with this cloth, making a Spanish flag, and in the middle of it they were planning to put a print of Christ that the doorman's wife had lent them.

"It doesn't look bad," said Guillermina, taking her glasses out of their case and putting them on. "Let's see what a good job you can do, Juan Antonio. Don't we have some flowers too?"

"Paper flowers . . . just a minute, I'll show you what we've got," replied Severiana, leading the lady into her bedroom and showing her some brushed gold flowers spread out on the table.

There were also some cigar bands and some roses with silver leaves like those used to decorate whistles people blow during the San Isidro festival in May.

"These are ugly," said the saint. "Don't you have any fresh flowers, or at least a branch of something?"

"Yes, Señora. The neighbor in number six, who has some job or other in la

---

* The correct name for this medicine is nux *vomica*, or poison nut. Galdo's reproduces Severiana's pronunciation.

Villa, has promised to bring me a few sprigs of pine and pin oak. Juan Antonio will put these up above to make a border at the top."

"Look for a pretty euonymus plant, child. Really! You seem to be at a loss for ideas," said Guillermina, going back into the living room. "And you could pin some paper flowers on the green branches—it would look very pretty. Come on, Juan Antonio, stop all that hammering—the curtains are nailed enough. Now: hang the Virgin of Sorrows under the Lord, and on either side—"

La Comandanta* came in with a big picture of Pope Pius IX blessing the Spanish troops at Gaeta. Juan Antonio suggested putting a print of the *Numantia* next to it. Guillermina hesitated before agreeing, but finally, with a chuckle and a wink, they resolved their doubts.

"Hang up the ship too—go on, hang it there. After all, everything in the sea belongs to the Lord."

Then she went out into the hall and, having already noticed that the staircase hadn't been swept, she called the doorman's wife:

"Where's your head, woman? Haven't you heard that the Lord is going to visit this house today? And with the hall looking like that! Get a broom, woman! If you don't sweep up, I will. What, do you think I won't do as I say?"

The woman saw that Doña Guillermina was taking off her cloak.

"No, Señorita. Don't get upset. It'll be swept. But just wait till you see how fast these pigs get it all dirty again."

"Then sweep it again."

The lady went down to the courtyard, where a blind man was playing the guitar and some children were imitating a bullfight.

"Hey, children! Today I want you on your best behavior. And mind you don't throw any trash in the hall or on the stairs. And gather up all that rattan and those rushes you've spread out and give them back to the owner."

The children listened without a word. At the back of the courtyard a chairmaker had set up shop. He made rattan chairs and stacked them up against the wall, some dyed red and set up to dry; others, undyed, were cut and stacked. The neighborhood kids were his sworn enemies; they specialized in stealing his rattan for their games and mischief. When he saw the saint speaking to them he came out of his little nook and, facing the infantile squadron, said:

"You heard what the lady said, you brats—behave, and keep your mouths shut, or she'll put you all in jail."

"Maestro Curtis is right, boys," said the founder, putting on the strictest face she was capable of. "You'll be tied up elbow to elbow and taken off to jail if you don't behave properly today, because today the Lord is going to—"

_____
* Severiana's housemate, who is a widow of a commander.

An old priest who was heading straight toward her interrupted. It was Father Nones.

"Good morning, Miss. So you're already up on a platform giving orders for the day."

"I've got to check on everything. If I didn't try to teach these people good manners, you'd come along with the Holy Sacrament and have to plough through all their filth."

"And what difference would it make?" Nones asked laughingly.

"None, naturally. But why shouldn't we have a clean and proper place for the Lord, even if it's only out of self-respect? If the house is cleaned for the lieutenant mayor and the doctor from Public Health with his tasseled canes, it's certainly not going to be left dirty for Our Lord. Stop that, man, for the love of God!"

This last was for the blind guitarist who, having heard about the lady's visit, wanted her to see that he was there, and he had drawn so close that he was practically poking his guitar into her eyes. At the same time he was playing and singing at the top of his lungs.

"Tone it down, for the love of God! You'll make us deaf," said the saint, taking out her purse. "Here, take this and go out in the street and sing. I don't want any fandangos around here today, do you understand?"

The persistent blind man left and the saint resumed her conversation with Father Nones.

"Go up and see if you can bring her around and give her the last blessing. I don't think she's ready for it. The condition of her body seemed worse, and as for her soul—it puzzles me more than ever. What strange notions she has! Go on up. I'll see you later. I'm not leaving till it's over."

Nones went up and the lady, after urging the chairmaker and other neighbors to sweep in front of their doors, was about to go upstairs too; but she was intercepted by two men on their way down. One was Don José Ido del Sagrario, but the witnesses of his romantic feats at the beginning of this story would hardly have recognized him, because he was so clean and well-dressed. From behind he looked like somebody else; but from the front his disjointed body, the warty squalor of his face, and his ever-growing Adam's apple declared his true identity. His companion was a miserable-looking musician who lived off the other courtyard in the same rat's nest that Izquierdo had occupied. The first thing one noticed about him was the enormous scarf wrapped around his neck to well above his ears and down over his chest. He was wearing a braided cap; from the neck down his clothes were skimpy and threadbare. He was shivering and had his right arm looped tightly around the bronze hoops of his trombone, which was pointed forward as if he wanted to yawn with its gaping mouth instead of with his own.

"This gentleman," said Ido as if to introduce him, "is a friend of mine, an Italian, Señora. His name is Señor Leopardi, and he's an unfortunate artist. He told me that if it would please you, he will stand by the staircase when the priest comes and he'll play the royal march."

The poor man murmured something in a strong foreign accent, raising his trembling hand to his cap.

"Why, the things that occur to this man! Holy Mary above!" exclaimed Guillermina benevolently. "Forget about royal marches. No, no; don't take off your hat, you'll catch cold. Gentlemen, the less music the better here, during the ceremony."

Ido and Leopardi looked at each other disconcertedly. The lady's observant eye had taken note of the state of the unfortunate artist's clothes, and she told him to go to his room, play the trombone there to his heart's content, and, finally—

"I'll see if I can find some trousers."

She went upstairs and stopped at every door to exhort the groups of women who were combing their hair.

"By noon I want these little groups broken up, hear? And sweep the corridor clean, all of it. Whoever has candles, put them out; whoever has flowers or pretty potted plants, bring them along . . . And all these rags that are hanging around: get them out of sight."

"Can you use these branches?" asked the tax inspector's wife, standing in her doorway.

"I certainly can. Bring them over. And you, Rita, comb your hair. You look like a madwoman. You must all look very proper."

The night watchman's wife was about to light her husband's lamp and hang it from its pole in the kitchen window grating. Another asked if a petroleum lamp would do. Manila shawls, the long kind, were worn by the little girls, who were to hold the candles at the doorway, and the ones who had new boots were told to wear them; the ones who didn't came as they were, in their rope-soled slippers full of holes.

"There's no need for luxury; just decency," said Guillermina, who imbued all the tenants with her feverish energy.

On her way back to Severiana's, she met Father Nones, who was just leaving.

"I've straightened her out, maestra; she's ready now," said the priest, who had to stoop because he was so much taller than Guillermina. "I'm going to church. We'll be back in forty-five minutes."

The founder went in and saw the altar, which looked very nice. Juan Antonio had nailed the paper flowers along the edges of the lengths of damask, making a sort of frame. They'd achieved a good effect, said the lady, putting on her glasses to see better. Then they covered the table with a very lovely spread which la Comandanta (who was very clever) had made for a raffle. It was checkered and alternated mesh squares with fluffy crimson velvet ones. On top of it was an altar cloth with beautiful lace from the parish church. Then some neighbors came in with pine boughs. They improvised vases by papering some little barrels that were used for storing olives and tuna fish. Juan Antonio, being a paperhanger, took charge of covering and decorating the barrels. With patience and a bit of paste he did wonders. The branches, candy boxes, and prints were arranged, and, last of all, the portraits of Juan Antonio's two brothers, sergeants in red pants and yellow buttons, very vividly painted, peered out from among the pine branches like real soldiers about to pounce on the enemy.

A little while later Estupiñá appeared in a green cloak, carrying under its folds a big bundle that he obviously respected. It was Guillermina's bronze crucifix, a beautiful and rather heavy piece of sculpture that Plácido was not prepared to entrust to anyone except the owner herself. The latter went out to the corridor and received the sacred image and, removing the silk scarf around it, she walked back into the living room looking very much like a real saint from biblical times, miraculously present at the picturesque altar, to be worshiped at that symbol of the ingenuous, firm belief that simple people have. She put the image of Christ in the appointed place, feeling very pleased by the admiration it caused in the onlookers, and then she went out to give Estupiñá further instructions.

"Go to the parish church and accompany the Holy Sacrament, and tell them to bring the candles as soon as they can."

Meanwhile Fortunata and her aunt-in-law had arrived dressed in black, looking very decent, and while the Jáuregui widow stepped in to have her say in Guillermina's group Fortunata went in to see Mauricia. She found her in a rather confused state, dazed. She replied to all questions very concisely because her fear of letting a bad word slip out made her answer strictly. She used only a third of her usual vocabulary, but she was still afraid that even the most common words would have some sort of infernal echo. What Fortunata heard plainly was this: "Oh, what a pleasure to be saved!" But upon uttering these words Mauricia frowned. She was afraid that the word "pleasure" sounded bad. She confided her fears to her friend, who reassured her with a smile and then said that if her intentions were good it didn't matter if she said a dirty word against her will. The sick woman agreed, somewhat calmed; but she wasn't quite in her right mind and seemed to be struggling against a great fear. She pulled Fortunata to her side and said tremblingly:

"Repent for everything, kid; everything. We're very bad, you and me. You have no idea how bad we are."

3

The time was approaching, and the courtyard was filled with the hushed murmurs that precede solemn occasions. The people stood in the space that is inevitably available to the curious; they didn't fit at the main door, where all the children of the neighborhood had agreed to meet, as if they believed the ceremony couldn't take place without them. Guillermina passed inspection, from Severiana's door to the main door, giving orders, checking on everyone's appearance, and sending to the back the ones who didn't look decent enough. An individual who looked like a sexton arrived from the parish church to deliver the candles. Guillermina ordered the girls in shawls to stand in the area of the corridor that the priest would cross and if they didn't already have candles, she saw to it they were supplied. La Comandanta marched over to her like an aide-de-camp to inform her that in the street, right in front of the door, there was a cursed street pianist playing polkas and popular music, which was irreverent and couldn't be tolerated. The saint's reply was that they didn't have to worry about what went on outside; but when she realized that the profane instrument was a nuisance and was beginning to prevent the common people from being edified because it made them feel like dancing, she headed for the main entrance and there spoke to the policeman on duty. All the members of the force who knew Guillermina obeyed her as if she were the governor himself. So the piano was trundled off and its arpeggios and trills could be heard dissolving and jumbling up, as if someone were sweeping notes down the street.

The beautiful moment of solemnity came. Massive murmuring welled up from the courtyard and then, in the heart of the silence that descended over the building like a cloud, a jingling bell rang, marking the entrance of the Sacrament and the retinue. The altar shone like a golden coal in the brilliant light; the gilded dust of the flowers reflected it in dazzling speckles. The windows had been almost completely shut, and there, before the glory of the altar, the people waited on their knees. The ringing sounded nearer and nearer; among the shuffling of feet, the priest's steps could be heard on the stairs, then approaching the door; the ringing grew more vibrant in the corridor, contrasting with the alcolyte's steady praying in Latin. Finally Father Nones appeared, so tall he seemed to touch the ceiling, slightly stooped, hair as white as the wool of an Easter lamb, clutching the chalice between the folds of his white cape. He kneeled in front of the altar and prayed. Mauricia looked at him and his bundle, her eyes half-open and lifeless, her face drained. Guillermina put her head next to Mauricia's. When the priest approached her, the saint whispered into the sick woman's ear as if delivering a secret from the angels: "Open your mouth." The priest said his Corpus Domini Nostri, etc., and all fell silent; Mauricia's eyelids fell shut, projecting the shadow of her long lashes over the circles under her eyes.

Shortly afterward the committee left, preceded by the ringing of the bell, and made its way down the aisle formed by the kneeling women, some with candles and some without. They could be heard going downstairs, out the main door, and down the street. When the ringing had faded away, Guillermina stopped praying and kissed Mauricia. All the others, whimpering or weeping, congratulated her noisily. Finally the saint herself had to order them to stop their rejoicing because it excited the patient too much and might cause a dangerous relapse. But with all the nervous gaiety Mauricia had stopped feeling any pain; it was as if she had been given a powerful anesthetic, the kind that produces unfailing—although short-lived—effects. She hadn't experienced anything like this since she was twelve, when they had taken her to Communion for the first time, and the impression was so vivid it had transported her back to her childhood; for a few moments she was even under the illusion that she was a pure, innocent child who had no notion of mortal sin.

Guillermina also ordered for the room to be cleared of the decorations and the lights put out. Among the many people who had come in were two very well-dressed colorful women wearing coffee-colored cloaks, blue aprons, plaid skirts, and loud scarves on their heads, their hair rising into crests with combs stuck in the top, their shoes perfectly made and fitted. They seemed to be anxious to talk to Mauricia but didn't dare approach her bed. As soon as the ceremony was over, Guillermina studied them carefully and finally decided to acknowledge them.

"Ladies," she said. "What are you here for? If you've come in good faith, that's all very well. But if you've come just to look around, I'm sorry to say that you'd better leave, because you're not needed."

The two in question hastened out and down the stairs, mumbling words that were incongruent with the Latin that had resounded in the same place a few moments earlier. All the women who heard Guillermina's innuendo praised her heartily, and Doña Lupe remarked on their way into the living room:

"You've certainly got a quick tongue, my friend. That's what I call backbone."

"One of them," said Severiana, "is Pepe la Lagarta,* a woman with a reputation, if you know what I mean. They say she killed her husband with a basket-weaving needle . . . a close friend of Mauricia's and she owes her five hundred reales. And she can't get her to pay them back. But do you think she's broke? Ha! I'd like to . . . She spends money like a duchess. Last month she paid for a novena to the Virgin and you should have seen it."

"A novena?"

"Yes, for el Clavelero,† a bullfighter friend of hers who got hit in the Leganés ring. Got the tip of the horn right in his can. Well, el Clavelero got well. So, Señora, you see what the Virgin can do!"

"She knows what's right, silly."

Guillermina left in a little while. The house went back to normal. The commandant's wife and Doña Lupe were in the living room talking about the raffle and the prize, the marvelous spread decorating the altar; Fortunata and Severiana

---

* Josie the Lizard.   † The Carnation boy.

were sitting with Mauricia, who was slowly sinking into a lethargic state because she hadn't slept at all the night before. Doña Fuensanta, who wanted to show Señora de Jáuregui samples of her clever work, invited her into the house next door. It must be confessed that Doña Lupe was somewhat disillusioned, for she thought that Guillermina was always accompanied on her charity visits by a regiment of ladies. "But then where are all those 'distinguished ladies' the newspapers talk about? From what I can see, I'm the only 'lady' here."

When Mauricia had fallen sound asleep, Fortunata went out to the living room. There wasn't anyone there. She went to the window and looked out at the street distractedly for a long time, her mind wandering until a noise in the hall snapped her out of her trancelike state. When she turned around she had a shock: it was Jacinta peering in from the door to see who was there. Holding her hand was a little girl dressed stylishly but simply, without the slightest touch of affected elegance. Jacinta stepped toward Fortunata inquiringly with an angelic smile that was unforgettable. Rubín's wife felt terribly upset; she didn't know how to react, but felt fear in the presence of such superiority. She blushed deeply, then turned white as a sheet. Jacinta must have asked her something; undoubtedly she wasn't able to reply. Señora Santa Cruz headed toward the door that led to the other room. Then Fortunata, who was behind her, said:

"She's asleep now."

Turning toward her again, Jacinta gave her that look and smile, which were devastating.

"In that case we'll wait for awhile," she said in an almost imperceptible voice, sitting down in one of the straw chairs.

Fortunata didn't know what to do. She didn't have the courage to leave so she sat on the sofa. At almost the same moment the Dauphine felt her chair wobble and moved to the sofa. The two were together, skirt to skirt. To avoid looking at her rival, Fortunata looked at the little girl, who was standing facing her, and took her hands. Rubín's wife observed Adoración's little blue dress, her boots, her whole decent outfit, and in the course of her prying inspection, her eyes me-Jacinta's several times. "Oh, if you only knew who you're sitting next to," thought Fortunata, and with this her fear faded a bit, letting her anger revive itself. "If I told you who I am, you might suffer more than me." Adoración wanted to say something, but Jacinta put her hand over the child's mouth and, looking at Rubín's wife, she smiled the ingenuous kind of smile that seems to say, "Let's talk to each other." The other understood it and said to herself: "No, I'm not going to help you start a conversation." The child, living proof of the Dauphine's kindness, couldn't help but stir new thoughts in Fortunata's mind. But her renewed hatred was trying to poison her admiration for her rival. "Oh yes, Señora," she thought. "We all know about your endless perfections. Why brag about them so much? In a little while, even the blind will be singing your praises. If we lived like you, around decent people and married to the man we liked, and had all our basic needs taken care of, we'd be the same. Yes, I'd be like you, if I could be in your place. So your virtues aren't anything out of this world, and there's no need for tooting your horn so much. And if you don't think I'm right, come take my place, the place I've had since *he* tricked me, and then we'd see what all your perfection looks like."

And the looks that Santa Cruz's wife gave her pierced her again. They were her silent comment on some silly or childish thing Adoración had said to her. For some reason or other the presence of the child and those looks from Jacinta made another thought flash through Fortunata's mind. She remembered that Jacinta had wanted to adopt another child thinking that he was her husband's son. "And mine! . . . Thinking that it was mine!" From the height of this reflection she plunged into a veritable abyss of confusion and contradictions. Would she have done the same? "Well, maybe not . . . or maybe so . . . or maybe so . . . I don't know." And if only Pituso hadn't been an invention of Izquierdo's; if at that very moment, instead of seeing Mauricia's little girl in front of her, she could see her poor little Juanín! She had such a strong urge to cry that in order to contain herself she summoned up her wrath, remembering all that she'd suffered, feeling certain that this would extricate her from the maze she was in. "Because you took away what was mine, and if God did justice, you'd put yourself in my place and I'd be in yours, you big thief . . ." She didn't continue in this vein because Jacinta, who could no longer resist the urge to start a conversation, looked at her and asked:

"How was Communion? And how is Mauricia?"

Once again, the fallen woman was abashed, not knowing how to reply.

"Fine . . . just fine. Mauricia's happy."

Fortunata was very thankful that the door to the bedroom opened softly at that moment and Severiana's head appeared. Adoración ran toward her.

"Shhh!" said her aunt, tiptoeing in. "Don't make any noise now, because your mamá's sleeping. She hasn't slept this long for some time. Oh, Señorita, what you missed! It was all so fine it was a pleasure."

While the Dauphine and Severiana talked, Fortunata, who was still seated, scrutinized *his* wife, getting a good look at her dress, her coat, then her hat. It didn't seem right for her to have come in a hat; but other than that, there was nothing to criticize. The coat was perfect. Rubín's wife decided she'd have one made just like it. And as for the skirt—what elegance! Where could she have found that material? It must have come from Paris.

Mauricia's hoarse voice could be heard. Her sister went running in and Jacinta looked through the door, which was ajar. When Severiana returned to the living room, Jacinta said:

"I'm not going in. You go in with the child. I'll stay here."

Even though her own faculties were disturbed, Fortunata was able to grasp why Jacinta was reluctant to go in with the child. It was out of modesty and delicacy. She wanted to spare the poor patient from having to express any gratitude, and also spare her the embarrassing role of neglectful mother.

"Could that be why she doesn't want to go in?" she wondered, looking at her from behind. "She's so finicky! When I say all this perfection really bothers me . . . Aren't we nice, though. Well, as for me, I'm going in."

Severiana went over to the bed, taking the child by the hand.

"Look, look who I've brought you. Which visit do you like the most, this one or the people who were here before?"

Mauricia flung her arms around her daughter and showered her with kisses. A bit scared, the little girl kissed her mother back, not affectionately, but rather the way obedient children kiss anyone their teacher tells them to kiss.

"Oh, how bad I've been!" exclaimed the sick woman, also uneffusively, like someone merely performing a duty. "My little darling, you do well to love the Señorita more than me, because I've been really ornery! Dmn—"

The word caught on her tongue and she made believe she was spitting. Then she cast longing looks every which way, saying:

"Severiana, or you, or anyone—if you'd only give me—!"

Doña Lupe and Doña Fuensanta had come in too.

"How do you feel, Mauricia? This is a happy day for you. You've received the Lord and you're seeing your little girl. And isn't she a pretty girl!"

But la Dura's whole being was caught up in her burning physical anxiety, and her eagle eyes were fixed on Severiana, who was pouring some of the contents of a bottle into a glass. The liqueur shone, shooting out rays like topaz set in gold. "Oh, just look at you craving for it, you witch," thought the skeptical and observant Doña Lupe. "That's the Eucharist that you like, good sherry . . ." And watching her drink it, the sharp woman mused: "Eh, go ahead and smack your lips. You didn't do this when you received the Holy Sacrament."

After the drink Mauricia seemed to revive, and her face shone with life and contentment. Then she proved that in the depths of her being she did have maternal instincts and feelings; she embraced and tenderly kissed the daughter she had carried in her womb. And she got so excited that the others began to fear she would faint, so they took her child away.

"Yes, let them take you away, away from me. I don't deserve you; you're afraid of me, baby. And if you ever act up, they won't say 'The bogeyman will get you' but 'Your mother'll get you.' Oh, what a pity! But I agree. They say I have to save myself. Won't that be good! And my daughter's better off on earth with the Señorita than in heaven with me. And that's all there is to it."

Adoración, upset and afraid, burst into tears. She had to be taken out of the room finally; the spectacle couldn't go on. Mauricia kept blowing kisses into the air and saying things that touched the others. "Oh, yes," thought Doña Lupe, who was moved too, "you really love your daughter. You'd drink her if you could!"

Fortunata didn't wait till the end of the scene. She felt so deeply disturbed that she was afraid she'd either burst out crying or explode. She retreated to the inner room and there, leaning on a trunk, she burst into tears. The feelings that gushed forth with her tears were not solely products of the circumstances; they came from a deep old sediment in her soul, her by now habitual misfortune, spite mixed with a vague wish to be good, "and yet not being able to" . . . "You really had to try it out to know what it meant."

She wept profusely when she heard Jacinta's carriage leaving, and then she went back into the living room. Doña Lupe was saying good-bye to Doña Fuensanta and offering to buy ten raffle tickets; she made a sign to her niece-in-law that it was time to leave. They took a last look at the patient, pressed her hand, and left. As they were walking along the street, Doña Lupe, who sensed what a vivid impression Fortunata had received upon meeting Señora Santa Cruz, tried to allude to it several times, but her innate prudence and delicacy kept her garrulous tongue in check.

4

At the door to her house they parted; Doña Lupe went upstairs and Fortunata continued on to the pharmacy where Maxi was all alone mixing a plaster. His wife told him in great detail all she had witnessed that day. She discreetly omitted Jacinta's visit. The pharmacist was pleased that his other half had had some part in a charitable affair, observed exemplary ladies, and seen for herself such deeply human pictures of suffering and death, for it was all undoubtedly more profitable to her soul than parties or some other form of light entertainment.

At mealtime they continued to talk about the same subject, Doña Lupe pondering on the moving solemnity of the ceremony. They debated over whether they should go back to Mira el Río that night or to Variedades to see a play, but since Fortunata couldn't stand theatrical performances the first idea prevailed and Maxi, who was very satisfied with his wife's interest in pious acts, promised to take them and then pick them up at eleven o'clock.

"And if there's no one to watch over her tonight I'll stay," said the widow, who couldn't be quite content until she gave Guillermina clear proof of her humility and abnegation.

Her nephew and his wife were both opposed to the idea. The former said that a good deed was well and fine but it shouldn't be carried too far. The Jáuregui woman answered with becoming modesty:

"But I'm not doing it for praise! There's no merit in it. I can take a night on my feet perfectly well; in fact I could stand two or three, so—"

It must have been nine o'clock when the three of them entered the main door to the tenement, and they were fairly astonished to see the courtyard ablaze; a bonfire had been lit, and torches with quivering flames gave the scene an awesome, fantastic look. What was all this? The neighborhood pranksters had set fire to a pile of straw in the middle of the courtyard and then stolen all the reeds (Maestro Curtis') they could get their hands on; and, lighting them at one end, they began to play "Viaticum," a game that consisted of lining up two by two, holding the reeds like candles and slowly marching "saying stuff in Latin" to the sound of a bell (which one of them imitated) and the royal march they all played on imaginary horns. The fun consisted of breaking up the procession unexpectedly and jumping over the bonfire. The boy who carried the ciborium, well wrapped up with a flannel undershirt tied around his neck, leaped about recklessly and even jumped like a goat, using all his skill to assume a reverent pose the second he regained a vertical position. In short, the scene gave one an inkling of what it must be like in those regions of hell that are used as playgrounds for Satan's children. Maximiliano and his wife paused a minute to watch, but Doña Lupe directed scornful looks and remarks at the troop of children, saying that it was their parents' fault for allowing such sacrilege.

They went upstairs, and when Fortunata went inside to see Mauricia, who was alone, Maxi left, saying that he would be back at eleven. That night the patient was extremely restless, and what little she did say was hardly an example of clarity. Her fear of using bad words seemed to have disappeared, because she spat out a few that shocked the ear. Her memory must not have been too reliable, because when her friend said, "Quiet now, and remember this morning," she retorted, "This morning! What happened?" And looking up at the ceiling with glazed eyes, she seemed to be making a painful effort to recall the events, reaching for memories as if she were swatting flies. The scene with her daughter stood out in her mind more than receiving the Sacrament. Oh, what a scene it had been!

"Did you see la Jacinta?" she asked Fortunata, rolling over onto her side and putting her hand on her friend's shoulder. "Did she talk to you? You're a dunce and you don't have any guts. If the same thing'd happened to me with that goodie-goodie; if one of those prudes tried to take away my man and got in my way, wow! They don't call me la Dura* for nothing. If I had her in front of me, I mean if she tried to come sweet-talk me, I'd grab her by the hair and pull! Pull it hard and slap her till I killed her."

---

* Hard as nails, or "hard boiled."

Mauricia's actions expressed her words; she went into violent contortions, threw off her covers, ground her teeth. Fortunata couldn't hold her down and called Severiana:

"Come here, please! She's talking nonsense. For the love of God, subdue her. Give her something to calm her down . . . a drink—"

"Nobody can keep me quiet," the wretched woman cried out, her eyes bulging from their sockets as she struggled against the four arms trying to hold her down. "I'm Mauricia la Dura, the one that punched a hole in the head of that thief that stole my shawls; the one that pulled la Pepa's hair out; the one that scratched up Doña Malvina's face, the *Protestant*. Let go of me you bitchy prude or I'll take off half your face with one bite. *You* decent! *You*—throwing over one soldier to take up with another. You've got a heart like the Alcalá Gate, so many men have been through it. Ha ha ha! You wolf-woman, filthy Jew. You drool like a mad dog. Spittoon-face, old bag! Just wait till I get my hands on you, I'm going to yank off your nose and spit in your eye. I'll rip out your guts—"

Eventually, what had been a human voice coming out of her frothing mouth turned into the roars of a cornered beast. Unable to free her arms from the vigorous ones restraining her, her fingers clutched with convulsive rage at whatever they touched, clawing at the sheets and furniture. Her moaning soon tired her, though, and her contortions grew less violent; finally she collapsed, exhausted. Sleep was an instant sedative and, indeed, looked more like death.

Señora Rubín was terrified. Severiana said to her:

"She's already had three of these attacks tonight and the night before last she had six. If the doctor came, he'd calm her by giving her one of those little pinpricks they call 'yections'—you know what I mean? A little drop of morphine."

No doubt due to the frequency of the attacks, Severiana took them relatively calmly, like a medical person who's used to seeing spectacles of human suffering in a clinic. Once Mauricia had quieted down, Severiana prepared the lamp for the night: a glass of water, oil, and a night taper on top.

The shrew dozed for about half an hour, every now and then uttering fragments of words and uncouth phrases like the remains of a storm that has passed. Then she woke up, and in a calm voice said to her friend:

"Are you still here? It's so good to see you! Of all the people here you're the one I like the most. I like you more than my sister. The first thing I'm going to ask of the Lord when I get to heaven is to make you happy by giving you what's yours and only yours; what they took away from you. His Divine Majesty can fix it up if He wants."

Nothing occurred to Fortunata as a reply to this nonsense.

"'Cause you've suffered, poor thing. Some mean tricks have been played on you in this life. The poor always underneath, and the rich women kicking us in the face. But don't you worry, the Lord'll fix things up; He'll do justice and give you back what they took from you. I know He will, I just dreamed it when I fell asleep and thought I was dying and being taken to heaven by a band of angels. They were so pretty! Believe me, I saw it all. And I personally will ask the Virgin and the Holy Trinity to make you happy and remember the hard times you've been through."

She fell silent for a moment, and after Fortunata sighed a few times, the sick woman continued:

"Have you seen Jacinta? She's the one that brought me my little girl. She's an angel, that woman. When I dreamed I was in heaven just now, I saw her on top of a cloud with a white veil. There she was, smack in the middle of all those angels. Do you suppose she's going to die? I'd be sorry for my daughter's sake. But God knows more than we do, right? And whatever He does, He's got a good reason for doing it. Tell me, did she talk to you? Did you say anything stupid? It would've been wrong. 'Cause it's not her fault. Forgive her, kid, forgive her; the first thing you got to do to be saved is to turn the other cheek. Look at me—all I do is obey Father Nones, and I've forgiven la Pepa, la Matilde—who wanted to poison me—and Doña Malvina the Protestant and everybody, dam——! Stop it mouth, you're doing it again. Yeah, forgive people. Listen to what I say. See how calm I am? Well, you'll be the same, and God'll give you your due, there's no doubt about it; that's the way it is. And by the holiness I've got in me, I tell you that if the Señorita's husband wants to come back to you and you take him, you wouldn't be sinning—"

Fortunata thought it best to cut her short, because this last notion didn't harmonize very well with the holiness she was bragging about.

"I think," she said, "that if Father Nones heard what you just said, he'd scold you because, uh, whoever rules, rules, and it's not right for things to change."

"What a laugh! What do you know about it? I've repented for all my evil deeds. I've forgiven everybody. What more do they want? What I'm telling you is just a flash I had. Can't I have ideas? When I die you'll see, God will tell me I'm right."

She stopped again, weary from talking, and Fortunata ordered her to stay quiet. Suddenly she grew restless again and, grabbing her friend's hand, she asked with fear in her eyes:

"What do you think—will I be saved?"

"Why doubt it?" replied Fortunata, reassuring her. "They say that even though a person's sins are too many to count, like grains of sand, imagine all the sand there must be in the sea."

"Oh, I know how much sand there is on all the shores and in all the sea!" echoed Mauricia in a pathetic voice.

"Well, even if someone's committed more sins than all the sand there is, God will forgive them if they really repent."

"And how about, say, an idea? Is that a sin too?"

"It depends. But you don't have any evil ideas. Don't worry."

"May God hear you. It breaks my heart to see you so sad, with a man you don't love. It's so sad for you! Die with me, kid; come with me. We'll be so much happier up there, you'll see. I love you so much! Embrace me, kid, and die with me."

"D—Don't push me," stammered Fortunata, who, very moved, caressed her friend. "I probably will die soon. The world doesn't need me . . . I don't know . . . It'd be better to . . . Oh, but I'm miserable!"

"D——! Bless your soul! The first thing I'm going to ask the Lord—I swear it on the cross—is to let you die."

The two of them started crying.

Meanwhile, Doña Lupe was engaged in a lively debate with Severiana.

"So. That's the end of it. There's nothing more to be said. I'm staying tonight so that you can rest a bit."

"Señora, I won't have it. There are neighbors who can stay."

"Neighbors! Fine hands the patient would be in. They're so clumsy and careless! They'd get all the medicines mixed up."

"No, Señora, I simply won't let you go to such trouble."

"And I repeat that I'm staying. There's no merit in it. It's no sacrifice for me. It doesn't bother me a bit to sit up all night. And besides, we've got to do something for others, don't we? So I'll sit with her, and don't mention your gratitude. It's ridiculous to make such a fuss over nothing."

Jáuregui's widow was not making any great sacrifice, and her determination was cleverly calculated, for one of the neighbors had told her that Guillermina was planning to take up a collection for her charitable projects the next day, and Doña Lupe had reasoned as follows: "If I spend the night tending the patient, I'll be doing my share; I don't care much about the collection, so I just won't show up tomorrow."

Severiana gave the Señora minute instructions on how to care for the patient and told her to send for her if anything came up. Another neighbor would stay to assist her. At midnight Fortunata went home with her husband. Their arms linked, they made their way home over the more winding than long stretch home, talking about alcoholism and domestic assistance, strongly doubting that Doña Lupe would be able to stay awake all night, because she was someone who, as soon as the clock struck ten, started to nod, even if she was visiting at a friend's or had callers at home.

The next morning Fortunata decided to find out how Doña Lupe had borne up under her sleepless night, and Maximiliano consented. After finishing the familiar duties that the head of the house had assigned her, Fortunata left with Papitos, and after directing her to do the marketing, she headed for Mira el Río. There she found her aunt-in-law in Doña Fuensanta's room in a truly sorry state—bags under her eyes, heavy-headed, and rather cross.

"Hurray for your courage!" said Fortunata. "So how did the patient behave?"

"Don't speak of it, child; I've never spent such an awful night in my life. She didn't let me nod off for even ten minutes. I'd swear she did it on purpose, to get even with me for making her be honest when she sold shawls for me. Imagine: she was delirious right up until dawn. I'd swear that all the alcohol she's ever drunk went to her head last night. She got up, she tossed around, she flung those big legs out of bed and waved her arms like windmills. And the shouting and screaming! Well, you know what her vocabulary's like. And then she huddled up like a cat ready to pounce—her eyes aglitter, mumbling on, and pointing at the table where the altar and the night light are—and she said: 'Look, look—there he is!' I was scared stiff. I'd rather hear her shout than that. Believe me, I was paralyzed with fear when I saw her point to the light and the little altar."

Doña Lupe started to drink the hot chocolate Doña Fuensanta had brought her, and after a few sips continued her tale, imitating the delirious woman's voice and gestures.

"And she said: 'There he is, look at him, Sor Natividad's Lord. The wretch has him locked up. Wretch, bitch . . .' Do you know who Sor Natividad's Lord is? The monstrance, child, the Holy Sacrament. And she went on saying: 'I'm going to get you; I'm going to take you out of there and throw you in the well.' The well! Can you imagine? Throw the monstrance in the well! You can see what evil thoughts fill her mind. Then she says she's going to be saved. If she could be saved . . . ! Severiana said that whenever she gets delirious, she always comes up with the same thing: that she's going to take the monstrance out of the ciborium and lock it up in her trunk or something like that. She burst out in such an eerie laugh my hair stood on end, and she said in a very hushed voice: 'Oh, how handsome you are with your white face, with your host's face in that jeweled frame. Oh, how *handsome* you are! Don't think I'm going to steal the jewels. I don't want them. I like you. I could eat you up! Don't tell me not to pick you up, 'cause I'm going to, even though I die and you send me to hell. Sor Natividad's cheating on you; with Father Pintado, if you want to know.' Anyway, child, it was horrid. I've left out the choicest bits; it would burn my tongue to repeat them."

Doña Lupe tried to half-lick, half-suck with her lips what was left in the bottom of the cup, and when she finally managed to, she ended thus:

"I spent the whole night listening to this sacrilegious nonsense, horrified; my stomach was upset and all I wanted was for day to come."

"I expected as much," said Fortunata, and then she told Doña Lupe what she had done at home and what she had instructed Papitos to buy.

"It feels as if I've been away for a year! I was afraid that the two of you wouldn't be able to manage without me, and that the little rascal would give you trouble. Let's go home now. We've done our duty here. Naturally this hasn't been especially saintly on my part, or any kind of heroism; but it's something, anyway."

Then they saw Guillermina heading for Severiana's, and Doña Lupe rushed out to receive from such an august mouth the praise she deserved.

"You're so good," said the saint, taking Doña Lupe's hands in hers. "To stay here and look after this poor woman! No, no; don't try to tell me it was nothing. It *was* something. To leave the comfort of your own home to stand watch over the sick bed of an unfortunate woman! Not everyone would do what you've done. May God reward you. This deserves more thanks than the donations others give while they stay tucked in their own beds. Yours is true charity, the kind that comes from the heart. But I see that I'm offending your modesty and I don't want to make you blush, my friend. Thank you."

Doña Lupe was very satisfied, but since she was afraid that the founder might produce the feared collection box, she said her farewells hastily.

"Dear friend, duty calls me at my humble home—"

"Yes, yes, I know," said Guillermina. "Duty comes first. Till later."

And taking Fortunata aside in the hall, Doña Lupe said to her:

"You stay for a little while; if there's a collection we're not going to make a bad show. Tell her to put down a *duro* from you and one from me. That's enough. She knows very well that we're not wealthy. I don't like collections, but I know what my obligations are at all times and I don't intend to shirk them. So a *duro* from each of us; don't forget now. Don't say whether or not that's all we can give. Just announce it, without apologizing or making a show of it. No matter how little you give her, she always thanks you for it with the same sweet little mouth. Oh, I can hardly believe I'll soon be inside my own four walls again."

5

When Fortunata, after chatting awhile with Doña Fuensanta, returned to the other house, she saw things that dumbfounded her. Guillermina had left her veil and prayer book on the sofa and was helping Mauricia with the most painful of the tasks involved in caring for the sick; she applied herself mechanically to the most repulsive of tasks, as if she were obliged to do so and used to doing it. Severiana tried to stop her, but Guillermina wouldn't give in.

"Let me do it, it doesn't bother me a bit. Go see what Juan Antonio wants; he's been shouting for some time."

The poor working woman wished she had three or four bodies so that she could attend to everything.

"Please, let me. How can I let the lady—?"

When Rubín's wife saw this commotion and the few people there were for so many tasks, she gladly offered to help. Guillermina's activity was enough to impress anyone. Fortunata didn't feel up to as much. But when she saw the illustrious aristocratic lady humble herself, she was ashamed that she didn't have the courage to imitate her and, summoning up what little strength she had, she offered to help. As a woman of the people, she didn't want to be less than a highborn lady in those lowly tasks.

"Get away, for God's sake, child," replied the saint. "I won't hear of it; I won't let you. Do you want to help us? Well, if you have such good intentions, sweep up the living room. The doctor's coming."

Fortunata had hardly picked up the broom when Severiana came in, and without even asking, took it away from her.

"That's the limit, Señora! You'll get covered with dust."

"For heaven's sake, let me help you. Do you want me to make your husband's lunch?"

"Imagine your doing—!"

"What, do you think I don't know how? An omelet goes in his lunch basket, and the roll should be sliced open with a sardine in it. I've made more workers' lunches than I've got hairs on my head."

"We've lit the fire in the neighbor's house. Doña Fuensanta's there, but she's going out to do the marketing. If you'd do us the favor . . ."

Fortunata didn't need to hear any more. She went back to the other house, where she found the commandant's wife in a state because there were three lunches to make: one for Juan Antonio and two for workers whose wives had gone to the factory and left her in charge.

"Go shopping," she said, "and I'll take care of the omelets."

Doña Fuensanta was very thankful for this; she put on her red shawl over her plaid dress and didn't change from her thick slippers, picked up a basket and her change purse, and went to ask Severiana, who was in a cloud of dust in the living room, what to buy.

"Bring me a pig's foot like the one you brought the other day, to salt it; a quarter of a pound of ribs . . . I have bacon . . . Oh, and don't forget the carrots, and a quarter of a hen. If you get any mutton brains, bring me some too. And if you see a good tongue, have it scraped for me and I'll salt it for both of us."

The widow limped out and down the stairs and shortly afterward Juan Antonio and the other two workers left with their respective lunch bags. Señora Rubín had done her task quickly and well, and as she was washing her hands, she let her mind wander to a subject that wasn't new to her. "This is what I'd like—work, be the wife of an honest worker that loved me! Don't try to get around it, kid: you were born with the common people and you'll be common all your life. It's in your bones; you can't change it. Good manners will never be in you."

When she went in to tell Severiana that the men's lunch was prepared, her friend had finished cleaning up the living room. Since there was such a bad smell there, they brought in a trowel of hot coals and, throwing in a handful of lavender, they took it through the whole house, from the hall to the kitchen. After the fumigation Fortunata went in to see Mauricia, whom she found in very poor condition—noticeably weakened and dejected. The doctor, who had just arrived, gave her a thorough examination and detected swelling in her legs and stomach. The disturbing paralysis was increasing at a terrifying rate. Before leaving, the doctor spoke with Guillermina in the living room; he said it couldn't help but end badly and that she would only live two days at the most. Fortunata was approaching them to hear his diagnosis when she suddenly saw a person at the door whose presence caused an electric shock in her. "Good God, it's *her* again! . . . I'm leaving."

Jacinta and Guillermina talked with the doctor for a moment and then he left.

"I'll go in to see her in a minute," said the Dauphine to her friend, sitting down on the sofa. "Are you going to be here long?"

"I have to go to the other corridor where the shoemaker lives. Poor man, he didn't want to go to the hospital. I've never seen a case of dropsy as bad as his. The poor man's belly was like a barrel last night, and they've already drilled him three times, but yesterday all they were able to get out was half a liter and they say that his body has no less than fourteen. What suffering people endure, Lord above!"

Fortunata went into the bedroom and returned in a few minutes, saying that Mauricia was sound alseep. Then the founder made a humorous remark. Turning to both of them, she said:

"Do you hear that trombone playing the royal march?"

Indeed, it was far away but very clear; they could hear the royal march being played frenetically by Leopardi, who upon repeating it was overly generous with his mordants and appoggiaturas.

"Ever since that poor man," added the saint, suppressing her laughter, "found out that I was here, he's been playing it for all he's worth. It's his way of reminding me that I promised to give him a suit of clothes; his lungs are in much better shape than his clothes, I'm afraid. Look," she proposed to Jacinta, taking her by the arm, "as soon as you get home today, see if your husband has some trousers he has outworn. He may not, because we've rifled his wardrobe so many times already . . . !"

"I don't know," and Señora Santa Cruz, trying to recollect. "Let me see, I think—"

"If he doesn't have any," Rubín's wife hastened to add, "I'll bring some of my husband's."

"May God reward you, child. It's really heartbreaking to see that poor man in this cold, wearing linen pants, the kind that the soldiers wear in Cuba."

Guillermina left for the lumberyard in La Ronda, and Jacinta escorted her to the outer corridor. Fortunata sat down on the sofa, thinking that both women had left; but after discussing several matters with her friend, Jacinta said:

"I'll wait for you here. Take my carriage and when you finish come back for me; we'll leave together."

She came back in immediately and sat down next to Fortunata.

Sitting beside her! Couldn't she read in her eyes that they could never be together anywhere! These were the thoughts that raced through Maxi's wife's mind; she felt an urge to escape, then shame and fear of doing it. If the other woman spoke to her, she'd have no choice but to reply. "If I told her who I am, she'd shake all over. Then we'd see who was afraid."

Jacinta looked at her. Her curiosity had already been stirred the day before by such expressive beauty. And when her eyes met those piercing black eyes, she felt a somewhat unpleasant sensation; a vague presentiment, as if she were coming into contact not with an object, but with the rush of air an object stirs as it quickly passes by.

"According to the doctor," said the Dauphine, who had resolved to break the ice, "poor Mauricia hasn't got a chance."

"She hasn't got a chance," Fortunata echoed rather awkwardly, for she feared that her language wouldn't be refined enough.

"If she doesn't improve, I'll bring her little girl to see her this afternoon. I should bring her in any case, don't you think?"

"Yes, bring her."

Jacinta knew that the stranger was not single, because she had offered a pair of her husband's trousers. So she naively asked what she always asked any married woman she met:

"Do you have any children?"

"No, Señora," Rubín's wife answered rather curtly.

"I don't either. But I like children so much you could even say I'm obsessed with them, and I wish other people's were mine. Believe me, I wouldn't have any scruples about stealing one if I could."

"I wouldn't either, if I could," declared Fortunata, who didn't want to be second to her rival in that maternal mania.

"Did yours die, or didn't you have any?"

"I had one, Señora . . . about four years ago . . ."

"And in four years you haven't had another? How long have you been married? Forgive me for being too inquisitive."

"Me?" Fortunata murmured hesitantly. "Five years. I got married before you did."

"Before me!"

"Oh yes, Señora. As I was saying, I had a child and he died; and if he were still alive, I'd—"

As the lady detected an unusual glimmer and shiftiness in her interlocutor's eyes, she began to wonder if the woman was mentally disturbed. The look in her eyes and her tone were very strange, in fact out of place in the calm conversation they were having. "I'd better leave this woman alone," thought Jacinta. "I won't ask her anything else."

They were silent for a while, their eyes downcast. Jacinta didn't think about anything in particular; Fortunata did: the story of her whole life blazed through her mind like a fire. Harsh words rushed to the tip of her tongue; she wanted to curse that "monkey face out of heaven" who had stolen her property. After all, wasn't it completely unfair? Insults crowded her mind and pushed their way recklessly to her lips, as they do in common people when they start to argue. "I'll grab her and—" she said to herself, digging her nails into her own arms. "So she's an angel? Well, let her be. And a saint? So what?" But she didn't unbutton her lips. "What a coward I am! With just a word, I could knock her down and have her so afraid of me she wouldn't dare ask me any more questions."

Meanwhile the "angel face," who was impatient because Guillermina hadn't arrived, went out to the corridor a minute. Once she was alone, the other woman thought she felt brave enough to make a scene. All her crudeness and stormy passion, which made her a typical woman of the people, the burning sincerity and lack of good manners that seethed in her soul, and an incredible self-inducement gave her the impetus to show herself as she really was, without the slightest trace of a hypocritical disguise. "What if she doesn't come back?" she mused, looking toward the corridor; and upon saying this she had a sudden insight into the reality of things: "She's a worthy woman and I'm not. But I'm right, whether I've been worthy or not, and justice is on my side, because she would be me if she was in my place."

At this the "monkey" returned. Seeing her was like being blinded. She lost control of her actions, and instead obeyed an impulse stronger than her will; like a hunting dog she pounced on her enemy. The two clashed in the narrow hall. The wicked woman dug her nails into her victim's arms and Jacinta looked at her in terror, as you would a wild beast. Then she saw a brutally ironic smile illuminate the stranger's face and she heard a murderous voice say clearly:

"I am Fortunata."

Jacinta was speechless. Then she uttered a sharp cry, like a person bitten by a snake. Fortunata nodded her head affirmatively, insolently, repeating:

"I . . . I am—"

But she was so breathless that she couldn't articulate the rest of her statement. The Dauphine lowered her eyes and, jerking abruptly, freed herself. She tried to say something, but couldn't. The other drew back, her eyes ablaze, panting, and, walking backward, she kept talking, although the words didn't come out clearly now: "I'll grab you and knock you down, because if I was in your place, I'd be—" She caught her breath at this point and was able to say: "Better than you, better than you!"

Santa Cruz's wife was the first to regain her serenity, and, walking into the living room, she headed for the sofa. Her attitude revealed as much dignity as it did innocence. She was the one who had been attacked, and now she was able not only to regain her composure more quickly but also be the first to forgive. The other woman, on the contrary, was filled with regret. Oh, but her actions weighed on her! She had lost all control, been so brutal! She felt as if the house had fallen down on top of her. She didn't have the strength to go back into the living room; she trembled to think what Severiana would say if she found out. And Doña Guillermina! She ran for cover to Doña Fuensanta's room, where she had left her veil and muff. Cowardice impelled her to run out to the street. Escape, yes, and not set foot again in that house or any place where she might have such an encounter. She left noiselessly, slipping out, and as she approached the door, looked back into the living room and saw her there, at the end of the long telescopic corridor. She saw her in profile, her hand on her cheek, very pensive; but Jacinta did not see her. She left, remembering one of the lessons Feijóo had given her: "Never lose control." Well, she'd certainly lost control today . . . "But actually," she debated, trying to calm herself, "what did I do to hurt her? Nothing. I only told her who I was, so she'd know me."

Then, strangely enough, she had an urge to wait for Jacinta, to see her leave. She stood watch on Bastero Street, and five minutes later saw the founder enter the house. "They'll go by way of Toledo Street," she thought. "From there I'll be able to see them without them seeing me." She headed for Toledo Street and once there picked out a spot on the opposite side of the street, next to a tavern. Fifteen minutes later the carriage with the two ladies appeared at the corner. "They're talking about me, and she's telling her what happened. She's imitating me, mimicking my movements when I grabbed her by the arms. Good God, what do you suppose they're saying? I can almost hear them: 'She's a dangerous character.' 'She should be sent to a reformatory.'"

6

As she climbed the stairs to her house, the young woman's conscience began to clearly reprove her for her actions. "It would have been much better," she thought, slowing her steps and pausing on every stair, "to have kept calm when I said, 'I am Fortunata,' so I could have watched her expression when she heard it. Then I could have just waited to see how she took it, and I could have thrown in a few other things, like telling her that I'm decent too, of course, and that her husband's a rat. To see how she would have reacted."

Entering the house she found that Doña Lupe was very cross with Papitos, on whose innocent shoulders she was depositing the bad mood that a sleepless night had caused. She found fault with everything that had been done in her absence and went so far as to say that she couldn't even leave on a charitable mission because whenever she turned her back things went wrong. Fortunata realized that she could be a target too, and since she had no desire to argue, she made no reply to her aunt-in-law's grumblings.

"What a blunder—to have ordered these flank muscles and loin that even the cat wouldn't touch! You must have a hole in the head. I know, as soon as I take my eyes off you, you make a mess of things."

Fortunata began to feel ill. She started to shiver, was getting a headache, and felt like yawning again and again. Doña Lupe detected signs of her perturbation in her face and inquired very solicitously:

"Do you feel nauseous or dizzy?"

"I don't know what's wrong with me, but I feel like lying down."

On her way to the kitchen, Doña Lupe reflected that Fortunata's symptoms might be a sign of the reproduction of a Rubín; but the young woman knew very well that her condition had nothing to do with that, and without further explanation she wrapped herself in a blanket and lay down on the sofa in her room. After the chill she felt sleepy and began to drowse, drifting into a quiet delirium, reproducing the scene in her mind and adding slight variants to it. Were they things she didn't get a chance to say, or were they merely ravings of her over-stimulated, feverish brain? "If that lady thinks she's the only decent woman in the world, humph! Forget it. What do you think you are, an example for the rest of us? Well I for one won't buy it. You know, if I decided I wanted to, I could be so decent and virtuous it'd make you sick. It's just a question of showing it. Yeah, and if I get mad, you'd better watch out. What did you think—that it'd be hard to take care of sick people and show what a good Catholic I am? Well, if I feel like it, I just might start one day: wash the most rotten sick patients there are and wear a cheap skirt and take in orphans. I can do all that and more. The little holier-than-thou can go to blazes! Don't try to convince *me* of your virtues. I'm just as much of an angel as she is. And if you really want to know, I can be more of an angel than you; a much better one. We all have a little bit of God in us."

After this she regained a clearer view of things; letting her eyes wander around the lonely, dim room she mused on the same subject, but with more insight into the reality of the situation. She turned things over in her mind repeatedly, and what stood out in her thoughts was her vivid desire to be not only equal to but better than her rival. The question was, how. "The first thing I've got to do is love my husband and behave better so they'll forget the awful things I've done."

Reviewing all the facets of the subject, her mind jumped from the most subtle to the most trivial things. "I've got to make a skirt exactly like hers . . . copy it, and make the same box pleats; if only I could find the same material. It's true that that little angel-face has a kind of grand air about her; a kind of . . . what is it? Majesty, yes. Bah! No, she doesn't. I'm just imagining it, the way anyone would after hearing that she's 'an angel.' I wonder if she really is. Who knows? Appearances can fool you."

Doña Lupe broke her chain of thought; she tiptoed in to say that she should eat something. Fortunata refused to eat anything and said that all she felt like was sucking on an orange. "Little cravings already?" her aunt said, smiling, and she sent Papitos out for an orange.

As she was sucking on the orange through a little hole and pressing it as babies press their mother's breast, another rush of anger, like the one that had determined her conduct that morning, swept through Señora Rubín's mind. "Your husband is mine and I've got to take him away from you. Snob! Fake saint! I'll tell you whether you're an angel or not. Your husband is mine, you stole him from me, just the way people steal purses. God's my witness, and if you don't think so, just ask him. Let go of him this minute or just watch out for me . . ."

She fell asleep and let the orange fall out of her hand. She awoke at the touch of her loving husband's hand on her forehead; he had come home for lunch and, when he heard that his wife was indisposed, was alarmed. Doña Lupe tried to raise his hopes for a successor, but he nodded his head skeptically and disconsolately and went into the bedroom to feel his wife's forehead.

"What is it, my darling?"

Upon hearing this tender expression and seeing before her the figure of her husband, Fortunata felt severely shaken inside. Just as a constitutional neurosis shows itself suddenly and without any warning, so, in the young woman's mind, did the aversion that her husband had inspired in her earlier in their marriage now explode. The first thought to cross her mind was amazement that the infamous plant of hatred, which she thought was dry and dead, or at least almost dead, could have blossomed again so suddenly. She looked at him, and the more she did so, the worse it got. She turned away and answered curtly:

"Nothing."

"Do you know what Aunt Lupe says? Listen . . ."

His aunt's opinion intensified her dislike and strong desire to be rid of her husband. Closing her eyes, she invoked the Lord and the Virgin, from whom she hoped to receive aid in curing herself of this insane dislike. But not even that worked. "I just can't stand the sight of him! I'd go to the ends of the earth to get away from him. And to think I thought I was getting fond of him! Some affection that was, that God put in my heart! I don't know what Feijóo was talking about. He was a fool, and I'm a bigger one to have listened to him."

Taking her pulse, Maxi spewed out a string of medical terms and concluded with the following:

"Tonight I'll bring home an anti-spasmodic, some orange blossom syrup, and maybe some quinine pills. You're running a slight fever. A bad cold coming on. You must have gotten chilled in that cursed tenement house, or gotten slightly intoxicated by a brazier."

Fortunata thought to herself how right he was: she had gotten intoxicated, although not from a brazier. Yielding to Doña Lupe's and her husband's pleas, she lay down, and when night fell she was quieter and wide awake, although she had no appetite; she listened peevishly to the noise of dishes and silverware clinking in the dining room where Nicolás was talking his mouth off as he ate.

"You'd be better off not eating anything if you don't feel like it," Maxi said as he came in chewing his dessert and carrying an overripe fig in his hand. "Just in case, I won't go back to the pharmacy tonight. I'll stay here and keep you company."

This was the worst medicine he could give her, because the young woman enjoyed being alone, entertaining herself with her thoughts. She tried to go to sleep; her husband tied a handkerchief tightly around her forehead and then stood next to the bed. After dozing off for a little while, she awoke and saw Maxi's spare figure pacing about the room. She looked first at him, then at his shadow gliding across the wall, long, angular, bending at the corners of the room. "Oh, Jacinta, would I like to see you married to him. *Then* I'd laugh; for years."

Maximiliano got undressed for bed. As he took off his vest, his shoulders appeared out of his shirtholes like the long wings of a bird that has had nothing to eat. Then his trousers delivered into view those legs, like canes being unsheathed. His joints moved jerkily, as if they were rusty, and his hair had gotten so thin that his head offered one of those undignified bald spots one finds on young men with thin, bad blood. When he got into bed and stretched his bony limbs he emitted an "Ah!" that could have been a cry of pain as easily as a cry of delight. Fortunata, pretending to be asleep, turned over, and by midnight she really was asleep.

At dawn she opened her eyes. The bedroom was still totally dark. She heard her husband's breathing—harsh, then wheezing, rising and falling in pitch, as if the air got blocked in that chest by gelatinous obstructions and metallic strips. Fortunata sat up, yielding to an inner movement that started in her while she was still asleep. What went through her mind was fairly unusual. The nonsensical thought—for it was sheer nonsense—that occurred to her was that she should slip out of bed, grope for her clothes, put on her underwear, go to the clothes rack, put on her dress. And her cloak—where was it? She couldn't remember. But she'd look for it in the dark too, and once she found it she'd leave the bedroom, pick up the key hanging on a hook in the entrance hall, and she'd be out, free! in the street. The idea of running away burned in her brain for a while like a flame of alcohol; she couldn't understand how it had been ignited. In her dress pocket she had half a *duro*, a *peseta*, and a few *cuartos*, the change from a *duro* that she had given Papitos to buy . . . she couldn't remember what. Well, she had enough. Why take more? And where would she go? To a rooming house. No . . . to Don Evaristo's. No, because he'd scold her. The thought that her "godfather" would scold her brought her to her senses again; the idea of running away was left over from a dream. "Am I awake or asleep?" she wondered, realizing her error, and she remained sitting on the bed, her cheek in her hand. The handkerchief around her head had slipped loose, and her hairdo had come out; her thick locks cascaded over her shoulders. "What a husband he is!" she thought, gathering up her hair. "Doesn't even know how to tie a handkerchief!" Then she fancied she saw eyes looking at her out of that pitch black darkness. "I must still be dreaming. What are you looking at? What are you saying? That I'm pretty? I know it. Prettier than your wife."

And she lay down again. As he turned over, Maximiliano's shoulder blade rammed into her. "Oh! I can see stars," Fortunata said to herself, retreating further to her side of the bed.

"Are you sleeping, dearie?" he mumbled, half-awake, making sucking movements with his mouth, as if he had a pill in it.

But without hearing her answer, he went back to sleep.

7

The next day Fortunata felt better, but she was still in bed when her husband, who'd already been to the pharmacy, came back to see her.

"How are you?" he asked, leaning over and planting a kiss on her forehead. "You can get up. It's a nice day. I'm not as healthy as you and I don't complain as much. Sometimes I feel so weak it's hard for me to move a finger. All my bones ache, and sometimes I feel as if my head were empty—with no brains in it. But it doesn't hurt me, and that's a bad sign, because migraines are a pillar in my life. I don't know what's wrong with me. Sometimes I get distracted; I get forgetful and feel sort of dazed; I forget where I am and what I'm doing. What I wonder is this: what if I lose my memory, and forget what I know best? You'll be better tomorrow; but who knows what will happen to me? Ballester says I should take a lot of iron— lots of it—and that it's due to a lack of globules in my blood; that must be it. This machine of mine has never been much, but now it's not worth two cents."

Fortunata looked at him and felt deeply sorry for him. Perhaps it was pity that revived the sisterly affection that had begun to die in her. But she wasn't sure. Looking at him as he left the room, she wondered whether the sickly plant of affection was dying; she knew she should make a colossal effort to keep it alive.

A little later, sitting in the parlor next to the balcony where the sun was streaming in, she heard voices in the hall; she couldn't tell whether they were happy or angry. But she didn't have time to be frightened, because suddenly Nicolás came booming in, waving his arms with joy, his face all lit up, his eyes aglow. He gave his sister-in-law a hearty embrace, saying:

"Congratuate me, everybody. It's finally happened. It wasn't a favor; I deserved it. But I'm very grateful to the people who—"

"Thank God! We've finally made a prebendary of him," said Doña Lupe who, after receiving a crushing embrace from him in the hall, followed him in, radiant at his good luck because she would now be relieved of feeding that monstrous mouth. "Where are they sending you?"

"Orihuela, Aunt," stated the clergyman, rubbing his hands together. "A bad cathedral, but maybe they'll let me transfer."

"Now that you've got a canonship, you'll be a pope in no time."

"I'm so happy for you," said Fortunata, just to say something, and she looked out the window for fear that the others might be able to read in her face the thoughts that her brother-in-law's canonship stirred in her.

"The ways of the world!" she thought. "Don Evaristo was right; there are two societies—the one you see and the one you don't. If it hadn't been for my bad conduct, this vulgar, stinking fool would never have gotten a canonship. And to see him so smug about it!"

"I'm leaving tomorrow to start in my new position. But first I want to celebrate with everybody. Juan Pablo doesn't know yet. He'll turn green! Yesterday he bet that they wouldn't give it to me. Villalonga's a great fellow, and Feijóo is a true gentleman; the minister is too. Do you know who gave me the news? Leopoldo Montes; he's with the Department of Justice and Ecclesiastical Affairs. I ran right over, and when the director of cathedral appointments told me it was true, I thought I would faint. He had my papers there and hadn't sent them because they didn't know my address. Again: I'm inviting everyone, anybody who wants to come—the Torquemada woman, Ballester, Doña Casta and her charming daughters—"

"Enough son, enough," said Doña Lupe, getting slightly peeved. "It will take you more than a year's salary to pay for all those guests, and if you think I'm going to pay most of the bill you're wrong."

Nicolás calmed down a bit and adopted the tone that befits a priest; he knew very well that it would help him to regain the composure he always lost when he got especially mad or happy.

"Yes, I'm satisfied, and even though I think I deserve this because of all the studying I've done and the service I've rendered in the confessional booth, I'm not proud of myself, and I'll say this from the start: I'll make every effort to get along with my colleagues; that's what counts. I like peace and harmony among Christian brothers. A quiet life; I'll say my Mass first thing in the morning, lead the prayers every morning and every afternoon, sit by the altar when it's my turn, go for a little walk in the afternoon, and handle whatever comes up."

While they were having lunch Fortunata couldn't banish the following thought from her mind: "If you did a good deed by making me decent, you stupid fool, I've paid you back, and I don't owe you a thing."

"I have to go to the pawnshop," Doña Lupe said a little while later. "The auction starts today. Keep an eye on Papitos; she's been getting out of hand lately. You spoil her with your kindness. Check up on her in the kitchen; don't let her off on her own. Make her put the codfish in soak, or you do it. And make sure the laundry's done when I get back."

Fortunata was left alone with the maid, but she couldn't watch her because visitors kept coming all afternoon. First Doña Casta Moreno, Samaniego's widow, came with her daughters, two very well bred (or so they thought anyway) young ladies. The mamá was a member of the Moreno family, which in the first third of the century had split into two main branches, the "rich Morenos" and the "poor Morenos." She had been born into the former but had ended up with the latter, and married Samaniego, a good man and very learned in pharmacology but with no knack for getting rich. On the Trujillo side Doña Casta was distantly related to Barbarita, who had been a childhood friend of hers, but they had drifted apart and hardly saw each other anymore; fortune and the vicissitudes of life had practically separated them. Sometimes when they saw each other they exchanged greetings; other times they didn't. What happens to many people who have known each other as children and then gone for years without seeing each other happened to them; namely, that when they meet they doubt whether or not to speak, and they end up silent, because neither wants to be the first to speak.

Casta's relationship with Moreno-Isla was closer and clearer. Although he was a "rich Moreno" he had kept up a family relationship with this "poor Moreno" and visited her from time to time. They still used the familiar form of address as they had during childhood, but their relationship was cold and served only to keep the family contact alive. The Moreno-Isla branch also made Doña Casta and Guillermina Pacheco distant relatives, but their relationship could hardly be called such. Guillermina and Samaniego's widow had never come into contact.

Doña Casta boasted about how well she had brought up her daughters. The elder, Aurora, who was an attractive-looking widow of a Frenchman, was naturally inclined to work. She had lived for some time in France and run a linens shop. She was an independent sort of woman and had a good instinct for business. The second daughter, Olimpia, had gone to the conservatory for seven years and won many prizes for her accomplishments on the piano. Her mamá wanted her to become a perfect teacher, and to this end she made her daughter work for good grades by forcing her to study a piece for months and even years, subjecting the neighbors to the torture day and night. The girl could count her suitors on her fingers, but as for counting proposals—there were none so far.

Fortunata liked Aurora very much, and Olimpia and the mamá very little. She was afraid that they snickered about her poor upbringing and had a low opinion of her because they knew about her past. Recognizing their superiority to her in their breeding and confident use of fine language, she sometimes felt disoriented during their conversations, so she merely echoed them. She always professed to agree with them, and even if she did think differently, she didn't dare express dissent. That afternoon Señora Rubín felt more inhibited than ever and wished they would leave. But unfortunately Doña Casta had never been more of a chatterbox. She was very sorry not to have found Lupe at home, because she had some extremely important news to tell her: Aurora was going to take a position as manager of a linens shop that was on a par with the best shops in Paris and London. What did she think of that?

Maxi's wife tried to disguise the boredom that this news inspired in her, and she responded to Doña Casta's hyperbole with cries of amazement and agreement.

"My daughter," added Samaniego's widow, "will be in charge of planning trousseaux, christening wardrobes, and all the other elegant merchandise, and she'll receive her salary plus a share of the profits. The owner of the grand establishment—and it will really cause comment—is Pepe Samaniego; my cousin, Don Manuel Moreno-Isla—who's the kindest, most generous man in the world— lent him the capital to set up the business, and let me tell you, it was quite a sum! He's a bachelor, you know; spends his time in London, bored with life. What I say is, he could have made one of the young girls in the family happy. Whenever he comes to see me, I give him a 'speech'* as he calls it, and he just laughs . . ."

---

* *Espich.* The character uses this word in English, pronouncing it with a Spanish accent.

"What do I care about all that!" thought Fortunata, who by now was having trouble playing her role; she was beginning to run out of monosyllables and smiles.

Finally, the Lord, with His never-ending compassion, decreed that the Samaniegas should leave; but not ten minutes had elapsed when Don Evaristo, supported by his servant, appeared, and Fortunata led him into the living room, where the old man sank heavily into an armchair.

"Doña Lupe?"

"There's no one at home," she said, as if to say, "you can speak freely."

"Oh, you're alone . . . And how are you? They told me that you* . . . you†‡ were a bit ill . . ."

After telling him that her illness hadn't been serious, she sat down next to him, intending to tell him about the real cause of her suffering, which was purely moral and quite severe. She wanted to ask her knowing friend and teacher why the few words she had exchanged with Jacinta had caused all that disorder in her soul. What relation did that woman have to her behavior and feelings? This wise connoisseur of the human heart and the world would surely have something substantial to say on the subject. She had racked her brains and had not been able to come up with the reason why that "angel-face" should upset her so. If she was an angel, then why did she bring out the worst in Fortunata? Why did she have the same effect as the devil has on earthly creatures, that of tempting them to evil? She must *not* be an angel. And there was another point she wanted to consult Feijóo about: her burning desire to be like her rival, be if not better at least as good as Jacinta. That meant that Jacinta wasn't a devil.

The hard part was to explain this so that Feijóo could understand it. As we know, she wasn't very adept at finding words to express complicated spiritual matters.

8

The worst of it was that the consultation hadn't even begun when Doña Lupe came in and invited Sr. Feijóo to stay for hot chocolate. The good gentleman didn't need to have his arm twisted, and so Doña Lupe went ahead and prepared it and then served it herself. As they drank, they talked about the visits the two ladies had made to Mira el Río Street.

"I," declared Doña Lupe, "admit that I don't have the heart or the stomach to do that much charity. I greatly admire our friend Guillermina, but I can't imitate her."

---

*Using familiar *tú*.   †Using formal *Usted*.

Feijóo made a few very knowing remarks on that philanthropic subject and then bid the ladies farewell, pressing their hands firmly.

That night Fortunata noticed something in her husband that put her on her guard. During dinner he hadn't opened his mouth; his face was very flushed and he was restless, sighing deeply, almost continuously. When he went upstairs to bed, his face had paled to an ashen color.

"Do you have a migraine?" his wife asked as she watched him collapse into a chair and sink his face in his hands.

Maxi replied that he didn't, that his head didn't hurt him at all, and that what terrified him was that his skull felt empty, "vacant," like a house with a For Sale sign up.

"A little while ago," he said rather bitterly, "I had such a total loss of memory that . . . I couldn't remember your name. I was coming up the stairs, and it made me so mad that I asked myself out loud, 'What is her name, what is it?' I remembered as I walked in the house. Today I was mixing a prescription for a man with eye trouble, and instead of putting in sulphate of atropine, I put in excedrin, which has the opposite effect. If Ballester hadn't noticed it—banish the thought!— I could have blinded him. I can't work. Something's wrong with my head. Imagine, sometimes—"

He shot her occasional glances as he talked, and Fortunata didn't know how to hide the terror that his eyes caused her.

"Sometimes I feel so stupid, so terribly stupid, that I think my head must be a piece of granite. I can't get an idea into it even though I bang it in with a hammer. And then there are other times when I'd swear I'm the brainiest man in the world. I get the strangest ideas! They're so sublime I can't express them; my tongue quivers and I bite it, then I spit blood. Then I feel as if I'd just fainted."

"Lie down and rest," his wife suggested, feeling sorry for him and frightened. "You're overtired, from thinking too much."

Maximiliano began to get undressed, pausing from time to time.

"Whenever I move my arms," he said, terrified, "the palpitations get so strong I can hardly breathe. Ballester says's its a nervous disorder, a cardiac hyperkinesia produced by dyspepsia . . . gases. But I say it's not; I think it's more serious. It's my aorta. I've got an aneurysm, and one of these days, bang! it's going to burst."

"Don't worry so much. If you didn't read all those big books on medicine this foolish stuff wouldn't occur to you," she said, helping him take off his trousers.

He stood there stiff-legged in his underwear waiting for his wife to help him pull off his boots too.

"May God reward you, my dear. Help me. Your poor husband needs you. He feels more miserable than ever."

Fortunata picked him up gracefully and put him to bed. She could have lifted an even heavier weight. They both laughed, but then Maximiliano sighed, saying in a terribly sad voice:

"You're so strong! And I'm so weak! And to think mine's called the stronger sex. Some example I am!"

"Go to sleep now, and don't bother your head with foolish thoughts," she urged him, moved by pity and convinced that the kindest thing was to stroke him.

"If it weren't for you," he said like a spoiled child, "I wouldn't care whether I lived or died. Life's not worth anything without love. It's the only meaningful reality there is; the rest is make-believe."

She lay down too, and chatted with him until he fell asleep. Poor boy! Fortunata's pity for him killed—or at least hid from view—her aversion. And the compassion she felt renewed her intermittent desire to attain sublime virtue. Her obsessive wish to imitate what she considered worthy examples led her to believe that if her husband became very ill she would be a veritable wonder, for she would take exquisite care of him. But in order for the triumph to be complete, Maxi had to have a disgusting, repugnant, pestiferous illness, the kind that scares off even the closest relatives. Then she would prove that she was as angelic as any other woman; she would show that she had soul, patience, courage, and stomach enough for anything. "And then Jacinta would see who's perfect, and what each of us is like. The bad part is that she won't get to see it, because she's never here."

Maximiliano distracted her from this meditation by whimpering in his sleep. His wife already knew the remedy for this, which was to turn him over gently.

"What a dream!" murmured Maxi, half-awake. "I dreamed that you'd left . . . and then I was holding onto you by your foot and you were tugging away, and I pulled you harder and then the aneurysm sac in my head broke open and the whole room was full of blood . . . the whole room, even the ceiling."

She rocked him back to sleep and fell asleep herself. She got up early the next morning because she had to work. After nine o'clock, when she went into the bedroom to see if her husband needed anything, he was getting dressed and he was in a very different mood from the night before. He not only seemed to have recovered from his weakness; he was restless and agile, as if he had just taken a powerful stimulant. As soon as his wife came in, he walked straight to her, buttoning his shirt collar, and in a bitter tone asserted:

"Listen, I was hoping you'd come, to tell you that I find those visits from that Señor Feijóo annoying. I was going to tell you last night and I forgot. So now you know. I heard he was here again yesterday and they invited him for hot chocolate and buns. My brother Juan told me; he was going by in the street as Feijóo was leaving, and they talked."

Fortunata was astounded by this rebuff, and more so by his tone. Maximiliano was usually a bit quarrelsome and peevish in the morning, but never that much. Turning toward the mirror to put on his tie, he continued:

"In this house, it seems that people do things on purpose, just to irritate me, to make me mad. Not only you; my aunt does too. You've all probably decided that you want me to get sick."

In the mirror, Fortunata could see Maxi's pale, contracted face; his nervousness showed up in a tic, a jerking of his head, which seemed to want to free itself of his body. She made what excuses she could, but he, instead of calming down, kept on complaining that they wanted to mortify him on purpose, that they wanted him to die. His wife remained silent; she suspected that her husband wasn't right in the head and that it would be worse to contradict him. From then on she observed that Maxi always awoke in that same excitable state, stubbornly insisting that everyone in the family was plotting against him. Sometimes what triggered him off was a tiny fault in his clothes—a missing button, a torn buttonhole, or some such thing. Other times that they'd made his hot chocolate taste awful, just to irritate him. As if they wanted to poison him! Or else that they'd left the balconies and doors open so a draft would kill him. These manias got progressively worse, putting Doña Lupe in a horrible mood, leading her to predict that a catastrophe of some sort was brewing. There came a day when Maxi began to speak with a violence that was completely out of character in him, and when they didn't contradict him he answered himself, fanning the flames of his anger even higher; finally, he left, grumbling, slammed the door, and rushed down the stairs four at a time.

At night the wolf became a lamb. It was as if his morning strength were gradually spent during the course of the day by his actions and movements, so that when night came he reached the opposite state and was exhausted, like a man who has worked very hard. Fortunata had already gotten used to this hot-and-cold, and none of her husband's extravagances surprised her. In the morning it was best to ignore him, to seem to yield to his requests. At night she had no choice but to cajole and pamper him a bit; anything else would have been cruel.

On a number of occasions, in private with his wife, Maximiliano had voiced that sadness so common among childless couples. Fortunata didn't like the subject; however, she had no choice but to accept it. One night she approached the subject with true enthusiasm, though, because she had had a very felicitous thought about it that day and wanted to communicate it to her husband.

"Look," she said, "if God doesn't want to give us a child, He must have His reasons for it. But we could adopt one—look for a little orphan and bring him home with us. I'd really like to, and we'd both be amused. Why shouldn't I—even though I'm poor—do the same as rich ladies that don't have children? A marriage without a little one around is very dull."

Maximiliano thought it was a good idea, but Doña Lupe, even though she didn't openly disagree, showed no enthusiasm. Children dirty up the house, made a mess of everything, and give one all sorts of trouble with their sicknesses and mischief. But she kept her thoughts to herself. Fortunata was crestfallen; she had taken it into her head the night before that it would be nice to adopt an orphan, and now that she had caressed the idea it was very hard to give it up. Her mania to imitate again!

9

Two days after Fortunata's clash with Jacinta, Doña Lupe invited the former to visit Mauricia again. What would Doña Guillermina say if they didn't return! Fortunata declined, making some excuse or other, and Doña Lupe went alone. It was Saint Isidro's Day and the pawnshops were closed. At about ten o'clock she came home, very much affected by the visit and, walking into the parlor where her niece was sewing, she said:

"Child, say an Our Father for poor Mauricia."

"She's not dead!" exclaimed Fortunata, shaken to the core.

"Yes, she died at nine thirty. It was as if she'd been waiting for me to get there to die . . . poor woman! I'm horrified. If I'd known, I wouldn't have gone. I can't take scenes like that. When I got there she was still in her right mind, and she asked after you with such concern! She said she loved you more than anyone else in the world, and that the moment she got to heaven she was going to ask the Lord to make you happy. When I heard that, I knew she was in a bad way, and then Severiana told me that last night they thought they were going to lose her several times. She was so overcome she could hardly breathe. I also noticed that her voice sounded as if it was coming up out of the bottom of a deep pitcher . . . it had a faraway sound to it. Her face had a peculiar wistfulness about it and her eyes were sunken, deep; but they shone. Guillermina was sitting at her bedside and was constantly embracing and kissing her, telling her to think of God, who suffered so much to save us . . . Then suddenly she fell apart and oh, what a shock it was! She turned livid and started to wave her arms around and spout all sorts of words. It was awful. Then Father Nones arrived—Guillermina had sent for him. But it was useless. That poor sick woman couldn't hear what they were saying to her and, anyway, her head wasn't fit for hearing religious things. The saint had a bright idea. She gave Mauricia a glass of sherry, full to the brim. Mauricia clenched her teeth, but the aroma must have gotten to her finally because she opened her mouth and downed it all at once. Oh, how she licked her lips, the poor soul! She calmed down, and then whosh!, her head fell on the pillow. Then Guillermina, putting the crucifix in her hands, asked her if she believed in God and entrusted herself to God, and the Holy Virgin, and this saint and that, and she nodded that she did. Father Nones was on his knees, praying away. They lit a candle, and let me tell you, the smell of the wax, the praying, and the whole scene turned my stomach and made me as nervous as a cat. I didn't want to look, but my curiosity got the better of me. Mauricia's eyes had sunken into the nape of her neck practically, and her nose—that pretty nose of hers— looked as sharp as a knife. Guillermina raised her voice and told Mauricia to embrace the cross, that God had forgiven her, and that she envied her for being able to go straight to heaven, and lots of other things; it was enough to make you cry. Mauricia's head was still, very still . . . then we saw her move her lips and stick out the tip of her tongue as if she wanted to lick them. She moaned something, and her voice sounded as if it was coming up out of a pipe from the cellar. I thought it sounded like 'More, more.' Other people claimed she was saying 'Now.' You know, like in 'Now I can see the everlasting glory and the angels.' Nonsense. What she said was 'More,' meaning 'More sherry.' Guillermina and Severiana put up a mirror to her face and held it there for a little while. Then everybody started talking in loud voices. Mauricia was already in the other world; her skin was a violet-bluish color. Ten minutes later her face looked so different you wouldn't have recognized her. But Guillermina—what a woman!" continued Jáuregui's widow after a sad pause, her eyes wide. "Would you believe that she herself shrouded her? She wouldn't have done more for her own daughter. She washed her, dressed her, put on the shroud—all very calmly. I would have liked to help, but frankly, I'm not much good at that sort of thing. It only seemed natural to offer my services. But I knew very well that the saint wasn't about to let anybody else lead the band; that's her job and that's how she likes it. I did offer to help, though. You've got to lend a hand whenever you can and put on a good show. And believe me, what little I did do deserves to be praised, because anything at all in those situations is a sacrifice for me, whereas it isn't for Doña Guillermina, because she's used to being involved with the sick and the dead, like the sisters of mercy. You should have seen her. Her little face always so rosy, moving about with that quick, lively step of hers. When she finished we had a long chat in the living room; we talked about Mauricia, about all the poverty there is in Madrid, and that thanks to good souls 'like you,' she said, a lot of wrongs were righted. 'And how about your niece—didn't she come?' she asked. 'The other day she promised me a pair of her husband's trousers.'"

"Oh, yes!" recalled Fortunata. "Don't think that I've forgotten. I've already put them aside. They're for a man who plays the horn or the trombone or something. We can send them to Severiana."

"I'll take care of it," said Doña Lupe, meaning that she planned to pay another visit.

"No, I'll take them, wrapped up in a shawl," said the niece, who suddenly felt like going to the funeral house. "And we can both take a *duro*, in case they're collecting for the funeral."

"That's not a bad idea. But the person to give our money to is Guillermina, who appreciates things. Oh, I almost forgot! She invited me to visit her orphanage. I mean, she invited us both. We'll go. I'll wear my new coat for the occasion, and you can wear the skirt you're planning to make. We'll have to make a contribution, but that doesn't matter. Other collections infuriate me, but I don't mind charity boxes."

Papitos came in, and her mistress asked her to make a cup of tea, because her stomach was upset. She hadn't even taken off her cloak and gloves yet; but as she chatted her spirits rose and she thought about changing clothes. She was carrying a little bundle that contained some delicacies she had bought on the way home to tempt Maxi. Ballester had recommended that he be given raw meat, but since he refused to eat it, Doña Lupe had decided to give him giblets and let him skip stews and starchy foods. For dessert she had brought him some Portuguese plums.

Fortunata didn't pay attention to any of this; she was engrossed in the thought of visiting Doña Guillermina's orphanage. That's where she could get the little orphan she wanted to adopt. Of course . . . And maybe, if the little boy her uncle Pepe Izquierdo wanted to sell Jacinta was still there . . . What an opportunity! What a blow *that* would be! She'd show them that they weren't the only ones who could—

But soon something happened that completely upset her plan to adopt an orphan. The next day, resisting Maxi's insistence on taking them to San Isidro, they went as planned to Mira el Río. Fortunata had misgivings about the visit for various reasons, not the least of which was the sorrow at seeing Mauricia's remains. Frightened and nervous, she stayed in the living room with Doña Fuensanta, who was wearing a black shawl over her shoulders. Severiana came in and out. Her eyes showed that she had been crying; she too was wearing a black shawl. Through a crack in the door Fortunata could see la Dura's feet in the coffin; she couldn't bear to get closer to see more. She was grief- and terror-stricken and couldn't forget her friend's last words to her: "The very first thing that I'm going to ask the Lord is for you to die too, and that way we'll be together in heaven." Although she considered herself unfortunate, Sra. Rubín mentally clung to life. What Mauricia had said was nonsense. Everybody dies when the time comes and that's all there is to it. Doña Lupe, who went in to see the deceased woman, was so profoundly affected by it that she could not remain in the room.

"Child," she whispered to her niece, "I can't stand seeing these morbid things. I don't feel well. Death terrifies me, and it's not because I'm apprehensive. There's no illness that scares me like this except a bowel obstruction. It's my one fear. Anyway, I'm going to the pawnshop. I need some fresh air. You stay, so that things will look right. The saint's in there. Take my money, just in case they do collect—they always do. As soon as they take the corpse away, go home."

When the Jáuregui woman left, leaving her niece by herself, the latter changed places so as not to see Mauricia's feet, which were shod in pretty, light-colored boots; beautiful feet that would never take another step. Doña Fuensanta came out and said a few words to her. A little while later the door to the death room opened and Fortunata shuddered nervously, thinking for a moment that it was Mauricia herself who was emerging. But no, it was Guillermina. From the moment she stepped into the living room she fixed her eyes on the frightened young woman. The saint walked straight up to her, staring as she never had before. Touching her arm lightly, she said:

"I must speak with you."

"With me!"

"Yes, with you." And saying this, she touched her again. The sensation that her touch produced ran through Fortunata's arm into her heart.

"Just a few words," added the saint, who corrected herself, saying: "Or maybe more."

Fortunata detected a certain severity in the saint's face; she was about to say something, but the saint didn't give her time, taking her arm as one would a man's arm, saying:

"Come this way. Are you in a hurry?"

"No, Ma'am."

"I hadn't left because I was waiting to see if you would come. Last night I waited for you too, but you didn't choose to come."

She led her next door, where Doña Fuensanta lived, and they went into a rather messy living room in which there were more trunks than chairs and two bureaus. Guillermina closed the door and, inviting Fortunata to sit down, sat down herself on a trunk.

10

Fortunata didn't know what to say or what expression to wear, she was so scared and overwhelmed by the presence of the respectable lady and her presumption of the serious reason for this meeting. Guillermina, who didn't like to waste time, broached the subject immediately:

"I have a friend who's very dear to me, so dear to me that I'd give up my life for her, and this friend of mine has a husband who . . . in a word, well, my friend has suffered terribly because of certain foolish things her husband has done; he's an excellent person too, you understand, and I'm very fond of him . . . but, well, men—"

Señora Rubín looked at the protruding objects in the room. She was undoubtedly looking for a piece of furniture to crawl under.

"Let me come to the point," continued Guillermina, clicking her lips. "I'm very straightforward in all matters; I don't like theatrical performances. I agreed to speak with you. First we decided that I'd go to Señora Jáuregui; but then I thought it would be better to attack the matter squarely—approach you and appeal to your conscience, because I thought if I knocked on that door, someone would answer from within. I don't believe there's anyone who's really evil. I've been surprised many times before. It's happened quite often that someone who was supposedly perverse suddenly did the most Christian deed, so it no longer surprises me to see virtue appear where I least expect it. So you've gone astray and done a few things you shouldn't have; everyone knows that. Why try to deny it?"

"Of course not!" murmured Fortunata, without realizing the full import of her words.

"I hadn't had the pleasure of meeting you. I'll admit that I was astonished when my friend told me who you were. I didn't have the slightest suspicion. It's all such a farce. Imagine, meeting here in this act of charity; two such different people—don't take offense if I say 'opposite'—due to their backgrounds and their way of living. I don't mean to belittle anyone. On the contrary: I don't quite know why, but I've got a hunch or an inkling that if someone shook you good and hard—just as when others are shaken, acorns fall—that if someone were to shake you, a flower would fall."

Fortunata nodded her assent, and the noose she felt around her neck seemed to loosen.

"Which is why I'm appealing to your conscience and asking you to tell me, with the utmost sincerity, if during these last few days, that is, if lately, you've had any dealings with my friend's husband. You see, this is what's troubling her; she's convinced of it. So, let's see—"

"Me!" exclaimed Fortunata, who almost forgot her fear in her thrust toward the truth. "Me, now? Are you dreaming? I haven't seen him in ages!"

"Really?" asked the saint, squinting her eyes. This mannerism of hers extracted the truth like a pair of tweezers. And indeed, the sinner felt the saint's eyes pierce her to the core, breaking up everything in their path.

"Don't you believe me? How can you doubt it?" she added. And forgetting her manners, she almost made a cross with her fingers to kiss and swear by.

The desire to be believed shone so brightly in her eyes that Guillermina couldn't help but see her clean conscience. She pretended that she did not, though, and kept up a cold, observant front, which made the other woman impatient, anxious to find a way to convince her.

"Why do you want me to swear it to you? Really, to even doubt it! I haven't seen him or even heard from him."

"Say no more," declared Guillermina with a certain solemnity. "That's enough. I believe you. If you had said the opposite, I would have asked you to do everything in your power to restore my poor friend's peace and quiet. But if nothing's going on, I'll save my request for the time being. All I'll do is ask it of you in general, shall we say, thinking of the future, in case what isn't happening now should happen tomorrow or the day after."

Señora Rubín looked down at the floor. She had her handkerchief in her fist and her chin rested on her hand.

"But now," added the saintly woman, "I'd like to ask you another little question. Be patient; dealing with me is like having a headache. Let's see now. If there's absolutely nothing between you and my friend's husband, if it's all over and past, then why do you have a grudge against someone who hasn't done anybody any harm? The other day in the hall—why did you treat her the way you did and call her some name or other? Frankly, child, this struck us both as very strange, because you're married and live peacefully with your husband, or at least so it seems. If all the mischief is over, why should you mistreat poor Jacinta with your words and even your actions? What you should have done was ask her to forgive you."

"It was because," mumbled Fortunata, crushing her handkerchief into a perfect ball, "it was because . . . uh . . . ."

And she couldn't get beyond this. Tears sprang to her eyes, and the lump in her throat swelled up again, blocking her breathing. In all her life, at no time had she found herself in such a spot. The person whom some had affectionately and familiarly dubbed "the ecclesiastical rat" inspired more respect in her than any confessor, bishop, or even the Pope himself. The "rat" squinted her eyes more narrowly yet, and out of kindness tried to open the way to confession.

"The truth is that you're harboring resentment and perhaps pretensions, and that's a great sin. You're not cured of the sickness in your soul, and if you're not involved at the present with the person in question, you're ready and willing to get involved again. Let's come out and say things clearly."

Fortunata made no reply.

"Am I right? Did I touch your sore spot? Be frank, my lady; this won't reach other ears. I take these liberties because I know you won't get mad at me. I know very well that I abuse people and that I can be unbearably persistent; but put up with me for a minute, it's the only way . . . So, let's see now."

She still said nothing. At last, unbunching her handkerchief and spurting out her words, she tried to skirt the issue:

"That day . . . when I said those things to that lady . . . I was sorry afterward."

"And why didn't you apologize?"

"Like I say, I was sorry."

"Yes, I know. But answer plainly: why didn't you apologize?"

"Because I left and went home."

"All right. But if you were to see her now?"

Complete silence. Guillermina had run out of patience waiting for answers, and, getting annoyed, she said the following:

"Don't you realize that that lady is that gentleman's lawful wife? Don't you know that they were married in the eyes of God and that their union is sacred? Don't you realize that it's a sin—a horrible sin—to desire another woman's man, and that the offended wife has the right to handle you as she sees fit, whereas you, with no fewer than two adulteries on your conscience, offend her merely by looking at her? And anyway, what do you think this is? Do you think you're among savages and that everyone can do as he pleases? That there are no laws, no religion, nothing? Well, *that* would be a fine state, wouldn't it! Don't be surprised if I get a bit angry; forgive me."

Fortunata felt as if a basket of stones had been emptied on her head. Every word Guillermina said was like a stone. Taking her handkerchief by two corners, she twisted it into a rope. It isn't clear whether bewildered spontaneity or deliberate reflection led her to say:

"I'm very bad, you see. You don't know how bad I am."

"Yes, yes; I'm beginning to see we're not all perfection," said the saint, sitting up erectly in her chair, as if to increase the distance between them. "Where there's repentance, the Lord forgives. But apparently these matters of morality roll right off you like water off a duck. I can't say I envy your blasé attitude. You're married. Even if your conscience doesn't bother you on one score, doesn't it bother you on another?"

"I didn't know what I was doing when I got married."

"What an angel! Didn't know what she was doing! What did you think—that getting married was as mechanical and meaningless as taking a drink of water? Can anyone possibly get married without realizing it? Child, save that argument for fools. It won't work with me."

"They married me off," added Fortunata, bunching her handkerchief into a ball again. "I don't know how, but they did. I thought it was the best I could do, and that I'd be able to love my husband."

"Isn't that amusing, though! What a darling little creature!" exclaimed the foundress in an amiably ironic tone. "These . . . girls who've sinned for all they're worth are very funny when they play innocent. So you thought you could love him! And what did you do to manage it? No, let's be frank. What *you* wanted was to get married so you'd have a name, independence, and freedom to run around. Do you want me to be even more blunt? What you wanted was a flag so that you could indulge in your piracy behind a legal front. Poor man who ended up with you! He really got the grand prize. And tell me this: did the affection you wanted to feel finally sprout up somewhere?"

"No, Ma'am," replied Fortunata, bursting into tears. "But if you keep talking to me like that, I won't be able to go on; I'll have to leave."

The saint slid across the trunk she was sitting on to get closer to the other woman's chair.

"Come now, don't cry," she said kindly, putting her hand on her shoulder. "Don't be offended by what I've said. I already told you that you have to be patient with me. You either take me or leave me. When I'm trying to pull out sins I'm unbearable. Naturally, it hurts. But then they feel better. And up until now you haven't said anything in your favor."

"But why am I to blame for not loving my husband?" asked the sinner between sobs. "I can't help it. I didn't get married for the reasons you say. I got married because I made a mistake; I saw things differently—not the way they are. I don't love my husband. I never will, even if all the saints in heaven command me to. That's why I say I'm bad, very bad."

Guillermina heaved a deep sigh. Confronted by that terrible antagonism between the heart and human and divine laws, an insoluble problem, her great mercy inspired in her a sublime idea.

"I know very well that it's hard to rule your heart. But that should give you the reason to stop being bad, as you say you are, and to acquire enormous merit. What have you been thinking, child, that this hasn't occurred to you already? Doing certain duties when love doesn't help make them easier is the greatest beauty of the soul. Just doing this would be enough to cleanse your soul of all its guilt. What is the greatest virtue of all? Self-denial, renouncing happiness. What purifies a creature more than anything else? Sacrifice. That's all I need to tell you. Open your eyes, for the love of God; open your heart, wide open. Fill yourself with patience, perform all your duties, resign yourself, make sacrifices, and God will call you one of His own, His very own creature. Do this, and do it clearly, so that it can be seen and felt, and the day that you become that person, I—"

Upon saying "I," Guillermina put her hand on her breast and her eyes filled with a most beautiful expression.

"On that day, I'll come confess to you, just as you're confessing to me now."

This left Fortunata so disconcerted that her tears dried instantly. She looked at the "ecclesiastical rat" in real awe.

"Don't be amazed, and don't gape like that," she continued. "I haven't had the chance to throw happiness out the window—or dreams, or anything. I haven't had to fight. I got into this way of life the way you walk from one room to another. There hasn't been any sacrifice on my part, or if there has, it's been so insignificant it's not worth mentioning. Laugh at me if you want to, but realize that when I see someone who has a chance to sacrifice something, to pull out something that hurts, I envy that person. Yes, I envy the evil because I envy the opportunity they have that I don't: to break away and give up a whole world, and I look at them and say, 'you fools, you've got all you need to make a sacrifice and you don't even take advantage of it.'"

In spite of its loftiness, this notion was intelligible to Fortunata. Guillermina drew closer to her and, putting her arm around her shoulders, pressed her gently. Never, not even in confession, had the sinful woman felt her heart so ready to overflow. The virgin and foundress' gaze alone seemed to evoke in her soul the ideal image that the wretched woman, like all of us, had formed of her actions and feelings, that image that, depending on the circumstances, brightens or dims before our eyes. On that occasion, it shone clearly, as if it were a focus of light.

II

The door opened, and Severiana came in crying loudly. The moment had come for Mauricia's body to be taken away; that this very sad event was about to occur was evident in the moaning and sobbing of all the women in the death house. When Guillermina and Fortunata left, the coffin had already been lowered on the shoulders of two burly men to be put in the humble cart awaiting it in the street. Curiosity and a wish to bid a final farewell pushed Fortunata toward the stairs. She managed to see the yellow ribbons on the black cloth as the coffin was rounding the corner, but she caught only a quick glimpse. Then she stepped onto the balcony and saw how they placed the coffin in the cart, how the latter moved forward with no accompaniment except a bleak-looking carriage in which Juan Antonio and two neighbors sat. She felt such a sharp impulse to cry and, indeed, wept so copiously that she couldn't remember when she had shed so many tears in such a short time. Her grief at seeing the final disappearance of a person of whom she was extremely fond sprang also from her need to weep over past sorrows that undoubtedly hadn't been fully wept over yet.

The cart soon vanished, and all that was left of Mauricia was a memory—still fresh, but destined to fade quickly. Ten minutes after the body had been taken away, Severiana came in swollen-eyed and opened all the doors, windows, and balcony doors to air the house. She was preparing for a thorough cleaning session and began by moving things out of place so as to sweep everywhere.

"Poor Mauricia!" Fortunata said to Guillermina, drying her tears quickly, for it didn't seem fitting that she should cry more than the others. "You know, that woman had a strange effect on me. I knew she was very evil, but I loved her. I just liked her; I couldn't help it. And when she told me the terrible things she'd done in her life, I don't know . . . I was happy listening . . . And when she advised me to do evil things, somehow it seemed, deep down inside that they weren't so bad and that she was right to advise me to do them. How do you explain it?"

"Me? Explain it?" replied the saint, somewhat perturbed. "The heart holds great mysteries, and as for our reasons for liking people—they're the most mysterious of all. Poor woman! If you could have seen how attractive she was when she was young. She grew up in my parents' house. Poor girl! Her elegant profile, her eyes, and her expression are about all that were left of her. She lost everything—her face got hard and mannish, and her voice got hoarse. They say she was the living image of Napoleon, and she was."

Guillermina looked at the prints of Napoleon and so did Fortunata, remarking on the resemblance. Then the saint bid Severiana farewell, indicating that she would return the following day. She recommended patience and, taking Sra. Rubín's arm, departed. Severiana and Doña Fuensanta escorted them to the main entrance.

"We have a lot to talk about," Guillermina said, once they were in the street. "A lot. We only scratched the surface today. Tell me, do you have any patience left to endure me? Because if you aren't sick of me by now, I'd like to request another audience with you. Would you be good enough to have another session with me?"

"As many as you want," replied Señora Rubín, who was enchanted by such indulgence and courtesy from this illustrious lady.

"Fine; we'll decide when and where later. Are you going home? We can go together because I have to go to Zurita Street to give my blacksmith a scolding, and you won't miss anything if you come with me. It'll only take a minute, and then I'll walk you to your door."

The proposal having been accepted with the greatest pleasure, the two of them took the winding, bumpy road that divides La Arganzuela from the Lavapiés ravine. They talked about matters that were far from spiritual, about how expensive everything was: boned meat—who would have guessed it!—at a *peseta*, milk for ten *cuartos*, crusty rolls at sixteen, not to mention housing—a room that used to cost eight *reales* was impossible to find now for under fourteen. They finally reached Zurita Street and went into a big blacksmith's shop; it was all black, the floor covered with coal, everything full of smoke and noise. The owner of the establishment came forth to receive the lady in his blackened apron, his face perspiring and charred, and, taking off his cap, he apologized for not having sent her the large round-headed nails.

"But how about the cramp irons—which is more necessary?" the lady asked, peeved. "You're going to be condemned, my good man, for all your white lies. Didn't you promise me that they'd be ready yesterday? What kind of promises do you make? Not even Job would have the patience to put up with you. The carpenters are held up because of your blooming slowness. I'm not surprised that you're so fat, Señor Pepe. And put your cap back on—you're perspiring and you could catch cold."

The blacksmith mumbled his apologies and finally swore that the cramp irons would be ready by Thursday; yes, definitely by Thursday. He'd had to fill a rush order, but he was almost finished and would go back to the lady's cramp irons right away and he'd have them for her on the day agreed, even if it was "over Christ's head." But the foundress gave him another sermon; she wasn't satisfied with promises. As she said good-bye she added that if they weren't ready by Thursday he could keep them. Señor Pepe followed her out, all courtesy, into the middle of the street, and the two ladies slowly walked toward Ave María Street.

"Well," declared Guillermina, "before we part, let's plan on something. Would you like to come to my house? Do you know where I live?"

Fortunata said yes. Santa Cruz had told her several times that the "ecclesiastical rat" lived next door and that she and Barbarita talked from their bay windows. Deciding on a day took some thinking because she didn't want Doña Lupe to get wind of the visit; she was afraid her aunt-in-law would want to stick her nose into things, so she thought that she had better choose a day when "the turkey woman" went to the pawnshop.

"Would Friday suit you? From ten to eleven in the morning?"

"Fine. Good-bye, child; take care." (They were already at the door of her house.) "I'll be waiting for you. Don't stand me up."

"Humph! That *would* be the last straw!"

Fortunata lingered in the doorway a moment, watching her go up the street, and then she walked in, slowly, pensively. For the rest of the day she couldn't get Guillermina out of her mind. What an extraordinary woman! She could feel her inside, as if she had swallowed her or taken her like a Communion wafer. The saint's eyes and voice stuck to her insides like perfectly assimilated substances. And at night, when Maxi fell asleep and she continued to toss and turn, unable to sleep, a thought that made her tremble crossed her mind. She could see Guillermina as clearly as if she'd been standing before her very eyes, but the odd part wasn't this; it was that she, too, looked like Napoleon, like Mauricia la Dura. And her voice? Her voice was exactly like that of her deceased friend. How could it be, when they were so different? Whatever it was, the mysterious liking she had for Mauricia had transferred to Guillermina. But why was she confusing the woman who was known for her shameless evil with the saintly lady who filled everyone with admiration? "I don't see how this can be," pondered Fortunata, "but there's no doubt about it—they do resemble each other. And their voices sound the same to me. Lord, what *is* this?" She racked her brains, trapped in the tourniquet of her sleeplessness, trying to figure out what it meant, and it dawned on her that from Mauricia's cold remains a tiny butterfly was emerging and somehow getting into the "ecclesiastical rat" and transforming her . . . It was so weird! Extreme evil recasting itself and reliving in the purest good! Mightn't it be that Mauricia, who had repented, confessed, and been absolved, had, upon dying, turned into a healthy, pure creature? A creature as pure as the saint herself . . . or even purer? "Lord, what confusion! And to think there's no one who can explain these things to me."

Later, she was chilled to the bone, envisioning Mauricia's feet. In the darkness, streaked by luminous rays, she could see the elegant boots on the deceased woman; the feet stirred, the body rose, it took a few steps, came toward her, and said: "Fortunata, my dearest friend, don't you recognize me? D———! I'm not dead, kid; I'm still here in this world—believe what I tell you. I'm Guillermina, Doña Guillermina, 'the ecclesiastical rat.' Take a good look at me: look at my face, my feet, my hands, my black cloak. I'm going mad with that blasted orphanage of mine. All I do is ask and ask and ask, every living soul that comes in sight. Señor Pepe, are you going to make those cramp irons for me or not? They must be rusty by now!"

VII. That Idea, That Crafty Idea

I

GUILLERMINA LIVED, AS I HAVE SAID, on Pontejos Street, next door to the Santa Cruz family. The Morenos had lived in the building before, and their bank had been located there for many years. It is still there, under the name Ruiz-Ochoa and Company. Because of its narrowness and height, the building looked like a tower. The present director of the bank didn't live there, but he did have his desk on the mezzanine. On the second floor lived Don Manuel Moreno-Isla (when he came to Madrid), his widowed sister Doña Patrocinio, and his aunt, Guillermina Pacheco. On the third floor lived Zalamero, who was married to Ruiz-Ochoa's daughter, and on the fourth, two elderly ladies, also members of the family; they were sisters of the bishop of Plasencia, Fray Luis Moreno-Isla y Bonilla.

Guillermina got home at nine-thirty that day, which was to be a memorable one. So early, and she had already walked all over Madrid—been to three Masses, visited both the old orphanage and the one under construction, and done errands on her way. She went into the parlor for a moment, thinking about the visit that was to take place later in the day, but her interest in it didn't distract her mind from other more personal matters, and, without taking off her cloak, she went from the parlor to her nephew's study.

"May I come in?" she inquired, gently opening the door.

"Yes, come on in, 'rat,'" replied Moreno, who had just taken his bath and was sitting at the desk writing in his bathrobe and sleeping cap, his gold-rimmed spectacles perched on the bridge of his nose.

"Good morning," said the saint as she came in. He peered at her over the top of his glasses. "I'm not going to disturb you. But tell me, how do you feel today? Have you had that tightness in your chest again?"

"I'm fine. I slept well last night. I can hardly believe I really got a good night's rest. I can take things patiently, but these sleepless nights are killing me. Today, as you can see, talking doesn't tire me."

"Dear me. It's your nerves, I guess, and also a result of the lazy life you lead. But let's get to the point. I only wanted to suggest that since you're not going to finish my ground floor for me, you could at least give me some old beams you have at your lot on Relatores Street. Yesterday I went to see them. If you give them to me, I'll have them sawed."

"What do you mean, *old* beams?"

"They're half rotten!"

"My foot they are! But anyway, they're yours, you wheedler," replied Moreno, going back to his papers. "When, for the love of God, are you going to finish your blessed orphanage and let the human race rest? You have no idea how unpleasant you make yourself with your collection drives. You're a nightmare for every family you approach. When people see you appear—and don't doubt it for a minute, even if they don't *seem* to mind—they're cursing you under their breath!"

To these serenely pronounced words, which sounded more playful than serious, Guillermina replied, sitting down next to his desk and leaning one elbow on it, looking at her nephew face to face and stroking his chin with her fingers, among which her rosary was still intertwined:

"You're saying all that just to get my goat. You're a tricky one. Come on, let me have those beams. You don't need them for anything."

"All right, they're yours; cart them off and see if you break a leg," replied Don Manuel, smiling.

"But that's not enough. You have to give your administrator orders to give them to me . . . here, on this scrap of paper. Since you've already got a pen in your hand, I'm not leaving without the order. Then you can finish your letter."

Saying this, she took a piece of his stationery and put it in front of him, moving the half-written letter out of the way.

"God have pity on me! And let the devil take these saints full of airs, these foundresses of establishments who aren't good for anything."

"Write, silly. All you're saying is stuff and nonsense. You're the kindest soul there is. And the most Christian."

"Me, a Christian!" the gentleman exclaimed, hiding his benevolence behind histrionic savagery. "Me, a Christian? *That* would be a sin! Listen, just to keep you away from me, I'm going to become a Protestant, or a Jew, or a Mormon. I want to scare you off as if I were the plague."

"Oh, go on; don't be silly. I warn you: you'll never be free of me, because even if you turn into the devil himself I'll ask you for money—and get it. Come on, write it for me."

"I don't feel like it."

And saying this, he began to write the order.

"That's it," said Guillermina, dictating to him. "Señor Don ____: Please be kind enough to give the sticks—"

"Sticks, yes; that's what you need: someone to take a stick to you."

In the silence of his writing, they heard a rustling of skirts, women's voices, and the sound of kissing in the hall. Moreno raised his pen and said:

"Who is it?"

"Don't interrupt what you're doing. What do you care? It's probably Jacinta. Go on."

"Well, tell her to come in. Why doesn't she come in?"

"She talking to your sister. Jacinta! Jacinta! Come in; the monster wants to see you."

The door opened, and there stood Jacinta and Patrocinio, Moreno's sister. The latter chuckled to see her brother in the saint's clutches and withdrew.

"Come in, Jacinta, for the love of God," said Moreno, signing the document, "and get me out of this Calvary. Your dear friend is crucifying me."

"Oh, be quiet, stingy," answered the young woman, advancing toward the desk. "You're the one who crucifies her, because you could give her all she asks for—and you've got plenty more—but you don't, and you're very wrong to torment her if you plan to give it to her in the end."

"Hmm, I see you've joined the enemy. There's no hope," he declared, taking off his glasses and rubbing his eyes, tired from writing so much. "We're lost."

"Well, how about it? Do I or don't I have good advocates?" queried Guillermina, picking up the paper.

"Stingy!" repeated Jacinta. "Refusing her three or four thousand miserable *duros* to finish her construction! A man without children who's swimming in money. You, who used to be so good and so charitable!"

"Well, you see I've become a Protestant—a heretic—and I'm going to become a Jew to see if I can get rid of this calamity."

"Oh, no, we won't leave you alone, will we?" insisted the saint. "Look, Manolo: Jacinta and I collect together now. Even if you become a Turk, you'll have a hard time with us."

"No. Jacinta doesn't get involved in things like that," said Moreno, looking at her fixedly.

"Oh yes I do. The orphanage is mine. I bought it."

"Really? Well, if you paid two *pesetas* for it, you did bad business. It's still only half built and it's already beginning to collapse."

"You'll fall first."

"It's mine," repeated Señora Santa Cruz, drawing closer and putting her hand on the desk. "So let's see how much you'll give for a work of God, you rich miser."

"Not again! I've already given her some valuable beams," said Manolo, looking dazedly, first at the beggar's face and then at her angelic hand, pink and plump.

"That's not enough. We have to finish the ground floor, and—"

"Yes, that's right," interrupted Guillermina. "But he won't give you a scrap. You see, he's going to become a Mormon and he needs the money for all the wives he'll have to support."

"Hey, wait a minute, ladies," remarked the rich miser, sitting back in his armchair. "This is starting to look different. Jacinta becoming a saint and foundress! What a bind! Now I really don't know how to get out of it, because now I'll be condemned if I try to refuse. There's no doubt about it—the hand that's asking comes straight from heaven—"

"That's right," added the Dauphine herself, shaking her open hand. "Make up your mind quickly, my dear gentleman. This is my first chance to be a saint. If you throw me a little something, you'll start me off."

"Oh?" he asked, wriggling very uncomfortably in his chair. "All right, all right—I'll give you something."

Guillermina began to clap, crying: "Hosannah! We've caught him." And with the liveliness of a young girl she grabbed the key that was in one of the desk drawers.

"Eh! No taking liberties, thank you," said her nephew, grasping her hand.

"His checkbook," said the "ecclesiastical rat" struggling to get free and suppress her laughter. "Here it is, you heretical dog. Take it out and fill it in with a few numbers and words and scrawl your signature. Jacinta, open it; don't be afraid."

"Order, ladies, order," argued Moreno, whose laughter interfered with his breathing. "This is a hold-up. Stay calm, because if you don't, I'll have to call in the police."

"The checkbook, the checkbook!" shrieked Jacinta, also clapping.

"Patience, patience. The checkbook isn't here. It's downstairs, in my other desk. So—"

"Bah! You're just trying to fool us!"

"Oh, no," said Guillermina ardently, "you can't get out of it now."

"I'm not leaving until I have your signature."

"My word," declared Moreno very solemnly, putting his hand on his heart, which was no longer worth much, "is worth more than my signature."

He was as white as the paper he was writing on.

"Really?"

"Say no more."

"That's true," said the saint. "He's a clever one, and a heretic, but as for keeping his word, no one can beat him."

After a few more jokes the two foundress-saints withdrew, leaving the heretic with his doctor. They were so pleased that when they got to the saint's room Guillermina almost danced for joy.

"Do you really think he'll send us a check?" Jacinta asked incredulously.

"It's as good as already sent. You were very clever. He knows me so well that it's hard to get anywhere with him. But he couldn't refuse you. Oh, what joy! We've got the ground floor now! Long live Saint Joseph! Long live the Virgin! Because we owe it all to them. Sooner or later, Manolo would have given me the money; I know him like the back of my hand. He's a perfect angel with a heart of gold, one of God's chosen."

2

Their rejoicing didn't last long, because they heard the clock at the Puerta del Sol strike ten; both suddenly altered their expressions.

"It's ten. I wonder if she'll come," said Guillermina, whose face still shone with happiness. "She promised to, but her word probably can't be trusted as much as Manolo's."

And standing still, the foundress said to her friend:

"I'm only doing this for your sake—getting involved in other people's lives! I got the impression the other day that *she's* not the one who's distracting him. If she is, she's a remarkable actress. If she comes today, we'll probe a little deeper and see if we can come up with something. In any case, I'll give her a good sermon so that she'll give him a poor reception if he tries to . . . Do you know something? That woman doesn't seem all bad to me."

"Maybe you're right. But if you could have seen the way she looked at me the other day . . . I've never seen such rancor in anyone's face, ever."

"She says she was sorry for it afterward."

"The wretch!" exclaimed Jacinta, pursing her lips and clenching her fists.

"Anyway, we'll probe her again today. No matter what she says I'll give her a little sermon. And in case she comes early—say between ten and eleven—you'd better leave. We don't want her to catch you here."

After a short silence the Dauphine said resolutely:

"I'm not leaving."

"Child, what are you saying? Are you mad?"

"I'm not leaving. I'll hide in the bedroom. I want to hear what she says."

"That I won't consent to. Theatrical scenes in my house? No, don't expect me to put up with it."

"Oh, you're so silly and overly scrupulous. What harm is there in it? I tell you, I'm not leaving."

"Well, then, stay here. No, don't. Leave, dear. Don't put me in such a bad position. These things aren't in me."

"Let me stay, please! What do you care? I'll go into the bedroom and stay hidden away like a lamb."

"But dear, scenes like this aren't even any good in the theater. Staying in there to spring out later and say in a dramatic voice: 'I heard it all.'"

"You won't hear a peep out of me. All I'll do is listen. Come on, Scruples, let me stay."

"I thought you'd come up with some foolish plan or other. You're a willful one. So that's how you thank me for what I'm doing for you?"

"But what harm will it do? Oh, you're so stubborn. Well, I'm not leaving." The doorbell rang.

"Do you want to bet it's her? I am sorry," said Guillermina, going to the door.

Jacinta thought it wouldn't be wise to argue any further and, without a word, she entered the bedroom, carefully closing the curtained glass door. Guillermina, not yet resigned to the idea of sheltering an eavesdropper, wanted to receive her visitor in another room, but fate decreed that her niece Patrocinio, upon seeing Fortunata appear, took her for one of the many people who came to beg for alms, and so she took her straight into the saint's parlor. The latter was somewhat disconcerted and did not know how to get out of the trap.

"Oh, was it you? I didn't expect you . . . Come in and sit down."

Fortunata, who was dressed very simply, came in like a laundress about to deliver clean clothes. She stepped forward shyly, pausing at every word from Guillermina, until the latter was forced to repeat that she take a seat in order to persuade her. Her humble air and inhibited manner, which were the best sign of her awareness of her inferiority, made her look fully what she actually was: a woman of the people who accidentally found herself with upper-class people. What particularly inhibited her was her fear of not knowing how to use language in harmony with the language her confessor would most probably use. Whenever she found herself in a difficult situation, she reverted to her innate coarseness and forgot the few lessons in speech and manners she had received during her short and troubled life as a lady.

But what was truly singular was that Guillermina, who was normally so sure of her speech, was also flustered that day and didn't know how to express herself. Knowing that her friend was eavesdropping filled her with confusion, because it was a fraud, a cheat, a prank unworthy of proper people. The first thing that occurred to the saint was to expand on what she had said the other day at Severiana's house.

"If you want us to be friends and me to give you good advice, you must trust me completely and not hold anything back, no matter how ugly or bad it is. There's a very obscure point in your life. You're married and you don't love your husband; you confessed it to me the other day. Believe me, it's kept me wondering. You also said that you didn't know what you were doing when you got married. An evasive explanation. Let's be sincere and speak plainly. Being sincere is hard; but just as children wouldn't confess their sins the first time unless the priest coaxed them out, I'm going to help you by asking and then throwing out a net to catch your answer. Let's see if you'll go along with it. When you decided to get married, did you do it with the mental reservation—somewhere in the back of your mind, I mean—that marriage would allow you to sin freely? I don't mean with anyone at all, but with the man you loved?"

Fortunata looked at the ceiling, trying to remember.

"Didn't you have that reservation? Let's see now. Search your soul; look in as far as you can."

"I might have," she said at last, in a very shaky, faint voice. "Maybe . . ."

"See how the dregs come up if you really look for them?"

"But I'll tell you something else, though: I didn't expect to see him again. I thought he'd forgotten me. I even got to thinking that I could be good and decent. I believed it. But how did it happen? Let's see . . . he came looking for me . . . yes, Ma'am; he looked for me and he found me. Suddenly—I don't know how—my marriage and my husband seemed to be hundreds of miles away. I can't explain it."

Whenever the conversation headed for the subject of Juanito Santa Cruz, Guillermina grew terrified. She tried to turn it away from that dangerous extreme and yet didn't know how to lead her penitent soul to a purely ideological realm.

"But your conscience—that's what I want to know about."

"My conscience! That's the strangest part. I'm telling you things the way they happened. My conscience didn't bother me when I committed those awful sins. And I'll tell you more, even if it horrifies you. My conscience approved of it. It said something that was really terrible: it said that my real husband—"

"Don't continue," interrupted the saint, who in a state of alarm by now feared she had heard a noise in the bedroom. "It's horrible. Don't go on. Mother of God! You're very corrupted."

"It seemed to me," continued the penitent woman, unable to repress her effusive sincerity, "that that man belonged to me and I didn't belong to the other one; that my wedding was a sham, an illusion, like something in a theater."

"Stop, stop, for heaven's sake."

"And that's not all. He'd given me his word to marry me—as sure as it's light—and he gave it to me before he was married. And I'd had a baby by him. And it seemed to me that we were tied to each other forever, and that everything that came afterward doesn't count."

Guillermina put her hands to her head. She decided that it would be best to postpone the session for another day, make the excuse that she had to leave.

"That's very serious. It must be examined slowly. It's true that a promise does mean something . . . I won't say that the young man behaved well toward you. But time, and society . . . And above all: you've lost the rights you might have gained, due to your bad conduct."

"I wouldn't have been bad," said Rubín's wife, plucking up her courage when she detected an inexplicable disturbance in her confessor, "if he hadn't ditched me with a baby in me."

The saint hesitated. She didn't know what course to take. Oh, if only she hadn't had a dangerous witness in Jacinta! She would have voiced her thoughts easily and told the bold woman a thing or two.

"You're upset, my child," she said, searching for a way to make the conversation insignificant. "The other day you seemed more reasonable. What's gotten into you?"

"What's gotten into me?" asked Fortunata, looking somewhat dazed. "What's gotten into me?"

"You're not realizing that time has passed; that that man is married to an angelic woman and that—"

The sinful woman's face suddenly shone very brightly. She looked as if she had a halo of inspiration around her. More beautiful than ever, she produced a staunch argument that hit the other woman like an explosive.

Boom! Guillermina was stunned when she heard this atrocity:

"Angelic! Yes, she's as angelic as you like. But she doesn't have any children. A childless wife isn't a wife."

Guillermina was so dumbfounded she didn't know what to say.

"What I think," continued the other with apostolic inspiration and the criminal audacity of an anarchist, "—and you can say what you like—what I think is, and nobody can change my mind, is that she's virtuous all right. Agreed. But she can't give him an heir. I could; I gave him one and I can give him another."

"For the love of God, don't go on. I've never seen anything like it. The idea! What nerve! You're wretched."

And the virgin and foundress plunged into such great confusion that she didn't know whether she was coming or going.

"I may be wretched, like you say, but, anyway, that's what I think. I'll take my idea wherever God sends me—heaven or hell. And it still has to be proved that I'm as bad as they say."

The saint looked at her in true horror. Fortunata seemed to have forgotten herself, like an exalted artist who doesn't know what he's saying or singing.

"Why should I be as bad as it seems? Just because of my idea? Can't you have an idea? You say she's an angel. I don't deny it—I don't want to try to rob her of her merits. I like her, I wish I could be like her in some ways; not in others, because she's as saintly as you want but she's less than me in one thing: she doesn't have any children, and when it comes to having children I won't stoop to her, no, I raise my head and hold it high. And she's not going to have any now, it's already been proved. And as for whether I can have them or not, that's proved too. So that's my idea. And I'll say it again: a wife that doesn't give children isn't worth a thing. Without us, the ones that have them, the world would come to an end. So we—"

"The woman's mad. I'll have to put her in the street," thought Guillermina. "And how bitter it must be for poor Jacinta to have to hear these gems!"

She detected a certain insane exaltation in her visitor, who wasn't the same woman she had spoken with two days ago. She was just about to send her off diplomatically when she heard a noise, like a hand rapping on one of the bay windows, and then a voice calling her. She went over to the window. Fortunata clearly heard Doña Bárbara's voice asking:

"Is Jacinta there?"

3

The saint hesitated before giving an answer. Finally, "Jacinta? No, she's not here."

The two ladies exchanged a few more words and Guillermina returned to her visitor. But the lie she had been forced to tell upset her so that she hardly seemed like her usual calm, composed self. Her friend's eavesdropping and now this lie put her in an extremely awkward position, for she was accustomed to the truth, so the poor lady felt like a fish out of water. A fearsome thought even crossed her mind: mightn't this be a mortal sin? It simply had to be brought to an end.

"Child, you're a bit excited today. I wish I could go on listening to you, try to console you, but you'll have to excuse me today. Another day."

"Do you have to leave?" the anarchist asked sorrowfully. "All right, I'll come back. I have something I want to tell you. If I don't tell you about it, I'll be sorry. Oh, it's awful, awful. It happened yesterday."

Guillermina stood there, wondering what it could be.

"If you persist," she added out loud, "in having those wild ideas, it'll be hard for me to console you. We'll never understand each other."

Just then the sinner stared hard at the saint. She was seeing Mauricia in her. The face wasn't the same, but the expression was. And the voice had gotten hoarse as it does in people who drink.

"What are you thinking about? Why are you staring at me?" asked Guillermina, impatient to end the session.

"I'm staring at you because I like to look at you. Last night and the night before, and every day since we talked, I've been seeing you in my mind. I see you when I'm sleeping and when I'm awake. Yesterday, when that thing happened to me, I said to myself: 'I can't rest till I tell the Señora about it.'"

Guillermina, moved by great curiosity, sat down and, taking Fortunata's hand, said in a low voice:

"Tell me about it. I can hear you."

"Well, yesterday," said the young woman, her eyes downcast except at the end of every sentence when she raised them as if to punctuate her words, "well, yesterday . . . I was going along calm as could be on Magdalena Street thinking about you, and I stopped in front of a store that sells pipes and faucets. I don't even know why I stopped there—after all, what do I care about pipes?—when I felt behind me, or rather here, in my neck, a voice. Oh, Señora, I could feel that voice right back here, where your hair starts to grow on your neck, and it was like a very thin, cold needle jabbing me. I froze in my tracks. Then I turned around and I saw him. He was smiling."

Guillermina put out her hand to cover Fortunata's mouth but wasn't able to keep her quiet.

"I couldn't speak. I was like a statue, and I felt like crying or running or something, I don't know."

"He didn't say anything special though, did he?" checked the saint, very frightened and trying to ignore how serious it was. "Just greeted you."

"Just greeted me? Not exactly. He said: 'What's become of you, baby?' I couldn't answer. I turned away and he grabbed my hand."

"Oh, come now. This is too much," declared Guillermina, getting up and feeling greatly disturbed. "You can tell me about it some other day."

"No—that's all there is to it. I pulled my hand away and left without saying a word. I didn't have the nerve to leave without looking back and so I turned around and saw him. He was following me from a distance. I walked faster and got home."

"Good, very good."

"But wait," said Fortunata, who was no longer exalted; she had sunken into a pitiful state of humiliation and her tone was that of afflicted sinners who cannot bear the burden of their sins. "You still haven't heard the best part. After I saw him I took it into my head . . . Well, I got this idea, a bad idea, Señora, but you're a saint and you'll get it out of my head. That's why I can't rest till I tell you about it."

"Enough, enough; I don't want to hear."

"Yes, you do," insisted the young woman, restraining her with both hands because the confessor had tried to move away.

"An awful idea. The idea of sinning again," stammered Guillermina. "Is that it?"

"That's it. But listen. I want to get rid of it, but sometimes it seems that I shouldn't try to, that I'm not sinning."

"Lord!"

"That's the way it should be, the way it was meant to be," added Señora Rubín, becoming exalted again and taking on the expression of an anarchist planning to throw a bomb to shake the powers of the earth. "It's this idea I have, a foul one I know, as black as the devil's eyes, but I can't yank it out of me."

"Be quiet!"

Guillermina was filled with consternation. She took several hesitant steps, like someone about to fall. The famous foundress hadn't been in such a predicament for a long time. She felt caught, deprived of her freedom, which was distracting and destroyed the sovereign serenity that was usually hers. Even so, she attempted to master the painful situation. Throwing alarmed looks at the glass door leading to her bedroom, she ventured:

"But you're not thinking of—"

She couldn't conclude this trivial sentence. The other woman, human weaknesses personified, nevertheless seemed stronger than the great doctor and saint and indulged in a smile as she listened.

"And what do I get from thinking? The more I think it over the worse it gets."

"I see that you have no control. With those ideas we'd soon be savages again."

With a sarcastic smile and an expressive shrug of her shoulders, Fortunata intimated that she wouldn't mind at all if everyone went back to being a savage again.

"You have no sense of morality; you'll never be able to have principles because you're uncivilized; you're a savage and you belong to a primitive race." This, or something similar, is what Guillermina would have told her if her spirits had been up to it. All she actually said was something vaguely resembling those ideas:

"You have all the brutal passions of the people; they're like rough-hewn rock."

This was the truth, because in our society it is the common people, the *pueblo*, who conserve basic ideas and feelings in their raw fullness, just as a quarry contains marble, the material for forms. The *pueblo* possesses truth in great blocks, and civilization, when it uses up the smaller pieces it lives on, goes back to the *pueblo* for more.

Suddenly Fortunata had a change of heart. It was as if her nervous energy had instantly subsided. Guillermina, on the other hand, suddenly rose in stature, responding to a call from her conscience.

"No more, now, no more lies. I can't, I can't—"

She raised her eyes to the ceiling, crossed her hands; her face brightened and her eyes lit up. The anarchist was astonished to hear her utter the following words in a strange, otherworldly tone:

"Dear God, save this soul that wants to destroy itself, and take all sin away from me."

Then she took Fortunata's hand, saying with deep pity:

"Poor woman! It's my fault that you've said these atrocious things. My fault. God forgive me for letting you. And the reason was a farce, a lie. But let the truth be told. The truth has always saved me and it will save me now. You've said infernal things that have broken my friend's heart, and you said them because you thought you were talking only to me. Well, I've betrayed you; Jacinta is hiding in that bedroom."

Saying this, she ran to the glass door and pushed it open. Fortunata, who was sitting facing the door, leaped up, speechless, paralyzed. Jacinta did not appear. All they could hear was her sobbing. She was sitting in a chair, resting her head on the saint's bed. Guillermina rushed to her side and entreated:

"Forgive her, my dear; she didn't know what she was saying. And you," she added, coming out of the bedroom, "must understand that you must leave. Please do me the favor—"

Perhaps it would have all ended peacefully, but the Dauphine suddenly got up, possessed by that dove's fury that at times took hold of her. Blessed souls! With a leap she was in the parlor. Her face was splotchy from crying and repressing so much anger. She couldn't even speak; she choked. She had to practically spit out the words, with intermittent screams:

"The wretch! She's got the nerve to think she's—! She doesn't understand that she hasn't been sent to a house of correction because justice . . . because there is no justice. And you!" (to Guillermina) "I don't know how you can consent . . . how you could have thought . . . What shame! A woman like her here, in this house. What an insult! Thief!"

In her first movement of fear and surprise, Fortunata took cover behind the chair she had been sitting in. Now, leaning her hands on the back of the chair, she crouched and wriggled her hips like a tigress about to pounce. Guillermina looked at her and felt more dread than she had ever experienced before. Fortunata lowered her head still more. Her black eyes, against the light coming in the balcony door, seemed to be turning green and shone with an almost electric light. And in a hoarse, terrifying voice she said at the same time:

"You're the thief! You! And this minute—"

The anger, passion, and uncouthness that characterize common people suddenly burst from her in a formidable explosion, revealing the instincts of her childhood, the time when, getting into an argument with some other young girl in the square, the two would grab each other by the hair and pull until the grown-ups separated them. She wasn't herself and must have been oblivious of what she was doing. Jacinta and Guillermina cringed for a moment, then the former let out a cry of anguish and the saint rushed out in search of help. Fortunata didn't have time to prolong the quarrel or come to her senses because Moreno's servant—who was a hulking Englishman—appeared at the door, and shortly afterward Doña Patrocinio and even Moreno himself came in.

Señora Rubín lost track of the rest. Afterward she thought she remembered that the Englishman's tough hand had grabbed her arm and pressed it so hard that it still hurt the next day, that they dragged her out of the parlor, opened the door, and left her to make her way downstairs to the street.

Everyone hastened to attend to Señora Santa Cruz, who had fainted, and Moreno, wearing an expression that mixed mockery and consternation, remarked:

"These things happen to my dear aunt for trying to save people's souls."

4

Fortunata went down the stairs laughing. It was senseless laughter sprinkled with interjections. "To tell *me*—! If they hadn't thrown me out I would have grabbed her and . . . but I don't know, I can't remember if I scratched her face or not. To tell *me*—! If I'd hit her I wouldn't have let her go. Ha, ha, ha . . ." Her legs were shaking so hard that when she got down to the street she could hardly walk. The light and air seemed to clear her head a bit and she began to take stock of the situation. Was it true, what she had said and done? She wasn't sure that she had hit her, but she was sure that she had said things to her. Why had Jacinta called her a thief? She went up Paz Street, crossing from one sidewalk to the other, oblivious of her actions.

"What have I done? Oh, was it done, though. Humph! Calling me a thief when she stole what was mine!" She turned back and, as if cursing, muttered between her teeth: "You can call me what you like . . . whatever you like, and you'll probably be right. You may be an angel. But you haven't had any children. Angels don't have them. And I do. That's my idea, yes. Get as mad as you want, good and mad, but you'll never have any and I will. Get as mad as you want."

Past the bank, she burst out laughing again. Her monologue ran like this: "The same as the other woman, the 'Señora' of the Holy Ghost! Doña Mauricia, I mean Guillermina la Dura . . . She wants to make us think she's a saint. Ha! Now that she's sick of frolicking around with priests she wants to be the bishop himself, the best Catholic in the world, and confess all our sins. You drunken hypocrite! Church slut, sleeping with all the priests. Even with the papal nuncio and Saint Joseph!"

Quite unexpectedly her thoughts took a new turn and, feeling a painful anguish in her soul that was rather like a horrible void, she thought this: "But who can I turn to now? Oh God, I'm so alone! Why did you die on me, my closest friend, Mauricia! No matter what they say, you were an angel on earth, and now you're having fun with the real ones in heaven and I'm here all by myself! Why did you die on me? Come back! What will become of me? What do you advise me to do? What do you say? Oh, I feel like crying, so hard. All alone, with nobody to say a word to console me. Oh, what a friend I lost! Mauricia, don't stay with the blessed souls anymore. Come back to life. Look at me, like an orphan. And me and all the orphans in your asylum are crying for you. The poor people you'd help are calling you. Please come back. Señor Pepe made you the cramp irons you wanted. I saw him at his forge this morning hammering away, bang, bang, bang! Mauricia, my dearest, come back, and we'll tell each other our sorrows; we'll talk about when our men loved us and what they used to say to us when they made love, and then we'll both drink because I like to too, just like you up in heaven, and I'll drink with you to make my sorrows go away, yes, so all my sorrows'll get drunk."

At last she reached her house. Thoroughly disturbed, she walked in automatically. Papitos, whom she saw but did not address, was the only one there. She shut herself up in her room, threw off her cloak, and stretched out on the sofa, groaning. After writhing like a wounded beast, she lay face down, pressing her stomach against the sofa springs, and dug her nails into a cushion. She soon sank into a painful lethargy full of nonsensical, horrible images, and she lost her sense of time. When she came back to her senses the room was dim. Struggling to see clearly, she made out Doña Lupe's scrutinizing face observing her.

"What is it? You frightened me. You groaned so! And then you started to laugh and said certain words . . ."

To her aunt's repeated and captious questions she replied evasively and very clumsily:

"Where were you today? You went out."

"I went to buy that material."

"And where is it?"

"The material? Uh, I don't know."

"You sound as if you're up in the clouds. Something's wrong with you. Get up."

But she wouldn't get up. The widow began to suspect that Fortunata was psychically disturbed, and she shook with fear. Past shame and misfortune came to mind, and she promised herself that she would keep a close watch. The lady was in a quandary all night, and Fortunata was in a worse one; she felt her aversion to the whole family gaining control of her soul. She couldn't stand them. They were her keepers, her enemies, her spies. Wherever she went in the house, Doña Lupe followed. She felt watched, and the creaking of her aunt's slippers infuriated her. The next day, after lunch and when Maxi had left for the pharmacy, Fortunata was so afraid of an angry outburst that she faked a migraine. Tying a cloth around her head, she shut herself up in her room and went to bed. Half an hour later she sank into that drunken state of the day before; her thoughts blurred in grief and pain and finally drowsiness overtook her.

She has a strong urge to go out; she gets up, gets dressed, but she's not sure if she has taken off the bandage yet. She goes out, heads for Magdalena Street, and stops in front of the pipe store, obeying that instinct that tells us that if we have a happy meeting at a certain place we can have it again if we go back to the same place. Pipes all over the place! Bronze faucets, spigots, and a multitude of things to conduct water. She stops for a while, looking and hoping. Then she goes on to Progreso Square. On Barrionuevo Street she stops at the door of a shop where there are bolts of material unwrapped and hanging in waves. Fortunata examines them and touches some with her fingers to feel their texture. "This cretonne is really pretty!" Inside there's a dwarf, a monster, dressed in a red cassock and a turban, a transitional animal, halfway along the Darwinian road, where the orangutans became men. The queer creature is performing all sorts of extravagant acts to attract attention, and in the street children are all huddled around to get a look and laugh at him. Fortunata continues on her way and passes by the tavern that has at the door a huge grill for roasting chops, and underneath it the enormous flames. The tavern holds memories that tear pieces from her heart . . . She takes Concepción Jerónima Street; then she takes a narrow little street, Verdugo, to Provincia Square; she sees the flower stands and, standing there, she doubts whether to head for Pontejos, as her mischievous idea impels her to, or Toledo Street. She decides on the latter—she doesn't know why. She goes along Imperial Street and stops in front of the door to the weights and measures office to listen to someone playing beautiful music on a piano. She feels like dancing, and maybe she does dance a step or two; she's not sure. Then something blocks her way, as occurs so often in Madrid. A big cart drawn by seven mules, strung together like rosary beads, comes up the street. The first mule rebels, clopping up onto the sidewalk, and the others use this as an excuse to stop pulling their load. The vehicle—laden with skins full of olive oil, a dog tied to the shaft, a frying pan hanging off the back end—comes to a halt just as a cartload of meat dripping cow's blood comes up behind, and the two drivers break out in the usual exchange of "compliments." There's no way to clear the road because the rosary of mules has encircled a hack coming from the other direction carrying two ladies. And as if there weren't enough of us, along comes a luxurious carriage bearing a very fat gentleman. "You move!" "No, you!" "Get out of my way, I can't get through." The meat driver gives God's name a spin. A stick to the mules, who are beginning to grunt, and one of the blows hits the hack and shatters it. Shouts, swearing, and the cart driver insists on fixing things up by making a verbal heyday of God, the Virgin, the Host, and the Holy Ghost.

And the little piano goes merrily on, cranking out popular tunes that with their piquant tone seem to ignite the blood of the mob. Several women who have set up their scarf stands on wheels in the gutter hastily gather up their merchandise, and the ones announcing "Close-out sale—bolts at a *real* and a half" do the same. One salesman, who's exhibiting a new way to cut glass on a folding table he has set up, has to leave at breakneck speed; another, who's selling the toughest pencils in the world (and to prove it he rams their points into a piece of wood without their breaking off) gathers up his bundles too because the first mule is tramping on everything. Fortunata looks at all this and laughs. The ground is damp and slippery. Suddenly, oh!, she feels as if she's been stabbed. Coming down Imperial Street, toward the crowd that has formed, is Juanito Santa Cruz. She stands on tiptoe to see him and be seen. It would have been a miracle if he hadn't seen her. He sees her instantly and heads straight for her. Fortunata trembles; he takes her hand, inquires about her health. Since the piano is still playing and the drivers are still shouting curses at each other, they both have to raise their voices to be heard. At the same time Juan puts on a very afflicted face and, leading her into the entrance to the Fiel Contraste office, reveals to her: "I've gone bankrupt and I'm working as a clerk in an office to support my parents and my wife. I'm applying for a job as a streetcar fare collector. Can't you see how badly dressed I am?" Fortunata looks at him and feels such intense pain that she might as well have had a dagger driven into her. Indeed, Señorito Santa Cruz's cape has a big snag in it, and underneath it his jacket trimmings are frayed, his tie is filthy, and his shirt collar looks two weeks old. Then she falls into his arms and says effusively, affectionately: "I'll work for you, dear; I'm used to it, you're not. I know how to iron, and clean, and serve tables. You don't have to work. I will, for you. As long as you're my delivery boy, that's enough. No more. We'll live in a garret, just the two of us, and we'll be so happy." Then she begins to see the houses and the sky fade out, and Juan isn't in a cape but a very smart-looking overcoat. Buildings and carts disappear from view, and in their place Fortunata sees something she knows very well: Maxi's clothes on a coat hanger, her own on another with a percale curtain over them; then she sees the bed and gradually recognizes her bedroom, and Doña Lupe's voice deafening the household, scolding Papitos because while she was cleaning the lamps she knocked over almost all the oil. "And you'd better be thankful it's daytime, because if it had been at night and the lights had been on, we would have had a fire for sure."

5

Señora Rubín's dream left such a vivid impression in her mind that it seemed real. She had seen him, she had spoken to him. She completed her thought, threatening an invisible being with her clenched fist: "He has to come back. After all, what do you expect? And if he doesn't come looking for me, I'll look for him. I have my idea, and no one's going to take it away from me." Then she sat up, leaning on her elbow and looking at the tiles. Her eyes fixed on a spot on the floor. With a quick impulse she leaped to that spot and picked up an object. It was a button. She looked at it sadly, and then she hurled it as far as she could, saying:

"It's black and it has three holes. Bad sign."

Back to her musings: "Because if I do run into him and he doesn't want to come with me, I'll kill myself, I swear it. I can't live like this, Lord. I tell you I simply can't go on like this anymore. I'll find a way to get some poison from the pharmacy, something to finish me off fast. I'll gulp it down and join Mauricia." This thought seemed to afford her a certain degree of composure, and she left the room. In a few words Doña Lupe informed her of Papitos' blunder.

"If she'd spilled the oil at night with all the lights on, here we'd all be, burned to a crisp. That girl's a nuisance. She's going to be the end of me."

Getting over her tantrum, she noticed her niece-in-law's face; she could see very obscure hieroglyphics in it, but could not read their meaning. "But don't worry; I'll figure you out . . . You're not going to fool me."

That night Maxi did one extravagant thing after another, and the next morning he was so stubborn and peevish he was unbearable.

"You have to be very patient," Doña Lupe told Fortunata. "Do you want my advice? Don't disagree with him on anything. You have to say yes to everything and then go ahead and do what you should. The poor boy isn't well. Ballester told me this morning that his brain's starting to go soft. God help us."

Fortunata felt a vivid urge to leave the house and didn't know what excuse to give to get away. She offered to do some shopping that Doña Lupe needed done, and she invented other errands. The cunning widow knew that it would be wrong to try to completely restrain her, and so she began to give her some freedom. One day she read her the rules in the following terms:

"You may go out; you're not a child and you know what you're doing. I don't think you'll do anything to upset us, and I think you'll protect the family's dignity as much as I do. Dignity, child, dignity comes first."

But Doña Lupe was beginning to make herself horribly unpleasant to Fortunata, who wouldn't have confided in her for all the world. What really annoyed Doña Lupe wasn't that Fortunata went out, but that she wouldn't tell her any of her thoughts or feelings. The thought that Señora Rubín was perhaps at that very moment playing a dirty trick on the family's decency mortified her, it's true, but not as much as seeing that her niece-in-law didn't consult her or ask for her advice on those shady events that were undoubtedly occurring. "Her sneaking around is what disgusts me. If I catch her, she's really going to get it. It was a black day when that mad hussy stepped into this house. No, I never fell for her; God's my witness. I smelled her out from the first. That goose Nicolás ruined things by making it a religious matter. If she'd at least come to me and say, 'Aunt, I've got this conflict; I've sinned, or I'm going to sin, or I might if somebody doesn't stop me . . .' She knows all too well that with my experience of the world and my gift for expressing things—thanks to God—I'd open up the way for her, to save the family honor. But no, the beast has to handle it herself. And what will she do? Some atrocious thing; something really rash. Sooner or later, we'll see."

Fortunata rushed out toward Progreso Square, where she saw lots of carriages. It was a funeral procession headed up Duque de Alba Street toward Toledo Street. The familiar faces she saw pass by made her realize that the funeral was for Arnáiz, who had died the day before. The Villuendas, the Trujillos, the Samaniegos, and Moreno-Isla all filed past. Don Baldomero and his son were probably there too, maybe in one of the carriages leading the procession. "Hmm! There's Estupiñá." From the cab he was sharing with one of "the boys," the great Plácido cast a scornful, indignant look at her. She followed the procession to the beginning of Toledo Street, where she turned right onto Ventosa Street and went to the esplanade at Portillo de Gil Imón, which overlooks the Manzanares River lowland. She knew the area like the palm of her hand, because when she had lived on Tabernillas Street she very often took afternoon walks to Gil Imón, sat on one of the big stones scattered there (no one knows if they're the remains or the beginnings of a municipal building project), and in a leisurely way enjoyed the pretty view of the river. Today she did the same. The sky, the horizon, the fantastic shapes of the blue mountains, and the drifting clouds awoke in her vague images of an unknown world, perhaps better than the one we inhabit, but in any case different. The landscape there is vast and beautiful, framed on the south by a row of cemeteries whose mausoleums whiten against the dark green of the cypress trees. Fortunata saw a long rosary of carriages that looked like a snake slithering forward, and at the same time another funeral procession was heading up the San Isidro ramp, and yet another up San Justo. Since the wind was coming from that direction she could distinctly hear the San Justo bells tolling the arrival of the hearse.

"He's probably with his papá," she thought, "and even if he sees me on the way back he won't speak to me."

After a long while there she visited the Virgin of the Doves—to whom she said a few things—and she was praying to her when her eyes, glancing down momentarily, spied an object shining on the marble stones. It was a button. "White and it has four holes! Good luck," she said to herself, picking it up.

She went home. The next day she went out to buy material for a dress. She went into two shops on the Plaza Mayor and then walked down Toledo Street, package in hand. As she was turning the corner of Colegiata Street to head home, she felt a voice like a pistol shot:

"Baby!"

God, what a shock! Running into *him* out of the blue, and it had to be at one of the few moments she wasn't thinking about him! She had been wondering what to get for the dress, blue or antique silver? She looked at him and turned white. Then he stopped a cab that was passing. He opened the little door and looked at his old friend with a smile, a smile that said, "Are you coming or aren't you? You're just dying to . . . Why hesitate?"

Her hesitation must have lasted two seconds. Then Fortunata plunged headlong into the cab, as if she were throwing herself in a well. He got in after her, saying to the coachman:

"Listen, head for Las Rondas; take Olmos Boulevard, then the Canal."

For some time they looked at each other, smiled, and said nothing. Sometimes Fortunata leaned back, as if she didn't want to be seen by passersby; sometimes she seemed perfectly calm, as if she were riding along with her husband.

"Yesterday I saw you. I mean, I didn't see you, but I saw the funeral and I figured that you were in one of the carriages up front."

Her eyes embraced him with a soft, affectionate look.

"Oh yes! Poor old Arnáiz's funeral. Tell me something: do you have a grudge against me?"

Her eyes grew moist.

"Me? None."

"In spite of how badly I behaved toward you?"

"I've already forgiven you."

"When?"

"When? What a joke! The same day."

"I've been thinking about you a long time, baby . . . a lot," Santa Cruz said in an affectionate tone that didn't sound fake, putting his hand on her thigh.

"Me too! I saw you on Imperial Street. No, I mean I dreamt I saw you."

"I saw you on Magdalena Street."

"Oh yes . . . the pipe store. Lots of pipes."

Even with this friendly language they didn't break through their reserve until they reached La Ronda. There the isolation invaded them. The carriage penetrated the silence and loneliness of the place like a boat making for the high sea.

"So long since we've seen each other!" exclaimed Juan, putting his arm around her shoulder.

"It had to be; it had to be!" she said, leaning her head on his shoulder. "It's my fate."

"You're looking so attractive! More beautiful every day."

"All for you," she declared, putting her entire soul in her words.

"All for me," he said, and their faces pressed together. "I don't deserve it, I tell you; I don't. Frankly, I don't know how you can even look at me."

"It's my fate. And I don't mind, because I have my idea of things, right here, you know?"

Santa Cruz didn't think of asking her to explain her idea. His was this:

"Oh, but you're beautiful. Have you gotten into any mischief since we last saw each other?"

"Me, mischief?" sounding very puzzled by the question.

"I mean, since you went back to your husband, have you had any little adventures?"

"Me!" she cried, the voice of offended dignity. "Are you crazy? I don't have adventures with anyone except you."

"How long do you have?"

"As long as you want."

"You might have trouble at home."

"Yes, that's true. But so what?"

And Feijóo's warnings quickly flashed through her mind. There was no need to lose her composure or be unfaithful to the religion of appearances.

"Well, I have an hour."

"And tomorrow?"

"Will we see each other tomorrow? Don't deceive me, please," she begged. "I'm used to your tricks."

"But not now. Do you love me?"

"What a question! You know I do, that's why you take advantage of me. I'm very stupid with you, but I can't help it. Even if you hit me, I'd still love you. What craziness! But that's the way God made me. It's not my fault."

This naiveté, with which the disbelieving Dauphin was already familiar, was one of the things about her that charmed him most. For a while now he had noticed a certain dryness in his own soul, and he longed to immerse it in the freshness of that savage, wild love, the pure essence of the common people.

"Will you deceive me again, you cheater?" digging her fingers into his knee as she spoke.

"Don't pinch so hard, it hurts. Let's just enjoy the present without thinking about what will or won't happen in the future. It depends on the circumstances."

"Oh, circumstances! They really bother me. What I want to know is, 'Why, Lord, are there such things?' All there should be is live and love."

"You're right," caressing her, excitedly now, and burying her in kisses.

"Live and love. You're the biggest heart in the world."

Fortunata remembered her friend and teacher Feijóo again: a big heart was a defect; it had to be trimmed down.

"I realize," continued the Dauphin, "that you're worth much more than I am, as a heart; much more. I'm very small compared to you, baby. I don't know what it is you have in those cursed eyes of yours. I can see all the dawns of celestial glory and all the flames of hell in them. Love me, even though I don't deserve it."

"I'd die for you!" pulling gently on his beard. "If you don't love me you'll go to hell. Just so you'll know: you'll go there with me; I'll pull you by your beard."

Laughter.

"I'm so happy, so so happy!" she cried, her face and eyes radiant. "I wouldn't change places with all the angels and seraphim frolicking around in heaven right in front of His Divine Majesty; no, I wouldn't, I tell you."

"Me either. I've been needing happiness for some time now. I was sad and said to myself, 'I'm missing something. But what is it I'm missing?'"

"I was sad too. But my heart's been saying to me for some time now, 'You'll come back, you'll come back.' And if you don't come back, why go on living? Living is waiting for a day like today to come. The rest is dying."

"It's late and I don't want you to get in trouble. Careful, baby. Let's not do anything foolish."

Remembering Feijóo again, she repeated:

"The main thing is, don't do anything foolish."

"So we'll—"

"Tomorrow, whenever's best for you."

"Driver: turn around."

"Leave me at the beginning of Valencia Street."

"Wherever you want."

"And the day after tomorrow too," the senseless woman said anxiously, after a pause.

"And the next, and the next . . . But don't bite."

She was thinking of the future, and her radiant happiness was clouded over by the thought that it wouldn't live up to this day she was experiencing.

"And you won't be so naughty this time, will you, my little rascal? You won't, will you, my little prize?"

"No, no. You'll see. You'll see for yourself."

"Swear it to me! Oh, what a fool! As if vows were any good. Anyway, this time I'll take my precautions. If my idea works out . . ."

"And what idea is it that you have?"

"I don't want to tell it to you. It's just an idea I have. If I told you, you'd think it was crazy. You wouldn't understand it. What did you think, that I'm not as clever as other people?"

"What you are, baby, is the tastiest bite in the world," kissing her romantically.

"Well, anyway, along with the charm there's the idea, and if my idea works . . . I don't want to say anything else now."

"You can tell me tomorrow."

"No, not tomorrow either. Next year."

"'And so the time has come!'"

"'Sylvia, for our farewell!' Leave me here. Good-bye, my little darling. Remember me! If only the minutes could be hours. Good-bye, I'm dying of love for you."

"Be sure to be there. And don't forget the number."

"How could I ever forget it? I'd forget my name first."

"At one on the dot. Good-bye, baby."

"Till tomorrow."

"Till tomorrow."

VOLUME FOUR

VOLUME FOUR

1. On Ave María Street

I

SEGISMUNDO BALLESTER (the pharmacist in charge of Samaniego's pharmacy) had frequent arguments with Maxi over the awful mistakes the latter made. He finally had to forbid him to prepare any strong medicines on his own. "Now look, son, if you're going to mix up the alcoholates with tinctures, let's call it quits! This flask is the alcohol for scurvy and this is the aconite tincture. Take another look at the prescription; read it carefully. If you don't improve, we'll simply have to tell Doña Casta to close down the business."

And with these words, uttered in a rather harsh, teacherly way, Ballester appropriated whatever was in his subordinate's hands. Then, sniffing the mixture Maxi had concocted, he asked angrily: "What the devil did you put in this? Either this is valerian or I've lost my sense of smell. I knew it—you're just not well today. Why not go home? I can get along better by myself. Take care, now, and here—take this laxative on an empty stomach. Then at mealtimes and bedtime take one of these hydrogenated iron pills with extract of wormwood. With this heat it's wise to watch your intake; not overdo it, you know? And above all, go out and walk. Don't read so much."

Relieved of his duties, Rubín went into the laboratory and, taking out a big book from under a chair, he began to read. His pinched, pimply face exuded deep sadness. He got so carried away reading he looked as if he'd fallen into a well where his eyes—and with them his soul—swam in a torrent of letters. He sat in strange, incredible positions. Sometimes he propped his crossed legs on a board much higher than his head; at other times he rested one leg on the low shelf between two decanters of drugs; or he drew his knees up to his chest and used one arm as a pillow for the nape of his neck; or he leaned his left elbow on the table; or he fitted his right armpit over the backrest of his chair as if it were a crutch; or he spread his legs out on the table like arms. The chair, supported only by its back legs, announced with pained creaking its intention of collapsing, and meanwhile the book adapted to these extravagant contractions of its reader's body. The book would appear up in the air, supported by a hand; grasped by both, under his knee level; or its open pages were fanned out as if it wanted to fly; or its covers folded all the way back, risking a break in their spine. What neither varied nor dwindled was the reader's concentration, always fixed and intense regardless of the muscular movements, like an underlying principle that outlives a revolution.

Ballester came and went, working incessantly, humming snatches of tunes from popular musical comedies. He was a likeable man with a careless air, not very clean, with an unkempt beard and a very thick nose, a face crowned by a bushy head of hair that must have had very little to do with combs, and a body ending in some well-worn corduroy slippers that he dragged across the bricks of the back room and laboratory floor.

"For the love of God, since you're not working . . . at least you could take care of the little things," he said, facing Rubín. "Look: that woman's been standing there for a quarter of an hour. All she wants is a penny's worth of diachylon. It's in that drawer over there. Come on, let's move now."

Rubín went out front and attended to the customers.

"Where are the flasks of Scott's Emulsion?"

"Right there—you're practically touching them. I tell you, you've got to take care of that head of yours. Reading again! All right, but mark my words: read, read, read, and your cerebral apparatus will go to the dogs. Humph! Ta tá, ta tée . . ."

He went on singing and his apprentice plunged back into his book.

"What are you reading, anyway? Let's see," said Ballester, looking at the book. "*The Plurality of Inhabited Worlds.* Some subject! The day I start worrying whether or not there are people on Jupiter . . . I tell you, Rubín, you're headed the wrong way. And anyway, just between the two of us: what do you care whether there are people on Mars or not? Is anyone going to give you a prize for finding out? Humph! I'd take a chance on betting," he added, crushing something in the mortar, "that there're people up there on the stars; I'd even go so far as to say so. And what if there are? They're probably as fed up as we are."

Rubín didn't answer. Some time later he left his book, putting it down on a corner of the shelf that stank of carbolic acid, between two jarsful of it; then he rubbed his eyes and stretched his arms and body, taking at least five minutes to conquer his drowsiness and get his blood—what little he had—circulating. He took his hat from the rack and headed for the street. It was a short walk home. He got there with his head hanging, frowning. His aunt told him that Fortunata hadn't returned yet and that they would wait for her to have dinner. Maxi took his place at the table; Doña Lupe put away his hat, returned quickly, and sat on the wicker sofa. They waited awhile in silence.

"Today she's later than ever," observed Doña Lupe. But since she detected signs of distress in her nephew's face, she hastened to make more pleasant conversation. "All day long I've been remembering the talk we had last night. If you weren't who you are, if you had any ambition, we'd be rich in no time. If a pharmacist doesn't make money these days, it's because he wants to be poor. You know quite a bit, and with a few tricks out back and lots of advertising out front— lots of it, that's for sure—you'd have it made. Believe me, I'd help you."

"Aunt, don't think I haven't considered it too. Yesterday it occurred to me that you could add a solution of iron to all sorts of medicines. I think I could come up with a new formula."

"Look, son, these things are done either on a big scale or not at all. If you're going to invent something, make it a panacea, something that will cure every-thing, absolutely everything, that you can sell in any form—liquid, pills, tablets, capsules, syrup, plasters, and even special cigars. With all the drugs that you and Ballester have in there, aren't there three or four that could mix well and be good for everyone? It really hurts me to see you with a fortune at arm's length and you not even reaching for it. Look at Dr. Perpiñá on Cañizares Street. He's made a bundle from that syrup . . . what's it called? Something like—"

"Refined lacto-phosphate of lime," said Maxi. "As for panaceas, pharmacolog-ical ethics don't permit them."

"What a fool! What do pharmacological ethics have to do with this? See? You're proving I'm right: you'll never be anything but poor. You're just like that simpleton Ballester; he gave me that business about 'ethics' the other day. Doesn't experience teach you two anything? And poor old Samaniego didn't leave his family any capital because he had the same dumb streak you have. Humph! In his time almost anything you bought at a pharmacy had to be mixed while you waited. Casta was exasperated, of course. She's hoping, too, that you and Ballester will come up with something to give the business a name and fill the registers with cash. A fine pair she's got running her business . . ."

Every now and then Doña Lupe interrupted her chatter to look at the dining room clock but did not express her impatience in words. Finally, the bell rang faintly. It was Fortunata who, when late, rang timidly and cautiously, as if she wished that even the doorbell would comment as faintly as possible on her tardy return to the home front. Papitos ran to open the door, and Doña Lupe disap-peared into the kitchen. Maxi's tone indicated that he was pleased to see her, but he rebuked her gently for not returning sooner. Her eyes were swollen, as if she'd been crying, and it wasn't hard to guess that she was hiding great sorrow. But Rubín didn't notice his wife's long face and sighs that night. For some time now his powers of observation had been waning; he lived within himself, and all his thoughts and emotions came from his ruminations. His objective impulses were almost nonexistent, and this resulted in a dreamlike state.

Doña Lupe, on the other hand, didn't miss a thing; she took note of every detail. At the table they talked about the weather, the terrible heat wave "that was so unseasonable" because it wasn't July yet, although it would be in a few days; about the trains coming and going and the many people leaving for the northern provinces. Rather timidly, Fortunata ventured that her husband should stop taking pills and make up his mind to go to San Sebastian for medicinal baths. Very apathetically, the poor boy said that it would do him just as much good to take them in Madrid with some Cantabrian seaweed, to which his wife replied energetically: "Seaweed doesn't have any value anyway, and even if it did, what matters most is the sea breezes."

Spearing the garbanzos on her plate one by one, Señora Jáuregui said to herself: "I know what you're up to . . . you snake in the grass. I know what 'breezes' you want. After playing around here, you want to keep it up there, because your friend's going. Yes, I know it for a fact; Casta told me. The family from Pontejos Square is leaving tomorrow. But you won't get away with *this* one. To San Sebastian, no less! Not on your life! Don't worry, I'll give you some good 'breezes.'"

Later on Doña Casta appeared with Olimpia to propose a walk to the Prado. Rubín vacillated, but his wife firmly refused. So Doña Lupe left with her friends and Fortunata and Maxi sat until midnight in the living room in the dark with the balcony windows wide open because of the heat, and they talked about things that had nothing to do with reality. He brought up truly morbid subjects, as, for example: "Which of us will die first? I'm very delicate, you know, but even so I may have quite a few years in me. Delicate constitutions last the longest, and robust types are the ones that collapse first." She made an effort to keep up this soporific and unpleasant conversation. Another of Maxi's propositions was: "You know, if I weren't married to you, I'd devote myself to a religious life. You have no idea how it seduces me, how it calls me. To go into retreat, renounce everything, completely annihilate exterior life and live only within—that's the only positive good there is; the rest is a rat race, running around in circles for nothing."

Fortunata agreed with everything he said and, feigning interest, privately turned to her own thoughts, rocking herself in the gentle, warm, dark atmosphere of the room. The light from the street lamps filtered in weakly through the balcony windows, reproducing on the ceiling the candelabra and the shadows of its branches, and this fantastic image, quivering on the smooth, white ceiling, attracted the sad young woman reclining in the armchair, head leaning back, eyes fixed on the ceiling. Maxi harped on his theme: "If it weren't for you, I wouldn't mind dying at all. In fact, the thought of death even pleases me. Death is the hope of carrying out somewhere else what was no more than an attempt here. If we were assured that we'd never die, we'd soon become brutes, don't you agree?"

"Yes. Who doubts it?" she responded mechanically, letting her own thoughts flutter about the ceiling.

"I've thought about it for a long time. You know, I'd certainly give myself up to the inner life if it weren't for the fact that one's tied to a cart of emotions that has to be pulled."

"Good God! I'd better brace myself for tomorrow!" thought his wife. Experience had taught her that whenever her husband fell into a kind of spiritual drowsiness at nighttime, the next day he was sure to become wildly suspicious and think that everyone was plotting against him.

Shortly after this, Maxi said that he wanted to go to bed. Fortunata lit the lamp and he headed for their bedroom, dragging his feet like an old man. While his wife undressed him, the poor boy shocked her with the following words, which hinted at infernal inspiration in a brain already possessed by the devil. "Well, let's see whether I dream the same thing I dreamed last night. Didn't I tell you about it? Listen. I dreamed I was in the laboratory and that I was busy measuring—by eye—potassium bromide into one-gram size packets. I was upset, and I was thinking about you. I had filled at least a hundred packets when I felt a strange thirst—a spiritual thirst—that not even fountains of water could quench. I went to the flask of morphine hydrochloride and drank all of it. I fell on the floor, and in that groggy state—listen carefully now—in that groggy state an angel appeared to me and said, 'Joseph, do not be jealous. If your wife is pregnant, it is the work of Divine thought.' Can you imagine dreaming such nonsense? You see, yesterday I got to reading the Bible and I read the passage about . . ."

Maxi stretched out in bed and, closing his eyes, fell instantly into a deep sleep, as if he had drunk all the laudanum in the pharmacy.

2

Fortunata did not go to bed because it was very hot. She lay down on the sofa half-dressed, and when it dawned, after she had dozed off a few times, she realized that her husband was awake. She could hear him grunting and sighing, as if rage were suffocating him. She heard him groping for the matches on his night table. The matchbox fell, and in the darkness Fortunata saw the livid glow of their phosphorescence. Maxi's hand reached out and finally managed to seize the box. Fortunata watched the bluish light of the matches rise and then disappear when he struck one and it instantly lit up the room. The young man's eyes squinted anxiously in search of her and, seeing his wife on the sofa, he said: "Oh! There you are. Don't you play the role well!"

To avoid such an untimely quarrel, the wife pretended to be asleep. But, squinting, she saw him light a candle. Maxi put on enough to cover his bareness and then cautiously got out of bed. Taking the candle, he went out to the hall. Fortunata heard him checking the lock, opening the door, rummaging around in the room where she kept her clothes, then going into the dining room and the kitchen. Maxi had done this so many times that his wife had gotten used to these extravagant acts. He was obsessed by the notion that somebody was entering or trying to enter the house to dishonor him.

When Maxi came back to their bedroom, day was breaking. "If I don't catch you today, I'll catch you tomorrow," he muttered. "Nothing's wrong, but I heard steps and whispering; you went out and came back, and now you're pretending you're asleep to fool me. Go on, try it. I've got a sharp eye, and even if it seems that I don't notice anything, I see everything. You don't know who you're dealing with. There was a man in the hall, there's no doubt about it. So it's no good swearing that there wasn't anybody there. Do you think I'm deaf? Or dumb?"

He said this as he sat on the bed, candle in hand and staring at his wife, who continued to pretend that she was asleep, all the while hoping that he would calm down. But it wasn't that easy. Once his insane mania broke loose, it meant there was trouble ahead. Putting on the rest of his clothes, he began to stride around the room, waving his arms and talking to himself.

"Oh, no. If they think they can fool me, they're wrong. The worst of it is that my aunt's covering up for her. After all, how could anyone get in unless she consented to it? And Papitos is mixed up in it too. Humph! She's probably getting a good payoff. But I'll fix you, you two-bit runner! And they'd better not try to give me any nonsense. Yesterday I noticed some footprints on the doormat that are from a refined person's boots. They say they're the water-carrier's. The water-carrier's, my eye! And the day before yesterday this room gave me the distinct impression that someone had been here. I can't explain it. It's as if there were footprints in the air, a sort of smell or shape of a body in the atmosphere. I know what I'm saying: someone has been here. Oh, but I have a choice role to play! Lord, what good does it do to put your honor above everything else? Someone comes in from the street and steps on it and covers it with filth. And it's not enough to watch, watch, watch. I don't even sleep at night and yet I've got to keep a closer watch. My wife, my aunt, Papitos—I can't let them out of sight for a minute. That damned Papitos is the one who opens the door, and I'm going to bash her head in."

At last Fortunata thought it was time to pretend that she was waking up. The odd thing was that in his crises the wretched young man never went beyond verbal extravagances to violent acts; the crises consisted of extremely bitter complaints, anguished concern over his honor, and threats that he was going to carry out.

"What nonsense are you talking?" asked his wife. "Why don't you go to bed? And if you're not going to sleep, at least let me sleep."

"Do you think that after what you've done a person can sleep? What a conscience, Lord, what a conscience you have! You'll deny it now. Who was out in the hall? The cat, of course. The poor beast gets blamed for everything. And why did you leave the room? To play with the cat, right? Sure. And you expect me to swallow that? What kills me is that my aunt consents to this; my aunt, who loves me so much. I know you don't love me. But my aunt! Really . . . And that sneaky Papitos with her monkey face. Really, you people are incredible. An honorable man has no defenses against so many enemies. Treachery surrounds him. Disloyalty stalks him. The people he trusts the most sell his soul. And where he least expects it, in his own family, a Judas strikes. There can't be any honor on earth. It can only exist in heaven, because God is the only one who doesn't deceive us, the only one who doesn't wear a mask of love and then stab us in the back."

Fortunata got dressed instantly. She knew from experience that the more he was contradicted, the worse he got. She sat on the sofa for a while listening to his ranting and raving, waiting for when she could warn Doña Lupe. Before going in to wash, she stopped at her aunt's bedroom—Doña Lupe was already getting dressed—and said: "It's awful today . . . poor thing. Maybe you could calm him down."

"I'll be right there. I can see that you two can't manage without me. If you didn't have me, I hate to think what would happen. Look—get Papitos up. Tell her to light the fire. We'll make him a hot chocolate, because not eating enough is what puts him in such a state. That poor body needs nourishment. Take the keys, here. Get out the chocolate that Ballester gave us, the chocolate fortified with iron. What a boy, the things he comes up with! I'll be right there."

When his aunt came in with the chocolate, Maxi was still spouting the same foolishness. "What I can't understand, Aunt," he said, flashing his eyes at her, "is why you consent to this and cover up for them and want to kill me, because you might as well hear this: for me, honor comes before life itself."

"My dear boy," answered Doña Lupe, putting his chocolate on the table, "we'll talk about this later. I'll explain everything and you'll be convinced that it's all in your head. Drink your chocolate first. You're very weak."

The young man gave in. Sinking onto the sofa and leaning toward the table where his breakfast was, he picked up a piece of pound cake and dunked it in the thick liquid. Before tasting it, his tongue started to wag again, although admittedly in a more subdued tone. "I don't know how you're going to convince me. I can see and hear, and when there's evidence you can't—"

He made a gesture to express his repugnance and horror when he tasted the cake dunked in chocolate.

"Aunt . . . Fortunata! What is this? What have you given me? This chocolate has arsenic in it."

"Son, for the love of God!" Doña Lupe exclaimed in great consternation just as Fortunata was coming in.

"Do you think you can hide the taste of arsenic?" he asked, his composure gone, his eyes wild. "They're not stupid, either. They put in a small dose, just a centigram, to kill me slowly. And I bet it was Ballester who gave them the arsenic . . . because he's against me too. What kind of hell is this, Lord?"

"Come, now. We can't stand for this. Saying that we've poisoned his chocolate!"

"It's arsenic all right; the taste couldn't be plainer."

He got up desperately and started pacing the floor again, venting his delirious apprehensions.

"I'll have to let myself die of hunger. It's horrible—my own house full of enemies. The people who used to love me the most want me to die now."

"So it's arsenic, is it!" exclaimed Fortunata, making a joke of it all, hoping to achieve a better result this way. "Just so you'll see how silly you are, *I'm* going to drink the chocolate."

And she immediately started to drink it. Her husband stared in astonishment.

"Let's see if I drop dead, once and for all. It may be poisoned, but it sure tastes good. Are you convinced now? I could drink another cup, right now. And it wouldn't be so bad if this stuff killed me, because then I could clear out of this world fast. Don't think it's any fun for me—all the headaches you give me, and the way you make us suffer."

Meanwhile, Doña Lupe had brought in an alcohol burner to prepare another hot chocolate before Maxi's eyes. Even so, it was a painful struggle to persuade him to drink it, because he insisted that this cup tasted of arsenic too. "Although I agree; the taste isn't so strong now." Then in a more conciliatory tone he declared:

"I think all this is Papitos' doing. You have no idea how malicious she is and the grudge she has against me."

"Oh, come now," said Doña Lupe. "You make me feel like spanking you. To say such things about poor little Papitos! Look—when you get these ideas, blame me for everything. I know how to defend myself and prove my innocence. Now. Why don't the two of you go out for a walk in the Retiro? It doesn't get hot till nine o'clock, and it's a lovely day."

Fortunata seconded this suggestion, but he didn't feel like going out. He remained on the sofa, his elbow resting on the end table, his head cushioned on his hand, staring at the floor as if he were counting the reeds in the mat next to the sofa. The two women exchanged looks, communicating their unfavorable impressions.

"Sure," he murmured thickly, distrustfully. "They want to get me out in the street so that—"

"For God's sake, Maxi, she's going with you."

"And where does she plan to take me? God only knows. Some trap or other. If it were just to murder me, it wouldn't be so bad. But if it's to attack my most sacred possession: my honor!"

"God help us."

"Didn't you know, Aunt, that three months ago . . . It was in *La Correspondencia*. A woman took her husband to the Retiro, and when they were strolling along one of the empty paths, the accomplice sprang out; yes, her accomplice, he was hiding in the bushes. And between the two of them they tied up the poor husband and threw him in the pond."

"Lord, how atrocious! Where did you hear such nonsense?"

"No such thing was in *La Correspondencia*," said Fortunata.

"You must have dreamed it."

"I did not dream it!" he cried, jumping up in agitation. "It's true; I read it in the paper . . . and . . . Now they call me a liar too! I always speak the truth. You're the liars. You're the ones who have so many crimes on your consciences."

Doña Lupe clasped her hands and looked up, imploring divine justice from above. Fortunata looked completely crushed, as if she were on the verge of losing all patience.

"Look," said the widow. "Go to the pharmacy; go to work, and your head will start to clear."

Señora de Jaúregui knew from experience that when her nephew had a severe attack the only person who could bring him back to his senses was Ballester, who alternated ridicule with stiff, even cruel, authority. The others in the family, whom he loved, were the most inept at controlling him, and they had to bear the brunt of his enraged suspicions. "All right, I'll go," said Maximiliano, picking up his hat. "I have a few things to say to Sr. Ballester. He's not going to laugh at *me* anymore. And if he does have something to say, let him say it to my face! I bet he won't dare. He's a coward, and a traitor—selling you friendship and stabbing you in the back."

Aunt and wife said nothing; they followed him to the door. Taking his cane from the rack in the entry, he walked out and slammed the door. He went downstairs quickly and talked for a while with the doorwoman. From the balcony the two ladies saw him walk out, cross the street, look back at the house . . . Then they hid themselves and, peeking cautiously from between the iron bars, they saw him continue on, gesturing and nervously twirling his cane. Along the way he made occasional stops to look back; he would take a few steps and then go on his way up the street. On one of those turns, he saw Ballester at the pharmacy door and heard him call out imperiously: "Come here, now. That's right! You come here."

Like a dog cringing and dragging its tail at the threat of its master's stick, Rubín entered the pharmacy with: "Good morning, my friend. I didn't see you. I was out for a bit of fresh air. And how are you?"

3

"Me? I'm fine. So you were out for some fresh air?" replied Segismundo ill-humoredly. "Your 'fresh air' can be to put some labels on these bottles of syrup. And be careful you don't make any mistakes. Red labels are for the bitter orange peel syrup with potassium iodide; the green are the same, except they're fortified with iron. If you mix up the labels I'll make hamburger out of you."

He set to work and, strangely enough (considering the chaos in his head), he didn't make a single mistake, not even when given six more kinds of syrup with their corresponding labels in different colors. Ballester, who had already been informed by a note from Doña Lupe of Maxi's bad attack that morning, watched him out of the corner of his eye, but not enough; on one of his trips to the laboratory, Maxi abruptly abandoned his work and left for the street without his hat. When Ballester came back in and noticed the young man's absence, he remained very calm and said only: "So he's flown off . . . and in what a state!" He took his colleague's extravagant acts in stride; he only wished that one of those escapes would be for good. "But I wouldn't have such luck," he said to himself. "They'll send him back to me, to tame him."

Maxi went home. When Fortunata opened the door, she wasn't surprised by his distraught air, because such unexpected appearances had become quite common. "I suppose," he stated, lips quivering, "that you won't deny it now. My aunt may try to—she's such a hypocrite! But you won't. You're bad, but sincere. When you strike a fatal blow, you say so, don't you? And now, with clear evidence in sight, what do you have to say?"

"Not again! But son . . . ," cried Doña Lupe, coming out into the hall.

"You, Aunt, will try to deny it, but *she* won't. I can't catch him, because he's probably already escaped from the balcony. But you can't deny that he was here. I saw him, I saw him go past the pharmacy. He left his footprints on the stairs; his footprints, traces . . . They're unmistakable."

"Well! So we're having a party, are we?" Doña Lupe said to Fortunata, who sighed as she looked at her husband with intense pity.

"And that little tramp Papitos is going to pay for this!" he shouted, stomping off to the kitchen.

"Papitos! She's out doing the shopping. Poor girl! Uff! Please, we're fed up with all this. Leave us alone, will you? We'll tell Ballester to tie you down. That's enough of your foolishness, son."

Saying this, Doña Lupe took him by the arm and shook him with corrective, maternal anger. "We won't be able to stand you if this keeps up. *Your* problem is that you're spoiled."

The miserable young man collapsed onto a bench in the entry hall, somewhat like a church pew, and, seated there, that insane mask of fury gradually gave way to a look of consternation. "Guarantee me, then, that my honor is . . . what they call intact . . . and I'll feel calmer."

"Your honor! But who the devil's bothered it? It's all in your head; you've conjured it up all by yourself."

"Me, conjured it up! Oh—"

"Yes, every bit of it," said Fortunata, putting her hand on his shoulder tenderly. "Don't think about it and you won't be afraid of anything. It's just your imagination, that's all. 'The crazywoman in the house,' as your brother Nicolás says."

"You know what we're going to do?" Doña Lupe suggested after a pause, taking advantage of the relative calm she observed in her nephew. "We're going to give him lunch."

His wife took him by the arm to lead him to the table, and he didn't put up any resistance. They were afraid that he wouldn't want anything, that he'd think the food was poisoned; but to their mutual surprise Maxi wasn't at all suspicious. He didn't have much of an appetite, and to make him eat something the two of them started a competition, using quite a number of affectionate words. They were so loving that Maxi ate more than usual without any remarks or complaints about how the food was seasoned. Then they made him coffee—the only thing he took willingly. After lunch Doña Lupe tried to cheer him up by chatting about things that had nothing to do with the gibberish about his honor; but he let it be known with deep sighs that the storm in his soul was not yet over. Nevertheless, the worst of the attack was over, and soon total serenity would ensue. Upon leaving for the pharmacy, he took his wife aside and beseeched her, "Promise me you won't go out this afternoon. Promise me you'll never go out without me."

"Me, go out! What nonsense! I hadn't thought of any such thing," she replied with a smile. "I'll be right here, waiting for you. Tonight we'll go to Doña Casta's, all right? Or we could take a walk."

As she was saying this, Doña Lupe, spying on her from a corner in the hallway, fixed an astute eye on her.

That afternoon Maxi was much calmer while he was at the pharmacy. Once, when he was free, he went into a corner of the laboratory where he kept his books and took one, intending to plunge into it. But Ballester grabbed a measuring stick, headed straight for him, and, knocking the book out of Maxi's hands, threatened to punish him. "Aah—let's forget all that book-learning; that's what confuses you. And anyway, what is this book? Oh, how sweet! *Errors in Egyptian and Persian Theology.* Or so the chapter heading says. For the love of God, do you always have to be sticking your nose in the wrong pie? What difference does it make to you if those barbarians—who've been dead for thousands of years anyway—adored lots of gods? You're just nosy about other people's lives. So they had gods by the dozen? So what! Do *you* have to worry about feeding them? It's like I say—you're just nosy. I can't stand this nonsense" (getting so exalted now he was almost angry). "I can't see why a Christian spends his time trying to find out about stuff he couldn't understand any more than geese would understand our sermons. I'm going to hide those books, or better yet, I'm going to burn them . . . I'll be right there!"

This last sentence was directed to a customer who was showing him a prescription.

"You blockhead" (meaning Maxi); "get a move on. Bring me the camphor, the saltpeter, and the licorice powder."

He concocted the medicine before you could bat an eye and was back with his stick and his invective, which ran like this:

"It's just like the other nonsense—that they're going to take away your honor; that men get into your house; that your honor's being ambushed from all sides. Aren't we melodramatic, though! It's hard to believe that you could think up such absurd things and be married to a woman who's as chaste and pure as the Virgin Mary; yes, sir, I'll say it again: as chaste as the Virgin Mary; a woman who'd sooner let herself be carved up than look at another man. And since you know it's so, why do you make such a fuss? Ah, if I had a woman like that—so beautiful, so virtuous—if I had a virginal creature like that at my side, I'd get down on my knees to worship her; I'd let myself be caned before giving her any reason to be upset. Your honor! You've got more honor than . . . well, I don't know what to compare it with. Your honor is brighter than the sun. No, not even the sun will do; it's got spots. It's cleaner than clean. And you still complain. Listen; I'm going to cure you with this stick. As soon as you mention honor, whack! It's the only way. You do these things because you're spoiled. An aunt who looks after you, a pretty wife who spoils you and lives only for you. That's the truth. Jiminy, if only I had a wife like her . . . "

When Segismundo reached this point in his reprimand, which he was delivering very sanctimoniously, Rubín had become so calm that he could almost listen benevolently, even jovially. And finally he did smile, and after a long pause said:

"Ballester. I'd like to invite you to the theater tonight. Will you come?"

"Would I like to? Sure. I wish rain like this would fall every day, my dear friend. Yes, we'll go—that is, if Padilla can tend the pharmacy in case there are any night calls. Now let's go, my dear colleague, and make those pills of iodide of mercury. You mix the mucilage of gum arabic and licorice. It's a tricky prescription; be very careful. I'll tell you, there's no science as sublime as pharmacology. It's so much more interesting than finding out if there were this many or that many dozens of gods. Well, let's get on with it. Be very careful with this mercury; it's very precious. The patient it's for must be badly off. I wouldn't want to be in his shoes . . . But he must have had a pretty good time in this world with beautiful girls. Well, if it's costing him a lot now, it's because he had a heyday in his time. Whoa! Be careful with the dose. Don't be so impetuous or you'll end up making the patient worse—he'd drool so much we'd see it. What a beautiful science pharmacology is! For me, there are two arts: pharmacology and music. Both cure humanity. Music is the medicine of the soul, and . . . vice versa. You know what I mean. After all, what are we if not the composers of the body? You, for example, are a Rossini, and I am a Beethoven. In both arts it's a question of mixing. They talk about notes; we talk about drugs, or substances; they have sonatas, oratorios, and quartets; we have metics, diuretics, tonics, etcetera. The point is, you've got to know how to touch the sensitive spot with a composition. What do you think of these theories? When we're out of tune, the patient dies."

In a little while the assistant pharmacist (who only worked nights at the pharmacy) arrived and, taking him aside, Segismundo said: "Padilla, today I'm going to propose to Doña Casta that you work during the day, because Rubín is a real calamity—he's got a head like a broken basket, and I'm afraid that if he's left alone he'll poison our customers."

4

That night after dinner they all went to Doña Casta's, where they had planned to meet before their walk. But shortly after entering, Ballester arrived, saying that an unpleasant wind had blown up and a storm was threatening, so it was unanimously decided that they would stay in. A light was lit in the living room, and Doña Casta told Olimpia to play her piece for Maximiliano and Ballester.

Olimpia was the youngest of Samaniego's daughters. She would have been greatly admired in the times when it was stylish to be consumptive or at least appear to be; thin, spiritual, circles under her eyes, a delicately shaped face with a romantic expression, the girl would have been an ideal beauty fifty years ago in the days of corkscrew curls and sylphlike waists. Doña Casta wanted her daughters to be able to earn a living in case some unforeseeable circumstance arose and left the family penniless, so Olimpia had been taken to the conservatory at an early age. For seven years she stayed at the keyboard, and then she continued on their own piano under the direction of a famous teacher who came twice a week. It was hoped that her exams would win a prize, and because of this the young girl spent no less than three years studying a certain piece that she had not yet managed to master. The famous piece, morning, noon, and night. By now Ballester knew it by heart and didn't miss a note. Olimpia hadn't yet been able to render the whole piece, from the *adagio patético* to the *presto con fuoco*, without making a mistake somewhere, and whenever she played for anyone she got all muddled, making such a mess of the notes that not even God would have been capable of unscrambling them. Doña Casta made her play whenever there were new visitors so that she would lose her fear of "the audience."

The agreement to call off the walk put the young lady in a bad mood because she wouldn't be able to talk with her fiancé, who at that moment was stuck to the corner of Tres Peces Street waiting for the family's exit in order to join them. He was a worthy boy, currently in his last year of I don't recall what subject, and he wrote (unpaid) criticism for various newspapers. In spite of his notable traits, Doña Casta didn't eye him favorably because, well, criticism wasn't the most lucrative work when it came to supporting a family. But Olimpia was his ardent admirer; she read all of her fiancé's articles, which he clipped out of the newspapers and glued onto separate sheets of paper; the reading was proving quite enlightening. She kept this bundle of esthetic pronouncements with his letters and locks of his hair. Doña Casta had not yet permitted the worthy young man in her house.

The girl played her piece, not without tiring, occasionally mauling the keys as if to punish them for some misdemeanor of theirs, and sometimes caressing them so they would emit gentle sounds, she pedaling and arching her body first this way, then that, and putting on a tortured or vexed countenance, depending on the passage. Her fingers were like mouths, famished mouths judging from the number of notes they devoured. On certain difficult scales some notes anticipated their predecessors; but when she came to an easy effect the pianist said to herself, "I'm sure to get this right," and she compensated for her earlier blunders. Exclamations of admiration didn't cease throughout this long martyrdom of the keyboard: "What hands that girl has! Guelbenzu's nothing next to her!" "And what artistic talent, what expression!" Ballester, the rascal, exclaimed. And Doña Casta: "This is the hard part, the one that's coming now. She plays it to perfection. What a clear touch! And she phrases so well!" Doña Lupe oohed and aahed too, and Fortunata felt obliged to express some enthusiasm, even though she didn't understand a word of this tin-pan serenade and inwardly wondered that it should be called "a sublime art" and that serious people should applaud music that sounded like noise from a boilermaker's shop. Any old musical tune being cranked out on a street piano pleased and moved her more.

Olimpia played with faith and feeling, presuming that the best of critics was out in the street listening to her performance. When she finished she was spent, perspiring, her bones aching—she could hardly breathe. She didn't even have the strength to thank the others for their compliments. Her sudden coughing seemed to be a sign of her hemoptysis. "My child," cautioned her mamá as she saw her heading for the balcony, "don't go out; you're perspiring. Here, put on this shawl."

So she put it on, and, unable to suppress her urge to be on the balcony, she went out with Fortunata, and the two of them looked at the suffering soul pacing the sidewalk across the street.

Shortly afterward Aurora came; she was the elder Samaniego, very different from her sister—black-haired, good-looking, yet not a beauty, one of those women who combine an anemic complexion with a bland strength and the luxuriance of colorless flesh. She had an oversized bosom, a short neck, a well-shaped bodice and hips, and the seams of her sleeves looked as if they were about to split, accommodating the plump fullness of her arms. Her head was pretty—not much hair, very well styled. She had a sharper mind than her sister and dressed with that graceful simplicity that characterizes foreign women who earn their living at the counter of an elegant shop or managing accounts for a restaurant. Her dress was always one color only—no combinations—and the cut was rather severe and efficient; the dress of a young woman who is alone on the street and has some sort of decent job.

A word on this. Aurora Samaniego was thirty, the widow of a Frenchman who had come to Spain as a representative of foreign drug companies. Soon after their marriage, in '65 or thereabouts, the Frenchman took his wife to Bordeaux, where he inherited from his parents a linens shop that he expanded by hard work and eventually turned into a small fortune. But between Bismarck and Napoleon III it was lost, because these two characters brought about the war of 1870, which was to nip so many hopes in the bud. Fenelón, an extremely good man with a business mind, had the defect of being a Chauvinist. He took up arms, joined the army, and was one of the first to fall when the Prussians started shooting.

A widow with scanty means, although she was childless, Aurora returned to Madrid, where her readiness to work and the experience she had acquired could not be employed due to our lack of "big stores," the few there are being already taken by those professional loafers, the salesmen, who usurp from girls their only respectable way of earning a living. Fenelón's widow had learned all there was to know about linens; she was good at bookkeeping; she had clear notions on what economic order and practices a well-built business should stick to; and she spoke French fluently. Nevertheless, all these merits would have been totally useless had it not occurred to Pepe Samaniego to establish a linens shop that "would have the latest creations from other countries" and employ someone as intelligent as his cousin, who was so appropriate for the shop. The project was huge. Aurora would be in charge of trousseaux, christening, children's and ladies' apparel. The capital for setting up this important industry had been supplied by Don Manuel Moreno-Isla, who had confidence in Pepe Samaniego's integrity and skill. The shop was to be in a new building near Santa Cruz Square, facing Pontejos, and its window displays were sure to be the most glamorous and elegant in Madrid. The inauguration was scheduled for September 1.

Samaniego was in Paris buying, and at the time we're referring to, boxes were beginning to arrive. In the makeshift store next door to the permanent one there was already a lot of work. Aurora, the center of a graceful pleiad of very clever assistants, laid out the models that were to be shown the first few days as samples of the shop's delicate garments. From dawn to dusk she lived in waves of batiste and the foam of exquisite lace, cutting and fitting, a stitch here and a little trimming there, leading her flock of seamstresses with as much intelligence as authority.

At night, when she came home exhausted, her mother liked for Doña Lupe, Fortunata, or her other friends to be present so that she could give free reign to her vanity. As soon as she saw her daughter return, her face lit up, and from that moment on their only subject was the new business and the unconceived wonders that Madrid's elegant set would admire there. The four women usually gabbed until midnight, so Ballester, seeing that a session was getting under way, took Maxi aside and said, "You and I are going to the theater." Olimpia, who shared neither her mother's presumptuousness nor her enthusiasm for business, stayed where she was, leaning on the windowsill in the parlor, following the melancholic shadow of her bored Aristarco, and occasionally casting him a word or two to sweeten his long wait.

"You must be very tired; sit down," said Doña Casta to her daughter as she rounded up the group. "How's it going?"

"They were testing the gas today in the new shop. It's going to be splendid. Shipments are already arriving and there are things that are so pretty there's nothing to match them in all Madrid. They just don't know how to do shop windows here. Wait till you see ours—full of the nicest things you can find. They'll catch people's eye and make them stop and come in to buy. Once they're in we'll show them more; we'll make them see things at different prices and they'll end up falling for the best. Shopkeepers here hardly know what the art of *étalage* is, and as for the art of selling—few have that. There are lots who still operate the way Estupiñá did: scold the customers who want to buy."

"I think," said Doña Lupe with a greedy look, "that Pepe Samaniego's going to do a stupendous business. Madrid's ripe for it. It's just a question of having the knack. When I think of the pharmacies alone, goodness me! They're a gold mine. I've been telling Maxi he should invent something, come up with some sort of panacea. But everybody's so moral and full of righteousness. That's why this country doesn't get ahead and foreigners walk off with all our money."

This last sentence brought the conversation back to where it had been when the panacea business got them sidetracked.

"That's just the reason," said Doña Casta, "that a business set up like the best ones abroad can't help but make a fortune. Once it's here, the ladies of the aristocracy won't have to go to Biarritz or Bayonne for the latest styles."

Aurora was wearing a light blue muslin dress, and a leather belt with a large buckle. Her attire had the fresh simplicity of an elegant working woman. She left the living room briefly to have the light supper or snack that her mother always had ready for her and came back with a dish in one hand and a spoon in the other. It was a plum compote and a piece of cake.

"Would you like a taste? . . . Well, as I was saying, there are boxes waiting to go through customs at Irún now that have some little knitted suits for children that are sure to be a sensation. The sample came yesterday by express, and there was a fichu with it that we're going to do a cheaper imitation of with ordinary lace. Just wait, you'll see. And the christening robe, for example, that we're doing with Valenciennes lace will have to cost at least five hundred francs." (Aurora had the habit of counting in francs.) "It's really charming. I'll bring it home when it's done so you can see it."

"We'd do better to go over there," said Doña Lupe. "That way we'll get a good look at everything before you open to the public."

Fortunata made an occasional comment too, although not very often, because the shop didn't particularly interest her. After finishing the compote, Aurora left again and came back with some sugared egg yolks. What a sweet tooth she had! She offered one to Fortunata, who accepted it, and Doña Casta went about preparing to offer her friends a glass of water. This lady drew on all her inventiveness to select good jugs for cooling the water, and she gloried in the thought that no other house had such cool, delicious water. After bringing in a dish of sugar wafers, she set about serving the precious contents of the jugs (there were several), first regulating the temperature of each by placing it, if necessary, on the balcony. Doña Lupe assisted her in the bringing of the waters, and meanwhile Aurora put her arm around Fortunata's waist and led her out onto the living room balcony. Each was eating a chocolate-frosted candied yolk, and after that they had coconut ones.

Far from the impertinent ears of Doña Lupe and Doña Casta, Aurora whispered to Fortunata: "They all left this afternoon. Their cousin Manolo's going with them too."

5

It would be suitable to mention here that Fortunata and M. Fenelón's widow had become good friends. The latter was very nice to Sra. Rubín in a way that encouraged trust and she was very tolerant when it came to her friend's faults, so tolerant that she gradually gained access to all of her friend's secrets. It goes without saying that these intimacies were exchanged only behind Doña Lupe's back and far from Doña Casta's ears; neither lady would have consented to such subjects being brought into the honest and proper conversations held in the Samaniego home.

Their arms linked, each encircling the other's waist, the two women stood in silence for a while eating the candied yolks and looking out at the street. Suddenly Aurora burst out laughing.

"Look at that fool Ponce—making faces at Olimpia. I think my sister's the only girl in the world who could fall in love with a critic. She deserves to marry him, just as a punishment. Except that I wouldn't wish that on her, because she's my sister."

"He's really in a spot, isn't he," said Fortunata, laughing too. "He's making signals for her to come down. Oh, now she's leaving. But you're not about to get what you want. He probably wants to give her one of those articles he writes where he tells you the plots of plays so you'll know what's going on. Oh come on, don't be in such a rush; you'll talk to her some other night. It can't be now. What a bore those two are!"

A little while later, when they had unlinked arms and were wiping their fingers with their respective handkerchiefs, Aurora said again: "Yes, they all left this afternoon, and their cousin Moreno was with them. I think they're going to Saint Jean de Luz."

Fortunata turned toward the parlor balcony where Olimpia was. Then she looked at her friend and said to her in a rather curt tone: "They're going to San Sebastian and Biarritz, and at the beginning of September they're going to Paris."

"Girls," said Doña Casta, tapping them on the shoulder, "which water do you want—the *Progreso* or the *Lozoya?*"

"It's all the same to me," replied Fortunata.

"Try the Lozoya; take my advice," suggested Doña Lupe, glass in hand.

"No matter what she says, the *Progreso* is a bit salty."

"That depends on your taste. And the water you're used to," argued Doña Casta with the assurance and formality of a winetaster. "Since I grew up on Pontejos water—which is the same as Merced water, which they call *Progreso* today*—any other water tastes like mud to me."

I won't dwell on this treatise on the various waters of Madrid. While the elderly ladies were gossiping inside, Fortunata and Aurora continued their session on the balcony. It must have been eleven thirty when they heard Ballester's voice. He and Maxi were looking up at them from across the street. "If you'll come down," said Rubín, "I'll wait here."

"Olimpia!" cried Ballester. "We just saw the play that opened two nights ago. It's awful! Have you heard about it yet?"

"Me? What do you mean?"

"Since you know the real critics . . ."

As he was saying this, the critic walked past him.

---

*The change in names reflects the change in emphasis on different parts of the Square over the years. The fountain is the same one.

"Listen, Olimpia. The play's trash, but certain friends of the author rave about it. I'd like to see them so they'd tell me why they want to deceive the audience."

"Leave me alone. What nonsense!" exclaimed Olimpia, reentering.

"Are you coming down or not?" asked Maxi, and his wife told him to wait in the pharmacy, that they'd be down soon. Aurora and Fortunata laughed as they saw Ponce escape up the street like a soul being chased by the devil.

The Rubín ladies took their leave, both with the satisfaction of seeing Maxi greatly improved from his deranged condition that morning; he looked like a new man. Favorable symptoms were that he obeyed whatever command he was given and made sensible and calm replies. That night he slept peacefully and there was nothing out of the ordinary. The next afternoon husband and wife decided to take a walk before dinner. She went to the pharmacy to meet him at the agreed time but didn't find him in. "He went to have his hair cut," Ballester told her as he offered her a chair. "With all his sulking, the poor boy didn't realize that he was starting to look like a long-haired poet. I told him to go get himself fleeced this afternoon. Remember—you have to lead him along, combat his tendency to be reading all the time, and don't allow him to get wrapped up in himself. It's better to make him mad than let him sink into those depressions. I always put things bluntly to him and believe me, he's scared of me. That's what he needs."

"Poor thing!" exclaimed Fortunata. "Have you heard what he's been saying? I've never seen such madness."

Segismundo, who didn't have much to do at the time, dropped everything to attend courteously to his friend's wife and please her in any way he could. He was a man who had to make a considerable effort to contain himself to not flirt and even be bold to any woman in whose company he found himself. He had permitted himself a joke or so with Fortunata in the past; this time he went further. Running his fingers through his unruly hair and using them like the teeth of a comb, he smoothed it over and, arching his body, leaned toward the lady and remarked playfully:

"You've been very sad since yesterday . . . No, no—don't deny it. Do you think I don't know what's going on? I can read your face like a book."

"Well, you must have read very little in mine."

"More than you think. I read very tender passages . . . stanzas of fond adieus . . . sighs of loneliness . . ."

"Oh, what a nerve!"

"I don't miss a trick. I agree that you have reasons to look pathetic. But there's something else. I like to get at the root of things, ask the whys, and, frankly, when I look at the why I can't help but lament the error you've been making for a long time now."

Fortunata smiled at him, thinking she should not reveal any anger.

"Yes, I can't help but deplore," he continued, swelling now, "that you should be so fair to people who don't deserve it. With so many loyal hearts in the world, you would have to go and look for the most fickle there is and—"

"What's the meaning of all this nonsense?"

"Oh, it's not nonsense," replied the pharmacist, taking a few steps in front of her and trying to make them as graceful as possible. "Please forgive my boldness. That's the way I am—I've always been John Clear Tongue, and when a thought wants to get out of me I open the door so it can go, because if I keep it inside I burst. Well, as I was saying: will you be mad at me?"

"No, of course not. Why should I be mad? Let it out."

"Well, as I was saying" (Ballester assumed a pose that he thought was aristocratic), "I was thinking that the person you should love is me. I don't beat around the bush, as you can see."

"Oh, isn't that funny! I like the way you can't speak up."

"I call a spade a spade. Loving me, you'll see what a really loving, passionate, tropical heart is. But I'm warning you of one thing."

"What?"

"If you decide to love me—you won't—but if you should, be careful not to tell me suddenly. The shock would kill me."

"Don't worry, I'll tell you little by little—prepare you for it, like when someone gives you bad news."

"Not that much!"

"Hmm! You really are naughty. With all these medicines around, don't you have some that could cure your head?"

"Well, if I did, my dear friend, if I did . . . And most people think the worst head in this place is poor Maxi's, when mine's like a zoo. The truth is that a word from you know who would make me the sanest, happiest man on earth."

Seeing Rubín come in as he was saying this, he took a new tack. "I was just telling your other half that I'm going to give her some pills that . . . God, what pills!"

"For her?"

"No, my friend, for you."

"What do they have in them?"

"So you want to know already. Heck, when you think up something new you've got to keep the secret. It's a formula."

"Segismundo is nuts," said Fortunata. "Let's go."

"I don't take pills unless I know what's in them," stated Maxi in good faith.

"These fellows who are happy are very impertinent. They want to know everything. And now he's going for a walk with his precious dove! What a lovey-dove! And then the poor boy complains" (pulling one of his ears), "whines over nothing, the boy that fate has spoiled. Go on now, leave; enjoy yourselves."

He accompanied them to the pharmacy door, stiffened up, and, standing on tiptoe in his slippers, craned his neck, following them till they were out of sight.

6

The tiresome summer days were passing and it was near the end of a season that is sad in Madrid because people hardly eat or sleep, society retires, and the people who do stay seem to be surviving on the bread of emigration. In the Rubín family nothing in particular happened; Maxi didn't get worse, although he did have his regular morning bouts, fairly noisy ones, but as long as he didn't reach the degree of furor of that famous morning with the arsenic the two women could bear it patiently. At night he showed slight signs of depression, sometimes none at all. Combining persuasion with severity, Ballester had managed to distract him from any and all reading that might be conducive to spiritual concentration.

Fortunata's and Doña Lupe's relations weren't all peace and harmony either, because Sra. de Jáuregui, observant and discerning, had sensed that from the beginning of June her niece was involved in something shady. All the people related to the Rubín family knew the story of Maxi's wife and the dramatic role that Señorito Santa Cruz had played in it. Some perhaps knew about the adventuress' third foray into the amorous field, but no one dared to tell the tale to "the turkey woman." She, however, knew it from sheer instinct, for she had a very sharp sense of smell. She tried once to spring it on Fortunata "just so she won't think," she reflected, "that she can pull the wool over my eyes and that I'm sitting around here like a ninny." But Fortunata, immediately recalling the lessons her friend Feijóo had given her, drew the dividing line that he had recommended and said something to the effect of: "From there to there, Señora, you rule; but from there to *here* is my turf, and you have no right to pry."

The proud widow of the halberdier did not give up at this. She made a few more stabs: "If poor little Maxi were well, he'd give you your due the way any man with self-respect ought to, but he's not well and I have to carry the burden of the family honor. I've said it to myself a hundred times: 'Should I explode or not?' In that poor boy's situation, my explosion would be his death. That's why I contain myself and swallow all this gall. Look—my hair's even turning gray since I've begun to witness such ignominies from this helpless position."

Fortunata turned aside to hide her tears. This scene took place in the parlor while they were sewing summer dresses.

"After what happened in November last year," continued the widow with a frightening severity, "after your real or fake reform, after you were forgiven (and if it had been up to me, you wouldn't have been forgiven), after we buried the horrible crime, it seems to me that you should have felt obliged to behave differently. Don't cry pretty little tears now—they only seem more hypocritical. Because I'll tell you one thing. Listen closely."

Doña Lupe dropped her sewing and prepared to speak as if she were a professional orator. "I can put myself in the place of a woman who feels a passion so deep-rooted it can't be removed. There are cases, and they have to be looked at carefully. If you had come to me and said, 'Aunt, something's happening. He's after me; I don't know if I'll be able to defend myself; I'm weak; help me out.' *Then* it would have been different. Because I would have guided you, I'd have given you courage, consolation . . . But no; you have to do it all your way, on your own, like a foolish girl. It's nonsense to act that way. It's the cause of all your misfortunes: not taking into consideration the people who should be guiding you. The result? When you come calling for help it'll be too late, and those people will say to you: 'Figure it out for yourself now; wallow in your shame, you can go to the devil.'"

Having delivered this eloquent invective, the lady continued to snort for a while; Fortunata didn't take her eyes off her sewing. She was reflecting on the strangeness of the widow's ideas; she sounded as if she might actually agree to certain weaknesses if only she were consulted and regarded as an infallible protector and sanctioner of the actions involved. "This woman wants to be the Pope," thought Fortunata, "and as long as she's made Pope she'll agree to anything. But as for me . . ." Doña Lupe's despotic morality revolted her; she sensed that it had more haughtiness than righteousness, or that the righteousness was Jesuitically adapted to the haughtiness. This admixture didn't settle well with the young criminal's absolute ideas. She wanted either complete absolution or complete condemnation for her acts. Heaven or hell, nothing else. She had her "idea" and she didn't need advice or protection from anyone. She could manage much better on her own, and no matter what cross she had to bear she didn't need a Simon of Cyrene to help her. Her actions were decisive, direct: she performed them as simply as a missile shot out of a cannon.

When Doña Lupe found out from her friend Doña Casta that the Santa Cruz family had left for the summer, she decided to use the information; she sprang another speech on her niece, although it was less severe this time.

Señora Jáuregui was essentially governmental; she built all her plans and judgments on the solid base of consummated facts. "Just listen to how we could arrive at an understanding," she said one afternoon when she'd decided it was a good time to bring up the subject again. "I've heard that the person who sets you on fire isn't in Madrid anymore. What better occasion do you want to start reforming? Remember, inside you're like a house in a shambles. I'm willing to help you all I can. I shouldn't do it, but I'm charitable and I take human weaknesses into account. Someone else would plunge right into this; I think that with such a deli-cate situation you have to proceed ve-ry tactfully. You should start by filling me in on the past; telling me even the little details (the littlest ones, mind you), catch-ing me up on what you're thinking and feeling, what temptations you have every morning, evening, and night—in a word, you should describe every last symptom of that cursed sickness and give me your word that you'll do whatever I say." Thus spoke the widow—as if she had pocket recipes for every pathological disturbance known to man's soul. To be polite (although not enjoying it), Fortunata deigned to say a bit, but naturally she kept to herself the most delicate parts. Doña Lupe was so enthused by this show of submission that she began to boast about her professional faculties, topping it all off with these words: "I assure you that if you obey me I'll get those ideas out of your head and you'll become what you aren't: a model wife. For the time being I'll commit myself to seeing that you don't fall again, even if you're tripped. Your gentleman friend, humph! The police ought to hear about him. Just let me take care of this. Leave the lawsuit to me, and you'll see. Do you want to bet I won't go to Doña Bárbara's house one day and spill the beans? You don't know who you're dealing with; you just don't know me. And to think you've been so stupid you haven't wanted to rely on me! You deserve what you got. And as for now, like it or not, I've got a hand in this game. You'll end up adoring me the way you adore a mother."

After all this, Doña Lupe was radiant. She practically gave her niece a moth-erly caress, so great were her pleasure and satisfaction. One thought flashed through her mind several times, but she kept it stashed away in the most hidden page of her book of tricks, not letting Fortunata so much as suspect its existence. She kept it to and for herself: "I wonder if he's given her money." Whenever she asked herself this, she answered in the affirmative. "He had to have given her some, maybe great quantities. But where the devil does she keep it? Why doesn't she give it to me so that I can invest it for her? I know why: she's ashamed to turn over money acquired that way. This delicacy does honor her. I'm sure that's what it is—she's embarrassed to tell me. But it'll all come out in the end."

And one afternoon when the couple had gone for a walk, the great capitalist, unable to repress her curiosity any longer, sent Papitos on an errand so that she could be alone and, with admirable determination, she searched Fortunata's dresser and trunk. With her countless keys she was able to open all the drawers and methodically inspect every one of them, being careful to leave things exactly as she had found them. She used this Jesuitic procedure whenever her prying hands had to touch what they should not. She looked here, then there, but in vain. Bills are so easy to hide, there's no way of finding them. But Doña Lupe had such a keen nose for money that she was positive she'd find the bills if there were any. "Could they be sewn into her clothes?" she wondered. "Maybe. That sly girl looks as if she doesn't know black from white and yet she knows more . . . !" There was nothing resembling money or letters in the dresser. She saw some jewelry and trinkets—souvenirs of a romance?—but as for the loot, there wasn't a trace of it.

"It's very odd," grunted the widow as she searched the trunk after her minute inspection of the dresser. "And it doesn't make sense—him so rich and her so poor!" The trunk, which contained only some old clothes, didn't yield anything either. "Well, there must be some," she muttered, "there must be some. There's a hiding place somewhere. Either there's money here or there's no money anywhere in this world."

Fatigued from her useless scrutiny, she put away her keys, a tight cluster worthy of storage in a thieves' arsenal, and she sat down to think. Putting one hand on her cotton breast, she caressed it, scratching her forehead with her other hand, right along the hairline, as if to stimulate a thought, musing, "Well, if he really *hasn't* given her anything, you've got to admit it: the man's indecent."

7

The heat was oppressive, and the scenes I have described were repeated, marked by the mannerisms that human life tends to acquire at certain times, like a weary artist who fails to revitalize his forms. The little evening walks, the rides on the neighborhood streetcar, excursions to some summer theater, *tertulias* at the Samaniegos' or the Rubíns', the budding critic pacing the street, the romantic figure of Olimpia hanging over her balcony like a sign saying "Ideal Love Here," Ballester's extravagances, Maxi's spasms—it all repeated itself from day to day like clockwork.

In August something that was not on the program occurred. One morning Torquemada went to see Doña Lupe on business. In his summer attire our worthy Don Francisco looked like a military man from Cuba, because besides his blue suit he was wearing a wide-brimmed straw hat. His multicolored striped shirt looked like the United States flag, and to top off this American look he was wearing a jeweled tie pin and an endless gold chain that swayed back and forth across his chest. His pants were so short you could see up to his knees when he sat down. The article had obviously been pawned by a diminutive owner. Everything he wore looked either inherited or legally seized or obtained through some sort of deal. On visits his hat served as a fan that also benefited whoever sat near him, for they received some ventilation from that well-handled tropical accessory.

Torquemada and Doña Lupe had been engaged in an interesting conference of some duration when the doorbell rang and Maxi appeared in the parlor. Fortunata was ironing. As soon as she heard her husband arrive she hastened to see what had brought him. At ten in the morning it had to be something out of the ordinary, because the poor boy never came home then. Throwing a shawl over her shoulders (because the heat from the iron forced her to dress lightly), she went into the parlor. She and her aunt were equally astonished to see an unusual happiness in his face. His eyes shone, and even in the way he greeted Don Francisco they noticed something strange that filled them with alarm. "Hi, Don Paco. I'm fine, and you? And Doña Silvia and Rufinita, are they still taking the baths at Manzanares?" This chummy language belied Maxi's temperament and timidity.

"What brings you here at this hour of the morning?" asked his aunt, hiding her surprise.

Fortunata examined him attentively from her seat, which was outside the main group's, in a chair next to the door to Doña Lupe's room. He didn't sit down and, after his bold greeting to the usurer, he stood with his back to the balcony, hands in his pockets, looking at them all like someone who's waiting to be congratulated. "Nothing, really," he said. "I've had some good luck."

"Well, what is it—did you win at the lottery?"

"No, not that. What do I want with the lottery? I don't need that. It's much more important. I've found what I was looking for. I've already told you that I thought I only needed one formula to complete—"

"The mixture! Don't tell me you've discovered the panacea?" his aunt asked incredulously.

"That's not a bad name, if that's what you want to call it," said the poor boy, more exalted at each word. "From pan, which means everything, . . . and akes, which is the same as saying remedy. It heals and purifies everything, it's—"

"Thank God you're doing something worthwhile!" declared Doña Lupe distrustfully, watching Maxi's expression, which by now had a feverish glow to it.

"Last night I didn't sleep a wink thinking about it; my brain was on fire, because all I needed for my plan, or rather the system, was a formula. A blasted formula! Finally, a little while ago, it came to me; I jumped for joy. Ballester, who doesn't understand this (and he never will) got mad and didn't want to give me any paper and ink to write it down. I'm afraid I'll forget it, that it'll escape. My memory's like an open cage and the birds—piff!"

Doña Lupe and Fortunata looked at each other sadly.

"All right," said his aunt, seeing that a cloud was forming. "Calm down. You'll write down the formula and you'll make your panacea; it'll be a great success and we'll earn lots of money."

"No," he replied, conveying the heaviness one associates with any burdensome task. "Don't think it's so easy. To set forth the whole system with enough clarity so that everyone will understand it you have to sweat blood. I'll lose many a night of sleep over this. But that doesn't matter. Once this thing gets started, you'll see: I'll have such a big reputation and so much glory that—"

"Good Lord, he's really gone," murmured Doña Lupe, and Fortunata thought something similar.

"The problem I still haven't solved," said Maxi, approaching his aunt and snapping his fingers, "is the emanation of souls. Where does the soul emanate from? Is it part of the divine substance that is incarnated in human life and disincarnated at death, when it goes back to its original state? Or is it an accidental creation of God's that subsists in an impersonal way? This was what I couldn't figure out."

Doña Lupe heaved a deep sigh, looking at Don Francisco, who was winking half-mockingly, half-sympathetically.

"For God's sake!" said Fortunata, drawing nearer. "Don't say such things, they give me a headache. Yes, it's fine, but everything that has to be found out about this has already been found out. Don't get so worked up."

"My dear," rejecting her gently and adopting an emphatic tone, "if in this *via crucis* of work and persecution that awaits me, if on the painful and glorious road of this apostleship you don't want to accompany me, I'll be sorrier for your sake than for mine; but you'll be with me in the end. How can you help but be, being a sinner? What I've been thinking about and want to propose concerns sinners and their redemption."

Fortunata returned to the isolated chair she'd been occupying and Doña Lupe, after throwing her hands to her head, made a gesture of Christian resignation. She was on the verge of tears. At this point Torquemada deemed it appropriate to intervene; he hoped that his discreet reasoning would set straight the twisted mind of the unfortunate youth. "Look, my friend Maximiliano: I think that all we should know has been taught to us already. And what we don't know we probably shouldn't learn; pushing things too far kills our faith. This life is just a matter of getting by—that's the way we found it and that's the way we'll leave it, and no matter how hard we look up to heaven, the manna's not going to come raining down. 'You'll earn your bread with the sweat of your brow,' as someone said, and that's all there is to it. What do you get out of wondering whether the soul is made of this or that? We all die in the end anyhow. So let's have a clean conscience, let's not do bad things, and on with it. And let's not be afraid of the materialism of death; we're dust, after all, and——"

"That's enough; don't go on," said Maxi, frowning, cutting short his speech. "If you're a materialist we'll never understand each other."

"No. What I'm saying is that the soul receives what it deserves, and since the body is no more than a shell, when it rots I'm not scared of the materialism of turning into dust."

"Yes . . . I understand," said Maxi, even more exalted and thereby emphasizing his disagreement. "You belong to the same school as my brother Juan Pablo:

'force and matter.' We'll discuss that later. I'll expound my doctrine, and Juan Pablo can expound his, and then we'll see who attracts Lady Humanity."

Saying this, he spun on his heel and left for his room. His wife followed him, deeply upset. Maxi sat at the table where he had some books and notes. Putting her hand on his shoulder, his wife looked at the scrawls he made with a feverish hand.

"Here are the main points," he babbled as he wrote. "Solidarity of spiritual substance. Incarnation is a penitent or trial state. Death is liberation—no, excuse me—it's true life. Let us try to attain it soon."

"Rest for a while now," said his wife, trying to take the pen out of his hand. "You've worked hard enough today on those difficult calculations. You can continue tomorrow. No, don't think I disapprove; I'll help you think. We'll talk about it. I have ideas too."

Surprisingly, Maxi didn't get irritated. His face had a seraphic expression, his manners were mild, and he looked more like an ancient mystic whose madness developed in the solitude of the cloisters than like a modern madman who's prepared for an insane asylum by the unleashed appetites of present-day society.

"You have ideas too," he said gently. "I know. You think because you feel; you understand me because you love. You've sinned, you've suffered, sinning and suffering are two sides of the same thing, and that's why you have a feeling for freedom. To use a metaphor, the bars of life are chafing against your wrists."

The entire sermon was lost on Fortunata, but so as not to contradict him she assented to everything.

"As for suffering, I've had my share. My whole life has been sheer torture. But don't trouble yourself about that anymore."

Doña Lupe peeked in through the door, which was ajar.

"You'll help me," continued Maxi, religious inspiration flashing in his eyes. "You'll help me preach this great doctrine, the result of so much thought, and that wouldn't have become fully mine without aid from Heaven. The great mystery of revelation has been reborn in me. What I know, I know, because He who knows all has revealed it to me."

Noticing his aunt watching him from the door, he gestured to her, saying: "Come in, Aunt. There are no secrets. You, too, will be with me in the immense and painful propagation. Which reminds me—I don't see how you can consent to having that materialist here."

"Don Francisco! Son! What harm can he do you?"

"A lot, Aunt, a lot. All the people in that infamous sect can't stand the sight of me, and if that man keeps coming into this house in such a familiar way he could try to discredit my system and dishonor me in no time."

He looked to Fortunata for some sign of support or agreement. Sensing his need, she hastened to corroborate: "He's right, Aunt. That materialist shouldn't come here anymore."

"Well, he won't, son; he won't. I'll tell him to go to the devil with his materialism."

"Do you feel well? Would you like something?" his wife inquired affectionately.

"I feel better than I've ever felt before, believe me," his tone indicating his soul's serenity. "Ever since I found the formula I was searching for so hard, I feel like a new man. Before, my life was a martyrdom; now, I wouldn't change places with anybody. Nothing hurts, I feel well, and to top off my happiness I don't even care about eating or sleeping."

"Well, you have to have something."

"I don't need anything . . . believe me. You'll see, I don't. I'm a new man; I don't have flesh anymore, and I don't want it for anything. All I have is a skeleton, and it's enough to carry my soul."

Fortunata's eyes grew moist. A little while later, when she went out for a minute, she found Doña Lupe fighting off tears. "He's gone," said Señora de Jáuregui, "completely gone . . . There's no way to mend this."

8

That afternoon the poor women had some very bad moments. He stayed on the sofa in the bedroom in a lethargic or an ecstatic state; his eyes were open but he didn't seem to notice anything that was going on around him. Fortunata picked up her sewing and sat down beside him, waiting to see what would happen. Doña Lupe went in and out, sighing or pouting. When it was time for lunch Maxi perked up a bit, but he refused food. They didn't feel up to lunch themselves, but they urged him to eat and tried to persuade him any way they could. At last Doña Lupe got results with this argument: "I don't know how you're going to stand that hardworking life without eating something. They say Christ fasted, but he didn't go for days on end without a bite. On the contrary; it was during dinner that he founded his most important institution, Holy Communion."

At this Maxi agreed to a bowl of soup and a little wine. But they couldn't get him beyond that. Afterward, he seemed more exalted again. Taking his wife's hands, he said:

"I am only the precursor of this doctrine; the real messiah will come later; he'll come soon—he's already on his way. He who knows all told me so."

Fortunata didn't understand an iota of this.

Doña Lupe sent word to Ballester, who arrived soon after dark. The pharmacist couldn't control his lively, jocose temper or be as tactful as the case required, and even though Fortunata tugged at his coattails to make him talk in less obtrusive tones, the blasted man simply could not contain himself: "The ideas you come up with, really, Maxi. What do you care if the soul comes from here or over there? What are you going to line your pockets with for finding out? Do you think they're going to give you something for discovering it? The day before yesterday you gave me a pain in the neck with that business of 'the thing in itself.' Well, suppose it was 'the thing beyond itself.' It's just a lot of malarkey. How about 'the thing of it, beyond the self'? Oh, what a silly boy, and what a busybody! Because you know, this business of sticking your nose into eternity and such must get on God's nerves. Nobody likes being watched, to see what he's doing. That's why whenever nosy, sly types sneak after Him and count His wrinkles He punishes them by making them dumb. So you draw your own conclusions. It's unbelievable that someone who could be the happiest man on earth, married to this Oriental pearl, and being a nephew to this aunt, who's another pearl, should rack his brains over things that don't matter at all. Nobody's going to thank you for it! If these ladies will allow me, I'll cure you with an extract of ashwood, rubbed on a switch that I'll use on you morning and night."

Maxi looked at him scornfully, and Ballester, seeing that his jokes didn't produce their usual results, grew serious and tried other means. On his way out, escorted to the door by the two ladies, he said: "I'm going to give him the hashish. It's marvelous for combating low spirits, which cause these gloomy thoughts and religious manias. Immediate results. You'll see—if you give it to a hermit, he starts to dance right off."

Since the new phase of Maxi's disturbance appeared peaceful, aunt and wife were on the lookout. During the night he didn't budge from his bed, and although it's true that he talked to himself he spoke in a low voice, in a tone children use when they're memorizing a lesson. In spite of this Fortunata was so nervous that she couldn't sleep all night, so she took catnaps during the day. The patient no longer went to the pharmacy or showed any desire to go anywhere; he seemed to have sunken into a profound apathy and compressed all his existence into the silent, recondite seething of his own thoughts. Except for walking around the dining room or bedroom, he did no exercise, and after losing his appetite for the first few days he developed a voracious one, which the two women considered a good symptom. A week later he showed signs of wanting to go out, but they both attempted to dissuade him. He was quiet, and whenever he talked about anything that didn't have to do with the emanation of the soul and the doctrine he was going to preach he expressed himself rationally, even wittily. Little by little, his deranged periods became more infrequent, and he would be completely sane and open to any subject in a natural way for hours on end. Fortunata had him help her with the clothes or winding skeins, and he submissively agreed to anything. Doña

Lupe entrusted him with checking her accounts, and this kept him busy; no one would have dreamed that anything was wrong with this very delicate part of the human machine.

At the beginning of September, having gone for three days without breathing a word of his gibberish about the soul, the two ladies were very pleased, thinking that the thunderstorm would soon be over. They took up their evening walks again, and soon they allowed him to go out alone, and he went back to work at the pharmacy, carefully watched over by Ballester.

Fortunata had additional reasons for deep sorrow. He hadn't written her a word, not a single letter; he had broken his promise. The ungrateful wretch! What trouble would it have been to write her a few lines saying, for example, "I'm well and love you as always." But nothing, not even that. She revealed her sadness to her sole confidant, Aurora, during the juicy sessions that the older ladies unwittingly allowed. The opening of Samaniego's shop, around September 15th, kept Fenelón's widow quite busy those days. Seldom had a business in Madrid been so full of life or shown clearer signs that it had impressed and appealed to the public. The exquisite novelties that Pepe Samaniego had brought from Paris attracted crowds of people; ladies swarmed around and quickly stuck to the honey. The sales clerks couldn't show their wares fast enough, and Aurora was soon exhausted, flooded with orders for trousseaux and sundry bridal apparel. Doña Casta wasn't content unless she walked over every day and stuck her nose into things too, so she could tell Doña Lupe all about the orders and what they were making for royalty and others who weren't royal but had lots of money. Fortunata hardly went at all, because she didn't feel like it and because Aurora advised against it.

The two friends spent Sunday afternoons together at either one or the other's house, and they whiled away the time eating sweets and exchanging little tidbits as they sat facing the balcony watching the young critic come and go down below, from Tres Peces Street to Magdalena Street. He might not have much judgment, but as for his legs . . .

One Sunday toward the end of September, Fenelón's widow brought important news again: "They're coming back tomorrow. Candelaria's been cleaning the house from top to bottom today."

What Fortunata felt was a mixture of pain and joy that left her speechless. Although she wanted him to come back, at the same time she had a presentiment that it would bring some new disaster. Really, not to have written her once, not even a word! Aurora agreed that he was really a cad. After a few more remarks on the subject, the Fenelón woman told her bosom friend something else that elicited extraordinary curiosity and attention from the latter. "Would you believe what's gotten stuck in my mind? It may not be true, but then again, maybe it is. Doña Guillermina was in the shop yesterday. Pepe had offered her a sum for her project if the inauguration went well, and so she'd come over to collect. Well, in talking about the family, she said that their cousin Moreno is returning with them tomorrow. He left with them and he's coming back with them. I know they spent the summer in Biarritz and then they all went to Paris together. What do you think? Their cousin Manolo doesn't come to Spain except, for example, in the winter; he's never come in September before. And as for sticking with the Santa Cruz family so long—him, the man who loves to be alone! It's probably not so; but there are so many things that seem impossible and then they happen! Before they left, it seemed to me, after a couple of things I saw and heard, that the 'good man' was a little bit too fond of Jacinta. Do you suppose there's anything . . . ? What do you think?"

Fortunata looked distracted, even dazed. What her friend was telling her sounded incredible.

"His following after them that way is very strange. Always with them, a man who hasn't made a home anywhere! I don't know. Do you suppose there's something to it? What do you think?"

"Well . . . ," said Rubín's wife very pensively, "I don't think so, no."

"Well, if there is, I'll get wind of it, because I'm right there 'on the lookout,' as they say. From my mezzanine window I can see the bay windows at the Santa Cruzes' and the Morenos'. If there are any telegraphs going back and forth, I'll be sure to spot their game. Do you suppose they're—?"

"No, I don't think so," repeated Fortunata, more and more pensively.

9

The news of the Santa Cruzes' return, which Doña Casta communicated to her, rekindled Señora de Jáuregui's desire to resume her campaign of redeeming her niece. Since she happened to be nearby that day, the widow sprang another speech on her: "It's now or never. The enemy's at bay. I'm at your command in case you want any advice or some fair strategy for self-defense." This said, she all but forced her niece to cough up whether or not she had ever received a large sum from her lover.

Fortunata didn't take her eyes off the clothes she was mending. "I understand," proceeded Doña Lupe in a parliamentary tone, "that you're bashful about confessing certain things to me, and for my part, I'll tell you frankly—I don't think you're worse than you are, I don't think, as other people might, that your weakness is selfish and that you love that man because he's rich and you wouldn't if he were poor. No, I don't do you that disservice. You can count on that. I feel sure that, as unscrupulous and foolish as you are, without a grain of sense in your head, your faults come from love, not selfishness, and that you'd do the same crazy things you do for a powerful man who gives you lots of money as you would for some poor chap who didn't have enough for cigarettes."

"What's all that about lots of money?" asked Fortunata, looking at her in awe, on the verge of laughter.

"No, I don't want to know the exact sum. Keep it to yourself, please. It's better to leave some things unsaid. Don't think that I want you to give me your capital so I can invest it. No; you probably know how to manage it yourself."

"But . . . what are you saying, Señora?"

"Nothing, nothing at all. It would be revolting to handle those funds, really."

"What funds? You must be dreaming."

"Oh, go on. You don't think I'm going to fall for a lie as big as this house! You can't mean to say that he doesn't give you—"

"Me!"

"Don't pretend to be so dumb—"

"I don't know where you got that idea . . . Look, for once and all: I have nothing. He'd give me something if he saw I needed it. He's offered before . . . but I didn't want to take it."

Doña Lupe was about to hurl another tirade at her. She thought: "Some plum you got, you big idiot. You're so naive, you don't even know how to be a fallen woman." But she contained herself and swallowed all her wrath, which she vented later in an agitated soliloquy: "I've never seen anyone like her. She has no idea of shame, or common sense either. What a tramp she is, and yet, what a dunce at the same time! If there were a hell for fools, you'd plunge straight into it."

Maximiliano gradually returned to his regular life, although this is not to say that he had banished all thoughts concerning that idea of his. He was completely transformed; just as in hepatic crises there is a discharge of bile, in that mental crisis there seemed to have been a discharge of feelings. Not only was he extremely calm, he was also very tender now, and his emotions had become more refined, like liquor that has passed through a still. The words of affection he had for his aunt and his wife were extraordinarily mild, even cloying at times. It pained him to cause any trouble and, thanking them for their lavish care, he nevertheless declined it as often as possible. He was beginning to show a tendency to impose privations and suffering on himself, and mortification, which had infuriated him before, no matter how slight, pleased him now. If in conversations or in those polemics with the family at mealtime he ever spoke an inopportune word, he later regretted having uttered it, and if he didn't take it back and apologize, it was only because his shyness stopped him.

One day, because Papitos hadn't cleaned his boots, he said to her: "What a nuisance you are, girl. You'll see!" And as he was leaving the house he so regretted his disdainful, angry tone that he nearly shed a tear. "When will I ever break this habit of insulting my inferiors! What difference does it make whether or not my boots are polished? What should shine is my soul, not my boots. It's hard to believe that we human beings attach so much importance to such childish things. I was unfair to the poor girl, the innocent, angelic creature! I'm a beast! But who in blazes from the stars down understands and practices justice? The supposedly fair man commits well over fifty barbaric acts every day. It takes some doing to get rid of this moral itch I've got; if you're born with it, you live with it till the hour of liberation comes."

"What are you frowning about so much? Do you want me to get out my stick?" said Ballester with that harshness that, according to him, was the most effective treatment. "Because it seems to me we're feeling very 'evangelical' today. Careful now. You know how I can get."

"Hit me; I don't mind," replied Maxi, leaving his hat on the hook. "I deserve it, and so would anyone who gets mad because his boots haven't been polished. Humanity is a bunch of imbeciles. Segismundo, my friend, death is beautiful."

"If you repeat that 'death is beautiful,'" retorted the other, grabbing the stick and wielding it comically. "I'll cover you with bruises. Imagine, saying that the wretch is beautiful! She's uglier than not eating, you fool! Look at her; look at that revolting face . . . Look at her, and if you so much as say she's pretty I'll pulverize you."

He was pointing to an emblem painted on the ceiling of the pharmacy depicting a decorative combination of the serpent of Aesculapius, Time's hourglass, a distilling flask, a retort, a bust of Hippocrates, and a skull.

"If you want to see all the grace in the world, look at me," said Ballester, putting aside his stick. He turned around, straightened the tails of his frock coat, and asked, "Now am I handsome or not?"

That day Ballester was sporting new shoes and a new flannel suit of the cheapest sort, and he had gone to the barber for a fleecing and curling.

"You certainly are elegant," said Maxi as he started to weigh some doses for pills.

"Well, I'll be even more elegant tomorrow, because tomorrow my little sister is marrying Federico Ruiz, a very talented boy. Do you know him? The newspapers are always talking about him, and they always put in some kind of praise or other before his name. Now they're calling him 'the distinguished thinker.' I bet nobody calls you that in spite of all your thinking. That's because you don't use your judgment the way he does."

That night Padilla and Rubín, the two assistant pharmacists, were at the pharmacy with Ballester. As soon as the famous critic appeared across the street, Segismundo was seized by a silly rage; the mere presence of that character, who had such unquestionable importance in the republic of letters, infuriated him. "I'm up to here, he said, "with the little gent, especially since he praised that awful play that opened last winter, saying that it 'posed the problem' or whatever. You know the one I mean? The moralistic piece that recommends marriage and good habits. It makes all us bachelors out to be delinquents, and just because a young man comes in late and spends his money on having some fun, they call him a monster and his papá curses him. There's a scene where they all swoon because one of them, who turns out to be a man of science, tells them outright that he doesn't believe in God and doesn't care if they shoot him for it. Anyway, when I saw it, I felt as if I'd drunk all the emetics I have in the pharmacy. The moral of the play is that without religion there's no happiness, which is why the saintly creature, who's the soul of pretentiousness, raves about it."

Night fell and Ponce came to exchange telegraphs with his beloved. A string was hanging from the balcony, and the young man was tying on a piece of paper.

"He's sending her his latest article," said the boss to his friends, spying from the pharmacy door. "Now she's lowering some candy on the string. Just like last night. Just wait till you see the gag I've got for them."

He rushed nervously to the back room and grabbed from a drawer an object the size of an egg yolk, white and sugary looking. Padilla burst out laughing and Maxi watched in amusement.

"But you have to help me. Padilla—you know him, so go out and make believe you've run into him by accident; talk about the theater with him, distract him, make him turn this way, and meanwhile, very carefully, I'll slip out and creep up when the string comes down with the candy. I'll take the yolk off, see, and then I'll tie this on. I whipped it up last night. It's strychnine, in a dose you'd give a dog; the flavor's neutralized with licorice and it's coated with sugar. He'll eat it and explode like a firecracker."

Padilla was doubled over in gales of laughter; Maxi thought Ballester was joking.

"Don't kill him, now," said Padilla. "If you'd made it of Aleppian scammony or something like that—"

"No, son. I *want* him to explode. I'll be sent to the penitentiary. That'll be the end of me. So what? I can't forgive him. Insulting men of science and bachelors!"

Carrying his joke to extremes, Ballester swore that the yolk was poisonous, but since the other man refused to be an accomplice in this "homicide," the exalted pharmacist went over to their side and confessed that the little ball was made of sugar and castor oil. Maxi, who had helped him concoct it, smiled to himself. Quite a while passed with all this quibbling, so when Ballester wanted to put his prank into effect the string had already come down with a coconut yolk and the critic was eating it. The schemer consoled him himself by thinking that another night he would consummate his tragic revenge. "He has to eat it," he said, putting away the ball. "As sure as my name is Segismundo, he's going to swallow it, and then I'll say like my theatrical namesake, 'Thank God he did!'"

10

When Maxi got home to dinner that night he found his wife not feeling well. She had a headache and nausea. Doña Lupe, who always kept an eye on her, thought her illness was an excuse to hide from the family the grief that was consuming her. "What you have," she thought, "is the urge to answer his call. You're fighting with yourself. You want to go and you can't make up your mind to." It must have been something of the sort, because Fortunata shut herself up in her room and refused food. Maximiliano didn't urge her to eat, because he thought his wife's attitude was a wish for self-privation born of some inner decay or an appetite for death and liberation. Doña Lupe, weary of fighting off so much nonsense from both sides, retired, leaving them to themselves, saying: "Do what you want. Figure it out any way you want. I'm pooped." She ate alone and via Papitos sent them some food that came back almost untouched. Then she went into their bedroom for a minute to ask how they were and left to rest herself. "I can't take this dog's life any longer," she said. "God have pity on me."

Fortunata would have liked for her husband to fall asleep and leave her in peace. But he didn't seem willing to comply with her. He was quite talkative that night, which really annoyed her, because rarely had she felt less like talking. Shortly after going to bed she noticed that her husband, seated at the table where the lamp was, was taking things out of his pocket—first a little package, then another, things wrapped in paper—and putting them in front of him like a man preparing to work. The faint crinkly noise of paper being unfolded, a noise that seemed louder in the silence of the night, irritated Fortunata and attracted her attention. The first thing Maxi did was to take out of an average-size bundle a multitude of small, very neatly folded packets, the kind with medicinal powder, predivided into separate doses. But then the young woman saw him untie another package, a long one, and—God above, it was a knife! He studied it for a while, first from one side, then from the other, and then he tested the point with the cushion of his finger, as if to feel whether it was sharp enough. His wife broke out in a cold sweat all over. She couldn't contain herself and, speaking as if she were waking up someone to free him from the imaginary horrors of an anguishing nightmare, asked: "Maxi, dear, what are you doing?" He looked at her very calmly.

"I thought you were asleep. Aren't you sleepy? Well, then, let's chat about pleasant things."

"Whatever you say. But I think it would be better for you to come to bed and leave those pleasant things for tomorrow."

"No . . . You're sure to like what I'm going to tell you. Wait a minute."

He gathered up all his packets and the knife and, moving to the chair beside the bed, put everything on the night table.

"Aha! Now you'll see," he said, smiling affectionately, like someone who's about to give his beloved a little present. "This, as you can see, is a dagger."

Fortunata shivered as if the cold blade were touching her skin; her teeth started to chatter.

"I bought it today at the shop behind Cañizares Street. Look, here it is: 'Toledo, 1873.' Nice, isn't it? I've been thinking for days about the best way to do my soul the big favor of sending it off to a better world. What do you think? I won't decide on anything without your advice; whatever you prefer, I prefer."

The unhappy woman was so filled with dread she was speechless.

"Put it away, for God's sake . . . It scares me out of my wits."

"Scares you!" he exclaimed, astonished and discouraged. "I thought I had managed to instill my idea in you, and that you'd gotten used to it by now. Scared of death! That's like saying you're scared of freedom and you love prison! Don't tell me you mean that? Why, I've told you hundreds of times that you have to look at death as the end of suffering, just the way shipwrecked people look to the shore when they've only got a piece of driftwood to hang onto and they're struggling in the waves."

"No, it's not that I'm scared," she said, hoping to calm him, because she noticed that he was getting exalted. "It's just that . . . it's better to talk about those things in the daytime. Let's go to sleep now."

"Sleep! There's more nonsense for you! What do you get out of sleeping? You only numb yourself and forget what's more important—detachment and evasion. Listen, my dear: either you're with me or you're against me. Make up your mind fast. Are you ready to grab the keys and escape with me? You are? Well, the first thing is not to be scared of death. It's a door; you should always be looking at it and know you could be ready to walk through it when the happy hour of liberation comes."

Fortunata pulled the covers around her more tightly to fight off the cold. Oh, was she scared!

"The moment of liberation is when one considers himself sufficiently purified to undertake the passing from one world to another and can take steps himself. Most religions prohibit suicide. They're so foolish! Mine orders it. It's a sacrament, the supreme alliance with divinity. And, well, people who attain purification by annulling themselves socially and cultivating their inner life sense when the moment to disappear has come. Liberation shouldn't be called suicide. The best way to put it is to call it 'killing off our beast of a jailer.' A time comes when the soul can't stand slavery any longer and has to be free. How? Watch."

Fortunata shivered, debating whether or not she should fetch Doña Lupe.

"This is a dagger . . . a well-sharpened one. You have to remember that the beast will try to defend himself, no matter how exhausted he is. Flesh is flesh, and for as long as it lives, it manages to hurt us. So that's why it's best to bring about liberation with as little pain as possible. You see, the soul, regardless of all its strength, starts to cower and feel sorry for the beast, and it even intercedes on its behalf. Look carefully now, and if you don't like the white weapon, tell me frankly. Would you prefer a firearm? Shots can miss, and then the soul gets impatient. What usually happens is that the bullet doesn't point the right way and the beast is only half killed. That's why I've brought you poisonous means—they're safe and silent."

He began to show her his well-made packets—neatly folded, each drug clearly identified. Fortunata felt unspeakable terror when he showed them to her and instinctively covered her nose and mouth for fear that inhaling such ingredients would poison her.

"Listen to what they are, now. This white substance you see here, in little crystals, is strychnine. A sure, convulsive death, and it causes a lot of anguish, so I don't recommend it. This is atropine and this is hemlock, see? White powder. Hemlock has an advantage, which is that Señor Socrates freed himself with it and that makes it venerable. Both of them are soporific poisons; that is, they put you to sleep and it all ends in a dream. But what I ask myself is, in the darkness of sleep, won't the beast's kicking make it an awful torture? What do you think? Should we choose digitalis, which kills by asphyxiation? Or should we use some type of mercury? Look, here they are: iodide of mercury, the red one; cyanide of mercury, the white one. I also have a phosphorus mix that kills by poisoning the blood. But the best is here, look—it's really the apple of the pharmacist's eye, a blessing from God. This one kills fast. See this gray powder? It's gelsemium, the wonder of all poisons. Just the sight of it makes the beast shake in his boots, because he knows it means business. Instant death."

"Enough, enough!" said Fortunata, who couldn't stand any more. "If you don't put all that away, I'm leaving."

He looked at her, his face a mixture of sinister despair and compassionate awe. This look augmented her fear, but, sensing that it was necessary to hide her feelings and instead humor his sick ideas in order to prevent a barbarous act on his part, she said:

"Everything's fine . . . I understand. Of course you have to kill the beast. But if you want me to love you, you have to promise me not to bring those poisons here."

"Oh, all right! If you'd prefer firearms . . . But if that's the case, we have to practice. You should die first, then me. But what if I miss and I get left alive and people come and grab me?"

"No, dear. That won't happen. We'll each take a pistol and one can aim at the other, like in duels. We'll give the signal and bang! You'll see what becomes of the two beasts then."

Maximiliano mused on this.

"Your solution doesn't sound very practical to me."

"Yes, it is. I tell you, it *is*. Do me a favor and gather up all those powders and throw them out the window. No, wait a minute. It would be better if you wrapped them up in a package and gave them to me. I'll keep them. I promise you, I'll keep them. What, don't you trust me? Thanks a lot, friend."

Indeed, he did distrust her. The minute she reached for the packets he hastened to defend them as if they were sacred property. "No. They're for me. Leave them here. I'll keep the—"

"All right. Put them in the night table drawer. The knife too. I promise not to touch it."

"Do you swear you won't?"

"I swear it. You'd think I'd already deceived you from the way you act. Really! Now, lie down—"

"I'm not sleepy, thank God. When I sleep at all I dream that I'm a man, I mean, that the beast gets hold of me and whips me and does whatever he wants, that infamous jailer!"

Impatiently now, Fortunata took the steps that serious cases demand. She got out of bed just as she was and, almost by force, blending affection with authority as one does with children, she made him go to bed. She took off his clothes, picked him up, and, after physically putting him to bed, she embraced him, holding him in place and lulling him to sleep. She murmured all sorts of nonsense about his "liberation"—the beauty of death, how good it would be to kill the beast, that awful jailer. "Every beast has to face his Saint Martin,"* she repeated along with other sentences that would have been funny except that the circumstances made them lugubrious.

She hardly slept a wink. At dawn, seeing him in a deep lethargy, she got up cautiously and took the dagger and packets from the drawer. Once she had hidden the former she emptied the contents of the latter into a newspaper that she had fashioned into a cone to take to Ballester. With help from Doña Lupe, who was horrified by what Fortunata told her of the night's events, she put into each packet a proportionate amount of salt or powdered sugar and, refolding them, they put them back in the night table drawer. The first thing he did when he woke up was to see if anyone had stolen his treasure, and since the dagger's absence surprised him, his wife said, "I've put it away. It's so nice. Don't worry, I won't lose it. Do you trust me or not? As for your powders—you take care of them. And

---

*Saint Martin's Day, at the beginning of cold weather, is the traditional day for slaughtering pigs.

if the time comes, I won't be the one to turn up my nose at them because, you know, when you think what life is—ha! always suffering for something, waiting and waiting, and every day another disappointment . . . Believe me, life's nothing but a bad joke."

"Embrace me," said Maxi, rushing toward her half-dressed. "That's the way I love you. You've suffered, you've sinned . . . so you're mine."

And since his aunt appeared then with his hot chocolate, he went toward her barelegged, wanting to embrace her too and saying:

"You've suffered too, and you've sinned too, my dear aunt."

"Me, sin!"

"So you're one of my kind."

"Whatever you like, as long as you drink your chocolate for me."

"I'll drink it, I'll drink it, even though I don't feel like it. You know, just because I should."

"That's right. It's one thing to fall in love with death, and another to do our duty till the time comes," said Doña Lupe naturally. "As for me, I can tell you this: I'm fed up with life—fed up—and if I haven't done anything about it, it's because I'm so busy I don't even have time to think about what I should do. But we'll fix things up, son, and you can count on me to give the beast a blow on the head when it's least expecting it. I can't stand it any longer."

Aunt and wife, pretending not to be sad, watched him as he drank his chocolate, awed by the spectacle of his thirst. He wasn't thirsty; the beast was.

II

At about ten o'clock Fortunata left to take the package of poisonous substances to Ballester. "Here's what your friend was preparing for us," she said curtly. "Some care you take! Look what he brought home!"

Ballester examined the terrible drugs. Then he grew very stern. "That fool Padilla's to blame. I don't know how he allowed him to get into these. Don't worry—I'll give him a good scolding today. The best thing is to fire him. He could get us into serious trouble any day. But sit down."

Upon offering her a seat, Ballester seemed to take special care to let his shiny new boots be seen, to let Fortunata admire his frock coat and hair that had been done in a curling iron and gave off a strong smell of heliotrope. She noticed everything and showed so by smiling mischievously.

"You're smiling at how handsome I'm looking today, right? Since you're used to seeing me look like a ditch digger . . . Well, I'll tell you why. My sister's getting married today to the fellow who's known as the 'distinguished thinker,' Federico Ruiz. I'm going to the wedding, and tonight I'll bring you some sweets."

Fortunata reverted to her subject. "We've got to make a decision on this. The medicines that you prescribe don't have the slightest effect on him. My aunt and I talked it over today. Before sending him to a mental institution we should try some other medicine. Don't you think you could try giving him the one you told us about—I don't remember what it's called—the one that sounds like a sneeze?"

"Oh, hashish! We'll make some up. You're boss here. You're the master and you rule me; if you asked me for a cataplasm made of my own minced heart, I'd whip it up in a second."

"Are you already joking again?"

"And now it's my turn to ask you a favor."

"Go ahead."

"Tonight I'll bring some sweets from the wedding. I'll send some up to the second floor and leave the rest here for friends who come. Will you be going upstairs to Doña Casta's or coming here?"

"We're going up. If we go for a walk, we might drop in. Depends on how he is."

"Fine. Tonight my critic friend's coming. Padilla will invite him in and offer him some sweets. I want him to eat one that I have ready for him. You have no idea how much I hate him."

Fortunata, whose head was buzzing with thoughts of poison, was startled. "What in the devil are you going to give that poor wretch? He's a good sort."

"Nothing. Don't worry. It's only a laxative. The fun will start when Doña Casta invites him up afterward and he goes up—"

"Don't be a brute. He's such a good boy! I've heard that he supports his mother."

"Supports his mother! With what, I'd like to know! His articles?"

"He gets two *duros* an article. So there you are. And he writes four a week."

"Yes, and it sure shows. But even if he does support his mother and his grandmother and the whole family and he's an excellent boy, I still want to play this innocent trick on him. Will you do me the favor I ask?"

"What?"

"I'm not going to ask you to kiss me, because if I asked for that much heavenly glory you wouldn't give it to me, and if you did I'd have to be put in a psychiatrist's hands, Ezquerdo's, immediately. My aspirations today, my dear friend, are that you—if you're here when the illustrious boy comes in—offer him the 'candied yolk' that I've got ready for him. If you give it to him he won't suspect anything. Besides, you could tell Doña Casta or Aurora to invite him up to hear 'the piece' . . ."

"Stop it! I won't have anything to do with those plots. Poor boy! I'm on his side. You're so mean!"

"You're meaner. And to repay you for your infamy I'm going to give you some good news."

"News for me?"

"It's so good that it will taste better than the sweets tonight. Oh! One thing consoles me, my friend, and it's that if you're ungrateful to me you are to others too. A lot have to suffer the same!"

"What are you talking about?"

"Well, they really walk the streets for you. And the little girl doesn't appear anywhere. The poor boy straining his neck to see up onto the balconies, and you tormenting him with your absence. Poor gentleman! All afternoon, going up the street, down the street . . . "

Fortunata paled, and in the sternest of tones inquired:

"Who and when?"

"Don't play dumb. Yesterday afternoon, when he left, he was in such a bad mood! He's never been stood up like that before. I watched him and said to myself: 'You more than deserve it. Bear it, chum. We're all alike.' Do you want some advice? Be rough on him. Let him sigh and pace the street till he knows it like the palm of his hand. Not all the gall should be for me. And do you want some more advice? What you need is a heart like the one I've got stashed away— virginal, completely virginal. Accept it, and stop loving ungrateful wretches."

Fortunata was so shaken she didn't hear the pharmacist's romantic confidings.

"Well, it's getting on," she said, rising. "I have to go home."

"Let's see. If he comes back this afternoon, what should I tell him?"

"Stop it," she said, disturbed now and hastening toward the door with him behind her.

"What should I tell him? I've never spoken to him, but if you order me to, I will. Should I tell him to not turn up around here again? Oh, what a woman! There she goes, like a gust of wind. She's touched in the head, just like her husband. And all because she won't fall in love with a worthy man like me, for example. Patience, Segismundo! Imitate a fisherman—wait, and wait, and wait, and finally she'll bite."

Doña Lupe, when her niece entered breathlessly from rushing up the stairs, was amazed to see her so happy. "God only knows," she said inwardly, "why this is such a happy occasion. The powders and Ballester were probably just an excuse to get out and see *him*. He probably told her that he'd be by at a certain time. And she's so flushed! Rubbing noses down at the main entrance, I'm sure of it!"

Maxi continued to be calm. He seemed more like a convalescent than a patient. He was very weak and wanted only to sit next to the parlor balcony windows and gaze blankly at the passersby. This didn't particularly please Fortunata because "if *he* feels like coming back this afternoon and Maxi sees him, he's going to get upset again." This made her very restless; she went in and out of the parlor constantly, trying to persuade her husband to go sit somewhere else. But *he* didn't feel like coming by that afternoon. What he did do was send a message to his friend, rescuing her from that purgatory of uncertainty and sadness. His go-between for the message was Fortunata's aunt, Segunda Izquierdo, who the previous May had beseeched her, in tears and rags, for money. Since then she had returned every week, and her niece had helped her, either with money, or leftover food, or some clothes. Santa Cruz protected her too, and she used her begging as a means of getting love notes into the Rubín home; she was so stealthy that even the shrewd Doña Lupe suspected nothing.

That afternoon, after having arrived empty-handed many times, she slipped a note into Fortunata's hand. Finally—it was incredible! When she could, the happy woman read the little piece of paper, which told her the time and place he wished to see her the following day.

At night they all went to Doña Casta's; the lady took Maxi under her wing, showering him with attention, offering him sweets, and trying to refresh his mind with a placid dissertation on the waters of Madrid and the qualities that distinguish Alcubilla, Abroñigal, and Fuente de la Reina waters from Lozoya water.

Fenelón's widow arrived at the usual time, and shortly afterward the delivery boy came up from the pharmacy with a tray of sweets sent by Ballester. It wasn't long before the tenants on the third floor (right side) appeared. By one of those ironical coincidences that are so common in life, his name was Don Francisco de Quevedo* (a brother of the priest Quevedo whom we met at the *tertulia* along with the Pater and Pedernero), and he was the most austere, cold, and disagreeable man in the world. His wife's elegance could compete with that of a buoy stuck in the sea for ships that need a place to stop. Her gait was difficult, slow and heavy, and when she sat down there was no way to get her up unless you helped her. Her round face looked like a lighthouse—all red and as if there was a light on inside, that's how much it shone. Well, Ballester called this monstrosity Doña Desdemona, because Quevedo was or had been very jealous; and I will refer to her with this nickname, although her real name was Doña Petra. The couple was childless, and while Don Francisco spent his time delivering mankind's children, his wife helped to deliver and breed birds, and she was very good at it. The house was full of cages, and in them diverse families and species of singing birds reproduced themselves. And to top off the contrasts, the male midwife's lady of the house was an extremely witty woman who knew how to make people laugh. On the other hand, Don Francisco de Quevedo was about as amusing as an alligator.

---

*Famous Spanish satirist of the seventeenth century.

12

Aurora and Fortunata, after briefly attending to the visitors and laughing at Doña Desdemona's jokes, exited to the balcony. The widow had things of great importance to tell her friend, and so their whispering started immediately. "I no longer have any doubts. Everything points to it. Do you know that their cousin Moreno never leaves the shop? That's where he goes in the morning, and he doesn't take his eyes off the door to the Santa Cruzes' house, just waiting to see if they come in or out. What a fool, and it's so hard for him to hide it! It's hard to believe that a man his age—because he must be close to fifty now—a sick man— because no matter what the doctors say, any day now he's going to keel over . . . And what proves his foolishness more than the fact that he's here? Why doesn't he go abroad the way he's done other years? A fine state he's in, poor fool. There's a man who, *par exemple*, could have made any decent girl happy, and he doesn't have love, or a family of his own; he's alone in the world, sad. Oh, I know him well! He's dissolute, immoral, completely corrupt. The only women who interest him are married ones. He told me so himself."

"But . . . you?"

"Wait a minute. Let me explain," Aurora added cautiously, making sure that no nosy member of the *tertulia* could overhear. "Well, this cousin Moreno— although he's a distant relative, and all the more distant because he's rich and we're poor, he used to visit us about thirteen or fourteen years ago. Mamá thought a lot of him, so whenever he came to call she rolled out the red carpet. She had hopes at one time—imagine what nonsense!—of marrying me to him. I was eighteen; he was slightly over thirty. You know?"

Fortunata listened very keenly.

"Do you want me to speak frankly? Well, I rather liked him, but he never said anything to me . . . He cut a good figure and had a gentlemanly air that very few men have. Mamá and Papá, poor dears, got carried away hoping. What dodos they were! That man's very sharp. Marry me! Sure, just my type. Months would go by and he wouldn't even show up around here. I remembered him and the times when he used to come calling—just the sight of him coming through the door would dazzle us, as if it were God Himself. Well, anyway, as I was saying, he stopped coming. Then · me. Fenelón; he became my fiancé and asked for my hand. Mamá still had her hopes; Papá didn't. We got married. Well, would you believe that a month after we were married, our cousin comes back to Madrid and starts to court me as nicely as you could wish?"

Fortunata looked as if she were listening to the most facinating tale imagin- able, judging from the interest and awe she displayed.

"It was like this. Fenelón was one of these people who are so good they judge everything according to the way they see it and couldn't recognize evil even if you dangled it in front of them. He didn't realize I was being pursued and having an awful time. Oh, what danger it was! Whenever I went out, bam! I met him. I don't know, it's as if he could smell when I was coming, like a hunting dog. One rainy afternoon he grabbed me and practically forced me into his carriage. I was an inch away from the abyss . . . half an inch . . . but I didn't fall in. Lord, what a man! It's absurd."

"But did you love him?" Rubín's wife asked, for loving solved all problems as far as she was concerned.

"I . . . well . . . it was kind of strange. I trembled whenever I saw him. But as I say: why didn't he marry me?"

"Sure."

"I would have loved him very much and wouldn't have been unfaithful for all the world. But men like him are evil, so evil! Listen to another one. I go to Bordeaux with my husband, months and months go by. Summer comes and we go to Royan for a short stay; it's a beach resort. Well, one afternoon I was at the wharf watching some passengers get off a steamboat from Bordeaux when I see Moreno. It made me—well, I can't describe what I felt."

"Was your husband with you?"

"No, that's the point. Fenelón had gone to Paris on a buying trip. Moreno was in Paris, saw him, and without a word to anyone took off for Royan, where he knew he could catch me off guard, all by myself. I wasn't careful enough this time, and I didn't manage to get out of it the way I did in his carriage. Oh! I tell you these things because I know you're very discreet and won't betray me. If Mamá ever found out . . . ! Anyway, the cad had as much fun as he wanted and then gave me the gate. Then it was 1870, and those vile Prussians killed poor old Fenelón. It was so painful. Ah, and to think it all happened just because he was courageous and insisted on going out on patrol! He was so patriotic that to save his beloved France he would have given a hundred lives if he'd had them . . . But let's get back to the other one, that depraved bachelor. When I became a widow I thought, 'Well now, if he really likes me . . .' Hah! I met him in Madrid the next year and it was as if nothing had ever happened. Do you think he had anything romantic to say? Do you think he remembered the promises he'd made? Let's hope God will remember for him. I've never seen anybody so cold. I tell you, I felt like, well, like sticking a dagger into him. It's true that he offered me whatever I wanted to establish myself; but I didn't want to take anything from those hands. The monster! When he gave his cousin Pepe money for the new shop, he gave it to him on the condition that I be put in charge of the employees. But I don't thank him for it, not in the least."

"So your cousin only likes married women. What a rascal!" said Fortunata, shaking her head like someone who's just understood what she should have understood before.

"Those idle, rich bachelors are like that. They're vice-ridden, depraved, spoiled. And since they're used to having their own way, they think they can even ask for noon at two o'clock in the afternoon, as the French say. Now he's bored and sick and doesn't know what to do with himself. He wants family warmth and he can't find it anywhere. He deserves what he got. I'm glad. Let him pay for his sins. And to make things worse, he's taken a fancy to Jacinta. What makes him fall in love is being resisted, so women with a reputation for decency excite him, and if besides having the reputation they really are decent, they drive him to distraction. He must have gone through a tremendous struggle for Jacinta, a tremendous one; but in the end she yielded to him, don't doubt it a second. I was Metz—I surrendered too soon; and she's Belfort, which defends itself but eventually surrenders too. The signs are as plain as day. Their cousin goes to their house every day and watches for when she goes out so he can pretend to run into her. Some afternoons he doesn't come to the shop. Do you suppose they meet secretly? That's what I think. And I swear that I'm going to find out. It's impossible for me not to find out. Even if it meant losing my job, losing every last cent I had . . . What infamy! And just look at her, the little goody-goody with her Baby Jesus face and her virtuous reputation. Sure, I know that kind of saint—they're a dime a dozen. I can assure you, the day this thing explodes and the big tragedy comes will be the happiest day of my life. What does he expect, anyway? That he can deceive, and deceive, and keep deceiving and make a laughing stock of poor honorable husbands? Well, now he's in for it, except that this time he's not up against my Fenelón, who was a saint and didn't suspect anyone except the Prussians. This time he's up against a harder man, your friend, who won't stand for this dishonor, will he? He'll tear down his little cousin, his meanness and foreign ways."

Fortunata sat speechless. This revelation had affected her like a heavy blow in the head.

Jacinta, good Lord above! The paragon, the angel, God's own child. What would Guillermina say? What would the "lady bishop," who was bent on converting people and seeing who sinned and who did not, think? What would she say? Ha, ha, ha! So there wasn't any virtue after all! The only law left was love! She could lift up her head now! Now they wouldn't confront her with a model that confused and troubled her! Now God had made them all equal, so He could forgive them all.

II. Insomnia

I

AT NOON ON A BEAUTIFUL DAY in October, Don Manuel Moreno-Isla was returning home after a short walk in Hyde Park—I mean the Retiro. My slip of the tongue reflects the kind that my dear character was making those days; Moreno, in his mildly troubled state, had begun to confuse immediate impressions with memories. That day, despite his fatigue, he began to make some mental comparisons which in turn led him to take stock of his real situation and the place where he was. "My machine must be in very bad shape when I'm only halfway down Alcalá Street and I'm already exhausted. And all I've done is walk around the pond. Blast this neurosis or whatever it is! I, who could walk all the way around the Serpentine and then go right on to Cromwell Road—it was nothing, and it was about ten times as long as today's walk. I, who'd get home and feel like walking some more, and here I am exhausted halfway down this cursed street! Maybe it's because of this cursed pavement—it's unbearably steep! This is a capital all right—the capital of the seven hundred hills! Oh, and there they are watering—what animals—I have to cross the street to keep from getting drenched by that beast with the hose in his hand.' 'Go on, you brutes—make a nice big puddle so there'll be plenty of mud and malaria!' And there are the street sweepers, who always sweep a cloud of dust at you. 'Have more respect for people!' . . . I prefer getting drenched. Oh, this uncouthness makes me sick; that's what's wrong with me. You just can't live here. There's another beggar. Didn't I say so? You can't take a step without being harassed by these hordes of beggars. And some of them are so insolent! 'Here, go on, take it. You too.' If I ever forget to fill my pockets with change, I'll certainly know it. There are no policemen, no beneficent organizations, no manners, no civilization here! Thank God I've made it up the hill. It's like going up to Calvary, and with the cross I have to bear, it's worse. What beautiful spikenards that woman's selling! I think I'll buy one. 'Give me one; just one. No, give me three. How much? Here. Good-bye.' She overcharged me. Everybody cheats here. I must look like Saint Joseph, but I don't care. 'I don't play at the lottery; leave me alone!' What do I care if tomorrow's the last day to buy tickets or if the number's a 'lucky one' or an 'unlucky one'? But I could buy a ticket for Guillermina. She's sure to win. I've never seen such a lucky woman! 'Here, I'll take that block of ten, little girl. Yes, you're right, it's a lucky number. And you—why are you so dirty?' What a town this is, and what a race, Lord help me! As I was saying yesterday to Don Alfonso: 'Don't fool yourself, Your Highness. Centuries will pass before this nation is presentable unless we crossbreed with some northern race by bringing in Anglo-Saxon women as mothers.' I don't have much left to go now. Frankly, I ought to take a cab. But no, I'll try to bear it; I'll be there soon . . . A funeral procession going through the Puerta del Sol. No, I'm not going to die here if I can help it. I don't want to be carried away in one of those hideous coaches. It's noon. There are the unemployed watching the clock drop the ball as it strikes twelve. I'd like to give you a thing or two to watch. Here comes Casa-Muñoz. But what's that I see? Is it really him? He doesn't dye his hair anymore. He must have realized that it's absurd to have white hair and black sideburns. He's not seeing me, he doesn't want me to say hello. It's really ridiculous, his situation—a man who dyes his hair being seen when he's decided to give it up because of his age or because he's convinced himself that he isn't fooling anybody. There goes the duchess of Gravelinas in a carriage. She didn't see me. 'So long, Feijóo . . .' What that man's lost! Well, I've made it to Correos Street. I wonder if my cousin's come for lunch yet? He's simply got to look me over, and thoroughly, because I feel awful. He should listen to my heart carefully; this poor heart of mine sounds like a broken bellows. Could this be a purely moral phenomenon? Perhaps. I know the remedy if it is . . . The grass is always greener on the other side. And the balconies look as sad as ever. Oh, there's Barbarita at the bay window to talk with the 'ecclesiastical rat.' 'Hello, I've just had my morning walk. I'm fine—not at all tired today.' What a lie I just told! I'm more tired than ever. Now, staircase: be kind to me. Up we go. Oh, curse this heart of mine! Slowly, now; there's time to climb up. If I don't get there today, I'll get there tomorrow. Six done and the rest to go. Good God, there are so many!"

When he reached the second floor, he found his sister waiting for him at the door. "Did you get very tired?" "More or less. Where's Tom? Tell him to come."

Moreno walked into his room followed by his servant, who was English and accompanied him on all his trips. The anti-patriot said that Spanish servants are so awkward they can't even close a door properly. His was one of those men who make an intelligent profession of service and know how to anticipate even the most trivial desires of their masters in order to please them. Moreno told him in English to fill one of the earthen vases in the room so he could arrange the spikenards, and without so much as releasing them from his hand he collapsed onto the sofa. The gentleman was wearing a dark jacket and checkered pants, a top hat, and those indispensable spats over his roomy, thick-soled boots. "Has my cousin arrived?" he asked Tom, giving him the flowers.

"The doctor is with Miss Guillermina in her parlor."

"Tell him I'm here."

He still felt fatigued from his walk and the stairs when he saw the most pleasant of doctors, Moreno-Rubio, come in radiating happiness as if it were a preservative against the sadnesses of medicine. A doctor of great knowledge and devotion, he had gained considerable fame and had a very brilliant clientele.

"Today you've got to look me over very carefully," said his cousin. "Imagine that I'm a stranger who's come to consult you. Don't tease me, and tell me the truth. I warn you—I'll discredit you unless you do."

"All right, my friend, don't worry; we'll look you over from head to toe," replied the doctor, smiling and sitting down next to him. "Are you very tired?"

"Can't you see what I'm like? You just feel like asking questions. As soon as we've finished lunch, I'll turn myself over to you like a corpse in a dissecting laboratory."

"Well, I think we'd better start right now," he said, taking out his stethoscope and adjusting it.

"All right, start now if you'd like," this as he took off his jacket. "Should I lie down? Yes, it would be better; I'll be just like a dead man with my hands crossed."

"No. Extend your arms. That's right."

The doctor unbuttoned his shirt and put the stethoscope on Moreno's chest, leaning closer to listen. "Don't move. Now. Breathe deeply. Sigh, a good deep sigh, the way lovers sigh."

"I'm beginning to think you're teasing me. This is serious, for God's sake, serious, Pepe. I haven't slept for ten nights, and your blessed digitalis doesn't help me at all."

"Shh, be quiet. Let me listen—"

"What do you notice? What is it?"

"Please, be patient. Wait a minute—this isn't sounding right. There's a ticking I don't like."

"What kind of sound is it? The systole is too loud and—"

"Something like that."

"My blood pressure—"

"Yes, but there's one symptom that I keep noticing, a very nasty one—"

"What is it, tell me? What's it called?"

"Love."

"Oh, go on! I'll call another doctor. You aren't any good to me, with your bad jokes. What could that have to do with it?"

"What?" Moreno-Rubio asked rhetorically, turning sober and putting away his instruments. "I don't know how you think things run. Do you want to destroy the harmony of the spiritual world and the physical world in one blow? You already know it; I've told you so a hundred times. I don't need to listen to your heart anymore. You have some disorder in your circulation, and it could be very serious unless you change your way of life."

"You'd think that I led a life of perdition." He got up and started to put his clothes back on.

"You lead an erratic life, which is worse. You need absolute quiet; you should give up violent desires and the mental anxiety that their being unsatisfied causes you. Travel less and control your body's appetite; it's too lusty. Give up all unhealthy stimulants. I'm referring not so much to coffee and tea as to those imaginary, idealistic stimulants; avoid emotions and end your romantic career, promising yourself you won't go back to it. Draw a line in your life and say, 'Christ didn't go beyond the cross, and I won't go beyond this.' If you were thirty or thirty-five I'd advise you to get married, but it would be more prudent to make believe that a judicial, or divine, decree has just been passed and caused all the women there are in the world—married, single, widowed—to disappear."

"Bah! It's always the same old story," said Moreno-Isla, taking it as a joke. "Are you a doctor or a confessor?"

"Both," stated his cousin in a serene, but firm tone. "If you don't do what I tell you, Manolo, if you don't do it you'll die, and soon. So now you know my opinion. Don't consult me anymore. I don't know anything else. I've used up what I know with you. If there's a colleague somewhere who can find a way to match your living habits and passions with orderly, sane vascular functioning, call on him and do what he tells you."

The servant announced that lunch was served.

"Let's go," said the sick man, taking his cousin by the arm. "Wait a minute. I want to ask you something."

They stopped for a minute and Don Manuel, wearing a very serious face, asked his cousin this: "Let's see now, joking aside. In my condition, be it good or bad; in my present condition, just as I am right now—could I have children?"

Moreno-Rubio burst out laughing.

"I wouldn't say you couldn't. You could have a school full of children."

"I mean . . . But answer me seriously, now. What I mean is, in my condition, with my valves half out of order—"

"Yes, I think you could, if it's a question of being *able* to—"

"I'm telling you this because after that I'd agree to accept what you've proposed to me—retirement, no more romance, etc."

"Look, Manolo. Don't worry about adding to the human race. The fewer born, the better. For what this life has to give . . ."

"I agree. But I'd like to have the assurance that . . . It's just in case. Don't think that I disapprove of your plan for a vegetable life. I'll adopt it all right; but when the time comes."

"Cousin," said the doctor, looking at him craftily, "if you wanted children, you should have thought of it sooner."

"No, no, silly. It's not that I want them. I don't need little kids. I'm only asking you hypothetically. It's enough just to know if I'm capable. A sick man's curiosity."

"Well, are you coming or aren't you?" asked Moreno-Isla's sister, appearing at the door.

"What a rush you're in! We're coming. And anyway, with this appetite, or should I say, this lack of one . . ."

"But I've got one, blazes," said the doctor.

2

Moreno called for his carriage that afternoon and went out visiting until seven. He had lunch with the Santa Cruzes, who found him gloomy, shockingly distracted, and so indifferent to everything that he didn't even muster up a strong defense of his principles and foreign tastes when Barbarita, to combat his brooding, brought up the subjects that usually promised an entertaining debate. He did say something, however, that livened up the dull conversation that night.

"Do you know what irritates me most in Spain among other things? The habit that servants have of singing while they work. You'd think that in my own home I'd be free of this torment. Well, I'm not. My Aunt Guillermina has a little maid who's got a mouth like a couple of street bands. It's useless to tell her to be quiet. She obeys for ten minutes and then suddenly breaks out again with her 'el señor alcalde mayor.' She says she forgets to keep quiet. Believe me, I feel like bashing her head in."

"You don't mean to suggest that in other countries—! But Manolo . . ."

"Oh, no, my lady. You may be sure that if a servant so much as dared to sing in London she'd be thrown out immediately. They wouldn't even think of it there."

"I believe you. They're such wet noodles, the English."

"This roguish race of ours simply doesn't value time or silence. You'll never be able to get it across to these people that whoever starts shouting or singing when I'm writing, or when I'm thinking, or sleeping is stealing something from me. It's a lack of civilization, just like any other. Taking over someone else's silence is just like stealing a coin from someone else's pocket."

These remarks amused the others, and that particular night they laughed more heartily to cheer him up. Juan invited him to the Royal Theater but he refused. There were very few people visiting that night—Guillermina in her corner, Don Valeriano Ruiz-Ochoa and Barbarita II. Barbarita I had conceived the mad plan of marrying Moreno to this niece of hers who was a very pretty girl, and when she confided this to Jacinta, the latter found the thought mere nonsense. "But Mamá, my sister's only eighteen and Moreno's almost fifty, and besides, the man is ill!"

"It's true there's a difference in age," the lady said, laughing. "But it would be a great match. If you keep having so many scruples, just watch what comes your sister's way—a second lieutenant, an officer from the rank and file. This man is a good-natured fellow, and rich. His illness is boredom, the bachelor's sickness, what the English call spleen. Marry him and he'll be ten years younger."

Jacinta wasn't convinced, and as for the illness, her opinion was very different from her mother-in-law's. That night there was an opportunity to give him a good dressing down. They were in the study, separated from the other two sitting groups (Don Baldomero, Ruiz-Ochoa, his wife, Pepe Samaniego, and someone else). Barbarita II and her sister had Moreno in front of them; at first he mused to himself, "If the young girl weren't around, I think I'd speak to her. That girl with her innocence and her pretty face irritates me. It's as if they put her there like a shield against me. What a fate I have—the few times I catch her alone I don't get anywhere. If I venture some delicate reticence, she plays dumb. She avoids meeting me alone, and now she always drags her scarecrow of a sister (who's an angel) with her to discourage me."

"Goodness, you're quiet," observed Jacinta, smiling. "Do you feel worse? Mamá says that if you'd get married you'd take off ten years. So why not make up your mind?"

The misanthrope's face glowed when he heard this unexpected recipe.

"I think so too," he said. "But look—there's a remedy that sounds so simple and yet it's impossible."

"Of course—no more women left in the world. You're right; there are no more women."

"For me, it's as if there weren't any. What did I tell you yesterday? You don't remember. Telling you something is like blowing words to the wind."

"I promise—I've forgotten. Do you remember, Bárbara?"

"Bárbara wasn't there."

"That doesn't matter. Everything you tell me I tell my sister, immediately."

"Yes, you're a tattletale, I know. And why do you tell your sister?"

"Because she always thinks it's funny."

Moreno was unable to hide the deep sadness overtaking him.

"Goodness, what's wrong with you tonight? Your 'spleen' seems worse than ever."

"Didn't you tell us yesterday that you'd left behind three girlfriends in London?" queried Bárbara, who liked to draw things out of him.

"Yes, but I don't love *them*," replied Moreno with childlike candor. And then, wallowing in that sadness of his that his social self couldn't cope with, he ran through another monologue: "I'm in my second childhood; foolishness and my inability to cope with things are beginning to get the best of me. This woman with her coldness and irony is stepping on me, just the way the Blessed Virgin stepped on the serpent. I'm beginning to look foolish."

"Why don't you tell my sister what you told her last week?" Bárbara II asked the melancholy gentleman.

"I . . . what?" frightened, like someone waking from a dream. "I . . . didn't tell her anything."

"Yes, last week, when we went to La Casa del Campo and you started to tell that story about the Englishwoman who wanted to shoot you because of something you'd said to her on the train."

"I don't remember," said the misanthrope, looking like an utter fool.

"When it comes to forgetting," remarked Jacinta, "nobody can beat this man. You told me that you'd get married if I found you a wife."

"Ah! Well, I have to take it back. If you've started your task, it's been useless. I'll reimburse you, if need be."

"You certainly shall! Well! And with all I've done. You're really formal, aren't you?"

The two women looked seriously at him. They noticed a deathly pallor in his face, an overall weariness, and a peculiar distractedness, unlike the usually constant attention he politely paid to ladies whenever he spoke with them. Jacinta leaned toward him, opening her fan over his knees, and said to him in a very affectionate tone: "You need to look after yourself, my friend, and watch your health more. This afternoon we saw Moreno-Rubio at Amalia's house and he told us that there isn't anything wrong with you, but that if you're careless and don't do what he says, you're going to have a bad time of it. You're not a boy, and you should realize this. Why don't you pay attention to what people who love and care about you are telling you?"

Moreno looked at her ecstatically. A few monosyllables left his mouth, but those broken pieces of his thoughts sounded more like acquiescence than protest. Jacinta continued talking to him in sweet, tender tones that made her seem more like a mother than a friend.

"We'd be so happy to see you strong and well, and it would be so easy for you if you'd only try! The only thing that's bothering you is bad thoughts. Your cousin told me so, and his opinion fits what I thought. It's a pity that, having everything to be happy, you're not. What else do you need?"

Moreno felt his heart crumble.

"You're asking me what I need? I need everything, absolutely everything. Oh, what a woman! If you go on in this vein, I think I'll look even more ridiculous."

"What do you lack? Nothing. If you didn't get it into your head to want what's impossible, you'd be as fresh as a daisy. What you are is very spoiled. You're like a little boy."

"That's precisely it! I'm like a little boy," thought the unhappy gentleman.

"Moreno-Rubio said so and he's right: you have your health and your life in your hands. If you lose them it's because you want to. It's incredible that a man your age can't listen to reason."

"Reason! She's an indecent one!" Moreno thought to himself.

"And you have to shake out those bad thoughts and temper your spirits—not desire what you can't have, and not live such an aimless life, insisting on upsetting things just to please and satisfy yourself. What's spleen if it's not haughtiness? Yes, what you are is haughty. Your infernal 'You' counts more than anything else. Those English think the world was made for them. Oh, no—you've got to take your place in line just like everyone else. Well! Are you going to take care of yourself? Are you going to do what your cousin and I order? Because you know, I'm a doctor too. And there's something else: here in Spain you're always criticizing and cursing. If you don't like it, then why do you bother to stay? Why don't you go back to England?"

"She already wants to throw me out, see?" said Moreno, looking at Barbarita and attempting to smile to hide his disturbance. "And then they don't want me to travel."

"No, we don't. It's not good for you to always be moving from one place to another like a traveling salesman. Go off to your dear London, stay there, and relax; and if you meet a nice English girl with a good character, marry her, put up with her, even if she's a Protestant. I hope Guillermina doesn't catch me saying this, but—get married, and you'll see how your sullenness will vanish, and you'll have children. I hereby promise to be the godmother of your first—I mean if you baptize him, that is. And I'd even agree to be the child's mother if you gave him to me. I'd take him even if he weren't a good Christian. I'll baptize him. But I shouldn't talk about that. I'll be content to be the godmother of the first little Moreno born, and I'll tell my husband to take me to London for the christening."

Moreno got up. He felt very ill, and the Dauphine's words excited him dangerously.

"What, are you leaving? Do you feel ill? Don't you like my sermons?"

"If I don't leave, it'll be all over for me," thought the misanthrope, pursing his lips. "This beguiling girl is killing me."

"Are you leaving, Manolo?" Don Baldomero called from the other side of the room.

"They're throwing me out, my friend. Your daughter wants to exile me."

"Oh, what a rascal you are! Quite the contrary."

Barbarita I stepped in, saying, "Come, don't exaggerate so. Take the girl's arm and walk to the parlor and back. Do you feel ill? It's only nerves. Relax a bit. Bárbara, come here."

Moreno gave his arm to Barbarita II and the walk began. Jacinta caught a few phrases from the couple's superficial conversation every time they passed her on their walks across the room. "Me? No, I promise you." "Really, the things that occur to you! You're so naughty!" "As soon as I get there I'm going to convert to Judaism." "Good Lord!" "I have a boy friend? Where did you get that idea?" "No, I don't like young boys much."

"If she were a bit more clever," said Señora Santa Cruz to her daughter-in-law, "I think she could catch him."

But Jacinta was very dubious about this, and she looked sadly at the couple when they walked past. As he was leaving, Moreno was able to speak to her for a second without any witnesses.

"I'll do just as you wish—all of it, even down to the baby. You'll have your 'Morenito.'"

Jacinta saw such gloominess in his eyes that she couldn't help but say to herself: "He's terribly confused."

Moreno left with an unsure step. His vision blurred, and as he was going downstairs he clung to the banister to keep from falling. "When I say I've gotten stupid, I mean it; I'm getting to be as stupid as they come. I don't know how to think anymore. I don't know what's happened to my reasoning powers. That woman has bewitched me. I'm becoming a real fool."

3

In the solitude of his bedroom my man gained more control of himself, having now overcome that inexplicable disturbance that afflicted him as he was leaving the Santa Cruzes'. He dismissed his servant after the latter helped him off with his clothes, and in his bathrobe now he stretched out on the sofa. During such long stretches of time he tried to trick his insomnia by alternating between walks around the room and short catnaps. When he did manage to inveigle sleep, memories of that day or previous ones (at times, very remote ones) crowded his mind. That night, strangely enough, his valet had just left when Moreno sank into a deep sleep on the sofa, without any dreams; but he woke up in half an hour, unable to tell how long his lethargy had lasted. Upon awakening, sleep deserted him so instantly and he felt so restless that he couldn't even accept as probable the idea of sleeping. Just as a chess player gradually arranges his men on the black and white squares of the board, he brought out his ideas. His opponent was himself in that game. "I move a pawn."

"A great move! Some campaign this is! How long have you been in Spain? A little over a year. What for? Nothing. Poor man! What seemed easy is not only difficult, it's impossible. And what makes it worse is that when I'm with that blasted, blessed woman I turn into the most insipid schoolboy imaginable. Why? And tell me something else, you idiot: what does that adorable woman have that makes you lose your head? Others are more attractive, wittier; there are women who are more elegant; and yet she's number one—she's the only number—for you. I've gone from liking her to being mad about her, and I'm beginning to notice something I'd never noticed before: a sort of happiness, a sadness; I feel like crying, and laughing, and even being a fool in front of her. Oh, well. It must be a premature second childhood. But I'm only forty-eight. And there's something else that had never happened to me either—I want to be daring and bold, and I can't. I intend to be gallant with her, and out comes some stupid expression. She makes me feel a respect I've never experienced. I follow her to Biarritz, to Paris, and just when I've gotten to know her better this cursed respect ties my tongue. I wish I could cut it off like a gangrened hand. Why should I feel so much respect? What does it mean? Whatever it is, that woman has made me think something that I've never said about any of them: if she were single, I'd marry her."

This agitated him so, he had to get up and start pacing the room again. "This world is a circus—I'm miserable, and she's miserable, because her husband's blind and doesn't realize what a jewel he has. From these two miserable states we could make happiness if the world weren't what it is—slavery, utter slavery. I can almost see her face when I said that to her. What sweet laughter, what serenity, and what an admirable reply! She left me speechless, so much so that I haven't gone back for more. And even when I do prepare something to say to her, it takes all my courage, and even then, the opposite comes out instead. I never dreamed anyone could be so stupid. Oh, Lord! If I die and thought lives on after death, I'll be seeing that adorable face with its heavenly expression for all eternity . . . Those serene, smiling eyes . . . that dark hair with those charming white strands . . . that mouth that can't speak without making my soul ache. Poor angel! Her only passion is motherhood, and it's an unquenched thirst, a terrible despair. I can feel her passion; it burns me. I want to have a child too. I can almost see him, he's here, on the brink of life, begging me to let him in, and that's all I have to do—bring him to life! He'd come, if she wanted him to. I'm sure he'd come, the thought's rooted in me. And what I'd say is, 'You could certainly give up virtue for a child . . .' Oh, not to have the courage to come out and say it. How, though? There simply aren't any words that will do."

The pounding of his heart was so hard that he had to sit down. He felt asphyxiated. In the area around his heart, or nearby, close to the center, he could feel the blood surging in a sharp, forceful rhythm. It was as if a blacksmith were hammering right next to his very heart, riveting a new piece onto it, in the fire.

"This is horrible. If it's going to break, I wish it would break once and for all. Oh, this is unbearable! If she loved me, my heart would be cured. It's not an illness that I've got; it's impatience, a constant tingling. What have I done to deserve this? Now I realize that I've never enjoyed myself. All my adventures were desire chasing after what was only boredom. And people think I've been a happy man, that I'm ill from overindulging myself. What fools!"

Without knowing how or why, certain impressions he'd had that day reproduced themselves in his mind. The least fleeting of them was this: That morn-

VOLUME FOUR

ing, on his way into the Retiro Park, one of those revolting beggars who are usually at the outskirts of the city but sometimes work their way into the center suddenly confronted him. He was in rags and was walking on one leg and a crutch; the other leg was a repugnant limb—the thigh swollen and scabby, the foot hanging there, dry, shapeless, and bloodstained. He showed it to stir up sympathy. His leg was his way of life—his farm, his business, what the guitar or the violin are for a penniless musician. Such spectacles made Moreno indignant, and when he was accosted by one of these professional exploiters of human misery he almost exploded with rage. When he turned aside in order not to see him, the cursed man dodged cleverly with his crutch and managed to confront him again, showing him the leg. This made the bored gentleman feel even less like giving him alms, but he finally did give the man something to free himself from such terroristic persecution. He walked away from the beggar cursing. "This isn't a country, this isn't a capital. There's no civilization here! Oh, how I wish I could cross the Pyrenees right now!"

Well, that night he envisioned the poor cripple so vividly that he could almost see him in the bedroom. There was a moment when Moreno's hallucination became so powerful that he sat up and reached for a book lying on a nearby chair, saying, "Look—if you don't leave with that rotten leg of yours . . ." Then his head fell back on the sofa again and he put his hand over his eyes. "The wretch has to make a living somehow. It's not his fault that there aren't any charitable institutions in this blasted country. If I see him tomorrow I'll give him a *duro*. My Aunt Guillermina will really envy him for it. Well, let's turn over now and see if we can get some sleep. That's right, close my eyes . . . No. It would be better to open them and make believe. I want to stay awake. You can never have what you want. Let's just pretend that I'm trying not to fall asleep. What do I want to sleep for? It's better to be like this—thinking about things. These lines on the paper, blue and green, break when you see them about a foot away. The gray flowers alternate with blue flowers . . . a pretty pattern. The man who invented it must have felt his head spinning afterward. And there's a small spot here. I think that if I looked at the light, I'd fall asleep sooner. Let's try turning over again."

He looked at the light on the table in the middle of the room; it was large, round, and covered with a thick cloth, an oil lamp made of two bronze burners that merged into one stand. Green shades, with green satin skirts hanging from them, covered them both. The light cast on the table and the rest of the room was shadowy and had the kind of greenish tinge you see on an old rug. On the table were some gloves, a few books, two portraits in pretty frames (one of them of Tubs Arnáiz), a writing paper case, a very fine porcelain tea service, a little ivory box, and other pretty objects. "That glove," said Moreno, "that's on the writing paper case looks exactly like a greyhound chasing something. What a solemn silence there is now! You can always hear the Pontejos fountain flowing, though, and an occasional hack going through Puerta del Sol, taking some merrymaker home. That used to be me in my cab, leaving the Piccadilly Club, except that my cab used to speed by and these old carriages sound as if they're falling apart on the cobblestones. The mere sound stirs up old memories . . . I can almost see the girl I happened to meet one night in Haymarket on my way out of that bar. Nothing like her since! She looks rather like that stupid Aurora Fenelón. Well, it's all over now; it's all falling by the wayside as I move on."

Suddenly he jumped up and started pacing the room.

"I'm leaving tomorrow," he said. "Yes, tomorrow. And I'm leaving for good. Die here and be carried away in one of those pretentious funeral carts? No! Thank God I'm making up my mind. This last one was strong—it happened so suddenly and was so overwhelming. I can hardly wait till dawn, when I can tell Tom to pack my bags. I'll do my shopping tomorrow. You can't leave Spain without a few trinkets—fans, tambourines. Oh, how happy the decision's making me! Leave! I should have thought of it long ago. What are you here for—to waste away? And she won't say I haven't obeyed her—her desires are orders. She said, 'Leave, my friend,' and I'm leaving. Will she love me after I'm gone? Will she think of me? She just might . . . If only she could see that loving her husband is like throwing roses to a donkey; if only she could see it! But who can wait till she does? It can't be. She's madly in love with that cad and she'll love him to her dying day. It seems to me that she despises him and loves him at the same time; oh well, the human heart has these dualisms. But what I wonder is—won't the thought of loving me ever cross her mind? I'd be happy with that, just knowing that the thought had crossed her mind once . . . or twice. It's very likely that she's said to herself, 'Moreno's a good man. If I were *his* wife, he wouldn't have made me suffer, and we would have had a child, or a couple of them.' Who knows. Do you suppose she has ever had thoughts like these? I don't know why, but I think she has. I can only guess. Inside I feel so persuaded, it's like having a seed of hope that hasn't blossomed yet but that's living and growing. If I knew for a fact that she thought these things, why, I'd become the most Catholic man in the world to please her, because she's very religious. There's no end to the Masses and ceremonies I'd pay for just to please her! And it wouldn't be hypocritical on my part either, because loving her would make faith come, yes faith. It has fled, and I don't know where to. I think it's almost dawn now. I'm not sleepy. I just can't sleep. Tomorrow I'll be leaving. I'd leave this afternoon if I could arrange the trip in time. And something else. Should I go say good-bye to her? Why not? I'll go. She told me to leave; she wants me to go. I'll love her just as much from a distance as I do right here, and maybe she'll love me too. I'll be like a dream for her, and dreams usually affect the heart more than reality."

He lay down again and entertained himself by gazing absently at the walls. On one there was a large painting of Saint Joseph; it was a family heirloom of small artistic worth, but Moreno esteemed it greatly because it had hung for many years in the room where he was born. He associated his childhood impressions with that good-looking saint who was reclining on a cloud with his staff, his child, and that yellow cape whose folds competed with the streaks of light in the cloudy sky. At that moment the good gentleman suddenly remembered his father so vividly he could almost hear him. He'd never known his mother, because she died when he was very little. He also recalled when he and his sister (the same widow who lived there) used to go to their grandfathers's house on Concepción Jerónima, and how they'd walked hand in hand. And one afternoon, going down Imperial Street they—or rather she—got lost, and he almost died of fright. And the day that he was in Provincia Square, when he saw the water vendor's donkey break loose; the owner was in a nearby tavern. Manolito felt like riding the animal and he did. But as soon as the damned donkey felt a rider he bolted, and although the boy tried to slow him down, he couldn't. He ended up on Segovia Street, very near the bridge, not because the donkey stopped but because the rider fell off and gashed open his head. He still had the mark. Luckily, the García brothers, craftsmen who made wineskins and had a shop underneath the Sacramento, saw him fall and, recognizing him, took him to his grandfather's house. What a scene! Don Manuel remembered the episode as if it had happened the day before. He could see his grandfather, Don Antonio Moreno, who still wore a shirt frill, a leather tie, and a dress coat all day long. He even wore his dress coat to the drugs warehouse. Then his papá came and couldn't decide whether to spank him or not. The worst was the donkey—there was neither hide nor hair of him and the family had to pay a stiff compensation. "It's as if it had just happened yesterday," said Moreno, touching the scar on his forehead.

When day was breaking he heard noise in the house, but he knew what it was in a second. "The ecclesiastical rat's up. She's on her way to at least half a dozen Masses, and to chat with the Holy Trinity. Poor thing—what's in it for her? But no matter what, it's a happy way to live."

4

Guillermina rapped twice on the door and, opening it slightly, she poked in her rosy face with its lively eyes. "Son, when I saw the light in your room I said, 'That poor dear is probably still up and hasn't slept a wink.' I see that I was right. What is it? Did you have another bad night?"

"Yes. Come in. I haven't slept a wink. And you?"

"Me? I wake up in the same position I go to sleep in. I only sleep four hours, but I sleep straight through. Can't you see how exhausted I am when I get home? And I do my musing in the daytime."

"Wonderful. Are you off to Mass?"

"Yes, and wherever I end up," replied the saint, and her newly washed face shone with freshness and contentment.

"And you're so calm! You're very calm, you know . . . with your Masses in the morning and then sponging hefty sums all day long. You know something? I envy you. I'd trade places with you any time."

"Well, you're silly," approaching him. "What I do is easy. What else is there to do but . . . do it?"

"Sit down a bit," said Moreno, sitting down on the sofa himself and patting a seat for her. "Attending half a dozen Masses is nowhere as saintly as practicing mercy by keeping the sick company and taking time to talk to someone who's spent a sleepless night. Tell me something: how's the work on your orphanage going?"

"Didn't you know?" sitting down. "It's going well. Thanks to charitable souls, the building's progressing like lightning. Jacinta has taken it up so ardently that she works more on it than I do now, and she can sponge so gracefully I'm nothing next to her."

"You have priceless friends. I've been thinking about you and your devotion during the night. You'd be amazed if I told you that since daybreak I've been experiencing a new feeling—something like wanting to be religious, to think of God, to devote myself to pious works—"

"Manolo! If you're going to start with your little jokes, I'm leaving," remonstrated Guillermina.

"No, it's no joke," he replied. And his face had such a dejected air that the saint looked at him in awe.

"Are you putting this on or . . . ? Manolo, what are you thinking? What's wrong with you?"

"There are hours in life that seem like centuries because of the changes they bring. Just a little while ago the strangest thing happened! I remembered a beggar who'd asked me for alms yesterday morning. He was a poor wretch with a deformed, repugnant leg full of ulcers. He asked me for alms and I threw him a copper coin, saying to him, and feeling horrified, 'Get out of my way, you rascal!' Well, tonight that man visited me here. I saw him as clearly as I'm seeing you. At first he filled me with repugnance, then sympathy, and I ended up asking him, 'Do you want to trade places?' Because you know, with his rotten leg and his crutch and his freedom, he enjoys a peace of mind that I don't have. His conscience is like a pool where not even the smallest pebble drops in. Poor me! I'd trade places with him. I'd exchange my wealth for his begging, my sick heart for his lifeless leg, and my anguish for his peace. What do you think?"

"I think God has touched your heart," said the lady, narrowing her eyes and putting her right hand—in which she held her missal and rosary—on the sad gentleman's head. "Your face doesn't have any signs of joking in it. Some great procession is passing through you. If you've said heretical things and made me mad in the past, don't think I ever considered you bad. You're a blessed soul, and if you had always lived with us instead of spending your life among Protestants and atheists, you'd be a different man."

"Don't you know that I'm leaving tomorrow?"

"You're leaving? Really?" sounding very disconsolate. "Bad business. Always looking for the cold, always running away from family warmth."

"But it's here that I'm not loved," Moreno declared somberly.

"We don't love you? Well! That's a fine statement. Don't say such foolish things, silly."

"My life is truncated, broken. There's no way of mending it now. You can believe that if I were loved I'd stay here; I'd be good, and to please you and your friends I'd become very religious—a very good friend of God's and the Virgin Mary's. I'd spend all my money on charitable works; I'd protect the devoted."

The saint's astonishment was so great she couldn't express it. Her mouth fell open in awe, as if she were witnessing a miracle. "Would you, really? Look, dear, if you want me to believe in the state of your soul, you'll have to prove it to me."

"How can I prove it to you?"

"Let's see," said the virgin and founder resolutely. "I bet you wouldn't do something."

"Do you want to bet I would?"

"I bet you won't go to San Ginés with me."

"I bet I will."

She got up and pulled the bell cord.

"I have to see it to believe it," said Guillermina, her eyes sparkling with joy. "No, don't bother; I'll call Thomas. The poor boy probably hasn't gotten up yet."

"I think he has. Tom!"

"I'll make your tea. Come, get dressed now."

That morning foray pleased him because it broke the tedious routine of his existence.

"I certainly am going to church," he said as he started some feverish activity. "I'll attend all the Masses you'd like and I'll pray with you. Tell me, doesn't Jacinta go to San Ginés now too?"

"Not this early. Bárbara usually goes a little later, after me."

"Well, I'm glad we'll be the first, the early birds, the most impatient to do our duty and be blessed . . . Tom!"

The Englishman appeared and, shortly afterward, when his master was already dressed, brought him his tea. Guillermina, serving him his breakfast, said: "Dress warmly—the mornings are chilly. Let's not start your new life with a case of pneumonia."

"It'd be better . . . I'm convinced that living is the most inane thing you can do," he said on their way downstairs. "What do we live for? To suffer. The poor man with the leg gets by all right because that doesn't hurt. He puts his leg out in front as if it were some pretty thing the public wanted to see."

"There's a lot of misery," observed the lady, approaching the subject from another angle, "and those of us who have enough to eat are wrong to complain. The more we suffer here, the more we'll enjoy ourselves there."

The misanthrope didn't counter this with anything. He was very pensive.

"The beggar with the leg will go straight to heaven with his crutch, and most of the rich who ride around in carriages will roll right down to hell in them. I wish God would give me the most revolting illness there is but . . . he doesn't want to; I'm always so healthy. Patience. He always grants what's right for us."

Moreno didn't respond to this either. They entered San Ginés, and Guillermina went straight to the Soledad Chapel, where the first Mass was starting. Although she didn't take her attention off the ritual, the illustrious lady noticed during Mass that her nephew was behind her participating like any other churchgoer—kneeling and rising whenever he ought to. But during the second Mass she noticed that he was distracted and restless. He walked from one part of the chapel to another, examining the altars and statues as if he were in a museum. This annoyed her, and she felt so out of sorts that she didn't dare to take Communion that day; she didn't feel that her soul was entirely serene and pure. By the fourth Mass the gentleman was not only distracted, he disturbed others in their devotion by walking in front of the altars where Mass was being said without so much as a genuflection or a sign of worship. "I'll have to tell him to leave," thought the saint. "That's no way to behave in church."

Moreno was contemplating a reclining statue in a luxuriant glass case when he heard these whispered words:

"Lovely, isn't it? It's the Christ we use in the Holy Burial procession."

He turned and found Estupiñá in his black wool cap, pointing to the statue with a Ciceronian gesture.

"The shroud's made of fine Dutch linen, the Micaela nuns embroidered it, and it's a gift from Doña Bárbara. A magnificent sculpture, and it's portable—we can stick it on the cross or take it down, depending on what we need."

But since the gentleman did not answer him, Plácido moved away, praying under his breath. He sat on a bench and, without disregarding the Mass, kept a sharp eye on Señor Moreno, baffled by his presence in the church. "That's the last thing I expected to see," he said to himself; "Don Manolo here. Him, the man with no religion! It must be because he likes the artwork. That's the way I got started."

The founder gave her nephew a good scolding once they were out. "Son, I couldn't even follow Mass, watching you stroll around the church. I knew you'd get bored."

"But Aunt, you can't complain. It's my first day in the course. It's all a question of getting started. I did hear one Mass. What did you expect—that I'd be like you? I can assure you, I found the experiment satisfying. I spent a very pleasant time, in a state of peace that's done me worlds of good. Didn't you like my walking around? When you're starting a new life you like to look around first, you know. I wanted to get a good look at the statues. Believe me, if I stayed in Madrid, I'd get to be friends with them all. I like to see them looking so beautiful, with their luxurious clothes and intent, staring eyes. It's as if they could see something that's coming but never quite comes. The ones that look at us seem to be telling us something when we look at them, and that they'll console us if we ask them for something. I understand mysticism, I can see it clearly now. Oh, if only I'd stayed here—!"

"Why don't you? What a fool you are, Manolo!" said the saint disconsolately.

"Impossible! I have to leave. And I'm going to be very sad there, I can tell."

"Well, then, stay. Do you want me to find something for you to do? That's just what you need. I hereby appoint you supervisor of my work, administrator of my accounts, and head sexton of my new chapel when it's finished."

Moreno burst into laughter at this.

"Head altar boy! I'd accept, I swear to you I would. I'm turning into an utter child. Head of the altar boys! I'd light the candles, dust the statues, and spruce them up a bit. I'd talk to the old ladies! You wouldn't believe it, but something that fits that humble job very well is starting to sprout in me."

"You're as good as they come. It's idleness, and all your merrymaking, and that English 'spleen' that have made you this way. I promise you that you'll be even more bored if you don't look up to God. Do what I do, Manolo: kick the world; become small to be big; come down to go up. You're not a boy anymore, you know; you're past marrying. And besides, it's bad for you to be always traveling around like a letter with the wrong address on it. And women: what do they do but ruin you? Be bold for a few minutes; think it over; and give up the rest of your life to God. I don't mean that you should become a priest. There are hundreds of ways to win eternal well-being. Listen to this: why don't you dedicate all your money, your activity, and your soul to a vast, holy project; not to some passing thing, but to one of those that add some good to humanity and testify to the glory of God? Start from scratch on a new building, an asylum of one kind or another, for example, a huge insane asylum that would take in and cure the poor people who've lost their minds—"

"You've got an obsession with buildings and you want to stick it on me."

"It's the first thing that entered my mind. Does it sound bad? A model insane asylum, like the kind you've probably seen in other countries. We're very backward in this. It would be an immense work of charity, and Madrid and Spain would bless you for it."

"An insane asylum!" said Moreno, smiling in a manner that petrified his generous aunt. "Yes, that's a fine idea. You and I would be its first patients . . ."

5

At the door to their house Guillermina said good-bye and left for her orphanage, and he went in. He noticed the strangest thing! He was hardly tired from the stairs. He felt very good that morning: his spirits comforted, the palpitations quieted, his appetite sharp. Upon entering he ordered more tea, and as Tom served it to him he said in Spanish:

"Tomorrow we leave. Pack the bags. Tell Estupiñá to please come, if he will, so that I can order a few things from shops. One can't go back to England without a few colorful souvenirs from Spain."

Then he continued talking to himself. "This is dizzying. If you don't bring tambourines with bulls or some other junk painted on them, they eat you alive. Let's see if I can find some watercolors. I need blankets too, and badges from fighting bulls, and maybe some original looking bric-a-brac. There's no worse fate than being a collector's friend." Estupiñá, who was cultivating Moreno at the time because the latter had entrusted him with managing his house in La Cava, was willing to bring him the contents of all the stores in Madrid for him to examine. He brought a succession of the most garish tambourines, fans, and little paintings all day long, and Don Manuel chose and paid as they went along. It was pleasant entertainment, and he chuckled, thinking of the happiness he would be bringing to his London friends. "This picador lancing the bull, with the horse stepping on its guts, is made to order for the Simpson girls, who are so mannish. This tambourine showing a *chula* playing the guitar, for Miss Newton. If she ever saw the originals, what a disappointment she'd have! This Andalusian couple— him on horseback and her twined in the grilled window talking to him—for the sentimental, novel-reading Mistress Mitchell, who got starry-eyed just hearing the word 'Spain,' the country of love, orange trees, and incredible adventures. Ah! and this Don Quixote slashing up the wine bags, for my friend Davidson, who calls Don Quixote 'Dawn Kwichotte' and prides himself on being a Hispanist. All right. We've got enough trinkets now. These jars are ghastly. Modern Spanish ceramics aren't worth anything. Let's see, Plácido: do you think you could find me a complete bullfighter's outfit? I want it for a friend who dreams about wearing one to a masquerade ball. He'll look hideous. But what do we care? Could you find me one?"

"Of course," said Plácido, for whom there were no obstacles when it came to shopping. "New or second-hand?"

"New, I think. But, well, whatever you find."

Estupiñá departed—on the wings of Mercury one might have said—and shortly afterward Moreno's manservant returned; his master had entrusted him to locate certain things too. Tom had become a real *aficionado* to bullfighting; he never missed a fight, and counted among his friends several eminences in the art of the horn. For this reason Moreno asked him to find a *moña*, * the kind *aficionados* save as venerable relics; and he'd asked for one that was bloodstained and had lots of hoofprints on it that recalled the tragic struggle. Very disconsolately, the Englishman entered with the news that there were none to be found, not even if he offered his eyeteeth in exchange.

"Well, don't worry," said his master. "Since there are no *moñas*, we'll take something else. Have you ever noticed that man around the Prado and Recoletos—that ugly chap who carries a basket with scads of windmills in it? They're attached to sticks, all stacked up to make a huge tree; there are scads of them— gold and silver and colored ones. You know the kind I mean? They spin in the breeze, and children buy them; they only cost a few pennies. Well, bring me a dozen. We'll take them instead and say that they're the *moñas* that are used on the bulls when they're sent into the ring. Ugh! Giving you the willies with those sharp horns they have. They'll fall for it, if I know my friends."

Tom laughed, but inwardly he rejected the hoax because of two scruples he had: his English moral rectitude and his ethical feelings as an *aficionado*. His master's fraud was a double violation; it was deceiving a nation and insulting the respectable art of *tauromaquia*, a truly tragic sport. I don't know the upshot of Moreno's proposal. Meanwhile, Rossini was filling the house with fans and tambourines that Moreno chose, paid for, and then amused himself with by wrapping up and putting stickers on to identify their recipients.

He had decided to limit his farewells, using as an excuse his poor health. After lunch he went down to his desk to liquidate and put in order his private accounts. He wasn't engaged in any business, and banking, which he had formerly enjoyed so much, bored him now. But that day his taste for business seemed to renew itself; he talked business for a long time with Ruiz-Ochoa, recommending that he not pass up any auction of gold bullion for the bank.

"This year I think I'll be buying some gold. You bankers better be more careful

---

* A knot of ribbons indicating by their color the breeder of the bull.

about coining so much silver, because it's going down and it's going to go down even further. With pounds costing what they do it's better to ship gold, and I for one am going to take as much as I can get." At this point Ramón Villuendas came in asking what they were taking for pounds, and the conversation fell back on the same subject. He was ordering more and more gold now.

"Give this amount to Guillermina," said Moreno when he came upon an extra sum he had not anticipated from the rents on his houses.

Other people came and started talking about various subjects. For as long as the conversation lasted Moreno pondered over whether or not he should say good-bye to the Santa Cruzes. If he didn't, his godfather might feel offended, but if he did, worse things might happen; he might regret his trip and postpone it. He had no choice but to go, though. When? At lunch time? He wavered, and on his way home, he pondered on when he should go. "Now that I've taken a stand," he cautioned himself, "it would be better not to see her in person again; as it is, I'm always seeing her in my mind's eye. What a silly boy I've turned into! Anyway, there's time to think about it from now to tomorrow; I won't go today, that's for sure."

At about five o'clock the misanthrope went to a shop on the Plaza Mayor to see some Granada blankets that he wanted to give to some English friends. He had been there for a quarter of an hour when the shopkeeper suggested sending his best ones with Plácido so that Señor Moreno might choose the ones he wanted. It was already almost dark, and it would be better to examine the fabrics in the daylight. They agreed and Moreno went home. Just as he was entering the main door he felt something tapping him on the shoulder. It was Jacinta with her umbrella. Our good man stood there as if he'd been shot. He tried to speak but could not. Jacinta took his arm, and once they were up the first few steps their dialogue began:

"So you're finally leaving?"

"Finally. It was high time—"

"What is it, are you very tired today? We can go more slowly if you'd like. Ah! Guillermina told me you were *very* holy today. That's how I like people."

"Why didn't you come to see me? I was a spectacle, I'm sure."

"I didn't know. Are you going again tomorrow?"

"Will you really come to see me? Oh, how you'll laugh!"

"Laugh! The things you say. I'll come follow your example."

"I bet you won't."

"I bet I will."

"Well, I'll be there competing with Estupiñá. You'll see, you'll see. Each day, more and more."

"More and more? But aren't you leaving tomorrow?"

"That's right. I'd forgotten. Well, I won't leave."

"No; none of that. You should leave, and you can continue your novitiate there."

"It's no good there."

"What do you mean, 'no good'?"

"Because some Protestant friends of mine will get ahold of me and whether I like it or not they'll make me start giving up religion again. It will be your fault; it'll be on your conscience. So. Should I stay or leave?"

"If my responsibility is that huge, I don't dare advise you. Do whatever seems best to you. Well. We've made it. Did the climb tire you very much?"

"A little . . . But as long as I'm with you, I'm happy. Shall we go back down?"

"Again?"

"Yes, to come up again. As if you had to go to the fourth floor."

"I wouldn't be able to forgive myself if walking with me meant that you'd get so tired."

They went in, and Jacinta went to the saint's room. Moreno went to his and collapsed onto the sofa, pushing his hat back. He thought he'd rest a bit and then go to Guillermina's room. "No, I won't. I don't want to see her anymore. Why torment myself? It's over. Let's put a gravestone over it." A little later he heard Jacinta leaving and he approached the door, hoping to see her. But he couldn't see anything. Since the vestibule light still hadn't been lit, all he could make out was a shape, a shadow, and he caught a few words of Jacinta's farewell to the ecclesiastical rat. The latter then came to her nephew's room and found him pacing the floor. "How do you feel, catechumen?" she asked affectionately.

"All right, almost well. I have hopes I'll be able to sleep tonight."

"Go to bed early."

"That's what I'm planning to do, and tomorrow . . . Listen—didn't Jacinta tell you that I was planning to go back to San Ginés tomorrow?"

"No, she didn't."

"Didn't she say that she'd go to see how devoted I was?"

"No. We didn't mention you."

"Didn't she say she'd come upstairs with me and that—?"

"No, not a word."

Moreno felt the awful pulsating in his chest flooded by a glacial wave. He had to sit down to keep from collapsing because his legs were shaking and his vision was blurred.

"If you want to go back tomorrow I'll call you. If you sleep well, that is."

"We'll go, to kill time," said Moreno in a morbid tone, "and to placate my despair with a little gaiety, just the way you keep a beast from biting by throwing him a scrap of meat."

"If you would ask the Lord—ask Him properly—to cure you of that 'spleen,' He'd cure you. Ask Him, son. I know what I'm talking about, I promise!"

"What do you know? What can you know about what there is on the other side of the black door?"

"Are you going to start that again? You may have lost some of your faith, but you'll never lose all of it. You say those things without believing them, foolishly. With all your jokes I still say that if someone were to scratch your surface a believer would show through."

"No, silly. I don't believe in anything, in nothing, you hear?" Moreno said emphatically, mortifying her on purpose.

"May God show us the way. Then why do you go to church with me?"

"To pass the time, to see you and Estupiñá, who are rare specimens of humanity, you know; you're eccentric, like all this stuff I'm taking back to London for people who are addicted to the typical local color of Spain."

Guillermina sighed. She didn't want to let it affect her.

"As for eccentrics, there's you," she said at last, bursting out laughing. "You're the one they should exhibit in side-shows—'ten cents a look, a nickel for kids and soldiers.' The man who put you on display would be sure to make money."

"With a big sign saying: 'The most unfortunate man in the world.'"

"And it's his own fault, his own fault; you've got to add that. To be unfortunate and not look to God: that's the last thing I thought I'd ever see. Go ahead—sink into your materialism, be more of a hedonist, and see if you find happiness that way. You're haughtiness personified; you're a fool. Look, nephew—I'm leaving, because if I don't I'll hit you with your own cane."

But he was so lost in thought that he didn't even hear her leave.

6

He ate, although his appetite was poor, with his sister and Guillermina. When they finished he informed the latter that he had left instructions to have whatever was left over in his personal accounts passed on to her; the news made the founder as happy as a couple of castanets and, unable to repress her joy, she went straight over to him and said, "I'm so thankful to my dearest atheist. Please keep giving me more proofs of your atheism and the poor will bless you. You an atheist? I wouldn't believe it even if you swore it to me!" Moreno smiled sadly. The saint was so overjoyed she kissed him. "Here—you Mason, Lutheran, and Anabaptist, in payment for your alms."

He was so impressionable now that when the saint's lips touched his forehead he felt anguished and almost said so. He pressed the saint to him in a fond embrace, saying, "One thing doesn't exclude the other, you know; even though I'm faithless, I want to keep my 'ecclesiastical rat' happy, just in case. Let's suppose that there is what I don't believe in . . . it could be. If so, my dear 'rat' would start gnawing at a corner of heaven and she'd make a little hole where I could get in too."

"And we'll all get through there," said Moreno's sister gleefully, for these jokes amused her greatly.

"I certainly will make the hole!" said Guillermina. "I'll gnaw away for a while in eternity, and if God catches me and raises the roof, I'll say to Him, 'Lord, it's to let my nephew in. He was very atheistic, or that's what he said anyway, but he gave me money for the poor.' The Lord will pause to think for a minute and then He'll say, 'Oh well, let him in. But don't tell anyone about it.'"

At ten o'clock the misanthrope was in his room preparing to retire. "Is there anything you need?" his sister asked.

"No. I'll try to sleep. Tomorrow at this time I'll be hearing them cry out 'Fresh milk!' Oh, this is a bore!"

"What do you care, Manolo? Just don't buy any if you don't like it. Those poor people live on that. Let them."

"I'm not against their living all they want," Moreno answered energetically. "But that doesn't mean their yelling doesn't bother me . . . a lot."

"For heaven's sake! There are worse things, and they too can be borne patiently."

Then Tom came and Moreno's sister left, just as Guillermina was coming in with the same song: "Do you need anything? Let's see if you can sleep now, because you've got a big day tomorrow. Remember—a telegraph from Paris so we'll know how you are."

She headed out, then turned around: "I'm not going to call you tomorrow morning. You need to rest. You have time, son; plenty of time for repentance. Health comes first."

"Tonight I know I'm going to sleep well," Don Manuel announced with that hopefulness of ill people whose joy is steeped in melancholy. "I'm not sleepy yet, but something inside tells me that I'm going to sleep well tonight."

"And I'm going to pray that you do rest. You'll see—when you're over there I'll pray for you so much that you're sure to be cured, and you won't even know what the remedy was. What you'd least expect, silly, is that your 'ecclesiastical rat' has taken you under her wing and is saving your soul without your even noticing it. And when you feel something new in your soul, and suddenly discover one morning that all those atheistic blemishes have disappeared for good, you'll cry, 'It's a miracle! a miracle!' and there won't have been any miracle; you'll just have pull with God, as they say. But I don't want to make your head spin. It's very late. Go to bed right away, and sleep for seven hours at least."

She patted him on the back and he watched her leave disconsolately. He would have liked for her to stay a little longer because her words comforted him greatly.

"Listen, if you want to call me early tomorrow, do. I promise that I'll behave better than I did today."

"If you're awake I'll come in. If not, I won't," said Guillermina. "Sleeping would do you more good than praying. Do you need anything? Would you like some sugared water?"

"It's already here. Go to bed now; you need to sleep too. Poor thing, I don't know how you can bear all this. You're always doing so much for others!"

He was going to add "And what's it all for?" but he contained himself. He'd never appreciated his aunt as much as he did that night; he felt almost magnetically drawn to her. Finally the saint left, and shortly afterward Moreno told his servant to retire. "I'll go to bed in a little while," said the gentleman. "Even though I feel sure that I'll eventually get to sleep, I don't feel at all sleepy yet. I'll sit here for a while and go over my gift list to see if I have them all. Oh! Don't forget the blankets. Morris' sister will be mad at me if I don't bring her something original." The thought of the blankets reminded him of something he'd seen that afternoon. On his way to the shop on the Plaza Mayor in search of the item, he had crossed paths with a blind woman begging for alms. She was only a girl, accompanied by an old guitarist, and she was singing *jotas* so gracefully and so masterfully that Moreno couldn't help but stop to listen. She was horribly ugly, ragged, and smelled awful, and when she sang, her coagulated eyes seemed to be bulging out of their sockets like those of a dead fish. Her face was all pockmarked. She had only two pretty things: her teeth, which were extremely white, and her vigorous, silvery voice, which throbbed with feeling and had a sad undertone that filled one with poignant nostalgia. "This is original," thought Moreno as he listened, and he stood bewitched for a while by those charming cadences, that warbling of love which famous theatrical singers cannot imitate. The words were as poetic as the music.

Moreno put his hand in his pocket for a *peseta*. But it seemed like too much, so he took out some small coins instead and left.

Well, that night the blind girl with her ugliness and beautiful song came to his mind's eye so vividly that it was as if she were actually there singing. The popular music echoed charmingly in his brain, sounding even better than it had in reality. And the *jota* exuded a sadness that seemed infinite but at the same time consoling, a balm being spread gently by a heavenly hand. "I should have given her the *peseta*," he thought, and this reflection filled him with remorse. His nervous susceptibility was such that all of his impressions were terribly intense, and the pleasure or pain they produced affected his innermost self. He felt something like an urge to cry. The music vibrated in his soul as if it were harmonious chords and nothing more. Then he lifted his head and said to himself: "Am I awake or asleep? I really should have given her the *peseta.* Poor thing! If only I had tomorrow, I'd look for her so I could give it to her."

The Puerta del Sol clock struck the hour and upon finishing made Moreno notice the deep silence around him; an awareness of solitude followed his mental experience of that music. He fancied that there was no one nearby, that his house was deserted, that the neighborhood was deserted, that Madrid was deserted. He looked at the light for a while, and as he was drinking it in other thoughts assaulted him. They were his "main ideas," as it were, rather like the tenants of his mind, or pigeons flocking back after a short flight through the sky. "She's the one who's losing out," he stated with rather emphatic conviction. "Scorn is its own penitence; she'll never be consoled as she hopes. I shall console myself with my solitude, which is the best friend there is. And who's to say that when I come back next year I won't find her in a different frame of mind? Why not? After all, it's conceivable. She'll have grasped that it's against nature to love a husband like hers, and her God, that worthy gentleman reclining in the glass case with his fine Dutch linen sheet, that very same God, Estupiñá's friend, will advise her to love me. Yes! Next year I'll be back . . . By April I'll be back. My aunt will see for herself how I become a mystic, such a great mystic that the others won't be able to hold a candle to me. My adorable girl is well worth a Mass. And I'll spend a million, two million, six million, on a charitable institution. For what kind of people, did Guillermina say? Oh, yes! For crazy people. Yes, that's what's needed most. And they'll call me 'the poor man's Providence,' and I'll shock the world with my devotion. We'll have a child or two, or more, and I'll be the happiest man alive. I'll buy that Christ with so many bruises, a silver urn and . . . and . . ."

He got up, and after a few minutes' pacing sat down again at the table where the light was, because he'd begun to feel a heavy oppressiveness in his chest. The pulsations, which had stopped momentarily, recommenced overwhelmingly, accompanied by a sensation of fullness in his chest. "Oh, how awful I feel now! But this will pass and I'll fall asleep. Tonight I'm going to sleep very well. The oppressive sensation's passing . . . Well, yes, I'll be back in April, and by then I'm sure that—"

He was forced to stiffen up; he could feel something swelling up, like a wave surging up into his chest and blocking his breathing. He stretched out his arm as if he were about to add a word to accompany the gesture; but the word, an expression of his anguish, perhaps, or a call for help, couldn't get beyond his lips. The wave swelled; he could feel it rising up to his throat, then higher, higher. He could no longer see the light. He put both hands on the edge of the table and, leaning over, rested his forehead on his hands, letting out a stifled moan, and remained like that, motionless, mute. And in that withdrawn, sad posture, the poor man died.

Life ceased in him as a consequence of a ruptured heart, which produced an instantaneous commotion that vanished as quickly as it had come. He was torn away from the great tree of humanity, a completely dry leaf whose imperceptible fibers had held him there. The tree felt nothing in its myriad branches. Here and there, at the same moment, leaves and more useless leaves were falling; but the next morning would reveal countless fresh new buds.

When it had already dawned, Guillermina approached his door to listen. She couldn't hear anything. The room was dark. "He's sleeping like an angel . . . It would be foolish to wake him." And she tiptoed away.

III. Dissolution

I

TOWARD THE MIDDLE OF NOVEMBER, Fortunata looked somewhat unhealthy. Observing her, Ballester said to himself: "She really ought to love me instead of wasting away because of that blockhead! What women will do! They're like donkeys—they can be walking along on a cliff, yet they'd rather be beaten to death than take another path."

From the storeroom where he was working he saw her pass in the street. "There goes the ship—always so punctual for her little 'appointments.' Doña Lupe furious, poor old Rubín off his rocker, and the pigeon's flying to a neighbor's roof. She'd never dream that I know about her hiding place. It took some doing, but I finally found it. Not that I want to report her . . . it wouldn't be fitting for a gentleman like me. I do it for my own knowledge; that's how I am. I like to trace the steps of a person who interests me. After all the billing and cooing she's sure to come. Oh, what a memory you have, Segismundo. You've completely forgotten that you promised to have the hashish pills ready for her today, the ones they want to give poor Maxi to see if they can lift his spirits and cure him of that gloominess. Let's get to it, and see whether my poor, miserable friend will react to this precious stimulant" (taking out a flask of an Indian hemp extract from a cabinet) "that's supposed to bring expansive happiness and a pleasant outlook on life."

Several hours later, Fortunata was on her way to the pharmacy. The pharmacist detected consternation in her features. She was undoubtedly suffering deep, deep sorrow; horrible sorrow, he felt, probably the kind that can only be described with the rhetorical image of a sword thrust through one's breast. "Don't be afraid, my friend," said Ballester, "that I'll mortify you with vulgar advice; but you're suffering today, and not over any trifle. What's bothering you is a real tribulation. No,—don't try to deny it. I can read your face like a book, the most beautiful book in the world. I can read everything that's going on inside you, so it would be useless to try fooling me. But don't get me wrong: I don't want you to confess your sorrows to me until you're convinced that I'm the doctor who can cure them."

"Please, Ballester," said Fortunata very crossly. "I'm not in the mood for jokes."

"I can see that. You look as if someone were trying to crush your heart."

"Oh, yes, yes!" the young woman exclaimed impulsively; she was clearly on the verge of tears.

"And you've been crying. Your eyes show it."

"Yes . . . yes. But stop this. Don't pry into what's not your business. You're very nosy today."

"I've always been. You may keep secrets from other people, but not from me. I know where you've just come from. I know the street, the number of the house, and the floor. And I can even tell you what just happened. An argument, it's your fault, no, it's yours; you don't love me, yes I do; come on, let's . . . no, not anymore; well, what about him? well, what about her? anyway, you're deceiving me, no, *you* are, and we're through, so long. And then the tears."

Letting her head droop over her breast, Señora Rubín plunged into the black lake of her sadness. Ballester, not daring to utter a word now, watched her, respecting her pain, which was so real she could not possibly attempt to conceal it. Finally, Fortunata rose from the chair as if she'd just regained her senses and asked:

"The pills—are they ready?"

"Here they are," giving her the box. "And by the way, it wouldn't be a bad idea if you took one."

"Me? Pills can't help me. Take care. I'm going home now."

"Console yourself," Segismundo said to her at the door. "That's how life is— sorrow one day, happiness another. You have to be calm and take things as they come; we can't bind ourselves to just one person. When one candle goes out, another has to be lit. So let's be strong and learn to despise. Whoever doesn't know how to despise isn't worthy of the delights of love. And one thing more, my dear, sweet friend: I'm at your service, and remember that you can count on me for anything that comes up. I'll be a diligent friend, entirely discreet, dependable . . . Good-bye."

The young woman went home. Doña Lupe wasn't in these days; she was unfailingly at the pawnbroker's public sales, and Maximiliano spent long hours in his office or the bedroom without so much as venturing out into the hall, lost in a meditation that was more like grogginess, stretched out on the sofa usually, gazing absently at a spot on the ceiling, like a visionary penitent. He didn't disturb anyone, he didn't refuse meals or medicines, quietly submitting to whatever orders he was given, as if this stage of his mental process required the nullification of his will: being nothing in order to become everything. Thinking she was alone in the house, Fortunata walked from one room to another in search of some activity that would distract and console her. Impossible. The more she worked, the more energetically and vividly her mind replayed the morning's events. "I'm going to go mad," she thought, putting the clothes in to soak. "I'm crazier than poor Maxi, and this is going to be the end of me."

Without interrupting her mechanical actions, the poor woman's mind continued to recreate the scene down to the very words, gestures, and most insignificant inflections in the dialogue. In the midst of this recreation, her present reflections on the subject arranged themselves like notations. Her mind's labor was a painful, frenzied mixture of judgment and memory that got all scrambled up, making brilliant flashes of thought and sensation illuminate her thoughts and then disappear.

"It was so stupid to tell him. He's been very cold to me for some time now, as if he wanted to break up. Tired of me again, always tired! And back in June—yes, I remember it was June because they were setting up the awnings for the Corpus Christi procession—he told me he'd never leave me again, and he was ashamed of having left me twice and Lord knows how many more lies. Now he's just looking for an excuse to take off. God, how his face changed when I said those things to him: 'Don't be so dumb, and don't trust your wife's virtue so much. What did you think, that she's not like everybody else? Well, for your information, your wife's been unfaithful to you with that Señor Moreno who died suddenly one night. You were just lucky he blew up. Hearts explode when they love so much, and believe me, as God's my father, your little "angel face" loved him too, and they had their rendezvous; I don't know where, but they had them. As smart as you are, you've been fooled too.' Good God, the way he looked at me! Wounded pride and haughtiness came bulging out of his mouth."

Then she clearly felt vibrating in her ear the reply that had made her tremble and still upset her because the words repeated themselves endlessly, like a music box whose cylinder no sooner strikes the last note than it starts the tune again. "Just what did you think? That my wife is like you? Where did you hear that vile story? Who put those ideas into your head? My wife is sacred. My wife is immaculate. I don't deserve her, and for that very reason I respect and admire her all the more. My wife—and get this straight, now—is above any sort of slander. I have absolute, blind faith in her, and not even the slightest doubt could trouble me. She's so good that on top of being faithful she has the habit of confiding all her thoughts to me for me to examine them. I only wish I could confide mine to her! And now, when you bring me those absurd stories, I see how far beneath her I am. I couldn't be any lower . . . Even you are punishing me by claiming that my wife's like you or could be. You're punishing me because you're showing me the difference; I compare you with her, and if you don't come out ahead, blame yourself. And finally, if you so much as say a word about my wife in my presence, I'll take my hat . . . and you'll never see me again for as long as you live."

Her comment: "And to think I'd had hopes that she wasn't honorable, and now I have no choice but to confess that she is! Could Aurora have been wrong? She sounded so convinced . . . I don't know. Maybe she was wrong. Maybe the gentleman was taken with her. But that doesn't mean she sinned; no, not at all."

Once again she heard his formidable words echoing in her ear: "If you so much as say a word, etc." This time her reflection registered simultaneously with his invective. "Oh, you trickster, you! You didn't talk that way before. Back in June it was 'I love you' and 'I adore you,' and we had laughs enough over 'Angel Face,' although it's true that we always thought she was virtuous. So she's sacred, is she? Then why do you cheat on her? Sacred! Now you come up with that. 'I'll take my hat and you'll never see me again.' That's exactly what you've been wanting for some time now. You were just looking for an excuse, so you grabbed onto what I said. 'I compare you with her, and if you don't come out ahead, blame yourself.' That's like telling me I'm a tramp, that I can't be decent even if I want to. It made my blood boil to hear that, and I'm furious again. I feel such an awful lump in my throat; it makes me want to cry. Say that to me, me, when I'm condemning myself on account of him. For God's sake, why should it be my fault if his pretty wife's an angel! Even virtue's an excuse to hit me on the head. Ungrateful wretch!"

Then a reproduction of part of her answer: "Look, don't take it so seriously. It might be a lie. What do I know? You don't think I made it up, do you? Just so you'll see I don't want any farces with you, I'll tell you this: I got that story that bothers you so much from Aurora."

And his reply: "If I catch her, I'll rip out her tongue. That woman's a snake. An envious, scheming snake. Be careful around her."

Her reflection: "It's true, I was very careless. You shouldn't say bad things about anybody unless you know what you're talking about. Ever since I said that he hasn't looked at me the way he used to. I hurt his pride. It's like when you sit down on a top hat by mistake: no matter how much you iron it afterward, you can't get it to look the way it did before. He won't forgive me this time."

"Are you mad?"

"Do you think I shouldn't be?"

"Pretend I didn't say anything."

"I can't; you've offended me; you've lowered yourself in my eyes. Since you don't have any morals you don't understand this. You have no idea how much someone degrades himself when he talks too much."

"Don't say that."

"I can't help it, it just comes out. Ever since you slandered my poor wife I worship her and love her more, and I see something else: I see how far beneath her I am; you're the mirror that shows me my conscience, and I can tell you this much—I look awful."

Reflection: "When he uses that special tone of his I feel like hitting him. It's like telling me I'm indecent. And whenever he brings out all his principles it's because he wants to leave me. I can't live like this, God; this is worse than death."

Reproduction: "Are you leaving already?" "Do you think it's still too soon?" "Are you coming on Monday?" "I can't promise you." "There you go with your tricks again." "You really can be annoying." "I don't want to argue. Say what you want to say." "If we break up, don't blame me; it's your fault." "Mine?" "Yes, yours, for letting out that vulgar gossip." "All right, whatever you want . . . You always have to be right." "Good-bye." "So long."

And after awhile her mind jumped to a new thought that shone into her despair like a ray of light streaming through the clouds unexpectedly, illuminating and gilding them with its brightness. "What in the devil is this business about 'virtue'? No matter how much I think about it, I can't get to it and get it inside me."

Then she noticed that she hadn't soaked the clothes. Her task was undone; the mound of shirts and dressing gowns and other garments was still sitting where she'd put it, in front of her. Papitos, who came in from the dining room with the knives already clean, was the shock that brought her back to reality.

2

On Saint Eugene's Day Doña Casta proposed a picnic at the Pardo, but the Rubín women didn't want to even hear about anything resembling fun. Their mood wasn't exactly fit for a picnic. The Samaniego women went, though, along with Doña Desdemona, Quevedo, and other friends. That night Doña Casta insisted on giving them some of the acorns she'd gathered. They were having the *tertulia* at the Rubíns'. The only one missing was Aurora, whom Fortunata was awaiting anxiously, so whenever she heard steps on the stairs she rushed to the door before the bell rang. At last M. Fenelón's widow arrived, totally exhausted. That month there had been quite a few orders; there was one aristocratic wedding after another, and poor Aurora couldn't keep up with them all, not to mention the fact that she'd brought some of the work home so as to have it ready on time. She usually stayed up till midnight or one in the morning. Rubín's wife offered to help her, and with the elderly ladies' leave they went next door. Fortunata wanted to be alone with her friend so she could talk at length about various subjects.

They lit the lamp in the parlor and began to prepare to work on the large cutting table; Aurora got out her equipment and started to cut. Fortunata helped by laying out patterns and basting them to the material. Aurora was constantly pulling out or sticking a threaded needle into her breast, which was her pincushion; she also kept a battery of common pins there. Looking the patterns over with artistic concentration, reaching now for the needle, now for the scissors, now leaning over the table, now standing back to get the effect from a distance, slanting her head this way or that to get an oblique perspective, she began to chat, throwing out words as if they were leftovers from the spiritual energy she was applying to her mechanical work.

"The funeral was today. Candelaria says it was really impressive—the catafalque as high as the ceiling, and the orchestra magnificent; lots of candles. That's how those egoistic bachelors end up using all their money. The Santa Cruz women were there, and Ruiz-Ochoa, and the Trujillo women, and Lord knows who else. Since I haven't seen you for days I haven't been able to tell you how it hit me that morning. It was like this. I was crossing Pontejos Square at about eight thirty on my way to the workshop when I saw his English servant come charging out looking aghast. Later I found out that he was trying to locate my cousin Moreno-Rubio, who lives on Bordadores Street. I was wondering what had happened when Samaniego came out of the store and asked: 'What is it?' 'What do you mean, "What is it?"' Then the Englishman, looking so terrified I couldn't begin to describe it, said to us: '*Señor muerto; señor como muerto.*'[*] Pepe ran over and I followed him. There were people clustered at the door—some were coming out and others were going in, and all of them looked very sorry. I went up with Pepe; the door was open. You could hear Patrocinio Moreno's cries from the stairs. Oh, what a bad moment that was! I was scared to death. I went up to the room little by little. There was the saint, wearing her cloak, prayer book in her hand. She looked like a religious statue. And Moreno—I'd rather forget it. Seated in a chair next to the table. They say they found him with his head resting on his hands, all stiff and rigid and bloodless. I can't tell you what a horrible sight it was. They had propped him up in the chair. His shirt front was all bloodstained and his chin had blood caked all over it. His eyes were open—" At this point Aurora suspended her work and devoted herself to her tale.

---

[*] Because it seems illogical to have this character use broken English, I transcribe the original text in this case. A literal translation: "Master dead; master like dead."

"I didn't want to go in. I turned back from the door and somehow or other got back to the workshop, stumbling my way back; I thought I would faint. You have to admit it: that man had to end badly, but that doesn't stop you from feeling sorry for him." She turned back to her work. "I felt ill that day, and sometimes I felt like crying. He treated me badly, very badly. Oh, now I see that you pay for everything in this life."

"Poor man!" exclaimed Fortunata. "I was sorry too, when I heard about it. But you know what? Today *he* and I had a big fight because I told him that business about—"

"About—?" asked Aurora, stopping work again and looking at her friend mischievously.

"Yes. He got so mad that we broke up. Oh, I'm so sorry. If it's slander, just imagine how awful it was, telling that story!"

"It's not slander," said Fenelón's widow, paying closer attention now. "It might be an error. Who in blazes knows what's going on inside 'Angel Face'? There's no doubting that Moreno was mad about her. What we don't know, *par exemple*, is whether she loved him too."

"You told me she did, and that they had rendezvous."

"Yes, but I only told you that I supposed they did," replied the astute woman rather warily, as if she wanted to change the subject. "You rushed things by telling him that story. Of course he left in a huff. You have to be tactful, my friend, and not hurt men's pride. You should have known he wouldn't take it well."

"And what do you think? Tell me as if you were confessing to a priest. What do you think? Is she really some kind of angel or what?"

Aurora put down her scissors and stuck the threaded needle in her breast. After planning her response, she phrased it as follows:

"Well, to tell you the truth, without reaching any final conclusions, mind you, I'll say this: I think she's virtuous. If my cousin had lived, I don't know what it would have come to. He was courting her in the most childish way. Who would ever have guessed it? Such an experienced man! She . . . I don't know . . . but I think she mocked him. And he deserved it; he was a rascal. Maybe she was fond of him. As far as rendezvous go, though, I don't think there were any, my friend. And if I said anything, it was just a maybe; I take it back."

She picked up her work, leaving her friend swimming in confusion.

"In the last instance," she said later, "what do you care whether she's faithful or not? What matters is whether he loves you more than her."

"Oh, no!" exclaimed Fortunata with all her heart. "If that woman wasn't faithful, I'd think there wasn't any decency in this world and that everybody could do as he pleased. It's as if everything holding you together came apart; do you know what I mean? Black would be white. Believe me, that doubt's nailed in my head now; I'm always thinking the same thing, and it makes me just as happy to know she's bad as it does to know that she's not bad. Oh, you have no idea how much I think in a day. What I have to live through doesn't have a name."

"Well, just so you'll be calm once and for all," the other woman said, looking away from her, "consider her honest, and when you talk with him, make him see that you believe it, and don't try to get him to respect you, be satisfied with his love."

"Stop it, Aurora," Fortunata jumped up nervously. "It's all over. He stands me up now! I've only seen that cad twice in two weeks. He always comes late, and as if he didn't want to come. Oh, I know his tricks—I know them by heart. He wants to dump me again, that's all. I can just feel it. Today I told him so and he didn't answer anything."

"So 'Angel Face' has to be congratulated."

"Oh, no. I think the plot's thicker than that. He's cheating on us with somebody else that neither his wife nor I know of. To put it in plain language, he's giving us both the gate, and it's killing me—I'm furious and jealous and I can't do anything. I won't stop trying till I catch him, and believe me, if I do, and if I catch the woman too, I'll fly off the handle. I'll get revenge for 'Angel Face' and for me both. I wouldn't want to die without having that pleasure."

"Tell me something. Have you noticed anyone special?" her friend asked, studying her closely.

"I don't know. Tonight I wondered if it might be Sofía la Ferrolana, or la Peri, or Antonia—the one that was with Villalonga."

"It's only natural; you think of the ones you know. What would you give me if I found out for you?"

Saying this, Aurora dropped her work and stood in front of her friend with an agreeable expression.

"What would I give you? Whatever you want. Everything I have. I'll thank you for it forever."

"All right. Leave it to me, then. If I get wind of something I'm sure to figure it out. Let me tell you why. In my shop there's a girl, a very charming one, to be sure, who just might be—"

"In your shop!"

"Yes, but don't jump to conclusions. Maybe it's not her. What I mean to say is that she'll put me onto something and then I'll be able to get closer. Just trust me, and don't do anything on your own account. Promise me you won't get into this. If you do, don't count on me."

"Well, all right. I promise. But you have to tell me everything you discover. I tell you, if I catch her . . . I don't care if they send me to a reformatory; not a bit. I can almost feel her in my clutches."

Doña Casta came in, opening the door with her key. It was late and Fortunata had to leave. Aurora stayed on to work a few minutes and said to herself, "These dumb girls are awful when they get angry. But she'll calm down. After all . . . ! *That* would be the limit . . . "

3

One afternoon Doña Lupe saw her niece arrive looking so desolate that she couldn't help but jump on her and give vent to all her irritability; she couldn't bear Fortunata's not confiding her sorrows any longer; she wanted to know about them, no matter what their cause. "Do you think this a proper hour to be coming home? And next time please leave your agony in the street and don't come in with that long face. We've got enough sad spectacles around here as it is."

Fortunata was so upset she couldn't contain herself and broke out in that childish anger that leads to wrangles in tenement houses. "Señora, leave me alone. I don't bother you and I could care less whether you've got a long face or any other kind of face. A fine state we're in! I can't even be sad, because troubled faces bother the lady. Would you like me to dance for you?"

Doña Lupe wasn't used to being answered like this and was disconcerted. After a silence she retorted: "Whether I make it my business or not isn't for you to decide. After all, what is this, women's emancipation? Humph! Do you think that self-pleasing life you lead is going to be tolerated? Humph! Your airs make me laugh! I'll fix you . . . I'll fix you."

Her niece was so furious and her nerves were so strained that when she was putting a chair aside she knocked it over, and when she put her muff on the dresser it knocked over a glass of water.

"That's it, break my chair. Look at the water you've spilled."

"Good."

"Oh? I'll fix you one of these days."

"You, Señora, can fix what you like, but nobody fixes me."

"I don't want to lose my temper or raise my voice," said Doña Lupe, getting up from her chair, "or that poor miserable soul will hear."

She went out for a minute, planning to close doors so their scene wouldn't be heard, and returned shortly, saying:

"He's fallen asleep. If you want to make a racket and keep the poor boy from sleeping, go ahead. Your behavior . . . Silence!"

"You're the one who's shouting. I didn't say a word when I came in. But you insist on trying to infuriate me."

"Go on, make a racket. You won't even let the poor boy sleep."

"As far as I'm concerned, he can sleep all he wants."

"And what infuriates me most is your stubbornness," said Doña Lupe, lowering her voice, "and that determination to rule yourself; yes, that stupid independence. You made your bed, then you had to lie in it. That's why it feels so awful. Everything that happens to you, you more than deserve."

Rubín's wife's soul was in such deep turmoil that the anger she was experiencing seemed to be precariously pinned in place; the slightest accident, even a mere trifle, caused it to slip and give way to sorrow, making her convulsive energy turn into the most despondent passivity. Something was breaking down inside her and, losing her composure, she burst into tears like a child whose mischief has just been discovered. Doña Lupe prided herself on that change of tone, which she considered to be the result of her powers of persuasion. Fortunata sank into a chair and sat there for over fifteen minutes without uttering a word, pressing her handkerchief to her face.

"Yes, Aunt, it's true that I should . . . tell you. I didn't confide in you because it didn't seem fitting. How awful! Bring home, to this house, stories of . . . I'm wretched, I shouldn't stay here anymore. Even to cry here about what I'm crying about is vile. But I can't help it. My soul's falling apart. I have to tell someone that I'm dying of grief, that I can't go on living. If I don't say it, I'll burst. Think whatever you want, but believe me, I'm terribly unfortunate. I know I don't deserve it, either. I'm bad, as bad as they come, but I'm very unfortunate too."

"You see," said Doña Lupe, gesturing with her right hand, the fingers very stiff, like a bishop's, "that's what you get for not doing as I say. If you'd followed the advice I gave you last summer, you wouldn't be in this spot."

Fortunata felt so suffocated that her aunt had to bring her a glass of water.

"Calm down," she said. "I'm not going to scold you, although you certainly deserve it. No, you don't have to tell me what's happened to you; it's God's just punishment. Do you think I'm dumb? All I have to do is look at you. It had to happen. Bad roads always lead to bad ends. What's happened is exactly what I predicted. Sin brings penance. That man's dumped you again, am I right?"

"Yes . . . What a wretch he is!"

"Come on, now, you were in it together, and you're both the same breed. Criminal relations always end like that. One punishes the other, and the one who does the punishing will get his due later on, somewhere else. Some position he left you in . . . What a pair, ha! And you in the lurch now!"

"What a wretch, though!" Fortunata repeated, looking at her aunt with tear-filled eyes. "And to think he had the nerve to insinuate with his jokes that I was involved with Ballester! Excuses, his 'principles'—that's all. I'm sure he doesn't really believe it."

"Bear it—you deserved it. And don't come to me for sympathy. If you'd come in time, I won't say I wouldn't have listened. But now it's too late: you open your eyes and discover that you're horribly alone—without a family or a husband or me."

In a panic, like what a drowning person feels, Fortunata grabbed Doña Lupe's skirt and burst out in a flood of tears again.

"No, no, no. I don't want to be left alone, poor me. Say something, even if it's only that I should be patient, or that I should behave better now. Yes, I'll behave, now I will, I *really* will."

"Now! Don't be such an early bird, child. The only time you think of God is when you need him. What would I get for consoling you and correcting you, when you'll only go back to your tricks when I least expect it?"

"Not this time . . . not this time."

"Give that story to someone who'll buy it. The way things are now it seems to me I shouldn't step in or have any part of it. It would even be unbecoming of me. It would seem as though I'd somehow been an accomplice to your crimes. No, child, you've come too late. I've surrounded you with tolerance and you chose to ignore it, and now that you're drowning you come to me. Oh, no, I can't."

And without another word she went to the kitchen, thinking that the woman couldn't be treated severely enough and that it would be a good idea to terrorize her to see if she'd bend once and for all.

Soon it was dark. The days were getting shorter, weighing on the spirits of those who were already sad for other reasons. At six thirty the house was dark, and Doña Lupe put off lighting the lamps for as long as she could. In her husband's room, which was almost dark, Fortunata went as far as the sofa where he was stretched out and asked him if he felt like eating; he gave no reply. She was listening to the poor man sighing when he took her hands and pressed them affectionately. There was something in Fortunata's soul which responded to this display of tenderness. Her affection for him was like that which a sick child inspires: an effusion of protective pity that asks for nothing in return.

Doña Lupe brought the light and, looking at the couple, their eyes shimmering in the light of the gas flame, she said (undoubtedly to cheer up Maxi with a joke): "Are you two billing and cooing again? It'd do you more good to eat, Maxi. Do you want her to eat in here with you?"

"Yes, yes—I'll eat here," his wife hastened to say. "And he'll eat too, won't you, dear? You'll eat with your wife, won't you? She'll cut up your meat for you and feed you."

"Well, then, I'll send your meal in," said Doña Lupe, putting the shade on the lamp and turning down the flame. "I've made some chicken livers and rice, which is what you should eat."

In the time they were alone, before Papitos came in with the table settings and the soup, Maxi sprang a few sentences on his wife that were related exclusively to the infernal subject of his madness. Fortunata supported everything he said, feigning a keen interest in the urgency of establishing the principle of solidarity of divine substance as a social reality. She said yes to everything, and while they were eating she noticed that the sick man was getting extremely excited, reaching the point of being happy, talkative, and enthusiastic about his apostleship projects. When she left the room for a minute, Fortunata asked his aunt, "Did you finally give him the pills?"

"Yes, I did. He took one this morning on an empty stomach, and at four I gave him another. Isn't that what Ballester prescribed?"

"Yes. So that's why he's so lively. Some medicine! But he's talking the same nonsense, except that now he doesn't see things so gloomily; he makes light of them."

She went back to him and fed him the chicken livers with a fork; he ate them hungrily, without interrupting his stream of talk and occasional laughter. His tranquil laughter didn't sound like a madman's.

Fortunata felt a slight consolation in her soul and thought: "If God would only make him well! But how is God going to do anything I ask Him? I'm the worst stuff that He ever threw onto this earth. My days in this house have to end. Where will I go? What will become of me? Wherever it is, I'll want to know about this poor boy, the only one who's really loved me, who's forgiven me twice and would forgive me a third time . . . and a fourth. I think he'd even forgive me the fifth time if he didn't have a head like that. And it's my fault. Oh Lord, what remorse! I'll carry this burden wherever I go, and I'll never be able to breathe freely."

After eating he was livelier than he had been in a long time, but his ideas were outlandish. Doña Silvia and Rufinita came to visit, so Doña Lupe went into the living room with them and the married couple was left alone. Maxi got up and stretched all over, raising his arms. His bones cracked, he did various contortions that looked like gymnastics, and then he sat down again, embracing his wife and staying there in front of her (she was on a stool in front of the sofa) in a pose that theatrical lovers strike when they're about to say something very nice in rhymed verse.

4

"My darling," he said in the sweetest of tones, "a thousand thanks for the consolation your words have given me."

Fortunata didn't know which words had consoled him, but it didn't matter. She made an affirmative sign and he continued:

"Because when you think the way I do, that's all I need. My aspirations are satisfied. Long live the grand principle of liberation through disinterestedness, through annulment!"

"Long may it live!"

"That's what crowds will shout when this doctrine is spread, but that doesn't concern us; it's for those who will follow. You and I, let us respect the law of death as we reflect that we've arrived at the perfect stage of purity. Let us kill the beast when its prisoner is completely untied from it and, like the well-ripened chestnut, our spiritual substance has come loose from the burr."

"All right, son, we'll kill it."

"I like to see you like this. Is there anything more beautiful than death? To die, end our grieving, fall free from all this misery, from so much pain and earthly filth! Is there anything that can compare with this supreme good? Can the soul conceive of anything more sublime?"

"And afterward?" asked Fortunata, who, although she knew very well who was speaking, listened to that way of viewing death with great pleasure.

"Oh, afterward one will feel absolutely pure, part of the divine substance, and one will be all mixed up with the great All. It's colossal happiness!"

"Not suffer!" murmured the sinner, resting her head on his chest. "Not be afraid that they'll play some dirty trick on you. Not to ever have to agonize; just pleasure, pleasure . . . !"

Her thoughts were transported by that sublime notion to invisible realms.

"To feel good radiating from yourself and be able to contemplate yourself in that ethereal, substantial ambience, infinitely perfect and sane, beautiful, transparent, and pleasurable!"

This was getting a bit metaphysical and Fortunata didn't understand very well. What was accessible to her was the first idea: dying, shaking off the torture of this world and then feeling exactly like the person you were when you were alive, enjoying everything that was made to be enjoyed and loving and being loved with an unending ecstasy.

"My dear," Maxi said to her, moving his head, his facial muscles twitching, "we'll both die when we've completed our mission. And just so you're sure you know what yours is, I'm going to tell you what I've learned through a heavenly revelation."

Fortunata braced herself for the sheer nonsense that her husband was about to announce and put on a grave, attentive face.

"Well, I know something you don't, although you may have had a hunch and you're sure to know soon. Maybe you've already begun to notice some symptoms, but your soul can't have more than a presentiment of this great event."

He looked at her in a way that scared her. Lord, what could it be, *what?* Maxi was silent for a while, driving eyes like arrows into her, and at last he enunciated words that made her tremble: "You're pregnant."

The poor woman was paralyzed by this. She tried to take it as a joke, she tried to deny it, but she didn't have the strength to do either. Immense terror filled her soul when she saw that Maxi was saying this with total assurance. But the last thing Fortunata was to hear was the following, which was said with the exaltation of an enlightened man and more atrocious nervous tics: "It was a revelation. The spirit that instructs me brought this idea to me last night. A terribly lovely mystery, isn't it? You are pregnant. And you presume as much, or rather, you know it; I'm telling you to your face; you've been hiding it because you don't realize that it won't cast any dishonor on you. The child you're carrying in your womb is the son of Pure Thought who wanted to become incarnated to save the world. You were chosen for this prodigy because you've suffered so much, because you've loved a lot, and because you've sinned a lot. To suffer, to love, and to sin: these are the three infinitives of existence. The true messiah will be born from you. All we are is precursors, do you understand? Only precursors, and when you give birth, you and I will have fulfilled our mission and we'll free ourselves by killing our beasts."

Fortunata leaped up and ran over to the other side of the room. She was in such a panic she almost ran out into the corridor to call for help. Maxi's face was awry and transfigured, and his eyes looked like burning coals. He didn't even notice that his wife had left his side; he kept on talking as if she were still there. The poor creature was scared to death and had crouched in a corner, her hands clasped, and, looking at her miserable, demented husband, she said to herself: "How could he tell? God, what a man! I wonder if all this 'craziness' is just an act? Do you suppose he's putting it on just so he can kill me and not be caught by the law? But how did he find out? I haven't told a soul! And it doesn't show yet. Oh, but he's tricky. That 'revelation' business is just to fool people. He probably guessed it, or was afraid of it happening, or else he figured it out from something. I wonder if I've talked about it in my sleep? But no—he probably guessed it with his own madness. Don't they say that children and madmen know the truth better than anybody? Oh, I'm so scared! Good God, free me from this suffering. This man wants to kill me and he's going through all these acts to take his revenge on me, to murder me and get away with it . . . ."

The enlightened man walked over to his wife and took her arm. She was so weak from fear that she had even less strength than her husband. "My little squirrel," he said, pressing her arm with nervous energy and looking at her in such a way that the unfortunate woman felt he was both her lover and assassin. "We'll free ourselves in a bloodbath as soon as your mission is completed. When will it be? In February or March?"

"It's probably going to be in March," thought Fortunata, "but you're not going to catch me around, I'll see to that. Kill yourself if you want. I have to live to bring up the baby . . . and I'm going to be so happy with him! He's going to be my one consolation in life. That's why I'm having him; that's why God gave him to me. See how I got my way with my idea? My son's a new life for me. Then there won't be anyone to sniff at me. Oh, if I didn't feel him here inside me, you and I would be the same, one as crazy at the other, and then we really should kill ourselves."

They could hear the murmur of Doña Silvia's and Rufinita's farewells in the hall. A few minutes later the Jáuregui woman came in and, seeing her, Maxi left his wife standing in the middle of the room and went back to the sofa.

"How are you two, sleepy? It's eleven o'clock," said Doña Lupe.

"Your arrival has disturbed our happiness," replied Maxi from his seat, moving his legs in midair. "My chosen one and I would like to be alone, all alone. The ineffable mysteries that she and I—"

"What are doing with your legs?" (not sure of whether she should laugh or be stern). "You look like a clown."

"Ineffable mysteries, I say, have been revealed to us and have transported us to a delicious ecstasy that ordinary people can't participate in."

"Calling me an ordinary person!"

"Being ordinary is being very attached to worldly goods, which is to say, spoiling the beast."

"What? Are you going to do somersaults too?" Doña Lupe asked in a frightened voice when she saw him brace his hands on the sofa and lean his head until it touched the gutta-percha.

"My movements are not the concern of a woman with almost no faith. It's cold tonight and I need to warm my extremities. An oven has been lit in my skull."

"You see . . . you see?" said Fortunata, not taking care to lower her voice. "It's the effect of those cursed pills. I think he shouldn't be given any more of them. Just look at what a state he gets into—his brain gets more disturbed and he guesses secrets."

"What do you mean, 'guesses secrets'? Son, what are you doing?"

Rubín sat down and got up repeatedly, bouncing in the seat like a rider who's mounting English style.

"Sometime in March it'll be, the big event, to be admired by all the world," he grunted as he rolled over. "It will be announced by a star that will appear in the West, and the heavens and earth will resound with hymns of joy."

"What are you talking about? Come on, child, please—be calm."

"What I'd like to know now is where my hat is," he said, looking under the table and the sofa.

"And what do you want your hat for?"

"I want to go out, I have to get out of the house. But I don't mind if my head's uncovered. It's awfully hot."

"Yes, let's go to the Retiro. Fortunata, get the candle, and you go first."

And taking the wretched young man by the arms, they took him to the bed-

room. Maxi went straight to bed, where from a lying position he raised his arms
and legs. Then he let his extremities fall heavily and lifted them again.

"A fine night he's going to give us!" exclaimed Doña Lupe, crossing her hands.

Fortunata, spiritless and brooding, fell onto the sofa.

"What do you two bet that you don't know where I am?" said the poor demented
soul. "I've fallen from the sky onto a rooftop. What's my wife doing over there
instead of coming to help me?"

"Yes, sir; a fine night!" repeated Doña Lupe, sighing at every word.

They tried to get him ready for bed, but it was impossible. He slithered out of
their grasp like a child whose agility at times seemed monkeylike. His laughter
horrified the two ladies, and they didn't understand a word of the many he was
spilling out all at once and pronouncing as if he were just learning to talk. Finally,
his nervous energy began to run out and he ended up lying quietly on the sofa,
with one leg on the table, the other on a chair, his head under a cushion, and his
arms stretched out, making him look like a cross. One hand was touching the
floor and he had the other underneath him, that arm twisted into a very unlikely
position. Neither of the women wanted to alter this difficult posture because they
were afraid that touching him might upset him again. Doña Lupe drowsed in a
chair next to the double bed, but Fortunata didn't sleep a wink all night. It was
already dawning when they were finally able to put him to bed. He hardly knew
what was happening, and he moaned whenever he moved, as if his puny, miserable body had been beaten black and blue.

5

I think it was on the day of the Holy Conception that Rubín came out of his
room with a knife in his hand, chasing Papitos and threatening to kill her. He
gave his aunt and Fortunata a great fright and it took some doing to wrench the
weapon away from him; it was a table knife, which wouldn't have made it easy to
take anyone's life. But the scene was terrible and Papitos' shrieks were heard by all
the neighbors. She bolted out of the Señorito's room aghast, and he came running
out behind her, cold and resolute as if he were about to do the most natural thing
in the world. Monkey-face sought refuge in her mistress' skirts, screaming, "He's
going to kill me, he wants to kill me!" and Fortunata rushed in to restrain him,
something she wouldn't have been able to manage, despite her muscular superiority, without Doña Lupe's help. His resistance was purely spasmodic, and as he
tried to defend himself against the four arms that wanted to control him and pull
away the knife, he said in a hoarse voice: "I'll slit her throat and I'll . . . !"
Afterward they learned that it was Papitos' fault; she had irritated him by stupidly

contradicting him. Doña Lupe had suspected as much, and while Fortunata was taking him back to his room, trying to calm him down, the lady took Papitos in hand, and after three or four persuasive pinches she made her confess that she was to blame for what had happened.

"Look, Señora," she replied, swallowing her tears, "*he* started it, 'cause I didn't say anything. I was clearing the table and he jumped on me saying all sorts of stuff. I didn't understand and I started to laugh. But then he started with that crazy stuff. You know what he said, Señora? That Señorita Fortunata's going to have a baby and things like that. I couldn't help but laugh out loud, and that's when he grabbed the knife and came running after me. If I hadn't of jumped he'd of gashed me for sure."

"All right. Go to the kitchen, and learn your lesson for next time. No matter what he says, no matter how crazy it sounds, you say yes, and only yes."

This event was perhaps a symptom of a new aspect of his madness, and the two ladies were about to jump out of their skins they were so scared. Not a week had elapsed when it happened again. Maxi got hold of a knife and went after his aunt, saying he wanted to "free her." Thanks to Señor Torquemada's presence it wasn't hard to disarm him, but nobody could relieve Doña Lupe of her fear; she made herself a cup of medicinal tea to calm her nerves. Incidentally, the lady considered herself the most unfortunate lady on earth because of the many afflictions she had weighing on her soul. It wasn't only the pitiful state of her most beloved nephew; other things were atrociously mortifying too and crushed her mighty spirit. She exchanged a few words with Fortunata that revealed that harmony would be impossible.

"So!" Doña Lupe remarked to her one night. "You're really admirably discreet! But why so reserved when the occasion calls for confidence? How did Maximiliano, who's demented, know before I did, being in my right mind? Why all this hide-and-seek with me?"

After a long pause and with great exertion, Fortunata finally gave her this answer:

"I didn't tell him. He guessed it. I couldn't tell it to anybody in this house, least of all him."

"Least of all him!" echoed Doña Lupe, narrowing her eyes on the delinquent as if to shoot at her.

"Yes, because he never should have found out," she continued, making a final effort. "I was planning to tell you but I was too ashamed. Now that you know, what I have to do is ask you to be sympathetic, pack up my clothes, and leave this house. And this time it will be for good."

Sr. Jáuregui's widow took her time to formulate an answer to these deathly serious words. A thousand thoughts rushed through her mind and bewildered her for some time; she didn't know where to start. A definitive break would literally tear out a strip of her heart, because it would mean that she wouldn't be able to retain the sums Fortunata had entrusted her with. The elasticity of her conscience was never so great as to allow her to appropriate something that was not hers, either directly or indirectly. Other people's property she considered sacred, so even though she might increase her own as much as possible at someone else's expense, she never reached the point of embezzling funds placed in her trust. She would return the sum that had been remitted to her plus the dividends that her good management had secured. This restitution would be a painful act indeed, something like separating from a son who's going off to war to be killed, because once the "manna" was returned to its owner, it would soon be lost in that life of disorder and vice.

But if this sorrow stimulated her to compromise once again, her decorum—and even more so her self-pride—rose in anger against the infamous woman who was bringing home a child that was not her husband's. It couldn't be done without bringing dishonor on them, and Doña Lupe was not about to tolerate that, even if she had to fork up not only someone else's money but even her own . . . Well, maybe not her own, but, anyway, that's the way she put it to emphasize how terribly angry she was.

What would people say! Her friends, before whom Doña Lupe officiated as the keeper of morality and good principles! It's true that in the eyes of the world the situation created by Señora Rubín's maternity would be a legal one as long as Maxi, sick and perhaps locked up in an insane asylum by then, did not proclaim the deception; but in that case the affront would be all the greater because it would be a lie too. And everyone would take Doña Lupe for an imposter, and they'd make mincemeat of her. She could almost hear them: "Look at her, so proud and righteous, covering up what that hussy sneaked into the house. She's probably getting something out of it. The kid's father is rich and he probably paid her a good sum to keep it quiet." The mere thought that they might say this brought to the widow's august forehead drops of sweat as large as chick-peas.

"She thought nothing of telling me," she reflected, "that poor Maxi's as innocent of this as I am. And she'll let everyone know it with that big mouth of hers. But at least the offense isn't so bad this way; since she tells the whole truth, people won't start making up stories or wondering if the child is or isn't . . ."

Doña Lupe's conclusion from all this was that the tramp had brought a curse upon their house, that she was to blame for Maxi's madness. Doña Lupe had predicted it when she said that Fortunata was too much of a woman for him. Naturally the poor boy had to die or lose his head. The best she could wish for now was for the sinner to get lost; for an unbridgeable abyss to open between Fortunata and the family; for the opportunity to say to their friends, "That woman is dead as far as I'm concerned." Jáuregui's shadow seemed to be there aiding the illustrious widow to take a stand; she felt that her husband was on the verge of stepping out of the frame of his portrait to admonish her with the following words: "If you don't throw that woman out of the house, *I'll* leave; I'll disappear from this canvas and you'll never set eyes on me again. It's either her or me." And when "that woman" repeated that she was leaving, Doña Lupe couldn't help but retort bitterly: "What's been keeping you? Frankly, it astonishes me that you have the gall to still be here. Nobody could match your nerve." Leading her into the parlor, she spoke to her about returning the money. Fortunata very coldly and calmly said that she didn't want the money; only the interest. "How would I invest it? Keep it; I'll keep the receipt and come four times a year for the interest."

Doña Lupe gaped enough for a fly to enter. Her first impulse was to refuse to manage funds for someone like *her*; but this show of confidence slayed her. She insisted on returning the money, the other woman insisted further on leaving it in hands that knew so well how to make it grow, and the matter rested there. The "turkey woman" feared that this would necessitate some relationship between them, a sort of telegraph cable that would connect the most immaculate honor to immorality. Keeping the money would be tantamount to keeping up a sort of family relationship. No! That would be trafficking with the affront itself. But at the same time, returning those blessed coins to their owner would be like throwing them away. Her lovers would spend them before you could blink . . . and it would be a pity to destroy such nice capital.

A lot was said on this, both of them voicing their delicate reasons for this or that; but finally the money remained in Doña Lupe's hands. It amounted to thirty thousand *reales*—twenty thousand from Feijóo and over ten thousand in profits that Torquemada had made on loans to military men. As a matter of fact, precisely when these events were taking place (in the last days of the year), nearly the whole sum was on hand and the Señora had it in the bureau waiting for a "big deal" that Don Francisco was hoping to make with a commandant. Fortunata's bank shares were being held in the same way because Don Evaristo had thus instructed her. Maxi's aunt kept the title to the shares in a nook of her gilt desk and she took it out only twice a year to collect the dividends at the bank. There was no dispute over this type of funds because Fortunata certainly planned to take them and Doña Lupe didn't like keeping money that she couldn't use in her ingenious financial operations. Having custody of the title annoyed her and caused her such fruitless worry that she wasn't at all sorry to see it leave the house. The thirty thousand *reales* she left where they were: neatly stashed away in a corner of the bureau. For Doña Lupe they were like an adopted son she loved like one of her own.

6

Maxi didn't notice his wife's escape (for that's what it was) the first few days. When he was cognizant of it, he became so restless that he subjected Doña Lupe to an even greater strain. She seriously considered putting her hapless nephew in an insane asylum. It grieved her to think of a separation and putting him in the hands of mercenary employees, but there was no choice. To discuss the matter and arrive at a suitable solution, she called on Juan Pablo, who at the time had transferred from the Justice to the Health Department and could perhaps get his brother into the "privileged persons" section of the Leganés asylum and arrange for reduced fees or no payment at all.

Meanwhile Fortunata, upon leaving her husband's home and before proceeding to her new one, headed for Don Evaristo's. He was the first person she had to consult in this critical situation. Informing him of the events was going to be the real punishment for her perversion; the mere thought of confessing them horrified her. She hated to think of how Feijóo would take it when he learned that his *chulita* had trampled on the practical doctrine that he had expounded to her so ardently and fondly when they agreed to separate! How much better it would have been if she'd never left that peerless man! She would have borne with him in his most advanced old age, and she would have been as happy taking care of him as she would an innocent child! When she reached Carros Square and saw Don Pedro Street, she felt that she didn't have the courage to tell her friend about her recent shenanigans. She trembled as she climbed the narrow staircase, carpeted and decked with flower pots in honor of the emperor's birthday, which had been celebrated with a big splash the night before at the embassy. This is what Doña Paca told Fortunata when the latter asked to see the master of the house. "He was very restless because there was a party and a reception downstairs and the carriages didn't stop making a racket until dawn. This house is usually very quiet, but when there's noise, it sounds as if the world's coming to an end. What do we care how old the confounded emperor is! A fine headache he gave us last night! Come in. You'll find him a little disturbed because of the bad night he's had."

Don Evaristo was by this time in a pitiful state. His legs were almost completely paralyzed, and when he did go out it was in a wheelchair pushed by his servant. He went to Vistillas to sit in the sun, or sometimes he went as far as Oriente Square, along the Viaduct. He never went downtown, so for the acquaintances and friendships he had in the liveliest part of Madrid this paralytic existence, beset by the ailments of old age and circumscribed within the boundaries of his immediate neighborhood, was like an anticipation of death; the real Feijóo, the man we knew, was only a shadow now. He was completely deaf and had to use an ear trumpet to catch whatever sounds he could, his intelligence was occasionally eclipsed, and his memory sometimes blanked out almost completely, leaving him in the sadness of the present, without any yesterdays, any history, as if he'd fallen from a cloud into the midst of life like a shooting star. His amusements now were totally infantile. He killed time playing bilboquet or entertaining himself with the many cats there were in the house. All of Doña Paca's beautiful cats' litters were kept, at least for as long as they had the charm of kittenhood. Sitting in the sun next to the balcony in a comfortable armchair, Feijóo was throwing out a ball tied to a string to his funny friends and entertaining himself by watching the little creatures leap and pirouette in the air. Or he'd throw the ball across the enormous room, or he'd tie a rag to the string and pull it in like a fisherman. When Fortunata arrived he had abandoned the ball-and-string game for a change and held a bilboquet in his hand. A couple of gray-spotted white kittens were frolicking on top of the worthy gentleman. One was crawling up the blanket over his legs; another was in his lap, on its haunches, licking its paw, which it then rubbed against its nose; a third cat had climbed up onto his shoulder, where it attentively studied the bilboquet ball's movements and marked them with its paw in the air. What it wanted was to touch the pretty ball.

Upon seeing his friend enter, the invalid began to smile with pleasure. He expressed all his feelings by smiling or laughing now. He told her to sit down beside him and even wanted to continue in his innocent solace, but he had to interrupt it to reach for his ear trumpet. Fortunata took one of the kittens to caress it.

"What's new?" asked Don Evaristo, looking at her in a way that suggested gratitude for the caresses she was giving the animal. "Oh, he's the biggest rascal of them all! He knows more tricks and games . . . Well, *chulita*, how are you?"

Fortunata didn't know where to begin. It annoyed her greatly to have to shout; she was afraid the servants, the neighbors, and even the ambassador with all his foreign staff would hear. And how could she talk about such a delicate subject at the top of her lungs, as if she were a night watchman calling out the time? Something she said led Don Evaristo to the conviction that his *chulita* was in a tight spot. Suddenly my friend burst out in childish, drooly laughter, saying: "Shall we bet there's been a 'deed'?* Exactly what I prohibited most, a 'deed.' They always bring trouble."

In her consternation the young woman was not sure whether her latest devilry deserved the name and rank implied by "deed," but it was undoubtedly something very bad. Above all, she had not paid the slightest attention to her friend's wise formulas for social life. To make him understand without having to go through a long explanation, she took out the document that she was carrying in an envelope wrapped in paper.

---

* Literally, *rasgo* means "flourish." Feijóo uses the word to mean feat, deed, or escapade.

"What's that, the document?" asked the old man, laughing again. "Don't tell me . . . hee, hee, hee . . . you've broken up with the poor man?"

And he put his trumpet to his ear to catch her reply:

"Completely off his rocker. He's . . . insane."

"He eats, satiated?"

"*Insane asylum!* They're going to put him in Leganés," she shouted.

"Oh! And Doña Lupe?"

"She and I—"

Fortunata put the tips of her forefingers together, as if pitting one against the other, thus expressing herself without words.

"Have you had a quarrel? Hee, hee, hee. Imagine! Doña Lupe—very sly."

The kitten on the gentleman's shoulder was most intrigued by the ear trumpet. Undoubtedly, he didn't know what it was and wanted to know at all costs, because he extended his paw as if to examine the mysterious object. The little animal's curiosity interrupted Feijóo's hearing, which was already quite pained. Feijóo took the document and asked: "What's wrong? Doña Lupe? Hee, hee, hee. She'll still go on claiming that I made love to her. Nobody can get it out of her head. And all because I used to stand on the corner of Tintoreros Street waiting for Inza's wife . . . hee, hee, hee . . . the man with the blanket store."

After this brilliant flash of memory the precious faculty went into an eclipse, and the past fled once again from the worthy gentleman's mind. He looked at his *chulita* stupidly, as if in doubt or surprised. Fortunata kept shouting, but he couldn't make out what she was saying; the little he heard was like the sound of the wind: it meant nothing to him. Tired of her futile efforts, the young woman fell silent and looked at her friend in deep sorrow. He was looking at her too when suddenly he broke out in his childish laughter again—the kitten was tickling his neck. "This little fellow's a rogue; he won't leave me alone!" Fortunata sighed, but the elderly man didn't even notice this expressive sign of her discomfiture. At last, realizing that it would be in vain to hope for consolation and advice from these ruins of her friend, she decided to leave. When she embraced him affectionately, the old man seemed to return to his senses, recovering his memory again. "*Chulita*, don't go," he said, slapping her thigh. "Ah! What a time we had! Do you remember? What happy days. A pity I wasn't twenty years younger. Then we *really* would have been happy." She nodded her assent. Then Don Evaristo appeared to have been instantly struck by a disturbing thought. After meditating for a minute, he made use of that momentary flash of intelligence; he took the envelope containing the document and, returning it to her, said: "Don't leave this here. I may die any minute, and your money would risk getting lost. It'd be better for you to keep it. Don't worry. The shares are made out in your name, and no one else can cash them in." And then, as if the only purpose of this clearing of his mind had been to permit this important warning, as soon as he had issued it his brain was clouded over again; he relapsed into the childish laughter and was more concerned about the bilboquet ball hitting the stick than about the matters affecting his desperate friend.

So Fortunata left after this sad visit with the feeling that she had lost forever that great and useful friend, the best man she had ever known and also undoubtedly the most practical, the wisest, and the one who gave her the best advice. It's true that his advice rolled off her like water off a duck; but that didn't keep her from recognizing its excellence and the knowledge that she should have followed it down to the last syllable.

7

Maximiliano Rubín's wife could no longer hope for any protection or moral support from that senile old man, more a child than an adult now. Only in his rare lucid moments was there any trace of the man he had formerly been. She wept over his death, she wept with the effusiveness of an inconsolable daughter, and she shuddered at the thought of being left an orphan when she most needed a judicious, discreet person's direction. Her sense of emptiness and loneliness—which the house had provoked—made her terribly sad, and when she heard a little street piano in the Cava Baja playing an enticing, romantic aria, the music touched her deeply. She stopped awhile to listen and tears sprang to her eyes. She felt as if her soul were peering up over the edge of the well in which she was trapped, glimpsing undiscovered realms. The music played on her skin, making her quiver with an indefinable feeling that she could express only by crying. "I must be very coarse," she reflected as she started to walk away, "because I like this kind of music from street pianos better than the piece Olimpia plays that they say is so good. When I hear her, it's as if somebody was beating the music into my ears with a pestle."

Fortunata had resolved with her Aunt Segunda that she would live with her again (in the Cava, for her aunt had moved back). She headed that way; before crossing the threshold of the main door that led to the poultry shop, the same door and the same building where the story of her misfortunes began, a neighbor told her that Segunda was at her stand at the square, eating with friends. She went there and found her aunt with two other haggish women at a little table eating lamb stew on Talavera plates. A jug of wine and a pitcher of water completed the service. The three ladies, hair in the wind, were all talking at once in loud voices with that pertness and independence that characterize street vendors who live outdoors and are used to crying out their wares. Segunda Izquierdo was a corpulent woman with a flushed face and graying hair. She looked quite a bit like her brother José, but she hadn't preserved as much of that beauty of "the race of handsome people" because poverty, sickness, and the dog's life she'd led the last few years had devastated her face and body. People who'd known Segunda at her peak hardly recognized her now, because her face was full of big seams and on her neck and the underside of her jaw she had marks that testified to surgical work on other abscesses. Her right eye was no longer as open as it should have been, due to a fistula, and the lower lid had acquired a notorious resemblance to a tomato since a closed fist had been applied to it, causing an inflammation that eventually hardened. Segunda hadn't even kept her beautiful teeth; the year before they had begun to emigrate one by one. Her body was beginning to look like that of a cow on its hind legs.

The minute she saw her niece coming she picked up a huge key lying on the table—it looked like the key to a castle—and, handing it to her, instructed her to go home if she wished. The other two hags looked at the young woman with impudent curiosity. Fortunata knew one of them, not the other. She sat down for a minute on a bench they offered her, for she was tired; but since her aunt's friends' impertinent questions were irritating she left for the room that was to be her shelter, for God only knew how long. The neighborhood and the places she passed were so familiar that she could have found her way among the crates blindfolded. And what about the house? From the main entrance to the highest place on the stone staircase she could see her entire childhood with all its episodes and accidents, just as in church one sees all the Stations of the Cross in succession. Every step had its story, and the poultry shop and the room between floors and then the room on the second floor had that "holy look" that belongs to places consecrated by religion or life. "The turns we take in life!" she thought, following the staircase's turns and conquering the steps wearily. "Whoever would have guessed that I'd end up here again! Now I realize that even though it isn't much, some class has rubbed off on me. I'm fond of all this; but it looks so vulgar! Those two old sharks . . . what characters! And for that matter, what about my aunt?"

The room Segunda occupied in the building was one of the highest. It was above Estupiñá's. Fortunata hadn't yet reached the second floor when she saw him coming down, and she felt like greeting him. He put on a stone face when he saw her; but despite the change the young woman still felt like speaking to him. She liked him. She knew what an appetite he had for gossip, and although his friendship with the Santa Cruzes made him one of her enemies, she considered him a harmless, kind man. "Even though you don't want to answer, Don Plácido, good morning." The great Rossini didn't deign to turn his parrot profile toward her, and, muttering something the new tenant could not understand, he continued on his way downstairs, making the stone steps sound unusually strident.

Fortunata saw the apartment. Lord, it was awful! So dirty and ugly! The doors looked as if they had an inch of grime on them; the wallpaper was covered with stains; the floors were very uneven. The kitchen was horrifying. Undoubtedly, the young woman had become quite decent and acquired the habits of a lady, because the dwelling struck her as being beneath her station, habits, and taste. She resolved to wash and even paint the doors and to clean up that rubbish heap as much as possible so as not to have to look for a more modern place, whether Segunda wanted to live with her or not. The tiny parlor that she was to occupy had as its living room an iron-grilled window facing the Plaza Mayor. She spent a short while mentally arranging the furniture—the bed, the dresser, a table, and two chairs. And she must buy all this, because no support would come from her husband's family. Walking around the room she reflected that if the owner would agree to do certain repairs it wouldn't look bad. The kitchen had to be white-washed; some of the holes and the enormous cracks had to be filled with putty; the parlor, which was to be her bedroom, had to be papered; the doors had to be painted. She was already thinking about the headaches she'd give the manager when she remembered (her glee fading fast) that the manager was Estupiñá. "As soon as I mention repairs, he's sure to flare up at me. Sure, he has a grudge against me. Well, what's he, except a lackey to the Santa Cruzes? Even so, I think I'll ask him, because if worse came to worst we could just leave and that would be it. And now that I think of it, this building belonged to Don Manuel Moreno-Isla, who made Plácido the manager last year. My aunt told me so. Don Plácido's such a tyrant he won't put on one single slab of putty unless they shoot him. I wonder who the house belongs to now. Do you suppose Doña Guillermina inherited it?" She dwelled for a while on the thought that fate would not release her from the circle of people who had surrounded her in recent years. It was like being caught in a net: whenever she tried to squirm out she found herself trapped again. "No. The Ruiz-Ochoas or Zalamero's wife probably inherited the house. And anyway, why should I care who got the place? I won't be inheriting it."

If she'd had a good supply of water, she would have set about cleaning the house top to bottom. She'd start the next day. She noticed that the grate gave onto a little balcony or terrace and decided at a glance to fill it with flowerpots. The view of the four sides of the square was pretty—clear and cheerful. The garden showed up nicely from above with its two little fountains and the big-bellied horse whose haunches looked like a fat hog's, and she could see the king on him too, with his little stick in his hand. Christmas was coming and they were already setting up the Christmas Eve stands. She could also see her aunt and the other two matrons who, assisted by a burly individual, were nailing boards and setting up an awning. A little later, looking at the sidewalk on the Panadería side, she got a glimpse of Juan Pablo sitting at one of the shoeshine stands reading a

newspaper while his shoes were being shined. Then she saw him cross the square
and walk to the corner were the stairs are, as if he were going to the Gallo Café.

8

As has been said, a few days after his wife disappeared, Maxi began to miss her;
he was suspicious and expressed his need of her company with a whining impertinence to Doña Lupe that made her furious. She and Juan Pablo discussed at
length what should be done, and at last the latter said that he would try to apply a
good therapeutic system to his brother before resorting to the extreme measure of
locking him up in an insane asylum. They still hadn't tried showers, or taking him
for walks in the country, or sodium bromide, which was having such good results
with various types of periencephalitis and meningitis, etc. . . . and he kept spewing out more medical terms, because he was going through a medicine fad and
read whole volumes; with one idea from one book and another from another he
concocted some incredible theories.

Said and done. Every morning Juan Pablo came to pick up his brother, whom
he sometimes deceived, at other times forced. He dragged him to San Felipe Neri,
where he made him take cold showers that would have revived the dead. Some
afternoons he took him for a walk in the outskirts and tried to entertain his
imagination with pleasant thoughts and anecdotes that were absolutely unlike the
medley of nonsense the poor boy had been storing in his brain recently. After two
weeks of this energetic treatment Maxi improved visibly, so his brother and doctor were highly satisfied. More than once on their walks, Maxi spoke like the
sanest man in the world. He never mentioned his wife, but if anything came up in
the conversation that was vaguely related to her, he lapsed into a gloomy brooding and heavy silence from which Juan Pablo could not, not even with all his
rhetoric, free him.

One morning, emerging from the shower (when the patient seemed to be in-
vigorated—agile and clear-headed), he stopped in the street and, gently taking
hold of his brother's overcoat, sprang this: "But let's get something straight: why
doesn't my aunt, or you, or anybody, want to tell me where my wife is? What's
become of her? Be frank, and stop being so mysterious with me. Has she died and
you don't want to tell me? Are you afraid the news will upset me?"

Juan Pablo didn't know what to reply. Seeing signs of nervous worry in his
brother's face and eyes, he tried to steer the conversation away from that subject.
But Maxi stuck to it, repeating his questions and stopping at every minute.

"Well, look," he finally replied with a careless gesture, "make believe she's
dead, because, after all, what difference does it make to you whether she's alive or

dead? What do you want a wife for? Women only give you trouble, kid. That's why I've never wanted to get married."

"Dead!" exclaimed Maxi without raising his voice but with an extraordinary gleam in his eyes. "Dead! So I can marry again."

As he said this he rebelled; he left the sidewalk for the street, where he continued gesturing with his hands and bumping into passersby. Juan Pablo got him into a cab and took him home. When his aunt heard about it, she confirmed Juan Pablo's news of Fortunata, saying:

"Son, we all have to die. Don't be so surprised that she was called before you. If God wanted to take her, what can we do about it? Accept it; have Masses duly said for her soul. There have already been four, I assure you; we'll have to console ourselves little by little, as well as we can."

After this, the gradual improvement from the new treatment seemed to disprove itself. The patient was not agitated, but he sank back into his deep brooding. Perhaps a new thought had crept into his brain, or perhaps some of the old ones, which he thought had fled or disintegrated, revived. For many days he did not mention his wife, until one night, when he was out walking with Juan Pablo, he stopped and asked him:

"Do you expect me to believe she's dead? What nonsense! If it's true, why aren't we in mourning for her?"

"You're really behind, aren't you? Didn't you know that a law's been passed prohibiting mourning clothes?"

"A law prohibiting mourning! You don't expect me to swallow that, I hope! Look—even though it may seem that I'm half-cracked, I see more clearly than any of you."

And no more was said on the subject. It may be of interest to note in passing that Juan Pablo's abnegation and deep concern for his brother's health would be absolutely inexplicable—given Sr. Rubín's egoism—if we ignored, in searching for the motive, certain thoughts of his that were related to economy or the science called finances. For quite some time now Juan Pablo had been considering a vast plan for converting his floating debts into assets, and the success of this plan depended on his receiving aid from the Rothschild—or rather, his aunt's—fortune. As for the urgency of the loan, there wasn't the slightest doubt: it was a matter of life and death. All that remained was for Doña Lupe to agree to it. Unfortunately, though, the moral guarantee of one of the two parties was hardly as solid as that which England or France would provide. So the firstborn of the Rubíns began by lending, in the delicate matter of Maxi's illness, the officious aid we have witnessed. His visits were constant, and his opinions, in his conversations with his aunt, were always identical to hers, whether it was on politics, the Treasury, or whatever. He had enthusiastic praise for Señor Torquemada, and he expanded warmly on the subject of his need to arrange his private affairs, tossing in phrases like "turning over a new leaf" and resolutions like "I'm going to keep such a scrupulous account of my expenses that not even the first lord of the English treasury could outdo me." Whenever he got a chance, he edged in a word for his case; but Doña Lupe was very foxy and knew how to play dumb . . . so dumb he felt like hitting her.

Urged by the terrifying growth of his debt, the philosopher displayed a more than brotherly constancy and willpower in caring for Maxi. By January of '76 he had managed to tame him enough to take him along to the office; once there, he kept him busy putting papers in order or taking notes. At night he usually took him along to the *tertulia* at the café, where the poor boy sat as attentively as if he were at Mass, listening to everything without uttering a word. Only rarely did he bring up his cursed old theme song on "voluntary liberation" and "the death of the beastly jailkeeper." But one night when they were alone at the café he brought it up, or rather out, like an old thing from the attic one brings down and dusts to see if time has deteriorated it or the rats have gnawed at it. Very serenely, in the manner of a philosophy professor, Juan Pablo said the following:

"Look—the dogma of the 'solidarity of substance' has been criticized for its pretentiousness by all the wise men of our times; they congregated just recently at an ecumenical council that was held in . . . Basel. Their conclusions were awesome. Since you don't read the paper you don't hear about these things. Well, anyway, it's been decided that anybody who believes in 'liberation through loosening soul from body' and 'giving the beast what it deserves' is an utter fool. And people who sustain the philosophical heresy that a new messiah is coming as the son of a good-looking woman, et cetera—they've been declared fit to be tied and condemned to survive on wood shavings."

"Now, look," said Maximiliano in the gravest of tones, as if he were about to confide something important. "That business about the messiah, just between you and me, I never believed a word of it, and it wasn't a dogma or anything like it. I said it because I had a dream, and when I woke up some of it chimed in my head like a bell. What happened was that during those days I got a wild idea—it must have started in the part of the brain where what they call jealousy ferments. What do you think it was? That my wife was being unfaithful and she was pregnant. Can you imagine such nonsense?"

"Holy Mary, how awful!"

"I could feel jealousy somewhere in the back of my mind; it was like heat burning me. To find out if that awful idea had any basis I went and—you know what I did? I concocted all that stuff about the messiah that was going to come, telling her she had him in her womb and that the messiah's father was pure thought. Anyway, I thought that if I put on a farce I'd be able to get her to confess. What happened? Nothing, because I got very sick that night; but later on

I realized that I was mad to try . . . I saw things clearly, very clearly, and . . . God forgive her."

He started to drink his coffee and, meanwhile, Juan Pablo said to himself: "Oh, but he's in a bad way tonight! God, it's bad!" Maxi repeated over and over "God forgive her;" and when Leopoldo Montes and another friend came in he fell silent. After an hour and a half of the *tertulia* he took to celebrating Montes' witticisms with extreme hilarity. Then he took part in the conversation, expressing himself so serenely and with such clear judgment that those present were in awe of him. Juan Pablo's thoughts ran as follows: "So he's not as 'touched' as we thought, and what he said before reveals a really sharp mind. Holy saints and the devil's nail! If I can make you well, my dear aunt—alias the Baroness Roth-schild—will have no choice but to lower herself and give me what I need.

IV. New Life

I

ON JANUARY 4TH, FORTUNATA HEARD the doorbell ring and went to open the door, first looking through the peephole, which was covered with an iron plate (the rudimentary kind). It was Estupiñá, peering through the opening in the most authoritarian way. The young woman opened, and the great Plácido, with a scornful gesture and a frown, showing in one hand the cane with the parrot head handle (a gift the Santa Cruz couple had brought him from Seville), handed her a stamped paper with the other.

"The rent receipt," he said like an Asian despot delivering a death sentence.

"Come in, Don Plácido," she smiled engagingly. "I have to talk with you."

"I'm not coming in. Hand over the money. I don't feel like talking."

That man saying he didn't feel like talking was like the sea saying it had no water. But his obstinacy overpowered his frivolous appetite.

"Lord, what a temper this man has! Don't worry, I'll give you the money. I bet you don't have any tenants better than us."

"Sure. That aunt of yours has given me a hard time more than once. No, I'm not coming in; don't be a nuisance."

"I want you to see the house so you'll be convinced that it's no place for Christians to live."

"Well, move, then."

"Oh, what a tyrant you've turned into! I've never seen such a bad manager.

Won't you even whitewash the kitchen for me? It looks like a coal mine. And the holes! I can't live with such filth. You know what I say? If you don't want to do the repairs I'll do them. So there!"

"That's something else again. As long as I do the supervising and . . ."

"Come in, come in and see for yourself."

At last Plácido deigned to step into the hall. He went to the kitchen and took a glance at the inner bedroom, which had a number of cracks in the walls.

"Repairs can't be done every time a tenant asks for them. There'd be no end to them. Suppose you two moved out tomorrow; the next person would see the fresh whitewash and start asking for something else. We can't do it. Last month I spent over twenty thousand *reales* on repairs alone. So get on with it. I'm in a hurry."

"Have you turned into a rocket or something? Sit down for a minute. Tell me something—"

"I don't have anything to tell. I'm leaving—"

"Oh, what a man, always on the go! You won't live very long that way, you know."

"That's fine with me. I've lived long enough already."

"Sit down. I'll give you the money right away. But tell me something I want to know. Whose house is this now?"

"That's none of your business. Do you think I've got time to waste? The house belongs to its owner. I repeat: I don't feel like talking. Do you want to buy the place? Come on, now, let's get back to business. You know I don't talk much."

"Don't talk much! Well, if that's what you call not talking much . . . You were born talking, talking more than seven men at once. Tell me—who does the house belong to?"

"To its owner. So . . . listen, we've talked enough already. In closing, I'll say this: it's magnificent. Appraised at thirty-five thousand *duros*. The rock in the foundation and the staircase are worth tons. And how about the walls. The other day when the carpenters made a hole in one they couldn't get the pick into it. Tools break on this old brick, 'cause it's as hard as diamond. And, well . . . I don't feel like talking. When Señor Don Manuel Moreno-Isla's last will and testament was opened—and the will was drawn up three years ago—it was discovered that he'd left the house and the site on Relatores Street to Doña Guillermina Pacheco, his aunt. The lady mortgaged them both to finish her orphanage and that's why they're working like the dickens on it. They'll have it done this year. So—"

He held out his hand, and with the other showed his cane as if were a staff of authority.

"Doña Guillermina, my landlady!" said Fortunata pensively, turning over the money. "Well, I'll ask *her* to have the repairs done. She's a friend of mine."

"What do you mean, a friend of yours! Humph, of course!" Estupiñá retorted sarcastically. "If you want to see her get furious, talk to her about work that isn't on the orphanage. Well, good-bye. Take care. Oh, I almost forgot: be careful with the flowerpots on the windowsill. If I see them dripping water I'll throw you out, you can be sure of that. Holy Mary, what a garden you've got there! It's too much weight, I think. What beautiful views. It's been a bad year for the Christmas stands. The poor vendors are ready to go under. With all this rain . . . And I think we'll be having some snow today. I've never seen a winter as cold as this one. Did you hear that the deaf man died, the one with the meat stand? Last night, suddenly. He looked so healthy and normal just the day before yesterday. What trials life has for us! Well, I'm going to see if I can collect from the people on the second floor, the ones on the left side. They owe me five months. If the Señora would let me, I'd put their things out in the street; but you know how she is; she doesn't want any dispossessing. 'For heaven's sake, Plácido—don't throw them out. The poor things will pay up; it's just that they can't right now.' 'But, Señora, if they'd just give me what they spend on alcohol and pastries from Botín.' When you've got an owner like mine, these nervy tenants do as they please."

The man gabbed so much that Fortunata, after having begged him to come in, had to ask him diplomatically to leave.

"But Don Plácido, you're going to be late."

"Oh dear, yes! It's your fault, for talking so much. Good-bye now."

Fortunata never went out. She prepared her meals herself, and Segunda, who had a stand at the square, did the shopping.

In the days following the house manager's first visit, the sinner found that the lady who had been her friend for such a short time was on her mind continually. "How would she ever have guessed, and how would I, that I'd live in her house! It's such a small world. In those days I never dreamed of coming here, and this house wasn't hers then anyway. And when Don Plácido tells her I'm one of her tenants, what will she say? Will she be furious and want to throw me out? Maybe not, maybe not . . ." When this thought or a similar one refreshed her memory of that unspeakable scene and quarrel in the saint's parlor, the poor woman's conscience tormented her and she couldn't placate it, not even by reminding herself that "she'd been provoked." "I was blind. I didn't know what I was doing. Really, if I had a chance, I'd ask Doña Guillermina to forgive me."

Her lonely life, which was conducive to this mental resurrection of the past, inspired her with a very clear judgment on her behavior and sentiments. She now saw everything in the light of reason, at a distance that permitted her to take stock of the true size and shape of things, just as the peace of cloisters permits its fugitives from the world to see the errors and evil they committed while they were out there. "And would I ask Jacinta to forgive me?" She wondered about this but couldn't decide on an answer. As soon as she thought she would ask her forgiveness she changed her mind. The Dauphine had offended and insulted her when she hadn't done anything except tell the saint about her sorrows and conflicts. At last, by dint of long meditation, fusing her thoughts with the sadness that enveloped her soul, she began to think she would. She certainly ought to apologize for trying to scratch her face—how awful of her!—and for the bitter words that had escaped her. But for this notion to triumph totally she had to clear up the following point:

Had Jacinta been unfaithful with Señor Moreno? If she *had* been, they were equals, and one was as good as the other. Señora Rubín could never, for all her musing, arrive at a definitive solution to this terribly obscure point. First she considered the "Eternal Father's Monkey Face" guilty, then she considered her innocent. "I'd give anything," she exclaimed, invoking the heavens, "to know the truth, which only God and she can know now, because the third person's dead. Jacinta's confessor probably knows too, if she confessed. But nobody else. I'd give anything to clear up this doubt. I'm just itching with curiosity. Small difference there is between one thing and the other. If she sinned, it's a different story; I wouldn't lower myself to asking to be forgiven; but if she *wasn't* unfaithful . . . Oh! that little 'Angel Face' has me right under her foot, just like Saint Michael has the devil."

This led her into another chain of thoughts: "And now we're the same breed. He doesn't love either of us. Some position we're in! We could console each other, because I'm virtuous for my part; I haven't been unfaithful to him with anybody. And if she knew it, she could come to me, and between us we'd be able to find the rat that's keeping him from us now, and we'd make mincemeat of her. After all, why shouldn't Jacinta and me, now that we're equals, be on friendly terms? No matter what they say, I've gotten more refined. When I'm careful I hardly ever come out with any foolish remarks. Unless something really gets to me I don't say any swearwords. The Micaelas cleaned me up some, and my husband and Doña Lupe rubbed me with a pumice stone and polished me up a bit. Why shouldn't we be friends and forget about the silly stuff we said? That is, if she's been faithful. If she hasn't, I wouldn't lower myself. A person's got her dignity."

Unconsciously she switched to another chain of thoughts: "But she won't want . . . She's very proud and she's got lots of cheek, especially now that she must be full of envy. And she'd better not come telling me about her rights. What does she mean, 'rights'? What I've got inside me isn't something you can sneeze at, oh no . . . I'm so happy! The day she hears about it she's going to be so mad it'll kill her. She'll say she's his legitimate wife. Ha! All they've got is some Latin the priest threw at them and the ceremony that's not worth a cent. What *I've* got, my dear lady, is more than Latin. So take that! Priests and lawyers—I hope they get struck by a plague! They'll say this is no good. But I say it is. It's my idea! When nature talks, men have to shut up."

And her conviction was so profound that it gave her strength to bear that terribly sad, lonely life.

2

One morning when she got up she saw that there had been a blizzard during the night. The square was a stunning spectacle: the rooftops, completely white; all the horizontal lines of the architecture and the iron gratings on the balconies were outlined by the sharp white edges of snow; the trees displayed masses that looked like cotton stuffing; and King Philip III wore an ermine cloak and a sleeping cap. After getting dressed she looked at the square again, intrigued by the magic spell of the melting snow—how the whiteness of the rooftops developed cracks, and the pine trees shook off their unfamiliar clothes, and how the snowflakes dripped into liquid running down the king's body and onto the bronze underneath. The ground, which had been so pure and snow white at dawn, was by noon a muddy puddle in which the street sweepers and cleaners splashed, thawing the snow with spurts of water and letting it mix with the mud so as to direct it all down into the sewer. The spectacle was entertaining, especially when the hoses shot out water and the boys rushed into the mud with huge brooms. Fortunata was watching all this when suddenly . . . Good God! She saw her husband. It was him, all right; Maximiliano, entering the square through the 7th of July Arch; he jumped back to avoid stepping in a puddle. Instinctively the young woman left her window, but then she peered out again, saying to herself: "He can't see me here. The last thing he'd expect is that he's so near me. Come on, now, he's turning around. He's gone under the arcade. He's undoubtedly going to the Gallo Café to see his brother, the other nut-head in the family. How could they have let him go out alone? I wonder if he's cured. Do you suppose he's better? Poor boy!"

And she didn't think of him again until that night when she was in bed, alone at home, for her aunt hadn't returned yet.

"It's terrible that they let him go out alone. Any day he might go off his rocker and do something foolish. Now that I've seen him on the loose, I'm scared, and I'll be constantly wondering if he's going to show up here some fine day. Luckily he won't know where I am; I'll see to that. But who can be sure of any secret nowadays? Some clown will probably tell him, and then there we'd go, all over again. Unless he plans to kill me! That'll depend. He'd have to catch me really off guard, because I can take care of him with a couple of blows. But what if he comes in on the sly and then springs on me and bang! shoots me dead? No. I'll have to be very careful. I won't even open the door to God. And I'm going to tell my aunt that I need a maid. A well-behaved, efficient girl like Papitos is just what I need.

Alone all day in this cage! Oh, thank God, I hear my aunt's key in the lock; she must be coming in. But I wonder if it's her or someone who's stolen her key and is coming to kill me?"

"Aunt, Aunt—is that you?"

"Yes. What is it?"

"Nothing. I'm fine. It's just that I get very scared when I'm alone and I think thieves or murderers are trying to get in."

She could never fall asleep until the clock at the Panadería struck twelve. She heard a few strikes very clearly; then the sound died out in the distance as if it were swinging away, only to return and strike against the windowpanes. In that twilight zone that her sleepy brain was crossing, Fortunata imagined that the wind was coming to the square to play with midnight. When the clock began to strike, the wind took midnight in its arms and carried it far, far away. Then it came back, making an enormous wave that crashed, so loudly that the sonorous metal seemed to be inside the house. The wind passed with the hour in its arms over the square and went as far as the Royal Palace, then even further, as if it were showing the hour to all the town and saying to its inhabitants: "Here is midnight in all its glory." And then it turned back. Gong! Oh! It was the last stroke. Then the wind drifted away muttering. Other nights the young woman entertained herself by fancying that the hour struck at the Puerta del Sol and the hour struck by the Panadería clock met and intertwined. One started and the other answered. The bell strokes blended so completely that not even night, which had invented the hour, would have been able to distinguish them clearly. Twelve o'clock there and twelve o'clock here sounded like a dispute among the bells. "You can even hear them ringing over at the Merced Church. So many of them telling time, you don't even know if it's twelve o'clock or what . . ."

In order to have company and service, she took as a servant a young girl, a daughter of one of Segunda's friends at the square. Her name was Encarnación and she seemed very trustworthy. Her mistress told her the rules the first day, saying: "Look. If somebody you don't know, for example a skinny gentleman with an unhealthy complexion, looking a little strange, asks you if I live here, you tell him no. Don't ever open the door to anyone who's not one of us. If they ring, look to see who it is; come and say, 'Señorita, it's a man or a woman who looks like such and such.' So listen carefully to what I'm telling you. Your aunt has probably told you the same. If you don't obey us, you know what we'll do? We'll put you in jail. And don't think anybody will get you out—you'd be there for three years at the very least."

The girl carried out her orders to a tee. One Sunday, someone rang the bell.

"Señorita, there's a man with a long beard; he looks like a real gentleman, and his voice is, well, sort of 'rispeckfel.'"

Fortunata looked through the peephole. It was Ballester.

"Tell him to come in."

She was glad to see him so she could find out what was going on in the family and he could tell her what Maxi was doing loose in the streets.

The good pharmacist was so pleased to be there he was a bit abashed. He was in his Sunday best, his hair just done at the barber's with a part very well made from his forehead all the way back to the nape of his neck, his black curls dripping with strong hair tonic, his boots new, and his top hat very shiny.

"I wanted to see you so much! I didn't dare come. But Doña Lupe urged me so much that I finally . . . No, no; don't worry about Maximiliano discovering where you are. We're very careful to keep it from him. Although he's so reasonable again you wouldn't believe it; everything he says makes sense and he never does anything foolish."

Fortunata felt somewhat inhibited, because despite her conviction that she could flaunt her legal status, she was ashamed that she couldn't hide her condition in front of a friend of the Rubín family. She blushed deeply when Segismundo said:

"I have a message for you from Doña Lupe. She told me to ask you if you'd like for her to get in touch with Don Francisco de Quevedo. He knows his profession very well; he's very careful and skillful."

"I don't know; we'll see. I'll think about it. It's still . . ." she stammered, lowering her eyes.

"What do you mean 'still—'? Doña Lupe told me it will be in March. This is February 20th. Oh, no—you can't be careless. You might be caught off guard. You have to prepare for things like this well in advance."

Taking a gallant attitude, he added:

"I have a genuine interest in you, no matter what, you know. I'm the same old Segismundo I've always been, and when you need a loyal friend you can count on, remember that you've got me."

And raising his tone almost to pathos, he suddenly blurted out:

"I don't take back anything I've said to you at other times."

As she didn't seem to be interested in this turn of the conversation, Ballester reassumed his brotherly tone:

"I'm going to take the liberty of speaking to Quevedo. We should be prepared. I'll tell him to come see you. You can trust him, and he already knows he isn't supposed to say anything to Rubín."

What surprised and even awed Fortunata was the Jáuregui widow's purported interest in her.

"I don't know why, my friend, but the 'organization woman' has asked me at least half a dozen times lately if I've seen you. 'I'm not going,' she said to me, 'but someone has to look after her. She can't be left like a dog.' That's why I decided to come, and now I'm glad I did, because you've received me and we'll continue to be good friends. So Quevedo will come, all right? Yes, let's be prepared, because sometimes these things turn out well, but sometimes they don't. You won't lack anything. Jiminy! You've got to stand up to situations and . . . Oh, what a memory I have! I almost forgot the best part" (reaching into his pocket). "The organization woman gave me this packet of money for you. The amount's written on the outside—one thousand two hundred fifty-two *reales*. It must be the interest on some funds that are yours. And finally, I want to say this: whenever anything comes up, no matter what it is, think about it first and then ask yourself, 'Who should I turn to? That nut Segismundo.' All you have to do is send me a message. Although I'll be coming anyway, some Sunday or whenever I have some free time; now that I'm alone at the pharmacy I have very little time. If I could, I'd come every morning and afternoon, if you let me. But in this tricky world you get as far as you can, and whoever tries to go past that simply because he wants to is heading for a fall."

He repeated his offer to help and then was on his way, leaving Fortunata with the impression that she wasn't as alone as she thought and that with all his nonsense and extravagances Segismundo was a generous and loyal heart. The unhappy young woman found it very strange that Aurora hadn't come to visit, and she was sorry she had forgotten during Ballester's visit to ask about the Samaniego women. But she'd be able to inquire next time.

With her change of life and address, Señora Rubín renewed some family relationships that had been completely cut off, notably the one with José Izquierdo, who started by coming to dinner at his sister's and niece's every now and then and ended—true to his congenially parasitic way—by spending all his free time there. Fortunata found her uncle morally transfigured, with a spiritual calm she'd never seen in him before, an easy talker cured of his crazy ambition and that black pessimism that had made him curse his luck constantly. Having finally found a rest from his vagabond life, the good Platón had settled down on a stone on the wayside in the shade of a leafy tree laden with fruit (may the metaphor pass) without anyone scolding him for eating his fill. There wasn't a better model than he at the time in all Madrid, and painters fought over him. Izquierdo's services were always being requested, beseeched; he received a steady stream of notes and messages, and it disheartened him not to have three or four bodies with which to serve art. And there wasn't a job in the world that would have suited him better: it was like not working! It was just "having your portrait done": the one who worked was the painter, who had to put heart and soul into it and stare at him as if he were his girl friend. In those days of February of '76, if he started telling his sister and niece about all the many works under way, he never finished. In so and so's studio he was doing an "Eternal Ladder" creating the light; in another, he was doing King James arriving at Valencia on horseback. Somewhere else, it was Nebuchadnezzar on all fours; here it was "some guy in his birthday suit that they call Aeneas" with his father. "But the best thing we're painting now—and it's coming out beautiful—is that scene where Hernán Cortés orders them to open fire on the bloody ships . . ." My good man earned enough for his needs and was happy; and his being tied down during the day was compensated for by the long sessions of talk and drink he enjoyed in the evenings in some café or other where he invited his friends. He lent his niece his services too, doing whatever errands his artistic duties left time for. She often sent him to her seamstress and depended on him to do some of the shopping. More than once she sent him to the Samaniego store after material or lace for the layette she was making; but she always told him not to let them know anything about her. Since Aurora had not come to see her—which was bad manners on her part, or to put it more bluntly, downright meanness—she didn't want to appear to be begging for her friendship; and if the Samaniego woman had her reasons for staying away, she had hers for not lowering herself. "She may be more refined than me, but she's not as proud."

v. The Logic of Illogical Thinking

I

MAXIMILIANO'S IMPROVEMENT CONTINUED, which led his aunt and brother to infer that the separation had been highly beneficial; without a doubt, the presence and company of his wife was what had driven him out of his mind. All winter long they continued the showers and sodium bromide treatment. At first, when Juan Pablo didn't take him out for walks, his aunt herself did, so she had the opportunity to note how sensible he was becoming. They observed, however, that in the young man's head there lurked a thought about his conjugal mate's whereabouts, and they feared that this thought, although it was presently contained by the harmonious rebirth of his cerebral life, might any day gain enough expansive strength to destroy the machine again. But these fears were not confirmed. In December and January his improvement was so marked that Doña Lupe was astonished and extremely pleased. By February they allowed him to go out alone again; he never bothered anyone now and his shyness and docility had become quite noticeable. It was like a regression to the stage he went through in his first years at pharmacy school, and it even seemed that thoughts he had harbored long ago had renewed themselves, bringing with them this inhibited manner, faltering speech, and lack of initiative.

His life was very methodical; he wasn't allowed to read anything, nor did he attempt to, and whenever he went out Doña Lupe stipulated at what time he was to return. Not once did he fail to return at the agreed time. To top off the resemblance between these days and his early student days, the only pleasure the young man indulged in was to wander aimlessly through the streets, lost in observations and thought. There was one difference between his earlier meandering and this present meandering, though. The former had taken place at night and had resembled sleepwalking with morbid thoughts; the latter took place during the day and, due to the favorable condition of the solar atmosphere, they were healthier and more conducive to health and mental stability. In the former his mind had worked in an illusory state, fabricating insubstantial worlds out of the foam of his well-beaten ideas; in the latter, it worked in the realm of reason, entertaining itself by doing exercises in logic, asserting principles, and obtaining consequences with admirable ease. In a word, during the course of this cerebral process he contracted "the fever of logic," and I say this because when he thought about something he had a maniac's insistence on applying to all subjects the most rigorous dialectics. He tenaciously rejected as repugnant anything that was not a product of logic and sheer calculation, and he stuck to this practice even when dealing with the most trival matters.

It goes without saying that shortly after recognizing this tic of his (using logic on everything), he proceeded to examine the obscure logical problem of his wife's absence. "There's no doubting that she's alive; that's an unquestionable premise that needn't be discussed. Now. Let's figure out whether she's in Madrid or away from Madrid. If she'd gone somewhere else, my aunt would receive letters from her from time to time. That's probably why the postman never comes to our house, and when he does, it's to bring a letter from one of my Uncle Jáuregui's sisters; that must mean . . . But let's suppose she addresses the letters to someone else so I won't find out about it. It's farfetched, but let's make that proposition. In that case, who would the person be? Logically thinking, it couldn't be Doña Casta, because Señora Samaniego doesn't like that sort of role. The logical one would be Torquemada. But the day before yesterday Torquemada went into my aunt's parlor and from out in the hall I clearly heard him asking her if she'd had any news of the Señorita. So it can't be Torquemada. Well, since it's not Torquemada, there's no go-between for the letters, and without a go-between there can't be any correspondence; therefore she's in Madrid."

These reflections satisfied him greatly and, after stopping for a while to see a window full of prints, he resumed his thoughts. "It could be doubted that there's any communication between her and my aunt, and in case there isn't any, the problem of her whereabouts remains wide open; but I maintain that there is communication. If not, what was the meaning of the scrap of paper I happened to see the other day on my aunt's bureau where I saw by chance that it said '1,252 *reales* belonging to F.' 'F' means *her*. Therefore, there *is* communication between them, and since the communication isn't by mail, it's clear as day that she's living in Madrid."

He spent long periods of time with these exercises in logic. Sometimes he mused: "Let's reject all fantasies. Let's not admit anything that's not based on logic. What does she live on? Does she live an honest life, I wonder? Let's not pass any premature judgments. She may live honestly and then again she may not. I'll discover the whole truth without asking anybody a word. Since they're all silent with me, I'll be silent with them. I see, I hear, and I think. This way I'll find out everything I want to know. How beautiful truth is! Or rather, these borders of the cloak of truth that we glimpse from earth, because the cloak itself, and truth, can't be seen from here! Good God, I'm astounded at how sane I am. People look at me with pity, as if I were sick; but deep down inside I take pleasure in how sane my mind is. Blessed is the man who knows how to think, for he is truly on the straight road."

He entered the Café del Siglo, where he expected to find his brother, but Leopoldo Montes informed him that since Villalonga had accepted the directorship of Health and Welfare he had commissioned Juan Pablo to do a very delicate, troublesome job, something to do with straightening accounts with some quarantine hospitals, and he kept the poor man in the office from sunup to sundown. His coffee was brought to him there. It didn't do Juan Pablo any harm to be commissioned extra work; it was a sign of confidence, and such confidence signified a promotion. They talked about political jobs, and Maximiliano made some cogent remarks.

Refugio, Juan Pablo's mistress, had a very shabby wardrobe that winter and did not frequent the Siglo; instead, she went to the Gallo, which, besides being much nearer (the couple lived on Concepción Jerónima), had a modest clientele that allowed her to wear any old thing or a cloak with a scarf on her head. Several people usually joined Refugio, people with whom she had an easy acquaintanceship, the type that springs up between neighbors or at a café. They were a doorman from the Academy of History with his wife and a city collector from the marketplace with his, or whatever she was. This couple usually appeared on Sundays with the whole family, to wit: a grandmother who had been a victim in the May 2nd massacre and seven younger members of the family.

The café consisted of two sections separated by a thick partition and connected by an arch. Yet despite this strange construction, which made it seem more like a Masonic lodge, the place didn't have a gloomy air. In the second room, where Refugio settled herself, there was always a familiar, lively, joking atmosphere, and since there's so little space there, the clientele ended up as one single *tertulia* group. Refugio reigned, like the star of an elegant salon. She gave herself airs and played the grande dame, boastful of her keen articulation and witticisms (which the others were forced to accept in amusement). She always sat in the corner which, due to the room's arrangement, had the honor of appearing to be the presiding area. When Maxi came she had him sit next to her and showered him with attention, feeling sympathetic and protective, taking the liberty of using the familiar *tú* form with him, and giving him advice on his health. He let her carry on and hardly participated in the *tertulia* unless one counted his mental syllogisms on every subject discussed. One night the poor boy was having his coffee very quietly at Refugio's table when he noticed two men at the next table, one of whom was not an unfamiliar face. Searching his brain, he finally recalled who it was: Pepe Izquierdo, his wife's uncle, whom he had seen only once: when he and Fortunata were on a walk near Las Rondas she had introduced them.

In the familiar atmosphere at the Gallo, people from nearby tables soon got to talking. First they discussed politics, then they speculated that the civil war would end for lack of money; and since politics and wars turn out to be the fibers of which history is woven, they talked about the French Revolution, a regrettable era when, according to the city collector, "many souls" had been guillotined. Hearing talk about history and not getting in his two cents was impossible for Izquierdo; ever since he'd started his modeling career he knew that Nebuchadnezzar was a king who ate grass, that Don Jaime had entered Valencia on horseback, and that Hernán Cortés was a very warm "charaktir" who "got his fun burning up ships." The nonsense that that man had to offer about the French Revolution made them all laugh, particularly the doorman from the Academy of History, who looked about disdainfully, not wishing to venture any opinions, because they would only be pearls thrown to swine. But Platón's companion, completely new to Maxi, must have been one of the most erudite characters to ever grace that place; when he took the floor, he attracted everyone's attention. He had a pimply face and a neck like a turkey's with an enormous Adam's apple and swabbed hair, and he expressed himself in terms very much unlike those used by his garrulous friend:

"Louis XVI and his queen Marie Antoinette," he said, "naturally had their heads cut off because they didn't want to give the people their freedom. That, of course, was the reason for the great Revolution and why they changed everything—even the names of the months, gentlemen—and they abolished the yardstick and switched to the metrical system, and religion was abolished too; they held Masses thereafter to the goddess called Reason."

Such knowledge impressed Maxi; he immediately struck up a conversation with Izquierdo's learned friend, who was none other than Ido del Sagrario, and they commented on the tragic events of '93.

"Because look—when the people rise up, citizens see that they're defenseless, and frankly, naturally, liberty is good; but living comes first. What happens? They all ask for order. So a dictator springs up, a man who starts carrying a big stick, and when it starts to work, they all bless him. Either there's logic or there isn't. So

Napoleon Bonaparte came along and started to buckle down on all of them. And he was right to do what he did, and I applaud him, yes, sir; he's got my applause."

"And mine, too," said Maxi, utterly sincere, for he observed that the man was reasoning keenly.

"Does this mean I'm in favor of tyranny?" proceeded Ido. "No, sir. I like liberty, but only as long as it means respecting the other fellow and letting everybody believe what he wishes without any uprisings. Obeying the law. Lots of people think that being liberal means shouting around and insulting the priests and not working and asking for abolishments and saying the authorities should be killed. No, sir. What do you get out of that? When you've got misconceptions about liberty and lots of abolishing going on, the rich get scared and leave the country and you can't find a *peseta* anywhere. And when money's not flowing the market's bad—nothing gets sold, and the laborer who was screaming so loudly about the constitution doesn't have anything to eat. It's like I always say: 'Be logical, liberals.' And nobody can get me to believe anything different."

"That man's very sharp," thought Rubín as he nodded his assent to these statements.

And when, upon leaving, Ido gave him his name (adding that he was a primary school teacher in the Catholic schools), Maximiliano reflected that the humble nature of his job didn't go with the knowledge and dialectic skill that he displayed.

The next afternoon Maxi went back to the Gallo. The only people he knew there were the city collector and José Izquierdo. The latter had left a package on the seat next to him. The young man looked at it unobtrusively and saw that it was clothes or shoes or something, wrapped in a scarf. The bundle was so poorly tied that when the chair was moved an elegant tan boot showed. Seeing it, Rubín felt a cold drop of something fall on his heart. "That's her boot . . . oh, God! I know it as well as if it were my own. He's not taking it to be fixed, because it's practically new. He's taking it as a sample for another pair to be made. She's very conceited about her shoes. She always liked to have three or four pairs in good condition. And why didn't she take it herself? Because she doesn't go out. That means she's sick. Sick . . . with what?"

2

Platón said good-bye to his friend and picked up the bundle, adding that he had to go to Arenal Street.

"Sure," thought Maxi, not saying a word. "That's where her cobbler is, 22 Arenal Street. What I still don't know yet I could find out by following that brute. But no . . . With logic and logic alone I'll figure it out. After all, what's this great sanity I have now for? With a head like this I can take care of things myself."

Later, when Ido, Refugio, and others came, he was most affable, commenting with admirable clarity on anything mentioned, whether it was the uprising in Cuba, the hike in the price of meat, how to choose a lucky number in the lottery, the frequency with which people jumped off the Viaduct on Segovia Street, the new streetcar that was going to be added, or any other topic.

Sometime in early March, on his way to the café, Maxi spotted Izquierdo under the arcade in front of the Panadería, and just as he was about to greet him, the city collector came along and stopped to chat. He and José exchanged a few words.

"I'll be right over at the café," said the model, showing various packages to his friend, who looked at them curiously. "I'm going to drop these off: yards of ribbon, soap . . . what the devil's this? Oh, dates. I've been packed like a blessed donkey."

Maximiliano continued on his way to the café, and, observing that Platón was heading for Ciudad Rodrigo Street, he looked at his watch.

"Dates! How often I've bought them for her! She has such a sweet tooth, she simply craves them," mused the reasoner as he entered the café, oblivious to his surroundings. "She's eating dates. Therefore she's not sick. Dates are very hard to digest. And since she's eating them, the reason for her not going out isn't sickness. Therefore it's something else . . ."

And seeing Izquierdo arrive, he looked at his watch again. "It took him twelve minutes. Therefore the house is nearby. Twelve minutes: let's say it took him four to go up the stairs, two to come down . . . And he's tired . . . there must be a lot of stairs. The house is near here. We'll discover it with logic. No questions, because nobody will tell me anything; nor will I follow that animal—it would be unworthy. Sheer calculation . . . by calculation alone."

Izquierdo and the city collector invited him to have a few drinks, but he didn't want to accept because alcohol revolted him. He listened to their conversation, pretending not to; but there was nothing of interest in it for him, because it was about whether or not the city council would remove a number of mules from the city gardens and walks and divide up the profits among the councilmen. Then the tax collector brought up some family business, complaining about his wife always getting sick, which Izquierdo snatched as his chance to throw in some absurd remarks on the advantages of not having a family to support. "We widowers do as we please," he said, turning to Maxi and giving him a slap on the back. The poor boy pretended to approve of the idea by smiling, meanwhile cranking the handle of logic a few more turns: "You've been told to keep it quiet; you've been told to be very careful with what you say around me, you ass; and like everybody else you're trying to make me think I'm a widower. You haven't realized yet that my head is a prodigy at reasoning and clarity. If you only knew who you're speaking to. Just wait, you'll see how I make hash of your sophisms and—what an enlightened brain can do! So I'm a widower, am I! Just like my aunt, who said to me yesterday: 'Ever since you've become a *widower* you're like a new man!' It'll be to my advantage to make them think that I've fallen for it. With my logic I can take care of things beautifully and laugh at the world. Oh, but logic's lovely! So lovely! And it's so beautiful to have a head like mine is now—free of all phantasmagoric illusions, attentive to facts, only to facts, so that I can stake my reasoning on solid grounds. But let's go home now; my aunt's waiting for me."

Three days after this, walking into the pharmacy, he noticed that Ballester and Quevedo, who'd been talking, suddenly fell silent when they saw him. Since he had acquired a facility for interpreting facts, this one seemed clear to him. Segismundo and the obstetrician were talking about something they didn't want Maximiliano to hear. To cover up, they inquired about his health and in a minute the latter asked: "Have you got the ergot of rye ready? That's all I need now.

"Well, and how've we been, young man? Walking a lot?" he added out loud, turning to Maxi and showing his alligator face, whose smile turned into an expression of ferocity. "We're doing fine, just fine. At last you'll be able to take on your daily duties. I always said so, that as soon as you were free . . . you know, 'once the dog dies, its rabies are gone,' as they say."

Rubín answered affirmatively and amiably. Then he saw Ballester taking a packet of medicine from a drawer and giving it to Señor Quevedo, stating:

"Take this to her; I pulverized it myself very carefully. I'll take her the antispasmodic."

The male midwife took the package and departed.

A few minutes later Doña Desdemona came in, inquiring about her husband, and the young man caught Ballester signaling to her that *he* was there, because the lady had opened with: "Has he gone to the Cava again?"

She stopped in time and then invited Maxi to escort her home, which he did very gladly, practically pulling her up the stairs. They talked for a long time, and Señora Quevedo showed him her bird cages: baby canaries, a linnet drinking from a little well and eating by pulling bird seed out of a box, and other ornithological curiosities—the house was full of them. At lunch time Quevedo came in, looking very tired, saying:

"Nothing yet—"

And seeing Doña Lupe's nephew, he said no more.

As Maximiliano was leaving, an extraordinary chain of reasoning started to take shape in his mind. "You see? I was right. What was flashing through my mind like a sinister glare in my delirium is now clearing, like light from a high peak, illuminating everything. Hmm, I'm even becoming a poet. But let's forget about poetry; poetic inspiration is an insane state. Logic, logic, and nothing but logic. How is it that what I've discovered today with purely logical proceedings founded on facts and real clues existed in my mind before as traces of a dream or as extravagant notions produced by an alcoholic delirium? This isn't new to me. I'd already thought of it; I conceived of it in the midst of crazy impressions and totally absurd ideas. Mysteries of the mind, I guess . . . disorders in our thinking! Poetic inspiration always precedes truth, and before truth can appear, led in by a healthy logic, it's revealed through poetry, a morbid state. Well, anyway, I guessed it, and now I know it for a fact. Heat turns into energy. Poetry turns into truth. It's so clear now! She lives in the Cava, in the same house where she lived before. She's hiding so that no one will see her. The day is coming. Quevedo's attending her. The ergot of rye and the anti-spasmodic are for her. Oh, but these imbeciles who think they're fooling me make me laugh! Fool *me*? I'm saner than sanity itself. God, am I smart! And do I know how to reason! I'm astonished at myself, and I'm sorry for my aunt and Ballester and everyone who's putting on this show. 'Nothing yet,' is what Quevedo said when he came back from the Cava. A mistaken presumption; false symptoms. Therefore, it's about to happen. It's March. Fine. All I have left to find out is which house it is. If I let myself be led by my inspiration, I'd say it was that same house, the one with the stone staircase. But no. Let's proceed logically. Let's not state anything that's not based on fact."

The next day he was with his brother at the Café Siglo, then at the Gallo with Refugio. It was March 19th, Saint Joseph's Day, so everyone named José was inviting everybody else to a round. Ido del Sagrario refused to drink, and his friend Izquierdo, who drank alcohol like water, laughed at the primary school teacher's sobriety. Ido said he had had a "big meal" and that his stomach didn't feel right. Little by little the poor man broke away from the group who made up the *tertulia*, moving from one chair back to another until Maxi saw him sitting at the table farthest away; he was lost in thought, his elbows resting on the marble and his head resting in the palms of his hands. Maxi walked over to him and asked what the trouble was. "Friend," said Ido in a hollow voice, the composure gone from his features, "do you see how my right eyelid is twitching? Well, it's a sign that I'm going to have an attack. And you have no idea how bad it can be."

"Oh, come now, Don José—you're being overanxious," he said, trying to draw him back to the main group.

"Leave me alone. They laugh at me because I talk a lot of nonsense. It's been quite some time since I've had an attack, but I can feel it coming on. It's starting, it's starting, and I can't help it. I'll have to leave so they won't make fun of me. I completely lose control. I start acting as if I'd been drinking a lot, and as you can see, I don't touch the stuff; I know you'll believe me—you're a gentleman. You're the only one who won't laugh at me; you understand my plight and have sympathy for me."

"Don José, you must get those ideas out of your head," said Maxi, playing the judicious, reasonable man.

"Ah! Well, then, take the facts out of my life," touching his friend's arm lightly. "We're slaves to other people's actions, and our own aren't the basis for our life. That's how the world is. It does you no good to be honorable if the malice in other people forces you to commit an atrocious deed."

"That's very well said."

"Oh, bad luck can make even a fool wise. No, we aren't the masters of our own lives. We're meshed into a machine, and our movement depends on the wheel next to us. The man who's foolish enough to marry gets caught, caught—do you understand?—and he's no longer the master of his movements."

"I understand, yes . . ."

"Well, don't accuse me if you hear that I've committed a crime" (whispering into his ear) "because those of us who have the bad luck to have an adulteress for a wife . . . we can't say we'll obey the commandment that goes 'Thou shalt not kill.' I think it's the fifth."

"Yes, it's the fifth," Maxi confirmed, feeling a cold arrow shoot down his spine.

"And as sure as I'm sitting here," he said, leaning back and continuing in a very low voice, "today I'm going to kill—"

Even though this was said very softly, Izquierdo overheard it, and, bursting out laughing, he retorted, "So this jerk Ido's gonna kill today! What bullring you gonna choose, buddy?"

The guffaws spread throughout the café, and Rubín approached the main group, stating in a benovolent, compassionate tone and with the greatest serenity imaginable: "Gentlemen, don't laugh at this poor man whose head isn't right. Mental illness is the worst kind there is, and it's not Christian to laugh at these things. Give him some water with a touch of brandy."

They offered it to him, but Ido didn't want it. He sat and sulked, his head on his crossed arms, and the owner of the establishment, looking at him sarcastically, remarked: "This is no place for a drunken snooze. Go out in the street if you want to sleep." Maxi tried to get him to lift his head. "Don José, it would help you to take a shower and some sodium bromide pills. Would you like me to mix some for you? It's the most effective treatment there is. I should know . . . I was in the same state for a while, except that I was much worse. I invented religions; I wanted all mankind to be killed off; I was waiting for the messiah. And here I am—all sane and well again." And turning to the main group: "Just leave him to himself. He'll get over it. Poor man—I feel so sorry for him!"

Suddenly Don José got up and charged out of the café amidst sneers and jokes from them all. Maxi wanted to follow him, but Refugio tugged at his coattails and made him sit down next to her. "Leave him alone. What do you care?" And the tumult grew, for more Pepes*—or Josés—had arrived, and the café owner, who had a José somewhere in his name, gave out cigars and rum with maraschino. Some of them insisted that Maxi have a drink, but he neither wanted one nor would Refugio have permitted him one, attentive as she was to his precarious health. What the excellent boy did was to laugh wholeheartedly at their jokes, even the coarse and downright gross ones; but he didn't really share their noisy happiness.

3

That night Rubín ate calmly with his aunt, telling her about what he had seen and heard at the café; the great lady's response was to express her desire that he not frequent the place anymore because it was very far away and because he would find ignorant, vulgar people there. The young man seemed to agree with this opinion, and he said that he would not return. Then he went to the Samaniegos' with his aunt, and for as long as the *tertulia* lasted sat by himself polishing up his idea: "It's the house with the stone staircase." After Izquierdo had made that stupid toast he had said something about crawling up to his sister's house and rolling all the way down on the stone staircase. "So now I know where she is. And I've got to proceed cautiously, taking firm steps. Now's the time for punishment. Honor obliges me to do it. I'm not a murderer; I'm a judge. That poor wretched man said so: 'We're cogs in a machine, and the wheel next to us forces us to move. Its teeth mesh in mine and I move.'"

"Why are you sighing, son?" his aunt asked him, seeing that he was brooding and sighing.

He answered evasively and soon they got up to leave, not without Doña Desdemona's first inviting the young man to spend the following morning with them. She would show him all their birds and give him lunch.

Having accepted her courtesy, Maxi appeared at the Quevedos' house the next morning at nine, when the lady was well into her morning activities—cleaning cages, checking nests, examining eggs, and carrying on very affectionately with one bird or another. Her obesity didn't prevent her from being agile and most diligent at her tasks. She was wearing a reddish-ocher housecoat, and since her figure was almost spherical she looked not so much like a person walking as an enormous Gouda cheese rolling through the halls or from room to room. She drew

---

* Pepe is the nickname for José.

Maxi into her procedures right away, showing him how to give birdseed to the whole family. With some of them Doña Desdemona had truly maternal conversations. "And what do you want to say, my little baby? Let's see, is the baby very hungry? Would you just look at how this child opens his little bird-mouth!" And their trills filled the air. With true zeal Maximiliano kept turning over in his mind the thoughts he had entertained the previous night. "I'll kill her and then I'll kill myself, because in these situations you have to put your case in the hands of God. Human justice can't solve it."

"What a naughty bird she is!" exclaimed Doña Desdemona. "You have no idea how naughty. She's already killed three husbands, and she doesn't pay the slightest attention to her children. If it weren't for the male—he's over there, and as you can see, a decent person—the poor things would die of starvation."

"You have to forgive her," Maxi said humorously. "She doesn't know what she's doing. And anyway, if we were going to condemn her, who could throw the first stone?"

"Let's go see the parakeets—they're getting all excited by now."

"Logic demands her death," thought Rubín, carefully hanging a cage crowded with nests. "If she continued to live, the laws of reason would be violated."

Changing the water and refilling the birdseed trays made those poor little charming beings wildly happy; they all started chirping and singing at once and it became impossible to talk in their midst. Doña Desdemona used signs instead. Maxi seemed happy enough; he would have started the daily ritual over again purely for the pleasure of it. By lunch time he'd developed a very good appetite, and the male midwife and his wife were very hospitable, saying they would appreciate more visits, every day if he wished. Quevedo had gotten over his jealousy, and ever since his wife had plumped out to the point of competing with a Gouda cheese, the good man had been cured of his sulking and no longer played Othello. Nevertheless, he didn't permit anybody except poor old Rubín to visit freely because, if the truth be told, he didn't consider Rubín capable of staining the honor of any home he entered.

Doña Lupe came in very cheerfully with: "Well, and how has my gallant nephew behaved?"

"Admirably, Señora. He's the most lovable . . . ," replied Doña Desdemona. And taking her aside, she added: "He's sane and sound, I tell you. If only you could have seen how happy and calm he's been! Like the most sensible person you could imagine."

"I think," said Jáuregui's widow, "that if he's not cured, it's just a question of waiting a bit more. And how about the other business?"

"Quevedo came back this morning. Nothing yet. Just waiting for the moment. She's very scared."

They chattered some more, but it's not relevant. Doña Lupe took her nephew to the public auction, but since the merchandise was of very little interest that day, they went home early, after having bought strawberries and asparagus at a stand on Atocha Street. That afternoon she asked her nephew to do some rather complicated accounts and he did them quickly and accurately, not one cent off. And when his aunt marveled at his arithmetical skill, the young man burst out laughing and said: "What did you expect? My head's never been this clear. I'm so sane that I've got extra sanity to give to the many people who pass as normal."

It had been a long, long time since Doña Lupe had seen the boy so clear-headed, so calm, and so inclined to be happy, all signs, unquestionably, of his recovery. "I don't doubt that you're well. And it's true, lots of people would be only too happy to . . . Anyway, I can't tell you how pleased I am to see you like this, and I only pray that God keep you in such fine health."

"I'll go on like this, believe me. I feel a new strength in my mind that was never there before. I can reason remarkably well, and I'm going to prove it to you right now. You'll be astounded when you see that while you've all put on a good show for me, I've put on a better one for you. The deceivers are the deceived."

Doña Lupe began to feel alarmed.

"Just listen," he said, staying at the table where he had done the accounts and keeping the paper in his hands. "My family, Ballester, and everyone I know outside home played their roles beautifully. And I kept quiet, playing the fool, while with sheer calculation, and calculation alone, I discovered the truth."

Doña Lupe was petrified. She had no reply.

"And just listen to how my mind outsmarted the best ones, even yours. Without a word to anyone or a question to a living soul, and basing my ideas only on whatever clues I picked up here and there, arranging facts and deducing the consequences, I've discovered the truth—all with logic, Aunt, pure logic. Listen. You'll be amazed."

The illustrious widow was, indeed, as amazed as somebody seeing a cow fly.

"Well, in the following order, I've gradually discovered these facts: Fortunata did not die; she's in Madrid, and she lives near the Plaza Mayor, in the Cava de San Miguel, in the house with the stone staircase. She's been due to give birth for a month now, and Don Francisco de Quevedo is attending her."

Doña Lupe didn't dare try to deny it—there were too many overwhelming truths. "Well, look . . . You shouldn't trouble yourself with all that. I concede that she's alive, but I don't know where. And as for the pregnancy—it's an error that you and your cursed logic have made. Some notions! The devil take your logic."

"If you insist, my dear Aunt, on making a farce, I'll start thinking that the one who's lost her mind is you, not me. I still assert what I've said, and I'm sure it's the truth. My logic doesn't deceive me, nor can it. Frankly, now: do you observe anything in me that remotely resembles a lack of judgment?"

Doña Lupe didn't know what to reply.

"Have I said anything foolish? Do you dare sustain that I have? Well, then we can hail a cab and go to the Cava. Ah! So you don't want to. Then I *have* spoken the truth, and the one who isn't speaking the truth—undoubtedly for a good reason—is my dear aunt. So who is sane and who isn't?"

"Well, I repeat: that business about her expecting is stuff and nonsense," said the widow, thoroughly confused by now. "Somebody wanted to play a joke on you and it was in very poor taste."

"I swear to you that I haven't mentioned this matter to anyone, not a soul. What knowledge I acquired was the result of pure calculation. And now, just in case anyone doubts that I'm sanity personified, I'm going to give everybody a final proof. How? By not bringing up the subject again. It's all over. Let's go back to ordinary life. Nothing's happened here, Aunt; just pretend we never talked at all. Didn't you say you had another account to balance? Bring it out. I'm ready for it, and I've got a mind like a steel trap when it comes to numbers, because they're the pure essence of logic."

And he went back to work on the arithmetical problems so serenely and so even-mindedly that Doña Lupe walked out of the room blessing herself and mumbling that if the four Evangelists had told her what she'd just heard she wouldn't have credited their story. But since her nephew's words indicated a prodigious intellectual capacity, the lady wasn't sure what to think about the state of his head. Alarm filled her as it had in the worst days and paralyzed her mind; she couldn't decide whether that business about his "logic" was a favorable crisis or whether, on the contrary, it would bring new complications.

And Juan Pablo wasn't very lucky to have chosen that particular day to propose a special loan to Doña Lupe; he found the capitalist in a foul mood. He was the unluckiest man on earth, all right—never could pick the right time. It was a great pity, because the speech he had prepared to convince his aunt was truly eloquent; even a rock would have softened at it. His aunt didn't let him get beyond the exordium, though, categorically refusing to give him any sort of loan, even under the most usurious conditions. In sum, Juan Pablo left the house cursing his unlucky star, his aunt, and the whole human race, concocting plans for revenge by suicide. The poor man was like a victim of a shipwreck—kicking desperately in the waves and giving out, giving out. He was drowning.

4

The night of that fateful day, which he thought he should mark with the blackest stone he could find, Juan Pablo sustained the most radical theories at the

Café del Siglo. To the great stupefaction of Basilio Andrés de la Caña (who had reincorporated himself in the *tertulia*), he attacked private property, making Don Basilio and others think he had done a lot of fast reading of Proudhon. Actually, he hadn't laid eyes on a single book, not even its cover; all his ingenious arguments sprang from his anger at Doña Lupe. It was a truly satanic rancor, enough to inspire an epic.

Since the great principle of private property had only Don Basilio as its defender in that unequal match, it came out quite badly. The marble table around which the opponents' faces made a lively circle was by the end of the session full of corpses decorated with spoons, coffee-ringed glasses, cigar ashes, newspapers, and the little metal saucers where Don Basilio's hungry hand had left only the powder of a few grains of sugar. Said corpses (horribly destroyed) were property, all kinds of property: the State, the Church, and as many institutions as derive from the two: marriage, the army, credit, etc. To everyone's admiration, Juan Pablo spoke out for free love, absolutely spontaneous relations between the sexes, and he transferred jurisdiction in family matters to the mother. He cut the Pope to shreds and papal authority was left trampled under the table along with scraps of newspaper, spit, and a chewed-up toothpick, for Don Basilio had at last, in the aftermath of his defeat, flung down the marker of his arguments. The royal crown was also on the ground, crushed by the soles of boots, and the all-powerful scepter had suffered the same fate. The ferrules of their canes, banging furiously on the dirty parquet, finished off the victims, who fell from the table agonizing. One would have thought that Juan Pablo was smashing them to death with his elbows after wounding them to the quick with his dialectics; and when he picked up a pencil and started writing numbers feverishly on the marble to prove that there should not be a budget, he looked like a Fouquier-Tinville signing death penalties and sending flesh to the guillotine.

How could the hapless Rubín do less than discharge his horrible anguish against social order and historical powers? He was lost; his aunt's cruel refusal had forced him to choose between dishonor and suicide. Before coming to the café he had had a violent quarrel with Refugio because she wanted him to take her to the Gallo; and this argument with his mistress, whom he was fond of, had increased his anger. His friends didn't know what to do with him; he was furious and on the verge of insulting whoever contradicted him. And his paradoxical inspiration was so exalted that he looked like a propagandist for the Holy Rollers. The one who refuted him best—believe it or not!—was Maxi, whose interest in the polemics had kept him at the café longer than usual. The young Rubín defended the fundamental principles of all societies with such ardor and serene conviction that he dazed them all. He didn't get angry like his brother; he argued coldly, and his nerves, which were absolutely calm, let his reasoning powers function freely and easily. The elder Rubín was lucky, though, because the younger Rubín left at ten o'clock; Doña Lupe had told him not to come home late, and he wouldn't have disobeyed this rule for anything in the world. He had regained his, shall we say, "antidiluvian" docility, his temperament previous to the catastrophe of his marriage.

Leaving his brother to fend for himself against the other defenders of public law, he left the café, planning to go straight home. He crossed the Plaza Mayor from Felipe III Street to Sal Street, and at that corner he couldn't help but pause for a minute and look at the building fronts on the west side of the square. But this suspension of movement was quickly overcome by his relentless logic, which dominated him, and he said to himself: "No, I'm going home. It's already ten o'clock . . . so I shouldn't stop." He continued along Postas Street and Vicario Viejo, and before reaching the hill to Santa Cruz he saw Aurora pass by; she was on her way out of the shop, heading home. "She's so late tonight!" he thought, following her toward Santa Cruz Square, not to follow her but because she was in front and didn't see him. Fenelón's widow was going at a brisk pace without looking about her, and she was carrying a package, perhaps some order she was taking home to work on the next day, which was Sunday, and Palm Sunday at that.

Since she was walking faster than he was, the gap between them widened quickly. Then, instead of continuing along Atocha Street to Cañizares, which seemed natural (that was Maxi's route), the young woman turned off onto a dark side street, Salvador. In the shadow of the Public Ministry a man was waiting for her; he stopped her for a moment, they took hands, and continued on together. "Well, well," Maxi said to himself, skulking nearby. "What's this all about?" And seeing them continue down the side street, a thought, or rather a suspicion, kindled sharp curiosity in him. Following them at a safe distance, he confirmed what had been an assumption, and the certainty made his soul shake violently. "It's *him*, that cad . . . He's waiting for her; they're going off together . . . and they've chosen the most deserted street; that means they're lovers. To deceive a poor woman! A married man!" At that moment the rancor he had felt in the past reasserted itself forcefully; it was a dense, subtle rancor, somewhat like a poisonous virus that may show itself as easily as lurk unseen until it rises to the surface, producing many different cerebral effects. At the same time, the miserable young man's soul was overflowing with a quixotic sense of justice, not as the law and men regard it, but justice as it appears to us directly, emanating from the divine essence. "Society tolerates and even applauds this. Therefore, society is shameless. And what defense is there against it? Laws don't give us any. Oh, good Lord, if I had a revolver here I'd use it immediately! I'd shoot him in the back and split his heart in half. He doesn't deserve to be killed to his face. Traitor, dog, thief! Stealing other people's honor! And that foolish woman, letting herself be deceived! She doesn't deserve death, though. She deserves the galleys, yes, the galleys."

Since the day after the pitiful incident near Cuatro Caminos Maxi hadn't been more worked up or rancorous than he was on this occasion. Since that fateful night in November he had seldom seen his offender, and always from a distance. He'd never had him so close, at shooting range. "Oh, why didn't I bring a revolver? I could have stopped him dead. If I saw an arms store, I'd buy one. But I don't have any money. Auntie only gives me enough for the café. Lord, what despair! If you give me the idea of justice—a logical idea, a perfectly logical one— why don't you give me the means for carrying it out? To see him gasping, rolling over in his own blood, and me not feeling any pity for him. And to think I won't see it, Lord! And the whole world won't! The whole world would rejoice."

After going down Barrionuevo Street and across Progreso Square, the couple took San Pedro Mártir Street, always looking for the most deserted route. "They're going to take Cabeza Street," said Maxi, "where you never find a soul at this time. Oh, you miserable cur, murderer, seducer. Justice will be done to you some day; if not today, tomorrow. What I regret is that it won't be my hand that does it." He pursued them without letting them out of sight, quite some distance behind. "The wounds I got that night feel just as fresh as they did then. You coward—you only fight weaklings, sick people who can't defend themselves. The answer you should get is a bullet. Bang! And you'd drop in your tracks. And I'd be so pleased if I could give you what you deserve . . . so pleased and satisfied . . . just like a person who's done a very good deed, and I mean *really* good."

When he reached Ave María Street, Rubín crossed over to the odd-numbered side and lay in wait on the San Simón corner. They stopped; Aurora seemed to be telling her escort to stop there. The advice was prudent, and the man said good- bye, pressing her hand. Maxi watched him head for Magdalena Street and he felt an urge to scream and jump him: "Stealing my honor, everyone's honor. Now you're going to pay for it all!" He felt as if his nails had sharpened and turned into tiger claws. For a split second it seemed that Maxi would actually jump on his prey. Logic saved him. "I'm much weaker and he'll destroy me. A revolver, or a rifle—that's what I need."

When the lovers were out of sight, Rubín entered his house. The oddest part was that the idea of his wife was completely absent from his mind during the incident; or perhaps she was personified by Aurora, the picture of disloyalty and female treachery. Alone in his room, he was overtaken by an awful doubt. "But this business that's keeping me awake now," he said to himself, rolling over in bed, "is it true or did I dream it? I know I came in, I know I fell into bed, I know I fell asleep, and now I have this awful image in my mind. Did I really see them— the cad and her—or did I dream it? It's beyond a doubt that I just dozed off into a deep sleep. I'm beginning to think that it was a dream. Yes, it had to be a dream. Aurora's virtuous. Goodness, the things one dreams! But no, by God—I saw it! I know I did. I can still see it; I've got a picture of them in my mind. This is enough to drive a man crazy! And it would be such a pity, now that I'm so sane!"

All the next day he fought against this confusion. Had he seen it or dreamed it? On Ash Wednesday his aunt sent him to the Samaniegos' with a message, and after being there quite awhile (hearing "the piece"), he noticed that Doña Casta was talking very heatedly with Aurora. "Well, Aurora, you certainly stood us up today! Three hours waiting for you. Why do you have to go to the workshop today if everything's closed? Just like Palm Sunday: all afternoon at the workshop and then Pepe comes and tells me you never showed up there or anywhere near it. Where were you! Visiting the Reoyos girls! And what were you doing so long at their house? I have to find out."

Aurora defended herself ingeniously and willfully, in the manner of a person who knows she's of age and can, whenever she wishes, send maternal authority packing; but things didn't reach this point. Maxi, pretending to be absorbed by Olimpia's piece, didn't miss a word of that domestic quarrel, thanks to the fact that it occurred while Olimpia was handling the *andante cantabile molto expresivo*, because if it had coincided with the *allegro agitato*, not even God almighty would have been able to salvage a letter of the mother-daughter talk. During the *presto con fuoco*, Maxi said to himself: "It's hard to believe that I could have doubted even for a moment that it was pure reality. And I thought it was a dream! What an imbecile! A fact taken from positive existence has removed all my doubts. Logic isn't enough now; I have to see more . . . and I'll see it. What a lesson for my wife! Oh, my God—now I have another horrible doubt: if I kill her, there won't be any lesson. Teaching is more Christian than death; more cruel, perhaps, and certainly more logical. Let her live so she'll suffer, and by suffering she'll learn. But I should kill him. Yes, kill him!"

Hearing the boisterous end of the piece, he fell into a soporific state momentarily and then snapped out of it, plagued by the following thought: "No. Not kill him. His evil is necessary for this great punishment. Life is what hurts and teaches. Death is for the virtuous. For the perverse, logic . . . logic."

The toccata was barely over when Doña Casta came in, saying: "Maxi, Señora Quevedo has just called me from the courtyard window to ask you to drop by for a minute. She has a message for Lupe." The poor boy went up, and Doña Desdemona kept him waiting awhile because she was helping her husband undress. He had come in exhausted; they had called him at noon and he hadn't been able to come home until just then.

"Dear," the spherical lady said to Rubín, touching him on the shoulder in a friendly way. "Do me a favor and tell Lupe that the bad bird hatched an egg this morning . . . a very beautiful baby bird . . . and it all went well."

Maxi scratched his ear, and from his depths there rose to his lips a strange smile whose meaning Señora Quevedo could not fathom. "The bad bird," he said like a pampered child; "show it to me . . . and the chick . . . show it to me too."

"No, no, not now," replied Doña Desdemona, nudging him toward the door. "You'll see them tomorrow. Go tell your aunt now."

<h1 style="text-align:center">5</h1>

Doña Lupe's interest in "the bad bird" and whether it was hatching its egg safely or not is not understandable unless we take into account the great ideas that were budding in the worthy lady's mind those days. Her remarkable intelligence suggested solutions for every case and ways of harmonizing facts with principles as well as possible. Her motto was: we should always start with reality and sacrifice what seems best to what is good, and what is good to what is possible. She had learned this from her business experience, which she applied successfully to moral issues, just as mathematics (and the gymnastic agility that it gives the mind) aids in studying philosophy.

Well, thinking of her niece, she arrived at certain basic conclusions that she herself argued against but finally accepted as irrefutable, namely: that the matter couldn't be remedied; that disgrace was inevitable, although *she* wouldn't have to bear the brunt of it, for everyone knew that she had neither encouraged nor condoned Fortunata's straying. The last dog on the block knew that much. Therefore, the lady could afford to rest on this point. The second point: Fortunata might be as bad as one liked, but she *had* belonged to the family, whose most important member could hardly do less than visit the misguided young woman to ascertain her present condition and try to prevent her from flinging worse ignominies at the illustrious Rubín name. The problem was serious, and its solution was not within the grasp of an ordinary mind. The little creature who was going to present himself to the world was by nature's laws the successor to the Santa Cruzes; he was the only direct heir to a powerful, rich family. True, written law would say that the child was a Rubín; but the strength of blood ties and circumstances would overpower the fiction of written law, and if Señorito Santa Cruz didn't hasten to declare himself the real father and seek a way to transmit to his successor part of the opulence that he enjoyed, he would deserve the title of monster.

"Oh, if what happened to that goose had only happened to me!" she thought. "Now, would I let him get away without first giving me child support? I've got a real temper when it comes to things like this. If only she'd listen to me and let *me* handle it! I can tell you this much: she'd be sure to get at least two or three thousand *duros* for an allowance. The very first thing I'd do would be take myself over to see Doña Bárbara and tell her what was what. And I'll do it; I'll do it, even if the stupid girl doesn't authorize me to. I can't help it; my urge to do something is just terrible. I'll burst if I don't act. And I feel sorry for the baby, because it will be a shame for him to be poor with such a rich father. Why, in no time (supposing it's a boy), when he grows up and it's time to get him out of doing his military service, what's he going to do? No, this can't be left as it is. Poor little creature! Something has to be done. It all goes to show that one's charitable when one least expects to be. Oh, no—I'm not going to keep this thing under cover; I'm going to see Doña Bárbara. With my tongue and my knack for explaining things I'll make her see how senseless it would be for her grandson to be worse off than an orphan. After all, what's he going to live on? The mother and son will eat up the bank shares in a couple of years, and with the interest on the thirty thousand *reales* they don't have enough for soup. And as for money from Maxi—they won't get a *peseta*, I'll see to it! That would be the last straw! So. I'll start ringing bells if that Señorito doesn't arrange an allowance for her within a month. And I'll really ring them. I'll put on my velveteen coat, my cape, my gloves, and, on with it! But it occurs to me that I should air this with my friend Guillermina first. She could administer justice in this case. Yes, that's a magnificent idea! Guillermina will speak to her and . . . Now that feather-brained girl will see the difference between acting on her own and having me for a counselor and director. Do you want to bet that if he doesn't give her a cent she'll go right on just as sluggishly, not daring to do a thing, swallowing her bitterness, and dying of hunger? Not me. When I do good, I do it come hail or high water, and I ram it right down the throats of stubborn, useless people who don't know how to do anything for themselves."

These thoughts, which fermented in the brain of that great diplomat and stateswoman during the month of March, led to little notes entreating Ballester to visit Fortunata, and others to Quevedo to deliver the baby (she didn't hesitate to tell the ugly and clever professor of obstetrics that his fees would not be overlooked). Maxi had disconcerted her a bit the day he showed that he knew the secret, because the Señora, in making all her beneficent plans for the Santa Cruz heir, was working on the assumption that her nephew was completely ignorant of the truth. She was extremely happy to see him so serene; but it drove her mad to think that he would keep becoming more reasonable until he felt sorry for his wife and decided to allot her a small income so that she wouldn't beg for alms or become a prostitute. No; the other one, the one who had broken the glass, was the one who should pay for it.

Her thoughts were revolving around this when Maxi gave her Doña Desdemona's message. The first thing to which she directed her intelligent attention was the expression on the young man's face upon giving her the news, and she was shocked by its composure, for he made it clear that he had penetrated the real meaning of Señora Quevedo's allegory. After repeating the message verbatim, he added:

"It was this morning. Don Francisco had just gotten home and he was going to bed."

Doña Lupe pondered in astonishment: "Isn't he taking it calmly, though? And thank goodness he is. Is this sanity or what? Maybe it's what they call philosophy. But Lord help us if he suddenly turns to the opposite kind of philosophy."

"Are you planning to go see her?" the boy then inquired, in a completely natural tone.

"Me? Gracious, the idea! I see it's useless to try to fool you. With this new cleverness of yours you don't miss a trick. Me see her! It was only out of curiosity that I wanted to know what I know. From now on, it's as if she didn't exist. Don't you agree?"

"Completely. You see how serene and cold I am?"

"That's what I like. That's what's called being a philosopher in the full sense of the word and transcending human misery," declared the widow with either real or feigned emotion in her voice. "Don't ever think of her again."

"And even if I did, Aunt . . . even if I did—"

"What for? You're not going to see her."

"And even if I did see her, Aunt . . . even if I did . . ."

Doña Lupe felt rather uncomfortable when she heard these words, uttered with a certain insane tenacity. But then Maximiliano hastened to relieve her with another argument:

"Don't you notice how sane I am? I've never been like this, not even when I was at my best. Anybody else would be only too happy . . ."

The Señora latched onto this to change the subject.

"Well said. You know, your brother Juan Pablo doesn't seem right in the head to me lately. Today he was here giving me a headache again: either I give him that loan or he'll shoot himself. He won't shoot himself. He's egoism personified. Really, he's got a nerve. Asking me for money when he's a man who when he owes *you* some you can't get a penny out of him and he gets mad at you for trying to get back your own money. He says they're going to make him the secretary in a government of a province and I don't know what all. Do you believe him? Civil servants are low, but I doubt if they'd sink to . . ."

After that second desperate attack on his aunt, Juan Pablo had left the house more dead than alive. His aunt was no longer simply a bad woman; she was a monster, a fury, a mythological dragon. That shot he had threatened her with—how much better if he'd used it on her! "About that shot: should I or shouldn't I? I have no choice; I've got to," he thought as he entered Magdalena Street. "I don't see the answer anywhere. As for shooting myself—yes, I'd do it. Except I don't have a gun. Maybe I just won't shoot myself after all. I'm like that—so lazy I just can't get started. I'm beginning to see that it's one thing to say you're going to kill yourself, even though you believe it, and another to go ahead and do it. But I'm sticking to my ideas; I'll have to shoot myself in the end; there won't be any choice."

6

He was in a foul, foul mood all Maundy Thursday and Holy Friday. On Saturday, just after arriving at the office, Villalonga called him in. Rubín entered excitedly. "God!" he exclaimed to himself. "Do you suppose it's to give me the secretaryship? What a blow if it's not for that, though, . . . what a blow! I couldn't take it. As soon as I leave the director's office I'm going to blow my brains out, as sure as there's a God up above. The trouble is that I don't have a gun. Well, I'll jump out the window. No, I won't; I'd end up like a pancake. And anyway, I've got a hunch that he wants to make me secretary. Keep your chin up, Juan Pablo; this is going to be your lucky day."

The director was a very expeditious man, and without so much as offering him a seat, said:

"Rubín, you're a smart man and I can use you."

The director struck Rubín for his close resemblance to the Eternal Father, whom painters depict surrounded by cherub-covered clouds.

"I can use you, and I'm going to get you started on a career."

"Thank you very much, Señor Don Jacinto. I'm at your service, as you know."

"Well, I'm going to give you a big surprise. I need a man; and since I gather that you would know how to handle yourself in the delicate job I've got in mind for you—"

"The secretaryship of—"

"No, my friend; it's more than that. When I find a person who appeals to me and who's right, I say 'I'll lay my bet' and I bring him to work for me. I swear that I can use you, comrade. So bombs away: you're going to be the governor of a third-class province."

Rubín was at a loss for words. He felt as if the ceiling and the whole ministry had opened up.

"Yes, sir—governor of my province. I want to see how I can arrange it. You'll only have to deal with me. The secretary will give me a free hand."

"Mr. Director," babbled Rubín, "I'm at your command."

"Well, you'll be part of a project that will be ready for the king's signature tomorrow. We'll be in touch about it, and I'll let you know how it's going. I think we'll do well on it."

Then they had a smoke and talked a bit about the state of the province, deflowering the issue. People began to come into the office, and Rubín retired to start on his preparations. He didn't know what had hit him; he thought he was dreaming and pinched himself to see if he was really awake. He wandered in the streets for a while, completely dazed; he laughed out loud; then he felt like buying a gun just to fire it into the air. Ah, but what he *should* do was stick a few bullets in Doña Lupe's body . . . Yes, for being so mean and stingy. But no; he should forgive everybody. Life is beautiful, and governing a piece of the country would be the greatest of joys. Whenever he met any policemen or similar officers he looked on them—already!—as subordinates and came close to ordering them to arrest his aunt and Torquemada.

The big show took place in the café that night. At first he didn't say anything, hoping to spring it on them, but his friends saw that he wasn't the same. He infused his words with an authoritative inflection; he measured them carefully; he drank his coffee more slowly than usual; and his comments were frequently tinged with a new protective tone. "But Montes, my friend—don't worry. We'll see what we can do for you. Don Basilio has to give me some facts that I need on collection in province X. Listen, Relimpio, don't rush on your report; this situation's going to last. Cánovas will be in for quite some time. He's nobody's fool." And whenever a serious debate got going on politics, Rubín sided with the defenders of the most reasonable, conciliatory, tempered thesis. "After all, what do you think—that society can survive if it's always dreaming about upheavals? Let's be practical, gentlemen; let's not confuse what a bunch of little politicians say with the country itself."

Meanwhile *La Correspondencia* had come; at the first conspicuous glance that the good Don Basilio took at its columns, he spotted a list of new governors and, uttering a cry of surprise, rubbed his eyes thinking he must have misread it. Then, convinced that it was not an error, he exclaimed more loudly, and in a moment everyone knew about it. Juan Pablo was the object of acclaim and congratulations, some of them sincere, some tainted with well-feigned envy.

"My friend Villalonga has wanted this for some time now. Today he hammered on it so much I couldn't say no."

"And to think you've kept it so secret!"

From all sides of the chamber—I mean, the café—people hastened to congratulate the governor, and the waiter, to whom Juan Pablo owed over five months' consumption of goods, was happier than if he'd won at the lottery. Even the café owner came over and shook his customer's hand, asking him if there might be a spot in the province's offices for a nephew of his whose handwriting was very good.

"I can't give you 'yes' or 'no' for an answer, Don José. We'll see. I have tons of commitments. But you know that I'll do everything in my power to help you."

My man's pleasure that night was compensation for the many months of suffering and sadness. Everyone nearby regarded him with astonishment and respect, as one looks at someone who is, has been, or is about to be somebody in this world. Whatever subjects the circle discussed that night Rubín approached judiciously. There was a need to restore the morals of provincial administrations, end all abuses; and he was very firm on this last point. His outline for his conduct was very political. Adapt himself and get along for as long as he could, push a conciliatory attitude to extremes, and when he was completely in the right, raise the stick and let anyone who so much as stepped out of line have it hard. After all, the institutions that support social order deserve respect. When corrupting materialism starts to take hold, you've got to stir up faith and support honest consciences. And as for *his* province, the "professional revolutionaries" would be risking their necks if they tried to preach certain ideas. Quite a temper, his! In short, some Spaniards had no breeding and one had to keep a few rascals from tricking the innocent. The majority are good, but there are always lots of dumb ones—you know, naive types—and the government should protect them, see that they're not tricked. As for the morals of the administration, there was nothing to say. He had not, and would not, stand for certain things. He'd already told Villalonga that he was accepting on the condition that he wouldn't be restricted in persecuting and exterminating the rascals. "A lot of jerks throwing their weight around now are going to be led personally, by me, to jail. That's how I am—take me or leave me."

Don Basilio was among those who were sincerely happy about Juan Pablo's "stroke of luck." The job wasn't "in his field," so he didn't envy him. If it had been an administrative post in the economy of a province, Don Basilio would not have rejoiced at his neighbor's good fortune. As long as his standing wasn't affected . . . As a matter of fact, the minister had given *him* a dizzying assignment—a project to regulate collections on industrial subsidies. "These plums always fall in my lap. It just so happens that over there in the secretary's office they don't know the background of this or that. 'Oh, of course! La Caña will know!' So they come to me. Or someone in Congress asks for a report on the state of codification in the Treasury. What a mess! No one has the faintest: 'Ah! Maybe La Caña . . .' And La Caña gets them out of the spot. Or else the minister wants to find out what's been done to set up a fiscal registry, which is the best way to uncover the wealth that's being hidden. Well, he turns the place inside out, looking high and low till it occurs to someone to say 'La Caña—he's the man.' And he's right—La Caña was the first one to do research on fiscal registry." In a word, if because of some catastrophe Don Basilio failed to appear at the Treasury, it would collapse, like a building without a foundation.

Leopoldo Montes hoped that Rubín would let him tag along as his secretary, but it wouldn't be easy. "I'll mention it to Villalonga, Leopoldo. But I think a secretary comes with the job. I'll see if I can get you in as a police inspector." Other members of the *tertulia* were envious, and although they congratulated and adulated the favored one, they also predicted the troubles that he would have in governing a province. But the fact is that flattery, envy, ambitious greed, curiosity, and a craving for novelty considerably augmented the group from the time Rubín was named governor to the day he departed for his new post.

These were very busy days for him; he had to take care of all his personal business and outfit himself with new clothes. And what interfered with his movements and bothered him were certain domestic dissensions. Refugio, who was already giving herself the airs of a governor's wife and had laced her farewells with offers to patronize everybody, was petrified when her master announced that he could not take her. Pouts, tears, cries, complaints, shouts. "But, my dear, try to understand the situation; don't be like that. Don't you see that I can't present myself in the capital of my province with a woman who's not my wife? What would high society say, and the others, and the middle class? It would rob me of my prestige, dear, and we wouldn't be able to live there. It can't be done. A fine state of affairs it would be if the governor, whose mission it is to supervise the morals of the public, set such an example himself. The man who's supposed to see that laws are respected, failing to obey the most basic ones himself! Some condition society would be in, if the representative of the State practically preached concubinage! Not even savages do that. So convince yourself; it simply can't be. You stay here and I'll send you whatever you need. But don't dare ever set foot in my capital, because if you do, your little 'lovey-dove' would have to nab you— and you know what a temper I have—nab you and turn you over to the police."

VI. The End

I

FORTUNATA HEARD A NOISE AT THE DOOR and then: "May I come in?" "Come in, Don Segismundo," she replied, recognizing the pharmacist's voice. And he came in with a cheerful face and an officious attitude, like someone who thinks he's useful. The young woman was sitting up in bed wearing a dressing jacket and a scarf on her head. "Isn't she sumptuous!" thought Ballester as he greeted her, pressing her hand warmly. "What a pity!"

"You weren't let in yesterday," she said amiably, "because I didn't know who it was and I didn't want any visitors. I'm scared to death, and at night I dream that someone is coming to steal him from me. Do you want to see him?"

Beside her, the newborn character was sleeping placidly, and she wanted to show his precocious charms to her friend, so, more proudly than timidly, she drew back the sheets, leaving in full view the little pink face and clenched fists of the tender infant.

"Well, he certainly is a pretty baby!" said Ballester, craning forward. "He has someone to take after on both sides."

"He's been in this deep sleep for two hours now. What an angel! And if you could only see what an appetite the little rascal has! He's come into this world to have a good life. If you could only see the way he looks at me. Poor little thing! He loves me very much. He knows that I love him more than my own life, and that my world revolves around him."

"Remember what we agreed on. I'm to be his excellency's godfather. You promised me so the last time we saw each other."

"Yes, yes, I know; and I won't go back on my word. You will be his godfather."

"And after his first name—which you'll choose" (swelling as he spoke) "he'll bear mine: Segismundo. What do you think?"

"Fine. His name is going to be Juan, then Evaristo, then Segismundo."

"All right; I'll settle for third place. But I won't be put back any further. If you try to push me to fourth place I'll protest."

They both laughed. Ballester had sat down on a chair next to the bed, his eyes glued to that woman whom he found more beautiful than ever. "I'd like to give her a few kisses," he thought, "friendly, purely Platonic ones, because this poor woman touches me. And no matter what they say, she's not as bad as people make her out to be." Then he began to give her news of the family and friends, which Fortunata received very curiously.

"Doña Lupe, despite all her ferocity, hasn't forgotten you. Every day she asks Quevedo or me for news, and she asks about the baby too—whether he's strong, if he's nursing well, if he has some physical defect—"

"Defect!" exclaimed the indignant mother. "He's beautiful. More perfect than perfection itself. I'll show him to you bare so you can see what a beautiful son I have. I'm crazy about him. But I'm afraid they're going to come and take him away from me. There are so many envious women around!"

After letting her streak of maternal enthusiasm run its course, Ballester continued with:

"But what will astonish you is to know that our friend Maxi is so much better that if you saw him now you wouldn't recognize him."

"Can it be true? No—it's just one of your jokes."

"No, dear. Whenever anything that's hard to solve comes up at home or in the neighborhood, they consult him. He's become a walking dictionary. Whenever

Doña Desdemona has any trouble in her bird kingdom she calls on him and does whatever he recommends."

"Well, you've got a lot to say today. I only hope it's true. I'd be very happy as long as he didn't remember me at all or even know that I'm alive."

"Well, I'm afraid you won't be granted that. He knows everything."

"Oh my God, you don't mean it!" very frightened and turning pale. "You have no idea how scared that makes me. I won't have a quiet moment ever again. Is it true? Don't play games with me, Ballester. Look—I'm trembling with fear."

"Fear? Of what? He's very reasonable and calmer than ever. All his thoughts revolve around benevolence and tolerance. He hardly talks, and if he does, it's to make some very good observation. He couldn't say anything silly, not even if you asked him to as a favor. As for you, I think that what he feels is indifference— that is, if indifference can be called a feeling."

"I don't trust him," she said thoughtfully, showing in her tone that her mind was not at rest. "You'll see, when you're least expecting it . . ."

The conversation went from Maxi to the Samaniego girls, and Fortunata showed her surprise that Aurora had not remembered her.

"It's because she has no manners. She knows very well where I am, and it's only a three-minute walk from where she works. And if she didn't want to come, what trouble would it have been to send one of the girls from the shop to ask if I was alive or dead? It really hurt my feelings. You know me—if someone loves me at all, I repay them a hundred times over."

Ballester answered with a deep sigh, which his interlocutor did not interpret correctly. Suddenly the pharmacist changed the subject.

"Oh—I almost forgot the best part. Did you know that the critic and I have become friends? Who would have guessed it! Hating him as I did. It was like this: Padillita brought him into the pharmacy one day and I started to pull his leg about his articles, telling him how much I liked them. Well, as it turns out, he's very modest and gets all flustered when he's praised. Little by little we've gotten to know each other better, and all my spite for him has vanished. Poor Ponce is so honest he can't write anything unless his conscience approves of it. Even when he praised that awful play that almost drove me mad he did it because that's what he felt. And even though the pay is bad or late or there isn't any he's just as happy with his 'priesthood'; he takes it very seriously and thinks that nobody will have an opinion on plays if he doesn't give his. He's taken the exams for a position in the Exchequer and he's been given it. And you know what? The poor guy has to support his mother, who's ill, so ever since he told me about his situation I don't charge him for medicines. We kid him about Olimpia and her 'piece,' telling him that his fiancée is very romantic and that he shouldn't be afraid to marry her, because she doesn't eat anyway, so they don't need a cook or a kitchen or even a basket for the shopping. I tell him he should give up the 'priesthood' and let all the authors and the audience take care of themselves as best as they can. He agrees with me, and he finally told me a secret: he's written a play, and the Teatro Español has it, and if it's put on, it's sure to be a hit. I plan to attend the opening with all my friends to make a show and clap for the author to come onstage for at least forty curtain calls. He wants to read it to me, and I told him to bring it over. Without reading it I'll tell him that it's magnificent, and a friend of mine who's a journalist will put in a blurb to the effect of 'in literary circles someone who's causing constant comment lately is . . .' I tell you, the poor boy interests me a lot; I'd like to do something for him if I could. I've already given him half a pint of salve and plenty of belladonna, because his mother had rheumatism. I've also made him a poultice, which costs quite a bit. That's the way I am; whoever I take a fancy to can have the shirt off my back. And if you could only see how fond he's grown of me! We have long chats about realist art and the ideal and esthetic emotions, and no matter what I say, even if it's pure nonsense (because I've never been caught in that spot before) he listens to me as if it were the Gospel truth, and I simply shine, talking away to him. Aside from all this criticism business, he's the milk of human kindness; he's very grateful, very considerate, and has no weaknesses, except loving Olimpia and thinking that a man with any brains can marry such a useless creature. I've decided to take it out of his head, and I think I'm beginning to succeed. I ask him 'What are you going to live on? The piano piece?' If they get married, there'll be four in the family—the couple, his mamá, who's ill, and a little sister who from what Ponce says must have an appetite like a horse. We talk this over at length at the pharmacy (which we call the 'literary circle') and I'm beginning to make him see it my way. Olimpia would tear my eyes out if she knew what I was saying to her fiancé; but let her get mad. I've seen her run through seven of them, and she's not going to catch this one either. I've taken him under my wing and I'm going to save him. Some prize he'd get, marrying her!"

"Oh, what laughs there are with you! Poor Ponce! I told you he was a good boy, and you insisted on trying to trick him."

"He escaped a good one, all right. I'm keeping the fatal yolk for somebody else; yes, for someone who attracts all my hatred. Don't ask me who it is, because I'm not going to tell you. I'll tell you after the person's swallowed it, because that person's going to eat it, as sure as this is day."

At that moment the sound of voices in the adjoining room amplified considerably, and the following words reached Ballester's ears: "I bet on the ace, and stake my whole hand."*

"It's my Uncle José," said Fortunata, "playing *mus* with a friend. I ask him to come over to keep me company while I'm in bed because I get very scared. And so

*This only roughly translates the text, which describes a move in a Spanish card game called *mus*.

he won't get bored I have a bottle of beer sent up and let his friend come keep him company."

Ballester walked over to the door to look at the couple. He didn't know either of them, but Ido del Sagrario's face wasn't new to him; he felt he'd seen it somewhere before, although he couldn't remember where or when.

2

The first time Ballester saw Izquierdo and his learned friend he spoke only a few polite words, but the second time there was such a crossfire of compliments, invitations, and frank exchanges that it wasn't long before friendship tied the three in a tight knot.

From her bedroom, where she continued confined to her bed, Fortunata laughed at Segismundo's witticisms, designed to coax out something from Platón and Ido del Sagrario, whom he usually called "maestro." Whenever the pharmacist came at night he inevitably found the two men there and he had a grand time joking with them.

The unfortunate girl was very thankful for those visits. Ballester had the most decent, generous heart in the world, and he took it upon himself to proudly perform duties that by all rights should have been performed by others but that had been shirked. And although he had long-term hopes of a romantic nature about Señora Rubín, his charitable acts were nonetheless pure and disinterested, and he would not have done less even if his friend had been frightfully ugly and devoid of any charm whatsoever.

Fortunata was beginning to trust him more and more, so she revealed some of her thoughts to him. There was one, however, that she dared not show for fear of being misunderstood. Segunda and José Izquierdo wouldn't understand it either. But she simply had to spill out those thoughts—which were already overflowing from her mind—so she was forced to tell them to herself to keep from drowning. "Now I'm *really* not afraid of comparisons. What a difference there is between her and me! I'm the mother of the only 'son in the family,' I'm the mother, it's very plain; the only grandson Don Baldomero has is this king of the world that I've got with me here. Would anybody dare try denying it? It's not my fault if the law says such and such. Laws are a lot of stupid nonsense and I don't have anything to do with them. Why did they make them like that? The real law is blood ties, or, as Juan Pablo says, nature, and because of nature I've gotten back the place that 'Angel Face' took away from me. I'd like to have her here *now* to tell her a few things and show her this son. Oh, what envy when she finds out! She'll be furious! Let her come to me with laws now—she'll see the answer I've got for her. But no,

I don't feel bitter about her; now that I've won the lawsuit and she's underneath, I forgive her; that's how I am.

"And him? When he finds out, what will he do? What will he think? I just can't imagine, Lord! He may be a cad and ungrateful, but when it comes to his own little boy he's got to love *him*. Hmmm, he'll be mad about him. And when he sees that he's the spitting image of himself . . . Christ! And if Doña Bárbara saw him, why. . . And she will, she'll see him . . . As sure as there's a God, she'll be nuts about him. Oh, I'm so happy, Lord, so happy! I know very well that I'll never be able to be on close terms with that family, because I'm very vulgar and they're all so refined; what I want is for it to be recognized, yes, Sir, recognized, that yours truly is the mother of the heir, and that without yours truly they wouldn't have a grandson. That's my idea, the idea I've been nurturing deep down inside for so long, keeping it safe till it pushed its way out, like a baby bird cracking open its shell. But God only knows, I didn't think of this because I wanted to get something. I don't want their money for anything in the world; I don't need it. What I want is for it to be recognized. Yes, Señora Doña Bárbara, you're my mother-in-law over Our Father's holy head, and no matter how hard you try to squirm out of it, I'm the mother of your grandson, your only grandson."

She was wholly convinced of it after uttering these arrogant affirmations, and her satisfaction made her so content that she started to sing softly, lulling her son; and when he fell asleep, she kept on humming, like a bird in a nest. Her pleasure from these thoughts kept her awake some nights, and she spent long hours toying with the idea she had turned into reality, juggling it the way Feijóo had done with the bilboquet ball.

Quevedo visited her daily, but although he found her in very good condition, he ordered her not to get up. What a bore, being a prisoner so long! Thanks to her little one she had some entertainment. At night, Segunda helped her bathe and dress him, and during the day, Encarnación did; she was quite capable. Whenever her mistress let her hold the tiny creature for a few minutes she was ecstatic. In her moments of delirious happiness, Fortunata thought very often of Estupiñá. "Aunt, haven't you met Plácido on the stairs? Tell him to come in, that I have to speak to him." Segunda replied that she had seen him not just once or twice, but at least twenty times, but that all the hints she'd dropped about a visit had been in vain. "When I told him the news, he looked at me like a judge. And yesterday he said to me: 'Get out of my way, you cheating woman! I'm going to throw you and your bragging niece in the street!'"

"He'll come around. What do you bet he does?" said the young woman, smiling. "I want him to come in here and see this star that has fallen out of the sky."

Segunda did so much and talked so cleverly that one morning Estupiñá came in grunting and pretending to be in such an awful mood that he had to contract all the muscles of his face to repress his indignation. He responded to whatever

Segunda and her brother said with a snort, and if Señora Izquierdo hadn't restrained him, he would undoubtedly have made a run for the stairs. "You can't talk to braggarts like these. Go to the devil. I hope you fry in hell." Venting his anger—true or fake—and so on, the fact is that he did not leave, and Segunda got him into the bedroom (almost by force). Obeying an instinctive impulse, Estupiñá took off his hat the minute he heard the Santa Cruz heir cry; he was sorely in need of his mamá's breast. Seeing the talker uncover his venerable head, Fortunata's soul was flooded with joy, and she said inwardly: "That's right. Greet your little master. He'll protect you just as his grandparents and his father have." Plácido leaned forward to look at him, and even though he wanted to act cold, this sentence slipped out: " 'Xactly . . . 'xactly like him."

"He's so ugly, isn't he, Don Plácido?" exclaimed the mother, radiant with joy. "Aren't you going to kiss him? Do you think you'll catch something? Don't worry, good looks don't rub off. You know something, Don Plácido? I think you're going to adore him, and he's going to adore you, too. Do you want to bet?"

The talker murmured something that was unintelligible.

For a moment he seemed caught between furor and gentleness. Then he broke out in a conversation with Segunda on whether or not she planned to set up a stand at the San Isidro festival that year, and at last he left, saying good-bye in a manner that could easily have been judged conciliatory. Fortunata was extremely content and reflected: "He's sure to go telling people now. That's what I want— for him to gossip." Associating freely, she thought about the pleasure she would derive from seeing Doña Guillermina, presuming at the same time that if she saw her she would feel most embarrassed. "I'll ask her to forgive me for how badly I behaved that day, and she'll forgive me, as sure as there's light. She'll give me a good scolding first, but I'd go through anything just to see her face when she looks at my son. I wonder what she'll say about my idea. What will occur to her? Something I won't understand; nobody will. No matter what she says and how she looks at it, God can't go back on what He's done; and even if the world comes to an end, this son of mine is the legitimate blood grandson of those people, Don Baldomero and Doña Bárbara. And as for her—she may be as angelic as you want, but she's not good at this; that's what I say. Let her show me a son like this. She won't; that's for sure. God said to me, 'You'll be the one who carries him,' and He didn't say anything of the sort to her. And if Doña Bárbara lost her head over the fake Pituso, what will she do over the pure gold one! I'm so happy I think I'm going to be sick. Estupiñá's sure to talk about it. What I want is for my friend 'the bishop woman' to know first. You want to bet she comes to see me? She'll be here, all right; she's not going to waste that sermon she's got ready for me. So it's a sermon! I don't care. Better. I'll tell her she's right. But I've got the child, and having the child makes you right."

She considered the visit an inevitable event; the saint relished reprimanding

and correcting anyone who had committed serious sins. Fortunata was so sure of
seeing her that whenever the bell rang she thought it was the saint and got ready
to receive her, fixing up the bed and trying to look as decent as possible, quivering
with emotion and hope.

3

The baptism was held most modestly at San Ginés Church one morning in
April, and the baby was given the names Juan, Evaristo, Segismundo, and a few
more. Ballester, in a magnanimous gesture, invited Izquierdo and Ido del Sagrario
to lunch at the nearby Café Levante. He urged the maestro to have a steak, but
Don José declined—although it wouldn't have pained him to accept. Just smelling the meat and seeing the juice run out of it into the grease on his friends' plates
was enough to upset him. His lunch was a cup of coffee with half . . . then
all . . . of a toasted roll. After coffee came the tantalizing drinks, and the professor stuck to his scruples again. Not "the model," though: he filled up on rum
until it practically ran out of him, and yet his solid head was unfazed by it; it must
have been a distillery. While they were eating, they saw Maximiliano Rubín go by
on his way out of the café; but since he pretended not to see them, they said
nothing. At about one o'clock Ballester left for the pharmacy and the two Josés
left too for the house in the Cava. It was Sunday, and neither man was busy.
Izquierdo sent Encarnación out for a big bottle of beer, and, taking the dominoes
out of a filthy box, he spread them out and mixed them up to start a game. And
according to the "Platonic" chronicles, the dominoes were abandoned halfway
through the second game. Ido had gotten up and started pacing around the room.
Izquierdo sank onto the sofa and slept like an animal, his hat pulled over his eyes,
his mouth hanging open, his four paws stretched out, limp. Señá Segunda took
Encarnación off to the square because there had been a fire there the night before
that had damaged several stands next to hers, and she spent all morning helping
fellow workers salvage the remains and repair whatever could be repaired.

Fortunata was terribly bored that day and wanted very much to get up. Out of
respect for Señor Quevedo's orders she stayed in bed, but she wouldn't be able to
bear that awful jail two days longer. After being brought home from San Ginés,
Juan Evaristo Segismundo looked so handsome and satisfied it seemed as if he had
comprehended his happy admittance to the family of Christians, and to celebrate,
as soon as he was restored to his mother's side, he searched for the pantry and
filled himself so full that he couldn't fit another drop into his replete little body.
Fortunata could hear the venerable Platón's snoring like the monologue of a pig;

she also heard Ido's pacing and an unintelligible monosyllable every now and then, sighs that sounded like sorrowful laments or poetic invocations, and when the professor's meandering took him as far as the bedroom door, she thought she saw his hands or part of an arm reaching up almost to the ceiling. Then the bell rang and Don José got up to open the door. Fortunata thought that it was Encarnación on her way back from the square, but she was mistaken. It wasn't long before she heard whispering at the door. Who could it be? Then she heard steps and a squeaking of boots that made her tremble; she was paralyzed by fear upon seeing Maximiliano standing in the doorway. It was he; she recognized the fact after doubting it for a moment. Her stupefaction hardly allowed her to cry out, and her first movement was to throw her arms around the baby, resolved to devour whoever tried to harm him or take him away from her. Rubín stood there for over a minute without taking a step, stuck to the doorway and standing out in that frame like a subject in a painting. And it was so odd! She didn't detect the slightest sign of hostility in either his face or his gestures. He looked at his wife seriously but not severely, and as he took the first few steps toward the bed, his expression was almost indulgent. She, however, was not in full possession of herself, and looked at him as if she were preparing to defend herself energetically, "Uncle, Uncle!" she cried, raising her voice. "Encarnación!" Since neither her uncle nor the maid replied, she tried to call the zombie who was pacing around in the other room. But just as she was about to pronounce his name, it vanished from her memory. "What the devil is that man's name? . . . Hey you! Come here! Ah, now I remember. Señor Sagrario, please wake up my uncle!" But her uncle didn't wake up; nor did Don José give any sign that he had heard her call.

"It seems that you're afraid of me and you're calling for help," Maxi said with cold kindness. "I'm not going to eat you up. You're wrong if you think that I've come with malicious intent. It's no longer a question of killing you or anybody else. That stupid idea left me long ago . . . luckily for everyone."

Saying this, he sat down on the chair, and, taking off his hat, he put it on the bed. Fortunata found him thinner, he looked balder, and his expression had a certain calmness that she found reassuring.

"Even though nobody breathed a word," proceeded Rubín, "I know everything that's happened to you; I figured it out with my own reasoning; I've come to sympathize with you and do something good. I lost my mind, as you well know. But I got it back. God took it away from me and gave it back to me so whole that I'm now saner than you and the rest of the family. Don't be astonished, dear; you'll soon see, from what I'm going to tell you, that my head is perfectly clear, better than it ever was, in fact. What, don't you believe me?"

Fortunata didn't know whether to believe him or not. Her fear had not subsided yet, and she suspected that after those calm words there would be other, angry ones that wouldn't make any sense. She didn't say anything and continued to protect her son as if she were defending him from the first attack. Maxi didn't seem to notice the baby. Very serenely, he began:

"I'm so sane now that I fully realize your situation and mine. There can't be anything between us anymore. We were married because of your weakness and my error. I adored you; you did not adore me. An impossible marriage. Divorce had to come and it did. I went mad and you freed yourself. Nature corrected our foolish actions. You can't protest against nature."

He looked at the protuberance on the bed caused by Juan Evaristo; but since his gesture had no hostility in it, Fortunata began to feel more relaxed.

"I already know what you've got there. Poor child! God didn't will it that he be mine. If he had, you would have loved me, at least a little. But he's not mine—everybody knows it, and I know it too . . . A consummated divorce. It's better like this. I shouldn't have married you. I certainly paid a high price for it, losing my mind. What should I do now that I have it back? See things from up above, and respect facts and observe the tremendous lessons that God teaches His creatures. First He taught me; now you. Prepare yourself. I haven't come to do you any harm, but to tell you the good news about the lesson, because these godsends heal and cure and strengthen."

"I wonder if this man," thought Fortunata, "is sane or crazier than he was before? Some headache he's going to give me! But as long as he doesn't go beyond this, I can take it."

She wanted to say something out loud, but he wouldn't let her get in a word edgewise; and as if he'd come with a prepared speech and didn't want to leave out any of it, he went right on with:

"Do you remember when I was crazy? You more than deserved the bad times I gave you, because after all, you were behaving very badly toward me. Your infidelity had seeped into my mind; I didn't have any facts to base my thoughts on, yet I couldn't help but feel convinced. I really couldn't say whether I dreamed that you were going to become a mother or whether my jealousy gave me the idea. Because I was jealous, you know; oh, was I jealous! I could hardly bear it. 'My wife's cheating on me,' I told myself. 'All she can do is cheat on me, that's the way it's got to be.' And since I loved you so much, I couldn't find any solution for your sin except death—that's why I got that notion of liberation, excuses, and tricks to justify murder and suicide. The thoughts grew on me like moss on a trunk. What it was, really, was a reflection of common ideas, collective thought modified and adulterated by my sick brain. Oh, was I sick! I tell you, when I invented that ridiculous philosophical system I was going through the worst phase. I hate to remind myself of it. I remember the crazy things I said the way you remember stuff that's said in novels you read when you were little. And now I can laugh at them, and I can imagine how much everybody else must have, too. Do you remember?"

Fortunata nodded her assent. She didn't take her eyes off him for a second, watching his movements attentively in case he lost his composure; she was prepared for any sort of aggression.

"Then I had an attack of what I call 'messiahnitis.' That was a mental version of jealousy too. The messiah . . . your son, the son of a father who wasn't your husband! First I got the idea that I ought to kill you and your descendant, and then this idea boiled up and decomposed, like a substance put in the heat; and in the foam that absurd business about the messiah started to bubble up. Examine it closely and you'll see that it was nothing but jealousy, jealousy fermented and putrified. Oh, but it's awful, being crazy! It's so much better being sane, even though when you come back to your senses you find the furnace of your affections cold—all the life in your heart dead, limited to a logical, cold, rather sad life."

Upon hearing this, which Maxi expressed quite eloquently, Fortunata felt disturbed again, and she called her uncle, who kept sending snores in reply. She got the same results when she called "Señor Sagrario . . . Señor Sagrario, please come here." Don José appeared at the door, threw the couple the kind of look a schoolmaster gives a classroom he's inspecting, and resumed his pacing without realizing anything at all.

Rubín drew his chair closer and Fortunata became more frightened.

"But all that nonsense about liberation and the messiah is over. Real facts have substituted for my brain's concoctions. God gave me back my reasoning powers in an improved state. That's why I could see the facts; that's how I discovered what my family was hiding from me; that's what let me reconstruct myself, as it were, after having endured so many cataclysms. With my new power I was able to grasp our divorce, and I discarded the idea of homicide several times; that's how I was finally able to consider you a stranger, the mother of children I couldn't have; and that's how I've clothed myself in serenity and conformity. Aren't you amazed to see me like this? You'd be even more astounded if you could read my mind and comprehend this elevation of mine when I judge things; the calm with which I can consider you, the indifference that I feel toward your child. Another person in the world! Since he's come, he must have his reasons. What right do I have to try to obstruct his life? What right to kill you because you've given him life? Remember, it's a very serious matter to go so far as to say, 'So and so should never have been born.'"

"My God!" Fortunata exclaimed inwardly. "Is this man sane or what? Is he talking sense or saying the most absurd things I've ever heard in my life?"

"What I ask is," added Maxi, drawing even closer, "is this: the right to be born—isn't it the most sacred of all rights? Who says I can obstruct a person's birth? A fine state of affairs that would be. Let them be born and live; they'll learn."

"As far as I'm concerned," thought his wife, "he's worse than before. What he says may be sane but I don't understand a bit of it."

"You seem to be afraid of me," he said, always serious and calm. "I don't know why. You must have seen that nobody could beat me at being reasonable."

"Yes, that's true . . . but—"

"But what?"

"You're probably thinking you don't want to be burned twice," he said, smiling faintly for the first time in that lecture. "And there's something else: show me your son."

Fortunata was terror-stricken again, and when she saw Maxi reach out to where the little creature was, she pushed him away, saying:

"You'll see him another day. Leave him alone—he's asleep and you'll wake him up."

"Well, you're certainly obsessed with him! I thought that after hearing me out you'd be convinced that my mind is running like clockwork and that you'd notice my new talent. What have you seen in me that seems suspicious? Absolutely nothing. My feelings are peaceful; I had my last evil thought some days ago, but I tore it out and I'm cleansed of anger and hatred. To say it all in a word: I'm a saint, Fortunata. This isn't bragging; it's the truth. Do you think I'm going to harm your son? Harm a defenseless creature! It wouldn't be humane. Let me see him, and I'll tell you something you'll enjoy knowing."

Finally, fearing that contradicting him might irritate him, she allowed him to see the baby—as long as he didn't get too close—protecting the child with her hands. He didn't say anything while he was looking. Then he returned to his seat and sat for a while, absently staring at the design on the bedspread, his brow knit.

"He looks like the man who has been your downfall. Evil never perishes—it engenders itself, and the virtuous are annihilated in sterility."

4

"Uncle, for God's sake, wake up!" Fortunata cried again. And when the flaccid, warty figure of Ido del Sagrario appeared in the doorway again, the young woman reproofed him: "Why haven't you woken up my uncle? The two of you have left me completely alone in here! And Encarnación staying away so long!"

Ido muttered something Fortunata couldn't hear. Looking at the professor piteously, Maxi said to his wife: "That good man is touched. I feel very sorry for him because I know what it's like to be wrong in the head. If he wanted to follow my plan, I'd commit myself to curing him."

And in a louder voice, seeing the miserable man approach the door again and look in stupidly, he said: "Señor Don José, calm down and learn to see life as it is. It's foolish to believe that things are what we imagine them to be and not what they happen to feel like being. Love can't be restricted by laws. If a wife's unfaithful, there's a divorce, and let logic work things out—it punishes enough without any sticks or stones."

Fortunata made the sign of the cross, full of admiration, saying to herself: "Can it really be, oh my God, that my husband's been given a privileged mind all of a sudden? Or are these things he says a farce to cover up an evil scheme? What can I do so he'll leave soon? He's apt to take me unawares and really give me a scare."

"He looks like your enemy!" repeated Maxi, picking up the idea that had excited him. "It's bad luck for him. And if he turns out to be a pure type morally, it'll be worse than worst. An innocent child isn't responsible for his parents' sins, but he inherits their bad traits. Poor child! I feel sorry for him. If he dies on you, you should be happy, because if he lives, he'll give you a lot of sorrow."

This idea made Fortunata indignant, but she didn't dare try to contradict it. Let him say all he wanted. Her plan was to keep quiet and see if he got bored and left soon.

"He's got some model to take after," Maxi added with mournful irony. "His father's a gem. You don't have to tell me that he has ignored you. I can guess as much. He probably hasn't even come to see you. I can imagine that, too. He won't come, either; you can count on that."

"Who knows!" slipped from the young woman, who felt a lump forming in her throat.

"I repeat: he won't come. I have my reasons for saying so."

"Of course not. Why should he? I don't need him anyway."

"You're right. I'm glad to hear you be philosophical about it. That man is busy with other amusements now."

Fortunata felt all her blood rush up to her face, and for a moment she felt asphyxiated. Rubín leaned his elbow on the bed lazily, taking the position he used when he read at the pharmacy.

"You should know soon. The longer you take to find out, the longer you'll be in recovering."

La Pitusa felt stifled, and, picking up a fan that was next to her pillow, she began to fan herself.

"You have to know about it," Maxi repeated with the implacable coldness characteristic of a man used to murder. "Your hangman has completely forgotten about you; he's having an affair with another woman."

"With another woman!" she said, echoing the phrase as if it were a crutch, but a useless one. Her eyes wandered vaguely about the design on the bedspread.

"Yes, with another woman. You know her."

The murderer gave his victim the words in small doses and watched the effect they produced. Fortunata tried to control herself during this torture, and, shaking her uncombed head, as if to scare off a conviction that was trying to take hold of her, she said: "What are these stories you're bringing me? Leave me alone."

"What I'm telling you isn't gossip or anything made up; it's the truth. That man is in love with another woman and you know her. So learn about it. That's the marvelous weapon of human logic, which I'm going to use on you. It will hurt, but then you'll be healed. It's better to die learning than to live not knowing. This terrible lesson can take you to sainthood, which is my condition now. And who's responsible for my blessed state? A lesson, a simple lesson. Listen, Fortunata: blessed be the knife that heals."

"What you claim has to be proved, though," said the victim in self-defense.

"You don't have to believe it, just the way a patient doesn't have to take the medicine his doctor prescribes for him. And this is the medicine for your conscience. Do you want more? Do you want the name of the woman who has stolen what you stole? Well, I'm going to give it to you."

Fortunata felt dizzy, and when she sat up, her head clouded over and the room started to spin. Covering her eyes, she said to her husband:

"You must tell me."

"She's a very good friend of yours."

"A friend of mine!"

"Yes, and her name starts with A."

"Aurora, it's Aurora!" she exclaimed, bolting upright in bed and looking at her husband like a respectable person who has just been dealt a blow.

"She's the one."

"For some time my heart's been trying to tell me, but very faintly, and I didn't want to listen."

"I'm as sure of my statement as a person could be."

"You're deceiving me, you're deceiving me," replied the young woman, looking like the Virgin of Sorrows. "You want to kill me, and instead of coming to shoot me you've come with that story."

"If you want to take it as a deathblow, go ahead," Rubín declared with inexorable coldness.

"Aurora . . . Aurora! Good God, what a hideous idea!" becoming very agitated. "But it can't be. This man is crazy and he doesn't know what he's saying."

"Me, crazy?" (unperturbed). "All right, try defending yourself with that. But you'll see, and then you'll be convinced. There's no way out. The truth will win. It's like a shot that never misses. Do you want more details? When Aurora leaves work, he's waiting for her on Santo Tomás Street and they go on together toward Ave María. On Sundays, Aurora tells her family she's going to the workshop and where she goes is—"

"Shut up. Shut up, I tell you!" shouted Fortunata, writhing now. "You're a liar, a slanderer."

"Well, what did you expect?" with a glacial smile. "You've got to take the good with the bad, dear. What did you want—to wound and not be wounded? Kill and not be killed? That's life. Today you're doing the stabbing and tomorrow you're getting it. Do you still have doubts?"

The victim was silent. She didn't doubt it, no; what that man, who sometimes sounded insane and sometimes not, was saying was based on a true fact. The miserable young woman felt something confirming it in her mind and inundating it with light. She recalled words and acts, tied together the loose ends, and . . . It was true. As sure as there's a God, it was true. The poor boy might be gone, but what he said was true.

"Do you still doubt it?" he asked again.

"I don't know . . . Suppose you're mistaken?" very restless now and in angry outbursts. "I don't know what to think. Oh Maxi, if you'd only shot me you would have killed me less! I swear to you that if it's true, that woman, that shameless hypocrite who came selling me friendship, isn't going to ridicule me. I swear that I'll stamp on her soul faster than you think," rolling over in bed now. "This can't be left like it is. I'll kill her, I'll tear out her eyes, I'll rip out her heart. Where are my clothes? Uncle, maid, I want to get up! They've completely forgotten about me!"

"I understand that it's a shock. It was for me too, but I've become a stoic. Learn from me. Don't you see how calm I am? I've been through every kind of crisis there is—anger, rage, madness—"

"Because you're not a man," she interrupted.

"Lessons have taught me something."

"Well, all right; because you're a saint. I'm not a saint and I don't want to be."

"Why shouldn't you be one, too?" taking her hands and trying gently to contain her angry movements. "Why shouldn't you aspire to the state I find myself in? I've reached this after going through rage and madness. Right now, just a little while ago, when I saw that devil of a man committing another infamous act, I felt the weakness I thought I had conquered; I felt like shooting him dead to free humanity of such a monster. But I was able to control myself; I thought: 'A logical consequence punishes better than a dagger.'"

"You mean you saw him with her and it didn't even faze you!" she shouted furiously, her eyes shooting sparks.

"No. It did affect me. It upset me quite a bit. But then I reflected on it. What matters, I told myself, is not his death, but that she learn. And you have learned."

"Well, if I ever see them—"

"If you ever see them, remember me. Be saintly, like me. Just look at them and be on your way."

"You're not a man. You're not anything," she exclaimed scornfully. "*She's* the one, that imposter; she's the one I'd like to fix. If I catch her, watch out. The sneaking cheat! To deceive me like that!"

"Think it over. Do you have the right to treat her that way?"

"*Do* I?" completely perturbed and unaware of what she was saying. "She stole my property. I may be bad, but she's much worse."

"I understand your exaltation. When I saw them—and I didn't have any motive except justice—when I saw them and was convinced that they were sinning, believe me, if I'd had a revolver I would have shot them in the back till they were stone dead."

"Good, good," said the wife ferociously. "Why didn't you do it? You're a fool. Even though you'd killed me next. You've got a right to."

"I saw them go into that house . . ."

Fortunata's eyes widened with terror.

"I waited to see them come out. Such and such street, number X. I hid in the doorway. They don't know how lucky they were I didn't have a gun."

"I'll buy you one. Today, right now." As she said this, she wriggled in bed and took hold of her son; then she let him go, and bared her breast; then she covered it up, not knowing what to do.

"Kill her! Teach her a lesson? And how about yours?"

"Mine? I've already learned it, you pest. Do you still want to teach me one? That treacherous woman is the one I'm going to teach a lesson—one she'll never forget."

"You'll be sent to the penitentiary if you kill her."

"Well, I'll go gladly."

"How about your little boy?"

Hearing this cut short Fortunata's wild idea, and, picking him up—for he was beginning to whimper—she put him to her breast.

The mother cried and so did the child, and Ido the Great appeared at the door again, staring blankly at husband and wife; his eyes looked like the hollow eyes of marble or plaster statues. Thanks to Segunda's entrance, the situation came to an end. The mere sight of Rubín sent her flying into the other room uttering curses in all colors and shapes, blaming her brother and his useless sponge of a friend; and Don José Ido, hearing himself insulted for no apparent reason, contracted his facial muscles in almost unbelievable ways, joining one eye to his mouth and making the other meet his hairline. "I don't know what it is," he said. "I don't know why; but my head simply isn't right today. If he came in, it was because he wanted to; *I* didn't tell him to come in. And if he kills her, he has his reasons, of course. What a temper this lady's got, and what a way to treat me! Doesn't she know who I am? Well, I'm Josef . . . the Edomite . . . professor of . . . intellectual births."

5

"Shut up, you sponger!" shrieked Segunda, who with threatening movements seemed ready to smash to smithereens the "Edomite professor's" fragile body. "The one who's to blame is this jerk that's dozin' through the whole business."

It was a colossal task to rouse the sleeping Plato; finally, his sister yanked one of his hind paws while Encarnación pulled the other, and the model's carcass, sliding across the sofa, landed with a thud on the floor. He stretched for a while, rubbing his eyes with his big paws and spitting out Vatican thunder rather than words. "Where's that fuckin' thief that got in here without my permission? Damn it! I'll split him in half." Segunda's language didn't compare unfavorably with her brother's in its refinement and cultivated tones, which Ido found extremely displeasing. Maxi entered the room and José Izquierdo cornered him, barking:

"Ah! Sho, it's you. Get outta here . . . brrr. And ya'd better look out for my temper—it's real sweet! If I'd a seen ya before, dadblammit, I'd a fucked you off in no time, right off that fuckin' balcony inta the gutter."

Without showing any fear whatsoever, Maximiliano smiled. Then such a noisy rumpus got under way that Ido had to step in with conciliatory words. Meanwhile, Segunda gestured wildly, laying all the blame on her chicken of a brother, who tried to shift it onto Encarnación, and the girl laid it on Maxi, and the shouting got so loud that it attracted Estupiñá to the open door. Rushing in like a policeman, he ordered them all to be quiet and threatened to call in some real policemen. "I told you there wouldn't be any peace in this house. If this keeps up, I'll put you all in the street." He left, grumbling. That evening, when Ido and Maxi had left and the Izquierdos were having dinner, he came up again, determined to command them despotically: "Quiet, now. The first one of you that makes any noise is going to jail."

"Why, Don Plácido, is the viaticum coming or something?"

"Just about," replied the talker, having been shown in and heading into the bedroom. "The owner of the house is coming, so let's be quiet, ladies and gentleman, and let's be on our best behavior."

The news of Señora Pacheco's imminent arrival made Plato so nervous that he lost his composure; he wolfed down his food and made for the street. He was so afraid of being seen by the Señora that he raced down the stairs; and his hair stood on end when he thought about meeting her there, because he wouldn't have anywhere to hide.

Ever since the interview with her husband, Fortunata was so restless that Segunda had to be angry to keep her from getting up; for she wanted to, no matter what. The little one must have noticed a change in his milk supply, too, because he was in a bad mood and acted as if he wanted to get up to stage his protest, too.

The news of the saint's imminent visit calmed the mother somewhat, but not her son, who didn't have the slightest idea yet of what saints were. The lady arrived at nine o'clock, escorted by Estupiñá, and after greeting Segunda as if the latter were the noblest lady in Madrid, she proceeded into the bedroom, and before saying a word to her former friend, she examined Juan Evaristo Segismundo. Segunda brought in a candle so that the lady could get a good look at the features of the baby, who did not seem at all enthused by this impertinent inspection or the brightness of the light held so close to his little eyes.

"What a bad temper he has!" said the saint, sitting down next to the bed while Fortunata comforted her son, putting the nipple of her breast into his mouth. Guillermina was very dry in her greeting and displayed very little emotion, and when Señora Rubín and the saint were left alone later, the latter said nothing about religion; nor did she mention virtue or sin or anything related to morality. She asked the young mother whether or not she had enough milk, whether she had any minor discomforts, and other such things concerning her present condition. Fortunata detected a certain studied severity in the saint's placid face, and to break the ice, remarked the following, which was not very timely: "He really is the legitimate Pituso, the real thing, isn't he, Señora? Ah! Didn't you know? As soon as my Uncle José heard that you were coming, he ran out of here like a bat out of Hell."

"Because he's afraid of me. Some trouble he gave us . . . But let him be. If I ever catch him, I have a few things to tell *him*."

And when the mother put her full and sleepy child back down at her side, Guillermina scrutinized him again, observing his features as a numismatist observes the blurred profile and inscriptions on an ancient coin to determine if it is authentic or counterfeit. She sighed, and then squinting to see Fortunata better, exclaimed: "We've really outdone ourselves, haven't we?" And the two of them stared at each other in silence for a while.

"Señora," broke out the new mother as if she wanted to confess a secret that had become a burden: "I have to apologize to you."

"Apologize, to me! Why?"

"For the awful things I did; for the atrocious things I said that morning at your house. I'd apologize to her too, if I saw her. I behaved badly, I know I did. I don't have a grudge against anyone. I mean, I don't have one against her because . . . oh, Señora! You don't know what's going on. You don't know that he's cheating on both of us! And I know who's keeping him from us—a snake, a hypocrite who came selling me friendship. This can't be left as it is, Señora; it can't go unpunished."

"Now, don't come to me with gossip—I'm not interested in it," she said gracefully. "What you need now is rest. There will be time to settle the score later."

And she looked at the baby boy again, silently taking in his beautiful, healthy face. Fortunata drank in the saint's expression, priding herself on guessing her real thought, which may well have been, "If Jacinta could only see him!" But how could she see him? That really would be impossible. "As for me," thought la Pitusa, "I don't have anything against it. But the poor thing would suffer so much if she saw him! And she might feel like . . . Oh sure, I know you'd like to have him. No, no, my friend—you've got to have your own. Now the saint's going to go tell her what he's like; she'll say: 'His mouth is like this, his eyes are like this; he looks like his father in such and such a way, and his mother, etc. God has never given the world a more perfect creature."

"When you're well, we'll talk," said the saint, preparing to leave. "I have an idea. You're not the only one who has ideas. The difference is that mine aren't bad, or at least I don't consider them bad. And before I leave, do you need anything? If you can't nurse him, don't worry—we'll find a nursemaid for the little gent; I don't think he'd turn up his nose at her. He must be well fed."

"I can nurse him myself," replied the irritated mother. "What did you think? I'm very strong. Nobody else is going to feed my son."

"Then feed him well," she said, recovering her sweetly authoritative tone. "And be careful about what you do. Let's not have any foolishness. Follow the doctor's orders. No temper tantrums or straying from your duties. Ah, I strongly doubt that you'll be good at this."

And with one of those flashes of inspiration that enhanced her, making her somehow sublime, she said in parting:

"I'll have you know that God has chosen me to be this child's guardian. Yes, my pretty girl. Don't look so astounded and don't make such big eyes at me. You're his mother, but I have some authority over him, too. God gave it to me. If he were to lose his mother, I'd take charge of finding him another, and a grandmother, too. You've come into this world with a blessing, my son, because no matter what happens, you'll never be alone. Let me see him again. My eyes can't get their fill. I want to take away a picture of him in my mind. Lord above, he's simply beautiful! He has someone to take after. Good-bye, now."

She left, escorted by Estupiñá, adding silently, as if in a prayer: "Let's respect God's will. He must have his reasons for having sent this angel into our midst. Jacinta's furious and says God must be senile because all He does is allow absurdities. Poor thing! What narrow minds we have! We don't understand anything, nothing of what He does, and we rack our brains to figure out the meaning of certain things that happen, and the more we ponder them, the less we understand. That's why I'm making a clean break and all my arithmetic comes down to 'Thy will be done.'"

That night Fortunata dreamed that Aurora, Guillermina, and Jacinta appeared armed with daggers and, wearing black masks and threatening to kill her, took away her son. Then it was only Aurora who was committing the nefarious crime, tiptoeing in and making her smell a blasted handkerchief soaked in a mixture from the pharmacy that left her paralyzed but able to witness the events. Aurora picked up the baby and carried him off without his mother being able to prevent it or even scream. She woke up in a state of terrible distress. She felt awful and started to feel drowsy again, prone to confused mental wandering, and very thirsty. Her thirst became so bad that, since she couldn't wake up her aunt by rapping on the headboard with her knuckles, she had to get up herself and go find some water. When she lay down again, she felt very cold, and this chill, alternating with a feverish state, lasted until morning.

6

Ballester came early that day, and she couldn't tell him about Maxi's visit and story fast enough. The pharmacist was most annoyed by what he heard, and, with a seriousness unusual in him, he hotly denied what his friend said about the Samaniego woman.

"Look, my friend," she said, "the more you try to deny it, the more I believe it. You never talk like this; and when you're serious you're always lying. What you want is for me to calm down. I appreciate it, but it can't be. And as for that disgusting French whore, she's not going to have a laugh on me."

Her good friend used all his logical skills to drive the idea out of her mind, but he didn't get anywhere. "And anyway," he said, using a jovial tone he'd tried on Maxi once, "why should we pay any attention to what that weakling says? We're becoming so romantic and tragic! My friend Rubín, for all the brainy show he's been putting on lately, is daffier than ever. He gets everything backward. The other day he tried to tell me Doña Desdemona was beautiful. If we keep this up, I'm afraid I'll have to bring over my yardstick."

These words didn't affect Fortunata. He observed her gravely and noted that she was obsessed with a very sinister, tenacious idea and that it wouldn't be easy to get it out of her head. He feared that her state of mind might have an unfavorable effect on her health, and, in order to prevent it, he tried to frighten her. "Quevedo said that we must watch you very carefully these days and that he's not going to allow you to get up till next week. An absurd act could be fatal at this point. So, my child" (taking her hands) "let's be ve-ry careful. I don't ask it for my sake. I know you don't pay the slightest attention to your poor little pharmacist friend. And why should you? I'm nobody to you. But do it for my friend Juan Evaristo, whom I love as if he were my own son; yes, and I hereby name myself his guardian. Do it for him, and we'll all be happy."

She seemed to be convinced, and Ballester left with a sense of triumph. She was quiet all morning, but at about midday when she woke up from a short nap she felt such an intense urge to get up and leave the house that she couldn't overcome this blind impulse. She got up, shocking Encarnación, the only other person in the house. She ran a comb through her hair and put on her dark wool skirt, a black crêpe shawl, a bright scarf on her head, her red mittens, her pale boots, and . . . But before leaving she devoted a long time to her son, who, having woken up while his mamá was getting dressed seemed to protest that he found her little exit most vexing. She persuaded him by giving him all he wanted, or all there was, and the little angel fell asleep in his wicker crib. "Look," Fortunata said to Encarnación, "I'm going out. I won't be gone long, because I'll take a cab and I'll be able to do my errand in half an hour. Don't you leave, and if the baby wakes up, sing to him and rock him to sleep, telling him that I'll be right back. Be sure not to leave him alone, now. And listen—while I'm gone, don't open to anyone. Or wait a minute; it'll be better if I close and lock the door and take the key. If Segunda comes, tell her to wait on the stairs." She kissed her son effusively—it was to be their first separation—and left, locking the door and taking the key. "I wouldn't want someone to come and . . . No, nobody's going to steal him; but there have been cases. My little angel is going to attract them like flies. And especially that envious Jacinta—she's the one that scares me the most. She's going to turn bright green with envy, and skinny as a wire. But what can she do except accept things? I've suffered enough already! Let her suffer now. Oh, I hear steps! Frankly, I wouldn't want anyone to see me because they'll start gossiping about me going out and I don't want any talk. It sounds like Don Plácido coming upstairs. I'll wait till he goes inside his apartment. Here he comes . . . he's opening the door. Now I'll sneak out and—God bless me! I should have brought something that hurts. Ah! The key. It's better than the pestle. With this and my nails, I swear I'll . . ."

She took a cab, and scarcely had she sat down when she felt dizzy from the movement and her own weakness; she closed her eyes and leaned back against the seat to avoid seeing the houses outside spinning around. "I should have had some soup before leaving. But this is a fine time to think of it. Oh well, this won't last." Indeed, it didn't, and the first thing she did when she recovered was to change the address she'd given to the hackman. She had told him 18 Ave María, but she had another idea and said "10 Cabeza," putting her head out the window and tapping him on the arm with the key she carried like a weapon. She was at the given address for about half an hour, and when she came out to the coach again, her pale face looked absolutely waxen and her lips colorless. "Where to, Señora?" the coachman asked her when he saw that she didn't say anything. "Up to Santa Cruz Square, the corner of Vicario Viejo Street." Having said this, the cab in motion, she started thinking: "Sure. It's just like I thought. Visitación wouldn't keep it from me. And then that dumb Ballester saying my husband's crazy! He's got a sharper mind than all of the others put together. He hasn't been wrong by a hair so far. I gave Visitación twenty *duros* to tell me the story. Sure, she wouldn't try denying it to me." And she went over and over these same thoughts, caught in painful circles.

She got off at Santa Cruz Square and walked up to the Samaniego workshop, entering by the main door on Vicario Viejo Street. She was so determined that she did not hesitate at any point. The door to the mezzanine was covered with an oilcloth screen that made a bell ring when it was opened. Fortunata had been there before the opening and remembered everything perfectly. You didn't have to ring—you simply had to push the screen, there was a loud *rrring* and you were inside. So she entered; she just crossed the short hall that led to the main room when she came face to face with Aurora, who at that moment was heading from the table in the middle of the room to one of the windows, carrying some materials. Fortunata saw about six or seven assistants sitting around the table sewing, and on a sofa next to the widest window (facing the street) were two ladies holding laces and materials up to the light.

"Good day," said the Rubín woman, pausing a moment and taking a fleeting look at all the faces around her. Seeing Fortunata was such a shock for Aurora that she didn't know what to say or how to look. "Oh . . . it's you, Fortunata. It's been so long!" Then she switched to a harsher tone. "Excuse me—I'm busy. If you'd like to come back some other time—" Then her tone changed again: "You've been making yourself scarce. Have you been sick?"

"How about you? How've you been? Always doing so well . . ." said Fortunata, drawing closer and putting on a fictitiously kind face in which it was easy to detect the cruel gentleness of a beast who licks its victim first before devouring it.

"Where have you been keeping yourself?" babbled Aurora, visibly shaken now, not knowing which way to turn.

At last she turned to the ladies sitting there, but she didn't know what to say to them. As she headed back to the table Fortunata crossed her path. "I had to talk to you. But since you're never around . . . Oh, what a friend! You could die and she wouldn't even say a word."

Aurora was somewhat reassured by this language, and, smiling, she replied: "With so much to do, kid, there's no time for visits. I was planning to go see you . . . But sit down."

"I'm fine as I am. This will just take a minute."

Aurora went over to the ladies again, and when she turned back her friend touched her arm. "I had something I wanted to tell you. Just a little thing I wanted to tell you. I was dying to see you. You ungrateful thing! Knowing how much I like your company!"

"You're right," replied Aurora, growing restless again because she detected something in her friend's face that put her on her guard. "I thought about coming every day—"

"Knowing how fond I am of you—"

"And I'm very fond of you. Why don't you sit down?"

"No. I'm leaving in a minute. I've only come to bring you something."

"Bring something . . . to *me*?"

"Yes. You'll see."

And saying "you'll see" she made a swift, energetic movement with her right arm and slapped Aurora in the face so resoundingly that Aurora couldn't contain herself; she cried out and fell to the floor. Fortunata said:

"There it is, you indecent whore, thief!"

There has never been such a tremendous slap. All the assistants ran out aghast to fetch the manager, but despite their speed they weren't back in time to stop Fortunata from clenching the key in her right fist and bringing it down like a hammer on the other's forehead; and then, with indescribable speed and wrath, she grabbed hold of Aurora's bun and pulled her hair with all her strength. Aurora's shrieks could be heard from the street. The two ladies ran out calling for help. Thanks to the assistants, the beast was held back the minute she started to dig her claws into the victim's hair; if she had not been, it would have been the end of Aurora. Restrained by so many hands, Fortunata nevertheless tried to break free and continue the attack, but eventually numbers—not a lack of courage—won out. She knocked one of the seamstresses down with one blow; she socked another in the eye. Panting, livid and sweaty, her eyes aflame, Fortunata let her tongue continue the tragic job her hands alone could not do.

"That's so you won't stick your fingers in somebody else's pie again, you slut. Cheat, hypocrite—you could deceive the Holy Ghost! Poor water that had to baptize you! Sneaky little snake. I'll squash your face, even though it's an insult to the soles of my boots."

And she made such a huge effort to break free that she almost managed to. Two of the girls had rushed to pick up Aurora; she was still crying out in pain. If Pepe Samaniego and a salesman hadn't appeared on the scene, Lord knows what would have happened.

"What is this? What's happened here? Who are you? What are you looking for?"

"Who am I?" Fortunata cried desperately. "A decent person."

"Yes, that's obvious. For God's sake, Aurora! What is all this?"

"A decent person who's come to settle the score with this snake in the grass who works for you. And she's a slanderer too."

"Shut up and get out of here. What is this, Aurora? Lord! Blood on your head! A wound! Listen to me, woman: you're going straight to prison. Call the police!"

The Fenelón woman was almost swooning and her helpers unbuttoned her dress to loosen her corset.

"*She's* the one that's going to prison" shrieked the aggressor in a frenzy, reverting suddenly to her old self: a low-class woman with all the passion and crudeness that her contact with society had temporarily disguised. "I haven't cheated on anyone. But someone *has* cheated on *me*. That imposter deceived me, she deceived both of us, because there are two of us that have been hurt by this, two, and you might as well know it. She's an angel and so am I . . . I mean, I'm not . . . But we've had a son, the son of the house, and this woman here is an ugly busybody, a nervy, scummy little cheat who's going to pay for this. I'm going to make her pay for it."

"If you don't shut up . . ." threatened Samaniego, advancing toward her. "If you weren't a woman, I'd give it to you this minute."

"You, hit me? Just try it. You'd do better to keep this woman here from doing such indecent things."

"I told you: if you don't shut up—I can't stand this any longer! Call in the police!"

The scene started to look even worse when Doña Casta made an unexpected appearance. As soon as she heard what was going on upstairs she came hobbling up and entered that theater of dramatic events crying:

"My dear daughter! What . . . ? They've killed her! Blood! Oh, my God! Aurora, Aurora! Who was it? Oh, that woman!"

"Yes, me. I did it," declared Fortunata from the corner where she was being held. "You'd be better off, you old witch, if you didn't cover up for your daughter's tricks."

Rushing to her daughter's aid, Doña Casta ignored the compliments. Aurora came to her senses moaning.

"Don't worry—it's nothing, Aunt," said Samaniego. "A slight contusion and the fright that comes with it. When will that beastly woman shut up? Call the police!"

"Never mind. Let her go," murmured Aurora with her eyes closed.

"To jail," Doña Casta shouted hoarsely.

"No, not to jail," remonstrated the victim, putting on a show of generosity. "Let her go, let her go. Pepe—don't do anything to her."

"I haven't. Let her tell her story to the judge."

"No, no. Don't bring a judge into this," the Fenelón woman hastened to say. "I forgive her. Let her leave and fast. Get her out of my sight."

Fortunata was implacable; she kept on talking, and the people surrounding the victim had different opinions on what should be done about the aggressor. More people clustered around, and with all the shouting and the coming and going the workshop began to look like a room in hell.

7

The first person who came to the house in the Cava during la Pitusa's absence was Guillermina. After she knocked twice, Encarnación's voice replied through the holes in the doorlock:

"The Señorita is out. She locked me in."

"Out! Lord help us. Is that the truth or doesn't she want to receive me?"

"No, Señora; she's not here. She said she'd be back soon. She turned the key twice."

"And the baby?"

"He's still sound asleep."

"I'll wait for a while," said the saint, heaving a sigh. And tired from standing, she sat on the top stair. She looked like one of the needy who sit waiting until the door opens, when they beg for alms. "Where in the world would that madwoman have gone? It's just what I said: no one can hold her back. She's not going to be able to nurse her baby. She does some good, sometimes; but when you're least expecting it, she takes off and gets into trouble. She'll abandon her child any day, or put him in an orphanage. But oh, no; we're not going to let her do that. If the poor little thing has a negligent mother, there'll be somebody else to take care of him."

As she was thinking this, she heard someone coming up the stairs. It was Ballester, who upon seeing her was rather abashed.

"Are you coming to this house?" the lady inquired. "Well, be patient. The bird's flown her nest. The "lady" has taken to the streets. The boy and the maid are inside; but since she took the key, we can't get in. Tolerate being stood up the way I am, if you're not in a hurry; she can't be long now."

"But we forbade her to go out!" very frightened and angry. "Last night, according to Don Francisco de Quevedo, she was a bit overexcited. That's why I came, to see—what foolishness she's capable of!"

"You can say that again! Do you have any idea where she might be?"

"None at all. Oh well, let's wait."

The pharmacist sat two steps below the saint, who squinted to see him clearly. Since she didn't have any qualms when she thought it was necessary to interrogate someone, she suddenly sprang this on Ballester:

"Tell me, my good gentleman—and forgive me if I'm too inquisitive—are you the person who has the most . . . influence now on this woman?"

"Influence? I don't believe I do, Señora. I've only known her a short time. I'm her friend; I'm concerned about her."

"I'm not trying to make you tell me what sort of friendship you have with her—"

"It's the purest there is. Don't you believe me?"

"Yes; I believe everything. As a matter of fact, I've got a lot of faith" (laughing pleasantly) "but it's not a question of that now. Why should I care? What I'm trying to say is, if you have any influence over her, you should advise her to . . . You know, any day now that woman may go back to her old ways and tire of taking care of her little boy. The best thing would be to find him a nursemaid and turn him over to people who would take better care of him than she will. Advise her to do this."

"I . . . what can I say? I really don't think she'll abandon him. She's very enthusiastic about him."

"Hmm, some enthusiasm! Look at her—out on a walk! What an overpowering urge she must have had to go out. I don't know how the little angel has gone for so long without being nursed."

She had scarcely said this when they heard cries from the poor baby. Unable to restrain herself, Guillermina got up and walked over to the door, firing away with: "Poor baby, and that madwoman still away! You're right; she's a rascal. Hold on just a little longer . . . just a little bit." She called the maid to the door and said:

"Listen, girl—try to distract him; your mistress can't be long. Rock the cradle, sing him a lullaby, silly."

And settling on the steps again, she remarked to her fellow in waiting:

"What a woman! Oh! My temper's so quick that I'm on the verge of knocking down the door to get the baby and take him to be fed. Are you a doctor?"

"No, Señora. I'm a pharmacist."

She fell silent because they heard steps, very near now, as if somebody were coming upstairs cautiously, and they looked down to the landing, expecting to see the person turn there. The person who appeared surprised them both. It was Maximiliano, who, upon seeing Doña Guillermina and Segismundo sitting on the steps, reasoned as follows: "Two people waiting who've sat down because they're tired. That means they've been waiting for some time and the house is locked."

For a minute he doubted whether to continue up or go back down. The pharmacist was laughing and Guillermina looked at him waggishly.

"You'll have to wait too," she said. "Do you have a key?"

"Me, a key?"

"Key, schmee," Ballester remarked ill-humoredly, thinking that they could do very well without Maxi around. "You'd be better off leaving, my friend Rubín, and coming back later. This is going to be a long wait."

"I'll wait too," he replied, sitting several steps below Ballester.

And when el Pituso's desperate cries were heard again, Guillermina didn't disguise her impatience and worry.

"You can just hear how hungry the poor little creature is. Imagine, getting up before she was well and taking off to the streets! I tell you, I feel like hitting her."

Maximiliano was silent, his eyes glued to the saint, whom he had never seen at such close range.

"Well, what a scene!" she added. "Now there are three of us. This is starting to get boring. I hear steps. Do you suppose it's finally her, that fickle girl?"

The steps didn't sound like a woman's. Who could it be? All three of them looked through the railing and they beheld José Izquierdo, who at the sight of Doña Guillermina got all flustered and looked down, as if he wanted to plunge downstairs head first. He would have given his right arm for a hiding place. The saint laughed in his face and finally said:

"Don't be scared of me, Señor Platón. Why are you looking so frightened? I don't eat people. We're friends, you and I . . ."

"Señora," said the model with a grunt, "when an individ'al *needs* somethin', he can't be a gent and he's apt to do anythin'."

"Yes, my friend; I know. And you're forgiven for that big swindle. If you could only see how handsome Pituso is!"

"Really? Oh, poor little flea. I loved 'im."

"Yes. He's growing up very well. And he's so bright and full of mischief he's got the whole asylum in an uproar."

"Well, that's his mother's blessed blood for you! She upset half the world. I knew that boy was gifted. I told you—"

"Well, now you're doing pretty well, Señor Platón, according to what they tell me—earning piles of money with painting."

"We keep bread on the table, Señora."

"I'm glad for a number of reasons, especially because now that you're high on the hog you won't be swindling people."

Izquierdo scratched his ear and would have surrendered it for the saint to change the subject.

"If the lady'd be so kind—let's not hash over the past."

"I'm not 'hashing over' anything. And be honest: if you were badly off now, you'd probably try another deal like that again. And not with fake stuff, but the real thing."

Ballester chuckled, but Maximiliano looked displeased, which the saint quickly remedied with:

"If it weren't for these jokes, how would we get through this waiting? I hate to have to wait, and when I'm waiting because of someone's stupidity, I completely lose my patience."

Juan Evaristo's plaintive protest was heard again and Guillermina rang the bell to say to the servant:

"Distract him; talk to him. Are you dumb or something? She's coming, my little baby! Just wait—I'm going to give her a good spanking for leaving you all alone like this, dying of hunger. Señores" (turning back to the step), "you'll have to excuse me, and if any of you gets tired, don't stay just to keep me company. Something must have happened to that woman; she's taking an awfully long time. I propose that a committee be named to go have a look in the street and find out where she might be."

Saying this, she looked at Maxi, implying that he be part of the committee. The youth gave no sign of moving and, staying in his lazy position, looking at his companions out of the corner of his eye, he said:

"Approximately an hour and a quarter ago she was riding in a coach going along Atocha Street; it had come from Cañizares Street. About three-quarters of an hour ago I saw the same coach cross Santa Cruz Square, heading toward Esparteros Street."

Ballester and Guillermina exchanged an alarmed look.

"Well, I suggest that a committee go to Esparteros Street. Did you see the coach make any stops?"

"No, Señora. I thought it was coming this way, because even though the most direct route from Atocha Street is by way of the Plaza Mayor, Ciudad Rodrigo, and Cava Streets, they're paving the Atocha entrance to the Plaza and it's closed, so I thought to myself: 'The coachman's going to take Mayor Street.' But apparently she hasn't come here. That means she's gone somewhere else. Maybe she's gone to visit some friend, Aurora, for example . . ."

Ballester and the saint exchanged another worried look.

"What this boy's saying," stated the pharmacist, communicating his fears to the lady, "sounds so logical that I'd almost go so far as to think he's right."

Steps were heard again, but they were very heavy and were accompanied by the panting and throat clearing of an older person that made all of them think it wasn't Fortunata.

"It's Segunda," Izquierdo said before seeing her.

And he was right. The square vendor looked quite impressed when she saw the multi-level *tertulia* there, and when she was able to see who was seated on the top stair, she almost dropped her jaw, expressing her admiration as follows:

"Blessed Lord above! The owner of the house just sitting there on the steps like a beggar hoping for scraps from somebody's meal! What's wrong—isn't that niece of mine in? Don't tell me she went out to the street! I was afraid of that. What a head! Last night she was so worked up! But Señora, why don't you wait at Don Plácido's? At least there would be chairs there, and you and the gentlemen could be more comfortable."

"Do me a favor and ring; see if Plácido's in. I'm sure he can find her."

Segunda rang, but Plácido wasn't at home.

"Would the lady like me to go look for her? But where?"

"I'll go," said Ballester, convinced that they would know something about the fugitive at Samaniego's shop. He was still confering with Guillermina when

Segunda, who had gone downstairs in search of a key or a picklock, shouted up from the first floor:

"She's back!"

"Oh, thank God for that!" exclaimed Guillermina without intending any double meaning. "The lost sheep is back. Let's see how she is."

"It could be one of two things," sighed Ballester. "Either her face is scratched or she's got blood and maybe human skin under her nails."

"She's a lot a woman . . ."

They all got up except Maximiliano, who remained apathetically reclined until he saw his wife. She came up breathlessly, exhausted, wiping the sweat from her face and lifting her skirts to keep from tripping on them, the key in her hand.

"You say I've been gone long? It didn't take but a minute. I was through right away. Doña Guillermina—you here too! I thought I'd finish sooner. And my prince is hungry . . . I can hear him crying. I'm coming, I'm coming, my own little son. Oh! I was afraid they wouldn't let me come home. If they'd taken me to jail, I don't know what . . . My poor little baby."

"Open the door, hurry up, now," said Guillermina, pushing her, "street walker, wench. It's very plain that you are not a good mother. Poor angel! He's been crying for two hours. If you don't mend your ways, we'll have to take care of him."

8

She opened the door and they all pushed through: Fortunata first, Guillermina holding onto her, Ballester behind them, Maxi, Izquierdo, and Segunda. The mother headed straight for the bedroom, where the little one was in his crib letting out cries that would have moved Philip III's bronze horse.

"Here I am, my tiny darling; here's your slave. Come, come here, and take the nice breast Mamá has for you. Oh! He's so hungry, and he's cried so hard! And I was wild to come back to my little angel. He's so happy now! My baby's not going to cry anymore now, is he? No."

Without even taking off her cloak she had picked up the baby and started to soothe him. She sat on the bed so as to leave the only chair in the room for Guillermina. The saint was concerned only about the baby, though; she watched him anxiously to see if the suckling satisfied him.

"I'm afraid that those angry fits are going to stop your milk."

"Bah! No, Señora. Don't worry—I have more than he needs. I think it's the other way around: if I hadn't gotten it out of my system I would have run dry. Last night I was almost beside myself. Getting my revenge was as vital as breathing and eating. Listen to what I did: after whacking her one that they must have heard clear across Madrid, I rammed the key at her and probably fractured her skull. Then I got my hands into her hair—"

"Stop it, for the love of God; you're horrifying me."

"They wanted to take me to prison, and they spent about an hour trying to decide if they should. The police came and I told them I had a baby to feed. Anyway, they finally let me go and I came running home. If you want people to respect you, you've got to be like me! If the blasted seamstresses hadn't of been around, I'd of walked right over her carcass as easy as I'm walking across this room. You know, she's *really* bad, Señora; just imagine, cheating on *two* of us— on me and on her—and according to what everybody says, she's an angel. You can tell her that the score's been settled with la Samaniega."

"You're overexcited, I think. So be quiet. Be quiet and attend to your son."

"I am taking care of him. Can't you see? My little glory, my prince! I can tell you this: if those pigs hadn't of let me come feed my son, I don't know what would have become of me! Samaniego himself is the one that let me go, saying 'Let her be on her blasted way.' Well, yes, Señora; I'm pleased. And don't think I've got any motives in this. What would I want the money for? Nothing. I'm happy to have the son of the house. Nobody can take that away from me. No priest mumbling Latin can take him away. Isn't that right, Señora? You're on my side now. And *she's* on my side too, isn't she?"

"I told you—your head's not right," quite alarmed. "Be quiet. And let's be serious, now," patting her on the shoulder, "because if you don't nurse him properly, we'll have to look for a nursemaid. And if worse comes to worst, we'll have to take him in to live with us."

"Bah! No, Señora. I'm not letting go." She said this in a terribly excited, dangerously ecstatic state. "I'm so happy! You'll love me, won't you, Señora? Will you love me? I really need for someone to love me. Just wait—you'll see how good I'm going to be. And men? I don't even want to see one. I don't want to have anything to do with them. Just my little son. Nobody else."

"Oh, yes. Save that for the birds."

"You don't know me, Señora! Do you think that . . . ? Ha, ha, ha! My little son and peace. Listen. We can get used to the idea that he's the son of the three of us, and he'll have three mothers instead of one."

The saint found that strange notion amusing.

"Look. Since God has given the son of the house to me, I don't hold anything against her. Because you know, I'm as important as she is—at least—if not more. But let's just suppose I'm the same. I don't have anything against her. In fact, I could even get to like her. This little treasure is going to have three mamás: me, the first mother; her, the second mother; and you'll be the third mother."

"Child, what nonsense you're talking! You're terribly upset," taking her pulse and noticing with alarm the gleam in her eyes. "I wonder how poor little Juanín can find anything in that breast . . ."

The other people who had entered the house were in the living room, not daring to interrupt that lively colloquy between the she-devil and the saint, whose muffled voices they overheard. Then Guillermina came out in search of Ballester, who was standing very mournfully by the window looking out at the square, and she said:

"That woman is in a very excited state and I'm afraid her milk is going to dry up. Is there an anti-spasmodic here?"

"Yes. I mixed one very carefully, but I'll bring more tonight. Did you say she's overexcited?"

"Terribly. Her head's disturbed. She's saying all sorts of absurd things. Come in."

When Ballester proposed that she take the medicine, the young woman replied:

"What I want is water. I'm terribly thirsty . . . my mouth's dry."

She drank avidly, and meanwhile the founder took Ballester aside and said to him:

"Listen: her husband, that poor soul—what does he want? What's he doing and saying? How has he taken all this?"

"Señora," answered the pharmacist, wavering between seriousness and laughter. "You say you don't understand him? Well, I don't either. He's timid at heart. So whenever I see him talking with people he hardly knows I feel suspicious. For some time now, everything that boy has said has been so right that it might as well have been stated by the seven wise men of Greece."

"But isn't he—?" asked the lady, touching her head with her index finger.

"Well, he was the one who brought her the story on the Fenelón woman. I don't trust that gentleman's sanity, and whenever I have him at arm's reach I search him to see if he's carrying a weapon. I don't like seeing him here at all."

Rubín and Izquierdo were sitting on the living room sofa in silence. Fortunata called Ballester and Plato to tell them what she had done, and meanwhile Guillermina went out to sit with Maximiliano, trying to coax him to talk by smiling benevolently. The lady wanted to speak and yet she didn't say a single word; with all her talent and knowledge of the world she nevertheless could not find the right chord to strike with him in this situation. What could she say? That really was a problem! What tone should she take? Was the man sane or not? It was hard enough if one considered him insane, but to treat him like a sane person was nearly impossible. Should she talk about the child? Lord, no—what a mistake *that* would be. Should she tell him his wife was a treasure? No, that would be awful! Should she take the bull by the horns? Heavens, no. Or should she take a religious attitude and talk about resignation? No. The mundane side of it? Oh! The good lady had never encountered such a fearful, involved problem of social science. This enigma outdid any and all she had met in her indefatigable life.

"Oh, well," thought the founder, "I bet I'll come out all right if I just plunge in. It's the best way; this system has always given me good results."

"Listen, my dear friend—"

"Señora . . . ?"

And the dialogue came to a halt here, because the saint did not dare continue. But God willed that the sphinx should clear the way, for the gentleman said:

"I knew you by sight and by name. But I had never had the pleasure of speaking to you. You're a saint, and when you die we'll canonize you and put you up on altars."

"Thank you; you honor me," she replied gracefully. "I think that you're the one who's a saint."

"Me . . ." without much awe at the compliment. "But there's a big difference between you and me. It's true that I've won a few battles against my passions, but I've never gotten anywhere near your degree of perfection. I'm still a long way off. If one got there by suffering I'd already be at the summit, because I've suffered a lot, Señora. You're probably amazed at my serenity. Everyone is, and they well might be. Because this serene man you see was crazy, dead crazy . . ."

"I know, I know. Oh, what pain!"

"And I've gone through all the phases. First, I had a persecution complex, then delusions of grandeur. I invented religions; I thought I was the head of a sect that would transform the world. I also suffered a homicidal furor and almost killed my Aunt Lupe and Papitos. Then there were horrible depressions; I felt like dying; religious manias, trying to be a recluse, my delirious self-denial and indifference. But God wanted to cure me, and little by little I got through those phases, and my reason—which was dead—began to grow and was born. First it was only a tiny little thing, but then it grew so, so much that it was as if I had a new brain and I was a new man, Señora. And then I discovered I had a talented mind (please forgive my immodesty), a great ability to judge things."

Guillermina was astounded; she couldn't think of anything to oppose his logic. He expressed himself with admirable serenity and with fluent, even, easy words, without stumbling or hesitating for a minute, features composed, his manner courteous and poised.

"And when I came back to life—because it was like being reborn—I felt like a man who has climbed a very high mountain and suddenly sees everything reduced to miniatures. 'Everything that used to look so big to me' (I said to myself) 'look at it: tiny.' I realized all that had happened to me during my illness (which was more like a dream) and I saw that pitiful woman's infidelity. I also saw that she had a baby; and the clarity of my strong new mind made me see how justice could be done, and I thought it was my duty to contribute to the extirpation of evil from humanity by killing that miserable woman, and that would be redeeming her, because I've always said, 'Blessed are they who go to the scaffold, because in their torture they repent, and by repenting they earn salvation!'"

Guillermina was about to reply something, but he didn't let her get a word in edgewise.

"Wait a minute; you haven't heard the second part. I was wondering how I'd carry out that act of justice when chance, or rather fate, gave me a better, more Christian solution than death. This poor woman didn't need my justice. God himself had planned her punishment and a tremendous lesson. Unfaithfulness punishes unfaithfulness. What could be more logical? So I decided to let logic handle it. I thanked God for helping me to see the light. God is the only one who punishes, isn't He, Señora? And we're so lucky He knows how! Why should we usurp His functions? Doing justice through events, logically, is the most admirable spectacle that the world and history can offer. So I wash my hands of it and let things take their natural course, and justice gets done. Is this 'being reasonable'? Is this 'being sane'?"

He folded his arms, asking this question, and, after hesitating slightly, Guillermina answered with:

"I'll say it is. Christ teaches us that we shouldn't take justice in our own hands because God punishes without sticks and stones, and He gives every creature what suits him best. When some injustice touches us because of other men's conniving, what we should do is fold our arms and say, 'Go on, use sticks. The more I'm humiliated, the higher I'll rise later. The more I'm beaten here, the healthier I'll be there.'"

"That's exactly what I think. I've conquered all the resentment I had in my heart. I consider the idea of killing anyone inefficient and absurd—like the wrong medicine. Only God kills, and He's the one who always teaches. I've experienced awful jealousy, and I've felt burning rancor; but even so, all that bad growth is falling away under the hatchet of reason. I no longer think about killing anybody, not even people I hated so much. I see God's admirable teachings; I see that the evil receive their due punishment; and I strive not to deserve it myself. This is my system; this is my life."

Segismundo had called Guillermina from the bedroom door. They whispered something about Fortunata, and he asked the saint her opinion of young Rubín's condition; the founder replied:

"What he's just said bespeaks wisdom and sanity itself, but—"

"—But he's not all there. I'm not, either."

9

Izquierdo came in with a bottle of beer, and behind him came a waiter from the Gallo Café with glasses, a large lemonade, and a punch bowl.

"The lady," he declared, trying to be gallant, "is going to have a little glass of beer with lemon."

"Pshaw!" replied the lady. "I don't drink that vile stuff. But I appreciate your bringing it."

They invited Fortunata too, but she didn't want any, either; she asked for milk. Ballester, heedful of her slightest desires, sent Encarnación out for the milk and Guillermina said good-bye, leaving just as Plácido was arriving; he had rushed up full of officiousness to put himself at her command.

Segismundo observed his friend and in truth did not find her in very good shape. Her fake joviality, which made her laugh at the slightest provocation, was not a good sign, and he would have liked for her to talk less. But her only concern was to retell the episode with Aurora, giving it tragic proportions; and once she'd finished, she started all over again, revealing an implacable rage against the woman who had been her friend. Ballester contradicted her diplomatically, recommending prudence, tolerance, and that "we forgive those who trespass against us." Finally, at wit's end, he brought in the case of Maximiliano, who was bearing his affronts with such Christian meekness. When the devil heard this she laughed even harder, saying that her husband was a saint, a true saint, and that if he was canonized and put up on altars she'd pray to him and spit on him. Rubín didn't hear this; he was playing checkers with Izquierdo.

They brought the milk, and when Encarnación served it to her mistress, the latter saw that two flies had fallen into it. In disgust, she called her maid a careless swine, among other things. The pharmacist ordered another glass of milk and said he'd drink the milk with the flies and that nothing disgusted him. He scooped the insects out with his little finger and his friend criticized him for it, saying he was dirty and recoiling from him. They brought the milk well covered the next time, and as Fortunata drank it, Ballester drank the other milk, making a few jokes and entertaining remarks, but they did not suffice to pull his young friend out of the depression she'd lapsed into after her noisy happiness. He ordered her to lie down; meanwhile, he went into the living room, pretending to follow their game of checkers. He couldn't feel at ease as long as Maxi was there; nor did he trust his resigned, philosophical appearance. Pretending that he was only teasing, he tickled Maxi so as to touch his pockets, for he was afraid he might be carrying a weapon. But he didn't discover anything. In any case, Ballester didn't want to leave unless Maxi was ahead of him, so he pushed the idea of leaving until he finally got results. And then the pharmacist left with plans to return, because his friend had him worried.

Plato also left when it started to get dark, but he came back at nine o'clock and lit the lamp in the living room. It wasn't yet a quarter past nine when Fortunata, who had begun to doze, heard steps and saw a man entering her bedroom.

"Who is it?" she asked alarmed, reaching to cover her son. "Oh! It's you, Maxi. I didn't recognize you. It's so dark in here."

Her uncle's canine cough reassured her; it was a reminder that she wasn't alone. She sent the girl out for a lamp because she wasn't asleep any more and José, on the lookout, appeared at the door every few minutes. Maximiliano sat down next to the bed as he had the day before and said kindly:

"There were lots of people here this afternoon, so I couldn't talk with you. That's why I've come back. I know that you and Aurora had a fight. Doña Casta is furious, and you have no idea what a rage my aunt's in because of you. This event has suggested something I'd like to tell you."

"Tell me, hurry up, what?" said Fortunata, who didn't know why, esteeming this man so little, she nevertheless hoped for strange and perhaps consoling thoughts from him.

"Well, what you did this afternoon favors your enemy," Rubín asserted with medical severity, watching for the effect his words would have on her. "Yes, it favors your enemy. You're dumb and you don't know human nature. Ever since I started going through this great crisis and discovered logic, I can see everything clearly and human nature doesn't hold any secrets for me."

Fortunata didn't understand.

"Let me make myself clearer. What I mean is, when you mistreated your rival, you gave her the victory. The man you both love might have doubted before in choosing which one deserved his love definitively. Now he won't. Between a woman who loses her composure and does the brutal things you did, and another who suffers and is mistreated, love has to prefer the victim. All victims are interesting, simply because they're victims. And villains are hateful because they're villains. In matters of the heart, the victim always wins. This truth is so general it might as well be written in the human heart, and I can read it as plainly as if it were a piece of news in the Imparcial. I know everything; nothing escapes me. You have plenty of proof of that."

These words had such a bad effect on Fortunata that she felt like grabbing the candlestick and flinging it at him. She retorted spitefully:

"Well, she can win, then. I don't give a hoot whether he loves her or not—"

"—And now he's going to love her so much," added Maxi impassively, "so much, that the lovers of Teruel will look like puppets next to them. He'll love her because she's been injured; victims always inspire love. Believe me; I know what I'm saying. He'll love her madly—more than he loves you or his wife, and he'll do for her what he hasn't done for either of you. He'll abandon his wife and his parents to live freely with her. And they'll be happy and have lots of children."

The Rubín woman's reply was no more than a moan. She reached out as if to grab the candlestick. Then she covered her face with her hand.

"I tell you these things because they're true. And I'm hitting you with the truth so you'll smart from the lesson as if it were a slap. That way you'll learn. A nice lesson, isn't it? Of course it hurts and it makes you bleed; but learning and suffering are synonymous. It's for your own good. Your conscience will be purified. And I wish you'd die from your grief, because you'd go straight up to heaven."

The young woman cried in anguish, but he didn't seem to feel any compassion for her.

"I see you believe me; you're right to. What I've told you has always been right. I know everything, and my mind shows me life like a panorama spreading out before my eyes. It's a gift that God has granted me. When I was crazy I guessed things, I was inspired, you could see that, and as you may recall, I foretold everything that would happen. Truth came to me then wrapped up in a sort of symbolism, the way it appears in the Orient. Then I entered the age of reason, and now the truth offers itself to me clearly and stripped of adornments, and that's how I'm giving it to you: clear and stripped. Didn't I find you when everybody told me you were dead? Didn't I discover the business about Aurora, down to the details of their rendezvous spot, times, et cetera? So now you see. Nothing escapes me, and what I've just told you is the gospel truth. You've given your enemy the victory, so stand by for the blow. Your victim and torturer—they'll be happy and have lots of children."

"Shut up, shut up or else—" cried Fortunata, brandishing her fist at him and trying to overcome the superstitious terror he inspired in her. "I know some truths too, and I'm going to tell you one."

"Go ahead, out with it."

"You're a man without any honor—"

Maximiliano trembled slightly; that was all. He kept listening.

"And what else?" he asked.

"Isn't that enough?" continued the devil whose mouth, in her fit of rage, had started to foam. "Well, Ballester and Doña Guillermina were saying just a little while ago: 'He's a saint, but he doesn't know what honor is.' So now you know. Leave me in peace. I don't want to see you anymore. Some people say you're sane and others say you're crazy. I think you're sane, but you're not a man; you've lost your masculinity and you don't have any . . . well . . . any self-esteem or dignity. So there's a lesson for you. Swallow that and come back for another. What did you think, that I was going to stand for your lessons and not give you some of mine?"

"What you're saying (with glacial stoicism) "is fitting for a creature ridden with weaknesses and impurities, whose reason is still in an embryonic state, and who always acts on impulse, a slave to her passions and vices."

"You and your diagnoses!" screamed Fortunata, becoming exalted and waving her arms like an actress during a dramatic passage. "If you'd had just this much dignity you would have shot me dead. You didn't. All the better for me. And I'll tell you something else; if you'd had a drop of manly blood, when you saw him with her you would've plugged them full of bullets and left them dead in the street. But you've got *water* in your blood. All that saint stuff and Christianity and your sickly 'logic' are the repulsive syrup that you've got in your veins instead."

Izquierdo, who could hear from the door, was alarmed and thought he'd better end the conversation that was taking such a bad turn.

"Hey!" he vociferated, coming in, "we've talked enough, now. And you, Señor Maxi, please be kind enough to beat it."

He took him by the arm and found no resistance. Rubín was somewhat perplexed, as if he were analyzing and mentally dissecting his wife's accusations before issuing the reply they deserved. All of a sudden, as if moved by an epileptic impulse, Fortunata sat bolt upright in bed, reached forward, and dug her fingers into her husband's shoulder so vigorously that he seemed to be in the grip of a pair of pliers, and, devouring him with her eyes, she said the following:

"My husband—do you want me to love you? Do you want me to love you with all my heart and soul? Say you do . . . I've behaved badly with you, but now, if you do what I ask, I'll be good. I'll be a saint like you. Say you want it."

Maxi gave her an inquiring look with his luminous eyes.

"Say you do. You'll see, I'll keep my promise. I'll be a model wife and we'll have children, you and me. But, first you've got to do what I'm going to say. I swear I won't go back on my word and I'll love you. You don't know what it's like—a woman who'd die for a man. Poor dear, you've never tasted that honey! Wouldn't you give something for me to love you the way you loved me? Do you remember when you adored me? Do you? Well, I adore you the same way and I've got you engraved on my heart, the way I used to be on yours."

Maximiliano began to react. His cold, stoical mask started to melt like wax in the heat, and his eyes revealed emotion that grew visibly, like a wave coming to a crest.

"Say you do," repeated the devil in delirious exaltation. "Forget about all that saint stuff and let's make up and love each other. You've never known what it's like. You don't know what it is, to be loved. You'll see . . . but on one condition: that you do what you should have done—kill that scurvy. Kill her, because she deserves it. I'll buy you the gun, right now."

Her quivering hands rummaged underneath the pillows in search of her change purse. She found it and took out a bank note.

"Here. Do you want more? Buy a gun, a good one. And then follow her, and bang! make her drop dead. And listen, there's something else: just so you won't be jealous anymore and you can defend your honor like a gentleman, kill both of them, hear? Her and him; he deserves it too. And when they're dead" (with savage sarcasm) "they can have children in the other world. So: will you do it? Do it for my sake, and for his poor wife; she's an angel. We're both angels, each in our own way. Tell me you'll do it. And then I'll love you so much! I'll live only for you. We'll be so happy! We'll have children . . . your children. What do you think?"

Maxi, mute, looked at her like a ninny. Finally, his eyes moistened. He was thawing. He tried to speak and could not. His voice was caught in his throat, gargling.

"Yes, love you," she added. "I don't know why you doubt it. Oh, you don't know me. You don't know what I'm capable of. Forget your 'diagnoses.' Love! I'll teach you what it is. You don't know, silly. It's so delicious . . . !"

"Hey, what are all these 'yections'?" exclaimed Izquierdo, tugging at Rubín's arm. "That's enough song and dance, you two. Out in the street, you. This girl's not well."

"Uncle, leave him alone; let him stay. He's my husband and we want to be together. Come on!"

Maxi let himself be pulled up from his chair as if he were a sack. He'd become inert. Then, quite unexpectedly, something occurred in his soul; he experienced it as a sudden turning upside down of things, so that those that had been on the bottom pivoted up to the top. His hands shook, his eyes were aflame, and when he said, "Kill them, kill them," his voice came out as a falsetto as it had that tragic night after he'd been a victim in the fight at Cuatro Caminos.

"Yes, let's kill them," added the devil, wringing her hands. "Her have children! In hell, maybe."

She fell back on the pillows, her head banging against the iron railing of the bed.

Maxi put out his hand and took the bill, which was still on the spread. And just as Izquierdo was leading him out, Juan Evaristo shrieked loudly and Segismundo came in, very surprised to find the philosopher there again.

10

"That devil of a boy!" he said to Izquierdo when he came back from escorting Señor Rubín to the door. "You've got to be very careful with him and never let him out of your sight when he's here. And how about her—how is she? Hello, my fine girl. Are you up to things?"

The young woman didn't reply. She was in a sort of lethargy. But the baby kept on crying, and made the mother open her eyes. Taking him in her arms, she put him to her breast. Ballester told the maid to turn down the lamp because it heated up the bedroom too much, and he sat down where Maxi had been. Then he took out a medicine box and a little bottle with a potion in it.

"I've brought you another anti-spasmodic. I made it up myself, and I've also brought the perchloride of iron and the ergotine, just in case. Take care now, child; you need a lot of rest so that all today's emotion and foolishness won't bring on a relapse. I bet that Maxi came to bring you more stupid tales. He'll have to be forbidden from coming."

Fortunata had closed her eyes again. The baby was quieting down now and you could hear him sucking at his mother's breast.

"Our little friend doesn't have any problems swallowing, does he?" remarked Ballester. And to himself, contemplating the devil, who was either asleep or pretending to be, he said: "How beautiful she looks! I feel like kissing her—with the purest motives in the world. Here's a woman who isn't worth anything morally today, but who would be worth so much if that damned Santa Cruz would drop dead. He's got her under his spell. What a waste, a heart like hers going to the dogs!"

The baby started to cry again, and the mother seemed as restless as he was.

"Friend Ballester . . . you know, I think my milk's dried up. My son keeps sucking and sucking and he's not getting anything."

"Don't worry. It won't last. Try to sleep. Let's see. Has Maxi been talking nonsense?"

"Nonsense, no. The truth."

"The truth!" bursting out laughing. "And how do you know it's the truth?"

"Because children and crazy people tell the truth."

"That's just a saying that doesn't make any sense. Crazy people only talk nonsense."

"But my husband's not crazy. He's very smart now. At least, I think so."

Juan Evaristo stopped crying again and latched onto his mother's nipple with savage determination.

"Drink some of this. I prepared it for you. It's delicious. You've got to calm your nerves."

The girl brought a glass and a spoon and Fortunata took the anti-spasmodic.

"You're so good, Segismundo! I'm so thankful for all you do for me!"

"You deserve much more," the pharmacist answered effusively. "We're going to be very good friends."

"Yes, friends. As for loving anyone—I'm never going to love anyone again except my husband, that is, when he does what I want."

"Your husband!" taking it as a joke. "That's fine. And now that he's become a saint—"

"No, not a saint. Really, you say such silly things!"

"A saint; that exactly what I meant. So you'll be a saint too. Well, I'll be your disciple. The three of us will go to a desert to do penance and live on weeds."

"Be quiet."

"You're the one who's going to be quiet and see if you can sleep and calm your nerves. Today's escapade won't have any consequences. Do you know what I was thinking on my way over? That if I found my good lass in poor shape I'd spend the night here. And when I left I told my mother that I might not be back. I've made up my mind to treat you as if you were my other half."

"But you don't have to go to all that trouble. I don't feel bad tonight, really I don't; last night I was worse."

"Well, I'll stay till midnight or one o'clock. I'll read the paper or play cards with Señor Izquierdo. And if I see that you're sleeping quietly, I'll leave. If not, I'll stay right here like a watchdog."

Which is what he did. When it was past midnight and he had not observed anything out of the ordinary he tiptoed out, leaving instructions with the square vendor to attend to the mother or child if either needed care during the night. The model left too, and Segunda withdrew to her little hole in the wall. She had hardly dropped off to sleep when Encarnación called her to say that the Señorita felt sick. The baby was crying for all he was worth and there was no way they could quiet him. He exhausted all Encarnación's and his mother's remedies— holding him, walking him, almost dancing him, and trying to persuade him with loving words that children shouldn't cry.

"I think," Fortunata ventured, terrified, "that I'm drying up."

"Well, if you do," replied her aunt, who had a peevish, unpleasant tone even when she was consoling someone, "if your milk does dry up, blast it! it'll be better; we'll find a wet nurse and start living again."

"Tell me, Aunt: has my husband come back?"

Segunda looked at her astounded.

"Your husband! Do you know what time it is? And what do you want that creep around for?"

"I have to talk to him . . ."

"Holy Jesus and curtains too! You certainly picked a nice time for your courtesies. God, only the devil could understand you! Asking for her husband now! For what you can expect from him, it'd be better if he didn't show up around her for a thousand years."

"I have to talk to him. He hasn't been here since last night."

Segunda looked at her again and burst out in rude laughter.

"Look, kid: he was here tonight, and he left at ten o'clock."

"Oh, was it tonight? I get the nights mixed up. I thought a day had gone by. When you're in bed you lose your sense of time."

The baby continued to fuss and his mother continued to complain of a restlessness she couldn't explain.

"I'm so sorry Segismundo left! He would have prescribed something, or at least he would have told me it's nothing and I'd have believed him."

Segunda offered to fetch him, but Fortunata didn't consent to it; she'd get through the night somehow. And so it was, and the truth is they spent a very bad night, even Encarnación, who fell asleep on her feet.

The next morning Estupiñá came up to inquire about the whole family, showing an interest that Segunda knew how to exploit. "How was Mamá's night? And the baby—how's he? I've already heard about the wet nurse business and I've found three very good ones: one's from the highlands of Santander, one's from Santa María de Nieva, and the third's from Asturias—she's got a pair of udders like a dairy cow. Excellent quality!"

"Well, you've taken steps in the right direction, Don Plácido, because she's about to dry up on us," said the vendor, relishing her role in this, "and if the Señora" (alluding to Guillermina) "wants a wet nurse, I'm of the same mind."

After gossiping a bit with Segunda at the latter's door, he went down to his apartment, where in the living room, which was papered with posters announcing novenas and other ecclesiastical functions, Guillermina was standing, holding her rosary and prayerbook. Owner and manager gossiped a bit more, and the outcome of this conference was that Rossini rushed back upstairs for some more scuttlebutt with Segunda, who was at the door. "Tell me, is she sleeping now? And the baby: is he nursing or not?" "Well, they're both quiet now. Seems they're asleep." "All right. Silence then. Be careful not to make any noise. And I'll keep after the brazier's boys; if they start acting up on the stairs, I'll break their backs."

And he went back down and came back up again with another message. "Señá Segunda, be sure to send for that Señor Quevedo today so he can take a look at her and tell us if we should get a wet nurse or not." "All right." "I'll be on the lookout. I've already briefed them, and I'll look them over at my place. Good women, and they don't care about making a lot of money. As for the milk, Señá Segunda, I think the one from Asturias would give us the best milk. I've got an eye for these things . . . Anyway, take care, now."

And he went down again with all his officious diligence, ready to go back up a hundred times, if necessary. Guillermina stayed a little while longer at her friend's house; he hardly knew what to do with himself, seeing his humble dwelling honored by such a lofty personage. He would have brought over the Virgin of the Rosary's throne from San Ginés if he could have, to provide a suitable seat for his friend. Well, when the doorbell rang and he went to open and beheld none other than Jacinta, the poor man thought the entire heavenly court had graced his house. The lady didn't say anything; all she did was smile in a way that meant "How strange it feels to be here!"

Guillermina raised her voice from the living room: "Come in. I'm in here." Estupiñá, always refined, withdrew to leave them alone. The saint seemed to be giving her friend a maternal reprimand: "I told you to leave this to me. I can handle it. If you insist on getting into things, I think you're going to spoil it. No, I won't let you go up. Do you think it's easy to see him without his mother finding out? You've gotten a bit bold. Tell them to bring him down? Really, the things you say! You'll have lots of time to see him. If we start doing foolish things and behaving like a couple of spies sticking our noses into other people's business, we'll deserve it if Ido puts us in his novels. Let's go to San Ginés now, and then we'll ask Señor Quevedo's opinion. Don't worry, he won't die of hunger on us."

They left, and Plácido escorted them to church; even though he had already been to Mass, he was quite pleased to escort the ladies now. They stayed for two, and before leaving, seated on the bench, the Dauphine said to her friend: "You know, I haven't been able to concentrate on Mass devoutly because I was thinking about that woman. I can't get her out of my mind. And the worst of it is that I think she did well to do what she did yesterday. God forgive me for the atrocious thing I'm going to say, but I think that that adventuress has redeemed some of her sins with her act of justice! She may be bad, but she's got a lot of courage. We should all do the same."

The saint made no reply because she did not like to openly discuss profane matters in church; but on their way out to Arenal Street she took her friend's arm and said: "A lovely show they put on. They're a couple of gems!"

"Well, believe me—when I heard about it I was so glad! I would have given anything to witness the tragedy."

"Hush! It's revolting to think of two women hitting each other."

"Maybe so, but ever since I heard about it, the old witch has grown in my eyes and she doesn't seem as bad as the new one."

"This world is full of evil, child. No matter where you look, all you see are sins—sins that are getting grosser and grosser because humanity seems to be getting more and more shameless and losing its fear of God. Who would ever have guessed that Aurorita, the girl who seemed so clever and so virtuous—! Well, she's clever, all right. But the other one's smarter. And what does Bárbara have to say about it? She was delighted with her, and she went to the workshop every day, just to see her work. But shhh! Here comes your mother-in-law now."

Barbarita and the pair met.

"You're too late for the padre's Mass. What a time to come!"

"They wouldn't let me leave all morning. Jacinta, your husband's there calling for you. I went in and . . . 'Where is she?' And then 'Why did you have to be out in the street so early?' So you'd better hurry."

"Let him wait. That would be the last straw," Jacinta replied tediously. "Let him be patient, the way other people are."

"Where have you two been?"

"Us? Seeing wet nurses," said the saint with a smile.

"Wet nurses!"

"Yes; it's not a joke—wet nurses."

"Aren't you peculiar today!"

"You don't mean this ninny hasn't told you yet that we've found another Pituso?"

Barbarita dissolved in graceful laughter.

"You mean they've swindled you again?"

"Ha! Not this time. This is the real thing—twenty-four carat, not just gold-plated like the other one you lost your head over."

"Bah! None of that, now," Barbarita replied in a festive mood. And she rushed off to reach her Mass on time.

"Wait . . . listen!" Guillermina called after her. "When you finish, go window shopping for a while. You'll find your buyer, Estupiñá the Great. Wait—buy a good cradle."

The lady laughed; they all laughed.

I I

Quevedo's report on the mother was not alarming, but he had bad news about the baby: his supply was going to be depleted very soon. That afternoon Plácido related to the lady that the woman refused to yield her baby to a wet nurse's breast, even if it came straight from heaven; she insisted that she had milk. The baby squawked, implying that his mamá was making a sham of the truth. "Anyway, Señora," Estupiñá added obnoxiously, "that woman ought to be killed. She's as evil as they come. What she wants is for the little fellow to die."

The founder went up and was glad to find Ballester in the living room. "Let's see if you can convince her that she shouldn't try to nurse him. Since the poor girl's head is a bit weak and confused, she thinks they're trying to take away her son. And that's not it; we're just concerned about his being fed properly."

"I've already told her. I used almost the same words, Señora. But you should see what she's like. She woke up in an apathetic, sad mood that I don't like at all. There's no way to get an answer from her about anything. She's got the baby in her arms, and when a wet nurse is mentioned, or we tell her that her milk is drying up, she squeezes him so hard I'm afraid she'll suffocate him."

"May God's will be done . . . I'll go in to see the wild beast and we'll try to tame her."

Without giving up her distrustful, frightened attitude, Fortunata nevertheless seemed glad to see Guillermina, who greeted her extremely amiably, showing great interest in both mother and son.

"What a pleasure to see you!" the sinner exclaimed without stirring. "I was hoping you'd come so I could tell you something."

"Well, don't waste a second because I'm only going to stay a minute."

The unhappy young woman put the baby down at her side, showing less distrust; but she put her arm around him protectively.

"Would you take him away from me? Tell me if that's what you wanted to do. Joking aside. I'll believe what you say."

"Thank you very much, my friend. So you take me for a kidnapper. I didn't know I was a witch—"

"No. It's just that . . . well, you'll see. I thought they were going to take him away from me because I've been so bad. But that doesn't have anything to do with it, does it? I'm much worse now. Oh, Señora! I've committed such a big sin I don't think God will forgive me."

"Shall we bet it's just some nonsense?" she asked, leaning forward and stroking her chin.

"Oh, Señora, I only wish it was just foolishness. I'm going to tell you. But don't scold me too much. Well, last night my husband was here, we talked, and I gave him twenty duros to buy me a gun. The gun's to kill him and her with. Especially her, that French whore . . ."

Guillermina was shocked by these words, but she made an effort to conceal it and appear serene. "That's a tall order, yes, my dear. But your husband won't do it. I talked with him and he sounded very reasonable."

"Reason is his theme song, but you can't trust him. And as for shooting them, he'll do it. I egged him on. I took all that new knowledge out of his head by what I told him. He went crazy again, Señora; I promised to love him the way he loved me, and believe me, I really meant it."

"You're giving me gooseflesh," growing alarmed. "You realize, don't you, that that sin's the worst there is. If he does kill them, he's sinned less than you, because you got him to do it by making those promises."

"That's exactly what I've been thinking, and that's why I've been scared all night."

"If you realize that you've behaved badly and beg forgiveness from God for your evil intentions and try to cleanse yourself of them, God will have pity on you, the sinner."

"Well, you see . . . I am only half sorry. Kill him? You know, that would make me sorry. No, he shouldn't be killed. But as for her—that dirty little liar. And being nervy enough to think about having his children! Children, *her*? Tell me: what would be lost by sending trash like her to the other world?"

She said this so naturally that Guillermina didn't know whether to be indignant or take it as a joke. "Well, well, what appealing thoughts you have. I'm beginning to think that your husband and you make good company . . . with your 'understanding.' If you don't take back all that nonsense immediately, I'm leaving and you'll never see me again. This is intolerable."

"So that monster of a woman shouldn't get punished? Humph! That'd be nice. And she'll go right on laughing up her sleeve at us. I don't get it."

"God is the one who punishes; it is for us to learn."

Both fell silent and looked at each other.

"I'll have to bring you a confessor. Your body and soul are both in poor condition. Because if death should take you—and may God not will it—when you're not ready yet, you're going to get the grand prize."

"If I die, I'm taking my son with me," said the devil, picking him up again and pressing him to her.

"That's another wild statement. You're full of them today."

"Well, isn't he mine? Wasn't it me, after all, who brought him into this world?" feverishly impatient.

"What! *You* brought him into this world? You certainly aren't short on pretentions, child. So now you want to compete with the Creator of the world and everything in it. Really, all I can do is laugh. We're sitting here talking like a couple of fools and things have to be settled. You have to send for your husband and tell him that in order for you to love him as God would wish, he mustn't kill anyone, no one, you hear? Will you do that?"

"If you order me to, yes. Oh! I thought that killing a person who deceived you wasn't a sin . . . well, I mean, not a very big sin. Last night I was out of my mind, I realize that; my bitterness went to my head. I'm so furious at her! It seems to me you can be furious at somebody and hope she's killed without being evil yourself."

She sat up so as to express more persuasively an argument that had just occurred to her and that she deemed very strong. "Let's see, Señora. I bet you won't have anything to say to this. I bet that with all you know, you still won't have an answer."

"To what?"

"To this; listen. Señorita Jacinta is what you call an angel, right? Everybody says so. All right. Well, with all her merit and holiness, wouldn't she be glad if somebody got rid of me?"

She leaned back on the pillows satisfied, waiting for an answer, feeling sure that the saint's only way out of this one was to lie.

"What are you saying?" Guillermina replied indignantly. "Jacinta wanting someone killed! Either you're a fool or you've lost your mind!"

"Well, all right; I'll put it another way," she said, backing up to a less extreme position. "Wouldn't the Señorita be glad if I died?"

"Glad . . . that you died? That God had taken you?" she floundered. "No, she wouldn't. Jacinta doesn't wish misfortune on others, and she knows that we should love our enemies and be kind to those who abhor us."

With a sad "ho, ho," Fortunata expressed her incredulity.

"What, don't you believe me?"

"That she wishes me well? That's a joke."

"Jacinta doesn't know what rancor is. She doesn't even remember you."

"But there's a big difference between that and liking me."

"The next thing you're going to ask for is that she be as fond of you as she is of me. And, indeed, the good little girl deserves what she wants. Listen—you ought to be satisfied if she forgives you."

"Has she forgiven me? Really forgiven me?"

"What makes you doubt it? Since you don't know what faith, or fear of God, or anything is, you couldn't understand it."

"And could she be my friend?"

"Well, child, as much as a friend . . . That's asking a bit too much," unable to suppress her laughter. "You don't stop at anything, do you? After all that's happened, you want her to be your bosom friend."

"Friends!" repeated the devil, knitting her brow. "No matter what you say, she can't stand the sight of me, especially now that I've had a son and she hasn't. And as far as that goes, she won't ever have one; that's clear. So she can forget about it."

When Ballester, hearing the saint laugh, approached the bedroom door, she beckoned:

"Come on in if you want to be amused. This is a regular comedy. Your friend still has to be subdued. What notions she has! That reminds me—I'm going to send her Father Nones. She needs a thorough cleaning. Well, I'll be on my way. With all this foolishness the morning's almost over."

She got up, but Fortunata tugged at her dress to make her sit down again. "I've still got a doubt, Señora. Please clear it up for me."

"Well, what is it? Probably another piece of nonsense. Oh, what a head!"

"Sit down for a minute. I'm going to ask you one more thing. Tell me," lowering her voice, "was Jacinta unfaithful with that gentleman or not?"

"Holy saints above! What gentleman?"

"The one that died all of a sudden."

"Be quiet, or I'll hit you."

"I don't believe it anymore. I used to. But since it was that indecent little

Aurora who told me, I stopped believing it. But I still had a tiny doubt in the back of my mind."

"That . . . ?" with supreme scorn. "And she dared—!"

"Oh, she's horrible. You have no idea how evil she is," very sincerely. "With all I've done, I'm an angel next to her."

"I believe it," smiling. "But let's not bother ourselves with such trifles. Jacinta unfaithful! Those hardened sinners think that everybody's like them."

"But I don't believe it, Señora; I never believed it," she hastened to add. "She was the one that said it and believed it. You know something?" attracting Guillermina to her as if to confide a secret. "And this is God's truth. One of the reasons I hit her was for making me swallow that stuff and think Jacinta was like us. And tell me this: didn't she deserve getting crowned with that key for insulting our friend? Didn't she? Of course she did."

Guillermina was nonplussed; she didn't know whether to approve or disapprove.

"So, we're agreed on one thing," she said, getting up. "Tomorrow Father Nones will come to call and there'll be an Asturian wet nurse for this little tyke. According to Estupiñá—"

"No, no wet nurse. What for? I can feed him. Haven't you seen how satisfied the king of the house is? Isn't it true, my little darling, that you don't need a wet nurse? His mamá gives him all he wants."

"Señor Quevedo is a better judge than you. Nothing that I don't command is going to be done here," declared the saint with that authoritarian tone and manner that no one dared oppose. "If Quevedo doesn't change his mind by tomorrow, the wet nurse will come. You obey and be quiet. I'll pay for any expenses and decide what's to be done. So. Take care of yourself and then we'll talk. Señor Ballester is hereby entrusted with carrying out my decree."

12

That afternoon Doña Lupe arrived in a panic searching for Maximiliano, whom she expected to find there. She didn't go beyond the living room, nor did she want to see Fortunata, for whom she expressed her sympathy but with whom she could have no sort of relationship, she said. The "organization woman" whispered to Segismundo, informing him of what had transpired. Maximiliano had done no less than buy a gun. But who in the devil had given him the money? The Señora had found out by chance. It had occurred to her when she saw him come in with something hidden under his papers. The worst part was that she hadn't been able to get it away from him. He ran out of the house and a little while later the blacksmith's assistants (on the ground floor) came up to tell her that they had seen him at La Ronda firing at the walls of the gas factory as if he were practicing. Oh! The "turkey woman" was terrified. All that logical knowledge in the poor boy's head had probably gone up in smoke. And he hadn't come home for lunch, either; she didn't have a clue to his whereabouts. "We'll have to inform the police, to keep him from doing some terrible thing. I thought he might have come here, so I came running over hoping against hope . . . Where the devil could he be? For the love of God, please find out, Ballester, and free me from this awful dilemma. You're the only one who can control him when he gets like this. Go out and see if you can find him, I beg you." The good pharmacist's reply was that he couldn't play the music and dance too. So the Jáuregui woman left in extreme desolation, intending to beseech Señor Torquemada, the luminous beacon who charted her course in the squalls of life.

Fortunata had heard Doña Lupe's voice, and when the latter retired, she asked Ballester to explain what had brought her there.

"Nothing, really. The 'organization woman' just wanted to stick her nose in the pie and see you and tell you things that probably would have made you dizzy."

"Well, don't let her in. I can't stand the sight of her. I think I'll be sick if I see her. And what did she say about my husband?"

"She didn't mention him."

"Well, I don't want to see Maxi either. You have no idea what a bad effect he has on me. He upsets me. Don't let them in. They can go to the devil for all I care. I'm so calm here, all alone with my son and friends who protect me! Please don't let them come. Do you promise me they won't?"

She requested this with supplicating fear. Ballester, who was outdoing himself in protective gentlemanliness and fraternal nobility, assured her that no Rubín—big or small, of flesh and blood or with cotton breasts—would darken that door except over his dead body.

All afternoon the young woman was obsessed with the thought of how unpleasant the Rubíns were and what she would do to avoid receiving them if they came to see her. Segismundo tried, good as he was, to calm her on this point, and once he observed that thinking about other people excited her spirits favorably, he talked about Doña Guillermina and her beautiful life. "You know what she said to me as she was leaving? That if you should need anything, Plácido has been instructed to carry out your wishes."

"Sure," said Fortunata, overflowing with innocent pride, "and Plácido's like one of the family; from the time he was a little boy he's spent all his time carrying messages and doing hundreds of errands for them. He's a good man and I like him very much. Do you know Doña Bárbara? I don't either. But when Jacinta and I make friends, I'll be friends with Doña Bárbara too. Frankly, I'm amazed at how fond I've gotten to be of 'Angel Face' when I remember that before just the thought of her made me sick. It's true I didn't get to hate her; I mean, I hated her but I liked her, too. Strange, isn't it? Now we'll be friends, we really will be. Do you doubt it?"

"Why should I doubt it, dear?"

"Well, it's just that you seem to smile a little when you hear me say it."

"Oh, you're just seeing things."

"Well, even if you're teasing me, we'll be friends. And nobody's going to have anything to say about me because I'm going to behave . . . It's going to be a new life: my son and my son and my son. Oh, come on, are you going to tell me that you're not smiling now?"

"Yes, but it's out of satisfaction from seeing you so regenerated. Nobody will dare sniff at you now, when you're surrounded by members of the heavenly court!"

"That's all. What did you expect would happen?"

She was so breathless that the pharmacist deemed it prudent to switch the conversation to a trivial subject. But Fortunata always managed to bring it back to the same subject: that she and the Dauphine were going to be like flesh and blood and that in the future her conduct would be worthy of a seraph. "This person you're looking at, friend Ballester, can be an angel too, if she sets herself to it. It's just a question of starting. And it's very simple. At least, I don't think it's going to take much effort. I can feel it in my bones."

"It also depends on the people you're with," he said very gravely. "Let's talk about something else now. I don't want to mention certain bold feelings I had and still have about you, because you're going to become a saint on us. And yet it could be feasible, it seems to me—being a saint and also loving one of God's creatures. But I'll close the book on that for now. Do you realize that if I'm not careful I could lose my job at Samaniego's pharmacy? If Doña Casta finds out that these absences of mine are so that I can come visit the person who cut her daughter down to size, she'll clean out my cupboards in no time. So I can't press my luck too much; that's why I won't be coming tonight. I have to tend the pharmacy. I'd make a clean break if it weren't for the fact that it would be hard to find another job right away; and believe me, unemployment would cripple me. I wouldn't mind myself, but I don't want my mother and sister to have to fast. The poor 'thinker,' my famous brother-in-law, isn't doing too well with his interest, and if I don't pull the cart, the sighs and cries for bread will reach all the way to Gibraltar."

"Don't be silly," said Fortunata with one of her characteristic bursts of generosity. "I've got some dough. If you feel like telling the Samaniego women where to go, do it. Let them stew in their juices and go broke. I'll give you what you need for your mother and the 'thinker' till you find another pharmacy. Trust me. With me it's all the way."

Ballester was so refined that merely hearing this proposition made him blush; he declined, expressing his gratitude. Shortly after dark he left, telling the Izquierdo pair in no uncertain terms what to do about visitors: If a Rubín, no matter which one it was, shows up, don't open. On the living room table he left an arsenal of medicines, and to Fortunata he recommended rest and that she "slam the door of her mind" to any lugubrious thoughts.

Izquierdo posted his watch in the living room with a big bottle of beer (he'd also brought a little one in case the first ran out during the night). Segunda came back at ten after her habitual hour of conversation at the meat stand, and, seeing her niece wide awake, gave her some chit-chat. "Guess who I saw? That woman, you know, 'the turkey woman.' She came looking for me at my stand, all offended because Señor Ballester didn't let her in to see you. She's out hunting for her nephew. He ran off on them this morning and still hasn't showed up. You know what she told me? I'm telling you to give you a laugh. She says the Samaniegas are furious at you and that the old hag—you know, that Doña Casta—won't be content till she sees you put in jail. What a laugh! It's all envy. Well, anyways, that swiny French Fenelona—she's worse than trash—says that the father of this son of yours isn't who it is and that it's really Don Segismundo. But laugh at her, silly. All it is is envy."

The sinner sat speechless; but it was quite clear that these words had had a disastrous effect on her soul. When she was alone again she could not repress her urge to get up. Rage seethed in her soul, and, unaware of what she was doing, she sat up in bed and reached out to the rack for her clothes. "I'm getting up this minute, *this minute*, and I'm going to bash in her face till her nose is flat . . . the pig! Saying that! A lie like that! What time is it? It's striking midnight! Well, no matter what time it is, I'm going out, I can't stop myself. I'll go right into her house and drag her out of bed and stomp on her soul. To say *that*! And I know she doesn't believe it. She's saying it to dishonor me! First she dirtied Jacinta's name. Now it's mine."

She sat up in bed envisioning, despite her troubled state, the difficulties of this undertaking. "If I leave it for tomorrow, I won't do it; they'll get the idea out of my head. And I'm going to squash her head in with the soles of my boots. If I don't, Lord knows, it'll be impossible for me to be an angel and I won't be able to be a saint. Unless I do this, I'll end up being bad again; I can feel it."

And she began putting on her clothes, then taking them off, experiencing an awful vacillation, caught between the formidable impulses of her desire and a sense of impossibility. Finally she finished dressing, and, entering the living room, she saw her uncle asleep, face down on the table, near the lamp, with the big bottle half-empty beside him. "I could leave without anyone knowing. Or I could wake up my uncle and tell him to come with me." The thought of associating Plato with her rash scheme made her realize how crazy her plan was. "But early tomorrow morning," she said to herself on her way back to the bedroom, "early in the morning, before she leaves for the shop, I'm going to grab her by the neck . . ."

When she looked at her son, the flame of her anger leaped even higher. "To say he isn't the son of his father! What infamy! I could rip out her guts and not feel a bit sorry. So innocent, so tiny, and already they want to dishonor him. But they're not going to, no sir, because his mother's here to defend him. And whoever tries to tell me he's not the son of the house is going to get his eyes torn out. *He* wouldn't have said it. But if I found out that he had, I swear by this cross" (making one with her fingers and kissing it) "by this cross they killed You on, my Savior, I swear I'll detest him . . . and I mean with heart and soul, not just my tongue. Oh, my God!" (flinging herself down on the bed, grief-ridden), "if they tell this big lie to Guillermina and Jacinta, will they believe it? Maybe so . . . People always believe the bad things they hear, and if it's about me, they're sure to. But no; maybe they won't believe it. It's a horrible lie. Nobody could believe it, nobody; first they'd have to believe that the world's turning inside out and that day is night and the sun's the moon and water's fire. And if anybody does believe it, he'll disprove it, I'm sure he will. I haven't been unfaithful, no, I haven't" (raising her voice) "and whoever says I have been is lying and deserves to have his tongue torn out with hot tongs. They want to see me fall, but no matter what those dogs do, they're not going to get it out of my head that I'm as much of an angel as anybody else. Let them be furious. I *will* be an angel."

She was terribly restless and rolled over and over in bed. Her son begged for and was given her breast, but he must not have found the supply very abundant, for he kept turning away to cry desperately. His cries of need and despair joined with his mother's as she queried plaintively: "My own little son, what is it? Isn't there any milk? That thieving witch is to blame; she took it from you. But just wait, you'll see how your mamá fixes it all up. Poor baby, so tiny and small and they already want to dishonor him. My little boy is the king of Spain and he doesn't have anything to do with Ballester, who's only his friend, that's all. My baby is who he is, and there's no other in 'the house,' and there won't be either, isn't that so? Isn't that so, my glory, my heaven, my happiness?"

13

All this was very pretty and tender, but the milk did not come and Juan Evaristo was far from satisfied by these words of such meager practical value. Neither the mother's nor the child's outcries awoke José Izquierdo; once he laid one on, not even thunder could wake him. But they did arouse Segunda from her lethargy, and she went to see what was wrong; finding her niece half-dressed, she virtually exploded and almost hit her. "I warn you—I'll bash your head in if you start any scenes on us," she said in her usual exquisite language. "Can't you see, you ass, that your milk's dried up and there's nothing for the poor thing to suck?"

Luckily, among the things Ballester had left for any and all possible mishaps there was a very nice looking bottle. Segunda quickly filled it with milk (which she happened to have a few glasses of) and tried it on the baby. At first he was puzzled by the hardness and coldness of the nipple they were forcing into his little mouth. He refused it several times; but eventually hunger won out over squeamishness and he reluctantly accepted the artificial teat. "Oh, look how fast the little angel has learned to take it. He's so noble! Poor sweets—we were starving, weren't we?" The mother looked at her son disconsolately, although content that they had found a way to overcome the difficulty. "You know something," said her aunt, putting her hand on Fortunata's forehead, "you've got a fever. That's what comes of thinking what you shouldn't. If you'd only pay attention to me now that you're going to be the queen of the world. Because they'll have to give you payments every month, you know. The 'turkey woman' and I were talking about it. Some lady you're going to be! Come on, don't be so humble; lift up your head. Don't you see that those ladies are putting one over on you? And you're the one with the power. If I was you I wouldn't make a move till Jacinta came and kissed your feet. And *him*—don't you realize he'll come too? He'll have to answer the call of his own blood. And the minute he sees this spitting image of himself, he's going to drool. Listen kid, we're even going to get a carriage out of this. What a laugh! We're in the big time now. He'll come, and I can tell you this: if he takes four days it'll be a long time. Can't you see—that family wants a baby to make them happy? They're just dying for one! You watch your step, because God's looked out for us by giving us this son of our own flesh and blood. I'm very proud, because as sure as there's a God he's a Santa Cruz; but nobody can take out the touch of Izquierdo in him—both families are lucky. I've started to brush off some of our dust already. This afternoon I started Plácido thinking about letting us live rent free. What do you expect? The Santa Cruzes are as excited about your son as a kid with new shoes. And I'll tell you something you don't know: yesterday la Jacinta was at Don Plácido's. She wanted to come up and see him but the other one, you know, the big saint, said that what if you got all riled up . . . So you see, there's stuff you should know. Who would've ever guessed it! I can even picture myself walking along with Don Baldomero for a stroll on the Castellana. And I'm going to flaunt it! This is really a riot. You be proud and don't be a ninny. If we play our cards right we might even get to be duchesses."

During her aunt's speech tears rolled down Fortunata's face; but when she heard the part about becoming a duchess, a streak of joviality cut through her sadness, and the young woman burst out laughing, her face still wet with tears.

"Stop laughing; we won't get as far as that, and anyways, what do we care about titles? But we will have our carriage. I can tell you this: if la Jacinta comes today, she'll have to come up. And just wait. You'll see how fast he follows her. When his wife's not here, of course. I think this time she's just going to have to go plant cabbages. You're the one that's going up on the throne now. Or else there ain't no justice on this earth. And they'd better not say you're married and that your son's gotta be called Rubín. What a laugh that'd be! You're a widow and you're free, and you can consider your husband out of it, up in heaven some- wheres. Everybody knows what went on here, and anyways, it's written all over the boy's face, so they'll have to give you money."

Fortunata stopped laughing and Segunda didn't say anything else that might induce hilarity. Her aunt stayed with her until daybreak when, seeing that she was relatively quiet, she left to catch a few winks before leaving for the marketplace.

Shortly after being left alone, Fortunata felt something strange happening in- side her. Her vision blurred and she could feel a mass breaking away from her that reminded her of when Juan Evaristo came into the world, except that this time there was no pain. She wasn't able to observe the phenomenon well because she fainted. When she regained her senses she noticed that it was midmorning and she heard the birds chirping in their barracks, which were the treetops of the Plaza Mayor and the bronze mane of Philip III's horse. She tried to pick up her son and could hardly hold him. She was completely drained of strength. She even seemed to be losing her sight; objects looked disfigured and she mistook them for things that did not exist. After calling out three times she started to call again and . . . this really was serious: she had no voice, it made no sound; her intended words stuck in her throat. She rapped on the wall with her knuckles, but her hand got so soft it felt like cotton; she knocked with her whole hand, but the blows were inaudible. Or perhaps they were audible and it was only she who couldn't hear them. But why didn't Segunda hear them from the other side of the partition? Then her arm felt like dead flesh; she couldn't move it. "Do you suppose I'm dying?" the young woman wondered, trying to see into herself. But she couldn't see much, for she found her interior either dark or glaringly bright. Her thoughts became feverish; the images in her mind seemed to be wearing disguises, like people who go to a masquerade dressed up as somebody else, and the only plain sensation she had in the midst of that disorder was immobility and rigidity; her involuntary movements had stopped and her voluntary ones were disobeying her wishes. She had the impression that she wasn't even breathing; every now and then her sight and hearing gave her some fleeting proof of exterior life, but these perceptions were like something going past her, always from left to right. She thought she saw Segunda and heard her talking with Encarnación; but they were talking at full speed, as if they were possessed by the devil, and they were passing by her toward some vague spot on the right into which they dissolved. And the birds' chirping pierced that gloominess, and so did Juan Evaristo's cries for his bottle.

After a certain length of time, indefinite for her, she regained her senses and her ability to move, thus perceiving reality more easily. "Who are you?" she asked Encarnación, the only person with her. "Oh, I know. How stupid of me! Isn't my aunt here?" The girl told her that Señá Segunda had gone to the marketplace, brought milk for the child, and left again. Fortunata's dizzy spell had left her with a conviction that she clung to as if it were a basic notion, namely, that she was going to die that morning. She could feel the wound deep within her, although she couldn't exactly pinpoint it; it was an incurable wound or decomposition, and her bodily awareness had revealed it to her in an infallible diagnosis that had come to her like an inspiration or a prophetic message. Her head recovered its serenity; breathing became easier, although she was short of breath; a debility was developing at an alarming rate in her extremities. But as her physical person began to be extinguished, her moral self, concentrating on a single idea, began to acquire an unusual vigor. All the good that she could think and feel emptied itself as if into a mold, into that idea, and on that idea she imprinted, quite simply, the most beautiful and perhaps the least human profile of her character so as to leave behind a clear, dynamic impression of it. "If I'm not careful," she thought extremely anxiously, "death will take me, and I won't be able to do it. What a grand idea! Having thought of it is a sign that I'm going straight to heaven. But quickly, quickly—I haven't got long to live." Calling Encarnación she said, "Little one, run down and tell Don Plácido I need him. Tell him I need him, and to come up. Hurry now, and don't stop on your way. He must be there, home from church, drinking his hot chocolate. Hurry up, child. I'll be very grateful to you."

While Encarnación was out, the devil did nothing but shower her son with kisses and tender words. The baby boy was awake, looking at her silently, and although he said nothing, she fancied that he was talking. "You'll be so well off, my son. They won't love you as much as I do, but almost as much, that's true. I'm dying . . . I have something or other . . . that medicine, I'd take it . . . where is it? Encarnación! Oh . . . That's right, she's gone downstairs. It feels like I'm losing blood. Oh, my son, I'm dying; life's flowing out of me like a river running into the sea. I'm still alive thanks to this blessed idea I have. Oh, what a gorgeous idea! I don't need any Sacraments with this; I know it, they've told me so from up above. I can hear the voice of the angel who's telling me, here in my heart. The idea came to me when I was lying here speechless, and when I woke up, I clung to it. It's the key to the gate of heaven. My little son, be nice and quiet please; if your mamá leaves it's because it's God's command. Oh, Don Plácido! Are you there?"

"Yes, Señora," answered the talker, entering the bedroom in the most officious manner imaginable. "What is it? The Señora asked me to—"

"Friend, do me a favor and bring me a pen and paper. Wait a minute; give me the medicine, that yellow powder. Which one? I don't know. But never mind; you've got to write a letter for me."

"A letter! But first—" rummaging through the night table. "Which medicine did you want?"

"None of them. At this stage, why bother? Hurry up, I'm giving out . . . I'm dying."

"Dying! Come on, don't joke like that."

"Don Plácido, if you won't help me with this, I'll find someone else. If I could just wait for Ballester . . . but no, I haven't got time."

"But child, there's no rush. I'll go find an inkwell." Within five minutes he was back, and he saw that Fortunata was sitting up in bed holding the baby in her arms; then, with Encarnación's help, she wrapped him warmly and put him in his wicker cradle that was more like a basket. They gave him his bottle so he wouldn't make a fuss, and they covered him with a fine silk cloth. Estupiñá didn't understand any of this; nor did he see any connection between the pen and paper and these proceedings. "Don Plácido," said Fortunata in a very excited voice, "do me a favor and write—oh, but there's no table in here—Encarnación! Bring him the chess board. Forget about the medicine. Why bother now? Well, Don Plácido, get ready for this; it's going to be a shock. I had an idea awhile ago. When I couldn't speak, I also got the idea that I was dying. Put down this:

"Señora Doña Jacinta. I—"

"I—" repeated Plácido.

"—No. It shouldn't start like that. I can't think what to say. What a dunce I am! Oh, yes! Put down: 'Since the Lord has seen fit to take my soul, and I realize now how evil I was . . .' How's that? Does it sound all right?"

"—How evil I was—"

"Well, anyway, keep writing what I say. 'I don't want to die without doing you a kind deed, and I'm sending you, in care of our friend Don Plácido, the little "angel face" that your husband gave me by mistake.' No, cross out 'by mistake' and put 'that he gave me, stealing him from you.' But no, Don Plácido, not like that; it sounds awful . . . because it was me who had him, me, and nobody took anything away from her. What I mean is that I want to give him to her because I know she'll love him and because she's my friend. Write this: 'To console you for the bad times your husband gives you, I'm sending you the real Pituso. This one's not fake; he's legitimate, the real thing, as you'll see in his face. I beg you—' "

"—I beg you—"

"Put it all down nice and clear, Don Plácido; I'm just giving you the idea. Well, where was I? 'I beg you to consider him your own son, and his father's too.

Yours truly—' How's that sound? Is it proper? Now I'll try to put my name to it. My hand's shaking so much. Bring me a pen."

She scribbled something, then ordered Estupiñá to open the bureau and get out the certificate of the bank shares. After a lot of searching, the document turned up. "Give it," said Fortunata, "to my friend Doña Guillermina."

"But they're no good unless you transfer them," replied the talker, examining the paper.

"Without what?"

"Without legal transference."

"Stuff and nonsense. It's mine, and I can give it to whomever I want. Take the pen, and write that it's my wish that the shares are for Doña Guillermina Pacheco. I'll put lots of signatures underneath and you'll see, it'll be good."

Although Estupiñá did not consider her way of making a will to be valid, he did what she ordered.

"Now, my friend," she said, gradually losing her command of language, "pick up my son and take him . . . Oh, let me kiss him again! Wait till I die . . . No. Take him before my aunt gets here, or my husband, or Doña Lupe; they're mean people. They might come and it wouldn't work. They won't let me have my way and I'll get mad, and then I wouldn't die in such a holy state, the way I want to."

That was all she said. Plácido, approaching to contemplate her, was terribly frightened. He thought she was dead or on the verge of death; he sent Encarnación out to look for Segunda and José Izquierdo, and, picking up the basket where Juan Evaristo was sleeping, put it in the living room. "I can't make up my mind to take him," thought the worthy old man. "But at the same time, if those brutes try to keep me from taking him . . . oh, no; I'm taking him with me. They can try whatever they want." He picked up the basket and took it down to his house as quickly as his legs permitted (they were rather weak), scared and wary like a smuggler; then he went back up again and to see the patient, looking at her at such close range that his face almost touched hers. "Fortunata . . . Pitusa," he murmured, whispering 'xactly into her ear. At the third or fourth call, Fortunata's eyelids fluttered, and, parting her lips, she barely uttered: "*Baby . . .*"

14

"Confound it, that woman's dying! And me here alone with her, and the kid downstairs! They're going to say I stole him. Humph—they'll be the thieves. Let them talk. What do I care? I'll just show them the paper, signed by her, that's all. Poor woman." He gazed at her, horrified. "Holy Virgin of Carmen, her blood's running cold! How could those pigs leave her at a time like this? Didn't they see the danger? And that doctor—what's his mind on? What a jam! What should I give her? There are some medicines here; I'll give her these. But what if I'm wrong? Careful with the drugs, Plácido; let's not botch it up. We'd better wait. But what if . . . by the time they get here, she'll be on the other side of the fence. God forgive her, and may He give her what she deserves. I've got to try to revive her" (speaking into her ear): "Fortunata, Fortunatita, don't die on us like this. I'll bring you the viaticum, or at least the Extreme Unction. Hey, girl, child! She doesn't hear me. This is the end! Child, think of God and the Blessed Virgin; call on them at this crucial moment, they'll protect you . . . It's no use—I might as well be speaking Greek. She can't hear, or else she's so bound up in evil she doesn't want to hear any talk about religion. I'm going to try another tack," he reflected maliciously. "Fortunata, sweetie, look who's here—wake up and see. Don't you know him? It's your Señor Don Juanito, he's come to see his . . . lady. Look, just look how upset he is to see you so ill." (Then to himself): "What a smile the devil's got now! Hmm, hopelessly in love with him. She's opening her eyes and looking around for him. It's like drunks—even when they're almost gone, you mention wine and they revive. Unless someone saves her, this woman's going to plunge headfirst into hell. What a way to repent! I speak of Our Divine Redeemer and the Blessed Virgin of Carmen and it's like water off a duck. Deaf as a doornail. But I mention the Señorete, and there she is—all excited and ready to live again, and no doubt full of intentions to sin, too. Her salvation's not going to be any short order! I think I hear her aunt coming up. I can hear her snorting like a seawolf. Yes, here they come," exiting to the corridor and talking to Segunda, who was coming up breathlessly, preceded by Encarnación. "You're certainly calm about things! She's in a very bad way, a very bad way."

Segunda had hardly entered the bedroom when she started to cry out: "My niece, my daughter—they've killed her on me, they've murdered her! Oh, what butchery! What a state she's in! They've killed her! And the baby? They've stolen him from us!"

"Attend to your niece, and see if you can save her," Estupiñá instructed, taking her by the arm, "and forget about assassinations and kidnappings, and don't act like an old fool."

"My darling dear . . . what is it? Fortunata—have they killed you, or what? Let's see, kitten, do you have any wounds? Looks like you've been stabbed a hundred times. But you're alive. Tell me what happened; who was it? And your baby, our baby, where is he? Did they take him away?"

"Call for the doctor," Plácido said angrily. "Where does he live? I'll get him. And don't worry about the baby—he's better than he could hope and has everything he needs."

"But where is he? Don Plácido, Don Plácido," exclaimed Segunda, furious and totally lacking any composure. "Seems to me your next stop's gonna be jail. I'm gonna report it to the police. You're a bandit, yes, sir, and I mean what I say. You snatched the kid from us."

"Blast it! You demon," recoiling for fear that Segunda would scratch out his eyes. "Will you shut up a minute? Can't you see your niece is dying?"

"Because *you* killed her on me, you miserable swine . . . you—"

"Go on, give me more garbage. What you need is a muzzle. I'm going to get the Emergency Service."

"Where *you're* going—is jail."

And at that moment José Izquierdo appeared, and his sister tried to get him to attack poor old Estupiñá. Plato vacillated, not crediting his sister as much as she thought she deserved.

"I'm fed up, and the one who's bringing the judge is me," declared the old man, stamping his foot. "The boy's where he should be and you know very well that I'm not lying. And if you don't think so, ask his mother."

"My own, my dearest!" shrieked Segunda, embracing and kissing her niece, who, if she was not yet a corpse, nevertheless looked like one. "Tell us what they did to you, tell me, dearie. Oh, what pain, what grief!"

"You," said Plácido to Izquierdo in an authoritarian tone, "run out and find that pharmacist gentleman who comes here, the one who's taking care of her. I'll find somebody else, and let's be on our way fast, because death's got a head start on us."

He slipped out without waiting to hear Segunda's opinion. Plato, whose instincts told him that Estupiñá's orders were more practical than the vendor's, left and rushed over to Ave María Street.

The first person to arrive was Guillermina, whom Plácido had informed along the way. Climbing the stairs, the saint said to her sexton: "Go into your apartment and wait for Jacinta, who'll be here any minute. Tell her I don't want her to come up. I'll be down as soon as I can. Jacinta isn't to move; tell her to wait for me."

When the founder entered, the patient was still in the same condition. In her deep consternation, Segunda had stopped talking about the assassination, and although she didn't understand "the kid being stolen," she didn't dare mention it in front of Guillermina. She had tried to make Fortunata take strong doses of ergotine but hadn't succeeded. The patient's teeth were clenched, and there was no way to bring her around. Guillermina was luckier, or used more effective methods, because she managed to make her drink some of the potent medicine. There was a great tumult, a hasty application of various remedies, external and internal. The saint and the square vendor labored with equal ardor to stop the life running out of her, but life did not want to stop; and, faced with the inefficacy of their efforts, the two women came to a halt, exhausted and disheartened. Fortunata looked gratefully at her friend, who took her hand; but when she tried to talk, she could hardly utter a monosyllable. So they communicated in silence.

"Father Nones is going to come," said the saint. "I left word with him on my way over. Prepare yourself, child, and start turning your thoughts to our Lord Jesus Christ, and if you beg forgiveness for your sins, and you're truly contrite, He'll forgive you. Have you asked Him yet?"

Fortunata nodded in the affirmative.

"My dear friend has been told about the present, and she's most thankful. It was a truly Christian gesture."

In the fogginess of her mind, the unfortunate young woman heard the word "gesture" and recalled Feijóo and his prohibitions; but this memory didn't make her regret her action.

"Jacinta asked me to give you her thanks. She bears you no ill will. On the contrary: you've done something that will leave her with a good memory of you. And besides, she's one of the few people who know how to forgive. Imitate her; it wouldn't do you any harm right now to stifle your passions, love your enemies, and do good to those who hate you. My child" (embracing her) "have you forgiven the man who's to blame for all your misfortunes and who dragged you to sin so many times?"

Fortunata nodded "yes," and her expression made it plain that this forgiveness was easy, because love was involved.

"Do you also forgive the woman you thought had offended you and whom you offended with your words and acts, either with or without justification?"

This was a really hard one. The saint fell silent and observed how uneasy the devilish woman was; her head was thrown back, and she moved it rather nervously as her gaze wandered over the ceiling.

"Are you doubtful? Well, you know if God's going to forgive us, first He has to know whether we've forgiven others. What do you want that petty hatred for now? What good is it? It's a dead weight that will keep you from getting up to heaven. That lead has got to be thrown out" (embracing her more affectionately). "Dear little friend, do it for me, and for your little tiny 'angel face,' who should be left showered with blessings, not curses."

Fortunata quivered from head to toe. Her heavy breathing indicated her urge to overcome the physical restraints that kept her from speaking. "You don't need to speak," the saint told her; "I can understand you if you nod your head. Do you forgive Aurora?" The moribund woman moved her head in a manner that could have been called affirmative, but it was a listless movement, as if part but not her whole soul were affirming it.

"More clearly, now."

Fortunata nodded again, a bit more firmly, and her eyes became moist.

"That's more like it."

And then something that resembled poetic inspiration or religious ecstasy shone in the face of the miserable Señora Rubín, and in a marvelous triumph over her prostration, she suddenly found the energy and words to declare this: "I am, too . . . Didn't you know? . . . I'm an angel."

She spoke a few more words, which became incoherent again, but in her face, that look of calm, ineffable happiness remained. The saint was bewildered for a moment, not knowing what position to take.

"An angel! . . . Yes," she said at last. "You'll be one if you're purified first. My dear friend—you've got to prepare yourself seriously. Father Nones is on his way, and he'll give you the consolation that I can't give you. And I've just remembered that you had a malignant idea, and it was the source of many sins. You've got to throw it out, stamp on it. Look into your soul very carefully; you'll find it. It's that nonsense about a childless marriage not being worth anything, and that you— because you'd had his children—were the real wife of . . . Come now" (with extraordinary tenderness), "admit that an idea like that was a diabolical error that was born out of ignorance, and promise me that you'll disown it and you won't forget it when you make your confession to Father Nones. Remember, if you take it with you, it will get in your way in the next world."

La Pitusa didn't express anything, which led her fervent friend to renew her attack more vigorously:

"Fortunata, my child, for my sake, for the fondness you feel for me, which I don't deserve, and for my fondness for you, which I'll feel the rest of my life, I beg you to root out that idea and put it here, like a decoration that sinners wear, like rouge or an artificial mole. It won't be any good to you there unless the devil uses it for his wicked schemes. Will you root it out, yes or no? Do it for my sake, so I'll rest in peace."

Fortunata's eyes brightened again, as if reflecting a cerebral illumination, and pleasure vibrated throughout her body as if a benign spirit had suddenly taken hold of it. Her will and words returned but only to say: "I'm an angel . . . Don't you see?"

"An angel, yes; fine, I like that conviction," disturbed. "But I'd like—"

The lady was interruped by the appearance of Father Nones, who had to stoop to fit through the door. The whole room filled with a sad, severe blackness. "Here I am, maestra," said the old man; and the lady got up to give him her seat. The two mumbled something before she withdrew. Nones spoke affectionately to the patient, who looked at him with cloudy eyes, not answering anything he said. At last she spoke, in a voice that sounded childlike; it was whining and pained, like that of a tender creature who has been wounded. What Nones thought he understood among those articulations of undefined emotion was: "Didn't you know? . . . I'm an angel . . . I am too; an 'angel face.'"

And the priest continued his exhortation, saying to himself: "It's useless . . . her mind's gone."

And out loud: "An angel, yes; but we must confess our faith in Christ, my child, and consecrate our last thoughts to Him and beg Him from our heart to forgive us. He's so, so good that He doesn't refuse shelter to any sinner who appeals to Him, no matter how hardened the sinner is. The main thing is to be pure inside, to—"

He looked at her in alarm. Had she said something? Yes, but Nones couldn't make it out. It was undoubtedly that same sentence—"I'm an angel"—then she let her head droop, like someone about to fall asleep. The priest looked at her more closely and out loud said, "Maestra, maestra—come."

Guillermina entered the room and they studied her.

"I think," said Nones, "that's she's gone. She couldn't confess . . . Her mind was disturbed. Poor thing! She says she's an angel. God will decide."

The maestra and the priest began to pray out loud. Segunda started to make a scene, and at that moment Segismundo (having been told the events on the stairs) entered the house and the bedroom more dead than alive.

15

While Father Nones was there, Ballester expressed only consternation, contemplating the pitiful scene with the respect the dead inspire and confining his grief to a composure that had a certain correctness about it. But when the only witnesses left were the saint and Segunda, the good pharmacist felt unable to restrain the impetuous surge from his heart, and, approaching the still warm body of his unfortunate friend, he embraced her and imprinted a multitude of kisses on her forehead and cheeks.

"Oh, Señora!" he said to the founder, drying his tears, "I see you're shocked to see me cry like this, and at this show of affection. I loved her very much; she was my friend . . . she was going to be my lover—I mean, no, excuse me—we were friends. You didn't know her well; I did. She was an angel—I mean, she should have been, she could have been. Please excuse me, Señora; I don't know what I'm saying, because this tragedy has struck me so deeply. I didn't expect it . . . It was carelessness. She herself, with the wild things she did. Because she was one of those angels who do crazy things, do you know what I mean? Poor woman, so beautiful and so good! The hemorrhage was undoubtedly caused because there was no involution. I was afraid of it. Getting up too soon, her overexcitement, and then the carelessness, and the lack of someone to watch over her and an authority who would have imposed himself. Oh, if only I'd been here! But I couldn't, I couldn't. My obligations . . . Oh, Señora, believe me—my heart's broken, and it will take me a long, long time to recover from this grief. I'd grown so fond of her. I always had her on my mind. My fate linked me to her, and we would have been happy; yes, happy . . . We would have gone to a foreign country, to a faraway country. With your permission I'm going to kiss her again. I never kissed her. I didn't dare, and she wouldn't have let me, because she was the most decent, honest person you could imagine."

Guillermina felt as much astonishment as pity at the display of this poor man, who expressed himself so frankly. Little by little, Segismundo's grief began to subdue, taking a quieter tone, and, seated next to the head of the deathbed, he spoke to the saint about a matter that necessarily and as a reality had to be discussed.

"Oh, no, Señora; please allow me. I'll take care of the funeral expenses. I want that satisfaction. Don't deny me that, for God's sake."

"But son," replied the founder. "You're poor. Why should you take on that expense? If there were no other way, it would all be well and good. Don't be silly, save your money—you need it enough as it is. The person who has that obligation is the one who should meet it. Not another word now."

Not willing to admit defeat, Ballester persisted; but Guillermina hammered away at him so hard that she finally got the idea out of his head. Segunda and her two vendor friends shrouded the unfortunate Señora Rubín, and meanwhile the pharmacist, with indefatigable activity, took care of the arrangements for the funeral, which was to be the next morning. He didn't abandon the death house all day long. At noon he was alone with her, and Fortunata's body, already dressed in the black habit of the Virgin of Sorrows, was laid out on the bed. Ballester couldn't get his fill of looking at her, observing the serenity in those features that death had marked but not yet devoured. Her face was like ivory, tainted around the eyes and on the lips with a wine-colored tone, and her eyebrows looked even finer, blacker, and more carefully drawn than they had in life. Several flies had settled on those withered features. Segismundo once again felt the desire to kiss his friend. What did he care about flies? It was like when they fell in milk—you took them out and then drank the milk. The flies flew away when his living face leaned over the dead one; and when it withdrew, they returned to resettle there again. Then Ballester covered his friend's face with a very fine handkerchief.

Guillermina came back later. She came up from Plácido's to tell Ballester something about the funeral. They talked for a while, and since she suspected that the deceased's husband might turn up and make a row, the pharmacist reassured her:

"Don't worry about anything. We were able to lock him up this morning. The poor man's furious, and we needed God's help and more to take away the blasted revolver he'd bought and was planning to use on the poor Samaniegas and someone else who's usually in the neighborhood. Doña Lupe was hanging by a thread. Padilla and I went over, and after a struggle we managed to disarm the philosopher and shut him up in his room where he was banging his head against the wall and shouting at the top of his lungs."

"I knew it. So much logic had to end badly. Well, so you know, then—at ten o'clock there'll be a Mass and then the responsory at the cemetery. And it's been decided by the person who should decide, that the funeral will be first-class—a luxury carriage with six horses; the children from the orphanage will be there too. Maybe you think it's too unsuitable a show."

"No, I don't object."

"I wouldn't be at all surprised if you did, because at first glance it's absurd. But complicated causes bring on complicated effects, and that's why we see so many things in this world that seem out of proportion and even comical. That's why I believe we shouldn't laugh at anything, and also, everything that happens, merely because it does happen, merits some respect. Do you see what I mean?"

She was about to add something else, but Plácido came in, hat in hand, and rather like an aide de camp announced to his general that Doña Bárbara had arrived.

So the saint went downstairs and found her friend a bit stern compared to Jacinta's lavish display of affection for the baby that had come into her power as instantly as if she had found it in the street or discovered it in a basket on her doorstep. The baby's features had their effect on the elderly Señora Santa Cruz, too; but having learned from that other painful experience to be more cautious, she contained herself to avoid the ridicule and embarrassment she had felt before. The lady was undecided; she couldn't quite permit herself to be enthusiastic; and the reasons Guillermina used to convince her did not unlock her from that reserved, suspicious attitude. The Dauphine was overflowing with emotion; it was a harmonious combination of happiness and sorrow due to the circumstances in which that tender creature had fallen into her hands. She couldn't take her mind off the person upstairs who had ceased to exist that same morning, and she was amazed to discover in her heart feelings beyond mere pity for the luckless woman; perhaps some sort of companionship founded on their mutual suffering. She recalled that the dead woman had been her archenemy; but the final stages of their enmity and the incredible case of her inheriting the Pituso implicated, even though her intelligence could not decipher the enigma, a reconciliation. With death in between, one of them in visible life and the other in invisible life, the two women may quite possibly have looked at each other from opposite banks and wished to embrace.

The three ladies said all at once:

"And what do we do now?"

A discussion ensued to decide where the precious acquisition should be taken. Guillermina obviated the difficulties by proposing that he be taken to her house. Estupiñá was given orders to escort the three wet nurses to the saint's house, where the one who was to bring up "angel face" would be conscientiously selected.

The night of that famous day there was a memorable scene at the Santa Cruz residence. Jacinta and her mother-in-law called in the Dauphin for a conference; they put him in a tight spot, relating the events to him, showing him the letter written by Estupiñá, and forcing him (causing his dignity to tarnish regrettably) to display his sincere consternation; the matter could not be made light of, nor could it be brushed off with a few phrases and a witty remark. His misconduct had been serious; he had wronged his lawful wife, abandoned his accomplice, and made her worthy of compassion and even likable due to a series of circumstances for which he alone was responsible. At last, in an effort to rebuild his shattered self-pride, Santa Cruz denied some of the facts, and others, the bitterest, he sweetened and glossed over admirably well to make them pass; he ended up affirming that the child was his, very much his, and that he recognized him as such and accepted him and was resolved to love him as though he had been born to his legitimate wife, whom he adored.

When the Dauphins were left alone, Jacinta dealt with her husband in her own way; and she was so right, so firm, and valiant that he could hardly retaliate, his petty tricks becoming mere laughable, impotent weapons against the truth that flowed from the lips of the wronged wife. She made him tremble with her steely judgments, and it was no longer easy for the clever gentleman to triumph over that tender soul whose dialectics had usually weakened under the force of his affection. Then it became evident that the continuity of Jacinta's suffering had destroyed her respect for her husband, and the ruins of that respect had destroyed some of her love, and then the greater part of it, until it was finally reduced to such miserable proportions that it was scarcely visible. The ungraceful position in which Santa Cruz found himself inflamed his pride all the more; and with this disdain—no longer disguised, but now real and effective—that his wife was showing him the poor man suffered horribly, because it was very sad for him that his blows could no longer hurt his victim. To be a nobody to his wife, not to find in her that periodic refuge to which he was accustomed, put him in a very bad frame of mind. And his confidence in the security of that refuge was such that, upon losing it, he experienced for the first time in his life that terrible sadness produced by irreparable losses and the emptiness of life; a sensation which in the prime of youth equals aging; when surrounded by one's family, equals loneliness; which convinces one that the best of life is behind, leaving one's back turned on the horizons that were once ahead. She told him so clearly, with expressive sincerity in her eyes, which never deceived.

"Do what you like. You're as free as the air. Your tricks don't affect me at all anymore."

These were not merely words; the Dauphin saw that this time she meant it.

For some time *le petit Dauphin* stayed at Guillermina's (where the wet nurse was) until Don Baldomero had been fully informed of everything and the baby could be brought into his parents' house. Jacinta was devoted to him body and soul, and she had the satisfaction of seeing everyone, even his father, love him. When she was alone with him, the lady entertained herself by building castles in the air with intangible towers and even more fragile cupolas that were the essence of her ideas. The inherited child's features weren't the other woman's; they were hers. Her flights of fancy were so lofty that the putative mother was even beguiled by an artificial memory of having borne the beautiful child in her womb, and she shuddered at the thought of the labor pains to bring him into the world. These games of her playful fantasy were followed by her reflection on how disorderly the world was. She, too, had her notions on lawful ties, and broke them, turning back the clock and changing people by giving this one that one's heart, and that one someone else's head, making such extravagant corrections on the world's work that God would have laughed if He had heard about them, and so would His skirted vicar, Guillermina Pacheco. Jacinta made this cyclone of thoughts and corrections spin on the angelic head of Juan Evaristo; she recomposed his features, attributing to him her own, but mixed and confused with those of an ideal being who might well have Santa Cruz's face but whose heart was surely Moreno's . . . the heart that adored her and even died for her. Moreno could very well have been her husband . . . still alive, not emaciated or sick . . . with the face that actually belonged to the Dauphin, that false, evil person. "And even if he didn't have the Dauphin's face, even if he didn't . . . Oh, *then* the world would be as it should, and all the bad things that happen wouldn't happen."

16

At Señora Rubín's funeral, the luxury of the hearse contrasted with the few carriages that followed: there were only two or three. Riding in the first was Ballester, who in order not to be alone, had asked his friend the critic to accompany him. On the long ride from the Cava to the cemetery (one of those in the southern part of the city), Segismundo told the good Ponce everything he knew about Fortunata's life, which was not a little, and he did not omit the closing episodes, undoubtedly the best parts. The response from the famous judge of literary works was that it had the makings of a play or a novel, although in his opinion

THE END

the artistic texture wouldn't be especially attractive unless it were warped in places so that the vulgarity of life might be converted into esthetic material. He didn't tolerate "raw life" in art; it had to be scrubbed, seasoned with aromatic spices, and then thoroughly cooked. Segismundo did not share his opinion and they discussed the matter, each party advancing its select reasons, but each sticking to its own convictions, so that in the end they agreed that well-ripened raw fruit was very good, but so were compotes, if the cook knew what he was doing.

Meanwhile, they arrived, and Señora Rubín's body was buried before the eyes of the four or five people who had accompanied it; namely, Segismundo and the critic, Estupiñá, José Izquierdo, and the husband of one of Segunda's marketplace friends. Ballester, overcome with grief, felt his heart breaking into pieces, and he was the last to retire. On his way back to Madrid in the carriage, there grew in his mind a fresh image of the woman who no longer was.

"This image," he said to his friend, "will live in me for some time, but it will fade, little by little, until it's finally gone. And the knowledge that I'll forget, even though it's still probably remote, mades me sadder than what I've just seen . . . But one has to forget, just as death has to exist. Without forgetting there wouldn't be any room for new feelings and thoughts. If we didn't forget, we couldn't live, because in our soul's digestive work there can't be any ingestion unless there's also elimination."

And later on:

"Look, my friend Ponce: I'm inconsolable, yet I can't fail to recognize—if I express my social egoism—that the death of that woman is better for me—the good and the bad always come in pairs in life—because, believe me, I was all set to commit foolish acts for that sweet girl; I was already committing them, and would have reached God knows what point . . . you can imagine how attractive I found her! I consider myself a reasonable man, and yet I was headed straight for an abyss. That woman held a power over me I couldn't begin to explain; I took it into my head that she was an angel, yes, an angel in disguise, you might say, all done up in a mask to scare off fools; and not all the wise men in the world could have convinced me to give up that notion. Even now it's firmly implanted in me. It may be delirious, an aberration, but that notion is fixed in me, and what makes me despair the most is that now, because of death, I can't prove whether it's true. Because you know, I wanted to prove it to myself . . . and believe me, I would have gotten my way."

The following week Ballester left the Samaniego pharmacy because Doña Casta had learned of his relationship (which she called immoral) with the notorious woman who had so rudely attacked Aurora, and she didn't want to have any more to do with him. Doña Lupe begged him several times to come see Maximiliano, who continued locked up in his room; they passed him his meals through a window. Neither the Señora nor Papitos dared enter, for the wretched boy's howls were a sign of dangerous, insane agitation. Segismundo was the first to enter the room fearlessly, and he found Maxi curled up in a ball in the corner, looking more like an imbecile than a fury, his face awry and his messy clothes unkempt.

"Well?" said the pharmacist, leaning down in an effort to pick him up. "Is it getting better? Since you wanted to bite us a few days ago when we took away your gun and you snarled and kicked and wanted to kill the whole human race, we had to lock you up. A fair punishment for foolishness. Well, what is it? Cat got your tongue? Look at me and stop making faces, they're very ugly. Don't you recognize me? I'm Ballester, and I've got a rod for spanking naughty children."

"Ballester?" said Maxi, staring at him, as if waking from a lethargy.

"It's me all right: so what? Would you like some news of the world? Well, promise me you'll be sensible."

"Sensible? I am, I am. Have I ever stopped being sensible, by even this much?"

"Bah! No, never. You, not sensible? That'd be the day."

"The thing is, I've been asleep, my friend," said Rubín with relative serenity, and getting up. "What I remember now is that I was sane, saner than anybody, and then I suddenly got in a frenzy about killing. Why, why was it?"

"Well, scratch your little head a bit and see if you can remember. It was because we can be very foolish at times. You were the picture of a philosopher and on your way to becoming a saint when you suddenly took it into your head to buy a gun."

"Oh!" his eyes widening, aghast. "Oh, yes; it was because my wife gave me her word that she'd love me, with true love, madly, you know? The way she knows how to love."

"Fine. So now you want to blame her, poor thing."

"Yes, it was her. She made me lose track of myself . . . and I still have. I've got an evil spirit inside me, and I can scarcely remember the virtuous state I was in before."

"What a pity, son! We've got to go back to the cold showers and the sodium bromide. It's the best way to become virtuous and philosophical."

"I'll come back," stated Maxi, wholly serious, "when I've kept the promise I made to my wife. I'll kill; then I'll enjoy that ineffable, infinite love I've never tasted that she offered me in exchange for sacrificing my sanity; and then we'll consecrate ourselves to doing penance and asking God to forgive us for our faults."

"Well, that's a fine program; yes, sir! A lovely contract! Except that it can't be signed because one party is missing."

"Which party?"

"The one that offered the love, that sublime . . . delirious love."

Maxi didn't understand, and Ballester, resolved to tell him the news without beating around the bush or soft-pedaling it, concluded thus:

"Yes, your wife no longer exists. The poor dear died eight days ago."

And saying this, he was so moved that his voice thickened. Maxi broke into raucous laughter.

"The same comedy again! But this time, just like last time, it won't work, Señor Ballester. How much do you want to bet that with my logic I'll discover where she is again? Oh, good God! I can already feel logic flooding my mind; it's rushing in fast, and my talent's back . . . yes! I can feel it coming. Blessed be God!"

Doña Lupe, who was listening to this conversation from the hallway (ear pressed to the door), gradually lost her fear when she heard her nephew's serene voice, so she cracked the door open, letting her inquisitive, intelligent face be seen.

"Come in, Doña Lupe," said Segismundo. "He's all right again. The fit is over. But he refused to believe that we've all lost his wife. Sure, since we deceived him last time . . . but he outsmarted us."

"And I will this time, too," asserted Rubín with maniacal insistence. "I'm going to start my observations and calculations right away."

"Well, you needn't get all worked up—I'll prove it to you; I'll show you what I've said. Doña Lupe, please bring me his clothes—he shouldn't go out looking the way he does."

"Where are you going to take him?" she asked in alarm.

"Leave it to me, Madam Organization. I know what I'm doing. Are you afraid I'll steal this jewel?"

"My clothes, Aunt, my clothes," said Maxi, as lively as he had ever been and showing no signs of emotional disturbance.

At last, Ballester's wishes were carried out; Maxi got dressed and they left. In the hall, Segismundo communicated his thoughts to Doña Lupe:

"Look, Señora; I have to go to the cemetery to see the tombstone I've ordered for the poor girl's grave. I'm paying for it; I wanted to have that satisfaction. It's a beautiful tombstone, with the name of the deceased and a wreath of roses—"

"A wreath of roses!" exclaimed the "turkey woman" who, for all her diplomacy, was unable to suppress a slightly ironic tone.

"Roses, yes. What difference does it make to you?" quite vexed. "Did you have to pay for it? I would have liked for it to have been made of marble, but it wasn't possible; it's made of Novelda stone, a modest, affectionate tribute to a pure friendship. She was an angel, yes—I won't take back my words, even if you do laugh at me."

"No, I'm not laughing at you. That would be the last straw."

"An angel in her way. Well, anyway, let's drop the subject and go back to the other matter. Since convincing this poor boy that his wife is no longer alive is bound to influence his mental state strongly, I plan to take him . . . so he'll see for himself, Señora."

Doña Lupe approved, so the two pharmacists left and hailed a cab. Maxi rode along with his head hanging low; the approach to the cemetery weighed on his soul with the gravity inherent in the idea of dying.

"Onward, son," his friend encouraged him, taking his arm and leading him into the cemetery grounds.

They crossed a large courtyard full of more or less luxurious mausoleums; then another full of niches; then a third full of open graves, others recently occupied, and they stopped in front of where some carpenters were still working, where they had just set a gravestone and were gathering up their tools.

"Here it is," said Ballester, pointing to the big Novelda quarry slab on whose upper part there was a fairly well engraved wreath of roses under the RIP and then a name and the date of death. "What does it say there?"

Maximiliano stood stock still, his eyes glued to the gravestone. It didn't leave any doubts! And added onto his wife's first and surname was "de Rubín." Both fell silent; but Maxi's emotion was more vivid and harder to master than his friend's. And in a little while, a quiet weeping, the expression of true, hopeless grief, streamed from his eyes in what seemed like an endless torrent.

"They're tears that come from my whole life," he was able to say to his friend, "the ones I'm crying now. All my sorrows are coming out through my eyes."

Ballester led him away, not without effort, for Maxi wanted to stay there, crying. As they were leaving the cemetery, a rather large burial procession was entering. It was following the body of Evaristo Feijóo. But the two pharmacists paid no attention to it. In the cab, Maximiliano voiced the following thoughts to his friend in a calm, sorrowful voice:

"I loved her with all my soul. I made her the crowning object of my life, and she didn't respond to my desires. She didn't love me. Let's view things from up above: she couldn't love me. I made a mistake and she did, too. I wasn't the only one who was deceived; she was, too. We defrauded each other. We didn't take nature into account, the grand mother and teacher who rectifies the errors of those of her children who go astray. We do countless foolish things and nature corrects them. We protest against her admirable lessons, which we don't understand, and when we want her to obey us, she grabs us and smashes us to bits, as the sea does to whoever tries to rule it. My reason tells me this, friend Ballester; my reason, which today—thanks to God—has illuminated me again like a magnificent beacon. Don't you see? Because you know, whoever claims I'm crazy is the one who really is. And if someone tells me so to my face, Holy Christ and all the saints! he's going to pay very dearly for it."

"Calm down, my friend," kindly. "Nobody's contradicting you."

"Because now I can see all the conflicts, all the problems of my life with a clarity that can only come from reason. And to make things plain, I swear before God and men that from the bottom of my heart I forgive that luckless woman whom I loved more than life itself and who did me so much harm; I forgive her, and I banish all rancor from my thoughts, and cleanse my soul of all evil growth, and I reject any thoughts that are not directed to goodness and virtue. The world is over for me. I've been a martyr and a madman. And may my madness—from which, with God's help, I have recovered—be counted as martyrdom, for what were my crazy acts, if not the external expression of the horrible agonies of my soul? And just so that nobody will be left with any doubts whatsoever about my state of perfect sanity, I declare that I love my wife as much as the day I met her; I adore what is ideal and eternal in her, and I see her not as she was, but rather as I dreamed and envisioned her in my soul. I see her adorned with the most beautiful attributes of a divine being, reflected in her as if in a mirror. I adore her, because we would have no way to feel God's love unless God revealed it to us through our idea that His attributes are transmitted by a creature of our human race. Now that she's not alive, I contemplate her—freed from the transformations that the world and contact with evil impressed upon her. Now I don't fear infidelity, a conflict with the forces of nature rubbing against us; now I don't fear treachery, which is the projection of shadows of opaque bodies as they approach us; now everything is liberty and light; the disgusting side of reality has disappeared, and I live with my idol in my mind, and we adore each other with sublime purity and saintliness in the incorruptible chambers of my mind."

"She was an angel," murmured Ballester, to whom that exaltation was somehow being communicated.

"She was an angel!" shouted Maxi, bringing his fist down on his knee. "And the wretch who tries to deny it or cast any aspersions on her will have to contend with me!"

"And with me, too!" echoed Segismundo, equally ardent. "Poor woman! If only she were alive . . ."

"No, friend. Life is a nightmare. I'd rather have her dead—"

"Me, too," said Ballester, beginning to realize that he should not contradict him. "We'll both love her as one loves angels. Blessed are they who have this consolation!"

"Blessed a hundred times over, my friend," Rubín exclaimed enthusiastically, "are they who have reached these serene heights in their minds. You're still tied to the senselessness of life; I freed myself and dwell in pure thought. Congratulate me, my dear friend, and embrace me—hard, harder, harder, because I feel very, very happy."

Upon entering his house, the first thing he said to Doña Lupe was:

"My dear Aunt: I want to retire from the world and enter a monastery, where I can live in seclusion with my ideas."

The sky opened up for the Jáuregui woman when she heard him express himself thus, and she replied:

"Oh, son—I've already arranged for you to enter a very private, beautiful monastery there is near Madrid! Just wait—you'll see how comfortable you'll be there. There are some very charming gentlemen priests who do nothing but meditate on the Lord and heavenly things. I'm so happy you've made this decision! Since I was anticipating it, I've been preparing the clothes you'll be taking." Ballester supported the idea that had occurred to his friend, and he spent all day talking it over with him, just in case he should have a change of heart. And taking advantage of Maxi's good disposition, he transported him in a cab, very early the next morning, to the quiet retreat that they had arranged for him. Maxi left very contentedly, without putting up any resistance at all. But upon arriving he said out loud, as if he were talking with an invisible being:

"These fools think they're deceiving me! This is Leganés, the insane asylum. I accept it; I accept it in silence, to prove the total submission of my will to whatever the world wishes to do with me. But they won't be able to confine my thoughts within these walls. I live among the stars. Let them put the man called Maximiliano Rubín in a palace or a dung heap—it's all the same to me."

Madrid, June 1887

READ MORE IN PENGUIN

In every corner of the world, on every subject under the sun, Penguin represents quality and variety – the very best in publishing today.

For complete information about books available from Penguin – including Puffins, Penguin Classics and Arkana – and how to order them, write to us at the appropriate address below. Please note that for copyright reasons the selection of books varies from country to country.

In the United Kingdom: Please write to *Dept. EP, Penguin Books Ltd, Bath Road, Harmondsworth, West Drayton, Middlesex UB7 0DA*

In the United States: Please write to *Consumer Sales, Penguin USA, P.O. Box 999, Dept. 17109, Bergenfield, New Jersey 07621-0120*. VISA and MasterCard holders call 1-800-253-6476 to order Penguin titles

In Canada: Please write to *Penguin Books Canada Ltd, 10 Alcorn Avenue, Suite 300, Toronto, Ontario M4V 3B2*

In Australia: Please write to *Penguin Books Australia Ltd, P.O. Box 257, Ringwood, Victoria 3134*

In New Zealand: Please write to *Penguin Books (NZ) Ltd, Private Bag 102902, North Shore Mail Centre, Auckland 10*

In India: Please write to *Penguin Books India Pvt Ltd, 706 Eros Apartments, 56 Nehru Place, New Delhi 110 019*

In the Netherlands: Please write to *Penguin Books Netherlands bv, Postbus 3507, NL-1001 AH Amsterdam*

In Germany: Please write to *Penguin Books Deutschland GmbH, Metzlerstrasse 26, 60594 Frankfurt am Main*

In Spain: Please write to *Penguin Books S. A., Bravo Murillo 19, 1° B, 28015 Madrid*

In Italy: Please write to *Penguin Italia s.r.l., Via Felice Casati 20, I–20124 Milano*

In France: Please write to *Penguin France S. A., 17 rue Lejeune, F–31000 Toulouse*

In Japan: Please write to *Penguin Books Japan, Ishikiribashi Building, 2–5–4, Suido, Bunkyo-ku, Tokyo 112*

In Greece: Please write to *Penguin Hellas Ltd, Dimocritou 3, GR–106 71 Athens*

In South Africa: Please write to *Longman Penguin Southern Africa (Pty) Ltd, Private Bag X08, Bertsham 2013*

READ MORE IN PENGUIN

A CHOICE OF CLASSICS

Jacob Burckhardt	**The Civilization of the Renaissance in Italy**
Carl von Clausewitz	**On War**
Meister Eckhart	**Selected Writings**
Friedrich Engels	**The Origins of the Family, Private Property and the State**
Wolfram von Eschenbach	**Parzival**
	Willehalm
Goethe	**Elective Affinities**
	Faust Parts One and Two (in 2 volumes)
	Italian Journey
	The Sorrows of Young Werther
Jacob and Wilhelm Grimm	**Selected Tales**
E. T. A. Hoffmann	**Tales of Hoffmann**
Henrik Ibsen	**A Doll's House and Other Plays**
	Ghosts and Other Plays
	Hedda Gabler and Other Plays
	The Master Builder and Other Plays
	Peer Gynt
Søren Kierkegaard	**Fear and Trembling**
	The Sickness Unto Death
Georg Christoph Lichtenberg	**Aphorisms**
Karl Marx	**Capital (in three volumes)**
Friedrich Nietzsche	**The Birth of Tragedy**
	Beyond Good and Evil
	Ecce Homo
	Human, All Too Human
	A Nietzsche Reader
Friedrich Schiller	**The Robbers/Wallenstein**
Arthur Schopenhauer	**Essays and Aphorisms**
Gottfried von Strassburg	**Tristan**
Adalbert Stifter	**Brigitta and Other Tales**
August Strindberg	**By the Open Sea**

READ MORE IN PENGUIN

A CHOICE OF CLASSICS

Honoré de Balzac	**The Black Sheep**
	César Birotteau
	The Chouans
	Cousin Bette
	Eugénie Grandet
	A Harlot High and Low
	Lost Illusions
	A Murky Business
	Old Goriot
	Selected Short Stories
	Ursule Mirouet
	The Wild Ass's Skin
J. A. Brillat-Savarin	**The Physiology of Taste**
Marquis de Custine	**Letters from Russia**
Pierre Corneille	**The Cid/Cinna/The Theatrical Illusion**
Alphonse Daudet	**Letters from My Windmill**
René Descartes	**Discourse on Method and Other**
Denis Diderot	**Writings**
	Jacques the Fatalist
	The Nun
	Rameau's Nephew/D'Alembert's
	Dream
Gustave Flaubert	**Selected Writings on Art and Literature**
	Bouvard and Pecuchet
	Madame Bovary
	Sentimental Education
	The Temptation of St Anthony
Victor Hugo	**Three Tales**
	Les Misérables
Laclos	**Notre-Dame of Paris**
La Fontaine	**Les Liaisons Dangereuses**
Madame de Lafayette	**Selected Fables**
Lautréamont	**The Princesse de Clèves**
	Maldoror and Poems

READ MORE IN PENGUIN

A CHOICE OF CLASSICS

Molière	**The Misanthrope/The Sicilian/Tartuffe/A Doctor in Spite of Himself/The Imaginary Invalid**
	The Miser/The Would-be Gentleman/That Scoundrel Scapin/Love's the Best Doctor/Don Juan
Michel de Montaigne	**Essays**
Marguerite de Navarre	**The Heptameron**
Blaise Pascal	**Pensées**
	The Provincial Letters
Abbé Prevost	**Manon Lescaut**
Rabelais	**The Histories of Gargantua and Pantagruel**
Racine	**Andromache/Britannicus/Berenice**
	Iphigenia/Phaedra/Athaliah
Arthur Rimbaud	**Collected Poems**
Jean-Jacques Rousseau	**The Confessions**
	A Discourse on Inequality
	Emile
Jacques Saint-Pierre	**Paul and Virginia**
Madame de Sevigné	**Selected Letters**
Stendhal	**Lucien Leuwen**
	Scarlet and Black
	The Charterhouse of Parma
Voltaire	**Candide**
	Letters on England
	Philosophical Dictionary
Emile Zola	**L'Assommoir**
	La Bête Humaine
	The Debacle
	The Earth
	Germinal
	Nana
	Thérèse Raquin

READ MORE IN PENGUIN

A CHOICE OF CLASSICS

Leopoldo Alas	**La Regenta**
Leon B. Alberti	**On Painting**
Ludovico Ariosto	**Orlando Furioso** (in 2 volumes)
Giovanni Boccaccio	**The Decameron**
Baldassar Castiglione	**The Book of the Courtier**
Benvenuto Cellini	**Autobiography**
Miguel de Cervantes	**Don Quixote**
	Exemplary Stories
Dante	**The Divine Comedy** (in 3 volumes)
	La Vita Nuova
Machado de Assis	**Dom Casmurro**
Bernal Diaz	**The Conquest of New Spain**
Carlo Goldoni	**Four Comedies (The Venetian Twins/The Artful Widow/Mirandolina/The Superior Residence)**
Niccolò Machiavelli	**The Discourses**
	The Prince
Alessandro Manzoni	**The Betrothed**
Emilia Pardo Bazán	**The House of Ulloa**
Benito Pérez Galdós	**Fortunata and Jacinta**
Giorgio Vasari	**Lives of the Artists** (in 2 volumes)

and

Five Italian Renaissance Comedies
  (Machiavelli/The Mandragola; Ariosto/Lena; Aretino/The
  Stablemaster; Gl'Intronati/The Deceived; Guarini/The Faithful
  Shepherd)
The Poem of the Cid
Two Spanish Picaresque Novels
  (Anon/Lazarillo de Tormes; de Quevedo/The Swindler)